SCOTLAND

Chester
Mold
Hawarden
Caer yn Arfon
Dolbadarn
Dolwyddelan
UPPER POWYS
Cricieth
BlancMinster
Llyn Myngul
Meifod
LOWER POWYS
Caus
Craig Adern
Tywyn
Montgomery
R. Dyfi

ISLE OF MAN

Irish Sea

Middleham

York

SEE SET

Conisbrough

North Sea

Môn
Aber
Chester
Dolwyddelan
CHESHIRE
Nottingham
Lincoln
Newark
Sleaford
Swineshead Abbey
The Wash
GWYNEDD
POWYS
Shrewsbury
Grantham
Holbeach
Long Sutton
Lynn
CrossKeys
Caus
White Ladies Priory
R. Wellstream
Wisbech
SHROPSHIRE

WALES
Buellt
Ludlow
Worcester
Silverston
Cambridge
Hereford
HEREFORD-SHIRE
Tewkesbury
Cardigan
DEHEUBARTH
Cirencester
Woodstock
Tenby
Carmarthen
Abergavenny
Abbey
Oxford
Windsor
London
Swansea
R. Thames

Bristol
Runnymede Meadow
Rochester
Dover
Guildford
Chilham
Salisbury
Winchester
Ewell
Southampton
Porchester
Portsmouth

Corfe

English Channel

Miles
0   50
0   50
Kms.

SHARON PENMAN

HERE BE DRAGONS

COLLINS
8 Grafton Street, London W1
1986

William Collins Sons & Co. Ltd
London · Glasgow · Sydney · Auckland
Toronto · Johannesburg

BRITISH LIBRARY CATALOGUING IN PUBLICATION DATA

Penman, Sharon K.
Here be dragons.
I. Title
813'.54[F]   PS3566.E4/

ISBN 0-00-222960-9

First published 1986
Copyright © Sharon K. Penman 1986

Photoset in Linotron Times by
Rowland Phototypesetting Ltd, Bury St Edmunds, Suffolk
Made and printed in Great Britain by
William Collins Sons & Co. Ltd, Glasgow

TO MY PARENTS

ACKNOWLEDGMENTS

I would like to thank the following people for their support and encouragement and understanding: My parents. Julie McCaskey Wolff. My American agent, Molly Friedrich of the Aaron M. Priest Literary Agency. My British agent, Abner Stein. My dear friend Cris Arnott, who helped me to track down the elusive Richard Fitz Roy. Betty Rowles and Jean and Basil Hill, who showed me so many kindnesses during my research trips to Wales. Olwen Caradoc Evans and Helen Ramage, who shared with me their knowledge and love of Welsh history. Above all, my editor at Holt, Rinehart and Winston, Marian Wood. And lastly, the staffs of the National Library of Wales, the British Library, the Caernarfon Archives, the University College of North Wales Library, the research libraries of Cardiff, Llangefni, and Shrewsbury, the Brecknock Borough Library, the County Archives Office in Mold, and in the United States, the University of Pennsylvania Library.

PROLOGUE

Theirs was a land of awesome grandeur, a land of mountains and moorlands and cherished myths. They called it Cymru and believed themselves to be the descendants of Brutus and the citizens of ancient Troy. They were a passionate, generous, and turbulent people, with but one fatal flaw. They proclaimed themselves to be Cymry – fellow countrymen – but they fought one another as fiercely as they did their English neighbours, and had carved three separate kingdoms out of their native soil. To the north was the alpine citadel of Gwynedd, bordered by Powys, and to the south lay the realm of Deheubarth. To the English kings, this constant discord was a blessing and they did what they could to sow seeds of dissension and strife amongst the Welsh.

During the reigns of the Norman Conqueror, William the Bastard, and his sons, the English Crown continued to gain influence in Wales; Norman castles rose up on Welsh soil, and Norman towns began to take root in the valleys of South Wales. As the Normans had subdued the native-born Saxons, so, too, it began to seem that they would subdue the Welsh.

Henry Plantagenet, King of England, Lord of Ireland and Wales, Duke of Normandy, Count of Anjou, ordered a wall fresco to be painted in his chamber at Winchester Castle. It depicted a fierce, proud eagle being attacked by four eaglets; as the great bird struggled, the eaglets tore at its flesh with talons and beaks. When asked what this portended, Henry said that he was the eagle and the eaglets were his sons.

And as the King's sons grew to manhood, it came to pass just as Henry had foretold. Four sons had he. Young Henry, his namesake and heir, was crowned with his sire in his sixteenth year. Richard, the second son, was invested with the duchy of Aquitaine, ruling jointly with Eleanor, his lady mother. Geoffrey became Duke of Brittany. The youngest son was John; men called him John Lackland for he was the last-born and the Angevin empire had already been divided amongst his elder brothers.

But John alone held with his father. The other sons turned upon Henry, sought to rend him as the eaglets had raked and clawed at the bleeding eagle on the wall of Winchester Castle. In the year of Christ 1183, the House of Plantagenet was at war against itself.

BOOK ONE

1

July 1183
Shropshire, England

He was ten years old and an alien in an unfriendly land, made an unwilling exile by his mother's marriage to a Marcher border lord. His new stepfather seemed a kindly man, but he was not of Llewelyn's blood, not one of the Cymry, and each dawning day in Shropshire only intensified Llewelyn's heartsick longing for his homeland.

For his mother's sake, he did his best to adapt to the strangeness of English ways. He even tried to forget the atrocity stories that were so much a part of his heritage, tales of English conquest and cruelties. His was a secret sorrow he shared with no one, for he was too young to know that misery repressed is misery all the more likely to fester.

It was on a Saturday morning a fortnight after his arrival at Caus Castle that Llewelyn mounted his gelding and rode north, towards the little village of Westbury. He had not intended to go any farther, but he was bored and lonely and the road beckoned him on. Ten miles to the east lay the town of Shrewsbury, and Llewelyn had never seen a town. He hesitated, but not for long. His stepfather had told him there were five villages between Westbury and Shrewsbury, and he recited them under his breath as he rode: Whitton, Stony Stretton, Yokethul, Newnham, and Cruckton. If he kept careful count as he passed through each one, there'd be no chance of getting lost, and with luck, he'd be back before his mother even realized he was gone.

Accustomed to forest trails and deer tracks, he found it strange to be travelling along a road wide enough for several horsemen to ride abreast. Stranger still to him were the villages, each with its green and market cross, its surprisingly substantial stone church surrounded by a cluster of thatched cottages and an occasional fishpond. They were in truth little more than hamlets, these Shropshire villages that so intrigued Llewelyn, small islands scattered about in a sea of plough-furrowed fields. But Llewelyn's people were

15

pastoral, tribal, hunters and herdsmen rather than farmers, and these commonplace scenes of domestic English life were to him as exotic as they were unfamiliar.

It was midday before he was within sight of the walls of Shrewsbury Castle. He drew rein, awed. Castle keep and soaring church spires, a fortified arched bridge spanning the River Severn, and the roofs of more houses than he could begin to count. He kept his distance, suddenly shy, and after a time, he wheeled the gelding, without a backward glance for the town he'd come so far to see.

He did not go far, leaving the road to water his horse at Yokethul Brook, and it was there that he found the other boy. He looked to be about nine, as fair as Llewelyn was dark, with a thatch of bright hair the colour of sun-dried straw and grass-green eyes that now focused admiringly upon Llewelyn's mount.

Llewelyn slid to the ground, led the gelding forward with a grin that encouraged the other boy to say, in the offhand manner that Llewelyn was coming to recognize as the English equivalent of a compliment, 'Is that horse yours?'

'Yes,' Llewelyn said, with pardonable pride. 'He was foaled on a Sunday, so I call him Dydd Sul.'

The other boy hesitated. 'You sound . . . different,' he said at last, and Llewelyn laughed. He'd been studying French for three years, but he had no illusions about his linguistic skills.

'That is what Morgan, my tutor, says, too,' he said cheerfully. 'I expect it is because French is not my native tongue.'

'You are not . . . English, are you?'

Llewelyn was momentarily puzzled, but then he remembered. The people he thought of as English thought of themselves as Norman-French, even though it had been more than a hundred years since the Duke of Normandy had invaded and conquered England. The native-born English, the Saxons, had been totally subdued; unlike us, Llewelyn thought proudly. But he knew the Normans had for the Saxons all the traditional scorn of the victors for the vanquished, and he hastened to say, 'No, I am not Saxon. I was born in Gwynedd, Cymru . . . what you know as Wales.'

The green eyes widened. 'I've never met a Welshman before,' he said slowly, and it occurred to Llewelyn that, just as he'd been raised on accounts of English treachery and tyranny, this boy was likely to have been put to bed at night with bloody tales of Welsh border raids.

'I'll show you my cloven hoof if you'll show me yours,' he offered, and the other boy looked startled and then laughed.

'I am Llewelyn ab Iorwerth . . .' Unable to resist adding, 'Ab Owain Fawr,' for Llewelyn was immensely proud that he was a grandson of Owain the Great, proud enough to disregard Morgan's oft-repeated admonition against such bragging.

But the younger boy did not react, and Llewelyn realized with a distinct shock that the name meant nothing to him. He seemed to want to respond to Llewelyn's friendliness, but there was a certain wariness still in his eyes. 'I am Stephen de Hodnet.' He hesitated again. 'You do not live in Shropshire, do you? I mean, if you are Welsh . . .'

The implication seemed clear; if he were Welsh, why was he not in Wales where he belonged? Llewelyn was more regretful than resentful, for this past fortnight had been the loneliest of his life. 'I'm staying at Caus Castle,' he said coolly, and reached for Sul's reins.

'Caus Castle!' The sudden animation in Stephen's voice took Llewelyn by surprise. 'Lord Robert Corbet's castle? You're living there?'

Llewelyn nodded, bemused. 'For now I am. My lady mother was wed a fortnight ago to Sir Hugh Corbet, Robert's brother. You know them?'

Stephen laughed. 'Who in Shropshire does not know the Corbets? They are great lords. My papa says they have more manors than a dog has fleas. In fact, he hopes to do homage to Lord Robert for the Corbet manor at Westbury.' And he then proceeded, unasked, to inform Llewelyn that he was the youngest son of Sir Odo de Hodnet, that the de Hodnets were vassals of Lord Fulk Fitz Warin, holding manors of Fitz Warin at Moston and Welbatch, that he was a page in Fitz Warin's household at Alberbury Castle.

Llewelyn was a little hazy about the intricacies of English land-holding, but he did know that a vassal was a tenant of sorts, holding land in return for rendering his overlord forty days of military service each year, and he was thus able to make some sense of this outpouring of names, places, and foreign phrases. What he could not at first understand was Stephen's sudden thawing, until he realized that the name Corbet was his entry into Stephen's world. It was, he thought, rather like that story Morgan once told him, a tale brought back by

17

the crusaders from the Holy Land, of a man who'd been able to gain access to a cave full of riches merely by saying the words 'Open Sesame!'

This realization gave Llewelyn no pleasure; it only reinforced his conviction that English values were beyond understanding. How else explain that he should win acceptance, not for what truly mattered, his blood-ties to Owain Fawr, the greatest of all Welsh princes, but for a marriage that he felt should never have been? All at once he was caught up in a surge of homesickness, a yearning for Wales so overwhelming that he found himself blinking back tears.

Stephen did not notice, had not yet paused for breath. '. . . and my papa says Caus is the strongest of all the border castles, that it could withstand a siege verily until Judgment Day. Tell me . . . is it true that Lord Robert has a woven cloth on the floor of his bedchamber?'

Llewelyn nodded. 'It is called a . . . a carpet, was brought back from the Holy Land.' He could see that Stephen was on the verge of interrogating him at tiresome length about a subject that interested him not at all, and he said quickly, 'But I know naught of castles, Stephen. Nor do I much like living in one. We do not have them in my land, you see.'

Stephen looked incredulous. 'None at all?'

'Just those that were built by the Normans. Our people live in houses of timber, but they're scattered throughout the mountains, not all clustered together like your English villages.'

It was obviously a novel thought to Stephen, that not all cultures and societies were modelled after his own. They were both sitting on the bank by the stream and he rolled over in the grass, propped his chin in his hands and said, 'Tell me more about the Welsh.'

Llewelyn no longer had any reservations about boasting of his bloodlines. Stephen was so woefully ignorant that it was truly a charitable act to enlighten him, he decided, and proceeded to acquaint Stephen with some of the more legendary exploits of his celebrated grandfather, giving his imagination free rein.

'And so,' he concluded, having at last run out of inspiration, 'when my grandfather died, his sons fought to see who would succeed him. My father was deprived of his rightful inheritance, and Gwynedd is now ruled by my uncles, Rhodri and Davydd.'

Welsh names were falling fast and free; to Stephen's unfamiliar ears, much like the musical murmurings of Yokethul Brook. But one fact he'd grasped quite clearly. A prince was a prince, be he Welsh or Norman, and he looked at Llewelyn with greatly increased respect. 'Wait,' he begged. 'Let me be sure I do follow you. Your grandfather was a Prince of . . . Gwynedd, and your lady mother is the daughter of a Prince of . . .?'

'Powys. Marared, daughter of Prince Madog ap Meredydd. My father was killed when I was a babe, and ere my mother wed Hugh Corbet, we lived with her kin in Powys . . .'

Llewelyn had not begun talking until he was nearly two, and since then, his mother often teased, he seemed bound and determined to make up for all that lost time. Now, with so satisfactory an audience as Stephen and a subject that was so close to his heart, he outdid himself, and Stephen learned that among the Welsh there was no greater sin than to deny hospitality to a traveller, that Welshmen scorned the chain-mail armour of the English knight, that Llewelyn's closest friends were boys named Rhys and Ednyved, and the ancient Welsh name for Shrewsbury was Pengwern.

The sun had taken on the dull red-gold haze of coming dusk as Llewelyn obligingly gave Stephen a lesson in the basics of Welsh pronunciation. 'Say Rhys like this: Rees. And Ed-nev-ed. Now try Gruffydd; it sounds like your Griffith. In Welsh, the double d is pronounced as th. So my little brother's name is spelled A-d-d-a, but we say it as A-tha, Welsh for Adam.' He paused, his head cocked. 'Do you hear that? Someone is calling your name.'

Stephen scrambled to his feet so fast he all but tumbled down the brook embankment. 'My brother! Jesu, but he'll flay me alive!'

'Why?'

'I coaxed him into taking me with him to Shrewsbury this morn. We agreed to meet at St George's bridge and I . . . I just forgot!'

'Well, cannot you say you're sorry and . . .'

Stephen shook his head, staring at the boys now mounting the crest of the hill. 'No, not with Walter. He . . . he's not much for forgiveness . . .'

The approaching boys looked to be about fourteen. The youngster in the lead had Stephen's butter-yellow hair. He strode up to Stephen and, without a word, struck the younger boy across the face, with enough force to send Stephen sprawling.

'We've been looking for you for nigh on two hours! I've a mind to leave you here, and damned well should!'

As Walter reached down and jerked Stephen to his feet, Llewelyn

19

came forward. He'd taken an instant dislike to Walter de Hodnet, but for Stephen's sake, he sought to sound conciliatory as he said, 'It was my fault, too. We wcrc talking and . . .'

Walter's eyes flicked to his face, eyes of bright blue, iced with sudden suspicion. 'What sort of lowborn riffraff have you taken up with now, Stephen?'

Llewelyn flushed. 'I am Llewelyn ab Iorwerth,' he said after a long pause; instinct was now alerting him to trouble. At the same time Stephen burst into nervous speech.

'He is a Welsh Prince, Walter, and . . . and he's been telling me all about Wales . . .'

'Oh, he has?' Walter said softly, and Stephen, who knew his brother well enough to be forewarned, tried to shrink back. But Walter still had a grip on his tunic. With his other hand, he grasped a fistful of Stephen's hair and yanked, until Stephen's head was drawn back so far that he seemed to be staring skyward, and was whimpering with pain.

'That's just what I could expect from you. No more common sense than the stupidest serf, not since the day you were born. So he's been telling you about Wales? Did he tell you, too, about the crops burned in the fields, the villages plundered, the women carried off?' Releasing Stephen, he swung around suddenly on Llewelyn.

'Suppose you tell him about it now. Tell my lack-wit brother about the border raids, tell him how brave your murdering countrymen are against defenceless peasants and how they run like rabbits when we send men-at-arms against them!'

Sul was grazing some yards away, and for several moments Llewelyn had been measuring the distance, wanting nothing so much as to be up on the gelding's back and off at a breakneck run. But with Walter's taunt, he froze where he was, pride temporarily prevailing over fear. He'd never run like a rabbit, never. But there was a betraying huskiness in his voice as he said, 'I have nothing to say to you.'

Walter was flanked by his two companions; they'd moved closer to Llewelyn, too close, and he took a backward step. But he dared retreat no farther, for the brook embankment was at his back and he did not know how to swim. He stood very still, head held high, for he'd once seen a stray spaniel face down several larger dogs by showing no fear. They stepped in, tightening the circle, but made no move to touch him. He was never to know how long the impasse might have lasted, for at that moment one of the boys noticed Sul.

'Damn me if he does not have his own mount! Where would a Welsh whelp get a horse like that?'

'Where do you think?' Walter, too, was staring at the chestnut, with frankly covetous eyes. 'You know what they say . . . scratch a Welshman, find a horse thief.'

Llewelyn felt a new and terrible fear, for he'd raised Sul from a spindle-legged foal, Sul was his pride, his heart's passion. He forgot all else, grabbed at Walter's arm as the older boy turned towards Sul. 'He's mine, to me! You leave him be!'

It was a grievous mistake, and he paid dearly for it. They were on him at once, all three of them, and he went down in a welter of thudding fists and jabbing elbows. He flailed out wildly, desperately, but he could match neither his assailants' strength nor their size, and he was soon pinned down in the trampled grass, Walter's knees on his chest, his mouth full of his own blood.

'Misbegotten sons of Satan, the lot of you!' Walter panted. 'Blood bastards, not worth the hanging . . .' And if the profanity sat self-consciously on his lips, flaunted as tangible proof of passage into the mysteries of manhood, the venom in his voice was not affectation, was rooted in a bias that was ageless, breathed in from birth.

'Know you what we mean to do now, Welsh rabbit? Pluck you as clean as a chicken . . .' He reached out, tore the crucifix chain from Llewelyn's neck. 'Spoils of war, starting with that chestnut horse you stole. You can damned well walk back to Wales, mother-naked, and just thank your heathen gods that we did not hang you for a horse thief! Go on, Philip, I'll hold him whilst you get his boots . . .'

Sul. They were going to take Sul. His bruised ribs, his bloodied nose, hurt and humiliation and impotent fury – all of that was nothing now, not when balanced against the loss of Sul. Llewelyn gave a sudden frantic heave, caught Walter off guard and rolled free. But as quick as he was, the third boy was quicker, and before he could regain his feet, an arm had crooked around his neck, jerking him backward. And then Walter's fist buried itself in his mid-section and all fight went out of him; he lay gasping for breath, as if drowning in the very air he was struggling to draw into his lungs.

'Walter, no!' Stephen had at last found his voice. 'He's not a nobody, he's highborn and kin by marriage to Lord Corbet of Caus! He's stepson to Hugh Corbet, Walter, and nephew of Lord Robert!'

Suddenly all Llewelyn could hear was his own laboured breathing.

Then one of the boys muttered, 'Oh, Christ!' and that broke the spell. They all began to talk at once. 'How do we know he's not lying?' 'But, Walter, do you not remember? Lord Fulk was talking at dinner last week about a Corbet marriage to a Welshwoman of rank, saying the Corbets hoped to safeguard their manors from Welsh raids with such a union.' 'Will he go whining to Corbet, d'you think?' 'Since you got us into this, Walter, you ought to be the one to put it right!'

After a low-voiced conference, they moved apart and Walter walked back to Llewelyn. The younger boy was sitting up, wiping mud from his face with the sleeve of his tunic. He was bruised and scratched and sore, but his injuries were superficial. His rage, however, was all-consuming, blotting all else from his brain. He raised slitted dark eyes to Walter's face; they glittered with hatred made all the more intense by his inability to act upon it.

'Here,' Walter said tersely, dropping the crucifix on the ground at Llewelyn's feet. The conciliatory gesture was belied by the twist of his mouth, and when Llewelyn did not respond, he leaned over, grasped Llewelyn's arm with a roughness that was a more honest indicator of his true feelings.

'Come, I'll help you up.' Walter's voice softened, took on a honeyed malice. 'You need not be afraid,' he drawled, and Llewelyn spat in his face. It was utterly unpremeditated, surprised Llewelyn almost as much as Walter, and he realized at once that his Corbet kinship would avail him little against an offence of such magnitude. But for the moment the incredulous outrage on Walter's face was worth it, worth it all.

Walter gasped, and then lunged. Shock slowed his reflexes, however, and Llewelyn was already on his feet. He sprinted for Sul, and the gelding raised its head, expectant, for this was a game they often played and Llewelyn had become quite adroit at vaulting up on to the horse's back from a running jump. But as he chanced a glance back over his shoulder, he saw he was not going to make it; Walter was closing ground with every stride. Llewelyn swerved, tripped, and sprawled face down in the high grass. There was no time for fear, it all happened too fast, Walter was on top of him, and this time the older boy was in deadly earnest, he meant to inflict pain, to maim, and his was the advantage of four years and fully forty pounds.

'Walter, stop!' The other boys had reached them, were struggling to drag Walter off him. Llewelyn heard their voices as if from a great distance; there was a roaring in his ears. His right eye was swelling rapidly, and an open gash just above the eyelid was spurting so much blood that he was all but blinded. Through a spangled crimson haze, he caught movement and brought his arm up in a futile attempt to ward off the blow. But the expected explosion of pain did not come; instead, the voices became louder, more strident.

'Jesus God, Walter, think what you do! Do you not hear your brother? The boy's not fair game, he's kin to the Corbets!'

'He's talking sense, Walter. You've got to let the boy be!'

'I intend to . . . as soon as he does beg my forgiveness.' Walter was now straddling Llewelyn, holding the boy immobile with the weight of his own body, and he shifted his position as he spoke, driving his knee into Llewelyn's ribcage until he cried out in pain. 'We're waiting on you. Tell me how sorry you are, and . . . whilst you be at it, let's hear you admit the truth about your God-cursed kinfolk, that there's not a Welshman born who's not a thief and cut-throat.'

Pain had vanquished pride; Llewelyn was frightened enough and hurting enough to humble himself with an apology. But it was unthinkable to do what Walter was demanding.

'*Cer i uffern!*' It was the worst oath Llewelyn knew, one that damned Walter to the fires of Hell. The words were no sooner out of his mouth than his face was pressed down into the dirt and his arm twisted up behind his back. He'd been braced for pain, but not for this, searing, burning, unendurable. The shouting had begun again. Walter's mouth was against his ear. 'Say it,' he hissed. 'Say it, or by Christ I'll damned well break your arm!'

No. No, never. Did he say that aloud? Someone was gasping, 'Sorry . . .' Surely not his voice. 'Welshmen are . . . thieves . . .' No, not him.

'Again . . . louder this time.'

'Enough, Walter! It was different when we did not know who he was. But Philip and I want no part of this. You do what you want with him, but we're going home . . . and straightaway!'

The pain in his arm subsided so slowly that Llewelyn did not at once realize he was free. Time passed. He was alone in the meadows now, but he did not move, not until he felt a wet muzzle on the back of his neck. It was Sul, nuzzling his tunic, playing their favourite game, seeking out hidden apple slices. Only then did tears well in Llewelyn's eyes. He welcomed them, needing to cry, needing the

23

catharsis, the healing, but it was not to be; this was a hurt beyond tears, and they trickled into the blood smearing his cheek, dried swiftly in the dying heat of the setting sun.

Priding himself on his horsemanship, Llewelyn had never felt the lack of a saddle before. Now, with his right arm all but useless, with no saddle pommel to grip, the once-simple act of mounting was suddenly beyond his capabilities. Again and again he grasped Sul's mane, struggled to pull himself up on to the gelding's back. Again and again he slid back, defeated. But Sul's placid temperament stood him in good stead; the chestnut did no more than roll its eyes sideways, as if seeking to understand this queer new game Llewelyn was set upon playing, and at last, sobbing with frustration, Llewelyn was able to pull himself up on to Sul's withers. He was promptly sick, clinging to Sul's mane while his stomach heaved and the sky whirled dizzily overhead, a surging tide of sunset colours spinning round and round like a child's pinwheel, until the very horizon seemed a-tilt and all the world out of focus.

He headed the gelding back towards Caus Castle; he had nowhere else to go. Village life ceased at dusk, for only the wealthy could afford the luxury of candles and rushlight, and the little hamlets were deserted, his passage heralded only by the barking of dogs. It was well past nightfall by the time he was approaching Westbury. He had a hazy half-formed hope that he might somehow sneak unseen into the castle bailey, and then up into the keep, to the upper chamber where Robert Corbet's three young sons slept. How he was to accomplish this miraculous feat he had no idea, and it was rendered irrelevant now by the sudden appearance of a small body of horsemen.

Llewelyn drew rein, for he'd recognized the lead rider. Hugh Corbet, his mother's new husband.

'Llewelyn! Where in the name of Jesus have you been, boy? Your mother's frantic and little wonder. We've been out looking for you since Vespers!'

The search party carried lanterns, and as Hugh reined in beside Llewelyn, a glimmer of light fell across the boy's face, only a flicker of illumination, but enough. Hugh drew in his breath sharply. 'My God, lad, what happened to you?'

There was some talk of summoning a doctor from Shrewsbury, but it was finally decided that Llewelyn's need was not so great as that.

24

As the lady of the manor, Emma Corbet was, of necessity, a skilled apothecary, as adroit in stitching up wounds, applying poultices, and brewing healing herbs as any physician. It was she who applied a salve of mutton fat and resin to Llewelyn's bruised ribs, bathed his swollen eye in rose-water, and washed the blood and dirt from his face.

No, his shoulder was not dislocated, she said soothingly. If it was, he'd be unable to move the arm at all. She did feel certain, though, that his wrist was sprained; see how it was swelling? She'd need cold compresses for the eye, hot towels for the wrist, and her cache of herbs, she directed, and her maids speedily departed the bed-chamber, leaving Llewelyn alone with Emma and Marared, his mother.

Voices sounded beyond the door. Llewelyn recognized one as his stepfather's; the other belonged to Robert Corbet, Hugh's elder brother. 'Do you not think you're making too much of this, Hugh? Boys will get into squabbles. Look at my Tom, how he –'

'You have not seen him yet, Rob,' Hugh said grimly and pushed the door back.

Robert Corbet, Baron of Caus, was only twenty-eight, but he was decisive by nature and long accustomed to the exercise of authority. At sight of Llewelyn, his face hardened. Kneeling by the boy, he said, 'Who did this to you, lad?'

Marared was standing behind her son. She reached out, let her hand rest on his shoulder. Emma shook her head, said, 'It is no use, Rob. He's not said a blessed word so far. Mayhap if we left him alone with Hugh and Margaret . . .'

Llewelyn's head came up at that. Her name is Marared. Marared, not Margaret. The words hovered on his lips; he bit them back with visible effort, and turned his face away, stayed stubbornly silent.

Servants had carried bedding into the chamber, were spreading blankets down on the floor by the bed, and Hugh smiled at Llewelyn, said, 'Margaret and I thought it would be best if you passed the night here with us. Now why do we not see about getting you out of those begrimed clothes?'

Llewelyn rose obediently, let his stepfather strip off the bloodied, torn tunic, his shirt, chausses, and linen braies, the knee-length cowhide boots. But as Hugh pulled the blanket back and the boy slid under the covers, he said, very softly yet very distinctly, 'My mother's name is Marared.'

25

Hugh stood looking down at his stepson. He did not say anything, but Llewelyn had an unsettling suspicion that he understood, understood all too well.

Left alone at last, Llewelyn sought in vain to make himself comfortable on the npallet. He held the compresses to his injured eye, tried not to think of anything at all. When the door opened, he did not look up, believing it to be his mother. But the footsteps were heavier, a man's tread. Llewelyn raised up awkwardly on his elbow, and his heart began to thud against his sore ribs, for it was Morgan.

Marared had been only fifteen when Llewelyn was born, widowed the following year while pregnant with his brother. With Adda, small and frail and maimed, she was fiercely protective, but she'd tended from the first to treat her eldest son as if they were playfellows rather than mother and child. Llewelyn adored the dark, beautiful girl who teased him, laughed at his misdeeds, and taught him to view their troubles with light-hearted abandon. But it was Morgan who set the standards that structured his life, it was Morgan's approval that mattered. Instinctively he knew that his mother would forgive him any sin, no matter how great. Morgan would not and that made his good opinion the more precious. He shrank now from revealing his shame to Morgan; that the youthful priest should look upon him with contempt was a greater punishment than any pain Walter de Hodnet had inflicted.

Morgan was carrying a platter. Setting it down, he tossed a cushion on the floor by Llewelyn's pallet, and spreading the skirt of his cassock as if it were a woman's gown, he settled himself beside the boy.

'The Lady Emma has sent up some broth, and your lady mother thought you might like a slice of seed-cake.'

Llewelyn smiled wanly at that; his mother's invariable remedy for any childhood hurt was to offer sweets. Morgan leaned forward, spooned some broth into Llewelyn's mouth, and then turned the boy's head to the side, his eyes moving slowly over the bruises, contusions, and swellings.

'You're likely to have a scar over that eye,' he observed dispassionately and, not waiting for a response, fed Llewelyn another spoonful of soup. Putting the bowl aside, he turned towards the tray, handed Llewelyn a fresh compress.

'Are you ready now to tell me about it?'

26

Llewelyn flushed, shot Morgan a look of mute entreaty. But Morgan's grey eyes were unwavering, expectant. Llewelyn could not lie, not to Morgan. He swallowed, began to speak.

Shrewsbury. Stephen. The meadow. Walter de Hodnet, his fear, and 'Welshmen are thieves . . .' He held nothing of it back, spared himself nothing. But he could not meet Morgan's eyes, could not bear to see Morgan's dawning disgust. He looked instead at Morgan's hands, linked loosely in his lap; they were beautifully shaped, fingers long and supple, a symmetry marred only by the bitten gnawed nails, chewed down to the very quick, an incongruous quirk in one with such a disciplined nature. Llewelyn kept his gaze riveted on those hands, saw them flex, tense, and then slowly unclench.

When Llewelyn had at last run out of words, one of the hands reached out, touched his hair in what seemed strangely like a caress. But Morgan's caresses were sparingly doled out and surely would not be given now, not after what he'd just confessed? And yet the hand had not been withdrawn; it was brushing the hair back from his forehead, lingering.

'Morgan . . .' Bewildered, utterly at a loss.

'I'm proud of you, lad.'

'Proud?' Llewelyn choked. 'I shamed you, shamed us all. Did you not understand? I did what he demanded, I dishonoured my blood, grovelled before him.'

'And would you rather he'd broken your arm, mayhap maimed you for life?'

'No, but . . .'

'Listen to me, Llewelyn. Courage is a commendable quality, and a true test of manhood. You showed that today, and may rightly take pride in it. But for a prince of our people, courage alone is not enough; it must be tempered with common sense. You showed that, too, today, lad, showed you were able to make a realistic recognition of superior strength. There's no shame in that, Llewelyn, none whatsoever. Be thankful rather that, in a world full of fools, Our Lord Saviour has blessed you with brains as well as boldness of spirit.'

'I was so ashamed . . .' Llewelyn whispered. 'Not for the apology, but for the other, for saying my countrymen are thieves and cut-throats . . .'

'And does saying it make it so?' Morgan shook his head. 'Do you know what the English say of us, Llewelyn? They say a Welshman's

27

word is worth spit in the wind . . . and they are right, lad. An oath given to an enemy is made to be broken; we understand that. We use what weapons we have available to us, and when we fight, we fight on our terms, not theirs.

'These are lessons you must learn, Llewelyn, and learn well. The day will come when you'll return to Gwynedd, lay claim to the lands your uncles now rule. You must be ready to win back what is yours by right, and above all, to deal with the English.

'We are not a numerous people. For every Welshman born, the Lord God has seen fit to beget twenty of English blood. Our princes have been forced to accept the English king as their liege lord. But we have not been subjugated as the Saxons were, we have not become a nation of serfs and bondsmen. These Norman lords who rule England, and would rule Wales if they could, hate us above all others . . . and still we live free, with our own princes, our own ways and customs.'

Llewelyn nodded eagerly, intent on a lesson he'd long ago learned.

'This is because when the English come on to our lands,' Morgan continued, 'our people drive their livestock up into the hills and then they hide themselves. The English burn our houses, but we are not bound to the land like the English peasants, and when they withdraw, our people rebuild. Nor do we despair when we fight the English and find ourselves outnumbered. When we see ourselves losing, we retreat . . . and hit them again on the morrow. When they send armies into our land, we fade away into the woods, and they cannot find us.

'If you understand this, Llewelyn, you must understand, too, that you've no reason to reproach yourself, no reason to feel shame.'

It seemed nothing less than miraculous to Llewelyn that Morgan could heal the worst of his hurts with so little effort, and he gave the priest a grateful smile. Morgan smiled back and then said briskly, 'Now . . . is it your wish that I tell the Corbets about this boy?'

Llewelyn hesitated. Although he was feeling more and more comfortable about the role he'd played in that frightening encounter by Yokethul Brook, he still did not relish the prospect of confiding in his Corbet kin. 'No,' he said slowly. 'No matter what they did to him, he'd just take it out on Stephen afterward. I'd rather we let it lie, Morgan.' For now, he added silently. Walter de Hodnet. Not a name to be forgotten.

Morgan watched as Llewelyn touched his fingers to the puffy, discoloured skin over his eye, to the swelling bruise high on his cheekbone, almost as if he were taking inventory of his injuries. And that, the priest knew, was precisely what the boy was doing, making a private acknowledgment of a debt due. Morgan sighed. Vengeance is mine, saith the Lord. On that, Holy Church spoke quite clearly. But his people parted company with their Church on this issue; they did not believe in forgiving a wrong, forgetting an injury . . . ever.

'Here,' he said, handing Llewelyn a brimming goblet. 'The Lady Emma mixed some bryony root in wine, to ease your pain and help you sleep. Drink it down and I'll stay with you till it does take effect. I have something of great importance to tell you. We learned this noon of a death . . . a death which will change the lives of us all.'

Llewelyn sat up. 'Who, Morgan?'

'Young Henry, the English King's eldest son and heir. We had word today that he died in France on the eleventh of June, of the bloody flux. He knew he was dying and pleaded with his father to come to him so they might be reconciled ere he died. But Henry did not believe him, feared it was a trick. They are an accursed family, in truth, the Devil's brood.' He shook his head, made the sign of the cross.

'What will happen now, Morgan?'

Ordinarily the priest would have insisted that Llewelyn be the one to tell him that. But it was late and the boy was bruised and sore, in no condition to be interrogated about lessons of history and statecraft. 'You know, Llewelyn, that the English give all to the firstborn son. Since young Henry had no son of his own, the heir to the English throne is now his brother Richard. So this means that Richard will one day be King.'

'That is not good for us, is it, Morgan? If Richard is as able a soldier as men say . . .'

'He is.'

Llewelyn swallowed some more wine. 'I'm sorry Henry died,' he said regretfully. 'Since he was to be King one day, you made me learn as much as I could about him. And now all that effort goes for naught and I have to begin all over again with Richard!'

That triggered one of Morgan's rare laughs. 'It is even worse than you know, lad. It is very likely that one of Richard's brothers might one day be King after him, so that means you must familiarize yourself with Geoffrey and John, too.'

'All three? But why, Morgan? Richard will surely marry and

beget a son. How, then, can Geoffrey or John ever be King?'

Morgan did not respond at once, seemingly lost in thought. 'Aye,' he said at last. 'I reckon you are old enough to know. I take it that your mother and her brothers have spoken to you of carnal matters, explaining how a woman gets with child?'

'Of course! Mama and my uncle Gruffydd told me what I needed to know ages ago.'

A youngster growing up around livestock could not remain sheltered for long, and Llewelyn's were an uninhibited people who viewed sex as a natural urge and a very enjoyable pleasure; nor was theirs a society in which the stigma of illegitimacy carried much sting. Morgan was not surprised, therefore, by the boy's emphatic answer.

Actually, Llewelyn knew far more about carnal matters than Morgan suspected, for he knew about Gwynora. The average parish priest, be he Welsh or English or French, was not a well-educated man; Morgan was an exception. Most were simple villagers, and the burden of celibacy was one not many could shoulder with equanimity. It was not at all uncommon for these lonely men to take to their hearths wives and live-in concubines, and while the Church officially decried these liaisons, they were tacitly accepted by most people as inevitable and even natural. Unlike so many of his fellow clerics, Morgan had never taken a wife or hearth-mate, and the occasions were few when he'd found his vow of chastity too onerous for mortal flesh. He was always quite discreet and it was purely by chance that Llewelyn had found out about Gwynora. He had told no one, and would never have dreamed of saying a word to Morgan; it gave him a warm glow of pleasure to keep a secret for this man he so loved.

'I know all about carnal matters, Morgan,' he said loftily. 'But what has that to do with one of Richard's brothers becoming King?'

Morgan hesitated. 'Richard is a brilliant battle commander, one of the best in Christendom. Nor, for all his tempers, is he an impious man. It is well known that he yearns to take the cross.'

'You mean go on pilgrimage to the Holy Land?'

Morgan nodded and then hesitated again. 'However, the fact remains that Richard has been known to indulge in an unnatural vice. He would rather satisfy his lust with men than with women.'

Llewelyn's eyes widened. 'But . . . but how?' he blurted out, saw Morgan frown and lapsed into a chastened silence. Men laying with other men? How was that possible? He'd seen enough animals mating to be able to envision a coupling between a man and woman, but when it came to coupling between men, his imagination failed him.

'Morgan . . . do Richard's brothers share this sin?'

'It is not a hereditary vice, Llewelyn, does not pass with the blood,' Morgan said dryly. 'Young Henry was happily wed, though childless. Geoffrey's sins are beyond counting, but he does confine those of the flesh to adultery. As for John, his wenching is notorious. As young as he is, he has at least one bastard and seems destined for a life of debauchery and lechery.' His mouth tightened.

'They are not admirable men, lad, but one of them will one day be England's King, and your lives will be inextricably entwined, yours and his. Know thine enemy, Llewelyn. I can teach you no more valuable lesson than that.'

'Lessons? At this time of night? Good God, Morgan, have you no mercy?' Marared had come quietly into the room. Laughing at Morgan, she bent over Llewelyn's pallet, enveloping him in a perfumed cloud.

'Here, darling, I thought you should have a pillow tonight. And I brought you this . . .' She opened her palm. 'See? It's a coral pater noster. You put it under your pillow and you'll not be troubled by bad dreams.'

She began to adjust the covers, tucking him in, all the while keeping up a running commentary about his 'battle scars', telling him of fights his father had got into as a youngster. He had reached the age where he'd begun to shy away from caresses, and she confined herself to a playful kiss on the tip of his nose, saying cheerfully, 'Get some sleep now, sweeting, and when next there is a full moon, we'll go out by the moat and catch a frog. Then we'll draw a circle around it, throw a handful of salt about, and you whisper to the frog the name of the wretch who gave you that fearsome black eye . . . and within a month, he'll find himself covered with loathsome, hairy warts!'

She got the response she was aiming for; her son grinned. But as she straightened up, Morgan touched her elbow, drew her away from the pallet.

'I do wish, Madame,' he murmured, 'that you would refrain from filling the boy's head with such fanciful thoughts. Superstitions of that sort are rooted in pagan rites, have no place in Christian belief.'

Marared laughed, unrepentant. 'Do not be such a stick, Morgan!' But then her amusement chilled as if it had never been. The dark

31

eyes narrowed, the full red mouth thinned noticeably. It was as if he were of a sudden looking at a different woman altogether.

'I want the names, Morgan.'

'Names, Madame?'

'The names of the hellspawn who did that to my son,' she hissed. 'I know he told you, he tells you everything.'

'He does not want you to know, Madame. It's better forgotten.'

'Forgotten? That is my son, flesh of my flesh! I'll not let –'

'Mama?'

They both turned back towards the bed. Marared leaned down, smiled at her son. 'Are you not sleepy yet, sweeting?'

'Yes . . .' The day's trauma and the medicinal wine had loosened Llewelyn's tongue at last. 'Mama, I do hate it here. So does Adda. I'm so homesick, Mama. I miss Rhys and Ednyved and Uncle Gruffydd and . . .'

'Ah, Llewelyn . . .' Marared's eyes filled with tears.

'Please, Mama, can we not go back where we belong? Can we not go home?'

'You will, lad,' Morgan said quietly. 'I promise you that the day shall come when you will.'

Llewelyn stared up at him and then turned his head aside on the pillow. 'You mean we have to stay here for now.'

'Yes . . . for now.' Morgan stepped back, stood looking down at the boy. 'But you will go back to Wales, Llewelyn. You will go home.'

June, 1187
Shropshire, England

'Think you, then, that there'll be war?'

Hugh Corbet hesitated. It was no easy thing to be a younger brother in an age in which all passed by law to a man's eldest son. But Hugh had been luckier than most. His was a family of considerable wealth; the Corbets held lands not only in Shropshire, but in Normandy, Warwickshire, Worcestershire, and Wales. Robert Corbet had inherited the barony of Caus, but there were manors to spare for Hugh, too, and his relationship with his brother was blessedly free of the poisonous jealousy that bred such strife between a fortunate firstborn and his landless siblings.

Much of the time they were in harmony, working in tandem for the common Corbet good. But in this they were at odds. In this they were a House divided, much like the rival royal masters they served, for Robert's loyalties lay with Richard, King Henry's eldest son and heir, and Hugh's sympathies went out to the beleaguered, aging King.

Hugh was silent, considering Robert's grim query. 'I would hope to God it will not come to that, Rob,' he said at last. 'Father against son – that is the ugliest of all feuds, goes against the natural order of things.'

Robert took this as a veiled jab at Richard, the unfilial son. 'It would never have come to this if Henry would but formally recognize Richard as his heir!'

Hugh had to concede the truth of that. Finding himself forced to defend the indefensible, he at once took the offensive, saying sharply, 'Be that as it may, Richard had no right to ally himself with the King of France – not against his own sire!'

'You know damned well why he felt that need, Hugh! With their brother Geoffrey dead in France last summer, that leaves but Richard and John in line for the succession, and Richard knows all too well that his father loves him not. He knows, too, that Henry has ever favoured John. What else can Richard think, except that his father means to raise John up to the place that is rightfully his?'

'And a right fine fear that be,' Hugh scoffed, 'one to cover a multitude of sins. You know fully as well as I that Henry could anoint John as the very King of Heaven for all it'd avail him. The lords of this realm would never countenance so flagrant a breach of the laws of inheritance. Nor can you doubt the outcome. Whatever John might be given, he'd not long hold – not against Richard. No, Rob, if that be the balm Richard uses to soothe his conscience, he is a man in need of absolution.'

Robert's face was mottled, splotched with resentful red. 'Richard is to be our next King, should God so will it, and I'll not have you speak ill of him in my hearing.'

Hugh sighed. By now he could recite the dialogue verbatim for these acrimonious exchanges. Rob was as blind as a barn owl in noon-bright sun, dazzled by Richard's celebrated skill with a sword. Mayhap it was true that he was the finest soldier in Christendom, but if he had in him the makings of a good king, Hugh had yet to see any signs of it. Like as not, he'd pawn London itself to raise the gold needed for his foreign wars. And John . . . would John be any better? Hugh thought not.

He came abruptly to his feet. Why offend Rob and unsettle himself . . . to what end? Let it lie.

They were sequestered in the uppermost chamber of the castle keep, alone but for a bored page and a dozing mastiff, Robert's faithful shadow. The window was unshuttered; in winter it would be screened with oiled and thinly scraped hide, but this was summer and it was open to sun and sound from the tiltyard below. Hugh went to it and watched for a while.

'What do you watch?' The question was polite in tone, conciliatory in intent; Robert thrived on family discord no more than Hugh.

'Llewelyn and some of his friends.' As Robert joined him, Hugh gestured towards a small group of youngsters gathered below. Llewelyn was mounted on a burnished chestnut gelding; as the boys watched, he lowered his lance, took aim, and sent the gelding cantering across the tiltyard. He hit the target off-centre and the quintain swung about in a wide arc, the sandbag slicing through the air like an opponent's counter-blow. It should have sent him tumbling from the saddle to the straw meant to soften youthful falls. But

Llewelyn twisted sideways in the saddle, leaned so far to his left that it seemed inevitable he'd be unhorsed, and the sandbag swept by harmlessly overhead.

Hugh grinned. It was a showy stunt, an undeniably impressive feat of horsemanship, one Hugh had seen before. Robert had not, however, and he swore in startled wonder.

'How in Christ did he do that without breaking his neck?'

Hugh laughed. 'You'd not credit what I've seen that lad do on a horse. I truly believe the Welsh do learn to ride even ere they're weaned.'

Below them, Stephen de Hodnet was taking his turn upon Llewelyn's gelding. He, too, hit the quintain awry and, seconds later, went sprawling into the straw, with a bruising impact that earned him no sympathy from the two watching men; they had suffered too many such spills themselves during their own years as knightly apprentices.

Reclaiming Sul, Llewelyn led it over to the fence, held out the reins to his brother. Adda shook his head, but Llewelyn persisted, manoeuvring the gelding up to the fence so the younger boy could mount. Once securely in the saddle, Adda shed much of his awkwardness, and while he did not attempt the quintain, he put the gelding through several intricate manoeuvres, showed himself to be a better rider than most of Llewelyn's friends.

Robert frowned. No matter how often he told himself that it was unchristian to feel such abhorrence of deformity, he could not control his distaste, could not keep his eyes from Adda's twisted leg. Thank the Lord Jesus that his Tom was sound of limb, that the younger boys, too, were whole.

'He lacks for spirit, that one. If not for Llewelyn's coaxing, I dare say he'd never stir from the hearth.'

'Well, it's hard on the lad, Rob, being lame. What future has he, after all? Under Welsh law, that crooked leg bars him from any claim to his father's lands.'

Robert shrugged. 'He's not like to starve. Their law also holds that he must be provided for.'

'True, but would you want to be taken care of . . . like a woman? At thirteen, Adda's old enough to feel the shame of it.'

'I suppose,' Robert agreed, without interest. It was not that he wished Adda ill, merely that he regretted his engrafting on to the Corbet family tree. It was fortunate indeed that Llewelyn was of

35

more promising stock. 'Tell me, Hugh, what plans have you made for Llewelyn's future?'

'Well, it is the custom in Wales for boys to be placed with a local lord when they reach fourteen or so. Whilst in his service, they learn the use of arms, the tactics of warfare, much like our youths do whilst serving as squires. Margaret thought to send Llewelyn back to her brothers for such training, but I think I've persuaded her that we should place him as a squire in a Norman household. I dare say the boy will balk at first, but I feel such a move would be in his best interest.'

'That is just what I'd hoped you'd say, Hugh. You see, when I was in London at Whitsuntide, I had the good fortune to encounter His Grace, the Earl of Chester. Naturally the conversation turned to our common interests, protecting our respective lands from Welsh raids. He was most interested to learn that your stepson is the grandson of Owain Fawr, and he suggested that he find a place for the boy in his household.'

'Jesu!' This was so far above Hugh's expectations that he was, for the moment, speechless, and Robert grinned, well pleased with himself.

'I see I need not tell you what an opportunity this will be for the boy, for us all. Chester is one of the greatest lords of the realm, and as shrewd as a fox for all his youth. He saw at once the advantage of befriending a boy who might one day rule in his grandfather's stead. Llewelyn has the blood-right, after all, and most assuredly the spirit. With luck . . .' He shrugged again, said:

'But a chance like this, to come to manhood in an Earl's household . . . Loyalties given in youth often last for life. As Chester's squire, the brilliance of Llewelyn's world cannot help but eclipse all he's learned in the woodlands of Wales. He'll find himself amongst the greatest Norman lords, at the royal court, and in time he'll come to embrace Norman values, to adopt Norman traditions as his own.'

Robert paused. 'Do not misunderstand me, Hugh. I know how fond you are of the boy, and I find him a likable lad myself. But I cannot help feeling a certain disappointment that, after four years, he clings so tenaciously to the teachings of an undeniably primitive people. Despite all the advantages you've given him, Llewelyn remains so stubbornly –'

'Welsh?' Hugh suggested dryly, and Robert laughed. He'd actually been about to say 'untamed' before thinking better of it, and he did not demur now at his brother's interpretation; they were, he thought, merely different ways of saying the same thing.

'Well, I shall talk to Margaret this forenoon, tell her about Chester's offer . . .' Hugh began, and then turned towards the opening door.

'Ah, Margaret, we were just speaking of you. Rob has – Margaret?'

Upon seeing Marared for the first time, Hugh had blessed his luck, suddenly found himself eager to consummate their political alliance in the marriage bed. Marared was a beautiful woman, if rather exotic by English standards, and after four years of marriage, he still took considerable pleasure in the sight of her. But she had no smile for him now, and the golden glow that owed so little to the sun was gone. Bleached of colour, her face was ashen, and her lashes were sooty thickets, smudged with the kohl bleeding into a wet trail of tears.

She paid no heed to Robert, crossed to her husband. 'Hugh, we must go home. We must go back to Powys at once. It is my brother Owain. He . . . he's been murdered.'

There was a word in Welsh, *hiraeth*, that translated as 'longing', but it meant much more, spoke of the Welsh love of the land, of the yearning of the exile for family, friends, home. Whenever he was claimed by *hiraeth*, Llewelyn would flee to the heights of Breiddyn Craig, and there he would spend hours in sun-drenched solitude, gazing out over the vales of the Rivers Hafren, Vyrnwy, and Tanat. Now he was back at last, sitting on Sul before the grey stones and slate roof of Llanfair, the church of St Mary.

This ancient church in the vale of Meifod was the traditional burial place for the princes of Powys; here his mother's father had been entombed and here his slain uncle would be laid to rest. He sought to summon up grief for this uncle he could little remember, but to no avail. He'd come back for a funeral, to mourn a man who was his blood kin, and yet as he looked upon the wooded hills that rose up behind the church, he felt only exhilaration, felt like a caged gerfalcon, suddenly free to soar up into the sun-bright azure sky.

Here he'd passed the first ten years of his life. Seven miles to the south was Castell Coch, the ancestral seat for the princes of Powys. His mother's family had a *plas* – a palace – less than a mile away at Mathraval. The woods of mountain ash and oak and sycamore, the

37

river teeming with trout and grayling, dappled by summer sun and shadowed by willow and alder – each stone was known to him, each hawthorn hedge rooted deep in memory. He was home.

He glanced sideways at his companion, one of his stepfather's squires. Should he tell Alan of his family's *plas*, he knew what the other boy would expect, a Norman edifice of soaring stone and mortar, for while most castles were timbered fortresses, the word 'palace' conjured up images of grandeur and luxury. Llewelyn had been to London, had seen the Tower and the palace at Westminster, and he'd heard of the splendours of Windsor Castle. He knew there was nothing in Wales to compare to the magnificence of the Norman court, and he cared not at all that this was so.

He laughed suddenly, and when Alan shot him a curious look, he slid from Sul, handed the squire'the reins.

'I'd be obliged if you looked after Sul, Alan. Should my lady mother or stepfather ask for me, concoct what excuse you will.'

Alan grinned. 'Consider it done. But are you sure you'd not want company?'

Llewelyn was tempted, but only briefly. He thought of Alan as a friend, but his were memories, emotions, sensations that no Norman could hope to understand.

The Vyrnwy was free of the mud and debris that so often polluted English rivers, for there were no towns to despoil its purity with refuse and human waste. Llewelyn could see chalk-white pebbles glimmering on the shallow river bottom, see the shadows cast by fish feeding midst the wavering stalks of water weeds. He forgot entirely that his uncle had died by this very river, his *plas* at Carreghova besieged by a man who was Llewelyn's own first cousin, Gwenwynwyn, Prince of southern Powys. He forgot his mother's tears, forgot his stepfather's ambitious plans for his future, forgot all but the here and now.

He'd walked these woods so often in memory, hearing the rustle of wood-mice and squirrels, the warning cries of overhead birds, sentinels ever on the alert for the intrusion of man into their domain. A fox come to the river to drink was slow to heed the alert and froze at sight of Llewelyn, muzzle silvered with crystal droplets of river water, black eyes bright as polished jet. Boy and fox stared at one another in rapt silence, and then Llewelyn snapped his fingers, freeing the fox to vanish into the shadows as if by sorcery; not a twig cracked, not a leaf rustled to mark its passing. Llewelyn laughed, walked on.

He felt no surprise when he broke through a clearing in the wood and came upon the boys by the river; somehow he'd known that he would find them here. The Vyrnwy had always been their favourite fishing stream.

Shyness was an alien emotion to Llewelyn, but he found himself suddenly ensnared by it now, reluctant to approach the youths who'd once been like his brothers. They were not talking, theirs the companionable silence born of the intimacy of blood and a bonding that had begun in the cradle. Watching them, Llewelyn felt an unexpected emotion stir, one closely akin to envy. He belonged here, too, fishing on the banks of the Vyrnwy with Ednyved and Rhys, but how to surmount the barriers built up by four years of English exile?

They were lounging on the grass in positions as characteristic as they were familiar: Rhys sitting upright, utterly intent upon the trout to be hooked, Ednyved sprawled on his back in the sun, fishing pole wedged into a pyramid of piled up rocks. And as ever, Llewelyn found himself marvelling that two boys so unlike could share the same blood. First cousins they were, but none seeing them together would ever have guessed the kinship.

Rhys shared with Llewelyn the pitch-black hair so common to their people, but while Llewelyn's eyes were dark, too, Rhys had the eyes of a Welsh mountain cat, purest, palest green. His unusual colouring, thick sable lashes, and features so symmetrical as to draw all eyes were, for him, a burden rather than a blessing. He loathed being fussed over, and yet his startling beauty of face doomed him to be forever fending off the gushing compliments and effusive embraces of his doting female relatives, who considered him quite the handsomest male child ever born and took great pride in showing him off to mothers and aunts of less favoured youngsters, to Rhys's utter disgust and the vast amusement of his friends.

It was possible to look upon his beauty – for there was no other word for it – and to note his slightness of build and conclude that there was a softness, a fragility about the boy. That was, Llewelyn had long ago learned, an impression so erroneous as to be utterly ludicrous, and not a little dangerous. Rhys was as hard, as unyielding as the flint of his native land; there was no give in him, none at all.

As for Ednyved, in all honesty he could only be described as homely. Lanky brown hair, deep-set eyes of a nondescript colour that was neither brown nor hazel but a murky shade somewhere in between, a mouth too wide and chin too thrusting, too prominent.

39

Big-boned even as a small boy, he seemed to have sprouted at least a foot since Llewelyn had seen him last, and Llewelyn had no doubts that when fully grown, Ednyved would tower head and shoulders above other men.

As he watched, Llewelyn suddenly found himself remembering a childhood game he'd long ago liked to play with his mother, in which they sought to identify people with their animal counterparts. Llewelyn had promptly pleased his sleekly independent and unpredictable mother by categorizing her as a cat. Hugh, whom he liked, he saw as an Irish wolfhound, a dog as bright as it was even-tempered. Robert Corbet, whom he did not like, he dubbed another sort of dog altogether, the courageous but muddle-headed mastiff. Morgan, too, was easy to classify, for Morgan was a priest with the soul of a soldier, a man who'd chosen of his own free will to fetter his wilder instincts to the stringent disciplines of his Church. Morgan, Llewelyn had explained to Marared, could only be a falcon, for the falcon was the most predatory of birds, a prince of the skies that could none the less be tamed to hunt at man's command. Adda, too, was a bird, a caged sparrow hawk, tethered to earth whilst his spirit pined only to fly; when he'd told his mother that, tears had filled her eyes. But when she wanted to know how he saw himself, Llewelyn grew reticent, evasive. From the day she'd taken him to the Tower of London to see the caged cats, he'd known what animal he wanted to claim as his own, the tawny-maned lion, but that was a vanity he was not willing to confess, even to his mother.

He had never tried to characterize Rhys or Ednyved, but it came to him now without need for reflection, for Rhys had the unpredictable edginess of a high-strung stallion and Ednyved all the latent power, the massive strength and lazy good humour of the tame bear he'd seen at London's Smithfield Fair.

Ednyved yawned and stretched, reaching for the woven sack that lay beside their bait pail. He shook several apples out on to the grass, tossed one to Rhys.

'I dare say you want one, too, Llewelyn?' he queried nonchalantly, and without looking up, sent an apple sailing through the air. It was remarkably accurate for a blind pitch, landed just where Llewelyn had been standing seconds before. He was no longer there, however, having recoiled with such vehemence that he bumped bruisingly into the nearest tree. Rhys, no less startled, spun around so precipitantly that he overturned the bait pail, and, as he cursed and Llewelyn took several deep breaths, trying to get his pulse rate back to normal, Ednyved rolled over in the grass and laughed and laughed.

'How in hellfire did you know I was there?' Llewelyn demanded, and Ednyved feigned surprise.

'How could I not, with you making enough noise to bestir the dead? Is that the English style of woodland warfare?'

He'd always been a lethal tease, and Llewelyn was not normally thin-skinned. But they'd not yet established the boundaries of their new relationship. Llewelyn opened his mouth to make a sharp retort, but Rhys was quicker. Rhys's pride was prickly and unpredictable, easily affronted, and he'd been embarrassed by his failure to take notice of Llewelyn. Glaring at his cousin, he snapped:

'And Llewelyn might well ask if this is the Welsh way of welcome!' Turning back to Llewelyn, he smiled, said, 'We thought you'd be home for your uncle's funeral, were watching for you.'

Llewelyn smiled back, and coming forward, he settled himself beside them on the grass. A silence fell between them, one that seemed likely to swallow up any words they could throw into the void. It was broken at last by Llewelyn; he heard himself making courteous queries about the health and well-being of their families, falling back upon all the obligatory conversational gambits to be shared between strangers. Nor did Rhys ease the awkwardness any by offering Llewelyn formal condolences for the death of his uncle.

Llewelyn would have liked to speak freely, to explain that he'd not known his uncle Owain all that well. But he felt constrained to respond with a conventional politeness, and thus found himself flying false colours, coming before them in the guise of a grief that was not his.

Rhys offered him an apple. 'Did your stepfather come with you?' he asked, as if he could possibly have had any interest in Hugh's whereabouts.

Llewelyn nodded. 'Hugh came on behalf of the Corbet family, as a gesture of respect to my mother's kin . . .' He stopped, for Ednyved had leaned forward, was regarding him with exaggerated attention.

'Why do you look at me like that? Has my face of a sudden turned green?'

'I was trying to decide,' Ednyved drawled, 'whether or not you'd picked up a French accent.'

Llewelyn tensed, but then he looked more closely at the other boy, saw that Ednyved's eyes were bright with friendly laughter.

41

'No French accent,' he said, and grinned. 'But I did spend some right uncomfortable days this spring worrying that I'd picked up the French pox!'

Ednyved's mouth twitched. 'Llewelyn!' With a frown towards his cousin. 'If you please, no bawdy talk – not before the lad here!' Ducking just in time as an apple whizzed past his head.

Seconds later, Rhys followed up his aerial assault with a direct frontal attack, and Ednyved, caught off balance, was knocked flat. Rhys's anger was more assumed than not, and their scuffling soon took on an almost ritualistic quality, for this was an old game, rarely played out in earnest, and likely to continue until one or the other of the combatants lost interest. In this case, the mock battle lasted until they noticed that Llewelyn had appropriated the rest of the apples and stretched himself out comfortably on the turf to watch, for all the world like a front-row spectator at a bear-baiting.

'Go to it, lads,' he said airily and, by common consent, they both pounced on him at once. For a few hectic moments all three boys were tumbling about on the river bank, until at last they lay panting in a tangled heap, lacking breath for anything but laughter.

After that, there seemed to be too much to say and not enough time in which to say it, and they plunged into the past as if fearing it might somehow be forgotten if it were not shared immediately, interrupting each other freely, trading insults and memories, laughing for laughter's sake alone.

Rhys had gone to the river to drink. Returning, he threw himself down in the grass, and broke into Ednyved's monologue to demand, 'When must you go back to England, Llewelyn?'

'I'm not going back,' Llewelyn said, at once capturing their undivided attention.

'You both know the history of my House, know how my uncles Davydd and Rhodri cheated my father and my other uncles of their rightful share of my grandfather's inheritance. They carved Gwynedd up between them as if it were a meat pie, forced my father, Owain Fawr's firstborn, into exile, brought about his death whilst I was still in my cradle. His blood is on their hands and they've yet to answer for it. I think it time they did.'

'You mean to avenge your father's death?' Rhys's green eyes were luminous, a-glitter with sudden excitement, but Ednyved seemed far more dubious.

'All know the English are born half-mad,' he said slowly, 'but I

42

wonder if the madness might not be in the water they drink or the air they breathe. How else explain that four short years amongst them could have so scattered your wits?'

Llewelyn was amused. 'Your faith in me is truly wondrous to behold, Ednyved. Think you that I'm such a fool as to challenge my uncles on my own, with only God on my side? I had a long talk this morn with my Uncle Gruffydd and he has sworn to give me his full backing, men who know war well and the money to pay them; he even offered the services of no less a soldier than Gwyn ab Ednywain. It is my intent, too, to join forces with my Uncle Cynan's two grown sons. They were denied their inheritance just as I was, giving us common cause against Davydd and Rhodri.'

'When you put it that way, it does not sound quite so crack-brained,' Ednyved conceded. 'But how in the name of the Lord Jesus did you ever get your lady mother and stepfather to give their consent?'

Llewelyn hesitated. 'Well, to be honest, I have not told them yet,' he admitted, and flushed when they both laughed.

'Can you truly blame me?' he protested. 'We'll be bound to have a God-awful row. I do not know whom my mother'll be more wroth with, me or my Uncle Gruffydd, for aiding and abetting me in this. As for Hugh, he's like to have an apoplectic fit. You see, he'd arranged for me to enter the household of a Norman Earl.'

Llewelyn shook his head in mock regret. 'Poor Hugh, how he has struggled to make of me a proper Norman. I once overheard his brother grumbling about turning a sow's ear into a silk purse, and I dare say Hugh has had moments when he's in heartfelt agreement!'

This last was said without rancour. Llewelyn never doubted that Hugh's fondness for him was genuine, but he'd come to understand that affection and bias could take root in the same soil. In this, he had the advantage of Rhys and Ednyved, and they looked so offended that he felt compelled to come to Hugh's defence.

'Yet he is a good man for all that. My mother has been quite content with him and I . . .' He grinned suddenly. 'I even came to forgive him for his greatest sin, that of not being born Welsh!'

But here they had no common meeting ground; neither Rhys nor Ednyved had English friends, English kin. Both looked blank, and then Rhys dismissed what he did not understand, said, 'You'll not let them talk you out of it?'

43

'No.' Llewelyn sat up, his eyes searching their faces with sudden sober intent. 'I shall have men to counsel me, men well lessoned in the ways of war. But no matter how much help I get from my Uncle Gruffydd or my cousins, I shall have to stand or fall on my own efforts. If I cannot convince people that my claim be just, if I cannot win their allegiance . . . Nor can I expect my blood to count for aught should I fall into Davydd's hands. And the risks will be no less for those who follow me.' He paused. 'My Uncle Gruffydd has agreed to speak with your fathers should you –'

'You want us to help you overthrow Davydd and Rhodri, to fight with you?' Rhys could wait no longer, burst out eagerly, 'Jesu, Llewelyn, need you even ask?'

Llewelyn smiled. 'What of you, Ednyved? Does Rhys speak for you, too?'

'I'd as soon speak for myself,' Ednyved said, sounding quite serious for once. 'I want to be sure I fully understand. We'd be camping out in the mountains of Gwynedd, harassing your uncles howsoever we could, living like outlaws, sleeping in the open, eating on the run, rebels with prices on our heads. Is that a fair summing up of what we could expect?'

'Very fair,' Llewelyn agreed, and a slow grin began to spread over Ednyved's face.

'Who could possibly turn down an offer like that?'

'It is settled then,' Rhys said briskly, never having doubted what his cousin's answer would be. As he spoke, he was rolling up the sleeve of his tunic. Before Llewelyn and Ednyved realized what he meant to do, he unsheathed his dagger and, without the slightest hesitation, drew it swiftly across the bared skin of his forearm.

'This is too important for mere words,' he explained composedly, watching the flow of his own blood with indifferent eyes. 'For this, we must swear in blood.'

It was a gesture as irresistible as it was melodramatic, at least to Llewelyn. Ednyved looked rather less enthusiastic, and when Rhys passed him the bloodied dagger, he took it with such reluctance that Llewelyn burst out laughing.

'Since you share the same blood as Rhys, mayhap you could swear, too, in his,' he gibed, and Ednyved grimaced, drew a few drops of blood.

'Here, my lord princeling,' he grunted. 'Your turn.'

Llewelyn made a far more modest cut than Rhys, saying, 'If I'm to spill my blood, I'd as soon spill it in Gwynedd.' And rising, he searched the clearing until he'd gathered a handful of rock moss. This he brought back to Rhys, and leaning over, he applied it to the other boy's arm.

'Hold this upon the cut till the bleeding ceases or you might well end up as the first casualty of my war,' he said and laughed again, realizing that he was as happy at this moment as he'd ever been in his life.

Hugh Corbet was surprised to find the great hall all but deserted; as in England, the hall was the heart of Welsh home-life. But then he heard the voices, angry, accusing, and he understood. At the far end of the hall his wife and her elder brother Gruffydd were standing, and even Hugh, who knew no Welsh other than a few endearments Marared had taught him in bed, could tell at once that they were quarrelling, quarrelling bitterly. Gruffydd's retainers and servants had wisely fled the battlefield; only Llewelyn, Adda, and Morgan ap Bleddyn, his wife's chaplain, were still in the hall.

As Hugh moved up the centre aisle, Gruffydd turned on his heel and stalked out of the door behind the dais, slamming it resoundingly behind him. Hugh was secretly amused that his wife should be giving her brother such grief. He had discovered early on in his marriage that Welshwomen were more outspoken and less submissive than their Norman sisters, and while he'd learned to accept Marared on her own terms, it pleased him to see Gruffydd reaping what he had sown. For certès, a society in which women were not taught their proper place was bound to lack harmony, a natural sense of order.

But he was taken aback by what happened next. Marared swung around on her eldest son, put a question to him, and when he shook his head, she slapped him across the face. Hugh was astonished, for he'd never seen her raise her hand to Llewelyn before, not even on occasions when the boy richly deserved it. He hastened towards them, wondering what sins would loom so large in her eyes.

Could Llewelyn have set his heart upon trading his gelding for an untamed stallion? No, Margaret was a doting mother, not a foolish one; she'd never sought to wrap the boy in soft wool. What, then? Had he got some village lass with child? That was likely enough. He was an attractive lad, and having discovered where his sword was meant to be sheathed, seemed set upon getting as much practice as possible. But no, why should Margaret fret over a peasant wench

45

ploughed and cropped? She was too sensible for that, would not blame Llewelyn for so small a sin.

Marared had turned away abruptly, sitting down suddenly on the steps of the dais. Llewelyn followed at once, hovering uncertainly at her side, his face troubled. But when he patted her shoulder awkwardly, she pushed his hand away. Hugh quickened his step, no longer amused.

'Margaret? What is wrong?'

'Ask Llewelyn,' she said tautly, and then, 'He says he's not going back to England with us. He wants to stay in Wales, to try and overthrow his uncles in Gwynedd.'

Her answer was so anticlimactic that Hugh felt laughter well up within him, dangerously close to the surface. He gave an abrupt, unconvincing cough, knowing she'd never forgive him if he laughed. But how like a woman, to let herself get so distraught over a boy's caprice, a whim of the moment that bore little relationship to reality. Doubtless, too, she'd been seeking to scare Llewelyn with horror stories of the hardships he'd be facing, the dangers and deprivations, the hand-to-mouth existence of a rebel on the run . . . and what could be better calculated to appeal to a foolhardy fourteen-year-old?

'Is this true, Llewelyn?'

Llewelyn nodded, but his eyes were wary and Hugh hesitated, recognizing the need to tread lightly, not wanting to trample the boy's pride into the dust.

'That is a rather ambitious undertaking, lad, too much so. In saying that, I do not mean to belittle your courage in any way. But courage alone is not enough, not when we are talking of rebellion.'

'I know,' Llewelyn slanted a sudden glance towards Morgan. 'Courage without common sense is the least of God's gifts.'

'It's glad I am to hear you say that, Llewelyn. For should you go up against your uncles now – on your own – I fear the only ground in Gwynedd you'd claim would be enough to fill a grave.'

'I know,' Llewelyn said again, and when Hugh smiled, so did he. Before adding, 'That is why I did appeal to my Uncle Gruffydd for advice and assistance. He thinks I'm of an age to lay claim to what is mine, has promised to help me do just that.'

Hugh's jaw dropped. 'He what?' Jerking around to stare at his wife. 'Your brother has agreed to this, to aid him in this madness?' he demanded, incredulous, and she nodded grimly.

Christ, no wonder Margaret was so wroth! Of all the damned

46

fool . . .' 'I am sorry, Llewelyn,' he said curtly, 'but you must put this scheme from your mind. There is no way on God's earth that I'd ever give my consent.'

'I'm sorry, too,' Llewelyn said softly. 'I should've liked to have had your approval.'

He'd spoken so politely that it was a moment or so before Hugh realised he'd just been defied.

'You're not being offered a choice, Llewelyn! I'm telling you that you're to forget this lunacy, you're to return to Shropshire with your mother and me, and that will be the end of it. As for your uncle, I'd not speak ill of a man in his own house, but he had no right to encourage you in this, to go against our wishes. You are not his son, after all.'

'I am not your son, either.'

Hugh stiffened. The boy's matter-of-fact reminder hurt, more than he'd have expected or Llewelyn had intended. It was a hurt that camouflaged itself in rage, and he clenched his fist, his face darkening with a sudden surge of blood. But while Llewelyn felt that his mother had a perfect right to hit him if she chose, he did not accord Hugh the same privilege, and he'd prudently put distance between them.

'No, you are not my flesh and blood. But when I wed your mother, your wardship passed into my hands. That means, Llewelyn, that you are answerable to me, and will be until you do come of legal age. Once you reach your majority, you may do what you damned well please, may sell your life as cheaply as you like. But for the next seven years, you'll do what I say. Is that clear?'

'Very.'

It was Llewelyn's composure that struck the first false note. The boy was too calm, was arguing more like an adult than a youngster with a head full of fanciful dreams, and Hugh said warningly, 'If you think to run away once we're back in Shropshire, Llewelyn . . .'

Llewelyn was shaking his head. 'I've heard you out, Hugh. Now I'd have you do as much for me. I'd not have you think me ungrateful . . . and I do not deny your right of wardship over me until I come of legal age. As we both know, in England that is twenty-one. But what you plainly do not know is that in Wales it is fourteen . . . and I did turn fourteen in February.'

Hugh stared at his stepson. Llewelyn's dark eyes were shining with triumph; a smile he could not quite repress quirked one corner of his mouth. Hugh caught his breath, swore softly. Little wonder

47

the lad had been so cocky; he'd known from the first that he was playing with loaded dice.

Hugh was swallowing bile, spat into the floor rushes. Rob was right; there was no reasoning with the Welsh, they were all mad, beyond redemption or understanding. What were they to tell Chester? The opportunity of a lifetime lost to them, all because a headstrong boy wanted to play the rebel!

'And what of your brother? Would you leave him without a qualm, knowing he has such need of you, knowing you go where he cannot follow –'

'Adda hears very well! Do not speak of him as if he were not even here!'

There was a strained silence. Adda had gone very pale, but he said, quite evenly, 'I want Llewelyn to go, want him to claim what is his. So would I, had Got not willed otherwise.'

Hugh felt a touch of shame; it was Llewelyn he'd wanted to wound, not the innocent Adda. Llewelyn was staring at him, accusing, defiant. Whatever chance he might have had of prevailing was utterly gone now. Llewelyn might, he knew, forgive a slight on his own behalf, but on Adda's, never. He'd not yield in this, knowing he had the full backing of his Welsh kinsmen. All their plans set at naught, their hopes of an alliance with Chester now gall and wormwood, ashes in his mouth.

'Go to Gwynedd and be damned then!' he said bitterly and turned away.

They watched in silence as Hugh strode from the hall. But when Marared rose to follow him, Llewelyn stepped in front of her. 'Mama . . .'

'No, Llewelyn. Do not expect my blessing. Do not expect my forgiveness, either.'

He'd won. But he could take no pleasure in it, not now. Llewelyn sank down on the dais steps, passed some moments disconsolately sliding his dagger up and down its sheath. The excitement he'd experienced in sharing his plans with Ednyved and Rhys had gone suddenly sour, tarnished by his mother's tears.

'Adda?' Marared let her hand linger on her younger son's shoulder. 'Are you coming, lad?'

'Yes, Mama.'

As Adda rose, Llewelyn looked up, said, 'Hugh did not mean that, Adda. He was angry, just did not think . . .'

48

'People never do, do they?' Adda smiled thinly. 'Yet we'd be apart, too, once you were sent off to serve as Chester's squire. Better you should follow your heart.'

Their eyes caught, pulled away. Marared was waiting. Adda reached for his crutch, angled it under his armpit. Watching his brother limp towards the door, Llewelyn felt a protective pang. What Adda had just said was true. It was also true that he was being left behind.

'Morgan . . . Morgan, am I doing the right thing?'

'If I said no, would you heed me?'

Llewelyn considered, and then gave the priest a rueful smile. 'No,' he conceded. 'Gwynedd is my birthright. But it's likely to take years to claim it. Years I can ill afford to squander in Shropshire. I have to do this, Morgan. I have to.'

Morgan nodded slowly; he'd expected no less. He more than anyone else had nurtured in Llewelyn a love for his heritage, his homeland, had moulded youthful clay into adult ambition. He was proud of what he had accomplished, proud of Llewelyn's resolve, his daring. But he could not help feeling fear, too, for Llewelyn was the son he'd never have.

'I cannot say I approve, lad.' And then, very softly, 'But I do understand.'

3

June, 1189
Chinon Castle
Province of Touraine

'What is your name, girl?'

'Lucy . . .' She added 'my lord' for safety's sake; a fortnight at Chinon had not been long enough for her to absorb the intricacies of the castle hierarchy. She knew only that this man was a bailiff, a being as far above her as stars in the firmament, and she was trembling with dread that she'd somehow displeased, that she might be dismissed in disgrace.

'Turn around,' he directed, and as she complied in bewilderment, he gave a satisfied nod. 'Yes, you'll do once you're cleaned up; he's right particular about such niceties. Agnes, see that she has a bath first. I expect it is too much to hope that you would still be a virgin?'

Lucy gasped so audibly that several men laughed, and the bailiff looked at her with the first flicker of genuine interest. 'Well, well. That is a stroke of luck for you, girl; how many wenches get to lose their maidenheads in a royal bed?' He laughed, moved on to other matters, and Lucy was forgotten.

She stood there, rooted, until Agnes stepped forward, slipped a supporting arm around her waist. 'Shall we get you that bath?' she said, and giving Lucy no chance to balk, she guided the girl towards the door. 'Do not look so stricken, lass. It'll not be as bad as you think; you might even enjoy it.'

'But . . . but he's so old and sickly!' Lucy shuddered. She'd seen the old King infrequently since his arrival at Chinon. There was in his face the haggard, grey gauntness of coming death; it would, she thought with horror, be like embracing a corpse.

'Old?' Agnes echoed and then laughed. 'You need not fear, Lucy, you're not for poor King Henry. God pity him, he's beyond feeling

50

that itch only a woman can scratch. No, his son rode in within the hour, and it is a rare night when that one does not want a wench to warm his bed.'

'Lord John?'

'Well, for certès not Richard!' Agnes giggled, but thought better of pursuing that particular brand of hazardous humour; instead, she took it upon herself to allay Lucy's fears. 'He's handsome, is Lord John. Not as tall as Richard, of stocky build like his father, although dark as a Barbary pirate. And young, one-and-twenty against his sire's six-and-fifty, a far better age for bedding!' But Lucy did not seem to appreciate her good fortune; she looked dazed. Agnes thought she knew why, and glanced about to make sure no others were within earshot.

'You must not believe all you hear, child. It is true John does have men about him who'd make even Hell the fouler for their presence. He might not rein them in as he ought, but he does not seem to be one for sharing their nastier sport. In the five years I've been at Chinon, I've never heard it said that he takes pleasure in a woman's pain, and whilst I cannot speak first hand, mind you, I've been told he has no quirks a woman would not enjoy, too. And he's ever been generous in the past, will be sure to give you something after.'

She hesitated. 'But in all honesty, his temper's like to be on the raw. God knows, he has reason and more, with his father ailing, with Richard and the French King encamped outside Tours, just a day's march from here. Richard has much to answer for, in truth. To war upon his own father . . .' She shook her head. 'At least John is loyal.'

Henry moaned, turned his face into the pillow. His shirt was soaked with sweat; so, too, were the sheets, damp and darkly splotched. A servant had removed his shoes and chausses, and his legs looked absurdly white and frail, utterly incongruous supports for that barrel chest, those massive shoulders. But even that once-mighty chest seemed somehow shrunken, diminished. It was impossible for John to recognize in this bedridden invalid the father who'd cast so colossal a shadow, larger than life, omnipotent, King of England, Lord of Ireland and Wales, Duke of Normandy and Gascony, Count of Anjou, Touraine, and Maine, liege lord of Brittany, Auvergne and Toulouse.

Henry was breathing through his mouth, gulping air as if each breath might be his last. Saliva had begun to dribble down his chin, but John could not bring himself to wipe it away, shrank from touching that wasted flesh. He was profoundly shocked that in a mere fortnight his father's illness should have made such lethal inroads; until this moment he'd not acknowledged that the illness might be mortal.

'John? Thank God you've come. He's done little but fret over you. Could you not have sent word that you'd got away safe from Le Mans?'

Two weeks ago, the town of Le Mans had fallen to the forces of John's brother Richard and Philip, the young French King. Henry and his followers had escaped the burning city just as the French army moved in, and in the confusion John had become separated from the others, had passed some harrowing days himself, in consequence. But he was not about to explain that now to the speaker, his illegitimate half-brother Geoffrey. Like all his brothers, Geoffrey was much older than John, well into his thirties, a tall, powerfully built man with sandy hair, Henry's flint-grey eyes, and an acerbic tongue. John did not feel for Geoffrey the consuming, corrosive jealousy that he did for Richard, but he had no more liking for this Geoffrey than he'd had for the dead brother who'd borne the same name. Ignoring the accusatory, querulous tone of the other's question, he said:

'Christ, but he looks bad. Is he in much pain?'

Geoffrey nodded. 'All the time,' he said bleakly, and then turned towards the bed as Henry stirred.

The grey eyes opened, focused on John. 'At last,' he said huskily, held out his hand. 'You did give me some bad moments this past week, lad.'

John was much relieved at the hot, dry feel of the hand in his, having steeled himself for a touch cold and clammy. 'You need not have worried, Papa. Are you not the one who always said I had more lives than a cat? Or was that the morals of a cat?' he added, coaxing from his father a grimacing smile, a cough masquerading as a chuckle.

'Johnny . . . I had William de Mandeville and William Fitz Ralph swear to me . . . swear that should any evil befall me, they'll surrender my castles to you and to you alone. Not to Richard, God rot him, not to Richard . . .'

To John, that sounded more like a concession of defeat than a declaration of trust. 'Surely you do not expect it to come to that, Papa?'

There was a wine flagon on the bedside table, and Henry gestured,

52

waited till John poured out a cupful. 'Of course not, lad. You'll never see the day dawn when I let them get the better of me,' he said, with a bravado that might have been more convincing had John not needed to help him up in order to drink. 'Le Mans was not the first town I've lost in my life, will not be the last . . .' He drank deeply, signalled for John to lower him back against the pillows.

'Johnny . . . listen, lad. I have not forgotten my promise to you, do mean to give you the earldom of Mortain, give you the revenues from Cornwall . . .'

John's mouth twisted. For how many years had he been hearing this? Promises he had in plenty, but little else. His brother Henry had been the heir apparent, Geoffrey Duke of Brittany, and Richard Duke of Aquitaine, Count of Poitou. But him? John Lackland. He'd been betrothed since age nine to his cousin Avisa, a bride to bring him the rich earldom of Gloucester, but that, too, was proving to be an empty expectation; the very least that could be said of a twelve-year-old betrothal was that his father was in no tearing hurry to have him tie so lucrative a nuptial knot. It was John's private suspicion that his father denied him incomes of his own for the same reason he'd refused to name Richard as his heir, to keep them close, puppet Princes who'd dance to his tune only.

'I think you should rest now, Papa,' he said, and Henry nodded; sweat was breaking out again on his forehead, trickling into his beard.

'The fever is worse at night,' he mumbled. 'Stay with me till I sleep.'

The chamber was heavy with the fetid odours of illness, with stifling summer heat. John soon began to sweat, too, began to yearn for a lungful of the cooling night air so fatal to the sickroom. At last Henry found relief in sleep; his hold slackened, fingers no longer clutched. John gently disengaged his hand, wiped his palm against the sheet, and came to his feet.

He stood for some moments, looking down at his father, until joined by Geoffrey.

'He's dying, is he not?'

'Yes.' Geoffrey gave John a thoughtful look. 'You surprise me, John, sound as if you care.'

John caught his breath. 'Damn you, of course I care!'

Henry groaned, fumbled with the blankets, and Geoffrey at once bent over the bed, making soothing sounds, lulling the older man back into sleep. John watched until Henry grew quiet again, then turned away with such haste that, to Geoffrey, it seemed not so much an exit as an escape.

Entering his own chamber, John was reaching for a wine flagon when he caught movement from the corner of his eye, spun around to see the girl cowering in the shadows.

'Who are you?'

'Do not be angry, my lord,' she pleaded, stumbling forward to make an exceedingly awkward curtsy. 'I . . . I am Lucy, and I am here because Master Randolph . . . he thought . . .'

Her painful stammer, her flaming face told John quite clearly what Master Randolph thought. His first impulse was to get rid of her, but even as the dismissal was forming on his tongue, he changed his mind. What better way to exorcize the horrors of the sickroom than with flesh that was smooth and whole and healthy? Moreover, he had ever hated to be alone. Tonight of all nights, even the company of this timid little maidservant was preferable to his own.

'Remind me to thank Master Randolph,' he said, and smiled at her. 'Be a good lass now and fetch me some wine.'

But the wine did not help as he'd hoped. Instead of dulling his anxieties, it acted as a stimulant, spurring his imagination into unpleasant excesses, conjuring up half-forgotten fears of boyhood and projecting them into a future that suddenly seemed fraught with menace.

'He's dying, Lucy. Did you know that?'

'Yes, my lord,' she whispered. Hastening to refill his wine cup, she approached the bed and then skittered back out of range, putting him in mind of a squirrel caught between trees.

He'd sent Lucy down to the buttery for another wine flagon when he heard a commotion in the stairwell. He sat up on the bed as Martin Algais and Lupescaire burst into the chamber.

'Look what we found in the stairwell.' Shoving Lucy forward into the room. 'What is that saying about a bird in the hand?'

John was not amused. Algais and Lupescaire were Brabançons, men who sold their swords to the highest bidder. In the past he had permitted, even encouraged, familiarity, dicing and drinking with them, treating them as intimates. But tonight he had no desire for their company, and he found himself resenting the way they were making free with what was his, Lupescaire helping himself to the

54

wine while Martin Algais backed Lucy into a corner, laughing at her ineffectual attempts to fend off his roving hands.

'I do not recall summoning you,' John said irritably, as Lupescaire handed him a brimming wine cup.

'The talk amongst our men is that the old King is in a bad way. You did see him, my lord; how does he, in truth?'

John could not, in fairness, fault them for their concern; their future, like his own, rose and fell with each laboured breath Henry drew. But they were servants, companions, handpicked hirelings – not confidants.

'Well enough,' he said, had his cup half way to his mouth when Lucy screamed. His hand jerked, and wine splashed on to the bed, splattered his tunic. John jumped to his feet with an oath. 'Damn your soul, Martin, look at this!' He stared down at the winespill in disgust, then turned to glare at Algais. 'Must you ever have your hand up a woman's skirts? If you want to tumble a wench, you can damned well do it someplace else than in my chamber. Let that girl be, and get a servant up here to change these bedcovers.'

But Algais did not move. Holding the weeping girl with one hand, with the other, he reached for the neck of her gown, jerked until the material tore, baring her breasts.

'Did you not hear me?' John demanded, astonished. 'I told you to let the girl alone.'

'Why?' Algais sounded sullen, defiant. 'We've shared women before; why not now?'

Lupescaire put his wine cup down, eyes suddenly a-glitter, cutting from John to Algais and back again. John's mouth went dry; never had either of them dared to defy him before. 'Because I say so, Martin. You take what I choose to give you, no more and no less.'

Algais had very pale eyes, an unblinking, feral stare. But after a few frozen breaths, he loosened his hold on Lucy. 'You want me to ask? Then I'm asking. I have taken a fancy to this one; let me have her for an hour.'

It would be so easy to agree, a face-saving solution for them both, and John was very tempted; he'd never had a stomach for confrontation. But he knew better, knew it had to be all or nothing with a man like Martin Algais.

'No,' he said.

Algais's fingers clenched, dug into Lucy's upper arm, and she sobbed anew. But then he pushed her away.

55

John's breathing slowed, steadied. 'Go down to the great hall,' he said; 'send a servant up to me. You need not come back after. I've no use for you tonight.'

He'd won. They did as he bade, if not docile, at least unrebelling. John moved to the table, poured the last of the wine with a shaking hand. He knew them for what they were, his pet wolves, but he'd never thought they might turn on him. He knew why, of course. For the same reason that Geoffrey had suddenly dared to voice his dislike. The scent of blood was in the air.

Lucy was still sobbing, and he snapped, 'Will you stop your whimpering, girl? You were not hurt, after all!' But as he turned towards her, he saw that was not true. There was an angry red welt upon her left breast; there would soon be an exceedingly ugly bruise.

'Do not cry, lass,' he said, more gently, and then she was on her knees before him, clinging to his legs, weeping incoherently. It was some moments before he could make sense of her sobbing, before he realized that she was feverishly, hysterically thanking him for saving her from Martin Algais. John choked back an unsteady, mirthless laugh, raised her up.

'Lucy, listen to me. Dry your tears and go down to the hall. Find my squire, tell him to get up here. Then go to the kitchen, tell the cooks I said to give you mutton fat for that bruise.' As he spoke, he was steering her towards the door. 'After that, lass, go to bed . . . your own.'

Giving him an incredulous look, she fled. Within moments, his squire was panting up the stairs. 'My lord, what is amiss? That girl acted so strange . . .'

'Get our men together. I want us ready to ride within the hour.'

'Ride where? My lord, it's full dark. Where would we go? At such an hour, we might well have to bed down by the roadside –'

'I was giving you a command, not inviting a debate. I want to be gone from here as soon as we can saddle up, and if you make me repeat that, you'll have more regrets than you can handle. Now see to it!'

Hastily the man said, 'I will, my lord, indeed. But . . . but what of your lord father? I've been told he sleeps; is it your wish that he be awakened ere you depart?'

'No,' John said. 'Let him sleep.'

*

'I know you Angevins have ever been short of brotherly love, but surely John is not as worthless as you think? Admittedly, I know him not well, but he never struck me as a fool.'

'Oh, John is clever enough. But what do brains avail a man if he lacks backbone?'

In Richard's lexicon of insults, that was the most damning accusation he could make, and to Philip, it cast a revealing light upon Richard's relationship with his younger brother. He found himself feeling a touch of sympathy for John, who'd been weighed against Richard's exacting standards of manhood and found wanting, for he knew that he, too, had failed to measure up in Richard's eyes; their friendship was never the same once Richard discovered that he had an irrational fear of horses, rode only the most docile of geldings.

'But to be fair,' Richard said grudgingly, 'my father has ever played the same game with John as he did with me and, whilst they lived, Geoffrey and Henry, promising all and delivering nothing. Although the one time he entrusted John with power of his own, sent him to Ireland, it was an unmitigated disaster. So badly did John bungle his rule that he achieved the all-but-impossible, he got the Irish chieftains to stop squabbling with one another and unite against him!'

'Surely that was Henry's blunder as much as John's. You do not send a boy of seventeen to do a man's work.'

'When I was seventeen, I was putting down a rebellion in Poitou,' Richard said pointedly, and Philip conceded defeat with a wry smile, signalled to a servant.

'We'll see Lord John now.'

John had rarely been so nervous; eleventh-hour allies were not always welcomed with open arms. He was much relieved, therefore, when the French King smiled as he knelt, at once motioned him to rise.

'Your Grace,' he said, with an answering smile that lost all spontaneity, all sincerity, at sight of his brother. Even in the dim light of a command tent, Richard's colouring had lost none of its vibrancy, eyes blazingly blue, hair bronzed even brighter now by a summer in the saddle. Most likely, John thought sourly, he did glow in the dark. 'Richard,' he said, as if they'd been parted just that morning, and Richard gave him an equally indifferent greeting in return.

'You did surprise me, John,' he said dryly. 'I'd expected you to turn up weeks ago. Cutting it rather close, were you not, Little Brother?'

57

Fortunately for John, hatred choked all utterance. He stared at Richard, reminding himself this was but one more grievance to be credited to Richard's account, promising himself that payment would be in the coin of his choosing.

Philip had been watching the Angevin brothers with covert amusement. Now he asked the question John most dreaded. 'John . . . how does Henry?'

John had given this a great deal of thought in the hours since his midnight flight from Chinon. He had no way of knowing if Philip and Richard were aware of the gravity of Henry's illness, could only hope they were not; an infidel who converted at knife-point had, of necessity, to count for less than one who willingly renounced his heresy.

'I do not know, Your Grace. I've not seen my father since we fled Le Mans.'

Richard and Philip exchanged glances, and then Richard said, 'Rumour has it he is bedridden, but I expect it's yet another of his damnable tricks; he could teach a fox about slyness.'

John said nothing, concentrated his attention upon a nearby fruit bowl. Picking out two apples, he tossed one to Richard, a sudden, swift pitch that disconcerted Richard not in the least. He caught it with the utmost ease, his the lithe coordination, the lazy, loose grace of the born athlete. John doubted if Richard had made a careless misstep, a clumsy move in all his thirty-one years.

Richard crunched into the apple. 'Let's talk about you, Little Brother. What is the going price for –' He caught himself, but not in time.

'Betrayal? What game are we playing now, Richard? If we are tallying up sins, I rather doubt you're in any position to cast the first stone.'

There was a silence, and then Richard gave a short laugh. 'Fair enough. I deserved that. Let me put it another way. What do you want for your support?'

'Only what be my just due,' John said cautiously, 'what I've been promised since boyhood. The county of Mortain, the earldom of Gloucester, the incomes from the lordship of Ireland, Nottingham Castle.'

Richard did not hesitate. 'Done,' he said, so readily that John regretted not asking for more. He murmured a perfunctory expression of appreciation, and then said:

'You might want to do something for our brother Geoffrey, too. If I were you, Richard, I'd keep Geoffrey in mind when it comes time to fill the next vacant bishopric.'

Richard frowned, but after a moment he began to laugh. 'An excellent thought, Little Brother. I shall do just that.'

Philip looked from one to the other in bemusement. 'I seem to have missed something. Correct me if I be wrong, but I never thought either one of you to be overly fond of Geoffrey. Why, then, do you want to make him a bishop?'

'Geoffrey has no more calling for the priesthood than I do,' Richard said with a grin. 'Some years ago, our father sought for him a career in the Church, tried to make him Bishop of Lincoln, but he balked, refused to be ordained. So we'd be doing him no favour.'

'Brother Geoffrey has ambitions ill-befitting his base blood,' John added softly. 'Too often have I heard him remind people that William the Conqueror was himself bastard born.'

Philip saw the light. 'And as a priest, he would, of course, be barred from ever laying claim to the crown. Clever, John, very clever. But risky. What's to keep Richard from concluding that Holy Orders might do your soul great good, too?'

Richard laughed until he choked, sputtering something unintelligible about 'Father John'. John laughed, too, but his eyes narrowed on Philip with sudden speculation. Philip, he decided, was one for muddying the waters. That would indeed bear remembering.

'You did arrive just in time, John. We are about to lay siege to Tours, for its fall is sure to force the old fox from his lair. This campaign has dragged on far too long. It's nigh on two years since I took the cross; I'd hoped to be before the walls of Jerusalem months ago.' Richard paused, said with sudden seriousness, 'Philip will be leading a French army, and we expect men to flock to our standards. You ought to give some thought to taking the cross yourself, John. What better quest can a man have than pledging his life to the delivery of the Holy City from the infidels?'

John was appalled, forced a strained laugh. 'The truth now, Richard,' he said with what he hoped would be disarming candour, 'can you truly see me as a pious pilgrim on the road to Damascus?'

Philip laughed; so did Richard. 'No,' he admitted, 'I confess I cannot, Little Brother. You'd disappear into some Saracen harem never to be heard from again!'

John smiled thinly, marvelling that Richard should dare to sneer at another man's sexual habits, given Richard's own vulnerabilities in that particular area. There were, he thought scornfully, worse vices than liking women overly well. But all at once he found himself thinking of that ugly scene at Chinon, remembering the fear he'd felt facing down Martin Algais. That would, he knew, never have happened to Richard. Men did not defy his brother. The foolhardy few who'd dared were dead. He had a sudden wild impulse to tell Richard that their father was dying, wondering what Richard would say or feel. Nothing, he suspected. Everything was always so damnably easy for Richard.

John was the youngest of the eight children born to Henry Plantagenet and Eleanor of Aquitaine. His sisters, who had been bartered as child brides to foreign princes, were little more to him now than time-dimmed memories. His brothers had been, by turns, indifferent and antagonistic to this last-born of the Angevin eaglets . . . with one exception. William Longsword was, like Geoffrey, a bastard half-brother. But Will had somehow missed his share of the Angevin temperament; his was a placid, unimaginative nature, sentimental and straightforward, an unlikely drab-grey dove in that family of flamboyant hawks. Will had been amiably interested in the little brother born within days of his own tenth birthday, had taken it upon himself to wipe John's nose, to pick him up when he fell, to be for John a good-natured guide through the pitfalls and passages of childhood. He'd become quite fond of the dark little boy so eager to please, had watched rather sadly as John was utterly ignored by his mother, overly indulged by his father, as the twig was bent, twisted awry, seeing the distortion but not knowing how to set it right. Yet the bonds of boyhood had proven to be enduring ones, and Will and John did to this day enjoy a relationship remarkably free of strain in a family notorious for its internecine rivalries.

It was nightfall by the time Will reached Rouen, was escorted up to John's chamber. John greeted him with a grin, with genuine pleasure, at once sent to the castle buttery for wine, even dismissed an uncommonly pretty bedmate so they could talk alone.

Richard had that day departed Rouen for Gisors where Philip awaited him, and John and Will joked now about the exorbitant price Philip was likely to claim for his support in securing Richard the crown. Will could not help thinking that John, too, had profited handsomely. Richard had wasted no time in investing his younger brother as Count of Mortain, John's marriage to Avisa of Gloucester was to take place on August 29, and Will had heard Richard meant to bestow upon John the incomes from the English counties of Cornwall, Devon, Dorset, Somerset, Nottingham, and Derby. Will thought Richard had been surprisingly generous, and said as much to John.

'That,' John said cheerfully, 'is because I am – by the vagaries of fate – Brother Richard's heir. And Richard's more peculiar proclivities do make it at least likely that I'll be the only heir.'

Will sighed, feeling much like a parent with a loved but wayward child. 'Bear in mind, lad, what Scriptures say about coveting,' he said mildly, and John laughed.

'What we need to do now, Will, is to get Richard to find an heiress for you ere he goes galloping off to find martyrdom in Messina . . . or was it sainthood in Syria? Can you believe the man, Will? He's not even set the date for his coronation yet, and all he can talk about is how he cannot wait to risk his life in some infidel hellhole. I truly think he must be mad,' John said, with such sincerity that Will had to laugh.

'If you can coax Richard into giving me a landed wife, I'll be much in your debt. But now we do need to talk. I rode in from Fontevrault with Geoffrey. He's right bitter, John, like to say that which would be better left unsaid. I thought I'd best get to you first, tell –'

'My lord? My lord, your brother –'

Geoffrey did not wait to be announced, shoved the servant aside, and strode into the chamber. 'I do want to talk to you, John.'

'How lucky for me,' John said coolly, signalling to the servant to pour them wine. 'What shall we drink to, Geoffrey . . . your good fortune? Did he tell you, Will, that Richard has ordered the canons of York to elect Brother Geoffrey as their Archbishop? Of course there is still a minor matter of taking vows, but that is a small price to pay to become a Prince of the Church, is it not?'

'I rather thought I had you to thank for that,' Geoffrey said. 'But that is not why I'm here, and you damned well know it, John. I'm going to tell you how our father died, and you're going to listen.'

'Am I, indeed?' John's eyes had gone very green. 'I think not. If you want to lay blame about, lay it where it belongs – on Richard's head. Not mine. If you have anything to say, say it then to Richard!'

'I did . . . at Fontevrault. He at least was man enough to hear me out. Are you?'

John had half-risen from his chair. With that, he sank back. 'Say what you have to say and then get out.'

'Gladly.' Geoffrey reached over and, without asking, helped himself to one of the wine cups. 'I would to God I knew what Papa saw in you. He kept faith to the end, you know. Even your cowardly flight from Chinon did not open his eyes. Almost to the last, he kept expecting you to come back, even worried about you . . . if you can credit that!'

'Geoffrey,' Will said uneasily, 'this does serve for naught . . .'

'Keep out of this, Will. On July 3rd Tours fell, and Philip and Richard summoned Papa to Colombières. He was sick unto death, made it only as far as the Knights Templar at Ballan. But when he sent word to Philip, Richard insisted he was malingering, playing for time. By then he could barely stay in the saddle, but he refused a horse litter, somehow got himself to Colombières. Even Philip was moved to pity at sight of him, even Philip, offered to spread a cloak on the ground for him. But he would not agree. He was too proud, you see . . .' Geoffrey's voice had thickened; he drank, keeping his eyes all the while upon John.

'They told him he was there not to discuss terms, but to yield to their demands. They dared to speak so to him, and he could do nothing about it. Then they told him what they wanted. He must do homage to Philip for his lands in Normandy and Anjou, accept Philip as his overlord. He must pay Philip twenty thousand marks, must have all his barons swear fealty to Richard, must promise not to take vengeance upon those who'd betrayed him. All this they demanded . . . and more. By then the noon-day sky was black as ink, sweat ran off him like rain, and how he ever kept to his saddle, the Lord Christ Jesus alone does know. But they were not through yet. He must publicly give Richard the kiss of peace, they said. Even that he did, even that . . . and then hissed in Richard's ear, "God grant I do not die ere I have revenged myself upon you." Of course you may already know that, John. I understand Richard told one and all at the French court, as if it were some droll joke!

'We brought him back to Chinon by horse litter, and I watched through the night as his fever burned ever higher. The next day Roger Malchet rode in from Tours with a list of rebels, those men

62

who'd gone over to Philip and Richard. Need I tell you, John, that your name did head the list?'

Geoffrey paused, but John said nothing. 'He did not believe it at first, cursed Roger, me, all within hearing, accused us of lying, of trying to poison his mind against you, his "dearest born". And when he could deny it no longer, he turned his face to the wall, said no more. Within hours he was dead. His last words to me were, "You are my true son. The others, they are the bastards."

'There were only a few of us with him at the last; most had already taken themselves off to Richard's encampment. Whilst I was in the chapel, his servants stripped his body, stole rings, clothing, whatever they could find. We'd have had to bury him mother-naked had not one of his squires let us wrap the body in his cloak, and as it was, we had not even money for alms.

'So died the greatest Prince in Christendom, our lord father. You think on that, John, think on how he died, and then tell me again that you bear no blame. Well? Have you nothing to say? Passing strange, neither did Richard.'

Geoffrey drained the wine cup very deliberately, turned and walked to the door. 'Richard forced him from a sickbed, broke his power, his pride. But you, John, you broke his heart. I truly wonder which be the greater sin.'

Will shifted uncomfortably as the door slammed, slanted a surreptitious look towards John. It may have been the dimmed lighting, but John seemed to have lost colour. He'd turned his head away; his face was in profile, utterly still, mask-like. Will fidgeted, opened his mouth, and then sat back, defeated. What, after all, was there to say?

4

February, 1192

Southampton, England

Will was frowning as he followed a servant up the stairwell to his brother's chamber, dreading the scene sure to follow. He was almost tempted to stand aside, to let John rush headlong to his own destruction. Almost.

His mouth softened somewhat at sight of the man and boy together on the settle. John was surprisingly good with children, could not be faulted when it came to the care of his own, and whenever Will found himself despairing of his brother's flexible measurements of morality, he took comfort in remembering how conscientious John was in acknowledging and providing for the children born of his bedsport. That was no small virtue to Will, himself born of Henry's passing lust for a green-eyed milkmaid with well-turned ankles.

He was as yet unnoticed. John was holding out his hands, fists clenched. 'Now tell me, Richard. Which hands holds the fig?' The little boy pointed. 'Sorry! This hand, then? No, wrong again. Where did it go? Ah, there it is . . .' Reaching out, he seemed to find the fig behind the child's ear, to Will's amusement and Richard's utter delight.

'One more time, Papa!' he pleaded, as John turned at sound of Will's chuckle. For an unguarded moment, his face showed sudden unease, and then he smiled, beckoned Will into the room.

'"One more time,"' he mimicked. '"One more time." Mayhap we ought to call you that rather than Richard!' He then plucked the fig from Richard's sleeve, while Will watched and wondered, not for the first time, what perverse impulse had prompted John to name his son after the brother he so hated. As with much of what John did, the answer eluded him. Will had long ago recognized that his imagination was rooted in barren soil; no matter how he strained, it brought forth only a meagre crop, never the sort of creative conjecture he'd have needed to track the twisting byways of his brother's brain.

Richard was munching on the elusive fig; now he offered the uneaten half first to John and then to Will, with a gravely deliberate courtesy that was both unexpected and poignant in one so very young. He was, Will knew, just shy of his third birthday, a date well etched in Will's memory because of the scandal attached to that birth. For Richard's mother, quite unlike John's other bedmates, was no impoverished knight's daughter, no Saxon maidservant. Alina was the daughter of Hamelin de Warenne, Earl of Surrey, half-brother to King Henry, albeit base-born.

That was the first and only time Will could remember Henry showing concern for one of his sons' sexual escapades. He had even taken it upon himself to rebuke John for seducing a first cousin, a girl of high birth. Unfortunately, his own moral armour was particularly vulnerable to that very charge, and he succeeded only in arousing in John an indignation that was, Will conceded, not altogether unjustified. John's involvement with Alina was of minor moment, after all, when compared to Henry's seduction of the Princess Alais.

Will did not like to think of Alais; he was by nature protective of women, and he could not deny that Alais had been ill used, first by his father and now by Richard. Sister to Philip, the French King, she had been betrothed to Richard in childhood and, at age seven, was sent to England to be reared at Henry's court in accordance with custom. It was hardly customary, though, Will thought grimly, for a man to bed his son's betrothed, and yet his father had done just that, had taken Alais to his bed when she was sixteen. It was scarcely surprising, Will acknowledged, that upon Henry's death Richard refused to honour the plight troth, telling Philip bluntly that he'd not wed his father's whore. Will saw no justification, however, for keeping Alais in close confinement, and yet for almost three years now, Richard had held Alais prisoner in Rouen.

But Will had troubles enough of his own without taking on those of a captive French Princess, and he shifted impatiently in his seat, waiting for John to send Richard off to bed so they could talk.

'You did that trick with the fig very adroitly. Where did you learn it?'

'From a juggler at the French court. He told me that I have a rare gift for sleight of hand!'

John looked at him, eyes alight with laughter, and Will felt a

65

dulled ache, a wrenching realization that he was too late, years too late. Yet he had to try, and as soon as Richard's nurse came to collect the boy, he said, very quietly, 'John . . . do not do this.'

'Do what, Will?'

'I know why you are here in Southampton. You mean to sail for France, to meet in Paris with the French King.'

'Is that why you came racing from London? Poor Will . . . you did bruise your bones for naught, in truth.' John's smile was wry, faintly reproachful. 'I am about to sail as soon as the weather does clear, but for Normandy, not France.'

He was more than plausible, he was thoroughly convincing, and he was lying. Will leaned over, grasped his wrist. 'John, do not play me for a fool. You owe me better than that. If I cared enough to make an eighty-mile ride in weather as foul as this, then you can damned well hear me out!'

'All right, Will,' John said slowly, taken aback by this uncharacteristic outburst. 'What makes you think I mean to ally myself with Philip?'

'Because Philip and Richard buried what was left of their friendship in the Holy Land. Because Richard is still in Acre and Philip is now back in Paris, nursing a mortal grudge. Because you'd barter your very soul for a chance to do Richard ill. Because Philip has of a sudden invited you to Paris. Need I go on?'

'If disliking Richard be grounds for accusing a man of conspiracy, I dare say you could implicate half of Christendom in this so-called plot,' John scoffed. 'Richard endears himself easiest to those who've yet to meet him.' Rising, he moved to the table, gained time to think by pouring himself a cupful of cider. He poured, too, for Will, stood for a moment looking down at the older man. So, he thought suddenly, must their father have looked at thirty-four, for Will had Henry's reddish-gold hair, his ruddy colouring, even the same scattering of freckles across the bridge of the nose.

'Just suppose, Will, that you are right, that I do mean to throw my lot in with Philip. If you had proof of that, what would you do? Go to my lady mother? Betray me to Richard?'

Will's shoulders slumped. 'No,' he mumbled, full of self-loathing. 'You know I could not.'

'Do not begrudge me your loyalty, Will. I deserve it more than Richard, for he loves you not and I love you well.' John thrust a dripping cider cup into Will's hand, took the closest seat. 'I even love you enough to trust you with the truth. Did you by chance see a monk in the great hall when you arrived? That is Brother Bernard de Coudray, Philip's man. You were right, of course; Philip has indeed made me an offer. "All the lands of England and Normandy on the French side of the Channel." I need only swear homage to him as overlord, and once we get his sister Alais out of Richard's power, take her to wife.'

Will choked on his cider, began to sputter. 'Christ Jesus, John! You cannot mean that? You'd truly agree to wed Alais?'

'Why not?'

Will drew a strangled breath. 'For one thing,' he snapped, 'you already do have a wife! Or did that somehow slip your mind?'

John drank to conceal a grin; his brother's ponderous attempts at sarcasm never failed to amuse him, but he did not want to offend Will by laughing outright. 'Have you forgotten that Avisa is my second cousin? Or that we neglected to get a papal dispensation for our marriage? Nor need your heart bleed for Avisa, the abandoned wife. We may not agree on much, but we do share a deep and very mutual dislike.'

'But Alais! She bedded with Papa for years and all know it, even bore him a stillborn son!'

John shrugged. 'Being Papa's concubine does not make her any less Philip's sister, and if she's the price for Philip's support . . . At least we'd be keeping her in the family!'

'That's not amusing, John! How can you jest about betrayal and treason, a marriage all but incestuous?'

John set his cup down with a thud. 'What would you have me do? It's been sixteen months since Richard named our dead brother Geoffrey's son as his heir, nine months since my lady mother coerced him into taking a Spanish wife. Nine months, Will. For all I know, she could already be with child. What if she is, if she manages a miracle, keeps Richard in her bed long enough to give him a son?'

'Ah John . . . you'd still be Count of Mortain, Earl of Gloucester, with an income of four thousand pounds a year. Can you not content yourself with that?'

John stared at him, and then gave a short, incredulous laugh. 'God help you, Will, I truly think you're serious!'

Until that moment, Will had been slow to see the magnitude of his mistake. Had he really thought he could talk sense into John?

All he'd done was to take on a share of the guilt, to compromise himself in the complicity of silence.

'Do not leave on the morrow, Will. Stay till week's end. How is your manor at Kirton? This was a bad year for crops; if you're in need of money . . .'

Will had no false pride, saw no reason to refuse aid from John, not when he had only the manors of Kirton and Appleby and John had the revenues from six shires. He made a point, though, of not abusing John's generosity, never asked unless there was a specific need. 'Thank you, lad, no. I do not –'

'My lord!' A flustered servant stumbled into the chamber. 'My lord, the Queen has just ridden into the bailey!'

John spilled his cider. 'That cannot be! My mother is in Normandy.'

'No, my lord, she's in the great hall.'

'You both are wrong,' a cool voice said from the doorway. 'I'm out in the stairwell.'

Will jumped to his feet. He was very much in awe of John's mother, for Eleanor of Aquitaine was more than the widow of one King, mother to another. She was a creature rarer even than the unicorn, a woman who, all her life, had been a law unto herself, as Duchess of Aquitaine, then as Queen of France, and finally as Queen of England. She had in her past two failed royal marriages, a crusade, scandal and lovers, even a rebellion, for when Henry betrayed her, she'd incited their sons to civil war, had spent sixteen years in confinement as a result. But she'd won in the end, had outlived the husband who'd shut her away from the world, from her beloved Aquitaine. Moreover, she had somehow survived those bitter years with her soul unscarred, her spirit unbroken.

Upon regaining her freedom, she had, at age sixty-nine, journeyed to Navarre to fetch a bride for her favourite son, brought the girl across the Alps to Richard in Sicily. She was now in her seventy-first year, and in the high, elegantly hollowed cheekbones, the posture that conceded nothing to age, and the slanting green-gold eyes, Will could still see traces of the great beauty she'd once been. He was both fascinated and repelled by this woman who'd dared to outrage every tenet of the code governing proper female behaviour, but he was glad, none the less, to see her now, for she was the one person John might not dare to defy.

He watched as John greeted her with guarded formality, did not mind in the least when she made it pleasantly yet perfectly plain that his presence was not required. In a contest of wills between John and his mother, he did not think John would prevail, indeed hoped he would not. But he did not care to be a witness to their confrontation; he suspected Eleanor's methods would be neither maternal nor merciful.

Eleanor snapped her fingers and the last of the servants disappeared. As John handed her a goblet of mulled wine, she sipped in silence for some moments, then confirmed his worst fears. 'I do hope you have not entangled poor Will in your intriguing, John? That would be rather unsporting, like spearing fish in a barrel.'

'Should I know what that means, Madame?'

She leaned back against the settle cushions, eyed him reflectively. 'Do you have any memories of Gwendolen, John? No, I see not. She was a young Welsh girl, nurse first to your sister Joanna and then to you. I liked her, found the Welsh to be much like my own Poitevins, a people passionate yet practical. There was one Welsh proverb in particular Gwendolen was fond of quoting: "Better a friend at court than gold on the finger." ' She smiled faintly, glanced down at her hands, at the jewelled fingers entwined loosely in her lap. 'As you can see, I have gold rings in profusion. But I also have friends at court, John . . . at the French court.'

She waited, but John continued to look at her blankly, with the suggestion of a quizzical smile. 'Why is it,' he asked, 'that I suddenly feel as if I've stumbled into the wrong conversation?'

'You do that very well, John. Honest bewilderment, with just the right touch of humour. I do not doubt your indignation will be equally impressive. And if you insist, we can play the game out to the end. I'll tell you exactly what my informants at the French court revealed, and you can deny any and all knowledge of Philip's intrigues. I'll confront you with the fact that I know you've coerced the constables of Wallingford and Windsor to turn over the royal castles to you, and you can then concoct some perfectly innocent explanation for that.

'But eventually, John, we'll get to the truth. It may well take all night, but we will, that I promise you. So why do you not make it easy on both of us? It has been a very long day. I'm tired, John, am

69

asking you to keep this charade mercifully brief . . . for my sake if not your own.'

John could not say with which precise word she hit a nerve; it may have been the tone as much as the content. But by the time she stopped speaking, he was rigid with rage. 'For your sake? There was a time when I'd have done anything on God's earth for you, just to get you to acknowledge I was even alive! But now? You're too late, Mother, years too late!'

There was a sudden silence. John rose, retreated into the sheltering shadows beyond the hearth, but he could not escape her eyes, could feel them following him all the while. What had ever possessed him? Fool! In lashing out like that, he'd only shown her where his defences were weakest, most vulnerable to attack.

'What would you have me say, John?' she said at last. 'That you are my flesh and blood, my last-born, that I care, care more than you know? It would be easy enough to say, and I admit I might be tempted . . . if I thought you'd believe me.'

'I would not,' he said hastily, and she gave him an unexpected smile, a look of sardonic and surprising approval.

'Why should you? You were not yet six when Henry confined me in Salisbury Tower, sixteen when next I saw you, twenty-one when Richard ordered my release. How could I love you? I do not even know you. You were ever Henry's, never mine.'

'That's a lie,' John said bitterly. 'You never cared for me, never! Not from the day I was born. You think I do not remember how it was?'

'You exaggerate,' she said, but there was that in her voice which he'd never heard before, a faintly defensive note. 'Mayhap I did not have you with me as often as I should in those early years; I'll concede that. I'll concede, too, that I could take no joy in a pregnancy at forty-five. Why should I? I had just found out about Henry and that Clifford slut. He'd even dared to install her at Woodstock – Woodstock, my favourite manor!' She stopped abruptly, and John saw that she, too, had been goaded into saying that which she'd not meant to share.

'It is a pretty fiction that mothers must love each child in equal measure . . . a fiction, no more than that. There is always a favourite. With me, it was Richard. With Henry, it was you.'

'No,' John said, too quickly. 'I was not his favourite. It was rather that I was the only son he had left. Have you forgotten? My brothers

70

sided with you.' Again, John had the disquieting sense that he'd have done better to hold his tongue. Eleanor's eyes were too probing, too knowing. Cat's eyes, ever on the alert for movement in the grass, he thought uneasily, not reassured when she shrugged, said:

'If that's how you'd rather remember it. But I did not mean that as a reproach. I do not, in truth, think less of you for having the common sense to abandon a ship once waves began to break over the bow. Nor, after sixteen years shut away from the sun, am I likely to find tears to spare for Henry Plantagenet.'

Without warning, she came abruptly to her feet, crossed swiftly to John. 'But Richard – that is another matter altogether, John. Did you truly think I'd stand idly by whilst you plotted with Philip to usurp Richard's throne?'

When he sought to move away, she caught his arm. 'Of my children, I have ever loved Richard best, have never made a secret of it. My first loyalties are to him, will always be to him. But what you do not seem to realize is that they are then given to you. You want to be Richard's heir. Well, I, too, want that for you, am willing to do what I can to make it so.'

She sounded sincere, but John knew how little that meant; neither of his parents had ever held veracity to be a virtue. 'Why?' he said warily. 'The soul of sentiment you're not . . . Mother.'

She laughed. 'To your credit, neither are you. I've always thought sentimentality to be one of the cardinal sins, second only to stupidity.'

That afforded John a certain ironic amusement, for it was his private conviction that his brother Richard was decidedly stupid, in all but killing, at which he excelled. But he said nothing, let Eleanor lead him back to the settle.

'Richard's marriage is not working out. Unfortunately, the girl is as insipid as she is innocent, and so absurdly sweet-tempered that I suspect if you cut her, she'd bleed pure sugar. She and Richard . . . well, it's been like pairing a butterfly with a gerfalcon. I do not think it likely she'll give him a son.'

'And if she does not, that leaves only me . . . or Geoffrey's son. Richard prefers the boy; why do you not, Madame?'

'Arthur is not yet five; you're twenty-and-four. That in itself would be reason enough to favour you. And you are my son; that's another. Lastly, I think you have it in you to be a better king than

71

your past record would indicate. At least you're no fool, and most men are.'

'Even if you do favour me over Arthur, what of it? Richard has already made his choice.'

'No choice this side of the grave is irrevocable. Richard named Arthur as a means of keeping you in check whilst he was on crusade. Once he does return from the Holy Land, he may well reconsider, especially if I urge him to do so. I'm sure you'll agree that, if there be one voice he heeds, it is mine. If I speak for you, he's like to listen. But it does cut both ways, John. If I speak against you, he's apt to listen then, too. So it is up to you.'

'What do you want me to do?'

'It is rather what I want you to refrain from doing. No intrigues with Philip. No pleasure jaunts to Paris. No conniving with the Welsh or the Scots.' She paused, hazel eyes holding his own. Satisfied with what she saw in them, she rose, stifling a yawn. 'I expect a bedchamber has been made ready for me by now, so I'll bid you goodnight. I'm glad we did reach an understanding. But I rather thought we would, Johnny.'

'Do not call me that!' John said sharply, startling himself even more than Eleanor. She stared at him, eyebrows arching, and he flushed.

'I'd almost forgotten,' she said softly. 'That was what Henry always called you, was it not?'

John said nothing, and she moved towards the door, where she paused, turned to face him. 'If you should happen to suffer a change of heart in the night, John, decide that Philip's offer is a better gamble than mine . . . I think it only fair to tell you that, on the same day you sailed for France, I would personally give the command to seize all your lands, castles, and manors in England, confiscate them on behalf of the Crown.' And closing the door quietly behind her, she left him alone.

5

January, 1193
Gwynedd, Wales

They left Hawarden Castle in the early hours of a cloud-darkened dawn. A week of unrelenting rains had reduced the road to a mere memory, and as they headed west into Wales, they found themselves trudging through mud as thick and clinging as molasses. It splattered their legs and tunics, squished into their boots, made them fight for every footprint of ground gained. Exhaustion soon claimed Edwin; so, too, did disillusionment. Stumbling after his companions, blinded by gusts of wind-driven rain, chilled and utterly wretched, he could only wonder where the glory had gone.

All his eighteen years had been passed in the Cheshire village of Aldford. He had never even seen Chester, a mere five miles to the north. But three months ago, his cousin Godfrey had come back to Aldford. Godfrey was a legend in their family, the youth who'd willingly abandoned home and hearth for the alien world waiting without. Godfrey was a solidarius, a man who fought for pay, and he told his awestruck kin that he was now being paid by no less a lord than Ralph de Montalt, Lord of Hawarden and Mold, Seneschal of Chester. And then he told them why he'd come back: for Edwin.

There was no question of refusal; any village lad would have pledged his soul for such a chance. Much envied, Edwin had accompanied Godfrey back to Hawarden, eager to learn about war and women and the world beckoning beyond Aldford. But at Hawarden, he'd found only long hours, loneliness, scant pleasure. Garrison guard duty was monotonous and dreary. But this was far worse, this was unmitigated misery, and as he tripped and sprawled into the mud, blistered and sore and soaked to the skin, Edwin wished fervently that he'd never even heard of Godfrey, that he'd never laid eyes upon Hawarden Castle.

Of their mission, he knew only that the young knight they were escorting had an urgent message for Davydd ab Owain, a Welsh

Prince who had allied himself with the Normans. Godfrey had told him the Welsh Prince was encamped at Rhuddlan Castle, some twenty-five miles from Hawarden, and he wondered how long the journey would take. He wondered, too, why they were no longer following the coast, why they'd swung inland at Basingwerk Abbey.

'Godfrey?' He quickened his pace, caught his cousin's arm. 'Godfrey, why did we change our route? Are we not more vulnerable to attack in the hills?'

'You'd bloody well better believe it!' Godfrey tripped, cursed as the mud sucked at one of his boots. 'But our guide told de Hodnet that this is a quicker way, a road made long past by the Romans. And that Norman whore-son is set upon getting us to Rhuddlan as fast as he can, no matter the risk.'

Edwin had been about to ask who were these Romans, but with his cousin's last words, he forgot all else, stared at Godfrey in amazement. De Hodnet was a Norman, a knight; to Edwin, that made him a being beyond criticism. He glanced ahead at the knight, his eyes lingering admiringly upon the man's roan stallion, the silvery chain-mail armour. He felt no resentment that de Hodnet should ride while they walked. That was just the way of it, and now he ventured a timid protest.

'But Godfrey, surely he knows what he's doing. After all, he's a knight.'

'So? Does that make him the Lord Jesus Christ come down to earth again?' Godfrey sneezed. 'Think you that no man Norman-born can be a fool? As for his Norman knighthood, that'll count for naught against a Welsh longbow.'

'Should you speak so?' Edwin asked uneasily, provoking a snort of derisive laughter from his cousin.

'You think he'll hear? Nay, he knows just enough English to order us about.' Godfrey reached out, grasped Edwin's arm. 'If a man is like to lead you over a cliff, Little Cousin, you'd best see him for what he is. De Hodnet wears a long sword, and sits a horse well, but he's no more fit to wage war against the Welsh than our aunt Edith. He's as green as grass, lad, and as arrogant as Lucifer, and there are no more dangerous traits known to man or God.'

Edwin stared at him, dismayed. 'But . . . but he's been taught the ways of war. All knights . . .'

'Aye, and I dare say he'd fare well enough on a battlefield in France or Flanders. But what does he know of the Welsh? He was in service with Lord Fitz Warin for a time, did garrison duty at Fitz Warin's manor of Lambourne in Berkshire. After that, he found a place with a Wiltshire lord. Then his lord took the cross like King Richard, and de Hodnet had no urge to see the Holy Land.' Godfrey sneezed again, spat into the road. 'Shropshire, Berkshire, Wiltshire. But not Wales, Edwin, not Wales.'

He shook his head, said bitterly, 'Giles tried to tell him, warned him that the risk be too great, what with Llewelyn known to be in the area. But what Norman ever heeded Saxon advice? He does not know his arse from his elbow when it comes to fighting the Welsh, but he gives the orders, we obey, and if we reach Rhuddlan Castle, it'll be only by the grace of the Almighty.'

Edwin glanced over his shoulder at the shadowed, wet woods that rose up around them, dark spruce and pine blotting out the sky, giving shelter behind every bush to a Welsh bowman. The Welsh scorned the crossbow, preferred a weapon called a longbow, and they used it with deadly skill. According to Godfrey, a Welsh bowman could fire twelve arrows in the time it took to aim and fire one crossbow; he swore he once saw a Welsh bowman send an arrow through an oaken door fully four inches thick. Remembering that, Edwin hunched his shoulders forward, suddenly sure that even at that moment a Welsh arrow was being launched at his back.

'Who is Llewelyn?' he asked at last, and at once regretted it, for Godfrey gave him an incredulous look.

'God keep me if you are not as ignorant as de Hodnet!' But Edwin's discomfort was so painfully obvious that he relented somewhat. 'You do know that Davydd ab Owain claims to rule most of North Wales? Well, Llewelyn ab Iorwerth is his nephew and sworn enemy. They've been warring for nigh on six years, and were I to wager on the outcome, I'd want my money on Llewelyn. He's not much older than you, I hear, yet he's been able to get the people on his side, has forced Davydd on the defensive. Davydd still holds a few strongholds like Rhuddlan Castle, but Llewelyn now controls the countryside, owns the night.'

Edwin decided he did not want to hear any more, lapsed into a subdued silence. The rain had ceased, but the small patches of sky visible through the trees were an ominous leaden-grey. Although it was unusually mild for January, Edwin shivered each time the wind caught his gambeson. Stuffed with rags, quilted like eiderdown, it suddenly seemed a poor substitute for de Hodnet's chain-mail hauberk. He ran his hand over the padding, tried to convince himself that it could deflect a lance.

As the men moved deeper into the woods, so, too, their sense of unease deepened. They werc bunching up, all but treading upon each other's heels, moving at an unusually brisk pace for men who'd been on the march all day. Edwin paused to fish a pebble from his boot, sprinted to catch up. Panting, he slowed, came to a bewildered halt. The men had stopped, were gathered around Giles. Edwin squeezed into the circle, straining to hear.

Edwin was very much in awe of Giles. A dark, saturnine man in his forties, laconic and phlegmatic, he was renowned for his icy composure, and Edwin was stunned now to hear the raw emotion that crackled and surged in his voice.

'We've taken too great a risk as it is, should have followed the coast road. But if we take this path, we are begging to be ambushed!'

'I do not agree. We're losing the light, are wasting time even now that we can ill afford to squander. I have an urgent dispatch for Davydd ab Owain, a message that comes from His Grace, the Earl of Chester. I swore to my lord Montalt that I'd get it to Rhuddlan without delay, and that is what I mean to do.'

Giles stepped forward, stopped before the roan stallion. 'Sir Walter, I urge you to heed what I say. You do not know the Welsh, you do not know how they fight. This is not war as you learned it. It is bloody brutal work, with no quarter given. Let me tell you about the battle of Crogen. The old King, Henry of blessed memory, led an army into Wales, went up against Owain Fawr. The Welsh won the day, and King Henry was forced to retreat back into England. But ere he did, he had a number of Welsh hostages brought before him, wellborn men all, including two of Owain's own sons. He ordered them blinded, Sir Walter.'

The other's face did not change. 'That battle was fought nigh on thirty years ago. Why tell me this now?'

'Because you may be sure the Welsh do remember. Because that's how war is waged in Wales . . . on both sides. I've fought in Normandy, in Scotland, even Ireland, and I tell you true when I say the Welsh do make the worst enemies. They do not play by your rules, they win when they are not supposed to, and they do not know when they're beaten. They're wild and cunning and treacherous, not to be underestimated. It's been only a week since we captured one of Llewelyn's men not a mile from Hawarden. When we put the knife to him, he admitted that Llewelyn was encamped in these woods. Knowing that, we'd be mad to take yon path, no matter how much time we'd save.'

'Our guide assures me that this rebel you seem to fear so much is not in the area, that he's known to be in Arfon. He also assures me that this is the quickest way to Rhuddlan.' Walter de Hodnet paused, his eyes moving from Giles to the encircling men. Although most of them spoke only rudimentary French, it was evident that they'd followed the argument; their faces were flushed, hostile. He stared them down, and turning back to Giles, said curtly, 'Give the order to move out.'

Giles had black eyes, flat and shallow-lidded. They flickered now, glittered with impotent fury. And then he nodded, signalled the men to fall into line. There was hesitation, but only briefly. From the cradle, they were taught obedience to rank; rebellion was utterly beyond their ken.

But although they obeyed, they did not like it any. Walter could hear them muttering among themselves in the guttural English he found so harsh upon the ear. Saxon swine. As a boy, he'd thought it was one word, Saxonswine. Stupid and sly, the lot of them. It was always his accursed ill luck to have such oafs under his command. Little wonder he'd yet to win the recognition he craved, to find his niche. But this time would be different. By getting Chester's message to Rhuddlan by nightfall, he'd stand high in Montalt's favour. It was not inconceivable that Montalt might even make mention of him to Chester.

A smile softened his mouth at that, and for a happy moment he indulged in a gratifying daydream, imagining himself summoned by the mighty Earl, friend to King Richard, one of the most powerful lords of the realm. A knight in Chester's service would be a made man. He'd have no reason then to envy his elder brother Baldwin; Baldwin might even envy him.

His smile faded; thoughts of Baldwin were always sure to sour his mood. There was less than a year between them, but Baldwin was the eldest born, Baldwin was his father's heir, would inherit all when Sir Odo died. For Walter, for his brothers Will and Stephen, there would be nothing, only what they could win with their wits or their swords. And a younger son's options were limited. If he was fortunate, he might find a place for himself in some lord's household. Or he might try his luck in the tournament lists, but that was a risky

77

way to earn a living. For those who'd failed to find service with a lord, or lost in the lists, there was little left but banditry. Of course one could become a clerk, like his brother Will. But a clerk had no social status; he was a nonentity, of no account. Walter's mouth tightened; was he any better off, in truth? What had he except his horse, his armour, and a shilling a day in wages?

But if he could do this for Montalt and Chester . . . he glanced back over his shoulder, at Giles's dark sullen face. He'd managed to infect them all with his damned-fool fears; they were shying at every sound, as jumpy as cats. As little as he liked to admit it, it was even getting to him. He tilted his head back, studied the sky with narrowed eyes. Dusk was fast falling. But if their guide was right, they were less than seven miles from Rhuddlan.

Walter slid his fingers under the nose-guard of his helmet, rubbed the chafed skin across the bridge of his nose. What was the guide's name . . . Martin? A quiet sort, half-Welsh, half-Saxon, an outcast in both worlds. But he knew these hills as few men did, and he –

'Sir Walter!' Giles had come up alongside his stallion. Keeping his voice pitched for Walter's ear alone, he said tensely, 'You hear it – the silence? Suddenly there is not a sound, no birds, nothing.'

Walter stiffened, listened. Giles was right. 'Oh, Christ,' he whispered. He swung about in the saddle, peering into the surrounding shadows, saw nothing.

'Martin!' he called sharply. A few yards ahead, the guide turned, his face questioning. But as he did, a low humming noise cut through the eerie stillness. Walter gasped, flinched as a rush of hot air fanned past his face. His stallion leapt sideways, and he jerked on the reins, turned the animal in a circle. Only then did he see Giles. The other man had dropped to his knees in the road. As Walter watched, he tugged at the arrow shaft protruding from his chest, and then fell forward, slowly slid into the mud churned up by Walter's stallion.

For a moment frozen in time, nothing happened. And then one of Walter's men, the one called Godfrey, dropped to the ground, rolled towards a fallen log, shouting, 'Take shelter!' An arrow struck the log, scant inches from where he crouched, followed by an ear-splitting, wordless yell, and Walter's men panicked, whirled about, slipping in the mud, crashing into one another in their haste to escape the trap.

Walter jerked his sword from its scabbard. Godfrey's action had been instinctive, but Walter knew it was also futile. The Welsh were firing from both sides of the road, with savage-sounding battle cries that only panicked his men all the more. The woods offered no refuge, only shafted death, and he shouted, 'Make haste for the castle!' An arrow burned past his thigh, grazed his stallion's mane, and he spurred the animal forward. The horse stumbled over Giles's body, righted itself and lengthened stride. In the fading light, Walter never saw the rope stretched across the road. It caught him in the chest; he reeled backward, hit the ground with jarring impact.

When he came to, dazed and disoriented, he did not at first remember where he was. He groaned, started to move, and a knife blade was at once laid against his throat. Behind the knife were the coldest green eyes he'd ever seen. The man was young, twenty at most. He said something in Welsh, and Walter said, 'I do not understand.'

The youth spoke again, harshly, and Walter shook his head, tried to sit up. His coif was jerked off, and the knife nicked into his throat; a thin red line appeared upon his neck. He froze, scarcely breathing, and the pressure eased slightly.

From the corner of his eye, he could see several figures huddled on the ground, a freckle-faced, frightened youngster, Godfrey, and a third man smeared with his own blood. Beyond them, a body lay sprawled in the mud, and nearby a young Welshman, seeking to soothe Walter's roan stallion.

Another man was now bending over him, a huge youth with a scarred cheek and deep-set brown eyes. He reached for the neck of Walter's hauberk and, as Walter recoiled, he grinned. 'Easy, English,' he said, in accented but understandable French. 'The Lord loveth a cheerful giver!'

He drew out the rolled parchment, eyes widening at sight of the Earl of Chester's seal. 'Chester,' he murmured, passing the scroll to his companion. 'Well, well. You fly high, English.'

Walter drew a deep breath, thanking God for this French-speaking, amiable giant. Surely he could reason with this one. But the other . . . he glanced at the glinting blade, swallowed and said in a rush, 'My name is Sir Walter de Hodnet, son of Sir Odo de Hodnet of Welbatch in Shropshire. My father is a man of means, and will pay dear for my safe return.'

'Indeed?' The Welshman smiled at him. 'Horses? Gold?'

'Yes, both.' Knowing his father would not part with so much as a shilling on his behalf.

'You hear, Rhys? We've a man of wealth in our midst. Tell me, English, what of your men there? Who ransoms them?'

Walter stared up at him, perplexed. Who'd pay money for men-at-arms? 'I do not see . . .'

'No, I know you do not. But I'd wager your men do.' He was no longer smiling, and Walter's mouth went dry. Giles's voice was suddenly thudding in his ears: he blinded them. Blinded them. Blinded them.

He was barely twenty, his face contorted with pain, sweat beading his upper lip, his temples. A dark stain was spreading rapidly across his tunic. Llewelyn knew few injuries were as dangerous as an upper thigh wound; all too often the man died before the bleeding could be checked. Drawing his dagger, he split the tunic, set about fashioning a rude tourniquet. It was with considerable relief that he saw it begin to take effect.

'You're a lucky lad, Dylan,' he said and grinned. 'Half a hand higher and you'd have lost the family jewels.'

Dylan was chalk-white, but he managed a weak smile at that, whispered, 'Jesu forfend.'

Two men were bringing up a blanket stretched across two poles, and Llewelyn rose, watched as Dylan was lowered on to it. A flash of movement caught his eye. He turned, saw the guide Martin standing several feet away. Llewelyn unfastened a pouch at his belt, sent it spinning through the air. Martin caught it deftly, tucked it away in his tunic. For a moment their eyes held; then he silently saluted Llewelyn and vanished into the wooded darkness beyond the road.

Ednyved was now at his side. He said, 'Well?'

'Three dead, including one gut-shot so badly that I thought he'd count death a mercy. Four captured. The rest fled. One horse taken. And this.' Handing Llewelyn the parchment roll.

Llewelyn, too, was startled at sight of the seal. 'Chester, no less!' He turned, beckoned to the closest man. 'Rosser, fetch a torch.'

'One of those taken is the lack-wit who led them right to us. A fool of the first order, but you might want to talk with him, none the less, Llewelyn. He says his name is de Hodnet. Is that not what an English friend of yours be called, too?'

Surprised, Llewelyn nodded. 'Yes, Stephen de Hodnet. Yet the last I heard, Stephen was attached to Fulk Fitz Warin's household, not Montalt's. Of course Stephen does have several brothers –' He broke off, and after a moment, laughed, shook his head. 'But no, I could not be that lucky!'

Godfrey was cursing under his breath. Edwin sat stunned and silent beside him. They both stiffened at Llewelyn's approach, watched warily as he stopped before them, and then moved towards Walter de Hodnet.

Walter waited, no less warily. The man standing before him was quite young, nineteen or twenty, dressed in the same homespun as his comrades, and Walter was startled when he said, in fluent French, 'I'm Llewelyn ab Iorwerth. Welcome to Wales.'

Walter flushed; even as frightened as he was, he did not miss the mockery in the other's voice. But he could not afford pride, not now, and he said hurriedly, 'It's glad I am that you speak French, my lord. If I may say so, you're young to have made such a name for yourself.' He summoned up a smile, was encouraged when Llewelyn smiled back. 'My lord Llewelyn, may I speak plainly? I can pay for my release; you need only name your price. My father –'

'You do not remember me, do you?'

Bewildered, Walter shook his head. 'We've met? My lord, I think not. I would . . .'

Llewelyn was still smiling. 'A pity your memory is so poor, Walter de Hodnet. For I do remember you, all too well.'

This was no pretence, Llewelyn saw; Walter was genuinely baffled. He stood looking down at the Norman knight, and then, abruptly tiring of this cat-and-mouse game, he said, 'I think you'll remember if you put your mind to it. Think back some years, to a summer noon and a meadow beyond Shrewsbury, to a chestnut gelding and a fearful ten-year-old boy.'

'I still do not –' Walter began, and then sucked in his breath. Llewelyn saw his face twitch, saw his eyes glaze over with horror, and he said:

'You see? You have not forgotten me after all.'

Rhys and Ednyved had been following this exchange with increasing curiosity. Now Rhys demanded, 'What is this English to you, Llewelyn?'

81

'A man who has long owed me a debt.' Speaking rapidly in Welsh, Llewelyn gave them a terse summary of that long-ago encounter by Yokethul Brook, concluding in French, 'So what do you say? What shall I do with him?'

Rhys's eyes flicked to Walter. 'Need you ask? Kill him,' he said, without hesitation. He'd answered in Welsh, for he used French only under duress, but it was obvious that Walter understood; he was ashen.

'Ednyved?'

Ednyved shrugged. 'This English is such a dolt, it would be almost a shame to lose him; never have I seen a man so eager to be ambushed. And he is the brother of your friend. Would his death grieve Stephen?'

'I very much doubt it,' Llewelyn said dryly, saw Walter flinch, and thought that Stephen had just unknowingly gained vengeance for a childhood of beatings and intimidation.

'Well, I can think of no other reasons to spare him, Llewelyn. There are too many English as it is; one less would be no loss. This grievance you hold against him, how deep does it fester?'

Llewelyn smiled at that. 'Is there ever a time when you do not go right to the heart of the matter? The answer is, of course, that it does not . . . not any more.'

He gazed down at Walter, his eyes thoughtful. And then he turned, for Rosser was approaching with a burning pine torch.

'Ah, at last.' Breaking the seal, he held the parchment up to the light. 'Let's see what message is worth the lives of three men.' Beginning to read, he laughed aloud, beckoned to those within hearing range.

'It seems King Richard had more to fear from his fellow Christian crusaders than he did from the infidels. On his way back from the Holy Land, he fell into the hands of his erstwhile ally, the Duke of Austria, is being held for ransom by the German Emperor!'

His men had gathered around to listen. They burst out laughing, too, began to exchange markedly unsympathetic quips about the English King's plight.

Llewelyn was rapidly scanning the rest of the letter. 'Wait, you've yet to hear the best of it. When word reached England, Richard's brother John did himself proud in the finest tradition of Cain and Abel, at once set about gaining the Crown for himself. He's sailed for France, where he means to ally himself with the French King

Philip. It seems they plan to offer the Emperor an even larger ransom not to let Richard go!'

Llewelyn was elated, for nothing better served Welsh interests than English discord. God had indeed been good to Wales, he thought, in giving Richard a brother as untrustworthy as John. With Richard languishing in some Austrian castle and John scheming to steal the throne, the English would be too taken up with their own troubles to have time to spare for Welsh conquest. That meant he'd have a free hand to move against Davydd, to force a battle that would break his uncle's power once and for all.

'One good turn deserves another, so I wish John well,' he said and laughed again. 'For although he does not know it yet, he's going to give me Gwynedd.'

'I do not doubt it, my Prince,' Ednyved said with mock servility, 'but at the moment you're a rebel on the run, and we'd best be gone ere any of those English soldiers reach Rhuddlan. Now,' jerking his head towards their captives, 'what mean you to do about them?'

'To tell you true, Ednyved, I have not made up my mind.' Llewelyn walked over, looked down at his prisoners.

Godfrey tensed, and then blurted out in broken French, 'My lord, spare my cousin. He's but a lad of eighteen; do not put him to the knife, I beg you.'

'Why should I put any of you to the knife? There are but two legitimate times for torture, when a man has information you must have or if he has committed a sin so great that justice demands he suffer for it.'

But Godfrey did not fully believe him, Llewelyn saw.

And what of Walter de Hodnet? A rare jest of God, in truth, that de Hodnet should fall into his hands now, years too late. Walter was mute; but his eyes pleaded with anguished eloquence.

'You fear more than death, do you not?' Llewelyn said slowly. 'You think I mean to extract every ounce of mortal suffering for a boyhood wrong. A pity, Walter, you know so little of the Welsh. You see, we have a saying amongst my people: *O hir ddyled ni ddylir dim*. From an old debt, nothing is due.'

Walter stared up at him, in utter disbelief. Rhys looked no less startled, but Ednyved laughed, as if at some private joke. 'I thought it was your ambition to be Prince of Gwynedd, Llewelyn. Are you seeking sainthood, too?'

'I know you're woefully ignorant of the Scriptures, Ednyved, but

83

even you must have heard: Vengeance is mine, saith the Lord.' Llewelyn paused, and then added in Welsh, 'Of course we do have another proverb I rather fancy: the best revenge, contempt.'

Ednyved nodded, eyes alight in amused understanding. 'Now that sounds more like you,' he said, as Walter found his voice.

'You truly mean to let me go?' He sounded more suspicious than relieved, for magnanimity to an enemy was an alien concept to him.

'Yes, I do . . . but I rather doubt you'll thank me for it. For I mean to release your men, too. I should think they'll have a most interesting tale to tell Montalt. You've hardly endeared yourself to them, have you?'

Walter opened his mouth, shut it abruptly, but he was unable to keep his eyes from shifting towards Godfrey. Llewelyn saw, smiled.

'Of course you will have time to think up an explanation for your appalling ineptitude . . . on your walk to Rhuddlan. For although you are free to go, we'll be keeping your horse and armour. Spoils of war . . . remember?'

Five minutes ago, Walter would have bartered anything on God's earth for his life and not counted the cost. But his were now the changed priorities of reprieve, and he gave a gasp of dismay. 'If I do reach Rhuddlan like that – naked, alone, on foot – Christ, I'll be a laughing-stock!'

'Yes,' Llewelyn agreed. 'I know.' And signalling to two of his men, he said, 'Strip him of his armour.'

Walter scrambled to his feet, began to back away. In that instant, his fear of humiliation was greater than his fear of death, and his eyes darted to the dagger in Llewelyn's belt. For a mad moment, he saw himself lunging for it, plunging the blade into Llewelyn's chest and racing for the woods.

But his was an easy face to read. Llewelyn felt a sudden urge of excitement. 'It is your choice, Walter,' he said softly, almost encouragingly.

Walter's throat muscles contracted; he had not enough saliva to swallow. The realization that Llewelyn wanted him to go for the knife was a lifeline back to sanity. Appalled by what he'd almost done, he sagged against the nearest tree.

'I swear by all the saints that you'll regret this day,' he said, choking on his hatred, and Rhys lost all patience. In three strides, he'd crossed the clearing, had his dagger poised at Walter's throat.

'Are you so eager to die, English?' he demanded. 'Think you that we need an excuse to claim your life?'

'He does not speak Welsh, Rhys,' Llewelyn said, amused, and Rhys smiled grimly.

'Mayhap not, but he understands me well enough.'

Walter had lost all colour; a vein showed at his temple, throbbed wildly against skin damp with sweat.

'Yes,' Llewelyn conceded. 'I dare say he does!' Glancing up at the darkening sky, he realized that they'd already tarried here too long, and he moved towards Walter's men. 'You understand what was said?'

Godfrey had been staring at Walter de Hodnet, eyes glittering. Now he looked up at Llewelyn, nodded, and then grinned. '*Merci,*' he said, and then gestured towards Walter, adding something in English which Llewelyn did not understand; he caught only a name, Giles.

But time was on his uncle's side; some of the fleeing soldiers might have reached Rhuddlan by now. He still held Chester's dispatch. Unsheathing his dagger, he slashed at the parchment until it hung in tattered ribbons. Handing it to the wide-eyed Edwin, he said in slow, deliberate French, 'Here, lad. Give this to Montalt. And tell him that Llewelyn ab Iorwerth has a message for Chester: stay out of Wales.'

Edwin could not envision himself giving a message like that to a Norman lord, and he was much relieved when his cousin said, 'I'd like nothing better, my lord!'

Edwin released his breath, clutched the shredded parchment to his chest. Godfrey would keep faith with the young Welsh lord, and he was glad, for they owed this man their lives. He doubted that the Earl of Chester would heed the warning, would stay out of Wales. But he would, he thought, with sudden resolve. He was going home. Home to Aldford.

May, 1194
Lisieux, Normandy

In January, 1194, Queen Eleanor reached Germany with the one hundred thousand silver marks demanded as ransom for her son's freedom. Richard was finally released on February 4, one year and six weeks after he'd been taken captive in Austria. By March he was once more upon English soil, where he set about extinguishing the embers of his brother John's rebellion. John's castles of Tickhill and Nottingham fell to him within a fortnight, and on March 31, he summoned John to appear before his great council. John was given forty days to answer the charges of treason. He defied the summons, did not appear, and on May 10, he was outlawed, declared to have forfeited any claims to the Angevin crown, and then stripped of the earldoms of Gloucester and Mortain, of his castles, estates, and manors in England and Normandy.

Two days later, Richard and Eleanor sailed from Portsmouth. Landing at Barfleur, they headed south into Normandy. Lingering a few days at Caen, they moved on to Lisieux, where they were greeted with excessive affability by Archdeacon John de Alençon, Richard's vice-chancellor, and there joined by Joanna Plantagenet, sister to Richard, daughter to Eleanor, young widow of William the Good, King of Sicily.

'. . . and after I set up a gallows before the walls of Nottingham Castle, hanged a score of John's men and left them for the ravens, the others lost their taste for treason, moved out even faster than the ravens moved in!'

'What of Johnny, Richard? Have you any word as to his whereabouts?'

'Oh, I know exactly where John is, Joanna – skulking about the French court. He fled to Paris months ago, after Philip sent him warning that my release was imminent. "Look to yourself; the Devil is loose,"' Richard quoted with relish, and then laughed.

Joanna laughed, too. 'This has not been one of Philip's better years, what with your return and his troubles with the Pope.'

'What is the truth of that, Jo? The garbled account I heard did not seem likely to me, that Philip sought to repudiate his Queen the day after their marriage?'

'Likely or not, it's true enough. They were wed at Amiens last August, and the very next day Philip disavowed the marriage, refused to recognize Ingeborg as his Queen. When she balked at being shipped back to Denmark like defective goods, Philip convened a council of French bishops at Compiègne, got them to declare the marriage null and void, then confined Ingeborg to a nunnery. But the Danish King did not take kindly to this, and he appealed to the Pope on his sister's behalf. I expect His Holiness will order Philip to take Ingeborg back, but Philip is nothing if not stubborn, and I'm not sure he'll yield even if the Pope does lay France under Interdict.'

'Jesu, the idiot, the utter idiot!' Richard shook his head in amused amazement. 'Mayhap I ought to ask him if he wants to send Ingeborg to me at Rouen. We could pen her up with Alais, split the cost of their upkeep!'

He laughed again. In the shadows behind him, Archdeacon Alençon could not hide his disapproval. After a moment, his eyes shifted from Richard to the woman at his side. Eleanor was watching her son, a faint smile curving her mouth. It was not a smile to give Alençon comfort, reminding him what an implacable enemy this woman made. Upon gaining her own freedom, one of her first acts had been to declare an amnesty for those imprisoned in English jails, declaring that she knew from personal experience 'how irksome it was to be a prisoner'. And yet she'd shown no pity at all for the woman confined for five years now at her son's command, the unfortunate Alais, who'd been raised at her court, had come to womanhood in her husband's bed.

But it was too late to worry about Eleanor's enmity. He'd chosen to gamble, could only hope he'd not made a fool's wager. Moving closer, he murmured, 'Madame, might I have a few moments alone with you? I've a matter most urgent to discuss.'

Eleanor felt no surprise. She had a sharp eye for the unease of others, and Alençon's overly hearty welcome put her in mind of a man whistling his way past a graveyard. She asked no questions, came unobtrusively to her feet, and followed Alençon from the hall.

The Archdeacon's manor was a substantial structure of stone and timber, rising up two storeys on the bank of the River Touques. It was to an upper chamber that Alençon led Eleanor, stepping aside so she could enter first. As she did, he closed the door quietly behind her. Eleanor stood very still, staring at the man by the unshuttered window, silhouetted against a twilight sky of soft, shadowed lavender.

'Mother,' he said at last, so low she could not be sure he'd spoken at all.

There was an oil lamp sputtering on a trestle table. She reached for it, took several strides forward into the room, held it up so that the smoky light fell across his face.

John blinked, flinched away from the sudden illuminating glare. His mother's face was impassive, but her eyes pinned him to the wall, amber ice in which he could read the reflection of his every sin, could read accusation and indictment, but no hint of absolution.

He forgot entirely his carefully rehearsed plea of explanation and atonement. When the silence had become more than he could endure, he blurted out, 'You know why I'm here. I need you to speak for me. You're the one person Richard would be likely to heed.'

'I dare say you're right. But whatever makes you think I would?'

Eleanor set the lamp on the table, turned back to her silent son. 'At least you've shown you're not the utter coward Richard thinks you to be; he was sure you'd not dare leave the sanctuary of the French court. Although how you'd have the nerve to face him after all you've done – allying yourself with your brother's sworn enemy against your own House, promising to wed your father's harlot and to cede the Vexin back to Philip in return for his support; hiring Welsh mercenaries and seeking to stir up a rising in England; doing your damnedest to sabotage the collection of Richard's ransom; and when all else failed, joining with Philip in offering to better Richard's ransom if the German Emperor would but hold Richard for another year. Have I left anything out?'

'No,' he said shortly, unwillingly.

'Well then, suppose you tell me why I should want to help you escape the punishment you so deserve, why I should raise even a finger on your behalf. And do spare me any maudlin pleas about you being flesh of my flesh; you'll have to do better than that, John . . . much better.'

John drew an uneven breath. 'Nothing has changed since that

night we talked in Southampton. Your hopes for an Angevin dynasty are not going to take root with Richard's seed. He's not laid eyes upon his wife in nigh on two years, did not even bother to summon her to England upon his return. Unless you are counting upon another Virgin Birth, Madame, I suggest that leads us right back to Arthur or me, a child of seven or a man grown of twenty-six.'

'Yes,' she said icily. 'But the child is as yet unformed clay; who knows what manner of man he may become? Whereas we already know the man you are, John.'

John was not as impervious to insult as he'd have her think; he betrayed himself with rising colour. 'Yes, you do . . . a man who knows what he wants and will fight to keep what is his. Can you say as much for Arthur? I might make use of Philip's help if it serves my need, but we'll see the Second Coming ere I'd trust him out of my sight. But Arthur? His advisers wax fat on French gold, look to Paris for guidance the way infidels do look to Mecca. He'd be Philip's puppet and you well know it, Madame. Just as you know I would not.'

'What I want to know,' she said, 'is how you can be shrewd enough to see all that and yet stupid enough to fall in with Philip's schemes, to so disregard my promise . . . and my warning.'

Her tone was barbed; each word carried a separate sting. And yet John sensed he'd gained some ground. 'For what it's worth, I fully meant to hold to our understanding.'

'Why did you not, then?'

'The truth? Because Richard's capture unbalanced the equation. I truly did not think he'd ever come back, not with the enemies he's made. I saw the crown up for the taking, and so . . .' He shrugged. 'I put in my bid. What more can I tell you?'

Eleanor's mouth twitched. 'Credit where due, you can surprise. I was curious as to what your last line of defence would be. But I admit I did not expect you to fall back upon honesty!'

With that, John no longer hesitated. 'Well?' he said. 'Will you help me, Mother? Will you intercede with Richard on my behalf?'

She gave him a look he could not interpret. 'I already have.'

John's relief was intense but ephemeral. So this whole scene had been yet another of her damnable games, he thought resentfully, a stupid charade as meaningless as it was malicious.

'Richard can be unpredictable, so there are no guarantees. But he did agree that if you came to him, he'd hear you out. It might help,' she added dryly, 'if you sought to appear somewhat contrite.'

She started towards the door, stopped when he made no move to follow. 'What are you waiting for? Richard's below in the great hall; now will be as good a time as any.'

'The great hall?' John echoed in dismay. He thought it penance enough to have to humble his pride before Richard, was not about to put on a performance for a hall full of witnesses. But as he opened his mouth to protest, he caught the contempt in his mother's eyes. She was like Richard, he knew, in that she, too, was one for setting tests and traps for people, measuring their worth by standards that made no allowance for frailties or failure. Richard judged a man by his willingness to bleed, to risk his life upon the thrust of a sword. With his mother, the test was more subtle and yet more demanding. She might forgive deceit and betrayal, but never weakness, would expect above all else that a man be willing to answer for the consequences of his actions.

'I suppose you're right.' He moved away from the window, gave her a crooked smile. 'What was it the Christian martyrs always said before they were thrown to the lions . . . *morituri te salutamus*?'

'Your command of Latin is not bad, but your grasp of history is rather weak. "We who are about to die salute you" was the battle cry of the Roman gladiators, not Christian martyrs. We can safely say you have no yearning whatsoever for martyrdom, but it will be interesting, none the less, to see how you handle yourself in the lion's den.' Eleanor's laugh was not in the least maternal, but John knew he'd pulled back from the brink in time, had scrambled to safety even as the ground seemed sure to crumble under his feet.

Men stared at sight of John, fell suddenly silent. Eleanor stepped aside so that he stood alone. Richard was sitting on the dais at the far end of the hall. John hesitated, then began the longest walk of his life. So quiet it was that he could hear the scuffling sound his boots made as they trod upon the floor rushes, hear the clinking of his sword in its scabbard, even, or so he imagined, the thudding of his own heart. Richard had not moved, was watching him approach, eyes narrowed and utterly opaque. John stopped before the dais, slowly unbuckled his scabbard and laid it upon the steps. Then he knelt.

'My liege.' In the brief time allotted to him for calculation, he'd decided that candour was his best hope. It had served him well with his mother, might, if he were lucky, appease Richard, too. In truth, what other choice did he have? For what could he possibly say that Richard would believe?

'I can offer you no excuses, Richard. I can only ask for your forgiveness. I know I've given you no reason to –' He stopped in mid-sentence, for he'd just recognized the woman seated at Richard's left, a slim woman with green eyes and reddish-gold hair gleaming under a silvery gossamer veil, a woman he'd not seen for eighteen years. His sister Joanna.

'I'm surprised to see you here, John. Frankly, I did not think you'd have the nerve. I was not surprised, however, by your treachery, by your willingness to snap at Philip's bait. You're as easily led astray as any child, have never learned to say no. It's lucky you were not born a woman, Little Brother; you'd have been perpetually pregnant!'

Richard laughed, and so did most of the others in the hall. The colour drained from John's face; he bit down on his lower lip until it bled, sought to focus upon the pain to the exclusion of all else.

Rising, Richard bent down, picked up John's sword. 'But you're here; that counts for something. And our lady mother would have me forgive you; that counts for much. I suppose I should just be thankful that, since you are so much given to treachery, you're so reassuringly inept at it!' He stepped forward, held out John's sword. 'Your betrayals are forgiven, Little Brother . . . if not forgotten. But though your blood buys you a pardon, the price is higher for an earldom, higher than you can pay. I've no intention of restoring your titles and lands, not until I'm damned well sure that you're deserving of them . . . if ever.'

John came to his feet, reached for his sword. Richard was some inches the taller of the two, and now, standing on the dais stairs, he towered over the younger man. As their eyes met, John said, quite tonelessly, 'I shall remember your generosity, Brother. You may count upon that.'

Supper was generally an afterthought, but that evening's meal was an unusually bountiful one; in his relief that his risky role as peace-maker had met with such success, Archdeacon Alençon emptied his larders, set before Richard a succession of meat and fish dishes, highly seasoned venison and salmon swimming in wine gravy. The salmon Richard dispatched to John's end of the table, with a good-humoured but heavy-handed jest about the Prodigal Son and the

91

Fatted Calf. To John, the taste was bitter as gall, and as soon after the meal as he could, he escaped the hall, out into the dark of the gardens.

He was alone but a few moments, however. Joanna had followed, came forward to sit beside him on a rough-hewn oaken bench. 'Here,' she said, thrusting a wine cup into his hand. 'I think you're in need of this.'

They'd got on well as children; she was only two years older than he, and he'd been sorry when their father had sent her off to Sicily as an eleven-year-old bride for William the Good. When he thought now upon his humiliation in the great hall, it was Joanna's presence there that he minded the most, and he said sharply, 'If you've come to offer pity, I do not want any!'

'You need not worry; I do not think you're deserving of any. You were not "led astray", knew exactly what you were doing . . . and got what you deserved.' But then she gave him a direct, searching glance. 'Does that offend you, Johnny?'

'No,' John said, surprised to discover that he actually preferred her matter-of-fact rebuke to Richard's contemptuous pardon, and when she smiled at him, he smiled back.

'I'm glad,' she said simply. 'I can tell you then, that I think Richard erred. A pardon should be generously given or not at all. For all that Richard has a fine gasp of tactics, he's always been woefully lacking in tact!'

And what was he expected to say to that, John wondered, agree and incriminate himself? But after a moment to reflect, he dismissed the suspicion as unwarranted. For all the love that lay between them, he could not truly see Joanna as Richard's spy. Nor, were he to be fair, was that Richard's way, either. Richard would not take the trouble.

'I'd rather not talk of that, Jo.' The childhood name came without thought, was curiously comforting, evoking echoes of an almost forgotten familiarity. 'You're beautiful, you know, you truly are. Not at all the skin-and-bones sister I remember! Joanna Plantagenet, Queen of Sicily, Duchess of Apulia, Princess of Capua. Were you happy, Jo, in Sicily?'

'Not at first. I was too young, too homesick. But William meant well by me, gave me no cause for complaint. He was some thirteen years older, treated me like a daughter until I was ready to be a wife. Yes, I was happy enough. But at thirty-six, he died leaving no heirs,

92

and as you know, his bastard cousin Tancred seized the throne. Tancred not only denied me my dower rights, he put me into close confinement at Palermo. I sometimes wonder what would have become of me, Johnny, if not for Richard. He landed at Messina on his way to the Holy Land, and when Tancred balked at releasing me, restoring my dower, Richard laid siege to the town, forced Tancred into submission.'

Yes, John thought, and then he took you with him to the Holy Land, where he offered you to the brother of the infidel Prince Saladin. But he said nothing.

'Richard's arrival at Messina was a godsend, in truth, and I will be ever grateful to him. Yet I do not doubt you'd have done as much for me, too, Johnny. So would our brother Henry. Even Geoffrey, provided it did not inconvenience him unduly. Any one of you would have come to my aid, I know that. And yet none of you would ever have come to the aid of each other. I've often thought on that.'

'When I was sixteen, Jo, Papa sought to persuade Richard to cede the Aquitaine to me. Our brother Henry was a year dead, and Papa promised to name Richard as his heir, but he thought it only fair that Richard should then yield up Aquitaine in return. Richard did not see it that way, flared into a rage and swore he'd be damned ere he'd agree. Papa flew into an equal rage, told me that Aquitaine was mine if I could take it from Richard. A sixteen-year-old boy has no money for troops. But the Duke of Brittany does, and Geoffrey offered to provide the men and money, told me this was the chance of a lifetime. So Geoffrey and I led an army into Poitou, and Richard burned damned near half of Brittany in retaliation . . . until Papa made haste to summon us all to London, told us he had not meant to be taken seriously.'

They were both silent for a time after that. John leaned over, plucked a primrose from the closest bush, and presented it to Joanna with self-mocking gallantry. 'Tell me, Jo, why did you follow me out to the gardens? What did you want to say to me?'

'Do you remember what I would call you whenever we'd have a falling out? Johnny-cat, because you were always poking about where you had no right to be.'

'I remember. I never liked it much.'

'I could not help thinking of that as I watched you and Richard in the great hall. You offered up your eighth life in there, Johnny-cat. You do know that?'

93

'Christ, Joanna, of course I do. Do you think anything less than that could have brought me to Lisieux?'

'Thank God you see that,' she said sombrely. 'I was so afraid you would not. Because I know Richard; he'd not forgive you again, Johnny. The next time you fall from grace will be the last time. For your sake, I do hope you never forget that.'

September, 1196
Yorkshire, England

Too excited to sleep, Joanna awakened just before dawn on the morning of her fifth birthday. Taking care not to disturb her mother, she slid from their bed, pulled her gown over her head, and ran a wooden comb through her tangled dark hair. She knew she should wash her face, clean her teeth with a hazel twig, but she could not wait; the day, her very own, was beckoning.

In the outer room, Maud still slept, rolled up in blankets by the hearth. Joanna tiptoed around her, searching for food to break the night's fast. The only furniture the room contained was a trestle table, a coffer chest, and several stools, but it was cluttered with household utensils: her mother's distaff and spindle, a pile of reeds Maud meant to plait into baskets, the hand-mill Maud used to grind their corn, several letten pots and pans. In the corner an armful of peeled rushes was being steeped in tallow fat; Joanna's nose wrinkled at the pungent smell. Reassured by Maud's steady snoring, she broke off a chunk of thick, black rye bread, smeared it with cheese, and headed for the door.

Outside, she paused by the hen roost, soothed her conscience by scattering a handful of seeds in among the chickens. Joanna very much wanted her mother to think her responsible, did not mean to shirk her household duties. But the morning sky was clear and cloudless, the brilliant blue of her mother's eyes, and the wind rippled through the moorland grass, stirring up a billowing green sea that swept all before it as it raced for the distant silver of the River Ure. Joanna let the wind take her, too; breaking into a run, she skimmed the grass, arms outstretched and hair streaming behind her like an ebony sail, and for a moment or two she actually was a small boat, bound for exotic, alien shores.

She slowed as she approached the cottage, home to Cedric, the young Saxon farmer who did for them those chores that required a man's hand. Cedric's cottage looked, at first glance, much like their own: thatched roof and timber framework, covered with clay, chopped straw, and cow-dung. But it was much smaller, contained a single room for Cedric, his wife Eda, and their three children. Joanna had once sneaked a look inside, knew they all slept on pallets around the hearth, lacking the straw mattress and wooden bedframe she shared with her mother. Nor did they have the feather pillows, the embroidered coverlets, or the hand mirror of polished metal, all of which Joanna's mother had brought with her from her home to the south, the home Joanna had never seen.

As early as it was, Cedric's family was already up and about. He was disappearing into the distance, on his way to the fields he worked with the other villagers. Eda was toting a bucket of milk towards the cottage, and the children were chasing the chickens out of the garden. They were making a noisy game of it, herding the hens in a circle, and Joanna felt a pang of envy, yearning to join in. She'd watched Cedric's children for months, knew the boy was called Derwin and his sisters Rowena and Elfrida, names strange and foreign-sounding to Joanna. She knew, too, that they were not proper playmates for her; Maud had warned her often enough of that. Saxon peasants, she'd said scornfully, bound to the land, who could be bought and sold and were born to serve. That had confused Joanna somewhat, for she knew that Maud, too, was a servant. Maud had nursed her mother, called her 'lamb' and 'sweeting' and yet she was still a servant; Joanna had heard her mother remind Maud of that more than once. So why, then, did she look upon Cedric and his family with such contempt?

No, Joanna did not understand. It mattered little to her that Cedric's children were serfs, that they spoke an alien tongue. She would even have dared her mother's wrath, so lonely was she, so eager for friends. But Rowena and Elfrida had shied away from all her overtures, stared at her with suspicious, wary eyes, and at last she'd stopped trying. Yet she still wondered why they would not play with her. Was it because she was Norman? Because Cedric addressed her mother as 'my lady'? Or because she was 'different'?

For as young as she was, Joanna was aware of the irregular aspects of her homelife. She had no family but her mother. They had no friends, no visitors, and the past was a forbidden terrain, a land of dark secrets, secrets Joanna instinctively feared. There was so much she did not understand, but she sensed that what was wrong in their lives was somehow her fault.

Now the other children had noticed her, were whispering among themselves, laughing. Joanna turned, walked away.

But her spirits lifted, as always, at sight of the castle. She spent hours here some days, watching the people passing in and out of the bailey. Four times a year Maud would mount the steps into the keep, would pay the rent for their cottage to Guy, bailiff for Robert Fitz Ranulf, Lord of Middleham. Joanna had begged in vain to accompany Maud on these quarter-day visits, and the world hidden away behind those timbered outer walls remained a mystery to her.

Stretching out in the grass, she picked up a stick and cleared a space. Her mother was different from the villagers in yet another way; she could read and write. Very few women had such a skill, she'd told Joanna one night when wine had loosened her tongue, but her father – Joanna's grandfather – had permitted her to be taught with her brothers. 'He was so proud of me, Joanna . . . once,' she whispered, and when she began to cry, Joanna cried, too; she dreaded her mother's tears even more than her slaps.

Now she patted the earth till it was smooth, took the stick and laboriously scrawled her mother's name in the dirt: CLEMENCE. Then she traced JOANNA below it. But that was the extent of her knowledge; Clemence had neither the patience nor the aptitude to instruct, and her sporadic attempts to teach Joanna the alphabet had come to naught.

A solitary child is more given to daydreaming, and Joanna was no exception. She lost track of time; the morning drifted away on an easterly breeze. Yawning, she sat up in the grass, and then saw how high the sun was in the sky. It was nigh on ten o'clock; she was perilously close to being late for dinner. Joanna scrambled to her feet, began to run.

Sprinting through the village, with several barking dogs at her heels, she raced for home. Maud kept a water bucket outside the door and, proud that she'd remembered, she conscientiously washed the dirt from her face and hands. But she'd splashed water about too freely, and looked with dismay now at the splotches darkening the skirt of her gown. She was always displeasing her mother and Maud, and yet she tried so hard to be good, she truly did.

She hoped the mud stains would pass unnoticed, but at sight of her, Maud set down her bowl with a thud. 'And where have you

97

been, rooting about in the pigsty? For the love of the Lord, look at the child!'

Clemence, thus appealed to, turned from the hearth. 'Oh, Joanna!' Ruefully. 'What a slovenly little beggar you are.'

There was no anger in her voice, though, and Joanna's tension dissipated in a rush of relief. But the bewilderment remained. The same misdeed which would, on one day, earn her a slap in the face might, at another time, be shrugged off with indulgent laughter. Her mother's erratic tempers were baffling to the little girl, but they were disquieting, too. There was a perverse security in the constancy of Maud's dour disapproval, none whatsoever in her mother's quick-silver moods.

A special birthday dinner had been cooked for Joanna: a rabbit stew, flavoured with onions, saffron, and wine, a thick bean pottage, stewed apples. There was cider for Joanna, red wine for Clemence, ale for Maud, and plum tarts for the final course. Sitting in the place of 'honour', Joanna was flushed with happiness. Their dinner usually consisted of soup or fish, bread and cheese, and she took this rich fare as proof that she was loved, in favour. She even dared to hope that her mother might have heeded her pleading, have got her the dog she so wanted. She held her breath in excitement now as Maud cleared away the stale bread trenchers that served as plates, as her mother rose, moved towards the bedchamber.

'Joanna, these are for you.' Her mother was smiling, holding out her presents: several scarlet hair ribbons and a wooden top.

Joanna bit her lip, blinked back tears. 'Thank you, Mama,' she mumbled, and Clemence frowned.

'I told you we'd be having no dogs in this house. I thought you understood that.'

Joanna swallowed. If only Mama knew how much she wanted a puppy. She'd tried so hard to make Mama understand.

'Joanna! Joanna, I like it not when you sulk; you know that.'

'I'm not sulking, Mama, I'm not,' Joanna said hastily, and after a long moment, Clemence nodded.

'See that you do not. Now come here and get your birthday kiss.'

Joanna did.

Joanna sat on a stool, watching in awe as her mother loosened her thick blonde braids, shook her head in a swirl of brightness. Joanna was fascinated; when unbound, her mother's hair cascaded down her

98

back in a silky tumble of light, reaching well below her hips. She smiled over her shoulder at Joanna, held out the brush, and Joanna reached eagerly for it; she loved brushing her mother's hair, took pride in making it gleam like gold.

'Mama . . . when is your birthday?'

'In less than a fortnight.' Clemence seemed to sigh. 'My twenty-first. I expect that sounds very old to you?'

'Yes,' Joanna admitted, and they both laughed.

'Then I was almost born on your birthday, was I not, Mama? Mama . . . was I not?'

She felt her mother stiffen. 'Yes,' Clemence said at last, a grudging one-word answer that thudded between them like a stone, and Joanna suddenly wanted to cry. Once again, she'd managed to say the wrong thing.

'You have pretty hair, Mama,' she said imploringly. 'So pretty; it is like looking at the sun.'

'That's sweet, Joanna.' Clemence reached over, patted Joanna's hand, and then picked up the mirror. As she shifted, Joanna saw her own eyes staring back at her. Not blue like her mother's, a strange colour neither brown nor green, what her mother called 'hazel', slanting queerly at the corners. Joanna hated her eyes, just as she hated the straight, coarse hair that even now was defying her birthday ribbons.

'Mama . . . why do I not look like you? Why do I have hair black like a crow?'

'Because you take after him.' Clemence turned on the stool, gazing upon her daughter; the blind inward look that Joanna most feared, for she knew it meant her mother was remembering, not seeing her at all.

'That was all I asked of God, that I need not see him each time I looked into your face. Little enough to ask, I should think.' She laughed suddenly, unsteadily. 'But we do pay and pay for our sins, it seems, and you grow more like him with each day that passes.'

Joanna shrank back. She knew who 'he' was, the father who had not wanted her, who had made Mama so unhappy. 'Mama . . .'

'Oh God, how like him you are!' Clemence's eyes were not blind now; they were riveted on Joanna's face with an emotional intensity that terrified the child; she thought she could read revulsion in them, and she sobbed,

'No, Mama, I'm not! Please, Mama, I'm not!'

99

This was not the first time her mother had accused her of this blood-sin, but for once her tearful denial proved stronger than the pull of the past. Clemence blinked, sagged back on the stool. 'Do not weep, Joanna,' she said, with an effort. 'Hush now. It matters not if you've his colouring, as long as you've not his accursed, evil soul.'

Joanna's tears dried; once more her mother had forgiven her for a sin beyond her understanding. But when she came back from the garden privy, she found the bedchamber door barred to her. Maud was already asleep, and she scratched softly on the door. 'Mama? Mama, it's me.'

There was no response. After a few moments she gave up, found a blanket, and dragged it over to the hearth next to Maud. This had happened before; there were times, Maud explained, 'when your lady mother needs to be alone'. But as she edged closer to Maud's bulky shelter, Joanna wished her mother had not felt such a need on this, her birthday.

The next morning, Clemence was moving about the kitchen by the time Joanna awakened. She was pale, hollow-eyed, and as she bent over to kiss Joanna, there was a sour wine smell on her breath. But she seemed to have laid her ghosts to rest, at least for a time, and Joanna asked for no more than that. Nor did Maud, who set about cooking breakfast with unusual cheer.

It was midmorning. Joanna was weeding midst their cabbages and onions, chanting under her breath, 'Plant a seed, pull a weed,' when she looked up and saw the cart moving slowly down the road.

The coming of the cart was an occasion in their lives, much like Christmas or Easter week, and she dashed to meet it. Three or four times a year a tight-lipped driver she knew only as Luke pulled up at their door. When Joanna had been younger, she'd confused him with St Nicholas, for like the celebrated saint, Luke brought riches, food and blankets and sometimes a pouchful of small silver coins. Dancing with excitement, Joanna sought now to see what the cart held. Two crated geese. Sacks of salt and flour. A barrel of salted pork. Bundles of flax stems; Maud would soak them to separate the fibres, and her mother would then spin them into linen for sheets and clothing. Jars of honey and flagons of wine.

'Mama! Luke's come, and with so much food! Can we have a goose for Michaelmas, can we, Mama?'

Clemence did not answer; she was staring at the object Luke was holding out towards her, a sealed parchment. Joanna slid down from the cart wheel. Mama had never got a letter before. She shivered suddenly, watched her mother break the seal with clumsy fingers.

'No! Oh God, no . . .' The letter fluttered to the ground, and Joanna grabbed for it. But her mother had whirled, was fleeing back into the house.

'Luke? Why did the letter make my mama cry?'

He rarely acknowledged her, generally acted as if she were invisible to adult eyes. But he looked down at her now, said, 'Her father is dead.'

The bedchamber door was ajar. Joanna gave it a push and it swung open. Her mother and Maud were on the bed, Maud cradling the younger woman as if she were no older than Joanna.

'I always thought . . . thought someday he'd forgive me. I had to believe that, had to . . . But he did not, died believing me to be a whore . . . and I'm not, I'm not!'

'I know, lovedy, I know.' Tears were streaming down Maud's face. 'My little girl, do not. I beg you . . .'

'And George . . . he'll inherit all, will not pay the rent on the cottage . . . you know he will not! And what will we do, Maud? Mother of God, what will we do?'

Joanna could bear no more. 'Mama . . . Mama, do not cry!' But her mother was beyond any consolation she or Maud could offer. She continued to weep as the day dragged on, sometimes silently, hopelessly, sometimes with deep, shuddering sobs that convulsed her in gasping spasms, until at last her body rebelled and she retched miserably into the floor rushes around the bed.

At dark, Maud made pallets for Joanna and herself by the hearth. But the bedchamber door could not completely shut out the sounds of sobbing. At last Joanna cried herself to sleep. She was awakened well past midnight by a dull thud. Sitting up, she saw her mother standing by the table, two of Luke's wine flagons clutched to her chest. She put her fingers to her lips, backed stealthily towards the door. Her face was waxen in the moonlight, her eyes swollen to slits, blonde hair spilling down her breasts and shoulders in a colourless, tangled snarl. Joanna's breathing quickened; this glassy-eyed swaying stranger was not her mother.

By the time she wriggled free of the blankets, Clemence had retreated back into the bedchamber. As Joanna reached the door, she heard the bolt slide into place. When Maud awoke at dawn, she found the little girl asleep on the floor, huddled against the bedchamber door.

The day seemed endless. Joanna wandered about the cottage like a ghost; not even Middleham Castle could lure her away from that closed bedchamber door. Maud made periodic attempts to coax Clemence out. Sometimes her entreaties provoked curses and slurred abuses; at other times, her pleas echoed into an eerie silence. At dusk, Maud set a plate of cheese and bread before Joanna, stood over the child until she choked down a few mouthfuls, and then put her to bed by the hearth. Exhausted, Joanna slept.

By the next morning, the bedchamber door was still bolted. Maud sent Joanna for Cedric, and as they hastened back up the path towards the cottage, they could hear Maud's fists thudding against the oaken door.

'My lady, I beg you, open the door. You've not eaten for two full days.'

Maud's hands were raw, knuckles bleeding, but she continued to beat futilely on the door until shouldered aside by Cedric. He tested the latch several times, and then said, 'Where is your axe?'

Maud gave a low moan and gestured, but a shudder passed through her body each time the axe connected with the wood. As the door gave way, Cedric put his shoulder to it, shoved inward, and stumbled into the room. Joanna heard him gasp, and then he had spun around, was seeking to block Maud's entry with an outstretched arm. She lunged past him, and then began to scream.

There was a strong stench in the room, of wine and vomit and urine. Joanna could see part of the bed, see the overturned flagon on the floor. Wine dripped from the rim, had gathered in a sodden pool midst the rushes. Her mother's blonde hair swept the floor; the ends were trailing in the wine, matted and dark. The wine looked like blood to Joanna. She tried to take a step closer, but her knees gave way.

'A doctor, name of God, fetch a doctor!'

A white arm dangled over the side of the bed, fingers tightly clenched. Cedric reached out, reluctantly grasped the wrist and quickly let it drop. 'Nay, we do need a priest,' he said huskily, and Maud fell to her knees by the bed, began a high keening wail. Cedric crossed himself, backed towards the door.

Joanna found herself sitting on the floor by the hearth. She slid along the ground until she reached the table, crawled under. There she crouched, putting her hands up to her ears to shut out Maud's screams.

Maud had yet to move away from Clemence's body. She looked up as Cedric re-entered the bedchamber, and her face contorted in fear, for he'd not summoned the village priest; the white-garbed monk at his side was John Brompton, Abbot of Jervaulx Abbey. He looked at the woman on the bed, shook his head slowly, and Maud sobbed, grabbed his arm.

'A mischance, Reverend Father, that is all . . . I swear it! She wanted only to sleep . . .'

He disengaged her clutching fingers, gazed down at the empty wine flagons. 'She did take a sleeping draught?'

Maud sobbed again. 'Her nights were so bad, Abbot John. Last spring I went to the castle leech; he gave me henbane and white poppy . . . But she meant no harm to herself. You must believe that, must let her be buried in consecrated ground, I beg you . . .'

Her voice rose shrilly, and the Abbot said hastily, 'Calm yourself, woman. You do disturb yourself for naught, I assure you. It is plain enough what happened. She was distraught, did misjudge the potion.'

Maud nodded dumbly, then snatched up his hand, and before he could withdraw, pressed it to her lips. He patted her shoulder, said, 'Do you wish Cedric to see the wainwright about building a coffin?'

She'd buried her face in her apron, only wept the harder, and he sighed, unfastened the crucifix that dangled from his belt and approached the bed. As he did, he happened to glance towards the outer room and, for the first time, noticed Joanna, cowering under the table.

'God in Heaven, did you never think of the child?'

Joanna watched as he knelt beside her, held out his hand. 'Come to me, little one. That's a good lass . . .'

He smelled of sweat and horses and garlic, but his voice was soft, coaxing. Joanna wrapped her arms around his neck. She was trembling so violently that her teeth were chattering, and she bit down on her thumb, tasting blood in her mouth. 'Mama . . .'

'She's in God's keeping now, lass. She's dead.'

Clinging to the Abbot's hand, Joanna entered into the bailey of Middleham Castle. Ahead of her rose the limestone ashlar keep.

She stared up at it, open-mouthed, for it seemed to reach straight towards Heaven. A wooden stairway extended out into the bailey, led up into the keep, and she hesitated, dizzy at the thought of scaling those heights, but the Abbot gently propelled her forward, and she grasped the railing, began a slow, cautious climb.

The great hall could easily have accommodated their entire cottage, so vast it was, with windows soaring towards the roof and an open hearth in the centre of the floor. A woman was moving towards them, dressed in the softest blue wool Joanna had ever seen.

'I've been expecting you, Reverend Father. Is this the child?'

'Aye. Joanna, this is the Lady Helweisa, wife to Lord Robert. Make your curtsy and then await me in the window seat.'

He watched as the child moved away, said, 'She has not cried, not even yesterday when we buried her mother.' Turning, he gratefully took the wine cup a servant was offering, followed Helweisa to the hearth.

'Tell me, Madame, what do you know of the girl's mother?'

'Nothing, if truth be told. Guy, our bailiff, rented them the cottage, and all their dealings were with him. Neither my husband nor I concern ourselves with such minor matters. I did assume that the woman was a young widow, or more likely a foolish girl who'd listened to the wrong man's blandishments.'

He nodded. 'An all too common tale, I fear. The girl was very young, and the man was married. When her family discovered she was with child, they cast her out in disgrace.'

'How, then, did she pay the upkeep on the cottage?'

'From what the old woman, Maud, told me, the girl's father paid the rent, saw that her needs were met. Not so much out of charity, I fear, as to keep her from bringing further shame upon the family name. He knew enough to realize that a girl turned out to starve will buy her bread with all she has left to barter, her body. But although they put food on her table, they denied her their forgiveness. The father said she was dead in his eyes, and held to that, even upon his deathbed. The elder son was no less rigid. The younger son was more sympathetic, but he could not gainsay his father and brother, although he did take it upon himself to write her of their father's death. The rest you know.'

'As you say, Reverend Father, a common tale, and likely to remain so as long as there be born men with glib tongues and silly chits willing to pay them heed. What mean you to do about the child?

A pity she were not a boy; it might be easier to find a family willing to take in a lad.'

'That is why I've come to you, Madame. You see, the girl was well born, of Norman stock. I got the family name from Maud: d'Arcy. The father held his manor from no less a lord than William de Ferrers, Earl of Derby.'

'Ah, that does put a different light upon it,' Helweisa conceded. 'If the child's mother be of gentle birth, then a villein's hut is no fitting place for her, bastard or no. What would you have me do, write to the family?'

The Abbot nodded. 'Aye, to the younger brother, Sir Roger d' Arcy. He should be told of his sister's death . . . and of her child's need.'

'I shall be glad to oblige you, of course, Abbot John.' Helweisa's eyes strayed across the hall to where Joanna sat, very still, in the window seat. 'Poor little lass, I wonder what shall become of her.'

'She is in God's hands, Madame. As are we all.'

There was no reality in Joanna's time at Middleham; it left little imprint upon her memory. She did as she was bade, spoke when spoken to, and when left to her own devices, sat for hours staring out at the dales, now burnished with bracken. To the other children of the castle, pages and playmates of Lord and Lady Fitz Ranulf's young son Ralph, she was a curiosity and, provoked by her eerie indifference, they baited her with words learned from their elders: 'bastard' and 'sideslip'. They were the first to put a name to it, to the sin of birth that somehow made her different from other children. A fortnight ago, she'd have been devastated by their mockery. But now their taunts had no power to hurt. What mattered it if they called her 'bastard'? She had so much more grievous wrongs to answer for. Mama was dead because of her. In her grieving, Mama had sobbed out the truth at last, had cried, 'If only she'd never been born!'

Mama had not wanted her, and now Mama was dead, and it was her doing, would not have happened if not for her. She did not wonder that Maud did not come to the castle to see her. How could there be forgiveness for a sin so great?

On her ninth day at Middleham, she was awakened by a young maidservant, and to her astonishment and apprehension, was told to attend Lord and Lady Fitz Ranulf in the solar.

She'd seen Lord Fitz Ranulf only in passing, was much in awe of him, a heavyset man in his fifties, with the brusque, no-nonsense manner of one who does not suffer fools gladly and prides himself inordinately upon that impatience. Lady Helweisa was more familiar to Joanna. A plump, complacent woman much her husband's junior, she would stop and talk to Joanna whenever they happened to meet in the bailey or great hall, but Joanna did not think Lady Helweisa truly heard her answers.

Her nervousness eased somewhat, though, at sight of Abbot John, for he had been kind to her. The fourth man in the chamber was young, dressed in starkest black, with a long sword at his left hip. But it was his hair that held Joanna's eyes; it was blond, the same sunlit shade as her mother's.

'Come here, Joanna.' Lady Helweisa beckoned her into the solar. 'There's one here to meet you, your uncle, Sir Roger d'Arcy.'

Joanna gasped, stared up at this man who was her kin, her family. As her gaze reached his face she saw he had her mother's sapphire blue eyes.

'Jesu!' His breath hissed through his teeth; the blue eyes widened. 'Christ, if she's not his very image!'

For the briefest moment, hope had flickered in the dark of Joanna's world. Her uncle had come for her. But with his words, that faint hope guttered, died. There was on his face the same expression that had been on her mother's the night she'd cried, 'Oh God, how like him you are!'

Seeing they all were staring at him, Roger d'Arcy drew a deep breath, said, 'I'd never seen her, you see . . .' There was a wine cup on the table, and he reached for it, drank until he began to cough. 'I expect you think my father was a hard man. Mayhap he was. He put family honour above all else, taught us to do likewise. He taught us, too, that a woman of rank must be chaste, must go to her marriage bed a virgin. When my sister confessed she was with child, he felt betrayed. Shamed.'

'And you?' Abbot John asked quietly.

'It was my duty to obey my father's wishes.' Roger drank again, not meeting their eyes. 'But . . . she was so pretty, my sister. So quick to laugh. And so young. Just fifteen when she came to court. Fifteen . . .' He turned back to face them, said tautly, 'I always did blame him, not her. She was such an innocent, such easy prey. I'd have killed him if I could.' His voice sounded suddenly muffled, as if he were swallowing tears. 'But I could not. I could only watch my sister suffer for his accursed lust.'

Helweisa and her husband exchanged glances. Roger d'Arcy had just unwittingly confirmed a growing suspicion of hers. Why had not the d'Arcys taken vengeance upon the man? As bitter as they were, one thing alone could have stayed their hand; the man had to be highborn. Very highborn.

'What of the child's father, Sir Roger? Would he do nothing for your sister?'

He shook his head. 'She'd have died ere she asked him for so much as a shilling. My sister was a d'Arcy, Madame; she, too, was proud.'

Helweisa hesitated, and then decided that the best tactic might be a direct frontal assault. 'Sir Roger, who is the child's father?'

He looked at her, then down at Joanna, and she said, "Your sister is beyond slander. If you keep silent now, you do but protect the man.'

'You're right,' he said abruptly. 'By God you're right. The man who seduced my sister, the man I blame for her death – he is the Count of Mortain.'

There was a shocked silence; even Helweisa had got more than she'd bargained for. Her husband whistled softly, as Abbot John echoed, incredulous, 'The Count of Mortain? John, the King's brother?'

Roger nodded. 'Mayhap you understand now why we could not . . .' His voice trailed off.

'Joanna,' Abbot John said hastily, 'go and sit in the window seat.' Holding up his hand for silence till she was out of earshot. 'That does explain much. But there is one thing I do not understand. For all his vices, Lord John has never failed to acknowledge his bastards. He may spill his seed without care, but he's then willing to claim the crop as his; he has at least five baseborn children, and they lack for little. Why would he not do as much for Joanna?'

'My sister hated him, Abbot John, blamed him for her plight. She took her vengeance the only way she could, by denying him his daughter. We gave it out that the child was stillborn.' Roger saw the Abbot's disapproval, added defensively, 'My sister feared, too, that John might take Joanna from her if he knew. Christ curse him, he had the power.'

He drained the wine cup, set it down. 'I am in your debt for what you did for my sister, Abbot John. I shall be taking Maud back with me. She nursed us all; we'd not have her starve. I shall send Luke for the furnishings of the cottage.' As he spoke, he was taking a pouch from his belt, spilling several silver pennies on to the table. 'Take these, Abbot John, and have Masses said for my sister on her month-mind.'

The Abbot nodded, but then realized that Roger d'Arcy meant to depart. 'Sir Roger, wait! What of the child?'

Roger seemed no less taken aback. 'Surely you do not expect us to take her in? John's spawn? My brother would sooner shelter a leper, and in this, I do agree with him. There are always villagers in want of children; place her with one of them.'

'Sir Roger, these be hard times; few of our serfs have food to spare for their own. And what of your sister? Joanna is her child, too.'

Roger was shaking his head. 'We cannot take her. My brother would never consent, and I . . . do you not see? Every time I did look upon her, I'd remember the Hell that was my sister's life these five years past. Christ, you cannot ask that of us. She'd be a living, festering sore in our midst, and we will not take her. We cannot!' But he did not move, and after a moment, he shook additional coins out on to the table.

'There; use that for her corrody, place her with the nuns at St Clement's. I can do no more than that.' Not waiting for their response, he moved swiftly towards the door, did not look back.

Abbot John approached the table, looked down at the silver pennies. 'Well, mayhap it is for the best. May the lass stay with you, my lord, until I can make arrangements with the sisters in York?'

Robert Fitz Ranulf nodded, then turned in surprise as his wife said, 'No, Reverend Father. We can put that money to better use. Why not send the child to her father, to John?'

'Madame, you would undertake that? Lord John is in Normandy, and to be truthful, I think such a journey would cost more than d'Arcy's grudging offering.'

'No matter, we will pay the difference,' Helweisa said placidly, and her husband stared at her in outraged astonishment.

'That is indeed a kindness, Madame, and you shall not go unrewarded for it. God sees . . . and approves.'

'I do not doubt it, Abbot John.' Helweisa smiled, shepherded the Abbot towards the door.

'Have your lost your senses, woman? Whatever possessed you to make an offer like that? You do not even know that John would accept her as his!'

'Ah, Rob, that is a false fear. Whatever other evils may be credited to his account, John does tend to his own, and that child is his. Once he sees her, he'd be the last to deny that.'

'Even so, you do not expect him to reimburse us for our trouble, do you? What prince ever paid back a debt?'

'That is true enough,' she conceded readily. 'But it will be a cheap price to pay for the favour of a king.'

'And what makes you so sure that John will ever be King?'

'My dearest, can you doubt it? It's been five years now since Richard's mother badgered him into taking a Spanish wife, and she's yet even to set foot in England! Richard will give England no son of his loins; nor is he a man to die peacefully in bed. He has but two possible heirs, his brother John or his nephew Arthur. Arthur is a child of nine. John is twenty-eight, and has Lucifer's own luck. Did we not all think he'd ruin himself with his scheming when Richard was taken by his enemies in Austria? Remember what happened when Richard's ransom was finally paid? John was banished from England, had the earldoms of Mortain and Gloucester taken from him. And then? He did meet with Richard in Normandy, somehow got Richard to forgive him, and within a year, even to restore his titles. Any man who could work a miracle like that is no man to wager against, Rob.'

Her husband nodded slowly. 'Mayhap I was over-hasty in objecting. Very well, you do have my permission.'

Helweisa, who'd never doubted that for a moment, none the less gave him a grateful smile, a dutiful kiss. 'I think I know just the one to escort the child, Rob. Simon, our bailiff's eldest. He's a likely lad, and can be trusted to keep his wits about him.'

Across the solar, Joanna sat, forgotten, in the window seat. She understood now why her mother had not wanted her, why her uncle and Maud did not want her. There was something shameful in her birth, so much so that her uncle had looked upon her with loathing.

'Joanna?' Lady Helweisa was standing by the window seat, smiling at her. 'I do have wondrous news, child. You are to go to Normandy, to go to your lord father.'

Joanna's breath stopped. She could only stare up at the woman, too stricken for speech, for more than a whispered, 'Please, no . . .' that none heard, or would have heeded.

Joanna's fear of her father was soon eclipsed by the utter misery of her journey. Perched precariously behind Simon's saddle, she slowly overcame her fearful conviction that each dip in the road would jar loose her hold on Simon's belt, send her sprawling into the dirt, to be trampled by the horses of Simon's escort. But the jouncing soon raised blisters and welts upon her thighs and buttocks. As Simon was under orders to make haste, some days they covered thirty miles, and Joanna's muscles would be so cramped and sore that she could barely crawl into bed at night. Bed was generally no more than a scratchy woollen blanket, and on those nights when they could find no monastery or inn to take them in, they bedded down in the fields, Joanna huddling against Simon in a futile search for warmth, for it was October now and the nights were chill.

The days blurred, one into the other. They would be on the road at dawn, moving south through ghostly hamlets and silent villages, for plague and famine were abroad in the land. Simon's men kept swords loose in their scabbards, for all knew that, in troubled times, the roads abounded with highwaymen and brigands. Joanna's anxieties were more immediate; too shy to ask Simon to stop when she needed to relieve herself, she suffered agonies of discomfort, and once, the ultimate humiliation, as urine trickled down her legs, stained her skirt. Her world was taking on more and more the aspects of a terrifying dream, one that offered no escape.

They reached London on the tenth day. Joanna had not thought there could be so many people in all Christendom. The streets were never still. Heavy carts rumbled by; men led over-laden pack animals; women rode sidesaddle and in horse litters; the activity never seemed to cease. Nor did the noise. She was glad when, after a night passed in a seedy Cheapside inn, Simon led her towards the wharves.

The docks were crowded with vessels, large galleys manned by oarsmen, smaller esneques rigged with canvas sails. It was one of these that was to convey them across the Channel, and Joanna found herself squeezed into a dark, foul-smelling canvas tent already overflowing with pilgrims, merchants, and mercenaries. Joanna had never even seen the sea, and she became seasick almost at once. Most of the passengers were experiencing the same distress, and the fetid, airless tent soon became unbearable for all entombed within.

It took several days to navigate the River Thames and turn south into the Channel. They reached the Seine estuary on the third day, began the slow passage upriver towards Rouen, not dropping anchor in the harbour until dusk on the following day. It was dark by the time they disembarked. Joanna had long since passed the limits of her endurance. She stumbled after Simon in a daze, clutching his hand as if it were her only lifeline. When he dragged her into a riverside alehouse, she simply sat down on the floor at his feet. Snatches of his conversation drifted to her. '. . . in Rouen for the wedding of his sister Joanna, the Queen of Sicily, to the Count of Toulouse . . . bringing his baseborn daughter . . .' Joanna at once was surrounded by strangers, suddenly the centre of attention. She heard someone say, 'He is at Le Vieille, at the castle.' That was the last thing she remembered. There on the dirt floor of the tavern, she fell into an exhausted sleep.

When she awakened, she found herself in a large torch-lit chamber, again encircled by strangers. The smoke from the hearth stung her eyes; she rubbed them with the back of her hand, tried to focus on her surroundings.

'I suppose we must take your word that there is a child hidden underneath all that grime. Has she ever, in all her life, had a bath?'

The voice was scornful, belonged to the most beautiful woman Joanna had ever seen, fair-skinned and flaxen-haired, a flesh and blood embodiment of ideal womanhood, as extolled in Clemence's bedtime chansons. But this bewitching creature was looking at her with such distaste that Joanna flushed, pressed back against Simon, who seemed no less flustered. He stammered something about the hardships of the road, and the woman laughed.

'I dare say you never even noticed how she looked. God knows you're filthy enough yourself!'

Joanna did not like this woman, not at all. 'My mama gave me baths,' she said, and was bewildered when those around her laughed.

But then the door was opening, and two enormous dogs were rushing at her, barking furiously. They towered above Joanna; when one lunged at her, hot breath brushing her face, her nerves gave way and she began to scream, could not stop, even after someone had lifted her to safety.

Joanna's screams soon gave way to choked sobs. Her rescuer let her cry, having silenced the dogs with a one-word command. His tunic seemed wondrously soft to her, fragrant with orris root. She rubbed her cheek against it, felt his hand moving on her hair.

'Do you not like dogs, lass?' he asked, stirring an immediate, indignant denial.

'I love dogs! But they were so big . . .' Peering down from his arms, she saw the dogs were not quite so monstrous after all, were merely large, friendly wolfhounds. 'I love dogs,' she repeated. 'But my mama would never let me have one.'

He laughed, and touched his finger to a smudge on her nose. 'Well, you are a surprise package, if a rather bedraggled one. How would you fancy a bath?'

A pallet had been made up by the bed; they stood looking down at the sleeping child.

'Do you remember the mother at all, John?'

'Yes, I do; does that surprise you? Clemence d'Arcy. A very pretty girl . . . and a very stupid one.'

Joanna's clothes lay on the floor by the bathing tub, and John touched them with the toe of his boot. 'Have these rags burned, Adele. I assume there is a seamstress in the castle? See that she has enough material, from your own coffers if need be.'

'But John . . . it's nigh on ten; she's abed for certès.'

'Not for long. I want a new gown for Joanna by morning, something soft, in green or gold.' Reaching for the corner of the blanket, he rubbed gently at Joanna's wet hair. She stirred, but did not awaken.

'I'm amazed, in truth, that she does not seem to fear me. I rather doubt that Clemence spoke tenderly of me. Until I can engage a suitable nurse, I'll expect you to care for her,' he added, and Adele's mouth dropped open.

'Me?'

'Yes, darling . . . you. Passing strange about the name. Joanna was Clemence's mother; I recall now. I think I shall tell her that she was named after my sister Joanna. She is my first daughter, Adele;

all the others have been sons.'

Adele laughed. 'I've never seen this side of you before, John. You remind me of nothing so much as a lad with a new toy!'

John raised his head, gave her a long level look. 'I begin to think you might be as stupid as Clemence,' he said, very softly, and Adele paled.

'I did not mean to offend you, my lord.'

'Well then, you'd best think how to make it up to me, darling,' he said, still softly and she nodded.

'It shall be my pleasure.'

'Not entirely yours, I hope!' He laughed then, and after a pause, she laughed, too.

Joanna slept till midmorning, awakening, bewildered, in a huge curtained bed as soft as a cloud. There was a fox-fur coverlet pulled up over her, and at the foot of the bed, the most beautiful clothes she'd ever seen: a linen chemise, an emerald wool gown, and a bliaut over-tunic of green and gold. But her own gown was nowhere in sight.

Wrapping herself in the fur coverlet, she moved cautiously from the bed, began to search the chamber for her clothes. Never had she been in a room like this. The walls were covered with linen hangings, glowed with colour. Thickly laid floor rushes tickled the soles of her feet, intermingled with sweet-smelling herbs of basil and mint. There was a table covered with a clean white cloth, an enormous oaken coffer, even a large brass chamber pot.

Joanna was at a loss. But she was remembering more now, remembered being bathed and put to bed, remembered a man with a reassuring smile, green-gold eyes, and the beautiful unfriendly woman he called Adele. She remembered, too, how, when she'd awakened in the night, not knowing where she was, he'd taken her into bed with him and Adele, and nestled between them, she'd soon slept again, feeling safe for the first time since her mother died.

The door opened; Adele entered. 'Well, you're up at last. John's awaiting you in the great hall, so hurry and dress.'

'My clothes are gone,' Joanna said reluctantly, suddenly afraid that she'd be blamed for their loss.

'They're right there on the bed.' Adele pointed impatiently when Joanna merely looked at her, uncomprehending. And only then did

113

Joanna reach out, timidly touch the soft lace edging the chemise, not truly convinced such clothes could be hers until Adele snapped, much as her mother had so often done, 'Are you going to tarry all day? Put them on.'

Following Adele down the winding stairwell, Joanna discovered it led to a great hall, much like the one at Middleham. Dogs were rooting in the floor rushes for bones; servants were carrying platters of food; men seated at long trestle tables laughed and joked as they ate, the overall atmosphere one of cheerful chaos. Joanna hesitated, daunted by the sight of so many people, but Adele pushed her forward, into the hall. 'Go on in. Would you keep him waiting?'

At the end of the hall a dais had been set up, and Joanna recognized the man who'd been so kind to her the night before. She was gathering up her courage to approach him when he beckoned to her. She came at once; realizing, with a jolt of astonished happiness, that he was as glad to see her as she was to see him. Within moments, she found herself seated beside him, being urged to share the food ladled on to his trencher. She was dazzled, both by the size of the portions and the amazing variety: roasted venison, lampreys in sauce, a rissole of beef marrow, pea soup, glazed wafers, pancake crisps, and sweet spiced wine he called hippocras.

John let her sip from his cup, named each food for her – even let her choose for herself which dishes she wanted to try, and by the end of the meal, Joanna was utterly captivated by him. He had a low, pleasant voice, never raised it, and yet was obeyed with celerity. It was obvious to Joanna that he was a man of importance. That made it all the more wonderful that he should take such an interest in her. She watched him closely, eating what he ate, laughing when he did, so intent she did not at first notice what would normally have claimed all her attention, the small spaniel puppy being led towards the dais.

'You said your mother would allow you no dog, Joanna. Well, I will,' John said, depositing the squirming spaniel in her lap. He heard her catch her breath; she looked up at him with eyes so adoring that he laughed. 'I think you shall be cheaper to content than the other women in my life; they yearn for pearls and silks, not puppies.'

'For me? Truly for me?' The puppy was a soft silver grey; it wriggled as Joanna ruffled its fur, swiped at her fingers with its tongue.

'Have you a name in mind, Joanna?' When she shook her head, John smiled. 'I've one for you, then. Why not call her Avisa?'

Joanna thought that a very pretty name, wondered why so many of the men laughed. One, wearing a priest's cassock, said, 'Despite your differences, the Lady Avisa is still your wife, my lord, in the eyes of both man and God.'

'And precisely because she is, Father, I can say for certès that Avisa is an uncommonly apt name for a bitch,' John said dryly, and again those around the dais laughed.

Joanna did not understand this byplay, but she reached out, shyly stroked John's sleeve. 'I do like Avisa for the puppy,' she said, seeking to please him, saw by his smile that she had.

After the meal was cleared away, the men sat down at one of the tables, unrolled a large map of Normandy. Joanna hovered in the background, playing with her puppy. When her curiosity drew her towards the table, John did not chase her away; instead, he sat her on his lap, spent several moments pointing out places on the map, showing her a French town called Gamaches and telling her how he had taken and burnt the town that August past for his brother the King. Joanna did not understand about battles or campaigns; what mattered to her was that he should take the time and trouble to explain.

She was so happy that she went quite willingly when Adele came to fetch her. Back in the bedchamber, she sat docilely on the coffer while Adele brushed her hair, wondering why Adele, who obviously did not like her, should care if her hair was combed or not. When Adele put the brush away, she went to the window, climbed on to the seat to gaze down into the bailey. And panicked at what she saw.

'Simon!' She'd actually forgotten all about him.

'Who is Simon?'

'He brought me here.' Joanna jerked at the shutters, tugged until she'd blocked Simon from view. 'When does he go?'

Adele shrugged. 'On the morrow, I expect.'

On the morrow. On the morrow Simon would take her away, to her father.

As soon as Adele departed the chamber, Joanna scrambled down from the window seat. Never before had she thought to rebel, but never before had so much been at stake. She quickly settled upon the coffer. Rooting in the hearth for a suitable stick of firewood, she tucked the puppy under her arm, lowered herself into the coffer, and

115

jammed the stick under the lid so she'd not be utterly in the dark. On the morrow Simon would search for her in vain, would have to leave without her.

'Joanna?'

She tensed, heard her name called again. Avisa had begun to whimper. She shivered, kept very still. And then the coffer lid was thrown back, her hiding place exposed.

'Why did you not answer me, Joanna? What foolish game is this?' But at sight of her tear-stained face, John's annoyance ebbed away. Reaching down, he lifted her out, set her beside him on the bed.

'Now, tell me what is wrong.'

'I was hiding from Simon,' she confessed. 'So he could not take me to my father.'

There was a silence. She slanted a glance through wet lashes, saw he was watching her, with a very strange look on his face. 'Please,' she entreated. 'Do not make me go with him.'

Still he said nothing. As hope faded, tears began to streak her face again.

'I thought you understood. Joanna . . . I am your father.'

He saw her eyes widen, pupils dilate with shock. He started to touch her, stopped himself. 'Joanna . . . what did your mother tell you of me?'

She swallowed. 'That you were wicked, that your soul was accursed, that you did not want me.'

The corner of John's mouth twitched. 'She lied to you, lass. I do want you.'

Joanna stared down into her lap. 'Mama did not want me,' she whispered.

'Did you love your mother, Joanna?'

She nodded, and then said, almost inaudibly, 'I was afraid of Mama sometimes.'

John reached out, tilted her chin up. 'Do you fear me?'

She did not answer at once, and he was later to tell Adele that he'd actually been able to see it in her eyes, that moment when loyalty given to a dead woman was given to him.

'No,' she said, and as the wonder of that realization registered with her, she shook her head vehemently. 'No, oh no . . .'

'You're flesh of my flesh, Joanna, of my blood. You understand what that means?'

'That I belong to you?' she ventured, and he smiled.

'Just so, Joanna. Just so.' And then she was in his arms, clinging, and he was laughing, hugging her back.

That was the beginning of the good times for Joanna.

January, 1199
Poitiers,
Province of Poitou

'So you've come. I was not sure you would.'

'Of course I came, Madame. You sent for me, did you not?' John's smile faded. 'What is wrong? Why do you look at me like that?'

'As if you do not know!' Eleanor had stood motionless by the hearth as John crossed the chamber. But as soon as he moved within reach, she took two quick steps forward and struck him across the mouth. 'You fool! You utter fool!'

John gasped, grabbed her wrist when she raised her hand as if to strike him again. His face was stinging; her signet ring had scratched his cheek. 'Christ Jesus, Mother, what is the matter with you? Why should you be wroth with me?'

'Why, indeed? Betrayal is as natural to you as breathing, is it not? More fool I, for imagining it could ever be otherwise!' Eleanor jerked her wrist free, began to pace. 'Five full years without a misstep, five years of fidelity. Besieging Evreux, burning Gamaches, taking the Bishop of Beauvais prisoner – all for one reason only, to win Richard's favour. And you were more successful than you know. Not that Richard would ever trust you again, in this life or the next, but you had shown him you could do more than intrigue, that you were not as worthless as he once thought. Five years, John, all for naught. Name of God, why?'

'Why what? Just what am I supposed to have done?'

'Oh, enough! We know, you see, know of your latest scheming with the French King. Philip told Richard all when they met on Wednesday last to declare a truce. And how fitting that you should be betrayed to the very one you did mean to betray!'

'And Richard believed this?' John was incredulous. 'What joy it must give Philip, that he has only to dangle the bait and Richard invariably lunges for it like a starving trout! But you, Madame, God's truth, I'd have expected better of you!'

'Philip claims to have a letter which proves your complicity in this intrigue, a letter in your own hand.'

'Oh, for the love of Christ! What better proof of my innocence could you ask for than that? If I were involved in some scheme to betray Richard, do you truly think I'd ever be so stupid as to incriminate myself in writing? Are you sure Philip does not have a convenient confession, too, that I somehow happened to sign and leave in his safekeeping?'

Eleanor felt the first flickers of doubt. 'Your denial has the ring of truth to it,' she said slowly. 'But then, your denials always do, John.'

'If you and Richard believe this lunatic accusation, it can only be because you want to believe it, Madame. You yourself said it; five full years I've devoted to regaining Richard's good will. Think you that I've enjoyed being at his beck and call, being subject to his erratic tempers, his every whim? Or that I'd gamble those five years on something so worthless as Philip's word? Jesus God, Mother! What would I gain by intriguing with Philip? We both know he has no hope of ever defeating Richard in the field.'

He was as angry as Eleanor had ever seen him, too angry for either artifice or discretion. His was not a defence calculated to endear, would have found little favour with Richard. But there was an ice-blooded, unsparing honesty to it that was, to Eleanor, more persuasive than any indignant avowals of good faith. It was the very amorality of John's argument that carried so much conviction. 'You're saying, then, that Philip was merely seeking to stir up trouble between you and Richard?'

'And succeeding, from the sound of it. Know you where Richard is now? Will I find him still at Castle Gaillard?'

Eleanor no longer doubted. There could be no better indication of John's innocence than this, that he would willingly seek Richard out. When he was in the wrong, the last thing he ever wanted was to face his accusers, to confront those he'd betrayed.

Eleanor's relief was inexpressible. Her easy acceptance of John's guilt had been prompted as much by fear as by her son's dismal record of broken faith and betrayals, the fear that she had misjudged him, after all, that he was not the pragmatist she'd thought him to be. Had he indeed been intriguing with Philip, that would mean to Eleanor that his judgment was fatally and unforgivably flawed, flawed enough to taint any claim he might have had to the crown. That was a conclusion she shrank from, for it would have signified the end of all her hopes for an Angevin dynasty, and that was the dream which had somehow sustained her even when she'd had nothing else to hold on to.

She sat down abruptly in a cushioned chair. 'Thank God,' she said simply, with enough feeling to soothe John's sense of injury.

'But of course I do accept your apologies, Mother,' he said, very dryly. Righteous indignation was not an emotion indigenous to his temperamental terrain; he had too much irony in his make-up to be able to cultivate moral outrage, and now that he no longer feared being called to account for a sin that truly was not his, he was beginning to see the perverse humour in his predicament. '"Be not righteous over much,"' he quoted, and grinned. 'But how can I help it? After all, how often have I been able to expose my conscience to your exacting eye . . . and live to tell the tale?'

Eleanor could not help herself, had to smile, too. 'By what strange alchemy do you manage to make your vices sound so much like virtues?' She shook her head, gestured towards the table. 'Fetch me pen and parchment. Better that I be the one to assure Richard of your innocence.'

The ancient river port of Rennes was the capital of Brittany. It was, as well, the favourite residence of Arthur, the young Duke who bore the name of a fabled Celtic king and never doubted that one day he, too, would be a king.

The April wind had suddenly shifted and servants were hastening to shutter the windows on the leeward side of the great hall. A juggler was making a manful attempt to entertain, but only Arthur was finding his antics amusing; the adults were far more interested in speculating upon the provocative presence of the man seated at Arthur's right. John had arrived in Rennes at dusk the preceding day, bearing lavish gifts for his 'dear nephew' and 'sweet sister-by-marriage'. While all agreed that he must have an ulterior motive in mind, none could agree upon what it was, and after twenty-four hours of unbridled conjecture, rumours were rampant, the Breton court was in turmoil, and John was enjoying himself immensely.

Growing bored now with the amateurish efforts of Arthur's

juggler, John appropriated a ruby ring from the prettiest of the women. Showing off the sleight of hand that never failed to delight his daughter Joanna, he soon had an appreciative audience, and when he at last pretended to find the ring in the girl's bodice, she blushed amidst all the laughter, but then slanted him a long-lashed look of unmistakable invitation.

'I want to learn how to do that trick, would have you teach me.' After a nudge from his mother, Arthur grudgingly added, 'if you will, Uncle.'

'It would give me great pleasure to lesson you, lad,' John said pleasantly. 'On the morrow, shall we say?' Knowing that Arthur was a typical twelve year old in that what he wanted, he wanted at once.

Arthur was not that much older than John's son Richard, but the two cousins had nothing whatsoever in common beyond a blood bond. Richard was an unusually introspective youngster, conscientious and cautious, but quietly stubborn, too; John was fond of his youngest son, but he never knew what Richard was thinking. Arthur was Richard's opposite in all particulars. Boisterous, cocky, imperious as only a cherished only son can be, Arthur was not accustomed to sharing the limelight, and he'd taken John's unexpected arrival with exceedingly poor grace. He could not comprehend why he must welcome his only rival for the Angevin crown, and at first he'd not even made a pretence of civility. But the ruder he was, the more courteous John became, indulgently affectionate, playful, answering insult with an exaggerated solicitude that stopped just short of parody. Arthur was spoiled, but by no means stupid, and he was not long in realizing that John was getting much the best of these exchanges. He was too young, however, to understand that he was, in effect, making a fool of himself. Now he opened his mouth to protest, thought better of it, and lapsed into a sulky silence.

But John had lost all interest in baiting the boy. A woman was approaching the dais. Making a graceful curtsy before Arthur, she then curtsied to John. She had utterly compelling eyes, the shade of purest sapphire; she looked, briefly, into his face, and turned away. John waited a discreet interval, announced he was retiring for the night, and made an ostentatious departure for his own chambers.

The gardens were deserted. Although early April, it was as if spring were being held in abeyance that year; the trees were barren, the grass still browned and sere. John hesitated, stepped off the path.

She was waiting for him in the arbour, came quickly into his arms. He slid his hands under her mantle, kissed her mouth, her throat, and she sighed, pressed close against him.

'I heard you'd come, but did not believe it. What devious game are you playing now, John? Why are you here?'

'To see you again, why else?' John said, in part because he thought it was expected of him, and in part because he was curious to see if she was naïve enough to believe him.

She laughed softly. 'How gallant! But have you forgotten how well I know you, my love? Have you some specific trouble-making in mind, or are you merely seeking to muddy the waters?'

'The latter,' John admitted; he, too, was laughing now. 'Philip could find conspiracy in a convent of Cistercian nuns, and his favoured pastime is jumping to conclusions. Need I tell you what dire plots he'll read into my visit to Arthur's court? And whilst Philip is convincing himself that Arthur and I must be up to no good, Arthur's advisers are unable to sleep for worrying over what I've got in mind. It's not often I've been able to sow so much discord with so little effort!'

'I cannot blame you for wanting to give Philip some grief. My husband told me about the good turn he tried to do you. There were more than a few here in Rennes who were right disappointed that Philip's ploy came to naught.'

'That I do not doubt, sweetheart. It's lucky, in truth, that Richard and I have such pure and perfect trust between us . . . is it not?' John began to kiss her again. 'I hear your husband is in Nantes; how long will he be gone?'

'A fortnight, at least. How long can you stay?'

'Till the week's end. Richard's been besieging some godforsaken castle near Limoges; one of his vassals found a Roman treasure on his lands and was then idiotic enough to refuse when Richard claimed it all as his liege lord. Richard expects to need just a week to wreak utter havoc upon the poor fool's lands, told me to meet him and our lady mother at Fontevrault Abbey for Easter. But ere I do, I want to pass some time in Rouen; I've a lass there most eager for the sight of me.'

'Indeed?' Feigning anger, she dug her nails into the back of his hand. 'If you think I came out into the cold to listen to you boast about your other bedmates . . .'

'She's my daughter, darling. I do not have her with me as often

122

as I ought, but I do try. With my sons, it is different. Save for Richard, they're old enough to fend for themselves. And bastard or no, many would envy Richard. He's highborn, after all; his mother is a Warenne. But Joanna is just seven, has no one but me. And now that I've satisfied you, when can you do the same for me? Can you come to me tonight?'

'John, it's so risky . . .' But after he devoted some moments to increasingly intimate persuasion, she sighed again, murmured, 'Yes . . . yes, I will. But we dare not tarry here any longer; we might be seen.' She pulled away, set about rearranging her clothing, and then turned back, gave him one last kiss, biting his lip and taking his breath.

John waited, giving her time to depart unseen. But as he emerged on to the garden path, a shrouded figure detached itself from the shadows, barred his way. The man was garbed all in black, his face hidden by a deep cowled hood. He was no apparition to encounter on a moonless night, a stark, spectral embodiment of the most irrational and elemental of mortal fears, and John recoiled violently.

'My lord, I must talk with you.'

John took a second look, recognized the habit and mantle of a Benedictine monk, and swore, fluently and with considerable feeling.

The monk listened in stolid silence, and when John had exhausted every abusive possibility in an uncommonly extensive vocabulary, he repeated stubbornly, 'We must talk, my lord.'

But as the monk moved closer, John happened to glance down, saw the dusty boots protruding from the hem of the monk's habit. For a moment he froze, and then jerked his sword free of its scabbard.

'Indeed, we'll talk. We'll begin by you telling me who you are, in whose pay, and just why you went to so much trouble to find me alone like this. And Christ save you if I do not like your answers.'

The man burst out laughing. 'And I thought I made a truly admirable monk! What gave me away?' He reached up, pulled back his hood, and John swore again.

'De Braose!' Slowly he lowered his sword. Suspicions were coming too fast for him to take them all in. 'I thought you were at Châlus with my brother Richard.'

'I was.' De Braose was fumbling at his belt. 'Your mother the Queen bade me give you this, so you'd not doubt I came at her behest.'

123

John stared down at the ring de Braose had pressed into his hand; it was indeed his mother's. Sheathing his sword, he followed de Braose off the path.

'My lord, you do not know how very lucky you are. Word has not got out yet. If it had, you'd not live to see the morrow.'

John caught his breath. 'Do you mean what I think you do?'

William de Braose nodded. 'I do . . . my liege.'

'Richard . . . he's dead?'

De Braose nodded again. 'He was near death when your lady mother commanded me to get to you, to warn you away from Rennes ere Arthur learns the crown is up for the taking. Too many of his men know my face; hence this monk's cowl. I've men and horses waiting, put them at your disposal, my lord.'

'I still cannot believe it. That it would happen like this, so sudden . . .'

'You're not alone in your disbelief, my lord. Your brother was so sure of victory that he had not even bothered to arm himself. He'd ridden out to inspect the siege progress with only a shield, took an arrow in his left shoulder. It was full dusk, and his men did not see him hit. He made no sound, turned and rode back to his tent, had his surgeon cut it out. He took the castle, ordered every living soul in it hanged – servants, women, children, all – sparing only the man who shot him for God knows what fate. But the wound festered. When he realized it was like to be mortal, he pardoned his killer and sent for your mother the Queen.'

'"Near death," you said. Are you sure he could not recover?'

De Braose's mouth twitched in a grim smile. 'My lord, I could scarce bear to enter the tent for the stench of rotting flesh.' He stiffened suddenly; so did John. But they'd heard only echoes on the wind, were still alone in the gardens. De Braose loosened his grip on his sword hilt. 'I think it best, my lord, if you do not return to your chambers, make no farewells. If we leave now, we can put a good thirty miles between us and Rennes by dawn.'

'Jesu, yes! My life would not be worth spit should this get out whilst I'm still in Brittany.' John gave an abrupt laugh, both exultant and unsteady. 'But you have no idea, Will, what I'll be passing up!'

'You still have not asked it, what I expected to be the first question you'd put to me – if Richard named you as his heir.'

'He did . . . did he not?'

'Yes,' de Braose admitted, and John grinned.

124

'You did say my lady mother was at his deathbed, no? Well, as soon as you told me that, there was no need to ask. For even if he had not named me, she would have told the world that he had!'

A woman was walking alone in the cloisters of Fontevrault Abbey, a frail, forlorn figure swathed in deep mourning. She turned at sound of John's footsteps, and he recognized Berengaria, his brother's neglected Queen.

He'd gone out of his way to befriend her, motivated as much by a malicious desire to vex Richard as by pity for her plight, and now he found himself cast in an unfamiliar role, giver of comfort and solace.

'Juan!' Berengaria held out her hands, gave him a shy, sisterly kiss, and burst into tears.

'*Calma, querida, calma.*' That was, however, the extent of John's Spanish, and he could do no more than pat her consolingly on the shoulder, wait for her to regain her rather uncertain grasp of French.

'Forgive me,' she sobbed. 'But it's been so hard . . . so hard. I was at Beaufort-en-Vallée, would have gone to him at once, Juan. But I did not know, not till he was dead. He sent for his mother, but not for me. Not for me . . .'

'But of course he would not! He was in great pain, *querida*. He knew you could never bear to see him suffer so, wanted to spare you that. Any husband would.'

'Truly you think it so?' Fawn brown eyes beseeched him to convince her. 'If I could but believe . . .'

Hugh of Avalon, Bishop of Lincoln, had followed John into the cloisters, reached them just in time to hear this exchange. His eyes softened, and he watched with approval as John gently disengaged himself from his sister-in-law's tearful embrace. But no sooner were they alone on the cloister walkway than John shook his head, said wryly:

'Damn me if those tears were not genuine. And yet she could count herself lucky that Richard even remembered her name from one day to the next! That girl is a born martyr if ever there was one. But to be fair, there's something to be said for Richard, too. All that Madonna-like purity and goodness would be enough to put any man off; who wants to bed a saint?'

The Bishop jerked his head up, gave John a look of poorly concealed dislike. 'Such talk is most unseemly, my lord,' he said, so stiffly that John laughed. He'd been almost continuously in the aged churchman's company on the ride from Chinon, and he was wearying of the Bishop's homilies on virtue, his exhortations about sin and salvation; it was all too plain that he thought John's soul to be in mortal peril, thought John to be the most ungodly of a family never noted for its piety, and John, who'd begun by good-naturedly seeking to placate, was now deliberately doing all he could to confirm the priest's worst fears.

'You seem to be labouring under a misconception, my lord Bishop,' he said cheerfully. 'I mean to be crowned, not canonized.' But by then they were entering the abbey church, and he sobered abruptly, did not at once move into the sunlit stillness of the nave.

Eleanor stood before the marble tombs of her husband and son, John's father and brother. Her face was tearless, all but bloodless; her grieving was painful to look upon, but intensely private, had in it a fierce pride that conceded little, asked for even less.

'Mother.' John stopped before her, hesitated, and kissed her on the cheek. He could discern the faintest stiffening of her body at his touch, an almost imperceptible pulling away, so slight he might have imagined it. Releasing her at once, he stepped back. For a long moment they looked at one another, and then he said, 'I am sorry I could not get here in time for the funeral.'

The others had tactfully withdrawn, giving them some degree of privacy, and he could risk asking, very low, 'Did Richard truly name me?'

'Yes . . . he did.' Eleanor glanced down at Richard's tomb, back to her surviving son's face. 'But that alone will not make you King,' she said tonelessly. 'You're likely to have to fight for the crown, John. Whilst you'll have no trouble winning acceptance in England and Normandy, the barons of Brittany, Maine, and Touraine will hold fast for Arthur. Already his partisans are moving on his behalf. We had word this morn that Angers has been taken in Arthur's name, that Le Mans is likely to fall to his forces, too. Angers is not ten leagues from here, John.'

'Your point is taken, Madame. You need not worry; I mean to head north on the morrow, to raise an army in Normandy if need be.'

Eleanor searched his face, found what she sought, and nodded. 'I've done what I could. It is up to you now.'

126

'Yes,' John said coolly. 'I know.'

Eleanor watched as he departed the crypt, pausing for only the briefest of moments before the tombs of their dead. She did not move until the Bishop of Lincoln came to stand beside her.

'Do you know why he missed the funeral, Madame? As soon as he learned Richard was mortally stricken, he rode straight for Chinon. Not Châlus, where his brother lay dying, or Fontevrault, where he would be laid to rest, but Chinon . . . where the royal treasury is kept.'

'I know,' Eleanor said wearily, and he presumed upon an old and enduring friendship to put a supportive hand upon her arm.

'Madame . . . I would not add to your griefs for the very surety of my soul. But I cannot deny my fears, not even for you. If John does prevail over Arthur, it will be in large measure your doing, Madame . . . and your responsibility. Are you sure you're making the right choice?'

'Choice?' Eleanor echoed, with such bitterness that he shrank back. 'Think you that I'm blind, that I do not see John as he is – as Henry's son?' She drew a laboured breath, then said softly, 'But he is still my son, too. And at least he'll not be Philip's puppet, as Arthur would. At least he'll not be that . . .'

April, 1199
Powys, Wales

Never having been in Wales, Aubrey de Mara looked about with
interest when Thomas Corbet informed him that they had just crossed
from Cheshire into Powys.

'I hear Wales is a wild, beautiful country, deeply wooded and
right mountainous.' But Thomas just grunted, and Aubrey cast a
sideways glance at the other man, a big-boned, burly youth in his
early twenties. He had no liking for Thomas Corbet, would not of
his own accord have chosen Thomas as a travelling companion. But
in his passage through Shropshire, he'd twice enjoyed the hospitality
of the Corbet family, first with Thomas's uncle Walter Corbet, Prior
of Ratlinghope Priory, and then with his father, Robert Corbet, at
the latter's castle of Caus, and when Thomas decided he would
accompany Aubrey into Cheshire, Aubrey could think of no graceful
way to escape Corbet's company.

He'd hoped Thomas would turn back once they reached Hawarden, but he showed no signs of homesickness, spent a month as
the guest of Aubrey's cousin, Ralph de Montalt, and when Aubrey
announced his intention to move on to the Montalt castle of Mold,
Thomas nonchalantly allowed that he, too, would stop at Mold.

'Your cousin at Mold, Lord Ralph's brother . . . you've never
met him, either?' Thomas now asked idly, and Aubrey shook his
head.

'No. Their grandfather and my great-grandfather were brothers,
but they settled here in England with William the Bastard whilst my
family kept to Normandy.' Turning in the saddle, he signalled to his
squire, was handed a wineskin. 'Are you sure, Tom, we needed no
escort from Hawarden?'

'Damned sure. Mold is but six miles from Hawarden. Moreover,
the Welsh dare not trespass in these parts; they're not ones to risk
their necks unless the odds are rigged in their favour. So you need

not fret, I'll get you there safe enough.' Thomas smiled, to signify that he was, of course, joking, and Aubrey smiled sourly back; he did not doubt that Thomas could merely wish a man good-morning and yet manage to give offence.

'Tell me of the Welsh,' he said. 'Who rules in these parts? Was there not a Welsh Prince named David, who was wed to a half-sister of old King Henry?'

'Yes, although the Welsh do pronounce that as Daý-ith. But Davydd was dethroned nigh on five years ago. The man who now wields the greatest power in Gwynedd is Llewelyn ab Iorwerth.'

'Ah yes, I recall hearing some talk about him. He sought to overthrow Davydd at a rather young age, did he not?'

'At fourteen.' Thomas was frowning. 'When he was twenty-one, he defeated Davydd in a bloody battle at the mouth of the River Conwy, and since then has ruled Gwynedd with his cousins and allies; they hold the lands west of the Conwy and he all that lies east . . . for now. Sooner or later, he'll find a pretext to claim all of Gwynedd. Nor would I – were I a prince of Powys – sleep well nights with him for a neighbour; I'd sooner bed down with a snake.'

Aubrey grinned. 'Still, though, few men gain so much so young. How old is he now?'

'Twenty-six this February past,' Thomas said flatly, and Aubrey's eyes shone with sudden curiosity.

'You seem uncommonly well informed about the man, even to his very birthdate.'

'He's my cousin,' Thomas said reluctantly, and then made haste to add, 'by marriage,' lest Aubrey think he had Welsh blood. 'My uncle Hugh did wed with Llewelyn's mother.'

'I gather there is no love lost between you,' Aubrey said wryly, and Thomas leaned over, spat into the road.

'What of Llewelyn's uncle Davydd? Was he put to death?'

'No,' Thomas said grudgingly. 'Llewelyn banished him into English exile.'

Aubrey was thoroughly enjoying the turn the conversation had taken. 'Most magnanimous,' he murmured, much amused when Thomas rose at once to the bait.

'Do not fool yourself,' he snapped. 'He knows no more of mercy than he does of honour. If he spared Davydd's life, it was only so as not to make a martyr of the man; I'd wager my birthright on that.'

Aubrey laughed. 'It sounds as if the poor man cannot win with

129

you, Tom. If he'd claimed Davydd's life, I dare say you'd have scorned him as a cold-blooded murderer; yet because he did not, you scorn him even more!'

'If that is a jest, I see no humour in it.' Thomas lapsed into a sullen silence, and they rode without speaking for a time, Aubrey congratulating himself upon having discovered so effective a burr for Thomas's saddle.

'Where mean you to go after our stay at Mold?' Thomas asked at last, and Aubrey, grimacing at 'our stay', shrugged.

'I thought I might venture down into South Wales, the lands under Norman control. Whilst serving with King Richard in Normandy a few years past, I became friendly with a Marcher lord, and I should like to renew that friendship, to spend some days with him at Abergavenny Castle.'

'Aber–Jesu, man, are you talking of William de Braose?'

'Yes, Lord of Brecknock and Upper Gwent. Why does that so surprise you?'

'Because de Braose's name stinks like a mackerel in the sun; I'd have thought the foul smell sure to have reached even as far as Normandy.'

'You speak of a man I call friend,' Aubrey said stiffly. 'I'd advise you to choose your words with care.'

'You are an innocent, Aubrey, in truth,' Thomas said impatiently. 'Ere you unsheath your sword, you'd best hear me out, hear how de Braose avenged the death of his uncle. The man responsible was a Welsh lord, Seisyll ap . . . whatever. De Braose summoned this Seisyll and his followers to Abergavenny to hear a royal proclamation, set out for them a rich table, as much wine as they craved. When the Welsh were off guard, de Braose's men fell upon them, killed them all. Then, ere word could get out, he dispatched others to Seisyll's camp, there abducted Seisyll's wife and, right before her eyes, murdered her seven-year-old son.' Thomas reined in, looked challengingly at Aubrey. 'I bear no love for the Welsh, but vengeance such as that does no man honour.'

Aubrey was shocked. 'But he had such an agreeable nature, was quick to jest, to open his purse to his friends. And he seemed truly pious, never passed a wayside cross without offering up a prayer . . .'

'Farsighted of him, I dare say, given how greatly he'll be in need of prayers come Judgment Day. Although to be fair, there are those who say de Braose was urged to it by his kin. There are even those who think the old King was not displeased. And that bloody night at Abergavenny is twenty years past. But none would deny that de Braose is a hard man, a man not over-burdened with scruples.' Thomas laughed suddenly. 'Little wonder his greatest friend at court is none other than Lord John!'

Aubrey was not surprised that Thomas should be so indiscreet, not after some six weeks in the latter's company. But he had no intention of compromising himself, of sharing his political prejudices with Thomas. 'Indeed?' he said coolly, and then, 'Tom, look at the sky. There must be a fire ahead.'

Thomas stared at the smoke spiralling up through the trees, and then spurred his stallion forward. Rounding a bend in the road, he came to an abrupt halt. Aubrey and the squire reined in, too.

'Christ Jesus!' Thomas sounded stunned, turned to Aubrey in disbelief. 'The whoreson's besieging Mold!'

Aubrey searched in vain for an identifying banner. 'Who?'

'Llewelyn, you fool! Who else would dare?'

Smoke from the smouldering palisades drifted across the outer bailey, set Llewelyn's men coughing. Most of the faces around him were well smudged with soot, but he saw only jubilant smiles, for they'd broken through the first ring of the castle defences. Ahead lay the deep ditch that separated the inner and outer baileys, and beyond, the castle curtain wall, a far more formidable obstacle than the timber palisades, which had been easily set afire with brushwood and flaming arrows. But the curtain wall was stone, the gateway shielded by a portcullis grille.

The drawbridge meant to link the two baileys still blazed, set alight by retreating soldiers. Llewelyn glanced about at his captains, said, 'We can do nothing till we fill in the ditch; see to it. But we'll need cover. Remember, their crossbows may be more cumbersome than our bows, but they have a greater range.'

As if to prove his point, behind him a man screamed, fell forward into the dirt. Up on the walls, an English bowman gave a triumphant shout. Encouraged, his comrades loosed their own arrows down into the valley. The Welsh drew back, retreated behind a wall of upraised shields.

When enough wood, sand, and faggots had been thrown into the ditch, Llewelyn signalled and the battering ram was brought up, a

131

huge tree-trunk capped in iron, sheltered by a large wheeled shed, fireproofed with raw cowhide.

Ednyved ducked behind the shed, gave the battering ram an approving pat. 'What are your orders?'

'Whilst we seek to break through with the ram, turn the mangonels upon the walls. Now I want every bowman we have aiming up at the walls. Have the scaling ladders ready.'

Ednyved gave a pleased grunt. 'Consider it done,' he said, crawled under the shed to confer with the men crouching within. Llewelyn raised his right arm, dropped it sharply. At once the air throbbed with the twanging of Welsh longbows, and the battering ram began creaking across the bailey.

By the time the shed reached the curtain wall, the castle defenders were raining every possible sort of missile down upon it: stones, lances, lit torches, even quicklime. But it continued to creep inexorably forward, like a huge shelled turtle, leaving a trail of deflected weaponry in its wake. Once within range, the men inside jerked on the ropes, straining until the massive log began to swing back and forth, gathering momentum and smashing into the portcullis. There was a splintering sound; the iron reinforcements held but the wood buckled, and the Welsh raised a cheer.

The capture of Mold Castle would be a signal victory for the Welsh, and Llewelyn had left little to chance; his army was equipped both with the huge crossbow machines known as ballistas and with the even larger mangonels, catapult-like devices capable of launching boulders of considerable size. He watched as his largest mangonel was dragged forward, as a windlass was wrenched to pull the beam back, as it was loaded with heavy rocks, and then released. The beam jerked back to a vertical position, propelling the rocks into a deadly overhead arc. Some shattered against the castle walls; others plummeted down into the inner ward. Not waiting to savour their success, his men were already reloading the mangonel. Llewelyn paused long enough for a 'Good lads!' and then sprinted across the open ground towards the lean-to being set up by the ditch. 'Bring out the second mangonel,' he panted. 'And keep your shields up. They're launching red-hot bolts from the walls; I just saw one go clean through a man's belly.'

So far all was going according to Llewelyn's expectations. The battering ram continued its relentless thrusting. Up on the walls, men were lowering large hooks, desperately fishing for the ram, but the arrow fire was too intense for any man to risk exposure for long, and they were grappling blindly.

'Llewelyn!' Rhys raced for the lean-to, flung himself down a split second before an arrow buried itself in the wood above his head. It had all but grazed his hair, yet he said only, 'Close, that one. Llewelyn, they signal from the ram. They've broken through the portcullis, have reached the door.'

'Now!' Again Llewelyn raised his arm, let it fall. 'Do not let up, drive them off the walls!' And as his bowmen obeyed, launching arrow after arrow with eye-blurring speed, he pulled his sword from its scabbard, brought his shield up.

With wild yells, the Welsh rushed the castle walls. Those up on the battlements threw down stones, flaming pitch; more than one Welshman was engulfed in fire, rolled screaming upon the ground. But Llewelyn's bowmen had achieved their aim, forcing many of the English to retreat, and the Welsh headed now for these exposed areas, threw scaling ladders against the walls and began to scramble up, trailing light thong ladders over their shoulders.

By the time Llewelyn reached the walls, the battering ram was smashing through the oaken door. He was among the first to plunge through, fought his way clear of the gatehouse to find many of his men already within, clambering down their thong ladders to head off the English retreat. Of the buildings ranged along the curtain walls, only one was not of wood, a squat two-storey tower. Seeing themselves overwhelmed by numbers, the English soldiers were running for this, their last refuge, and Llewelyn shouted, 'Christ, cut them off!'

But even as he raced for the keep, he knew they'd be too late. Men with torches were standing in the doorway. When most of the soldiers had made it to safety within, they scattered brushwood upon the stairs, tossed their torches on to the pile. The stairs ignited at once. One of the torchbearers was too slow, took a Welsh lance in his chest and tumbled down into the flames, but the other ducked back inside; the door was slammed and bolted behind him.

Smoke hung heavy over the inner ward; the wooden buildings had been set afire. Llewelyn and his captains had gathered in the gatehouse, were measuring the keep with speculative eyes.

Rhys gestured towards the charred ruins of the wooden stairway. 'Even if we built a platform and then forced the door, all the advantages would lie with them; they could smite us down one by one as we sought to enter. Better we should build a mine, tunnel under the wall and bring it down about their ears. Or else use the battering ram to smash into the cellar.'

'The River Alyn sinks underground here; the ground is like to be too wet for tunnelling.' Ednyved took up a flask, drank, and passed it around. 'But we could use the battering ram, though it'd be slow going. What say you, Llewelyn?'

Llewelyn considered. 'If we go across the battlements, we can enter on to the roof of the keep. If we then stuff burning brushwood down the louvres, mayhap we can smoke them out. But ere we decide, I'd see if I cannot talk them out.'

Moving to the door of the gatehouse, he raised his voice. 'I would speak with your castellan or constable!'

There was silence, and then a shutter was cautiously drawn back. 'I am Sir Robert de Montalt. Identify yourself.'

Llewelyn and his friends exchanged surprised looks; they'd not expected to hook so large a fish. 'I am Llewelyn ab Iorwerth, Prince of Gwynedd below the Conwy.'

The silence was even longer this time. 'What would you say to me?'

'Just this. I shall take your keep. If nothing else, I need only wait, starve you out. You can neither escape nor hope for succour. Your overlord, the Earl of Chester, is in Normandy with your King. The Lord de Montalt, your brother, is known to be ailing; nor has he the men to break my siege. Remain mewed up within the keep and you do but prolong your own suffering, do only delay what is writ in blood. Yield now and with honour. Your lives shall be spared, and you may ransom your freedom, with no shame to you, for a fight well fought.'

The shutter opened wider. 'And if I refuse to yield?'

'Need you ask? You know full well what's like to befall a besieged garrison which persists in holding out after all hope is gone. My people call this place Yr Wyddgrug: the burial mound. If need be, I'll turn this ground into a burial mound in truth. I shall take this keep, easy or hard, but take it I shall, and when I do, all within shall be put to the sword. So the choice is yours. I do give you two hours to decide.'

Llewelyn passed the next hour conferring with his captains, getting reports on the casualties suffered, the prisoners taken, and planning

134

for their assault upon the keep should it become necessary. There was still an hour remaining upon his deadline when Ednyved appeared at his side.

'Well, my lord, once more your silver tongue triumphs!' Pointing towards the keep. The door was opening. As they watched, elated, a ladder was slowly lowered over the side.

'My grandfather took Mold Castle, too, Rhys. The garrison held out for three months before yielding, and he later said it was his sweetest victory ever.'

'My lord!' Llewelyn and Rhys turned from the window, towards the man just entering the solar. He was carrying a large bolt of emerald velvet; this he held out to Llewelyn, saying, 'As soon as I saw this, my lord, I knew your lady should have it. Nothing better becomes a woman with red hair than the colour green.'

Llewelyn fingered the cloth. 'Indeed, you are right, Dylan. It shall please her greatly to make a gown of this.'

'Llewelyn?' Ednyved paused in the doorway. 'Is it your wish to see de Montalt now? And our men captured two English knights up on the road. I'll fetch them, too.'

Sir Robert de Montalt had advanced well into his fifties, time enough to have acquired a philosophical approach to the vicissitudes of fortune. If he felt any resentment now at being ushered, a prisoner, into his own solar, he was too politic to let it show in his face.

'My lord Llewelyn,' he said, stiffly correct. 'I assume, of course, that you mean to raze the castle.'

'Of course,' Llewelyn agreed politely, secretly amused, as always, at the Norman insistence upon preserving the proprieties. As if war were a game of sorts, to be played according to recognized rules.

Robert de Montalt gestured towards the table. 'I will, with your permission, write to my brother, tell him that our men shall be set free once your forces withdraw. May I ask what price you mean to put upon my freedom?'

Llewelyn calculated rapidly. 'I think seven hundred marks to be a fair sum.'

It was steep, but not exorbitant, and de Montalt nodded. 'You will take partial payment in cattle and horses, I trust?'

'Naturally,' Llewelyn said, no less gravely, not daring to meet Ednyved's eyes lest he laugh, reveal what a charade he thought this to be.

135

The other men were now being escorted into the solar. The first was a flaxen-haired youth, expensively armed. He did not look particularly pleased by his predicament, but neither did he look all that worried. Here, Llewelyn saw, was another games-player, confident that men of rank would always make common cause against those of inferior birth, acknowledge their membership in an international aristocracy of class. They would never understand, Llewelyn knew, that he felt a greater kinship to the least-born Welshman than to the highest-born Norman lord.

His eyes narrowed, though, at sight of the second man. 'Well, Tom,' he said coolly, 'you're a long way from home.'

Thomas was not cowed. 'So are you,' he shot back. 'This is Powys, not Gwynedd.'

Aubrey decided Thomas Corbet was, indeed, mad. All knew the Welsh were as unpredictable a people as could be found in Christendom, and common sense dictated that a man did not bait a bear in its own den. 'You are, of course, Prince Llewelyn,' he said hastily. 'I am Sir Aubrey de Mara of Falaise, cousin to Lord Ralph and Sir Robert de Montalt.' He turned then to de Montalt, smiled ruefully. 'I regret I must impose upon our kinship, Cousin, must request that your brother pay my ransom. My lord father will naturally reimburse you.'

With such a victory, Llewelyn could afford to be generous. 'Add another hundred marks for your cousin, Sir Robert, and I shall be content.'

Aubrey grinned. 'I do not know whether I should be thankful to escape so cheaply,' he confessed, 'or insulted that you do not value my worth more highly!'

Llewelyn laughed, raised Aubrey in his estimation; generally, when a man was bested in combat, his sense of humour was the first casualty.

'Well, you two can barter what you will for your freedom, but I'll be damned ere I pay so much as a penny for mine,' Thomas said truculently, and Aubrey and de Montalt jerked their heads about, stared at him in astonishment. There was on Aubrey's face grudging admiration for so bold a stance, yet resentment, too, for his own easy acceptance of his plight suddenly seemed less than honourable when contrasted with Thomas's defiance.

Llewelyn was regarding Thomas with unconcealed contempt, but it was to Aubrey that he said, '*Mwyaf trwst llestri gweigion.* In your language that translates: Empty vessels make the most noise. Your heroic friend knows full well that his release is already secured, bought with his Corbet blood. I do owe Hugh Corbet too much to claim the life of his nephew and, as ever, he trades upon that.'

Thomas had flushed angrily. 'I accept no favours from Welshmen!'

Llewelyn, too, was angry now. 'You're an even bigger fool than I once thought . . . Cousin. That does not, however, alter the debt I owe your uncle. But come the day when he's gone to God, I shall be sorely tempted to burn Caus Castle around your head. I'd think on that if I were you.'

Thomas opened his mouth, and Aubrey jabbed him with an elbow. 'For Christ's sake,' he hissed, 'do not stretch your luck!'

'My Prince!' It was Dylan again, pushing before him a fearful youngster of eighteen or so. 'This one ran right into our scouts, claims he has an urgent message for de Montalt.'

The boy fumbled within his tunic and withdrew two rolled parchments. With an apologetic glance towards Robert de Montalt, he knelt and handed the messages to Llewelyn.

De Montalt had stiffened. He watched tensely as Llewelyn broke his brother's seal. He saw surprise upon the latter's face; Llewelyn said something in Welsh, and the others looked no less startled.

'Cousin?' Aubrey had sidled closer. 'See the second dispatch? Does it not bear His Grace of Chester's seal? The news then is from Normandy.'

The Welsh were still talking among themselves, with considerable animation. Several were smiling, but Llewelyn looked suddenly pensive. He walked towards them, said to de Montalt:

'Your brother has just received a letter from the Earl of Chester. Your King Richard was sore wounded whilst besieging Châlus Castle; he died on the sixth of April.'

Thomas did not appear overly affected by the news of his King's demise, but de Montalt was stunned and Aubrey stricken. He sagged back against the wall, whispered, 'Jesu have mercy upon his soul.'

Thomas dutifully crossed himself at that, then blurted out, with the single-mindedness of the true pragmatist, 'Whom did he name as his heir, John or Arthur?'

'His brother John.' Llewelyn's eyes flicked from the letter to the ashen-faced de Montalt. 'If you wish,' he said, 'your chaplain may offer up prayers for Richard's soul.'

De Montalt swallowed, nodded. 'He . . . he was a great soldier.'
Llewelyn nodded, too; that he could acknowledge in all honesty.

As soon as the Welsh were alone in the solar, Llewelyn's companions crowded around him. 'What of Arthur, Llewelyn? Did he not put in his claim, too?'

Llewelyn glanced again at the letter. 'Indeed he did, Ednyved. Chester says rebel barons of Brittany and Touraine laid siege to Angers and Le Mans, proclaimed Arthur as Richard's rightful heir. He says John almost fell into their hands at Le Mans, but he was able to reach safety at Rouen, and there the Norman lords rallied to him, answered his call to arms. He led an army back into Anjou, razed the castle at Le Mans and burned the city. Arthur escaped, fled to the French court, and John seems like to prevail. Chester writes that he was invested as Duke of Normandy on the 25th, that he sails for England within the fortnight.'

'Llewelyn?' Rhys was frowning. 'What does this mean to us? Are we the better or the worse for his death?'

'I would that I knew, Rhys. For certès, I'd rather have seen Arthur crowned over John; a twelve-year-old lad would cast no great shadow in Wales. As for John . . . I hope I am wrong, but he may well prove to be more troublesome than ever his brother was. For all his vaunted skill with a sword, Richard never bothered much with Wales. Or with England, either, if truth be told. He was King for ten years and how often was he even on English soil? Twice, I do believe! But John has no interest in crusades or foreign campaigns, is likely to make England the central jewel in his crown. And he knows our ways better than most, was, as Earl of Gloucester, himself a Marcher lord. No, I suspect we've no reason for rejoicing that John is to be King.

'King John,' Llewelyn repeated softly. 'Morgan is a better prophet than even he knows. Once, years ago, he told me our lives should entwine, John's and mine. And, so it now seems, they shall.'

June, 1200
Fontevrault Abbey, Province of Anjou

The royal abbey of St Mary of Fontevrault was young in years when measured against the timeless span of stone and mortar, but few religious orders were as influential or as wealthy. Matilda de Bohème, the proud, pious woman who ruled as Abbess, was related both by blood and marriage to the great Houses of Champagne and Blois, and the thriving community within Fontevrault's walls included a convent for well-born nuns, a monastery for monks and lay brothers, a hospital for lepers, a home for those nuns and monks grown too old to serve God in other than prayer, even a shelter for penitent prostitutes. At Fontevrault the Plantagenet dead of Henry's House were buried, and Eleanor was often an honoured guest of the Abbess. Taken ill that spring, she had chosen to convalesce in the white-walled stillness of the abbey, lingered weeks later, having found an unexpected contentment in the cloistered and placid peace, so utterly lacking in the turbulence and high drama that had marked her life for almost eight decades.

The Abbess Matilda welcomed her with heartfelt gladness; theirs was a friendship of genuine affection, if not genuine intimacy. She wondered, though, how long it would be before Eleanor's restless spirit would begin to yearn for the pleasures of the world that was truly hers, the glittering court at Poitiers, where for almost sixty-five years she had reigned in her own right as Duchess of Aquitaine. Eleanor was not, she knew, a woman ever to renounce power, no matter the accompanying pain . . . and pain there had been in plenitude.

Looking pensively at Eleanor's sculptured profile, at the face so familiar and yet so unrevealing, Matilda found herself thinking of all the griefs Eleanor had endured in recent months. Death had claimed four of her children in a heartbreakingly brief span. Both the daughters born of her marriage to the French King were now dead; Richard had died in her arms, and not five months later, she'd stood a ghastly vigil over yet another child, as Joanna died giving birth to a stillborn son. She had, Matilda thought, been no luckier as a mother than she had as a wife. Of the ten children she'd borne, she'd buried eight, had only a daughter in distant Castile and the son she was even now awaiting, the last of her eaglets – and the least-loved.

And yet Matilda knew she had laboured tirelessly for that same son to gain for him the Angevin crown, had then exhausted herself seeking to win recognition of his right. She'd traversed the length and breadth of her domains on his behalf, formally designated him as heir to her duchy of Aquitaine, and lastly, undertaken for him a gruelling journey that would have daunted a woman half her age. This past January, Philip and John had come to terms, sought to secure peace with the marriage of Philip's son and John's niece. Eleanor took it upon herself to fetch the young Spanish bride, child of the daughter sent so long ago to wed the King of Castile. Daring a dangerous winter crossing of the Pyrenees, she'd brought her granddaughter to Normandy for the wedding that would one day make her Queen of France. But however indomitable her spirit still was, her body was in its seventy-ninth year, and she'd fallen gravely ill upon her return, had been forced to miss the royal wedding she'd done so much to bring about.

Eleanor rose, moved restlessly to the window and back again. John had sent word that he'd be arriving at noon; he was already two hours late.

'This will be the first time that you've seen your son since the wedding, will it not, Madame?' Matilda would have liked to discuss the controversial peace that the wedding was meant to warrant. The treaty was not proving popular in England, where men long accustomed to Richard's readiness to wage war for honour and profit looked askance at any resolution not bought with blood. Among those most eager for plunder and among those who'd have cheered the campaign on from the battle lines of London alehouses, John had earned himself a derisive sobriquet, one utterly at odds with the admiring 'Richard Lion-Heart' that had been bestowed upon his brother: 'John Softsword'. But Matilda knew better than to broach the subject; Eleanor did not share confidences, least of all about her youngest son.

'Madame . . .' A young novice nun stood in the doorway. 'Madame, the King's Grace has just ridden into the garth.'

'. . . and we celebrated the wedding the day after Philip and I concluded the treaty. We had to hold it across the border in Normandy, of course, what with France being under Interdict, and Philip had to get a second-hand account of the ceremony, since he's barred from all the Sacraments.'

At that, John and Eleanor exchanged identical, amused smiles, for the French King's marital troubles had only grown more tangled with time, had now embroiled him in a confrontation with the Holy See. It was seven years since he'd rejected Ingeborg, four since he'd defiantly wed the Duke of Meran's daughter, and the Pope had at last lost patience. Six months ago he had turned upon Philip one of the more effective weapons in the papal arsenal, laying France under Interdict until the King agreed to set aside his present wife and recognize the long-suffering Ingeborg as his Queen.

'A pity you had to miss all the festivities, Madame . . . especially that memorable moment when Philip compelled Arthur to do homage to me for the duchy of Brittany, to acknowledge me as his King and liege lord. If I'd gained nothing else from the treaty, the look on Arthur's face would be recompense enough!'

This last was said with the trace of defiance. John knew what was being said in alehouse and army encampment, that his brother Richard would never have made such a peace, and he'd come prepared to defend himself with irrefutable logic and common sense. But his relationship with his mother was too tenuous, too fraught with ambivalence and inconsistencies to be governed by the dictates of reason. Instead of citing the very material advantages of peace with Philip, he found himself saying sarcastically:

'But I'm discovering that a truce not won at swordpoint is somehow suspect. People crave glory. I give them peace, and they fancy themselves the poorer for it. What of you, Madame? Do you, too, fault me for renouncing glory in favour of crops in the fields and money in my coffers?'

Eleanor gave a startled laugh. 'Good God, no! Do you know me as little as that? War is the least productive of men's pastimes and the most indulgent. Why should I want you to fight for what you can gain at the bargaining table?'

John was pleased, but still wary. 'I yielded to Philip only that which I could not hope to hold in the field,' he said cautiously. 'The truth of it, Mother, is that I could not afford a war. The money is just not there.'

They both knew why, because Richard had depleted the royal treasury with his wars, his crusade, his ransom. Eleanor said nothing, and John, disarmed by her unexpected approval, forbore for once to criticize the son she still mourned.

'Not that I expect the peace to last,' he admitted. 'But it will give me the time I need to replenish my coffers, to checkmate Arthur, and to deal with trouble from a source I had not expected – you have heard? Despite years of rivalry and bad blood, the Count of Angoulême means to wed his daughter to that whoreson de Lusignan. It is a marriage guaranteed to give me naught but grief.'

Eleanor's mouth twisted; in their dislike of Hugh de Lusignan, she and John were in rare and full accord. That past January, as Eleanor was setting out for Castile, she'd been intercepted by Hugh de Lusignan, compelled to accept the hospitality of his stronghold at Lusignan Castle. Just as de Lusignan's invitation could fairly be termed an abduction, the favour he sought from Eleanor was more in the nature of extortion than appeal: that she yield to him the county of La Marche. Eleanor was proud, but hers was a pride tempered by pragmatism; making a grimly realistic assessment of her predicament, she acted to cut her losses, gave de Lusignan what he demanded, and within hours, was free to resume her journey westward. John, on the verge of making peace with Philip, could do little but acquiesce in the *fait accompli*, accept de Lusignan's homage as the new Count of La Marche. But he knew that de Lusignan would never have dared to commit such an audacity while Richard lived, and that was a raw, ulcerous sore, a grievance beyond forgiving.

'Yes,' Eleanor said flatly, 'I heard. That is why I summoned you to Fontevrault. We know what Hugh de Lusignan is; the man has the scruples of a snake. But the Count of Angoulême is another malcontent who serves only his own interests, and both of them are hand in glove with Philip. Should they put an end to their feuding, ally their Houses in this marriage, that would one day give Hugh both Angoulême and La Marche. We cannot allow the marriage to take place . . . although I confess I'm at a loss as to how to prevent it. You dare not forbid it outright; as jealous as my barons be of their rights, every lord in Aquitaine would rally to their support.'

'If I forbid it, yes.' John leaned back in his chair. 'Yesterday I summoned the Count of Angoulême to do homage to me on July 5th . . . at Lusignan Castle.'

'You what?' Eleanor's eyes widened. 'The three of you under one roof? That is a volatile mix if ever I heard one! What do you mean to do, John?'

'I mean to stop the marriage.'

'But how? I do not see . . .'

'I'd rather not say just yet. I will tell you this much, that if I succeed, Aymer of Angoulême and Hugh de Lusignan will be blood enemies till the day of mortal reckoning and beyond, and I'll have made of Aymer a steadfast ally, which is more, Madame, than Richard could ever do. And if it also happens that Hugh de Lusignan should find himself a laughing-stock, the butt of every jest from Poitiers to Paris – well, that's not likely to break my heart; nor yours, either, I'd wager.'

Eleanor did not respond as he had expected. After some moments of silence, she said thoughtfully, 'If you are asking whether I'd like to see Hugh de Lusignan humiliated, of course I would. If you are asking whether I think it would be wise, I'd have to say no. With all the enemies you have, John, vengeance is an indulgence you can ill afford right now.'

John was irked, disappointed, too. 'Life at Fontevrault is making you very pious, Mother. Next you'll be quoting Scriptures.'

'I'm talking of foresight, not of forgiveness,' Eleanor snapped, but John was already on his feet. She tensed, but did not protest. With Richard, she could have insisted that he stay, hear her out. She had no such leverage with John, and well she knew it.

'I do not know what sort of devious scheme you have in mind. I can only tell you this. Whilst stupidity may indeed be a sin, it is also possible to be too clever. I sometimes fear, John, that you are too clever by half.'

John shrugged. 'At least,' he said, 'you might wish me luck.'

Will Longsword was seated at a table in his brother's chamber, labouring over a letter to his girl-wife. He wielded the pen awkwardly, for his was a hand more accustomed to grasp a sword hilt, swearing under his breath as he searched for words to put to parchment.

Done this 6th day of July in the year of Our Lord 1200, at the castle of Hugh de Lusignan, Count of La Marche and Lord of Lusignan and Couhé. To the Lady Ela, Countess of Salisbury, my dear wife, greetings.

And that was as far as he'd got. Will had no idea why they were at Lusignan. Neither, he suspected, did Hugh de Lusignan. It was well known that John never forgave a wrong, forgot a grudge, and Hugh had made ready for his lord's goodwill visit with sceptical wariness, much like a man who'd just been assured that the wolf wandering midst his flocks was in fact a domesticated dog. But whatever John's ultimate intentions, he was presently on his best behaviour. Even his enemies never denied he had a certain scapegrace charm when he cared to exert himself, and he'd been drawing upon that charm so lavishly that Hugh had begun to relax somewhat, to let down his guard. The workings of Hugh's brain were too broadly meshed for subtlety. He knew Richard would not have rested until his head rotted on a pike over his own gatehouse, until his castles were reduced to rubble and his lands to charred embers, his women-folk despoiled and his brother hanged. But John drank with him, diced with him, swapped bawdy jokes and hinted at royal favours to come. Such a man was not to be feared. Once Hugh reached the fateful conclusion, he was hard put to hide his disdain; there was a bluff heartiness in his manner that was a shade too familiar, a swaggering assumption of intimacy that filled Will with foreboding.

Now Will sighed. Even if he had been privy to John's plans, he could not have shared them with Ela. She was just fourteen, all elbows and knees and sudden blushes, a sweet child, he thought fondly, who'd brought him an earldom and deserved in turn to be sheltered and protected until she outgrew her little-girl awkwardness. But what to tell her, then? Will gazed at the parchment as if willing words to materialize of their own accord, at last gave up and elected, instead, to watch the game of tables in progress between John and Aymer Taillefer, Count of Angoulême.

Aymer was staring down at the game-board with unblinking blue eyes. He played as he did all else, with a competitive intensity that knew no quarter, and he sucked in his breath when the dice roll gave the game to John, paused too long before saying, 'What do I owe Your Grace?'

'Shall we play again? Only this time let's double the stakes.' John smiled as if oblivious of the other man's ill humour, and reached for the wine cup by his elbow. 'Hugh tells me you've set a date for the wedding.'

'August 26th.' Aymer tossed the dice on to the table. His were eyes as hard as stones, empty of all save suspicion. 'Shall we speak plainly, Your Grace? Hugh de Lusignan may be a fool, but I am not. I know full well that Hugh's coming marriage to my daughter is not to your liking, that you would prevent it if you could. It is your right as my liege lord to speak against it, and if it is your wish, I will hear you out. But I think it only fair to tell you that I shall not change my mind, that I mean to see Isabelle as Countess of La Marche.'

John drank, studying Aymer all the while. 'It is said that your daughter is uncommonly pretty. Is that true?'

'She is a beauty, Your Grace. Why?'

'Your daughter is a great heiress, will one day inherit all of Angoulême. And she is of high birth, her mother a first cousin to the King of France. Now you say she is a beauty into the bargain. What escapes my understanding is why you would waste such a girl on Hugh de Lusignan. I should think you'd aim higher – much higher.'

'Your Grace?' Aymer was no longer feigning disinterest. 'Just what are you saying?'

'I am saying that you'd be doing your daughter a grave disservice if you settled for Hugh de Lusignan.' John paused; there was a faint mockery now in his smile. 'Unless, of course, you have no interest in seeing her as Queen of England?'

Aymer's intake of breath was audible even to Will. He hastily cast his eyes down, but not in time; John caught the sudden hot light, the glimmer of bedazzled greed. 'You overwhelm me, my liege, and do my daughter great honour. But you already have a Queen, have you not?'

'No,' John corrected amiably, 'I have a wife, not a Queen. Do you think that I neglected to have Avisa crowned with me through sheer oversight? It has long been my intent to end the marriage; I've merely been awaiting the opportune time.'

Aymer swallowed, so caught up in John's spell that he absent-mindedly helped himself to John's wine. 'You do not foresee any difficulty in casting off the Lady Avisa?'

John laughed. 'Unlike Philip, who's likely to be yoked to the martyred Ingeborg for all eternity, I happen to be able to satisfy the most scrupulous papal conscience. Avisa and I are second cousins, you see, well within the prohibited decree of consanguinity, and we never did bother to get a papal dispensation for our marriage. Need I say more?'

Aymer laughed, too, in that moment vulnerable as only a man could be who suddenly found reality exceeding all expectations, even the fantasy world of dreams. 'It will afford me great pleasure, Your Grace, to give you my daughter. But what of de Lusignan? He makes an ugly enemy, is one to nurse a grudge to the grave. How shall we manage it?'

'Easily enough, I think. I understand the girl is now at Hugh's castle of Valence, no? Well, after you depart from here, you need only ride to Valence, tell the de Lusignans you wish to take her back with you to Angoulême for a final visit with her mother ere the wedding. In the meantime, I shall find some distant task for Hugh and his kin to undertake on my behalf. I dare say you've noticed that Hugh's acting much like a cat that got into the cream. He's sure that he's basking in my royal favour, will see this charge as proof positive that he's truly won my trust, my friendship.'

'Indeed,' Aymer said approvingly. 'And then?'

'From here I go to Bordeaux, where I'll have the Archbishop declare my marriage void *ab initio*. As you know, I plan to pass the summer on progress in my lady mother's domain. What would be more natural than to accept your hospitality when I reach Angoulême, at which time I shall right gladly plight troth with your pretty daughter . . . on the 26th of August, mayhap? After that, we need only decide whether we want to invite de Lusignan to the wedding!'

This time, however, Aymer did not join in John's laughter. 'A plight troth,' he echoed sharply. 'Why not a wedding?'

John hesitated. This was the only weakness he could see in his scheme. A plight troth would give him all the political benefits of a marriage; would, as well, enable him to disavow Isabelle without difficulty should a better marital prospect appear at a later date. But the advantages of a plight troth were so blatantly one-sided that he was not at all sure Aymer would ever agree.

'Because of your daughter's extreme youth,' he said earnestly. 'She's but twelve, is she not? I think it only fair to give her time to adjust. It will be bound to come as a shock, to arrive in Angoulême expecting to marry Hugh, a man she knows well, only to be told she's to wed a total stranger.'

Aymer reflected upon this in silence, then gave John an oblique smile. 'Your concern for my daughter is commendable.' He rose as John did, made a perfunctory obeisance, and suddenly burst into malicious laughter. 'Damn me if de Lusignan's not going to look a right proper fool when word gets out!'

'Yes,' John agreed complacently. 'I expect he will.'

He waited till they were alone, at once turning to Will and demanding, 'Well? What think you?'

'It is brilliant, John,' Will said admiringly, 'in truth, it is. That marriage would have been a disaster for us, and you've hit upon the one way you could stop it. But . . . but would it not be better to let Hugh de Lusignan save face? You need not do it this way, could let Aymer end the betrothal, then wait a discreet interval ere you claim the girl. I fear that if you steal her out from under Hugh's nose –' John was smiling and Will stopped in mid-sentence. It had baffled him that a man as bright as his brother could be so blind to conse- quences; now John's sardonic smile brought it all into focus for him. 'You want to humiliate Hugh de Lusignan, do you not?' he said slowly. 'Fully as much as you want the girl, if not more. John . . . are you sure you've thought this through, that the game is worth the candle?'

'Shall I tell you, Will, why you always lose to me when we play at hazards or tables? Because you're so cautious it damned near cripples you! Poor Will, just once in your life have you never wanted to risk all upon one throw of the dice?' John moved back to the table, gestured for Will to pour them wine.

'Only one thing does puzzle me,' he confessed. 'Aymer is right; he's no fool. So why then, did he agree to a plight troth? Why did he not insist upon a wedding?'

From Bordeaux, John had moved south into Gascony, and then began a slow circuit back into Poitou. On Wednesday, August 24, he crossed the River Charente, and the next morning was welcomed into the walled capital city of Angoulême.

The great hall of Aymer's ancient castle had been swept clean, strewn with fresh rushes and sweet-smelling herbs, hung with em- broidered wall hangings of red, green, and gold. Aymer's countess, a striking, statuesque woman who bore no resemblance to her cousin the French King, insisted upon personally acting as John's guide, proudly pointing out her favourites among the hangings: the Five Joys of the Blessed Mary and the Story of Paris and Helen. John made the proper admiring responses, but he was impatient to see the girl he'd one day be taking to wife and, sensing that, the Lady Alice excused herself, went to fetch Isabelle.

'You have told her, I assume?' John asked, and Aymer nodded.

'But of course. She was both awed and honoured that Your Grace should think her worthy of a crown, and she vowed that you would never repent your choice.'

John gave Aymer a sceptical smile, and winked at Will. He had enough experience with children to know that no twelve year old was likely to harbour such lofty sentiments, much less express them aloud. He only hoped the girl was truly reconciled to the plight troth; England must seem as distant as Cathay to a girl who'd never been anywhere but Angoulême and Valence. Will's little Ela had been a twelve-year-old bride, too, and remembering how fearful she had been, approaching the altar like a lamb led to the slaughter, John hoped Isabelle would be of sturdier stock. But the memory of Ela's unease gave him an idea, and he beckoned to Will. 'Why do we not send the lass to Ela at Salisbury?'

Will beamed. 'An excellent thought. I dare say she'd be less homesick with Ela and me than at your court. She'd be good company for Ela, too . . .'

He stopped, for John was no longer listening. He'd taken an involuntary step forward; Will heard him murmur, 'Good God.' Turning to see what had so transfixed his brother, Will found himself staring, too, at the girl coming towards them. His mouth dropped open; the shock was all the greater because he'd instinctively cast Isabelle in Ela's image. Expecting an endearing, coltish clumsiness, bitten nails and shy, sidelong glances, he saw, instead, a slender vision in turquoise and silver silk, a delicate, oval face framed in a cascade of shimmering light. Will had occasionally seen young girls who'd matured too early, overly-ripe and knowing beyond their years. Isabelle d'Angoulême was not one of these, had not forfeited the touching and poignant appeal of innocence. And yet she held the eye of every man in the hall. It was the first time in his life that Will had ever seen a woman who could truly be called 'unforgettable', and it was with a vague sense of shame that he acknowledged the sheer physical impact of the girl, reminding himself hastily that she

148

was not a woman, was, for all her startling beauty, still a child of twelve.

What amazed him even more than her appearance was her poise. She approached John without a trace of nervousness, sank down before him in an eye-pleasing curtsy. But after a moment to reflect, Will realized why; no girl who looked as this one did could long remain ignorant of her advantages. For the first time he glanced towards his brother. John was staring at Isabelle so avidly that Will decided John, too, needed to be reminded of Isabelle's extreme youth.

'Your Grace,' she said, her French attractively enhanced by the soft accents of Provençal, the *langue d'oc* spoken throughout Eleanor's domains.

'No, darling, the grace is yours,' John said huskily. 'I'd have you call me John.'

Aymer had been standing to one side, watching with an odd little smile, one Will had seen once before, that July night at Lusignan Castle. Stepping forward now, he said, 'I explained to Isabelle that you thought it would be a kindness to delay the marriage. She assured me, however, that will not be necessary, told me she would like to be wed at once. Is that not so, Isabelle?'

'Yes, Papa.' Isabelle gave John a dazzling smile. 'That is indeed my wish.' But only Will noticed as she then surreptitiously wiped the palms of her hands against her elegant silk skirt. Poor little lass, he thought; so she was not so different from his Ela, after all. And his heart went out to her in a surge of protective, paternal tenderness.

'Is that agreeable to Your Grace, then? Have I your permission to make plans for the wedding? As the Archbishop of Bordeaux is in your entourage, he could officiate. On the morrow, shall we say?'

John had yet to take his eyes from Isabelle. 'By all means, Aymer,' he said and smiled at Aymer's daughter. 'The sooner the better.'

'Oh, how beautiful! It is truly for me?'

John smiled. 'Truly. Here, turn around and I'll fasten the clasp for you.'

Isabelle did as he bade, sitting beside him on the garden bench. Because of her youth, she wore no wimple or veil, let her hair fall free down her back. John brushed it aside, fastened the necklet about

149

her throat; even in the moonlight, the stones glowed, opals the shade of twilight and amethysts of deepest purple. 'Emeralds would suit you better, I think. Do you like emeralds, Isabelle?'

'They are green, no? I've never owned much jewellery. I do have a betrothal ring from Hugh. But I suppose I must give it back now, must I not?' she said impishly, and John laughed.

'Indeed not; consider it a keepsake. You have no regrets, then? About not marrying Hugh?'

'Oh no! I would have tried to be a dutiful wife, truly I would. But . . . but I did not want to marry him.' Isabelle hesitated, not sure if such candour was permissible. 'He was so much older than me, older even than my papa. He had salt-grey hair, not black and glossy like yours, and his eyes were always bloodshot and he . . . he made me uncomfortable sometimes, the way he looked at me . . .'

'As if he were starving and you were on the menu?' John suggested, and she gave a startled giggle. 'But I look at you that way, too; have you not noticed?'

'I do not mind it with you,' she said softly, lowering her lashes to cast silky shadowed crescents upon skin so perfect it looked like porcelain. John reached over, stroked her cheek. When she did not pull away, he leaned closer still, touched her mouth with his. Her breathing quickened; he could see the rise and fall of her small breasts, budding against the bright silk of her bodice. He kissed her again, this time as a man would kiss a woman, and found that the entrancing flirt who'd invited such intimacies was but an illusion born of the moonlight and his own desire, found himself holding a fearful little girl. She submitted docilely to his embrace, let him explore her mouth with his tongue, but her body had lost all pliancy, was rigidly unresponsive under his hands. John released her, frowning, and tears filled her eyes.

'I did not please you?' she faltered. 'Papa said I must, said I –'

'Isabelle, hush. There is nothing about you that does not please me. I do not expect you to know how to pleasure a man, will teach you all you need to know.' He began to caress her hair, let his fingers trail across her throat. 'And they'll be lessons much to your liking, that I can promise you.'

There was no anger in his voice, and Isabelle was emboldened to confide, 'Papa told me I must not let Hugh touch me till we were wed, but . . . but he said I should let you do what you will. And I was so afraid . . . because if we bedded together and then you did

150

not want me as a wife, Papa would have blamed me for that, would have been so wroth . . .'

'Isabelle, listen to me. Forget what your father told you; it does not matter. You do not belong to him any longer. You belong to me and I do want you. I want you as my Queen, I want you in my bed, and right now I want you on my lap.' John smiled, but she reacted as if to a command, at once settled herself upon his knee, and put her arms shyly about his neck.

Her obedience delighted him, and he realized suddenly that he wanted her as much for her youth as in spite of it; she was still unformed, as malleable as she was beautiful, soft clay to be moulded and shaped as he desired. 'You are so fair to look upon,' he murmured, then began to laugh. 'And I've done Hugh de Lusignan an even more grievous hurt than I dared hope for!'

The great hall was in utter chaos, as the entire household of the Count of Angoulême laboured to make ready for the wedding on the morrow. When Will could abide the confusion no longer, he escaped out into the gardens. It was becoming increasingly apparent to him that this wedding had been planned weeks in advance, so sure was Aymer of his daughter's power to enchant. He wondered briefly if he should mention this to John, decided it was pointless; John was not being shoved to the altar at swordpoint, after all.

He was approaching an intricate arbour of whitethorn and willow, walled by trellises and fragrant with summer honeysuckle. As he came nearer, he heard a man's voice, low and coaxing. 'You have to trust me, love. You do, do you not?' The girl's voice came even more clearly to Will's ears, an innocent accomplice in her own seduction. 'Oh, but I do, truly I do.' Will was genuinely shocked; he'd recognized the male voice at once as his brother's, but he found it almost impossible to believe that John could be so reckless, so unforgivably ill-mannered, as to debauch one of Aymer's womenfolk on the very eve of his marriage to Aymer's daughter. What if it had been Aymer who'd come upon them? he thought, and strode forward, a warning hot on his lips, only to stop, dumbfounded, at sight of Isabelle.

Isabelle gave a little gasp of dismay, flushed bright red. It was one thing to tell herself that John had every right to fondle and caress her as he chose, that it was proper to allow him such intimacies. It was quite another for his brother, the Earl of Salisbury, to discover

151

her sitting on John's lap, her hair in telling disarray and her bodice partially undone.

She came hastily to her feet, jerking at her gown, so flustered she might have fled had John not reached out, caught her hand. Rising unhurriedly, he said soothingly, 'You've no cause for embarrassment, love. It is not for Will – or any other – to pass judgment upon you.'

And with that, Isabelle suddenly and fully comprehended just what marriage to John would mean. That she would get to wear a crown and enjoy unknown luxury, that a son of hers would one day be King of England, all that she'd already grasped, though it was not quite real to her, not yet. The awareness that came to her now was more immediate, and therefore more easily understood. All her life she'd been taught it was her duty to obey, to please others, first and foremost the father whose expectations she could never quite satisfy. But no more. She need not ever worry again about her father's anger. Nor about her mother's sharp-tongued reprimands, or Hugh de Lusignan's hot rages, or the jealousy and spite of girls less favoured than she. She had only to please one man and one man alone, and as long as she was secure in his approval and affections, no one else's disapproval mattered.

Isabelle drew a deep breath, giddy with the realization that she who'd had so little power would now have so much. When I am Queen of the English, she thought in awe, it will be Papa who'll have to please me – me! And she looked at John in wonderment, Will all but forgotten.

They could hear other voices in the gardens now, women's voices. Isabelle cocked her head, listening. 'My mother . . . she's calling for me.' But she did not move, looked to John for guidance. 'Would you have me go to her?'

John nodded, bringing her hand up to his mouth and kissing her palm. 'It is late; you'd best be in.' Watching as she gathered up her skirts and ran lightly up the garden path, he said admiringly, 'Lord God, what a beauty she's going to be, Will! To think she almost ended up in Hugh de Lusignan's bed; talk about casting pearls before swine!'

He was turning to follow after Isabelle when Will grasped his arm. 'John, wait. I want you to tell me I misinterpreted what I just saw. I want you to tell me that you do not mean to bed that little girl.'

John's eyes narrowed, took on sudden green glints. 'Are you worrying that I shall dishonour her ere the wedding? How quaint. But you can put your mind at ease. I do intend to wait till the morrow . . . though that is no small sacrifice!'

'Christ Jesus, John, she is but twelve years old – a child! You do not think I'd have touched Ela, do you? Nor will I, not till she's of a proper age for bedding. As you must wait with Isabelle. Her father would expect no less; he's entrusting her to your care, your keeping. If he even suspected you –'

John gave an angry, incredulous laugh. 'There are times when your innocence truly defies all belief! Who do you think sent us out into the gardens? You fool, I could lay with Isabelle at high noon atop a table in the great hall and Aymer would cheer us on!'

But John did not truly want to quarrel with Will. Those very elements of Will's nature that made him champion Isabelle so stubbornly were also those that made him the only man John had ever been able to trust. He paused, then said impatiently:

'Will, you are my brother, companion, even confidant. But my conscience you are not, and thank God for it. I suspect you'd put a saint to shame! Good Christ, man, what do you think I mean to do, go after her like a stag in rut? You know me better than that, Will, or you bloody well should! I admit I've forced a woman or two in my life, but you name me a man who has not. I'm no Will de Braose, and you know it. I prefer a willing bedmate, prefer a woman who wants what she's getting.'

He grinned suddenly. 'I assure you, Isabelle will be in good hands. I had my first woman at fourteen, have long since lost count. You think I did not learn from all those couplings? That I'd not make Isabelle's deflowering as easy for her as I could? She's more woman than you know; I'd wager it'll take no more than a fortnight ere she's not only willing, but eager.'

'John, you must not –'

'Sweet glory of God, enough! Better me than de Lusignan. Now let that be an end to it.'

Will knew his brother well enough to read the danger signals, but he felt honour-bound to persevere. 'I do not doubt that de Lusignan would have wasted no time dragging the lass into bed. But you know better, John. The very fact that you feel the need to justify yourself proves that. It would be wrong to bed a twelve-year-old girl, no matter how fair she is. It's not . . . not decent. And it's dangerous, as well. What if you get her with child? I need not tell you how many women die in childbirth . . . and the younger the mother, the greater the risk.'

John caught his breath and then swore. 'Will, I'm warning you for the last time! You've pushed to the very limits of my patience. I'm heartily sick of this, will hear no more on it.'

But as he swung about, Will followed him on to the path, hastening to keep pace. 'What of your own daughter, what of Joanna? Can you tell me you'd want to see her as a man's bedmate at twelve, a mother at thirteen? John, I know what I'm saying! My Ela could not have –'

'Pox take your Ela, and you, too! I see nothing noble in your forbearance; I've met Ela, remember? I do not wonder that you're in no hurry to claim her maidenhead. But I doubt you'd be so saintly if it were Isabelle naked and eager in your bed!'

Will recoiled violently, backed away. John did not wait for a response, stalked up the path. He did not look back, but Will watched, unmoving, until he was out of sight.

As deeply offended as Will was, even greater was his sense of hurt. Never before had he felt the full lash of John's Angevin temper. His was a uniquely privileged position; he alone dared speak his mind utterly and freely to his brother, with no fear of incurring the King's disfavour. Will was honest enough to admit to himself that he relished the many tangible benefits he derived from John's kingship, but even more did he relish his special status as the King's brother and confidant. He prided himself on his candour, told himself that even if John did not always heed his advice, at least John was always willing to hear him out, liked to think he alone knew how to appeal to John's better instincts, and in consequence, he'd been slow to feel the ground shifting under his feet.

He stood there alone for a time in the darkness, half-expecting John to return, seeking to make amends. But John did not come back, and Will was left with the envenomed echoes of that last lethal exchange, with the unhappy understanding that his influence over John was more illusory than not, that he must take John on his own terms . . . or not at all.

Picking up a brush, Joanna parted her hair, and then began to plait it into two thick braids. Impatience made her clumsy, and the strands kept slipping through her fingers. But she persevered; she was nine now, too old for wild, unkempt hair, especially on the day of her father's return from Normandy.

Never before had he been gone so long, five lonely months. Always before, he had taken her with him; in the past four years, Joanna had learned to look upon a Channel crossing as nonchalantly as a Londoner viewed an outing across the Thames into Southwark. But when John had sailed for Normandy that past April, he'd left Joanna at Conisbrough, the Yorkshire castle of his uncle Hamelin de Warenne, Earl of Surrey, home, too, to Hamelin's grandson, her half-brother Richard.

Now it was October and Joanna was back at Westminster Palace, awaiting John's arrival. All around her, women were sleeping; she shared a chamber with the ladies in waiting to the noblewomen of John's court. Snapping her fingers to attract Avisa, she unlatched the door, moved into the stairwell, the spaniel at her heels.

Emerging out into the sunlight of the New Palace yard, she was just in time to collide with a man coming around the corner of the old hall. He stumbled, caught her as she reeled backward.

'I'm sorry, my lord.'

'No matter, Joanna. If I cannot sustain a bruising from a little lass like you, I'd best retire to my hearth and give my lands over to my sons,' he said and smiled at her. William de Braose, Lord of Brecknock, was an attractive man, fit and sun-browned, blond hair and beard only lightly touched by grey although she knew he was well into his fifties. He was one of her father's closest friends, and was unfailingly pleasant to her. There was no reason why she should be so ill at ease with him, and yet she was. It was with relief now that she saw de Braose was not alone, was accompanied by her father's half-brother Will, Earl of Salisbury.

Will was family; with him, she need not stand on formality. 'Papa's come?'

Will nodded. 'We rode in from Freemantle late last night, so I expect he's still abed.'

'I'd wager the surety of my soul on that!' de Braose said and laughed.

Will frowned and Joanna edged closer. 'Uncle Will . . . Papa's new wife, is she comely?'

'Very comely, Joanna.' Will looked intently into her face, and then put his arm around her shoulders, drew her aside. 'Does it bother you, lass, that John has wed again?'

Joanna shook her head swiftly. 'No, but . . . but I did not think he would wed again so soon.' She fidgeted and then blurted out, 'Uncle Will, I heard some men talking last month after we had word of Papa's marriage. They . . . they said Papa's new wife was plight-trothed to another lord, that Papa stole her away from this lord. That is not true, is it?'

Will did not answer at once. Joanna was, he knew, normally well insulated from rumours and gossip; no rational man would dare criticize the King in the hearing of his daughter. But this marriage had been virtually guaranteed to stir up controversy. It was said that Hugh de Lusignan had gone berserk with rage, raving and ranting and swearing to avenge himself upon John if it took a lifetime. And Hugh found some sympathizers among the Poitevin nobility, men who disapproved of the clandestine, underhanded nature of the marriage, others who'd willingly seize upon any pretext for rebellion. The result was that a marriage which should have solidified John's hold upon Poitou was in itself proving to be a source of dissension, while John had alienated the more pious of his subjects by his lustful infatuation for a girl of Isabelle's tender years.

Will shook his head slowly, wondering just how to answer Joanna. 'Yes, it is true, lass. Isabelle was betrothed to as untrustworthy a man as you could find in all of Christendom, and her marriage would one day have put into his hands all of Angoulême. Your father could not let that happen.'

Joanna was quiet. 'Is Isabelle truly only twelve?' she asked at last, and Will nodded.

'I think I do know what frets you. But she is a lively, good-natured lass, and I'm sure you will like her.'

That was not what was fretting Joanna at all. She was quite prepared to like Isabelle, although she did think it distinctly odd to have a stepmother only three years older than she. Her fear was that Isabelle would not like her. She had long since accustomed herself to her father's women. Most were kind to her, sometimes cloyingly so; Adele alone had not been friendly, and Adele's reign had been brief. One day she was gone and Joanna had learned a valuable lesson; whilst Papa's ladies came and went, her place in his heart was constant. But a wife . . . a wife was not like a mistress.

Brooding on this as she crossed the bailey, she was pleased to see Richard coming towards her. She'd gained more than a father at Rouen, she'd gained six brothers, too. Most were well into their teens by now, and she saw them but seldom. With Richard, it was different. He was only two years older than she, and from their first meeting, had appointed himself as her protector, as her guide and mentor. She could ask Richard what she could not ask Will, and as he fell in step beside her, she said, 'Richard . . . what if she does not like us?'

Richard was eating manchet bread glazed with honey. He took a large bite, handed what remained to Joanna. 'Papa will not love us any the less if she does not, Joanna. My mama says not to worry, that Papa is no man to be swayed by a woman's cajoling.'

It occurred to Joanna that Richard was not as confident as he sounded, else he'd not have felt the need to consult his mother. But she took comfort, none the less, from his assurance. His mother was more than a one-time mistress. Alina was John's first cousin, and had remained on friendly terms with him to this day, was often at court. Hers was a voice to be heeded.

'Richard . . . when your mama's family found out she was with child, were they shamed?'

'Angry, yes, but shamed . . . no. After all, Papa was a Prince. And then, too, my grandpapa Hamelin is baseborn himself; he was a bastard brother to King Henry. Mama told me that Grandpapa and my uncle did berate her somewhat at first, but they know women are weak vessels. They could hardly blame her for being true to her nature.'

'My mama was not so lucky,' Joanna said softly. 'Her family shunned her for her sin.' She hesitated. 'I told you that my mama died. But I never told you that I did think that it was my fault.'

Richard had been reaching to reclaim the honeyed bread. He stopped, gave her a look of sudden interest. 'You did? Why?'

The memories of her mother's death were so fraught with pain even now that Joanna had never been able to share them with anyone but John, and she said evasively, 'Oh, because she was so unhappy. But Papa explained it all to me, told me that the blame did lie with my mama's family, not with me.'

Richard's interest waned. 'Well, you're – Joanna, look. There's Uncle Will.'

Will raised an arm, beckoned. 'Joanna, Richard, make haste. Your lord father is ready to see you now.'

St Edward's chamber had been for well over a hundred years the traditional bedchamber of the King, was still used even though it was part of the old palace of the Confessor. John was sitting on a coffer as his barber carefully trimmed his beard, but he waved the man away at sight of his children.

Joanna ran to him, into his arms. 'Papa, I missed you so!'

'I missed you, too, sweetheart. But keep your voices down. Isabelle is still asleep.'

Joanna and Richard quieted at once, cast subdued glances towards the curtained bed. John smiled at them, gave Richard a playful poke. 'You need not act as if you're in church! Come over here and see what I brought back for you.'

Lifting the coffer lid, he fished around, at last unearthed their presents: spurs for Richard, a carved ivory comb for Joanna. 'I do have a second gift for Joanna, lad, but that is because I missed her birthday. Here, sweetheart.'

Joanna gave a delighted gasp, slipped the ring on to her finger. It was a perfect topaz, set in silver, but too big, sliding over her knuckle until she made a quick fist.

'John . . . John, where did you go?' The voice was young, sleepily content. Richard and Joanna turned as a tousled head poked through the bed hangings. Joanna felt a sharp pang of envy; as she'd suspected, Isabelle's hair was a lustrous swirl of sunlight. She yawned like a lazy kitten, blinked at them with long-lashed, lavender-blue eyes. Joanna could not, of course, begin to comprehend the complicated sexual cravings that made this beautiful child-woman so desirable to a man with jaded sensibilities, a man in need of novelty. But she could see how undeniably lovely Isabelle was, and her fear came rushing back. How could Papa not be influenced by Isabelle?

'You must be Joanna and Richard.' Isabelle jerked the bed hangings aside, and wrapping herself in the sheet, accepted a servant's offering, a cup of watered-down wine. 'I suppose I'm now your mother!' She laughed suddenly. 'But do not dare call me Mama!'

'What shall we call you, Madame?' Joanna asked, at a loss, and Isabelle gave a comical grimace.

'How serious she is, John! I am Isabelle, of course. Come, sit beside me on the bed and I shall tell you of my first meeting with your father. I can tell her, can I not, John? It is six weeks to the day; we were wed without even posting the banns! John said he knew as soon as he saw me, knew he would have me for his Queen and no other.'

Joanna and Richard exchanged bemused glances. Both quiet by

nature, they were overwhelmed by Isabelle, who seemed able to talk without even pausing for breath. But her friendliness set their fears at rest, and Joanna gladly did as Isabelle bade, settled herself upon the foot of the bed. She should have had more faith in Papa, she thought, should have known he would not have chosen a wife who'd scorn his children.

11

August, 1201

Gwynedd, Wales

After passing the night at Basingwerk Abbey, Baldwin de Hodnet and his brother moved cautiously westward, keeping to the narrow coastal road. The sea was frothed with whitecaps, the sky flaming to the east in the sunburst dawn that promised a day of surpassing beauty. But Baldwin had no eye for God's wonders; he was too taken up with manmade troubles.

'How do you know where he is, Stephen?'

'I do not. The Welsh court moves about no less frequently than John's. Llewelyn has palaces at Aber, at Aberffraw on the isle of Môn, at Caer yn Arfon, has palaces and hunting lodges scattered throughout the Eryri Mountains.'

'Well, then, how shall we find him?'

'We will not. He'll find us,' Stephen said, and withdrew from his saddle pouch a brightly painted silk banner: quartered lions passant, red on gold. 'Llewelyn's arms. What better way to make known that we seek him?'

'Clever,' Baldwin said grudgingly. 'But to what avail? I'm damned if I know why I let you talk me into this. We'll find no welcome at his court, Stephen. How can we? Just last month, he signed a truce with King John, agreed to do homage to John as his overlord and, in return, was recognized as ruler of Gwynedd. Why should he risk angering John by aiding men branded as rebels?'

Stephen laughed. 'You do not understand the Welsh, Baldwin. You share all the common misconceptions about Llewelyn's people. Ask any lord at John's court to describe the Welsh character, and what is he likely to say? That the Welsh are impulsive, quick-tempered, easily stirred by passion. That may well be true. But it is also true that in matters of statecraft, no people in Christendom are as pragmatic as the Welsh princes. They have to be, with England more than twenty times the size of Wales. Since the reign of Owain

Fawr, their princes have sworn allegiance to the English kings, because they were shrewd enough to see they had no choice. The Welsh are realists, Baldwin, and an oath of allegiance is cheaper than blood as the price of sovereignty. Do not ever think, though, that Llewelyn sees himself as a vassal of John's. He does not.'

Stephen grinned. 'The great weakness of the Welsh has always been their penchant for fighting amongst themselves, a weakness our kings have been quick to exploit. But Llewelyn has a rare gift for fishing in troubled waters. John may well find —'

'I'd as soon you spared me a lesson in Welsh history,' Baldwin interrupted impatiently. 'All that does concern me at the moment is whether we're likely to find refuge at Llewelyn's court. And you've yet to convince me that we will.'

Now it was Stephen who showed impatience. 'We always knew it might come to this, Baldwin. When Fulk Fitz Warin rose up in rebellion against John, and we decided we could not do otherwise than support him, as our kinsman and liege lord, we had no illusions about the risks, or the likely outcome. Tell me, would you rather seek exile in France?'

'No,' Baldwin conceded. 'I ought not to be taking out my foul temper on you, Little Brother. As you say, better Llewelyn than Philip. How long has it been since you've seen him last?'

'Three or four years, I think,' Stephen said, and Baldwin let out an explosive oath.

'Blood of Christ! You expect him to incur John's wrath for a man he has not even seen in years?'

Stephen was unperturbed. 'The Welsh make bad enemies, better friends. Your trouble, Baldwin, is that you have so little faith!'

'My trouble is that I have a price upon my head, and an ingrate of a brother set upon laying claim to my inheritance,' Baldwin said sourly.

'What else would you expect from Walter?'

'Better than this. Did I not persuade Fulk to give him a place in his household? And when he came to me, claiming he'd had his horse and armour stolen, did I not lend him the money for another mount and hauberk?'

'And I thought you were mad to do it; I still do. As the eldest, you never knew him, Baldwin, not as Will and I did.'

'What else could I do, Stephen? He's still blood kin.'

'If he were drowning, I'd throw him an anchor,' Stephen said flatly, and Baldwin gave his brother a surprised, speculative look.

'You truly mean that, do you not? I did not realize –' He stiffened suddenly, and then said softly, 'Stephen, to your left.'

'I know. I think we're about to be welcomed into Wales.'

There was a flash of movement through the trees; a lance thudded into the path a few feet ahead, quivered like a snake coiled to strike. They both drew rein, waited.

A man emerged from the woods, came to a wary halt. Stephen tilted his lance up so that Llewelyn's banner caught the breeze. *'Tangnefedd,'* he said loudly. *'Rydu i Stephen de Hodnet, cyfaill o Llewelyn ab Iorwerth, o Tywysog Gwynedd.'*

There was a silence; other men were now coming out of the shadows. Stephen ventured a few more sentences in halting Welsh, then turned to Baldwin, smiling. 'Did I not tell you? These are Llewelyn's men, will take us to him. I told them that I am his friend, that he will want to see me.'

'So you hope,' Baldwin said.

They were travelling south, through a well-wooded river valley. Stephen was carrying on a disjointed conversation with their guides, partly in his rudimentary Welsh and partly in their fragmented French, and from time to time he'd translate for Baldwin's benefit. 'We have to ford the River Conwy up ahead, and then veer west.'

'Did you, by any chance, think to ask where we're going?'

'Dolwyddelan Castle.' Anticipating Baldwin, Stephen grinned, said with exaggerated precision, 'Dole-with-éllan. I'd hoped Llewelyn would be at Aber or Aberffraw, wanted you to see the Welsh court. But Dolwyddelan should be of interest, too; it's one of the few Welsh-built castles, belonged to Llewelyn's father Iorwerth.'

That did interest Baldwin. So, too, did the countryside once they were across the River Conwy. It was far more mountainous now; on all sides the sky was silhouetted by snow-capped crags. Baldwin was impressed in spite of himself, forbore to mock as Stephen shared the knowledge gleaned from their guides. 'They say snow is sometimes found all summer long upon the highest peaks. The steepest is that one to the south, Yr Wyddfa. And over to your right is Moel Siabod, which all but overshadows Dolwyddelan.'

'Little wonder the Welsh are so hard to dislodge,' Baldwin said, and shook his head. 'Their whole wretched country is a fortress of sorts!'

They reached Dolwyddelan Castle at dusk. It appeared without warning, seemed to spring suddenly from the rough-hewn rocks overlooking the River Lledr. Baldwin, appraising it from habit, with an eye to assault, saw at once that it would be no easy prize to take. On the south, the ground fell away sharply, and deep ditches had been cut into the rock to the west and east. But what impressed Baldwin was the high curtain wall. Most castles were enclosed by timber palisades, but Dolwyddelan was encircled by stone.

Stephen, too, was regarding the curtain wall with surprise. 'When I was here last that was a wooden enclosure.'

'He's doing right well for himself if he could undertake an expense like that,' Baldwin said thoughtfully, and Stephen frowned.

'He's not just another Marcher lord, Baldwin. He's Prince of Gwynedd. Power is power, be it Welsh or Norman; you'd best bear that in mind.'

Passing through a gateway in the north wall, they dismounted in the bailey. Baldwin's eyes surveyed the wooden buildings clustered along the walls, focusing upon the two-storey rectangular keep, its entrance protected by a wooden forebuilding. He noted with satisfaction that the stairs leading up into the forebuilding were of stone; a miscalculation for certès. But as he reached the top, he abruptly revised his opinion of the keep's defences. A wide pit lay between the stairs and the door of the keep, a gap that could be spanned only by drawbridge.

'Clever,' he murmured to Stephen. But his brother was already hastening across the drawbridge, utterly sure of his welcome within. Following more slowly, Baldwin discovered that the entire first floor of the keep contained one large chamber. By the hearth, his brother was kneeling. As Baldwin watched, Llewelyn raised Stephen to his feet, and the two men then embraced. Stephen turned, gave Baldwin a smile shot through with triumph.

Baldwin leaned back in the window seat, only half-listening to his brother's conversation with Llewelyn. He was more interested in his surroundings than in Stephen's boyhood reminiscences, glanced about with frankly curious eyes. They were in Llewelyn's bedchamber; a large curtained bed stood at the far end of the room. The furnishings startled Baldwin, in that they were so familiar: rushes for the floor, a trestle table, coffers, even a privy chamber tucked away into the thickness of the south-east wall. He could, Baldwin mused in surprise, quite easily have been in the bedchamber of any Norman lord.

He did not realize how nakedly his thoughts showed upon his face until Llewelyn looked at him, said, 'Did you think to find us living in caves?'

Although said with a smile, it carried a sting, none the less, and Baldwin flushed. He was honest enough, however, to acknowledge he'd been fairly caught, and he summoned up a smile of his own. 'To tell you true, my lord, I knew naught of how the Welsh live.'

'We have our own ways, but we are not too proud to learn from others.' Llewelyn grinned, gestured towards the bed. 'Take yon feather bed. That is one Norman custom I'm quite willing to adopt for Wales.'

'Papa even sleeps on a pillow,' a voice said, right at Baldwin's elbow, and he jumped, turned to find himself under the unblinking scrutiny of a small boy. He looked to be about five, an unusually handsome youngster with dark red hair, wide-set green eyes, and a rather remarkable assurance for his years, volunteering now without waiting to be asked, 'I'm Gruffydd ap Llewelyn.'

Llewelyn laughed. 'My son Gruffydd, who delights in giving away all my guilty secrets!'

Gruffydd thrived upon attention, and he moved closer to Baldwin, confiding, 'Papa has two pillows. But he lets my mama use one.'

Baldwin was not comfortable with children. 'Does he, indeed?' he said lamely. Adding, since the boy was obviously cherished, 'You speak French very well, lad.'

'I know,' Gruffydd said. 'Are you English? Do you know what Papa says of the English? He says, "Poor Wales, so far from Heaven, so close to England!"'

'Gruffydd!' Llewelyn frowned, sought without success to look disapproving. 'Where are your manners, lad?'

Not in the least amused, Baldwin managed a thin smile. Stephen, who was amused, diplomatically piloted the conversation towards safe waters, saying swiftly, 'How is your lady? She's not here with you, I take it?'

'No, she's at Aberffraw. Her babe is due next month . . . our fourth.' A man now leaned over Llewelyn's chair, murmured a few words, and he rose.

'Alun will escort you to the great hall, where our cooks have set out a meal for you. I'll join you directly I put this hellion to bed.' Gruffydd at once darted for the door, but Llewelyn was quicker, grabbed the boy and swung him up into the air, making him shriek with laughter.

Baldwin signalled for another helping of stewed eels. 'Your friend does feed his guests well,' he admitted. 'But tell me – whilst we're alone – you asked after his "lady". A concubine, not a wife?'

Stephen hesitated. 'Llewelyn is not wed to Tangwystl. But do not be misled by that, Baldwin. Tangwystl is highborn, daughter to Lord Llywarch of Rhos. Less than a wife, mayhap, but much more than a mere bedmate. Theirs is looked upon as an honourable liaison. The Welsh have their own ways, as Llewelyn told you, and I confess I find none stranger than their attitude towards bastard-born children. They see no sin attaching to the children; under Welsh law, Gruffydd is fully equal to any sons Llewelyn may later have in wedlock.'

Baldwin was shocked. 'You mean that even though he's a bastard, he's Llewelyn's heir?' And when Stephen nodded, he could only shake his head in astonishment. 'The Welsh are mad, in truth. You've met her then, this Tang . . .?'

'Tang-oo-iś-til.' Seeing Llewelyn enter the hall, Stephen smiled a welcome, said, 'I was telling Baldwin; Tangwystl does mean "pledge of peace", does it not?'

'And never was a woman more aptly named, Stephen. She claims I like to ride the whirlwind, but she's managed to make of our home a veritable haven of peace.' Llewelyn tasted the mead set before him, and then said, 'I understand Fulk Fitz Warin has rebelled against King John; a dispute over a castle, I believe?'

Baldwin stiffened; he'd not expected so abrupt an exposure of their need. Stephen seemed untroubled, however. 'Yes,' he said. 'John did unjustly deny Fulk's claim to Whittington Castle. Baldwin and I . . . we felt honour-bound to support him. But John has passed Bills of Attainder against us all, and we've been hard pressed these weeks past, Llewelyn. Will you help us?'

'Of course. You are welcome at my court, for as long as you wish. So, too, is your lord, Fulk Fitz Warin. Did you doubt that?'

Stephen shook his head. 'No, I know you too well, know the ways of Welsh hospitality.'

Baldwin was still unable to believe salvation was being offered so casually. 'Why?' he blurted out. 'Why should you risk John's enmity for us?'

Llewelyn looked amused. 'Scriptures set forth Commandments for all Christians to honour. But my people honour other commandments, too, those that speak to the difficulties of dwelling in England's shadow. Let not an enemy be thy neighbour. It is no deceit to deceive a deceiver. And the enemy of my enemy is my friend.'

Baldwin nodded slowly. 'So you see John, then, as your enemy?'

Llewelyn smiled. 'I said that?' Reaching over, he clinked his cup against Stephen's. '*Croeso i Gymru, Steffan*. Welcome, Stephen, to Wales.'

The man seated at Baldwin's left had been introduced to him as Rhys ap Cadell, but he seemed little inclined to polite conversation. The man on his right was Gwyn ab Ednywain, Llewelyn's seneschal; he was friendly enough, but at the moment was concentrating all his attention upon the food being ladled from chafing dishes: venison baked in coffyn pies; boiled pears flavoured with honey, dates, and cinnamon; oatcakes; roast heron. It was, Baldwin acknowledged, a meal fit to grace any Norman table. He was beginning to think his stay in Wales would not be so great a hardship after all.

He glanced around the hall with interest. Except in that it was a ground-floor structure, it looked exactly like any Norman hall: three parallel rows of wooden pillars, the side aisles occupied by beds and partitioned off by screens. He and Stephen had slept here last night, as comfortably as ever they had in Fulk's Alberbury Castle, had been given places of honour near the hearth.

Llywarch, Llewelyn's court bard, now moved towards the centre aisle, carrying a small harp. The hall quietened at once. Men laid down their knives and spoons to listen as he began a haunting ballad, not a word of which Baldwin understood. He was rather surprised that Llywarch had so much standing at Llewelyn's court, being treated by all as a man of importance. Bards and minstrels enjoyed no such privileged status in England. There was much Baldwin found odd in Llewelyn's world, but gratitude was proving stronger than bias, and he was determined to adapt as best he could. The song ending, conversation resumed again, and he leaned forward with interest when he heard Stephen say, 'You expect war with your cousin, Meredydd ap Cynan, my lord Llewelyn?'

'It may well come to that. When my cousin Gruffydd – Meredydd's brother – died last year of a wasting fever, I laid claim to his lands. As that gave me most of Gwynedd above the Conwy and all of Gwynedd below the Conwy, Meredydd took it amiss, and there's been naught but discord between us for months now.'

Llewelyn did not sound particularly grieved about this, and Baldwin smothered a smile with his napkin. He did not know Meredydd ap Cynan, but he had a strong suspicion that, having snapped at the bait, Meredydd was about to bite down upon the hook.

Llewelyn drained his wine cup. 'I was sorry to hear of your lord father's death, Stephen.'

'Thank you, my lord. His death was a tragedy twice over for us, as Walter is now laying claim to my father's estates, lands that should by rights have passed to Baldwin.'

'How like Walter, to wait until his foe is crippled ere he strikes.'

Stephen nodded glumly. 'And there is little we can do to stop him.'

'Mayhap not. But I rather think I can. Shall I?'

'You mean that? Jesu, we'd be ever in your debt! Baldwin, did you hear?'

Baldwin did not share Stephen's excitement. 'That would be very kind of you, my lord,' he said slowly, 'but in truth, I do not see how you can help.'

Llewelyn's smile was suddenly cool. 'You'd not care to wager upon that?'

Stephen laughed. 'I'd not take him up on that, Baldwin. You see, Walter has long owed him a debt!'

Llewelyn laughed, too. 'Not so, Stephen. That debt was discharged in full some eight years ago; did Walter never tell you? No, this I do for you.'

Stephen did not reply; he was staring across the hall, at the man standing in the door. A slender silver-haired priest in his mid-forties, he looked somehow familiar to Stephen. 'My lord Llewelyn, I may be wrong, but is that not your chaplain, Morgan ap Bleddyn?'

Llewelyn turned at once. 'Yes, it is. Strange, he knew I'd be back at Aberffraw by week's end. I wonder what could not wait . . .'

'My lord . . .' Morgan knelt, rose stiffly to his feet. 'A word with you, if I may . . . alone.'

Llewelyn pushed his chair back. 'Morgan, are you ill? I've seen corpse candles with more colour. Here, take some wine . . .'

'Llewelyn . . .' The priest waved the cupbearer away. 'If we might retire behind the screen . . .'

Llewelyn moved around the table, grasped the older man by the arm. 'Tell me,' he said. 'Tell me now.'

'It happened yesterday morn. Tangwystl was entering the chapel; somehow she stumbled, fell upon the stairs. As soon as your doctor saw her birth pangs had begun, he summoned the midwives.' Morgan stopped, drew a deep breath. 'You have a daughter, Llewelyn. I'll not lie to you; she's fearfully tiny and frail. But with our prayers . . .'

'I'll leave for Aberffraw as soon as the horses can be saddled. You told Tangwystl you were coming to fetch me?'

'Llewelyn . . . she began to bleed. The midwives, they did what they could, but . . . they could not save her, lad.'

'She's dead?' Llewelyn's was the calm of utter disbelief. He stared at Morgan, saw tears well in the priest's eyes. He was aware now of the others. The hall was very quiet, but all else looked as it had only moments before. Dogs still lurked under the tables, snarling over bones. Summer sun still spilled through the unshuttered windows. Out in the bailey a curlew cried, a rising mournful plaint that went unanswered.

Morgan pressed a crucifix into Llewelyn's hand. 'Come with me to the chapel. I'll say a Mass for her soul, and afterwards, we'll talk . . .'

Llewelyn looked at the crucifix, let it drop into the rushes. Turning away from Morgan, from them all, he walked rapidly across the hall.

Unlike Baldwin, who'd been listening in utter bafflement, Stephen had grasped enough for appalled understanding. He took a quick step towards the door, but Ednyved caught his arm.

'No,' he said. 'Let him be. There is nothing any man can say now that will ease the pain. I know; I did lose my wife in childbed, too.'

Morgan retrieved the crucifix. 'It is God's will,' he said, sounding very tired, and Ednyved turned upon him with something much like anger.

'I can tell you, Father, that is but little comfort to a man who's just lost his wife!'

'It is all we do have, Ednyved,' Morgan's grey eyes met Ednyved's brown ones, held them steadily. 'I know Llewelyn, better even than you do. All his life he has always got what he wanted, has shrugged at obstacles that would have daunted other men. It has been his strength, that utter assurance, the certainty that he can shape his own destiny. But you see, he's never learned to deal with defeat. He's never had to – until now.'

Ednyved nodded. 'Yes,' he said softly. 'You do understand.'

The air was cool and damp against his face. Llewelyn slid from the saddle. The sky was no longer visible, stars hidden by leafy clouds of oak, birch, and hazel. Here was no woodland quiet; the night echoed with the sounds of river raging against rock. Llewelyn could see a ghostly gleam of white through the trees as the cliffs rose up above the bank. The roaring was louder now. Rhaeadr Ewynnol, his people called it, the Foaming Fall. Even at midday the water was always dark near the rocks, lightening to a paler green in the shallows. Now it was the blackest of blacks, faintly silvered by moonlight. Above the pool surged the River Llugwy, spilling down on to the rocks in a wild, white cascade of foam.

Llewelyn did not know how long he stood there, scant inches from the cliff. Instinct alone had drawn him to Rhaeadr Ewynnol, where he'd so often come with Tangwystl, just as instinct had guided him during those hours alone on the heights of Moel Siabod. He had no memory of where he'd been, merely a blurred awareness of time passing, darkness blotting out the light. There was only numbness, an inability to accept Morgan's words as true. Tangwystl was dead. He knew that. And yet how could she not be waiting for him at Aberffraw? How could she be gone forever from his life?

Exhaustion at last led him back to Dolwyddelan Castle. They were watching for him; the drawbridge was lowered by the time he rode up the north slope, and a groom was waiting to take his stallion. He crossed the bailey, noting with dull surprise that the sky showed pale grey along the horizon. Mounting the steps into the keep, he all but stumbled over his son.

'Gruffydd? Gruffydd, lad, what are you doing out here?'

The boy blinked sleepily, looked about him as if he, too, wondered why he was not in bed. His face was puffy, streaked with dirt from the stairs. 'I was waiting for you, Papa.'

Lifting Gruffydd in his arms, Llewelyn carried him into the keep. Rushlights burned in wall sconces, the bed coverlets were turned back, a large flagon of mead and a loaf of manchet bread had been set out on the table. But the chamber was empty; the servants who normally slept on pallets were nowhere to be seen. Mead and solitude – all his friends could think to offer him.

169

'Sit beside me, Gruffydd. There is something I must tell you, about your mother.'

Gruffydd had Tangwystl's green eyes; they were, Llewelyn now saw, swollen and rimmed in red. 'Uncle Rhys told me, Papa, told me Mama is dead.'

Llewelyn touched the boy's cheek, stroked his hair. 'You understand what that means, lad?'

Gruffydd nodded. 'That I will not see her any more.' Tears escaped his lashes, smudged a grimy path down his face. 'Uncle Rhys said Mama's soul has gone to God. But . . . but when my dog died, Papa, you buried him in the ground. Will Mama be buried, too? I do not want her buried, Papa, do not want her in the ground . . .'

'Oh, Christ . . .' Llewelyn stumbled to his feet, backed into the table. Gruffydd had, with those few words, made Tangwystl's death real at last. The merciful numbness, the stunned sense of disbelief gave way before the image now burning into his brain – Tangwystl covered with dirt, lying alone under cold, dark earth, Tangwystl who'd so loved light and summer warmth.

The flagon rocked as he bumped the table, and his fingers closed of their own accord around the handle. The earthenware jug shattered on impact against the hearthstones, scattered clay fragments into the rushes. The flames sputtered and hissed; fingers of fire shot upward, feeding upon the sudden surge of air.

Gruffydd still sat upon the bed, staring wide-eyed at the wreckage strewn about the floor. And then he scrambled down, ran to Llewelyn. 'Do not cry, Papa, please . . .'

Llewelyn knelt, and Gruffydd wrapped his arms around his father's neck, sobbed into his shoulder. 'Hush, lad, hush. I did not mean to frighten you.' Gruffydd's tears were wet upon Llewelyn's face; his son's breath, hot and gasping, rasped against his ear. 'It is all right to weep for her, Gruffydd. But the pain will ease, I promise you . . .' And in seeking to comfort his stricken son, Llewelyn finally found a small measure of comfort for himself.

12

June, 1202
Rouen, Normandy

'When do you depart for Fontevrault Abbey, Joanna?'

'At week's end, Papa, said.' Joanna sat on the bed, began to brush her stepmother's long, silky hair. 'Will you tell me about her, Isabelle?'

'About Eleanor? What could I add that you have not long since heard by now?'

'But I have not . . . heard that much, I mean. People rarely tell me about scandals,' Joanna said regretfully.

Isabelle needed no further coaxing. 'You do know, of course, that she was the greatest heiress of her time, Duchess of Aquitaine and Countess of Poitou. So great a marital prize was soon taken, and when she was fifteen, she became Queen of France. They say Louis doted upon her, could deny her nothing, even to allowing her to accompany him on crusade.'

'In truth?' Joanna asked, having learned the hard way to be rather dubious of Isabelle's more extravagant claims, and Isabelle crossed herself with a dramatic flourish.

'Upon the soul of Blessed Mary, ever Virgin, I swear it so. And whilst in the Holy Land, she did bring great scandal to her name. Her uncle Raymond was Prince of Antioch, a most handsome man only eight years older than she. Eleanor had not seen him since childhood and he welcomed her right lovingly . . . too much so, men thought. Whilst none can prove they did bed together, it is known that Eleanor told Louis she wanted to end their marriage. But he was still besotted with her, had her taken from Antioch by force!

'Theirs had always been a marriage of fire and milk. Eleanor was once overheard to say she'd thought to marry a King, but found she'd married a monk! The Pope sought to reconcile them, but when Eleanor gave birth to a second daughter, even Louis began to think their union was not blessed in the eyes of God. And then, in the fall

171

of 1151, Henry Plantagenet, Duke of Normandy, came to the French court. Eleanor was eleven years older than he, but still surpassingly beautiful. We do not know what passed between them, but as soon as Henry left Paris, Eleanor again besought Louis to annul their marriage. This time he agreed, and the marriage was declared invalid in March, 1152. She at once withdrew to her own lands in Poitou, and there stunned all of Christendom by taking Henry Plantagenet as her husband.

'Louis would never have let her go had he suspected her intent, would rather have seen her wed to the Devil, so deeply did he fear Henry's ambitions. And with cause. With Eleanor's backing, Henry pushed his claim to the English crown, and within three years of their marriage, Eleanor became the only woman ever to wear the crowns of both France and England.'

Joanna was, as usual, proving to be a highly satisfactory audience, and Isabelle plunged ahead, scarcely pausing for breath. 'In fifteen years as wife to Louis, Eleanor had given him but two daughters. But as Queen of England, she bore Henry a rich crop, eight children in fourteen years. Four healthy sons she gave Henry; what king could ask for more?'

'How, then, did she fall out of favour with Henry?'

'I'd say, rather, that Henry fell out of favour with her! He'd never been faithful, but that is a wife's lot, and she'd turned a blind eye to his straying. Rosamond Clifford, however, could not be ignored. He brought Rosamond into his bed, even to his table, honoured her as if she were Queen, not concubine. Most husbands are more discreet than that, praise God, for the truth of it is, Joanna, that even if a man sets up his harlot right in the keep, there is little his wife can do about it. But Eleanor . . . Eleanor was not like other women; when Henry shamed her so, she left him, withdrew to her own Poitou, and raised the standard of rebellion against him!'

Joanna had been listening, open-mouthed. Indeed, her grandmother was not like other women! 'What happened then?' she prompted, as if listening to some improbable minstrel's tale.

'John was just a little lad, but their other sons were well nigh grown, and they sided with Eleanor. So, too, did Louis, the French King, who was only too eager to turn Henry's own sons against him. In the fighting that followed, Henry ravaged Eleanor's lands, took her prisoner. She was,' Isabelle said with relish, 'not waiting meekly by the hearth for capture, had dressed as a man and was seeking to escape into Anjou. Henry sent her back to England under guard, imprisoned her in Salisbury Tower, kept her closely held until his death . . . nigh on sixteen years, Joanna.'

'Oh no!' Joanna had utterly forgotten these were events from a long-gone past; her sympathy for Eleanor, the captive Queen, was as immediate as it was unlawful. She knew she should feel only disapproval towards a wayward wife, a rebel Queen, but she was aware, instead, of a sharp piercing regret, an ache for that wild spirit caged at last within Salisbury Tower.

'They were bitter years for Henry, too,' Isabelle conceded, 'years of strife with his sons. Henry, the eldest-born, died of a bloody flux. Geoffrey was killed in a tournament in France, leaving his wife with child, that wretched boy Arthur who now gives John such grief. Richard allied himself with Louis's son Philip, and between them, they brought Henry to bay, forced him to accept their terms for peace. He died days later, muttering, so they say, "Shame upon a conquered King."'

But Joanna's imagination was still fired by Salisbury Tower. 'What of Eleanor?'

'Oh, Richard at once dispatched William Marshal to free her. They were always close; when Richard was taken captive by the Holy Roman Emperor, she laboured day and night to raise his ransom.'

'Have you ever met her, Isabelle?'

'Yes, two years ago. John took me to Fontevrault soon after our marriage. She was most generous, dowered me with the cities of Niort and Saintes. But I confess I am ever so thankful that she divides her time between Poitiers and Fontevrault, that she does not dwell at John's court!'

Joanna had heard few fables as enthralling as this factual account of a flesh and blood woman, her own kindred. But she had noted one strange omission in Isabelle's narrative. 'But where was Papa in all this, Isabelle? Did he not help to raise the ransom, too?'

Isabelle laughed. 'Oh, indeed! He and Philip pledged one hundred thousand silver marks – if the Emperor would but hold Richard for yet another year. Does that shock you? It should not; you know John loved Richard not.'

Joanna nodded slowly. While her father spoke only rarely of his family, he did occasionally relate sardonic stories about his brother, stories that were far from flattering to Richard: how, when he and the Saracen Prince Saladin failed to come to terms over the ransom of prisoners at Acre, Richard had given the command to slaughter them all, some twenty-five hundred captives; how it had cost every man in England one-fourth of his year's income to pay Richard's ransom; how, when Issac, the Emperor of Cyprus, had surrendered to Richard, he'd done so on the promise that he would not be put in irons, only to have Richard fetter him in chains made of silver.

'Papa had no reason to love Richard,' she said defensively. 'He was not a good King. Papa is a better one.'

'I can guess who taught you that!' Isabelle teased.

'And do you find fault with it, Isabelle?'

Isabelle turned a startled face towards the door, said hastily, 'Of course I do not, John! I think you're a far abler King than your brother; surely you know that, my love?'

Joanna waited as Isabelle crossed to John, sought to placate him with a long, lingering kiss. Then she, too, rose, moved to greet her father.

'Isabelle was telling me about your lady mother, Papa,' she explained, watching him all the while with anxious eyes. Never had she seen him so tense, so quick to take offence as he'd been in recent weeks. Since the spring, since the outbreak of war with France.

Watching unhappily as her father's nerves frayed under the dark strains of the coming campaign, Joanna sought to cheer him in small ways, engaging him in talk of his cherished falcons, memorizing a verse he'd much admired, obeying his every whim with the alacrity of a command. But all her efforts had so far gone for naught. She knew her father to be deeply troubled, and every night she prayed for God to smite his enemies, Philip, King of the French, and the youth Isabelle always referred to as 'that wretch, Arthur'.

Three years ago when her father had claimed the crown, Joanna had been too young to realize how close a thing his prevailing over Arthur had been. Now she understood all too well. The Angevin empire remained dangerously divided over the succession, with England and Normandy favouring John, and the barons of Brittany, Anjou, Maine, and Touraine preferring Arthur. Time had not reconciled them to John, and Arthur, Breton-born, was casting a long shadow indeed. He was fifteen now, old enough to assert his own claims to what he'd been taught was his birthright, and he had a valuable ally in the calculating King of France. Just as he'd once sought to advance his own interests by turning Richard against Henry and later, John against Richard, Philip now saw in Arthur the means of John's downfall. In May he'd accepted Arthur's oath of homage, had betrothed his five-year-old daughter to the young Duke of Brittany. And that meant, Joanna knew, the stakes for her father were all or nothing. A loss to Philip and Arthur would cost him his crown, his realm, his life.

She hastened now to pour a cup of wine, offered it to him with exaggerated care. 'What is she like, Papa . . . your lady mother?'

John was quiet for so long that she thought he was not going to reply. 'A legend,' he said softly. 'A living legend . . . like my illustrious brother, the Lion-Heart.' His eyes, shadowed by weariness, shone with a hard green glitter.

'You want to win her favour, Joanna? Talk to her of Richard, then.' He'd drained the cup already, set it down with a thud. '"I have lost the staff of my age, the light of my eyes." Those are her words, are what she cried out upon his capture. Yes, talk to her of Richard.'

Joanna did not know how to answer him. Nor, she saw, did Isabelle. They looked at each other helplessly.

'I would rather talk to her of you, Papa,' she ventured, and John gave a sudden laugh, a staccato sound that had in it little of mirth.

'I'd not advise that, lass. My mother has never been one to feign interest where she has none.'

Joanna's eyes filled with tears. She was aware by now that he was drunk, and that only made her all the more uneasy, for he generally had a good head for wine.

Isabelle, no less at a loss than Joanna, reached out to steady his hand as he refilled the cup. 'Come to bed, beloved,' she coaxed, knowing no other comfort to offer, knowing only what he'd taught her.

He touched her cheek, brushed aside the bright hair falling free about her face. 'You're such a child, Isabelle, a lovely child. I do not want you tonight. Go away. Both of you, go away.'

Isabelle started to speak, and he put his fingers to her mouth. 'I would not take out my demons on you, Isabelle. But if you stay, I shall. Take Joanna and go.'

She nodded, retreated towards the door, pulling Joanna after her. In the antechamber, she sank down, white-faced, upon the nearest coffer. 'Mayhap I should not have left him . . . Joanna, Joanna, was I wrong? Should I have stayed?'

Joanna was accustomed to Isabelle asking her questions better

175

put to an adult, but that did not make the answers come any easier. 'I do not know,' she confessed. 'I never saw Papa like that before . . .'

'He's afraid,' Isabelle said, almost inaudibly. 'God knows, he has reasons enough for fear. So many enemies. So few he can trust.' She shivered. 'He's afraid, Joanna . . . and so alone.'

The Benedictine abbey of Fontevrault was situated in the province of Anjou, not far from the crossing of the Rivers Vienne and Loire. It was a rich land, famed for its vineyards, lush and green in the summer sun, and Joanna's journey from Rouen should have been a pleasant one. But the threat of war overhung the countryside, hovering like woodsmoke along the horizon, and Joanna soon discovered that distance did little to ease her fears for her father's safety. She was nervous, moreover, about meeting her grandmother.

Eleanor was entering her eighty-first year, an age no less vast to Joanna than that of the ancient, gnarled oaks shadowing their path. Joanna's craving for family, for belonging, was the mainspring of her being, but as Fontevrault Abbey came into sight, she found herself beset by misgivings. She had no right to her father's name, was accepted at court only on his sufferance. Would Eleanor welcome a grandchild born of sin?

The room was in shadows, shielded from the sun by heavy linen hangings. Joanna groped her way forward, blindly, knelt before the woman sitting in an oaken, upright chair, much like a throne.

'Come closer, child, so I might see you.' The voice was not at all the croaking whisper Joanna had been expecting; it was clear, perfectly pitched, made her long to hear it again.

Joanna rose shyly, took the hand outstretched to her. It was hot and dry, so frail she could think only of the time she'd held a captive bird within her palms; her grandmother's bones seemed no less fragile, to be broken by a breath. But then the fingers, long and tapering, ablaze with emerald and opal and turquoise, closed around her own, firmly, drawing her forward. For a moment, she felt a cheek pressed against her own; it, too, was hot, crinkled like parchment. An exotic, beguiling fragrance perfumed the air; as her grandmother embraced her, she heard the whisper of silk. She lifted her lashes, looked into hazel eyes much like her own.

'So you are Joanna,' Eleanor said, and when she smiled, Joanna, caught like so many others before her by the potent pull of that sudden, capricious charm, gave up her heart with reckless and innocent abandon.

July skies were cloudless, shimmered metallically above vines scorched beyond renewal by the unrelenting sun. Joanna rarely ventured out into the midday heat, having adapted her habits to those of her grandmother. Eleanor was that rarity in an age of dawn risers, a creature of the night. She flowered in those hours after dusk, not going to her bed until the world was long stilled and hushed, sleeping away the bright, hot afternoons under the soft swishing of her ladies' fans. That was, she told Joanna, one of the advantages of age, that she could at last follow her own inner clock.

'What other advantages does age offer, Madame?'

'Precious few, child. The sweet satisfaction of outliving all my enemies, of burying my mistakes, of remembering and savouring my triumphs. Memory is merciful, Joanna, more so than man. It fades past pain, yet holds bright the colours in recalled joy.'

Joanna was not long in discovering that Eleanor's memory was no less remarkably preserved than her small white teeth. It was rare to reach such an age without gaping blank spaces in the mouth and mind; most ancients were reduced to gruel and muddled memories in which time blurred all boundaries. But Eleanor had somehow triumphed over the vagaries of age, just as she'd somehow triumphed over the confines and constraints of womanhood. Her past was very much with her, vivid and precisely drawn, a treasure trove of memories ripe for sharing. And share them she chose to do, in those sultry summer nights when sleep would not come and her yesterdays seemed so very close, just beyond reach.

She told Joanna of her long-ago girlhood, conjured up the ghosts of her marital bed: Louis, so mild, so pious and softspoken, so utterly unlike the Angevin great-grandson of the Conqueror, the youth who'd dared to seek her out at her husband's court, caressing her boldly with hot grey eyes as he talked of empires. 'I was twenty-nine and Henry was eighteen, but more of a man than any I'd ever known, in bed or out,' Eleanor said softly, startling Joanna by the nonchalance with which she confessed to adultery, but then she gave the girl a self-mocking smile not entirely free of bitterness. 'I must

177

have loved him, in truth, or I could not have hated him so much after.'

She told Joanna of Henry's bitter quarrel with Thomas à Becket, how Henry had sealed Becket's doom by crying out in a fit of rage, 'Will none rid me of this turbulent priest?' Told her the legend that the royal House of Plantagenet came from the Devil; told her, too, how her sons had laughed at their Angevin heritage, turned aside criticism with jests about the demon Countess of Black Fulk of Anjou.

Some of her memories were tragic; her daughter Joanna's death in childbed at thirty-four. Richard's foolish and fatal bravery before the walls of Châlus. Others were fraught with menace: Eleanor's perilous journey from French territory into her own lands in Poitou after her divorce from Louis; two separate attempts had been made to ambush and abduct her, for landed women were often forced into marriage against their will and Eleanor was the greatest heiress in Christendom.

And some of her stories were tales of horror, none more so than the massacre of the Jews the year before Joanna's birth. 'Richard had forbidden all Jews to attend his coronation, but some wealthy merchants brought gifts to the banquet following. Members of his court, the worse for wine and having no liking for Jews even when sober, expelled them from the hall, and the citizens of London took this to mean all Jews in the city were fair game. Rioting broke out, the ghetto burned, and many died. Other cities were soon caught up in the same violence, as it swept like plague across the realm, but nowhere was the outbreak worse than in York. There the Jews had sought refuge in the castle keep, and when it appeared they'd be taken by the besieging mob, the men, women, and children trapped within, numbering in the hundreds, killed themselves.'

Joanna dutifully crossing herself, felt no real surprise; death seemed to follow her uncle Richard like a lover. The thought was not her own, of course, had its seeds in a caustic comment once made by John, that Richard's lust was sated on the battlefield, not in the bedchamber.

But in these weeks at Fontevrault, slowly another image of Richard was taking shape. Richard loomed large in his mother's memories. From Eleanor, Joanna learned that Richard, having to withdraw from the Holy Land, denied himself even a glimpse of Jerusalem from the heights of Nebi Samwil, saying, 'Those not worthy

178

to win the Holy City are not worthy to behold it.' She learned of the celebrated exchange between Richard and Philip, the French King, over Richard's great fortress, Castle Gaillard, Philip boasting, 'If its walls were made of solid iron, yet would I take them,' and Richard's mocking rejoinder, 'If its walls were made of butter, yet would I hold them.' Richard had indeed been a great soldier, Joanna reluctantly acknowledged. But she did not understand why her grandmother should have preferred him above her other children, and wished she could summon up the nerve to ask Eleanor why she spoke so often of Richard and so rarely of John.

She never did, though, sensing such a question would not be to Eleanor's liking. As bedazzled as Joanna was by Eleanor, she was very much in awe of her, too, and uneasily aware of the fragile foothold she'd gained in her grandmother's life. There was indeed iridescent magic in Eleanor's spell, but no security. Eleanor could be amusing, indulgent, utterly captivating. She was also impatient, unpredictable, easily bored. On any given evening, Joanna might find herself welcomed into Eleanor's presence with genuine pleasure; Eleanor would share confidences both intimate and adult in nature, tutor Joanna in the intriguing complexities of politics and statecraft, and at such moments, Joanna knew happiness in full and abiding measure. But on the morrow she might find her grandmother preoccupied, pensive, with no interest whatsoever in a child's companionship. Joanna did not resent Eleanor's mercurial mood swings; her sense of self was too tenuous, too vulnerable, to allow for the indulgence of wounded pride. She only tried all the harder to earn her grandmother's good will, and when she did not, she accepted the failing as her own.

On this particular night in late July, Eleanor was in markedly good spirits, relaxed and responsive to Joanna's eager queries about times long past and people long dead. But as midnight approached, Joanna's energy began to ebb; she sought to stifle a yawn, was relieved when Eleanor said, 'You'd best get to bed.'

Joanna rose obediently. 'May I go and light a candle first for the French Queen, Madame?'

'If you wish.' Joanna's impassioned partisanship for Philip's unfortunate Queen was a source of some amusement to Eleanor, but she was touched, too, suspecting that Joanna's pity for Ingeborg's plight could be traced to her own years of confinement, that it was the captive Eleanor Joanna was mourning as much as it was the hapless

179

Ingeborg, whose luck had yet to change for the better. Philip had held out against the Pope's Interdict for seven stubborn months, and then agreed to set aside his second wife, to recognize Ingeborg as his Queen. But he'd then confined her in Étampes Castle, and rumour had it she was not being treated kindly.

Joanna's sympathies went out to the Danish Princess, Queen of France in name only, being made to suffer for no sin of her own, and she'd been lighting nightly candles on Ingeborg's behalf. Now she hastened back from St Magdalene's chapel, undressed and crawled into the pallet made up for her at the foot of her grandmother's bed.

Lights still burned, and the constant murmur of conversation sounded around her; Eleanor's ladies could not retire until she did. But Joanna had learned to block out background noises, and she fell at once into a fitful sleep. Her dreams were troubled, reflecting the tenor of her waking hours. Eleanor had recently had a letter from John, in which he'd told her that he'd broken Philip's siege of Radepont, just ten miles south-east of Rouen. But that was the only good news the letter held. Isabelle's father Aymer, Count of Angoulême, had died suddenly that past month, but John had not dared to risk her attendance at the funeral; Angoulême bordered upon La Marche, and Hugh de Lusignan still nursed a bitter grudge over Isabelle's loss.

Tossing and turning on the pallet, Joanna attracted the attention of the Abbess Matilda. Matilda was intrigued by her friend's unexpected rapport with Joanna; she'd never before known Eleanor to show more than the most perfunctory interest in children. It was, she decided, probably because Joanna was such a serious child. The questions she asked were invariably sensible, of the sort Eleanor had always encouraged in her own daughters; she had nothing but scorn for the prevailing viewpoint that women should abjure interest in such masculine concerns as power, policy, and tactics.

Matilda was surprised, too, that Eleanor should suddenly evidence a hitherto unexpressed interest in looking back, in dwelling upon yesterday, at last attributing it to the twin crosses of age and illness, for Eleanor was not well, had not been well for months. Her spirit still blazed so brightly that those around her did not always notice how frail the shell enclosing the spirit had become. Matilda did. For all that Eleanor was fiercely private about her ailments, Matilda saw with sorrowing eyes how easily she tired in this summer of her eighth decade, how she'd begun to lean upon a companion's arm when walking, to place a hand over her breast as if willing away the heart palpitations she would not acknowledge. And as Matilda watched her friend and grandchild on recent evenings, Eleanor piecing together her past with the gossamer strands of memory as Joanna listened, intent and enthralled, Matilda found herself wondering if Eleanor was not reaching out to right a wrong, seeing in this hazel-eyed, dark-haired granddaughter the son she'd never loved.

This was sheer speculation, she knew; Eleanor was the least fanciful of women, little given to regrets. The thought lingered, none the less, and she laughed soundlessly now, envisioning what Eleanor's reaction would be should she be so foolish as to confess what she suspected. Joanna sighed, mumbled something unintelligible, and Matilda stooped, touched her hand to the sleeping child's forehead. 'She does not feel feverish, but her sleep is not a restful one.'

Eleanor sat down on the bed. 'She fears for her father.'

'As well she might, poor lass. She's utterly devoted to him.'

Eleanor looked up at that. 'Need you sound so surprised?' she said dryly. 'Or think you, as do John's enemies, that he is incapable of loving or being loved?'

'No, Madame, indeed not. I would not presume upon our friendship to speak ill of your son. But I must admit to being troubled by some of his acts, such as how infrequently he does partake of the Holy Sacraments.'

'That is rash of him, I agree, and I dare say he'll pay a high price for it.'

'I would hope, Madame, that he will repent in time; God forbid that he should go unshriven to his Maker,' the Abbess said with fervour, and Eleanor gave her a thin, ironic smile.

'Indeed. But I was not thinking of his immortal soul, Matilda. I was thinking that history is chronicled by monks.'

Joanna had begun to whimper in her sleep, and Eleanor leaned over, shook the girl's shoulder. Joanna awoke with a gasp, eyes wide and staring. She had been dreaming of her father, abandoned and alone before Philip and Arthur, but she was reluctant to admit it; it seemed somehow disloyal to John, almost as if she'd be revealing his own fears. She hesitated, and then turned aside Eleanor's query with the first lie to come to mind. 'Yes, a bad dream . . . of Ingeborg.'

'You must not dwell upon her, Joanna. Hers is a sad fate, yes, but common to women of rank. Would you pity the swan that ends up swimming in gravy upon your father's table? Well, princesses, too, are bred to be sacrificed, as pawns in the marital game. That is just the way of it. Be grateful, rather, that you were spared such a fate, that you need not fear a foreign marriage in a far-off land. Unless, of course, you do yearn for a crown . . .' Eleanor smiled, shrewdly certain that Joanna did not.

Joanna had long been thankful that her tainted birth so severely reduced her value on the marriage market; her ambitions rose no higher than a manor and children of her own, a husband of respectable rank, ideally a knight of her father's household so that they might be often at court.

'No, I would not want a crown, Madame. I would that Papa did not have one, either, would that he were still Count of Mortain. Mayhap then, he'd be safe . . .'

She was hoping for some sort of assurance from her grandmother, an expression of faith that all would go well for John. But Eleanor was turning away, frowning at the woman standing in the antechamber doorway.

'Your Grace, Sir Aubrey is without, requests an urgent word with you.'

Joanna sat up on the pallet, pulling the sheet up to her chin. Aubrey de Mara was the captain of her grandmother's guards, but Joanna had never known him to seek Eleanor out at such an hour. She watched uneasily as he entered the chamber, knelt before the Queen.

'Madame, forgive me, but a courier has ridden in, sent by your son. The King's Grace wants you to leave Fontevrault on the morrow, to withdraw with all speed into your lands in Poitou.'

'Arthur and the de Lusignans?'

'They've been encamped at Tours, not forty miles to the north, are now known to be on the road south. The King has left Queen Isabelle in Rouen, is heading for Le Mans. But he fears for you, Madame, as well he should. You'd be a most tempting prize, in truth.'

Eleanor nodded slowly. 'My son is right. We depart for Poitiers at first light. See to it, Sir Aubrey.'

Their journey south proved to be a slow, arduous one. The road was rutted and rock-strewn, the soil cracked and seared by weeks of burning sun, and their horses churned up clouds of thick, red dust.

Jolted from side to side in her swaying horse litter, Eleanor at last called for a halt. As her servants began to set up a tent so that the Queen might shelter a while from the heat of high noon, Joanna slid from her mare, hastened to join Eleanor in the shade of several elms. In addition to his midnight message for her grandmother, her father's courier had carried two letters for her, a brief dispatch from John instructing her to accompany Eleanor south for safety's sake, and a longer communication from her brother Richard. Clutching this letter, she settled herself in the grass next to Eleanor.

'Shall I fan you, Madame? I've a letter from my brother; may I read it to you? Richard is serving as squire to the eldest son of Lord de Braose, is with his household in South Wales. He says there is trouble between the two de Braose sons and a Welsh Prince, Gwenwynwyn of Powys, that Gwenwynwyn – what queer names the Welsh have – is set upon war.'

'I'd say, rather, that the de Braoses are the ones set upon war.' Eleanor leaned back against the tree, closed her eyes. 'Your father granted them the right to any Welsh lands they can gain by conquest. And they know that there has been a shift in our Welsh policy, that John has decided it is more to his advantage to back Gwenwynwyn's chief rival, Llewelyn, Prince of Gwynedd.'

'Richard makes mention of him, too . . . Prince Llewelyn. He says Fulk Fitz Warin is still in rebellion against Papa, that he has taken refuge at this Llewelyn's court. He says, too, that Llewelyn has been pulling strings in Shropshire on behalf of the rebels, that he prevented a younger brother of one of Fitz Warin's vassals from laying claim to his father's manors. The family – de Hodnet they're called – hold land of the Corbets, and Robert Corbet, as overlord, refused to recognize the younger de Hodnet's claim. Richard says all know the Corbets were acting at Llewelyn's behest, he being kin.'

Joanna frowned. 'I met Lord Corbet once, when we were at Worcester two years past. Papa granted him the right to hold a weekly market at Caus. I do not think he should be so quick to do a Welsh Prince's bidding, not when that Prince is aiding men outlawed, men who are Papa's sworn enemies.'

Getting no response, she glanced up, saw that Eleanor was no longer listening. Sweat was glistening at her temples; her face was bleached of colour, as white as the linen wimple that hid her hair. 'Two years ago,' she said, bitterly amused, 'I rode a mule across the

183

Pyrenees, and in the dead of winter, too. But who'd believe that, seeing me now . . .'

'Madame!' Aubrey was coming towards them at a run. 'Madame, our scouts report a large armed force on our trail. I'd wager my life it is the Duke of Brittany and the de Lusignans, that you are the prey.'

Joanna was amazed by how rapidly her grandmother seemed to shake off her fatigue. She at once held out her hand for Aubrey's assistance, came quickly to her feet. 'If my memory serves,' she said coolly, 'we are but a few leagues distant from Mirebeau. It's not much of a refuge, but beggars, as they say, cannot be choosers.'

Aubrey nodded grimly. 'Madame, can you ride astride?'

'I shall have to, shan't I?' Some of her servants were struggling now to dismantle the tent they'd just erected, and Eleanor said impatiently, 'For Jesu's sake, let it be!' Seeing Joanna still standing immobile, she gave the girl a push. 'Go on, child, make haste to mount. Sir Aubrey . . . which of your men do you most trust?'

Aubrey did not hesitate, beckoned to a slight bandy youth, one who looked to have been born in the saddle. 'Edmund, take my stallion. Kill him if you have to, but get to Le Mans, get to the King.'

Edmund did not even pause to acknowledge the command. Vaulting up on to Aubrey's roan, he set off across the fields at a dead run, within moments was lost from view.

Mirebeau was a walled town in the marches between Anjou and Poitou, having sprung up around a small border castle. It was little more than a village, and the sudden arrival of the Queen created a sensation. Men and women abandoned their daily work, crowded into the street to catch a glimpse of the legendary Eleanor of Aquitaine. Aubrey at once set about conscripting men to guard the walls, gave orders to bar the town gates as the Queen and her party passed on into the castle bailey. There, the exhausted Eleanor was assisted from her mare, up into the keep.

Relief at having reached Mirebeau was not long in giving way to dismay. Even to Joanna's untrained eye, it was all too clear that the castle was in a ruinous state. The moat was clogged with debris and weeds, silted and foul-smelling. The outer curtain walls were constructed of aging timbers, looked likely to tumble down in a stiff wind. The keep itself was a stone and mortar tower, but it, too, showed the effects of long neglect. Aubrey, assuming command in the name of the Queen, put the small garrison to work shoring up the walls as best they could, sent men into the town to appropriate food supplies. The women sought to convert the solar into a suitable bedchamber for the Queen. And then they waited for the inevitable to occur, waited to be found by the pursuing army, an army led by Eleanor's own grandson.

They appeared before the town gates as summer twilight slowly darkened the Poitevin countryside, flying the banners of Arthur, Duke of Brittany, Hugh de Lusignan, Count of La Marche, and his uncle Geoffrey, Lord of Vouvant. A peremptory demand for surrender was rejected with equal dispatch by Aubrey. Negotiations dragged on for a time under a perfect crescent moon, and then both sides settled down to pass the night.

Soon after sunrise the next day, the negotiations resumed. Arthur and the de Lusignans wanted Eleanor alive, and she exploited that, her only advantage, to the fullest, feigning belief in their good will, playing desperately for time. They, in their turn, promised whatever they thought likely to lure her out, swore she could continue un-molested on her journey, that she need only agree to cede Poitou to Arthur. Back and forth the lies flew, until Hugh de Lusignan lost patience and gave the command to assault the town walls. The townsmen, unwillingly impressed into a quarrel not of their making, put up only feeble resistance, and by day's end Mirebeau was in enemy hands. The ancient castle alone held out, ripe for the taking.

The keep was stifling, shuttered windows barring entry to cooler night air. Joanna huddled on a bench in the great hall, a plate of food untouched upon her lap. It was quiet now, but her ears still echoed with the cries of the wounded and dying, the screams of the women claimed as spoils of war by Arthur's jubilant soldiers. When the assault was first launched, she'd climbed with Eleanor up to the battlements on top of the keep, had watched as the town's defenders sought to push aside the scaling ladders, as men plunged screaming to their deaths. Hours later, the horror of it was still very much with her; unable to sleep, she kept inconspicuously to the shadows, watching as her grandmother and Aubrey sought a viable plan of defence.

It was very late when Aubrey rose, sent a man to the kitchens for his first food of the day. Joanna slipped from the bench, crossed to Eleanor.

'Madame . . . what will happen on the morrow?'

'They will assault the castle.'

'Can we hold?'

'No, child, we cannot, not for long.'

Joanna swallowed, sought to emulate her grandmother's composure. 'But . . . might not Papa come in time?'

'No, Joanna. I'd not give you false hope. We cannot be sure my courier reached John's camp. And even if he did, Le Mans is well over eighty miles away. John could not get to us before Friday, Thursday night at the earliest . . . and by then, it shall be too late.'

Joanna knelt on the floor by Eleanor's chair. 'Aubrey is a brave knight. Surely God will not favour Arthur over Aubrey, Madame?'

Eleanor did not reply.

Wednesday dawned hot and overcast. The sky was leaden, and for a time, it did seem as if God meant to favour Aubrey. A rainstorm swept in from the east, denying the attacking army the potent weapon of fire. Aubrey's outmanned force struggled to keep the enemy off the walls, casting down boiling water and stones from the curtain battlements. The de Lusignans responded with mangonel bombardments, set about filling in the overgrown moat so they could make use of a battering ram.

On the top floor of the keep, Eleanor stood at an arrow loop, watching as Aubrey waged a gallant, futile battle below. His courage was contagious and his men offered up their lives with desperate abandon, until overwhelmed at the last by the sheer numbers of their attackers. Forced off the walls, they fell back towards the keep. Eleanor, hastening down into the great hall, signalled the guards to stand ready. As Aubrey and the surviving defenders plunged into the hall, they set the stairs alight, bolted the door.

The great hall was overflowing with exhausted men. They lay sprawled in the rushes, some seeking sleep while they could, others clutching wine flagons close. There was little eating, less talking. In the corner, one youth sat alone, softly strumming a gittern. Aubrey, grey-faced with fatigue, was slumped in the window seat. He raised his head only after Joanna plucked repeatedly at his sleeve, regarding her with bloodshot blue eyes.

'Sir Aubrey, when they take the keep, what will they do to us?'

'They want the Queen . . . only the Queen. They might let my men go . . . or they might put them to the sword.' Aubrey was slurring his words like one drunk, yet he still thought to add, 'But not you, not a little lass like you . . .' He leaned forward, cradled his head in his arms, and Joanna backed away.

Taking a candle, she groped her way up the stairwell. The solar door was ajar, but as she reached for the latch, she heard her grandmother's voice.

'The de Lusignans must not know that Joanna is John's daughter. I've already discussed this with Aubrey, mean to claim her as a niece of the Abbess Matilda.'

'But Madame, might it not be a greater protection for her . . . that she is the King's daughter?'

'Are you truly as naïve as that, Cecily? I should not think I'd need to remind you that Hugh de Lusignan is not a man of honour. They do need me; I shall not be harmed. But they might well see John's bastard-born child as . . . fair game, shall we say? And that is a risk I am not prepared to take.'

Joanna sank down upon the stairs. She sat there for a long time, alone in the dark, not wanting them to know she wept.

Joanna awoke in her grandmother's bed, with only a vague memory of how she got there. Had she fallen asleep upon the stairs? She still wore her chemise, but someone had removed her gown and bliaut, folded them over the foot of the bed. She reached for the gown, pulled it over her head. As she did, she saw the light filtering through the unshuttered solar window. For a moment, her breath stopped. They'd lost the night, their last shield. Even now men might be gathering below, preparing for the final assault upon the keep.

All around her, her grandmother's ladies slept on makeshift pallets. Threading her way between their bodies, she reached the window, climbed up on to the seat. Although to the west a few stars still glimmered, the sky was slowly and inexorably paling, taking on the dull pearl colour of coming dawn. The bailey was enveloped in an eerie quiet, men just beginning to stir, to crawl, groaning, from their bedrolls. A few castle dogs prowled about. A sleepy soldier relieved himself against the chapel wall, provoking curses from some of the blanket-clad forms downwind. Up on the curtain wall, guards dozed by empty wine flasks. The aroma of roasting pigeon wafted across the bailey from the gatehouse, where Arthur and the de Lusignans had set up their command post. The scene below her resembled not so much a siege as the morning after a drunken carouse, and that, Joanna knew, was what the night had been. So sure of victory were these men that they'd already begun to celebrate their triumph, for they, no less than those trapped within, knew there could be but one outcome. The only question as yet unanswered was how many men would die in the capture of the aging Queen.

Footsteps sounded behind Joanna, and she turned as her grandmother and Aubrey de Mara entered the solar, joined her at the window. The soldier who'd just urinated glanced up, saw them standing there, and raised his voice in a mocking shout. 'We've been wagering upon the hour when the keep falls. Think you that you can try to hold out till noon? If so, you'll win me a right fair sum!'

The window was faced with an iron grille, but Joanna shrank back, grateful when Aubrey reached out, jerked the shutters into place. 'I've set men to bringing up water buckets from the cellar well, Madame. I expect they shall seek to fire the outer door, so I had it well soaked. I had additional bolts attached, too, but the wood is so warped and rotted that I do not doubt even the little lass here could force it.'

As Joanna watched, marvelling at the lack of emotion in his voice, he walked over to the solar door, tested the bolt's strength. 'You'd best barricade yourself here within the solar, Madame. We'll hold them as long as we can below.'

Eleanor nodded. 'I expect we've a few hours' wait. They do not seem in much of a hurry, do they?'

'Why should they be? Does a cat rush in for the kill when it has its prey secure within its paws?' Aubrey's mouth twisted. 'I would to God that –' He broke off abruptly, as a shout echoed from the battlements. Joanna flinched, started to tremble. Was it to begin as soon as this? They heard now a clatter upon the stairs. Aubrey reached the door just as a man lurched into the solar, all but fell into his arms.

'Under attack . . .' he gasped. 'Hurry . . .'

Aubrey whirled towards the window, and the soldier caught his arm. 'No,' he panted, 'not the keep . . . the town!'

The stairs were in a dangerous state of disrepair, and Eleanor had to lean heavily upon Joanna for support, compelled to caution when they both yearned to run. Emerging at last out on to the battlements, Joanna froze for a moment, grappling with her fear of heights, and then edged along the walkway. The men were leaning recklessly over an embrasure, suddenly heedless of enemy bowmen, gesturing towards the town. The wind was gusting; Joanna found herself blinded by her own hair. Clutching Eleanor's hand, she nerved herself to look over the battlements, down into the bailey.

Men were stumbling to their feet, shouting groggy questions none could yet answer, groping hastily for weapons. Dogs were barking frantically as soldiers staggered, bewildered and bleary-eyed, from the buildings ranged along the curtain walls; a riderless horse galloped in panicked circles, adding immeasurably to the confusion. The more wide awake were running for the gatehouse, only to encounter comrades retreating from the town, where a wild mêlée had broken out.

'Could it be des Roches, Madame, and the garrison from Chinon Castle?'

Eleanor, no less bemused than Aubrey, shook her head. 'He has not the men to raise a siege. I confess I do not –'

Joanna could wait no longer, tugged at her arm. 'It's Papa, is it not? He's come for us!'

'I do not see how it could be John,' Eleanor said slowly, 'and yet –'

'It is Papa,' Joanna interrupted. 'I know it is!'

'She's right, look at the banner they fly!' Aubrey gestured towards the armed knights now surging into the narrow streets of Mirebeau, cutting off escape into the castle. 'Gules, three lions passant guardant in pale or – the Royal Arms of England, Madame!'

Aubrey's soldiers raised a cheer as the door was unbarred, squabbling good-naturedly over who should lower the ladders, reaching out eager hands to assist the men climbing up into the keep. Joanna squirmed among them, hopelessly hemmed in, until one young soldier swung her up into the air, and she found herself passed from man to man to be deposited, breathless and dizzy, within sight of the door, just as William de Braose scrambled up into the keep.

She almost did not recognize him. De Braose had always prided himself upon his elegance, and this man looked as if he'd not had a bath in months, so grimy and dishevelled was he, blond hair matted and dark with dirt, eyes reddened and dust-swollen. But his smile was a dazzle of radiant white, and when he demanded, 'Good Christ, give me a drink,' fully a dozen flasks and flagons were thrust at him from all directions.

The next man up was William des Roches, Seneschal of Anjou and Touraine. But then the soldiers surged forward, shoving and pushing, and Joanna could no longer see the door. By the time she'd managed to squeeze through the press, her father had mounted the ladder into the keep. Like de Braose, he was utterly filthy, and like de Braose, too, his smile was blinding. Joanna had meant to curtsy, but John held out his arms to her. The chainlinks of his hauberk scratched her cheek, and he was holding her so tightly that it hurt, but she made no objections; it was only when she saw the dark wet stain across his surcoat that she recoiled, with a cry of fright.

'Papa, you are bleeding!'

'No, sweetheart, it is not mine,' he said soothingly. 'There's nothing wrong with me that a bath and a week in bed will not cure!'

There was a sudden stir among the men; a path was opening. John set Joanna back on her feet, moved towards his mother. For a long moment they looked at one another, and then Eleanor said incredulously, 'You're truly here; I know my eyes do not lie. But eighty miles . . . how in God's name did you do it, John?'

John laughed. 'I dare say that's what Arthur and the de Lusignans are asking themselves, too, about now! Your man caught up with me late Tuesday, outside Le Mans. We set out at once for Mirebeau, rode day and night, spurred our horses till they foundered, till men reeled in the saddle like drunkards, stopping only at Chinon for William des Roches and fresh mounts.' Someone handed him a flask; he drank deeply, all but choked. 'They'd barred all the city gates but one, which they left open for supplies . . . and for us. By the time their besotted guards awoke, we were in the town. Upwards of two hundred knights captured, none escaping.'

Eleanor had never seen him so elated; there was about him an intense, surging excitement, an intoxication of the senses bordering upon euphoria. 'And Arthur? What of Arthur, John?'

John's eyes showed suddenly gold. 'Arthur and Hugh and Geoffrey de Lusignan, all taken. They were breakfasting on pigeon pie, had not even time to draw their swords. And their faces . . .' He laughed again. 'Ah, Madame, to see their faces!'

'You have indeed won a great victory,' she said, then put her hand upon his arm. 'Come now, sit and I'll send for food. Do you even remember when you've last eaten?'

'No,' he admitted. 'Why? Think you that I'm in need of sobering up?' He grinned, let her lead him towards the table, and then stopped without warning, swung about to face her. 'Arthur and the de Lusignans were not alone in their disbelief . . . were they?' he challenged. 'You never expected me to come to your defence, never expected me to reach you in time, never expected much of me at all, did you . . . Mother?'

Eleanor saw now how exhausted he truly was; his voice was slurred, husky with fatigue, his eyes hollowed and feverishly bright, at once triumphant and accusing. 'It was not a question of faith, John,' she said carefully. 'Do you not realize the extent of your victory? You have done what most men would swear to be impossible, covered some eighty miles as if you'd put wings to your horse, arrived in time to save me from capture, to take the town, all your enemies. That is a feat more than remarkable, it is well nigh miraculous.' She paused, and then said that which she knew he'd waited all his life to hear, what she could at last say in utter sincerity, 'Not even Richard could have hoped to equal what you did this day.'

John looked at her, saying nothing for a time. 'I should have known that the highest praise you could offer would be a comparison with my sainted brother. Well, that is an honour I think I'll decline, Madame. I've no longer any inclination to compete with a ghost.'

'Ah, Johnny . . .' Eleanor was suddenly and overwhelmingly aware of her own exhaustion, of the toll these last days had taken. 'I am proud of you, I swear it,' she said softly. But she'd waited too long; John had already turned away.

John's triumph was even more conclusive than he had at first thought, for his nephew Arthur was not the only prize to be taken in Mirebeau. Arthur's sister had been with him when he joined forces with the de Lusignans, and rather than risk leaving her behind in Tours, he'd chosen to have her accompany him, for safety's sake. As ill-fated as was his decision to besiege Mirebeau, this was to be an even greater blunder, for he thus delivered into John's hands both remaining heirs of the Angevin House, the two people with a rival claim to the English crown.

Joanna watched with sympathetic interest as the girl was escorted into the great hall. Ironically named Eleanor after the grandmother Arthur had been seeking to capture, she was slender and blue-eyed, looked to Joanna to be about seventeen or so. She also looked terrified. Approaching the dais, she sank down before John in a deep, submissive curtsy, but he at once raised her up, drew her towards him. He spoke softly and earnestly for several moments, and then smiled at her, pulling from his own finger a topaz ring. Topaz, he

191

murmured, was a known talisman against grief. It would please him greatly if she would accept it, as his niece and kinswoman.

None knew better than Joanna how reassuring her father could be when he so chose, and she was not surprised now to see colour coming back into Eleanor's face, to see Eleanor's hands were no longer shaking as she let John slip the ring on to her finger. Pouring a cupful of madeira from the sideboard, Joanna carried it across the hall, presented it to her father. He already had a cup, but he set it aside, accepting Joanna's, instead.

'Thank you, lass,' he said, and then smiled at her. 'What say you, Joanna? Should you like to meet your cousin Arthur?'

Joanna was shocked by her first sight of Hugh de Lusignan. A huge shambling bear of a man, stout and greying, he seemed the least likely of mates for the exquisite Isabelle, and Joanna decided her grandmother was right. There was great risk in being born a swan.

Both Hugh de Lusignan and his uncle seemed stunned by the sudden reversal of their fortunes. Shoved forward, shackled at the wrists, they knelt awkwardly before the dais, watching John warily, as if they still could not fully credit their own senses.

If Hugh de Lusignan did not fulfil Joanna's expectations, her cousin Arthur did. He truly looked like a prince, she conceded grudgingly, taller already, at fifteen, than her father, with bright chestnut hair and blue eyes like his sister. He, however, showed none of her fear; unlike the de Lusignans, he refused to kneel, had to be forced by his guards.

John continued to drink, measuring his nephew with thoughtful eyes. 'Well?' he said at last. 'Have you nothing to say to me?'

'No,' Arthur said sullenly.

'Do not be a fool, boy,' Hugh de Lusignan said, out of the corner of his mouth, and Arthur gave him a scornful look.

'I am no boy. I am a belted knight, Duke of Brittany, Count of Richmond, rightful heir to the Angevin crown, and I ask no man's pardon for seeking what is rightfully mine.'

'Boldly spoken,' John said, very dryly. 'That speech might sound more effective, however, if you were not fettered in irons, having just bungled an assault upon your own grandmother.'

There was laughter at that, and Arthur flushed. 'At least I was open and honest in my quest for the crown. Unlike you, Uncle, you who'd have sold his own brother to the Saracens if he could, who did betray his dying father –'

'That is quite enough, Arthur!' Eleanor said sharply. 'For all your posturings, you are very much a child, and I, for one, am weary of listening to you.'

'So am I.' John's voice was quite even, devoid of emotion. He raised his hand, and guards at once stepped forward, dragged Arthur from the hall. Eleanor ignored the struggles of her defiant grandson, kept her eyes riveted on John. Her husband's most dubious legacy to his offspring was the wild Angevin temper; his sons were notorious for the violence of their rages. But she had learned that John was most dangerous when he did not shout or threaten, and she leaned forward, laid her hand upon his arm. As she feared, the muscles were corded, rigid with tension.

'He's a stupid, wilful boy,' she said softly, 'foolish and headstrong. But he is a boy, John . . . and blood kin.'

John exhaled a breath too long held, slowly unclenched his fingers from the stem of his wine cup. 'As you say, Madame, a foolish boy.'

Hugh and Geoffrey de Lusignan still knelt stiffly before the dais, and John's eyes now came to rest upon Hugh. Hugh's face was streaked with sweat and grime, an unhealthy ashen grey; under John's mocking gaze, colour began to stain his cheekbones, the dull, blotched red of impotent rage. But he was forty-five, not fifteen, knew enough to hold his tongue.

Geoffrey de Lusignan cleared his throat. 'Your Grace, what mean you to do with us?'

'What would you do if you were in my place?' John asked, saw the other man flinch. 'So . . . as bad as that? I can see we're going to have a great deal to talk about, and I'll make time for it, you may be sure. But you're luckier than you deserve, for you happen to be worth more to me alive than dead. If not, I'd have hanged you both higher than Haman, and might yet.'

He signalled, did not bother to watch as his guards pushed the de Lusignans towards the door. Glancing about the hall, he beckoned to William de Braose. 'Since you had the honour of taking my nephew prisoner, Will, you shall have the honour of looking after him. I hereby remand him into your custody.'

De Braose did not appear surprised. 'As it pleases Your Grace.'

William des Roches, however, appeared distinctly taken aback. 'But . . . but my liege!' He stepped forward, towards the dais. 'You

193

did assure me that the Duke of Brittany would be put into my keeping. Your Grace . . . you gave me your word!'

'Did I?' John sounded quizzical. 'I recall no such promise. Do you, Will?'

'No, Your Grace,' William de Braose said blandly, and des Roches opened his mouth, shut it again. But he seized his first opportunity to speak to the Queen, drawing Eleanor aside as servants began to set up trestle tables, to prepare the hall for John's victory dinner.

'Madame, I did not lie; upon my oath, I did not.'

'No one has accused you of lying, my lord.'

'Your Grace . . . may I speak plainly? I did support your son against Arthur, have been his loyal subject. But I do understand the loyalties your grandson commands amongst many in Anjou, in Touraine, in Brittany. I sought to explain this to the King, to make him understand the risk, and he promised me I should have the care of his nephew. I do not think it wise to give the lad over to de Braose, Madame, in truth I do not.'

Eleanor agreed with him, but she responded with so glacial a stare that des Roches's warning froze in his throat; he swallowed, not daring to say more, realizing he'd already said too much.

Joanna, hovering within earshot, wondered why Lord des Roches should be so concerned about Arthur. Each time she remembered the outrageous way he'd dared talk to her father, she felt anger stir anew. Arthur was arrogant and hateful, deserved to be punished for his malice. She hoped her father kept him close, for a long, long time. She did feel sorry, though, for Arthur's sister, and pushing through to John's side, she waited patiently till she caught his eye. He leaned down, listened as she whispered in his ear, then nodded. 'If that be your wish, sweetheart, by all means.'

Joanna did not wait, made her way across the hall towards the girl sitting forlorn and forgotten in the window seat. Eleanor was staring down at her lap, twisting the ring John had given her. She did not look up, not until Joanna said, 'Lady Eleanor? I am your cousin Joanna, the King's daughter. My father wants you to dine with us, says you shall have a place of honour, as his kinswoman.'

'That's most kind of him,' Eleanor said tonelessly.

Joanna had hoped to cheer Eleanor, was disappointed by the girl's tepid response. 'I know you are afraid. I was afraid, too, when I thought we'd be taken by your brother. But there's no need to fear, in truth there's not. My father does not blame you for what Arthur did, would not ever maltreat you. Please believe me, he would not.'

Eleanor studied the child. 'I do believe you, Cousin Joanna,' she said, managed a wan smile, even as her eyes filled with tears. 'But what of my brother? What of Arthur?'

195

April, 1204
Southampton, England

Following a servant into the solar, Will found his sister-in-law conferring with her almoner. Isabelle was always friendly, but now she greeted Will with such unfeigned delight that he flushed with startled pleasure. He was not at ease with lovely women, and Isabelle's beauty was particularly intimidating and ethereal to him. Try as he might, he could not imagine her afflicted with such ordinary, mundane ailments as chilblains, blisters, or cramps, could not envision her nose red with cold, her eyes swollen with sleep, her hair in uncombed early morning disarray – as he'd so often seen Ela, who was not glamorous or exotic, but reassuringly real.

'John and I broke our Lenten fast by eating meat yesterday, and so today I've instructed our almoner to feed one hundred of the city's poor,' Isabelle explained, linking her arm in Will's and drawing him towards the privacy of a window recess. 'How glad I am that you've come, Will. Have you seen John yet?'

'No, I was told he'll be hearing appeals from the shire courts for the rest of the day.'

'You'll sup with us, of course, and you must stay awhile with the court, Will. John has need of you, and so have I. I am relying upon you to cheer his spirits. He's in a right foul temper, has been brooding for more than a fortnight about the fall of that wretched castle.'

'Well, Castle Gaillard is of great defensive importance, guards the approach to Rouen . . .' Will began, quite willing to educate Isabelle in the finer points of military strategy.

His efforts were wasted. Isabelle heard him out, but murmured only a tepidly polite, 'How very interesting.' She glanced about to make sure all others were out of earshot. 'Will . . . tell me in honesty. Is Normandy well and truly lost to John?'

'We still hold Rouen and Falaise, Chinon Castle . . .' Will hedged. 'But even if the tide continues to run against us, and Normandy, too, falls to Philip, you must not fear, lass. Angoulême, Gascony, and Poitou still hold fast for John.'

He waited glumly for her to remind him, though, that Maine, Anjou, Brittany, and Touraine had all been lost to Philip within the past twelvemonth. He could recite the reasons why it had happened, a litany of ill luck, blunders, and betrayal: John's chronic and crippling lack of funds; the disloyalty of his Norman barons, who thought it safer to defy a distant English king than a neighbouring French one; John's errors of judgment and his indecision, his unfortunate penchant for turning allies into enemies; William des Roches had ridden away from Mirebeau as a rebel. But to understand why Philip had prevailed was not to accept it, and Will did not want to discuss their disastrous Normandy campaign with anyone, least of all with his brother's wife.

Isabelle fidgeted with her rings; John might be short of money to pay his troops, but he still found the means to indulge his young Queen's love of jewels. 'I suppose,' she said, 'that it was a great mistake for John to have ever let Hugh de Lusignan buy his freedom.'

Will winced. When John had decided to set the de Lusignans at liberty, he'd encountered opposition from an unexpected source, from his mother. Eleanor had been adamantly against the idea, insisting that the time to make peace with Hugh de Lusignan had been before John's marriage to Isabelle, that it was now too late. Will had not agreed with her, unwilling to believe it was ever too late to right a wrong; while he cared not a whit for Hugh de Lusignan's sense of injury, he hoped a conciliatory gesture on John's part would favourably impress other Norman lords wavering in their loyalty. Convinced that they could keep Hugh in check by demanding hostages for his good faith, Will had added his voice to those arguing for release. Hugh and Geoffrey de Lusignan had been freed five months after their capture at Mirebeau, had at once joined William des Roches and the rebel barons of Brittany and Anjou, leaving Will a legacy of guilt out of all proportion to his small share of the responsibility.

'The de Lusignans offered up such an extravagant sum for their freedom that John could not afford to turn it down,' he said defensively, 'not with so pressing a need for money.'

'I know; John explained it all to me at the time. But shall I tell you what I think, Will? That John was goaded as much by his mother's opposition as he was swayed by the money. It's said she can be right clever at getting men to do her bidding, but with John, she's always been brutally blunt. They had a fearful row about it, and I think that was when John truly made up his mind to set Hugh free, to prove to Eleanor that he was in the right.'

Will stared at her, all at once seeing Isabelle with new insight. John had never been known for constancy, and Will's expectations for his marriage were minimal. Greatly to his surprise, John's passion for his girl-wife had not been slaked by possession; Isabelle was his constant companion and bedmate on his travels around his realm. Will had attributed Isabelle's continuing bewitchment of his brother to her uncommon beauty. Now he suddenly wondered if he'd under-estimated her.

'I think,' he said slowly, 'that you content John so well because you understand him so well,' stating the obvious with such a solemn sense of discovery that Isabelle had to stifle a giggle.

'I doubt that anyone understands John all that well! But I do know when he is troubled. I truly think he'd not mourn for long the loss of his continental domains in and of themselves. He has always seen England as the heart of his inheritance, has oft told me how easy it is to safeguard an island kingdom, how difficult to defend a far-flung empire. But that empire was Richard's, and so he cannot bear to let it go.' Isabelle leaned forward, put her hand on Will's sleeve. 'I would help him if I could, but I do not know how. I was so hoping that you do,' she said, giving Will a look of such irresistible appeal that he felt a lump rise in his throat.

He'd wondered if Isabelle loved his brother, was pleased now to conclude that she did. And yet he felt a certain surprise, too. He had few illusions about John, knew what John had done and what he was capable of doing, but the bond of brotherhood was one to last from the cradle to the grave. The bond between husband and wife he believed to be more fragile. Women were known to be the lesser sex; Will thought they were also the purer sex, softer of heart and more innocent of mind than men. As Isabelle lay with John in their vast marital bed, was her sleep never disturbed by uneasy thoughts of Arthur?

Will could not be sure, of course, that the rumours were true, that Arthur was dead. But his suspicions were strong enough to keep him from confronting his brother, from insisting that John tell him what he'd rather not know. It was not that he was shocked; while he would never have chosen himself to claim Arthur's life, he recognized John's right to do so. Treason warranted death. Scriptures said that plainly, said rebellion was as the sin of witchcraft. And Arthur had remained defiantly unrepentant. Will had been present when John confronted Arthur at Falaise in January, 1203, had come away from that turbulent, ugly encounter with the grim realization that Arthur was doomed; if he would not bend, he'd have to be broken. The French King had been putting about lurid rumours for months, contending that Arthur had been murdered in a number of grisly ways – drowned, stabbed, blinded and castrated – rumours that found ready believers among Arthur's Bretons, but few in England, where Arthur's fate was a matter of supreme indifference. But that past Easter John had paid a second visit to Arthur, then being held at Rouen Castle, and soon after, rumours again began to circulate that the sixteen-year-old Duke of Brittany had been put to death at his uncle's command; some even said by John's own hand. That last, Will dismissed as nonsense; he knew John too well, knew his brother had always preferred to keep distance between himself and his darker misdeeds. Yet the sinister silence that descended over Rouen Castle after that Easter visit convinced Will that these rumours were well grounded in reality, and he could only wonder at John's genius for self-sabotage. However much Arthur's death was deserved, it was still a drastic, Draconian step to take, and even a political novice like Will understood that it had to be done in the fullest light of high noon – or not at all.

'Will . . . why are you staring at me like that?'

Will blinked, lost Arthur's ghost in the deep blue of Isabelle's eyes. She was truly a sweet lass, he thought, and not for the world would he see her lose her faith in John. 'It gladdens my heart to know that you are happy in your marriage, and I shall indeed do what I can to ease John's discontent.'

'Why would I not be happy in my marriage?' Isabelle echoed, surprised. 'John denies me nothing. Richard's poor Berengaria might well have been invisible for the notice people took of her. But when I enter a chamber, all conversation hushes, all eyes are upon me – because people know John cares whether I am content or not. Oh, I grant you he is not always an easy man to live with, has tempers and black moods and shadowy places in his soul where I cannot follow. But we'll be wed four years come August, Will, and not once has my womb quickened with life. Yet not once has John ever reproached me for that. How many barren wives could say as much?'

Will was both embarrassed and touched by the unexpected intimacy of this glimpse she'd just given him into her married life. 'I am sure you'll conceive in God's time, lass,' he said awkwardly, and Isabelle smiled.

'So am I,' she assured him, sounding faintly amused. 'But it is kind of you to try to ease my mind. You are a good man, Will, you truly are. John . . . John is good to me,' said with just enough emphasis on the last two words to tell Will that she was not so innocent as he'd first thought, as he'd like to believe. He looked at her, at the wide-set eyes utterly clear and untroubled by ghosts, at the mouth so soft and sweetened by laughter, and decided he must have misread her meaning.

'You must not fret,' he said soothingly. 'I'll stay as long as John has need of me, I promise you.'

'It is your move, John,' William de Braose prompted, sounding so smug that John gave him a cold stare before resuming his very deliberate study of the chessboard.

Will shifted in his seat. He was a mediocre chessplayer at best, but even he could see that John had allowed himself to be manoeuvred into an utterly untenable position. That realization gave Will almost as much exasperation as it did John, for Isabelle had not exaggerated; he'd rarely seen his brother in such a grim mood, a mood not likely to be improved by a loss to William de Braose. De Braose was as ungracious a winner as John was a loser. Already there was gleeful anticipation in his grin. He would win, then magnanimously waive payment of their wager stakes, gloating thinly guised as jest; Will had seen de Braose win before.

Will had known de Braose for some ten years, for he was one of the few men who'd managed to be friendly with both Richard and John. Will had watched disapprovingly as de Braose insinuated his way into John's inner circle, becoming, in time, one of John's favourite carousing companions. He'd never lacked for confidence – as shy as a timber wolf, as scrupulous as a Barbary pirate – but Will had noted an increasing familiarity in his friendship with John, a familiarity that Will found offensive, that seemed to go beyond their mutual pursuit of what de Braose jokingly called 'the three aitches . . . hunting, hawking, and "horing".' A familiarity that Will had first noticed in the past year, in the weeks after John's Eastertide visit to Rouen.

Will was not alone in his critical appraisal of the chess game's unhappy consequences. Joanna knew how her father hated to lose. Lord de Braose would revel in his victory, she knew, and Papa would be in ill humour for the rest of the night. It was not fair. Papa was so disquieted, much in need of distraction. Joanna thought it only just that he should be able to forget his troubles for a few hours. She knew suddenly what she must do, took a moment or so to nerve herself for it. Rising, she reached for a bowl of candied fruit, carried it across the chamber to John.

'Would you like a fig, Papa?' she asked, and then bumped into the trestle table, upsetting the chessmen and knocking the board on to the floor.

'Papa, I'm so sorry! I truly do not know how I could have been so clumsy.'

'Divine Providence?' John suggested, straight-faced, but his eyes were laughing.

'That is one explanation, I suppose,' William de Braose said, favouring them both with a sour smile, and Joanna saw that he, too, knew her action had been deliberate. But John was looking at her with such amusement, such affectionate approval that nothing else mattered to her. She groped hastily for a topic of conversation likely to hold his interest, to exclude de Braose.

'Did you hear any uncommon appeals today, Papa?' she asked, knowing as soon as she spoke that her question was inspired, for John shared his father's fascination with the law. He genuinely enjoyed hearing court appeals, arguing points of law with his justices, issuing writs to right perceived wrongs, and he saw to it that the Exchequer published his itinerary weeks in advance so that petitioners might know where he'd be on a given day, so they could appeal to the royal court for justice denied in the shire courts.

'Indeed I did, Joanna. A youth not much older than you, calling himself Roger of Stainton. He'd been amusing himself by throwing stones across a stream. By ill luck, one struck a young girl. She died and he was sentenced to be hanged.'

'Shall you pardon him, Papa?' Joanna asked, pleased when John nodded.

'How could I not? It was death by misadventure; a man should not hang for that.' John paused, looking up as an usher came into the chamber.

'Your Grace, a courier has just arrived from Fontevrault.'

John tensed; his good humour chilled into icy wariness. He'd been dreading this, his mother's reaction to the loss of Castle Gaillard, Richard's pride and joy, the castle he'd boasted he could hold even if the walls were made of butter. John did not want to be reminded of this by Eleanor; even if she did not reproach him directly, he did not doubt her disappointment would echo between every line. It was with considerable reluctance, then, that he said curtly, 'Send him in.'

The monk was young and visibly ill at ease. The black habit of the Benedictines camouflaged the grime of his journey, but the parchment he clutched was soiled from much handling, slashed and threaded through with a braided grey cord that might once have been white. He knelt, thrust the letter at John as if he longed only to be rid of it.

John looked down at the wax sealing the cord ends; it was intact, but unfamiliar. 'This is not my mother's seal.'

'The letter is from the Abbess Matilda, Your Grace. She bade me tell you . . .' The monk swallowed, no longer meeting John's eyes. 'Your lady mother . . . She is dead, my liege.'

John heard his daughter cry out, plaintively denying death with an indrawn breath that broke on a sob. No one else spoke. John found himself staring at the monk's clasped hands; they were rawboned, knuckles roughened, nails caked with dirt. Never had he been so aware of detail; he saw a sheen on the man's habit, where kneeling had worn the material thin, saw the damp splotches under his armpits, the telltale signs of sweat, of fear. But he felt nothing, only a stunned sense of disbelief.

Utterly unnerved by John's silence, the monk squeezed his knees tightly together to stop his trembling, and stammered, 'It . . . it did happen on Thursday last, soon after Vespers. But it may comfort you, my lord, to know that hers was a peaceful and Christian passing. She died in God's grace, with our lady Abbess and Abbot Luke of Turpenay at her bedside; he'd been with her when your brother King Richard died, you may recall, and when she knew her end was nigh, she sent to St Mary's Abbey for him.'

Still John said nothing, and the monk drew several shallow breaths, speaking now almost at random. 'It was your mother's wish that she be buried at Fontevrault with King Richard and your sister, the Lady Joanna. Our Abbess saw that it was done. I hope that meets with your approval, my liege . . .'

'Did she leave any word . . . any message for me?'

'No, my lord.'

Another silence fell. John crumpled the letter, unread, let it drop into the rushes at his feet. The monk made an instinctive grab for it, then jerked his hand back as if burned. Will cleared his throat, seemed on the verge of speech. John forestalled him, said without any intonation whatsoever, 'Leave me. All of you.'

The men did not need to be told twice; even Will obeyed at once. But Joanna's discipline took her only as far as the door. There she whirled, ran back and knelt by John's chair. 'Let me stay, Papa,' she pleaded. 'Please . . .'

The face upturned to his was waxen, wet with tears. John put his arm around her, and she began to sob in earnest. He drew her closer, let her weep against his shoulder, and after a brief time, her sobs subsided, gave way to sighs and hiccups. Joanna's first flow of tears had been for herself, for her own loss. But now she wiped her face with her sleeve, ready to share that loss, recognizing that her father's sense of bereavement might be even greater than hers.

'Papa . . . I'm so sorry.' Joanna remembered, too vividly, what it had been like to lose her mother, remembered not so much her grieving as her sheer terror. Did men and women grown ever experience blind, suffocating panic like that? She did not know. Her father's face was shuttered, unreadable.

'Papa . . . you have not said a word, not one. Do you not want to talk? How do you feel?' She looked up at him anxiously, no longer a child, not yet a woman, tears still glistening in the slanting hazel eyes, Eleanor's eyes, and John was suddenly glad he'd allowed her to stay.

'How do I feel?' He found that was not an easy question to answer, at last said, 'Alone . . . very alone. And angry, so angry I can think of nothing else.'

Adult emotions were no longer as mysterious or inexplicable to Joanna as they'd once been, but this was utterly beyond her comprehension. 'Angry . . . at your mother? Because she died? But why? I do not understand, Papa.'

'Neither do I, Joanna.' And in that moment John sounded no less bewildered than his twelve-year-old daughter. 'Neither do I.'

203

14

September, 1204

Winchester, England

Summoned by her father, Joanna left London on Tuesday morning of Michaelmas week. Travelling in the company of her aunt Ela, Countess of Salisbury, they reached Winchester at dusk on Thursday. There they found other ladies of the court; like them, summoned to attend the King. But John had not yet arrived from Clarendon, had still not come by noon the next day.

With so many people to be sheltered, beds were scarce, and Joanna's aunt was given a cramped chamber musty with the rancid odours rising up from the castle moat. It was a far less desirable room than those taken by Maude de Braose and Isobel, Countess of Pembroke, but Ela voiced no objections. Although she had brought her husband an earldom, his fief was neither large nor lucrative; Will held only fifty knights' fees, and no castles, although John did allow him to make use of Salisbury Castle. In contrast, William de Braose held no less than three hundred and fifty knights' fees and some sixteen English and Welsh castles. Ela, a shy, self-effacing young woman, accepted the realities of power without a murmur of protest, would never have dreamed of contesting wills with so aggressive a personality as Maude de Braose. It did occur to Joanna, who liked Maude not at all, but her youth and illegitimacy effectively rendered her mute.

Joanna was standing now on the stairs outside their bedchamber, frozen with rage. The door was only slightly ajar, but the voices within came quite clearly to her ears, so audibly that she recognized the speakers without difficulty: Maude de Braose, Maude's daughter Margaret de Lacy, wife to the Lord of Meath, and Isobel, wife to the powerful William Marshal, Earl of Pembroke. She had yet to hear her aunt's voice, however, and while that did not surprise her, it did anger her. Ela was her father's sister by marriage; common courtesy, if not loyalty, should compel her to speak up for him.

'I had a letter from my husband today, Mama. Word reached Ireland a fortnight ago that Poitiers fell to the French on August 10th, but Walter refuses to believe it.'

'After the defeats of the past year? After losing all of Normandy in less than a twelvemonth? You could tell me tomorrow that Philip had taken London itself and I'd not think to doubt you!'

'Ah, Maude, that's not strictly fair. I grant you the King made some grave errors of judgment. My husband warned him it was folly to release the de Lusignans, no matter how many hostages they offered up as pledges for their loyalty. Nor did John help himself by relying upon so brutal a captain as Lupescaire; a man does not gain himself a name like "The Wolf" without cause, and I doubt not he affronted many who might otherwise have stayed loyal to John. But –'

'Yet men such as that do have their uses. In Wales we –'

Most people found themselves at a distinct disadvantage when competing with Maude de Braose for conversational control, but Isobel of Pembroke was a remarkably single-minded woman, little given to self-doubt. 'If I may finish, Maude,' she said, placidly overriding Maude's interruption with one of her own, 'not all of his troubles were of the King's making. His lack of money; you know as well as I that Richard drained the royal treasury dry. And in all honesty, some of John's difficulties with his Norman barons can be traced, too, to his brother's reign. Richard laid a heavy hand upon the land, and there were many who chafed under it.'

'I dare say there's some truth in what you say, Isobel. But that does not change the fact that within two years of his triumph at Mirebeau, John lost Normandy, Anjou, and Touraine, and now most of Poitou. Say what you will about Richard, but do you think that he would have stayed in England whilst Castle Gaillard was under siege? Not if he had to swim the Channel with his sword in his teeth! Mayhap he, too, would have lost Normandy, but we may be sure that Richard would have lost his life as well, would have died ere he'd yield up so much as a handful of Norman soil to Philip. You can scarcely say the same for John!'

Joanna had not meant to confront them; girls of thirteen did not challenge their elders. But with Maude's taunt, she forgot all else, grabbed for the door latch. The women within turned startled faces towards her; even Maude looked somewhat disconcerted. Recovering quickly, however, she said curtly, 'I trust you were not eavesdropping, Joanna.'

'I need no lessons in manners, Madame. Not from you.'

Maude's mouth tightened. 'If you were my daughter, I'd slap you silly for that,' she snapped. 'No child of mine would dare speak so insolently to her elders.'

'But I am not your daughter, Madame. I am the King's daughter,' Joanna said, and saw that she'd achieved the all but impossible, had the last word in an argument with Maude de Braose. Never had she been so rude to an adult, but now she turned her back upon Maude, crossed to her coffer chest. No one spoke, watching in silence as she knelt, retrieved a willow basket. She could feel their eyes upon her, all the way to the door.

The lower bailey was awash in sun. A postern gate in the north curtain wall opened out into the gardens, and it was towards this door that Joanna hastened, almost running in her need to put the bedchamber scene behind her. Reaction to her rage had set in, and she was flushed, trembling. But she was proud, too, that she had stood up to Maude de Braose.

Joanna had long since passed the stage where she thought every adult was all-knowing. Some were quite clever. Others were not. And some could be remarkably shrewd and yet surprisingly foolish, too. Joanna was slowly realizing that her young stepmother was one such, insightful about that which interested her – relationships between men and women – and unabashedly uninformed about all else. Now, as much as she disliked Maude de Braose, Joanna did not dismiss Maude as a fool. No, Maude and Isabelle were reverse sides of the same coin. Maude was quick-witted about that which interested Isabelle least. She could add up long columns of figures in her head, knew the names of all her vassals, could talk of Welsh border warfare as well as any man. But she had no understanding of people's hearts.

Joanna smiled. Precisely because she was so ignorant of emotional needs, Maude would be sure Joanna would repeat all to her father, would have some uneasy moments in consequence, for even Maude, who prided herself upon her outspoken, careless candour, even she would not want such a tale to reach the King's ears.

Not that she would ever tell Papa. He had burdens enough, needed no more. He was – Joanna calculated rapidly – only in his thirty-seventh year, but his hair was increasingly flecked with grey, and there were lines around his mouth that had not been there a year ago. Worst of all, his temper was honed to a sharp edge. He rarely shouted, as his father and brothers had done, but sarcasm, too, could scar. Even in good humour, he'd always trod that fine line between jest and mockery, and these days he was all too quick to turn upon others the sardonic lash of an unbridled tongue.

Joanna sighed. Papa was so good to her, so good to Isabelle. And he was very clever, in truth he was. So why, then, did he offend people so needlessly? For he did: he was too suspicious, too quick to read the worst into men's motives. Not, she added loyally, that he had not cause for mistrust. Many of the Norman barons had gone over to Philip at the first chance.

Joanna had spent much time in the past year seeking to puzzle it out, how her father's luck could have soured so swiftly in the months after Mirebeau. She'd even attempted to discuss it with John, but had been rebuffed with unwonted sharpness. And Isabelle had been no help whatsoever. She was interested only in consoling John for his loss, not in analysing the whys and wherefores.

It was from her uncle Will that Joanna had got most of her answers. He'd admitted that John had blundered in freeing Hugh de Lusignan and in alienating William des Roches. But he told her, too, that John's mistakes were threads woven into a larger pattern. 'In some ways, Joanna, John is reaping the crop Richard sowed. Mayhap Richard could have held on to the lands for a while longer, but that is all. What is writ is writ. You remember that, lass, whenever you hear ignorant tongues wag.'

Joanna did remember, sought now to dismiss Maude's mockery as her uncle had advised. But anger was not so easy to subdue; resentment remained, and regret that others could not see into her father's soul, could not know him as she did. Yet there was, as well, a realization which had no place within the borders of childhood, which was rooted in an adult understanding: that her father could make mistakes, could suffer from uncertainty and indecision, could share all the failings of mortal men. He was not a saint, after all, not the all-powerful knight without peer, Lancelot and Roland and Gawain, a child's champion in the lists, her favour on his lance and her name on his lips.

'He was a burning and shining light,' Joanna murmured, with some self-mockery, but not much. Why should she scorn the be-dazzled child she had been? She had loved Papa when, in her innocence, she'd thought him to be perfect, and she loved him no less now that she knew he was not.

Winchester had been a favourite residence of Joanna's grandfather, the old King, and in days gone by, when he'd still cared about pleasing his Queen, he'd built for Eleanor vineyards to remind her of her native Poitou, chains of fishponds, a garden arbour. It was to these gardens that Joanna had retreated.

From her basket she fished out her lesson tablet and the bone stylus she used to mark the wax coating. But this was not just a sop to her conscience, for she did not intend to study. Unrolling a sheet of scraped parchment, she smoothed it with a pumice stone, then dipped her pen into her inkhorn.

> To the Lady Eleanor, my cousin, greetings.
> I write to you from the gardens at Winchester Castle, on this, the Friday after Michaelmas, whilst I await my lord father the King to ride in from Clarendon. I have not seen him since he did meet last month with the Welsh Prince . . .

Here, she paused, having no idea how to spell Llewelyn. After some thought, she opted for a phonetic spelling, although she was not even sure if her pronunciation was correct.

> . . . Lliwelin. He had sworn to do homage to my father more than three years ago, but he was not over-eager to make good his word, did only this summer agree to meet with Papa at Worcester. I hope their meeting did go well, hope, too, that I shall have more time with my father now. I saw him but little this twelvemonth past, as you know. He was occupied in defending his lands against the French King, and I spent part of the year with my grandmother in Poitiers . . .

Again she paused, remembering that her cousin, too, was Eleanor's grandchild. Inking out 'my', she wrote 'our' above it, and then added in an uneven hand, 'may God assoil her.' It was one day short of five months since Eleanor had died at Fontevrault, but Joanna's grieving was still green, her loss still keenly felt.

She sat for a time, staring down at the parchment. Letters to her cousin were never easy, invariably written with a faltering, hesitant pen. But she felt compelled to persevere, knowing how lonely Eleanor must be. And then, too, Joanna liked to write letters. There was something almost mystical to her about the process. She enjoyed signing her name with a flourish, using large blobs of sealing wax, paying couriers with the silver pennies hoarded for such a purpose, remembering the little girl who could do no more than draw her name in the dirt with a stick.

Did you get the saddle my father ordered for you? I do not yet know where Papa will keep his Christmas court, but I am sure he will want you to join us. Since I saw you last, I have acquired a dog. I had one once before; she died when I was ten, was run over by a cart, and I swore I would never have another. But my stepmother the Queen gave me a puppy for my New Year's gift. She is no bigger than a cat, with long, silky fur, comes from the island of Malta. My father suggested I name her Sugar because she was so costly!

What to say now? Should she mention Arthur? Was Eleanor aware of the vile lies put about by Papa's enemies, that Arthur was dead? It was so unfair. He'd been nothing but kind to Eleanor, saw that she had every comfort, even brought her occasionally to his court. Why, then, would he put her brother to death? Joanna shook her head, reaching for the inkhorn. Pray God Papa would soon be able to mount his campaign to win back Normandy and Poitou, to punish Philip as he deserved.

'Joanna!'

The voice was Richard's. Joanna scrambled to her feet, ran to meet him. 'Richard, how glad I am to see you! Has Papa come, then? Did the council with the Welsh Prince go well? Did you meet him?'

'Yes, to all your questions. Hurry now, get your things together. Papa is asking for you, wants to see you straightaway.'

'Indeed?' Joanna was delighted. Her father's arrivals were inevitably chaotic; sometimes hours passed before she had the chance to see him alone. 'He truly wants to see me first?'

Richard nodded. 'You know, it was rather queer. When Papa asked after you, Aunt Ela and the other ladies acted right peculiar, almost as if they were reluctant to have you found. Even Lady de Braose professed ignorance of your whereabouts, and she most generally has an opinion on everything!'

'Lady de Braose has a viper's tongue,' Joanna said emphatically, 'and I care not a pin for her good opinion. Need I comb my hair first?'

209

'No, but your face is dirty.' Richard spat on his fingers, wiped away a smudge on her cheek, and then pleased Joanna by giving her a quick, awkward hug.

'The last time I remember you doing that,' she laughed, 'I'd spilled ink on Papa's favourite book, was about to be called to account for my sin!'

Richard gave her a look she could not interpret, reached down for her basket. 'Come, I'll take you back to the castle.'

Joanna fumbled with the cloth, unwrapped an exquisitely engraved ivory case. At the touch of her fingers, it flew open to reveal a thin sheet of glass over brightly polished metal.

'Papa, what a beautiful mirror!' Setting it down beside her other present, a bolt of deep blue linen, she gave John a grateful kiss. 'But you sent me a book for my birthday, do you not remember?'

'And can I not give you more than one gift? A pity my men in the Exchequer are not as frugal as you; mayhap I'd not then be so deeply in debt!'

They were alone in John's bedchamber. Much to Joanna's surprise, her father had dismissed all others upon her arrival, even Richard, who seemed strangely reluctant to leave, glancing back over his shoulder with the same enigmatic look he'd given her in the garden.

'I think, lass, that you're now old enough to have a lady in attendance, to assist you in dressing and the like. So I've told Isabelle to choose someone suitable for you.'

'Thank you, Papa!' Joanna wondered if this was how Richard had felt when he'd learned he was to be squire to William de Braose the younger, was to take that first step over the threshold towards manhood.

'I have one more gift for you, sweetheart – a crown.'

Joanna giggled. 'And a halo, too, Papa?'

John laughed, shook his head. 'I'm not jesting, Joanna. I've made a brilliant marriage for you. I've agreed to betroth you to Llewelyn ab Iorwerth, Prince of Gwynedd.'

'Papa?'

'In truth, sweetheart. I've offered the castle and manor of Ellesmere in Shropshire as your marriage portion, will yield it to Llewelyn next spring, although I would not have the marriage take place till after you pass your fourteenth birthday.' John reached over, took

Joanna's hand. 'You realize what this will mean, Joanna? You'll be a Princess, lass. This goes so far beyond what I ever hoped to gain for you. It is a rarity, indeed, when needs and wants do mate in such harmony. But . . . but have you nothing to say to me? I would have thought you'd be besieging me with questions. Are you not curious about the man you shall marry?'

Too stunned for coherent thought, Joanna could only stare at her father in dazed disbelief. 'He . . . he does speak French?' she whispered at last.

That was not what John had been expecting. 'Of course, and quite well. He knows much of our ways, lived in Shropshire as a lad.'

'Is he . . . is he a Christian, Papa?'

John frowned, torn between amusement and annoyance. 'What sort of foolish question is that, Joanna? Wales has been a Christian country since the days of St David. To whom have you been listening?'

To you, Papa. How often I've heard you say the Welsh were barbarians, that theirs was an accursed land fit only for mountain goats, that the Welsh were as bad as the Scots and worse than the Irish. Joanna said nothing, though, watched as John rose, moved to the table. Her hands were icy; she laced her fingers together, locked them around her drawn-up knees.

'This Welsh Prince . . . how old is he, Papa?'

'I'd reckon about thirty or thirty-one.'

Joanna could not hide her dismay. 'As old as that?' she gasped.

'He happens to be at least five years younger than me, Joanna,' John said dryly. He was smiling, but Joanna remembered, just in time, that her father was fully twenty years older than Isabelle.

'I . . . I did not mean it like that, Papa,' she stammered, and then a sudden thought came to her, a faint glimmer of hope. 'But Papa, I am your natural daughter. What prince would want a wife born out of wedlock?'

'A Welsh prince,' John said, and laughed. 'The stigma of illegitimacy counts for little amongst Llewelyn's people. If a father recognizes a child as his, that child then enjoys full rights under Welsh law. Llewelyn had his son with him at Worcester, a lad about eight or so, born of a Welsh concubine, and yet looked upon by all as his heir. In fact, if a Welsh woman swears a holy oath that a certain man fathered her child, he must then deny her charge under oath, too, or the child is held to be his. Moreover, even if he does make such a denial, if she can show he gave her money for the child, her word counts against his! I have to admit, they do have some queer customs, but . . .'

Joanna was no longer listening, was trying to envision herself as a stepmother to an eight-year-old boy. She could not, and with that realization, some of her panic began to ebb. She could not make this marriage. She could not. To leave Papa, Richard, Isabelle, all that was known and familiar to her, to live out her life amongst strangers, an exile in an alien land . . . No, she was not strong enough, had not the courage. Somehow she must make Papa see that, make him understand that he asked too much of her.

John had poured wine into two cups, gave one to Joanna. 'Ah, lass, I cannot tell you how pleased I am about this marriage. Mayhap I should not say this to you, but of all my children, you are the dearest, the closest to my heart. I can think of no greater gift to give you than this, a crown.'

'Papa, you have been so good to me, and I would do anything for you, I swear I would. But this marriage –'

'– is the answer to so much, Joanna.' John leaned forward, his eyes shining; it had been months since she'd seen him so animated, so enthused. 'Before God, it was an inspired solution to the Welsh problem. I gain a gold coronet for you and a secure border for England, all for the price of one castle and a wedding ring. Rarely has a war been so cheaply won, sweetheart!'

'A war . . .' Joanna echoed numbly. 'Is the marriage as important to you as that?'

John's smile faded. 'Yes, it is. You want the truth, Joanna? I do not know if I shall ever be able to reclaim the lands lost to the French – Normandy, Anjou, Touraine. Now Poitou is slipping away, being swallowed up by that whoreson on the French throne. I'll not let it go, not lose the lands that were my mother's, that Richard held before me, by Christ I will not. But I cannot fight a war on two fronts, cannot deal with the Welsh and the French, too.'

He rose abruptly, began to pace. 'They are a strange people, the Welsh. Man for man, the best fighters in the world, for you cannot defeat a foe who has not the sense to know when he's beaten! We'd never have been able to keep them from laying claim to Shropshire and Cheshire, much less conquer so much of South Wales, had it not been for their one fatal weakness, that they are such a quarrelsome, passionate people. They kill one another as readily as they do Normans, engage in blood feuds, nurse grudges for years, and thank

God, but they have ever lacked a prince capable of uniting them against England . . . until now.'

Joanna stared down at her wine cup as if at some utterly alien and exotic object. Raising it to her lips, she took a tentative swallow; the wine was warm, so sugared that she all but gagged.

'There are men who be born lucky. All their lives, fortune does favour them, does play the whore for them. My brother Richard was one such. Llewelyn ab Iorwerth is another. And he is clever enough, ambitious enough, and ruthless enough one day to rule all of Wales if he is not reined in. Already he looks beyond Gwynedd, dares to send envoys to the French court, to treat with Philip as if they were brother sovereigns. Should he ever forge an alliance with the French . . .'

John had wandered to the window, speaking almost as if to himself. He turned now, back towards his daughter, gave her a sudden smile of coaxing charm. 'Are you not pleased, sweetheart, that you shall be Princess of Gwynedd?'

Joanna swallowed. 'Indeed, Papa,' she said tonelessly. 'If it be your wish that I wed with Prince Llewelyn, I am content.'

Leaving her father's bedchamber, Joanna stood for a moment in the darkened stairwell, not knowing where to go. So caught up was she in her own thoughts that she did not at once notice the young page.

'Lady . . . lady, will you come? The Queen wants you.'

Joanna looked blankly at the child. 'Yes,' she said with an effort. 'Of course.' But the summons was not all that unwelcome. Isabelle might be the one person who could understand how she felt.

Isabelle was awaiting her in her bedchamber, welcomed her with a perfumed embrace. 'Ah, Joanna, how happy I am for you, love! Is it not wondrous? Think, you shall be a Princess!'

'A Welsh Princess,' Joanna said, and with that, tears welled in her eyes, began to spill silently down her face.

Isabelle blinked. 'Are you as unhappy as that? Ah, Joanna . . .' Putting an arm around the younger girl, she led Joanna towards the bed.

'You just need time to accustom yourself to it. Do you not think I felt the same qualms when my father sent me to live in Hugh de Lusignan's household? Of course that marriage was not to be, and glad I am for it. But if fate had decreed otherwise, I do not doubt I could have learned to be content as Hugh's Countess. As you will be

213

content with Prince Llewelyn. Once the surprise of it fades, you'll be quite reconciled, you'll see.

'Now, sit on the bed, and I'll tell you all about your husband, tell you what John should have and likely did not, men having no sense for what is truly important. He is dark, of course, like most of his people, with blackest hair, brown eyes, and a smile no woman is like to soon forget. He is taller than John, and well made, with truly beautiful hands . . . I always notice a man's hands; do you? He is well spoken, and when he listens, he keeps his eyes upon your face all the while. And he has a wicked sense of humour. When I asked him about Wales, he told me that his people were Druids, that they worshipped the oak and mistletoe and made virgin sacrifices!'

Isabelle laughed. 'In truth, love, there are many women who would envy you, and not just for that circlet of gold. Oh, but there is one thing you should know; he is clean-shaven!' She began to giggle. 'The Welsh do keep their moustaches, but they shave off their beards. I confess it did look right strange to me at first. I wonder what it would be like to kiss a man without a beard? You must be sure and tell me, Joanna.'

Joanna turned away, rolling over and burying her face in the pillow. Her tears had dried, but her breathing was still uneven, ragged, and she did not want Isabelle to hear. She supposed she should be thankful for what Isabelle was telling her, but she was numb, unable to make sense of anything. What was he to her, this Welsh Prince she'd never even seen? There was no reality to this conversation, none at all.

'My marriage was in haste, with little ceremony. But we'll give you a lovely wedding, Joanna, a wedding to remember.'

Joanna roused herself at that, murmured a meaningless 'thank you'. A year, Papa had said, not until she was fourteen. A year seemed so far away, seemed in itself an eternity. Time enough for Papa to change his mind. Or for the Welsh Prince to reconsider. He might even die. All betrothals did not end in the marriage bed. She must hold on to that thought, must not despair . . . not yet. Much could happen in a year.

May, 1206

Chester, England

'Which brooch shall you wear, my lady?' Blanche was holding out an open casket, and Joanna turned, took it upon her lap. Her choice was limited; she had only a few pieces of jewellery of any real value.

'The crescent brooch, I think.' As she spoke, Joanna could not keep from fingering the other contents of the casket, the letters from the Welsh Prince she would wed on the morrow. Four in eighteen months, polished and polite and utterly unrevealing. If she were alone, she might have taken them out again, re-read them for clues, so desperately did she need to know what manner of man he was. But she was surrounded by inquisitive eyes: Blanche, Isobel of Pembroke, her aunt Ela, Maude de Braose, the Countess of Chester, and the Lady Lucy, Prioress of St Mary's, the Benedictine nunnery where Joanna had been awaiting the arrival of her betrothed.

Blanch was positioning the brooch. 'There, my lady. You do look right elegant. How proud your lord father would be; how sad that he must miss the pleasure of seeing you wed.'

'It could not be helped, Blanche. In less than a month's time, my father will lead an army into Normandy. He must, of course, remain in the South, to make sure that the fleet will be ready to sail as scheduled.' Joanna had told herself this so often that the words came quite naturally to her tongue, sounded perfectly plausible even to her ears. But the hurt remained. She'd been counting so on her father's presence. In fact, her disappointment was such that she had put aside her pride and begged John to reconsider. Could not the wedding be held, instead, in Winchester? She would, she pleaded, write herself to Prince Llewelyn, entreat him to agree for her sake. Remembering that now, Joanna's face shadowed, for she had received a truly chilling reply. John had been both sympathetic and regretful. 'Even if you somehow did get him to consent, and I think that unlikely, Joanna, it is too late. The safe-conduct I gave him is for

215

Chester; there would not be time to issue a new one for Winchester.' It had never occurred to Joanna that Llewelyn would need a safe-conduct to enter into England. That brought home to her, as nothing else could have done, that she was marrying a man her father could not trust, that she would be living out the rest of her life in a country hostile to England.

Blanche fastened Joanna's wimple under her chin, reached for a rose-coloured veil. 'As soon as I attach this, my lady, you will be ready to meet the Prince.'

'Have you not another veil? With such sallow skin, rose is a colour she should ever avoid if possible.'

Joanna jerked her head around in surprise. There was more than feline spite in that remark, there was venom. She had not realized that Maude de Braose bore her such a grudge. She flushed in spite of herself, had to fight the urge to ask Blanche for another veil. 'Rose suits me well, Madame,' she said, as steadily as she could, and came to her feet. How unfair life was. Was it not enough that she must wed a stranger, a Welshman? But no, their first meeting must take place before an avid audience, for all the world, she thought bitterly, like the crowds who'd throng to a bearbaiting, hoping for blood.

St Mary's had been founded by the present Earl's grandfather; the Prioress Lucy was reputed, in fact, to be his natural daughter. The convent was situated just to the north-west of the castle, and all too soon for Joanna, she found herself passing into the inner bailey, mounting the stairs up into the great hall. So great was her tension that she had begun to suffer a slight queasiness, and she felt a surge of gratitude at sight of her brother, waiting at the door to escort her into the hall.

'I'm late, am I not?'

'You are worth waiting for,' Richard said loyally. 'But no matter. The Earl and Isabelle have given him a right proper welcome, Isabelle in particular. Indeed, to see them together, you'd swear they'd been friends all their lives long.' There was a faint edge to Richard's voice; Joanna was becoming aware that he no longer looked upon their stepmother as he once had, with uncritical, adoring eyes. But she felt only a throb of envy, at that moment would have bartered her soul for Isabelle's bright, breezy chatter, her insouciant ease of manner.

'Dearest, at last!' Isabelle was, as ever, encircled by laughing men. She held out her hand to Joanna, turning towards the man standing at her left. Joanna had a fleeting impression of a sun-browned face, alert, dark eyes, as she sank down in a hasty curtsy. He raised her up at once; she was thankful when he released her hands as soon as she was on her feet, made no attempt to touch her.

'Is she not sweet? I told Your Grace you were a fortunate man, did I not?' Isabelle smiled fondly at Joanna, who wanted to go right through the floor. Nor was her embarrassment lessened any when Llewelyn murmured a conventional gallantry in reply. For Jesu, what else could the man say? She gave Isabelle a reproachful look, but worse was to come. They would, of course, wish to be alone, Isabelle said gaily, and made a great show of shepherding them into the comparative privacy of the nearest window seat, withdrawing so ostentatiously that she virtually guaranteed they'd be the centre of all eyes.

Joanna had been relying upon Isabelle to ease the awkwardness of this first encounter, and now she was utterly at a loss, could not think of a single conversational gambit. All she could do was to blurt out her greatest fear.

'My lord . . . there is a favour I would ask of you, if I may. I do have a pet dog. I am very fond of her, and it would grieve me greatly to have to part with her. May I take her with me into Wales? I have a travel basket for her, and she'd be no trouble, in truth she –'

'Of course you may take your dog. Or whatever else you desire.'

'Thank you, my lord!' Joanna's relief was such that she dared look him fully in the face for the first time. What she saw took her breath. His eyes were very dark, a midnight brown, were measuring her in troubled appraisal. In that instant before their eyes met and his face changed, she read quite clearly his dismay.

Until now, she'd never given a thought to his expectations, had never thought of him at all, except as a shadowy figure outlined against an alien landscape foreboding and bleak, a stranger mysterious and somewhat sinister. But this man was no phantom threat; he was all too real, and all too disappointed. Colour rose in Joanna's face; she quickly looked away, stared down at her clasped hands, at her betrothal ring. She need not offer apology to him for what she was . . . or was not. She was the King of England's daughter, and he had wanted this marriage, had been no less eager than her father to make the match. And yet . . . and yet why should she feel such surprise? She had a mirror, had she not? Did she truly need to be told once again that beauty was to be found in skin lily-white, in hair like flax, in eyes like Isabelle's? Not in slanting cat eyes, ink-black hair, and the dusky skin of a Saracen . . . sallow skin.

'My lord? You asked me . . . what?'

'If you have always lived with your father the King.'

'Since I was five,' Joanna said swiftly, grateful that he seemed willing to do what she could not, to exercise some control over the conversation.

'And your lady mother?'

Normally, Joanna was very reluctant to discuss her mother; those memories were like imperfectly healed wounds, painful if probed too deeply. But now she was quite willing to talk of Clemence, so great was her dread of silence, and she answered readily. He continued to feed her questions, about her childhood, her father, and slowly she began to relax somewhat, to follow his lead.

'. . . and then these enormous dogs rushed in, barking fit to wake the dead. I was so fearful, but my father picked me up, all dirty and ragged as I was, held me out of harm's way. I did not yet know, of course, who he was, but –' Joanna stopped suddenly, in some confusion. What had ever possessed her to tell this man something so very personal? Isabelle was right; he was indeed, a good listener, too good.

'I did not mean to talk so much of myself,' she said, suddenly self-conscious again. 'Will you not tell me about you, my lord?'

'What would you most like to know?'

Joanna considered. She knew next to nothing about him, but there was one question in particular she yearned to ask. 'I would like to know about your children, my lord. Would you tell me of them?'

'With pleasure. I have six, two boys and four girls . . . by two mothers,' Llewelyn added, with a faint smile, and Joanna blushed, taken aback that he should have read her thoughts so easily. Her father's seven children had all been born to different women.

'Do they all live at your court?'

'The four eldest do. Gruffydd, my firstborn, is ten. Gwladys is eight, Marared six, and Gwenllian nigh on five.' Llewelyn paused, and then again answered an unspoken question. 'Their mother is dead.'

'And the other two?'

He smiled. 'Tegwared and Anghared, the twins. They lack but a fortnight of their first birthday.'

Joanna raised startled eyes to his face. It was a rather common belief that for a woman to give birth to twins, she must have lain with two men. Yet Llewelyn seemed neither embarrassed nor defensive. Was it, she wondered, that he had such faith in the woman? Or in himself?

'I was most fortunate in that my lord father married a woman who showed me naught but kindness. I shall not do less for your children, my lord,' she said earnestly.

She'd sought to please him, was bewildered to see that she had not. He looked suddenly sombre, pensive. For the first time, a prolonged silence fell between them.

'Tell me, have you begun to learn Welsh, as I suggested in my last letter?'

Joanna tensed again. 'No, my lord,' she admitted reluctantly, watching him anxiously for signs of anger.

'Well, there will be time enough.'

Indeed, she thought bleakly. A lifetime.

'Joanna.' It was the first time he'd called her by name. 'Now that I've satisfied your curiosity, I would have you do the same for me. I should like to see the colour of your hair. Will it distress you if I remove your veil and wimple?'

Caught completely off balance, she could only shake her head mutely. She willed herself to sit very still, not to flinch as he leaned over, unpinned her veil. His fingers were quite sure, barely touched her cheek. Joanna continued to stare down into her lap. After a time, she felt his hand under her chin, gently forcing her face up to his. As their eyes met, he smiled. 'You do look very Welsh.'

'Do I?' she whispered. He was much more sympathetic than she'd expected him to be. He'd been kind to seek to put her at ease, and he was being kinder now in trying to mask his obvious disappointment. But she could think only that in less than twenty-four hours he would have the right to strip away her clothing as he had just stripped away her veil, to bare her body as he'd bared her hair.

'My lord . . . would you think me unforgivably rude if I asked your leave to withdraw? I . . . I have so much still to do ere the wedding . . .'

'I understand, Joanna,' he said slowly. He rose as she did, brought her hand up to his mouth. 'Until the morrow.'

Ednyved ap Cynwrig made his way across the great hall, to where Llewelyn stood by the window seat. 'What, has the bride fled so soon, and ere I could get more than a glimpse of her? Well? Is she fat, thin, plain, pretty? From the look on your face, I'd wager that she was not much to your liking.'

'And you'd lose.' Llewelyn was frowning after Joanna's retreating figure. 'She has the makings of a beauty. But Jesu, how very young she is! I'd not expected that, in truth.'

'To thirty-three, fourteen is bound to seem close to the cradle.' Ednyved gave Llewelyn a shrewdly appraising look, said, no longer flippant, 'Many girls are wed at fourteen, Llewelyn, are ripe for the marriage bed even at that age.'

'Not this one. She's a child, Ednyved, a child being forced into a marriage she greatly fears.' Llewelyn glanced down, saw that Joanna had, in her haste, forgotten her veil and wimple. He picked up the veil, fingered the fragile silk weave. 'Poor little lass, trying so hard to do what her elders expect of her . . .'

Joanna's bridal clothes were the loveliest she'd ever had. Everything was new, even the garters for her stockings. Her chemise was of soft white linen, the gown of finest Florentine silk, as was the embroidered bliaut. Joanna knew they were becoming. Isabelle had insisted upon choosing the colours herself, and Isabelle had an unerring eye, selecting a deep emerald for the gown, a much paler shade of green for the tightly laced bliaut, delicately threaded through with gold. Since Joanna would wear her hair loose and flowing down her back, to proclaim she came to her marriage bed a virgin, there was no wimple, merely a thin, circular veil, as light as air, to be held in place by a gold circlet.

Joanna smoothed the skirt of her gown, remembering another outfit of green and gold, laid out at the foot of John's bed that first morning she'd awakened in Rouen. She stood for a moment, staring into the mirror Blanche was holding for her inspection, and then turned towards Isabelle and Ela. 'I am ready.'

Custom decreed that a bride's father or guardian be the one to lead her mount to the church. Since both John and Joanna's uncle Will were in Winchester, the Earl of Chester had offered to act in John's stead, and it was he who lifted Joanna up into the saddle. The mare, a glossy, small-boned chestnut, was Llewelyn's bride's gift to

Joanna. She'd never had a horse of her own before, and such a gift would normally have transported her into a state of high excitement. Now, however, she felt nothing. The prancing mare, the crowds lining Bridge Street, the sunlight so bright upon the banners above her head, all lacked reality for her. There was a strange dreamlike quality to the day, as if she were watching from afar as a girl very like her rode to her wedding with a Welsh Prince.

The precincts of the abbey of St Werburgh were already filled to overflowing with the people of Chester, eager for the spectacle of a royal wedding. Llewelyn was awaiting Joanna by the south door of the church, for it was there that their wedding vows would be exchanged; weddings were traditionally performed out in the open before as many witnesses as possible. He came forward to meet her, smiling. Time took an abrupt lurch forward, and with bewildering suddenness, she found herself standing before Geoffrey de Muschamp, Bishop of Chester, holding hands with a stranger.

Almost before she knew it, Llewelyn was pledging her his troth. She drew a deep breath, said in a clear, carrying voice, 'I, Joanna, do take thee, Llewelyn, in holy Church, as my wedded husband, forsaking all others, in sickness and health, in riches and poverty, in well and in woe, till death us do part, and thereto I plight thee my troth.'

The Bishop having blessed the ring, Llewelyn took Joanna's left hand, slipped the ring in turn upon each of her fingers, saying, 'In the name of the Father and of the Son and of the Holy Ghost.' Sliding it then upon her third finger, he gave her hand a gentle squeeze. 'With this ring, I thee wed.'

The crowd was cheering, surged forward as Llewelyn and Joanna dipped into the alms dish, scattered coins in their midst. Joanna was then embraced in turn by Isabelle, Ela, and the Countess of Chester. But it was Llewelyn now, not Chester, who led her into the church, for with her marriage she had passed from her father's control to that of her husband.

As little as she remembered of the wedding ceremony, Joanna remembered even less of the Mass of Trinity that followed. It was cool and dark within, pleasantly scented with incense. At one point, she heard the Bishop intone, 'Let this woman be amiable as Rachel, wise as Rebecca, faithful as Sarah,' and she realized, with bemusement, that he was speaking of her. She was shamefully ignorant of the Scriptures, could not for the life of her remember what Rachel,

221

Rebecca, and Sarah had done. She could think only of Ruth, Ruth, who'd gone forth into an alien land, who'd said, 'Whither thou goest, I will go, thy people shall be my people, and thy God my God.'

Llewelyn was approaching the altar now, to receive from the Bishop the kiss of peace. And then he was back at her side, lifting her veil. She raised her face obediently for him to transmit the kiss to her, felt his lips upon hers, a light, warm touch, almost impersonal.

Chester had always suffered a reputation as one of the most violence-prone cities of the realm; Cheshiremen were notorious for their thin skins, their ready swords. The Welsh were no less renowned for the touchiness of their tempers, for the ease with which they took affront. It was a volatile mixture, and Llewelyn and the Earl of Chester had done what they could to minimize the dangers. It was for this reason that Ascension Day had been chosen for the wedding; men who'd care little about breaking the King's Peace might think twice before breaking God's Peace as well. For the same reason, the wedding feast was served immediately upon their return from the church, in hopes that men well wined and dined would be lulled into good will, be less likely to yield to age-old antagonisms.

Joanna had never before eaten from the dais, except on that long-ago day in Rouen, sitting on John's lap. Now she sat between Llewelyn and the Earl of Chester, did her best to feign interest in the food being offered her, venison and roast partridge, fresh herring, each course crowned with an elaborate sugared subtlety. She was grateful that the conversational demands being made upon her were minimal. Llewelyn was being monopolized by Isabelle, seated at his left, and Chester, a dour, taciturn man, already balding although only in his thirties, was not much given to small talk. Joanna knew he'd only recently been restored to her father's favour; John had suspected him of conspiring with the Welsh Prince, Gwenwynwyn of Powys. If it were true, he could not be deriving much pleasure from playing host to Llewelyn, Gwenwynwyn's chief rival. But mayhap it was not true; Papa's suspicions were not always grounded in fact. Pray God his campaign would go well. Joanna laid down a tart, untasted. How would she even know? Whilst he was fighting a war in Normandy, she would be deep in Wales, utterly isolated from those she most loved.

Across the great hall, voices rose suddenly. Joanna saw both Llewelyn and Chester stiffen. Sharing a trencher and wine cup with

Llewelyn, she was not long in becoming aware that her husband was not drinking. Joanna was puzzled; such abstinence was highly unusual at a wedding feast, where male guests seemed to feel a social obligation to drink themselves into oblivion. Her unease grew as she realized that Chester, too, was cold sober.

The voices were growing louder. A bench was tipped over; a woman screamed. Joanna gasped as a man pushed away from the table, fumbled for the hilt of his sword. Llewelyn was already on his feet, shouting in Welsh. The man turned, reluctantly let his sword slide back down its scabbard. By then, Llewelyn had reached them, with Chester right on his heels. A brief angry exchange followed, with Llewelyn tongue-lashing the Welshman and Chester berating the Norman. The offenders lapsed into a sullen silence, but tension gripped the hall, spread by murmurs of discontent, voiced in two tongues. Joanna bit her lip, watched as Llewelyn took Chester aside, spoke in an urgent undertone. Chester nodded, stepped back, and sent a servant hastening from the hall.

Joanna gave Llewelyn a questioning look as he resumed his seat, but he said only, 'I thought it time for a diversion.'

Joanna was not long in finding out what he had in mind. Servants were entering the hall, carrying several huge baked pies. As all watched, they cut carefully into the crust, freeing more than a dozen small birds. The birds soared upward, circling and swooping over the tables as the men and women below laughed and cheered, eagerly awaiting the finale, the release of three sleek sparrow hawks. What resulted was utter chaos, with dogs barking in berserk frenzy, and men clambering up on benches to better view the kills, laying tipsy wagers upon the outcome, animosities forgotten in the excitement of the hunt.

'That was indeed clever, my lord,' Joanna said approvingly, and Llewelyn laughed.

'It was my man's fault. There is a hamlet across the Dee called Hanbridge, but it's been taken so often by the Welsh that we call it Tre-boeth, the "burned town". It is one thing to do so amongst ourselves, quite another to do so amidst a hall full of Normans . . . as Rosser should have known.'

'I see.' Joanna watched as a feather wafted slowly downward, came to rest in a tureen of sorrel soup. If the Welsh had such a hatred for Normans, how would they ever accept her as Llewelyn's wife?

Once the trestle tables were cleared away, there was dancing, but after there'd been two spills, caused by over-exuberant dancers whose coordination was rather the worse for wine, Chester signalled for less risky entertainment: jugglers, a man with trained marmosets, several minstrels eager to sing for their supper. The song requests were becoming increasingly bawdy, and Joanna was once more growing tense. It was not that she found the suggestive lyrics objectionable in themselves, but that they reminded her of what still lay ahead, the bedding down revelries and the consummation of her marriage.

Turning away from a group clustered around the wittiest of the minstrels, she collided with Maude de Braose, spilling some of her drink upon the sleeve of Maude's gown.

'I am sorry, Madame. I did not see you.' It was a listless apology, indifferently offered, but the best she could do in the circumstances.

'Obviously.' Maude's voice was tart, her eyes unfriendly. 'You've been wandering about the hall like a ghost. Can you not at least make a pretence that this marriage is to your liking?'

The unfairness of that took Joanna's breath away; she'd been trying so hard to hide her true feelings. 'I assure you this marriage is very much to my liking, Madame.' Even had she believed Llewelyn ab Iorwerth to be the veritable Antichrist, nothing on earth could have induced her to admit that to Maude. But she was never to know what imp then took possession of her tongue, was even more startled than Maude to hear herself add, 'Your advice I can well do without Madame. I do, however, need a fresh cup of wine.'

Maude's eyebrows shot upward. 'You want me to fetch it for you?' she demanded, openly incredulous.

'Yes.' But Joanna had never in her life given an order to a man or woman of rank, and there'd been a brief hesitation, a hesitation that did not escape Maude.

'I think not,' she said coolly, and turned away.

'Lady de Braose!' Joanna's voice had carried; others were looking her way. Still not sure how she'd got herself into such a predicament, she stared helplessly at the older woman, knowing neither how to enforce her command nor how to extricate herself without loss of face. Maude was looking at her mockingly, and she crimsoned, going hot with humiliation and impotent anger. She opened her mouth, having no idea what she was going to say, and then saw Maude's face change, saw her smile splinter into frozen fragments. Joanna spun around, to find Llewelyn standing just behind her.

'What are you drinking, Joanna? Hippocras?'

She nodded, watched wide-eyed as he held the wine cup out to Maude. 'Lady Maude, if you will,' he said, smiling. Maude was of a sudden as deeply flushed as Joanna, but she managed a stiff smile of her own.

'As it pleases Your Grace, it would be my pleasure.'

'No, Lady Maude. As it pleases my wife.'

Joanna wanted nothing so much as to sit down in a quiet corner; she felt as if her knees had turned to butter. She drew several uneven breaths, nerving herself to look up into Llewelyn's face. No matter how harshly he might treat her in time to come, she'd always be grateful for what he'd just done, would never forget it. But what must he think of her, that she would make such a fool of herself? If he were furious, she could scarce blame him, and she said, very low, 'Thank you, my lord. I'm so sorry, in truth I am. I did not mean to make a scene. I just wanted to . . .'

'To settle an old score?' he suggested softly, and as she raised her eyes to his, she saw in them only amused understanding.

If the Normans were indifferent and the Welsh aloof, there were wedding guests present who were absolutely elated by the marriage, the Marcher lords with Welsh holdings. One by one, they sought Joanna out, to wish her well, to express the hope that she'd soon bear Llewelyn a son, to praise her father's wisdom and foresight in making of Llewelyn an ally. She was surrounded now by a group of these men, one of whom was, to her delight, none other than Aubrey de Mara. He had fallen into Prince Llewelyn's hands when he took Castle Mold some years back, he explained, and whilst waiting for his ransom to be paid, a mutual regard had developed. He did indeed think of the Prince as a friend, would never have missed his wedding to a girl he remembered with such fondness.

Joanna had no interest, however, in reminiscing of Mirebeau. Her concern was more immediate, was in learning all she could of the man to whom she was now wed. She was most interested, therefore, in what Llewelyn's Corbet kin had to say, listened attent- ively as Hugh Corbet obligingly related anecdotes of Llewelyn's Shropshire boyhood. Hugh gave her more comfort than even he knew; the mere fact that he'd remained on such friendly terms with Llewelyn, although his wife, Llewelyn's mother, was five years dead, was to Joanna reason for reassurance.

But she did not like Hugh's nephew, Thomas Corbet, not at all; she'd been greatly offended by several snide remarks he'd made, revealing a deep-seated dislike for Llewelyn. To make such remarks in her hearing was in the worst of taste, was to imply that she was ignorant of the most basic loyalties a wife owed her husband, and she soon made an excuse to escape the Corbet company.

A man lurched towards her, so unsteady on his feet that he could not stop in time, pushed Joanna back against the wall. She'd been introduced to him earlier in the evening, remembered him only because he was surely one of the last men she'd have expected to find at her wedding, Fulk Fitz Warin, the Shropshire baron who'd led an abortive rebellion against her father. He'd eventually capitulated, sued for John's pardon and, to the surprise of many, had received it. That seemed to be what was on his mind; he launched into a rather incoherent speech of gratitude, although she could not be sure whether he was praising her father for pardoning him or Llewelyn for giving him refuge.

Joanna was more amused than affronted; the man was so obviously besotted. She was glad, none the less, when several of his companions, slightly more sober, came to her rescue. They, too, had earlier introduced themselves as friends of her husband, Stephen and Baldwin de Hodnet; with extravagantly elaborate apologies, they sought now to distract Fitz Warin. But he, with the peculiar obstinacy of the inebriated, was determined to continue his disjointed conversation with Joanna, assuring her solemnly that he wished only the best for her, that Prince Llewelyn was indeed a lucky man, and then, to Joanna's horror, that it was surely time to escort her and her lord husband to the bridal chamber.

Joanna stared at him in dismay. His voice was overly loud, carried. At any moment, others might hear, pick up the chant, and she was not ready yet, needed more time. Her fear of the marriage bed was not a fear of Llewelyn himself, for he had given her no reason to think he'd be brutal or abusive. Her fear was rather of the unknown. She could not imagine what it would be like, other than that there would be pain, and she shrank from the thought of being used so intimately by a man who was, in all respects, a stranger to her.

But if her aversion to the bedding itself was rooted in ignorance, her fear of the bedding revels was grounded in experience. She'd been to countless weddings, knew all too well what to expect. The women would take her up to the bridal chamber, where she would be undressed and made ready for her husband. The men would then follow with Llewelyn, would see that he was stripped and put into bed with her. Even under ideal circumstances, the bedding ceremony was an open invitation to unseemly and bawdy behaviour, to raunchy, crude humour; at worst, it could degenerate into a drunken brawl. Joanna dreaded the bedding revels even more than she did the actual consummation of her marriage, and she pleaded now with Fitz Warin, 'Do hush, please! Not so loud!'

He merely blinked at her in bleary incomprehension, but at that moment, much to Joanna's relief, Llewelyn sauntered over and not only managed to quiet Fitz Warin, but was able to send the man reeling off in search of the Earl of Chester.

'Thank you,' Joanna said, as soon as the de Hodnets went weaving off after Fitz Warin, vowing to keep him out of trouble. Thanking Llewelyn was, she thought, getting to be a habit. But he did have a most convenient sense of timing, in truth. It occurred to her suddenly to wonder if he could possibly be keeping an eye on her, but she had no time to ponder the unlikelihood of that, forgot all else when he said:

'I could not help hearing. I gather you'd as soon shun the bedding revels?'

Joanna gave him a startled look, quickly averted her eyes. She was not accustomed to having her face read as easily as this, did not like it in the least. But she was too dispirited to lie. 'Yes, I would,' she admitted, offering no further explanation. She was tired of struggling to camouflage her reluctance, to play her part. Let him think what he would.

Llewelyn was pleased, for she'd touched in him a protective chord from their first moments together in the window seat. He welcomed this opportunity, wanting to ease her qualms if he could, to see the fear fade from her eyes. Nor would he deny that the challenge of seeking to outwit an entire hall full of people had in itself an almost irresistible appeal.

'In a few moments, Joanna, I want you to make your way towards the south end of the hall . . . without attracting attention. Once you reach the door, just wait there for me. Can you do that?'

'Yes, but . . . but why?'

'Did you not say you had no taste for the bedding revels?'

'I do not understand,' Joanna said slowly. 'We could never hope

227

to escape the hall unseen. Nor could you forbid the revelries. Too many men are drunk, beyond reason.'

'I can see your father never told you much of his campaigns, did he? You're woefully ignorant of battle tactics,' Llewelyn said, and grinned. 'No more questions. You must take me on trust, love, or not at all!'

The unexpected endearment so flustered Joanna that she abandoned further argument, did as he bade. By the time she'd taken up position near the door, she'd managed to guess what he had in mind; a quick glance back over her shoulder caught him in whispered collusion with two of his men. But even though she was expecting what happened next, the realism of the brawl took her by surprise. A shove, a snarl, and suddenly they were rolling about on the floor, pummelling one another with enough verve to draw all eyes. Joanna, too, found herself straining to see, did not even notice Llewelyn's approach until he grabbed her hand, pulled her through the doorway.

'Make haste,' he warned, 'ere we be missed,' hurrying her across the solar, towards the corner stairwell. They were only half way up when they heard the sudden noise rising from the hall. Llewelyn swore, quickened his pace, all but dragging a breathless Joanna after him. By the time they reached the top of the stairs, they could hear a hue and cry below, but by then Llewelyn had the door open, pushed Joanna inside. He was laughing so hard that he could hardly get the bolt into place, managed it only moments before the first of their pursuers lurched against the door.

Joanna sank down, panting, upon a coffer. 'My lord, that was wonderful!' she exclaimed, looking at Llewelyn with shining eyes.

Still laughing, Llewelyn moved to the table, reached for a wine flagon. 'Do you not think it time you began to make use of my given name?' he asked, and with that, Joanna's excitement congealed into ice. 'Do you want wine?'

Joanna shook her head, at once regretted her refusal. Mayhap wine would have warmed, have thawed this frozen feeling that seemed centred in the pit of her stomach. Unable to meet Llewelyn's eyes, she glanced nervously about the chamber. Isabelle and the other ladies had done their work well. There were fresh rushes for the floor, a plentitude of candles, wine and wafers, a well-stoked fire, for May nights could be chill in Cheshire. The enormous bed was one of Chester's best, curtained and piled high with coverlets; there were even flower petals strewn over the turned-back sheets.

'Oh no!' Joanna was on her feet, staring at the bed. 'My lo – Llewelyn, the blessing! I did not think of it before, but in shunning the revels we'll forfeit, as well, the priest's blessing of our marriage bed!'

'Well, that can be remedied easily enough. We need only open the door.'

Joanna's hesitation was brief. From the noise in the stairwell, it sounded as if half the wedding party was congregating outside the door. No longer pounding for admittance, they'd begun to serenade the bridal couple with ribald good humour, interspersing the song with rather explicit encouragements and instructions.

'No, let's make do without the blessing,' she said hastily, and Llewelyn bit back a smile. Setting the wine cup down, he said:

'Joanna, come here.'

She did, slanting one swift look up at him through her lashes, a look of involuntary entreaty.

'Your veil is askew.' Tossing it on to the table, he let his hand linger upon her hair. Her lashes now shadowed her cheeks. She scarcely seemed to be breathing, so still was she, but her body was rigid under his touch; sliding his fingers along her throat, he could feel the wild throbbing of her pulse.

When had he first realized he could not take this little girl to bed? When she'd fled from the window seat, leaving behind a rose-coloured veil? Or was it when she'd begged him to let her keep her dog, sounding for all the world like one of his own daughters? He leaned down, brushed his lips against her forehead. He could find in himself no desire to bed a child. Mayhap if she were naked under him in bed . . . But why should he force himself to a coupling that would give him little pleasure and her none at all? It had been only two days, after all, since he'd lain with Cristyn. He felt no particular need for a woman tonight, would as soon sleep; in truth, it had been no small strain, seeking to keep his men and Chester's from each other's throats. But how to explain it best to the lass, to keep her from seeing his restraint as rejection?

'I would not have you fear me, Joanna. I would not ever hurt you, God's truth, I would not.'

'I shall do my best to be a good wife,' Joanna said, almost inaudibly, sounding so young that Llewelyn felt a sharp pang of pity.

'Joanna, listen. You need not deny your fears, not to me. It is

229

only natural that you should have such qualms. I think, though, that I can ease your mind. We have time enough and more, need not consummate our marriage this first night. There is no reason why we cannot wait until I am not such a stranger to you.'

Joanna stared at him open-mouthed. She did not know what to say, almost thanked him, realizing just in time how insulting that would sound. He'd turned away, moving to extinguish the candles. She watched until he began to undress, then retreated to the other side of the bed, fumbling with the lacings of her bliaut. Unlike Llewelyn, who undressed with casual haste, letting his clothes drop where they lay, she took her time, carefully folding each garment in turn, not approaching the bed until he was already settled under the coverlets. Sliding in on her side of the bed, she tensed as Llewelyn leaned towards her, but he merely kissed her lightly on the cheek, murmured, 'Sleep well, Siwan.'

Only then did Joanna relax, stretch out on the sheets. She lay very still for a time, listening to Llewelyn's even breathing beside her in the dark, utterly bewildered by the perversity of her own emotions. She should be so thankful, so grateful for this reprieve. And she was . . . So why, then, was there this strange sense of . . . almost of let-down? Why was there such a flat, empty feeling? It was not at all uncommon for a man to wed a very young girl, not laying with her until she was of age. But she was not a child. She was fourteen, fully two years older than Isabelle when Papa had bedded her. No man would ever have abstained from Isabelle's bed, that she knew for certès. How little to Llewelyn's liking she must be.

Without warning, tears filled her eyes. She blinked them back angrily, wiped her face on the corner of the sheet. She would not give in to self-pity. She had no cause to feel sorry for herself. Llewelyn could have been so different, could have been arrogant, crude, even cruel. But he was none of those things. Had he not been Welsh, had he only been a Norman lord, she would have been thanking God for her good fortune. And the worst was now over, their first meeting, the wedding, the bedding revels, the – 'Oh, Jesus God!'

Sitting upright in bed, she reached over, shook Llewelyn's shoulder. 'Llewelyn, Llewelyn, wake up . . . please!' He awakened at her touch, but looked at her so blankly that she realized he did not at once remember who she was. 'The sheets . . . come morning, the wedding party will enter our chamber, will examine the sheets to see if they be bloodied, to see if I came to my marriage bed a virgin.

But the sheets will be clean! They'll be clean, and I . . . I'll be shamed, shamed before all . . .'

Llewelyn swore under his breath; the words were Welsh, but his tone needed no translation. Joanna shrank back. For a long moment his eyes rested upon her face; even in the firelight, her pallor showed all too clearly. And then he threw the covers back, rose from the bed. Joanna heard him bump into the table, curse again, and she pulled the sheet up under her chin, having no idea what he was searching for in the dark.

There was a sudden flare of light; Llewelyn had at last found flint and tinder. He lingered by the table long enough to drink what remained in his wine cup. Now that he was fully awake, his sense of humour was beginning to reassert itself, and he was laughing quietly to himself by the time he returned to the bed; this was, after all, hardly the way he had expected to pass his wedding night.

'Hold this,' he said, thrusting a candle towards Joanna. Her eyes widened at sight of the slender dagger blade, and he could not help laughing again; what in God's name did she think he meant to do with it? 'I hope you do not mind, love, if you lose your maidenhead with only modest bleeding? I've been fighting for nigh on twenty years, and have had my share of hurts, but I can say for certès that never will I get a stranger scar!'

Joanna said nothing, watched as he drew the blade against the underside of his forearm, staunched the bleeding with the sheets. She was very close at that moment to hating him; what was to him such a source of obvious amusement was to her an acute humiliation. How could he laugh at her like this, be so cruel? Did he not realize how it shamed her, that she must fake the loss of her virginity, when other wives, no matter how plain, were wanted, bedded, even cherished?

Llewelyn was leaning over, concealing the knife under the bed, and she breathed upon the candle. When he would have kissed her cheek, she averted her face, and he gave her a sudden thoughtful look, but he said only, 'You'd best sleep now, Siwan. We do depart for Wales on the morrow.'

'You did call me that before . . . Shé-one. What does it mean?'

'Siwan?' Llewelyn yawned. 'It is Welsh for Joan or Joanna.'

'I am Joanna! Not Siwan, Joanna! I'll not lose my name, too!' No sooner were the words out of her mouth than Joanna froze, appalled by what she'd done. A wife had no right to speak so to her husband.

231

Women were beaten for much less. Llewelyn had raised himself up on his elbow, was staring at her, his face unreadable in the shadowy light. She swallowed, whispered, 'I am sorry, my lord, so sorry –'

'No, Joanna, you owe me no apology,' he interrupted, and then added something utterly incomprehensible to her. 'You see,' he said softly, 'my mother's name was Marared . . . not Margaret.' There was a pause, and then he rolled over, reached for his pillow. 'Joanna it shall be. But I ought to warn you: I do not know what my people will make of it. Most of them speak no French . . . and there is no letter j in the Welsh alphabet.'

The chamber was quiet. Feeling somehow as if she'd won the battle but lost the war, Joanna slid over, until the width of the bed was between them. It was only then that the full impact of his words registered with her. On the morrow, he'd said, they would depart for Wales. She'd been wrong, so very wrong. The worst was not over.

16

May, 1206
Aber, North Wales

Wales, Llewelyn explained to Joanna, was divided into cantrefs and commotes, similar in nature to the English shires. His favourite palace was at Aber, the royal seat of the commote of Arllechwedd Uchaf, fifty-three miles west of Chester. It was a journey of two days; they rode into Aber at dusk on Saturday.

'We're home, Joanna.' Reining in beside her, Llewelyn smiled. 'Aber Gwyngregyn – mouth of the white shell river.'

'A beautiful name,' Joanna said faintly. Only now was her breathing and heartbeat getting back to normal. She'd never been so frightened as in the past few hours, clinging dizzily to her mare's saddle pommel as the horse picked its way along an alpine trail of truly treacherous dimensions; so narrow no two horses could ride abreast, so close to the cliff that Joanna could hear the pounding of surf against the rocks below. The pass of Penmaenmawr, Llewelyn called it, Welsh for 'end of the large stone'. By then, alerted by Joanna's chalk-white pallor, he'd taken the mare's reins himself and, as the trail wound ever upward, Joanna had at last simply closed her eyes, sought to concentrate only upon the reasssuring murmur of Llewelyn's voice. She was embarrassed at showing her fear so nakedly, although at least she'd retained more dignity than Blanche, who, when not whimpering, was sobbing prayers to every saint in the Church calendar. Joanna belatedly understood why Llewelyn had declined the Earl of Chester's offer of a baggage cart. She could only marvel at the nonchalance of the Welsh, who braved these heights with the ease of eagles, and she was grateful when Llewelyn, after assuring her that Aber was not perched upon a mountain peak, confessed that he had no liking himself for the sea, never set foot on shipboard without feeling his stomach lurch, sink like a stone.

She was indeed lucky, Joanna reminded herself now, had no

233

cause for complaint in the husband God and her father had given her. And she would do her best somehow to make his world her own. With that resolution, she drew rein for her first look upon Aber.

Llewelyn's palace was encircled by a deep manmade ditch, fortified by wooden palisades, much like John's favourite hunting lodges at Freemantle and Clipstone. Passing through the gatehouse into a bailey packed with people, Joanna saw wooden buildings such as she'd expect in any Norman lord's manor: stables and barn, a kiln and kitchens, privy chambers, kennels for Llewelyn's hunting dogs, quarters for those not bedding down in the great hall. Joanna was not sure what she'd thought to find, but she felt relief, none the less, that her surroundings were so familiar, were neither alien nor exotic.

Llewelyn had no sooner dismounted than he was engulfed by well-wishers. For the moment forgotten, Joanna watched as a young boy and several girls ran forward, flung themselves into Llewelyn's arms. Joanna was taken aback by the exuberance of their welcome; she would never have given her father so uninhibited a public greeting. But she was not as startled as she might have been twenty-four hours earlier. In that brief span, she'd seen ample evidence to document a Norman aphorism, that there was not a Welshman born who did know his proper place. For certès, she thought, none of her father's subjects would have dared approach him as these Welsh men and women were crowding around Llewelyn.

Llewelyn had remembered he was bringing back a bride and, moving towards Joanna, he reached up to lift her from the saddle. Acutely aware of all eyes upon her, she slid to the ground, smiled at her husband's children. They were attractive youngsters, but solemn, unsmiling, and remembering her own nervous unease about meeting Isabelle, Joanna's heart went out to them.

Seated beside Llewelyn upon the dais in the great hall, Joanna received the acknowledgments of her husband's subjects, now hers, too. While the chief officers of Llewelyn's court spoke French of necessity, few of their wives did, and relieved of the need to make polite conversation, Joanna felt free to let her thoughts wander as they would. The gowns of the women were much like those at her father's court. But on their hair, they wore only thin veils. Would Llewelyn want her to put aside her wimples? The men looked rather like Papa's nobles, too, though not so finely garbed. She slanted a sideways look towards Llewelyn. His tunic was shorter than the gown in which he'd been wed, the long lavishly furred robe of a highborn Norman lord; both tunic and chausses were a subdued shade of green, his boots higher than was fashionable at her father's court, reaching to the knee. She was glad he'd dressed so richly for their wedding, would not have wanted Chester and the other lords to scorn him for the strangeness of his Welsh ways.

Mayhap life would not be as harsh and austere as she'd first feared. Looking about the great hall, she might well have been at Windsor or Winchester. And her bedchamber was in no way inferior to the royal apartments set aside for Isabelle's use. The rushes were sweet-smelling, the walls whitewashed, the bed hung with curtains, and the mattress filled with down, not straw. She'd not dared to ask Llewelyn if she would have her own quarters, like her stepmother and the queens on the Continent, and her relief had been intense and overwhelming upon finding it was so. But mingled with that relief was a reluctant sense of shame. No matter how often she told herself she had no reason for self-reproach, she flushed every time she thought of what she'd done at Rhuddlan Castle.

Llewelyn had taken Rhuddlan some ten years ago, and there they'd passed the second night of their marriage. They'd covered thirty-six miles, and Joanna was very tired. She was also utterly wretched, longing for what she'd left behind and dreading what lay ahead. Excusing herself soon after supper, she retired to their bedchamber, and when Llewelyn came to bed, she lay very still, pretending to sleep. Remembering that now, Joanna bit her lip, twisted her wedding ring until it chafed her finger. For a wife to deny her husband his marital rights was a sin of no small proportions. Not that she'd actually refused him, of course. But she could not stifle an uneasy suspicion that she'd violated the spirit, if not the letter, of her marriage vows.

Across the hall, her stepchildren had withdrawn into one of the window recesses. Joanna had been awaiting just such an opportunity to speak to them alone and, picking up Sugar, she made her way towards them. They rose at her approach, the girls staring more at Sugar than Joanna, for such small dogs were a rarity in Wales. Gruffydd, however, kept his eyes focused upon Joanna's face; they were a vivid sea-green, fringed with thick golden lashes. He was a handsome lad, Joanna thought, if very unlike his father. His sister Gwenllian shared his colouring, had pale skin and auburn hair, burnished curls spilling down her back in a cascade of copper, while Gwladys and Marared were as dark as Gruffydd and Gwenllian were fair. They were a striking quartet, but as wary as fawns, would need gentle handling. Joanna smiled, held out the dog towards Gwenllian, the youngest.

'Would you like to pet her?' The child reached out, her fingers brushing Sugar's long, silky fur, but Gwladys hissed something in Welsh, and Gwenllian jerked her hand back.

'You need not fear; she'll not bite,' Joanna said reassuringly. Getting no response, she tried another approach. 'As I do not speak Welsh, I should like to make sure that I am saying your names correctly. Griff-ith, is it not? And Glád-is? Your lord father told me that is Welsh for Claudia . . .' Her voice trailed off, for a disconcerting thought had just come to her. 'You do speak French?'

The little girls were now looking, not at Joanna, but at their brother. Gruffydd drew an audible breath. Joanna caught but one word of the outburst that followed: *Saeson*. As ignorant as she was of Welsh, she knew *Saeson* to be a contemptuous term for the English. But even had she not known its meaning, she would have needed no translation. It was there for all to read in the defiant jutting of Gruffydd's jaw, in Gwladys's black eyes, Gwenllian and Marared's shocked giggles.

'Gruffydd!' The voice was angry, was so like Llewelyn's that Joanna was startled to see a stranger. No, not a stranger, she amended, for this man's kinship to her husband was emblazoned upon his face for all to see. He had Llewelyn's colouring, the same finely-chiselled bone structure, the same deep-set dark eyes. But his mouth was not Llewelyn's; thinned and rigid, it spoke not of laughter, but of pain denied, of secrets never to be shared. He snapped a command in Welsh, and Gruffydd's colour faded. Not looking at Joanna, he mumbled:

'I ask your forgiveness, Lady, for my bad manners.'

'Of course,' Joanna said automatically. The boy's French was flawless. She watched as he fled the hall, his sisters in flustered pursuit, and all she could think of was her own first meeting with Isabelle, of how little it had taken to win her heart.

'You must pay my nephew no mind, Madame. Ten is a troublesome age.'

'You must be Lord Adda, Llewelyn's brother.' Joanna ventured a smile, and he nodded gravely, shifted his crutch so he could bow

236

over her hand. Joanna almost implored him not to make the effort, checked herself just in time.

'Do call me Joanna.' She hesitated, but who else was there to ask? 'My lord . . . Adda, will you tell me the truth? There was not much sentiment amongst your people for this marriage, was there?'

He did not reply at once, but she got the impression not that he was weighing his words, rather that he was weighing her, assessing her ability to accept honesty. 'No,' he said at last. 'Most of Llewelyn's subjects would rather he'd wed a Cymraes . . . a woman of our blood. But a Welsh wife would bring few political gains, so they'd reconciled themselves to a foreign marriage. It was thought Llewelyn would wed the daughter of the Manx King, but then your father offered you in her stead. Llewelyn would have had to be utterly mad, of course, to refuse. But not all are as clear-sighted as he, and some were affronted that he would take an English wife. I do not mean to offend you, but the Welsh have been given little reason to love the English.'

Joanna had never thought of herself as English; in fact, to one of Norman-French descent, that qualified as an insult. She did not quibble at Adda's inaccuracy, however, realizing that to the Welsh, the distinction drawn between Norman and Saxon was irrelevant. But that understanding only intensified her sense of isolation, her awareness that she was a political pledge, a hostage for England's amity.

'I thank you for your honesty, Adda. Be honest with me now, too. Tell me if you believe Gruffydd will come to accept me as his father's wife.'

Adda was silent for some moments. 'He's a headstrong boy, thinks the world of Llewelyn . . . and for five years has not had to share his father's love. It is only natural that he should resent you, see you as a rival, an intruder . . .' But Joanna was, after all, very young herself, and Adda compromised his candour with a half-truth, adding, 'Mayhap with time . . .'

'Yes, with time,' Joanna echoed, lowering her lashes to hide her hurt.

Joanna's life as Princess of Gwynedd was not utterly devoid of compensation or satisfactions. Never before had she her own private bedchamber. Never before had she had money of her own. All her life, she'd been dependent upon the generosities of others. But as

Llewelyn's consort, she had her own privy purse, was entitled to one-third of his private incomes. As far as she knew, English law made no like provision for English queens. Nor had she ever before experienced the sweetness of giving commands, of having them obeyed at once. She'd been greatly pleased when her father had engaged Blanche for her. Now she had her own household: a chaplain, seneschal, chief groom, handmaiden, candlebearer, doorkeeper, page, even her own cook and food-taster. If she wanted to write to her aunt Ela, she need only dictate to her chaplain, and within the hour a courier would be dispatched to Salisbury Castle. Bread, a staple of the Norman diet, was not as often found upon Welsh tables; they were herdsmen, not farmers. Joanna had casually confessed to a longing for wheaten bread, making but idle conversation with Blanche and Enid, her Welsh maid. The next day a freshly baked loaf was laid out by her trencher, and at every meal thereafter.

For the first time in her life, Joanna understood what a potent drink power could be. And she realized, too, that she'd not known herself as well as she once thought, that she was not so lacking in ambition, after all. It seemed that she was Eleanor of Aquitaine's granddaughter in more ways than one, a thought that gave her, in equal measure, amusement and astonishment.

But these pleasures were of fleeting moment, fireflies in the dark. The summer that followed her marriage was the most miserable of her life. Unable to speak Llewelyn's language, she felt herself an isolated island in a sea of Welsh. As she had no duties to perform, her days were unstructured, endless. She was not blind to the beauty around her. Aber faced on to the sea, offered spectacular views of the Eryri Mountains. But at night she lay awake longing for the sounds of the city, shivering at the distant howling of a wolf pack on the prowl. London, York, and Winchester seemed as far away as Jerusalem. Her husband's domain held neither towns nor cities. Nor fairs or markets. It was, to Joanna, a wild and awesome land, and she knew that Gruffydd was not alone in thinking her an intruder.

She was desperately homesick in those first weeks. Her yearning for her loved ones, for what was known and familiar to her, was a constant, unrelenting ache. She so wanted to go home, and knew that what she most wanted was now forever denied her.

The worst of her loneliness was that she did not feel connected to any other living soul. Her father and Isabelle were in Gascony. So, too, were Richard and her uncle Will. Blanche, never a comfort in the best of times, had become all but insufferable; she hated Wales, looked askance at the Welsh, drove Joanna to distraction with her whining, her constant complaints. Enid's French was inadequate for other than the most rudimentary conversation. Most of the women at Llewelyn's court spoke no French at all. One of the few who did was the Lady Gwenllian, wife to Llewelyn's friend, Ednyved ap Cynwrig. But Gwenllian offered no friendship; even her courtesy seemed grudgingly given.

Nor did Joanna have any better luck with the men. She'd hoped for a time to find an ally in her husband's brother. But Adda did not encourage her overtures. Aloof and reserved, he went his own way; only with Llewelyn did he thaw, let his defences down. Ednyved, Joanna avoided if possible. She realized his sarcasm was not meant to be spiteful, but all her life she'd been wary of sardonic tongues. Rhys ap Cadell, her husband's other intimate friend, was rarely at court that summer; his wife was in the last stages of a troublesome pregnancy, and Rhys stayed upon his own estates, awaiting Catrin's time. Men like Morgan ap Bleddyn, Llewelyn's chaplain, and Gwyn ab Ednywain, his Seneschal, were well into their forties, had little in common with a girl of fourteen.

As for her stepchildren, all Joanna's fears had come to pass. Gruffydd was not to be won over. Every smile Llewelyn bestowed upon her, Gruffydd begrudged. Each time he heard her addressed as 'Madame' or 'Your Grace', his face shadowed. Gwladys, the most devoted of disciples, loyally followed her brother's lead, and between them, they effectively curbed any conciliatory inclinations Marared or Gwenllian might have harboured. To Joanna, this was the most bitter disappointment of all.

Perversely enough, that which she had most reason to be thankful for – Llewelyn's solicitude – was yet another source of anxiety. Because he was so very good to her, she despised herself all the more for her discontent. Each time she thought of the French Queen Ingeborg, thought of the wives who'd have bartered their very souls for a husband like hers, she felt an utter ingrate. When compared to women who were beaten for trifles, treated as chattels, used only as brood mares, what had she to complain of, in truth? Isabelle had been right; many women would indeed envy her.

Not that Llewelyn was without flaws. In fact, the qualities she most admired in him, his easy self-assurance and his intelligence, were virtues with the potential to become vices. His self-assurance was occasionally flavoured with arrogance, and like many quick-witted people, he was often impatient when others were slow to follow the swiftness of his thoughts. He had a tendency to lose sight of the immediate in pursuit of the long-range goal. And his ambition was frightening to Joanna. For if her father aimed to prevent a Welsh-French alliance, Llewelyn had aims of his own. He saw their marriage as a way to keep John out of Wales, enabling him to deal with his old enemy, Gwenwynwyn of Powys. But Joanna did not think her father would give Llewelyn the free hand in Wales he seemed to expect. She remembered all too well her father's remark upon the day of her betrothal, that Llewelyn needed to be 'reined in'. She could imagine nothing worse than conflict between the two, to find herself torn between her husband, to whom she owed her loyalty, and her father, to whom she owed her love.

But Llewelyn's faults seemed of little consequence when she thought back to Chester's aloof moodiness or William de Braose's suave brutality. And in the three months of her marriage, Joanna had found much in him to admire. For all that he expected – and got – prompt obedience, he was not arbitrary, and he was rarely unfair. Once, when he'd flared up at his clerk, Hwfa ap Pilthe, in an unjustified public rebuke, he'd later sought Hwfa out and offered apology; Joanna could not remember her father ever apologizing to anyone for anything. But Llewelyn was much more easygoing than her father. He was quick to laugh, even at himself, had been amused, not affronted, when Joanna could not resist teasing that she wished she could be as sure of one thing as he was of all things. And he was unfailingly kind to her.

It was true that he did not treat her like a wife. His was more the casual, affectionate playfulness of an older brother for a much younger sister. But he never failed to smile at sight of her, saw that she was accorded all due respect as his Princess, just as he'd done on their wedding day, when he'd backed her up before Maude de Braose; she was convinced now that there was nothing coincidental in his providential appearances that night. And since their marriage, he had always been there when she most needed him, as on that dreadful day when her dog chased a squirrel on to the wooded slopes of Maes y Gaer, and she'd coming running to him in panic, for Sugar was all she had of home. He had soothed her, sent men out to search for the dog, had even forborn to tease, at least until after the animal was found.

Above all, Joanna appreciated Llewelyn's kindness in not flaunting his concubines at court. Even had she been sharing his bed, she would not have expected him to be faithful; fidelity was a marriage vow for women. She did not doubt that Llewelyn had a mistress. But he did not, as so many Norman lords did, parade his conquests before one and all, uncaring of his wife's discomfort. Not all men did swagger over their sins, of course. Her father had amazed many with his unexpected discretion after taking Isabelle as his bride. He was not faithful to Isabelle, but for a man notorious for his wenching, he showed a surprising sensitivity to Isabelle's pride. Joanna alone had not been surprised, for she knew that, in his way, her father loved Isabelle. But Llewelyn did not love her, and that made his consideration all the more remarkable to her, made her all the more grateful for it.

Llewelyn was her one comfort in a world that frightened her, and she regretted deeply that he was so often gone from Aber. He was a man always in search of additional hours in the day, juggling innumerable interests like so many coloured balls, presiding over the *Uchel Lys*, his High Court, fortifying his various mountain strongholds, consulting with vassal lords, with his *rhaglaws* and *rhingylls* – bailiffs and court officials. Like John, he travelled extensively about his realm. But John always took Isabelle with him, and Llewelyn never offered to take her.

The great hall was lit by rushlight; torches were used sparingly in Wales, pine and fir trees being less common than in England. It was a cool night for August, and a fire blazed in the centre hearth. Of all that Joanna found foreign in Wales, the altered dinner hour had been hardest for her to accept. Dinner, the main meal of the day, was served between ten and eleven in the forenoon, followed by a light supper at five. But the Welsh ate just one meal a day, and that in the evening.

The food and trestle tables had been cleared away. Llewelyn was sitting by the hearth, picking out a plaintive melody on a finely tuned harp. Joanna knew no people who loved music as the Welsh did. Every house, no matter how poor, had a harp; it passed by law to the youngest son, could never be seized for debt. Remembering how her father's lords had sneered at the Welsh passion for music, claiming that every pigsty held a harp, Joanna frowned. The unfairness of that gibe rankled. Whatever their faults, the Welsh were not at as

Normans saw them; that she could say with certainty after three months in their midst.

Llewelyn was the focal point of all eyes. While that was normally the case, there was an emotional intensity in the looks he was getting tonight, for he had given them all a bad scare. Five days ago, he and a few friends had gone off for a day's hunting. Because it was not an official circuit or *clych*, had no purpose but pleasure, he had been accompanied by only a token escort, and when the second day passed without word from him, a sense of unease began to spread. By the third day, all pretence was gone, and people were openly voicing their concern. Joanna found her sleep haunted by visions of twisting mountain trails; she could not stop thinking of the wolves that roamed the lower slopes of the Eryri Mountains, nor of the tusked wild boars that could disembowel a horse, rip apart a man with such murderous ease. But it was not until she talked to Enid that she became aware of a more sinister undertone to their fears. Fumbling for words, Enid drew upon enough broken French to convey Llewelyn's true danger, that he might have strayed too close to the Powys border. She need not say more; Joanna understood all too well. Gwenwynwyn would gladly risk war for a chance to catch Llewelyn off guard, for with Llewelyn's death, Gwenwynwyn would stand alone as the unchallenged power in North Wales.

On the fourth day, Rhys had ridden in from his own estates on the island of Môn, at once ordered out search parties. That night Joanna could not bear to withdraw to her own chambers, remained in the great hall, where word would first come. Ednyved's wife, Gwenllian, was there, too, and she made Joanna feel as if she were somehow intruding where she had no right to be. But for all the resentment smouldering in Gwenllian's eyes, Joanna was utterly unprepared to hear her remark: 'I marvel that she does pretend to such concern. Who does not know, after all, that Llewelyn's death would give her what she most craves – widowhood.' Joanna had been too shocked for anger, and thinking back upon it later, she'd sought to find excuses for the other woman, reminding herself that Gwenllian's husband was missing, too. Yet no matter how she tried to mitigate Gwenllian's malice, she knew the woman had meant for her to overhear; she'd spoken in French.

Soon after midnight, a courier from Llewelyn had ridden in. After that first surge of relief, Joanna blessed her husband's good manners, for he'd addressed the message to her, and she had the satisfaction of telling Gwenllian and the others that he was safe. There'd been a mishap, as feared, but the trouble had befallen one of Llewelyn's men; he'd taken a fall, broken a leg, had to be carried on a makeshift horse litter to the nearest shelter, the mountain priory at Beddgelert.

Remembering that now, Joanna was remembering, too, how she'd once hoped most fervently for Llewelyn's death. Not that she'd actually prayed for it; such sinful prayers were all too likely to rebound upon the one seeking them. But she had wished for his death, would willingly have bought her freedom with his blood. Yet during the past four days, she had felt only anxiety. Not once had it even crossed her mind that, with Llewelyn's death, she would be a widow, free to return to her world, her people. Why had it not? She found herself watching Llewelyn's fingers move nimbly over the harp strings; he did, as Isabelle noted, have beautiful hands. Was the answer truly so difficult? She had not known Llewelyn before; it was easy enough to wish for the death of a stranger. But now . . . now he was very real to her, a flesh and blood man with a passionate love for life, a man who'd shown her only kindness, a man she liked, liked very much.

No, she did not want Llewelyn to die, most assuredly not. She was not even sure she wanted to end their marriage. This alliance was no less important to Papa now than it had been nearly two years ago. Nor was it likely that she'd be so fortunate in her father's selection of a second husband. Moreover, in the eyes of the Holy Church, she was Llewelyn's wife, for better or worse. Mayhap if she were not wife in name only . . . mayhap then she would not be so unhappy, would not feel so utterly alone. It was not the first time this thought had occurred to her. And why not? She was old enough to be a wife, in just a month would be fifteen. Nor had she any reason to shun Llewelyn's bed. Isabelle said a woman's pleasure depended upon the man. Watching her husband, Joanna felt colour creeping into her cheeks. Llewelyn was not a man to abuse a woman, in bed or not. She had nothing to fear from him, was sure he'd be gentle, tender even.

But what did it matter that she was now willing to be a true wife to Llewelyn, when he showed no desire to take her to his bed? She could scarcely go to him, after all. She could only wait, until his need for an heir would bring him to her bed. For now she did remain in limbo, a wife and yet not a wife. Just as at her father's court. The King's bastard daughter, not truly belonging there, either.

*

243

Llewelyn put aside the harp, studied his friends with exasperated amusement. 'Jesu, to hear you all talk, I'm in need of a keeper! What did you think, that I'd go blundering into Powys like some green stripling? You should only see the day dawn, Rhys, when I do get lost in Gwynedd!'

'Not lost,' Morgan interjected dryly. 'It did cross our minds that you might have deliberately sought to lure Gwenwynwyn into breaking the truce.'

'Well, what better bait? That is a thought well worth exploring. But you should have known I'd not have been such a fool as to try it with only ten men.'

'How many have you in mind?' Adda asked laconically, and Llewelyn laughed.

'It'll not take as many as I once thought . . . thanks to my father-in-law, the English King. If Gwenwynwyn expects John to pull his chestnuts from the fire, they'll be well roasted, in truth.'

Rhys's eyes kindled with sudden interest. He knew that Llewelyn's dislike of the Powys Prince was as much personal as political; Gwenwynwyn was responsible for the murder of Llewelyn's uncle Owain at Carreghova, and a blood-debt demanded blood payment. 'Are you sure that John will not interfere?'

'As sure as any man can be when dealing with a snake. John and I came to an understanding at Worcester; it was that which he used to sweeten his offer of marriage. He gets what he wants, me as ally . . . expecting, I dare say, that a son-in-law will be easier to keep on a short leash. I get what I want, Powys. And Gwenwynwyn gets . . . trouble.'

They all laughed at that, but Ednyved could not help cautioning, 'Assuming, of course, that John can be trusted.'

Llewelyn grinned. 'I know what you're thinking, that it's risky, indeed, to sup with the Devil. But rest assured; I do plan to use a very long spoon!'

Glancing across the hall, Llewelyn's gaze was drawn to his girl-wife. Such an innocent-looking lass, a sweet bird in the hand, so unlikely an instrument of Gwenwynwyn's downfall. But there was a sadness about her that he'd never before noticed; how forlorn she seemed, a flower put down in alien soil. Rising, he crossed to her, leaned over to murmur, 'It occurs to me, lass, that you've yet to see much of my homeland. Shall we remedy that? On the morrow, should you like me to take you into the Eryri Mountains, to show you those sights closest to my heart?' He'd spoken on impulse, and it was an offer that would cause him no small inconvenience, would result in the utter disruption of his plans for the week, but he thought himself more than repaid now by the delighted smile that lit up Joanna's face.

It was to be one of the happiest days Joanna had known in months. Although both Ednyved and Rhys chose to accompany them, Llewelyn rode at her side, devoted his attentions to her alone, speaking with animation and at length of that which men rarely discussed with women.

He explained why he thought the bishopric of St David's should be independent of Canterbury, why he wanted a Welsh-born bishop for the See of Bangor. He was in the process now, he confided, of codifying Welsh law, that which had been passed down from the tenth-century Prince of blessed memory, Hywel the Good. Not that he thought Hywel's code to be sacrosanct, come down from Mount Sinai carved in stone. Laws needed to be flexible, to reflect the changing needs of changing times. For example, under the old laws, an act of violence was a crime against only the victim. If the offender made proper restitution to the victim's kindred, he was absolved of further liabilities. That was no longer enough; Llewelyn would have the man held accountable to his Prince, too. In that way, society could be better served, made safer for those dwelling under the law. But he was encountering some resistance. There were those who clung mindlessly to the old ways. As it was once done, so must it always be done, till the memory of man runneth not to the contrary, he said, and laughed ruefully.

Joanna listened intently, awed by the realization that Llewelyn was even more ambitious than she had first thought. But his ambition went well beyond what most men sought, power and land, entailed no less than a transformation of Welsh society. She'd never before met anyone who dared to dream on such a scale, and she found herself hoping that he'd not be disappointed, that his dreams would indeed come to pass.

She was no less interested in personal than in political revelations, listened with fascination as he talked of his mother, with such obvious affection that she felt a rush of empathy, thinking that his abiding love for Marared was very like her own love for her father. He spoke but briefly of Marared's death, saying only that he thanked God she'd

245

lived to see him in sovereign control of all of Gwynedd, and then he gave Joanna a deliberately light-hearted account of the rebellion begun at fourteen . . . 'just your age, lass.' It seemed perfectly natural to Joanna to tell him, in turn, of her own life, to tell him what she'd never before told anyone but John, of her mother's despairing last days, even of that brutal rejection in the solar of Middleham Castle. Llewelyn reined in abruptly at that, with an exclamation of incredulous outrage.

'Christ of the Cross! He turned his back upon a child, his own sister's flesh and blood, not knowing or caring what evil might befall you?' He shook his head. 'These d'Arcys, where are their lands? Are they near the Welsh border?'

'No, in Derbyshire, I think.'

'A pity,' he said, flashed her a sudden smile. 'If ever there were people who do deserve a little trouble in their lives . . .'

'Almost, you sound as if you mean that!' Actually, it mattered little to Joanna whether he meant it or not. It was enough for her that he'd said it, that his first impulse had been to avenge her wrong, to inflict punishment for her pain. It was, she thought, as great a gift as anyone had ever offered her.

'Do you know what Eryri means? "The haunt of eagles." Apt, is it not? Tell me, Joanna, what do you think so far of Wales?'

Joanna hesitated. It was indeed a beautiful country, but awesome, foreboding, not a land to submit tamely to man's control. Stark grandeur it had, but Joanna yearned for a softer harmony. 'Everywhere I look, I see a sight to take my breath, see mountains that might in truth serve as stepping-stones to Heaven. But . . . but it makes me feel very small, Llewelyn, as if I do count for naught.'

Llewelyn nodded. 'Yes,' he said approvingly. 'But in time you'll come to see the splendour of it, too.' Glancing back over his shoulder, he gave the signal to halt. 'Rhys, hold the men here. I want to show Rhaeadr Ewynnol to Joanna.'

The sudden coolness of the air took Joanna by surprise. The woods were shaded with summer green, suddenly hushed and still as Llewelyn led her forward. She could hear the river now, glimpsed the fall of white water through the trees. But she hung back, no longer following as Llewelyn moved towards the edge of the cliff.

'I . . . I have an unease of heights,' she said apologetically.

'So I've noticed,' Llewelyn said and smiled at her. 'But I'll not let you fall, do assure you that not one Princess of Gwynedd has ever drowned in Rhaeadr Ewynnol. That's it . . . lean back against me. See how much better the view is from here? This has ever been my favourite place. And Dolwyddelan is but nine miles to the south; we'll pass the night there and return to Aber on the morrow.'

Joanna was no longer listening. She felt no fear, for she was oblivious of the surging cataract, the wind-driven spray. Llewelyn was holding her back against his body; she could feel his encircling arms, pressing against the underside of her breasts, feel his breath upon her cheek, the soft tickle of his moustache against her temple, his hand warm on her wrist.

'You can let me go, Llewelyn. I am all right now,' she said, but her voice was so muffled that he at once drew her back from the cliff.

'You're trembling, Joanna; were you as fearful as that? Your face is flushed, too . . .' He put his hand to her cheeks, and Joanna gasped, wrenched free of his embrace, stumbling in her haste to put space between them.

Backing away, she leaned against the nearest tree. 'I . . . I'm sorry, but I . . . I was afraid . . .'

'Yes, so I see,' he said, and the coldness in his voice brought her eyes up to his face in utter dismay. As flustered as she'd been by his touch, that was as nothing to the way she felt now, with the wretched realization that he'd read fear into her confused recoil. She opened her mouth, but the words would not come. It was not that she'd liked his embrace too little; it was that she'd liked it too much. But how could she ever tell him that?

Ednyved crossed the great hall, sloshed a dripping cup into Llewelyn's hand. 'Here. Whenever I am wroth with Gwenllian, I find mead to be a great restorative.'

'Why should you think I'm wroth with Joanna?'

'Why, indeed? The lass spoke not three words at dinner, fled ere the tables could be cleared away, and now you keep to the hall like a man in search of sanctuary. But you have not quarrelled – not you.'

'I did not say that. I said I was not angry with Joanna. Well . . . I admit I did lose my temper this afternoon. I should not have, but I keep forgetting how very young she is. It is for that reason that I've kept to the hall, my way of making amends. You see, Joanna did not realize there is no lady chamber here at Dolwyddelan. She took one look at our bed, and her face took on all the colours of sunset. So

247

. . . I thought to give her time to get to sleep first . . . my good deed for the day!'

'She's nigh on fifteen, is she not?' Ednyved asked, his voice noncommittal.

'But she still has the emotions of a child, Ednyved, is not yet ready to be a wife.'

'You know her better than I. But there are women who shrink from the marriage bed, from a man's touch. Are you sure that your Joanna is not one such?'

'As to that, I cannot be sure till I bed her. But I think not, think she merely needs time.'

Ednyved looked at the other man, startled by a sudden surge of envy. It was obvious it had not even occurred to Llewelyn that Joanna simply might not find him to her liking. Just as it had not occurred to Rhys to worry whether Catrin would want him, would share his sudden passion. Ednyved reclaimed the cup of mead, wondering what it would be like to be so free of self-doubt. With only one woman had he felt it, with his first wife. Tangwystl, daughter of Lord Llywarch of Bran; he and Llewelyn had often joked about it, the confusion that resulted from their women sharing a Christian name. In the early years of their marriage, she'd come quite eagerly to his bed. But then the pregnancies began. Six sons she'd given him in less than nine years, had died giving birth to their last-born. Four years ago, he'd married Gwenllian, heiress of Dyffryn Clwyd, daughter of Lord Rhys, Prince of South Wales. It was a brilliant match, but a loveless marriage. Most of the time, he did not feel the lack. But there were nights, like this one, when he remembered the gentle, dark-eyed Tangwystl, felt the dull throb of an old grief.

'So what mean you to do, Llewelyn . . . wait for Joanna to grow up?'

'Why not? If a wife is not worth taking some trouble with, who is? Besides, I like the lass, would rather she be content than not.' Llewelyn half-rose, beckoned to a cupbearer. 'Nor is my forbearance all that unselfish. What man would choose an indifferent bedmate over an ardent one? If Joanna needs time to reach womanhood, I'm willing to give her that time. It's not as if I need her now to warm my bed, after all.' Llewelyn smiled at that, thinking of Cristyn.

'Indeed, I'd say not,' Ednyved agreed, so emphatically that Llewelyn knew he, too, was thinking of Cristyn.

*

Dawn light was spilling through the open shutters. For a confused moment, Joanna did not remember where she was . . . not until she saw Llewelyn lying next to her in the bed. At that, she remembered all too well. She'd lain awake for hours, waiting for Llewelyn, desperately trying to decide what she could say to him. But when he'd finally come to bed, her courage had failed her again, and as on that night at Rhuddlan Castle, she'd taken refuge in feigned sleep.

Llewelyn was sprawled on his back; even in sleep, he sought space. He was only partially covered with the sheet, and Joanna saw now what he'd meant when he'd spoken of his 'share of hurts'. A knotted, faded scar seared the skin across his ribcage; another, more recent, zigzagged from armpit to collar-bone.

Reaching for the sheet, she took care in tucking it about him. He had a third scar, almost invisible, a faint white mark just under his right eyebrow; she'd never noticed it before. Her eyes lingered upon his face, traced the sleep-softened curve of his mouth. Was it so much to have asked for? A husband she could respect, a marriage of mutual affection. She could have been well content with that. But this . . . She could take no joy now in what she was feeling for the man asleep beside her. All her life, she'd had a horror of making a fool of herself; what could come of this passionate yearning except hurt? And humiliation. Again, she reached out; her fingers stopped just short of Llewelyn's cheek. In her innocence, she'd once thought the worst that could befall a woman was to find herself wed to a husband she did not want. But what of the wife wed to a man who did not want her?

September, 1206

Aber, North Wales

The air was cool and crisp. Like cider, Joanna thought; it carried a snap. A fleet of rain-swollen clouds sailed across the sun, casting sudden shadows upon the sand. Even the sea seemed to lose colour, to take on the chilled grey of darkest December. Joanna shivered, pulled her mantle closer. And then the sun broke through again, resurrecting all the glories of an afternoon in early autumn.

The unexpected resurgence of warmth and light took Joanna by surprise. It was almost, she acknowledged wryly, as if she wanted leaden skies and biting winds, wanted a world that mirrored her mood. Snapping her fingers for Sugar, she walked closer to the water's edge. Yr Afon Fenai, the Welsh called it, the narrow strait that cut off the island of Môn from the mainland. It was, Llewelyn had told her, a deceptively dangerous stretch of water, for the currents ran very swift, forming sudden eddies and undertows, and where the tides came together, a lethal whirlpool, Pwll Ceris, that had taken more than a few men to a death by drowning. Llewelyn had palaces on Môn, at Aberffraw and Rhosyr. But she'd yet to see them; like so much of his life, that, too, was closed to her.

A piece of driftwood lay at her feet. On impulse, she knelt, patted the sand smooth and scrawled her name in the path of the incoming tide. Beneath it, she wrote: LLEWELYN, and then watched as the waves washed their names away. A dim memory stirred, took on substance. So had she passed the time on another birthday, ten years past, lying in the heather before Middleham Castle and laboriously tracing CLEMENCE and JOANNA in the dirt.

Birthdays had never been joyous occasions for her. Beneath the surface celebration lurked a lingering unease, a vague foreboding that she could neither identify nor yet ignore. She wondered suddenly if her aversion might not be rooted in that long-ago Yorkshire birthday. How vivid it still was: her desperate desire to please her mother, her futile yearning for a dog, the water stains upon her skirt, that closed bedchamber door. Two days later her mother was dead, leaving her with only the memory of a tear-splotched, swollen face, ghostly white in the moonlight.

Getting to her feet, Joanna tossed the stick out to sea, began to brush the sand from her mantle. Foolish to dwell upon a birthday ten years gone, to prod and prick at old hurts until they bled. Of all she least liked about herself, her weakness for self-pity must for certès lead the list. Nor was she going to squander what remained of this, her fifteenth birthday, in feeling sorry for herself. If truth be told, she was to blame, too. Why had she not told Llewelyn plainly that her birthday fell in mid-September? He would surely have marked the day in some way, might even have taken her with him to Cricieth Castle. But no, she'd had to be clever, had to test him, making just one deliberately casual mention over a fortnight ago. Had her words even registered with him? Or was it that he had not thought her birthday important enough to remember?

How right she'd been to be afraid, that night at Dolwyddelan Castle. She did not want to love Llewelyn. But she did not know how to stop. He had only to appear, and all others ceased to exist for her. So far she'd managed to cling to the shreds of her pride, but how long ere she well and truly singed her wings? She was so . . . so obvious, after all. Seeking him out on the slightest pretext, contriving reed-thin excuses to keep him in her company – only to freeze as soon as their eyes met, to find herself flustered, hopelessly tongue-tied. Joanna did not know which she feared more, that he should now think her an utter fool, or that he had not even noticed her peculiar behaviour. She did know that she'd have given anything in her power to have him with her this day, that she missed him as she'd never missed anyone in all her life before.

Alerted by Sugar's barking, Joanna turned, saw her husband's two youngest daughters standing a short distance away, watching her with grave, wary eyes. Joanna started to speak, stopped; that road led nowhere. Instead, she knelt, and using a shell as a shovel, began to scoop up handfuls of damp sand. Within moments, she had a castle motte, ready to receive the keep. She dug in silence, as if utterly intent upon her handiwork, not looking up until a small voice said, 'Is that a Welsh or an English castle?'

251

Marared and Gwenllian were now close enough to touch. Joanna felt much the same pleasure she would have if a wild bird had suddenly alighted upon her hand. 'I do not know yet,' she said thoughtfully. 'What do you think it should be?'

'Welsh,' Marared said, coming closer still, and when Joanna offered her the clam shell, she took it without hesitation. With four small hands to help, the castle was not long in taking on impressive dimensions: an inner and outer bailey, a thick curtain wall, a lopsided gatehouse that Gwenllian insisted she alone should build. Joanna deferred to their decisions, let them place the towers where they would. Nor did she try to draw them out in conversation, as she had in the past. And within the hour, she had her reward.

Marared had settled back on her haunches to inspect their creation. She drew so sharp a breath that Joanna at once looked up, saw on the child's face an expression of sudden dismay. Turning, she saw Gruffydd moving towards them. He stopped abruptly, all but stumbled over his dog. Since Adda's reprimand on the day of her arrival, he had not let his hostility blaze forth again. But it smouldered in his eyes, showed now in the rigidness of his stance, the set of his shoulders.

Always before, he had only to appear for his sisters to shun Joanna as if she were a leper. But Gwenllian and Marared so far showed no sign of flight, and Joanna took heart. 'If we dig a moat,' she suggested, 'we can fill it with sea-water,' and saw at once that she'd said just the right thing.

From time to time, Marared cast nervous glances over her shoulder, but she stayed put; Gwenllian seemed to have forgotten Gruffydd altogether, so absorbed was she in deepening the moat. At last it was ready to be filled, and the little girls grabbed their clam shells, ran towards the water, Joanna following. She allowed herself one look back at Gruffydd. He was still standing some yards away, watching.

'Would you like to help us?' Joanna asked, knowing she did but waste her breath. When he did not reply, she turned back towards the water. It was then that she heard Gwenllian cry out. Joanna spun around, in time to see Gruffydd's alaunt hound smash into the castle. Within the span of seconds, the big dog had wreaked utter havoc, flattened walls and towers, sprayed sand in all directions. Grabbing for the driftwood Gruffydd had thrown, he tossed it playfully up into the air, caught it deftly again, and carried it triumphantly back to his young master.

Gwenllian had begun to sob. Marared flung down her clam shell, as if it were something suddenly shameful. Joanna did not move, watched as Gruffydd whistled to his dog, slowly sauntered away. She was as angry as she'd ever been in her life, and it helped not at all to remind herself that he was only a child. She saw nothing childlike in what he had done; it was both deliberate and malicious, not to mention clever. How to prove, after all, that he had not simply misjudged his throw? She could not, of course, as he'd well known.

'We can rebuild the castle, Gwenllian,' she said, as evenly as her anger would allow. But their fragile camaraderie had collapsed with the sand castle. Gwenllian sniffed, shook her head. Marared was already edging away.

Joanna made no move to keep them. It would, she knew, have served for naught. But as she stared down at the wreckage of their rapprochement, her rage hardened into resolve. She would not let that wretched boy win. For four months now, she had been seeking to gain his friendship. No more. Let him hate her; she no longer cared. But she would not give up on his sisters. Today she had made the first breach in their defences. If a direct assault would not work, mayhap infiltration would.

Walking up the slope to Aber, she paused to watch as a small flock of bleating ewes and lambs was herded into a pen. Shearing had already been done early in the summer; today the clipping would be confined to the greasy wool at each ewe's neck and udder. This wool, Joanna knew, would be washed in cold water, and then boiled. As the grease rose to the surface, it would be skimmed off the water, reheated and then strained through linen. Once cool, vegetable oil and scent would be added, the resulting concoction being a highly effective ointment.

Joanna was rather pleased that she now knew something of the process. In fact, she'd learned much in these months in Wales, had watched with interest as goatskins were stretched taut on square frames, scraped with strickle knives, the first step in the making of parchment; watched as hides were soaked in lime vats to remove hair, preparatory to tanning; as mutton fat was boiled with wood ash and caustic soda to make soft soap, and whitethorn bark soaked in water, boiled, and left to thicken into ink. At her father's court, such activities were done behind the scenes; at Llewelyn's court, Joanna

253

found herself closer to nature, living a less insulated life, much like the vast majority of her father's subjects.

She watched until the sheep were penned, then moved indecisively away. She did not want to return to her chambers, was in no mood to put up with Blanche's carping. She hesitated, and then remembered what Llewelyn had told her, that there was an impressive cataract at the end of the glen. It was, he said, a sight well worth the seeing, for the River Coch cascaded over one hundred feet down a sheer cliff.

It proved to be a very pleasant walk. On her left rose the heights of Maes y Gaer, on her right thickly wooded hills. As the path wound upwards, she could look back and glimpse the sea. She'd been walking for about half an hour when she saw a glimmer of light through the trees. She quickened her step, some fifteen minutes later came to a sudden halt. Llewelyn had been right; Rhaeadr Fawr was well worth the walk. It had none of the wild surging power of Rhaeadr Ewynnol, but there was a stark elegance, none the less, in that narrow ribbon of white water. The stream was wider here, so clear she could count the mossy rocks lining the river bed, and wherever she looked, she saw wild flowers: golden rock-roses, purple bell heather, fragrant meadowsweet blossoms, daisies, others she could not name.

Joanna had turned aside to gather honeysuckle when she saw the man standing at the base of the falls. He turned a startled face towards her, then began to climb nimbly up the rocks. By the time he reached her, Joanna had recognized him as her husband's friend, and she said with a smile, 'Lord Rhys, you did take me aback! I'd not expected to see another soul here but a stray sheep or two.'

Rhys was frowning. 'Madame, you should not be wandering about on your own. What if you'd slipped, fallen upon the rocks? May I escort you back to Aber?'

It was phrased as a question, but given as a command. Joanna bridled a bit, but curiosity won out, and she fell docilely in step beside him. She knew this man hardly at all, had spoken to him so rarely that for a long time she'd thought he knew no French. He put a hand firmly on her elbow, but made no attempt at small talk, seemed to be one of those rare individuals not in the least disconcerted by lengthy silences. Joanna studied him covertly through her lashes. He was, she decided, surely the most handsome man she'd ever seen. So why, then, did she find Llewelyn more attractive, why was it Llewelyn whose touch caused her pulse to race, her imagination to take fire? Mayhap because she'd never known a man who derived so much joy from life, a man so at one with his world, doing exactly what he most wanted to do, doing it very well, and taking such abiding pleasure in it all. But why seek out hurt like this? Must her every thought be of Llewelyn, when he had nary a thought for her?

'I understand Llewelyn returns from Cricieth in a fortnight, and then the court moves to Môn?'

Joanna nodded. 'He has a . . . a *plas* at Aberffraw, does he not?'

'Aye, but he'll go to Rhosyr. He has no liking for Aberffraw, not any more.' Joanna had not realized her curiosity showed so nakedly until Rhys added matter-of-factly, 'The Lady Tangwystl died at Aberffraw.' He did not pause for her response. 'The Lady Catrin, my wife, did give birth just a month ago, was stricken afterwards with the milk fever. She is better now, God be thanked, but she's not yet able to travel. She is very eager, though, to meet you, and I would ask a favour of you.' He stopped, turned to face her, and Joanna realized he had not been making idle conversation, after all.

'When the court moves to Rhosyr, would you come to my manor at Tregarnedd? It would mean much to my Catrin, Madame, in truth it would.'

Joanna could find in herself no enthusiasm for meeting the Lady Catrin, not after making the acquaintance of Ednyved's wife. But she could think of no graceful way to decline, and she said, 'Yes, of course.'

They walked the rest of the way in silence. As they approached the gateway, they saw Blanche pacing back and forth distractedly. She gave a glad cry at sight of Joanna, ran to meet her.

'Madame, thank God you've come! Sir Hugh Corbet has just ridden in, is awaiting you in the great hall!'

'Oh, sweet Lady Mary!' Joanna tried to collect her thoughts, tried to remember all she must do for an honoured guest. Give orders for a special meal, one of several courses, ask Llywarch to sing for Hugh. See that a chamber was prepared for his stay, that his men were bedded down, too. What else? Jesu, what of a bath?

Joanna came to a sudden stop. It was customary of course, to offer a bath to any guest planning to pass the night. If the guest was of high rank, it was expected that the lady of the manor herself would assist him in bathing. To neglect so basic a courtesy would be no small insult. But Isabelle had never performed such tasks; was a

255

princess, too, exempt? Nor did she even know if this ancient Norman custom was followed amongst the Welsh. It would be dreadful to slight her husband's stepfather. But neither did she want to embarrass Llewelyn by turning her hand to a task better left to her maids. If only she knew what was expected of her, if only there was a woman she could ask.

Well, she must blunder through as best she could. Mayhap Hugh would give her some hint as to what he expected. Why was it that, the first time she had to act on Llewelyn's behalf, the guest must be one so important, must be her husband's kin?

Hugh resolved her dilemma, however, in a way she'd not anticipated. He could not pass the night, he explained regretfully, for it was urgent that he reach Llewelyn as soon as possible.

'I fear Llewelyn is some miles to the south, in the commote of Eifionydd. He is building a seacoast castle at Cricieth, wanted to judge the progress for himself. If you are set upon departing in such haste, we will gladly provide you with an escort and fresh mounts.' Trying to hide her relief, Joanna racked her brains to recall what little she knew of Welsh geography. 'You could pass the night at Dolwyddelan, or at Beddgelert Priory should you get that far.' She hesitated, for the first time seeing the fatigue already well etched into Hugh's face.

'Sir Hugh, may I ask why you are in such a rush to see my husband? Is there trouble?'

'Of a sort.' He drew her towards the privacy of the window seat, said in a low voice, 'Prince Gwenwynwyn of Powys has been a widower since the spring. Two days ago he was wed to my niece Margaret Corbet, my brother Robert's daughter. I want to get to Llewelyn ere he hears of it from anyone else.'

Joanna needed to hear no more; after four months as Llewelyn's wife, she had no doubts whatsoever as to what his reaction would be. 'It sounds rather as if it were something of a hole-and-corner marriage,' she said coolly. 'Why? To keep Llewelyn from finding out beforehand?'

'Exactly.' Hugh grimaced. 'My brother can be a fool at times. Had I only been consulted, I'd have told him Llewelyn would be sure to take such a marriage as a personal insult. But he pays too much heed these days to my nephew Tom, and Tom is no great thinker. Neither he nor Rob seems to realize that times have changed. It worked well once to play off the Welsh princes, one against the other. Fifteen years ago such a marriage would have been a shrewd manoeuvre. But those days are gone. Gwenwynwyn's good will counts for little against Llewelyn's. I only hope they do not have to learn that to their cost.'

'What will Llewelyn do?'

'For the moment, nothing. It's done and beyond changing. But he's not likely to forget, even less likely to forgive. Stupid and shortsighted, both of them. They have yet to get it into their heads that Llewelyn is not just another Welsh prince, to be bought off or duped as their need dictates. I've told them that the day may well come when he'll hold all of Wales, but they laugh. Fools. I only do hope I'm wrong, for Llewelyn's sake as much as ours. No English king could ever permit a Welsh prince to wield so much power; John would have no choice but to break him. I for one would not want –' He stopped suddenly, having remembered too late to whom he was speaking.

Joanna had gone very white; her eyes suddenly seemed enormous, so dark they were almost black. 'Do not say that,' she pleaded. 'That must never happen.'

Cursing himself for his clumsiness, Hugh made haste to repair the damage done. 'Indeed it will not, Lady Joanna,' he said soothingly. 'When I am tired, my tongue tends to outrun my brain; such talk means nothing. Your husband and father are more than allies of the moment; you are the living link that binds them together.'

Joanna nodded; colour slowly began to come back into her face. Hugh gave her shoulder a reassuring pat, wondering for whom she feared, John or Llewelyn.

As eagerly as she awaited Llewelyn's return, Joanna felt some anxiety, too, remembering her father's rages, his dark, moody silences. But however violent Llewelyn's initial reaction might have been, he had his temper well in hand by the time he got back to Aber, made no mention whatsoever of his Corbet kin. Joanna began to wonder if she had misjudged him; she'd been so sure he would take the marriage as a mortal affront. She had to know, at last asked him point-blank how he felt about it.

He looked at her with a faint smile. 'My cousin Tom has ever been one for gazing on both sides of the hedge. That is his misfortune.' And Joanna saw that she had not misjudged him at all.

*

257

It was a mild October afternoon four days after their arrival at Rhosyr. Joanna was in no hurry to reach Tregarnedd, had covered the eight miles at a leisurely pace. She only hoped the Lady Catrin spoke some French. On the other hand, if she did not, that would be as good an excuse as any to cut the visit short. At least it was a delightful day for a ride. And she would confess to some curiosity about the woman Rhys had married, wondered if Catrin would be a mirror image of her handsome husband.

Tregarnedd was an agreeable surprise; it was much like a village, for Ednyved had a manor here, too, and, as in England, there were people who preferred to dwell, for safety's sake, in the shadow of a lord. But the real surprise waited within, a smile of welcome upon her face.

'I am Lady Catherine, Madame. How good of you to come to me like this; in truth, you honour our house. I've so longed to meet you. For the first time in my life, I regretted that I did not know how to write. Of course I could have dictated a letter to our chaplain, but . . .'

Joanna stared at the other woman, astonished. It was not Catherine's appearance that so startled her, although she was not the ravishing beauty Joanna had been expecting. She was a buxom pretty woman with fair, creamy skin, thick, golden lashes and hair so blonde it was almost white. It was her speech, however, that riveted Joanna's eyes upon her; her French was not only fluent, it was colloquial.

'You are Norman!' Joanna blurted out, and then blushed. But Catherine merely laughed.

'Indeed, did Rhys not tell you? Ah, that man!'

On reflection, Joanna realized there was no reason for such surprise. Intermarriages were not that uncommon, after all; the Corbets were not the only Marcher lords to see the advantages in a Welsh connection. It was just that Rhys, so proudly, defiantly Welsh, seemed the last man to choose a Norman wife.

As if reading her thoughts, Catherine said, 'I know no people who value bloodlines as do the Welsh. But they have never balked at accepting foreign wives, for a woman takes on her husband's nationality, and any children of such a union have full rights under Welsh law. It becomes rather more complicated when a Welshwoman does wed with an *alltud* . . . a man of

258

foreign blood. But I expect Llewelyn has explained all this to you . . .'

Ushering Joanna into the great hall, she at once sent for wine and wafers, settled Joanna in the seat of honour by the hearth, and beckoned a nurse forward to show Joanna a small dark-haired infant swaddled in folds of soft linen.

'My daughter Gwenifer. Rhys always hopes the girls will have my colouring, and always in vain. This is the fifth time I've been brought to childbed, and each one has hair black as sin.'

Joanna laughed. She'd all but forgotten how wonderful it was just to sit and talk, to make inconsequential, easy conversation. She had, of necessity, learned to tune out the disgruntled Blanche's litany of complaints, and her encounters with Llewelyn were so fraught with sexual tension that she could take little pleasure in them.

'Now . . . do tell me how you like Wales. Llewelyn is well? I must confess that I'm half in love with him, do not know a woman who is not, in truth! My husband may turn all female heads, but yours is the one they'd run off with if . . .' Her words trailed off, for Joanna's colour had deepened, dark patches showing high on her cheekbones. Catherine realized she had trod amiss, but she was puzzled as to how. Surely the girl knew she was but joking? Unless . . . unless she knew about Cristyn? Catherine was now the one to be embarrassed, sought hastily for safer subject-matter.

'Should you like, my lady, to hold Gwenifer? You do know, I'm sure, that you have all our heartfelt prayers that you may soon have a babe of your own. It must weary you, in truth, to have the women ever measuring your waistline, whispering if you so much as miss a meal! But it is always so with newly wedded wives, and when your husband is our lord Prince . . .'

Joanna came to her feet so abruptly that she knocked her wine cup on to the floor. Would she never learn? This woman was even more malicious than Maude de Braose and Gwenllian, for they at least had pretended no friendliness. But Catherine drew blood with a smile, and for that, Joanna would never forgive her. 'Your jest is little to my liking,' she said, all the more furious that her voice was not as steady as she would have wished.

'But Madame . . . what have I said? How have I offended you?' Catherine, too, was on her feet now. Her distress seemed so genuine that Joanna felt the first glimmer of doubt.

259

'The entire court does know. Surely your husband would have told you . . .'

'Rhys never gossips,' Catherine said simply. 'I do not know of what you speak, my lady, I swear I do not.'

For a long moment, Joanna stared at her, and then sat down again. 'If I did missay you, I am indeed sorry. You see, I thought you were mocking me. Llewelyn and I . . . we do not share a bed, and there is not a soul at Aber or Rhosyr who does not know that . . .'

'I did not know, Madame,' Catherine said, after some moments of silence. 'That is not something Rhys would think to mention. It is not that unusual, after all, when the wife is quite young and her husband some years older than she.'

Some of Joanna's shame gave way to gratitude. Whether Catherine believed that or not, it was kind of her to say so, and she was very much relieved when Catherine began tactfully to talk of other matters.

Joanna was never able to pinpoint the exact moment when she let her defences down. For the first time in five months she had a sympathetic ear, and it was perhaps inevitable that she would find herself confiding in Catherine, Catherine who spoke her own tongue, who knew what it was like to be a bride in a foreign land, Catherine who offered friendship. She did not lower all the barriers, spoke of Llewelyn in only the most conventional, cautious banalities. But she did speak of her loneliness, her homesickness, spoke of the utter isolation and the cries of wolves on the wind and a forgotten fifteenth birthday.

There was a great relief in sharing; hers were secret sores much in need of healing balm. But there was unease, too, once she realized just how much she'd revealed. Isabelle was the only female confidante she'd ever had, and entrusting a secret to Isabelle was rather like toting water in a sieve. Very thankful that her tongue had not completely run away with her, that she had not betrayed the one secret that truly mattered, Joanna watched as Catherine bathed Gwenifer, then turned the child over to the wet nurse for suckling. She'd always nursed her own, Catherine admitted, although the Lady Gwenllian and others mocked her for it, would have suckled Gwenifer, too, had her fever not dried up her milk.

Catherine was emerging as more and more of an enigma to Joanna. She was, by her own admission, not educated. She'd made a self-disparaging remark about marriage portions when their conversation had turned to Margaret Corbet and Gwenwynwyn, laughing and saying she'd brought Rhys naught but headaches. Joanna had been distinctly taken aback; it was almost unheard of for a Norman lord to take an undowered wife. And if she were, in truth, no heiress, how in the name of Heaven had they even met, much less married?

'Catherine . . . would you think me rude if I asked how you came to marry Rhys?'

Catherine smiled. 'I'd not mind in the least, Joanna. That is a story I never tire of telling. My first meeting with Rhys goes back some thirteen years, to the autumn of the year after King Richard was taken captive on his way home from the Holy Land. My father was bailiff on Lord Fitz Alan's manor of Middleton in Shropshire. I was the youngest of six, the only girl. My mother died when I was four, and my father made rather a pet of me; so, too, did my brothers. That spring I did turn fifteen, and it was more or less understood that, come winter, I'd be wed to a neighbouring knight, Sir Bernard de Nevill. He and my father were talking of a betrothal at Martinmas, a wedding after Advent.'

'Were you willing, Catherine?'

'I was not offered a choice, Joanna. I felt it was my duty to do as my father bade me. And it was indeed an advantageous match. Sir Bernard held his own manor of Lord Fitz Alan; I'd be lady of the manor, with my own household, servants. And since Sir Bernard had no children by his first marriage, a son of mine might one day inherit the fief; not many second wives could say as much. Moreover, he seemed to be a good man, a devout Christian, well thought of by all. But . . . he was also nigh on fifty, and balding, with breath rank enough to stop a mule in its tracks. So I'd not say I was counting the days till the marriage!'

'What prevented the marriage?'

'A sunlit September day,' Catherine said, and laughed. 'My brother Adam was taking an oxwain into Blanc Minster, had a load of wool skeins to deliver to Will the weaver. Blanc Minster was only three miles away, but I was never allowed into town without one of my brothers. On that particular day Adam agreed to take me along, and so it happened that I was sitting out in the oxwain at noon as Rhys rode by. The Welsh often came into Blanc Minster to trade for goods, and even in war I never saw a merchant turn down their money. I did not know then, of course, that Rhys was Welsh. I knew only that he was the handsomest man I'd ever hoped to see in this life!'

'He is that,' Joanna agreed generously. 'What happened then?'

'He drew rein right there in the street, stared at me, and when he smiled, I . . . I fell in love. But then he dismounted, and I realized he meant to speak to me. At that I panicked. If Adam had ever seen me talking with a stranger, I'd have been beaten black and blue. As for Rhys, Adam would have run him through . . . or tried to. You can always tell if a man be handy with weapons, and Rhys had that look about him. So when he started towards me, I scrambled off the oxwain, fled into the weaver's. I was terrified that he might follow me in. He did not, but he was still there when Adam and I came out. Thankfully, he did not say anything; he just looked at me. I could feel his eyes on me all the while Adam was joking with Will, was never so aware of anyone in all my life as I suddenly was of Rhys.'

'Yes,' Joanna said softly. 'I do know the feeling. When did you see him next?'

'Adam had to return the following day, and I coaxed him into letting me go with him. I did not truly expect Rhys to be there again, but he was – almost as if he was waiting for me. Much later I learned he was; Will had told him Adam would be coming back that afternoon. What followed was the most unnerving, exciting hour of my life. I knew what a dangerous game we were playing, for at any moment Adam might take notice. But I could not help myself. I sat there on the cart, and each time our eyes met, it became harder and harder to look away. And then Adam's business was done, we were on our way home, and I knew I'd never see him again. I did not even know his name, had never exchanged a single word with him, but I cried half the night . . . Does that sound foolish to you?'

Joanna shook her head.

'I thought of him every waking moment in the days that followed. What I did not know was that he was keeping a close watch all the while on Middleton, waiting for the chance to find me alone. He later confessed he'd even thought of riding up to the manor house, asking my father for me. Thank Jesus he did not, for there'd have been a killing for certès.

'I gave him his opportunity at week's end. It was a Saturday, just at dusk, as hot as Hades, and I decided that, whilst the light held,

I'd walk to the spring, wash my hair. I brought my towel, hairbrush, and a sliver of soap, sat down in the grass to unbraid my hair. I never heard a sound, not even a twig snap, not until he was behind me, put his hand over my mouth. I've ever been an utter coward, Joanna; I made it very easy for him, fainted dead away!

'When I came to, I was all trussed up in a blanket, being held before him on his saddle.' Catherine's smile faded; she said quietly, 'I was terrified, and with reason. It is common enough to abduct an heiress, to force her into an unwanted marriage. What woman does not know that?'

Joanna nodded. 'Even so great a lady as my grandmother, Queen Eleanor, was held to be fair game. Two such attempts were made upon her after she divorced the French King.'

'But you see, Joanna, I was no heiress. I was a bailiff's daughter, had nothing to offer a man except my body. And yet if he had rape in mind, why did he not just take me there by the spring? The more I tried to make sense of it, the more fearful I became. I must have made some sound, whimpered or sobbed, for he realized I'd recovered my senses, at once sought to comfort me. He knew my name, called me Catrin, swore he'd not hurt me, that I had no cause for fear. That might have helped some, had it not been for "Catrin". For as soon as I knew he was Welsh, I was even more terrified; all knew the Welsh were half-wild, capable of any madness.

'It was full dark by then. Not that I could see a blessed thing; I could barely breathe, wrapped in that blanket like a cocoon. I've no idea how long we rode; after a time we stopped and he lifted me from the saddle. Do you know what a *hafod* is? It is a summer hut, used by the Welsh herdsmen when they move their flocks to higher ground for pasturing. It was to a *hafod* that he took me, empty now since it was September, a most convenient place for a . . . a tryst. It was too dark inside to see much; I just lay there shivering on the blanket. He'd already laid in firewood, and it took but a moment to get a fire going. He lit a candle from the flames, carried it back to me and, for the first time I saw his face.'

'You had not known it was Rhys?' Joanna interrupted, startled, and Catherine shook her head.

'No, not till he lit the candle; how could I? He sat beside me on the blankets – you'll find no proper bed in a *hafod* – and touched my hair, very gently. Then he began to talk. He told me he'd known from that first moment in Blanc Minster that I was his and only his, but I must not fear, for he did not mean to dishonour me, would have me for his wife, had taken me by force only because he'd known no other way.'

Catherine's voice had softened. Her eyes were no longer acknowledging Joanna, were gazing into a private vista of her own. Joanna suddenly had the fanciful thought that, if she but leaned forward, she could see captured in the pupils of Catherine's eyes the firelit image of a fifteen-year-old girl and a nineteen-year-old boy upon a pile of blankets in a summer *hafod*.

She hesitated; as candid as Catherine had been, it somehow seemed wrong to question her now, an unwelcome intrusion into a past not for sharing. At last she said shyly, 'Catherine . . . when did you stop being afraid? Do you remember?'

Catherine's eyes shifted to her face, no longer clouded, remote. 'Oh yes, I remember – when Rhys first struck that candle.'

She glanced down at her wedding ring; it was of an unusual, almost primitive design, a heavy gold studded with gemstones. 'We sent the priest who married us to my family. My father swore he'd never forgive me. But within a year Llewelyn had won that brilliant, bloody victory at the mouth of the Conwy, had laid claim to half of Gwynedd, and Rhys was always at his right hand . . . was his right hand. My father died nigh on ten years ago, but he lived to see his first grandson. And my brothers come often to Tregarnedd.'

'You've been very lucky,' Joanna said slowly.

Catherine's smile was radiant, innocent. 'I know,' she said.

Joanna found herself looking, too, at Catherine's wedding band. It did not surprise her in the least that Catherine should have been so easily seduced. What girl would have chosen an aging, ungainly neighbour over a reckless, love-struck youth with the nerve of a highwayman and the face of a dark angel? But beneath the undeniably romantic appeal of Catherine's tale, Joanna felt the tug of common sense. What if Catherine had, indeed, cared for her greying knight? If she had resented being carried off as a prize of war? What might have happened then?

No, for all that Catherine had obviously found all she'd ever wanted in that deserted *hafod*, Joanna could not but think Catherine's luck had been stretched to the very limit and beyond. And yet she was aware of an undercurrent of envy. For Catherine had one treasure beyond value, had what she'd have given anything in the world to have herself – the rare and precious certainty that her husband loved her, not for what she could bring to his coffers, not for castles or bloodlines or connections, but for herself alone.

November, 1206
Rhosyr, North Wales

'Catrin, my love!'

Llewelyn turned, swept Catherine up in a lover's embrace, then gave her a chaste kiss on the forehead. Laughing, she hugged him back.

'Have you some moments to spare? I need to talk, Llewelyn.'

'For you, always . . . day or night.' As he led her towards the window seat, it occurred to Catherine that her relationship with Llewelyn – teasing, affectionate, mildly flirtatious – was one an insecure, jealous young wife might possibly misconstrue. She would, she thought regretfully, have to strive for greater decorum. A pity, for as much as she liked to flirt, that was a game she dared play with Llewelyn alone. Having led an all but cloistered life prior to her marriage, she'd then made the belated discovery that it could be fun to talk and tease and coquet – a little – with other men, to her an innocent diversion that did not in the least diminish her love for Rhys. But she'd also discovered that her husband was intensely possessive, begrudged her any and all male companionship, no matter how innocent . . . save only for Ednyved and Llewelyn. Ednyved was little inclined to flattery, even less so to gallantry, but in Llewelyn, Catherine had found a kindred spirit, and they'd established a rapport from their first meeting. In the beginning, an unsettling misgiving had imperilled Catherine's peace, the suspicion that, if her husband tolerated Llewelyn's banter and familiarity while bristling if another man so much as glanced in her direction, it must be that Rhys trusted Llewelyn, but did not truly trust her. That was so disturbing a thought, however, that Catherine had swiftly buried it deep; hers was not a nature to probe for that which she'd rather not know.

'How is my godson and namesake?'

'As much of a hellion as you were at his age . . . and still are.'

'Do not be cruel, Catrin,' Llewelyn said and grinned. 'It is good to have you back at court. Joanna tells me your newest babe is as beautiful as her mother; how does she?'

'Gwenifer is fine.' Catherine paused. 'I just wish I could say as much for Joanna.'

'What do you mean?'

Catherine did not reply at once. Having already plunged into the water, it was no time to be worrying if she'd got in over her head. But she could not suppress a nervous qualm or two. As fond as Llewelyn was of her, he was not likely to thank her for pointing out all his shortcomings as a husband.

'We've been friends for nigh on thirteen years. I must hope that our friendship gives me the right to speak plainly . . . about Joanna and you. You've not done right by her, Llewelyn; I know no other way to say it than that.'

'Indeed?' Llewelyn was both surprised and annoyed. Leaning back in the seat, he gave her a distinctly cool look. 'I do not know to whom you've been listening, Catrin, but you are wrong. I think I've been very good to Joanna. Even ere we were married, I spared no expense in having her chamber made ready for her. Nor have I denied her anything since we've been wed, have given her whatever she asks for, have made sure that none speak disparagingly of her father in her hearing, that she's accorded the respect due her as my wife. I've been patient, too, keeping in mind her youth, have not forced her against her will, and I've taken care that my liaison with Cristyn should not cause her hurt. Now if that is not "doing right" by her, what more would you have me do?'

Catherine bit her lip. Rhys had an unfortunate and infuriating tendency to stalk out whenever he was irked with her; she felt sure that, even if he refused to act upon her advice, Llewelyn would at least hear her out. But she was not getting off to the best of starts; the last thing she'd wanted was to put him on the defensive.

'I did not mean you've been unkind,' she said hastily. 'I was speaking, rather, of sins of omission. I do not deny what you've done for her, but Llewelyn, do you ever think of Joanna, truly think of her as a woman, as your wife? Do you know how unhappy she is? How homesick? Do you know that she has been trying for months now to befriend your children, but to no avail? Or that she turned fifteen more than two months ago?'

Llewelyn was listening intently, his face thoughtful now rather

267

than irritated, and Catherine gathered up her courage, concluded bluntly, 'I suspect . . . and please do not take this amiss; I do not mean it as a criticism, for I know how heavy your burdens are. But I suspect you forget about Joanna altogether when she's not right there in front of you.' And then she held her breath, waiting.

'Yes,' he said at last, 'I suppose there is some truth in what you say. I am fond of the lass, Catrin, but she's not all that often on my mind, I admit. Is she truly as unhappy as that? I thought she'd adjust in time . . .'

'She tries, wants so much to do what is expected of her. But she's very young, and very alone. She speaks no Welsh, and how many at your court speak French? She cannot even communicate with her maid, Llewelyn, and with you so often away, there are days when she has no one at all to talk to. She's lonely and homesick, finds herself an alien in a land not her own. Can you not imagine how that would be?'

Llewelyn drew an audible breath. 'Yes,' he said slowly. 'I can imagine quite well; I've been there.'

Catherine leaned over, kissed him on the cheek. 'Joanna is a lucky girl, and someday I shall tell her so,' she said, smiled at him. The puzzle lacked but one piece now, and since he'd been the first to make mention of it, she felt no compunction in saying, 'You said you were being patient with Joanna, because of her youth. Then that is why you've not yet bedded her?'

Llewelyn nodded. 'Why else? I knew, of course, that she was fourteen. But to tell you true, Catrin, it came as rather a shock to find out just how very young a fourteen she was.' He gave a rueful laugh, thinking back upon his wedding night. 'Not having a taste for rape, I thought it best to give her time –' He broke off abruptly. 'Surely you do not think I was wrong?'

'Indeed not! I think your forbearance was much for the best, was as clever as it was kind. But as fearful and reluctant as Joanna may have been on her wedding night, Llewelyn, that was over six months ago. How long do you mean to wait?'

She saw amusement in his eyes, saw sudden interest, too. 'Did Joanna speak to you of –'

'No!' she interrupted, quite indignantly. 'Do you truly think I'd betray her confidence if she had? I would never tell you what she'd confided to me in trust; you ought to know that. It is because she did not that I felt free to come to you like this, to tell you what I think.'

'Which is?'

'That Joanna is not the child you think her to be. And I'd venture to guess that, if you were to stop neglecting the girl and pay her some long overdue attention, you might be pleasantly surprised!'

Putting down Richard's letter, Joanna began to re-read her father's. These were the first letters she'd had since their departure for La Rochelle in late May. She'd expected such a silence, for John would have little time for letter-writing in the midst of a campaign, Isabelle was a notoriously poor correspondent, and Richard had not the funds to engage a courier of his own. It had been a long, lonely wait, but the news was good, was all she could have hoped to hear. Her father was coming home.

Reaching for her mantle, Joanna hastened from her chambers, out into the bailey. She knew Llewelyn was conferring that morning with Iorwerth ap Madog, the lawyer he'd chosen to compile the ancient law code of Hywel the Good, and she headed for the great hall. Catching sight of her husband in the window seat, she started towards him.

'Llewelyn, I've had a letter from my father! He –' Coming to an abrupt halt, staring at Catherine.

The window was covered with oiled linen, casting the seat into sun and shadow. Llewelyn positioned a cushion behind Joanna's back, sat down beside her. He was so close that she felt his breath upon her cheek as he leaned over to unfasten her mantle, so close that she could think of nothing else, sitting in silence until he prompted, 'Are you not going to tell me what your father wrote, Joanna?'

'He . . . he has won signal victories against the French, did take Montauban Castle in just fifteen days.' Joanna raised her eyes to Llewelyn's, found she could not look away. 'He writes that he has secured his hold upon Poitou, that he and Philip have agreed to a two-year truce.'

'It does sound as if his campaign was indeed a success,' Llewelyn agreed politely, forbearing to tarnish John's triumph by pointing out that he might have regained Poitou, but Normandy was still lost to Philip.

Joanna nodded. 'Not even Charlemagne could take Montauban, but Papa did,' she said proudly. 'He took Angers, too.' She hesitated

269

then, before saying with studied casualness, 'What were you and Catherine talking about?'

Llewelyn had, however, caught her inadvertent look of dismay at sight of them together. Having long ago learned that a half-truth was often far more effective than an outright denial in allaying suspicions, he said, with equal nonchalance, 'As it happens, we were talking of you. Catrin was taking me to task for having forgotten your birthday.'

'Oh,' Joanna said, much relieved. She was not sure what she'd feared, for even had Catherine repeated verbatim every one of their conversations this month past, would that have been so dreadful, after all? Actually, she was glad that Catherine had told him about the missed birthday; she wanted him to know.

'I expect it's best that you find out the truth about me early on.' Llewelyn's smile was wry. 'You see, love, I do have an appalling memory for dates, be they birthdays, name days, saints days, whatever. Tangwystl finally resorted to laying out tally sticks in our bedchamber, to remind me of the days remaining until her birthday. And my children take no chances, talk of nothing else for fully a month beforehand.'

'Alas, and I thought you were without flaw,' Joanna said lightly. She was suddenly very happy. They'd often sat and talked, but this conversation was somehow different, Llewelyn was somehow different. She could not have articulated the change, knew only that there was an intimacy between them that she'd never felt before.

'Am I forgiven? I should like to make amends, though, so you may ask of me what you will.'

'Anything? Anything at all?'

'Well, anything within reason,' Llewelyn hedged, but then laughed, realizing she was teasing.

Joanna laughed, too. 'I shall have to give it some thought. An opportunity such as this is not to be wasted, must be . . .' And then her eyes fell upon the letter in her lap. Very much in earnest now, she put a hand imploringly upon his arm. 'Did you truly mean it, Llewelyn? For there is something I do want, more than you could ever know. My father wrote he expects to land at Portsmouth within the fortnight. I've not seen him for nigh on seven months, and . . . and it would mean so much to me to be there on the dock, waiting for him. May I, Llewelyn? May I go home for a visit?'

She did not, Llewelyn saw, even catch her slip of the tongue, the use of 'home'. Catrin had been right; he'd not done all he could for the lass. 'Of course you may go to Portsmouth, Joanna, if that is your wish.'

'Thank you, oh, thank you!' For a moment he thought she was about to fling her arms around him; she made an indecisive movement, and then jumped to her feet. 'May I go now? Today? It'll take a week to reach London, after all, and I do not know when he's sailing. I could stay with my Aunt Ela, and we could travel together to Portsmouth. And . . . and if you'd not mind, I could remain for Papa's Christmas court?'

'I'd not mind in the least. What could be more natural than that you'd miss your father, your family? Now if you truly want to depart this noon, you'd best set your maids to packing. Meanwhile, I'll see about getting you a proper escort.'

Joanna had begun to thank him again, and he rose, put his arm around her waist. 'Why do you not,' he suggested, 'ask Catrin to help you pack? You did look rather . . . taken aback at sight of her earlier, and I'm sure you'd not want her to think she'd somehow displeased you. She's a good friend, Joanna; they do not come any better. You need never fear that she'd betray a confidence, share your secrets.'

'Was I so obvious as that?' Joanna asked softly, and Llewelyn nodded, gave her waist a gentle squeeze.

'So you admit, then, that you have secrets from me?' he murmured, and Joanna's eyes widened. On the surface, it could have passed for his usual banter, but the undercurrent carried an altogether different message. He was, she thought in utterly amazed delight, flirting with her.

'That,' she said impishly, 'is for me to know and you to find out.'

Llewelyn burst out laughing, more than a little intrigued. It was a child's answer, the sort of flippancy that any of his daughters might have uttered, but there was nothing at all childlike in the look she gave him, a look impossible to misread, for he'd had it from too many women in the past not to recognize it on sight for what it was – an invitation to further intimacies.

Blanche was even more excited than Joanna at the prospect of returning to England, and she completed the packing in record if disordered haste. Within the hour, Joanna found herself out in the bailey, watching as her coffers were loaded on to pack horses. Enid

271

came forward, made a quick curtsy and retreated as if she feared Joanna might change her mind, make her accompany them to the English King's court, after all. But Joanna merely smiled, and then startled Enid by giving her an utterly inappropriate hug. Embracing Catherine next, she waited until Sugar was safely settled into her travelling basket, and then moved towards Llewelyn.

He was standing with her seneschal, turned at her approach. 'Dylan and I have just been determining your route. You'll be ferried across the strait at Abermenai; Dylan will swim the horses across. Ordinarily, I'd have you pass the night with the monks at Aberconwy, but you're getting a late start, and I'd as soon you crossed Penmaenmawr in full light. So you'd best halt at Aber tonight.'

He drew her away from the others then, put something into her hand. 'Here, this is a gift for your father. I had it looped upon a chain so you could wear it around your neck, for safety's sake.'

It was, Joanna saw, a square-cut ruby ring, set in heavy gold. 'I shall present it to Papa with your compliments,' she promised, and Llewelyn shook his head.

'No, Joanna. I've arranged for a falcon from Ramsey Island as my New Year's gift. This will be from you, and you alone.' He smiled, for the ring had been taken in one of his grandfather's wars with the English, and it amused him to think of the English King wearing booty from a border raid.

Joanna was staring down at the ring. Her father had a passion for jewels, but she had never before been able to indulge that passion, to give him a gift so sure to please. 'How generous you are, how good to me,' she said, and reached up, kissed him quickly upon the cheek.

On impulse, Llewelyn stepped closer, took her in his arms. Curious as to what her response would be, he bent his head, touched his lips to hers. He was half-expecting her to recoil, as she had at Rhaeadr Ewynnol but he was, just as Catherine had predicted, very agreeably surprised. Far from shrinking back, Joanna at once put her arms around his neck. He tightened his hold; there was a fluid feel to her body, as if she'd flowed into his embrace, so yielding was she, so softly supple and pliant, so utterly unlike the girl who'd once gone rigid at his lightest touch. Her breath was sweet, her mouth opening under his like a flower. When he probed it with his tongue, she clung all the closer, showed herself to be a quick student, responding with timid tongue-flickerings of her own. It was, for a kiss born of curiosity, one that offered infinite and unexpected promise for the future, and it was with genuine regret that Llewelyn released her, ended their embrace.

He'd noted before that Joanna had unusually beautiful eyes; they changed with the light, her mood, reflected colour like crystal, hazel brown to gold-flecked emerald within the span of seconds. They were very green now, a misty, glowing green, wide with wonderment. She was quite flushed, was running the tip of her tongue over her lips, as if she were still savouring his kiss, and Llewelyn suddenly laughed. Was this how Eve had looked upon first tasting the forbidden fruit?

'Do not,' he said, 'be gone too long.'

December, 1206
Portsmouth, England

'How long must we wait, my lady? I'm so cold, am like to catch my death if we . . .'

But Joanna was not listening to Blanche, for she'd caught sight of her father. He had emerged from the sheltering tent, was watching as sailors secured their moorings. Beside him, Joanna recognized Peter des Roches, Bishop of Winchester, one of the few churchmen her father seemed inclined to trust. Isabelle was now out on deck, too, looking improbably beautiful in a hooded mantle of silvery fox fur, cuddling a small dog that might have been Sugar's twin. Joanna could wait no longer, pushed her way to the forefront of the small crowd assembled upon the dock.

John was half way down the gangplank when he saw Joanna. He paused, then smiled, kept his eyes upon her all the while the city fathers bade him welcome. As the wind was biting enough to curb even the most effusive tongues, the official greetings were mercifully brief, and within moments, Joanna was curtsying before her father. He raised her up, then drew her to him in a warm, enveloping hug.

'I could ask for no more agreeable surprise than this. But how did you manage it, lass? You are not a runaway wife, are you?'

His banter did not ring altogether true; for all that it was playfully posed, the question articulated a genuine concern. What did Papa fear – that she was unhappy as Llewelyn's wife? Or that her unhappiness might jeopardize his alliance with Llewelyn? Probably both, Joanna acknowledged, but without resentment. Papa would be counting up political gains and losses even upon his deathbed. So, she suspected, would Llewelyn.

'You need not worry, Papa,' she said, and smiled at him. 'I have a very indulgent husband.'

*

'Will you be coming to me tonight, John?'

Isabelle's ladies were preparing her for bed, and she was clad only in her chemise, her hair loose and flowing down her back. A lovely child, she was maturing into a breathtaking woman; John never tired of looking at her, had yet to tire of sleeping with her. Crossing the chamber, he drew her to him, into a possessive embrace. 'Does that answer your question? But it'll not be till late, so you need not wait up for me. I'll wake you.' He kissed her again, then turned towards Joanna.

'How about a kiss from you, too, sweetheart?' he said, and Joanna smiled, came quickly into his arms. Stepping back, he looked for a long moment into her face, and she thought he meant to ask for assurance. But he did not, and she wondered why; was it that, since he could not change what was writ, he'd rather not know if the price had been too high?

Isabelle was dismissing her ladies. 'That will be all. The Lady Joanna can see to my needs.' As soon as they were alone, she beckoned Joanna towards the bed. 'Well? Are you not going to tell me about Llewelyn?'

Joanna nodded. 'Yes,' she said slowly, 'I am.' She'd given it a great deal of thought in the last fortnight, had concluded that she had no choice but to confide in Isabelle. She was not blind to the risk; Isabelle was not the most reliable of confidantes. Yet there was no one else. For a time, she'd considered her aunt Ela, for Ela was a pious, earnest woman who'd go to her grave before she'd betray a trust. And like Joanna and Isabelle, Ela had been married very young, to a man much older than she. But there'd never been true intimacy between them; no matter how she tried, Joanna could not envision herself discussing so sensitive a subject with Ela. Nor did she think Ela was a likely source for the sort of advice she needed; Ela was too passive, too docile, too . . . good. Ela would not have understood. But Isabelle would. That Joanna never doubted.

'I do need your counsel, Isabelle. Things are not right between Llewelyn and me, not as they should be. But ere I say one blessed word, you must swear to keep secret whatever I tell you, swear upon your very soul.'

'That is insulting, Joanna. Do you think that I cannot keep a secret?' Joanna merely looked at her in significant silence, and Isabelle yielded, said reluctantly, 'Very well, I do so swear. You surprise me, though. I was so sure you'd take to Llewelyn . . .'

'I did that, in truth,' Joanna said ruefully. 'I love him, Isabelle. I did not want to, but I do. And now I'm frightened . . . because for the first time I think he's starting to see me as a woman. I want so much to believe that, but if I'm wrong . . . I do not think I could bear it. I'm afraid to go back, afraid to find out. And I'm afraid, too, that when I do, I'll say or do the wrong thing, that I'll –'

'Joanna, I want to help, I truly do. But I do not know what you're talking about. If you love him, what then is the problem?'

'That he's not yet taken me to bed,' Joanna said, before she could lose her nerve.

Isabelle's brows rose. 'Why not?'

'I think . . . think I'm not to his liking, not the way a man wants a woman.'

Isabelle did not make the conventional polite denial. For several moments she said nothing, and then she shook her head. 'That's not likely, Joanna. I grant you your colouring is unfortunate. But no man thinks of such matters in bed. Now if you were rail-slat thin or partridge plump . . . But you're not, have high breasts, a waist a man could span with his hands –' She broke off, began to laugh. 'I sound as if I'm tallying up the finer points of a filly I hope to sell; fifteen hands high, with a gait smooth as silk!'

Joanna laughed, too. Isabelle was unpredictable and irreverent, but she could be perversely comforting, too, and Joanna very much wanted to believe her. 'Why, then, Isabelle?'

'Well . . . sometimes a man can be so besotted with one woman that he has no desire to bed with any others,' Isabelle said, rather dubiously, and at once wished she had not, for Joanna looked stricken. 'But such men are as rare as unicorns. And you'd know if he were so smitten with a mistress; all the court would know, as when old King Henry doted so shamelessly upon Rosamond Clifford.' She signalled for Joanna to pour them wine, added thoughtfully, 'Of course it may just be that he thinks you're too young for bedding . . . or unwilling. Have you given him cause for that, Joanna?'

'Yes . . . I suppose I have,' Joanna admitted, startled. 'He did not seem to want me, you see, so I . . .'

'So you returned the favour. Foolish . . . but not fatal. I dare say you can mend the damage easily enough. You need only let him know, Joanna, that you want him in your bed; what could be simpler?'

'But how do I do that? I cannot very well tell him, can I?'

'Why not? I assure you no man ever took a woman's admission

276

of desire as an insult. But there are any number of ways to let a man know you want him. Make an excuse to seek him out in his bedchamber, invite him into yours, look upon him with loving eyes, talk softly, tease . . . Dearest, it is so easy, in truth!'

'For you, yes, but not for me!'

'You may be an innocent, Joanna, but your husband is not. He'll take your meaning quickly enough. In the morning we'll go through my coffers, pick out colours that become you. Now I want to show you what John gave me for my name day, a necklet of sapphires and silver . . .'

Joanna lay back against the pillows, only half-listening to this accounting of Isabelle's newest acquisition; Isabelle already had, she knew, jewels enough to bedazzle any queen in Christendom. But where men were concerned, Isabelle's instincts were sound. She must somehow dispel Llewelyn's doubts, let him know she was now most willing to be his wife . . . if, in truth, she had not already done so, out in the November sunlight before half his court. And closing her eyes, she gave herself up to remembering the feel of Llewelyn's mouth upon hers, that kiss so sweet, so hot and so surprising.

John had returned to England in good spirits, pleased with the fruits of his summer campaign. His sense of satisfaction had done nothing to curb his innate restlessness, however, and he let neither heavy snows nor the grumbling of his courtiers slow his pace. Landing at Portsmouth on December 12, he held court in the fortnight that followed at Beer Regis, Clarendon, Lugershall, Marlborough, Winchester, and Farnham.

This constant, almost compulsive movement set most tempers on edge, for roads were bad, the weather was worse, and accommodations hard to come by for those dragged along in John's wake. Joanna was one of the few to accept the chaos and inconvenience in good humour. For the first time in her life, she had money to spend, and she did so with abandon, purchasing bolts of the finest Lincoln wool for Catherine, a magpie and wicker cage for Gwladys, dolls with dyed hempen wigs for Marared and Gwenllian, wooden tops for Tegwared and Anghared, the twins she'd yet to meet, a sachet of orris root and anise for Enid. She'd even selected an ivory-handled eating knife for Gruffydd, although she felt herself a hypocrite for doing so, knowing she had bought the knife, not for the boy, but because she did not want Llewelyn to know she disliked his son. But her greatest joy was in choosing gifts for Llewelyn: a chess set of jasper and crystal, ivory dice, a pellison of soft vair to wear over his tunic. She had even, with some misgivings, purchased two pairs of chamois skin gloves; gloves were still something of a novelty, were worn only by men of the very highest rank, and she was not altogether sure that Llewelyn would be willing to adopt this new Norman fashion.

The Thursday after Christmas found the court settled at Guildford in Surrey, some thirty miles south of London. Joanna was delighted, for Guildford was a noted centre for the cloth trade. With Richard in patient attendance, she'd lingered over the wares so eagerly spread out for her inspection, eventually selecting a ruinously expensive length of Spanish cotton, a deep russet velvet, sindon linen fine enough to see through and, despite his token protest, a rich Coventry blue for Richard.

Richard watched in amusement as the merchants all but fell over themselves in their zeal to please his sister. 'You shall have to buy additional packhorses to get all your purchases back to Wales, you know,' he gibed, moving forward to help her mount her mare. 'But are you still set upon departing on the morrow, Joanna? We thought sure you'd stay through Epiphany, and I do not doubt Llewelyn did, too.'

'Wales is not at the back of beyond, Richard. I'll come again.'

'I just do not understand your haste. Nor does Papa, I'd wager.'

'No, he does not. And I confess I am surprised, Richard. I'd have thought Papa would be pleased that I miss the husband he chose for me. But when I told him I was leaving, he gave me the strangest look. As foolish as this is going to sound, I suddenly felt guilty, although why I do not know.'

A light snowfall was powdering the ground by the time they reached the King's manor. Hastening into the great hall, Joanna came to an uncertain halt. Something was amiss; she sensed it at once. So, too, did Richard. He took her arm, followed her towards the dais. Isabelle was standing at John's side, her face turned imploringly up to his, speaking softly, placatingly. He did not seem to be listening, but as she persevered, he shook her hand off his arm, snapped, 'Be still, Isabelle. I'd not have you meddle in that which you do not understand.'

Isabelle recoiled. 'I did only mean to comfort you,' she said,

278

sounding hurt. But John had already turned upon his heel; men hastily moved aside to let him pass.

'Isabelle, what has happened?'

'I've never seen him so angry, Joanna. When he first read the Pope's letter, he went so red I truly feared he might be stricken with a palsy. And then he blistered the air itself with his oaths. I'd have begged him not to blaspheme, but I had not the courage. And when I did say –'

'The Pope has given his decision, then?' Richard interrupted, with such urgency that Isabelle forgave his rudeness, nodded bleakly.

'I cannot believe what he has done, Richard. He declared Reginald's election invalid, just as he earlier repudiated Bishop de Grey's election. But then he instructed the monks to elect a man of his choosing, Stephen Langton, cardinal priest of St Chrysogonus, a member of the papal court. They did as he bade, of course, and he now writes that John must recognize Langton as Archbishop of Canterbury, says that since the election was held in Rome, there is no need for John to give his assent!'

Richard was stunned. 'Christ Jesus help us all,' he breathed, turned away. Joanna followed, clutched at his arm.

'Richard, I do not understand. What does this mean?'

'You truly do not know?' He stared at her in such surprise that Joanna blushed.

'No,' she confessed, 'I do not. I knew, of course, that the Archbishop of Canterbury had died, but to be truthful, Richard, I thought of little last year except my own troubles. I was, after all, facing a marriage I dreaded. And I've been in Wales since May. Will you tell me what has happened?'

'The trouble began last year, with Archbishop Walter's death. A faction of the Christchurch monks held a clandestine midnight meeting, elected Reginald, their sub-prior, as Archbishop, sent him secretly to Rome to secure the Pope's confirmation. When Papa got word of this, he was understandably wroth. The King has ever had the right to have his own man as Archbishop; for more than a hundred years, so has it been. Papa confronted the monks at Canterbury, and they repented their folly, disavowed Reginald's election. Last December they chose an Archbishop more to Papa's liking, John de Grey, Bishop of Norwich.'

Richard frowned. 'This past March the Pope declared Bishop de Grey's election invalid, ordered the monks to send a new delegation to Rome. And now he has dared to handpick his own man as Archbishop of Canterbury! Papa can never ratify Langton's election, never. No English king would.'

'Oh, dear God!' Joanna sat down suddenly in the window seat, staring up at her brother in dismay. 'The Pope will not back down either, Richard. If Papa will not recognize Langton as Archbishop of Canterbury, he may well lay England under Interdict!'

Joanna bit her lip, remembering how the innocent had suffered when the Pope laid France under Interdict six years ago. Few papal weapons were as effective, and few were as unfair, inflicting pain upon the many to punish the few, denying to the faithful all Sacraments save the Last Rites, denying them Mass, confession, burial in consecrated ground. Philip was a monarch noted for his inflexible nature, his unimaginative obstinacy. He had capitulated in seven months. But Papa will not, Joanna thought with sudden certainty. Even if the Pope does lay all England under Interdict, he'll not yield. And then the Pope will have no choice. To compel earthly obedience, he will sacrifice Papa's immortal soul, will lay upon him the anathema of excommunication.

Joanna had been present when the Bishop of Lincoln excommunicated a baron who'd run afoul of Church law. She'd never forgotten it. The church had been hung with black tapestry. Moving with a slow, measured step, the Bishop and priests had entered the chancel, each holding aloft a flaming candle. And then the Bishop had cried out in a truly terrible voice, a voice that carried to Joanna the shiver of thunderbolts and the smell of sulphur, 'Gilbert de Rémy! Let him be cursed in the city and cursed in the field; cursed in his granary, his harvest, and his children; as Dathan and Abiram were swallowed up by the gaping earth, so may Hell swallow him; and even as today we quench the torches in our hands, so may the light of his life be quenched for all eternity, unless he do repent!' An appalled silence had fallen over those watching, and then they had flung their candles to the ground, casting the church into darkness.

'Papa will not yield, Richard. You know he will not. And if he does not . . .'

'If he does not,' Richard said bleakly, 'God pity England.'

20

January, 1207
Aber, North Wales

'Is Aber much further, Madame?' Alison's face was hooded by her mantle, but her voice was slurred with fatigue. Joanna felt a prick of remorse, for she was responsible for their punishing pace, having overruled Dylan and insisted that they push on for Aber instead of passing the night in comfort at Aberconwy Abbey. She knew she was being unfair to the others, especially to Alison. But she'd had six weeks to nurture her hopes, to hone her expectations to a fine edge.

Moreover, there was an element of calculation in her insistence; she wanted to arrive at Aber after dark. It was well and good for Isabelle blithely to advise her to lure Llewelyn into her bedchamber, for Isabelle's shyness had not survived her first glance into a mirror. But Joanna did not think she had either the experience or the assurance to carry off an amorous ambush, to play the coquette with such obvious intent. If she were to reach Aber at night, however, what would be more natural than that she'd go to Llewelyn's chambers to let him know of her arrival? If he responded as she hoped, her journey would end in his bed; if not, she could at least protect her pride, would be able to make a dignified departure for her own chambers. The more Joanna thought about it, the more foolproof it seemed – and the more appealing, a private reunion in soft firelight, with a bed so invitingly available for more intimate conversation.

Winter travel was always a dubious proposition; men who might easily cover thirty miles on a summer's day in June would find themselves lucky to make half that distance come January. But Joanna had allowed for that, felt sure they would still reach Aber soon after dark. What she had not allowed for was the snowstorm. It slowed them to a walk, for a time halted them altogether, and when at last they rode into Aber, it was well past midnight.

Joanna's disappointment was not as acute as it might otherwise

281

have been; by then she was so tired and so cold that she yearned only for sleep, and as soon as a fire was lit in her chamber, she and Alison fell, shivering, into bed. She awoke just before dawn, to find Alison already up and dressed; when she offered apologies for the harshness of Alison's introduction to Wales, the other girl said with a grin:

'If those mountains are as fearsome as you said, Madame, I think it was probably a mercy that I was spared the sight of them!'

Joanna grinned, too, remembering her first glimpse of Penmaenmawr Pass. 'I dare say you're right!' Alison was a genuine jewel, she thought fondly, blessing her luck in having thought to mention Blanche's sulks to Isabelle. In one brief afternoon Isabelle had resolved the problem, finding Blanche a position with the Countess of Surrey and finding Alison for Joanna. A Yorkshire knight's younger daughter, Alison was ambitious enough to jump at the chance to serve a royal household, and plucky enough to look upon a sojourn in Wales as an adventure. She was, Joanna now saw, holding out the most becoming of Joanna's new gowns. Joanna had been dubious of the colour, a dark wine-red, but Isabelle brushed aside her qualms, and as always, her fashion sense was flawless; when worn with a rose-coloured bliaut, the effect was pleasing even to Joanna's hypercritical eye.

'You seemed so eager to be back with your husband, my lady, that I thought you would wish to go to him upon waking.'

Suddenly Joanna was wide awake. She stared at the gown; it glowed with soft, seductive colour, and her pulse began to quicken. 'Yes,' she said, 'I do.'

Dressing with nervous haste, she fidgeted as Alison combed out her long, dark hair; she'd made the daring decision to leave it unbound, free-flowing down her back. And then Alison was holding out her mantle, saying with a smile, 'How pleased Lord Llewelyn will be to see you, Madame.'

The snow had ended in the night, but the bailey was blanketed in drifts and a chill, damp wind was sweeping off the sea. Clutching the most elegant pair of Llewelyn's new gloves, Joanna cautiously made her way towards her husband's quarters; never had the Welsh partiality for separate buildings seemed so ill advised. The sky was just beginning to lighten, but the mountain peaks were crowned with clouds, warning that the sun's sovereignty was likely to be brief.

She knew Llewelyn was an even earlier riser than most, but this morning he seemed to be lingering abed, for his squires were still asleep, bundled under blankets in the outer chamber. The guard, too, was dozing, but he jerked upright as Joanna closed the door, blinking at her as if she were an apparition. 'Holy Jesus, Madame, where did you come from?' he blurted out, with such a guileless disregard for protocol that Joanna had to laugh.

'You're dreaming; I'm still in London,' she said teasingly, moved past him into her husband's bedchamber. The room was in semi-darkness, shutters drawn and candles as yet unlit, and she paused in the doorway, hesitant until she heard Llewelyn's voice. There was a smoky sound to it, a lazy languor that warmed her like a physical touch. She'd never before realized how musical a language Welsh was; it had a lilt and cadence all its own. The bed curtains were partially pulled back; she took a step forward, saw the woman first. She was propped up on an elbow, her face in shadows, but as Joanna watched, she leaned over, spilling dark-honey hair on to Llewelyn as their mouths met. He said something that made her laugh, kissed her again, and started to sit up. As he did, he turned his head, saw Joanna standing frozen in the doorway.

'Joanna?' He sounded utterly incredulous, as if doubting his own senses, and that broke the spell. Joanna spun around, fled into the antechamber, out into the snow. She fell twice; the second time her ankle twisted under her and she lost Llewelyn's gloves, but she regained her feet before any of the startled spectators could come to her aid, at last reached the refuge of her bedchamber.

'My God, Madame, what happened?'

Joanna pulled the bolt into place, stumbled towards the nearest coffer. Her ankle had begun to throb. Raising her hand to her hair, she found it wet with snow; so, too, were the skirts of her wine-red gown.

'Madame, you're trembling so! Can you not tell me what is wrong?'

'No,' Joanna said. 'No.'

At a loss, Alison did what she could, cleaned the snow from Joanna's gown, removed her mantle, poured her a cup of wine. Joanna set it down untouched. She seemed oblivious of Alison's awkward attempts at consolation, but she jumped to her feet at sound of footsteps in the antechamber.

'Joanna, we do need to talk.'

Alison was reaching for the bolt when Joanna shook her head vehemently. 'But Madame, he is your husband!'

283

'Joanna, open the door.'

Alison looked helplessly to Joanna for guidance. Joanna said nothing, staring at the door.

In the outer chamber, Llewelyn, too, was staring at the door. His demands for admittance were accomplishing nothing except to attract an audience. Turning, he slammed the antechamber door in their faces, again tried the latch in vain. He was not accustomed to being defied, nor to being made to feel foolish, and at this moment he felt very foolish indeed. It was almost a relief, therefore, to have Joanna present him with a legitimate grievance, to be able to ease his discomfiture in anger.

'Joanna, I'll not tell you again. If you do not open this door, I swear by Christ that I'll fetch an axe and force it!'

There was a long silence. Just when he'd begun to fear he might have to follow through on his threat, he heard the bolt slide back. The girl who opened the door was unfamiliar to him, obviously frightened. Joanna was standing by the trestle table. She took several backward steps as Llewelyn strode towards her, said:

'Do not ever lock a door against me again.'

She flinched, and he saw then that she was no less frightened than her maid. Norman men were, he knew, free with their fists, apt to follow up a verbal reprimand with physical reinforcement. That realization took some of the edge off his temper. So, too, did the tears glistening behind her lashes.

Llewelyn took a deep breath, remembered he was here to redress a wrong, not to inflict new ones. 'I did not want to hurt you, lass, in truth I did not.' But when he put his hand on her arm, she said stonily:

'Go away. Just go away and leave me be.'

She was, Llewelyn thought, making this needlessly difficult. 'Joanna, I am sorry,' he said, to Joanna not sounding sorry at all. 'But this was not all my fault. I did not expect you back for a fortnight, at least. How was I to know you'd return so suddenly, or that you'd make a dawn appearance in my bedchamber? For most of our marriage, you've acted as if that was the last place you'd ever want to be!'

Joanna crimsoned. Her humiliation was, for the moment, even stronger than her hurt; she could think only of what a fool she'd made of herself. If only she had it to do over, if only God would give her back those shaming moments before his bed. 'You need not

284

worry,' she said, much chagrined by the sudden tremor in her voice, 'I'll not intrude upon you again. You can go back to your bed, back to your slut, finish what I so rudely interrupted.'

'Cristyn is no slut,' he said coldly. 'She is Tegwared and Anghared's mother.'

Cristyn. Did he call her 'beloved' and 'darling', did he murmur Welsh words of endearment whilst making love? 'Forgive my innocence, my lord husband, but even amongst the Welsh I'd not think bearing two bastard children would be a testament to a woman's virtue!'

Llewelyn looked at her without speaking for an unbearably long moment. '"Even amongst the Welsh," we do honour those who gave us life. The slurs you cast upon Cristyn can as easily be turned against your own mother, can they not?' He did not wait for her response, turned and walked out.

Joanna's anger ebbed away, to be replaced by desolation. She sank down, trembling, upon the nearest stool. Llewelyn was right. In seeking to belittle Cristyn, she had indeed besmirched Clemence, too. Far worse, she had affronted Llewelyn beyond forgiving. He would hate her now, would never want her as his wife.

So caught up was she in her own misery that it was some time before she became aware of Alison. The other girl was kneeling by her stool, looking up at her with eyes full of fear.

'Ah, Madame, what have you done?' she whispered. 'Go after him, beg his forgiveness ere it be too late!'

'It is already too late,' Joanna said wretchedly, but Alison shook her head.

'He is angry, yes, but his heart has not had time to harden against you. You must seek him out ere it does. Madame, listen to me. I do know what it is like to live in a house without love. My mother had too sharp a tongue, and then, too, my father blamed her for failing to give him a son . . . Well, the reasons count for naught. What does is that he did not use her well, Madame, made of her life a Hell on earth. A man can do that, my lady, can treat his wife no better than the meanest serf, and who is to gainsay him? She is his, after all, to be lessoned as he chooses. And in this we all are sisters. High birth did not spare Philip's Danish-born Queen. Nor your grandmother, Queen Eleanor of blessed memory. And your husband is a Prince, is a man to expect obedience above all else. I was astonished, in truth, that he did not take his hand to you, but you're not likely to be so lucky a second time. Go to him, tell him you're sorry. Would you have him hate you for all your married life?'

'No,' Joanna said, 'oh no!' And before she could repent of her resolve, she snatched up her mantle, ran from the chamber.

The bailey was now astir with people; they turned to stare as Joanna passed. There was no one at all, however, in Llewelyn's outer chamber. Joanna leaned for a moment against the door, sought to catch her breath. She'd not yet thought what she was going to say to him, knew that if she dwelt upon it, she'd lose her nerve. Tapping lightly on the door, she said, 'Llewelyn, it's Joanna. May we talk?'

She heard footsteps, and then the door swung open. Joanna stiffened at sight of Cristyn. She'd not dreamed Cristyn would still be there; surely if the woman had any decency at all, she'd have withdrawn at once. Yet Cristyn had not even bothered to dress, was clad only in a linen chemise. This was the first real look Joanna had got at her husband's mistress. She saw before her a tall, poised woman in her mid-twenties, with rather unusual and striking colouring. Cristyn had very white skin, masses of dark-gold hair, and brown eyes. She was not beautiful; her mouth was too large, her nose too tip-tilted, but there was about her an unstudied sensuality, a provocative earthiness more alluring than mere prettiness. Joanna could understand all too well the appeal Cristyn might have for a man, for Llewelyn.

For a heartbeat they stared at each other, and then Cristyn said, in passable French, 'Llewelyn is not here. This morn he was to meet Bishop Robert and the Bishop of St Asaph in Bangor, and rode out directly after he talked to you.'

Turning away, she moved back towards the bed. 'You will excuse me whilst I finish dressing?' she said, reaching for her stockings.

'I do not recall giving you leave to sit in my presence,' Joanna snapped, saw a resentful flush rise in Cristyn's face and throat. She came reluctantly to her feet, making it quite clear that she thought Joanna was not playing fair. Joanna did not care; fairness was the furthest concern from her mind. If she'd thought her command would have been obeyed, she'd have banished Cristyn then and there into English exile, even into Ireland if she could.

Cristyn was waiting, brown eyes suddenly wary. 'Madame?' she said icily, and Joanna felt so much hatred that it frightened her. She stared past Cristyn at the bed; it was still unmade, rumpled and warm where they had lain, Llewelyn and Cristyn, making leisurely love through the night. Whirling about, Joanna crossed the threshold, beckoned to one of the men loitering without.

'Madame?'

'Take that bed out into the bailey, and there burn it,' she said, saw the man's jaw drop.

'Jesu, Madame, I cannot do that! It is my lord's bed, is worth –'

'And I am your lord's wife, am I not? I have just given you a command, so see to it . . . now.'

Cristyn had followed Joanna to the doorway of the antechamber; she, too, looked dumbfounded. The man's eyes flicked from her to Joanna, and then he nodded. It took four men to wrestle the mattress out into the bailey; cursing and panting, they dragged it a safe distance from the building. By now a large, curious crowd had gathered. Someone brought out a torch; there were loud murmurings among the onlookers as the bed coverings ignited, burst into flame.

Joanna stood motionless, watching as the bed burned. After a time the wind shifted, blew smoke into her face, and she coughed, turned away.

'What of the bed frame, my lady? Shall we burn that, too?' The voice was young, the face friendly, lit by an engaging grin.

'No,' Joanna said, startled to see that most of the other faces were friendly, too. She'd not expected that. They were watching her with amused interest, even approval, seemed to take her action as a great joke. To Joanna, it was anything but that. She was just beginning to realize what she'd done. She must have been mad, in truth, for Llewelyn would never forgive her now, never.

Although Alison had managed to infect Joanna for a time with her panic, it soon passed. Llewelyn wanted an alliance with her father, would do nothing to jeopardize it. He'd not send her back to England in disgrace. Nor would he ever abuse her as Philip abused Ingeborg. She felt sure that was not Llewelyn's way.

He might well beat her for burning the bed, though. Even the most indulgent husband was likely to react with rage to folly of that sort. Each time Joanna thought of facing him with such a sin on her conscience, she shivered. She'd once seen a knight strike his wife in the great hall at Westminster, before a score of well-born witnesses; blood had gushed from the woman's nose, stained her gown and wimple. And while the man's action had been greeted with almost universal disapproval, it was not his brutality that earned him such scorn, but rather that he'd been so ill-mannered as to punish her in public. Even men who never hit their wives would still, Joanna knew, defend in principle their right to do so. Women were the lesser sex, after all, and even Holy Church said they were born to be ruled by man. Alison was right; she had indeed been lucky that morning.

But what she feared far more than a beating was the loss of Llewelyn's friendship. How could she bear to have him look upon her with distaste, to shun her company, treat her with chill politeness? And how could it be otherwise now? Even when he finally took her to his bed, it would be without affection or tenderness; he'd not make love to her, would make use of her to beget an heir. He might even install Cristyn openly in his bed, at his table. And it was her fault. She had allowed her jealousy to rob her of what she most wanted.

The six-mile ride from Aber to Bangor Fawr yn Arfon had done much to cool Llewelyn's anger, as he'd known it would. He'd always had a happy faculty for concentrating upon one problem at a time, and by the time he arrived at the great cathedral church of St Deiniol, he had as his primary concern the upcoming meeting with the Bishops of Bangor and St Asaph. He was never able to put his quarrel with Joanna completely from his mind, but he did succeed in focusing his attention upon the matters at hand, by day's end was satisfied with what he had accomplished.

It was dusk as he made ready to return to Aber. His escort was augmented by Ednyved's force, for the latter had been a guest of Bishop Robert's, and was now planning to move on to his own manor at Llys Euryn in Creuddyn.

'I assume you can find me a comfortable bed for the night at Aber?' Giving Llewelyn a mischievous, sidelong glance, Ednyved added, 'Or should I be offering you a safe bed at Llys Euryn?'

Llewelyn could not hide his surprise. 'What have you – second sight?'

Ednyved grinned. 'Just an ear for choice gossip. One of your men – who shall remain mercifully nameless – was kind enough to tell me about all I'd missed this morn. Did your girl-wife truly walk in on you and Cristyn? Jesus wept! What did you do? Mind you, that's not mere morbid curiosity, but in case I ever find myself in a like predicament!'

'I did what any man would do when caught in the wrong. I lost my temper.'

Ednyved laughed, then nudged his mount closer to Llewelyn's. 'Does Joanna know, Llewelyn, that you've given her grounds for ending the marriage? Is there any chance she's on her way home to England even as we talk?'

Llewelyn shook his head. 'Joanna knows naught of Welsh ways, even after some months in our midst. Moreover, Joanna knows that John wants me as ally, and as hard as it may be to fathom, she has found in him much to love.'

Llewelyn was aware that he was a magnet for all eyes, but it did not bother him unduly; he'd lived most of his thirty-three years on centre stage. He was bothered, however, by Joanna's failure to appear for the meal. Each time he glanced at her empty seat, he felt a twinge of guilt; nor was his conscience eased to be told she'd eaten nothing all day, had not ventured from her chambers since the morning. He sent a servant to the kitchen, and by the time dinner was over, a platter was waiting, mead and wafers and venison pasty. Ednyved sauntered over, drawled, 'As peace offerings go, you'd get better results with moonstones and amethyst,' accompanying Llewelyn as he left the hall, stepped out into the icy dark of the bailey.

'My lord . . .' A man emerged so unexpectedly from the shadows that they both started, instinctively dropped hands to sword hilts. But as he stepped closer, Llewelyn recognized Aldwyn, his silentiary.

'My lord . . . after you rode out this morn, your wife went to your chambers in search of you. The Lady Cristyn was there and they had words.' He paused, said unhappily, 'My lord, I know not how to tell you, but . . .'

'But what?' Llewelyn said sharply.

'Princess Joanna . . . she ordered us to burn your bed.'

'She did what?' Turning, Llewelyn looked at Ednyved, and then, of one accord and to Aldwyn's indescribable relief, they were shouting with laughter.

'Lord Jesus,' Ednyved gasped, wiping his eyes. 'Just count yourself lucky you were not in it at the time, my lad!' Sobering somewhat, he said, 'I've a confession, one that'll make me sound an utter ass. But when Aldwyn gave that pregnant pause, the damnedest thought crossed my mind, that Joanna knew more of Welsh law than you think, knew that, catching Cristyn in your bed, she had the right to claim Cristyn's life without paying a blood-fine!'

'Ah, but only if she did it with her own hand. Can you truly

289

imagine Joanna stabbing Cristyn . . . or anyone else?' After a moment, Llewelyn began to laugh again. 'But then, I never thought her capable of burning my bed, either!'

Llewelyn found himself hesitating before the door of Joanna's bedchamber. He was perfectly willing to placate his young wife, to offer her the balm of smiles and soft, soothing words. He was not so willing to humble his pride, to play a role for which he'd had so little practice, that of penitent, and it was with an unexpected sense of unease that he beckoned to his servant, reached for the door latch.

He forgot his reluctance, however, with his first sight of Joanna. Her face was pinched and drawn, a mirror for such misery that he no longer begrudged her an apology, would give it gladly if that would but heal her hurt.

He gestured for the servant to put down his burden, waiting until they were alone to say, 'I was told you'd eaten nothing all day, Joanna.'

Joanna was staring at the platter in disbelief. 'You . . . you are not angry with me?'

'Ah, Joanna . . . I'm sorry, love, I swear I am.'

To be offered absolution when she'd been expecting damnation was, to Joanna, nothing less than miraculous, and when Llewelyn took a step towards her, she more than met him half way, flung herself into his arms with a choked cry.

'I thought you'd never forgive me, never. Llewelyn, I am so sorry. I had not the right to speak to you as I did, no right to reproach you. It is not a wife's place to question her husband's action. I know that. But I . . . I was so jealous, so very jealous . . .'

Llewelyn stroked her hair, tightened his arms around her. 'Joanna, you had every right. Let's sit on the settle and talk about it.'

Joanna accepted a cupful of mead and, when urged by Llewelyn, even took a few bites of a cheese-filled wafer, but she tasted none of it. She still could not quite believe Llewelyn was here, sitting beside her on the settle, sharing her mead cup, for the first time calling her 'love' as if he meant it.

'I think you need to know how we look upon women. It is true, lass, that a Welshwoman cannot inherit her father's lands, whereas she would have a right of inheritance in England. But that is for the same reason that our laws exclude men maimed, deaf, crippled, or stricken with leprosy. It was feared, you see, that women, and men so afflicted, could not hold their lands against attack. But we do not claim that womanly weakness on the battlefield should make her subordinate in all else, too, as you Normans do. Our women cannot be wed against their will, and a Welsh wife has no less right to walk away from an unhappy marriage than does her husband.'

'But Llewelyn . . . the Church does recognize only three grounds for voiding a marriage: a previous plight troth, kinship within the seventh degree, or spiritual affinity such as acting as godparent.'

'Well, to tell you true, Joanna, when the Church's teachings conflict with the old customs, we tend to go our own way. As in our preference for marrying cousins. We have a saying, love: "Marry in the kin and fight the feud with the stranger." So when it comes to interpreting the marriage bond, we follow Hywel the Good rather than the Pope.'

Llewelyn laughed suddenly. 'I've been told that some Norman churchmen see my success as divine proof of the power of legitimacy. My father Iorwerth was a child of Owain Fawr's first marriage; when Owain later married his cousin Crisiant, the Church refused to recognize the union, and when he would not abjure Crisiant, Thomas à Becket excommunicated him. So they see my triumph over my uncles Davydd and Rhodri as ordained, they being sons of the so-called incestuous marriage. The only flaw in that theology is that my mother and father were themselves first cousins!'

He handed Joanna back the mead cup, said, 'But we were talking of how we end a marriage. It may always be done by mutual consent. And then, a husband may disavow his wife if she claims to be a virgin and he discovers on their wedding night that she is not, or if he finds her in compromising circumstances with another man, of course, or if her marriage portion falls short of what was promised.'

Llewelyn had been, for some moments now, playing with her hair; the feel of his fingers on her throat was so delightfully distracting to Joanna that she was not fully concentrating upon what he was saying. But at that, she smiled up at him, murmuring, 'Then you have me for better or worse, since my father handed Ellesmere Castle over to you months ago, I would never be unfaithful, and I am indeed a virgin.'

'For much too long, I think,' he said softly, dark eyes promising enough to bring a blush to Joanna's face. 'But do you not want to know how a wife may shed an unwanted husband? There are four grievances that will gain her freedom: if the man contracts leprosy, if he has foul breath, if he is incapable in bed . . . or if he does three times dishonour their marriage vows.'

Joanna all but choked on her mead. 'Now you are teasing me!'

'No,' he said, 'I am not, love. The first two times that a Welsh wife discovers her husband has bedded with another woman, she has the right to demand from him payment of a *gowyn* – a fine, if you will – for his adultery. With his third fall from grace, she may leave him, although if she does not, she then has no further cause for complaint.'

Llewelyn paused. 'There is one more reason for ending a marriage, Joanna – if a husband does ever bring another woman under his wife's roof.'

'As you did with Cristyn?' Joanna whispered, and he nodded.

'Yes, as I did with Cristyn. Amongst our people, that is one of the three great scandals, and the wife may at once disavow the marriage, disavow the husband who has so wronged her.'

'I . . . I would never do that, Llewelyn.' Joanna was stunned; in her world, laws such as these were more than radical, they were revolutionary. She was silent for a time, trying to take in this astonishing new insight, that Llewelyn, not she, had been in the wrong.

'I thank you for telling me. You did not have to, you know . . .' It came to her then, the reason for Llewelyn's remarkable restraint, and she cried, 'Now I understand! Why, as angry as you were this morn, you did not touch me. It was because I was in the right, was it not?'

'Joanna, I've never hit a woman in my life. You've not been listening to me, love. Did I not tell you we do not treat our women as the Normans do? Amongst my people, we do not take out our bad tempers upon our wives just because they happen to be handy. Welsh law allows a husband the right to discipline his wife for three offences only: if she is unfaithful, if she gambles away the family goods, or if she casts slurs upon his manhood. Should he strike her for any other reason, he is then obligated to play her a *sarhaed* or honour-price.'

Joanna had been listening in astonishment. '"A woman, a serf, and a willow tree, the more you beat them, the better they be,"' she quoted, and shook her head. 'But do men truly abide by these laws, Llewelyn?'

'Not all men, love. More do than not, however. You see, an

292

abused wife has the right to appeal to her male kinsmen for succour, and if they fail to protect her, the shame then falls upon them. Knowing a careless slap will bring down upon his head the wrath of his wife's kindred, might even give rise to a blood feud, well, that does act to curb all but the most heedless of men.'

Llewelyn drew her still closer, and Joanna shifted so that she could pillow her head against his chest. 'I begin to think the greatest gift the Almighty could give any woman would be for her to be born Welsh!'

'Or to marry a Welshman,' Llewelyn suggested, and kissed her. For Joanna, it was as it had been on that November noon at Rhosyr; she experienced again sensations exciting and unfamiliar, found her body responding to his touch like a flower starved for sun. All her senses seemed suddenly to have intensified, and when he slid his hand into the bodice of her gown, began to caress her breast, she gave a gasp, sought his mouth with hers.

Llewelyn was delighted. Brushing aside her fall of thick, ebony hair, he put his lips to the pulse in her throat, with his free hand unfastening the side lacings of her bliaut. 'Sweet . . . very sweet. I must have been well and truly out of my mind not to take you to bed ere this,' he murmured, utterly taken aback when Joanna abruptly went rigid in his embrace, then recoiled as violently as on that day at Rhaeadr Ewynnol.

For a startled moment Llewelyn did not move, staring up at her in amazement. He could not have mistaken her willingness, the way her body warmed under his caresses. She was not merely acquiescent, she was eager. That had been no pretence, he'd wager his life on it. Yet there was no pretence, either, in the stricken look on her face, no denying her sudden fear. He could only assume he'd gone too fast, fondled her too intimately too soon. Coming to his feet, he said, 'What is it, love? You've no cause for fear, Joanna, not with me.'

'But you do not know what I've done!'

'What you've done?' Whatever Llewelyn might have been expecting to hear, that was not it.

On the verge of tears, Joanna nodded. 'I went to your chambers this morning to ask your forgiveness. She . . . Cristyn was there, and I . . . Oh, Llewelyn, I burned your bed!'

Llewelyn bit down on his lower lip, pulled her back into his arms. 'Yes, love, I know.'

'You know?' Incredulously. 'And you're not angry?'

'Well, I'd rather you did not make a habit of it.' But with that, Llewelyn's gravity shattered into a multitude of mirthful splinters, and he laughed until he, too, was on the verge of tears.

Giddy with relief, Joanna began to laugh, too, until Llewelyn kissed her again. 'Now,' he said, with a grin that caught at her heart, 'ere I take you to bed, have you any other sins to confess?'

Joanna found herself longing to admit how much she loved him. But she did not, for it was not fair to burden him with a love he might never be able to return. She shook her head, looking up at him with eyes so soft and glowing, such utterly trusting eyes, that Llewelyn caught his breath.

'It will be good for you, Joanna,' he promised. 'I'll give you as much time as you need; we do have all night.'

'Do you know what Isabelle told me? That a woman will find the greatest pleasure in an older man's bed. She says a youth of twenty or so will pounce upon a girl like a dog on a bone, will be done and dying away almost ere he begins. But a man of a more seasoned age knows well how to – in her words, not mine – mount a mare and prolong the ride!'

'I'm almost afraid to ask, but how did Isabelle come to be so worldly, so knowing in carnal matters? John gave her a crown; did she give him horns?'

'Of course not! She knows that older men make better lovers because Papa did tell her so. Llewelyn . . . why are you laughing at me?'

'Because I suspect, my darling, that you're three swallows short of tipsy.'

Joanna peered at her half-empty cup of mead, trying to remember if this was her second or third. 'I believe,' she said thoughtfully, 'that you might well be right. I do feel . . . strange.'

Llewelyn moved his hand caressingly up her thigh. 'How, Joanna?'

'Feather light, as if all the bone and marrow in my body weighed no more than gossamer, as if your arms alone anchored me to the earth.' She shivered as Llewelyn tugged at the bodice of her chemise, freeing her breasts. His breath was hot on her skin, and she watched with fascination as her nipples swelled, became hard and taut. 'Oh, Llewelyn, love, you're right, I am tipsy! What I do not know is whether it is the mead, or whether it is you.'

'Let's find out,' he said, and when she put her arms around his neck, he lifted her from the settle, carried her across the chamber to the bed.

Llewelyn had never before understood the appeal virgins had for other men, had always looked upon a woman's maidenhead as more of an impediment to pleasure than a proof of purity. But now with Joanna, he found virginity need not be embarrassing or inhibiting, that it could even be enhancing. There was something very exciting in Joanna's wonderment, in her surprise, and her satisfaction. As she sighed, twisted against him, he knew she was experiencing sensations utterly new to her, experiencing all the urgency and pleasure that the body could give – for the very first time. To diminish her pain and prolong their enjoyment, he sought to keep physical needs under mental thrall, making use of all the tricks he'd learned in the twenty years since he had, as an awed fourteen year old, discovered how sweet fruits of the flesh could be, drawing out their lovemaking until he dared delay no longer. She stiffened under him, but did not cry out, and he felt the barrier give way with his second thrust. Joanna was gasping his name. He covered her mouth with his own, and she clung tightly, then turned her head from side to side on the pillow, shuddering, all but blinding them both with the wild tossing of her hair. Yielding to his own need, he let it take him towards satisfaction, towards that ephemeral moment of release, so fleeting and yet so overwhelming in its intensity, in its peculiar union of pleasure and pain.

Joanna awoke with an enormous thirst, a dull headache, and a profound sense of wonder. Alison at once approached the bed, offering a cup of watered-down wine. Reaching for it eagerly, Joanna drank in grateful gulps. 'What time is it?' she yawned, and winced, for she'd suddenly discovered that her thigh muscles were stiff and sore.

'Nigh on noon, Madame. My lord Prince said we were to let you sleep, and to give you this.' Holding out an unsealed parchment.

This speaker was a stranger to Joanna, was a slender, young woman with a delicate heart-shaped face and thick chestnut braids. 'Who,' Joanna asked, 'are you?'

The girl made a shy curtsy. 'I am Branwen, Madame. Lord Llewelyn wanted you to have a handmaiden who spoke French, thought I might suit you better than Enid. I would have been here yesterday to welcome you back, but we did not expect you for nigh on a fortnight. That will not happen again, I promise.'

'That is all right, Branwen,' Joanna said absently. Llewelyn's message was a let-down, a brief two lines: 'Cariad, I do have to meet again with the Bishops in Bangor, will be back by dark.' No more than that, unsigned but for a large scrawling double l.

'Branwen . . . what does *cariad* mean?'

'*Cariad?* Why, that is Welsh for "beloved", Madame,' she said, and Joanna sank back, smiling, upon the pillow.

Never had an afternoon passed with such excruciating slowness. Never had Joanna so begrudged daylight its domain. But with the coming of dusk, had come, too, the snow. Joanna's spirits plummeted. When it was evident even to her that Llewelyn was not going to return in time for dinner, if he returned at all, she went off to preside over a glum meal in the great hall. The snow slackened somewhat as the evening dragged on, and twice the arrival of late-comers sent her flying to the window, watching hopefully as they dismounted in the bailey. The third time that horsemen rode in, she did not even bother to look, having at last accepted the obvious, that Llewelyn had decided to pass the night in Bangor. But then Alison exclaimed, 'Madame, I see lights in your lord's chambers!'

Joanna's excitement was contagious, and Alison and Branwen enthusiastically set about making her ready for Llewelyn, brushing out her hair, applying strategic daubs of perfume. Looking into the mirror Alison held up, Joanna was, for once, pleased with what she saw. Her eyes reflected the colour of her moss-green gown, and she was becomingly flushed, a flush that seemed to be spreading through her entire body, the throbbing languid warmth that claimed her each time she let herself think upon their lovemaking.

'My lady . . .' Alison turned slowly from the window. Not looking at Joanna's face, she said, 'The lights . . . they've gone out.'

Joanna put the mirror down. 'Of course,' she said steadily. 'I did not stop to think; after a ride in such foul weather, my lord husband would be exhausted, in truth.' But the reasonableness of that did little to ease her hurt. Could he not at least have come in to bid her goodnight?

Once in bed, she found it difficult to sleep. The memories of what she and Llewelyn had done last night in this bed were too vivid, too real. At last she dozed, only to be awakened with a shock, with the feel of an icy breath against her cheek. Llewelyn was sitting on the bed, shook snow on to them both as he leaned over to embrace her.

'Not even a lantern left in the window for me, and sound asleep into the bargain,' he complained, caressing her all the while with his eyes, and Joanna, fully awake now, threw herself into his arms.

'I thought you came back hours ago, had gone to bed!'

Llewelyn grinned, started to remind her of the burned bed, but something eager and innocent in her face stopped him, and he said instead, 'Now why ever would I want to sleep alone when I could sleep with you?'

Alison and Branwen had discreetly disappeared. Joanna sat up, reached for her bedrobe. 'Where are your squires?'

'I sent them off to bed, thought I might persuade you to offer a hand.'

Joanna was as compulsively neat as Llewelyn was not, and she snatched up his mantle and tunic almost before they hit the floor, folded them conscientiously across a coffer chest. By now he was pulling off his shirt, and she gave a concerned cry, 'No! Over by the fire, or you'll catch your death of cold.'

'I do not recall you caring where I undressed last night,' he said, and Joanna blushed and then laughed.

'To tell you true, I do not even remember undressing last night,' she confessed, kneeling before him to help unfasten the cords binding his chausses to his braies. 'It just seemed to . . . happen.' He smiled down at her, and marvelling how her body's needs suddenly seemed to exist independently of her conscious control, she reached for the nearest cord, saw that Llewelyn's passions were kindled as quickly as her own. Her touch had been light, inadvertent, but as her fingers brushed his upper thigh, his reaction was immediate, pronounced.

'Women are lucky,' she teased shyly, 'for they can hide their desire so much more easily than men,' and Llewelyn laughed.

'Who wants to hide it?' he said, stripped off his chausses and braies. Joanna had often seen naked men, as a child had occasionally entered John's bedchamber as he was dressing, had assisted Ela in bathing more than one highborn guest at Salisbury Castle, had passed serfs bathing in the river in summer. She'd long ago mastered that which was essential in a society so lacking in privacy, the elusive art of seeing and yet not seeing. Now, however, she let her eyes linger upon her husband's body. He was taller than most Welshmen, his the lean wiry strength of stamina rather than muscle and sinew. He

297

had an insignificant amount of chest hair, his skin dark and smooth, marred only by the scars of old wounds, scars that now took on a new and sinister significance to Joanna, one tracking across his ribcage, another angled towards his collar-bone, a third slanting in a thin, white line from his pubic hair down his thigh. Joanna reached out, traced its path with gentle fingers.

'That must have been a frightening injury.'

'That, my darling, was not the half of it!' he said wryly. 'There is nothing like a groin wound to make a man repent his sinful past.' He did then what Joanna had wanted him to do all along, put his hand on hers, showed her how best to give a man pleasure.

It was to Joanna enormously gratifying, to find that Llewelyn wanted her caresses and kisses even as much as she wanted his. 'It is easy to understand how people came to use the term "manhood",' she said, rather breathlessly, 'but how explain "privy member"?'

'How explain any of them, Joanna; cock, shaft, codpiece, pizzle, sword, and in Welsh: *bonllost, gwialen, cal* . . . and those are just the polite terms.'

'*Bonllost,*' she echoed, amused by the unfamiliar phrasing, and then began to giggle. 'I do hope none of our children ever ask me which Welsh word I did learn first!' Llewelyn had taken her into a closer embrace; she could feel his hands under her bedrobe, and she sighed, said softly, 'I think, though, that I shall call it Merlin, in honour of the miracles it did work last night.'

Llewelyn laughed, and drew her towards the bed. 'And I begin to think,' he said, 'that I do owe the English King a far greater debt than I first realized.'

'Llewelyn . . . whilst we were making love, you did call me *breila*. What does that mean?'

'A *breila* is a dusky wild rose. It does suit you, I think.'

Joanna was touched almost to tears. '*Breila* . . . that's lovely.' She lay back against him, cradled her head in the crook of his shoulder. 'I know I was a disappointment to you at first, but –'

'Disappointment?' Llewelyn raised himself up on one elbow, saw with surprise that she was neither teasing nor fishing for flattery. 'Has no one ever told you, Joanna, that you're beautiful?'

Now it was Joanna's turn to doubt him. 'No,' she said at last, 'but when I was about twelve, I do remember hearing Maude de Braose say I looked verily like a Saracen.'

'Who in Christ cares what Maude de Braose thinks?' Llewelyn reached for a long strand of Joanna's hair, pulled it across his throat. 'If Saracen women do indeed have hair like black silk, eyes like emeralds, and blood hotter than Greek fire, little wonder men are so eager to take the cross, to reach the Holy Land.'

'Oh, love . . .' Leaning over, Joanna gave him a lingering kiss. 'That is blasphemous,' she said huskily, 'and the most memorable compliment any woman ever got.'

In reply, Llewelyn dropped a kiss on the tip of her nose, then yawned. Joanna chose to disregard the hint, not yet willing to relinquish the utter euphoria of the moment. 'Llewelyn . . . will you tell me of Tangwystl? Did you love her?'

'Yes, I did.' Llewelyn did not open his eyes, but the corner of his mouth curved in a smile. 'Tangwystl was a flaming redhead, and she did fret over her colouring fully as much as you do over yours, red hair being thought accursed since the days of Judas. But like you, she was fair to look upon . . . very fair.'

Joanna did not begrudge Tangwystl that echo of past passion. She felt no jealousy for a dead woman; all her anxieties were for a rival very much alive, for Cristyn. Did he love Cristyn? That was the question she dared not ask.

'Did you never think to wed Tangwystl, Llewelyn?'

'I had not the right, had to make a marriage that would be to Gwynedd's good.'

Joanna wondered why she'd asked a question with so obvious an answer. However lovely Isabelle was, she knew her father would not have married her had she not also been heiress to Angoulême, and Llewelyn was no less ambitious. 'Llewelyn . . .'

He yawned again. 'Joanna, had I known you were one for talking all night, I might have thought twice ere I told Aldwyn to move this bed and all your belongings into my chamber.'

Joanna stared at him, momentarily rendered mute. He was so nonchalant, as if unaware of what he was offering her. Sleeping every night in his bed, she'd be a true wife in every sense of the word, not just a consort, a political pawn. And Lady Mary, what it would mean, to be able to fall asleep in his arms, to reach out and touch him in the night, and most blessed mercy of all, never to have to lie awake wondering if he were in Cristyn's bed.

'I thought we'd use this chamber for well-born guests . . .' Llewelyn paused, belatedly remembering that a private chamber was no small luxury. 'Or would you rather keep it for your own, Joanna?'

'Oh, Llewelyn, beloved, need you ask? I'd rather sleep with you in a hut than alone in a palace!'

Llewelyn could not help laughing at the extravagant innocence of that avowal, at once regretted it, for he felt Joanna tense. She'd turned her head aside on the pillow, and he leaned over, touched her cheek. Her lashes lifted, their eyes met, and then she said, 'You knew?'

'Let's say I hoped,' he said with a smile, and Joanna flushed.

'That is why I did not want to tell you, so you'd not feel you had to . . . to be gallant. It's not fair to you.' She bit her lip, all too aware that she was floundering. 'What I'm trying to say, Llewelyn, is that I . . . I'm willing to settle for what you can give.'

Llewelyn did not answer at once. He'd been rather bemused by her obvious affection for John, had finally conceded that, whatever his other failings, John had at least done right by Joanna. Now he found himself thinking that, however much John had done for her, it was not enough. Not nearly enough.

'You hold yourself too cheaply, *breila*,' he said gently. 'It is true that when I came to Chester last spring, it was to wed with the English King's daughter. But I did ride back through a snowstorm tonight for Joanna.'

21

November, 1207

Tewkesbury, England

John leaned over the cradle, gazed down at his sleeping son. He felt no particular tenderness for the child, not yet; he'd never had any interest in infants. But he did feel a deep sense of wonder.

'Wherever did he get such red hair? I'm right glad that you are not a suspicious husband, love!'

'My father had reddish hair,' John said absently, only half-listening to his wife. But then he caught the scent of rosemary, felt her arms slip around his waist. For more than six years, she'd been unable to conceive, to give him the heir a King must have. Had she ever despaired? Had she feared that he might put her aside, find grounds to disavow the marriage? He did not know, for they had never discussed it. He'd shrunk from ever saying it aloud, gripped by an irrational belief that to admit his fear would be to make it fact. Turning now, he looked at the lovely face upturned to his. How fair she was. But that had only served to feed his fear. For as the years passed and her womb failed to quicken, he'd begun to suspect that God had played a macabre and sardonic jest upon him, giving him as wife and Queen the most beautiful woman he'd ever seen, the most desirable bedmate he'd ever had – only then to make her barren.

When she'd suddenly announced that she was pregnant, he'd been stunned, and then wary, not letting himself hope. She could still miscarry, could give birth to a daughter; God might well see that as the ultimate ironic jest. But her pregnancy had been utterly uneventful, and on the morning of October 1, she had given birth to a healthy son.

'Geoffrey, Richard, Osbert, Oliver, Henry . . . and now Henry again, for our babe. Why have you not named any of your sons after yourself, John?'

John shrugged, glanced across the chamber at the monk hovering in the doorway. 'What is it?'

'Your son has returned from Wales, my liege. May he enter?'

John nodded, and a moment later Richard strode swiftly into the chamber. 'You've given me a devil of a chase, Papa. I reached Winchcombe this morn, only to be told you'd departed for St Mary's Abbey, was not at all sure I'd be able to overtake you.'

'Never mind that. What news of Joanna?'

Richard grinned. 'The best news, Papa. On All Saints' Day, Joanna gave birth to a black-haired baby daughter.'

'Did she now?' John smiled. 'She and the babe, they are all right?'

'Indeed, Papa,' Richard said without hesitation. In truth, Joanna had not had an easy time; the birth had been a difficult one. But Joanna was now convalescing, was rapidly regaining her strength, and Richard, ever a pragmatist, saw no need for his father and Isabelle to know.

'A girl . . .' Isabelle was staring at Richard in dismay. 'Was Joanna very disappointed?'

'She was not disappointed at all.'

There was a pause, and then Isabelle said, 'I'm so glad,' but without any conviction. She knew that, had she given birth to a daughter, not all the balm in Gilead could have healed so grievous a hurt. Linking her arm in John's, she murmured, 'A January return, a November birth; our Joanna did not waste any time putting my advice into practice, did she?' John looked at her so blankly that she prompted, 'Do you not remember, love? What I told you about Joanna and Llewelyn . . .'

John gave a noncommittal grunt, and she fought an urge to laugh. One of the traits she most liked in John was their shared love of gossip. He was no less interested than she in court scandal, enjoyed regaling her with bawdy stories and ribald jests, with invariably accurate accounts of who was sinning with whom. But not once had she ever heard him mention the most scandalous stories of all, those lurid rumours of his mother's youthful indiscretions. And he was of a sudden showing the same reticence about his daughter's love-life. It amused Isabelle in no small measure, but the lesson was not lost upon her. Seeing now that Richard was regarding her with uncomprehending curiosity, she gave him a meaningless smile, having no intention of enlightening him, for by her lights, secrets shared in bed did not count and her faith still remained unbroken.

302

John moved away from the cradle, settled himself comfortably in a cushioned window seat. 'Do not keep me in suspense, Richard. What unpronounceable Welsh name did Llewelyn inflict upon that innocent babe?'

'Elen, which is Welsh for Helen.'

John pondered that for a moment and then conceded, 'Well, I grant you it could be worse. But is it true that Llewelyn is making Joanna learn that lunatic language of his?'

Richard laughed, before realizing that his father was not joking. 'I do believe it was Joanna's idea, Papa,' he said mildly, and John frowned.

'Indeed? It's well and good to be a dutiful wife, but . . .'

'Dutiful wife?' Richard echoed, much amused. 'Papa, Joanna does –'

'John, love, did you not say you'd promised to spare some moments for Abbot Walter ere we sup?' Isabelle's intercession was adroitly done, her query conveying no more than a commendable wifely concern. But Richard was not slow; he gave his stepmother a probing look, then wandered over to the cradle to study his baby brother.

John was in no hurry to depart; it was some moments before he reluctantly went off in search of the Abbot. As soon as the door closed behind him, Richard demanded, 'Why did you cut me short like that, Isabelle?'

'Because, my dearest, you were about to say that Joanna is hopelessly besotted with her husband . . . or words to that effect, were you not?'

'And if I was? It is true enough, after all.'

'Of course it is true. But to say so would have done neither John nor Joanna a kindness, and least of all, Llewelyn.'

Richard started to protest, stopped, and reflected upon what she seemed to be saying. Isabelle was only a year older than he, and when he'd first begun to feel the sexual stirrings of manhood, he had, for a time of brief and exquisite torment, believed himself to be in love with his father's beautiful wife. So shamed had he been by these wayward yearnings that he'd fought them the only way he knew how, by scorning the object of his sinful lust, by convincing himself that Isabelle was a frivolous little fool, vain and flighty. As an amputation of the soul, it proved to be an effective if drastic cure, and in time he'd outgrown both the desire and the disdain. Within the past year

303

or so, he found his sense of perspective returning, and he was once again able to look upon his stepmother without distortion, to see her for what she was and what she was not.

It would never occur to him to discuss with Isabelle the ramifications of John's ongoing quarrel with the Pope. Richard knew well that Isabelle gave little thought to the threat of Interdict and excommunication. But Isabelle knew his father as no one else did, was the first woman to hold his affections, in and out of bed. That was no small feat, earned her the right to be heard, and he said, 'Why do you say that, Isabelle? Papa wants Joanna to be happy; surely you do not doubt that?'

'Yes, he does,' she agreed indulgently. 'He wants her to be safe and cared for and content. He does not want her to be utterly and passionately in love with Llewelyn ab Iorwerth. Ah, Richard, do you know your father as little as that? Do you not know that John needs always to come first with those who love him? Is that so surprising? Why do you think John did not attend Joanna's wedding? Oh, I know the reasons he gave why he could not. But if he'd truly wanted to be there, he would have. He did not, and so he was not.'

Joining Richard by the cradle, she began to rock it gently back and forth. 'Trust me, Richard, in this. Do not speak to John of Joanna's abiding love for Llewelyn; he does not want to hear it. I think Joanna must sense that, for her letters to him are unlike those to me. To me alone does she go on at length about the unlikely perfections of her Welsh Prince.' She laughed suddenly, giving Richard a look that was amused and affectionate and faintly flirtatious. 'If he is half as good as she thinks, she's found herself a rare man indeed, one well worth the keeping! Now tell me . . . we know Joanna's heart. But what of Llewelyn? You've seen them together, Richard; does he love her?'

'That is a woman's question if ever I heard one! How would I be likely to know that, Isabelle? I can only tell you that he seems fond enough of her.' Richard paused, considering. 'He has a hunting lodge at Trefriw in the River Conwy valley. The nearest church is at Rhychwyn, about a two-mile walk up a mountain path too steep for horses, and when Llewelyn learned Joanna was with child, he ordered a church built at Trefriw to spare her that walk.'

'He loves her, then,' Isabelle declared with satisfaction, and Richard hid a smile, for he'd known she would be quickest to comprehend tangible expressions of caring.

'Madame?' One of Isabelle's ladies stood in the doorway. 'Madame, the Lady Margaret de Lacy is without, seeks some moments with you.'

Isabelle's face was suddenly still, remote. 'No,' she said. 'I do not wish to see her.'

As the woman withdrew, Richard gave Isabelle a pensive look. Like most people at John's court, he had been shocked by William de Braose's abrupt and unexpected fall from favour. The purported reason given for the estrangement between John and de Braose was money; de Braose owed the Crown a considerable sum, for in 1201 John had allowed de Braose to purchase the Irish honour of Limerick for five thousand marks, yet de Braose had unaccountably ignored the set schedule for payment, paying only a meagre hundred marks to date upon the debt. John had suddenly demanded payment in full, and when de Braose was unable or unwilling to comply, he found himself in political limbo, no longer welcome at John's court.

Richard did not doubt that Margaret de Lacy was here on her father's behalf, but what interested him now was the finality in Isabelle's refusal. Although she rarely interceded with John on behalf of petitioners, she generally accorded them a careless courtesy, was willing to hear them out. That she would deny Margaret de Lacy even the briefest audience was in itself significant to Richard, told him that de Braose was in much deeper disgrace than he'd realized.

There could be only one logical explanation for this surprising rupture of a relationship that had endured for fully half of Richard's lifetime, an explanation to be found within the shadowed silence of Rouen Castle. Richard was sure that Arthur was the key to the mystery of de Braose's downfall. Just as de Braose was the key to Arthur's disappearance.

Richard was, even at eighteen, a realist. He loved his father, but it had been more than four years since any man had laid eyes upon Arthur. Now he hesitated, but the temptation was irresistible. 'Isabelle, have you never asked Papa about Arthur?'

'Jesu, no!' She was looking at him as if he were mad. 'Indeed I have not!'

'But are you not curious? Do you never wonder, never want to know the truth of it?'

'No, she said flatly. 'I do not wonder. I do not ask.' The blue eyes were guarded, almost hostile. 'I do not want to know.'

305

March, 1208

Aber, North Wales

In Llewelyn's absence, Joanna had presided over the evening meal in the great hall. Now servants had dismantled the trestle tables, and she'd seated herself upon the dais, was making a request that Llywarch sing for them. Her halting Welsh grated unbearably against Gruffydd's ear. He hated how she mangled his language, hated her alien French accent, hated the way her clumsy efforts won his father's uncritical praise.

Feeling a tug at his sleeve, Gruffydd looked down, saw his little sister Marared holding out a thick strip of leather. 'My dog's collar,' she explained. 'Make it fit tighter, Gruffydd.' He obligingly cut another hole with his eating knife, and she went off, content. Gruffydd waited a few moments, and then moved casually in the direction of the hearth, stopping before the cradle. Seeing that no one was watching him, he leaned over, stared down at his baby sister.

He'd expected to hate her as he hated her mother. But each time he looked at her, he felt only relief, only an intense, abiding thankfulness that Joanna had not given birth to a son. For nine years he had been Llewelyn's only son and heir; the birth, three years ago, of his brother Tegwared had been a severe shock to Gruffydd. But Tegwared did not live at Llewelyn's court, was born of a concubine, and Gruffydd had gradually come around to a grudging acceptance of Cristyn's son. Joanna's son would be a far greater threat, a far more dangerous rival; although Welsh law did not distinguish between legitimate and illegitimate offspring, Holy Church did, would have to favour a child born in wedlock. If that woman ever bore Papa a son, he might lose all, even Papa's love.

Gruffydd drew an uneven breath, tried to fight back his fear. He knew she would poison Papa's mind against him if she could. But he had to have more faith in Papa. He had to – suddenly warned by a sixth sense of awareness, he raised his head. For the span of several hostile heartbeats, his eyes held Joanna's, and then she looked away. Hot colour flooded Gruffydd's face. He'd seen her look at him that way before – every time he came within two feet of Elen. Damn her, did she think he'd ever hurt a baby? He reached defiantly for the rattle, held it within Elen's range of vision. Elen was his sister, was not to blame for her Norman blood, and he would somehow see that she was raised right, raised Welsh. He'd not let that foreign woman win.

'Take care, Gruffydd. Yours is too easy a face to read,' a voice cautioned behind him, and he spun around to face two of Ednyved's sons, Hywel and Tudur. Tudur was the same age as Gruffydd; they'd both celebrated their twelfth birthdays within the past week. Hywel was two years older, was the one who'd spoken.

'So? As long as I am not rude to her, what right has she to complain? She cannot fault me for what I'm thinking . . . at least, not yet.' Across the hall, Joanna was thanking Llywarch and, as he listened, Gruffydd's mouth twisted scornfully. 'Did you ever hear anyone sound so peculiar? She makes a mockery of our tongue every time she opens her mouth!'

Tudur gave a sympathetic nod, but Hywel shrugged. 'I seem to remember you blaming her last year because she insisted upon speaking only French.'

Gruffydd's eyes narrowed. 'Elen was named after one of the most celebrated of Welsh heroines, the Elen of the Hosts acclaimed in the Triads. But do you think she knows that? That she even knows what the Triads are? She asked Papa one question only, what Elen meant in Norman-French!'

'I do not deny that she is ignorant of our history, of our ways,' Hywel conceded, then jerked his head in the direction of the Lady Gwenllian. 'But I'd still trade our stepmother for yours any day!'

'That shows how little you know, does it not?' Gruffydd snapped, and Hywel's good humour vanished. For a moment the two boys glared at one another; although Hywel had the advantage in years, Gruffydd was only an inch shorter than he, and in their one brawl a few months back, they'd fought to a bloody draw. Now Hywel was the first to look away.

'Have it your own way. Why should I care?' He turned on his heel, but his brother caught up with him after a few steps, said placatingly:

307

'Do not be angry, Hywel. Gruffydd's been in a bad mood these past days. Lord Llewelyn did forget his birthday, you see.'

Hywel paused, willing to be mollified, and Tudur lowered his voice, said in confidential tones, 'All Friday Gruffydd expected a courier to come, and when none did, he was sorely hurt. He sought to hide it, but all could see it plain in his face, and the Lady Joanna . . . well, she just made things worse. She tried to make excuses for Lord Llewelyn, told Gruffydd how busy his father was, how preoccupied with Gwenwynwyn's border raids. Gruffydd was wild, as wroth as I've ever seen him. But he dared not say anything to her, not after Lord Llewelyn warned him to mend his manners, to show her respect. So you touched a raw spot with him, and that's why he flared up.'

'But why did her remarks anger Gruffydd so? It sounds as if she meant well.'

'Mayhap she did. But there were others around, and Gruffydd thought she was deliberately calling it to our attention, that his father had forgotten him. And I know he much resented her offering apologies in Lord Llewelyn's name, saying she had no right, that his father did not need her to make amends for him. I can understand that, Hywel, in truth I can. Would you want our lady stepmother to make excuses to us for Papa?'

'No,' Hywel admitted. 'I would not. If Gruffydd – Tudur? You hear the dogs?'

Tudur nodded and, turning, he yelled, 'Gruffydd! I think your lord father has ridden in.'

Gruffydd was already moving eagerly towards the door. But Joanna was closer, and, as Llewelyn strode into the hall, she reached him first, flung herself into his arms. Gruffydd stopped abruptly, watched as Llewelyn and Joanna embraced, watched as Joanna then took Llewelyn's arm, pulled him towards the cradle. As if he had no other children, Gruffydd thought bitterly. Joanna was claiming most of Llewelyn's attention, holding up their baby for his inspection, and Gruffydd's sisters, Marared and Gwladys and Gwenllian, were clamouring, too, for notice. It was some moments, therefore, before Llewelyn missed his son.

He found Gruffydd leaning against one of the wooden screens that blocked off the side aisle, moved towards the boy with a smile. 'Have you no greeting for me, lad?'

'Indeed, Papa. Welcome home,' Gruffydd said, quite coolly. But

308

when he saw his father's smile fade, he was caught up in a welter of painful and confusing emotions, no longer sure why he'd wanted to punish Llewelyn, for having forgotten his birthday or for loving King John's daughter.

'Are you angry with me, Gruffydd?' Llewelyn studied his son, and then grinned. 'I see. You think I forgot your birthday again. Not this time, lad. Come, see for yourself.'

Men with torches stood outside in the bailey, and when Gruffydd saw what was evoking their admiring murmurs, his breath caught in his throat. The stallion was young, a pure milky white, the luckiest of colours, and bred for speed. Gruffydd whirled to face his father, entreating, 'Say he's mine, Papa!'

'You surely do not think he's for Elen, do you? But he's newly broken to the saddle, so take it slow . . .' Llewelyn's cautionary words were lost; Gruffydd was already reaching for the reins. The stallion bucked half-heartedly under his weight, and Gruffydd guided him in a semi-circle, grinned back over his shoulder at Llewelyn.

'He's begging to run, Papa!'

'Do not give him his head till you reach the shore. And remember . . . I paid a fortune for him, so if you have to break a neck, better yours than his!' Llewelyn laughed, and the wind carried back to him the answering echoes of his son's laughter.

Still laughing, Llewelyn re-entered the hall, looked around for his wife. 'Where did Joanna go?'

'To put your little Elen to bed.' Ednyved pulled a chair closer to the hearth, and Llewelyn sank down gratefully in it, pushed away the more importunate of his dogs.

He'd been gone for a fortnight, a guest of his cousin, Madog ap Gruffydd, Prince of upper Powys, and because Powys shared a border with Cheshire, Llewelyn was at once bombarded with questions about the two topics currently dominating English conversations: the threat of a papal Interdict and William de Braose's fall from favour.

'I heard nothing new about John's quarrel with the Pope. It does seem to be a stand-off; the Pope's man wears the mitre of Canterbury, but dares not set foot in England.' Llewelyn accepted a cup of mead, drank, and said, 'But I did hear something interesting about de Braose. His friends and family have prevailed upon John to grant him an audience; they are to meet at Hereford on the 25th of April. Not that I think it'll do him much good. There are few ruptures so bitter as a falling out amongst thieves.'

'What do you think is behind it, Llewelyn? It cannot truly be the money; de Braose has owed that for years.'

'This is just a guess, Rhys. But I think de Braose pushed his luck once too often. The more John gave him, the more he wanted. I heard he'd been pressuring John for an earldom, and I think John finally ran out of patience. Either that or de Braose went too far, moved from implied to explicit extortion, mayhap made an out-and-out threat about what he knew of Arthur's death.'

'I've never been able to understand why they did not give Arthur even a sham trial,' Adda confessed. 'Men might not have liked it much, but John had the law on his side. By resorting to a secret killing, he played right into Philip's hands. John's silence just gives credence to the more lurid rumours put about by the French: that Arthur was tortured, blinded, even slain by John's own hand. It was a stupid way to rid himself of a rival, since none can be utterly sure the boy is dead, and I do not see John to be a stupid man.'

'He may not be stupid, but he has no liking for the light, has a natural affinity for shadows and silence and deeds done in the dark,' Ednyved said dryly.

'Do you want to know what I've always suspected?' Llewelyn set down his mead cup, pausing instinctively for dramatic interest. 'That Arthur's murder was an act of impulse, was not premeditated. I think John confronted the boy, and they quarrelled; we know they'd done so in the past, that confinement had not broken Arthur's spirit. It is my belief that Arthur said or did something which so enraged John that he gave the command without fully thinking it through.'

Ednyved looked sceptical. 'Why unpremeditated, Llewelyn?'

'Because if Arthur's murder had been planned out in advance, John would never have been within a hundred miles of Rouen that night, would have put as much distance between himself and the crime as possible –' Llewelyn stopped abruptly, and an uncomfortable silence fell as Joanna came towards them. Not sure if she'd overheard, Llewelyn rose, moved to meet her.

To his relief, she smiled, 'Elen's begun teething, and I do not know how well she'll sleep – but she's abed now.'

'That,' he said, 'sounds like a right appealing idea.'

'What . . . sleep?' Joanna murmured, and laughed softly when he answered, as she'd known he would:

'No . . . bed.'

*

310

Joanna stretched, gave a small sigh of utter contentment, and Llewelyn leaned over, kissed her softly on the mouth. 'You're purring like a cat, you know that?'

'Little wonder. That was a very satisfactory homecoming, my lord.' She smiled at him. 'I missed you so much. And I love you so much.'

'I love you, too.' He kissed her again, gently, tenderly. 'But my darling, I'd love you so much more if you were to fetch me some wine.'

Joanna gave a splutter of indignant laughter, hastily culling her meagre Welsh vocabulary for the proper putdown. '*Digrin*,' she chided, gratified to see Llewelyn's eyes open wide.

'Joanna . . . what did you want to call me?'

'A sluggard.' She saw him bite down on his lower lip, said uncertainly, 'Why? *Digrin*, it is not . . .?'

'*Diogyn* means sluggard, love.' Llewelyn was openly laughing now. '*Digrin* . . . *digrin* means unwithered!'

Joanna's first reaction was one of mild embarrassment and frustration. She was coming to envision Welsh as a tide beyond her control; it was always sweeping in, inundating her in alien sound, and just when she thought she was getting her head above water, it went roaring out again, stranding her high and dry. But after a moment or so, she began to see the humour in it, and joined ruefully in Llewelyn's laughter.

'Sometimes I despair of ever learning your language,' she confessed, and he slid his arm around her shoulders, drew her closer.

'You'd learn it faster, Joanna, if we were to speak Welsh, not French.'

'But as tongue-tied as I am, we'd never be able to communicate at all, then. Except in bed!' She settled back in his arms, and then, before she could lose her nerve, she said, 'You were talking about Arthur before, were you not?'

Llewelyn did not answer at once. 'How much did you understand?'

'You were all talking so fast . . . just Arthur's name and Papa's. It was not hard to guess the rest. Llewelyn . . . do you think Arthur is dead?'

'Yes, love, I do,' he said quietly, and after a moment, she sighed.

'So do I,' she admitted. 'It's been nigh on five years. Logically, he . . . he must be dead. But Llewelyn, could he not have sickened, died through mishap? Papa might well have feared to make it known

311

after the way his enemies have lied about him in the past. And if Arthur tried to escape . . .' She looked at Llewelyn in mute appeal, and he said, with all the conviction he could muster:

'It may well be, Joanna.' But the day would come, he knew, when she would not be so readily reassured, when her faith might not be strong enough to prevail over fact. He smoothed her hair away from her face, said, 'I'd rather not talk of John's nephew, *breila*. But I never tire of talking of his daughter.'

That coaxed a smile from Joanna. 'You just earned yourself that drink of wine,' she said, reached for her bedrobe. The first time Llewelyn had said he loved her, soon after Elen's birth, she'd been convinced that was the happiest, most fulfilling moment of her life. But later, doubt had crept in. Llewelyn had been known to handle the truth with less than scrupulous care; how could she be sure he was speaking from the heart, not merely saying what he knew she needed to hear? Bringing the wine cup back to the bed, she watched as he drank, and then, as he leaned over to put the cup on the floor, the words seemed to come of their own accord. 'Llewelyn . . . why do you love me?'

'Why? Because in appearance and demeanour, you seem the perfect Norman lady, modest, reticent, aloof even. And then I get you in my bed, and you all but scorch the sheets!' He laughed, ran his hand caressingly along her back, down her thigh. 'Not to mention your admirable good taste in loving me beyond all reason!'

Joanna could not help herself, felt a throb of disappointment. But she should have known better, in truth, should have known he'd not take such a question seriously.

Llewelyn reached up, drew her down beside him again. 'No, you are not at all as you seem to be, *breila*. You are a constant surprise to me, and not just in bed. When I was a lad, my mother would often tell me the legend of the bird with the resplendent plumage; shall I tell it to you now? When it nests in the grass, it is not easily seen, for it takes on the drab protective colouring of the earth that gives it refuge. But when it takes flight, soars up into the sky, its wings burst into flame, reflect all the glories of Heaven itself. As a boy, I spent hours searching for that bird . . . in vain, of course. Passing strange, that I should find it after all these years . . . and in my own bed.'

Joanna had listened, mesmerized. 'Me?'

'You're like that mythical bird, love. You cloak yourself in the muted colours of a well-born Norman lady, seem soft-spoken, shy and obedient. But that is not you, Joanna, not truly, and when I least expect it, your spirit takes flight like the bird with the sun-bright plumage, as when you did defy Maude de Braose on our wedding day . . . or when you burned my bed.'

'You'll never let me forget that, will you?' Joanna laughed. 'But I need never explain why I do love you. How could I not, after hearing you say that? You are a man of many parts, in truth, Llewelyn, my love: Prince, war lord . . . and poet.'

'That is merely to be Welsh, *breila*.' But she was not deceived by the playfulness of his reply, knew how deeply she'd pleased him, for she'd learned by now how highly eloquence was valued in his world. He'd begun to caress her again, and she wrapped her arms around him, soon forgot all else but the here and now, the feel of his hands upon her body and his mouth upon hers.

The sensual spell was a powerful one; only belatedly did they become aware of the noise in the antechamber, of the pounding on the door. Llewelyn jerked upright, swore. But then he pulled the sheet up over Joanna, said curtly, 'Enter.'

Joanna's reflexes were slower; she reoriented herself with greater difficulty, lay back against the pillow as Ednyved, Morgan, and Gwyn ab Ednywain hastened into the chamber.

They wasted no time with apologies for the intrusion, knowing none were needed. 'Llewelyn, a messenger has just ridden in from the Bishop of St Asaph. The Bishop would have you know that on Passion Sunday a proclamation is to be read in churches throughout England and Wales, laying both realms under Interdict until John agrees to yield to the Pope.'

The news was not unexpected. Llewelyn felt no surprise, only rage. He cared little whether John or the Pope prevailed in their war of wills; their quarrel was nothing to him. But the pain of his people was, and he was deeply resentful that the Welsh must suffer with the English, that the papal punishment should fall equally upon both lands.

'Damn them both to Hell,' he said, with bitter blasphemy. 'Why should the Welsh have to suffer because a Norman King and a Roman Pope disagree over an English diocese?'

Morgan felt compelled at that to say, 'His Holiness had no choice but to do what he did.' But his heart was not in his defence, not when he thought of how long the churches might stand silent and dark, or how long the devout might be denied the Sacraments.

313

'Philip held out for seven months. But John . . . John could hold out for years,' Ednyved said grimly. 'It's nothing to him whether he can attend Mass or not. He's not like to care even if the bodies of the dead are stacked up like kindling in the churchyards. Not when he's found a way to turn the Interdict to his profit. Bishop Reiner says he has ordered the confiscation of all church property in retaliation, is using the Interdict as a licence to loot!'

'Llewelyn . . .' The sound of his wife's voice startled Llewelyn; he had, for the moment, forgotten she was there. Turning towards her, he saw she'd paled noticeably, and the hand she put upon his arm was cold as ice.

'Llewelyn, you keep saying *gwaharriad*. That means Interdict, does it not?' And when he nodded, she drew a sudden sharp breath. 'Oh no!'

'Joanna? Surely you knew it was likely to come to this . . .'

But she was not listening. 'Morgan, Morgan, I know an Interdict means there can be no Masses said, no burials in consecrated ground, no confessions. But what of christenings, Morgan? May a newborn child still be christened?'

'Yes, my lady, you may rest easy on that. Holy Church would not damn an innocent soul if it could be saved.'

'Thank God!'

'Joanna . . .' Llewelyn was staring at her. He started to speak, stopped, and glanced back towards the men. 'We'll discuss this on the morrow,' he said, but they were already retreating.

As the door closed, Llewelyn tilted Joanna's chin up, looked intently into her face. 'Joanna, are you with child?'

'I think so,' she whispered. 'My flux did not come this month. But it is too early to know for certès, and I did not want to tell you till I could be sure . . .' She averted her eyes at that, lest he guess the truth, that she'd been hoping she was wrong, that she was not pregnant. She wanted his children, wanted to give him a son. But not so soon. Elen was not yet five months old, and her memories had not had time to fade. Whenever she found herself remembering the pain-filled day of Elen's birth, she remembered, too, her fear. But she was ashamed that she could take so little pleasure in this pregnancy, and she forced a smile. 'If I am right, I may well give you a son ere the year be out. Would that not please you, Llewelyn?'

'Yes, of course.' He took her in his arms, rested his hand against her belly, so deceptively taut and flat, caressed the slender body that seemed such a fragile receptacle for a new life, repeated, 'Indeed, Joanna, I am well pleased.' But as she raised her eyes to his, she saw in them no pleasure, saw only the reflection of her own anxiety.

April, 1208
Hereford, England

William de Braose was surprised and disconcerted to find himself
hesitating before John's solar door. He'd spent a lifetime facing down
lesser men, men who lacked his cold-blooded courage, his utter
indifference to the rules of fair play, his intoxication with high stakes
gambles. Never before had he shrunk from confrontation. But never
before had he so much to lose.

A moment passed, and then another. De Braose stared at the
oaken door. And then he reached for the latch, shoved inward, and
strode into the chamber, his the assured loose-limbered gait of a man
equally at home in the saddle or on shipboard, a man with nothing
to fear. But he broke stride abruptly at sight of the others: the Earls
of Salisbury and Pembroke, the Bishop of Winchester, a shadowy
fourth figure beyond the range of hearth-fire.

De Braose was genuinely shocked, too shocked to hide his dismay.
He knew John as few men did, had never made the mistake of
underestimating him. But even he had never imagined John would
take such a chance, that he would risk witnesses for their war of
wills.

He had no conscious awareness of coming forward, kneeling
before John; the action was automatic. 'Your Grace, I think it best
if we speak alone,' he said warningly, never taking his eyes from the
man who was his sovereign, one time carousing companion, friend,
and benefactor. 'What I have to say be for your ears alone.'

'Indeed? I can think of nothing you could say that would warrant
a private audience. Be thankful, rather, that I was willing to grant
you any audience at all.' John's voice was cool, impersonal, utterly
at variance with what de Braose read in his eyes. 'What would you
say to me?'

And in that moment de Braose understood. He had underestimated John, after all. They might indeed share a bloody secret, but

they were not – and this was his fatal mistake – partners in crime. He'd not thought John had the courage to call his bluff, and in this he had been wrong, too. The twisted, dark road they'd travelled together since that Eastertide at Rouen had come to an abrupt end here in the shadow-filled solar of Hereford Castle. John had thrown down the gauntlet in irrevocable and unmistakable fashion, before a roomful of witnesses. Now the choice was his. He could subject himself to his King, make a total and humiliating and costly surrender to a man not noted for generosity towards fallen enemies. Or he could make use of what he knew, could damn John and doom himself.

John showed no emotion, but his son Richard drew a sharp, audible breath, stepped from the shadows as if to forestall de Braose. For Richard, too, understood what was occurring. When he'd first realized what his father was doing, daring de Braose to speak of Arthur, to make a public accusation, Richard was appalled; until that moment, he'd not recognized how much he preferred not to know Arthur's fate. Now he stared not at de Braose, but at his father, awed by the risk John was willing to take.

But . . . but was the risk in truth all that great? As the silence spun out, Richard's eyes flicked rapidly to the faces of the other men, to his uncle Will, to the aging Pembroke, to the elegant Peter des Roches, one of the only two Bishops not to follow their brethren into French exile in the wake of the Pope's Interdict, and some of his anxiety began to ease. No, not so great a risk after all. His uncle would be loyal to the grave and beyond. Like Will, Pembroke was a man of rock-ribbed integrity, little imagination, and moderate ambitions, a man who had devoted the whole of his life to the fortunes of the House of Plantagenet. Whatever personal repugnance he might feel at hearing a confession of royal murder, it would not shake his loyalty, for his loyalty was to the Crown, to the man anointed by God to reign . . . even if that man be revealed as Cain. And Peter des Roches was no rebel priest, was a worldly, accommodating, and ambitious Prince of the Church, not one to be shocked by the dark underside of men's souls. Even if the worst came to pass, and de Braose blurted out an admission of conspiracy and murder, none of the men in this room would ever act upon it; instead, they'd do their best to bury their unwelcome knowledge beyond recall.

But even as Richard realized that his father had shrewdly acted to minimize his political risks, he realized, too, that the personal risk John was willing to take was considerable. He could be sure that his

317

brother and son would never betray him, no matter what they heard in this solar at Hereford Castle. But how could he be sure that they would forgive him?

'Well?' John demanded. 'Have you nothing to say to me?' There was defiance in the query, but there was triumph, too, for he'd correctly interpreted de Braose's continuing silence as surrender.

De Braose did not answer. Once the initial shock had ebbed, he'd seen what Richard had, that John had picked his audience with a sure hand, an artful understanding of the men he'd chosen as witnesses. But if John was bluffing, so was he. He would never have made a public accusation of any kind. The day that he accused a reigning King of murder was the day he signed his own death warrant, and he knew it. But knowing what he had to do did not make it any the easier.

'I do owe Your Grace five thousand marks. I am here to promise payment.'

'Promises are cheap. You've made them before. And there are other considerations now. In the past year, you've given me reasons enough to doubt your loyalty. As you know, a fortnight ago I dispatched the sheriffs of Gloucestershire and Shropshire and five hundred men-at-arms into the West Country. I thought their presence there might serve to prod your memory, to remind you where your interests lie. It would seem they did. But men-at-arms need to eat, expect their two pence a day. So in addition to the five thousand marks you do owe me for the honour of Limerick, you now owe me another thousand marks for the cost of that campaign.'

De Braose was truly taken aback by the utterly outrageous gall of that demand, that he should be assessed for the expenses of an army sent to ravage his own lands. 'I serve the King's pleasure,' he said at last, with such bitter irony that John smiled.

'Just so,' he said softly. It was a warning as oblique as it was economical, but there was no need to say more. De Braose understood.

Of all his grandfather's castles, Will de Braose liked Abergavenny the best. He'd been born there, and had recently celebrated his twelfth birthday within Abergavenny's massive stone walls. On this Tuesday in late April he was alone in the uppermost chamber of the polygonal tower. The chamber housed the de Braose family chapel, but Will was not there to pray; he was leaning recklessly out of the unshuttered window, watching the road that wound off towards the north, towards Hereford where his grandfather was meeting with the King. He'd sent word that he would be returning this Tuesday noon, and Will had been keeping an impatient vigil as the day dragged on.

Down in the bailey, he saw his father, Reginald de Braose, conferring with his uncle, William de Braose the younger. His young cousins were playing a rough-and-tumble game of ball with an inflated pig's bladder, under the watchful eye of their mother Matilda. There'd been a full gathering of the de Braose clan at Abergavenny; only Will's aunt Margaret and his uncle Giles, Bishop of Hereford, were absent, Margaret having sailed for Ireland to rejoin her husband Walter, Lord of Meath, and Giles having gone into foreign exile in obedience to the Pope's Interdict. All were waiting anxiously for word from Hereford.

Will did not share their concern; he could not imagine any man getting the better of his grandfather. Moreover, he knew that his grandmother fully expected the King to restore her husband to favour, and Will needed no greater guarantee than that. As far back as he could remember, his grandmother had been the family linchpin. Imperious and earthy and blazingly outspoken, she'd always utterly eclipsed the Lady Gracia, Will's mother, a timid, passive personality who was reduced to wraithlike incompetence in the presence of her formidable mother-in-law.

Now Will decided to seek her out, to renew his faith in Maude's reassuring certainty that the bad times were over. The disgrace that had so suddenly come upon their family had been hard on Will. Since the age of seven, he'd been serving as a page in the household of Lord Fitz Alan, and when he was taunted by the other pages about his grandfather's fall from favour, Will had responded with hot, heedless rage, had got into so many bloody brawls that his training at Clun Castle came to an abrupt end. His father had been predictably furious; Will could not recall a time when he and his father had not been at odds. But his grandmother once again came through when it counted, saying cuttingly, 'Christ Jesus, Reg, let the boy be. Just be thankful he has the pluck to stand up for himself, that he has the backbone you too often lack!' Her acerbic intervention had spared Will a beating, but added yet one more drop of poison to a relationship already soured beyond salvaging.

Will was remembering that as he entered the great hall, saw Maude sitting upon the dais, attended by the submissive daughters-in-law who never dared stray out of beckoning range. She frowned at sight of him, gestured for him to approach.

'I saw your cousin Jack's eye; your handiwork?'

Will was not troubled by the scowl. 'He ran into my fist,' he said, saw her mouth twitch.

'Do not make a habit of it,' she said, but when Will grinned, she grinned back.

Settling down on the steps of the dais, Will began to occupy himself in carving a whistle. Within moments, he'd attracted an admiring audience, his little cousin Philip. Will was quite contemptuous of his cousin Jack, whom he considered a weakling and tattletale, but he liked Philip, who was only seven. Now he made room on the steps for the youngster, and turned obligingly so Philip could watch him whittle.

'Will . . . was it truly in this very hall that Grandpapa killed that Welsh lord and his men?'

Will nodded, cast Philip a sideways, searching look. Philip's eyes were wide; he was looking about him as if still expecting to see the floor rushes soaked in blood, the walls splattered with gore. Will understood, for he remembered his own confusion when he'd first been told of the Abergavenny massacre. Will had given to his grandfather all the love and respect he did not give to his father, and he'd been shocked to discover that his grandfather had so violated every tenet of the chivalric code. There was no way he could reconcile what his grandfather had done on that December day in 1175 with the accepted standards of knightly conduct, with the tales told by minstrels and bards of Roland and Arthur and the knights of the Table Round, for his grandfather had lured his enemies to Abergavenny under the guise of friendship, murdered them while they ate and drank at his table, then abducted Seisyll's wife and put her young son to death before her eyes.

Will had been troubled enough to go to his father with his qualms, but his father had laughed at him. Apparently the Welsh were not covered by the chivalric code. That was not good enough for Will. He'd often heard his family jeer at the strange ways of the Welsh, heard them called 'reckless' and 'untamed' and 'half-mad'. By Norman standards, he supposed they were, but those were the very qualities that most appealed to him. Wales was to Will a wild, mystical land of legend and blood feuds and stark grandeur, and he loved it as if it were his own. Most of his twelve years had been spent within its borders; he spoke fluent Welsh, had friends named Rhys and Ifor and Garwyn. He needed a better explanation for the killings at Abergavenny than merely that the victims were Welsh.

He'd got that explanation from his grandmother. 'Those men were your grandfather's enemies, Will. The enemies of our House. We do not forgive a wrong done us, not ever. You are old enough to understand that, lad, to learn that in this world we have to look after our own, to do whatever is necessary to safeguard what is ours. Learn that if you learn nothing else, and never forget it.'

Now Will gave his young cousin the same bleak, uncompromising answer his grandmother had once given him, saying tersely, 'They were the enemies of our House, Philip.' An answer that said all that needed to be said, that he had long since taken to heart.

He handed the completed whistle to the boy. 'You can have this if you like.' And then, because Philip was so young, because there was time yet before he had to learn the lessons of being a de Braose, Will drew Philip's thoughts away from that long-ago and bloody December day. 'Life must have been right lively back then, Philip. Seisyll's surviving sons besieged Abergavenny seven years later and burned all but the keep; luckily for Grandpapa, he was elsewhere at the time of the attack! And then, some years after, Gwenwynwyn attacked our castle in the Machawy River valley, the one the Welsh call Castell Paen. Our grandmother put up so successful a defence that people started calling it Castle Maude!'

Philip laughed. 'Which Welsh Prince is Gwenwynwyn, Will? I can never keep them straight.'

'You'll have to learn; you're old enough now. Gwenwynwyn is Prince of lower Powys; he's the whoreson who's been making raids upon our manors. South Wales is divided now between the sons of the Lord Rhys – Maelgwn and Rhys Gryg. And the North is ruled by the man Grandpapa says is the most dangerous one of the lot, Llewelyn ab Iorwerth, who is married to a bastard daughter of King John.'

As soon as John's name had crossed Will's lips, he swallowed, grimaced as if he'd tasted something sour. In the past year he'd come to nurture a deep and abiding hatred for the English King who was giving his family such grief. He started to speak, and then stopped, head cocked expectantly to the side. 'Philip, you hear? Grandpapa has just ridden in!'

*

Will's excitement congealed at first sight of the men accompanying his grandfather: Thomas Erdington, sheriff of Shropshire, Gerard d'Athie, sheriff of Gloucestershire, and Falkes de Bréauté, to whom William de Braose had been forced by John to yield up Glamorgan and Gwyllwg. The first two had in the past fortnight led an army on to de Braose lands, the third was a bitter and open enemy of their House. Will knew his grandfather would never have chosen their company of his own accord. He ran for the nearest window, looked out to find the bailey filled with men-at-arms, men who wore the red and white colours of the King.

Maude had risen, was staring at her husband in dismay. 'Will? Will, why are they here?'

Will knew his grandfather was no longer young, was in his sixties, but he was so energetic, so fit that Will never gave his age any thought. He was shocked now to see how haggard his grandfather suddenly looked, exhaustion etched into the smudged hollows under his eyes, impotent and embittered fury in the rigid set of his mouth.

'Not now,' he snapped, giving his wife a look that would have daunted all but the most intrepid or reckless, a look that made no impression whatsoever upon Maude.

'Name of God, Will, what has happened? Did you not see the King?'

'I said not now!'

But his unlikely escorts were not so reticent. It was Falkes de Bréauté who told Maude what her husband would not, saying with conspicuous relish, 'Ah, indeed he saw the King, Madame, and made many and varied promises to the King's Grace, amongst them to make payment of six thousand marks.'

'Six thousand!' Maude's eyes narrowed, cut sharply towards her husband. 'We do not have it,' she said flatly, defiantly, and de Bréauté grinned.

'You'll be relieved then, Madame, to know you need not pay it all at once. A thousand marks are due today, but the balance may be paid in instalments. Of course you will have to surrender to the King's Grace your castles at Hay, Brecknock, and Radnor as a pledge for payment –'

'Jesus God!' Maude whirled around to confront her husband. 'What have you done, Will?'

'What I had to do!' he snarled. 'But we're damned well not going to talk about it here . . . or now!'

322

'Hay Castle is mine, to me! I'll not give it up!'

'Your husband has already done that, Madame.' Gerard d'Athie spoke up for the first time. Sounding as if he were enjoying himself no less than de Bréauté, he said cheerfully, 'He gave the order two days ago to turn them over to the King's constables. We are here only to collect the thousand marks . . . and the hostages, of course. Not surprisingly, the King feels that your husband will be more likely to keep faith if he is keeping your grandsons!'

Maude gasped, and her husband took two swift steps forward. But even as he warned, 'Maude, no!' she was swinging back towards Gerard d'Athie, her face flushed, mouth contorted.

'Are you mad? Do you truly think I'd ever agree to that? Give my grandsons up to the man who murdered his own nephew? Never in this lifetime!'

Will's throat had closed up, cutting off an involuntary cry of protest. But his fear lasted only until Maude began to speak. He found himself blinking back hot tears; never had he loved anyone as much as he loved his grandmother at that moment, his grandmother who would dare to defy the King of England for his sake.

And then he became aware of the utter and absolute silence, then he saw the looks of horror on the faces of the adults. His grandfather had gone grey under his tan; even his lips were bloodless. His grandmother was standing very still. Will could not see her face. But he could see the faces of Falkes de Bréauté and Gerard d'Athie. Astonishment had given way to exhilaration; they both wore the jubilant grins of men unable to believe how fortune had favoured them.

William de Braose at last turned away from his wife, turned fathomless grey eyes upon Erdington, d'Athie, and de Bréauté. All three men reacted as one, dropped hands to sword hilts. Falkes de Bréauté said coolly, 'We'll be rejoining our men. You do remember the men-at-arms awaiting us in the bailey? You need not offer us your hospitality for the night, after all.'

De Braose said nothing. They departed the hall with enough haste to compromise their dignity, hands still on sword hilts. Only then did William de Braose move. Crossing the space that separated him from his wife, he struck her across the face.

Maude's head rocked back; she stumbled, put up a hand to staunch the sudden gush of blood. No one spoke. Her sons looked away. Will alone took a shocked step towards her.

'You stupid bitch.' William de Braose's voice was low, raw with rage, but it carried clearly to all in the hall. 'Do you know what you've done? You and your accursed, unbridled tongue, you've destroyed us all!'

October, 1208
Shrewsbury, England

Soon after Maude de Braose publicly accused John of murder, William de Braose and his sons made a desperate attempt to regain possession of the castles de Braose had surrendered to John. Failing in these assaults, they plundered and burned the market town of Leominster. John proclaimed de Braose a traitor to the Crown, and on September 29 he freed de Braose's vassals from all allegiance to their fugitive lord.

Gwenwynwyn, Prince of lower Powys, at once sought to take advantage of the resulting chaos by launching raids upon the de Braose lands and those of neighbouring Norman lords. John responded with more force than the Welsh Prince could hope to equal. The two agreed to meet at Shrewsbury to discuss peace terms.

Shrewsbury Castle had been held by the Crown for more than two hundred years, and the great hall had been rebuilt in stone by John's father. John's son was thinking of that as they awaited the arrival of the Welsh Prince, wondering if his grandfather would have done what John meant to do. Probably so, Richard decided; his father's lessons in cynical statecraft had been learned under Henry's tutelage.

Now he glanced about the hall, at the other men: Ranulf de Blundeville, Earl of Chester; Thomas Erdington, sheriff of Shropshire; Lord Robert Corbet and his son Thomas; Robert de Montalt. There was no one else in the hall; Chester had cleared it of retainers, servants, and men-at-arms. Richard knew why, knew Chester was seeking to make Gwenwynwyn's capitulation as painless as possible. No easy task, given the surprise they were about to spring upon him. But he gave Chester credit for trying; tact was an attribute Richard appreciated.

Richard had only recently joined the knights of Chester's household, but the past weeks had caused him to revise his earlier unfavourable opinion of the Earl. He was not a particularly likable man, was of a reserved and taciturn nature, but he was an astute judge of character, shrewd and surprisingly subtle, and he had soon won Richard's respect. Richard knew this coming confrontation with Gwenwynwyn had to be awkward for Chester; the two men had once been allies. But nothing showed in Chester's face or demeanour. There was in his manner only the dispassionate resolve of a man set upon doing his duty, upon carrying out the King's command . . . however little he might like it.

Richard wondered if the Corbets shared Chester's reluctance to do what John wanted done. Theirs was an even more awkward position, for Gwenwynwyn had taken Robert Corbet's daughter to wife. But they'd voiced no protests, raised no objections. With the fate of William de Braose still uppermost in all their minds, few of John's barons were eager to incur his displeasure in this, the tenth year of his reign.

'Richard?' Thomas Corbet was looming over him. Without waiting to be asked, he sprawled down beside Richard in the window seat. Richard retreated as far as he was able, but not in time to avoid Thomas's elbow in his ribs. He was not comfortable with such close physical proximity, even with those he liked, and he did not like Thomas Corbet. For all his self-professed contempt for Llewelyn, Thomas was showing himself quite willing to trade upon Llewelyn's marital connection with the Crown and his own tenuous connection with the Welsh Prince to establish an unwelcome familiarity with Llewelyn's brother-in-law, and his sensitivity was such that he was utterly unconscious of Richard's measured recoil.

'Have you had further word on de Braose's whereabouts?'

Richard was tempted to deny Thomas the pleasure of being one of the first to know. But all would know soon enough, and he said grudgingly, 'De Braose and his family fled to Ireland on Thursday last, are seeking refuge with his son-in-law, the Lord of Meath.'

'Indeed? And will your lord father the King now . . .' But Richard was spared further conversation by the arrival of Gwenwynwyn. Richard had never met the Prince of Powys, but he was quite curious about this man who was Llewelyn's avowed and embittered rival, and he watched with considerable interest as Gwenwynwyn was escorted into the hall. He was a good ten years older than Llewelyn, appeared to be in his mid to late forties; a short, dark-complexioned man, stocky and sinewy, he bore a surprising resemblance to the swarthy, thick-set Earl of Chester. And like Chester, Gwenwynwyn had black eyes ablaze with keen intelligence, sharp with suspicion.

Chester was advancing to greet him. Gwenwynwyn's eyes flicked past the Earl, encompassed the hall. 'I was summoned to meet with King John,' he said in fluent Norman-French. 'Why is he not here?'

'The King's Grace has instructed me to act on his behalf.' Chester's voice was neutral, matter-of-fact. 'He has been grievously affronted by your recent incursions into Norman lands in South Wales. No man, be he Welsh or Norman, may violate the King's Peace with impunity. The King has therefore directed me to take you into the custody of the Crown, to detain you here in Shrewsbury Castle.'

Richard saw the looks of incredulous outrage upon the faces of Gwenwynwyn's Welsh followers, saw hands drop to sword hilts. Gwenwynwyn looked no less outraged, but he showed now that he resembled Chester in more than colouring, showed himself to be the same sort of hard-headed realist. Having walked trustingly into John's trap, he could accept defeat with as much dignity as he could muster, or he could cast his life away in a gesture of grand defiance. He chose the former, snapped a command to his men, and then turned back to face Chester.

'I came here in good faith,' he said, with such scalding contempt that suddenly none of the Normans could meet his eyes; even Thomas Corbet looked somewhat discomfited.

'You came here to answer charges brought against you by Marcher lords like Peter Fitz Herbert, that you've been raiding Norman manors, running off livestock and burning crops,' Chester said, quite flatly, and Gwenwynwyn's lip curled.

'*Y ci a fyner ei grogi dywedir ei fod yn lladd defaid,*' he said scornfully.

Even Marcher lords like the Corbets had never bothered to learn Welsh; Chester alone spoke the language. It was he who translated for the benefit of his companions. '"The dog we would hang is said to devour sheep." If by that you mean the King has contrived an excuse to seize your lands . . .?'

'What else would I think? I would like to know, though, where this pretty plot was first hatched . . . Westminster? Or Aber?'

'Aber? You think the King is obliging Llewelyn ab Iorwerth in this?' Chester shook his head, even smiled faintly, as though at

Gwenwynwyn's naive misreading of English aims. 'Your suspicions are understandable, but unwarranted. I assure you the King has no desire to see Powys fall under Llewelyn's control. Royal couriers are even now on their way to Gwynedd and to the courts of Prince Maelgwn and Prince Rhys Gryg in South Wales, forbidding them to take advantage of your troubles with the King, telling them to keep out of Powys.'

'And you truly think Llewelyn will heed such a command?' Gwenwynwyn was staring at them in bitter disbelief. 'You fools. Your poor bloody fools. It would be laughable, in truth – if I were not to be the one to pay the price for your stupidity!'

No one answered him. Chester gestured abruptly and men-at-arms emerged from behind the screen, moved to escort the captive Welsh Prince to his confinement. In the silence that followed, Thomas Corbet stepped towards Chester, began to assure the Earl that he knew Llewelyn well, that he would not dare to defy the King's command. No one asked Richard for his opinion, and he did not volunteer it. He admittedly did not know Llewelyn as Thomas Corbet did, had only met him twice. But he suspected that Gwenwynwyn knew Llewelyn better than any of them, and if Gwenwynwyn was right, he thought uneasily, there would be Hell to pay. For his sister's sake, he could only hope that Thomas was right and the Welshman wrong.

Greying dawn light was illuminating the snow-drifted peaks of Eryri, turning the crystalline lakes of the high mountain reaches to glistening blue ice, bringing day to the River Lledr valley and the castle standing stark sentinel in the shadow of Moel Siabod.

Joanna stood by the hearth in their bedchamber, watching her husband dress. As always when he was in a rush, Llewelyn lacked patience, preferring not to summon his squires to do what he could more quickly do himself. It was cold and Joanna pulled her bedrobe close, sought with chilled fingers to fasten the belt over her swollen abdomen.

'I still cannot believe it,' she said when she could keep silent no longer. 'I cannot believe you'd do this, leave me when my time is nigh. The babe is due in six weeks, Llewelyn. You would truly leave me when I do need you the most . . . and for what? A bloody border raid!'

'Joanna, you are not hearing me, not listening to what I say. I know you are distraught, and I am sorry for that, love. But a chance like this will not come again. With Gwenwynwyn caged in Shrewsbury, all of Powys lies open for the taking. You think Maelgwn and Rhys Gryg are not planning to carve it up between them even as we talk? You know what I want for Wales, know what it would mean to hold both Gwynedd and Powys. Can you truly expect me to forfeit such an opportunity? I cannot do that, Joanna, not even for you.'

'My father will not forgive you,' she said, saw him shrug.

'I expect I can live with that,' he said, and his indifference only served to fan Joanna's fury all the higher. In the night she'd clung to him, put aside her pride and confessed her fear, her need to have him with her when the babe was born. And he'd been very tender, very loving. But he'd not weakened in his resolve to depart on the morrow, to lead an army into Powys, and when she said her father would not forgive him, she was in fact warning that she might not be able to forgive him either.

Llewelyn buckled his scabbard, felt the familiar weight of a sword at his left hip, sheathed a razor-edged dagger, and then crossed the chamber, put his hands on Joanna's shoulders.

'You say the babe is not due for six weeks, *breila*. That means there still will be time enough. Once I'm entrenched in Powys, neither Maelgwn nor Rhys Gryg is likely to mount any sort of challenge to my suzerainty. If all goes as I expect, I'll leave Ednyved in temporary command and come back for the birth.' He smiled at her, a smile to break her heart, said, 'I promise, love, promise to be back in time,' and she wrenched free.

'Think you that I'm a child to be mollified with sugared words, placated with promises? You're not God, cannot give me an assurance like that. How can you be sure the babe will not come early, before its time? That you'd not be delayed by foul weather, reversals of the campaign? Or that you'd not get so caught up in that campaign, in the killing and the conquest and whatever it is that makes men lust so after war, that you'll forget all else? Who is going to remind you that you've a wife in need of you, a wife about to bear your child?'

'Joanna, I have to do this.'

'Was that what you told Tangwystl, too?'

Joanna at once regretted it; there were taunts not even the most justifiable anger could excuse. She knew Llewelyn's grieving had

329

been all the greater for not having been with Tangwystl when she died, and she said hastily, 'I am sorry.'

'You damned well should be!' He turned away from her, strode towards the door, only to stop with his hand on the latch. Wheeling about, he came back, reached out and jerked her towards him. He was not gentle, pulled her into an angry, ungainly embrace, made awkward by the unwieldy burden of her pregnancy. 'I will be back, Joanna.'

She wanted to fling his grudging promise in his face, to say she'd see him damned and in Hell ere she'd beg him again to stay. Instead, she wrapped her arms tightly around his neck, for a moment buried her face in his shoulder. But there was no healing in their embrace. Llewelyn stepped back, again turned towards the door.

'Llewelyn.'

He paused, but she saw he was impatient to be gone, his mind already upon Powys and plans of conquest. 'Take care of yourself,' she said, and even to her own ears, her voice sounded strange, made flat and toneless by her fear. 'Take care,' she repeated bleakly. 'I would look dreadful in black.'

Upon arriving at Aber, Richard was disheartened to be told that his sister was awaiting her confinement at Dolwyddelan Castle, more than a day's journey to the south. But the winter was so far proving to be a mild one, and the passes were still clear of snow. With Welsh guides who knew every rock and crevice of the Eryri heights, they encountered no difficulties, rode into the bailey of Dolwyddelan soon after dark on November 18th.

This was his first visit to Dolwyddelan, and Richard was looking about with interest as he followed Dylan, Joanna's seneschal, up the stone outer stairs into the keep. But as soon as he stepped across the threshold, he sensed that something was very wrong. Morgan ap Bleddyn, Branwen and Alison were clustered awkwardly to one side, barely glanced his way. In the centre of the chamber Joanna and Gruffydd were standing. At sight of his sister, Richard felt a throb of alarm; she looked ill, eyes hollowed and swollen, skin showing a greyish pallor even in the warming, reddish glow of hearth-fire. She had yet to notice him, had all her attention focused upon her stepson. Richard spoke no Welsh, but it was obvious that the conversation was a strained, laboured one. Joanna paused frequently, fumbled for

330

words, and at last switched into French, saying in a very low voice, 'What more can I say than that I am sorry?'

Gruffydd had been staring past her into the hearth. At that, he raised his head, and Richard took an instinctive step forward. He did not dismiss the passions of the very young with indulgent amusement. At nineteen, he was still young enough himself to remember; he knew that a child's hatred might be even more intense than that of a man grown, for the man's emotions were likely to be tempered with painful adult experiences in the arts of compromise and conciliation. The child's passions were more pure, and more primitive, and the hatred of a child could easily get away from him, take on dimensions and depths he could not hope to control. Such a hatred was now naked upon Gruffydd's face, a helpless soul-scarring hatred for his father's wife.

Gruffydd somehow fought back the words rising up to choke him, whirled and bolted for the door. Joanna signalled to Morgan, and the priest swiftly followed the boy from the chamber. It was only then that she saw Richard. 'Oh, Richard, thank God!' she cried, with such an intensity of emotion that what was meant as a welcome became an involuntary confession of despair.

Richard was not normally demonstrative, but he came forward quickly, gave her a prolonged hug. Waiting until they were together in the window seat nearest the bed, he watched her fidget with the lap robe Branwen had tucked around her, and finally said quietly, 'Are you not going to tell me what that was about?'

She did not want to tell him; that was evident. She fidgeted a while longer, lavishing undue attention upon the small dog curled up beside them. 'Poor Sugar, she cannot comprehend why I no longer have a lap for her to sit in.' She sighed, then she said with obvious reluctance, 'I'll tell you. But you must understand how it has been. My nerves are so on the raw these days that I find myself always on the edge of anger, much too quick to flare up, to take offence. But I cannot seem to help it. In truth, I have been feeling wretched for months with this babe, even before Llewelyn left me, and these five weeks that he's been gone . . . Well, I'd not ever want to relive them, Richard, not even for the surety of my soul!'

He waited without prompting, for he was that rarity, a Plantagenet with patience to spare, and Joanna sighed again. 'This morn Sugar ran off, disappeared without a trace. I was so fearful for her, sent servants out to search, to no avail. Then . . . then the child of one

331

of the grooms told me that he'd seen Sugar down by the river-bank, ere he knew she was missing. And he said she was with Gruffydd.'

'Ah, Joanna, surely you did not . . .?'

Joanna flushed. 'Yes, I did,' she admitted, with a trace of defiance. 'I accused Gruffydd of chasing Sugar away.' From the way she averted her eyes, Richard suspected she'd accused Gruffydd of even worse. He said nothing, and she stroked the dog until the heat had faded from her face. 'I was in the wrong, I know that. I had no proof, should not have . . . But I did, and within the hour, Sugar came back of her own accord, muddy and matted and unhurt. I apologized to Gruffydd, but as you saw, he will not forgive me. I knew he would not, not the way he cherishes a grudge!'

'Joanna, you can hardly blame him for being hurt and resentful. How old is he now, not thirteen till the spring, no? Well, you have to –'

'Richard, you do not understand. I should not have said what I did, would to God I had not. But you do not know what a wretched, hateful boy he is. Believe me, he's quite capable of harming a dog out of spite!'

'Have you ever talked to Llewelyn about him?'

'No. At first I thought I should be capable of handling him myself. As Llewelyn's wife, I owed it to him to make peace with his children; a man should not be burdened with problems of the hearth. And . . . and it would serve for naught, would only cause Llewelyn hurt. With the girls, I think I've finally managed to gain their trust. Even Gwladys. I asked her to stand as Elen's godmother, and since then, she's been slowly – ever so slowly – warming towards me. But Gruffydd has given me naught but grief from the moment of my arrival at Aber. I detest him, Richard, I truly do. He's wild and perverse and dangerously unpredictable, has none of Llewelyn's strength and every damned one of his failings!'

Richard glanced up sharply. 'Do you want to talk about that – about Llewelyn's failings?'

Joanna hesitated, and then confessed, 'Yes, I think I do. We had a truly dreadful quarrel when he left, by far the worst of our marriage. I was so angry with him, Richard; I still am. He knows how fearful I've been about this baby, he knows, but it was not enough to keep him with me. That's hard for me to understand, harder still to forgive.'

'We heard he was encountering little resistance, found Powys was his for the taking. Is that true?'

Joanna nodded. 'Llewelyn has few peers on the battlefield,' she said, with a perverse pride in that which gave her so much anxiety. 'Men say he is a brilliant commander.'

That, Richard thought grimly, was precisely the trouble. 'Think you that he'll stop at the borders of Powys?'

'You have not heard, then? He has crossed into Ceredigion, into the lands of Maelgwn ap Rhys, has pushed as far south as the River Ystwyth.'

'Jesu! But how can he hope to hold it? Maelgwn is no man to yield up what is his. I know the man, Joanna, met him often when I served in South Wales with William de Braose's son. His past is a bloody one, includes the murder of a brother and the imprisonment of his own father. He makes a bad enemy.'

'I know. Ednyved's wife Gwenllian is sister to Maelgwn and Rhys Gryg; they paid a visit to our court last year. After meeting them, I found it easier to understand why Gwenllian is such a bitch! But to answer your question, Llewelyn does not mean to hold Ceredigion for himself. He means to turn most of it over to Maelgwn's nephews. They've been feuding with their uncles for years, are more than willing to acknowledge Llewelyn as their overlord in return for his backing against Maelgwn.'

'Yes,' Richard said slowly, 'I expect they would be.' Joanna could not have given him a more disquieting answer. Had Llewelyn merely acted to seize what lands he could for himself, it would be much easier to dismiss him as just another of the power-hungry princes and lords of the Welsh Marches, a region that seemed to spawn more than its share of renegades, outlaws, and rebel barons. They could be troublesome, the de Braoses and Maelgwns and Fulk Fitz Warins, but their aims were understandable, their vision was limited, and sooner or later they overreached themselves, were undone by their own greed. But a man who would voluntarily yield to others land he had himself won at swordpoint, such a man had ambitions above and beyond filling his coffers, plundering his weaker neighbours. Such a man posed a genuine danger to England's interests, would have to be dealt with.

'Joanna . . . what does Llewelyn want for himself, for Wales?'

She surprised him then, said, 'Are you asking for yourself, Richard? Or for Papa?'

'For myself,' he said, and she smiled, reached out to brush the hair back from his temples. But she did not answer his question.

Branwen approached with mulled wine, retreated discreetly out of hearing range. Richard drank, studying his sister. Despite the fact that John's mother had one of the best political brains in Christendom, or perhaps because of it, he had never encouraged Joanna to take an interest in statecraft. He'd pampered her and protected her, indulged her and lavished love upon her, but he'd never asked her what she thought, never showed any curiosity in the workings of her brain. Her political education had come from her grandmother, during those months she'd spent with Eleanor in Poitiers. And, it was becoming disturbingly apparent to Richard, from Llewelyn ab Iorwerth.

Richard drank again, spat out sediment that had not settled on the bottom of the cup. He found himself wishing that Joanna was not becoming so quick to comprehend the subtleties and consequences of power, to grasp that which women need not know. Far better for her if she were like Isabelle, if she cared only for womanly whims and the joys of the moment, if she were not aware of the gathering clouds.

Suddenly he felt very dispirited, felt caught up in currents beyond his control. He knew his father had no liking at all for Joanna's husband, that he distrusted the Prince and disliked the man. But he did like Llewelyn, for he could not help but see the changes marriage had wrought in Joanna. Neither he nor his father had been able to give Joanna what she most needed, a sense of belonging. Llewelyn had somehow succeeded where they had not, and Richard was grateful to him for it. He knew Joanna had found more than contentment in her marriage, that she'd found a rare and real passion. He knew how deeply she loved Llewelyn, and he wished that she'd never laid eyes upon the Welsh Prince, wished that he had the power to blot the past thirty-one months from her mind and memory, for he did not think her present happiness was worth the suffering sure to come.

She had refused to answer his question, but he knew what her answer would have been, knew all too well what Llewelyn ab Iorwerth wanted. He wanted a Wales free of all English influence, wanted a united country under his own rule, a sovereign, independent kingdom like Scotland. And Richard knew his father would never allow it to be. No English King could.

'Richard . . . was Papa very wroth with Llewelyn for laying claim to Powys?'

'Yes, I fear so,' he said reluctantly, hoping she would not interrogate him further, not wanting her to know the true extent of John's rage when he was told that Llewelyn's red and gold lions were flying over much of mid-Wales.

'I knew he –' Joanna gave an audible gasp; her wine cup splashed its contents on to the window seat cushions.

'My God, Joanna, is it the babe? Do not move, I'll fetch your women . . .'

Joanna's breath was coming back. 'You need not panic,' she said, sounding faintly amused. 'It was just a stray pain. They come and go in the last days, mean only that my time is growing nigh.'

Richard's relief was considerable. Like most men, he knew next to nothing about the birthing process, was quite content to keep it that way. 'You'll have a midwife, of course, and women to help, to do whatever . . . whatever must be done?' he asked awkwardly.

'Two midwives, Dame Rhagnell and Dame Meryl. And Branwen and Alison, of course. I should have liked Catherine to be with me, but her youngest has been ailing.' Joanna frowned; having Catherine with her would have gone far to allay some of her anxieties. 'I wish I were not so fearful, Richard, wish I did not dread it so, for when a woman is tense and fearful, the pain is worse. If I did not remember Elen's birth so vividly . . . But I will not be so afraid if I know Llewelyn is here. As long as he is close at hand . . .'

Joanna's voice trailed off; after a moment, she looked up, gave Richard a shy smile. 'I never knew it was possible to be so angry with a man and yet want him so much, too. But right now, I think I'd gladly forgive him any sin on God's earth if only he'd walk through that door, if only he comes back for the baby's birth . . .'

Richard would never have admitted his doubts to Joanna, but he thought it very unlikely that Llewelyn would return in time. Richard had known few husbands all that eager to endure long hours of waiting outside the birthing chamber, and he found it hard to believe a man would interrupt a military campaign because of a young wife's fears. Mayhap for a first child, but Llewelyn already had seven children, already had a son. He said nothing, however, did what he could to raise his sister's flagging spirits, and was never so pleased to

335

be proven wrong as when Llewelyn rode into the castle bailey just before Vespers on November 20.

Richard awoke with a start, a sleepy sense of disorientation. After a moment or so, he remembered where he was, in the great hall of Dolwyddelan, and glanced over at the pallet where his brother-in-law had been sleeping. But Llewelyn's pallet was empty. Despite the hour, Richard felt no surprise; several times in the night he had heard Llewelyn rise, go out into the rain, and each time he returned, wet and shivering, he answered Richard's low-voiced queries with a shrug, a shake of his head.

Pulling on his boots, Richard moved to the heavy oaken door, opened it a crack. It was just before dawn, a blustery, cold Monday; the wind was still gusting, and after a night of unrelenting rain, the bailey was ankle deep in mud. Llewelyn was mounting the stairs up into the keep. He'd not be given entry, Richard knew; men were strictly barred from the birthing chamber. But Branwen or Alison would join him on the drawbridge in the forebuilding, would give him word on Joanna's progress.

Richard retreated back into the hall, sent his squire for a chamber-pot, and then a cupful of ale. It was a quarter-hour before Llewelyn returned. Moving at once to the centre open hearth, he stood as near the flames as he could, blew on his hands to combat the crippling cold, and rejected an offer of bread and cheese to break his fast. In the harsh morning light, he looked to be a different man from the one who'd come back in such triumph just three days ago, jubilant after six weeks of successive victories. He suddenly seemed a stranger to laughter; lack of sleep and a failure to shave gave him a haggard, unkempt look. And remembering how he'd doubted that Llewelyn would return for Joanna's travail, Richard wondered how he could ever have been so stupid.

'How does she?' he asked, again got a weary shake of the head in reply.

'No change, or so they claim.' Llewelyn accepted a cupful of ale, swallowed without tasting. 'Eighteen hours it's been,' he said, and Richard realized he did not even know if that was an excessive length of time.

'Is that overly long?'

'Not if the pains are light, feeble. But Branwen says Joanna's pains are right sharp, and coming close together. She got no rest at

336

all last night. If the birth drags on . . . So much can go wrong, Richard, so much. If the babe is lying in the wrong position, the midwife has to reach up into the womb and try to correct it. If she cannot, both mother and child are like to die. Or the babe can be too big. Or the pains can go on so long that the woman's strength gives out. There's always the danger that she'll lose heart, the danger of sudden bleeding. And afterwards, the danger that she'll not expel the afterbirth.'

Richard looked utterly blank, and Llewelyn said impatiently, 'That is the skin that held the babe when it was in the womb. If it does not come out of its own accord, and the midwives cannot pull it out, the woman will sicken and die. And even if she gives birth safely and then expels the afterbirth, there is still the risk of milk fever. They say as many women die from that as from the birthing itself.'

Richard already had been told more than he'd ever wanted to know about childbirth. 'How in God's name do you know so much about it? The midwives I've met have been as close-mouthed as clams.'

'I asked Catrin to tell me.' Llewelyn was staring into the fire, caught up in memories of a woman with hair the colour of the flames, in memories of a summer seven years past. After a long silence, he said, 'I wanted to know why Tangwystl died.'

For Llewelyn, those hours just before a battle always passed with excruciating slowness. But nothing in his past had prepared him for the way time fragmented and froze as he waited for Joanna to give birth to their child. When it had become clear that Joanna's delivery would be neither quick nor easy, he'd sent for Catherine, hoping that her presence might give Joanna comfort. But although she was only twelve miles away at Trefriw, she had yet to arrive, and he did not know whether to attribute the delay to the rain-swamped roads or to the continued illness of her child. Each time he made that grim trek across the bailey, sought scraps of information from an increasingly evasive Branwen, he was aware of a new and frightening feeling, a sense of utter impotence.

The rain fell intermittently all morning. Just before noon, the cloud cover began to break over the mountains; patches of sky became visible. Llewelyn at last humoured his ten-year-old daughter, agreed to Gwladys's pleas that he allow the cooks to prepare a meal

337

for him. He was making desultory conversation with Adda and Richard, relating how Maelgwn razed three of his own castles in Cercdigion rather than have them fall into hostile hands, when Branwen appeared without warning in the doorway of the hall.

Her hair was falling about her face in wind-whipped disarray, her gown mudstained to the knees, and when Llewelyn reached her, he saw that her eyes were filling with tears.

'The baby will not come,' she whispered. 'We do not know what else to do, my lord. We've massaged her belly and anointed her private parts with hot thyme oil, laid agrimony root across her womb, given her bark of cassia fistula in wine, even given her pepper to make her sneeze. The pains are coming very quick now, very sharp, but the babe is no nearer to delivery than it was three hours ago. My lord . . . she cannot go on like this much longer. Her strength is all but gone and she has begun to bleed.'

To Llewelyn, that was a death knell. It showed on his face, and she said quickly, 'No, my lord, bleeding need not be fatal, God's truth! She's lost mayhap a cupful, no more. But she's losing, too, her will to endure, losing all hope. And once she begins to believe she and the babe will die . . .'

She was weeping openly by now. 'My lord, Dame Rhagnell sent me to tell you that we do need a vial of holy water. Will your chaplain –'

'Holy water? No! No, I forbid it!'

'But my lord, you do not understand! It is for the babe. By pouring holy water on to a baptismal sponge, we can insert it up into Lady Joanna's womb, baptize the babe whilst it still lives!'

'Are you mad? You've just admitted that Joanna now despairs of delivering this child. You tell her you want to baptize the child whilst in her womb and you'll be passing a death sentence upon her!'

'I know,' she said, and sobbed. 'But if we do not, if the babe dies unbaptized, its soul will be lost to God! What choice have we, my lord, what choice?'

'Llewelyn, she is right.' Morgan, Richard, and Adda had come up behind them. 'She is right, lad,' the priest repeated softly. 'If a child is not baptized, it is forever denied Paradise, may never look upon the face of God. Your child, Llewelyn. Can you risk that?'

When Llewelyn did not answer, Morgan reached out, put his rosary into the younger man's hand. Llewelyn's fingers closed tightly around it; he could feel the beads digging into his palm. He brought

338

them up, touched them to his lips, and then handed them back to the priest. 'If I must choose between Joanna and the child,' he said huskily, 'I choose Joanna.'

Alison opened the door just wide enough to allow her to slip through to join Llewelyn out on the drawbridge. When he grabbed the latch, pushed past her into the bedchamber, she cried out in shock, 'My lord, no!' but made no move to stop him. Nor did Branwen, a mute, miserable ghost trailing him across the bailey and up the stairs. Both midwives, however, reacted with outrage.

'My lord, you cannot enter the birthing chamber! You must go from here at once!'

Llewelyn did not even hear them. He stood immobile for a moment, staring at Joanna. Although the chamber was chill, she was clad only in a chemise. It was linen, not a clinging material, but it had moulded to her body like a second skin, so drenched was she in perspiration. Her head was thrown back so far that her hair was sweeping the floor rushes, and the taut, corded muscles in her throat told Llewelyn more of her pain than any scream could have done.

Dame Rhagnell had stepped in front of him, barring his way. He thrust her aside, knelt by Joanna. The contraction was easing; she was no longer writhing upon the birthing stool, no longer gasping for breath. He murmured her name, and she turned her head towards him. Sweat ran down her face like rain, soaked the bodice of her chemise; he was close enough now to see that her skirt was filthy, soiled with mucous and urine, stained with blood. But what appalled him was the expression in her eyes, the hopeless, despairing look of an animal caught in a trap.

'Llewelyn . . .' He'd never heard so much gladness compressed into one word, had never before heard his name invoked as a prayer. Her lips were cracked and bleeding; he touched them with his fingers, and she reached for his hand, clung tightly, desperately.

'I've sent for Catrin. She'll be here soon, love,' he said, saw her try to smile, and found himself blinking back tears. He'd long ago learned to freeze feelings until he could deal with them. If he had not, he'd not have been able to survive twenty years of border warfare, to see death claim men who mattered to him and not mourn them until the battle was won. But the lessons of a lifetime now served for naught; he could not dissociate himself from Joanna's pain. He watched the red stain widening over her skirt, and could

339

think only of Tangwystl, bleeding her life away in the bed they'd so often shared.

The midwives were by no means reconciled to Llewelyn's alien presence in a female sanctum. But they temporarily abandoned their protests, turned all their attention to Joanna as her pain began anew. Dame Rhagnell knelt before the birthing stool, poured oil on to her hands, and began to probe under Joanna's skirt. She withdrew her hand only when the pain subsided, beckoned the other midwife aside. When Dame Meryl continued to shake her head, Dame Rhagnell turned away from her, said abruptly:

'From what I could feel, the mouth of the womb is fully open. But her waters have not broken and the membranes of the water bag are blocking the babe's passage from the womb.' She'd not even glanced at Joanna or the other women, was speaking to Llewelyn and Llewelyn alone.

'Do you understand?' Challengingly.

He nodded. 'Yes. You're saying this water bag should have broken of its own accord by now, but has not. Can you break it?'

'Yes. But there are risks in doing so. Oft-times a woman's delivery will be hastened by breaking her waters. But once the bag is broken, the pains become more severe, and if the birthing is prolonged, she'll suffer more. Dame Meryl thinks we should wait for the bag to break on its own. I would rupture it myself. The mouth of her womb has been open for hours; the babe should have come by now. So . . . you tell me, my lord. Since you are here, you decide. What would you have us do?'

Llewelyn knew what she was doing, acting to protect herself should the wrong choice be made, should Joanna die. He knew, too, that she was also taking vengeance the only way she could, trying to punish him for his intrusion into her domain. What he did not know was which choice was the right one. How could he know? If he guessed wrong . . . He looked at Joanna in an agony of indecision. She was already exhausted, could not survive many more hours of this, that he did not doubt. Still he hesitated, but with him the need to act would always prevail in the end. He swallowed, opened his mouth to tell her to go ahead, when Joanna forestalled him. She'd not grasped all of what was said, but she did understand that the midwife was forcing upon Llewelyn a choice no man should have to live with.

'It is my decision to make,' she said, speaking slowly and very carefully in her faulty Welsh. 'I want you to break the water bag, Dame Rhagnell.'

The midwife studied her for a long moment, and then nodded. 'It is the right choice, Madame, I am sure of it.'

They all watched tensely as she anointed her hands again in oil, seized a goose quill, and lowered herself on to her knees before Joanna. 'My lord, sit behind her on the stool and put your arms around her, high over her belly. We must wait for the next pain.'

Llewelyn did as she instructed, straddled the wooden plank protruding from the end of the stool, and braced Joanna back against his own body. She had closed her eyes tightly, was whispering rapidly, 'Mary, holy mother of our Lord Jesus Christ, into thy hands and those of thy blessed Son now and forever I commit myself, body, soul, and spirit.' Llewelyn stroked her hair until he felt her stiffen, twist against him.

The midwife at once jerked up Joanna's skirt, leaned forward. Joanna continued to writhe in Llewelyn's embrace. And then the midwife was pulling back, and suddenly there was liquid gushing on to Joanna's skirt, on to the floor rushes, even splashing over Llewelyn's mud-caked boots.

Llewelyn could tell almost immediately that Joanna's discomfort had been eased somewhat; her breathing was no longer so rapid and shallow, and when Branwen put a wine cup to her lips, she drank in gulps.

Dame Rhagnell let Joanna's skirt drop. 'The bleeding has ceased,' she said triumphantly, and Llewelyn forgave her all.

'So, too, has the pain.' There was wonder in Joanna's voice at first, and then, returning fear. 'What does that mean, Dame Rhagnell? Why have the pains stopped?'

'It often happens after the water breaks, my lady.' The midwife had regained her professional poise, said now with calming certainty, 'Soon the pangs will begin again, and when they do, the child will come quickly, and with surprising ease.'

Whether she was lying or not, Llewelyn had no way of knowing. But Joanna was free of pain for the first time in many hours. Her queasiness had mercifully abated, too, and with Branwen's help, she was even able to walk the few steps into the privy chamber. When she emerged, Llewelyn put his arm around her, slowly steered her towards a chair. She leaned so heavily upon him that his fears came rushing back; as weak as she was, how much more could she endure?

341

'Llewelyn, I'm afraid . . .'

'I know, love, I know.'

'. . . afraid you shall be disappointed. You see, I think the babe may be a girl. Dame Meryl said sons are more easily birthed than this.'

He could not answer her at once, made mute by the utter intensity of his relief. His greatest fear was that she would lose heart, would begin to look upon death as a release; he'd watched too many men die because dying was easier than suffering. But if Joanna had indeed been teetering upon that precipice, she had pulled back in time, had found new reserves of courage to draw upon, to see her child born.

'I expect we can make do with a daughter if we must,' he said, tenderly teasing, and kissed her swollen eyelids, the corner of her mouth.

The respite was brief; as Dame Rhagnell had predicted, Joanna's pains soon resumed. As the contractions increased in frequency and intensity, Dame Meryl stripped off Joanna's bloodied chemise, began to massage her abdomen. Joanna was groaning, taking deep gulping breaths, but she was not fighting the pain, was going with it, so intent upon her body's inner directives that she no longer seemed aware of Llewelyn and the midwives. She gasped, digging her nails into Llewelyn's wrist, and suddenly he could see the child's head. Joanna's body convulsed again, and the baby's shoulders appeared; it slid between her thighs into the eager waiting hands of the midwife.

It happened so quickly that Llewelyn was taken almost by surprise. He had only a fleeting glimpse of a small dark shape, skin puckered and covered with what looked like slime, bloodied and bruised, and he felt a sick horror that Joanna should have suffered so, only to give birth to a dead child. But then the infant made a mewing sound, and the midwife held it up with a cry of triumph.

'A man child,' she exulted. 'You've a son, my lord, a son!'

Llewelyn reached out, touched one of the tiny waving fists, and laughed. The midwives did, too, for the birth of a male child called up instinctive and ancient loyalties, and they rejoiced in being able to present a son to the man who was their Prince. Joanna was all but forgotten until she demanded weakly, 'Give me my son.'

Dame Meryl started to do so, instead handed the wet, squirming infant to Llewelyn, and it was he who laid the baby against Joanna's breast.

Joanna had never before felt for anyone, not even Elen, what she now felt as she held her son for the first time, a fierce, passionate tenderness, love immediate and overwhelming. 'He's so beautiful,' she whispered, and Llewelyn laughed again, for he thought the baby could not have been uglier, splotched and red and smeared with his own faeces, with his mother's blood. Joanna looked up as he laughed, and smiled at him, a smile he would remember for the rest of his life. But then she jerked spasmodically, groaned.

One of the midwives grabbed for the baby, at once tied and cut through the naval cord, while the other pressed upon Joanna's belly. Blood was spurting down Joanna's thighs, clotting on the floor. But Branwen was already at Llewelyn's side, Branwen who knew Tangwystl had bled to death, saying hastily, 'It is not what you fear, my lord. The afterbirth does come, that be all.'

He saw she was right, soon saw a soft, spongy mass expelled into Dame Meryl's outstretched hands. She caught it deftly, scooped it into a waiting blanket. 'It must be kept, must be properly buried,' she explained, 'lest it attract demons;' adding, with more mischief than malice, 'Should you like to look at it, my lord?'

'Not really,' Llewelyn said, and when he grinned, she grinned back.

Dame Rhagnell now laid the baby back in Joanna's arms. 'You may hold him for a few moments, Madame, but then he must be cleaned and rubbed with salt, must have his gums rubbed with honey.'

Llewelyn stood watching his wife and son, not aware of Branwen until she had twice touched his arm. 'Here, my lord,' she said, handing him a goblet full of mead. 'Is it not wondrous thing, to see your child born?'

He nodded. 'Indeed. But I'll tell you what is no less wondrous to me right now. That after a woman endures all this, why she is then willing to let any man ever again get within ten feet of her bed!' And while he spoke partly in jest, he was partly in earnest, too, and the women recognized it, legitimized with lusty, approving laughter his brief incursion into a secret inner realm, the world within a world of women.

When Joanna awoke, the chamber was deep in shadows. She started to sit up, grimaced, and sank back weakly against the pillow. At once, Llewelyn was beside her, leaning over the bed.

'How do you feel, love?'

'I ache all over.' To her dismay, she was suddenly shy with him,

343

suddenly fearful that he might feel differently towards her now. 'I wanted you so much,' she confessed, 'even begged the midwives to send for you when the pains got too bad. They said they could not, that it was not seemly, that a man would be sickened by the birthing –'

'Joanna, I was fifteen the first time I killed a man. In the years since, I've seen men gutted, beheaded, hacked to pieces. I rather think there is more blood on the battlefield than in the birthing chamber,' he said wryly, and when she raised herself up awkwardly on her elbows, he gathered her gently into his arms.

'The baby . . . where is he? Has he been fed?'

'He is fine, *breila*.' Seeing the doubt in her eyes, he beckoned, and a wet-nurse approached the bed, gave Joanna her sleeping son.

'You've arranged for the christening, Llewelyn?' she asked anxiously, not wanting to wait a moment longer than necessary to put her child under God's protection, and he nodded.

'This evening in the chapel; I'll tell you about it after. Catrin has come; she rode in just after you fell asleep. I've asked her to stand as godmother, and as godfathers, Adda and Richard. Does that please you?'

'Very much.' Joanna cradled the baby, touched a finger to his cap of dark, feathery hair. 'But ere he can be christened, we must pick a name for him. Have you one in mind?'

'If you like, we could call him Sion.'

Joanna drew a sharp breath. 'Ah, love, you'd truly do that for me? Let me name him after my father?' She reached for his hand, saw the scratches she'd inflicted, sought feverishly to think, to give him a gift of equal generosity. What name would be most likely to please him? It was not a common custom amongst the Welsh to name a son after the father. Iorwerth? Morgan? And then she knew, and she smiled at him, and said softly:

'I do thank you, beloved. But there can be but one name for our son, for a Welsh prince. We must name him after the most cherished of your saints, we must name him Davydd.'

Beyond the castle, the world was utter blackness, the sky a vast, starless void. Gruffydd was blinded by the night, kept stumbling, and his face and the palms of his hands were soon scratched from sprawling falls into the tangled underbush. But he did not slow, did not halt his headlong flight into the dark.

He ran until his body could absorb no more abuse, and he staggered, fell to his knees, struggling to fill his lungs with the ice-edged November air. A sharp, pulsing pain was pressing against his ribs, and he dropped down upon the ground, lay panting, his face pressed into the earth. The ground was damp, cold, scattered with dead and decaying leaves. He could feel sweat trickling down his neck, and then tears, seeping through his lashes and searing his skin. He beat his fist against the hard, unyielding earth until his knuckles were raw and bleeding, until he wept.

25

October, 1209
Woodstock, England

'Harri, throw the ball to me. *Brysiwch, Harri!*'

Joanna, listening to her children play with Isabelle's two sons, found herself smiling, amused both by her small daughter's queenly commands and by the way she switched back and forth from French to Welsh. Henry was, at two, the oldest of the quartet, but he did Elen's bidding no less promptly than her brother. Davydd was normally Elen's favourite playmate, but he showed no resentment at being supplanted by Henry, played with his own ball until Richard crawled over, made an awkward grab for it.

Isabelle sighed, bracing herself for the inevitable squabble, to be followed by tantrums and tears, but Joanna knew better; she felt no surprise when Davydd good-naturedly rolled the ball towards the younger boy. 'He has always been like that,' she said proudly, 'always been willing to share. Unlike Elen, whose first word was "mine"!'

'She is rather an imp, is she not? Not like you at her age, I'll wager!'

Joanna laughed ruefully, gave her dark-haired little daughter a look of bemused affection. 'Lord, no. She must take after her father, for she surely does not take after me. You'd not believe the trouble she gets into, and still a fortnight from her second birthday. But she is clever, Isabelle, so clever; do you know she talks to me in French and Llewelyn in Welsh?'

The children's wet-nurses had now entered Isabelle's chamber, and the game was forgotten; all four were still suckling, and would be until past their second birthdays. Joanna watched as they were ushered towards the far end of the chamber, said, 'This has been such a good year, the best I can remember. Llewelyn agreeing to pass Easter with Papa at Northampton. Getting to see you and Papa again just six months later. Above all, Papa forgiving Llewelyn for

346

going into Powys as he did. As much as I dread to see Llewelyn ride off to war, I was almost pleased when Papa wanted him to join the campaign against the Scots. I felt that might well mend the rift between them. And it did, showed Papa that Llewelyn does mean to hold to his oath of allegiance.'

'That was a marvellous war, was it not? The best kind, brief and bloodless and oh, so profitable! John was right pleased, says those who call the Scots King "William the Lion" ought better to call him "The Lamb"!'

'What shall be done with William's daughters, Isabelle? The ones he was forced to yield up to Papa as hostages?'

'They shall be well treated, kept at court. John never maltreats women; look how he provides for his niece, Eleanor of Brittany, sees that she has whatever she wants.'

'All save freedom,' Joanna said sadly. 'She was about seven years older than me, which would now make her twenty-five or so. By that age, most women have husbands, children . . .' She did not go on. She did not blame her father, understood he had no choice. But it hurt, none the less, to think of her cousin's gilded confinement at Bristol Castle, and she sought hastily for another topic of conversation. She'd been somewhat taken aback by the luxury of Isabelle's chamber. She and John were not at Woodstock all that frequently, yet the walls had been wainscoted with fir shipped from Norway, painted a brilliant green and gold, and the windows were glazed, set with costly white glass panes. 'Your chamber is a marvel, Isabelle. Papa does right by you, in truth.'

'Dearest, nothing comes to a woman unless she asks. You ought to coax Llewelyn into having your chambers done over. If you're clever, he'll not refuse, will even come in time to think it was his own idea.'

Joanna laughed. 'How little you know of Wales. Llewelyn could never hope to raise the revenues that Papa does; his country is so much smaller, so much poorer. In fact, I wonder that Papa could afford all this either. From the way he talks, he is ever hard pressed for money.'

'John refuses me nothing these days,' Isabelle said, backed up her boast by opening an iron casket, lifting out a magnificent ruby necklet. 'What will it avail him to have peace with the Scots if he has no peace at home?'

Joanna opened her mouth, shut it abruptly. She'd only been at

347

Woodstock for two days, but it was time enough to become conscious of the whispers, the knowing smiles, the way her father's eyes followed the young, pretty, blonde wife of one of his household knights. Joanna was sympathetically sure that Isabelle was aware of what was occurring; Isabelle, of all women, would never have missed the subtle yet significant indications of infidelity. Joanna knew a blithe, worldly spirit like Isabelle's was not likely to be lacerated by a husband's adultery, but she had not expected her stepmother to react with such nonchalant sang-froid.

'It . . . it does not grieve you any?'

'Ah, Joanna, you are such an innocent. Would it matter if it did? Would John then repent, forsake all other women? What cannot be changed must be accepted, no?' Isabelle held the ruby necklet up to the light, looped it over her fingers. 'If we are supposed to profit from our own mistakes, why should we not, as well, profit from the mistakes of others, from the indiscretions of erring husbands?' She reached over, draped the necklet around Joanna's throat. 'You may wear it at dinner if you like. Surely I have not shocked you, darling? You do not truly think your Llewelyn is faithful, do you?'

'Yes,' Joanna said, and then, seeing Isabelle's smile of pitying disbelief, she added hastily, 'Oh, I am not so naive as to believe he has never strayed. I do not doubt he finds women to warm his bed when we are apart, as when he was away in Scotland and England for two full months this summer. Whatever the Welsh laws may hold on fidelity, Llewelyn is no man to live like a monk. But I know how little such encounters mean to him, and I know that he does not lay with another woman when he can lay with me.'

'No mistresses, no concubines? Not even that woman who bore his twins?'

'No,' Joanna insisted, so resolutely that Isabelle said indulgently, if still sceptically:

'It's glad I am for you, then.' She removed the circlet anchoring her veil and wimple, handed Joanna a brush, confiding, 'I had a scare this spring, thought I might be with child again. I do not mind having more, think I'd like a daughter. But I've borne John two sons in fifteen months, have no desire to drop a litter a year! So . . . to give myself some breathing space, I've been taking brake-root in wine.'

'But Isabelle, that is a sin. You know what the Church says, that nothing must be done to prevent a child's conception.'

Isabelle shrugged. 'I know, too, who gets to bear that child – not

348

His Holiness the Pope. But you cannot be all that eager yourself to face the birthing chamber again, Joanna. At the least, you should put a jasper stone under your pillow when you lay with Llewelyn. Ask him to get you one; you need not tell him what it is for.'

'Of course I would tell him! Do you think I'd do that without his consent?'

'And what if he balks? If he is one of those men who judges his manhood by his wife's protruding belly?'

'Not Llewelyn,' Joanna said, and smiled. 'The midwives think it unlikely that I'll be able to carry a child again to full term, think I might not even conceive again. When I told Llewelyn that, he said, "Thank the Lord God!" He has always –' Breaking off in mid-sentence, she jumped to her feet, ran to console her son. Davydd had begun an unsteady trek across the chamber towards his mother, only to lose a precarious balance and fall upon his face. Picking him up, Joanna soothed and teased until his sobs ceased, until he settled contentedly in her lap, began to suck upon a sticky little thumb.

'Joanna, I confess I still do not understand Welsh laws of succession. John says illegitimacy is no bar, that Gruffydd has the same rights as your son. Is that true? Does that make him Llewelyn's heir, as the firstborn?'

'Under Welsh law, all sons share equally in the father's estates. It is a fair system for the common people, fairer for younger sons than Norman primogeniture, which gives all to the eldest son. But it has one dreadful drawback, Isabelle; how do you divide a kingdom? What inevitably happens when a prince dies is that his sons fight amongst themselves, winner-take-all to the survivor.'

'You're saying that when Llewelyn dies, Gwynedd would be partitioned between his two bastard-born Welsh sons and your Davydd?'

Joanna nodded grimly. 'And the very thought terrifies me. It is not just a question of preserving Davydd's rightful inheritance. Should evil befall Llewelyn ere Davydd reaches manhood, it would become a question of Davydd's very life.'

'Is there nothing you can do, Joanna?'

'There must be.' Joanna brushed her lips to her son's pitch-black hair. 'Blessed Mary, but there must be.'

'I think not, have no desire for an English knife at my throat.'

'Do not be insulting; I am Norman, not English. And you let me cut your hair, do you not? So why should I not shave you? Unless you truly want to trust your throat to a barber so greensick from wine that he seems stricken with palsy? Now lie down. I'll be right careful, have no wish to get blood all over the bed!'

'Why am I so sure I am going to regret this?' But Llewelyn did as Joanna bade, lay back and rested his head in her lap.

'There now,' Joanna said with satisfaction some minutes later. 'Almost done and I've yet to draw blood.' She cocked her head to the side in playful appraisal. 'Have you never wondered how you'd look without your moustache?'

Llewelyn's eyes snapped open. 'You would not dare!'

'Ah, Llewelyn, how I wish you had not said that. Now I feel obliged to prove to you that I would!' She let the razor hover tantalizingly close to its target, laughing, and when he grabbed her wrist, sought to pull her down beside him, she wriggled free, defended herself with the pillow. Neither realized how close they'd rolled towards the edge of the bed, not until it was too late, until their struggle carried them over the side, tumbling down on to the floor rushes.

Joanna was breathless but unhurt; in falling, Llewelyn had managed to twist away, to keep from landing on top of her. She rose to her knees, pulled her skirt down. 'Are you all right?' she asked, stopped laughing when he admitted reluctantly:

'No, I think not . . .'

'Oh, love, you did not hurt your back again?' She leaned towards him solicitously, then gave a muffled scream when he pounced, rolling over and pinning her under the weight of his body.

Joanna found herself utterly helpless, unable to move. 'I should have known; you're so untrustworthy,' she scolded, smothering her laughter against his shoulder. 'Now let me up. Papa is awaiting us in the great hall.'

'Make it worth my while and I might.'

'If I were to say I was sorry, that I do love your moustache?'

He considered gravely, shook his head. 'Not good enough.'

'Well, that was my best offer.' Squirming under him, she made an intriguing discovery. 'When Gwenwynwyn and Maelgwn call you hard, they do not know the half of it, do they? So it's not true, then, that when a man gets to be your age his powers begin to wane?'

'My age?' he echoed, with mock indignation. 'I'm but six and thirty!'

350

'That is, after all, twice as old as me,' she pointed out gleefully, and deliberately shifted her hips to make the most of his erection.

'Wanton,' he murmured, his mouth against her throat. 'If you do not stop tempting me, we are going to bypass the great hall altogether, are going to continue this conversation in bed. So do not say you were not warned.'

'Love, you know we have to be there.' Joanna sighed, with real regret. 'Otherwise, I'd like nothing better than . . . conversing with you. You're such a deep, penetrating conversationalist, after all,' she said, all but choked in trying not to laugh at her own weak pun.

She'd never yet bested him at wordplay, and she waited expectantly to see how he would improve upon her effort. Instead, he said, 'Do come in, John.'

'You'll have to do better than that,' Joanna scoffed. 'You played that trick upon me once before, remember? Looking up and saying, "Yes, Morgan?" at a moment when we most definitely had no need of witnesses!' The memory made her laugh; Llewelyn did, too. But then he sat up.

'I was not jesting, Joanna,' he said, and Joanna turned her head, saw her father standing in the doorway of the bedchamber.

John's face was impassive, showed absolutely nothing of what he was thinking. 'I trust I'm not interrupting anything of urgency?'

Llewelyn grinned, but he could see the embarrassed blush rising in Joanna's face and throat; taking pity on her, he held his tongue, showed his amusement only in the exaggerated gallantry with which he helped her to her feet. Privacy was an unknown luxury, and Joanna had long since become accustomed to people intruding into their bedchamber at inopportune moments, surprising her on Llewelyn's lap, in his arms, once in the midst of a soapily erotic shared bath. But never before had she felt as she did now, flustered and thoroughly discomfited.

'The last of the Welsh Princes have arrived, and they are awaiting us now in the hall.' For the first time, John looked directly at Joanna, his eyes opaque, utterly unreadable. 'I thought we would enter together.'

'We would be honoured, Papa.' Joanna hastily snatched up her veil, crossed to her father. Laying a hand upon his arm, she looked searchingly into his face. She still thought him to be a handsome man, but she thought, too, that time was not treating him kindly. She knew he would not be forty-two until December, yet the ink-black

351

hair was liberally flecked with grey; his eyes were bloodshot, shadowed by suspicions beyond satisfying, the mouth thinned, inflexible, not as open to laughter as Joanna remembered.

What could she say? That she ached for him, grieved that he had so much and so little? 'I love you, Papa,' she said, saw his mouth soften, and put her arms around his neck.

'I love you, too, sweetheart,' John said gently, for a moment held her in a close, comforting embrace. But he was not looking at his daughter, was gazing over her shoulder at the man she'd married.

Joanna watched as Llewelyn knelt before her father, did homage to John as his King and liege lord. The hall was quiet; Llewelyn's voice carried clearly to all, his matter-of-fact tones revealing none of the distaste Joanna knew he must feel.

John was now making the obligatory response, promising to do all in his power to guarantee Llewelyn's peaceful possession of Gwynedd, raising his son-in-law up to give him the ritual kiss of peace. Llewelyn then declared, 'In the name of the Holy Trinity and in reverence of these sacred relics, I swear that I will truly keep the oath which I have given, and will always remain faithful to you, my King and seigneur,' and then it was over, and Joanna took more comfort from the ceremony than she knew it warranted, tried to convince herself that there could indeed be a true and abiding harmony between the two men she loved.

Gwenwynwyn alone was absent, a prisoner of the Crown for the past twelve-month. But Madog ap Gruffydd was there, Prince of upper Powys, Llewelyn's first cousin and ally. So, too, were the Princes of Deheubarth, of South Wales, Maelgwn and his brother Rhys Gryg, and one by one they followed Llewelyn to the dais, knelt to do homage to the English King. After them came the younger Welsh lords, Llewelyn's cousin Hywel and Maelgwn's estranged nephews, Owain and Rhys Ieunac; all three were in their mid-twenties, and all three were Llewelyn's sworn men. It was Hywel who was to give a deliberate and dramatic demonstration of where his loyalties lay. No sooner had he done homage to John than he crossed the hall, knelt before Llewelyn, and swore oaths of homage and fidelity for the lordship of Meirionydd.

The Welsh system of inheritance did not promote family unity; all too often it fostered fratricide, set brother against brother in a bitter battle for supremacy. So it had been with Llewelyn's father and uncles. So, too, it had been in the South, where Maelgwn and Rhys Gryg were the survivors of a long and bloody war of succession. Owain and Rhys Ieunac were a rarity, therefore, brothers who were not rivals, who acted as one. In the silence that settled over the hall after Hywel's acknowledgment of allegiance, Owain and Rhys exchanged wordless looks of perfect understanding. Then they, too, crossed the hall, did homage to Llewelyn for Ceredigion.

A man could, and very often did, owe allegiance to two or more liege lords. In choosing to do homage to Llewelyn, the Welshmen were well within their legal rights. But Joanna wished fervently that they had not done so, had not acted to tarnish her father's moment of triumph. Maelgwn was standing just to her right, close enough to touch. He was a striking-looking man in his early forties, no taller than John, with a thick head of tawny hair and the blue eyes of the true Celt; those eyes were the coldest Joanna had ever seen. She watched his face as his nephews did homage to Llewelyn for lands once his, and shivered, suddenly and uncontrollably.

'Did Llewelyn plan that?' a voice murmured at her ear. When she shook her head, Richard swore under his breath. 'Papa will not ever believe he did not, Joanna,' he said sombrely.

Richard took a seat as inconspicuously as possible, not entirely comfortable to be in the company of these men, the most powerful lords of his father's realm. As he glanced about the table, it was with a distinct shock that he realized how few of them bore his father no grievances, how few were not in some sort of disfavour.

Chester seemed to have weathered John's earlier suspicions. And his uncle Will, of course, still stood high in John's favour. So, too, did John's mercenary captains, Falkes de Bréauté and Robert de Vieuxpont. Richard thought them to be men without honour, men who whored for the lord who'd pay the most, but their very practicality would keep them loyal; none could pay better than the King. Peter des Roches had proved his loyalty even to John's exacting satisfaction, remaining in England despite the Pope's Interdict. The same could not be said, though, for the others.

William de Ferrers, Earl of Derby, had the bad luck to be a nephew of William de Braose. The northern baron Eustace de Vesci was suspect because of his links to the Scottish Crown; he was wed to a bastard daughter of King William. The Earl of Huntingdon's predicament was even more acute; he was the Scots King's brother.

353

Richard de Clare, Earl of Hertford, was twice damned in John's judgment; he had welcomed John's accession to the throne with less than wholehearted enthusiasm, and his daughter was wife to William de Braose's eldest son.

William de Braose was casting a long shadow indeed, Richard thought bleakly. Even the faithful, upright Earl of Pembroke had stumbled over it, had foolishly taken pity on the fugitive de Braose family, briefly given them shelter on his Irish estates, for which John had yet to forgive him. The truth his father did not want to face was unpleasantly clear to Richard, that there was a growing groundswell of sympathy for de Braose among his fellow barons, not because he'd been liked, but because he'd been so powerful, so apparently invulnerable. There was not a man in this chamber, Richard knew, who had not thought to himself: the same thing could happen to me, to mine, should the King ever turn against me as he did de Braose.

This was the first council meeting since they'd left Woodstock for John's hunting lodge at Silverston. Richard knew what his father wanted to discuss, his coming campaign in Ireland, with its dual purpose of capturing the de Braoses and punishing those lords who'd dared to harbour them, an expedition he meant to finance with the fifteen thousand marks he'd extorted from the King of Scotland.

The council meeting began on an entirely different and discordant note, however. Eustace de Vesci leaned across the table, said with poorly concealed relish, 'I've news Your Grace should know. The Pope has given the order for your excommunication.'

Suddenly the chamber was very quiet. The Interdict was causing no small degree of suffering for John's subjects, but so far it had not had the effect the Pope desired, had not undermined the allegiance of the English. A large majority still supported John's position, that it was the King's right to choose an Archbishop of Canterbury, and not for the Pope to force his own man upon them. It was only to be expected, therefore, that the Pope would resort to excommunication, which made of John an outcast among all men of faith. No Christian was to break bread with an excommunicate; he was to be shunned as a moral leper, as a man doomed to eternal damnation.

John looked at de Vesci for a long moment, then smiled coldly. '"When I was a child, I spake as a child, I understood as a child, I thought as a child, but when I became a man, I put away childish things."'

Richard heard more than one indrawn breath, and looking

354

around, he saw that his father had profoundly shocked most of the men. Even the cynical de Vesci seemed taken aback.

How much bravado was there in John's blasphemy? Richard did not know. The sentence of excommunication had come as no surprise to John; he'd been privately warned days ago by Peter des Roches that the decree was imminent, had time enough to come to terms with it. Richard knew, of course, that his father was not the most pious of men, but what man could contemplate damnation forever and aye without recoil, without an inner shudder of the soul?

It was the pragmatic Chester who at last ended an acutely uncomfortable silence, saying calmly, 'Have you thought, my liege, of the problems this will pose for you . . . for us? How the common people will react?'

'The common people are not likely even to know. Let the Pope proclaim it from now till Judgment Day – in France, Brittany, Normandy. But who's to proclaim it for him in England? My lord Bishop of Winchester is the only prelate still on English soil.'

Peter des Roches smiled imperturbably, confirming what all already knew, that he'd chosen his King over his Pope, ambition over obedience. 'Your Grace is, as ever, quite right,' he said blandly. 'Shall we speak now of Your Grace's Irish expedition?'

'Not yet.' John signalled for wine, said, 'I've had word from Shrewsbury. Gwenwynwyn is offering no less than twenty hostages for his freedom, as a pledge of future loyalties.'

That was of little interest to de Vesci and the Earl of Derby; theirs were not Marcher lands. It was of enormous interest, though, to border lords like Chester and de Clare. And to Richard, for altogether different reasons.

'Do you intend to release him, Your Grace?'

'I expect so . . . sooner or later.'

'You do know that will mean war?' Chester's eyes were suddenly speculative. 'Once Gwenwynwyn is free, he'll seek to regain what was his.'

'You think he can?' John asked, and Chester considered, shook his head.

'Against Llewelyn? No, Your Grace, probably not. Not unless he gets help.'

'I agree with you,' John said, no more than that, but Chester was sensitive to nuance, to the unspoken.

'You would aid Gwenwynwyn, my liege?' he asked, and John

355

acknowledged his percipience with a faint smile. But it was Will who answered him, saying with some indignation:

'No, he would not! Llewelyn is his daughter's husband, my lord Chester. Moreover, he has proven his loyalty in answering my brother's summons for war against the Scots. I grant you he erred in disobeying John, in attacking Powys, but what's past is past, forgiven and forgotten, and he –'

'Whatever makes you think I've forgiven him, Will?'

'Why, because . . . because you made him welcome at court, John, showed no sign that you bore him any ill will –'

'I do not ever forget a wrong done me, Will. Not ever,' John repeated softly, and again Richard heard someone catch his breath. Only the men whose swords were sold to the highest bidder, Falkes de Bréauté and Robert de Vieuxpont, appeared unaffected by the threat. Every other man in the room seemed to have taken John's ominous admission to heart. Will looked troubled, Chester inscrutable, de Vesci grim, expressions of unease flickering from face to face, the awareness that John's warning was meant as much for them as for his Welsh son-in-law.

'You were all at Woodstock, saw what happened, saw what he dared to do.' John's colour had deepened; there was in the low, precise voice echoes of remembered rage. 'For those of you who are not that well acquainted with Llewelyn ab Iorwerth's predatory past, he seized power from his uncle at twenty-one, and in the intervening fifteen years has steadily increased his holding – always at someone else's expense. He'll eventually swallow up all of Wales . . . if left to his own devices.'

Richard bit his lip, much disquieted. He knew Joanna had spoken privately to their father, had left for Wales confident she had convinced John that Llewelyn had not known what his young allies meant to do. It bothered Richard that John had not been honest with Joanna, bothered him that John had been nursing a grudge for more than a year, bothered him that the other men were so quick to nod agreement. He knew he owed it to Joanna to object, to defend her husband. But he knew, too, that he was there only on John's sufferance, that there was no voice in council for the King's twenty-year-old bastard son, and that silenced him, that and an instinctive reluctance to move from the sidelines to centre stage, to abandon the protective colouring developed during a solitary, introspective childhood, the unquestioning, fatalistic acceptance that had enabled him to look upon his father's darker side and neither approve nor condemn.

It was Chester who unexpectedly did what Richard felt he could not, offer a measured, unimpassioned protest. 'You understand the Welsh quite well, my liege, better than your brother ever did. And making use of one Welsh prince to checkmate another is indeed a shrewd and proven strategy for dealing with Wales.'

John, too, was responsive to insinuation. He frowned, said challengingly, 'But not this time?'

'Llewelyn ab Iorwerth is an unusual man, Your Grace. He is exceedingly ambitious, just as you say, but he is intelligent, too. I think he understands the limitations of power . . . of Welsh power. And because he does, I would prefer to keep him as an ally, even if it means giving him a free hand in Wales. I fear that if we do not, we risk pushing him into open rebellion.'

'And what if we do? Are you saying a Welsh rebel could prevail against the English Crown?' John's voice was scornful, but Chester refused the bait.

'No, Your Grace, of course I am not. He could not hope to defeat you. But I am not sure if you fully realize what victory might cost. It is too late, you see, to use a Gwenwynwyn or a Maelgwn to rein him in; the balance of power has already shifted too far in his favour. If you do not come to terms with him, it would not be enough to defeat him. You'd have to destroy him.'

Chester paused, waiting. But John made no response.

'As I said, Your Grace, I do not doubt the eventual outcome. But it would be a drawn-out, bloody, and brutal war. Wars with the Welsh always are. They disappear into inaccessible mountain retreats, phantom foes we cannot find. But they have no trouble finding us, my liege; they excel at ambush, at surprise attack and counter-attack upon the morrow. There is no glory in wars against the Welsh, only blood-splattered rocks and shallow graves, and once you win, you find precious little for the plundering. I would not undertake such a war merely to rid myself of a man I could more easily befriend, Your Grace.'

'Would you not? And if I were to order you to do just that, order you to lead an army into Gwynedd, what then? Would you balk, beg off from a duty you find so distasteful?'

The sarcasm was savage, utterly undeserved, and Richard winced. Chester had gone rigid in his chair; Richard was close enough to see

357

how the muscles clenched along his jaw line, how the tendons tightened in his throat. 'I serve the King's pleasure,' he said, quite tonelessly. 'When Your Grace commands, I obey.'

'How very reassuring,' John said dryly. His gaze shifted from Chester, moved slowly from face to face. The other men averted their eyes, guarded their thoughts. All save Will, who leaned across the table, put his hand upon John's sleeve, and asked what Richard so needed to know.

'John, Llewelyn is wed to your daughter. What of her? What of Joanna? I cannot believe you'd want to see her hurt.'

John exhaled a deep, drawn-out breath, stared down at his clenched fist, at the imprints his nails had left in the palm of his hand. 'No, I would never want that,' he said, 'never.' He looked up then, raised troubled hazel eyes to his brother's face. 'But I fear that marriage was a mistake, Will, a great mistake.'

August, 1210
Cricieth Castle, North Wales

William de Braose turned from the window, from the shimmering blue expanse of the bay. 'It is good of you, my lord, to make my grandson and me welcome at your castle of Cricieth.'

'To the Welsh, hospitality is a binding obligation. We never turn away a man in need of shelter, offer him food and a bed, guarantee his safety as long as he remains a guest at our hearth. I understand that Normans have different customs,' Llewelyn said, very dryly, saw the older man's face mottle with colour, saw his barb bury itself in the scar tissue of an old shame. He was not surprised when de Braose made no effort to defend himself; to de Braose, the Abergavenny massacre required neither explanation nor expiation. Nor was he surprised when de Braose forbore to take offence, for he knew how much the Norman lord needed his help.

'I hear John has been laying waste to half of Ireland. Have you no fears for your wife, your family?'

'There is no need. As soon as John moved into Ulster, my wife and sons took ship for Scotland.'

'A wise decision,' Llewelyn conceded. 'John makes a bad enemy.'

'You should know.'

'Should I?'

De Braose closed the space between them, stopped before Llewelyn's chair. 'Can you not feel the noose tightening about your neck? John had to delay his Irish expedition to deal with the Scots King, and he now delays your destruction whilst he settles a grudge against me and mine. But your turn is coming, my lord. Can you in truth doubt it? After John took Ellesmere Castle from you?'

Llewelyn tensed. It was months since John had abruptly reclaimed the castle he'd yielded to Llewelyn as Joanna's marriage portion, but the mere mention of Ellesmere was enough to ignite a still smouldering anger, anger which gave the lie to his affectation of indifference. De Braose saw, and smiled.

'I have friends still in Wales, in England, am kin by blood or marriage to Derby, de Clare, Mortimer. To a man, they hate John, and with cause. They'd heed a call to rebellion. So, too, would Maelgwn and Rhys Gryg, especially if you come in with us, my lord. With John occupied in Ireland, this is a Godgiven opportunity; we'd be fools not to take advantage of it. At the least, we could then treat with him from strength, pressure him into buying peace on our terms. And with luck, we might be able to do more than maim, we might even be able to bring him down. You do not fear him as most men do, so you do not realize the extent of their hatred. Let them scent blood, and they'll react like a pack of hounds with a live hare in their midst. Think what it would mean, my lord. With John shackled, one way or the other, Wales would be yours for the taking. And of course you'd have my full support, that of my kindred.'

'Of course,' Llewelyn echoed cynically. But the thrust of de Braose's argument could not be dismissed as easily as his self-serving promises. Llewelyn was quiet for some moments, at last shook his head. 'I'll not deny there is truth in what you say. And if I truly thought we had a chance to succeed . . . But the risk is too great. I've never been so hungry that I was willing to lick honey off thorns.'

'If rashness is a flaw, so, too, is an excess of caution. Sooner or later, a day of reckoning is coming between you and John. Better you should be the one to pick when and where. Think on what I've said, that is all I ask. Think on it.'

The sun was sliding into the sea by the time Joanna returned to the castle. So great was her sense of outrage that she'd been unable to remain under the same roof with William de Braose, gathering up her children and taking them down to the beach for a day in the sun, out of sight and sound of the man who was her father's avowed enemy.

Davydd and Elen had been thrilled with this break in their daily routine, splashed in the shallows and dug in the sand. But Joanna was utterly miserable. How could Llewelyn do it, how could he make welcome a man outlawed, a traitor to the Crown? Did he not realize – or care – what her father would make of that? Alys, Davydd's wet-nurse, had packed a basket full of food, but Joanna could swallow no more than a mouthful of cheese. In the months since Woodstock,

360

she'd watched helplessly as her life careened out of control, as her father and husband moved closer and closer to an irrevocable break. She'd been deeply hurt by her father's seizure of Ellesmere, saw the revoking of her marriage portion as a denial of her marriage, felt that her father had somehow betrayed her. That Llewelyn would receive William de Braose was, in a different way, no less of a betrayal.

Once they were within sight of the castle, Joanna felt free to dismiss Alys and the three men she'd taken along as an escort, knowing Llewelyn would have been furious with her if she'd gone off without them. She was in no hurry to climb the slope up to the castle, not when William de Braose might still be within, and she loitered for a time by the water's edge, watching gulls squabble over the last of her bread. When Elen came running up, brandishing a dead crab, Joanna made the obligatory response, delighted her daughter by shrinking back in mock horror, not confiscating the crab until Elen tried to stuff it down the front of Davydd's tunic.

Elen burst into thwarted tears, sobbing pitifully and resisting with all the strength of her small body as Joanna pulled her away from the water, in the direction of the castle. Just when Joanna's frayed patience was about to give way, Elen wriggled loose, sprinted forward with a glad cry of 'Gruffydd!'

A short distance away, three boys were sitting upon a log, throwing knives at a much smaller piece of driftwood. Joanna was now close enough to make a grudging recognition of her stepson and Ednyved's son Tudur. The third youngster had sun-streaked blond hair and a deep tan; she only belatedly recognized him as William de Braose's grandson and namesake.

He rose politely, if briefly, to his feet at sight of her; so did Tudur. But Gruffydd did not move, managed to make of his slouching pose a deliberate provocation. In the five months since he'd attained his fourteenth birthday and his legal majority, Gruffydd's relationship with Joanna had deteriorated rapidly. No longer sullenly mute, he was becoming openly antagonistic, almost as if defying Joanna to fall back upon her weapon of last resort, to complain of his rudeness to Llewelyn. Joanna did not know whether he was testing his newfound manhood or testing her, knew only that they were racing headlong towards a confrontation, and she watched grimly as Elen flung herself on to her brother's lap, wrapped her arms around his neck and entreated, 'Make me fly, Gruffydd!'

361

Coming to his feet, Gruffydd obligingly swung the little girl up into the air, high over his head, making her shriek with laughter, as Davydd watched wistfully. But while envying his sister's swooping flight, he stayed where he was, for he was somewhat afraid of Gruffydd. His every overture had been rebuffed so brutally that he now avoided Gruffydd whenever possible; although his awareness was still only on an unconscious level, he'd begun to sense that when his brother Gruffydd looked at him, it was with loathing.

Setting Elen down upon the sand, Gruffydd sprawled back upon the log. 'I hope you have an explanation for your disappearance. My father is less than pleased with you for running off as you did.'

'That is hardly your concern.'

As always, their conversation sounded discordant, somehow off-key, for Gruffydd refused to address Joanna in Welsh, and she just as stubbornly renounced French. Will was beginning to look amused, and it was to him that Gruffydd said:

'A Welsh-born wife would rise even from a sickbed to make welcome a guest in her husband's house. There was a time, in fact, when women did not come and go just as they pleased. In the reign of Hywel the Good, a prince's wife shunned the great hall in his absence, kept to the women's quarters until her lord returned. But then you Normans invaded England, brought queer and outlandish customs with you like some noxious foreign pox.'

'I find it passing strange that you would choose to boast of the more backward aspects of your heritage,' Joanna snapped, and Will laughed aloud.

'Check and mate,' he pronounced, with a mocking grin that endeared him neither to Joanna nor Gruffydd.

'Sugar!' Joanna whistled for her dog. With Davydd holding on to her skirt and Elen dawdling behind, she started towards the castle. She'd taken only a few steps, was still within earshot when Will laughed again.

'So that is your father's wife.'

'That,' Gruffydd said, quite clearly and distinctly, 'is my father's whore.'

Joanna froze, disbelieving, and then spun around. 'I want an apology from you, and I want it now. If not, I shall go to Llewelyn, tell him the way you dare to speak about his wife.'

Gruffydd's eyes narrowed. 'Go ahead. I'd deny it.'

'Do you truly think he'd believe you over me?' Joanna said, and he rose, took a sudden step towards her. He was taller than she, as tall already as Llewelyn, and for the first time she was aware of a physical menace, aware that a boy's raw, raging passion was now contained within a man's body.

Will moved to Joanna's side. '"My father's whore,"' he drawled. 'Did you forget, Gruffydd, that I heard you, too?'

Gruffydd was taken aback, but not for long. 'You keep out of this!'

Will smiled. 'Make me,' he said.

'Stop it,' Joanna said sharply. Will had shifted his weight, bracing himself; a hand had dropped to the dagger at his belt. Gruffydd, too, wore a dagger, and he was, Joanna knew, utterly fearless. They were, both of them, too old for boyhood squabbles that left only scratches and bruises, but not old enough to judge what was worth fighting or dying for, and Joanna was suddenly frightened. 'Stop this foolishness,' she repeated, knowing even as she spoke that they were not likely to heed her.

It was Elen who stopped it, Elen who was tired of being ignored and sought to call attention back to herself by quoting parrot-like, '"Father's whore." Is that you, Mama?'

Gruffydd drew a quick breath, looked down at the little girl, and Joanna saw in his eyes a sudden shame. His hand unclenched from his dagger hilt; he flexed his fingers, rubbed his palm against his tunic. He obviously did not know what to say to Elen, at last mumbled, 'You must forget that, lass, must not say it for others to hear –'

Joanna interrupted hastily, knowing nothing would be more likely to brand the word into Elen's brain. 'It is just another word for . . . for Norman, Elen.'

As Elen wandered away, satisfied, Gruffydd looked at Joanna. 'I was wrong to say that,' he said, very low. 'I never meant for my sister to hear. It will not happen again.' The apology cost him dearly, but in making it, he unexpectedly achieved a certain bleak dignity, which not even Joanna could deny.

Gruffydd's eyes flicked briefly to Will, back to Joanna. 'I owe my lord father better than that,' he said, turned and walked away.

Joanna paused on the wooden stairs leading up to her chamber in the Great Tower, looked thoughtfully down at Will. 'Thank you for escorting us back to the castle. But tell me, why did you take my side against Gruffydd?'

'I'm naturally gallant,' he said and laughed, then shrugged. 'Mayhap because you're Norman, a woman. Or mayhap because I was not much taken with your stepson.'

'I was surprised, in truth, to see the two of you together. I'd have thought Gruffydd would sooner befriend a *caeth*, a bond servant, than one of Norman blood.'

'Well, I expect it helped that I speak so much better Welsh than you! And we did discover a common bond, a shared loathing for the King of England.'

'I see,' Joanna said slowly. She knew his candour was a deliberate challenge, but how could the boy not blame her father for the downfall of his House? 'You know, of course, that I am King John's daughter. I take it you do not believe, then, in blood guilt?'

'Now you are mocking me,' he said composedly. 'But yes, I do believe in blood guilt . . . for men, for sons. Not for a woman, though, at least not a woman who looks like you do!' There was in his grin both impudence and a certain cocky charm, and Joanna had to laugh.

'For your sake, Will de Braose, I hope you learn to curb your tongue; you cannot trade upon being fourteen forever!' She turned to go, paused again. 'You remind me of someone, and I've just realized who. I think my husband must have been much like you at fourteen.'

Will looked pleased. 'If I can win as much with my sword as Llewelyn ab Iorwerth has won with his, I'd be well content.' He backed away from the stairs, stood looking up at Joanna. 'I shall remember you, my lady. And to prove I am generous as well as gallant, I have some free advice for you. Talk to your lord husband about his son.'

Joanna knew Will was right, but she knew, too, that now was not the time. Her relationship with Llewelyn was strained enough this summer, needed no more pressures brought to bear upon it.

Pushing open the door of her chamber, she came to an abrupt halt at sight of William de Braose. That Llewelyn should have brought de Braose here, to their private chamber, was more than she could forgive, and when de Braose moved towards her, kissed her hand, she was hard put not to snatch it from his grasp. She managed a grudging nod, but no more, and as soon as they were alone, Llewelyn said curtly:

'When I make a man welcome at my hearth, I expect my wife to treat him with courtesy. Is that clear, Joanna?'

'Yes.' But the mutinous set of her mouth belied the dutiful submission. Crossing to her clothes coffer, she jerked the lid up, let it drop with a slam. 'How can you allow that man at your table? You know what he is, a traitor, a fugitive from the King's justice. Why must you do this? Why must you antagonize my father to no purpose?'

'Joanna, I cannot shape my life around what will or will not please your father. Even if I were willing to do that, to turn myself into his puppet, it would avail me naught. For some months now, John has been looking for excuses to find fault, to curtail my authority in Gwynedd.'

'That is not fair! Nor is it true!' Branwen had hung a gown on the wooden wall pole; Joanna pulled it down, began to fumble with the lacings of her bliaut. The knots defied her fingers, and she was finally forced to ask Llewelyn's help. He had no more luck with the ties than she, jerked impatiently until one of the laces broke off in his hand.

'Thank you so much, that I could have done myself!' Joanna managed to get the bliaut over her head, flung it to the floor. She started to remove the gown, but then she paused, glanced at him, and retreated around the curtained bed to strip off the dress.

'Joanna, just what secrets do you think you could have from me after nigh on four years of sharing my bed?' Llewelyn sounded both amused and exasperated. But when she re-emerged, he said, quite seriously, 'I am bone-weary of these constant quarrels, bone-weary of having to defend to you every decision I make. You are my wife as well as John's daughter, but there are times when you seem to forget that.'

'That is so unjust, Llewelyn! You know I do love you. But I love my father, too. What would you have me do, choose between you?'

He did not give her the reassurance she expected. 'I would hope it will never come to that, Joanna,' he said quietly, and she stared at him in dismay, at a loss for words.

There was a sharp rapping on the door and Ednyved entered.

'Llewelyn, a messenger has just ridden in from the south. John landed at Fishguard in South Wales three days ago. And he brought with him Maude de Braose.'

Will swallowed. 'My parents?' he said. 'My little sister? Were they taken, too?'

William de Braose seemed not to hear. It was Llewelyn who reassured the boy, said, 'No, lad, they were not.'

'How . . . how was my grandmother taken? I thought they'd got safely into Scotland.'

'They did, but at Galloway, a Scots lord took them prisoner, held them for John. Your parents escaped; so did your aunt Margaret and her husband, de Lacy. But Maude was taken, and so was her daughter Annora, her son Will and his four young sons. They were sent under guard back to Ireland, to John at Carrickfergus.' Llewelyn looked from the boy to the still silent de Braose. 'What will you do?' he asked, and de Braose bestirred himself with an obvious effort, shrugged.

'What can I do? You said John is heading for Bristol. I shall have to go to Bristol, too, try to come to terms with him.'

The Welsh murmured among themselves at that, looked at the Norman lord with the first glimmerings of respect. Even Llewelyn was somewhat impressed. 'I wish you well,' he said and meant it, thankful that he would never be facing de Braose's dilemma, that his own wife had nothing whatsoever to fear from John.

De Braose seemed to have aged years in a matter of hours. He ran a hand roughly through greying blond hair, said heavily, 'My lord Llewelyn, I have a favour to ask of you. I know we are not far from the port of Pwllheli. Can you provide a guide for my grandson, get the lad safely there?' And when Llewelyn nodded, he turned to Will, said, 'At Pwllheli, you can take ship for one of the southern ports, Tenby or Swansea, and from there, sail with the tide for France.'

Will had lost most of his youthful bravado; he looked shaken and, although he tried to hide it, fearful. Joanna had so far listened in silence, but with that, she came forward, said, 'That would be a dangerous voyage for a boy of Will's years to undertake alone. Would it not be safer to leave him here, at my husband's court?'

'No, Madame, I think not.' William de Braose shook his head, said very evenly, 'Whilst that is a kind offer, I would not rest easy as long as there is any chance my grandson might fall into the King's hands.'

Joanna felt as if she'd been slapped. 'My father would never harm a fourteen-year-old boy!'

De Braose did not dispute her. But neither did he believe her, and it showed. Far worse, she could read the same scepticism on her husband's face, on the faces of the others in the hall. She looked about her, saw only disbelief, derision, and pity, and whirled, fled the hall.

When Llewelyn followed, he found her in their bedchamber, standing by a window opening on to the sea. 'Joanna,' he said, and as she turned, he saw tears streaking her face.

'My father is not a monster. He's not!'

'Ah, lass, I never said he was.'

'But you do think he would hurt Will, do you not?'

'I do not know, Joanna. I can only tell you that, if it were my son, I'd not be willing to gamble his life on John's sense of justice.'

'Llewelyn, listen to me. For once, please hear what I am saying. I know my father has flaws; what man does not? You've your share, too. But Papa has never been anything but kind to me, and to my brothers. He treats his wife far better than most men do. And he is a good King. When he travels, he is always willing to halt by the roadside, to let the common people petition him for redress of grievances, and no king within memory has worked so hard to provide all free men with access to his courts. He even sits himself when cases are tried. When poor crops caused the price of bread to rise beyond the ability of many to pay for it, he ordered that large quantities be bought, be offered to the people for a pittance, and he often gives money for alms, for –'

'Joanna, there is no need for this, love.' There was in Joanna's frenzied recital of her father's benevolences a desperation that told Llewelyn she was not as free of doubts as she would have him believe. 'Joanna, what you say is true; I know that. John can indeed be very generous, can be merciful and just . . . but only to the poor, the powerless. To those whom he sees as a threat, he is utterly without mercy.'

'You are wrong, Llewelyn, so very wrong.' Joanna brushed away tears with the back of her hand. 'You do not know him as I do. Why

367

will you not believe me? Why will you not at least try to allay my father's fears? You know he is of a mistrustful nature, know how quick hc is to suspect the worst. He has never truly trusted you after you defied him and seized Powys, we both know that. And now, when he learns that you gave shelter to an enemy like William de Braose –'

'You do not understand at all, do you, Joanna? You still do not see. This is my land, the land of my father and his father before him and his father before him. I am of the House of Cunedda, who ruled in Gwynedd in the fifth century after the birth of the Lord Jesus Christ. Can your Norman kings trace their ancestry back seven hundred years? I think not, yet they dare to sneer at our customs, to mock our heritage and our language.

'I am Welsh, Joanna, and even now you cannot comprehend what that means. Normandy, Anjou, England – it is all the same to you of Norman birth. Your people have dwelt in England for over a hundred years, yet you do not think of yourselves as English. You do not sicken when uprooted or exiled, you do not recognize the kinship of the tribe, which goes beyond the *cenedl*, the kinship of blood. You know nothing of *hiraeth*. And you will never understand what I feel when I see Norman castles guarding Welsh mountain passes, when I hear French spoken instead of Welsh in the valley of the Rhondda, knowing French might one day be heard in the valleys of Gwynedd, too.'

Joanna had listened in stricken silence. Their most heated quarrels had not frightened her so much. Not since the first days of her marriage had she felt as she did now, as an alien in a world that would never make her welcome, that she could never under-stand.

'You are right, Llewelyn,' she said softly, wretchedly. 'I do not understand. I would to God I could, but I do not. I love you, though. Does that count for nothing?'

'I know you love me, Joanna. But you believe your father is in the right and I am in the wrong, believe all would be well if only I'd act as a proper vassal, submit myself unto the King's will.'

She could not deny it, and that frightened her all the more. How much strain could a marriage absorb, how many quarrels before the foundation cracked, split beyond repair?

'I know of a sudden we seem to be arguing all the time, and I hate it, I do. I will not lie to you. There have been times this summer when I have not liked you very much. But I never stop loving you, Llewelyn, no matter how angry I get. You must believe that.' She paused for breath, forced herself to ask. 'You . . . you do still love me?'

'Ah, Joanna, how young you still are . . .' He crossed the chamber, stopped before her. 'When I married you, you were an appealing, courageous child. You've grown into a beautiful, courageous woman, and I have learned to love you, *breila*. But –'

'No,' she entreated, reaching up and laying her fingers against his mouth. 'You say you do love me. Let's stop with that, let's not talk any more . . . please. Love me, Llewelyn. Make me forget all but you.'

He tilted her face up, kissed her, gently at first, and then he lifted her in his arms, carried her to the bed, where he did make her forget . . . for a time.

When William de Braose, under escort, entered the solar of the King's castle at Bristol, he felt no surprise at sight of so many highborn witnesses: the Earls of Salisbury, Derby, Surrey, and Chester, Eustace de Vesci and Geoffrey Fitz Peter, John's Justiciar. De Braose understood all too well. There was no longer need for caution, no longer need to fear betrayal, not with de Braose's wife, son, and grandsons under close guard in this very castle.

De Braose was actually glad of an audience. Derby and Chester had intervened on his behalf, had persuaded John to issue a safe-conduct, and de Braose thought John would be more likely to honour it in the blaze of full noon. He knelt, said, 'I have come to beg my King's pardon, to ask what I must do to make amends, to regain your trust.'

'Indeed? Shall I tell you how to mend a broken trust? Pluck the feathers from a goose, scatter them to the four winds. Then gather them all up, each and every one, and put them back on the goose. It is as easy as that.'

John had won triumph after triumph during his two months in Ireland, had scattered his enemies, brought the ever-rebellious Irish barons to heel, had Maude in his hands and her husband on his knees. But he did not look like a man savouring his victories; he looked drawn and tired, almost haggard, and de Braose could take no comfort from what he read in those narrowed hazel eyes.

'I have offended you, and for that I am well and truly sorry. But

369

I am loyal to you, my liege, would never betray you. Let me prove myself. Set for me a task, I'll not fail you.' De Braose sought to slow his breathing, added very softly, 'Christ, John, it never had to come to this, I swear it.'

John's favourite falcon was perched upon his left arm, talons digging into the padded leather wrist-guard. It was unhooded, made harsh, guttural sounds low in its throat, and John stroked the sleek feathers with a gloved hand, spoke softly and soothingly until it quieted. 'My lords of Chester and Derby, amongst others, have urged me to show mercy. I would not want it said that I was arbitrary, unjust. Mayhap we can yet reach an accord. If you were to pay a fine, one large enough to discharge your indebtedness to the Crown, and to cover the costs I have incurred because of your rebellion, I would be willing to overlook your past offences, to give you and your sons full pardons.'

De Braose was stunned. 'And my wife? What of her?' he demanded, even as he sought feverishly to detect where the snare lay.

John smiled mirthlessly. 'I've no wish to have her on my hands for life, that I assure you. She would be released into your custody.'

De Braose was still struggling with disbelief; he might have found it easier to believe John had he not shared John's summary way with enemies. 'I do accept your terms, Your Grace, am speechless, in truth,' he said, without irony. 'Have you an amount in mind?'

'I think forty thousand marks to be a fair sum,' John said, and then de Braose understood.

'Indeed,' he said tonelessly. 'When do you want payment, my lord?' And there was no surprise whatsoever when John said:

'You have a fortnight to raise the money. Will that be acceptable?'

'Quite acceptable.' At John's gesture, he rose to his feet, took the wine cup John was offering, his own. Their eyes held as he drank, as he drained the cup. And then John gestured again, this time in dismissal.

Maude kept squeezing her husband's arm, as if to reassure herself of the reality of his presence. 'When they told me you were here, I could scarcely believe it!'

'What of Will, Annora, the lads? Are they all right?'

She nodded. 'Fearful, but unhurt. I'll confess, Will, that I've been none too easy myself.' And even that understated admission surprised him; hers was a haughty spirit that made no allowances for frailties, that would never acknowledge weaknesses in herself. 'Well? For the love of God, Will, tell me! What did John say?'

'That we can buy absolution . . . for forty thousand marks.'

'Forty thousand! You must be joking! We could never raise that, no one could. Did you not tell him so?'

'He already knows.'

She stared at him, then sat down suddenly on the nearest coffer. 'We . . . we could raise four, mayhap even five thousand. You could borrow from Derby, and de Clare. Pembroke might even –'

'Maude, it would not matter. Even if by some miracle, we begged and borrowed the entire amount, it would not matter. Can you not see that? He deliberately demanded a sum he knows we can never pay. He is not going to give any pardons, and he is not going to let you go, not for forty thousand marks, not for twice that amount.'

Her face did not at once show full comprehension; it came only in degrees, as if she were clinging as long as she could to the illusory security of denial. 'Christ have mercy,' she whispered. 'He'll keep me caged till I rot.' She rose, began to pace. 'God in Heaven, how I hate that man! May his misbegotten, cankered soul rot for aye in Hell everlasting!'

She raved on like that for some moments, abusing John in language even her husband could not have improved upon, at last turned back to face him, said tautly, 'What mean you to do now, Will?'

De Braose looked away, stared into space over her head. 'There is a ship sailing at dawn for Barfleur. For the right sum, the captain will smuggle me on board.'

'You mean to flee to France? To abandon me and your children to John? Jesus wept, Will!' There was so much shock in her voice that he flushed, lashed out savagely.

'I did what I could for you, more than you deserve, for none of this would have happened if not for you! What would it serve to share the same dungeon? I cannot help you, Maude, can only save myself now. And I'm damned if I'll feel guilty about it!'

Her mouth twisted. 'Do you want to tell our grandsons that, or shall I?' she jeered, and he almost hit her. Unclenching his fist, he swung away from her, towards the door. 'I suppose I should wish you luck! It will not be easy, you know; I dare say John has you

371

under close surveillance. It'll be a miracle if you even make it to the wharves.'

He paused, hand on the door latch. 'You still do not see, do you, Maude? It was not me John wanted. It was you. It has been you from the beginning, from the day you opened your damned fool mouth and doomed us all.'

May, 1211
Aber, North Wales

Catherine was being escorted across the bailey towards Joanna's chamber when she heard the screams, screams of such total terror that she gathered up her skirts, began to run. In the ante-chamber Branwen was retching into a water bucket, with Alison hovering helplessly nearby. The screams were abruptly choked off as Catherine reached for the door latch. Within the chamber, Llewelyn was braced against a high-backed chair, while Joanna knelt beside him, trying frantically to comfort the screaming child he held upon his lap. As Catherine watched, sickened, Llewelyn's barber straightened up, holding a pair of pincers and a small bloody tooth.

Elen writhed against Llewelyn's restraining hold, let out a high, keening wail of pain, fright, and outrage. Almost from the time she could walk, she'd shown a decided preference for her father, but now it was for 'Mama' that she sobbed, and Joanna gathered her into a close embrace.

Elen's face was beet-red, her eyes swollen, her bodice stained with saliva and blood and vomit, but her parents looked no less stricken. As Joanna crooned to the weeping child, heedless of the blood smearing her own clothing, Llewelyn rose, poured himself a full cup of mead with a hand that shook.

'Christ, Catrin,' he said softly, 'I do not think I could go through that again for the very surety of my soul.'

Catherine understood exactly how he felt; a child of hers had once been subjected to the same ordeal. 'You tried cloves, betony?' she asked, and he nodded wearily.

'Every remedy we could think of, and then Joanna lit candles at St Apollonia, but to no avail.' Elen's screams had yet to abate; he reached out, stroked the heaving little shoulder, and then retreated, leaving Joanna to minister to their daughter's pain.

It was a long time before Elen quietened, even longer before she slept. Joanna slumped down upon a coffer, already dreading the moment when Elen would awake, when her suffering would begin again. 'I do not know when I've ever been so tired, Catherine . . .'

She did look utterly exhausted, and Catherine felt a throb of pity, for she knew how bad a year it had been for Joanna. A bad year for them all, but above all for Joanna, who loved both John and Llewelyn, who was caught between anguished, irreconcilable loyalties.

Soon after William de Braose's flight to France, the Earl of Chester and the Bishop of Winchester had led an army into Gwynedd, advancing as far as the east bank of the River Conwy, where Chester rebuilt Deganwy Castle, which Llewelyn had razed in a futile attempt to keep it out of Norman control. At about the same time, John released Gwenwynwyn from his two-year confinement, giving him money and men-at-arms to mount a challenge to Llewelyn's hold upon his domains. Llewelyn thus found himself fighting a war on two fronts, and by December, he'd been forced to withdraw from most of southern Powys. But he struck back hard at Chester, making raids of reprisal into Cheshire, burning the Earl's manors and running off his livestock. Christmas that year had seen smoke-filled skies on both sides of the border, and Joanna, then in the second month of a stressful pregnancy, had miscarried on Epiphany Eve.

With Easter, a fragile, false peace settled over the Marches. All knew it would not last. Chester's men were still entrenched in Deganwy, and Llewelyn would never accept an alien presence on Welsh soil. Gwenwynwyn was now back in power in Powys, with a blood score to settle. And John had spent the spring forging alliances of expediency with Maelgwn and Rhys Gryg. What should have been a season of rebirth and renewal was now no more than a time of uneasy waiting, was to be but a brief prelude to a summer of war.

'Joanna . . . how is it between Llewelyn and you these days? Are you getting on better?'

'Yes, we are,' Joanna said, then gave Catherine a sad smile. 'But that is because he has been so often gone fom Aber this spring.'

'You argue about John, about your father? Catherine asked tentatively, and Joanna nodded.

In the past year, her life with Llewelyn had fallen into a disquieting pattern: sudden, sharp quarrels during the daylight hours, later reconciled in bed. 'I love him, Catherine, and I believe he still loves me. But . . . but we find little to laugh about these days, and I remember how we used to laugh together all the time . . .'

She rose, reassured herself that Elen still slept, and then turned back to Catherine. 'When all began to go sour between my father and Llewelyn, I blamed Llewelyn for much of it, Catherine. I kept thinking if only he'd try harder to earn Papa's trust, if only he were not so set upon having his own way, so prideful . . . But then my father sent the Earl of Chester into Gwynedd, gave Gwenwynwyn the means of making war upon Llewelyn. Oh God, Catherine, how could he? However angry he was with Llewelyn, did he never think of me? For my sake, could he not have found another way?'

Joanna was alone in their bedchamber, waiting for Llewelyn. Branwen had unbraided her hair, and she reached for the silver-backed brush Llewelyn had given her just four days ago, on their fifth wedding anniversary. As she did, her eyes fell upon a small crystalline stone, mottled with bronze streaks. Picking up the jasper pebble, she fingered it pensively. The stone was no talisman, was a goad to memories she'd rather not recall, memories of her January miscarriage.

But brake-root was not any more effective than jasper as a contraceptive. Isabelle had become pregnant within days of their confidential conversation at Woodstock, had given birth to a daughter while John was pursuing Maude de Braose in Ireland. That, too, was a memory Joanna preferred not to dwell upon, for she'd had an utterly unexpected reaction to the birth of her half-sister. She'd never realized how much it mattered to her – being John's only daughter amongst eight sons – not until it was no longer true, until Isabelle had given John a fair-haired baby girl and he'd given her Joanna's own name.

It was a common if confusing Norman custom to have legitimate and base-born children share the same name; John had twice christened a son Henry and Richard. But Joanna could not keep from reading a superstitious significance into John's choice of names, could not keep from being hurt by that choice.

She'd had ten months to accustom herself to the loss of her privileged status, no longer felt jealous of the baby sister she'd yet to see. But she had not heard from her father for months, not since the past autumn, and on this warm night in mid-May, she felt forlorn and forgotten and very much afraid of what the future might hold.

375

Suddenly sensing she was no longer alone, she looked up, saw Llewelyn standing in the doorway. 'I did not hear you come in. Have you been there long?' She gave him a self-conscious smile, for she did not like to be watched unaware. 'I finally had to give Elen a mild sleeping draught, the pain was so – Llewelyn? Llewelyn, what is wrong? What has happened?'

'What was bound to happen. Your father is gathering a large army at Chester.'

She came to her feet with a choked cry, and he said bitterly, 'You cannot be all that surprised. It has been obvious for months that John wanted war.' But even as he spoke, he saw that her shock was unfeigned, that she'd somehow managed to convince herself the inevitable could be defeated merely by refusing to acknowledge it.

'No, it must not come to that, it must not! Llewelyn, please, you must act whilst there still be time. Go to my father, seek his pardon. Oh, please, I beg you!'

'Seek his pardon?' he echoed, incredulous. 'For what, putting him to the inconvenience of an invasion?' He swung about, too angry to risk remaining, but she was already at his side, clutching frantically at his arm.

'No, you do not understand! I'm not saying Papa is right. He's not, he's not! But there cannot be war between you. When I think of you and Papa facing one another across a battlefield, I – Llewelyn, please, please do not let it come to that!'

'Joanna . . . Joanna, I cannot lie to you, cannot pretend this is just one more border skirmish. John wants as much of Gwynedd as he can conquer, wants my head on a pike.'

'No, Llewelyn, no. He'd not go as far as that, not if he loves me. And he does, he –'

'I know you love him, Joanna, but do not defend him. Not tonight, not to me.'

She stared at him, her eyes slowly filling with tears. 'My God, Llewelyn, what are we going to do?'

He reached out, traced a tear's path with his thumb, brushing it away before it could reach her mouth. 'I do not know if it will comfort you any, Joanna, but you need not fear a battlefield confrontation. I have no intention of taking the field against John.'

She drew an audible breath, and her hand tightened upon his arm. 'Oh, my love, my love, thank you!'

Although the temptation to lie to her was overwhelming, he shook

376

his head. 'I do not do it for you, Joanna. John can call upon all the resources of the English Crown, has the support, as well, of most of the Welsh Princes. He can put ten, twenty times as many men under arms as I ever could. I'd have to be out of my wits to engage him on the field in open battle.' Llewelyn paused. 'And if he thinks I'm that big a fool, thinks my pride will utterly vanquish my common sense, he's made the greatest mistake of his life.'

The night was so unseasonably warm that no fire had been lit in the hearth. But Joanna had begun to tremble. 'I'm so cold . . .' she said, and when Llewelyn turned towards the table, thrust a wine cup into her hands, she had to lock her fingers around the stem to hold it steady. 'What . . . what do you mean to do, Llewelyn?'

'I mean to instruct John how wars are waged in my country.' He reclaimed the wine cup, took several swallows. 'In England and France an army is expected to live off the land, off the spoils of war. But Wales . . . Wales has no towns lying open and easy for the taking. Aside from the few settlements that have grown up around the church in Bangor or my palaces at Aber and Rhosyr, my people live scattered about the hills. They're hersdmen, hunters, not farmers, Joanna. Much of Gwynedd is virgin soil, has never felt a plough. John's men will find no crops in the fields, no villages ripe for the plundering, no women for the taking, and nothing to fill their bellies. I'd wager that within a fortnight they'll be eating their own horses,' he said, with such savage satisfaction that Joanna shuddered.

He saw, and put an arm around her shoulders, drew her to him. But he offered her no words of comfort, no assurances that all would be well, no lies.

Most of the Welsh lived in circular timber-framed houses with earthen floors, wattle-and-daub walls, and thatched roofs, simple structures that could be abandoned without regrets. In hasty obedience to Llewelyn's command, they gatherd up their bedding, their kitchen utensils, their chickens, drove their livestock ahead of them as they fled into the deeply wooded hills, lost themselves in the formidable heights of Eryri.

On May 18 the English army moved out of Cheshire, crossed the border into a ghost country, exceedingly beautiful and eerily still. The few huts their scouts found were deserted, stripped bare. The only signs of life were distant spirals of smoke high up in the hills. They advanced warily along the coast road, advanced farther and

377

farther into an alien land of ominous silence and unseen eyes.

By the time they reached the east bank of the River Conwy, morale was at a dangerously low ebb. Soon their supplies were, too. As rations were cut and cut again, men began to appraise their neighbours' shares, began to dice for larger portions, and then to fight for them. While John and his captains argued whether to attempt a crossing of the Conwy, word spread through the ranks that scouting parties sent to search for the Welsh had not returned. Men began to sicken. Others riding out to hunt for game disappeared without a trace into the dark, foreboding forests that rose up on both banks of the river. John consulted urgently with Chester and Pembroke, calmed the camp by announcing that men were being dispatched back into England for wagons of flour, bacon, and cheese.

The supply party set out the next day at dawn. At noon, the few survivors staggered bleeding back into camp. With the realization that the man they were hunting had become the hunter, that Llewelyn had swung around behind them and cut off access to England, John's captains were hard put to maintain order. By month's end, Llewelyn's grim prediction had come to pass; they'd begun to butcher their horses.

Richard was standing by an open window in the keep of Deganwy Castle, gazing down at their encampment spread out upon the slopes below. To his right flowed the fluid barrier of the Conwy, and beyond, the whitewashed buildings of Aberconwy Abbey. Richard knew the white-robed monks would be moving about their daily chores, as if oblivious of the fact that only the width of the river lay between them and an enemy army. He wondered if the monks realized just how lucky they were. The abbey had flourished under Llewelyn's patronage, reason enough in his father's eyes to have treated the monastery as spoils of war.

The silence in the chamber was oppressive, utterly disheartened. His uncle Will and the Earl of Pembroke had unrolled a crude map of North Wales. No one else was making even a pretence of productive activity. Richard's older half-brother Oliver was sprawled in a far corner, trying to sleep. So, too, was Oliver's uncle, Fulk Fitz Warin. John's mysterious magnanimity in pardoning Fitz Warin's treason had been resolved for Richard upon learning that Oliver's mother was Fitz Warin's sister. He could not help thinking upon that now, wondering at the perverse inconsistencies in his father's nature, that the same man who'd forgive a rebel for the sake of a onetime bedmate would also undertake the destruction of a loved daughter's husband.

The door opened and Eustace de Vesci entered, followed by Robert Fitz Walter and Henry de Bohun, Earl of Hereford. They squatted down in the rushes, began to pass a wineskin back and forth. But they kept their eyes upon John all the while; Richard could not help noticing how many of his father's barons did that, watched John whenever he was not looking.

De Vesci had left the door ajar. It was jerked back now with a violence that spun all heads around. Ranulf de Blundeville, Earl of Chester, strode into the solar. Ignoring the others, he addressed himself to John, with a complete disregard for preamble or protocol.

'There've been three more stabbings today.'

John got to his feet. 'What of it? Soldiers are bound to brawl amongst themselves.'

'Indeed, that's so. But in the past when my men fought, it was over a wench – not over bread!'

'I hardly need to hear again about the shortages!'

'I think you do. We're running out of more than food, we're running out of time. Do you know a man with an egg can sell it for a penny and a half? That'd buy him an entire chicken back in England! There's not a dog or a hen left alive in the castle, and the pantry, larder, and buttery have been emptied to feed your men, supplies that were to maintain my garrison for months. It took me two months to fortify Deganwy, fighting off the Welsh almost daily. How in Christ do you expect me to hold this castle now?'

John did not reply, and Chester took a step closer. 'How much longer do you mean to deny the truth, that this is a war we cannot win? You need proof? Just go out and take a walk through the camp! So many have taken sick that you cannot get within ten feet of the latrine pits, the stink be so vile! What are you waiting for, until the bloody flux kills off those who do not starve?'

The chamber was utterly still. It had been years since any man had dared to defy John like this. Both Will and Pembroke had come to their feet. Richard took one look at his father's face and he, too, moved forward. But Chester was beyond discretion or prudence.

'You cannot say you were not warned, my liege, because I told you it would likely come to this! I told you this man would be no easy fox to snare, that he'd be too shrewd to take the field against

379

you, that you'd find your quick, clean war of conquest being fought on his terms. Now do you believe me? Now are you ready to admit defeat, to cut our losses whilst we still can?'

'You've said enough, more than enough! I'm beginning to wonder just where your loyalties lie. You've never had any stomach for fighting this man. Why? It could not be that the two of you have reached a private accommodation, could it?'

Chester's eyes glittered, black pools of utter outrage. 'I do not deserve that, have served you faithfully. If you call me disloyal for daring to speak my mind, to be honest with you, so be it then. But answer me one question, my lord. Have you so many men whom you can trust to tell you the truth that you can afford to spare even one?'

'Ah yes, and Scriptures tell us to "rejoice in the truth", do they not?' John said mockingly. But it was a surprisingly restrained response, showed Richard that Chester had unexpectedly hit a nerve. Chester sensed it, too, was quick to press his advantage.

'I'm not saying Llewelyn ab Iorwerth could not eventually be run to earth, though I still think it'd be a Pyrrhic victory. But there'll be no victory at all this time. He's won, you have to face that. It is done, my liege, done.'

John turned away, walked to the window. He stood there for some minutes in silence, staring out at Llewelyn's alpine citadel, the remote cloud-crested peaks of Eryri. 'No,' he said. 'Not yet.'

The hill the Welsh called Mynydd y Dref rose some eight hundred feet above sea level, offering sweeping views of Conwy Bay, the river, and Deganwy Castle. Joanna moved cautiously towards the edge of the cliff, was grateful when Llewelyn slid a supportive arm around her waist.

A high wind was gusting, but the sea was a brilliant sapphire blue, and the light was resplendent upon the grey stone church below; the monastery looked prosperous and orderly and utterly at peace. But the encampment on the far side of the river was a scene of disorder and desolation. Some tents were still standing, flapping forlornly in the wind; the area was littered with debris, scarred by ditches and smouldering camp fires; bones and rotting carcasses of dead horses were piled at the water's edge, and when the wind shifted towards the west, it brought to them a sickening stench of death and decay.

'My lord! It's true, they're gone!' Several horsemen were coming up the slope at a gallop. The lead rider was soaked from the river crossing, shivering and short of breath, but he was exultant, stammering with excitement.

'They've pulled out, all of them, even the castle garrison!' He glanced then towards Joanna, said in a lower voice, 'You'd best not let your lady cross the river, my lord. The English King left his dead for you to bury.'

'That much ground I'm willing to yield up to John,' Llewelyn said, and the other men laughed, began to crowd around him, gesturing towards the deserted encampment, interrupting one another freely, making boisterous jests and sardonic puns, theirs the grim gallows humour of the suddenly reprieved. Joanna turned, walked away.

Finding a sheltering boulder some yards from the cliff, she stood gazing out to sea, watching as gulls skimmed the wind-crested waves of the bay, circled above her father's abandoned castle keep. She could still hear Llewelyn's laughter, as buoyant and soaring as the birds wheeling overhead; if sunlight were not silent, she thought, it would sound much like Llewelyn's laughter. It had been so long since she'd heard him laugh.

After a time, Llewelyn broke free from the encircling men, came to stand beside her. His hair was blowing about wildly, and she raised her hand, brushed it back from his eyes. As she did, he caught her hand in his.

'I understand that you cannot rejoice in my victory, Joanna, but I hoped you'd not begrudge me the joy I take in it.'

'I do not, God's truth, I do not!'

'My poor Joanna; no matter who won, you had to lose. But it's over now, *breila*.' He reached for her other hand, drew her towards him. 'You can await me at the abbey whilst I cross over to the camp. Then we'll go home.'

Joanna swallowed, rested her head for a moment against his chest. 'It is not over, Llewelyn,' she said, her voice so muffled it was all but inaudible.

His eyes had seemed full of light, showed golden glints in the sun. But as she looked up at him now, she saw all the light had been completely quenched; his eyes were utterly opaque, bleak and chill.

'You think he'll come back,' he said flatly, and she nodded.

'I know he will, Llewelyn.' She moved back into his arms, whispered, 'I know he will . . .'

*

Llewelyn knew that Joanna's love for her father blinded her to what others saw in John. Yet for all that she was disbelieving of his darker impulses, she still knew better than most the intimate workings of his mind. Llewelyn accepted her anguished certainty as grim gospel. But neither one of them expected John to act with such ruthless, single-minded resolve, or with such stunning speed.

He at once set about making ready for a second Welsh campaign, and because he was both willing and able to subordinate all else to this aim, by early July a large army was assembling at the border town called Blanc Minster by the Normans and Croes Oswallt by the Welsh. This time he'd provided for packhorses heavily laden with salt, beans, cheese, flour, sides of bacon and beef. He'd also summoned carpenters and craftsmen, brought along labourers as well as soldiers, packed spades, axes, picks, and nails.

On the second Friday in July, they moved into upper Powys. Llewelyn's cousin and ally, Madog ap Gruffydd, prudently offered no resistance, let the English army pass unmolested through his domain. At the same time, John's allies, Maelgwn and Rhys Gryg began a well-coordinated plan of attack from the south.

Swinging up the Vale of Llangollen, John crossed into Gwynedd, pressed on towards the River Conwy. And as he pushed west, he began to build Norman castles on Welsh soil. They were hastily erected fortresses, constructed of Welsh timber by conscripted English carpenters. But they were also symbols of power, of the might of the English Crown, and each one cast a foreboding shadow over the countryside it now controlled.

Llewelyn was hopelessly outmanned, was forced to fall back before the inexorable advance of the English army, to withdraw into the deepest reaches of Eryri as John swept all before him. First Rhuddlan Castle and then Deganwy were reclaimed, and in the fourth week of July, John's men crossed the River Conwy. It was the first time in well over a hundred years that an English invasion force had penetrated this far into Gwynedd.

After sacking the Cistercian monastery at Aberconwy, John encamped his army upon the west bank of the river, then dispatched a large raiding party up the coast. With Welsh guides provided by Gwenwynwyn, they made their way through the pass of Penmaenmawr, on to Llewelyn's deserted palace at Aber, which they put to the torch. From Aber, they rode for Bangor Fawr yn Arfon, the episcopal see for the diocese of Bangor, where they dragged the

Bishop from the High Altar, brought him back a prisoner to John's camp by the Conwy. But before they did, they set fire to the cathedral church, burned every house in Bangor to the ground.

At dusk, Llewelyn's young allies, Owain ap Gruffydd and his brother Rhys Ieunac, rode up from the south. Her private chamber having been appropriated for a council of war, Joanna was at a loss as to where to go, unwilling to subject herself to the stares in the great hall. She'd thought her husband's countrymen had long ago reconciled themselves to his alien English consort, but during the past weeks, she'd come to realize how tenuous that acceptance was. As her father's army moved into the very heartland of Llewelyn's realm, there were many who looked upon Joanna and saw not Llewelyn's wife, Davydd and Elen's mother, saw only John's daughter.

Joanna finally climbed the stairwell up to the battlements that enclosed the gabled roof of Dolwyddelan's keep, her need to be alone prevailing over her dislike of heights. Even this refuge she had to share with several sentries, but they seemed to sense her mood, kept prudently to the other side of the walkway.

The keep towered more than forty feet up into the twilight sky. By daylight, the view was breathtaking, affording panoramic vistas of the River Lledr below and the mountains beyond. But as darkness descended over the vale, Joanna's attention was riveted upon the horizon. A pale reddish glow lit the sky to the north. She knew what it was; Llewelyn had received word hours ago that Bangor was burning.

Joanna set her lantern on the embrasure, unable to take her eyes from that eerily streaking sky. By dawn, all of Bangor would be reduced to ashes and charred rubble. Aber still smouldered. How long, she wondered, ere Dolwyddelan, too, fell to her father's army?

By now it was full dark. So absorbed was Joanna in her own purgatory that she failed to hear approaching footsteps, started violently when Morgan touched her arm.

They stood in silence for some moments, Joanna studying him through her lashes. She knew he was in his middle fifties, although he looked much younger, for he had a magnificent head of silvered hair and sculptured cheekbones that aging only enhanced. In every sense but the biological one, he was a father to Llewelyn, and Joanna had tried repeatedly over the years to break through that cool, disciplined exterior, to bypass the priest and befriend the man, but to no avail. He kept others at a distance no less effectively than did Adda. Only with Llewelyn did he permit himself the luxury of emotional intimacy, and Joanna often wondered if he'd acknowledged even to himself how deep the bond between them was, that Llewelyn was a son in all but blood.

'Owain ap Gruffydd brought news, Madame, that I think you should know. Lord Hywel of Meirionydd and Prince Madog have deserted Llewelyn, have gone over to your father.'

'Jesu, no! But they are Llewelyn's cousins, his blood kin!'

'They are also frightened men trying to save what is theirs. They see Llewelyn as doomed, do not want to be dragged down with him.'

Joanna stared at him in silence, trying desperately to get her fear under control, trying not to panic. Maelgwn and Rhys Gryg and Gwenwynwyn were already fighting for John. With Prince Madog's defection, Llewelyn would be utterly isolated, surrounded, facing enemies on every side.

'If what you're saying be true,' she whispered, 'then Llewelyn is trapped, trapped with no way out.'

'Yes,' he said dully, 'I know. And so does Llewelyn.'

Joanna could hear angry voices while still in the stairwell. But as she followed Morgan into the chamber, a sudden silence settled over the room. All eyes turned towards her, and in many of them she read a chilling suspicion, a doubt none would dare to voice in Llewelyn's hearing: can we speak freely in front of her? Feeling like an intruder in her own bedchamber, Joanna settled down as inconspicuously as possible in the nearest window seat.

Llewelyn and Owain ap Gruffydd were standing by a trestle table partially covered by a crude map of Wales and the Marches. Joanna's unexpected entrance had thrown Owain momentarily off stride. Turning back to Llewelyn, he gestured towards the map.

'You need look no farther than this, my lord, no farther than Eryri. What better stronghold could you find? You know these mountains as few men do; they'd never be able to take you.'

'What would you have me do, Owain, live like a rebel on the run?'

'There are worse fates, my lord,' Owain said evenly, and Llewelyn shook his head.

'You look at the map, but you still do not see. How can you be so blind?' Unsheathing his dagger, Llewelyn made a slashing cut in

384

the parchment. 'John has erected a castle here.' Again the blade flashed. 'And there. There, too. At Bala, Treffynnon, Mathrafal, Deganwy, Rhuddlan. Fourteen at last count, Owain, fourteen! Given time, he'll refortify each and every one in stone and mortar, put down roots so deep we'll never be able to dislodge him. Christ, man, do you not understand? He means the complete conquest of North Wales, means to turn all of Gwynedd into a God-cursed English shire!'

None could deny it. Nor could they meet his eyes. Owain mumbled, 'I know, my lord, I know. But you've got to think of saving yourself now. It is too late to save Gwynedd.'

'No,' Llewelyn said violently, 'no!' He stared down at the map, and then, with a sudden, swift thrust, he plunged the dagger downward, impaling the map and burying the blade deep in the soft pine table-board.

It was so quiet that Joanna could hear the slight scraping of Adda's crutch as he dragged it through the floor rushes, limped to Llewelyn's side. 'Llewelyn, I understand how you feel; how could I not? If I thought you had any chance at all, I'd say yes, go to the English King, seek to save what you can. But we're talking of John, Llewelyn, John who nurses a grievance till it festers. Not two months ago you made him look a proper fool, cost him money, men, and no small loss of face. He's gone to a great deal of trouble to get you just where you are this night, and the only terms he's likely to offer will be a generous bounty to the man who can bring him your head.'

'He'd listen to me.' Joanna stood up, found her knees suddenly weak; her heart was beating so rapidly that she felt slightly queasy. She had a blurred glimpse of faces, most expressing shock at the very thought of entrusting all to a woman, and then she'd crossed the chamber, had her hand on Llewelyn's arm.

'Let me go to him, Llewelyn,' she pleaded. 'He cares for me, and I can make him listen. I know I can.'

His face was hard to read; she could not immediately tell what his reaction was. Nor was she given a chance to find out, for Gruffydd could keep silent no longer.

'Papa, do not listen to her! You cannot trust her to speak for you; she's his daughter, of his befouled blood. She'd betray you, I know it!' The boy was too agitated to guard his tongue, pleaded with no less passion than Joanna, 'You cannot do this, cannot yield to him. Think how he'd humiliate you, make you grovel –'

'That will be enough, Gruffydd!'

'I'd die ere I'd do that, Papa! And if you go to him, shame yourself like that, you shame us all!'

Llewelyn took a swift step towards Gruffydd. Although he'd clenched his fist, he did not hit the boy. But Joanna saw him draw a deep unsteady breath, saw how close he'd come to it. 'Be thankful, Gruffydd,' he said scathingly, 'that I remember I, too, was a fool at fifteen.'

Gruffydd flushed to the roots of his hair, and Joanna suspected he'd rather have been struck. 'Papa . . .' he whispered, but only Joanna was close enough to hear him. Llewelyn had turned away, was already moving towards the door.

When Rhys would have followed after him, Morgan stepped from the shadows, said, 'No, let him be. He needs time to be alone, to think. Whatever price is to be paid, he must be the one to pay it. So the decision, too, must be his, his and his alone.'

Even dulled by moonlight, the stallion's coat shone like bronze; although white was the preferred colour for horses, Llewelyn's memories of Sul had given him an unfashionable fancy for red-gold chestnuts. No longer grazing, the stallion had begun to nuzzle his tunic, but now it jerked its head up, nickered softly. Llewelyn reached for his sword, faded back into the shadows.

A black-clad figure emerged through the trees, and he lowered the sword, watched as Morgan swung from the saddle. Morgan was unsure of his welcome, said, somewhat awkwardly, 'Joanna guessed you might be here. You've been gone so long we grew worried. But I'll go if you'd rather be alone.'

'I've not been alone. I've been keeping company with Arthur of Brittany, Hugh de Lusignan, Walter de Lacy, William de Braose, all the men in the last twenty years who made the fatal mistake of underestimating John Plantagenet.'

Walking to the edge of the cliff, Llewelyn gazed down at the cataract. Although rain had been scarce that summer, as if even nature were favouring John's campaign, the river still surged against its banks, plummeting over the jutting rocks and turning the pool below into a seething cauldron of froth and spume, an impersonal and awesome affirmation of infinity.

'We're our own worst enemies, Morgan, God's cursed truth we are. The Gospels say every kingdom divided against itself shall be made desolate; that could well serve as the epitaph for Wales. Since the time of William the Conqueror, we've allowed the English kings to play the same damnable, deadly game with us, to set our princes one against the other. And we never learn. Christ knows I did not, I fell into the same time-worn trap. If I'd found a way to come to terms with Maelgwn and Rhys Gryg, they'd be fighting the English now instead of collaborating with them. If we'd banded together at the outset, all offered resistance, we could have stopped John dead at the Conwy.'

'That is the great weakness of the Welsh, Llewelyn. We've never learned to act for the common good. I sometimes suspect that unity is not a word native to the Welsh tongue. It has ever been that way, ever will be.'

'No, Morgan, you're wrong. The day must come when our people will unite around one man, around one prince.' Llewelyn paused, then gave Morgan a twisted smile. 'But I always thought it would be me.'

Morgan made no facile disclaimers, offered no polite, empty assurances. But Llewelyn knew him far too well to expect any. Moving away from the cliff, he said, 'You did not ride all this way without fetching me something to drink, I hope?'

Morgan managed a smile of his own. 'Indeed not,' he said, handed Llewelyn a flask. 'I was watching you when Joanna offered to go to her father. You were the only man in the room who did not look surprised. It had already occurred to you to have her intercede with John?'

'Of course. What could be more obvious?' But Llewelyn then lowered the flask, revealed his own ambivalence. 'Why?' he challenged. 'You see it as sheltering behind a woman's skirts?'

'I see it as the only action open to you. What matters it if she's a woman when she is also the only one in Christendom with any chance of swaying John? But can you trust John, Llewelyn? Even if Joanna can somehow persuade him to offer terms, can you be sure he'd honour them? That he'd not agree to a safe-conduct merely to get you into his hands?'

'He might well refuse Joanna's pleas, but I do not think he'd use Joanna as a lure, as bait. Not even John would do that, not to his own daughter.' Adding dryly, 'But then, I'd have to believe that, would I not?'

Llewelyn drank again, passed the flask back to Morgan. 'I was at

Norham Castle with John when the Scots King came to surrender, to buy peace on John's terms. John demanded far more than money, left him nothing, neither pride nor manhood.'

He looked at the priest, suddenly dropped all defences and said with anguished, unsparing honesty, 'I do not know if I can face that, Morgan. There is a part of me that feels as Gruffydd does, that I'd rather die ere I let him do to me what I saw him do to the Scots King.'

Morgan found himself blinking back tears. 'I do not know what to say to you, lad, would to God I did.'

'Do you remember what you once told me? You assured me that accommodation to superior strength is no shame. That helped ease a boy's hurt, taught me a truth I thought I'd taken to heart. But . . . but it avails me little now, Morgan. Not when I think of John, and what he will demand of me.'

Joanna had finally fallen into a fitful doze. She awoke at once, though, when Llewelyn closed the door, sat up as he approached the bed.

'Did Morgan find you?'

'Yes. How did you know I'd go to Rhaeadr Ewynnol?'

'I remembered you told me you'd gone there when Tangwystl died.'

He made no comment. She felt the bed shift as he lay down. He was still fully clothed, had not even taken his boots off. As she'd lain awake waiting for him, Joanna had decided to take her cues from him. If he wanted her to comfort him with her body, she would. If he wanted silence, she'd keep still. If he wanted to talk, she'd listen. But now that he was here beside her, she found herself so afraid of saying or doing the wrong thing that she could do nothing at all.

His rage seemed to have burned itself out; she could see only exhaustion in his face. Leaning over, she touched her lips to his forehead. He opened his eyes, looked at her, and then reached out, grasped a handful of her straight black hair. 'You do in truth look Welsh,' he said, let her hair slip through his fingers.

'Llewelyn, please. Let me go to my father.'

He raised himself up on his elbow, and then he nodded. 'Tomorrow,' he said. 'Tell him that he's won, that . . . You know what to tell him.'

She was no longer so sure of that. She'd prayed that he would agree, but now that he had, she was suddenly terrified. He was putting his life in her hands. What if she failed him? If Adda was right, if her father would not listen to her?

'I'm frightened, Llewelyn,' she said, and he put his arm around her, held her close.

'I know, Joanna.' After a long time, he said, very softly, 'So am I.'

August, 1211

Aberconwy, North Wales

Once she had ridden into the English camp, Joanna was separated from her small Welsh escort, taken into the outer parlour of the abbey. Too tense to sit for long, she paced the confines of the small chamber as if it were a cage, until she could endure the waiting no longer, escaped out into the west walkway of the cloisters.

The Cistercian monks had fled before John's army; more than a dozen soldiers now lounged on the grassy inner garth. Joanna's unexpected appearance momentarily stopped all conversation; heads jerked around. Of all the privations peculiar to campaigning in Wales, the one the soldiers found most difficult to accept was the utter lack of women. Theirs was the most uncommon of army encampments, one in which there were neither willing harlots nor unwilling captives.

They were watching Joanna with avid interest, but warily, too, for her gown was a finely woven wool, her veil a gossamer silk. She could hear them murmuring among themselves, speculating whether she was a 'Crogin', a contemptuous slang term for the Welsh; that would, she realized, have made her fair game. At last one of the men rose, sauntered towards her. 'What can I do for you?' he asked, and while the words themselves were innocent enough, both his smile and his tone were slyly suggestive.

'Nothing whatsoever,' Joanna snapped. Although he was already backing away, warned off by the jewelled rings adorning her fingers, she added maliciously, 'But I shall tell my father the King of your concern,' and had the dubious satisfaction of seeing him blanch. The men could not have retreated any faster had she revealed herself to be a witch; within moments she was all alone on the walkway, filled with a rage as unfocused as it was impotent, that what should now matter most in Llewelyn's own realm was not that she was his wife, but that she was John's daughter.

A man was emerging from the monks' frater. He came to an abrupt halt at sight of Joanna, then limped towards her. She was no less surprised to see him. For several years Hugh Corbet had been suffering from the disease known as the 'joint evil', and his health was no longer up to the rigours of a military campaign.

'You've come on Llewelyn's behalf?' he asked, and she nodded.

'Yes. And you?'

'At the King's command.'

Joanna felt a chill. How would she ever get her father to listen if he were as vengeful as that, enough to make Llewelyn's ailing stepfather an unwilling witness to his downfall?

'Joanna . . . when you see the King, weigh your words with care. He is in a foul temper this morn. He got word, you see, that William de Braose has been stricken with a mortal sickness. It's said he's sure to die.'

Joanna's eyebrows rose. 'I'd have thought my father would be gladdened by news like that!'

'I expect he was. But he was not so glad to hear that Stephen Langton was at de Braose's deathbed, that he means to officiate at de Braose's funeral.'

'Good God, no wonder Papa was wroth!'

'With cause,' Hugh conceded. 'It is Langton's way of spiting the King, of course. For all that the Pope has anointed him as Archbishop of Canterbury, he dare not set foot on English soil. But de Braose was formally outlawed, declared a traitor to the Crown. It's not fitting for Langton to pay such honour to a rebel.'

'It may not be proper, but it certainly is political!' Joanna shook her head, bemused. 'I wonder if my father will release Maude de Braose once her husband is dead. I'd think he – Hugh? Whatever ails you?'

'I thought you knew. Maude de Braose is dead.' Hugh hesitated, no longer met Joanna's eyes. 'She . . . died in prison.'

'No, I did not know.' Joanna frowned. 'Strange, that Llewelyn never mentioned it. Surely he must have heard?' But then she forgot all about Maude de Braose and her dying husband, even forgot about Hugh, for a familiar figure was coming down the north walkway. Gathering up her skirts, she ran to meet her brother.

'Thank God, Richard! I prayed you'd be here. Papa . . . he will see me?'

'Did you ever doubt it?' Richard had his mother's pale blue eyes,

391

often remote, not easily read; she saw in them now only pity. 'He sent me to fetch you, awaits you in the small parlour next to the Chapter House.'

'Richard . . . tell me the truth. Do you think he'll heed me?'

'Ah, Joanna . . .' But as reluctant as he was to answer, when he did, it was with uncompromising honesty. 'No, I do not.'

John did not say anything, merely held out his arms, and for a few brief moments Joanna tried to take refuge in memories, sought to find again in her father's embrace the protected peace of childhood.

'I've been so frightened, Papa,' she confessed, finding it as easy as that to revert back to the role decreed for her so long ago at Rouen. John, too, seemed reluctant to let go of the past, speaking softly and soothingly as if hers were still childhood hurts, of no greater moment than scraped knees or a lost doll, hurts to be healed with smiles and the promises of sweets.

'I know, lass. But all will yet be well for you. I'll make it so, I swear. Come now, seat yourself at the table. I've food set out for you; you can eat as we talk.'

Joanna did as he bade, watched as he acted as cupbearer for them both, but not for Richard or Will. She had no appetite, though, merely toyed with the bread and cheese put before her. John took a seat facing her, said:

'You've been much on my mind, Joanna. I'd not have you suffer for sins not yours, think I have found a way to make certain you do not. Tell me of your son, of David. It's lucky, in truth, that he's too young to understand what's been happening.'

'I would that were so, Papa. But Davydd now wakes in the night whimpering, has begun to talk about creatures lurking out in the dark, hiding under the bed. And Elen, too, senses something is amiss. She has –'

'When will he be three . . . November? And the age of majority amongst the Welsh is fourteen, no? Of course he'd need guidance and counsel long after that, would need –'

'Papa, what are you saying?'

'I am saying, sweetheart, that you need not worry, that I mean to protect your son's inheritance. I shall have to take much of Gwynedd under the control of the Crown, but I'll leave David a fair share, that I promise.' He leaned across the table, with a smile of familiar, fond charm, the smile that invariably heralded the giving of

392

a memorable gift. 'And I see no reason, Joanna, why you should not act yourself as regent until David comes of age.'

Joanna sat very still. She was aware of perspiration trickling clammily down her throat, between her breasts, along her ribs, rivulets of cold sweat that seared her skin like ice, set her to trembling. Richard had moved behind John's chair, and when she opened her mouth, he gave a swift, warning shake of his head. She let her protest ebb away on an uneven, laboured breath, grabbed for a wine cup and drank without tasting.

John had been watching her intently. 'I see,' he said at last, quite coolly.

'No, Papa, I do not think you do.' Joanna set the wine cup down, reached at random for something she could not spill, clutched at a thick slice of bread. 'It would not work, you see. The Welsh would never accept a woman as regent. It is true that in most ways their women enjoy greater freedom than ours, but those freedoms are personal, not political.'

'Then we need only select a regent amenable to our wishes, eager to cooperate with the Crown. You'd still act as regent, in all but name. Does that frighten you? It need not, for you'd not be alone, lass. I'd see that you had advisers you could trust, men who –'

'Your advisers, Papa? Men of Norman blood? How do you think the Welsh would react to that? No, you still do not understand. It's not just that the Welsh would never accept me. They'd not accept Davydd, either. He is a babe, half Norman – and your grandson. Those would be liabilities to cost him the crown. Should aught befall Llewelyn, his people would not look to Davydd, they'd look to Llewelyn's other son, his Welsh son.'

'Gruffydd?' he said, showing her he was all too familiar with Llewelyn's court. 'And if he were not available?'

'It . . . it would not matter. Llewelyn has another son, Tegwared. He's still a child, but the Welsh would prefer him to Davydd. They'd even prefer Llewelyn's cousin Hywel. Davydd must earn the acceptance of his father's people, must prove to them that his heart and soul are no less Welsh than Gruffydd's. I've given this much thought, Papa, from the very day of his birth. I do think he can eventually win their allegiance. But he'll need time, time to grow to manhood. Until then, only his father can safeguard his inheritance, only Llewelyn.' Joanna had unwittingly been tearing at the bread as she spoke; the tablecloth was littered with crumbs. She put the crust

393

aside, said, 'That is why I have come, Papa. To beg you to spare Llewelyn . . . for the sake of my son.'

'You are saying, then, that all your concern is for David, none of it for Llewelyn?'

John sounded so sceptical that Joanna blushed, remembering the bedchamber scene he'd witnessed at Woodstock. 'No, Papa,' she said as steadily as she could, 'I am not saying that. I do care for Llewelyn. How could I not? He treats me quite well. I've been his wife for five years, have borne him two children, would not want to see him harmed.'

She reached across the table, caught at John's sleeve. 'If I owe Llewelyn a wife's loyalty and Davydd a mother's love, I owe you much, too. I told you at the time I agreed to wed Llewelyn that there was nothing I would not do for you. I meant it, Papa, proved it by making a marriage I dreaded. Did you know that, know how much I feared it? But I did it for you . . . and then found in that marriage an unexpected and abiding contentment.'

John shifted in his seat, drew back out of reach. 'Does it matter so much to you, Joanna, being Llewelyn's wife?'

'Not his wife, Papa . . . his consort.'

That was an answer he was not expecting. He leaned back in his chair, subjected her to a troubled appraisal. 'In truth, Joanna? At the time of your marriage, I seem to remember you counting a crown of little worth.'

'At the time of my marriage, I was only fourteen. The truth is, Papa, that I'm pleading not just for Davydd, but for myself, too. Even now it often seems no less than a miracle to me, that I could be bastard-born and yet wear a crown. I do not think I could bear to give it up. You of all men should be able to understand that.'

'Yes,' he admitted, 'I can. I only wish I'd known . . .' He rose abruptly, moved to the window. 'I am sorry, lass, I swear I am. But you ask too much of me.'

'Not if you love me.' Joanna had risen, too, stumbled over her skirts in her haste to follow John to the window. 'Papa . . . you do still love me?'

He swung around, stared at her. 'Jesu, do you doubt it?'

'I . . . I do not know. God knows I do not want to! But you led an army into my husband's lands, my lands, too. Your men even burned Aber, and that was my home, Papa, mine no less than Llewelyn's. What if my children or I had still been there, if we'd not –'

'Ah, Joanna, do not! This is between Llewelyn and me, has nothing to do with you. I'd not hurt you for the world. You have ever been my dearest child, do you not know that?'

'Help me then, Papa. You're the only one who can. For Davydd and for me, I beg you . . . please!' Joanna's voice broke; she started to kneel, and John stopped her, pulled her almost roughly to her feet.

'Do not, lass. There's no need.'

Joanna caught her breath. 'Does that mean you'll do it, Papa? You'll pardon Llewelyn?'

There was a long pause, and then he nodded. 'It seems I have no choice.'

Joanna had often heard Llewelyn quote a caustic Welsh proverb, one that spoke of a borrowed smile. She could feel just such a smile twisting her mouth, a counterfeit coin to pay a debt of dishonour. She could take no pride in what she had accomplished. Gratitude, too, was an alien emotion to her at that moment. Even her sense of relief was curiously muted. She was aware only of her utter exhaustion, and when John led her towards a bench, she sank down upon the hard wood as if it were a cushioned settle.

She'd once seen a swimmer collapse upon the beach after battling the sea back to shore; he'd lain panting in the shallows, digging his hands deep into the sand as if to anchor himself to the earth, too weak to do more than marvel at his reprieve. She felt much the same way now, wanted only to sit and be left in peace, if only for a little while. But John had seated himself beside her on the bench, and he was saying grimly:

'If Llewelyn comes to me here at Aberconwy, I will accept his surrender – for you, Joanna. But more than that I cannot do. He has much to answer for, and if he wants peace, it must be on my terms. You do understand that?'

She nodded, and John relaxed somewhat, sought then to swallow a noxious draught with grudging grace. 'I expect you'll want to send word at once? How many hostages will he want as pledges for his safety, five? Ten?'

'No, Papa. He wants but one . . . your brother, Will.'

John stiffened. 'Christ Jesus!'

'John, I do not mind, in truth I do not,' Will interjected mildly, as Joanna had known he would; it was one of God's minor miracles that Will had somehow survived more than fifty years without compromising his faith, without forfeiting his innocence. 'It is only a formality, after all. I'm glad to do it for you, and for the lass here.'

Joanna could endure no more. Jumping to her feet, she kissed first her father and then her uncle. 'I shall never forget what you're doing for me,' she said huskily, 'never.'

But once she emerged out into the cloisters, she faltered. The sun seemed hot enough to blind, to burn all it touched; even when she closed her eyes, she could not squeeze out the light. She leaned for a moment against one of the stone columns, and then felt Richard's supportive hand on her elbow.

'Come,' he said, 'there's a bench in the garth.'

They were alone in the sunlight. Richard had a soldier's flask at his belt. He drank, then passed it to Joanna. 'He was so set upon vengeance,' he said wonderingly. 'You need never again doubt that he loves you, Joanna.'

'I know.' Joanna drank from Richard's flask, found it filled with a pungent, spiced wine. She gasped, sputtered, and then blurted out, 'I do not know how I can ever look Uncle Will in the face again.'

'You were just acting as your husband's messenger. Uncle Will understands that.'

'No . . . I was not. Llewelyn told me to insist upon hostages of high rank, men Papa would be loath to lose. But he did not demand Uncle Will as one of the hostages. He would never have done that, for he knows how dear Uncle Will is to me.' The blood rose in Joanna's cheeks so swiftly that her skin seemed on fire. 'I do love Uncle Will, Richard. That's what is so unforgivable. For I never hesitated.' Joanna's voice trailed off. After a long silence, she confessed:

'But I suddenly knew that I was not willing to risk Llewelyn's life on my father's word alone.'

Llewelyn drew rein on the crest of the hill, stared down at the English encampment. Seventeen years ago he'd won a decisive battle on this very site, had defeated his uncle and made himself ruler of half of Gwynedd at age twenty-one. All of Gwynedd had been his before he was thirty. But the banner now flying over the abbey was emblazoned with the royal arms of England.

The sun was hot, the hill infested with horseflies and mosquitoes, but none of the men complained. They waited in sympathetic silence for Llewelyn to nerve himself for the ride down the hill, for his surrender to the English King. When he finally moved, it was sudden, swift, took them by surprise. He gave the chestnut its head, and it plunged down the slope, mane and tail taking the wind like flame, blazing into the English camp as if it had somehow seen into its rider's heart, shared his fettered rage, his fear, and his defiant despair.

His men spurred their horses to overtake the chestnut, some of them shouting as if on the trail of a wild boar, and the resulting entrance of the Welsh into the camp was a tumultuous one. But as they gazed about them, realized what John had in mind, they fell silent, lost much of their bravado. A few swore under their breaths, most tightened grips on sword hilts, and all looked towards Llewelyn.

The chestnut was fractious, fighting the bit, but Llewelyn scarcely noticed. For days now he'd been morbidly reliving the scene in the great hall at Norham Castle, putting himself in the place of the discomfited Scots King. But once again he'd underestimated John's capacity for imaginative reprisal. For his was to be a very public humiliation, to be no less a spectacle than a bearbaiting or the hanging of a notorious highwayman. His surrender was not to be made in the abbey hall, nor in one of the English command tents, but out in the open in the glare of high noon, witnessed by all John's troops and those of his Welsh allies.

One of the Abbot's high-backed chairs had been brought out for John; to his right were gathered the lords of his court, to his left the Welsh Princes. Llewelyn could count his enemies like rosary beads: Gwenwynwyn, Maelgwn, Rhys Gryg, Thomas Corbet. Men who'd long hungered for this day, men who watched him with mocking eyes and smiles like unsheathed daggers. Even worse were the faces of his friends, his stepfather, Stephen and Baldwin de Hodnet, his conscience-stricken cousins Madog and Hywel. They averted their eyes, like men too polite to look upon another's nakedness, offering him the lacerating balm of their pity, and Llewelyn's resolve faltered. For several harrowing seconds he found himself overwhelmed by emotions he'd never before experienced – a physical fear of entrapment and a shattering sense of his own helplessness.

Dismounting was an act of utter faith, the most difficult one of his life. With an intense effort of will, he blotted out the audience, focused his thoughts solely upon the man in the Abbot's oaken chair. And then he walked forward, knelt and handed John his sword.

397

'I submit myself unto the King's will,' he said, and John smiled.

'Surely you can do better than that. Not even the Lord God will forgive a man unless he first confesses his sins and then repents of them.'

Llewelyn had known John might demand this of him, had known, too, that he could never bring himself to do it. His mind raced, but he could think of no way to satisfy John while still salvaging his pride, and at last said with the candour born of desperation:

'What would be the point? No matter how convincingly contrite I was, you'd not believe me, would know I did not speak from the heart. Would it not make more sense to speak of hard, irrefutable facts, of power? You've won. I admit your victory, acknowledge your authority as my King and liege lord. That I am here proves it beyond question, as does my willingness to do homage, to swear oath of allegiance as your vassal lord and liegeman.'

John laughed. 'To put it in your own words, what would be the point? Twice in the past seven years you've done homage to me, have you not? So all you've "proved beyond question" is that a Welshman's sworn oath is worthless.'

Llewelyn was unnerved by the intensity of his rage, by the realization of how close he was to losing control of his temper, his tongue. He stared at John, his ears filled with the derisive laughter of John's soldiers, his heart filled with such hatred that he knew it must show on his face for all to see.

'Should I gather from your silence that you're loath to ask for absolution? Surely your pride is not as tender as all that. It did allow you, after all, to send a woman to plead for you?'

Llewelyn was livid. 'And would your brother Richard have pardoned you at Lisieux if not for the intervention of your lady mother?'

This time the laughter came from behind Llewelyn, came from his own men. He saw John's face twitch, saw he'd drawn blood. John had got to his feet so abruptly that the chair tilted, and Llewelyn instinctively started to rise, too, only to freeze as John swung the sword up. The weapon was three feet long, honed to a razor edge, tapered for thrusting. It had been custom-made for Llewelyn, and he knew better than most its killing capabilities. Now, with that naked blade levelled at his throat, his mouth went dry, he dared not even blink. He heard a woman cry out; although it did not sound like her, he knew it could only be Joanna.

The sword's point was pressed against his windpipe, but

Llewelyn's pulse was slowing, his breathing steadying, for he'd realized that John did not mean to kill him. He would never know what had stayed John's hand; Joanna's scream? Fear for Will? He could not even be sure John had ever meant to follow through on that first thrust. He knew only that John's eyes did not mirror the passion of a man provoked beyond all reason; his was a rage more glacial than volcanic, utterly implacable but controlled, icily deliberate, the rage of a man willing to wait for his vengeance.

It was not the first time Llewelyn had seen his death foretold in another man's eyes, but never had the threat carried so much lethal conviction, all the more chilling in eyes eerily like Joanna's. He felt the pressure increase, felt a stinging sensation, knew that John, too, had drawn blood. And then the sword was withdrawn, John stepped back, beckoned to one of the watching men.

'Take this,' he said, 'and break it.'

The man looked dubiously at the sword, uncomfortably aware how much pressure the blade was meant to bear. But he made haste to obey, grabbed the sword and withdrew, shouting for a hammer and anvil.

Llewelyn was becoming aware again of their audience. Gwenwynwyn looked like a man at peace with himself for the first time in three years, a man who'd just received payment for a long overdue debt. Thomas Corbet, too, was gleefully jubilant, Chester his usual impassive self, Hugh Corbet haggard, obviously ailing, while Eustace de Vesci ignored Llewelyn altogether, watched John with unblinking intensity. Surprisingly, Maelgwn had lost his smile; his eyes held Llewelyn's for several moments, but his thoughts were masked, utterly his own. Joanna, however, was not within Llewelyn's range of vision. He'd have given a great deal had she only been back at Dolwyddelan, been anywhere but here, witness to his shame.

'Your Grace!' Grinning triumphantly, a man was hastening towards John, holding out Llewelyn's sword. But it was no longer a weapon, was no more now than two twisted pieces of jagged metal.

John reached out, took the hilt in one hand, the sundered blade in the other. 'As easily as I broke this sword, so could I have broken you . . . and would have if it were not for my daughter. But do not count upon her to save you a second time. From this day forth, the Virgin Mary herself could speak for you and it would avail you naught.'

399

He flung the sword fragments to the ground. 'Now you may withdraw,' he said contemptuously, 'and wait until I have time to speak with you about the terms of your surrender.'

Llewelyn got slowly to his feet. His pride was already in shreds; he knew that if he allowed John to dismiss him as if he were a serf, the memory would haunt him for the rest of his life. But he saw no way out of the trap. He stared down at his broken sword, and then looked up, saw his wife.

Joanna's face was ashen, wet with tears, but her eyes were a brilliant, blazing green, and her mouth was contorted with rage. Richard was beside her, was gripping her arm, but as her eyes met Llewelyn's, she jerked free of her brother's restraining hold.

Llewelyn stood very still, watched as she moved towards him. All were watching her now. John took an involuntary step forward, said her name. She seemed not to hear, never took her eyes from Llewelyn. Coming to a halt before him, she said loudly and very clearly, 'My lord husband,' sank down on the grass in a deep, submissive curtsy.

It was more than a clever face-saving stratagem, it was an avowal of loyalty, of love. Llewelyn raised her up, looked for a long moment into her face, and then kissed her, kissed her as if they were alone, as if nothing mattered but that moment and the woman he held in his arms. Even he could not have said which meant more, that he was kissing John's daughter or kissing his wife.

Joanna could hear the erratic hammering of his heart, could feel the tremor in his arms, and behind her closed eyelids she could still see the sun glinting on the blade of his sword. She touched her fingers to his throat; they came away bloodied, and she shuddered, raised up and kissed him again.

Llewelyn smiled at her; she'd never seen his dark eyes so soft, so tender. And then she saw his smile change, saw it twist with triumph. She turned slowly and, like Llewelyn, looked at her father.

John's face was burning with colour, but his eyes were blank, utterly without emotion. Joanna could read nothing in them, not even recognition. Although she and her father were only some ten feet apart, it suddenly seemed to Joanna that the distance was widening with each silent second that passed. And then John had turned away, was walking rapidly towards the abbey, not looking back.

Joanna watched, and there was a part of her that wanted nothing so much as to run after him, to try to make things right. But she did not move; she could not.

She looked so desolate, so achingly vulnerable, that Llewelyn put his arm around her shoulders. She had, he thought, burned more than a bed this time; she had burned a bridge.

He said nothing, but Joanna knew it, too. 'He'll never forgive me,' she said softly, 'never.'

It was dusk before John summoned Llewelyn to the monks' frater. He watched as the Welsh entered the dining hall, waited until Llewelyn and Joanna approached the dais, and then said cuttingly, 'A woman has no place in the council chamber. Have your wife await you outside.'

Joanna flushed, and John discovered that hurting her did nothing to ease his own hurt. She curtsied, looked first at her father and then her husband, and John was swept with rage when Llewelyn nodded, as if he had the right to confirm a royal command. He saw now that the younger man had not washed away the dried blood on his throat, knew that was no less deliberately done than his own refusal to see Llewelyn for more than six hours, and at that moment there was nothing he would not have given to revoke Llewelyn's reprieve – save only the life of his brother.

The hall was crowded. John was flanked by the Earls of Chester and Pembroke, was accepting a wine cup from his cousin, William de Warenne, Earl of Surrey. Llewelyn recognized most of the Normans gathered around the dais. Eustace de Vesci looked, as ever, like a man nursing a perpetual toothache. Beside him stood his cousin Robert Fitz Walter, whose friendship with de Vesci was mystifying to those who knew them best, for Fitz Walter was a swaggering, jovial prankster and braggart, utterly unlike the aloof, sardonic de Vesci. Fitz Walter, whose estates were primarily in Essex, looked no happier than de Vesci to be embroiled in John's vendetta against a Welsh Prince. But Llewelyn noted that even the Marcher lords like the Earl of Hereford and Richard de Clare did not appear to be savouring John's triumph. To Llewelyn, that was dramatic and intriguing evidence of the growing estrangement between John and his barons, that they could take no pleasure in any victory that strengthened the Crown.

With a start, Llewelyn realized what he was doing, standing midst the burning embers of a charred ruin and envisioning it resurrected from the ashes and rubble, no less ambitious in design, far more impregnable to attack. It was heartening to discover that he had not yet lost all hope, even now as he braced himself for what was to come, for the price he would have to pay for John's truce. He knew, just as John did, that it was not a peace.

John wasted no time. 'I expect to be compensated in full for the cost of this campaign. But I am not vindictive. Since I know what a poor, wretched country Wales is, how limited your resources are, I am willing to take payment in livestock. I shall want some of your best horses, hawks, and hunting dogs for my own use, will let you know how many. But you are to pay tribute to the English Crown in cattle – twenty thousand head.'

'Christ!' Llewelyn was staggered. 'You do not understand how dependent we are on cattle. If you reduce our herds by twenty thousand, my people will starve!'

'You're the one who does not understand. You're not here to argue, to negotiate. You're here to listen whilst I tell you what I want from you. And what I want are cattle . . . and land. All of Gwynedd west of the River Conwy, the four cantrefs you call the Perfeddwlad.'

With one stroke, he'd just cut Gwynedd in two, gained half of North Wales for the English Crown. Llewelyn stared at him, saying nothing, taking what meagre consolation he could from a grim resolve, that claiming the Perfeddwlad would be easier than holding on to it.

It was not difficult for John to guess the tenor of his thoughts, for he'd made no effort to dissemble, and everything about him, from his stance to the set of his mouth, spoke of silent defiance. More than ever, John regretted what he'd done for love of his daughter. But he had one great advantage over most men, a lesson learned at bitter cost during those years he'd dwelt in the shadow of a brother he hated, in the shadow of the Crown. He knew how to wait.

'Whatever my other faults, naïveté is not amongst them. I know, of course, that you cannot be trusted out of my sight, that an oath of honour means no more to a Welshman than it would to an infidel Saracen. Therefore, I shall have to take measures to make sure you keep faith. I want thirty hostages as pledges for your fidelity to the Crown. They are to be well-born, the sons of your Welsh lords, scions of noble Houses.'

Llewelyn knew it was a common Norman custom to take hostages, knew John had in custody not only the daughters of the Scottish King but the sons of those of his own lords who'd fallen into disfavour. Even the powerful and respected Earl of Pembroke had been forced to yield up two of his sons to allay John's feverish suspicions. But knowing that did nothing to ease Llewelyn's sense of outrage. 'As you will,' he said tersely, not trusting himself to say more.

'You are to select them, to take upon yourself the responsibility for their fate. But of the thirty, one must be your son Gruffydd.'

Llewelyn's head came up sharply. 'No!'

There was a sudden, tense silence. Chester glanced towards John, then took it upon himself to say, 'Need I point out, my lord, that you're in no position to refuse anything the King might demand of you?' – making it a simple statement of fact when another man might have turned it into a mocking taunt.

'He's holding two sons of mine,' a voice close at hand said in Welsh, and Llewelyn turned, stared for a startled moment into the ice-blue eyes of an old enemy. Maelgwn seemed surprised himself, as if his words had somehow come of their own volition. He shrugged, murmured coolly, '*Mae yn rhy hwyr edifaru ar ol i'r ffagl gyneu.*'

It was an oft-quoted Welsh proverb, one Llewelyn knew well. It is too late to repent after the flame is kindled.

He looked from Maelgwn to Chester, realizing that these two men, the most unlikely of allies, were, nevertheless, trying to do him a good turn, to remind him of the wretched realities of defeat, the likely consequences of refusal. He realized, too, that they were right. But how in Christ's blessed name could he ever do what was being demanded? How could he give up his son to John, to John of all men?

John was smiling faintly. 'The boy is in the camp; it would be easy enough to take him. But I've a question to put to you first, my lord Prince of Gwynedd. You speak with such passion of your concern for your people, speak as if you truly care whether they have meat to put in their bellies. Tell me then, how you can agree to offer up other men's sons, whilst refusing to yield your own.'

Llewelyn sucked in his breath. He no longer looked defiant, looked shaken, and John took some satisfaction from that, but it was not enough, not nearly enough.

He rose from his chair, and Llewelyn took a step towards the dais. 'Will Your Grace spare me a few moments . . . alone?'

John frowned, but curiosity won out, and he nodded, waved

403

the other men away from the dais. They retreated with obvious reluctance, no less curious than he. As soon as they were out of earshot, he demanded, 'Well? What have you to say to me?'

'Just this,' Llewelyn had advanced to the first step of the dais. 'I want you to remember,' he said, 'that if Gruffydd is your hostage, Joanna is mine.'

John's eyes widened. 'What mean you by that? You'd never hurt Joanna!'

'No, I would not. I care very deeply for her. And I'm willing to concede that you care, too.'

'Of course I care!' John snapped. 'What of it?'

'You know now that Joanna loves me. But she loves you, too, and however angry you are with her, I do not think you want to lose that love. Am I wrong?'

John was frowning again. 'Go on,' he said curtly. 'Get to the point.'

'As I said, Joanna still loves you. But there are things she does not know, that I've kept from her. Mayhap they'd make no difference to her if she knew. Mayhap they'd make all the difference in the world. Do you want to risk it?'

'You expect me to believe you'd do that to Joanna, use her as a weapon against me?'

Llewelyn gave a harsh, bitter laugh. 'You expect me to believe you would not?'

John bit back a hot retort. 'What do you want?' he said at last.

'I want you to remember that your quarrel is with me, not my son.'

'He is a hostage, not a scapegoat. You have nothing to fear for him as long as you keep faith.' John paused. 'In a very real sense, his fate is in your hands, not mine.'

The Chapter House was lit by a single, smoking rushlight, cluttered with overturned benches and the debris of soldiers who'd been using it as a barracks. It was a sombre setting for what Llewelyn had to say, but it did offer privacy. When he'd left the frater hall, he'd found Joanna and Gruffydd waiting in the cloisters. They'd followed him obediently into the Chapter House, showed themselves to be sensitive to his mood by asking no questions. They watched as he wandered about the chamber, kicking aside empty wine flasks, until Gruffydd could stand the suspense no longer.

'Are you not going to tell us what happened, Papa? What does he want?'

'All of Gwynedd west of the Conwy, twenty thousand cattle, and thirty hostages.' Llewelyn had half-hoped his son might guess the truth, but Gruffydd's face showed only outrage. Whirling about, he glared accusingly at Joanna.

'I tried to tell you, Papa, that she was not to be trusted!'

'Do not talk foolishness, Gruffydd. If not for Joanna, there'd have been no terms at all.' Llewelyn glanced over at his wife. 'I owe her a great deal. We all do.'

He knew no easy way to tell the boy, and the longer he delayed, the harder it would get. 'John demands that you be one of the hostages, Gruffydd.'

Gruffydd gasped, stared at him, eyes dark with disbelief. 'And . . . and you agreed?'

'I had no choice, lad.'

'No . . .' Gruffydd backed away. 'She got you to do this! So her son will be your only heir, so he'll –'

'That's not true! I did not know my father would –'

'Liar! He did it for you, for you and your God-cursed son!'

'Gruffydd, that is enough!' In the silence that settled over the chamber, Llewelyn faced a very ugly truth, one he'd sought for five years to deny. He'd long known that Joanna and Gruffydd did not get along, but he'd succeeded in convincing himself that it was no more than the natural strain between a stepmother and a child not hers, that their relationship would mend as Gruffydd matured. Now he looked at Joanna and Gruffydd, and was forced to acknowledge that the son he loved and the woman he loved would never be reconciled, would never be other than implacable enemies, each one begrudging the other a place in his heart, in his life.

Standing there in the dimly lit Chapter House, he could, for the first time, comprehend how it must be for Joanna, caught between the conflicting claims of a father and husband. But for the moment, nothing mattered more than Gruffydd's need. 'Ednyved and Rhys are outside in the cloisters. They'll escort you back to our camp, Joanna.'

She gave him an anxious look that made him conscious of just how exhausted he truly was, but she did not argue, slipped quietly from the chamber. Llewelyn crossed to his son, put his hand on the

405

boy's arm. Gruffydd jerked free, with such violence that he lurched against one of the benches.

'How could you do it, Papa? How could you ever agree to turn me over to John?'

'Agree? Good Christ, Gruffydd! Does a man dragged to the gallows agree to the hanging? If you'd not insisted upon coming with me, if you'd stayed at Dolwyddelan as I wanted –' Llewelyn broke off in mid-sentence. After a long pause, he said, very quietly:

'Gruffydd, listen to me, lad. I'd give anything on God's earth to spare you this. But I cannot. You must somehow try to understand that. You keep telling me you've reached manhood, you're no longer a boy. You have to prove that now, Gruffydd, by accepting what has to be.'

Llewelyn had always known his son had uncommon courage, an unrelenting pride. Gruffydd had lost much of his colour. A few freckles not usually noticeable stood out in sudden, sharp relief across his cheekbones, the bridge of his nose; he'd rarely looked so much like his mother as he did at that moment. He swallowed with an obvious effort, but when he spoke, he'd got his voice under control.

'Where will he send me? To London, to the Tower?'

Llewelyn winced. Jesu, no wonder the boy seemed so fearful! 'Ah no, lad! You're to be a hostage, not a prisoner. You will not be caged, will not be shut away from the sun. John will treat you kindly, will keep you at his court.' He could see Gruffydd's doubt, said, 'He always does with hostages of high birth, has even allowed the younger ones to act as pages in his Queen's household.'

This time when he reached out, Gruffydd did not pull away. He put his arm around the boy's shoulders, and for a moment or two, no more than that, Gruffydd clung, held tight. But then he drew back. 'How long,' he asked tautly, 'shall I be held hostage?'

'I do not know,' Llewelyn admitted, and Gruffydd retreated even farther into the shadows.

'I want to be alone now, Papa.' Gruffydd did not wait for Llewelyn's response, but at the door, he suddenly stopped, swung around to face his father again.

'Tell me, Papa. Would you have given Davydd up as a hostage, too, had John demanded it?'

'Yes,' Llewelyn said, 'I would.'

Gruffydd's face was utterly in shadow. 'I wish I could believe that.'

'Gruffydd, wait!' Llewelyn reached the door in four strides, but still was not in time. The cloisters lay dark and deserted, and Gruffydd was nowhere in sight.

The sky was overcast, the sea dulled to an ashen shade of grey, the air so heavy and humid that Joanna felt as if she were filling her lungs with pure vapour. It must be like this to be caught in a cloud, she thought, and let herself indulge in a moment of fanciful whimsy, gazing up at the sky and wondering what it would be like, drifting within a world soft and wet and utterly opaque, a floating womb.

'Whatever are you thinking of, Joanna? You've the oddest look on your face!'

'When I was little, Richard, and out of favour with my mother, I would go out on the moors and play what I called my "pretend" game. Sometimes I'd become a bird, sometimes a boat bound for Cathay, sometimes just a leaf in the wind. I'd almost forgotten about those games.'

She glanced across the encampment, towards her husband and his son. Llewelyn was talking, Gruffydd saying very little. He was close enough for Llewelyn to touch, but even from where she stood, Joanna could see he was beyond reach. She turned back to her brother, said abruptly:

'Richard, promise me something. Do what you can for Gruffydd.'

He nodded, as ever, too discreet to pry. And because he did not, she felt obligated to explain. 'For Llewelyn, not for Gruffydd. I will not lie, not to you. When I learned what Papa meant to do, I was glad, Richard, I was truly glad. I only hope Papa keeps him in England for a thousand years. But if anything should happen to him whilst he is in Papa's hands, it will be the end of my marriage. Llewelyn might think he'd not blame me, but every time he'd look at me, he'd remember. How could he not? So try to . . . to keep an eye on Gruffydd, see that he does not do anything foolish, or provoke Papa into doing anything . . . rash.'

'Joanna, I'll do my best, but I'll not lie to you, either. I cannot be the boy's guardian angel, cannot be Papa's conscience.'

'No, I suppose not,' she conceded. 'Do you know if Papa is still within the Earl of Chester's command tent?'

'I think so. You mean to talk to him again? You've tried twice, Joanna; it might be best to give him time . . .'

407

'Time?' she echoed bleakly. 'Now who's lying, Richard? You know as well as I that time is running out even as we talk.'

Joanna curtsied, but did not wait to be summoned. Moving forward, she said, 'My husband is making ready to depart. May I speak with Your Grace ere we go?'

'I think it best if we do not. I do not see what we have to say.'

Joanna had no more warning than John. Never had her temper taken fire so suddenly, flaring from embers to inferno in the span of seconds. 'Well, I do have something to say to you, and say it I shall!'

John was staring at her as if at a stranger, for it was the first time he'd ever seen Joanna truly angry. He hesitated, then made a gesture of dismissal. The other men in the tent withdrew, leaving him alone with his daughter.

'I did not betray you, Papa. Yes, I love my husband, but I am not going to feel guilty about that, not any more.' Joanna drew several unsteady breaths; regaining some of her composure, she said, more calmly:

'Ah, Papa, do you not see? The human heart is not like a loaf of bread; if I give a large portion to Llewelyn, it does not follow that I must then give you a smaller slice. I love you both, in different ways. If I stood with Llewelyn on Sunday, it's not that my love for him was greater, but rather that his need was greater.'

John said nothing; she could not tell if her words were reaching him or not. 'Papa, you told me once that your mother and father had ever used you and your brothers as weapons against each other. You said you could not please the one without first damning the other. I'm asking you – no, I'm begging you. Do not do to me what they did to you.'

'Joanna . . . that's not what I ever meant to do. Surely you know that?'

'What I know, Papa, is that I love you and I love Llewelyn, and the two of you are tearing me apart!'

John flinched. 'I never wanted that, lass,' he said softly, 'I swear it.'

Joanna moved around the trestle table, moved into his arms. He hugged her close, then stepped back and smiled at her. 'I think it a good thing I had sons. Daughters are much too resourceful at getting their own way, are much harder on the heart!'

Joanna took her cue from him, did her best to echo his wry,

teasing tone. 'I do not know about that, Papa. I'd wager most daughters are more docile and biddable than a man's scapegrace sons.'

'So would I, until this morn. In truth, Joanna, I never suspected you had such a temper!'

'I am your daughter, Eleanor of Aquitaine's granddaughter. Are you not the one always telling me that a pure-blood horse breeds true?'

John laughed, and it was as if their estrangement was forgotten, as if all were as it had been. But as much as Joanna wanted to believe that, she knew it was not so, for either of them.

As she followed John from the tent, Joanna discovered that the Welsh were waiting for her. Llewelyn was already astride his chestnut stallion. He watched as John escorted Joanna towards her mare, as they embraced and John helped her to mount. He raised his hand then, gave the signal to depart. But John still retained his hold on Joanna's reins.

'Be sure,' he said, 'that you take care of my daughter.'

'Your Grace need not worry about my wife. You take care of my son.'

Joanna saw the look that burned between them; the very air seemed charged with static. She had no illusions left, knew their truce would not last. There would be a reckoning. There would be another war, and there was nothing she could do, 'for both men wanted it so.

March, 1212
Cambridge, England

John rode into the riverside town known as Cantebrigge at dusk on
Good Friday, settled himself and his court in the stone and timber
castle built by William the Conqueror.

Cantebrigge was a sprawling unwalled town of some two thousand
inhabitants, like most of the English towns Gruffydd had seen in the
past seven months in that it had a market place, a leper hospital, a
disproportionate number of stone churches, a Jewish ghetto called
the Jewry, and a gallows, stocks, and pillory. But Cantebrigge was
also home to a university with a large, raucous student population,
in consequence of which it had more than its share of alehouses and
bordellos.

Passing through the town, Gruffydd's companions took enthused
notice of the latter, began to make plans for a night of disreputable
pleasures. As always, it struck Gruffydd as strange, indeed, that in
some ways he should have greater freedom as a hostage of the English
King than as the son of Gwynedd's Prince. In Wales, he'd been
conscious at all times of his rank; as Llewelyn's firstborn son, he was
accustomed to being the focal point of stares, the target of whispers.
Unable to escape his identity, he could only do his best to live up to
it, and his dread of being made to look ridiculous had imposed upon
him an unwilling chastity. He'd known there were women of easy
virtue, women of the brake and bush who'd lay with a man for
money. But each time he was tempted, he would begin to fear that
he might not know what to do, that the woman would laugh at his
inexperience and, far worse, then tell everyone about his inept
fumbling, his greenness.

But once in England, he discovered that, for the first time in his
life, he was not the centre of attention, not known by sight to all.
The sudden anonymity was unsettling, but liberating, too. On a night
in mid-November, he'd accompanied some of his fellow hostages to

a Hereford bawdy house and had lost his virginity to a plump Saxon whore named Edwina, who smelled of sweat and garlic and charged him half a penny, but called him 'love' and put to rest any lingering doubts about his manhood.

Now, when his friends Collen and Emlyn pressed him, he fell in with their plans willingly enough. He was beginning to want more than hurried couplings on fetid, scratchy straw, to want a bedmate he did not have to buy. But he did not see the likelihood of forming an attachment of the heart at the English court, and if he could not ease his loneliness, his heartsick yearning for Wales, he could at least relieve his body's needs.

It was dark by the time a fasting-day fish supper had been served, before Gruffydd and his companions were able to find beds for themselves in the side aisles of the great hall. Madoc ap Maelgwn sauntered past, nodded coolly. Gruffydd gave an equally cool greeting in return, was glad when Madoc moved on; he was not good at dissembling, found it awkward to be in such close proximity with the son of his father's enemy.

He knew Collen's father had not sent him any money for some weeks, and he was counting his own coins to make sure he could pay for them both, when a man clad in the red and white livery of the King stopped before his pallet.

'I've been sent to escort you to the King's Grace,' he said brusquely, and Gruffydd's heart skipped a beat. He could think of very few reasons why John should be summoning him, none of them reassuring.

The room was circular, lit by smoking wall cressets, cluttered with open coffers and clothing. Gruffydd found it almost intolerable to be in John's presence, sometimes thought he might choke on his hatred, and it was with the greatest reluctance that he came forward, knelt.

But in the next moment the English King was forgotten. Gruffydd got abruptly to his feet, stared open-mouthed at the woman standing next to John. He would never have believed he could be so glad to see one he so detested, but now he stepped towards her, said eagerly, 'Do you bring a message from my father, Madame?'

Joanna shook her head, and he felt his throat close up with disappointment. But then he heard a familiar voice say, 'Why should

411

I give Joanna a message I can better deliver myself?' and he spun around, disbelieving.

'Papa?' He sounded stunned, and Llewelyn laughed, came swiftly across the chamber.

'I wanted to surprise you, lad, not send you into shock!'

Gruffydd still could not believe his father was here, on English soil, in John's private chamber, not even when he found himself gathered into an affectionate embrace. His sense of unreality went spinning wildly out of control when Llewelyn turned, said with the utmost nonchalance, 'John, I'd like to take Gruffydd back to my own chamber now, so we can talk.'

And when John replied composedly, 'By all means; Joanna can stay and talk to me, giving you time alone,' Gruffydd decided that the world had gone mad and all in it.

He somehow managed to hold his peace as they crossed the bailey, entered the north-west tower, mounted the spiral stairway to the chamber allotted for Llewelyn and Joanna's use. But as soon as the door closed behind them, he blurted out, 'Papa, what in God's name are you doing here?'

'Just what it looks like,' Llewelyn said blandly. 'I am celebrating Easter with my wife's family.' And then he gave a sardonic laugh, added, 'Of course this reunion required a safe-conduct and an exchange of hostages!'

'Are you sure that you're safe here?'

'As safe as Salisbury's life can make me. John sent his brother again as a pledge of faith.'

Gruffydd's anxiety abated somewhat, although not his bewilderment. 'But if he did not lure you to England to imprison or murder you, what has he in mind? Why is he being so polite to you?'

Llewelyn laughed again. 'He cannot very well do otherwise as long as I am a guest at his court. Ostensibly, he summoned me so he can see Joanna, whilst magnanimously giving me the chance to talk to you. The reality, of course, is that John wants something from me. Sit, and we'll talk about it. Do you know what has been happening in Wales?'

'Not much,' Gruffydd admitted. 'Just what we manage to overhear. I know that John sent Falkes de Bréauté and Maelgwn into Ceredigion, that they defeated Owain and Rhys Ieunac, forced them to surrender, to come to London and make a public submission to John.' That was a distasteful memory to Gruffydd. He grimaced,

412

said, 'They were thoroughly cowed, Papa, showed no spirit at all . . . not like you.'

That was, Llewelyn realized, Gruffydd's oblique way of making amends for those earlier accusations of cowardice. He smiled at the boy, said, 'But John then made a fatal blunder. Rather than turning Ceredigion back to Maelgwn, he claimed it for the Crown, set Falkes de Bréauté to building a castle at Aberystwyth.'

Gruffydd gave a low whistle. 'Maelgwn must have thrown an apoplectic fit!'

Llewelyn nodded. 'I cannot say John is his own worst enemy; the competition for that honour is too fierce! But he does have a decided tendency towards self-destruction. He has always to push his advantage to the breaking point and then beyond. As a result, his victories, no matter how brilliant, are always ephemeral, of fleeting moment. Maelgwn and Rhys Gryg, no fools, soon realized that John means to claim as much of Wales as he can, their lands as well as mine. Whatever their other failings, they are not men to become puppets of the English Crown. They besieged John's new castle at Aberystwyth, burned it to the ground. At the same time, John gave Robert de Vieuxpont a free hand in lower Powys, so Gwenwynwyn, too, is growing restive. For months now, all South Wales has been in turmoil, and I suspect John is worried lest I throw in with Maelgwn and Rhys Gryg. My guess is that he's sent for me to try to ferret out my intentions and, if need be, to use threats, even promises, to fetter me to the Crown.'

'And will he, Papa? Will he fetter you to the Crown?'

'What do you mean, Gruffydd?'

'You say Maelgwn and Rhys Gryg are in rebellion, that South Wales is ablaze. But not Gwynedd. It has been more than seven months since John took from you the Perfeddwlad. Passive acceptance is not like you, Papa. You have stayed your hand because of me, have you not?'

'Yes.'

'You cannot do that, Papa. The longer you allow John to hold the Perfeddwlad, the harder it will become to dislodge him. You cannot give him the time he needs to entrench himself – not without losing our lands forever.'

'That is what I want to talk with you about, Gruffydd.' Llewelyn rose, began to pace. 'What we feared is coming to pass. John is refortifying in stone those timbered castles he erected last summer.

His men patrol the roads, the passes, cross the Conwy into my domains at will, as if seeking to provoke a confrontation. And he is planning to bring in English merchants and their families, to charter towns as the Normans did in South Wales.' He swung around to face Gruffydd, said with sudden passion:

'The Normans would never have been able to steal so much of Deheubarth if not for towns like Swansea, Pembroke, Fishguard, Tenby. They are towns on Welsh soil, but no Welshman may become a citizen, or bear arms whilst in the town, or sit on a jury in any lawsuit between a Norman and one of Welsh blood. The Welsh in much of South Wales are intruders in their own land. But I'll not let that happen in Gwynedd. Christ forgive me, Gruffydd, I cannot!'

Gruffydd swallowed with some difficulty. In arguing that Llewelyn must try to reclaim the Perfeddwlad, he'd spoken from the heart; he truly believed every word he'd uttered. But it was no less true that he had not expected his father to agree with him. Now, he found himself approving what Llewelyn meant to do, while at the same time feeling a shocked sense of betrayal that his father would put anything, even Gwynedd's sovereignty, above his own safety. He'd have been put on the rack, though, before he would have admitted it, and he made an enormous effort, said as calmly as he could:

'I suppose, then, that we should think upon what I might expect from John. I know he has not harmed Maelgwn's elder son; Madoc is still at court. What of the younger son? Was he made to suffer in any way for Maelgwn's rebellion?'

'No, the lad is quite safe in Shrewsbury.'

'Well, that is reassuring.' Gruffydd managed a smile, but he had to ask. 'Papa . . . has John ever harmed a hostage?'

'No, Gruffydd, he has not. Not even when Hugh de Lusignan offered up hostages for his freedom after Mirebeau, only to betray John within days of his release.' Llewelyn moved back to the settle, sat down beside the boy. 'John is utterly without mercy to those who have offended him, but he has never avenged himself upon the innocent. His quarrel is with me, and it is with me that he'll settle it, not you, lad.'

Gruffydd was showing more courage, more maturity than Llewelyn had dared hope for; he was making it almost too easy. Llewelyn had never been so proud of his son, or so aware of his own failings as a father.

'Gruffydd, I want only the best for you. But I'd not blame you if you did not believe me, lad.' He hesitated, then said, 'I've done a great deal of thinking these months past, found out things about myself that I'd rather not have known. I wish I could say that nothing mattered to me but those I love. I cannot.'

Gruffydd was not sure what response was expected of him; he could not recall ever talking with his father about intangibles or imponderables, about emotions and doubts, secrets of the heart. 'I know you love me, Papa,' he mumbled, and flushed.

'Yes, I do. I loved your mother, too, lad. I loved her very much. But I could not allow myself to marry her, for there'd be no political advantage to the marriage; Gwynedd would have gained nothing from such a match. I was willing to wed Joanna, though, to take her sight unseen, to yoke myself for life to a woman I might find both undesirable and unlikable, because she was the King of England's daughter, brought me what Tangwystl could not, a border castle and a political alliance with the English Crown.'

Gruffydd was silent for some moments. 'You're saying, Papa, that you've always put Gwynedd first. I understand that, in truth I do. You see, that is the way I feel, too. There is nothing I would not do, nothing I would not give up if only you'd name me as your heir.'

Gruffydd's words had come without calculation. His was an uncomplicated, elemental nature, one not attuned to subtleties, still less to subterfuge. But the expression on his father's face was a revelation to him. He suddenly realized that Llewelyn's decision to break faith with John could work to his advantage and Davydd's disadvantage, that he would have a powerful claim indeed upon his father's conscience, that his would be a wrong much in need of redress.

'No man could have a son with greater courage, Gruffydd,' Llewelyn said softly.

'It means much to me that you think so, Papa. But what I need to know now means even more. Did you forget my birthday again?'

Llewelyn grinned. 'Brace yourself, lad. This time I remembered!'

They both laughed. Neither mentioned what Llewelyn's decision could mean – years of confinement for Gruffydd – the boy because he did not fully comprehend the risks, and the man because he'd managed to rationalize those risks, to convince himself that John's past generosity towards the innocent and the unoffending was an adequate guarantee for his son's safety.

*

415

Joanna crossed the crowded hall, slipped her arm through Llewelyn's. 'Papa wants to talk to you, love.' She hesitated, then murmured, 'He does seem to be trying, Llewelyn. It's not so impossible to believe, is it, that he might truly want peace?'

'John's peace is rather like the peace of God – in that it passeth all understanding.' But there had been so little conviction in Joanna's voice, so much wistfulness, that Llewelyn added, 'I will admit he's made this visit far more tolerable than I expected.'

John beckoned them up on to the dais, gestured for a page to serve them wine. For several moments, they made desultory conversation, bland in form and banal in substance. But then John directed his attention solely to Llewelyn, said:

'A strange rumour has reached my ears, that a papal nuncio has been travelling in Wales, that he was, in fact, received at your court. I should like you to tell me if this be true and, if so, the purpose of that visit.'

So that was why he was in Cantebrigge this Easter Sunday! Llewelyn smiled, said with complete sincerity, 'I should be right pleased to do so, Your Grace. I fear His Holiness the Pope is losing patience. You spurned his last offer to compromise your differences, did you not? If I'm not mistaken, you even went so far as to promise to hang Stephen Langton should he set foot on English soil . . . or words to that effect.'

'Those very words exactly,' John said coldly. 'But we were not talking of the Pope and myself. We were talking of you and the papal nuncio. What did he want from you?'

By now the hall was quieting; people were drifting towards the dais. Llewelyn pitched his voice for their growing audience, said, 'The Pope has lifted the Interdict from Wales. He has also absolved all the Welsh Princes from their oaths of allegiance to you, my liege, and urges us to join together in a holy crusade to depose you, claiming you to be a man beyond God's grace, no longer deserving to wear the Crown of a Christian King.'

John's war of wills with the Pope had been dragging on for four years, but the Pope had just dramatically and dangerously raised the stakes. John caught his breath. He would not give Llewelyn or the others the satisfaction of seeing that he was shaken, though, and he summoned up a taut, derisive smile.

'Tell me,' he challenged, 'do you, as a good son of the Church, mean to follow the Pope's directive?'

Llewelyn was enjoying himself. 'If I were truly such a good son of the Church, I would not be here at Cantebrigge, at your court. Your Grace is excommunicate, after all, and a man excommunicated is to be shunned by all Christians, to be treated as an Ishmael, as one facing eternal damnation.'

There was a strained silence. Joanna gave Llewelyn a look that was half-resentful, half-reproachful, and leaned over John's chair, whispering something meant for his ears alone. Llewelyn glanced around the hall, saw on other faces confirmation of his own belief, that he'd taken the honours in that exchange.

With those whom he knew well, Llewelyn could sometimes communicate without need of words, most often with Joanna, occasionally with Ednyved. But he experienced now just such a moment of shared, silent understanding with a virtual stranger. His eyes happened to catch Eustace de Vesci's; for several seconds the two men looked at one another, and in that brief span they reached an unspoken accord, one to be explored further at a more opportune time.

There was a sudden commotion at the end of the hall. Llewelyn turned, saw an extraordinary apparition stumbling through the doorway. He was uncommonly tall, so gaunt he looked almost skeletal, clad in a long, ragged gown of unbleached sacking, his feet grimy and bare, his hair drifting about his shoulders like dirty, windblown snow, his beard wild and unkempt. But although he'd obviously reached his biblical three-score years and ten, his face was curiously unlined, untouched by time, and his eyes, a startling shade of blue, were utterly without guile.

Joanna turned towards her father. 'Whoever is that strange old man?'

'A crazed hermit who has been wandering about Yorkshire for some weeks, prophesying my death. When reports first reached me, I did not pay them any mind. If I concerned myself with every lunatic roaming about the countryside, I'd have time for little else. But this lunatic,' John said dryly, 'is beginning to attract crowds.'

The old man seemed bewildered by his surroundings. He had to be shoved forward by his guards, and when he reached the dais, he stood there, blinking, until one of the men put a hand on his shoulder, directed him to kneel.

John leaned forward. 'Are you the one they call Peter of Wakefield?'

'Yes, lord.' He did not sound frightened, just confused. He

squatted back on his heels, waited patiently for John's will to be revealed.

'I was told you've been preaching that I'm to lose my crown by Ascension Day. Is that true?'

'No, lord!' The astonishing blue eyes opened wide. 'Not this Ascension Day, lord. The Ascension Day next to come.'

John gave an abrupt, incredulous laugh, one that did not sound very amused. 'God tells you this, I suppose?' he said sarcastically, and the hermit nodded.

'Yes, lord,' he said, so calmly that John lost all patience.

'Who put you up to this, old man? Who's paying you?'

Peter blinked. 'No one, lord. I am an instrument of the Almighty. He has given me second sight.'

There was something unexpectedly compelling in the utter simplicity of that statement. People murmured among themselves; a few surreptitiously made the sign of the cross. Llewelyn had less than the normal amount of superstition in his make-up, but even he was affected by the old man's composure, by his eerie certainty, and he was suddenly glad that the hermit's prophecy was not directed at him. He glanced curiously over at John, but the latter looked more angry than uneasy.

'You try my patience, old man, in truth you do. Go back to Wakefield, keep your foolish babblings to yourself, and I'll overlook the trouble you've caused me. But you'd best not expect me to be so lenient a second time.'

'I am sorry, lord; I do not mean to displease you. But I cannot do that. My visions are not my own. They come from Almighty God. He has chosen me to spread His word, and I cannot fail Him.'

The hall was very still. John stared balefully at the elderly hermit, shabby and emaciated and perplexingly tranquil; he met John's eyes quite placidly, as if his own fate was a matter of utter indifference to him. He did not flinch, did not react at all as John said grimly, 'As you will, old man.' He gestured to the waiting guards. 'Take this "prophet of God" to Corfe Castle, confine him there until Ascension Day of next year.'

They seized the hermit, dragged him to his feet. He offered no resistance. 'I shall pray for you, lord, when your time is nigh.'

John looked about the hall, saw he was suddenly the object of morbid speculation. He did not doubt that many among them would

418

lay grisly wagers on this madman's prophecy, that they'd count the days till Ascension-tide, 1213, with unholy glee. Few faces showed any sympathy; far more showed covert, cautious amusement. His son-in-law alone was making no attempt to hide his mirth, was openly grinning. John stared at Llewelyn, and for a long moment his brother Will's life hung in the balance.

'He amuses you, this pitiful lunatic?'

'Actually,' Llewelyn said coolly, 'I found him to be surprisingly convincing, found myself wondering if he might, indeed, be one of God's chosen.'

Joanna was close enough to hear her father's sharp inhalation of breath. She put her hand imploringly upon his arm, but he shook it off, keeping his eyes on Llewelyn.

'Sooner or later,' he said, very softly, 'you will make a misstep. And when you do, Christ Jesus Himself shall pity your fate.'

Joanna knelt, hugged in turn her four-year-old half-brother Henry, three-year-old Richard, and her namesake and half-sister Joanna, who was not yet two. None of them had their father's dark colouring; Henry and Richard were redheads, like their grandfather, and little Joanna had inherited Isabelle's blondeness. They accepted Joanna's kisses shyly, for she was a stranger to them, then approached the bed to receive good-night kisses from their mother.

Isabelle smiled fondly, ruffled Henry's untidy, bright hair, forbore to scold when her daughter left a dirty little handprint upon the skirt of her gown. But after a few moments, she signalled to the nurses, and the children were shepherded from the chamber.

The sight of them, the feel and smell of their sturdy little bodies had stirred up Joanna's longing for her own children. Never before had she been separated from Davydd and Elen for more than a few days, and she did not understand how Isabelle could be content to see her children so infrequently. Isabelle seemed proud of them, bragged about them often enough, but she reminded Joanna of Elen, who lavished much love upon her dolls, but only when she wanted to play at being a mother.

As the children departed, Joanna rose, too. 'I want to see Papa tonight, think I'd best go ere it gets too late.'

Isabelle, too, had been a witness to that scene in the great hall. She gave Joanna a wryly sympathetic smile, shook her head. '"Blessed are the peacemakers, for they shall be called the children of God." That may be true in Heaven, but they get precious little credit here on earth, darling.'

'What would you have me do, Isabelle? Just stand by, watch and do nothing? What would you do if you were in my place? If you were the one being torn between husband and father?' But even as she asked, Joanna realized the futility of expecting Isabelle to experience another's pain. She was coming to see that Isabelle's emotion landscape was an alien world to her, a world in which flowers bloomed upon the surface in generous, dazzling profusion, but nothing was rooted deep.

Isabelle was frowning; the blue eyes were soft with pity. At last deciding that she could best serve Joanna by helping her to face the realities of her predicament, she said candidly, 'I would be as loving a wife and daughter as I could. I would try not to let their hatred for each other poison their love for me. I would try to make each one see that I understood his grievances against the other. Above all, Joanna, I would try to reconcile myself to a bitter truth – that there can be no happy ending.'

'The hearth fire is almost out, Papa. Shall I fetch a servant to stoke it?'

'No, do not bother. But you can get me another cup of wine.'

Joanna obeyed, although she suspected that he'd already had more than enough wine that night. As soon as she'd been given admittance into his chamber, found him sitting all alone in shadowed gloom, she'd abandoned her intention to talk to him about his latest clash with Llewelyn. This was not the time for it.

'Isabelle tells me that you mean to give Uncle Will custody of Cantebrigge Castle. That's most generous of you, Papa.'

'I suppose,' John agreed absently. He was gazing into the dying fire, so absorbed in his own thoughts that Joanna made no further attempts at conversation. When Llewelyn drank too much, he tended to get playful, laughing a lot and making atrociously bad puns and eventually becoming amorous. But John's drinking had a darker, more disturbing texture to it; she'd never seen him well and truly drunk, knew she did not want to.

'You do not think he could actually have second sight?'

'No,' Joanna said hastily, if not entirely truthfully, 'of course not! Why would the Almighty bestow so great a gift upon one so unworthy?'

'Why indeed?' he echoed. The only light came from a single wall cresset; she could not see his face. She rose from her seat, moved towards him. But he rose, too, began to wander aimlessly about the chamber, picking up and discarding items at random.

'Do you believe in God, Joanna?' he asked suddenly, so shocking her that she was momentarily rendered mute. In all her life, she had never heard anyone ask such a question.

'Yes, I do. Surely you do, too, Papa?'

He shrugged, again said, 'I suppose . . .'

Another silence fell. John stopped before the hearth, reached for the fire tongs, and tried to prod the embers back into life.

'Talk to me, Papa,' Joanna entreated. 'Tell me what you're thinking. I'm here, I want to help, if only you'll let me.'

'What makes you think I need help?'

'Even a blind man could see that you're troubled! Is it the Pope? His meddling in Wales?'

John thrust the fire tongs aside, called the Pope an imaginatively obscene name. 'You know what he'll do next, Joanna? He'll announce to all of Christendom that I am not longer fit to be King of England, then anoint that grasping hellspawn Philip to lead a "holy crusade" to depose me. And as Philip's reward for acting as the papal catspaw, he'll bestow upon him the Crown of England, if he can take it from me. Do you know what that would mean? Every whoreson in England with half a grudge or half a brain would flock to the French banners.'

'Then come to terms with him, Papa . . . ere it be too late.'

'No,' he said, 'no, I will not. I'll not yield, not when I'm in the right.'

'It seems to me, Papa, that the relevant question is not who's in the right, but whether this is a war you can win.' Joanna crossed to him, laid a hand on his sleeve. 'I fear for you,' she confessed. 'Not just for your Crown, for your soul, too. If you die excommunicate, you're damned to Hell for all eternity. What could be worth so great a risk, Papa?'

'I'm damned whether the Pope absolves me or not. The things I've done . . .'

Arthur, she thought numbly. She swallowed, said, 'What things, Papa?'

He looked at her, and for a moment she truly thought he was going to answer. But he said only, 'Things God could never forgive.'

'That's not so, Papa. There is no sin so great that God cannot forgive it.'

He took her hand in his, raised it to his lips, and then he laughed, backed away. 'Do not believe it, lass, not for a moment! There is no forgiveness, either in this world or the next.'

'You're wrong, Papa.' Joanna drew a deep breath, said, 'I could forgive you any sin.'

John gave her an odd smile, shook his head. 'No, lass,' he said. 'You could not.'

He moved to the table, with an unsteady hand poured himself another cupful of wine. 'If that mad old man be right, I'll have reigned for fourteen years. Passing strange, for it seems longer, much longer.' He turned back to face Joanna, still with that strange smile. 'There is but one lesson worth learning, one you must teach your children, Joanna. That nothing in life turns out as we thought it would, nothing . . .'

On a cloudy, cool day in late May, the Welsh Princes came to Aber. Llewelyn greeted them in the great hall, but he then led them into his own chamber for the privacy such a volatile gathering required. He had not been entirely sure that they all would come. But he knew that if Maelgwn came, so too, would his brother Rhys Gryg. There was no love between them, but they had finally reached a grudging accord, more than a truce, less than an alliance. There was no question in his mind that his cousins Madog and Hywel would come, for he knew neither one was proud of the part he'd played in last summer's campaign. And Gwenwynwyn would come if the others did, for he had far too suspicious a nature to allow such a council to take place without him.

'I thought Aber was burned, compliments of your wife's father.'

There was mockery in Gwenwynwyn's smile, but Llewelyn ignored it, said evenly, 'I had it rebuilt . . . on a larger scale.'

Maelgwn took a seat next to Ednyved, giving him a cool nod; they were brothers by marriage, but not friends. 'What of my renegade nephews? Did you not invite them?'

'Owain and Rhys were unwilling to come,' Llewelyn said regretfully. 'Their defeat at John's hands seems to have left lasting scars upon their souls.' He saw no reason not to come straight to the point.

'I expect you've guessed why I asked you to Aber, to talk about forming a league of amity. I think it time we put aside our differences, band together against a common enemy, the English King.'

'You expect us to forget years of bad blood, mistrust, betrayals?' Gwenwynwyn's voice was scornful. 'Nor do I believe you've suddenly become such a bloody saint yourself, willing to overlook the part we played in your defeat at Aberconwy.'

'I've no claims to sainthood, but I like to think I'm capable of learning from past mistakes. What about you, Gwenwynwyn? Can you say as much?'

'You think I could ever trust you? I'd sooner deal with the Devil!'

Llewelyn shrugged. 'You think you could ever trust John?'

Madog had yet to take a seat. Now he moved towards Llewelyn, stopped in front of him. 'Your mother and my father were sister and brother; that makes ours the most significant of bonds, one of blood. It gives me the right to speak plainly. You're making a great mistake, Cousin. John's hatred for you is mortal. You move into the Per- feddwlad, and you'll see an English army in Wales within a fortnight. He'll take all Gwynedd this time, Llewelyn, and then he'll burn every hut, every tree if need be, in order to run you to earth. Need I tell you what befalls a man charged with treason? He's dragged behind a horse to the gallows, hanged and cut down whilst he still breathes, gelded and disembowelled ere he's finally – and mercifully – be- headed. And there are even worse deaths. You need only remember Maude de Braose's fate.'

Llewelyn had heard enough. 'You're overlooking something, Madog. Whether I keep the truce or not, sooner or later John would find an excuse to move against me. Besides . . . this time I do not intend to lose.'

Madog shook his head; there was on his face an expression of genuine regret. 'As you will. But I want no part of this. If I must come to terms with the English King in order to hold on to my lands, so be it. I know the limits of my power, would that you did yours.' He walked to the door, paused. 'I wish you luck, Cousin. I very much fear you'll need it.'

With Madog's departure, a pall had settled over the room. Llewelyn sought to dispel it by saying defiantly, 'Of course we can do nothing, can go on as we always have, fighting one another, allowing the English kings to play their sport of divide and conquer.

Is that what you want, Maelgwn? You want to wait until John has the time to deal with your rebellion, until you find yourself facing an English army?'

'You made a mistake in taking Ceredigion,' Maelgwn said coolly. 'And then I made one in backing John. I expect that makes us even . . . at least for now. You do not have to talk me into an alliance. I might not like it any; for certès, I do not like you. But it makes sense.'

Llewelyn grinned, looked towards the others. 'What do the rest of you say?'

Hywel nodded, grinned back. Rhys Gryg glanced over at his brother, then rose to his feet. Maelgwn was by far the more physically impressive of the two. Rhys was balding, freckled, with bloodshot blue eyes and a harsh, rasping voice, the result of a throat injury which had earned him the name Rhys Gryg, Rhys the Hoarse. As Llewelyn thought him to be fully as capable as his brother, although less trustworthy, he waited tensely for the older man's verdict.

'It seems to me,' Rhys Gryg said slowly, 'that you could act verily as a magnet for disaster, could draw John's wrath down upon us all. You did not have much luck against John last summer. What makes you think this time it will be different?'

'I made it easy for John, let him cut me off from my natural allies – other Welshmen. This time he will not be able to play us off against each other. This time we're not acting as rebels, but at the urging of the Pope. And this time we'll have allies. I've sent envoys to the French court; even now they are negotiating an alliance with Philip.'

Rhys Gryg looked startled, then impressed. 'That alone would sign your death warrant with John,' he said. 'I see you've been thinking about this for a long while.'

'I've had nine months in which to think of little else. We seem to agree that the English kings have had great success in exploiting our weaknesses. But two can fish in those troubled waters, and John's enemies are beyond counting. When I was at the English court this Easter, I spoke with some of them. They're men who hate John even more than they fear him, men who want him dead. If he leads an army into Wales, that will give them the opportunity they've been waiting for. If he crosses into Gwynedd, he'll find that he has as much to fear from his own lords as he does from the Welsh.' Llewelyn paused. 'Need I say more?'

'No,' Rhys Gryg said succinctly and, for the first time, he smiled.

By common accord, all eyes then turned towards Gwenwynwyn. He looked so perturbed that Llewelyn could not keep from laughing.

'It's rather like being asked to choose between dwelling in Sodom or moving to Gomorrah, is it not?' he gibed, and Gwenwynwyn scowled. But when the other men laughed, he, too, managed a very sour smile, a grudging nod.

Joanna's hair was unbraided, fell loose and free to her hips. Llewelyn entwined a long strand around his fingers, made of it a soft noose for his throat, entangling them both in its coil. 'Your hair always smells of lemon,' he murmured. 'Did I ever tell you how much I like that?'

Joanna said nothing. She could feel his breath on her cheek, and then his mouth was on hers. It was an unhurried, easy kiss, strongly flavoured with wine. He'd released her hair, and his hands were wandering at will over her body, his mouth tracking the curve of her throat. Joanna did not move, not even when he loosened the bodice of her gown, cupped and caressed her breast with a warm, knowing hand. He kissed her again, exploring her mouth as he was exploring her body, and then stepped back, abruptly ended the embrace.

'That kiss, Madame, could well give a man frostbite. What ails you, Joanna?'

'This afternoon I entered the antechamber, found that Madog had left our bedchamber door ajar. I listened at that door, Llewelyn, listened as you and the other Welsh Princes made plans for war.'

'I see. Just what did you hear?' When she did not reply, he said, 'Joanna, tell me!'

'I heard you talking of Norman barons who mean to betray my father. I heard Rhys Gryg say these men wanted my father dead, and I heard him ask if you, too, sought Papa's death. You said you did.'

'Not so, Joanna. I said that I would gladly see him dead, but I seek only to reclaim what is mine. I do not forget the vast and sovereign powers of the English King. Nor that you are of his blood. If he stays out of my lands, I shall be content. But if he leads an army into my realm, I will defend myself and mine as best I can, and make no apologies for it . . . not even to you.'

'My father has given you cause to hate him; I find no fault with you for that. I do not want to quarrel with you, not with so much at stake. I know you so well, Llewelyn, know the secrets of your heart, your soul. You have always been decisive, little given to self-doubts,

425

but you are not impulsive. I must assume, then, that you have thought on this long and hard, that you are fully aware of what the consequences might be. And that is what I find so difficult to understand. You do realize what you are risking? Our son's inheritance. Our marriage. Your son Gruffydd's freedom. Above all, your life. You do know that?'

'Yes,' he said. 'I know.'

She took a step towards him, held out her hands, palms up, in a gesture of despairing entreaty. 'Why, Llewelyn? Sweet Jesus, why?'

'Joanna, I would that I had an answer for you, one you could accept. I do in truth understand the risks. There are nights when I lie awake, when I cannot keep my thoughts from dwelling upon disaster, upon all I have to lose. I think of my son as a prisoner of the English Crown, and I think of you, a widow at the age of one-and-twenty.'

'But you still mean to do this, you are still set upon war.'

'Yes,' he said bleakly.

After some moments of silence, he moved to her, pulled her into his arms. This time she did not stand rigid and unresponsive in his embrace; she clung tightly. 'You are rushing headlong to your own destruction,' she whispered, 'and I do not know how to save you.'

August, 1212
Nottingham, England

Nottingham Castle was one of John's favourite residences, for it was all but impregnable to attack, situated on a cliff above the River Leen, with three baileys encircled by deep, dry moats. But Richard knew they would not be long at Nottingham; in just five days John was assembling an army at Chester.

John had gone at once into the great hall, but Richard was still loitering out in the middle bailey, watching as their baggage carts were unloaded. He was in no hurry to join his father, for John's temper was very much on the raw during this the fourteenth – and if Peter the Hermit were to be believed the last – summer of his reign.

His victories in Scotland, Ireland, and Wales had encouraged John to look towards the Channel. Time had not reconciled him to the loss of Normandy, and in the spring he'd begun making plans for an invasion of France. The summer of 1212, he assured Richard, was to be a season of retribution.

And indeed it was proving to be just that, Richard thought grimly, but not precisely as his father had anticipated. John was at the Scots border when word reached him of his son-in-law's rebellion. Llewelyn had chosen his time with care, and within a month he'd retaken all of the Perfeddwlad, save only Deganwy and Rhuddlan Castles.

Richard had never seen his father in such a violent rage, a rage that fed upon itself, gained ground with each passing day until John began to seem obsessed, so intent was he upon exacting vengeance. Philip was reprieved, the French invasion abandoned. There would be war, but the battlefield would be Wales. John gave orders for his vassals to gather at Chester, gave orders to recruit more than two thousand carpenters and six thousand labourers, men to follow in his army's wake and erect castles across the conquered land. None doubted that this was to be much more than a punitive campaign of retaliation. It was to be war with no quarter given, a war that would end only with Llewelyn's death and the conquest of his country.

Turning back towards the great hall, Richard saw his uncle Will standing on the outer stairs; Will, too, had begun to avoid John whenever possible. They stood in silence for some moments, their thoughts tracking the same bleak trail.

'When your uncle Richard was at war with Philip, they took to blinding each other's soldiers.' Will grimaced. 'I fear, lad, that this war shall be just as bitter, just as bloody. Know you that John is now offering a bounty for Welsh heads? He paid one man six shillings for six heads last week.'

'Yes,' Richard said, 'I know,' very much wishing that he did not.

'For a time I'd hoped that the London fire would turn John's mind from this war. Much of Southwark is but ashes and rubble, and I heard it said that more than a thousand people died. The homeless have to be sheltered, the injured tended, and John generally takes a personal interest in making sure that fire or flood victims are cared for. But not now. Now he can think of nothing except making his daughter a widow.'

Just then, Richard's other uncle, William de Warenne, Earl of Surrey, appeared in the doorway behind them. 'John wants you both,' he said. 'He's just learned that Llewelyn ab Iorwerth and the French King have entered into a treaty of alliance.'

Richard and Will exchanged looks of dismay, for they both knew that had always been John's greatest fear, that his enemies should unite against him, that he should find himself fighting a war on two fronts.

John was striding up and down before the open hearth, clutching a crumpled parchment. He thrust it at Will, saying, 'Read for yourself, see what that Welsh whoreson has dared to do!'

Richard, reading over Will's shoulder, saw that it was a letter from Llewelyn to Philip, one that spoke of a treaty 'between the kingdom of the French and the principality of North Wales', that promised Llewelyn would be a friend to Philip's friends and an enemy to his enemies.

'How did you get this, John?' Will asked, and John gestured impatiently.

'How do you think? I've paid informants at the French court.' Snatching the letter back, he scanned it rapidly. 'Listen to this.

". . . by God's grace, I and all the Princes of Wales unanimously leagued together have manfully resisted our – and your – enemies, and with God's help we have by force of arms recovered from the yoke of their tyranny a large part of the land and the strongly defended castles which they by fraud and deceit had occupied, and having conquered them, we hold them strongly in the might of the Lord."'

The more John read, the angrier he became. 'God rot his wretched soul for this,' he spat. 'But if he thinks Philip is going to save his skin, he's in for a bitter shock. What was it they said of the Romans, Will, that they made a desert and called it peace? That will be Wales, too, by Christ it will, and Llewelyn ab Iorwerth will go to his grave knowing that he brought destruction upon his people, he and he alone. Let him look out over the burning crops and smouldering woodlands, let him count the bodies and then say it was worth the price!'

He swung about, beckoned to the nearest man. 'I want a gallows built in the bailey, and then I want to see Llewelyn's Welsh hostages hanging from it, each and every one. Maelgwn's, too. See to it . . . now.'

His fury had dulled his perception, and it was several moments before he became aware of the utter silence. He turned, found they were all staring at him.

'My liege.' The Earl of Chester stepped forward, said quietly, 'My liege, I would advise against that. I do not deny Llewelyn has given you cause. But you kill the hostages and your war will become a blood feud. You'll find yourself fighting the Welsh for the next twenty years.' He lowered his voice still further, said, 'Even more to the point, how are your own lords likely to react? If you hang these Welsh hostages, what do you think will happen the next time you ask a man to yield up his son? He might well prefer rebellion.'

'Or do exactly what he's told, knowing now what will be at stake.'

Chester was first and foremost a realist. He'd done what he could to dissuade John from committing an act that he saw as neither morally justifiable nor politically expedient. Having failed, his concern now was to dissociate himself from the killing to come, and he was quite willing to defer to the Earl of Pembroke.

If Chester's objections had been coolly rational, dispassionate, Pembroke's plea was unashamedly emotional. 'My lord, listen to me. When I was a little lad, my lord father rose up in rebellion against

King Stephen. My father had given me as a hostage, and the King warned him that I'd be hanged if he failed to keep faith. My father sent back word that he had the hammer and anvil with which to forge other sons, and I was taken out to be hanged. I was but six and I did not understand. I thought it was all a game, and I laughed even as they put the noose about my neck. King Stephen watched, and was moved to mercy. He stopped the hanging, with his own hands removed the rope.'

He paused, but John said nothing. If he were moved, like Stephen, by pity, it did not show in his face. Pembroke walked towards him, said, 'Some of those Welsh hostages are just lads, have not yet reached manhood. My lord, I ask you not to do this. Do not take your vengeance upon the innocent.'

'You'd do better to tell that to Llewelyn ab Iorwerth,' John said coldly. 'He's the one who chose to gamble with the innocent, not I. If his son's life means so little to him, why should it mean more to me? No, my lord Pembroke, he set the stakes for this wager. I'm merely collecting what's due me.'

Will had been listening in appalled silence. He'd known this war would be a brutal one, but the cold-blooded killing of helpless hostages, many of them young boys, far exceeded his worst expectations. 'John, I beg you . . .'

'Do not, Will. Do not.'

Their eyes locked, held until Will could bear it no longer, had to look away. 'At least,' he mumbled, knowing how ineffectual his protest was and despising himself for it, 'at least spare Llewelyn's son . . . for Joanna's sake. If you murder the boy, Llewelyn will be bound to blame her. Do not do that to her, John.'

'It matters little whether Llewelyn blames her or not. He'll be dead ere the summer is out.'

Richard waited to see if Will would argue further. When Will did not, shoulders slumping in demoralized defeat, eyes averted from that which he'd fought a lifetime against acknowledging, Richard realized that Will's moment of truth was his, too. His every instinct told him to keep silent, to distance himself as he'd always done, even as he moved towards his father.

'I think it could work to your advantage to spare Gruffydd, Papa,' he said softly. 'Llewelyn would be half-crazed with fear for the boy. You could make use of that fear, hold it over his head like the sword of Damocles. To have leverage like that over an enemy . . .'

He saw John's eyes narrow and he dared to hope he'd hit upon the one argument that might stay his father's hand.

'There is much in what you say, Richard,' John conceded, 'and I'd agree with you – but for one thing. Llewelyn ab Iorwerth is a dead man, and there is no need to seek leverage over the dead.'

John glanced about the hall, saw that no one else meant to speak. 'I want it done this forenoon,' he said. 'The sooner they die, the sooner word of their deaths will reach Llewelyn.'

The first one to suffer from Llewelyn's rebellion had been his son. Gruffydd's status had been changed overnight from that of highborn hostage to prisoner of state. As yet, he was not being abused, and his confinement was in castle chambers, not the dark, airless dungeons that filled him with such fear. But his days and nights were passed under guard, and he was finding it harder and harder to keep at bay his most persistent enemies: boredom and loneliness.

Soon after their arrival at Nottingham, he had been escorted to the uppermost chamber in the Black Tower, and then left alone. The room was sparsely furnished, containing only a bed, trestle table, bench, and chamber pot. He wandered about rather aimlessly for several moments, indulging in the fantasy that occupied most of his waking hours, thoughts of escape. A pity the window was not large enough to squeeze through; mayhap he could have knotted the bed sheets, lowered himself down into the bailey once dark came. He never passed a church now without thinking of sanctuary, never picked up an eating knife without evaluating it as a weapon.

His meal had already been laid out for him; there was a glazed clay flagon brimming with ale, a round, flat loaf of bread marked with a cross, a chunk of goat's cheese, and a baked pigeon pie. Gruffydd would have liked to believe that his friends were eating as well as he, but he had no way of knowing. In these six weeks of his captivity, his isolation had been complete.

He was reaching for the clay flagon when the door opened. At sight of the three men, Gruffydd stiffened. It may have been the way they moved towards him, hands on sword hilts, saying nothing. It may have been the rope coiled from one man's belt. Or it may have been a more subtle indicator, an inborn sense of sudden danger. Gruffydd did not pause to puzzle it out; his reaction was as instinctive as it was immediate. He got to his feet, and as the first guard

431

approached the table, he swung the flagon in a wide, deadly arc. It shattered against the man's face; he screamed and staggered backwards.

They had not been expecting resistance, and that gave Gruffydd a momentary advantage. He overturned the table on to the second man, dived for the doorway. Had the third guard been slightly slower in his reflexes, he would have made it. But the man was cat-quick; slamming the door, he flung himself at Gruffydd.

He at once regretted it, for he could match neither Gruffydd's strength nor Gruffydd's desperation, and he found himself in a savage no-holds-barred brawl in which he was getting much the worst of it. Unable to unsheath his sword, he soon stopped trying to keep Gruffydd from reaching the door and concerned himself only with keeping Gruffydd from killing him.

After what seemed a lifetime to him, his comrade untangled himself from the wreckage of the table, came to his aid. Even then, it took the two of them to subdue Gruffydd, and the struggle ended only when one managed to draw his sword, put the blade against Gruffydd's throat and snarl, 'Give me an excuse, go on, just blink!'

They forced Gruffydd to kneel, jerked his arms behind his back, began to bind his wrists tightly together, cuffing him about the head and shoulders when he resisted.

The third man had taken no part in the fight, was slumped, moaning, against the wall. But now he stumbled to his feet, and his companions swore in startled sympathy. His face was already swelling rapidly, bloated and bloodied, his mouth so distorted and puffy that it resembled nothing so much as the grotesque grimace of a scarecrow. He bent over, spat into his hand, stared incredulously at a bloody tooth. With that, he lurched towards Gruffydd.

For a moment he stood over the boy, looking down at him. And then he grabbed Gruffydd's tunic collar, struck him across the face. 'You hear that hammering in the bailey? They're building a gallows for you and the other hostages. The King wants the lot of you to hang ere he dines. And you, you misbegotten Welsh bastard, you shall be the very first to die, I'll see to that!'

'No, my lord Salisbury said we're to wait with this one, that he's to be last.'

The man swore, discovered another loose tooth, and hit Gruffydd again, this time in the stomach. 'Mayhap that is even better. This way he'll have time to think on it, to imagine how that rope'll feel about his neck, how it'll feel to be choking for air, and not getting any!'

Gruffydd could not breathe; each breath was more constricted, more laboured than the last. It was partly the blow he'd just taken, but mainly it was panic. Not only was hanging a dishonourable, shameful way to die, but it was, he knew, also a particularly painful death. Only if a man was hanged from horseback did the fall break his neck; otherwise, he slowly strangled.

Never had Gruffydd known fear like this, terror made all the more intense by his utter helplessness. He strained against his bonds, tried frantically to free himself, while the men watched and laughed at his futile efforts. Out in the bailey, the hammering continued.

John stood at the window of the great hall, watching as the Welsh hostages were hanged. Some tried to fight, had to be dragged cursing and kicking up on to the gallows. Others, especially the younger ones, were too stunned to offer resistance. A few wept, a few pleaded. Richard had seen executions before. Nor had he thought he was particularly squeamish. But this had been too much for him; he'd turned away, unable to watch.

The hangings were still going on when dinner was served. The cooks had prepared one of John's favourite dishes, stewed lamprey eels in saffron sauce. It was a favourite of Richard's, too, but he found he could not swallow more than a mouthful. Some of the hostages being hanged were no older than the young pages serving the lamprey and roast peacock. He laid his knife down, did not pick it up again.

The pages were bringing in the subtlety, a spun sugar creation sculptured to resemblc a flame-breathing dragon. On their heels came the marshal of the hall. Kneeling before John, he said nervously, 'I thought it best not to wait till the meal's end, Your Grace. A courier has just ridden in from Wales, bearing an urgent message from your daughter, the Princess Joanna. Shall I send him in?'

John nodded, and a moment later a young Welshman stumbled into the hall. He was unshaven, his clothing stained with sweat and the dust of the road, and at first Richard thought he was drunk; his eyes were glazed, slid blankly past John without seeing. But then he saw how the young man's gaze kept coming back to the window, and he understood. Not drunk; in shock.

When prompted by the marshal, the Welshman knelt, held out a

433

folded parchment. 'My lady entrusted me with this. She said . . .' He swallowed, tried to remember, to blot out for a moment what was happening in the bailey. 'She said I must give it into your hands and yours only, that none but you must read it . . .'

John reached for the letter, made sure that the seal was indeed Joanna's and had not been tampered with. Only then did he break it open, begin to read. When he glanced up, he had paled noticeably.

'Someone give this man a shilling for his trouble. My lords of Chester and Pembroke, you stay. Will and Richard, you stay, too. The rest of you out . . . now.'

Men set down their wine cups, stared at him in astonishment, mouths full of unchewed food. But one look at his face and they pushed resentfully away from the tables.

Within moments, the hall was cleared. John rose, but he was suddenly reluctant to share the contents of Joanna's letter. He hesitated, and then said abruptly:

'Joanna has written me that some of my own lords are plotting with Llewelyn and the other Welsh Princes. She says that they mean to rebel once we're in Wales, either to kill me or to turn me over to the Welsh.'

As he spoke, his eyes moved intently from face to face, assessing the impact of his words. He did not truly suspect Chester or Pembroke, but he was relieved, none the less, to see that their surprise was unfeigned. At least these two could be eliminated as suspects. But that still left so many, half his court. How could he trust anyone? How could he ever be sure, ever be safe?

'John, what mean you to do?'

'I do not know, Will,' John admitted. 'I need time, time to think.' He began to pace. 'Christ, it could be any of them. De Vesci has always been a malcontent. De Clare never wanted me to be King; he thinks I've forgotten that, but I have not. Derby is de Braose's blood kin, and Huntingdon –'

The Earls of Huntingdon and Derby were Chester's brothers-in-law and he interrupted hastily, 'My liege, this serves for naught. We need more than suspicions. First of all, we must look to your safety. Thank Jesus for your daughter's warning.'

John nodded. 'My God,' he said softly, 'I'd have walked blindly into their trap. If not for Joanna . . .'

'She saved your life, Papa,' Richard said, and again John nodded.

'Yes, lad, I think she did.'

'Then give her a life in return, Papa – her stepson's life.'

John frowned. 'Joanna has reason to want Gruffydd dead,' he said impatiently, 'good reason.'

'But she does not want him to die, Papa. I know, for she asked me to protect him if I could.'

John turned to stare at his son; his surprise was genuine. 'You truly think she'd want me to spare him?'

'Yes, Papa, she would.'

'I cannot for the life of me understand why! I do owe Joanna a debt, but . . .' He fell silent, began to re-read his daughter's letter. He was remembering Llewelyn's surrender at Aberconwy, envisioning himself in Llewelyn's place, delivered into Llewelyn's hands by his own barons. It was a thought to make him flinch. Richard's words came back to him now: 'To have leverage like that over an enemy . . .'

'Has Maelgwn's son been hanged yet?' he asked unexpectedly, and Richard gave a baffled nod.

'I think so, Papa. Why?'

'I was just wondering how the Welsh Princes would react, if their sons were hanged and Llewelyn's alone was spared. I'd like to see him try to explain that to Maelgwn, in truth I would!' John said and laughed grimly. 'Very well, Richard. Mayhap you're right, mayhap there's more to be gained by keeping the whelp alive. Tell the hangman this one fish is off the hook. For now.'

'Blood of Christ!' Richard stood motionless in the doorway, shocked at the sight of Gruffydd. The boy's face was covered with welts and bruises; one eye was swollen shut; dried blood had encrusted a gash across his forehead, matted his hair. He shrank back as the door opened, struggled to sit upright.

Richard had once come across a snared wildcat, crouched to earth, spitting fear and defiance as the huntsman moved in for the kill. He saw that same terrified rage now on Gruffydd's face, knew it would be a memory to trouble his sleep in nights to come. He had always prided himself upon his analytical turn of mind. But however neglected his imagination was in consequence, he did not need to be told what the past three hours must have been like for Gruffydd, listening as his comrades were dragged to their deaths, expecting at any moment his own summons to the gallows, and he said furiously:

435

'Who told you whoresons to maltreat him like this? And why is he gagged?'

'We had to, lord. It was the only way to shut him up. He got right abusive. As for his hurts –' the man pointed to his own blackened eye – 'in truth, he gave as good as he got.'

'Hand me a flask,' Richard demanded, and he knelt by Gruffydd, removed the rag they'd stuffed into his mouth. 'Here,' he said, 'drink.'

Gruffydd did, swallowing in gulps as if he could never get enough. At last he took one final swallow, raised up and spat it into Richard's face.

Richard recoiled, and then raised his arm, slowly and deliberately wiped his face on his sleeve. 'I came to tell you,' he said, 'that you will not be hanged.'

Gruffydd did not react like one reprieved. His lips were drawn back from his teeth, and his swollen eye blazed with such feverish hatred that Richard realized further conversation would be pointless. There was nothing he could say that Gruffydd would believe, and he sighed, reached for his dagger.

Gruffydd gasped, tried to squirm out of range. Richard had no liking for Gruffydd, but at that moment he found himself pitying Llewelyn's son as he'd never pitied anyone before. 'I'll not hurt you, Gruffydd. I mean only to cut your bonds.'

Leaning over, he slashed at the ropes binding the boy's wrists, and then hastily backed away. 'I'll see that you're given balm for your bruises . . . and some wine.'

Gruffydd made no response, and Richard beckoned to the guards, moved to the door. 'I do not expect you to believe me,' he said slowly, 'but you'll not be harmed.' Knowing that he lied, that Gruffydd had already suffered harm beyond healing.

Gruffydd did not move, did not reply, and Richard lingered a moment longer, then closed the door quietly behind him. At that, Gruffydd scrambled to his feet, grabbed for the table boards and tried to barricade the door. But it was a futile effort and he knew it. He slumped down on the bed, massaged the rope burns on his wrists, and listened for returning footsteps.

It was a long time before he let himself believe that Richard had not lied, that they would not be coming back for him. It was even longer before he could nerve himself to stand up, to walk to the window.

Below him, the bailey was drenched in hot summer sun. A breeze had sprung up from the east, and the bodies swinging from the gallows were swaying gently back and forth. Gruffydd stood motionless, stared down at the slowly twisting bodies until the gallows blurred in a haze of hot tears.

John moved over to a table, selected a morsel of meat, and tossed it to one of the castle dogs. He and his son were alone in the hall; he had not even allowed the servants to clean up, and the tables still gave cluttered testimony to their interrupted meal. He threw the dog another titbit, said:

'You might as well be the first to know. I'm calling off the Welsh campaign . . . at least for now. I cannot risk going into Wales until I'm sure I'd not be betrayed.'

'I think that's most wise, Papa.' Ah, Joanna, you truly did it, lass. You won a war. But not a victory the Welsh will ever want to celebrate. Richard glanced over his shoulder, towards the bailey. Jesu, no.

A glimmer of silver caught Richard's eye. Bending down, he scooped up a handful of pennies, for a moment studied them in puzzlement. And then he understood. This was the money John had ordered given to Joanna's messenger. He fingered the coins, and then let them drop, one by one, back into the floor rushes.

'Since you mean to delay the Welsh invasion, you will not have any need of me for a while, then?'

'Mayhap not. Why?'

'Conisbrough Castle is but a day's hard ride from Nottingham. I should like to visit with my lady mother. Have I your permission to leave the court?'

'I see.' John subjected his son to a thoughtful, probing scrutiny. At last he said, with obvious reluctance, 'If that be your wish.'

Until that moment, Richard had not admitted to himself just how much he wanted to get away. 'Thank you, Papa,' he said, adding as casually as he could, 'It'll not be dark till well past nine. I think I'll make use of the hours of daylight remaining, and leave now.'

John merely nodded. But as Richard reached the door, he said suddenly, 'Richard . . . you do mean to come back?'

Richard's hand tightened on the door latch. 'Yes, Papa, of course I do.' Wondering if he had a choice. Wondering, too, if he truly wanted one.

437

John moved to the window, watched Richard cross the bailey. He did not like this request of Richard's, not at all, but something in his son's face had warned him not to refuse. Not once had Richard met his eyes, not once.

Mayhap he should have tried to explain, to make Richard see why it had to be done. But why was it not obvious to Richard? Of what earthly value were hostages unless men knew they'd be sacrificed if need be? Now when he demanded hostages from Huntingdon and de Clare, from all those he suspected, they'd take great care to please him, to stay loyal. They'd learn from Llewelyn's fatal mistake.

He glanced over at the gallows. A moment later he was at the door, shouting for a messenger. He had not long to wait; he'd never been obeyed with such haste as he was in these hours after the hangings.

'I have a message for you to deliver, one of great urgency. You're to leave now for Wales.'

The courier paled, guessing what was coming. 'Wales, my liege? Llewelyn ab Iorwerth?'

John was indifferent to the man's alarm. 'Yes. I want you to tell him of the hangings. I want him to know that his hostages are dead.'

31

August, 1212
Dolwyddelan, North Wales

Joanna had moved a stool close to the bed, and for more than an hour, she watched Llewelyn as he slept. His was the sleep of utter exhaustion; he'd not stirred for the past three hours, not even when Joanna removed his boots. The longer he slept, the more difficult it was for her to keep still. The urge to awaken him was becoming all but overwhelming, for they'd been apart for more than a fortnight, and never had her need to talk to him been so urgent.

But she dreaded it, too. What if she could not make him understand? In warning her father of the conspiracy against him, she'd been thinking of Llewelyn's safety as much as John's. Hers had not been an act of impulse. It was born of despair and fear and an anguish of spirit that only one who'd faced her choices could ever understand. If she did nothing, there was a very real possibility that her father might be walking into a lethal trap. Yet if she warned him of the danger, she might be taking from Llewelyn his only edge, the advantage that might spare his life, his realm. For she knew that if her father won this war, Llewelyn would die.

In the end, she'd sent the most trusted of her servants to John, because she could not do otherwise, because she loved her father, because there was a chance that her warning might stop a war. But now she had to tell Llewelyn what she'd done, and she was not at all sure if he would forgive her.

Llewelyn's lashes flickered, and she leaned over, kissed him on the mouth. He opened his eyes, smiled at her. But then he glanced down, saw how shadows were chasing sunlight across the floor rushes.

'Why did you not awaken me ere this, Joanna?'

As he sat up, she slid her arms around his waist. 'Do not get up, not yet.'

There was nothing either of playfulness or seduction in her voice;

she sounded so plaintive that he turned, held her close for a moment.

'I do not understand it, Joanna. I know John gave the command to gather at Chester on the 19th. Three full days ago. Yet my scouts report no movement on the roads, nothing.' He had his boots on by now, and as he rose to his feet, Joanna's hand tightened convulsively on his arm. He gave her a quizzical look, and her fingers unclenched; she let him go.

He picked up his sword and scabbard, buckled it at the hip. 'Did I tell you the latest word from the south? Rhys Gryg has taken and burned Swansea.'

'Does it matter, Llewelyn? My father is not leading his army against Rhys Gryg or Maelgwn. It is Gwynedd he means to invade. It is you he means to destroy.'

He glanced towards her, but said nothing. She knew she should have kept silent. That was not what he wanted to hear. He truly believed this was a war he could win. He had to believe that. She would to God she could believe it, too.

Llewelyn had reached the door. But something in Joanna's face made him pause, come back to her. 'I know how you're hurting,' he said, and Joanna put her arms around his neck, clung tightly. She'd rarely seen him look so tired; his dark eyes were bloodshot, swollen from lack of sleep, and his skin was rough and scratchy against her throat. She did not mind, but Llewelyn rubbed his chin, said ruefully, 'I expect you'll want me to shave ere we go to bed tonight?'

'That depends upon what you do have in mind,' she said, and he grinned.

'After a fortnight apart, need you even ask?'

Joanna managed an answering smile, but it was as strained as her banter. Mayhap she should wait, not tell him until after they made love. But the longer she delayed, the harder it would get. And if he ever found out from someone else . . . That thought was frightening enough to give her courage, and she said abruptly, 'Llewelyn, we must talk.'

'It will have to wait till night, *breila*. I've lost too many hours of daylight as it is.'

Joanna did not argue; a delay not of her own making was a reprieve she could accept in good conscience. 'Tonight, then,' she agreed. 'You still have not told me how long you'll be at Dolwyddelan.'

'That will depend upon John,' he said, and opened the door just as Ednyved came through the porch entranceway.

'Llewelyn, an Englishman has ridden in with a flag of truce and a right strange story. He says he has a message of urgency for you, that it comes from John.'

'A royal courier?'

'No, that is what be so strange about it. He is not a courier at all, is a blacksmith from Shrewsbury. He claims he met John's courier in a Shrewsbury alehouse, that the man paid him to deliver John's message. Moreover, he insists upon telling his tale to you and only you. Do you want me to send him away?'

'No. Either he is telling the truth, or he is willing to risk his life for a preposterous lie. Whichever it is, I want to know.'

Ednyved nodded. 'I rather thought you would. He is waiting below.'

The man looked to be Llewelyn's age, in his late thirties, with the calloused hands and heavily muscled forearms that were the inevitable badges of his trade. What was most distinctive about him was his extreme nervousness. He knelt and, when Llewelyn gestured for him to rise, he shifted awkwardly from foot to foot, darting sidelong glances from under lashes matted with dust and sweat, and then blurted out:

'I thank you for seeing me, my lord. Men call me Ralph the smith, for I've a smithy in Shrewsbury, not far from the church of St Alkmund.'

The information appeared gratuitous, but was not; Llewelyn understood that the man was seeking to establish his credibility, showing that he was, as a man of property, one deserving of belief. 'I understand you have a message for me?'

'My lord, I must ask you to bear with me, let me tell it my way. I fear you'll not believe me unless I explain how I happened to come by what I know. This past Saturday I'd stopped in a riverside tavern for a few tankards of ale. There was a stranger there . . . half-drunk, a talker. He said he was King John's courier, and indeed, he was wearing the King's livery. He was telling anyone who'd listen that the King had entrusted him with a message for you, a message he was loath to deliver. He was offering two pence to the man who'd take it for him, half now, half afterwards. That was a day's wages, and I was not the only one who took an interest. But . . . but when he told us what the message

441

was . . .' He paused, for the first time looked Llewelyn full in the face.

'It was not just the money, my lord. Not after I heard the message. You see, my first wife . . . she was of your blood. I am telling you this because . . . because I want you to understand. It seemed to me that you had a right to know. I kept thinking of my own boy . . .' His eyes were small and close-set, all but obscured by thick, shaggy brows, eyes brimming over with so much pity that Llewelyn's breath stopped.

'For Christ's sake, man, what do you have to tell me? Just say it!'

'Your son, my lord – he's dead. All the hostages are dead. King John hanged them last Tuesday at Nottingham Castle.'

For a merciful moment, the words had no meaning for Llewelyn. But then his numbed brain absorbed the full impact of what he'd just been told. Gruffydd was dead. They were all dead. He'd given them up to John, and John had murdered them.

He turned away, without purpose or direction, stumbled against the table. The trestle boards tilted, spilled over on to the floor. He stared down at the wreckage, at the shattered flagon, and then picked up one of the broken clay shards. It was sharp-edged, sticky with wine, beyond mending. He tightened his fingers around it, squeezing until Joanna's hand closed over his own.

'My love, you'll cut yourself,' she pleaded, and he opened his fist, let the shard drop back into the floor rushes.

'He died because of me. They all did.'

'No, Llewelyn, that's not so!'

'Gruffydd was sixteen,' he said, as if she'd not spoken at all. 'Some of them were even younger. Twelve, thirteen. I thought . . . thought their youth would protect them, that John would be less likely to maltreat youngsters –' His voice thickened, broke. He pulled away from Joanna, walked rapidly from the chamber.

'Llewelyn, wait!' But when Joanna would have followed after him, Ednyved stepped in front of her, blocking her way.

'Let him go, Joanna. You are the last one who can help him now.'

'I'm his wife!'

'You are also John's daughter.'

Joanna took a step backward, stared at him. 'I see. So you believe it, too. Well, it is not true, Ednyved. It is not true!'

Ednyved said nothing, but she saw his disbelief, and her eyes narrowed. 'There is no evidence to support this man's story, none whatsoever. Have you not learned by now not to accept alehouse babble as gospel? You need only think upon the wild rumours that have been circulating all summer long. First we heard that the royal treasury at Gloucester had been plundered. But that turned out to be false, did it not? And then we got word that my father's Queen had been abducted and raped, their baby son killed. But that was not true, either. It was no more than vicious gossip, tales spread by men with nothing better to do than give grief to the unwary.' She drew a bracing breath, said, 'And this ugly accusation is no different, Ednyved. This is no less of a lie.'

'I know there has never been a true friendship between us, Joanna. But believe me now, that I am speaking as a friend. For your sake as well as Llewelyn's, leave him be.'

'"Leave him be?"' she echoed incredulously. 'My husband thinks that his son is dead, and it's not true. I will not stand helplessly by whilst he breaks his heart over a lie, I will not! Now please move away from the door.'

He did. 'I hope you will remember,' he said, 'that I did try to stop you.'

It was unnaturally still. The birds had muted their songs at Llewelyn's approach, and he heard only the sound of his boots on the wet gravel of the riverbank. It had been a dry summer, and the river was shallow and slow-moving; mossy rocks jutted up towards the sun, seeming to offer a safe passage to the far shore for those willing to take the risk. How many youths had stood on this bank, gathering up their courage to put those beckoning stepping-stones to the slippery test? For risk-taking was the measure of a man. Had he not taught Gruffydd that from birth?

Llewelyn knelt, cupped his hands and splashed river water on to his face. Yes, he'd taught Gruffydd about risk-taking and manhood and pride. But he'd not taught him how to die on an English gallows. Gruffydd would have fought them, knowing no other way, would have spat defiance until the rope choked off all breath. Llewelyn could hear his own breathing grow ragged; it was coming in harsh, uneven gasps, filling the quiet woodland clearing with strangled sound.

For a time he knelt, motionless, on the riverbank, and there burned behind his closed eyelids a gallows laden with bodies, bodies left to rot in the summer sun, because he had been a risk-taker.

443

His instincts for self-preservation had long since become second nature to him; when a branch snapped underfoot, his head jerked up. The sound came again. Someone was following the trail he'd taken from the castle. He rose swiftly, hand on sword hilt. A moment later a large black alaunt broke through the underbrush, bounded joyfully towards him.

At sight of the dog, Llewelyn's eyes filled with tears. Math was his son's dog, had been Gruffydd's veritable shadow, and when Gruffydd went away, the big dog's grieving had been heart-rending. When he'd begun to refuse food, Llewelyn had taken over the dog's feeding, slowly coaxed the alaunt back to health, and in the past year, Math was never willingly far from his side.

Llewelyn bent down, gathered the dog to him. Math began to bark, swiped at his face with a rough, wet tongue, and he pulled back. Only then did he see his wife standing at the edge of the clearing.

Llewelyn was the first to speak. 'Go back to the castle, Joanna. This is not the time to talk.'

There was no emotion in his voice; he sounded like a stranger. Joanna hesitated, and then stepped towards him. 'Llewelyn . . .'

'Not now,' he said, much more sharply this time. He turned away, began to walk along the riverbank.

'Llewelyn, wait!' Hastening after him, she found she could not match his pace, and caught his arm, forcing him to stop.

'My love, you must listen to me. This one time you must believe me. Your grieving is for naught. Gruffydd is not dead.'

'Joanna, no!' But she clung to his arm with surprising strength; he could not free himself without hurting her.

'You must hear me out, Llewelyn. Please, beloved, please listen. My father is not a good man. Mayhap not even a kind one. But he would never murder Gruffydd and the other hostages. He is not capable of a cruelty like that, Llewelyn. I know he's not, know –'

'No, you do not know! You've never known John, never!' Llewelyn jerked free, saying bitterly, 'But I did. I knew how vicious he could be when cornered, how merciless, for I knew what he'd done to Maude de Braose. I knew all too well, and yet, God forgive me, I still turned my son over to him –' He broke off abruptly, turned to stare blindly out at the sun-glazed water.

'"What he'd done to Maude de Braose." What do you mean by that, Llewelyn?' Raising her hand to her forehead, Joanna found it

444

damp with sweat. She was suddenly aware of the hot, humid air, utterly still, as all-enveloping as a shroud; the sun had begun to hurt her eyes. 'What do you mean?' she repeated. 'Your stepfather told me Maude de Braose died in prison. Are you saying he lied?'

Llewelyn swung back to face her. 'Maude did die in prison. What Hugh did not tell you was how she died.' He paused, and then said, 'All right, then, the truth. Mayhap I should have told you long ago. John had Maude de Braose and her son cast into a dungeon at Windsor Castle, and then he starved them to death.'

He'd never seen anyone lose colour so quickly. Joanna's face was so ashen, her eyes so wide and unseeing that he took an instinctive step towards her, put his hand on her arm. But then she raised her chin, swallowed, and said, 'I do not believe you.'

His hand dropped to his side. 'Christ Jesus, Joanna, do you truly think I'd lie to you about that?'

He did not wait for her answer, turned and walked away. Like most huntsmen, he knew how to make the woods his own, left no trace of his passing. Math had vanished, too. Joanna stood alone in the clearing.

Within his chamber, Llewelyn found Ednyved and Morgan awaiting his return. They rose as he entered; he was grateful when neither offered expressions of sympathy or commiseration.

'I must have been gone several hours. Has there been any further word from our scouts?'

'Nothing. More and more, it looks as if John means to delay the invasion, Llewelyn.'

Ednyved was holding out a large goblet. Llewelyn caught the strong odour of fermented honey, and shook his head. 'No mead. Not yet.' After some moments of silence, he said, 'On the morrow I must begin telling the parents of the hostages that their sons are dead. It would mean much to me, Ednyved, if you were with me.'

Ednyved drew a sudden, sharp breath. 'Ah, Llewelyn . . .' He coughed unconvincingly, and then said brusquely, 'You do not have to do that. I'll take care of it for you.'

Their eyes met, held. Llewelyn slowly shook his head. 'No, Ednyved, I do have to do that,' he said, and the other man nodded.

'I've sent for Rhys and Catrin.' He hesitated. 'Did Joanna find you?'

'Yes,' Llewelyn said, 'she did.' He sank down in the closest chair,

445

began to fondle Math's thick sable fur. The dog had been swimming in the river, and his legs were caked with dried mud, his tail matted with burrs. Llewelyn found himself remembering how Gruffydd would groom the alaunt by the hour, wielding his brush until Math's coat shone like ebony. 'Morgan . . . fetch my daughters.'

'Would you rather I told them, Llewelyn?'

'No. This, too, I have to do.' Llewelyn glanced up at the priest. 'It was in this same chamber that I had to tell Gruffydd that his mother was dead. He was just five.'

Morgan's throat constricted. 'I know there are times, lad, when God's ways must seem –'

'No, not God, Morgan . . . John.' No more than that, but on his lips a common Christian name became an unspeakable obscenity, became a vow of vengeance rooted not in reason, but in blood.

As Morgan opened the door, they heard footsteps on the outer stairs. Llewelyn stiffened at the sound. It was a shock to realize that the person he most loved was suddenly the person he least wanted to see.

But it was not his wife who entered; it was his fourteen-year-old daughter. Gwladys was panting so, she could hardly speak. She stumbled into the chamber, clutched at a chair for support.

'Papa . . . there's an Englishman in the great hall. I overheard him saying . . . saying that . . . Papa, it's not true? Gruffydd, he's not dead?' Her eyes searched Llewelyn's face. 'No . . . no, Papa, no!'

Llewelyn reached her as she began to scream, caught her to him and held her as she wept. But he had no comfort for her, no more than on the morrow when he would have to face the parents of the other murdered boys.

'Madame, thank God Almighty! I've been so uneasy. Where were you?'

'Where?' Joanna gestured vaguely. 'I think . . . down there. By the river.'

'Madame . . . are you all right?'

Joanna nodded, not convincing Branwen in the least. Her shyness notwithstanding, Branwen could be very stubborn. 'Are you sure, Madame? In truth, you look ill.' But Joanna seemed not to hear. She was turning away as Catherine and Rhys rode through the gateway into the bailey.

446

Catherine did not wait for her husband's assistance. Sliding from the saddle, she ran towards Joanna, disregarded protocol, and embraced her as a sister.

'Joanna, what can I say?' Catherine's fair skin was splotched, the blue eyes reddened and puffy. 'I still cannot believe it. Where is Llewelyn?'

Joanna was reluctant to admit she did not know, and she was grateful when Branwen said, 'He is in his chamber, Lady Catrin.'

By now Rhys had reached them. Tragedy had not made him any the less taciturn; he greeted Joanna with his usual economy, moved towards the stairs. Catherine started to follow, and then stopped, looked back over her shoulder.

'Joanna, are you not coming?' And when Joanna shook her head, she hastily retraced her steps. 'Dearest, I do not understand. If ever Llewelyn needed you, it is now.'

'He . . . he does not want me there, Catherine.'

The other woman stared at her. 'Joanna, what are you saying?'

'He believes it, Catherine, truly believes my father hanged Gruffydd and the other hostages. I could not bear to see him hurting so, and I tried to tell him, to make him see it was not true. But then he told me . . . he told me, Catherine, that my father starved Maude de Braose to death.'

She saw first horror on Catherine's face, and then pity, and she said tautly, 'You need not look at me like that, Catherine. It is not true.'

'Joanna . . . Joanna, I know naught of politics. If you say it is not true, I want to believe you. But would Llewelyn lie?'

Joanna shook her head wearily. 'He is not lying, Catherine. He believes it to be true. I know it is not, but I cannot convince him of that.' Tears were spilling down her face. She made no attempt to wipe them away.

Joanna awoke with a gasp, did not at once remember where she was. She sat up, feeling queasy and disoriented. Beside her, Davydd and Elen slept soundly; in the other bed, Catherine lay between Joanna's stepdaughters, Marared and Gwenllian. Joanna rose quietly from the bed, stood looking down at Catherine. Catherine's coming had been a godsend; she'd been remarkably successful in consoling Gruffydd's sisters. Joanna had ached for the bewildered children, but she knew she'd been of little help to them. In the past twelve hours, her sense of reality had become hopelessly distorted; she felt as if her emotions were somehow sealed off, under glass and beyond reach.

She did not remember the dream that had so frightened her, was thankful she did not. Moving to the table, she poured herself some wine, noting with odd detachment that her hands were shaking. She wore several rings; without stopping to think what she did, she slipped one from her finger, laid it upon the table. It was topaz and silver, a long-ago gift from her father. She stared down at it, telling herself that her gesture had no significance. She did not believe Llewelyn. She could not.

Elen stirred, whimpered in her sleep. Joanna stood by the bed until she was sure her child slept, and then she moved silently towards the nursery door. Outside, all was dark and still. The air was surprisingly cool against her skin. She crossed the bailey with quickening steps, gripped by the uneasy, irrational certainty that she was being watched, that the darkness was alive with hostile, unseen eyes.

Upon the table a candle was burning down towards the wick. Gwladys was curled up at the foot of the bed, having at last cried herself to sleep. Llewelyn was sprawled in a nearby chair, his head pillowed awkwardly upon his arm. There was an empty mead flagon on the table, another on the floor by his chair. From a shadowed corner, Math's eyes glowed like embers; his tail tipped slightly in acknowledgment of Joanna's right to be in the bedchamber, even at such an hour.

Joanna moved closer to Llewelyn, stood beside him for several moments. His face was in shadow. Only his mouth was touched by the candle light; it was tautly drawn even in sleep, communicated so much pain that Joanna began to cry again, silently, in utter despair. At last she dried her tears upon her sleeve, backed quietly towards the door.

When Joanna returned to her bedchamber, the sun was rising above the hooded silhouette of Moel Siabod, dispelling the dawn mists that overhung the valley like fallen clouds; already, the day gave fair warning of what was to come, vagrant winds and sweltering heat. Gwladys was sitting on the bed, listlessly pulling a brush through her tangled dark hair. She looked up as Joanna entered, said tonelessly:

'My father is not here. He has gone to see the families of the murdered hostages, to tell them that John hanged their sons.'

448

Joanna was appalled, tried not to let Gwladys see it. Gwladys was the most passionate of Joanna's stepdaughters, the most like Gruffydd. It had been a slow and tentative endeavour, making a friend of this prideful, spirited girl, but Joanna had eventually coaxed from Gwladys what she'd never got from Gruffydd, acceptance. Her heart twisted with pity now at sight of the girl's grieving, and she said helplessly:

'Gwladys, if only there was something I could do . . .'

'But there is.' Gwladys flung back her hair; her eyes were as black as jet, and just as cold. 'You can write to your father, Madame. You can ask him to return the bodies of those he murdered. Ask him to return my brother's body for decent burial.'

Never had Joanna so wanted a day to end; never had one seemed so sure to drag on into infinity. She passed the hours as best she could, with her children, rising every ten minutes or so to stare out into the bailey. But by duskfall, Llewelyn still had not returned.

'Joanna . . . do you want me to talk to Gwladys?'

Joanna gave Catherine a grateful look. She'd been badly shaken by her stepdaughter's hostility; that it was understandable did not make it less hurtful. 'Thank you, Catherine, no. She is still distraught. I can only wait till we get word from Nottingham, till it is proven that Gruffydd and the other hostages are safe and well. But Catherine, if it is not soon . . . Jesus wept, the suffering this evil rumour has caused!'

She rose, moved restlessly to the window. 'Gwladys is not the only one blaming me, Catherine. I see it on other faces, too.'

'I know,' Catherine conceded. 'But not all do feel that way, Joanna. Llewelyn's people know that John would never have agreed to a truce if not for your intercession. And what you did that day at Aberconwy, defying your father on Llewelyn's behalf, that won you more favour than you realize. There are many who do not blame you, Joanna, who are sorry for your pain.'

'But I do not want that, either. I do not want them pitying me because they think my father is the . . . the Antichrist!'

Catherine did not know what to say to that. She watched in silent sympathy as Joanna turned from the window, began to pace.

'I find myself haunted by what Llewelyn said. I know it is not true, but I cannot stop thinking of it. It is such a vile accusation, Catherine; how can Llewelyn believe it? We are alone, and I can

449

speak the truth with you. I think it very likely that my father did have Arthur put to death, as his enemies charge. Men do things in anger, give commands they might later regret. I think it happened that way with Arthur.'

She stopped before Catherine. 'But it would take hours to drag thirty hostages to the gallows, Catherine. There'd be time to relent. Even if my father had given such a command in a moment of rage, he'd not have carried it out. As for the other, what Llewelyn said about Maude de Braose, that could never be. Such a dreadful death as that would take days, even weeks . . .' She shuddered, for she had the imagination to envision the full horrors of a death by starvation, Maude's slow realization that food would never be forthcoming, that none would heed her screams, that her dungeon was to be her tomb.

A silence fell. Joanna moved back to the window. Almost at once, she tensed. 'Llewelyn,' she breathed, and suddenly she was very frightened.

Llewelyn had dismounted by the time Joanna reached the bottom of the keep stairs. She started towards him, then stopped at sight of Cristyn. Cristyn had ridden in that afternoon with Tegwared and Anghared, her seven-year-old twins, and her presence was just one more goad to Joanna's unravelling nerves. Even though she believed Llewelyn's physical intimacy with Cristyn was over, their continuing friendship occasionally gave her some uneasy moments; she would always be jealous of Cristyn, if only because the other woman had the power to make her remember what it was like to be fifteen, awkward and innocent and so desperate to please.

Cristyn was looking up intently into Llewelyn's face, her hand on his arm. Saying all the things I cannot, Joanna thought. Llewelyn put his arm around Cristyn; they stood for a moment in a quiet embrace. It was, Joanna knew, just what it looked to be, but she felt a pang, none the less, found herself resenting Cristyn for being able to offer the comfort she could not.

Llewelyn had begun walking towards the great hall. He stopped when Joanna said his name, waited for her to reach him. She started to speak, but her words caught in her throat. His eyes were hollowed, his skin grey with fatigue; there was a bleak, bitter desolation in his face that went beyond grieving, that Joanna could not bear to look upon.

For a long moment, Llewelyn studied her face, searching for something he could not find. 'You still do not believe me, do you?'

450

'Llewelyn, I . . . I cannot!'

'No,' he said slowly, 'I do not suppose you can. But to tell you the truth, Joanna, I do not know where that leaves us.'

'Do not say that,' she whispered. 'You cannot mean that. Jesu, Llewelyn, we have to talk!'

'What would we say? I've just come from telling a man and his wife that their eleven-year-old son has been hanged, the son I took from them as a hostage. Do you truly think this is the time to defend John to me?'

'I'm not defending him, I'm not!' But he was no longer listening; he'd turned away.

Joanna stood as if rooted. She could feel eyes upon her, curious, gloating, pitying; they no longer mattered. At last she followed Llewelyn into the great hall, not knowing what else to do.

She paused uncertainly in the doorway. And then she saw the self-appointed courier, the Shrewsbury blacksmith.

'Why are you still here?'

He was flustered by her tone, and stammered, 'The priest . . . he said your lord husband might have additional questions for me, said I should wait for him . . .'

'Wait for payment, you mean, wait for your blood money! Tell me, how much do you think my husband should give you? You've seen the grief you've brought upon us; what price do you put upon it?'

Joanna heard her voice rising, shrill, accusatory. Llewelyn was suddenly at her side, saying, 'Joanna, that is enough.'

'No, it is not! This man goes into a tavern, hears a drunken stranger babbling in his cups, and suddenly he becomes a man with a mission, suddenly he cannot rest until he's made sure that we've heard the latest alehouse gossip. Well, you've delivered your poisonous offering, you've had your moment of acclaim. But look around you and then tell me if it was worth it!'

'You're not being fair! It was more than gossip. I know the man spoke the truth.'

'How could you possibly know that?' Joanna said, so scathingly that the man's face flushed a resentful shade of red and he said:

'The day the courier reached Shrewsbury, Robert de Vieuxpont hanged Prince Maelgwn's younger son. He was just a lad, not yet seven, and he died at the King's command. Why would I doubt, then, that the other hostages, too, were dead?'

451

The emotional upheavals of the past two days had left Llewelyn without the capacity to feel shock, outrage, to feel anything at all . . . or so he'd believed. 'Are you saying John had a seven-year-old boy hanged?' he demanded, incredulous, and the blacksmith nodded.

'I saw the boy's body with my own eyes, my lord.'

Their voices were echoing strangely in Joanna's ears, growing faint and indistinct. The people, too, seemed to be receding, faces blurring, slightly out of focus. The scene before her had lost reality; she was in it but somehow no longer part of it. She turned, without haste, began to walk towards the door.

'Joanna!' Llewelyn caught up with her in two strides, but she did not stop until he put his hand on her arm. She looked up at him, her face so still and remote that he felt an inexplicable throb of fear. 'Are you all right?' he said, very low.

'Yes.' He'd shifted his hands to her shoulders; she had to resist the urge to pull away, not wanting to be held, to be touched. 'I want to be by myself, Llewelyn. I just want to be alone for a while.'

He hesitated, and then stepped back. 'We'll talk later.'

'Yes,' Joanna agreed politely. 'Later.'

Joanna slid the bolt into place. Only then, with the world shut out, did she begin to tremble. Moving to the bed, hers and Llewelyn's, she lay back against the pillows. It came upon her without warning. Suddenly sweat broke out on her forehead, her face began to burn, and she was overcome by nausea. When it did not abate, she stumbled into the privy chamber. After some wretched moments, she vomited weakly into the privy hole.

She heard knocking on the door; Catherine called her name. Then it grew quiet again. After a time she was able to return to the bedchamber, where she washed her face, rinsed her mouth out with wine. But the more she tried to make sense of what she'd been told, the more agitated she became. Her thoughts took flight, too swiftly for coherence, ricocheting wildly off the outer parameters of belief. She thought desperately to seize upon fragments of fact, to patch them into an intelligible pattern, one that would enable her to understand. But the raw, graphic horror of the images filling her brain blotted out all else. A bewildered child being led up on to a gallows. A woman screaming alone in the dark.

A kaleidoscope of faces seemed to spin before her eyes. The florid, heavy face of the Shrewsbury blacksmith. Llewelyn's, lean and dark and terrifyingly aloof. John's, mouth quirking as if at some secret and very private joke. When she was little, their eyes would meet across the chamber, he'd wink, and she'd be flooded with happiness, revelling in the reassuring intimacy of their shared smiles. Had he smiled, too, as he gave the command to hang Maelgwn's son? He was just a lad, not yet seven. John had Maude de Braose and her son cast into a dungeon at Windsor Castle, and then he starved them to death. He hanged the hostages; they're dead . . . dead. She sank to her knees by the bed, but the voices would not stop. When she could endure them no longer, she fled the chamber.

Catherine was waiting out on the porch. 'Ah, Joanna, I'm so sorry . . .'

'I want Llewelyn. Please, Catherine, bring him to me.'

'I will, dearest,' Catherine said swiftly, soothingly, 'I will. But a man has just ridden in, and he . . . he was there, Joanna, at Nottingham the day the hostages were hanged. Llewelyn is with him now. I know he'll come to you as soon as he can.'

'No!' Joanna shook her head vehemently. 'No, I cannot wait!' She could hear her voice rising again, as it had in the hall. Her need for Llewelyn was an instinctive, blind groping towards the light, towards the only haven left to her, and she repeated, with the stubbornness born of shock, 'I cannot wait. I must see him now.'

Her eyes were clouded over, unfocused; they held a look Catherine had seen before, the dazed, defenceless look of a child half-awakening from a nightmare. Catherine had always been able to dispel childhood horrors with hugs and lit candles, but she had no comfort to offer Joanna, for her fears were not fantasy. She knew that Llewelyn would have no comfort, either.

Llewelyn was standing by the dais; men had clustered around him, intent eavesdroppers upon this eyewitness account of the August 14 hangings. Joanna did not yet know what she would say to him. In truth, she did not want to talk at all, for there was nothing he could say to change what was – that the whole fabric of her life had been founded upon lies. She asked no more now than to be held, asked no more than the reassurance of physical closeness, the familiar feel of his embrace.

She had almost reached Llewelyn when her gaze fell upon the man kneeling before him. Marc, the most trusted member of her household. Marc, whom she'd sent to Nottingham with a warning for John.

'Morgan . . .' Llewelyn's voice was husky, almost inaudible; he sounded stunned. 'Tell my daughters.' And then he was moving away from the dais, moving swiftly towards the door. He passed within several feet of Joanna, but seemed as oblivious of her as he was of the others in the hall. She stood, in stricken silence, as the distance between them widened; she'd begun to tremble again.

'Madame!'

Marc had risen to his feet, was hastening towards her. He started to speak, but she did not give him the chance. 'You told him. You told him about my letter.'

He nodded. 'Madame, I had to tell him. We're at war with John. Why would I be in England . . .'

Joanna was no longer listening. For a moment she closed her eyes. How could she face him? He might have understood yesterday, but now . . . Lady Mary, what was she to do?

'Madame . . . did you not hear what I said about your stepson? He is not dead, Madame. He is not dead.'

Llewelyn was standing by the window. He heard the door open behind him, but he did not turn, not until Joanna said his name.

'Marc told me,' she said softly, 'that Gruffydd is safe.'

'Safe? Safe . . . oh, Christ!'

Joanna had never heard so much raw emotion in his voice, so much fear. Tears began to burn her eyes.

'Why did John spare him? Why?'

'I . . . I do not know, Llewelyn.'

'Hanging is not an easy death. But there are worse ways to die, much worse.'

They looked at each other, and the same thought was in both their minds: Windsor Castle and the agony of Maude de Braose's last days.

'I have no way of knowing if Gruffydd is even still alive. John could have had him put to death yesterday . . . or tomorrow. Gruffydd will never know which sunset might be his last. And I can do nothing for him, nothing.'

'Beloved . . .' But the right words eluded her. He'd spoken only the truth; how was she to dispute it? The silence was fraught with tension, with all that still lay unsaid between them. Moving to the

454

table, she poured out a cupful of mead, all she could think to do for him. He took it from her, drank slowly, keeping his eyes upon her all the while, and then he said:

'Do you want to tell me now what was in the letter you sent to John, the urgent letter that was for his eyes alone?'

Her voice was little more than a whisper. 'I . . . I warned him that he faced betrayal by his own men if he led an army into Wales.'

She might have been a stranger of a sudden, a haggard, frightened woman looking up at him with eyes full of entreaty. 'I trusted you,' he said. 'I've never trusted a woman as I trusted you.'

'It was all I could think to do, Llewelyn. If my father feared treachery, there was a chance he'd not come into Wales, that he'd abandon the invasion. I did it for you. Beloved, I swear it!'

'Was this the first time? Or have you been keeping him informed all along? Have I been underestimating your talents? Loving wife, ardent bedmate – and John's spy?'

'No, Llewelyn, no!' Her voice broke and she began to weep.

He watched, saying nothing. He'd taken the mead on an empty stomach, and it was beginning to have an effect; so, too, was the lack of sleep, the guilt, the grieving. His anger ebbed away, leaving only exhaustion in its wake. Joanna's denial rang true, but it mattered little. Nothing mattered now but Gruffydd and what he faced at John's hands.

'Llewelyn, I would have told you, in truth I would. I meant to . . .'

'I do not want to talk about it. Not tonight.'

'But you do not understand, you've not let me explain –'

'Joanna, not now!'

The world had become a bewildering place to Davydd. His brother was dead. But then he was not. His sisters had been weeping continually. For three days now, his mother had been sleeping with Elen and him in the nursery. His father seemed no happier after learning that Gruffydd was alive, while his mother wept quietly in the night, and near dawn she'd awakened them all with her screams. Davydd did not understand.

Sitting on the edge of his bed, he watched as his mother and Aunt Catrin folded his clothes into an open coffer. He was anxious, wanting to make sure they packed his favourite toys, his wooden horse and his whipping top.

'Mama had a bad dream,' he told Catherine. 'I dream about wolves sometimes.'

'We all do, sweeting.' Catherine straightened up, said softly, 'Joanna, are you sure about this? I truly think you should wait till Llewelyn comes back . . .'

'I cannot, Catherine.' Joanna drew Catherine aside, out of her son's hearing. 'He might not let me go, and if I do not, I think I may truly go mad. I dreamed about her last night, about Maude . . . Catherine, I have to go.'

She moved over to the table, picked up a letter. 'I want you to give this to Llewelyn, Catherine –'

'Madame!' Branwen was standing in the doorway. 'Madame, Prince Llewelyn just rode in. When he saw your coffers being loaded on to the packhorses, I . . . I had to tell him.'

'I understand, Branwen.' Joanna leaned back against the table, gripped the edge for support.

'Papa!' Davydd scrambled from the bed, ran to his father. 'We're going away, Papa, we're going to England! Did Mama tell you?'

'No, Davydd, she did not.' Llewelyn's eyes flicked down to the open coffers, up to Joanna's face. 'Catrin, would you take Davydd outside?'

'I was going to leave you a letter.' Joanna held it out, as if in proof; he made no move to take it.

'Where were you planning to go . . . to your father, to John?'

'No!' She took a step towards him. 'I'm not going to my father, Llewelyn. You must believe me. I could not do that . . . not now. I'm going to my brother . . . to Richard.'

'For how long?'

'I . . . I do not know yet. Mayhap a month. Llewelyn, I have to go. I have to find some way to live with what I've learned. Nor can we continue like this. If we had some time apart, it . . . it might help.'

She'd feared that he might forbid her to go. Yet suddenly she wanted him to do just that, to tell her to stay, that their problems could be worked out, that he could forgive her.

A splash of red midst the floor rushes caught Llewelyn's eye; bending down, he retrieved his son's whipping top. He turned it over in his hand, fingering the wooden point, and when he looked back at Joanna, his eyes were bleak.

'I think you're right,' he said. 'It is probably for the best that you go. I'll see that you have a safe escort.'

Not trusting her voice, Joanna could only nod.

'You may go, Joanna, if that be your wish. But not my children. They stay with me.'

'They are my children, too, Llewelyn!'

She sounded so panicked that he found himself relenting. 'You may take Elen, then,' he said reluctantly. 'But not Davydd. Not my son.'

'But why? Do you want to hurt me as much as that?'

He slammed the wooden toy down upon the table. 'Do you think I'd ever willingly deliver up a second son into John's hands?'

She shrank back. 'But –'

'But what, Joanna? Are you going to assure me again that I've no cause for concern, that John would never harm a child?'

Joanna flinched, no longer met his eyes. 'No,' she whispered, 'No . . .'

Llewelyn found he could not be impervious to her pain, however much he willed it. 'I do not want to quarrel with you, Joanna.'

'I'm not going to my father's court, Llewelyn, I swear I'm not. Davydd would be safe with me.'

His mouth hardened again. 'No. You may take Elen . . . for one month, no longer than that. But not Davydd.'

He moved towards her, seemed about to speak, and then reached, instead, for the letter. Their fingers brushed, the meaningless, impersonal intimacy of strangers, and Joanna drew an audible breath. When she raised her eyes to Llewelyn's, her lashes were wet, fringed with tears.

'What I did was not an act of betrayal. I would never betray you, Llewelyn.'

'I want to believe you,' he said at last. 'But even if I can, is that enough? Could we live with John's shadow ever between us?'

And Joanna had no answer for him.

457

September, 1212
Grantham, England

Richard stood by a window in his bedchamber, staring out into the rain-drenched dark. The storm had swept in from the north, scattering the manor livestock and soaking the oats and barley harvested and left out to ripen in the late summer sun. Lightning had seared the aged yew tree in the village churchyard, and the villagers were sheltering before their kitchen hearths, cheated of daylight hours precious to a people dependent upon rushes dipped in tallow and fires that gave off more smoke than light.

'Sweetheart, are you not coming to bed?'

'Soon.' But he moved, instead, to the table.

Eve sat up, stifling a yawn. 'Are you reading again that letter from your lord father?'

'Yes.'

Another woman would have wanted to know if he planned to return to court. Eve was quite content to wait until Richard chose to tell her, and it was that which he valued even more than the pleasure she gave him in bed. That Eve was lacking in perceptiveness, even in simple curiosity, mattered little to Richard; what did was that she made no emotional demands, that she was placid and good-natured and easily relegated to the fringes of memory during their long separations.

He glanced down at the letter, at the phrases he already knew by heart. '. . . only twelve, so a plight troth might be advisable . . . bring you a barony, lordship of Chilham . . . an advantageous match . . .' Richard silently mouthed the words; an advantageous match, indeed. Marriage to Rohese de Dover would make him lord of Chilham Castle. With his lineage blemished by the bar sinister, with no lands of his own, he was no great matrimonial prize. And yet his father was offering him a barony.

'My lord.' A servant stood in the doorway. 'There's a woman seeking admittance out at the gate.'

'I'd not turn anyone away in such foul weather, least of all a woman. Give her shelter for the night.'

'My lord, you do not understand. This woman says she is your sister!'

Joanna had stripped off her wet clothes. Wrapped in one of Eve's bed-robes, she stood as close to the hearth as she could get, and when Richard handed her a goblet of hot mulled wine, she drank in deep, thirsty gulps. He watched uneasily, saying nothing. They were alone; Elen and Joanna's maids had been bedded down in an upper chamber, and Eve had uncomplainingly withdrawn so Richard might speak privately with his sister.

'How did you know I was at Grantham, Joanna?'

'I went to Conisbrough Castle. Your mother told me.' Joanna set the goblet down, began to dry her hair with a towel. There was an exaggerated and painstaking deliberation about her movements that Richard had occasionally seen in those who'd had too much to drink or too little sleep. He moved closer, close enough to see Joanna's face was free of all cosmetics, that the skin was discoloured and smudged under her eyes, stretched so tightly across her cheekbones that it put him in mind of silk strained to the breaking-point. It was an unsettling thought. Her tension was contagious; Richard could feel it constricting his muscles, eroding his composure. How much did she know?

'It worked, that warning you sent Papa. He has called off the invasion of Wales. He was truly shaken by your revelation, Joanna. He demanded hostages from all those he suspected. Most complied, how reluctantly you can well imagine. But Eustace de Vesci and his cousin Robert Fitz Walter fled the court, de Vesci to Scotland and Fitz Walter to France. To Papa, that is all the proof needed of their guilt. But he suspects that others, too, were involved in the plot, and as long as he does, I think it unlikely that he'll risk going into Wales.'

A fortnight ago that would have been the answer to Joanna's every prayer; now it was salvation come too late. She could not rejoice, felt only a numbed sense of relief.

'Joanna . . . did you hear what I just said?'

'Yes, I heard.' She turned from the hearth. 'You were at Nottingham, Richard. You saw the hangings.'

It was not a question, but he nodded, said reluctantly, 'Yes, I saw them.'

'I did not believe it, Richard. I tried to comfort Llewelyn by assuring him that it could not be true. I kept faith with my father, and all it cost me was my marriage.'

'Joanna . . .'

'Papa had Prince Maelgwn's younger son hanged in Shrewsbury. Did you know that, Richard?'

'Yes . . . I heard.'

'He was not yet seven. Did you know that, too?'

Her voice was low and so brittle that Richard sensed any answer would be the wrong one. 'Papa gave the command to hang Prince Maelgwn's son; I cannot deny that. But he may have forgotten how young the boy was. He may not even have known –'

'Richard, no!' Joanna had begun to tremble again. Richard pulled a blanket off the bed, draped it about her shoulders. As their eyes met, she said softly, 'Why did you not tell me about Maude de Braose?'

Richard expelled his breath in a sound much like a sigh. 'I hoped you would never have to know.'

'You should have told me, Richard. I had the right to know.'

'I did not tell you, Joanna, for the same reason that Llewelyn did not. We wanted to spare you if we could.'

'I know what Llewelyn told me is true. I have to accept it, to learn to live with it. But I do not know if I can ever understand it. How do I reconcile my memories with what Papa did at Nottingham . . . at Windsor? How, Richard?'

'I do not know,' he admitted, and she reached out, grasped his arm.

'But you must. You've done it . . . somehow. Tell me, Richard. Tell me how you've done it.' When he was silent, she cried, 'For God's sake, help me! Papa never raised his hand to me, not once. He was often moved to pity at sight of a crippled beggar and he never refused alms to the needy. He liked to play with his dogs, and I once saw him rein in to berate a drover who was whipping his cart horse. Yet now I must believe that same man sent children to the gallows, gave the command to starve two people to death. How could he do it, Richard? Did he never awaken in the night, thinking of them? Did Maude's shadow never once fall across his table?'

'Joanna, do not do this to yourself.'

'How can I stop? There are reasons beyond counting why men murder, but there can be only one reason for a death such as Maude's. Papa had to want her to suffer. He had to want to prolong her agony as long as possible.'

'No,' he said, 'no.'

'No more lies, Richard. Do you not think it time I faced the truth?'

'I'm not lying, Joanna. I've had months and months to think on this. All his life our uncle Richard did as he damned well pleased, with explanations or apologies to no one. But Papa is not like that; he needs to justify his actions, even to himself. He wanted Maude dead, but he had no right to execute her, and he knew it; all knew it. If he'd had her beheaded, there could be no doubt that it was done at his command. But prisoners are often neglected, often sicken and die. I truly think that is why he chose starvation and not the axe. Not to see Maude suffer. To enable him to deny responsibility for her death, to be able to claim it was not of his doing.'

'Maude's guards misunderstood their orders? Forgot to feed her? Christ Jesus, Richard, who could ever believe such a fable?'

'Uncle Will believes it. He's managed to convince himself that Maude and her son died through neglect. He has to believe that. How could he continue serving Papa if he did not?'

'How then –' Joanna stopped herself in mid-sentence, but he finished it for her.

'. . . can I continue to serve him? I do not often ask that question. And when I do, I tell myself it's because he is still my father. Because he is still the King. Because the only difference between Papa and other men is that he has the power to do what they cannot.'

'You cannot truly believe that, Richard,' she said, and he shrugged. 'What of Isabelle?' she asked, after a long silence. 'Do you think that she knows?'

'About the hostages, yes. About Maude, not likely; who'd dare to tell her? You need not fret about Isabelle. She has very selective senses, sees and hears only what she wants to know.'

'Was I . . .' Joanna swallowed. 'Was I like that, too?'

'You loved him, Joanna. I doubt that anyone loved him the way you did.' Richard hesitated. 'When Papa decided to delay the invasion of Wales, he moved up into Yorkshire. But he expects to be back at Nottingham within the fortnight, wrote and requested that I join him there. I mean to do that, Joanna. Would you be willing to go with

461

me? Mayhap if you talked to Papa?' Feeling no surprise, only a sad sense of futility when she said in a wretched whisper:

'I cannot, Richard. I cannot . . .'

'I know,' he conceded. 'This is a de Warenne manor. You're welcome here as long as you like.'

'I'll stay until you return to court. After that, I shall go to stay at the White Ladies Priory in Brewood forest.'

The White Ladies Priory was a small Augustinian nunnery in Shropshire that had occasionally benefited from John's largesse. Richard knew Joanna had twice visited it with John, at age eight and then again a few months before her marriage to Llewelyn. He thought her choice of sanctuary a very telling one, and he ached for her, thinking it ironic that he, who had always valued competence as the highest virtue, should now feel so utterly ineffectual, able to offer such meagre comfort.

'Joanna . . . you have not left Llewelyn?'

She slowly shook her head. 'No. I could never leave Llewelyn. But I'm not at all sure, Richard, if he wants me back.'

'Mama, look!' Elen balanced precariously on the tree-stump, and when she was sure she had Joanna's eye, she dived like an otter into the October leaves heaped about the stump. Joanna hastened to the rescue, anticipating scraped knees and sobbing, but Elen was already sitting up. She had dirt on her dress, leaves in her hair, and a satisfied smile on her face.

'Did you see me jump, Mama, did – Ohhh! What is that?'

Joanna followed the grubby little finger, saw two twitching ears protruding from a nearby thicket. 'That is a rabbit or coney, Elen,' she said softly. 'Be still so you do not frighten it away.'

'It's smaller than a hare,' Elen observed, with the knowing eyes of a country child. 'Do we have them back at home? Can I pet it, Mama? Can I keep it?'

'I do not know if there are coneys in Gwynedd, Elen,' Joanna admitted. 'It is not native to England, was brought over some years back by the Normans for their sport.'

Elen's other queries now became academic; the rabbit fled as soon as she moved. 'Oh, Mama, it's gone!'

'I'm sorry, sweetheart.' Joanna was, sorry for so much. These weeks at Brewood had not been happy ones for her daughter. Not a day passed that Elen did not ask when they were going home.

Sometimes she sounded fretful, petulant, at other times unbearably plaintive, and at no time did Joanna have a satisfactory answer for her. 'Soon' meant little to a homesick five year old who missed her father. It was coming to mean less and less to Joanna, too.

Several nuns were passing, lugging heavy oaken buckets of well water. They paused to beam upon Elen; she was a great favourite with them all, and when Sister Avelina offered to take her into the kitchen for bread and honey, she accepted readily. But she'd taken only a few steps when she stopped, whirled and came running back to Joanna.

'Kiss me, Mama,' she directed, and Joanna knelt, for a moment hugged her tight. Elen grinned, and then she was sprinting after the nuns, while Joanna stood very still, fighting her fear. If Llewelyn could not forgive her, she'd lose more than his love; she'd lose her children, too. When a marriage broke apart, the husband kept the children, and if he chose to deny his wife the right to see them, she had no legal recourse. Her own plight was even more perilous than that of most rejected wives, for her husband was a Prince, a Prince with the power to banish her from his domains, from their children's lives.

Joanna did not move until Elen's small figure was no longer in sight. And then she turned, began to walk away from the priory, under the leafy, rustling clouds of autumn oak and dappled elm. When her grandmother had divorced the French King, their two little daughters had remained with Louis. They were six and two then, and Eleanor did not see them again until they were women grown, in their twenties. Eleanor had apparently accepted the loss of her children as the price she must pay for Henry and the Crown of England. But Joanna knew her own grieving would be beyond hope, beyond healing. The loss of her father she could, in time, accept. She could even learn to accept the loss of her husband. But not her children. Not Davydd. Not Elen. Not ever.

More than four weeks had passed since she'd come to the priory, six weeks since she'd ridden away from Dolwyddelan. Soon after her arrival in Brewood, she'd dispatched a man with a stilted and terse letter for Llewelyn, asking his permission to keep Elen in England beyond the month's grace he'd given her. In the weeks since, there'd been numerous sleepless nights when she'd laboured over a second letter to her husband, a letter in which she sought his understanding,

463

his forgiveness. At dawn, she'd gather up her splotched and futile handiwork, feed it into the fire.

She was no less homesick than Elen. Her yearning for Davydd was like a physical ache, one no herbs or ointments could ease. Her need for Llewelyn was no less intense; her body's thwarted cravings robbed her of sleep at night, and her memories wreaked havoc upon her daylight hours. But as much as she wanted to return to Llewelyn, she was terrified of doing do, terrified of having to face him and hear him say that their marriage was over. It was easier to do nothing, to cling to her shreds of hope and tell herself that all would somehow work out if only she gave them enough time.

In her despair, she'd convinced herself that Richard would have the answers she needed. But Richard had failed her, and she knew she was now failing herself. Unable to face her future, unable to come to terms with her past. Grieving for the father she'd lost, not to death, but to merciless, recurring dreams in which she was walled up with Maude in that Windsor dungeon and the bloated little body swaying from a Shrewsbury gallows became Davydd's.

The woods were alive with the interior rhythms of their wildlife, echoing to soft rustles and muted trills. Joanna stopped under a maple tree and the wind rained russet leaves down upon her. One leaf spread its wings, revealed itself to be a butterfly mottled in black and gold. The butterflies at Aber were the colour of the sky; from May to September, they hovered over wildflower and marsh-grass, flickering blue flames to be extinguished at the first frost. Joanna leaned back against the tree's gnarled trunk, and closed her eyes. Did Llewelyn, too, lie awake till dawn? How was he dealing with his grief, his guilt? Had he learned to live with his ghosts?

'Madame!' The scream was shrill, fraught with fear, utterly out of place in a setting of such peace. Joanna tensed; the cry came again, and she turned towards the sound. She soon saw a blur of white, found a woman on her knees beside a fallen log. She looked up as Joanna reached her, and Joanna recognized one of the young novice nuns. Her habit was torn and dirtied, her face scratched by her flight into the woods, and she had no breath for speech, not even when Joanna grasped her shoulders, shook her frantically.

'Has my daughter been hurt? For God's sake, tell me!'

'Oh, Madame, thank Jesus I found you!' The girl was on her feet now, but had to lean on Joanna for support. 'They took us by surprise, rode into the priory as bold as could be. We thought it was a raid, and Sister Avelina tried to hide your Elen in the chancel. But one of the men called to her and she ran to him, Madame, ran right to him. He demanded to see you, my lady, and then our Prioress. We were so very frightened, Madame; all know how godless the Welsh are. But . . . but they did not hurt us. They talked to Prioress Alditha, then rode away, and . . . oh, Madame, they took with them your daughter. They took away your little girl!'

The quarter-hour it took Joanna to reach the priory was the most terrifying time of her life. Running through the woods, she caught her gown repeatedly upon protruding branches, tripped over exposed tree roots and rocks, fought her way free of the thickets looming up in her path, seemingly set upon entrapping her forever in the midst of this God-cursed forest. By the time she was in sight of the priory walls, she was scratched and bruised and thoroughly dishevelled, her ears echoing to the sobbing sounds of her own breathing, to the cry of 'Elen' that came to her lips of its own volition, that went unanswered in the strange silence that had enveloped the priory.

The guest house was to the north of the church, set apart from the nuns' dormitory and infirmary. It was there that Joanna shared a chamber with Elen. It would, she knew, be empty. She reached the latch just as the door opened, and she all but fell into the room, into Llewelyn's arms.

He put his hands on her waist to steady her, said, 'Are you hurt?'

She shook her head, and he released her. She was suddenly dizzy, and leaned back against the door. There was a sharp pain pressing against her ribs, cutting off her breath. 'Elen . . . where is she?'

'On her way back to Gwynedd.'

Joanna was too appalled for anger. 'Jesus God, Llewelyn, did you have to do it like that?'

'I was thinking of her safety. I did not want her here should word get out that I'm at the priory.'

The common sense of that could not be denied; some of Joanna's panic began to subside. But then Llewelyn said, 'I made a mistake in letting you take her, Joanna. I thought she would be safe because of her sex. But the more I thought on it, the more uneasy I became. The risk was just too great. I'll not allow her to leave Wales again.'

Pride had always been of paramount concern to Joanna. But not now. 'I know you have the power to take Davydd and Elen from me.

I can only beg you not to do that, to remember how much I do love them –'

'Whatever happens between us, I'd not deny you the right to see our children. I would still provide for you, would allow you to remain in Gwynedd to be near Davydd and Elen if you did not want to return to England. How could you think I'd do less than that?'

Joanna had no answer for him, for she could not explain her fear even to herself, an instinctive, elemental fear that had nothing whatsoever to do with logic or even love. She drew several shaken breaths. 'Are you saying that our marriage is over?'

'I do not know, Joanna,' he said, and there was in his voice a sadness that she found far more chilling than anger.

'Is it not dangerous for you to be here, on English soil?' she asked abruptly, and he shrugged.

'Probably. But I have no plans to tarry longer than necessary.' He saw that she was not reassured, and added, 'The borderland is quiet at present. John has ordered his army to disperse.'

He was close enough to touch; Joanna's fingers brushed his sleeve, came to rest upon his arm. 'Richard told me that twenty-eight hostages were hanged at Nottingham, all those who were being held at my father's court . . . save only Gruffydd. But there were others, mayhap a handful, who were being held elsewhere, and they still live. Richard promised me he would seek out their identities, then pass on that information to you.'

'And he did, a fortnight ago. A curious letter, Joanna, for an English King's son to write to a Welsh Prince. He was cautious, made no promises that might compromise him, but he implied, none the less, that he would speak for my son if he could.' Llewelyn reached out, traced the path of a scratch that marked her throat; at the unexpected touch, so like a caress, Joanna began to tremble. 'He told me, too, that your warning saved Gruffydd's life.'

'And do you believe him?'

'Yes,' he said, 'I do.'

'Then . . . then can you not forgive me?'

'It is not a matter of forgiveness, Joanna. I would that it were.' For a moment longer, his fingers lingered on her throat, and then he stepped back. 'Did you see John? Did you see your father?'

'No! I swore to you that I would not. I did not lie to you.'

'We have to talk about him, about John. I have to know what you feel towards him now. Joanna, I have to know.'

466

She twisted her hands together, gripping her wedding ring as if it were a talisman. 'I loved him, I believed in him. I married you to please him. And now . . . now I think of that little boy in Shrewsbury, I think of our Davydd and . . . and I know that I could not face him again. I cannot love the man he is, I cannot. But I remember how much I loved the man I thought he was . . . and it hurts more than I can bear. If he'd died, I'd still have had memories. But now even my memories are false. They do not comfort, they only torment . . .'

She closed her eyes, and then felt Llewelyn's fingers on her face, slowly wiping away her tears. She sobbed, and moved into his arms. She'd lost her veil, and he stroked her hair, smoothed the untidy ebony braids, brushed back stray wisps from her temples.

'You must not ever think,' he said, 'that I do not feel your pain.' She made a wordless murmur, pressed closer. He caught the familiar fragrance of her perfume, felt her hands sliding up his back, and damned himself for a fool, for an unwary moment in which he'd almost believed that he meant only to comfort her, to hold her as she wept.

Joanna had raised her head from his shoulder. Her eyes no longer shone with tears; they were luminous, filled with sunlight, with such naked need that he caught his breath. Taking his hand in hers, she kissed each finger in turn, bit down gently on his thumb; her tongue circled his palm, and his free hand tightened on her hair.

For a moment that seemed endless to Joanna, he did not move. And then he lowered his head, brought his mouth down hard upon hers, not ending the kiss until they both were breathless. He'd begun to fumble with her clothing, swearing when the lacings of her bliaut resisted his impatient fingers. She raised her arms so he could pull the gown over her head; the chemise quickly followed. He kissed her again, caressing her belly and thighs until she moaned, arched against him. Pushing her down upon the bed, he unbuckled his scabbard.

When he lowered his body on to hers, he was not gentle, but neither was Joanna. That was not what she wanted from him now. For more than two months, she'd slept as chastely as a nun, and her body had taken fire with the first touch of his fingers on her throat. She had no need of prolonged foreplay, and she entwined her arms tightly around him as he parted her thighs. 'Now, love, now . . . oh, yes, now . . .' She climaxed almost at once, with his third thrust, and then again when she felt him tense, groan and jerk convulsively, gasping 'Siwan' against her ear.

After a time, Llewelyn raised himself up, rolled over on to his back. Joanna was not yet ready to move. She knew it was a common belief that a woman's lust was greater than a man's and, for the first time, she wondered if there might not be truth to that folk wisdom. She could only marvel now at the fevered urgency that had so utterly consumed her so short a time before. But she knew that she had given Llewelyn pleasure no less intense than he had given her. His breathing was still uneven and shallow, a pulse was beating rapidly in his throat, and his body glistened with perspiration. She leaned over, touched the tip of her tongue to a droplet of sweat trickling towards his chin. He did not respond and, a moment later, rose from the bed, reached for the clothing scattered about the floor.

Joanna's sense of languid well-being dissipated in the span of seconds, in the time it took Llewelyn to turn away from her. She was suddenly cold, confused, afraid. 'Llewelyn . . . are you angry with me?'

'No, not with you, *breila*.'

The endearment gave her little comfort; it was too obviously offered as a courtesy. Nor did his denial carry conviction. 'You are angry,' she said slowly, 'and you were not angry ere we made love. Beloved . . . beloved, I do not understand. You cannot deny that you still want me, not now –'

'Of course I still want you,' Llewelyn said sharply. 'Our problems did not take root in our bed.' He was already dressed; moving to the table, he pulled the laver towards him, splashed cold water on to his face, and then gave an abrupt mirthless laugh. A pity he'd not thought to do that sooner!

He'd spoken the truth; he was angry with himself, not Joanna, and disconcerted by the realization of just how much he did still want her. In the six weeks since her departure, he'd had few restful hours, no peace of mind. Night after night, he found himself lying awake in the bed he'd shared with Joanna, thinking of his son, thinking of the youths hanged at Nottingham, thinking of his wife – John's daughter. And in time he'd come to a decision, that if Joanna could not give him the answers he had to have, it would be better to end their marriage. To walk away from Joanna would be the most difficult act of his life, but he knew he could do it. However much it hurt, he could do it. But he could not send her into English exile against her will; he could never deny her the right to see their children. He'd sought to reassure her of that, promised she could stay in Wales, and now the full implications of that rash promise were all too clear to him. What would it be like to have her in Gwynedd, to have her so tormentingly close at hand and yet no longer his?

Joanna hastily drew her chemise over her head, followed him to the table. 'What is it, then? Is it that you no longer trust me?'

Surprisingly, he shook his head. 'I do trust you, Joanna. You told me you'd never meant to betray me. As hurt and angry as I was, I think I believed you even then. I must have, else I'd never have permitted you to take Elen. I know you were not choosing between us when you sent John that warning. You wanted to save your father's life, but you also wanted to stop a war, a war you thought I'd lose. And you did, *breila*.' His mouth softened. 'I might quarrel with your methods, but I can hardly take issue with your results. The English King's banner does not fly over Gwynedd . . . because of you. And my son has had a two month reprieve . . . again because of you.'

'You do not know how I've wanted to hear you say that, Llewelyn. But now you have, and it seems to count for naught. If you still trust me, what is it, then, that is keeping us apart? My love, I do not understand . . .' And then it came to her, the only possible answer, and she caught his arm, moved so she could look into his face.

'Unless . . . unless you can no longer love John's daughter? My God, Llewelyn, is that it?'

'Yes . . . it is,' he admitted, and heard her indrawn breath, sharp as a blade. 'Joanna, Joanna, listen and try to understand. John is going to kill my son. I've had to face that. It is only a matter of time; sooner or later, he will give a command and Gruffydd will be dragged out to an English gallows . . . or worse. Gruffydd is going to die, and there is nothing I can do to stop it. Even if there was, I could not do it. I cannot buy Gruffydd's life with Gwynedd's sovereignty. Twenty-eight hostages died at Nottingham because I could not keep faith with John. I cannot bargain for Gruffydd over their dead bodies.'

His voice was quite even, tautly controlled. But Joanna saw what that control cost him, saw the way the tendons suddenly stood out in his throat, saw the toll these past weeks had taken in the newly-chiselled lines around his eyes, his mouth, and she was both awed and appalled by the strength of will that enabled him to forge such a resolve. There was nothing on God's earth that she would not have sacrificed for Davydd or Elen.

'For more than six years, Joanna, you have been torn between us, between your love for John and your love for me. You've never been able to give me all your heart, never been able to pledge your loyalty to me utterly and unreservedly. No, lass, I am not blaming you for that. I understood, and I did my best to accept it. I taught myself to curb my tongue, to leave much unsaid. But no more. We can never go back to the way it was, Joanna.'

'I know that, Llewelyn, but . . .' Joanna's voice trailed off. This was the nightmare that had held her in Brewood. So often had she anticipated this moment that it was as if they'd played out this scene before, as if she'd always known the time would come when she'd be listening to him explain, kindly but implacably, why their marriage had to end.

'For all our marriage you've defended John, offered excuses for his cruelties, blinded yourself to the unholy truth about him. But I can no longer indulge your love for this man. I'd learn to resent you, and in time I might even learn to hate you, *breila*. Rather than have it come to that, I'd sooner end the marriage now, whilst we can still salvage friendship from it.'

'But it does not have to be like that, Llewelyn. I would not defend John. How could I? My loyalties are no longer divided, I swear it.'

Never before had Llewelyn heard Joanna call John by his Christian name; it was always 'my father' or 'the King' or, with intimates, 'Papa'. Was it an unconscious, anguished attempt to distance herself from John? Or a desperate denial of a blood bond she knew he found abhorrent? He put his hands on her shoulders, said quietly:

'Joanna, you do not understand how much I'd be asking of you. Do you truly think you could disavow a lifetime of love? That you could remember the frightened five year old who was taken to John at Rouen and then harden your heart against him?'

'Yes,' Joanna whispered, and he tilted her face up, kissed her on the forehead.

'Beloved, I think not. I'm not even sure I'd have the right to expect that of you.'

'I give you the right. You are my life, you and our children. Why will you not believe me?'

'Ah, Joanna . . . I want to believe you. But I know what we'd be facing. I know what our future would be likely to hold. You do not think that John has abandoned his plans to claim Gwynedd for the Crown? There will never be peace between us, *breila*, not until one of us is dead. For now, John fears to cross into Wales, but he's dispatched the English fleet to blockade our coastal waters, and he's seeking to overthrow me with the aid of the sons of my uncles, Davydd and Rhodri. They've been dwelling in English exile, and he hopes to make puppet Princes out of them, promising them most of Gwynedd if they lead a rebellion against me.'

'He offered them most of Gwynedd?' Joanna echoed, sounding so shocked that he felt the need to reassure her.

'You need not fear. There is a world of difference between being invested with possession in London and then taking possession in Gwynedd. John's grant is more symbolic than substantial, but it does show how utterly intent he is upon vengeance, upon seeing my head impaled on London's new bridge –'

Llewelyn broke off, for Joanna was no longer listening. She was staring past him with glazed amber eyes, and when he touched her shoulder, he found that her body had gone rigid with rage.

'Liar!' she spat. 'That double-dealing liar! He promised me, he swore on his oath of honour that he'd safeguard Davydd's inheritance, that I need never fear for Davydd's future. And fool that I was, I believed him!'

'Does it truly surprise you so, Joanna? Davydd is my son.'

'He is my son, too . . . and John's grandson.'

To Joanna, it was the final betrayal. She turned away, moved to the window. Several of the nuns had gathered at a discreet distance. They were casting uneasy yet curious glances towards the Welshmen who were now loitering near the guest house, keeping an anxious vigil for Llewelyn. So turbulent had this past hour been that she'd all but forgotten the danger Llewelyn could be in, the risk he'd taken in coming into England. But the sight of his waiting men brought her fear back in a rush.

'Llewelyn, you must go!'

'I know.' But he made no move to depart. Instead, he stepped towards her, pulled her away from the window. 'I do not mind you bedazzling my men, but I'd hate for you to disconcert those poor nuns!'

It was not the realization that she was clad only in her chemise that brought the blood up into Joanna's cheeks, it was the unexpected amusement in Llewelyn's voice. She started to ask him how he could be joking now, of all times, when she saw what he had in his hand, her discarded gown.

'You'd best make haste to dress, *breila*. We've a long ride ahead of us.'

471

She raised her eyes to his face, and then closed the space remaining between them. He drew her into his arms, for a brief moment held her close.

'My love, you will not be sorry. You will not ever be sorry.'

Llewelyn could not share her certainty. 'We'll try, Joanna,' he said softly. 'At least we'll try.'

May, 1213
Dover Castle, England

Somewhere a dog was howling, a forlorn, haunting plaint that echoed eerily upon the sea-misted air, rending the fabric of Gruffydd's troubled dreams and jarring him into abrupt, uneasy wakefulness. He dreaded nights like this, dreaded the solitude and the silence, the hours alone with his ghosts.

He could think of few sounds as mournful as a dog's howling . . . or as disquieting. All knew it to be an ill omen, a harbinger of coming woe, and he instinctively fumbled for his talisman, the agate stone that gave the wearer strength, valour, the fortitude to prevail against his enemies. His guards had long since stolen his rings; he'd managed, though, to conceal the agate in his clothing and, in the months since Nottingham, it had been a secret source of comfort, a tangible link with Gwynedd. But his fingers plucked in vain at the torn wool tunic, the begrimed shirt. Fully awake now, he remembered. The agate was gone, lost on the road to Dover.

It was of no matter, he told himself resolutely. Dogs barked and men died, but the one happening need not presage the other. He lay back upon the pallet, began to whisper rapidly, 'Sweet Lord Jesus defend me, gránt me remission of all my sins and keep me from all peril. Lord, save me waking, save me sleeping, that I may sleep in peace and awake in Thee in the glory of Paradise.' He felt better at that; soon after, he slept.

When he awakened again, sun was seeking entry through the arrow loops high above his head, and two men were standing over his pallet with drawn swords.

In answer to John's urgent summons to arms, the men of England began to gather in early May at Barham Downs in Kent. The response was heartening; the impending French invasion had vitalized public opinion in John's favour, and those unmoved by patriotism were motivated by the knowledge that to refuse to bear arms was to risk 'perpetual servitude'.

For the past week John had been staying with the Knights Templar in Ewell, and it was to Ewell that Richard was returning on this Tuesday morning in mid-May. Chilham Castle was less than twenty miles from Ewell, and Richard had taken advantage of his proximity to pay a courtesy call upon his young betrothed.

He invariably enjoyed his visits to Chilham. It was gratifying to spend a day riding about the manor demesne, to see the green fields and well-fed livestock and know it would all eventually be his. That Rohese de Dover was a gentle, biddable girl, shyly eager to please, only made his marital prospects all the more alluring.

But he'd had an ulterior motive for this particular visit to Chilham, to escape, if only for a few days, the oppressive atmosphere of his father's court. What John had most feared was at last coming to pass: the circle was closing.

Sparing Gruffydd had not sundered Llewelyn's alliance with the other Welsh Princes. The hangings of the hostages had unified the Welsh as nothing else could have done. Rhys Gryg had fallen into John's hands, was being held captive at the royal castle of Carmarthen. But Maelgwn and Gwenwynwyn were ravaging Norman settlements in South Wales, and Llewelyn had retaken the only two castles still in Norman control; he had now regained all of the Perfeddwlad, regained all he'd been forced to yield up to John at Aberconwy. The Welsh were a God-cursed, stiff-necked and utterly vexatious people, John said bitterly, but they did have an inexplicable ability to rise Phoenix-like from the ashes of defeat, to soar upward on wings too scorched for flight.

As troublesome an enemy as Llewelyn was proving to be, he did not pose a serious threat to John's sovereignty. But as winter thawed into a verdant spring, John found himself facing a more dangerous foe, one who had the power to do what Llewelyn could not, to bring his reign and his life to an abrupt and bloody end.

At Christmas, the Pope had at last invoked his ultimate weapon, dispatched Stephen Langton to the French court with letters formally deposing John as King of England and freeing his subjects from their oaths of allegiance. Philip was more than eager to show himself a good son of the Church, and he immediately announced plans to invade England and claim John's Crown for a more worthy aspirant, his own son Louis.

With a French fleet being rigged at Boulogne, John was forced to acknowledge that time had finally run out, and he hastened to send envoys to Rome. This eleventh-hour capitulation gained him an extension of the Pope's deadline; the papal legate Pandulf was now in England to accept his submission to papal authority.

By coming to terms with the Pope, John had thus been able to deny Philip the opportunity to cloak himself in the mantle of the Church, to sanctify his invasion as a holy war of retribution against a renegade King. But if Philip's pretensions had been sabotaged, his ambitions remained intact; the French fleet would sail with or without the Pope's blessings. Which meant, Richard thought bleakly, that his father would soon be fighting a war on two fronts, trying to repulse a French landing in the south whilst Philip's Welsh allies turned the Marches into a wasteland of smouldering manors and charred fields. And if it came to that, how long would John's disaffected barons hold fast? How long ere men like Derby and Huntingdon and de Clare elected to throw their lot in with Philip?

Upon his arrival at Ewell, Richard was surprised to find Isabelle walking in the garden with her two youngest children. He had not seen much of Isabelle in recent months, still less of his little half-brothers and sister, for John had become obsessed with fears for their safety. After learning of de Vesci and Fitz Walter's intriguing, he'd required armed bodyguards, not only for himself but for his family, too; he'd even gone so far as to give orders that no one be admitted to the presence of his eldest son and heir without written permission.

Isabelle greeted Richard with unfeigned warmth, for they were long-standing allies in a conspiracy of self-interest, one dedicated to John's weal.

'Did my father meet with the papal legate?'

'Yes, they met yesterday in Dover.' Isabelle gestured for the nurses to take the children on ahead. 'It did not go well, I fear. Will told me that Pandulf was aloof, unable to conceal his doubts, his suspicions that John was not acting in good faith. And the terms offered were the very ones John had scorned for these five years past. He had to agree to receive Stephen Langton as Archbishop of Canterbury, to reinstate the clergy who'd gone into exile when the Interdict was declared, and to recompense the Church for its losses.

But what I think John found hardest to swallow was the Pope's insistence that he pardon Eustace de Vesci and Robert Fitz Walter, restore them to favour.'

From their respective exiles in Scotland and France, de Vesci and Fitz Walter had been loudly and persistently proclaiming themselves martyrs to conscience, Christians who could not serve an excommunicate King. Richard had not expected the Pope to give credence to so spurious a rationale for treason, and he could only shake his head in wonder, conclude that the name this particular Pope had chosen for himself was uncommonly apt: Innocent III.

'I thought I knew John so well, Richard, but I've never seen him like this . . . never.'

'What man would not be distraught, sore crazed with wrath?'

'But that is just it; he's not in a tearing rage. Richard, he is . . . well, there's but one way to describe his mood. Do you remember when Reginald de Dammartin gave John those weighted dice? Remember how he kept winning every toss, until he finally relented and showed us the trick? He is acting now just as he did that day, like a man who knows he cannot lose.'

Isabelle glanced about, reassured herself that none were within hearing range. 'He has called a council meeting for this forenoon, and he means to summon Pandulf back to Ewell on the morrow. I do not know what he has in mind. I can only tell you what he said, that he has thought of a way to thwart Philip's invasion plans, whilst gaining His Holiness the Pope as a steadfast ally.'

'Papa is more than clever; at times, he can be utterly ingenious. But not even Merlin could manage that. The Pope would never trust Papa again. Nor would he intervene on Papa's behalf unless the Church had a stake in the war, and it does not.'

Isabelle shrugged. 'I dare say you're right. But John is strangely calm for a man beset on all sides. He – Richard, look. The prisoner being escorted through the gateway . . . is that not Llewelyn's son?'

Richard spun around. Gruffydd's guards were pulling him from his horse. He stumbled, nearly lost his balance, and looked in Richard's direction. Richard saw recognition on his face and, for the briefest of moments, an involuntary appeal.

John glanced around the table at the few men he did not suspect of complicity in the de Vesci-Fitz Walter plot. They'd listened intently, without interruption, as he explained what he planned to do, and why.

476

and he'd seen their initial shock slowly give way to understanding, and then approval.

'Well?' he said. 'Now that you know, what say you?'

'It ought to work,' Chester conceded, and then added, with uncharacteristic enthusiasm, 'For certès, Philip will be caught utterly off guard.'

'So, too, will His Holiness the Pope.' Will was beaming; it had been some years since John had seen such unqualified admiration in his brother's eyes. Pembroke, too, was nodding appreciatively. But it was Reginald de Dammartin, the fugitive Count of Boulogne, who echoed John's own opinion of his desperate ploy. Dammartin was a newcomer to John's inner circle; he'd fled to England the preceding year after a bitter dispute with the French King. Aggressively independent, not overly scrupulous, and possessed of a brutally candid tongue, he had not found many friends at John's court. But as he was also utterly without self-pity, undeniably quick-witted, and a raconteur par excellence, with an inexhaustible supply of boisterous, bawdy tales as uproarious as they were unseemly, John had conceived a genuine liking for the man, quite apart from Dammartin's considerable value as a political ally. For not only was Dammartin Count of Boulogne by right of his wife, he also held the Norman fiefs of Aumale, Domfort, and Mortain, which John had lost to Philip in 1204.

Dammartin was grinning. 'There is but one word for such an underhanded stratagem – brilliant.'

The other men laughed. They were still laughing as the solar door opened and Gruffydd was thrust into the chamber.

His guards shoved Gruffydd forward, forced him to kneel before the English King. John pushed his chair back from the table, watched Gruffydd in unnerving silence, his eyes speculative, not easily read.

'You're looking rather bedraggled these days,' he said at last, and some of Gruffydd's fear was lost in a sudden surge of hatred.

'I'll not beg. No matter what you mean to do.'

'What I mean to do,' John said blandly, 'is to instruct your guards that you may have a bath upon your return to Dover.'

Gruffydd's jaw dropped. To be offered the promise of future tomorrows when he'd been measuring his life in minutes was a shock not easily absorbed. 'Why would you want to do a kindness for me?'

The corner of John's mouth twitched. 'I see you have your father's impeccable manners. As it happens, I mean to do you a greater

477

kindness than that. I've decided to allow you to write a letter to your father.' He beckoned to one of the guards. 'Cut his bonds, but make no mistake; he's not to be trusted. There is parchment and pen and inkwell on the table, Gruffydd. You do know how to write? If not, you can dictate to one of my scribes.'

Gruffydd flushed. 'I can write. I'm a Prince's son.'

John's smile was sardonic, but he said only, 'You may write what you please, within reason. I think you should assure Llewelyn that you are well, that you are not being maltreated or abused. You may tell him, too, that I am willing to let him send Joanna to my court in order to verify the truth of your assurances.'

Gruffydd was surreptitiously rubbing his wrists, while trying desperately to make sense of John's sudden benevolence. In the nine months since the Nottingham hangings, he'd dwelt in death's shadow; not a day dawned when he did not wonder if it would be his last. What enabled him to endure was the intensity of his yearning for freedom – and for vengeance. But if a beneficent spirit had offered to grant his lesser wishes, he'd have asked for a hot bath and contact of some sort with his family. It seemed almost diabolical to him that John should have pinpointed his vulnerabilities with such uncanny accuracy.

'Well?' John was regarding him with amused impatience. 'What are you waiting for? The sooner you write the letter, the sooner you'll get word from home.'

Home. To Gruffydd's horror, tears suddenly filled his eyes. 'No,' he said huskily. 'No. I'll write no letter for you, now or ever.'

It had never occurred to John that Gruffydd might refuse. 'Why ever not?' he demanded, sounding more astonished than angry.

'Because you want it written. I admit I do not know why. But if it serves your interests, it cannot be to my father's advantage. So I'll not do it.'

It was suddenly quite still. Even to Gruffydd, his words rang hollow, not so much defiance as doomed bravado. John was slowly shaking his head. 'Do not be a fool, boy. Surely you know I can make you write that letter.'

Gruffydd's stomach knotted. 'You can try.'

John pushed his chair back still farther; wood grated harshly on the flagstones. 'I cannot decide if you're an utter idiot or merely foolhardy beyond belief.' He made an abrupt gesture and the guards jerked Gruffydd to his feet. 'Take him back to Dover, where he can think upon his lunacy.'

Reginald de Dammartin was the first to break the silence that followed Gruffydd's departure. 'Are all the Welsh as mad as that?'

'I would that they were,' John said tersely. 'If so, Wales would be an English shire by now.' Rising, he moved away from the table and, for the first time, noticed his son. Richard had entered unobtrusively some moments before, after a futile attempt to coax Isabelle into interceding on Gruffydd's behalf; she'd parried with a cynical and unanswerable, 'If John indulges me, it is because I ask only for what I know he's willing to give.'

Gruffydd's intransigence had not surprised Richard any, but his father's forbearance had. He reached John just as Will said approvingly, 'Your patience with the boy was commendable, John, in truth it was.'

'That was not patience, Will. He called my bluff, pure and simple. The joke is that I doubt if he truly knew what he was doing even as he did it!'

'What do you mean?'

'Think upon it, Will. How would you have me explain to my daughter that Gruffydd's assurances of good health were extracted under torture? Even if I resorted to more subtle means of persuasion, withheld food or sleep until he agreed to cooperate, there'd be no way to keep him from regaling Joanna with all the gory details afterwards. It should be obvious by now that the damned fool is too simpleminded to scare!'

While there was understandable exasperation in John's voice, he seemed to be taking Gruffydd's defiance with remarkable equanimity. Isabelle was right, Richard decided; something was definitely in the wind.

John was shaking his head again, in disbelief. 'I dare say if I'd told him he was free to return to Wales, he'd then have insisted upon staying in England! I ought to have reminded him of the fate of his grand-uncles; mayhap that would have shaken some sense into him.'

'I know about as much of Wales as I do of the heathen kingdoms of Cathay,' Dammartin drawled, 'and I confess I find them of equal interest. What befell the boy's kin?'

'After my father lost the battle of Crogen to Llewelyn's grand-father, Owain Fawr, he took vengeance upon his Welsh hostages.

479

Two of them were Owain's sons, Llewelyn's uncles. Their eyes were put out with red-hot awls.'

Dammartin was not shocked, for Philip had been known to do the same to captured English soldiers; while Norman knights and men of rank were routinely ransomed, it was not unheard of to mutilate common soldiers, thus rendering them unfit for further combat. But for Will, that was a jab into an old wound.

'I've never been able to understand how our father could have done that,' he muttered. 'It was not like him.' He hesitated. 'John . . . you'd never take vengeance of that sort upon Llewelyn, by blinding Gruffydd?'

Will saw at once that he'd made a monumental blunder. John's eyes were suddenly opaque; a muscle jerked in his cheek. 'I told you why I hanged those accursed hostages! It was necessary to set an example, to remind my barons how much was at stake. I did what had to be done, and I'm bone-weary of being criticized for it.

'Christ, the utter hypocrisy of it all! Who spoke up for those blinded Welsh hostages? Or those hapless souls hanged by my sainted brother Richard at Châlus? He took his deathbed vengeance upon men, women, and children alike, and none called him "butcher" for it. As for that double-dealing hellspawn on the French throne, his hands are as bloody as Richard's. I may treat my Jews like milch cows, milk them for all they're worth, but they've not been slaughtered by rampaging mobs as they were in Richard's reign, and I've never burned Jews at the stake the way Philip has – eighty at Brie-Comte-Robert when a Christian was found slain.'

John paused, breathless, realizing too late just how much he'd revealed. 'Leave me,' he said, in tones that brooked no argument. Richard alone braved his displeasure by remaining.

'Why did you want Gruffydd to write to Llewelyn, Papa? What would you gain by that?'

John was standing by the window, watching as Gruffydd and his guards rode through the gateway, on their way back to confinement at Dover Castle. 'Llewelyn warned me, Richard. He told me plainly that Joanna was his hostage as Gruffydd was mine. But I did not believe him, not then.'

Richard was suddenly sorry he'd stayed. 'And now?'

'Twice in the past six months, I've summoned Joanna to my court, and twice he has refused to let her come. The last time I even offered to provide hostages if it would ease his qualms. Hostages . . . for my own daughter! And all I got in return was a stilted letter from Joanna, saying it was not possible for her to leave Wales, a letter she obviously wrote at Llewelyn's direction.'

Richard had learned to pick his way through conversations about his sister as if each one were a quagmire. But never had he so dreaded making a misstep. Knowing that John was too adept at reading faces, he busied himself at the table, pouring wine for them both. 'So you thought Llewelyn might relent if you made it worth his while?' he ventured cautiously, and John nodded.

'But I did not reckon with his son's lunatic yearnings for martyrdom! It might be foresighted to look after that lad, Richard; what could better serve England than to have Gruffydd one day reigning as Prince of Gwynedd? Can you envision him ever humbling his pride to an English King as Llewelyn did at Aberconwy? When pigs fly and monks no longer like their wine!'

Richard was relieved that they seemed to be edging away from the precipice. To banish Joanna into the peripheral reaches of memory where she could do John no harm, he said hastily, 'How long are you going to keep me in suspense, Papa? Isabelle says you've a scheme to outwit Philip and foil his invasion plans. What do you have in mind . . . a miracle?'

John laughed. 'I am merely taking a page from Philip and Llewelyn's own book. Philip has had great sport these months past posing as a pious champion of the Church; to convince the Pope that he was acting in good faith, he even went so far as to release the long-suffering Ingeborg from Étampes Castle! And Llewelyn, too, has had his fun at my expense, turning treason into a crusade for Christendom, all with the Pope's blessings. You ask what I mean to do, lad? I mean to show them that I can play that game, too, and with far greater skill.'

Philip was currently holding court in the sleepy village of Gravelines, and his restive barons were forced to seek livelier sport in the sea-coast town of Calais, just twelve miles to the west. Hugh de Lusignan, Count of La Marche, and his younger brother Ralph, Count of Eu, rode into Calais just before dusk, headed for their favourite wharfside alehouse.

'Three days till Ascensiontide.' Hugh shoved a drunk aside, claimed the table closest to the door. 'Think you that John is keeping count?'

'I am, for certès. I've a wager with our cousin Geoffrey, am hazarding one hundred marks that the old hermit is right.'

'Wishful thinking, Ralph. I'd have to be able to spit into John's open coffin ere I'd believe he was well and truly dead. He may have the scruples of a Scotsman and the morals of a rutting swine, but he has Satan's own luck.'

'Anyone using the words "swine" and "Satan" in one sentence can only be talking about John Plantagenet. John Lackland. John of the Devil's brood. John, the Pope's sworn man.'

The room was hazy with smoke from hearth and reeking tallow candles, and Hugh's eyes were stinging. He blinked up at the man weaving towards their table, said trenchantly, 'In your cups already, Fitz Walter?'

Robert Fitz Walter straddled the bench, sat down without waiting to be asked. 'I'm nowhere near as drunk as I hope to get. Since you're both still sober, I take it you have not heard yet? The papal legate Pandulf landed at Wissant on Saturday, wasted no time joining Philip at Gravelines. He carried a right interesting message for Philip, told him the Pope demands that he abandon the invasion of England. He said if Philip does not heed the warning, the Pope will lay France under Interdict again and, if need be, will excommunicate each and every man who sets foot on English soil.'

Hugh and his brother exchanged startled glances. 'If that's an example of your English humour, it's not much to my liking.'

'Philip did not find it very amusing, either.'

Hugh set his goblet down, sloshed red wine on to the table. 'You are not jesting, are you?'

'In truth, it does sound like a diabolical jest of sorts, but it is not mine; John's the one who is laughing. Do you not want to know why the Pope is of a sudden backing John, taking such a protective interest in English affairs? England is now a papal fief, part of the patrimony of St Peter.'

They were staring at him, dumbfounded. Hugh found his tongue first. 'You're daft or drunk, or both!'

'Pandulf told Philip that on Wednesday last John did freely surrender to God and the Holy Mother Church of Rome the kingdoms of England and Ireland, to hold them henceforth as the Pope's vassal.'

Fitz Walter helped himself to Hugh's wine, drank too deeply and gave a harsh, spluttering laugh. 'All know those tales told of men who sold their souls to the Devil. But John must be the first to turn a profit by selling his to God!'

'Wrath of God, man, how can you laugh about it?'

'What would you have me do? Rant and rave and sicken on my own bile like Philip? When I left him, he was venting his fury upon God, John, Innocent, his servants, his dogs, all within reach. But it'll change nothing. He's already learned what a confrontation with the Church can cost, is not likely to go that route again. I'll wager that he calls off the invasion as the Pope demands, and turns his rage, instead, upon a safer target, John's ally, the Count of Flanders. Whilst in England, John will continue to rule as arbitrarily as ever, except that the Pope will now have a vested interest in John's survival.'

'You're taking this rather well for a man who can now expect to live out his remaining days in French exile,' Hugh said suspiciously, and Fitz Walter grinned.

'Did I forget to tell you? My cousin de Vesci and I are included in the Pope's peace. I will be returning to England as soon as my safe-conduct does arrive.'

Hugh snorted. 'And of course John will welcome you back with true Christian forgiveness in his heart! Just how long do you expect this papal "peace" to last?'

Fitz Walter rose unhurriedly to his feet. 'Long enough to serve my purposes.' His eyes fell upon a large tortoiseshell cat, curled up contentedly upon an empty footstool. He kicked the stool, dumped the startled animal into the fetid, sodden floor rushes.

'You see,' he said. 'Not even a cat lands on its feet every time.'

Pope Innocent III to John, King of England: 'Who but the Divine Spirit . . . directed and guided you, at once so prudently and so piously, to consult your own interests and provide for the Church? Lo! You now hold your kingdom by a more exalted and surer title than before . . .'

On Ascension Eve, a large pavilion was set up on the Kentish downs, and there John celebrated Ascension Day with impressive pomp and grandeur. Trestle tables were lavishly laden with food; jugglers and minstrels entertained the crowds that flocked to the meadow, and the day rapidly took on the festive atmosphere of a fair or market day. At sunset, the pavilion was taken down and John returned in triumph to the Knights Templar at Ewell. It was, for many, a day of bitter disappointment.

It remained for Peter of Wakefield to serve as an object lesson for false prophets, would-be rebels. Five days later, the aged hermit was escorted to Wareham in Dorset, where he was dragged to the gallows behind the sheriff's horse, and there hanged.

January, 1214

Porchester, England

As she rode through the Land Gate into the outer bailey of Porchester Castle, Eleanor heard the murmurs of the watching soldiers, heard herself identified as the 'Breton wench,' as the 'King's captive niece'. None accorded her the titles that were hers by right, Duchess of Brittany and Countess of Richmond, the titles that had passed to her on the death of her brother Arthur.

Upon her entrance into the keep, she was greeted warmly by her uncle's wife, and although she sensed that Isabelle's affection was a counterfeit coin, no more than good manners, she was grateful, none the less, for such a welcome. John saw to it that she had soft linen sheets, gowns of velvet and silk, dinner tables laden with fine wines, richly spiced venison and fresh fish, but she was starved for friendship, for love.

Following Isabelle up the stairwell into the solar, she knelt submissively before John, steeled herself for his kiss. August would mark the twelfth year of her comfortable confinement at Bristol Castle, and in all that time not once had John ever raised his voice to her. He did not have to; he could chill Eleanor to the depths of her being with his smile. She sometimes wondered if he knew how much she feared him, but she found it impossible to read those enigmatic hazel eyes.

She recognized most of the men attending her uncle: her baseborn cousins Richard and Oliver Fitz Roy, the Earl of Pembroke, the swarthy Earl of Chester, who had for a brief time been her stepfather, for the old King Henry had compelled her mother to wed Chester after her father's tournament death. But they had never lived as man and wife, and Eleanor had no childhood memories of Chester, knew he was indifferent to her fate. She had no champions at her uncle's court, had none anywhere. Her brother and mother were dead, her friends silenced. She had a younger half-sister Alice, child of her mother's third marriage to a Poitevin nobleman, but Alice had wed a cousin of the French King, and they now ruled Brittany at Philip's pleasure, had a vested interest in Eleanor's continuing captivity. There was no one to speak for her, and well she knew it.

'I've heard men called you the "Pearl of Brittany", and now I know why.'

The speaker was unknown to Eleanor, a dark raffish-looking man with bold, appraising eyes that tracked the curves of her body with obvious intent. Eleanor felt her face grow hot; she was as flustered as a shy seventeen year old, for time had frozen for her on an August afternoon at Mirebeau, and at an age when other women had long since been wedded and bedded, she still knew no more of men and the world than a young novice nun.

The man seemed amused by her embarrassment. Before she could pull back, he caught her hand and brought it to his mouth. 'Since your uncle the King swears I'm not to be trusted with any woman who has not taken holy vows, I doubt that he'll introduce us. So I'd best do it myself. I am Reginald de Dammartin, Count of Boulogne. Welcome, my lady, to Porchester.'

'And now that you've met her, you may bid her farewell,' John said dryly, thus sparing Eleanor the need to reply. Rising, he linked his arm in Eleanor's, led her towards the window seat. 'Come, Nell, sit here beside me so we may talk.'

The familiar family name stung. So, too, did his protectiveness. He never teased her, never turned upon her the sarcasm, the mordant black humour that she'd so often seen him turn upon others. And Eleanor found his kindness harder to bear than cruelty.

'Have you heard that I sail next week for La Rochelle?'

Eleanor nodded. 'Your daughter Joanna writes to me from time to time. She told me that you mean to regain Normandy and Poitou from the French King.'

'You've heard from Joanna? She is well?'

Eleanor was surprised by the urgency of the query, but again she nodded. 'Quite well, and thankful for the truce that exists between her husband and Your Grace.'

John's mouth thinned, for the truce with the Welsh Princes had not been of his choosing, had been brought about at the insistence of Stephen Langton, Archbishop of Canterbury. But he'd had just one terse letter from Joanna in the past twelvemonth, and he

486

interrogated Eleanor now at some length, seeking reassurance that his daughter was truly well, that her prolonged silence was indicative only of Llewelyn's rancour.

Eleanor caught the undertones of unease, but she did not comprehend the cause. She wondered why he had sent for her. She wondered, too, if she would ever find the courage to confront him about her brother's death, to demand that he tell her how Arthur had died.

Satisfied at last that she had no more to tell him about Joanna, John said, 'My brother Will has already sailed for Flanders, where he'll be joined by Dammartin and my sister's son Otto, the Holy Roman Emperor. For my part, I shall land at La Rochelle. Once I've secured Poitou and Anjou, we'll be able to move against Philip on two fronts.'

'God grant you victory, Uncle.' Why was he telling her this?

Reginald de Dammartin sauntered over, held out a dripping wine cup to John. 'When you begin husband-hunting for her, John, remember that I put in my bid first.'

'I would, Reg,' John said and grinned. 'But I think your wife might take it amiss.'

Eleanor was dumbfounded. 'Husband-hunting?' she echoed. 'Uncle, what does he mean?'

John did not reply at once, studying her over the rim of his cup. She shared Arthur's colouring, he thought, but little else. Arthur had been too brittle to bend, but Nell was malleable clay; rebellion was not in her. 'Well, you can hardly expect to rule Brittany without a husband to give you support and guidance, can you?'

Eleanor seemed dazed; she could only stare at him in disbelief. 'You . . . you mean to recognize my claim to the Breton throne?' No sooner were the words out of her mouth than the full implications of her question hit her; if he admitted she was the rightful heiress to Brittany, he was admitting, too, that Arthur was dead.

John smiled. 'Your claim is for certès superior to your half-sister's,' he said, adroitly sidestepping the trap.

She could still ensnare him, she knew. She need only ask: What of Arthur's claim? But John's gaze did not waver; his eyes held hers quite steadily, hypnotically.

'Your sister and her husband have been French puppets; Philip pulled the strings and they danced at his whim. After I prevail against Philip, I shall want a more reliable regime in Brittany. Naturally, I thought of you, Nell.'

487

Eleanor swallowed. She was not so innocent that she did not understand what was being offered and what was not. It might sound as if John was opening the door of her cage, but she'd still be tethered to his will. If her sister was Philip's puppet, she would be John's.

She laced her fingers together, sought without success to still their tremors. His advisers would govern in her name. He'd pick a husband for her, and she'd be given no say in it. But she'd have a measure of freedom. And she was still young enough to have children, to have the family she'd thought forever denied her. She closed her eyes, and Arthur's name hovered on her lips, like an unspoken prayer.

'Well?' John put his hand on her arm, felt her quiver at his touch. How fearful she was, as timid as a trapped doe. Her vulnerability stirred his pity, her lack of pluck his contempt. He tilted her chin up, forcing her to meet his eyes. 'What say you, Nell? If I make you Duchess of Brittany, will I regret it?'

'No, Uncle,' she whispered. 'You'll not regret it. I'll do whatever you want.'

On February 14, John landed at La Rochelle. Taking advantage of an early spring thaw, he moved into Isabelle's Angoulême, and then the Limousin. When the de Lusignans scorned his offer of a truce, he led his army into Hugh de Lusignan's county of La Marche. Philip had been forced to split his army, dispatching his son Louis against John while he headed north in an attempt to halt Will and Dammartin's depredations in Flanders. But Louis was an overly cautious commander, and March gave way to April and then May and it began to seem as if the lost Angevin empire was John's for the taking.

On Whitsun Eve, May 17, John captured the de Lusignan castle at Mervant. The next day he moved on to Vouvant, where Hugh's uncle, Geoffrey de Lusignan, had taken refuge with his sons. Upon their refusal to yield, John's men surrounded the castle, and the siege began.

After filling in the moat with brushwood and dirt, they succeeded in setting fire to the wooden palisade, soon gained control of the outer bailey. John then ordered his siege engines brought up, and from dawn to dusk on Tuesday, the mangonels sent heavy rocks slamming against the castle walls and keep. While in La Rochelle, John had secured a relatively new siege weapon; called a trebuchet, it was a high trajectory sling, larger and more accurate than the mangonels, and by Tuesday afternoon, this, too, was in operation, hurling enormous boulders and the dreaded Greek fire and even the rotting carcasses of dead horses into the inner bailey of the besieged castle. By nightfall, John's soldiers were wagering upon the hour of the castle's fall, and John's was the sound sleep of a man already savouring the victory to come.

After breaking his fast the next morning, John summoned the Earl of Chester and together they went to inspect the siege tower that had been completed soon after sunrise. Fashioned from tree-trunks, it soared more than sixty feet into the sky. As John and Chester watched, hides doused in vinegar were tacked in place, and then, at John's signal, the huge belfry began to roll slowly across the bailey.

Up on the walls, the defenders were shooting flaming arrows, but they glanced off the hides, failed to ignite. Under cover of their shields, men clambered down, knocked off the belfry wheels, and then lowered its drawbridge, settling it against the castle wall. De Lusignan's soldiers began to throw torches, but men were already scrambling across, leaping on to the wall. Others were emerging from the lower storeys of the belfry, hastening to join their comrades on the drawbridge. The fighting was now hand-to-hand combat. Men grappled with each other, swearing and gouging and panting; some lost their footing, fell or were pushed off the walls to their deaths. But as more and more men crossed the drawbridge, the castle defenders were forced to give ground. Already some of the attacking force had lowered thong ladders, were climbing down into the bailey.

'Look!' John gave a jubilant shout, pointed. 'Our men have the inner gatehouse; the portcullis is rising!'

By noon, the de Lusignans and their surviving men had walled themselves up in the keep, and John's soldiers were readying themselves for the final assault. John had decided not to dig a tunnel to undermine the keep; while that was the surest method, it was also the slowest. 'We'll try the battering ram first,' he concluded, after a painstaking appraisal of the keep. 'Remember, though, that I want the de Lusignans taken alive if possible. I promised myself I'd have the pleasure of hanging the whoresons,' he added, and his captains laughed.

'Your Grace!' The Earl of Derby was gesturing. 'A rider is coming in under a flag of truce, and damn me if he's not wearing Hugh de Lusignan's livery!'

Within moments, an exceedingly nervous youth was kneeling in the dirt before John. 'Your Grace, my lord Count of La Marche most urgently requests a meeting with you. Will you grant him a safe-conduct so he might enter your camp?'

'Indeed I will,' John said, and smiled. 'Tell Hugh if he makes haste, he'll be in time for the hangings.'

They met in John's command tent within the hour. Hugh de Lusignan had not aged well in the twelve years since Mirebeau. His hair and beard were the shade of sea salt, his skin as splotched and sun-browned as well-worn leather, and his eyes put John in mind of his favourite peregrine falcon. But he came forward without apparent hesitation, knelt and said,

'I thank Your Grace for seeing me. I think it time we talked.'

'I offered to talk in March, as I recall. You said you'd sooner break bread with the Devil . . . or words to that effect.'

'I was in the wrong,' Hugh said stonily. 'I seek your pardon, seek peace between us.'

So did John. He needed the powerful de Lusignan clan to make good his conquest of Poitou. But he took his time, let Hugh suffer the suspense until he finally nodded, said, 'So it shall be, then.'

Hugh's eyes glittered. 'I shall give you faithful service, my liege. Now . . . what of my uncle and cousins?'

John smiled coolly. 'I'd planned to hang them, Hugh,' he said pleasantly. 'But if you can talk them into surrendering, I'll pardon them . . . as proof of the friendship I now bear you.'

Hugh sighed audibly, 'Again, I thank Your Grace.'

John signalled for wine. His ploy had worked even better than he'd expected; Hugh's uncle had proved to be irresistible bait. He'd bought a truce with the lives of Geoffrey de Lusignan and his sons, a truce for today. But what of tomorrow? What was to keep Hugh from disavowing his oath once his kinsmen were safe? He needed more, needed some way to bind the Lusignans to him, to make his fortunes inextricably entwined with theirs. And after careful consideration, he thought he knew how to do just that.

'There has been bad blood between us for far too long, Hugh. Let's pledge a new beginning, bury our grievances here and now.'

Hugh's smile was sour. 'Is that not what we are doing?'

'I mean what I say, Hugh. But words are hollow. So I'll give you living proof of my good faith – my daughter.'

'Jesu!' Hugh sat back, staring at him. 'Are you serious?'

'Very serious. Isabelle and I have a daughter; you have a son.

What better way to heal old hurts than to cleanse them in a bond of blood?'

There was no need to say more. This time Hugh's smile was genuine, even reached his eyes. He held his wine cup aloft. 'To the wedding,' he said. 'And to new beginnings.'

Isabelle was growing bored. Rising, she glanced about the chamber. They'd come to Parthenay for John to accept oaths of homage from the de Lusignans, and to secure their precarious peace within the sanctity of marriage. That morning Hugh de Lusignan's grown son and namesake had been betrothed to John and Isabelle's young daughter Joanna.

The little bride-to-be, still two months shy of her fourth birthday, had no comprehension of the ceremony that linked her life to Hugh de Lusignan, and she was now playing contentedly in a corner with a new doll. Across the chamber, Hugh de Lusignan and John were exchanging faintly barbed courtesies, while Eleanor was in animated conversation with Ralph de Lusignan and Hugh's son. Isabelle could not help noticing the changes four months at John's court had wrought in Eleanor. She'd shed much of her shyness; she was even flirting a little with Hugh's handsome son.

When she caught John's eye, Isabelle blew him a playful kiss, and then moved towards the door. Wandering out into the gardens, she picked a bouquet of white violets, settled herself upon a turf seat in the shadow of a flowering peach tree. She felt no surprise when, after a few moments, she saw the younger de Lusignan coming towards her; she'd noticed the way his eyes followed her when he thought no one else was watching.

'May I join you?'

'Why not?' Isabelle reached for her flowers, cleared a space on the turf seat. 'How did you get away from Eleanor? She's rather taken with you, you know. When you're there, she loses that air of martyred melancholy, becomes almost vivacious.'

He grinned. 'How sharp your claws, Madame! A man who was the vain sort might begin to wonder why.'

To Isabelle's surprise, she was not affronted. Mayhap it was his smile, she decided; it was disarming, boyishly endearing, appealingly at variance with the knowing blue eyes. She wondered how old he was: thirty-three or four?

She laughed and, at his questioning look, said lightly, 'I was

491

just thinking that, if fate had been different, I'd have been your stepmother!'

Hugh laughed, too. 'You'd have been wasted on my father.' Taking her hand in his own. 'Just as you've been wasted on John.'

'That is dangerous talk,' Isabelle said coolly. But she did not pull away.

'But true.' He turned her hand over, tracked her lifeline with his thumb. 'You're so very beautiful, far more beautiful than I remembered. How is it that John has not locked you away from the world? I'd have thought he'd sequester you behind the highest walls, veil you like a Saracen woman.'

Isabelle opened her mouth to say John trusted her, that she'd never given him cause for jealousy. Instead, she heard herself say softly, 'Is that what you'd do if I were your woman, Hugh?'

'If you were my woman . . .' he echoed, and for an unguarded moment, the game-playing was forgotten. Isabelle was accustomed to court flirtations. She was both flattered and amused that men invariably found her so desirable, but it was never more than a harmless diversion; she never forget where the boundary lines were drawn, had never been tempted to cross over. She was shaken now by what was happening with Hugh de Lusignan, shaken to realize that she was responding to this man's smile, to his touch. She looked down at the lean sun-browned fingers caressing her own, and then jerked her hand from his, forced a brittle smile.

'I dare say others might think this a rather peculiar conversation for a woman to be having with her daughter's betrothed!'

He did not return her smile. 'I'll settle for the daughter if I must,' he said softly, 'but I'd rather have the mother.'

When their eyes met again, Isabelle found she could not look away. 'I'm afraid the mother is already spoken for, Hugh,' she murmured, taking refuge in flippancy, while longing to reach out, to trace the curve of his mouth with her fingers. She fought the urge, kept her hands tightly clasped in her lap, and then a shadow fell between them, and she turned, saw her husband standing several feet away.

'John!' Isabelle was on her feet before she could realize that she'd have done better to remain sitting. Hugh's reaction was just as instinctive; he, too, sprang up, backed away from Isabelle. Isabelle recovered her poise first, summoned a dazzling smile. 'John, love, we were just talking about you!'

To her relief, John returned her smile. She moved hastily to his side, linked her arm through his. 'I remember you telling me your sister used to call you Johnny-cat. Now I can understand why; you approached us as quietly as any cat could, made no sound at all!' She was talking too much and too fast, but she could not help herself. She was suddenly panicked at the prospect of silence, and she chattered on brightly and aimlessly for several moments, while Hugh shifted uneasily, and John listened with an indulgent smile. After an interminable time, Hugh mumbled an excuse, made a swift departure. Only then, alone in the garden with John, did Isabelle begin to relax.

'So you were talking about me? What were you saying, Isabelle?'

'Oh . . . nothing out of the ordinary, love. We talked about Joanna, the betrothal and –' Isabelle cried out as John grasped her wrist, jerked her roughly towards him.

John had been neither surprised nor perturbed when he saw Hugh de Lusignan rise, follow Isabelle out into the gardens. He was gratified, not threatened, by the awareness that other men desired his wife, that they envied him so. It was not jealousy or unease that had motivated him to join them, but rather a sense of prideful possession; he enjoyed claiming Isabelle as his before a man so obviously bewitched by his beautiful wife.

The shock was all the greater, therefore, for being so unexpected. It was not the sight of Isabelle and Hugh sitting under the peach tree that jolted him so; it was the look on his wife's face. It was not the look of a woman engaging in an innocent flirtation; it was a look of yearning, a look both erotic and intimate, the look a woman would give her lover.

He tightened his grip on her wrist. 'Tell me, Isabelle. What was de Lusignan saying to you?'

'John, you're hurting me!'

'Tell me!'

The pain was radiating upward from wrist to elbow; tears filled her eyes. 'All right! I'll tell you . . . He was flirting with me, that's all. No more, I swear it!'

He released her so abruptly that she staggered backward, sank down on the turf seat, cradling her wrist. She'd always been scornful of women who cringed before abusive husbands, wondering how they could be so lacking in pride. But she had never been hurt before, had never been subjected to violence of any kind. Now she wept soundlessly, flinching as he stepped towards her. 'Why are you so

493

angry? Men always flirt with me; it means nothing. You know that, John, have never minded before.'

'Mayhap I should have.'

Isabelle forgot her pain in a sudden surge of fear. 'My God, John, what are you saying? Surely you do not think I've been unfaithful to you? Never, John, never; I swear on our children's very lives! You must believe me!'

'Must I? Why? Why should you not have betrayed me, too? Why should you be any different from the others?'

Isabelle was terrified. 'I would never betray you, never. John, I swear it. I'd have to be an utter fool to take such a risk!'

She saw his mouth twist, and realized she'd blundered; that was not what he wanted to hear. He was turning away, and she stumbled to her feet. 'Oh, listen to me, please. There has never been any man but you. John, I love you, I do!'

'Do you, Isabelle?'

'How can you doubt it? I've been your wife for fourteen years; when have I ever failed you? I've shared your bed and your troubles, and I've given you three children.' She wiped her face with the back of her hand, choked back a sob. 'And . . . and there's something I have not yet told you. I was waiting till I was sure, but . . . John, I think I am with child again.'

John did not react as she'd hoped. He gave her a cold, measuring look, a look that frightened her even more, and then said, very evenly, 'Is it mine?'

Isabelle gasped. Tears streaked her face, smeared the kohl outlining her eyes. She sobbed again, caught his sleeve. 'How can you ask that? How?'

Neither of them had heard the approaching footsteps, and they spun about as Hugh de Lusignan coughed. 'Your Grace, do forgive me. I did not realize you and your lady were quarrelling. I am indeed sorry for the intrusion.' The words were properly remorseful, and Hugh ducked his head, as if embarrassed. But he was a poor actor. John had seen how he stared at Isabelle, knew Hugh hated him not just for that long-ago affront to his pride. His grievance was a festering, thwarted passion; he'd wanted Isabelle in his bed, he still wanted her, and could not hide the poisoned pleasure their quarrelling gave him, his envenomed satisfaction that there seemed to be a snake in John's Eden.

Behind Hugh, John now saw Hugh's wife Matilda, the wife he'd

494

taken as substitute solace for Isabelle's loss. She was Isabelle's first cousin, but she'd not been blessed with Isabelle's beauty, was not a woman to make Hugh forget what could have been his, Isabelle and Angoulême. John drew a deep, deliberate breath, as Isabelle said in a muffled voice:

'We were not quarrelling.'

'There is no need to lie, Isabelle. We can be honest with Hugh.' John's smile felt wooden, utterly artificial, but the words came of their own volition, even carried conviction. 'We were indeed arguing, and I fear it was my fault. You see, Hugh, Isabelle just told me she is with child again. Naturally, I was delighted. But had I known of her condition, I'd never have allowed her to come with me to Parthenay, would have insisted she remain in La Rochelle, and I was disturbed that she did not tell me sooner.'

The sudden fragrance of damask rose told John that Isabelle was now standing just behind him. He turned, slid his arm around her waist. She murmured, 'You are sweet, love, to worry about me, but in truth there's no need.' John could feel the tension in her body, but her voice had steadied, and now she smiled defiantly at Hugh, asked, 'Are you not going to congratulate us, Hugh?'

'Indeed.' Hugh's voice was toneless. 'May God grant you a son, Madame.'

When Hugh and Matilda withdrew, John at once released Isabelle, turned away from her. At the far end of the gardens was a large fishpond or stew, shaded by ancient yew trees. He walked towards it, stood for a time staring down at the sluggishly moving carp. His rage had ebbed away; he felt only emptiness, only a dulled sense of disbelief, of loss.

His faith in Isabelle's fidelity was born of circumstance: her extreme youth and innocence at the time of their marriage. As she matured into womanhood, he'd been her guide and mentor, shaping her thoughts and fantasies to fit his own needs. She was more than his wife, she was his creation, utterly unlike the other women in his life, and when she said she loved him, he'd taken it as his just due, had never thought to doubt her. Not until the moment he came upon her and the young de Lusignan seated on a turf bench and suddenly saw her, not as his, but as a beautiful, passionate woman of twenty-six, a woman with a husband more than twenty years older than she.

'John.' Isabelle had followed him. Stopping a few feet away, she pleaded, 'John, please, we have to talk. You have to tell me if you

495

truly meant what you said, if you truly doubt that this babe be yours.'

John had picked up a handful of pebbles. Now he let them drop, one by one, watched the pond's peaceful surface fragment, ripple outward in ever-widening circles. 'No,' he said at last, 'I did not mean it. I know the babe is mine.'

Isabelle had not realized she'd been holding her breath. 'Thank God,' she sighed, utterly without irony. Her fear had been too great to allow her now the indulgence of resentment or outraged innocence, not when she thought of Eleanor's sixteen bitter years as Henry's prisoner, of Ingeborg's twelve wretched years in Étampes Castle, of the sinister silence that seemed to fall whenever mention was made of Maude de Braose and her disappearance into a Windsor dungeon.

'If the babe is a girl,' John said, after some moments of strained silence, 'we'll name her Isabelle.'

Isabelle smiled wanly. 'I should like that.' Her fingers encircled her wrist, lingered over the darkening bruises, and then she moved towards him, into his arms.

'Promise me, John, that you'll never again doubt my love for you.'

'I want to believe you,' he confessed. She seemed about to speak; as her lips parted, he brought his mouth down on hers. 'If I thought you'd ever taken another man to your bed, Isabelle . . .'

'I love you, only you.' Her voice was husky, beguilingly soft. But her lashes had swept downward, veiling her eyes, her thoughts, and John felt a throb of fear. How would he ever know if she were lying or not? How could he ever be sure?

The dawn sky on Wednesday, July 2 was a sun-glazed, boundless blue in which a solitary eagle soared, high above John's siege encampment at Roche-au-Moine. As men rolled, yawning, from their blankets, they gazed upward, took the eagle's flight as a good omen, for all knew that the eagle was king amongst birds, that old King Henry of blessed memory had oft-times spoken of his sons as his eaglets. The sudden appearance of a golden eagle over the King's camp could only mean that he would prevail against the French King's son, that the day's victory would be theirs.

For a fortnight now, John had been besieging the castle of Roche-au-Moine, just a few miles to the north of Angers. Barricaded within its keep was William des Roches, Philip's Seneschal for Anjou, the same William des Roches who'd turned against John after Mirebeau.

496

John's campaign had met with unqualified success to date; he'd won over the de Lusignans, captured castles and the strategic city of Angers, and his army had been swelled by the ranks of the Poitevin barons. When word came that Philip's son Louis was hastening north to des Roches's rescue, he chose not to lift the siege, chose instead to meet the French forces on the field of battle.

His scouts had reported that the French were approaching from the south-east, and the men now staring up at the circling eagle knew that battle was likely to be joined under that cloudless summer sky, that some among them would never see another dawning day. They were much heartened, therefore, when the eagle swooped lower, hovered for a moment above the tent of the English King.

Within, John was trapped in a dream of familiar horror, in which the very real fears of day merged with the secret terrors of the night, and he found himself naked and defenceless before his enemies, abandoned even by God.

'My liege?'

His eyes flew open; he looked up into the frightened face of a young squire. The boy backed away from the bed. 'Forgive me, my liege, but you cried out . . .'

'No matter, Simon, no matter.' As John started to sit up, he found he was entangled in the bedcovers. He signalled for wine, wiped the sweat from his face with the corner of the sheet. He wondered if his servants gossiped among themselves, swapped stories of the King's troubled dreams, knew they did. Rumour was a servant's coinage, lavishly spent.

He could hear voices beyond the inner partition, the excited, uneasy laughter of men girding themselves for battle. He shared their unease, but not their excitement, for he had no love of war, no lust for battle glory. He had never been able to comprehend what perverse pleasure his brother Richard found on the battlefield, and when he fought, it was only because he could get what he wanted no other way.

The squire was back, offering bread sopped in wine. 'An eagle alighted upon your tent this morn, lord, in sight of all!'

'Did it, indeed?' John grinned, and the lingering darkness of his dream fled before the sunlight flooding his tent. 'When Louis sent me his challenge, Simon, I replied that the sooner he came to Roche-au-Moine, the sooner he'd regret it. Today I shall make good my promise.' And while there was a touch of bravado in that, it was

497

also the pragmatic assessment of a battle commander who had picked the site, made the enemy come to him, and knew that numerical superiority was his.

The Earl of Chester was waiting for John, shared his breakfast as John was being armed.

'I understand couriers arrived with letters last night. Did Your Grace hear from Flanders, from your brother Salisbury and Dammartin?'

John shook his head. 'I regret not, can only assume that they are still waiting for Otto and the Rhineland Princes to join forces with them. I did hear from England, though.'

'From Pembroke?'

The Earl of Pembroke had remained behind in England; he and Peter des Roches, Bishop of Winchester, now John's Justiciar, had been entrusted with the government. Now John shook his head again. 'No, the last letter I had from Pembroke spoke of his suspicions that Fitz Walter and de Vesci were stirring up trouble with the malcontent barons of the North. No surprise, that; when they refused to take part in our campaign, we knew they'd try to take advantage of my absence from the kingdom. But I think Pembroke and Winchester will hold them in check until I can return to deal with them myself. No, the letter was from my son.'

Chester had developed a regard for Richard, and he smiled. 'I know Your Grace wanted him to look to your interests in England, but I confess I'd have liked to have him with us today. He's a good lad, can be relied upon to keep a cool head.'

John smiled, too. 'That he can. Well, he'll be joining us next month, after his marriage to the little Chilham heiress.' His squires had pulled his hauberk over a padded tunic, and were buckling his scabbard. 'The truth, Ranulf. What are our chances?'

Chester could not recall John ever calling him by his Christian name. 'Well, I'd not trade places with Louis for the surety of my soul!' he said, and John laughed. He was reaching for a wine cup when the shouting began.

'The King, where's the King?'

John yanked the partition aside just as the Earl of Derby burst into the tent. 'Your Grace, you'll not believe it, what Thouars and the barons are doing —'

'Stop babbling and tell me, then!'

'The Poitevin barons, they're pulling out, my lord, deserting us!'

498

'Oh, Christ . . .' For a moment John froze, unable to distinguish between daylight horrors and those of his dream. And then he shouldered Derby aside, ducked under the tent flap.

Men were clustered around the tent; they moved aside, quickly cleared a path. The Poitevins were already mounted, preparing to depart. John recognized Aimery, Viscount of Thouars, began to move towards him. They knew each other well; Thouars had long swung like a weathercock in a high wind, pledging fealty to John or Philip as circumstances seemed to dictate. He did not look defiant now, just uncomfortable, and before John could speak, he blurted out:

'We were willing to join you in laying siege to Roche-au-Moine, but not to fight the French. That was never our agreement. Philip is our liege lord, too; we owe him –'

'You lying bastard! You've known for a fortnight that I meant to do battle with Louis, and you said nothing, raised no objections. No, you waited, waited till the day of the battle. Tell me, how much did the French pay you, Aimery? Did you get your thirty pieces of silver?'

Thouars flushed, began to bluster, but John was no longer listening. Even as he'd raged at Thouars, as embittered accusations and invective took shape upon his tongue, an inner voice was sounding an instinctive warning. Something was very wrong. Thouars was unscrupulous and unreliable, but he was also weak-willed, shrank from confrontation. He'd have fled in the dark of night, on his own would never have found the courage for this diabolically timed desertion. John's eyes slid past Thouars, searched the faces of the others. And then he saw the de Lusignans, then he understood. His eyes locked with Hugh's. Hugh smiled and then leaned over, spat into the dust.

'You English have a proverb I've always fancied, John, the one that says revenge is a dish best eaten cold.'

John jerked his sword from its scabbard. 'You craven, cocksucking whoreson! God rot you, but you'll pay for this, I swear you will, if it takes me till Judgment Day!'

Hugh laughed. 'Ah, but today is Judgment Day – for you. Good luck with the French.'

With that, the de Lusignans spurred their mounts, signalled to their men. The other Poitevin barons followed, galloping out of the encampment to the jeers and taunts of the outraged English.

Chester came forward, stopped beside John. He waited, and

after a time, John said softly, 'And I gave him my daughter, my Joanna . . .'

'Your Grace!' The Earl of Derby was shoving his way towards them. 'Your Grace, what mean you to do? The French will be upon us, and how can we fight now? We've just lost half our army!'

John turned, and then sheathed his sword. 'We cannot fight. Give the command to retreat. Tell my captains to head for the Loire.'

'But what of our siege weapons, the mangonels and trebuchet? What of our tents, your baggage carts, your –'

'Leave them.' John's voice was without emotion, utterly flat, but Derby did not dare to argue. One look at John's face and he spun about, began to shout orders. The anger of their soldiers was now giving way to alarm, to the first stirrings of panic. Men began to run for their horses, and those without mounts began to scuffle with those who did. A few took advantage of the pandemonium to loot the tents of their commanders. Tempers flared, brawling broke out, and John's captains tried in vain to maintain some semblance of order. But the men had only one thought now, to flee before the French army arrived.

John did not move, even when his agitated attendants brought up his stallion, implored him to mount. He stood alone midst the chaos and confusion, watching the disintegration of his army.

Withdrawing to La Rochelle, John wrote urgently to his barons, earls, and knights, most of whom had remained in England, requesting that they cross the Channel and join him without delay, even promising that '. . . if any of you should have understood that we bore him ill will, he can have it rectified by his coming.' His son Richard, landing at La Rochelle in late July, caught up with John on August 2 at Limoges, where he had the unhappy task of telling his father that reinforcements were not coming, that John's hopes for regaining his continental empire now depended upon his brother Will and Reginald de Dammartin and the army they were assembling in Flanders.

It was a subdued gathering in the Abbot's solar that night. Eleanor was sitting in a window seat with John and Isabelle's five-year-old son Richard; young Henry, as the heir to the throne, had remained in England, and little Joanna had been turned over to the de Lusig-nans for rearing at the time of her betrothal in May. Isabelle was moving restlessly about the chamber. When Richard appeared in the doorway, she held out her hand, beckoned him towards the settle.

'I'm so glad you've come. John is much in need of cheer.'

Richard had noted his stepmother's pallor, the sleepless nights etched in the shadows smudged under her eyes, and he said, 'I suspect that you are, too. Tell me about Joanna. The de Lusignans will not give her up?'

'No, of course not. They mean to honour the betrothal, Richard. She's their hostage, you see. As long as they have her, John cannot move against them, cannot punish them as they deserve.'

Richard swore with unusual savagery. 'Misbegotten, treacherous hellspawn, may the curse of God be upon them all.'

Isabelle's lashes flickered. 'Hugh's son was not at Roche-au-Moine. It may be that he was not privy to their plans, did not know what they meant to do.'

Richard's surprise was considerable. He might have expected such naïveté from Eleanor, but never from Isabelle, Isabelle of all women. 'Have you been well? When is the babe due?'

'Not for months yet, not till December.' Isabelle nodded to her son's nursemaid, who rose to take the child off to bed. Eleanor at once rose, too, offered to take him herself.

'You've been kind enough to read to Dickon all evening, Nell; you need not act as his nursemaid, too.'

Eleanor smiled at the child, who grinned back. 'Oh, but I enjoy it, Madame,' she said, and did in fact look regretful when the nurse led the little boy from the solar. She seemed about to join Isabelle and Richard on the settle, but drew back into the shadowed window seat as John entered the chamber.

Isabelle at once became solicitous, finding a cushion for him, acting herself as his cupbearer. John accepted her ministrations without comment. Richard was startled by how much he had aged in the six months they'd been apart; the jet black hair was rapidly going very grey.

Giving Isabelle an oblique look Richard could not quite interpret, John said, 'I expect Isabelle has been telling you about the de Lusignans and our Joanna.'

Richard nodded. 'You must not blame yourself, Papa. Many a blood feud has been reconciled in the marriage bed. How could you know what would happen?'

'I should have, though, for this was not the first time I gave away a Joanna. And did marriage to my daughter bind Llewelyn to me? Did it make of him an ally? I gained nothing, and lost a daughter. No, Richard, I should have known . . .'

Neither Richard nor Isabelle knew how to answer, how to comfort. Isabelle slid closer, began to massage the taut muscles in John's neck and shoulders, but after only a few moments, he impatiently signalled for her to stop. 'Did you tell Isabelle, Richard, of the news you brought me? This past May I instructed Pembroke to levy a scutage tax of three marks per knight's fee upon all those who'd balked at taking part in this campaign. Scutage has always been paid in lieu of military service, since the days of my great-grandfather. Yet Richard tells me that many are now refusing to pay it, claiming they owe no service for wars fought on foreign soil.' John paused, before adding bitterly, 'And for this I can thank my great and good friend the Pope. Had he not insisted I pardon de Vesci and Fitz Walter –'

Breaking off as the door opened, John turned, saw the Earl of Chester standing in the doorway. 'Come in, my lord. We were just discussing the benefits of being the Pope's anointed. Since I became reconciled with God and the Church, nothing has gone right for me. What conclusion might I draw from that?'

But his sarcasm stirred no rejoinder. Chester had not yet moved from the doorway. He stood in shadow, saying nothing, and there was something about his stance, his utter stillness, that alarmed them all.

'Well?' John's voice was suddenly husky, full of foreboding. 'What is it?'

'I've news, Your Grace. News from Flanders.'

'Tell me,' John said, and Chester came forward, knelt before the settle. 'Your nephew Otto finally joined his army with that of your brother Salisbury. They were at Valenciennes, preparing to march on Paris when their scouts reported that Philip had circled around, was now behind them. They swung about, and the two armies met on Sunday last near the village of Bouvines.'

John's hand jerked; wine splashed upon his sleeve. 'And the victory?'

'It went to Philip, Your Grace. The victory was Philip's.'

John closed his eyes, gave himself up to the dark. But Chester's voice droned on relentlessly. 'It was bloody work, my liege. Philip burned the bridge over the River Marque, so his men could not retreat. By battle's end, the dead numbered in the thousands. Your nephew fled the field when it became clear all was lost. But your brother and Dammartin scorned flight, fought to the last. Your brother led a desperate charge across the field to reach Dammartin's men. It was an act of great courage, Your Grace, and almost carried the day.'

Chester's loyalties were not personal, were pledged to the monarch, not the man. But as he looked now at John's face, his dark eyes softened, and he said, with some pity, 'At least I can tell you that your brother still lives. He and Dammartin were both taken, are Philip's prisoners.'

Isabelle reached over, gently pried the wine cup from John's fist. 'Beloved, I'm sorry, so sorry . . .' When he did not respond, she tried to put her arms around him, but he pulled away, rose to his feet.

'It's over,' he said, almost inaudibly. 'It's all over.'

'For now, yes. But there'll be other chances. Papa, other –'

'No, Richard. It's done.'

John moved to the table, picked up an hourglass, put it down again. 'Find out what Philip wants to ransom Will and Dammartin. Whatever it is, I'll pay it. Whatever it is . . .'

'I'll be honest with Your Grace. Philip may not be willing to free them – for any price. That's a possibility you may have to face, my liege.'

John's head jerked up. 'No! There must be a way to secure their release. You find it, Chester. No matter what it takes, you find it.' What had begun as a command, even a threat, ended up quite differently, came as close as John could get to entreaty. 'I cannot lose them, too,' he said, and then turned abruptly, walked rapidly from the room. After a moment's hesitation, Isabelle followed.

Richard rose, too, but then glanced back over his shoulder. 'Is my father right, my lord Chester? Are Normandy and the other provinces well and truly lost to England now?'

Chester nodded. 'Nor is that all we lost at Bouvines. Your lord father may have been defeated at a distance, Richard, but he was defeated all the same. You may be sure his barons back in England will seek to take full advantage of it.'

Neither spoke after that; there was nothing to be said. The silence was at last broken by Eleanor. She'd sat, frozen, in the darkened window seat as Chester spoke of defeat and death. Now as she began to comprehend what the battle of Bouvines would mean to her, she covered her face with her hands, wept bitterly.

December, 1214
Aber, North Wales

Joanna often dreamed of Llewelyn when they'd been apart for a while, but rarely had a dream been so vivid, so explicitly erotic, and she awoke with regret, reluctant to find herself alone in a cold, empty bed. But as she sighed and stirred, she felt Llewelyn's breath on her throat, felt his hands on her body, and she sighed again.

'Now I understand why my dream was so wonderfully wanton,' she said drowsily. 'But you're taking a great risk; my husband is expected back at any time.'

He gave a low laugh. 'Then I'd best make haste.'

'If you do, I'll never forgive you.' She slid her hands up his back, wrapped her arms around his neck. 'Beloved, I'm sorry, so sorry. It was all my fault . . .'

'Later,' he said, and kissed her lashes, her eyelids, and then her mouth. 'Later . . .'

Rising from the bed, Llewelyn pulled a towel from a wall pole, rubbed himself vigorously. Returning to the bed, he pulled back the damp, rumpled sheet, and began gently to pat Joanna dry. 'You know more than one way to set a bed afire,' he said, and Joanna stretched provocatively, gave him a lazy, satisfied smile.

'We did strike some sparks,' she agreed. 'I truly missed you.'

He smiled too, and she touched her hand to his cheek. 'How did your meeting with your cousin Madog go? Were you able to win him over?'

'Yes, quite easily. I think he's wanted for some time to disavow the English and throw his lot in with us. He just needed to know we bore him no grudge.'

'You've been gone longer than I expected, fully a fortnight.'

'After Madog and I came to terms, I got word that a Genoan

merchant ship bound for Ireland had gone aground near Pwllheli. I decided to see for myself what cargo had washed ashore.'

'I see.' Joanna sat up, wrapped her arms around her knees. 'I know that as Prince of Gwynedd you claim dominion over any ship that founders off your shores. But in the eight years we've been wed, Llewelyn, not once have you chosen to visit a shipwreck yourself. Was this merchant ship truly as richly laden as that?'

'No,' he admitted. 'But I thought it best if we had some time apart.' He reached over, let his fingers follow the curve of her throat. 'Else I might have been sorely tempted to throttle you, my love.'

'I gave you cause. I'll not deny that I acted like the worst sort of shrew. The truth is that I think I wanted to provoke a quarrel with you.' She smiled sadly. 'And by God, that I did.'

'Your father's letter?'

'Yes.' Joanna put her hand on his arm. 'I fear you'll not like what I have to say, but I ask you to hear me out.'

When he nodded, she drew an uneven breath. 'I'd never had such a letter from my father before; I doubt if he'd ever written to anyone as he did to me that night at Woodstock. It began as a factual account of what has been happening since his return to England. He wrote that de Vesci and Fitz Walter met last month at Bury St Edmunds with the Earls of Clare and Norfolk and other barons who've refused to pay the scutage tax. He told me that they've changed their tactics, that they're now talking of a charter supposedly issued by the first King Henry. They claim this charter sets limits upon the King's authority, and they are demanding that John agree to be bound by its provisions. He is greatly troubled by this new stratagem, for he says it is like to find widespread support amongst his barons, even those who've so far held aloof. Hc thinks Stephen Langton's is the guiding hand behind it, for he says it is too subtle, too shrewd a manoeuvre for minds like de Vesci and Fitz Walter.'

Llewelyn had been listening with some impatience, for she was relating facts already well known to him. With that last, though, he silently saluted John's insight, for he had been in contact with the rebel barons for several months, and this sudden emphasis upon a charter of liberties was indeed Langton's doing.

'It was not until he made mention of my uncle Will and Reginald de Dammartin that the letter's tone changed, that his despair broke through.'

Llewelyn did not give a damn for John's despair, and he could

505

not keep the coolness from his voice as he said, 'I thought you told me John had been able to arrange Will's release.'

'He did. When he besieged Nantes last summer, a cousin of the French King was amongst those taken captive, and Philip has agreed to exchange Will for his cousin. But he flatly refused to release Dammartin. He said Dammartin was a traitor, owed a debt of dishonour that was now due and payable. When my father wrote to me, he had just learned what Dammartin's fate is to be. Philip has confined him in a cramped, dark cell, chained to a log, and he shall be kept in that hellhole until he dies.'

Joanna's voice faltered. 'I know what you're thinking, Llewelyn, that my father has forfeited the right to sit in judgment upon Philip. There's no denying that he'll face Our Maker with sins no less grievous upon his soul. But Reginald de Dammartin was his friend, and I know how deeply he mourns, for I read his letter.

'I read his letter,' she repeated, 'and I wept. I knew how heartsick he was, sore beset on all sides. I knew, too, that he was ailing, for Richard had written me that he'd suffered a severe attack of gout, so painful that he'd been bedridden for days. Yet shall I tell you what I did, Llewelyn? I dried my tears, found pen and parchment, and wrote him an answering letter as cold as death. I'd have shown greater charity to a stranger on the roadside. I offered my condolences with lethal courtesy. I said I could not come to his Christmas court. And then I told him that if he truly loved me, he would prove it by releasing your hostages.'

'Ah, Joanna . . .' Llewelyn had never hated John so much as at that moment, had never felt such utterly futile, frustrated anger. 'God damn him,' he said savagely, 'damn him forever and aye!'

'I think he is damned,' Joanna whispered, 'and . . . and if only I did not care! But I do, Llewelyn. I hated myself for writing that letter. And unfairly, unforgivably, I began to blame you.'

She could feel tears burning behind her lashes, but she blinked them back. 'Llewelyn, I swear I did not lie to you that day at the White Ladies Priory. I truly thought I could do what I promised you, that I could cut him out of my heart. You were right, and I was wrong; I can never fully forget that lost little girl at Rouen Castle.'

'I know.'

'I cannot forgive him, Llewelyn. I cannot forget those children he murdered at Nottingham Castle. Until the day I die, there will be nights when Maude de Braose and a seven-year-old boy steal away my sleep. And yet . . . and yet I still cannot be indifferent to his pain. Not even for you.'

Llewelyn felt no surprise, only a sense of weary wonderment that it had taken them so long to face the truth. She'd never be free of John. In a strange sort of way, she was as much John's prisoner as that poor lass, Eleanor of Brittany. Had he truly thought he could break that bond?

'Llewelyn? Llewelyn, talk to me. Tell me you understand, that you're not angry with me. Tell me what you're thinking . . .'

'I was thinking,' he said, 'that there's much to be said for marrying an orphan,' and Joanna gave a shaken laugh, not far removed from a sob.

'I was afraid,' she confessed, 'so afraid you'd say that I'd broken my word, that you'd tell me again what you said at the priory, that you did not think you could love John's daughter.'

'You were not the only one lying to yourself that afternoon, *breila*.' He brushed her hair back from her face, breathed in the faint fragrance of lemon, the sandalwood scent of her perfume.

'Not that it's always easy loving you.' His smile was at once both tender and wry. 'Welsh and Norman make for a spicy stew. And John casts a long shadow. I've never felt as close to any woman as I do to you, but I know that for all we share, there will always be secrets between us, drawbridges we dare not lower, because you are John's daughter.'

Sliding his arm around her waist, he drew her into a closer embrace. 'Yet I know, too, that I might not be alive right now if you were not John's daughter. He had me well and truly trapped when you came to him at Aberconwy. And still he offered a truce – because you asked it of him.'

That was not a memory Joanna wanted to dwell upon. She did not doubt that her father loved her. It was a millstone around her neck, one that scraped her conscience raw.

'No more talk of John,' she entreated. 'Let's talk rather of our Norman-Welsh mélange. You like your food both sweet and sour; why not your woman?' Reaching up, she kissed him upon the mouth, a kiss at first soft and then seeking. 'It's not always easy loving you, either. But it's worth the effort, my lord husband, well worth the effort.' She made a protective sign of the cross over his heart, began to track with gentle fingers the scars of old wounds. 'In truth, I'd

507

lower my drawbridge for you any time,' she murmured, and Llewelyn grinned.

'Scriptures talk of Heaven's gate, but for now I'd gladly settle for yours. Alas,' he laughed, bringing her hand down, catching it between his thighs, 'as you can see, if I were a flag, I'd be at half-mast.'

Joanna laughed, too, slid lower in the bed. 'I'd wager that I can raise a flag even faster than I can lower a drawbridge,' she said, and was not long in making good her boast. This time their lovemaking had none of its earlier urgency; it was leisurely, playful, and curiously comforting in its very lack of intensity.

Joanna was drifting towards sleep; she stirred reluctantly as Llewelyn sat up, threw the covers back. 'Can we not stay abed a while longer?'

'No, my lazy love, we cannot. I hear appeals from the commote courts this forenoon, afterwards meet with my council.' In council they would discuss an offer of alliance made by the rebel barons of England, discuss the resumption of war against his wife's father. Llewelyn pushed that thought from him. 'A pity I cannot go riding this day; I should've liked to make use of my new saddle.'

Joanna sat upright. 'What saddle?'

'The saddle with ivory pommel and cantle, a silver girth buckle. The saddle over in yon corner, covered with a blanket.'

'You wretch, that was to be your New Year's gift!' Joanna grabbed for a pillow. Llewelyn was laughing too much to defend himself, and she was able to deliver several blows before he could pin her down against the mattress.

'My lord, my lady, I'm so sorry!' Branwen was standing in the doorway, looking so flustered that Llewelyn and Joanna could not help laughing. But their laughter stilled abruptly at sight of the man standing behind Branwen, for he wore the colours of the English King.

Branwen was still blushing. 'I did knock, in truth,' she said faintly, stepping aside so the courier could enter.

Kneeling, he held out a sealed parchment. As Llewelyn reached for it, he said hesitantly, 'It . . . it is not for you, my lord, but for your lady.'

Llewelyn glanced towards Joanna. She'd lost colour, made no move to take John's letter. After a moment, Llewelyn claimed it, laid it on the bed beside her.

'Are you not going to read it?'

Joanna shook her head. She rolled over, clutched the pillow to her breast. She heard the door shut, heard one of Llewelyn's wolfhounds whimpering for admittance. She closed her eyes. What more did he want of her? Why would he not let her be?

'Joanna, I think you ought to read it. He must have answered you within a day of getting your letter. That speaks of urgency, *breila*.'

'I cannot. I know that sounds foolish, but in truth I cannot. You read it for me, Llewelyn . . . please.'

She felt his hand touch her hair, and then he said, 'As you wish,' broke the seal.

But as he scanned the first line, 'To my beloved daughter Joanna, Lady of Wales, greetings,' Llewelyn was suddenly reluctant to read further, to read a letter never meant for his eyes. 'Joanna . . .'

'Please,' she said, surreptitiously drying her tears against the pillow, not wanting him to know that she could be so unnerved by just the sight of John's handwriting.

Llewelyn was staring down at John's letter; he'd had to read it twice before he could banish disbelief. 'Jesus God,' he breathed, and there was in the look he now gave his wife no small measure of awe. 'He's agreed to your request, Joanna. He's agreed to release my hostages.'

'He did that . . . for me?' Joanna gasped, grabbed for the letter. John's words soon blurred; the writing wavered, bled black ink wherever her tears touched the page. Looking up at last, she said softly, 'But not Gruffydd.'

She put her hand on his, half-fearful he might pull away. He did not move; he was staring past her, dark eyes blind to the morning sunlight, the familiar furnishings of the chamber. For four Welsh families this would be a Christmas never to be forgotten, a time to give fervent thanks for the manifold mercies of God. Their sons would be coming home.

But his son would not. Gruffydd would pass yet another Christmas in an English castle, his fourth as a prisoner. Shut away from the sun and sky, how long could a wild, free spirit survive? How long could he live on hope? How long ere he began to look upon death as a friend, as deliverance?

March, 1215

Rhosyr, North Wales

On January 6, 1215, Eustace de Vesci, Robert Fitz Walter, and the more recalcitrant of the English barons came armed to John's council in London, where they demanded that John confirm their traditional liberties, as embodied in the ancient laws of Edward the Confessor and the charter of Henry I. John played for time, refusing to give them his answer until Low Sunday, April 26, and the barons reluctantly agreed to wait. John at once dispatched a trusted agent to Rome. Eustace de Vesci followed soon after, for the barons, too, understood just how critical the Pope's support would be. Both sides then began to prepare for war.

Joanna leaned over her daughter's bed. Elen turned her face into the pillow, mumbled, '*Nos da, Mam.*'

Joanna hesitated, but decided it was best to allow Elen her aggrieved sense of injury; Elen was seven, old enough for pride. 'I bid you good night, too, dearest,' she said gently, and then crossed the chamber to her son.

Davydd was wide awake, primed with questions to forestall bedtime. 'Tell me why Papa has gone, Mama.' His French was flawless, but Joanna knew that Welsh came more readily to his tongue, that Welsh formed his thoughts, and that realization had been a surprisingly unsettling one for her, as if a barrier had somehow been erected, leaving her on one side and her children on the other.

'Your father and the other Welsh Princes have gone to Rhyd y Groes to meet with the new Bishop of Chester and Coventry, who brings an offer of alliance from the English King.'

The English King. But what else could she say? Your grandfather? When not a day passed that Davydd did not hear John villified as a child-slayer, as Herod? Davydd was so young; how could she expect a six year old to understand what she herself could not at twenty-three? Was it not better to wait until he was older, until he began to ask questions? Mayhap by then she'd have some answers for him. Joanna reached out, playfully rumpled Davydd's dark hair, and hoped she was being honest with herself, that she was truly thinking of Davydd and Elen's pain and not her own.

Llewelyn returned that same night, shortly after Compline. As glad as Joanna was to see him, she was not eager to hear what he had to say, so sure was she that he'd spurned her father's olive branch. She delayed the inevitable with feigned cheer, with an animated account of all that had happened in his absence, and while he ate sparingly of smoked herring and rice, she told him that his Seneschal was still ailing, that Ednyved's wife had given birth to a daughter, and Elen had fallen from a tree, knocking out a tooth.

'Luckily, it was one of her baby teeth. But I felt I had to punish her, Llewelyn, if only to keep her from breaking her neck, and now she's sulking.' Joanna smiled ruefully. 'I can always tell when I'm not in her good graces; she'll talk to me only in Welsh!'

Llewelyn laughed, pushed his trencher aside; they were less than a month into Lent, and already he was heartily sick of fish, yearning for forbidden foods: butter, milk, cheese, eggs, and, above all, meat. 'I'll warn Elen that tree-climbing is one of the seven deadly sins.' Rising from the table, he moved towards Joanna. 'We need not talk about it, *breila*.'

'How well you know me. But no, I was being childish. Tell me what happened. What did my father offer for your support against the northern barons?'

'Everything but eternal life everlasting. As always, John is profligate with his promises.' Llewelyn turned back to the table, picked up a dried fig. 'But you'll not believe what John's new Bishop told us. It seems that John is of a sudden afire with crusading fever, and on March 4th, he took the cross!'

Joanna stared at him, open-mouthed. 'My father?' But after a startled moment to reflect, she realized how clever a stratagem that was, and said so.

'More than clever, Joanna. To give the Devil his due, it verges upon brilliance. Whatever else John lacks, it's not imagination. Nothing could be better calculated to win the Pope's goodwill; Innocent has been striving for fifteen years to prod Philip and John into another holy war against the Saracens.'

'I know,' Joanna said, and for an unguarded moment, there was in her voice the echoes of indulgent affection, of the love she'd once given to John in such free and abundant measure. 'I remember the Pope's letters, but my father never found the prospect of dying for the Holy Land all that alluring!'

'Well, he's now seen the light . . . at a most opportune time, in truth. Since a crusader's person and possessions are inviolate, that puts his foes at a distinct disadvantage – the most Christian King and the infidel barons. De Vesci would have done better to bypass Rome, to spend these weeks fortifying his castle at Alnwick. For as long as John talks of Jerusalem, the Pope will buy whatever he has to sell.'

It was a cynical assessment, but Joanna could find no fault with it. 'What of Gruffydd? Did my father offer to release him?'

'Of course . . . after I help him prevail over the rebels.'

'And . . . and you do not believe he would keep his word?'

'Do you, Joanna?'

'I do not know.' Joanna averted her gaze. 'Mayhap he might,' she ventured, and Llewelyn's eyes narrowed.

'I see. Do you also believe that unicorns can only be caught by virgins? Do you believe, too, that the barnacle goose is spawned in the sea like a fish and may be eaten during Lent?'

'Llewelyn, stop! You asked me what I believed, and I told you. It's not fair to blame me because you did not like my answer. Would you rather I'd lied to you?'

A moment passed, and then another, before Llewelyn was able to summon up a taut smile. 'How do you expect us to get a satisfactory argument going if you fall back upon logic?'

He stepped closer, let his hands rest upon her shoulders. 'I know you want to believe that John would keep faith, set Gruffydd free. I would to God I could believe it, too, Joanna. But I know better. John promises gold and delivers dross. He'll never let Gruffydd go, never. Not unless he's forced to it.'

Joanna said nothing. Llewelyn's way was not hers. She'd have bargained all that Heaven held, would never have risked the war that brought about twenty-eight deaths at Nottingham Castle. But Gwynedd was not her homeland, and Gruffydd was not her son.

'Joanna . . . there is something else I must tell you. William de Cornhill was John's sworn man long ere he was made Bishop of Coventry and Chester. He spoke for John, at John's bidding, offered to free Rhys Gryg, to buy our swords and let the dead bury their dead. But he warned, too, what we might expect should we make of John an enemy and not an ally. He was quite blunt, said that if I join with the rebel barons, I will be excommunicated.'

Joanna gasped. 'And you'd risk even that?' She knew that her father had not been greatly troubled by his own sentence of excommunication. But she knew, too, that Llewelyn's faith was not as tenuous as John's. 'Llewelyn, beloved, think what you do. When you ride into battle, you'll be offering up more than your life. You'll be offering up your soul.'

'I do not believe that, Joanna.'

'But to be excommunicated is to be cast into darkness, eternal damnation –'

'For the sin of not supporting John? In my eyes, that is no sin, Joanna, and nothing the Bishop of Chester or the Pope says can convince me otherwise. Am I to believe that John Plantagenet is now the anointed of the Lord, the chosen of God? Not my God.'

While Joanna shared Llewelyn's sense of outrage, she could not accept the comforting dichotomy he'd drawn between the stringent teachings of their Church and the infinite mercy of the Almighty. She believed in the Pope's power to damn her husband, however unjustly, for she was not like Llewelyn, not a rebel, and in despair, she wondered how she'd find the strength to endure what lay ahead.

'So it will be war,' she said softly. 'War yet again.'

On April 26, Robert Fitz Walter and Giles de Braose, Bishop of Hereford, led an armed force to Northampton. But John did not appear as agreed upon, and the next day the barons moved on to Brackley, where Saer de Quincy had a manor. At Brackley, they set forth their demands in writing, calling for a return to the 'old laws and customs of the realm', and warning that if John did not agree to their terms, they'd resort to force. John's reaction was pithy and predictable, 'Why,' he snapped, 'do they not just ask for my kingdom?'

With John's refusal, events seemed to take on their own momentum. The arrival of letters from the Pope did nothing to diffuse the tension, for he commanded the barons to abandon conspiracies and render their customary service to their King. On May 3, the barons formally renounced their homage and fealty to John, and chose Robert Fitz Walter as the 'Marshal of the Army of God and the Holy Church'.

John did not respond as they expected. He stayed his hand, offered to submit their differences to the Pope and a jointly picked council for arbitration. Despite the grandiloquent title they'd bestowed upon Fitz Walter, the barons were well aware that John had already pre-empted the high moral ground in this coming war. Few were willing to gamble upon a papal judgment against a crusader King, and their answer to John's offer was to lay siege to Northampton Castle.

John had so far trod with great care, had shown unexpected restraint, and he now began to reap the benefits of his forbearance. The vast majority of the English baronage were neither royalists nor rebels, and while many were sympathetic to the idea of a charter of liberties, these same men were not as enthusiastic about a civil war. The siege at Northampton was an embarrassing failure. On May 12, John commanded his sheriffs to seize the lands of all rebels. But just five days later, the political landscape was changed beyond recognition. For on Sunday, May 17, as Londoners were at Mass, Robert Fitz Walter's friends opened the city gates, and London, the 'capital of the crown and realm', was surrendered to the rebels.

Although Shrewsbury was perilously close to the Welsh border, its citizens trusted to the security of the Severn, for the town was sheltered in a protective bend of the river. On three sides, the Severn acted as a formidable barrier, as a deep, natural moat; on the north, the one land approach was blocked by the stone walls of Shrewsbury Castle. But the borderland was in turmoil that May, and when rumours spread of a Welsh attack, people panicked.

They had no luck in getting help from the sheriff of Shropshire, for Thomas Erdington was a trusted agent of the English King, and these days John's needs took precedence over all else. Nor could they rely upon neighbouring lords; Fulk Fitz Warin, the de Hodnets, and the powerful Corbet clan were all allied with the rebel barons and Llewelyn. Shrewsbury's common council met in urgent session, took the only action open to them, the fortification of the bridge that spanned the west bank of the Severn.

Known as St George's or the Welsh bridge, it was an imposing structure, would not be easily assaulted. A tower blocked the eastern entrance off the bridge on to the town's Mardevol Street; a gatehouse with massive looped hole battlements barred entry from the west. Trenches had been dug behind the bridge, sandbags piled up.

Frankevile, the little settlement on the opposite bank of the river, was all but deserted. Frightened villagers had long since driven their livestock into the hills, abandoned all they could not carry. St George's and St John's, the two hospitals on the wrong side of the river, had been evacuated. To the men gathered now upon the bridge, all seemed in readiness, but the eerie stillness was not conducive to confidence. Each time birds broke cover along the riverbank, men flinched, tightened grips on sword hilts.

Richard Pride and his brother Walter had both served as provosts and thought it only natural that they should assume control of the town's defences. The deputy constable of Shrewsbury Castle thought otherwise, and there'd been several heated exchanges. When the constable demanded that more men be deployed in defence of the castle, Richard Pride accused him of wanting to sacrifice the town for the castle, and they nearly came to blows. It took the intervention of Hugh de Lacy, Abbot of the influential Benedictine abbey of St Peter and St Paul, to restore order.

'Need I remind you whom the enemy is? It's madness to squabble amongst ourselves when Llewelyn ab Iorwerth and his cut-throat Welsh could come into sight at any moment.'

The Abbot's acerbic rebuke sobered them all. John de Hibernia said uneasily, 'Ought we not to send our women into the castle for safety's sake?'

No one answered him, for at that moment they heard the shouting. It came from behind them, from the town. The streets had been empty for hours; shops were boarded up, families barricaded within their houses. But as they turned, they saw a man running up Mardevol Street, running towards them.

'That's Lucas de Coleham,' the constable said, needlessly, for Coleham was known on sight to all. The Pride brothers were already hastening to intercept him, with John de Hibernia and Hugh de Champeneys right at their heels.

'The Welsh . . .' Coleham was sobbing for breath; he reeled to a stop, grabbed at Richard Pride for support. 'Llewelyn . . . he's at the bridge!'

'Lucas, are you drunk? We hold the bridge, hold –'

'The stone bridge . . . the English bridge! He's swung around to the east, is attacking from the other direction, from England!'

He saw horrified comprehension upon their faces. Someone swore; John de Hibernia muttered, 'Holy Virgin Mother,' and made an instinctive sign of the cross. The Abbot had reached them by now, clutched at Coleham's arm.

'My abbey,' he panted. 'What of my abbey?'

Coleham's throat was raw, his mouth parched. 'It's afire, Abbot Hugh. It's burning.'

'Spare the church!' Llewelyn's stallion shied as the wind sent sparks and cinders flying. He wheeled the horse in a semi-circle, gestured to his right. 'Burn the other buildings!'

Fire arrows had already embedded themselves in the thatched roofs of the laundry, the servants' dorters, the stables. Horses bolted in panic, several even floundering into the abbey fishpond. The Abbot's lodging had begun to burn; the guest house was already in flames. Dogs were barking frantically, and freed livestock milled about, but no monks were to be found, no resistance was offered. Most had fled as the Welsh rode into the abbey precincts; some had taken refuge in the nave of the church.

The Welsh had no time for the terrified monks. Just three hundred yards away was the English bridge, guarded by only a handful of men, men who were seeking desperately to raise its drawbridge. But they were too late; the Welsh were already on the bridge. Swords flashed, blood splattered upon the red grit stones. The one surviving English soldier whirled, plunged into the river; he did not surface again.

Llewelyn's stallion was maddened by the smoke, the scent of blood. It reared up wildly as a man darted into the street, swinging a chained mace. Llewelyn gave the horse a free rein; it plunged forward, and the man went down, under those flailing hooves.

Other men were emerging into the street, but the resistance the Welsh were encountering was sporadic, half-hearted. Women were screaming; some of the houses nearest the bridge were on fire. By the time Llewelyn reached Haystrete, he knew that Shrewsbury was his for the taking.

The High Cross was now in sight; ahead lay the sandstone walls of John's castle. A small group of men were clustered below the Cross. Their swords were sheathed, and they held up a makeshift flag of truce. Llewelyn recognized Hugh de Lacy, and he reined in his mount.

The Abbot came forward cautiously; his comrades kept a more prudent distance. 'My lord, I speak for the Holy Roman Church, for the provosts and common council of Shrewsbury. We will surrender the town to you, offer no resistance if you'll give us your sworn word that no further harm will come to our people.'

'What of the castle?'

The Abbot was close enough now to see the blood smears on Llewelyn's sword. He could not bring himself to look towards the east, towards the billowing black smoke that overhung his abbey. What they were offering in peace this man could take by force, and then turn their town over to his men for their sport. 'The castle, too, will yield, my lord. We ask only that no more lives be lost, that you spare the innocent.'

'I'd not see men die for a prize already won. Your offer is a fair one; so are your terms.'

The Abbot's shoulders sagged. His relief was such that he could not speak, could only sigh a fervent, 'Thank God Almighty!'

Richard Pride was not as easily assured; he knew from first-hand experience what could befall a conquered city. 'I do not mean to give offence, my lord, but are you sure you can control your men?'

'Yes,' Llewelyn said laconically, 'I'm sure.'

No more than that. But Richard Pride was suddenly sure, too. Reaching for his sword, he held it out, hilt first, to the Welsh Prince.

'What now? Shall we take you to the castle?'

'First I think we'd best see to those fires,' Llewelyn said. 'I find I suddenly take a very personal interest in Shrewsbury's survival.'

By noon, the Welsh had gathered in the inner bailey of Shrews-bury Castle, where they watched as the royal arms of England yielded to the red and gold lions of North Wales. As Llewelyn's banner fluttered aloft above the keep, they cheered.

Llewelyn could have cheered, too. He felt the same excitement, the same jubilant triumph as he gazed upward, and he did not move until Rhys came to stand at his side.

'Shrewsbury was once the capital of the Princes of Powys. You've retaken what was ours, Llewelyn.'

'We cannot hope to hold it, Rhys; I know that. But I can hold it as long as it truly matters, until we've forced John to come to terms with us.' Llewelyn reached out, impulsively embraced his friend.

'Passing strange,' he laughed, 'that the first English town I ever saw should have been Shrewsbury. I was just a lad of ten, but I remember it well, even after thirty years. And now . . . now

Shrewsbury shall be my bargaining counter, Rhys. I shall make use of Shrewsbury to set my son free.'

On June 10, John rode to the meadow called Runnymede, between Windsor and Staines. There he gave grudging consent to the demands of his rebellious barons. The articles drawn up by the barons were affixed with John's great seal, as proof that a preliminary accord had been reached. It was then agreed upon that negotiations would resume on Monday, the 15th, using the articles as the basis for a final settlement, a charter of liberties that would also serve as a treaty of peace between the embattled King and his disaffected subjects.

It was dark by the time John returned to Windsor Castle. He dismissed his attendants, withdrew to his private quarters in the upper bailey, and none dared to intrude upon his seclusion, to brave the Angevin temper on this, surely one of the most desolate days of a troubled kingship.

It was Richard who finally resolved to breach John's defences. He was no more eager than anyone else to serve as scapegoat for Fitz Walter and his Army of God and Holy Church, but he felt honour-bound to offer his father some small measure of comfort, if only a sympathetic ear.

'I'll go if you'd rather be alone, Papa.'

There was in John's face the exhaustion of a man who'd lived too long on nerves alone, and fury all the more intense for being impotent. But he beckoned Richard into the bedchamber, said, 'No . . . I'd have you stay.'

Several sheets of parchment lay scattered about the table. Richard picked up one headed, *'Ista sunt Capitula que Barones petunt et dominus Rex condedit.'* That, he thought, said it all: 'These are the clauses which the barons seek and which the lord King concedes.'

'The charter of Henry I that the barons set such store by, Henry never held to it, Papa. He granted it and promptly disregarded it. Might it not be possible to treat the barons' charter in the same way?'

'You're not familiar with all its provisions, are you? Look upon the last page of the articles.'

Richard had only a passing boyhood acquaintance with Latin, and it took him some moments to make a laborious translation of the clause dealing with 'The form of security for the preservation of the peace and liberties between King and Kingdom.'

The more he read, the more astonished he became. The articles

518

provided for a committee of twenty-five barons to act as a court of appeals against breaches of the charter provisions. If they decided John was acting in defiance of the charter, they had the power to seize his castles, lands, and possessions in order to force him into compliance, to do him injury in any way they could, sparing only his person and those of his family. Furthermore, all men were to be required to take an oath of obedience to these twenty-five barons, an oath to take precedence over oaths of allegiance to the King.

To Richard, this was an unheard-of constraint upon the inherent God-given powers of the Crown, and a formula for disaster. He did not need to be told that Fitz Walter, de Vesci, and their supporters would constitute a majority on this committee of twenty-five. But it was the last sentence that shocked him so. It forbade John to seek the charter's annulment from the Pope and held that the Archbishop of Canterbury, the other Bishops of England, and the papal legate Pandulf must agree to deny John's right of appeal to the curia in a matter already before it, to compel John to forswear his own liege lord, the Pope.

As Richard looked up, his disbelief clearly showing on his face, John said grimly, 'So you see, lad, whatever options I have, ignoring the charter is not amongst them.' He joined Richard at the table, read again that last coercive clause, and then crumpled it in his fist, flung it to the floor.

'Much of what they want in the charter I could live with. In fact, many of their demands can be found in a charter granted the city of Bristol nigh on twenty years ago, a charter that eased distraint for debts, gave citizens the right to marry without the licence of their lord, limited a lord's right of wardship. Do you know who granted that Bristol charter, Richard? I did, as Earl of Gloucester.'

'I know you've oft-times granted borough charters, Papa, and with generous privileges.'

'Including one to London giving them the right to elect a mayor . . . less than a week ere they opened the city to Fitz Walter!' John's rage was mounting; so was his sense of injury. 'I may not always have dealt fairly with men I could not trust; I'll concede that much. I'd have been willing to redress individual grievances. But I'll not submit to force. I'll not surrender the traditional and ancient rights of sovereignty, rights that were my father's before me and will be my son's after me. I'll not turn my kingdom over to the likes of de Vesci and Fitz Walter!'

519

'But you put your great seal to this document, Papa. You agreed to grant them their charter of liberties.'

'What else could I do? Fitz Walter holds London. Llewelyn razed Shawardine Castle to the ground, and then took Shrewsbury. There have been outbreaks in Northampton and Exeter. Lincoln is now in rebel hands. In South Wales, Reginald de Braose is laying siege to the castles I seized from his father. In the North of England, the Scots King dares to give open aid to the rebels. Christ, the country is in a virtual state of war! For nigh on a month, my revenues have been cut off, my government hamstrung. And each day sees more defections to the rebels. I'm no longer sure who's with me, and who's not, and I do not know whom I can trust. Yes, I agreed to grant them their charter. At swordpoint! But the game is not over yet.'

'I've not read these articles, Papa. You say you can live with most of the provisions. Mayhap you could live with the charter, too, if you tried –'

'Never. This so-called peace treaty is utterly one-sided. There's no equity in it. They give up nothing, whilst I am compelled to free all hostages, to banish my foreign mercenaries and Poitevin bailiffs, to dismiss Peter des Roches as Justiciar. And then . . . then to submit to the judgment of five-and-twenty over-Kings, men who'd barter with the Devil to see me dead. But I am King by God's will, not Eustace de Vesci's. As King, I am responsible for my subjects, not responsible to them. I'd rather lose my kingdom fighting for it than to see it whittled away piecemeal by men like de Vesci and Fitz Walter, Llewelyn ab Iorwerth.'

'What will you do, Papa?'

'Whatever I have to do. I'll give them what they want, their Runnymede charter, and then we'll see; then they'll fly their true colours. Why do you think I've shown such forbearance, Richard? When have you ever known me to be so tender with traitors? But I've had to play to a larger audience than de Vesci and Fitz Walter. There are one hundred and ninety-seven baronies in the realm. As far as I know, thirty-nine are in rebel hands. A like number holds fast for the Crown. That still leaves well over a hundred that are unaligned, that have not committed themselves to either side. I dare say most favour a charter in some form or other, but how many of them would be willing to fight for it, to fight both Crown and Church? Especially when they see how Fitz Walter and his five-and-twenty use their charter, as a means of feathering their own nests and settling old grudges . . . not all of them with me.'

'You mean then to ask the Pope to annul the charter?'

'If I have to, yes.'

'But what of this provision in the articles, the one expressly forbidding you to appeal to the Pope?'

'The Church will never accept such a stricture. It was naïve of Fitz Walter to think otherwise. However sympathetic Langton is to the concept of a charter, he cannot in conscience agree to foreclose a papal appeal. To do so would be to put the charter above the Church. I've talked to Langton and to Pandulf. The price the barons will have to pay for this great charter of theirs is to omit any mention of the Pope.'

John sat down suddenly in the nearest chair. 'Shall I foretell the future for you, Richard? It does not take a Peter of Wakefield to predict what is to come. I shall give them their accursed charter, for I have no choice. But they will not keep faith, with it or with me. The Pope will intervene on my behalf, invalidate the charter as an act of naked extortion.'

John paused, glanced over at his son, and Richard saw that for once, he was being utterly honest. 'And then,' he concluded bleakly, 'we will have what none of us truly wanted – war. War to the death, no quarter given, and God pity England.'

June, 1215

Dolwyddelan, North Wales

When Llewelyn rose to fetch Gwladys, Joanna experienced a moment of near panic. Ever since his arrival at Dolwyddelan, she'd been dreading the time when she would find herself alone with Reginald de Braose. Taking a bracing swallow of wine, she cast about frantically for a neutral topic of conversation, for a way to keep Maude's ghost at bay.

'I know your son Will. He once stayed at my husband's court. How does he? Will he be attending your wedding?'

'Not likely, Madame. As far as I know, he's still in France. Will's ever had a mind of his own, and now that he's nineteen . . .'

'His mother's death must have been hard on him,' Joanna sympathized, trying all the while not to think of the deaths that must have truly devastated Will. Had Reginald been the one to tell him? How could you tell a fourteen-year-old boy that his grandmother and uncle had been starved to death?

'In truth, Madame, they were not that close.' Reginald signalled for a servant to refill his cup; he did not seem to share Joanna's unease. 'My daughter Matilda is a good lass, does what she's told. But Will and I . . . well, we always seem to be at odds. Part of the trouble, I think, is that he was my mother's favourite, and she – Jesu! Madame, are you all right?'

Joanna stared down at her broken cup, at the wine soaking the rushes. When she raised her eyes to Reginald's, they were blinded by tears. 'I'm sorry,' she whispered, 'so sorry . . .'

Reginald was suddenly as flustered as she. 'How stupid of me,' he said at last. 'I was thinking of you as Lord Llewelyn's wife, had all but forgotten you are John's daughter.'

'I do not know what to say to you. I pray for Maude's soul, and for your brother's, but –'

'Madame, do not distress yourself so. I do not blame you. We are none of us answerable for the sins of our fathers.'

That was not the creed of his House; few Marcher families had so bloody a history as the de Braose clan. But Reginald sounded sincere, and even if he was speaking only out of his need to gain Llewelyn as ally, Joanna was grateful for his assurance, was willing to take absolution upon any terms she could get.

She was spared the need to respond, for Llewelyn had just re-entered the hall, was escorting his daughter towards them. Gwladys showed no embarrassment at being the object of all eyes. At seventeen, she had poise a much older woman might envy, a sure sense of her own worth as a Prince's daughter. We must get her a wedding gown of purest emerald silk, Joanna thought, a colour vivid enough to set off those dark gypsy looks. Gwladys would make a very handsome bride, and thank God, a willing one. Joanna knew the girl would have preferred to wed a *Cymro*, one of her own people. But even the independent Gwladys would never have claimed the right to choose her own husband, and she seemed content enough with Llewelyn's choice.

Joanna, however, had yet to be reconciled to the match. She could see the shrewd political logic in such an alliance. She could even see why the union was advantageous for Gwladys. Reginald de Braose was an attractive man, not yet forty, with polished manners and a reputation for being more moderate and reasonable than most of his tumultuous kindred. And the bulk of the de Braose lands were situated in Wales or the Marches, so Gwladys would be spared the fate that had so daunted Joanna, the prospect of a life in exile. But to Joanna, all else was overshadowed by a bond of blood.

Llewelyn had sympathized with her reluctance to see her step-daughter wed to Maude de Braose's son. But he had not been deterred from making the alliance. Joanna knew he had balanced her discomfort against the good of Gwynedd, and she'd come up short.

'What are you thinking of, *breila*?' Llewelyn was smiling at her. She linked her arm in his, let him lead her aside.

'I was thinking,' she said, 'how thankful I am that we have years yet ere we must give our Elen away in marriage.'

'What is this?' Joanna looked up as Llewelyn dropped a parchment scroll into her lap.

'I thought you might be curious about the Runnymede charter.'

'Indeed, I am, but I do not read Latin . . .' Unrolling the parchment sheets, Joanna stared in wonder at what she held, a French translation of her father's charter. 'Llewelyn, you did this for me?'

'Well, one of my scribes did.' Llewelyn pretended to stagger backward as Joanna jumped to her feet, flung her arms around his neck. 'Had I only known I could gladden you so cheaply with a few pages of parchment, I might have saved a small fortune over the years, need not have given you all those moonstones and garnets and gold necklets.'

'Laugh if you will, but the world is full of men who'd as soon share this charter with their serfs as with their wives, men who think a literate woman to be the Devil's handiwork.'

'And with good reason, *breila*. Teach a woman to read and write, and ere long, her head will be overflowing with unseemly and unwomanly ideas. She might even think to enter an enemy encampment, to negotiate peace terms on her husband's behalf.'

'Have I ever told you,' Joanna murmured, 'that you have very taking ways?'

Llewelyn laughed. 'I dare say the citizens of Shrewsbury would agree with you.'

Joanna laughed, too, and sitting down upon the settle, she began to thumb through the document, reading at random. 'I doubt my father was much troubled to agree that fish-weirs be banned from the River Thames! Nor by this provision that no free man shall be imprisoned or outlawed except by the judgment of his peers or by the law of the land; he offered that himself in his compromise proposal of May 10th. In fact, Llewelyn, much of this charter seems to state existing law. Take this clause: "No one shall be taken or imprisoned upon the appeal of a woman for the death of anyone except her husband." I thought that was already the law of the land, that a woman could testify only to the murder of her husband or her own rape.'

'It was, but apparently John has been somewhat lax about enforcing it, and his courts have been more responsive to women's pleas than the barons liked.'

'That's true. I remember one case in which he even allowed a woman to testify against her own husband! She claimed he was in collusion with the plaintiff to defraud her of her land, and John found in her favour.' Joanna very much needed to recall acts of compassion,

524

equities she could balance against the horror of Nottingham Castle, the merciless vengeance taken upon Maelgwn, Maude de Braose. But Llewelyn was not the ideal audience for a testimonial to John's better nature, and she glanced nervously in his direction, seeking to gauge the extent of his forbearance.

Quarrels had been kindled by much less. But Llewelyn's mood had been euphoric for days now, ever since they'd got word of the settlement upon the meadows of Runnymede. He could not begrudge Joanna such meagre solace, and he nodded agreeably. Reassured, Joanna returned to the charter.

'I know men think it unfair that a woman has the right to engage a champion whilst an accused man must fight for himself. But I find this provision no less unfair, Llewelyn, for it could conceivably be interpreted to deny a woman the right to bring a rape charge. How glad I am that we have our own laws, that we are not subject to trial by ordeal or combat and a Welshwoman's oath is conclusive as to whether she was raped or not.'

'When you said "we", did you speak from the heart? Have you come to think of yourself as Welsh, *breila*?'

Joanna hesitated. 'No,' she admitted. 'I think of Wales as home, but that is because of you, our children. In all honesty, I have not your love of the land; people are all that matter to me. I do not have any attachment to England, either, have never felt the . . . *hiraeth* that you do away from Wales.'

Llewelyn would have preferred another answer, but had not truly expected one. 'I'd wager that most of Norman-French blood feel as you do. But I think that will change in time. The loss of Normandy casts a long shadow.'

Joanna was intrigued. 'You're saying that, having lost their Normandy estates, men will come to give greater worth to their English lands?'

'Already, you can see signs of it, Joanna. You Normans may not yet think of yourselves as English, but you've begun to draw distinctions of birth. One of the complaints against John's Justiciar, Peter des Roches, was that he was born in Poitou, not England. It was the loss of his Angevin empire that brought John to Runnymede. But that same loss will one day forge a sense of unity amongst the English, Norman and Saxon alike. I only hope it will not be at the expense of the Welsh.'

He sounded suddenly grim, and Joanna reached up, laid her hand

525

on his arm. 'Have you forgotten the story you told me, Llewelyn, of the Welsh sage and King Henry? Henry wanted to know if the royal army would prevail, and he said . . .'

'He said, "Lord King, I do not think that on the Day of Direst Judgment any race other than the Welsh, or any other language will give answer to the Supreme Judge of all for this small corner of the earth."'

'I do not think the Welsh need fear the future, beloved, not as long as the House of Cunedda rules in Gwynedd. But why do you link Normandy and Runnymede?'

'Because, Joanna, this charter is aimed as much at John's father as it is at John. John's government is not that different from Henry's. Granted, his word is worthless, but Henry was not slow to dissemble either, when it served his purposes. Henry's barons chafed under his rule, too, fully as much as do John's. No lord wants an overly strong king, a government that truly governs. John is hated because men feel – rightfully – that they cannot trust him. But he might have been hated less had he been less effective a King . . . or had he not lost Normandy. Henry and Richard both ruled with a heavy hand, but they were gone from the kingdom for years at a time, occupied by events in Normandy, Anjou, Poitou. Those absences gave their English barons a needed respite, some breathing space. But for nigh on ten years, John has been anchored in England, riding the length and breadth of the realm, bringing his courts and his constables, collecting taxes, levying scutage, making enemies. To his hard-pressed barons, he must have begun to seem as ever-present as God, as inevitable as death . . . and about as welcome!'

Joining her on the settle, he stretched out, pillowed his head in her lap, and she leaned over, gave him a playful upside-down kiss. 'This charter could only have been drawn up by lawyers, with their passion for complexity. The wardship of minors, debts to the Jews, bridge-building, intestate deaths, uniform measures of wine and corn; is there any subject they did not seek to address? So much of it seems unnecessary to me. Here it states that a widow shall not be compelled to marry again, provided she offers security that she'll not marry without the King's consent. I agree with the principle, Llewelyn, but it already is the practice. Widows often petitioned my father for the right not to remarry, and he almost always allowed them to purchase that privilege.'

'Yes, he did. But that privilege depended upon the King's whim,

526

his convenience. Now it will depend upon the charter. As a widow, which would you rather rely upon, Joanna?'

Joanna did not need to consider. 'The charter,' she conceded. 'I see your point. You're saying that the true significance of this charter is that it changes privileges into rights?'

'And that it goes beyond the rights of individual petitioners. It's rather like a borough charter, one granting certain privileges to the citizens of a particular town. Except that this charter encompasses the entire realm. That is a novel concept. A pity it shall be as short-lived as the peace it warrants.'

'Are you so sure that the peace cannot last?'

'Read the last clause of the charter, Joanna. Then read the list of names affixed to the charter, the barons elected to the committee of twenty-five. And then tell me if you think John will ever accept their governance.'

Joanna did as he bade. 'God's wrath, look at these names! Eustace de Vesci, Robert Fitz Walter, Saer de Quincy, the Earls of Hereford and Clare – I count fully fourteen to be my father's sworn enemies, only two to be men he can trust. Llewelyn, they want war; it's as simple as that.'

'Nothing is ever that simple, love. I grant you that they mean to press their advantage to the utmost. They are not likely to keep faith with the charter . . . but I find it hard to fault them for that, for they know that John will not, either. He's bound to appeal to the Pope, and when he does, he will prevail. It cannot be otherwise, for his legal position is unassailable. Canon law holds that an oath given under duress is not binding. The Pope must annul the charter. John knows it, I know it, and I expect most of the barons know it, too.'

Llewelyn sat up, reached for the charter. 'You asked what I see as the true significance of the Runnymede charter. For me, it lies in two brief provisions, *breila*. One compels John to make restitution of Welsh lands, liberties, and rights seized unjustly by the Crown, recognizes the supremacy of Welsh law in Wales. And the other . . .' He did not bother to glance at the parchment, for the words had long since been committed to memory.

'"We will restore at once the son of Llewelyn,"' he quoted, '"and all the hostages from Wales and the charters delivered to us as security for peace." That is the heart of John's great charter, Joanna. My son is coming home.'

*

It was early morning; the July sun had not had time to assert dominion, and the air still held some of the dampness of night. Joanna's ladies were helping her to dress, and Llewelyn was about to submit himself to his barber's razor. It was then that the shouting began in the bailey, the sounds of celebration.

The scene that greeted Llewelyn was one of pandemonium. The bailey was thronged with men and women, barking dogs, excited children. In the midst of all the uproar, Gruffydd was struggling to control his stallion. He'd obviously not expected so joyful a welcome, and he smiled shyly at his well-wishers, acknowledging the greetings of friends shoving to reach his side. He was wearing a finely woven new tunic, but it was streaked with dust and sweat, offered Llewelyn poignant testimony to the urgency of his son's journey.

The crowd now took up Gruffydd's name, chanted it in triumphant unison. Gruffydd flushed under the acclaim, and then glanced up, saw Llewelyn standing on the stairs. As he slid from the saddle, the crowd hushed, parted before him. He moved towards the keep, stood looking up at his father.

'Gruffydd.' Llewelyn's voice was suddenly husky. He came down the stairs, stopped when the space between them could be breached by an outstretched hand.

'It's really me, Papa.' Gruffydd tugged self-consciously at his beard. 'I must look like a right proper Norman. But they would not trust me with a razor, and once I was free, I was not willing to wait a moment longer than need be.'

'I do not think,' Llewelyn said slowly, 'that a single day has passed in these four years when I did not envision this moment, imagine what it would be like, what I'd say to you. I meant to tell you how much I've missed you, and how very proud I am of you. And now you're here, and that's not enough. Christ, it does not even begin to be enough.'

'It is enough for me, Papa.'

Joanna had followed Llewelyn out on to the stairs. She stood very still, watching as her husband and his son embraced. She'd long had an unease of conscience where Gruffydd was concerned, for she remembered with uncomfortable clarity how she'd welcomed Gruffydd's banishment to the English court. It was a memory that often came back to haunt her in the months after Gruffydd's harrowing ordeal at Nottingham Castle, and she'd resolved that if the boy was ever given his freedom, she'd try to make peace with him. Not just for Llewelyn's sake. She owed it to Gruffydd. This was yet another of John's debts that she was somehow honour-bound to repay.

But her good intentions faltered now at sight of Gruffydd. Her pity had blurred Gruffydd's memory, and she'd had almost three years to recast her recollections in a more sympathetic mould, to convince herself that she could befriend Gruffydd if given a second chance. It was a shock, therefore, to confront reality, the flesh and blood man standing on the stairs. With his bright beard, broad shoulders, and flowing hair, he did not look like a proper Norman to her, more like a Norse pirate chieftain. She'd forgotten the aura of danger that clung to Gruffydd. Even as a boy, he'd had it, and he was no boy now, was very much a man.

Neither Llewelyn nor Gruffydd had seemed to want to end their embrace. When they'd finally moved apart, both had tears in their eyes and both were laughing. Only then did Joanna start down the stairs.

'Welcome home, Gruffydd,' she said, and smiled at him.

Gruffydd did not return her smile. She was his father's wife, he could not forget that. But he could not forget, either, that he'd forfeited four years of his life because of her, because she would see her son as Llewelyn's heir. 'Yes, Madame,' he said softly. 'Gwynedd is indeed my home.'

Gruffydd entered the stables, set his lantern upon a stall gate, and knelt, holding out a savoury beef bone. Math's tail twitched; he snatched the bone from Gruffydd's hand, retreated with it into the shadows. Gruffydd rose, but made no move to go. The raucous celebration of his return had not died down with the day's end, and after three years of solitary confinement, Gruffydd was overwhelmed by all the noise, the press of people. He'd once seen a young deer on the loose in Shrewsbury; he could better understand now the panic a woodland creature might feel in such alien surroundings, and he was not eager to return to the hall, to take centre stage again. Gruffydd did not feel like a hero, not at all, just very tired, confused, and curiously let down.

The stable door creaked and he glanced up, saw a small boy peering in at him. But he did not mind sharing his solitude with a child, and he gave the boy an encouraging smile.

'See that alaunt in the corner? Math was my dog once; I was sure

529

he was the best dog in all Christendom! I truly hated to leave him, and whenever I'd get too homesick, it would help to think of Math, to think how he'd welcome me home.' Gruffydd settled back upon a bale of hay. 'But I was gone four years. He does not even remember me.'

The child came closer. He was a thin youngster, with a thatch of untidy black hair, a shy smile, and a smudge of dirt on his nose. 'Here,' he said, thrusting something into Gruffydd's hand. 'This is for you.'

Gruffydd held it up towards the lantern light. 'A penny?'

'It's my lucky penny.'

'Then I cannot keep it, lad.'

'But I want you to,' the boy protested, and squatted down beside Gruffydd. 'I do not remember you, not at all,' he confessed, after some moments of companionable silence. 'I was too little when you left. But I'm six and a half now.' He paused, waited expectantly. 'Do you not know who I am? I'm Davydd – your brother.'

Gruffydd's hand jerked; the coin fell into the straw. Davydd at once scrambled to retrieve it. 'Here, you dropped your penny.'

Gruffydd ignored Davydd's outstretched hand. Getting hastily to his feet, he stared at the boy. His brother. Joanna's son.

'I do not want it,' he said roughly, saw Davydd's mouth quiver, saw only a small child, bewildered and hurt. But then Davydd stepped forward, and the lantern light fell full upon his face, upon the slanting hazel eyes. Accursed cat eyes. John's eyes.

Gruffydd drew an uneven breath. 'Jesus wept, you even look like him! You may speak Welsh better than she does, but you've still got his eyes, his blood. God grant that I never forget it.'

Gruffydd was badly shaken, and he took refuge now in rage, rage that would enable him to blot out memory of that moment, however fleeting, when he'd identified with Davydd's pain. If he ever gave in to weakness like that, he was lost, and so was Gwynedd. This was Joanna's son, John's grandson. 'Go away,' he said. 'You had no right to do this, to seek me out. I do not want you here.'

Davydd stood rooted. 'Why are you so angry with me? What have I done? I've never hurt you –'

'You've never hurt me? I spent four years in an English prison because of you, you and your mother! Why do you think John wanted me as hostage? Because he means to make you Prince of Gwynedd, a puppet English Prince to dance to London's tune!'

Davydd was struggling not to cry. 'I did not want you to be a hostage! I was glad you were coming home, gave you my penny. And my mama was glad, too, when the English let you go; she told me so. You say such strange things, and they make no sense. Papa is Prince of Gwynedd. So why would the English King want me to be Prince? And I'm Welsh; how could I ever be an English Prince?'

'No, you are not Welsh,' Gruffydd said bitterly. 'They may give you a crown, but they cannot give you that. Welsh you'll never be.'

Davydd gasped. 'I am so Welsh! You take that back!'

'Ask your mother, your Norman-French mother. She was born in England, the daughter of the English King. If I mate Math to a spaniel, the pups will be neither alaunt nor spaniel, but mixed-breeds, curs. Neither one nor the other. That's you, too, neither English nor Welsh, and you'd best learn to live with it.'

Davydd was alone in the stables. Gruffydd had gone, taking his lantern, and the dark was not friendly. Davydd still clutched his penny; now he flung it away, into the blackness beyond him, and moved closer to Math. The dog growled low in its throat. 'I do not want your bone, Math,' Davydd said, but the dog growled again. He'd find Mama, that's what he'd do. Mama could tell him if there was truth in what Gruffydd said.

The great hall was overflowing with people. Davydd had to squirm his way between them, trying not to tread upon the long, trailing skirts, trying to avoid jostling elbows, spilling wine cups. His neck began to ache as he craned upward, searching for familiar faces. He could not find his mother, and he began to feel a suffocating sense of panic. He wanted to get away from the smoke and loud laughter, the bodies walling him in on all sides. He wanted his mother.

But it was not Joanna that he found; it was Llewelyn. It had never occurred to him to seek out his father for comfort. He loved Llewelyn very much, but he was very much in awe of him, too. His need was now so great, though, that he could wait no longer. He had to know, and he edged his way forward until he could pull at the sleeve of his father's tunic.

Llewelyn glanced down. 'Should you not be abed, lad?' He was turning back to the adults encircling him when his son tugged again at his arm.

'Papa? Papa, am I Welsh?' he said, and saw with relief that he'd

531

succeeded in catching his father's full attention, for that was not always easy to do.

'Come with me,' Llewelyn said, and led Davydd up the steps on to the dais, sat the boy down in his own seat. 'Now,' he said, 'what would make you ask a question like that? Of course you are Welsh.'

'Is Mama Welsh?' Davydd asked, very low.

'No, lad. Your mother is of Norman-French descent.'

'Then . . . then I'm not Welsh,' Davydd concluded despairingly, and Llewelyn swiftly shook his head.

'You are Welsh, Davydd. You are my son, and under our law, that makes you Welsh, as Welsh as anyone in this hall, me included.'

Llewelyn smiled at the boy, but Davydd ducked his head. He'd begun to pull at the embroidery decorating the seat cushion. 'If Mama is Norman, I must be half Norman.'

'That's right, you are. Welsh by law, and half Welsh and half Norman by blood.'

'But the Normans are your enemies, Papa.'

'Yes, some of them are. But not all. I have many English friends, Davydd, men I'd trust far more than a Welshman like Gwenwynwyn. To have Norman blood is no shame, lad. After all, you are not ashamed of your mother. Surely you do not think less of her for being Norman?'

'No! I love Mama more than anything. But . . . but what of me, Papa? Mama is Norman; what am I? If I'm not fully Welsh and fully Norman, then I'm nothing!'

'Ah, Davydd, no. You could not be more wrong. Most people have only one heritage. But you have two, your mother's and mine. That gives you more than my other sons, makes you doubly blessed.'

Davydd was silent for a time, plucking absently at the cushion threads. 'I had not thought of it that way,' he admitted. 'But what of Math, Papa? If you mate him to a spaniel, the puppies will be curs.'

Llewelyn reached out, brushed the hair back from Davydd's eyes. He did not doubt now that Davydd was mouthing something he'd overheard; no six year old would ever have drawn such an analogy on his own. 'You know that roan stallion of mine, the one I bought at Michaelmas? I got him in Powys, because they are celebrated for the fine horses they breed. Horses of Spanish stock, crossed with sturdy Welsh mares. Crossbreeding can bring out the best of two strains, Davydd. In horses . . . and in men.'

Had he said what the boy needed to hear? He was not yet sure, for Davydd's was not an easy face to read. 'We should have told you ere this. But your mother finds it painful to talk about her father, and so we kept waiting . . .'

'The English King is truly Mama's father?' Davydd had absorbed too many shocks this night for one more to have much impact. 'He's a bad man, Papa.'

'Yes, lad, he is. That's why it hurts your mother so.'

'I'm glad, then, that I did not talk to Mama, that I talked to you.' Davydd then astonished Llewelyn by saying, 'To be both Welsh and Norman, is it like . . . like being a bridge, Papa?'

'Yes, Davydd, exactly like that.' Llewelyn was that rarity among parents, one capable of making a realistic assessment of his offspring, tallying up both strengths and shortcomings. He was very fond of Tegwared, but saw him for what he was, a good-natured, amiable youth, both generous and feckless, equally lacking in ambition or malice. Marared and Gwenllian were eager to please, easy to content, neither as clever nor as stubborn as Gwladys. Elen was his free spirit, his secret favourite. And Gruffydd was his firstborn, the son wild and reckless and courageous and wronged.

But Davydd had remained an enigma. A quiet, self-contained child, he was little given either to confidences or complaints, and he was so well-behaved that Llewelyn sometimes found himself wishing the boy would break free, put frogs in his sister's bath, or ink in the holy water. Such pranks were an exasperating but expected part of the rites of passage through boyhood, and it baffled Llewelyn to have a son so sedate, so unlike himself. This sudden glimpse into Davydd's mind was a revelation, therefore, the first intimation he'd had that this son could be special.

'Your brother Gruffydd is back in the hall. Let's go over and talk to him,' he suggested, not noticing when Davydd lagged behind.

'Papa . . . Papa, will Gruffydd go away again?'

Llewelyn turned, smiled reassuringly at the boy. 'No, lad, he'll not go away. Not ever again.'

Davydd stopped on the steps of the dais, stood watching as his father crossed to Gruffydd. Davydd's sisters were already there, clustered around Gruffydd in an admiring circle. At the sight of Elen in Gruffydd's lap, Davydd felt a sharp surge of a hitherto unfamiliar emotion, jealousy.

Something nudged his leg, and he looked down to see Math,

533

gratefully wrapped his arms around the dog's ruff. 'I wish you'd bite him,' he whispered, but without any faith that Math would. Gruffydd would give him bones and win him over. Why should Math be any different from Papa, or Elen and Gwladys? They all thought Gruffydd was wonderful, that he could do no wrong. He was the only one in all of Dolwyddelan who was sorry that Gruffydd had come home.

He heard his father say, 'And you actually refused to write the letter? You turned John down?' He sounded so amused, so proud, that Davydd felt tears prick his eyes. Never had he felt so alone. But at that moment he saw his mother. Joanna was standing by one of the hall screens. She, too, was watching Gruffydd and Llewelyn. Davydd's unhappiness had honed his insight, and the look on his mother's face gave him sudden, surprised comfort. He was not alone, after all. Mama was sorry, too, that Gruffydd was back.

July, 1215
Aber, North Wales

'If it were me, I'd spit on his summons! Why should you be at John's beck and call? You're Prince of North Wales, not a lackey of the English King!'

It was suddenly very still in the hall. Llewelyn swung around in surprise, turned thoughtful brown eyes upon his eldest son. 'For certès, I do not see myself as John's lackey. But the fact is, Gruffydd, that the Princes of Wales are vassals of the English crown, and John is within his rights in summoning us to his court to renew our oaths of homage. That is the price we must pay for the concessions he granted us in the Runnymede charter. I'll not lie to you, lad. I'll not pretend that I like it. But I have to do it, none the less.'

'I would not.'

'You would,' Llewelyn said evenly, 'if you were Prince of Gwynedd.'

Gruffydd's eyes flickered. 'I should think a Prince could do as he pleased.'

There was so much innocence in his son's arrogance that Llewelyn no longer had to strive for patience. 'I'm doing this, too, lad, because the Archbishop of Canterbury asks it of me. I owe him, Gruffydd; he assumed personal responsibility for assuring your release. He's a good man, and Lord help him, but he truly believes a peace can be made between John and his barons. Which brings me to the third reason why I shall go to Oxford, because it will afford me an opportunity to judge for myself how much time we have ere war breaks out.'

'Well, it is your decision, Papa,' Gruffydd said, managing to make a statement of simple fact sound as if he were making a concession of sorts. Llewelyn looked faintly amused, Ednyved pensive, while

Joanna drew farther back into the shadows of the window seat so none could read her face.

'Ednyved, I'll need you with me, and Rhys, too. Morgan? Have you any yearning to see Oxford?'

The priest smiled, shook his head. 'My bones are getting too old and brittle for journeys like that.'

'What about you, Gruffydd? Would you be willing to come with me?'

Gruffydd raised his head. 'The next time I cross the border into England,' he said, 'it will be at the head of an army.'

It had grown very quiet again. But Llewelyn said only, 'As you will.' He turned away, crossed the hall, and stopped before Joanna.

'What about you, *breila*?' he said softly, and with so much understanding that Joanna suddenly found herself blinking back tears.

'I cannot, Llewelyn. I just cannot face him – not yet.'

As shadows began to spill out of the corners, John called for torches. Dusk was settling over the city, and the sight of that darkening sky filled him with dread. The pain was bad enough during the day, but at night it became intolerable. And there seemed to be little his doctors could do. They mumbled that gout rarely struck in summer, admitted they knew neither its cause nor its cure, had no greater comfort to offer than their assurances that such an attack usually ran its course within ten days.

With infinite care, John shifted position. He was among men he trusted: his Justiciar Hubert de Burgh, the Earls of Chester and Pembroke, his cousin Warenne. But even with them he was unwilling to show weakness, to reveal the full extent of his suffering. 'It's been over a month since we met at Runnymede. In that month I've released hostages, dismissed some of my Poitevin captains, granted Hertford Castle to Fitz Walter, Fotheringhay to the Earl of Huntingdon, Mountsorrel to that turncoat de Quincy. And what have they done? They've fortified their castles for war, defied officers of the Crown, refused to give me a written pledge of their loyalty. And still they hold London!'

'We may be able to reach a compromise there, Your Grace. The Archbishop of Canterbury is sorely distressed by their intransigence, but he still thinks he can persuade them to yield control of the city in August, on the feast of the Assumption . . . provided that all have taken oaths of obedience to their twenty-five by then, and that you have satisfied their claims for disputed castles.'

'You call that a compromise, Hubert? By those terms, they could justify holding London till Judgment Day! "Satisfy their claims", you say? There's no way on God's earth that I can ever do that. But what I can do is stop this charade.'

John picked up a letter, threw it on to the table. 'This arrived at noon. The Pope has commanded all Christ's faithful to support me, and he directs Langton and Pandulf to excommunicate the barons if they do not come to terms in eight days. Langton is balking, contending that the Pope's letter was written without knowledge of the Runnymede charter. But he'll not be able to make that claim for long. I've appealed to the Pope, advising him of the shameful settlement I was forced into making at Runnymede and formally requesting that he annul the charter.'

'John, I must talk –' Isabelle was already in the room before she took notice of the other men. 'I did not know you were in council, will come back later . . .'

John shook his head. 'No, we'll continue this on the morrow.' Her entry could not have been better timed, for his foot was beginning to throb again, and he was grateful that Isabelle had given him so plausible an excuse to cut the meeting short. All knew a pregnant woman had to be humoured, and he'd far rather appear as an indulgent husband than as a crippled King.

As soon as they were alone, John pulled aside the blanket, stared down at his afflicted ankle. It was swollen to twice its normal size, so discoloured by a dark purple rash that his skin seemed covered with blotched ugly bruises; even the veins were distended, protuberant. John covered it with the blanket again, sagged back in his chair.

Isabelle placed a wine cup on the table within his reach, then lowered herself on to a nearby bench. This was the first of her five pregnancies to cause her so much discomfort. She felt bloated, her back ached all the time, and her queasiness was continuing although she was well into her fourth month. She wondered if it was because she'd become pregnant so soon after Isabella's birth. At the time, she'd welcomed this pregnancy; what better way to offer John tangible proof of her fidelity? But in the sweltering heat of high summer, the child she carried was becoming more and more of a burden. She'd never felt so ungainly, so vulnerable.

John had closed his eyes and, as she studied his face, she felt a new and chilling fear. John, too, looked vulnerable. What if he was? What if he lost this war? What would happen to her?

'When we leave Oxford, I mean to send you and the children to Corfe. It's the strongest of my castles; you ought to be safe there.' John reached for the wine cup, pushed it away after one swallow. 'Send down to the buttery for hippocras; I cannot drink this swill. But first, what have you to tell me?'

'John . . .' Isabelle braced herself. 'The Welsh Princes have ridden in,' she said, and winced at his sudden smile. 'My love, I'm so sorry, but . . . but Llewelyn did not bring Joanna with him. John, he came alone.'

Whenever he stayed in Oxford, John held court in the palace known as the Domus Regis, the King's House; it was his birthplace and a favourite royal residence. But it was also situated outside the city walls, and for his July confrontation with the charter committee of twenty-five, he bypassed the more comfortable King's House for the greater security of the eleventh-century castle. It was there that he welcomed the Welsh Princes, and there that he accepted their oaths of homage and fealty.

As Llewelyn glanced about the chamber, at the men mingling in apparent harmony, his sense of unreality intensified. Almost, he could believe he'd stumbled into some lunatic land in which nature's laws were mocked and madness reigned. The committee of twenty-five had been in session all week, hearing appeals of men who felt themselves wronged by John, and Oxford seemed populated by John's enemies. Giles de Braose alone was absent; he and his brother Reginald had balked at taking part in the Runnymede settlement, at making any peace with John.

Llewelyn was turning as a voice murmured just behind him, in Welsh. 'Would you care to wager how long their Runnymede peace lasts?'

'Till Michaelmas?' Llewelyn hazarded, and Maelgwn gave a shrug, a twisted smile.

'I've just heard a story I can scarce credit, but Saer de Quincy swears it to be true. John was to arrive on Thursday last from Woodstock, but he did not reach the city till the morrow, and sent word that his illness would prevent him from leaving the castle. He wanted the barons to hold their council in his chamber, but they refused, insisted that he come to them.'

Maelgwn drained his wine cup. 'I would,' he said, 'have given a great deal to witness that.'

Llewelyn would never think of Maelgwn as a friend, but in the three years they'd been allies he had developed a grudging respect for the other man. He'd watched as Maelgwn knelt before John, received the kiss of peace from the man who'd murdered his sons, and wondered if he'd have found Maelgwn's resolve had Gruffydd, too, died at Nottingham Castle.

'I said Michaelmas, but it could be even sooner. John has as many enemies as he has barons, and I truly think that at last he is going to reap what he's sown. And when he does, Maelgwn, Christ Jesus, what an opportunity for the Welsh! Once John is hopelessly bogged down in a war with his own barons, we move into South Wales, move against the Norman enclaves in Deheubarth and Powys.'

'"We?"' Maelgwn echoed, cocking a sardonic brow. 'So the Prince of Gwynedd will lead an army south to fight with us against the Normans? Most magnanimous, my lord, but I wonder what Gwenwynwyn will think of your generosity. I suspect he'd say we might be exchanging one army of occupation for another.'

'I dare say he will. But what of you, Maelgwn? What say you?'

'Oh, I expect I will give you the benefit of the doubt. But what I will not give you is Ceredigion.'

Llewelyn laughed. 'I prefer to make new mistakes, not to keep repeating the same ones over and over. I learned a hard lesson four summers ago at Aberconwy, but I learned it well. Welsh disunity is the most potent weapon the Normans have, and we alone can deny it to them.'

'My lord . . .' A servant was approaching, clad in the King's livery. 'My lord, the King wants to speak with you. Will you follow me to his chamber?'

This was a summons Llewelyn had been expecting. 'Like all here in Oxford, I serve the King's pleasure,' he said dryly, and Maelgwn laughed for the first time since arriving at the English King's court.

'I want no war with the Welsh. I want this peace to last.' John spoke slowly, drawing his words out for emphasis, to stress his sincerity. 'I would hope you believe that.'

Llewelyn did; even John could handle only one war at a time.

539

This was the first close encounter he'd had with John since the oath-taking, and he was startled to see what ravages three years had wrought. John's eyes were bloodshot and puffy, his waist thickening, his gestures abrupt. He looked more than ill, he looked haunted, and Llewelyn suddenly remembered the judgment he'd once heard an Augustinian monk pass upon the English King. A great prince, the monk had said, but scarcely a happy one.

A silence had fallen between them. John knew he had more dangerous enemies than the Welsh Prince, but there were few he hated as much, and rarely had anything come harder to him than this overture of peace. 'To prove to you that I mean what I say, I am granting you two English manors, Bidford in Warwickshire and Suckley in Worcestershire.'

Llewelyn was not impressed. How much English land did John think the lives of twenty-eight Welsh hostages were worth? 'I shall hold the manors for my daughter Elen,' he said coolly, 'to be part of her marriage portion when she's of an age to wed.'

John nodded. Assuming he'd been dismissed, Llewelyn rose, made an obeisance as meaningless to him as the oath of homage he'd had to offer to the English King. But as he reached the door, John could hold back no longer.

'I freed your son, just as I promised. So why, then, did you not bring Joanna with you? She's not seen me for three years; how could you keep her away?'

'I did not forbid Joanna to come. That was her choice.'

'You expect me to believe that?'

'I do not much care what you believe.'

'I know you've tried to turn Joanna against me. But I know my daughter, know she'd not believe your lies, your –'

'Lies?' Llewelyn moved away from the door. 'There are twenty-eight families to testify to the truth of Nottingham Castle. To you, a Welsh death might count for less. But to Joanna, a child is a child. You murdered my hostages to take vengeance upon me, and you did. But you hurt Joanna, too. She still dreams of that lad you hanged at Shrewsbury, Maelgwn's son. Only in her dreams, it is Davydd, her son, on your gallows.'

'I'll tell you who I blame for Joanna's pain – you! If you'd let her come to me, I could have explained, could have made her understand that I only did what I had to do. I hanged those hostages because you broke faith. They'd still be alive now had you not betrayed them.

540

Once you did, I had no choice. I had to set an example, but you forced me to it.'

'It does not surprise me that you find it so easy to justify the deaths of children. But what of murder done in the dark? How do you justify starving a woman and her son to death?'

To Llewelyn's surprise, John flushed. Only then did he realize that this might well be the first time that John had been held accountable for Maude's murder, for her family and friends had been exiled or intimidated, and John's family and friends did not truly want to know.

'They died in one of my prisons,' John said, after a lengthy pause, 'but I did not seek their deaths. Despite what you and others think, I am not responsible.'

For a man nurtured on parental falsehoods, a man to whom lying was now not so much habitual as reflex, it was a surprisingly unconvincing defence. Llewelyn slowly shook his head. 'Is that what you truly want me to tell your daughter?'

For once John could think of nothing to say. The look on Llewelyn's face was one he'd seen before. The man who'd come to tell him that Maude and her son were dead was a trusted servant, a man who'd shown himself to be immune to conscience, impervious to scruples. Yet there'd been in his eyes something John had never expected, a look of judgment, of involuntary revulsion. And it was only then that John had realized the full measure of what he'd done.

He'd given in to Angevin rages before, said things better forgotten, given commands he later regretted. But he'd never done anything he could not afterwards justify to himself. Not until he'd allowed himself to take an unforgivable vengeance upon Maude de Braose and her son. Not until he'd seen the truth in a soldier's eyes, that there were some acts nothing could justify.

He felt no grief for Maude, no remorse. What he did feel was harder for him to admit, to deal with – shame. He did not think he was any more cruel, any more vengeful than other men, than his brothers, his enemies. But he could not defend what he'd done to the de Braoses, could only put the memory from him, as an aberrant act, a tragic mistake. All men have thing in their past that they'd change if they could. All men. But that was not an argument he could make, not to Llewelyn ab Iorwerth. The Welshman's eyes had taken on the glitter of dark ice. If he was seeking absolution, he'd come to the wrong church.

541

'I should never have given my daughter to you. Of all the mistakes I've ever made, that must rank amongst the biggest.'

'Is that the message you'd have me give Joanna? That our marriage was a mistake?'

'No, damn you, it is not! Tell Joanna . . . tell my daughter that she will always be that, my daughter, and she will always be welcome at my court.'

In mid-August came a second letter from the Pope, castigating Stephen Langton and some of the English bishops for not giving John greater support against his barons and ordering the Archbishop forthwith to excommunicate all 'disturbers of the King and kingdom'. When Langton refused to comply, the papal legate Pandulf suspended him as Archbishop of Canterbury.

It was late September when the papal bull *Et Si Carissimus* reached England. Condemning the Runnymede charter as 'shameful and base and illegal and unjust', as 'concessions thus extorted from a great Prince who had taken the Cross', it declared the charter to be 'null and void of all validity forever'.

On September 30, a disloyal castellan surrendered the great royal fortress of Rochester to the rebels. On October 13, John seized the city, and laid siege to the castle. By then, Fitz Walter and his cohorts had already opened negotiations at the French court, had offered the English crown to Louis Capet, the eldest son of the French King.

January, 1216
Tywyn, North Wales

Llewelyn led his army into South Wales in early December. Joined by the other Welsh Princes, he laid siege to the Norman fortress of Carmarthen, which had been for more than seventy years the centre of royal power in the Tywi Valley; it fell to Llewelyn in just five days. The castles of Cydweli, Llanstephan, St Clears, Laugharne, Narberth, and Newport were taken in rapid succession. On the day after Christmas, the Welsh added Cardigan and Cilgerran castles to their list of conquests, and a jubilant Welsh chronicler recorded that, 'The Welsh returned joyfully to their homes, but the French, driven out of all their holds, wandered hither and thither like birds in melancholy wise.'

Rarely had a winter been so mild. The sea was a placid blue, and the beach glistened like powdered crystal, more than justifying Tywyn's name – a shining seashore. Alison spun around in an exuberant circle, arms and skirts flying. 'It feels verily like spring, Madame!'

Joanna, too, was enjoying the warmth of the sun on her face. 'Davydd? Would you like to help me build a sand castle? Davydd . . . what's wrong?'

Davydd was cradling his arm at an awkward angle. 'I fell, Mama.'

Joanna experienced a dizzying jolt of panic at first sight of the blood soaking her son's tunic, but a hasty examination of his injury reassured her that although the cut was deep, it was not serious. Alison was already unfastening her veil, and Joanna's bodyguard was holding out his dagger. Slitting Davydd's sleeve, Joanna tied a makeshift bandage and then, seeing that Davydd was on the verge of tears, she said swiftly, 'Do you know why you bled when you cut yourself on that shell? There are conduits in your arm, called veins, which carry the blood from your liver.'

As she had hoped, that interested Davydd. 'Where's my liver, Mama?'

'I'm not truly sure; near your stomach, I think. I do know it is the source for love and carnal lust.' She had an inspiration then, and jerked off her own veil. 'Here,' she said, and fashioned for her son a sling. 'Now you look like a soldier coming home from the war. Do you think you can walk back to the monastery? If not, I can send Marc to fetch your pony.'

'I can walk, Mama.' Davydd handed Alison his collection of shells, and they started across the sand. Joanna had laughed when Llewelyn once asked her if Davydd was not too quiet for his age; with her, the boy was rarely still, was a veritable fount of questions and queries and curious non sequiturs. His injury had not bridled his tongue at all, and he soon transformed their walk into an inquisition, wanting to know what caused high tide, why blood was red, why love sprang from the liver and not from the spleen, as laughter did.

'Show some mercy; one question at a time!'

Davydd grinned. 'All right. Are there elephants in England?'

Joanna sighed; elephants were Davydd's newest passion, and he could happily discuss their odd ways for hours on end. 'No, I think not. Elephants live only in far away lands like Ethiopia and India.'

'Are there dragons in England, then?'

So it was not elephants at all; it was England. 'There have been reports of English dragons, but I've never met anyone who actually saw one, Davydd.'

'Uncle Rhys told me he heard of a place in England, called Stroke or Stripe, where men are born with tails. Is that true, Mama?'

Joanna laughed. 'You mean Strood, in Kent. That's but a folk tale. Strood is close by Rochester Castle, and I was often there with my father. But I saw nary a single tail!'

Davydd looked disappointed. 'Mayhap they hide their tails in their tunics.' He stopped to pick up a shell. 'Rochester Castle . . . is that not where the fighting was?'

Joanna nodded. 'But the fighting is over now at Rochester.' The castle had been surrendered to the King after a seven week siege. 'The King has headed north, into Yorkshire. The rebels are allied with Alexander, the Scots King, and some of them even did homage to him for lands in Northumbria. Alexander has been raiding over the border, and my father wants to drive him back into Scotland; also to punish the rebels.'

How much more should she tell him? She'd vowed that she'd not keep anything from her children again, but how much truth could a seven year old handle? Did Davydd need to know that John's army was wreaking a bloody vengeance upon the North? Did he need to know that rebel manors were being burnt, livestock slain, that terrified towns were offering John lavish sums to be spared the fate of Berwick upon Tweed, burned to the ground, its citizens slaughtered?

'Is it a bad war, Mama?'

'To me, all wars are bad, Davydd, but that is a woman's view. In war soldiers sometimes do great evil, and the innocent suffer. It need not always be that way, though. Your father controlled his men at Shrewsbury. But my father would not – or could not – control his men at Berwick, and many people died.'

'Will the King win his war with the barons?'

'I'm not sure, Davydd. Your father says the odds are in his favour, since his army is made up of mercenaries, routiers. They're seasoned solders, you see, men who earn their living by their swords. Llewelyn thinks my father is likely to prevail, unless the French give substantial aid to the rebels. They have offered the Crown to Louis, the French King's son, but Philip is loath to incur the Pope's wrath again. Whilst he did allow Louis to send seven thousand French troops to London, he is discouraging Louis from coming over himself, and that is what the rebels truly need, a Prince they can rally around.'

Davydd slanted her a sidelong glance. 'Mama . . . do you want the King to win?'

It had not escaped Joanna that Davydd invariably referred to John as 'the King', never as 'your father'. She knew the little boy was confused by her relationship to John, but she did not want to lie to him, and she said slowly, 'You know that John has committed grievous sins. But he is still my father, Davydd, and so I have to say yes, that I do hope he will prevail over the rebels.'

'But . . . but what if he wins, and then he makes war on Papa?'

He'd gone unerringly to the heart of Joanna's dilemma. But as she looked into his upturned face, she suddenly realized what he was really asking, realized how threatened he felt by her kinship to the English King. 'I would hope it never comes to that, Davydd. But if it did, I would want your father to win. You and Elen and Llewelyn are my family, and Wales my home.'

That was what Davydd needed to hear, and he reached up, slid his free hand into hers. 'Papa would win,' he said confidently.

545

'He took all those castles from the Normans. He's a good battle commander, is he not, Mama?'

'The best, love. This was the first time, Davydd, that all the Welsh Princes banded together, offered a united front to the Normans. And it was your father's doing, as is this conference on the banks of the River Dyfi. All the Welsh Princes have gathered in answer to Llewelyn's summons, and that, too, is a first. Your father is seeking to make a lasting peace in the south between Maelgwn, Rhys Gryg, and their nephews, and to bring it about, he has proposed an equitable partition of Deheubarth amongst them.'

'What of all they won from the Normans? Is Papa not going to keep any of that land?'

'No, Davydd, he made no claims for himself. Do you know why? Because your father is a very clever man. He's gaining something from this peace that is of far greater value than land or castles, something of historic significance. That is why he sent for us, so that we could witness what is to happen.'

Davydd's eyes had widened. 'What, Mama?'

Joanna smiled. 'You'll find out,' she said, 'on the morrow!'

A man standing on the bank of the River Dyfi could look north into Gwynedd, south into Ceredigion, and Llewelyn had selected the river estuary as an appropriate site for his peace conference. It had taken all his diplomatic and political skills and nearly a week of wrangling among the participants, but in the end Llewelyn had prevailed, and on a mild sunlit morning in January a formal partition of Deheubarth was proclaimed.

Joanna had chosen an inconspicuous spot near Llewelyn's tent, one that none the less afforded an unobstructed view of the ceremonies taking place upon the white sands of Aberdyfi. As the agreed-upon division of the various cantrefs and commotes was read aloud to the assembled lords, Davydd lost interest, began to fidget with his sling. Joanna had been unable to convince him that he did not need it; he'd even managed to fasten his mantle so that the sling was still visible.

'If you do not stop squirming,' she murmured, 'you are going to miss the surprise.'

'Well, when will it happen, Mama?'

'Now,' Joanna said. An expectant silence had fallen; men were jostling to get closer to their Princes. As all watched, Maelgwn crossed the sand, knelt before Llewelyn, and swore an oath of homage and fealty to the Prince of Gwynedd. Rhys Gryg, who'd been freed from an English prison some months earlier; Llewelyn's cousin Hywel; his cousin Madog, Prince of upper Powys; Maelgwn's rebellious nephews, Rhys Ieunac and Owain – one by one, they followed Maelgwn, acknowledged Llewelyn as their liege lord.

Gwenwynwyn was the last to approach Llewelyn. High colour had mottled his cheekbones, and his eyes were slits of resentful rage, but he, too, knelt, did homage to the man who'd been his lifelong rival. Llewelyn half turned, and for a moment his gaze met Joanna's, a moment in which they exchanged a very private message.

'Do you know what this means, Davydd? The other Welsh Princes have just acknowledged Gwynedd's suzerainty, have just acknowledged Llewelyn as their liege lord . . . their Prince. He's too shrewd to lay formal claim to the title, knowing that would but alarm the English and stir up the jealousies of his allies. But from this day forth, your father is, in effect, Prince of Wales.'

Davydd did not fully comprehend the significance of what he'd just witnessed, but he responded to the echoes of pride and jubilation in his mother's voice. 'I'm glad Papa wanted me here, glad he's to be Prince of all the Welsh. Mama . . . will I be Prince of Wales, too, one day?'

Joanna did not answer at once, and as he glanced up at her, he saw that she was no longer watching Llewelyn. She was staring at the tall youth standing by Llewelyn's side, staring at his brother Gruffydd.

'Yes, Davydd,' she said softly. 'If I have any say about it, you will indeed be Prince of Wales.'

Gwenwynwyn soon recanted, swayed by his jealousy of Llewelyn and the beguilements of the English King. A thirteenth-century Welsh chronicle set forth the denouement of this embittered rivalry:

'In that year Gwenwynwyn, lord of Powys, made peace with John, King of England, scorning the oath and pledge he had given . . . And after Llewelyn ab Iorwerth had learned that, he felt vexed; and he sent to him bishops and abbots and other men of great authority . . . And when that had availed him naught, he gathered a host and called the Princes of Wales together to him, and made for Powys to war against Gwenwynwyn, and he drove him to flight into the county of Chester and gained possession of all his territory for himself.'

June, 1216
Corfe Castle, England

By spring, John's war seemed all but won. In three months, he had brutally and effectively suppressed rebellion in the North and East of England. He was receiving formidable support from his brother Will, who'd led a punitive expedition into East Anglia, and the two most powerful lords in the realm, the Earls of Chester and Pembroke, were holding fast for the Crown. The rebels still controlled London, but they were losing heart. By April, a number of them were seeking to make peace with John; even Eustace de Vesci was asking for terms.

It was not the prospect of fighting for John's kingdom that had discouraged Louis Capet from joining the rebels; it was his father. While Louis was quite willing to risk excommunication for the English Crown, Philip was not. It took Louis until Easter to coax a grudging consent from the French King, but on April 24, Philip summoned the papal legate Guala to a council at Melun. There the French monarch and his son contended that John was no rightful King, having been charged with treason by his brother Richard and having been condemned by a French court for the murder of his nephew Arthur. Guala was not impressed, warned that John was the Pope's vassal and England part of the patrimony of the Holy Roman Church. But Louis was deaf to all but the seductive sirens of kingship, and he declared his intent to claim the Crown that was his by right, his wife being niece to John and granddaughter to Henry.

John remained sanguine in the face of the impending French invasion, for he, more than any other English king, had appreciated an island kingdom's need for naval supremacy and had spared no expense in building England's first fleet. He felt confident that his ships would be able to keep Louis bottled up within Calais harbour. There was one aspect of successful kingship, however, that John had always utterly lacked – luck. Fortune now delivered a stunning blow. On the night of May 18, a sudden storm raked the Kentish coast, and John's galleys were scattered, driven on to the rocks or out to sea.

When coast watchers at Thanet reported sails on the horizon two days later, John allowed himself the indulgence of optimism, allowed himself to hope that some of his fleet had ridden out the squall. But the ships that sailed into Pegwell Bay flew the golden fleur de lys of France.

Pembroke and Chester advised against an immediate confrontation; too many of John's mercenaries were French, and John owed them too much in back pay to trust them in an encounter with their liege lord's son. John agreed, unwilling to risk all upon a single battle, one that might be decided by treachery, and he withdrew towards the west.

He'd hoped that the invasion of a foreign Prince would rally his subjects to his side. The opposite happened. Louis's presence upon English soil acted as a catalyst for the rebel cause. Men flocked to his banners, even men who'd so far been loyal. John's support began to bleed away. To stave off a lethal hæmorrhage, the papal legate Guala invoked the moral authority of the Church on John's behalf, and on Whit Sunday, he publicly excommunicated Louis and his followers, placed London under Interdict. But that did not deter Londoners from giving Louis a joyous welcome just four days later.

Stunned by the acclaim and acceptance the French Prince was encountering, John abandoned Winchester as Louis moved into Hampshire. On June 14, Louis took the ancient city of Winchester, set about besieging the royal castle. John retreated south, reaching the security of Corfe Castle on June 23. That was the day he learned of the defections. The Earl of Arundel, the Count of Aumale, and John's own cousin, William de Warenne, Earl of Surrey, had gone to Winchester, where they had disavowed allegiance to John and acknowledged Louis as their King.

Corfe Castle dominated the Dorsetshire peninsula known as Purbeck Isle. Its history was a grim one, for it was often used as a royal prison. Here the ill-starred prophet Peter of Wakefield had passed the last months of his life. Here twenty-two knights taken captive after John's victory at Mirebeau, had overpowered their gaolers, barricaded themselves within the keep, and starved to death rather than surren-

549

der. Here, too, John held four of Maude de Braose's grandsons, children of the son who'd died with her in a Windsor dungeon. But Corfe was also a favourite residence of the Angevin Kings. John had constructed lavish living quarters in the inner bailey, just east of the great keep, where Isabelle and their children awaited his coming.

Isabelle stirred, reached sleepily towards John's side of the bed. 'John? Why are you not abed?'

John turned from the open window, from the summer dark. 'It has begun to rain,' he said, and then, 'Go back to sleep.'

Instead, she sat up, wrapped herself in a sheet. 'I've missed you so. We've never been apart like this, not in all the years of our marriage. Pour me some wine, love, and talk to me. I just do not understand why this is happening, John. It makes no sense. Louis has no right to the English crown. His claim is a . . . a bad joke. What is he, after all? The husband of a daughter of one of your sisters!'

John paused in the act of pouring her wine, slammed the cup down on the table. 'Did I tell you what lame arguments they offered Guala at Melun? Whilst it's true Richard charged me with treason, that was five full years ere he died! All Christendom knows that we were reconciled, that Richard named me as his heir. As for that out-and-out lie about Arthur, no French court ever sat in judgment upon me. Since when am I accountable to the French King?'

'You're not, love,' Isabelle said hastily. 'Of course you're not.'

'Do you know what the Pope said when he was informed of Philip's claim? He said that Arthur was a traitor who'd invited whatever end he might have met. And he did, in truth. Whatever regrets I might have, Arthur is not amongst them.'

That was, she knew, as close as he'd ever come to a confession, to an admission that Arthur had died at his command. But she did not care; Arthur's fate had never preyed upon her peace. 'John . . . is it true that Rochester Castle has been lost?'

He nodded. 'It held out against me for nigh on two months, but yielded to Louis without offering any resistance at all. Which makes me wonder what will happen when Louis lays siege to Windsor Castle, to Dover. Will they try to hold out? Or will their castellans betray me, too?'

He swung about, back towards the bed. 'Have I been such a bad King, Isabelle?'

550

'John, no!'

'Then why,' he asked, very low, 'have my subjects forsaken me? Why are they so willing to support a foreign Prince?'

'John, that's not so. Many of your subjects are still loyal. For certès, the townspeople are. What king ever did as much to promote trade? Or granted as many borough charters? Let craven lords like Arundel and Surrey barter their honour to Louis. The towns will still hold fast for you.'

'As London did?' he asked bitterly, and she had no answer for him, could only entreat him to come back to bed. After a time, he did. But he did not sleep.

John was seated before a table cluttered with parchment sheets, ink, maps, books. He was surrounded by people – several scribes, a mud-splattered courier, Peter des Roches, Robert de Vieuxpont – all competing for his attention. He scrawled a hasty signature for one of the scribes, reached for the courier's message as he said to de Vieuxpont, 'I want you to go north again, Rob, am counting upon you to hold Cumbria and Westmorland for me.'

Seeing him so preoccupied, the boys hesitated, but Isabelle prodded them forward into the chamber. 'John, can you spare some moments for your sons?'

John had not seen his children for months. As he pushed back his chair, beckoned them to approach, he could not help noticing their shyness, their lack of ease. His baby daughters did not know him at all. Even to his sons, he was a stranger. Henry was eight, Richard seven, but he'd never been able to find much time for them, to make them part of his life as he had with the children now grown, born out of wedlock and before his kingship.

Isabelle took her youngest from the nurse, held the baby out towards John. Nell was entering her seventh month, and John had seen her for the first time yesterday, upon his arrival at Corfe. All Isabelle's three daughters had inherited some of their mother's beauty; Nell had dark blue eyes and hair like cornsilk. John smiled at the child, but she ducked her head, hid her face against Isabelle's shoulder.

John was still holding the courier's letter. Breaking the seal, he rapidly scanned the contents, and at Peter des Roches's questioning look, said, 'It's from the Earl of Chester. Gwenwynwyn has died.'

Henry edged closer. 'Who's that, Papa?'

551

'A Welsh Prince, Henry, an ally of mine. But he's been living in exile in Cheshire since the spring, when Llewelyn – your sister Joanna's husband – drove him out of Powys.'

'But . . . but I thought Joanna was living in France, Papa.'

'Not France, Aquitaine. I expect you're too young to remember your older sister. I lost two Joannas, lad, one to the de Lusignans, the other to Llewelyn.'

A servant had followed Isabelle into the chamber. 'My liege, your son, Lord Richard of Chilham, has just ridden in. Will you see him?'

'At once.' John glanced towards de Vieuxpont and des Roches. 'I sent Savaric de Mauléon to Winchester with an offer for Louis, that I'd order the castle garrison to surrender if Louis would agree to spare their lives. Richard was with him, will be bringing word.'

Richard had not waited for a servant's summons; he was already standing in the doorway. One glance at his face, and John stiffened.

'What is it?' he said sharply. 'You might as well tell me straight out; I'm getting used to bad news.'

'It is bad, Papa, as bad as it could be. I do not know how to tell you . . .' Richard was not easily discountenanced. John had never seen him so shaken. It was with relief, then, that he heard Richard say haltingly, 'At Winchester . . . amongst those who've gone over to Louis –'

'I know already, Richard, know that your uncle Warenne has broken faith, has done homage to Louis. But I do not want to talk about it, not now.'

'No . . . no, you do not understand. I'm not talking about my uncle Warenne. It's . . . Oh God, Papa, it's , . .'

John's mouth went dry. 'Not Chester?'

'No, not Chester.' Richard swallowed. 'It's your brother. Papa, it's Will.'

'No,' John said. 'No, you're lying. Not Will.'

'Papa . . . Papa, I saw him at Winchester with Louis. I saw him!'

Isabelle gave a choked cry, thrust her baby at the nurse. John was on his feet. He turned as Isabelle moved towards him. His eyes were blind, focused upon her without recognition. but she was too panicked to be able to respond to his pain, to be aware of anything except the ground giving way under her feet. 'Will would never betray you unless it was truly hopeless, unless he knew you could not win! What shall we do now? What will happen to me? John, I'm so frightened! What if they besiege Corfe? If you lose . . .'

She'd caught his arm, was clinging as if he were her only anchor. But her words struck John like stones. He jerked free, shoved her away with such force that she stumbled backward, careened into the table.

'Mama!' But Henry did not move. He stayed where he was, petrified. The other children had begun to cry. None of the men moved, either.

'If you're so fearful for your future, why wait? Why not go to Louis now, strike your deal with him? That's what you want to do, is it not? Get out, all of you! I do not need Will, do not need any of you. Go to Louis and be damned!'

The servants had already fled, and the nurses now gathered up the weeping children, hastened them from the chamber. Peter des Roches put his arm around Isabelle's shoulders; she had begun to sob, offered no resistance as he led her towards the door. Richard had gone very white, but he stood his ground. 'Papa, I'd not betray you. Nor would Isabelle. She loves –'

'Get out . . . now!' John's voice cracked. He spun around, fighting for control. When he turned back, Richard, too, had gone.

There were two large clay flagons on the table. He reached for the closer one, pulled it towards him. It was filled with a strongly spiced red wine; he drank directly from the spout, until he choked and tears burned his eyes. Picking up the second flagon, he hurled it towards the door. It shattered against the wood, sprayed dark wine all over the wall, the floor. He drank again, cleared the table with a wild sweep of his arm.

The rain had ended before dawn, and sunlight was pouring in from every window. He moved from one to the other, pausing to drink from the flagon as he jerked the shutters into place, as the room darkened.

The floor was littered with debris, with books and documents and broken clay fragments. He stumbled over a brass candelabra, sank to his knees midst the wreckage of his morning's work. The flagon was half empty by now; his head was spinning.

'Why, Will?' he whispered. 'Name of God, why?'

Johnny.

He froze, the flagon half way to his mouth.

Thank God you've come, Johnny. Thank God.

He could not see into the shadows. 'Papa?' he said softly. 'Papa?'

553

Stay with me, Johnny. The pain is always worse at night. Stay with me.

He grabbed for the flagon, drank deeply, spilling as much as he swallowed. 'I did not understand, Papa.' His voice echoed strangely in his own ears, sounded muffled, indistinct. 'I was but one-and-twenty. At that age, we think we'll live forever . . .' He set the flagon down, waited. But no one answered him. His voices were silent, his ghosts in retreat.

He was never to know how long he knelt there on the floor of his bedchamber, alone in the dark. When at last he lurched to his feet, he moved unsteadily towards the windows, fumbled with the shutters until the room was once more awash in sunlight.

A book lay open, almost at his feet. He reached down, picked it up. He took an uncommon enjoyment in reading, always carried books with him, even on campaigns. This was one of his favourites, a French translation of the Welsh legend of King Arthur; but several pages were torn, the cover smeared with ink. He blotted the ink as best he could with his sleeve, replaced the book upon the table.

'Damn you, Will! I trusted you. More fool I, but I truly trusted you. You think I'm beaten. You think Louis has won. Well, not yet. As Christ is my witness, not yet.'

September, 1216
Cirencester, England

'I understand you will not be staying with us, after all, Madame?'

Isabelle did not enjoy the company of clerics. Too often, she found them dour and disapproving, for if women were all daughters of Eve, born to lead men astray, a woman as worldly as Isabelle must be the very incarnation of Jezebel. But Alexander Neckam was no unlettered village priest. He was Abbot of the prosperous Augustinian abbey of St Mary, a man erudite and cultured, a man entitled to royal courtesy, and she found a smile for him.

'No, I regret not. My lord husband the King has decided it is too dangerous for me to accompany him any farther, and my son and I will be returning to Corfe whilst he goes to raise the siege of Windsor Castle.'

'We heard the King spent part of the summer along the Marches. Was he able to win over the Welsh?'

'He hired some Welsh men-at-arms, but he had no luck with the Welsh Princes, with Llewelyn or Maelgwn. Nor with Reginald de Braose.'

Neckam seemed to sense her preoccupation, for he made no attempt to prolong their conversation, murmured, instead, of duties elsewhere. She was not long alone, however; Richard was coming up the pathway. Falling into step beside her, he followed her into the abbey gardens.

Some yards to their right, John was walking with his son. When Richard started towards them, Isabelle laid a restraining hand on his arm. 'No,' she said. 'Give them time to say their farewells. And whilst we're still alone, tell me the truth. Can John win?'

'Had you asked me that in June, I'd have had said no. Now . . . now, I'm not so sure. There are straws in the wind, a growing discontent with the French. Some of the rebel barons are belatedly beginning to recognize reality – that should Louis prevail, they'll have a French King, a French court. Already, they're seeing what that would mean; each time Louis has taken a castle, he's given it to one of his French followers. Lastly, I know no man more dangerous to underestimate than my father.'

Isabelle nodded. 'When I'm with John, I cannot but believe that he will prevail against his enemies, that all will be well for us. But when we're apart, I . . . I lose faith. I think of what could happen to us should evil befall John, and I become so frightened, Richard, so –'

'Mama!' Henry was running towards them. 'Papa says he's going to give me one of his falcons! Papa, you'll not forget?'

John, following at a more sedate pace, smiled and shook his head. 'I'll give the order tonight, Henry. Richard . . . I've decided I do not want you to come with me. I'd rather you escort Isabelle and Henry back to Corfe, then return to Wallingford Castle, hold it for me till further notice.'

'If that is truly your wish, Papa.'

Turning, then, towards the child, John smiled again at his son. 'Henry, stay here and talk to your brother. I want a few words alone with your lady mother ere you depart.'

Taking Isabelle aside, John led her towards a trellised arbour. As soon as they were within, Isabelle moved into his arms. The air was sun-warmed, fragrant with honeysuckle; almost, she could convince herself that summer was not dying. 'I'm so glad I had these ten days with you. But . . . but when will we see each other again?'

'I do not know,' John admitted. 'Louis has been besieging Dover Castle for some six weeks now, but to no avail. Windsor, Lincoln, and Barnard Castles are also under siege. If they can hold out for me . . .'

Isabelle shivered. 'You must promise me, promise you'll take care. John, I . . . I'd be lost without you!'

Her fear was more than disheartening, it was contagious. John tightened his arms around her, kissed her on the mouth, the throat. She clung to him, but without passion, and when he kissed her again, he tasted her tears.

'Papa!' The voice was Henry's, high-pitched, excited. John and Isabelle moved apart, moved back into the sun. Henry was sprinting towards the arbour, gesturing. 'A courier, Papa, with urgent news from the North!'

556

One of the black-garbed Augustinian canons was standing a few feet away. 'There's a man seeking to talk with you, my liege. He says he's from Barnard Castle, from Hugh de Balliol. May we bring him to you?'

'At once.' John had paled. As Isabelle clutched his arm, he said tautly, 'If Barnard Castle has fallen . . .'

A messenger was being ushered into the abbey gardens. He was dishevelled and travel-stained, but John saw only his smile, the triumphant smile of a man bearing tidings sure to please. 'The Scots King and his army assaulted the castle, my lord, but we drove them off.'

'Thank God!'

'In truth, my liege. Shooting down from the battlements, one of our bowmen loosed an arrow at Eustace de Vesci. The Almighty guided his aim, lord. It struck de Vesci in the head; he was dead ere he tumbled from the saddle.'

John caught his breath. And then he began to laugh. 'I want the name of the bowman. That arrow of his is worth its weight in gold to me!' As he swung around, back towards Isabelle and Richard, they saw his eyes were ablaze with light. 'What better omen than this? I think my luck is about to change for the better – at long last!'

The Wash was a wide bay of the turbulent North Sea, fed by four rivers, extending more than twenty miles inland into the counties of Lincoln and Norfolk. The seaport of Lynn had grown up where the River Great Ouse emptied into The Wash. In early October, its citizens were alarmed when they got word of an advancing rebel force. But by then John had reached Lincolnshire. He swung south again, detoured towards Lynn, and the rebels fled at his approach. On Sunday, October 9, the grateful townspeople of Lynn welcomed their King, and on the following day a feast was given in John's honour at the Benedictine priory of St Mary Magdalene, St Margaret, and All Virgin Saints.

However boundless their good will, their resources were limited; they could not hope to equal the exotic fare that had been set before John in happier days. But they did what they could with what they had, and John, whose expectations were minimal, was pleasantly surprised. Ample helpings of stewed pomegranates and pears were served, to much jesting, for all knew such fruits were aphrodisiacs. Tarts filled with marrow, sugar, and ground pork were offered next, followed by a roasted peacock; the cooks had laboured hours to strut the bones and refit the skin and feathers so as to give the illusion of life everlasting. A pig had been slaughtered, and cut in half, the hind-quarters stuffed with suet and egg-yolked breadcrumbs, then carefully sewn together with the head and forepart of a capon, thus creating a wondrous beast to delight both the appetite and the eye. But what amused John the most was the subtlety, a sensual mermaid sculptured of marzipan, tail dyed green with parsley juice, her flowing hair a spill of saffron.

As entertainment, there was an acrobatic act and an alarmingly inept juggler who seemed continually in danger of stabbing himself with his own knives. But for the townspeople, the true attraction of the evening was the presence of their King, and they listened, spellbound, to a rare first-hand account of the momentous happenings in the world beyond the marshy Fens, beyond Lynn.

'Upon reaching Windsor, I found I did not have enough men for a direct attack, but I was able to end the siege by acting as bait. As I moved north out of the Thames Valley, the French abandoned the siege and set out in pursuit. Rather halfheartedly, since they soon gave up and returned to London. Which surprised me not in the least; Louis seems willing to fight to the last Englishman.'

As John expected, that drew laughter. 'I continued north, for we knew that the Scots King had come to Dover to do homage to Louis. It was my hope that I could intercept him on his way back into Scotland. Unfortunately, he managed to elude our scouts, but we were able to wreak havoc upon the lands of our enemies in the shires of Cambridge and Lincoln.'

Swallowing the last of his wine, John pushed aside the stale trencher that had served as his plate. 'Does your almoner save these for the poor?'

'Yes, Sire.'

Glancing about at his men, dining at the lower tables, John said loudly, 'Let no one throw his trencher to the dogs,' and signalled for more wine before resuming. 'On the Thursday ere Michaelmas, we entered the city of Lincoln. I know there were those who thought Nicholaa de la Haye no fit castellan for Lincoln Castle, but she has shown herself to be as steadfast, as stalwart as any man in holding the castle for the Crown. The townspeople had not her courage, however, and yielded the city to the rebels. They had no stomach for fighting, though, fled even as we approached. We pursued them north, and then headed back when we heard you were in need.'

'And thankful we are for it,' the Prior said fervently, and others in the hall took up the refrain, expressed their gratitude in terms so sycophantic that one of the young monks laid his bread down in disgust, his appetite utterly gone.

Brother Thomas was incensed that his Prior should make welcome a blasphemer, a man with such mortal sins upon his soul. The Angevins were ungodly, evil men. Thomas, who had been named after the holy martyr, Thomas à Becket, did not doubt that Henry and his sons were burning in Hell. John, too, would feel the flames of perdition. Nothing could save him, for there was no contrition in his heart. When the land was laid under Interdict, he had shamelessly mocked the clergy, men of God, arresting the hearth-mates and concubines of village priests, demanding that the priests ransom their illicit loves. He had heaped scorn and contempt upon Stephen Langton, a man of Thomas's own Lincolnshire and, like Thomas, of Saxon blood. Nor had John mended his ways after making peace with the Holy Father. Thomas had been appalled to hear that John had allowed his soldiers to stable their horses in St Andrew's priory church during his siege of Rochester Castle. And not three weeks ago, he had burned and plundered the Benedictine abbey at Croyland.

No, such a man was damned forever and aye, as surely as if he were a Jew or infidel Saracen, and Thomas cursed his own cowardice, the fear that froze his tongue and kept him from crying out in ringing, clarion tones that liars are loathsome to the Eternal and the wrath of God is fearful to behold.

'I shall have to depart on the morrow, but I'll leave one of my most trusted captains, Savaric de Mauléon, in Lynn to see to your safety. Not that I expect the rebels to threaten you again,' John nodded, sounding so cheerful, so confident that Thomas could endure no more.

'You said a number of disloyal lords had returned to their true allegiance, disavowed the French,' he blurted out, half-rising from his seat. 'Was one of these lords your brother Salisbury?'

His words seemed to echo endlessly in his own ears. All heads turned in his direction. Those seated beside him drew back so precipitantly that, in other circumstances, their recoil might have been comical. Thomas sat alone, seeing through a blur the shocked and outraged faces of his Prior, the townspeople, aware – as he'd never been aware of anything before – of the sudden and utter stillness of the King.

It seemed forever to those watching before John moved, completed an action frozen in time and space at mention of Will's name. Bringing his cup up to his mouth, he took a swallow of verney. The sweet white wine burned his throat like vinegar. Setting it down, he glanced towards Thomas, saw only a fearful youngster, beet-red and speechless, as if in belated realization of his gaffe.

'No,' he said, his voice very measured and remote, 'the Earl of Salisbury was not amongst them.'

There were relieved murmurings among the people at that. The Prior, who knew Thomas as John did not, gave the errant monk a scorching look that promised retribution at the earliest possible moment, and fumbled for a more suitable topic of conversation. It was John's old friend and comrade, Peter des Roches, who came to their rescue. He was not deceived by John's icy demeanour; he knew the monk had lacerated anew a wound that had yet to show any signs of healing, and he acted now to turn attention away from John and to himself, saying swiftly:

'We shall need your help, Prior Wilfrid. We encountered some difficulty in crossing the River Wellstream yesterday. Can you suggest a safer passage?'

'Indeed, my lord Bishop. The safest way is to ford the river at Wisbech, fifteen miles to the south. There is a castle there, so the King's Grace will have suitable lodgings for the night. But since your baggage train is so much slower and cumbersome, I would suggest you dispatch it by the shorter route, between the villages of Cross Keys and Long Sutton. It's some four miles across the estuary, but when the tide is out, much of the sand is exposed and with local guides who know where the quicksands lie, it can be safely forded.'

John had been only half-listening to the Prior's long-winded explanation. He looked up, though, as a man rose, approached the high table.

'My liege, might I have a word with you? I am Roger of the Bail, and I –'

'I know a Lincoln man by that name, Peter of the Bail. At Michaelmas, I appointed him as city bailiff. Are you kin?'

'We are cousins, Your Grace.' Roger beckoned, and two other men brought forward an iron coffer. As he lifted the lid, the torchlight fell upon a multitude of shimmering silver coins. 'This is for you, my liege, from your subjects in the township of Lynn. It's not as much as we could wish – one hundred marks – but we wanted to give you tangible proof of our loyalty. Use it, with God's blessing, to fight the French invaders and drive them back into the sea.'

John was touched, for that was no small sum for these merchants and fishermen to have raised. 'I thank you; your offering shall be well spent.' He gazed about the hall, heartened by sight of so many friendly faces. 'In the past, I've granted many a borough the right to elect a mayor, London and Lincoln amongst them. A while back, it pleased me to confer such a privilege upon Lynn.' Rising, he unsheathed his sword, handed it, hilt first, to the young merchant. 'Here,' he said when Roger made no move to take it. 'Your mayor shall need a ceremonial sword.'

Whatever else he might have said was lost in the sudden explosion of sound, the wave of cheering that engulfed the hall. When John could make himself heard again, he laughed and signalled for silence. 'I will drive the French invaders into the sea,' he said, 'and then I shall come back to Lynn, and celebrate my victory with those who stood by me when my need was greatest.'

The sun rose at 6.20 a.m. on Wednesday, October 12, but heavy mists overhung the marshes, did not begin to burn away until mid-morning. John crossed the River Wellstream at Wisbech, turned north along the embankment towards the village of Long Sutton. The cold was damp and penetrating, and the wind whistled eerily through the billowing salt grass. Birds cried mournfully, invisible in the mist, and occasional splashes heralded the passage of unseen animals.

'I hate the fenlands,' John said grimly, 'hate these barren, accursed swamps. What man in his right mind would live here of his own free will? Only a water snake could thrive in these stinking bogs.'

He'd been in a vile mood all morning, but his companions understood why. He'd been taken ill the day they left Lynn, had spent a sleepless night at Wisbech. He was still queasy this morning, and at Peter des Roches's troubled queries, finally admitted that he felt as if one fox were gnawing at his belly, another at his bowels. But he'd refused to lay over at Wisbech, or even to slow their pace, although he'd twice had to dismount while he vomited into the marsh grass.

'It's no surprise to me that you're ailing, John. I've been with you these six weeks past, have seen first-hand the way you've been

561

abusing yourself. It's a rare day when you do not cover forty miles; there've even been a few fifty-mile days! And then you spend half the night tending to matters of state. You keep burning a candle down to the wick, my friend, and it gets harder and harder to light.'

'How profound,' John said caustically, and spurred his stallion forward to ride beside John Marshal, the Earl of Pembroke's nephew. They began to trade marshland folklore, arguing whether it was true that men born in the Fens had webbed feet, whether the flickering swamp lights known as will-o'-the-wisps were truly the souls of unbaptized babies. Peter des Roches started to urge his mount to catch up with them but, after a few strides, let his horse slacken pace. What good would it do? John was not about to listen.

When they reached the village of Long Sutton, the tide was out, and the sands lay naked to a pallid autumn sun. Hungry gulls circled overhead, shrieking. The few houses huddled by the estuary did nothing to lessen the bleak desolation of the scene. There was no sign as yet of John's baggage train. But the wind was biting, and John's stomach was churning, and he let Peter des Roches persuade him not to wait, to press ahead towards Swineshead Abbey.

They turned west, and after a few miles, John consented to stop for his first food of the day. The little hamlet of Holbeach was no less dismal than Long Sutton. The awestruck villagers shyly offered John shelter, what meagre hospitality they could. But as soon as he stepped inside one of the wattle-and-daub huts, he was assailed again by nausea; the second room of the cottage was used as a stable, and the rank animal odours sent him reeling back into the icy sea air.

One of the peasants produced a blanket, and John's servants unpacked a basket of wheaten bread and cheese. John could manage just a mouthful, but even though the villagers could offer only ale and goat's milk, he could not get enough to drink; he was as thirsty, he said bemusedly, as if he'd gorged himself all week on nothing but salted herring.

Sitting back on the blanket, he studied the cottage. 'Cruck frame, thatched roof. As hard as it is for me to believe it, my daughter Joanna passed the first five years of her life in a house not much better than that one.' He waved away a proffered chunk of bread. 'What were you telling me about the tides, Jack?'

John Marshal took the bread John spurned. 'The Prior told me low water is at noon, high water at six. The half-tide comes in about three or so, so they'd have to cross between twelve and two.' He squinted upward, shook his head. 'I've yet to see enough of the sun to hazard even a blind guess as to the time now. But I see no cause for concern, Your Grace. The local guides know these waters better than the fish do, know where the sinkholes and quicksands lie.'

John yearned to lie back upon the blanket; his body ached for rest. But the wind was blowing sand about with such abandon that it had even begun to encrust the rim of his cup. 'I want to go to Nottingham next week to confer with Philip Marc. And when we reach the abbey tonight, I ought to send a courier to Hubert de Burgh.'

'You need not vex yourself over the Dover siege, John.' Peter des Roches had no liking for Hubert de Burgh, who'd replaced him as Justiciar, but his wish to ease John's mind prevailed over jealousy, and he said, quite truthfully, 'I know men call Dover "the key to the kingdom". But de Burgh has one hundred and forty knights and a full garrison at Dover Castle. I'd wager he can hold out against Louis till Judgment Day if need be.'

'My lords!' One of the villagers was pointing. 'A rider comes!'

The men were already on their feet, swords half-drawn. The rider wore John's colours, was one of the men left behind to wait for the baggage train. At sight of John, he jerked his lathered stallion to an abrupt halt, spraying sand in all directions.

'I waited and waited, my liege, and then ventured out on to the sands in search of them . . .' He swung from the saddle, leaned against his horse, sobbing for breath. 'They – Oh, Jesus, my lord, they're bogged down! They're out there in the river, caught in the quicksand, and the serfs say the tide is coming in!'

The villagers of Long Sutton were clustered upon the bank of the Wellstream, kneeling as their priest offered prayers for the souls of the doomed men trapped out in the estuary. They scattered as the horsemen came galloping out of the mist. The priest waved his arms frantically, ran after them, shouting that the incoming tide would turn the sands to quickmire and they'd all drown. John swerved his stallion just in time to avoid trampling the man, but he did not slow down; the horse plunged on to the sands. Most of John's companions followed.

The sounds reached John first, as the wind carried to him the cries of fear and rage, the shrill neighing of the sumpter horses. But until he saw the trapped wagons and animals, he did not – could

563

not – realize the full extent of the catastrophe. The heavy carts and wagons were hopelessly mired down in mid-river; the more the terrified horses struggled, the deeper they sank. John knew at once what had happened. The vanguard had become bogged, but the baggage train was more than two miles long, and those coming up behind were unaware of the disaster until they stumbled on to the lead wagons. And by that time, retreat was made impossible by the rearward. As more and more carts became bogged down, men and horses began to panic, and the sight meeting John's horrified eyes was one of utter and complete chaos.

Rescue was beyond mortal men; the tide was already sweeping in from the north. John could not see it yet, but he heard it, a low relentless rumble, getting louder. 'Cut the traces!' he shouted. 'Free the horses!'

John Marshal was beside him now, gesturing. 'We've got to turn back! Or we'll drown too!'

Some of the men had heard John's shouts, were slashing at the harness traces. Most had abandoned the wagons by now, were floundering in the river. John gave one despairing backward glance, and then swung his mount about, followed after John Marshal as they raced the tide for shore.

Their horses were battlefield destriers, bred for stamina; but they were capable of great speed in short bursts, and they were within yards of safety when Peter des Roches's stallion splashed into quicksand. The horse lurched to its knees, scrambled desperately to free itself as its rider clung helplessly to the saddle pommel. Des Roches had enough presence of mind, however, to wave John away when he saw the other man turning back. 'No, John, no! Go on!'

'Jump clear and I'll pick you up!'

'Your horse cannot carry us both!'

John Marshal had also wheeled his mount about. 'Go back, Sire! I'll save him, I swear!'

But by then, it was too late; the tide was upon them. John had time only to turn his horse so the water did not strike them sideways. As he was swept downstream, he caught a last glimpse of Peter des Roches. The force of the surging waters had freed the stallion, only to engulf both horse and rider. John saw Peter's head break the surface, but the current was too swift to fight. His stallion was swimming strongly now, striking out for the embankment; he could do nothing but give the horse its head.

John's stallion came ashore several miles south of Long Sutton. As he slid from the saddle, John found himself alone in a vast, empty marshland. The ground squished under his boots, his footprints filling with water. He shouted, in vain. Even the swamp birds were suddenly stilled. After a time, he heard a cry, saw a man struggling towards shore. Wading back into the shallows, he helped the man scramble up the embankment. Then they both slumped down upon the muddy ground, too exhausted even for speech. Out in the river, men and horses were drowning, but their death cries were muffled by the tide, muted by the rising wind. An unearthly silence blanketed the Fens.

John Marshal was the first to find them, followed by some of the villagers. John accepted the mantles they offered without comment, ignored their pleas that he come back with them to Long Sutton. But within the quarter-hour, he saw Peter des Roches limping slowly along the embankment. The elegant Bishop of Winchester was covered with fetid swamp mud and slime; even his hair was matted with it. But he was alive and smiling, and he and John embraced like brothers.

'The Almighty never showed me greater favour, John. I grabbed my horse's tail, held on so tightly that I could scarcely unclench my fists once we reached the shore!'

He gratefully accepted a wineskin, drank in deep, noisy gulps. 'There are some of our men downstream. A few who knew how to swim. A few more who had the wits to clamber up on to loose sumpter horses. They told me those in the rear of the train may have made it back to Cross Keys ere the tide came in. But most of the horses drowned, for certès, and too many men. How many we'll likely never know; only Christ All-merciful can say where or when their bodies will wash up.'

'What of my treasure?' John said huskily. 'Think you that any of it can be recovered at the next low water?'

No one spoke; he had his answer in their averted eyes. The village priest at last said, 'Some of it might be salvaged eventually. But most of it is gone, my lord.'

He spoke so matter-of-factly that it was obvious he had no idea what John had just lost. His treasure, jewels, gold plate, coronation regalia and crown, his wardrobe, his chapel, holy relics, tents, furniture, siege weapons, supplies, his books, documents of state, written records of his reign – all lay buried in the quicksands of the Wellstream. It was as if his very history were blotted out, his past

565

swallowed up by the rising tide that had claimed his ill-fated baggage train.

'John . . .' Peter des Roches touched his arm, lowered his voice for John's ears alone. 'We'll leave men here to do what must be done. But we've got to get you to shelter, and with no delay. I beg you, do not argue with me on this. You're soaked through, and half-frozen. A night out here in the Fens could be the death of you.'

John was not about to argue, for never had he been so cold. He clenched his jaw until it ached, but even that did not stop his teeth from chattering. The pain in his intestines, a constant throughout this day of horrors, was now as piercing as a knife blade, as penetrating as the wind blowing off the marshes. For the first time since he'd been stricken at Lynn, he remembered that his brother Henry had died of such a flux of the bowels, and when Peter suggested that they ride back towards Wisbech Castle, he shook his head, said reluctantly:

'I think it best if we head for Swineshead Abbey, Peter. It's more likely they'll have a doctor there.'

By the time he reached Swineshead Abbey, John was burning up with fever. He grew steadily worse on Thursday, but insisted, none the less, upon continuing the next morning to Sleaford Castle. Hearing that the Abbot of an abbey of White Canons at Croxton was skilled in the arts of healing, Peter des Roches sent urgently for the man, passed some anxious hours until his arrival at Sleaford on Saturday afternoon. He was with John now, while Peter and John Marshal waited in the solar for word.

'If only he'd rest!' Marshal burst out suddenly. 'But no, he lies in there, as weak as a mewing kitten, and what is he doing? Dictating letters, giving pardons, acquittances, safe-conducts. Mayhap if you talked to him . . .'

'He's never been one for listening,' Peter said dryly, spun around as the door opened.

'Well? How does he?'

The Abbot appeared to be choosing his words with care. 'I bled him, and that seemed to ease him somewhat. I'm going to prepare a mustard poultice now to draw off the pain.'

'You can speak plainer than that, can you not?'

The Abbot flushed at the peremptory tone. 'Very well, my lord. The truth is that I can attend to the King's spiritual needs. But more than that, no; it's too late.'

566

'You were not with him very long. How can you be so sure?'

'He is passing clotted blood,' the Abbot said bluntly, and they no longer doubted, stared at him in bleak silence.

As he entered John's chamber soon afterwards, Peter des Roches wondered why he'd needed a stranger to tell him John was dying. He had only to look into John's face. The shocking gauntness, the relentless wasting away of flesh, the ominous ashen cast to his skin – the signs were there for all but the blind to see, attesting to an illness that was mortal. Only the eyes were still John's, hollowed and feverish but utterly lucid, all too penetrating.

John struggled to sit up at sight of Peter. 'I'm not overly impressed with Abbot Adam. But I expect you'll want him to accompany us to Newark on the morrow?'

'Newark? Jesus God, John, you cannot! That's twenty miles from here!'

'And a damned sight safer, so let that be an end to it. Now fetch me some wine, Peter. You'd not believe the noxious concoction your Abbot would have me drink – egg yolk in rose-water!'

Peter laughed, approached the bed. As he did, John reached up, grasped his wrist. 'Tell me,' he said, 'what you're keeping from me. I heard servants talking, know a courier arrived from Hubert de Burgh. Why did you not want me to see him, Peter? What message did he bring?'

Peter hesitated, but John had never been easy to lie to. 'The news is bad, John. Hubert de Burgh has asked Louis for a truce whilst he consults with you. Their supplies are running out. He says if you cannot come to his aid, he may have to surrender Dover Castle to the French.'

John's grip loosened; he sank back upon the bed, and then turned his face towards the wall. He heard Peter's footsteps retreating, heard the door quietly close. He shut his eyes, but the tears squeezed through his lashes, seared his skin like hot rain.

To the Abbot, Adam of Croxton, the world as he knew it was encompassed within the white walls of his abbey of St John the Evangelist. If his was a narrowed focus, he felt no lack, had never yearned to break free of the familiar, to embrace the unknown. He had not welcomed the summons from the Bishop of Winchester, for he was not a man of worldly ambitions, and his every instinct warned him that no good could come to him at the King's court.

His instincts were sound. He found himself treating a dying man, while fearing that he might be held accountable for that death. His medical experience had been confined to the treatment of the canons and lay brothers of his abbey, local villagers, people who were in awe of his expertise, docile and submissive. Nothing had prepared him for a patient like John. Arrogant, irreverent, wilful, he had yet to show any of the virtues that the Abbot expected of a dying Christian. He was not humble, not noticeably repentant, and he seemed thoroughly preoccupied with secular concerns, seemed to be devoting all his waking thoughts to his earthly kingdom at a time when he should be concentrating only upon the Kingdom of God.

The Abbot had been appalled by John's determination to ride north to Newark Castle. He'd have sworn John was too weak even to mount a horse, but John did, somehow managed to stay in the saddle for more than four miles. Even after he collapsed, he remained stubbornly set upon reaching Newark, and his men had finally cut willows by the roadside, woven them into a makeshift litter, for however weakened his body was, John's will was not to be thwarted. Go to Newark he would, and go to Newark he did, at a cost in pain the Abbot preferred not to dwell upon.

Newark Castle was nominally in the hands of the Bishop of Lincoln, but in actual fact, it was a royal stronghold, and its constable, Robert de Gaugi, did all in his power to make the King comfortable. John was lodged in the Bishop's private quarters on the uppermost floor of the three-storey gatehouse. For two days now, the Abbot had divided his time between John's chambers and the chapel of St Philip and St James. As he entered John's bedchamber, he was not surprised to find a scribe at John's bedside, to find John dictating a letter to Falkes de Bréauté, instructing him to free some servants of William de Warenne, Earl of Surrey.

'Witness ourself at Newark on Tuesday, the 18th of October, in the eighteenth year of our reign,' John concluded, and glanced over at Peter des Roches to explain, 'Rumour has it Warenne is ripe for switching sides again. A gesture of good will costs us little and might just push him off the fence.'

The Abbot watched in silent disapproval as John turned back to the scribe, began another letter, appointing Nicholaa de la Haye and Philip Marc as joint sheriffs of Lincolnshire. It both baffled and troubled him that John should be squandering his last hours in sordid political dealings, and he marvelled that a man in such intense pain

568

could be so coherent, so cynical, and so single-minded. In all respects, he was finding John utterly beyond his ken.

John was still dictating, this time to Engelard de Cigogne, his constable of Windsor Castle, directing him to accept his son Henry as liege lord and to hold the castle for him. His voice had weakened over the past hours, for he'd been dictating similar letters since dawn to his sheriffs, constables, and castellans. The effort he was making to talk was obvious to all in the room, and when he paused for breath, the Abbot stepped forward, held out a cup of dark liquid.

'Drink this, Sire,' he entreated, and tried to mask his annoyance when John demanded to know what was in it. 'My own mixture: sumac, gall, pomegranate rind, and opium. It will ease your pain, my lord.'

John was panting, but he shook his head stubbornly. 'It'll make me sleep, too. And time is all I have.' When the Abbot would have protested, he flared into sudden rage. 'My son is nine years old. Are you so stupid that you do not know what that means? A child King and a kingdom at war, with half the realm under French control. A right loving bequest to leave my son, is it not?'

The Abbot shrank back, speechless. Peter de Roches moved towards the bed, said with as much conviction as he could muster, 'John, I understand your fear. But you must not despair. I truly believe men will rally to your son. He's but a child, has offended no one. Even men who are your sworn enemies might well forsake the French, return their allegiance to Henry.'

Almost, John could believe him – almost. 'To hear you tell it, Peter, the best thing I can do for my son is to die.' His outburst had exhausted him; he lay back against the pillows, fighting nausea. When he opened his eyes, the Abbot and Peter were bending over him, and he saw in their faces their relief that he still breathed. He swallowed with difficulty. He'd known for days that he was dying, but death was so very close now, was in the chamber with them, no longer willing to wait.

'I always thought, Peter, that I'd . . . I'd fear to die . . .' His tongue seemed to have swollen, was so rough and dry that he had to labour just to shape his words. 'But . . . after a week of this pain, I'm beginning to see it as . . . as a release . . .'

Peter reached for a wine cup, held it to his lips. 'Shall I hear your confession now?'

John managed a ghostly smile. 'I think not. Better the Abbot be the one to absolve me of my sins. You see . . . you know me too well, would not . . . not believe me when I said I forgave my enemies . . .'

The Abbot looked shocked, but Peter was smiling through tears. John waved the Abbot away from the bed, plucked at Peter's sleeve. 'You must take messages for me . . . Tell Pembroke that I entrust Henry into his care, that he must safeguard my son's crown. Tell Isabelle that she can rely upon Pembroke and Chester, that she can trust them . . . and you. Tell Pembroke, too, to reward those who . . . who were with me at the last.'

Peter could barely hear him now; he leaned forward, his ear to John's mouth. 'Tell Llewelyn ab Iorwerth . . . tell him to take care of my daughter. And tell Will . . .' John's voice trailed off, and Peter prompted gently:

'Tell him what, John?'

John closed his eyes. 'Nothing,' he whispered. 'Nothing . . .'

As the afternoon ebbed away, the sky darkened long before dusk and the wind intensified. The Abbot stood by John's bed, watching the uneven rise and fall of his chest. He was amazed that John still lived, for he'd been fearful that John might die before he could hear his confession, give him the holy Viaticum, and perform the rite of Extreme Unction. But John had rallied briefly, had once again shown an inner resilience that somehow defied all claims upon mortal flesh. Having administered the Sacraments, the Abbot had to believe that John was now in a state of grace. Yet dark doubts he could not acknowledge gnawed at the outer edges of his faith.

John had given the correct answers to the Seven Interrogatories, had received the Body and Blood of Christ, had shown the proper contrition. But after he was absolved, shriven of his earthly sins, he'd said softly, 'Do not Scriptures say there shall be greater joy in Heaven over one sinner that repenteth than over nine and ninety just persons?' Then he'd slept, and the Abbot did not know if he'd been sincere and seeking solace, mocking himself, or even mocking God.

John awoke to blackness and burning pain, to panic. He could not see, and when he cried out, no one answered him. His mind clouded by sleep and the Abbot's draught, he could not remember where he was or why he was suffering, and he tried to rise from the bed but

570

had not the strength, lay there helplessly in the dark until the door opened and the Abbot entered.

He saw at once what had happened, began to offer profuse apologies. 'The shutter blew open, my lord, and the candles guttered out. I went to fetch a lamp, did not think you'd awaken.'

The lamp was a crude one, no more than a wick floating in a bowl of fish oil, but its feeble light was the most welcome sight John had ever seen. For once he submitted willingly to the Abbot's ministrations, let the monk squeeze water on to his swollen lips, bathe the sweat from his forehead.

'Fetch the Bishop,' he whispered, saw the Abbot look away in sudden distress.

'My liege, he . . . he's gone. He and John Marshal left hours ago. They said it was urgent they reach my lords of Pembroke and Chester as soon as possible, in order to see to the safety of the young K – of your son.' He flushed, added remorsefully, 'You were so ill, my lord, and it seemed so unlikely you'd recover your wits . . .'

'I understand . . .' And John did. Peter des Roches was his friend. But when a king died, his power died with him. He mumbled something too low for the Abbot to hear. He could not be sure, but it sounded as if John had said, '*Sic transit gloria mundi.*' Thus passes the glory of the world. He gave John a look of surprised approval, glad that John seemed to be focusing his thoughts now as he ought, upon the Hereafter, and then stammered:

'Your Grace, I . . . I have a great favour to ask of you. Not for me, but for my abbey.'

That came as no surprise. How tired he was, so very, very tired. He roused himself with an effort, said, 'Ask then. Let yours be the last favour I grant . . .'

'My liege, if you only would . . . I know that you said you wanted to be buried in the Benedictine priory of St Mary at Worcester, before the shrine of St Wulfstan. But I wondered if . . . if you might consider . . . if we could have your heart and bowels for burial at Croxton?'

John's eyes opened – wide. 'What?'

'If you'd consent, my lord, it would be such an honour. We'd bury them at the High Altar and say Masses for your soul –' He broke off, dismayed and bewildered, for John was laughing. His laughter was unsteady, rasping and harsh, but it was unmistakably laughter.

571

'If only I'd known there'd be . . . be such a demand,' he gasped, 'We could have auctioned off the . . . the choice parts . . .' The horrified look on the Abbot's face only made him laugh all the more, until he could not laugh and breathe at the same time, began to choke.

Thoroughly alarmed, the Abbot propped him up with pillows, hastened to give him wine. As the spasm passed, he lay back, closed his eyes. 'I think I always knew . . .'

'Knew what, my liege?'

John turned his head, looked at him for a long time without answering. 'I always knew,' he said, 'that I'd die alone . . .'

Joanna reached the Benedictine priory of St Mary at Worcester shortly after dark on Friday, November 18. The hospitaller was awaiting her at the priory gateway; so, too, was her brother. Richard helped her to dismount, kissed her cheek. The hospitaller was looking askance at Joanna's Welsh guards, but when she asked if he could accommodate her men, he nodded. 'But of course, Madame. It is an honour to serve the sister of King Henry.'

Joanna said nothing, but Richard saw her flinch. He took her arm as the hospitaller assured her that all was in readiness to commemorate the late King's month-mind with a solemn Requiem Mass. 'Joanna, do you want to go to your chambers now?' he asked, and she shook her head.

'I want to go to him first. Will you take me, Richard?'

They walked in silence for a while. It had been snowing sporadically throughout the day, began again as they crossed the courtyard. Joanna's hood fell back; she seemed not to notice as droplets of snow dusted her hair, melted upon her mantle. As they entered the south walkway of the cloisters, she said, 'Tell me,' and Richard did, told her all he'd learned of their father's final days.

'A violent windstorm struck Newark ere he died. That's not uncommon for the season, but the fool servants took fright. Word spread that the Devil was coming to claim Papa's soul, and some even fled.' They'd stopped by the church door. He saw the anguished question in her eyes and shook his hed. 'No, Papa never knew. The Abbot who tended him wrote to Isabelle, said that by the time the storm reached its height, Papa was no longer conscious. He died soon after midnight.'

572

'And did they strip his body of his clothes and rings? Did they take all of value as they did when his father died at Chinon?'

Her bleak insistence upon knowing the worst troubled Richard, but he did not lie. 'Yes. But his soldiers kept faith, the routiers whom men scorned as base mercenaries, paid hirelings. They alone did not forsake him, Joanna, escorted his body to Worcester. Bishop Silvester officiated at the burial, but it was done without much ceremony, and in haste. The main concern was with getting Henry crowned as quickly as possible.'

'I heard it was done at Gloucester. You were there, Richard?'

He nodded. 'On the 28th. The Bishop of Winchester crowned him, since the Archbishop of Canterbury is still in Rome, under suspension. But then, even were he not, Westminster is in rebel hands. They did not even have a crown, Joanna, had to use a gold circlet provided by Isabelle.'

'Where are they now?'

'The younger children are still at Corfe. Henry and Isabelle are at Bristol with Pembroke. They reissued Papa's Runnymede charter last Saturday, with some of the more objectionable provisions deleted, that committee of twenty-five being the first to go. It is a shrewd concession, allows the barons to save face, and I think all but the very proud and the very embittered will come to terms with Pembroke and Chester. Peter des Roches told me that during Papa's three days at Newark more than forty couriers arrived from rebels seeking to make peace with Papa. But by then it was too late . . .'

They were still standing in the cloisters. Joanna's face looked chalky in the lantern light; nor had Richard liked the flat, brittle tone of her voice. 'Joanna . . .' He sighed, not knowing what to say. 'I am truly sorry you had to come alone like this to Worcester.'

'I had no choice. My husband is at war with England.' Joanna drew an audible breath. 'Nor do I think I would have wanted him with me . . . not here.'

He started to speak, but she'd turned away, was moving ahead of him into the nave of the church. Vespers was done, and the monks were now at supper in the refectory; Joanna and Richard found themselves quite alone. Torches flared in the choir, and a dark object before the High Altar was ringed with white syze candles, with flickering light. Joanna moved up the aisle, until she was close enough to touch her father's stone coffin.

573

'But he wanted to be buried with St Wulfstan,' she whispered. 'He often told me so . . .'

'Bishop Silvester and the Prior assured me that his wishes will be honoured. They plan to move the shrines of St Wulfstan and St Oswald from the crypt, to place them on each side of Papa's tomb.' Richard smiled sadly. 'Papa would have liked that – sleeping with saints.'

Joanna was still staring at the tomb. 'Richard, would you mind leaving me alone for a time?'

He started to object, thought better of it. 'I'll await you back at the Prior's lodgings.' He turned towards the shadowed nave, then stopped. 'Peter des Roches told me something I think you'd want to know, Joanna. He said that whilst Papa was at Lynn, he made a grant to Margaret de Lacy, Maude de Braose's daughter. He gave her one hundred and eighty acres of land in the royal forest of Acornbury, to found a religious house in memory of Maude, her husband, and her son.'

The candles encircling John's tomb wavered, swimming before Joanna's eyes in a dizzying blur of brightness. She stood very still, listening as Richard's footsteps faded. And then she moved forward. She knelt in the coffin's shadow for an endless time, until her knees ached and she trembled from the cold. But she could find no comfort in prayer.

'You're proving to be a merciless ghost, Papa. I should have expected it, knowing you as I do.' Her tears were coming faster now. 'What do you mean to do, Papa? Shall you haunt me for the rest of my days?' Her voice broke; kneeling on the icy tiles before John's coffin, she wept bitterly.

BOOK TWO

1

September, 1217
Windsor, England

At the time of John's death, Louis exercised authority over half of John's realm. London was his, and his ally, the notorious pirate and freebooter Eustace the Monk, claimed dominion of the seas, operating at will from his base in the Channel Islands. But an anti-French antagonism was taking root in the country, and John's death gave many disgruntled rebels the excuse they needed to abandon Louis. Among those who acknowledged the boy-King as their sovereign was John's brother Will, Earl of Salisbury.

John's alliance with the Church now stood his young son in good stead. Wales had been under Interdict since November. Louis and the rebel barons had been declared excommunicate, and the papal legate Guala did his best to elevate the conflict into a holy war, encouraging Henry's supporters to wear the white crosses of crusaders. Coming under such intense pressure from the Holy See, Philip was fast losing enthusiasm for his son's English adventure. But Louis was not, and the war dragged on through the winter and early spring.

It began to seem as if neither side could score a decisive victory. Then, in mid-May the Earl of Pembroke learned that Robert Fitz Walter, Saer de Quincy, and a French force were besieging Lincoln Castle. Pembroke saw his opportunity to engage them while Louis was occupied in another siege of Dover Castle, and by dawn on May 20, a royalist army was in sight of Lincoln's city walls.

Although the castle's hereditary castellan, Nicholaa de la Haye, had been waging a gallant defence, the town was securely in rebel hands. But Nicholaa sent her lieutenant constable out to the royalists with the welcome word that she could give them entry into the castle through a small postern door. Once in the castle, Peter des Roches made a daring reconnaissance into the city itself and discovered a

577

gate along the western wall, blocked but unguarded. Returning to his companions, he shared this discovery with Chester, Pembroke, and Will, the leaders of the expedition.

While the royalist vanguard sought to batter down the north gate, another force gained entry through Peter's hidden gateway, and soon the steep, narrow streets of Lincoln had become a battlefield. By 3.00 p.m. it was over. The French commander was dead, Fitz Walter and Saer de Quincy were taken prisoner, along with three hundred French knights, and the rest of the French were in flight.

Amazingly enough, only five men were slain in the actual fighting. More died, however, on the chaotic retreat back towards London. And when the triumphant royalists sacked the city, many women and children drowned, trying to flee in small boats that capsized in the River Witham.

Their victory was so complete that the jubilant English dubbed it the 'Fair of Lincoln', as if it had been a tournament. But it did not end the war. Louis still believed the English crown was within his grasp, was not willing to concede defeat.

Joanna reined in, shocked, at first sight of Windsor Castle. She remembered apple orchards, groves of hazelnut and filbert, lush vineyards nurtured since the days of her grandfather's reign. But she saw only scorched, mangled tree-stumps, barren and pitted earth where rocks launched from mangonels had gone astray. As she passed into the lower bailey, there, too, she found scars of the castle's three-month siege. There were gaping holes in the ground, the outer timber palisades were blackened, and the stone walls of the middle and inner baileys were gouged and battered.

Even the great hall had not been spared; a section of the roof had suffered a direct hit. Joanna stopped her mare. It had been more than eleven years, but she even remembered the day of the week: Tuesday, May 2, in God's year, 1206. She'd stood with her father here in the bailey, struggling to bid him farewell without tears, still unable to believe that in just nine days she would be the wife of a Welsh Prince. She'd thought she had managed to hide her fear from John, but when they embraced, he hugged her tightly, saying, 'You'll have no regrets, sweetheart, I promise.'

'No regrets,' Joanna echoed now, a lifetime later, and then she laughed, a laugh so strained, so lacking in mirth that her men gave her looks of curiosity, even of sympathy. After a time, her mare began to fidget. Only then did she bestir herself, shake off her father's spell, and cross the drawbridge into the middle bailey.

The timber buildings constructed by Henry II for his Queen's comfort were ranged along the north wall of the upper bailey, and they alone seemed unscathed. Joanna was escorted across a grassy courtyard and into the chamber where Isabelle awaited her.

They were alone; Isabelle had dismissed her own attendants and Joanna's maid. There was genuine affection in their greetings, animation in their first moments of sharing, but there was a slight wariness, too, as if their intimacy needed to be rediscovered, to be tested anew after a five-year separation.

'Henry had an earache, so I had to put him to bed with a vervain poultice. He is so excited by your coming, so eager to see you,' Isabelle said and smiled. 'Being an only child myself, I confess I cannot comprehend his passion for siblings. But nary a day goes by when he does not make wistful mention of Dickon, even Nell and Isabella, and they're just babes.'

'They're still at Corfe?' Joanna's disappointment was sharp, for she'd yet to meet her little sisters.

'Yes, for safety's sake. In fact, dearest, I was not at all sure Llewelyn would allow you to come halfway across England, safe-conduct or not.'

'Llewelyn does not know. He's waging war in South Wales, was besieging Haverford the last I heard from him.'

'Well, whatever enabled you to – Joanna, you do not yet know, do you? How could you, being on the road all week? There was a great sea battle fought on St Bartholomew's Day. The war is done, for Louis's hopes sank with his ships. And one of the heroes of the day was your brother!'

'Richard? Or Oliver?'

'Richard. Ah, Joanna, it was a glorious triumph. Robert de Courtenay was bringing reinforcements to Louis; they had a fleet of ten galleys and seventy smaller craft, under the command of Eustace the Monk. They meant to sail up the Thames to London, but our ships caught up with them at the mouth of the estuary. Richard brought his ship alongside Eustace's, and a cog commanded by John Marshal came up on the other side. The Monk had an enormous galley, but it was carrying horses and a heavy trebuchet, and was riding so low in the water that the deck was almost awash. Our cog was to windward, and the sailors threw down pots of powdered quicklime on to the French, temporarily blinding them. Richard and his men at once boarded the galley, and in the fighting that followed, all the French knights – thirty-six – were taken captive. Eustace the Monk was found hiding in the hold. He offered a thousand marks for his life, but Richard had him beheaded on his own deck.

'After that, it was a total rout. Although we were greatly outnumbered, the French panicked once the Monk's ship was taken. Some of the galleys made it back to Calais, but all the smaller ships were sunk or captured. Only the highborn knights were spared, all others being thrown into the sea. Much booty was taken and shared amongst our sailors afterwards, with some set aside by the Earl of Pembroke to found a hospital in honour of St Bartholomew. The day's glory belonged to Hubert de Burgh, who commanded our fleet – and to Richard.' Isabelle at last paused for breath. 'John would have been very proud of him.'

'Yes,' Joanna agreed softly, 'he would.'

'Pembroke sent Robert de Courtenay to Louis.' Seeing Joanna belatedly react to the name Courtenay, Isabelle nodded, said dryly, 'Yes, he's my uncle, my mother's brother. He brought back word from London that Louis is now willing to make peace, to depart from the kingdom. He meets Pembroke and Hubert de Burgh on Tuesday to discuss terms.'

'I'm glad.'

'Are you truly, Joanna? After all, Llewelyn is allied with Louis –'

'But Henry is my brother. Of course I want him to win.'

'What is troubling you, then? Is it that you think Llewelyn may not be willing to make peace with Henry?'

'No, it's not that. Llewelyn will eventually come to terms with the English . . . once they make it worth his while.'

Isabelle had rarely heard Joanna sound so cynical, but she was amused, none the less. 'Your husband can charm, but he can also calculate finely enough to split hairs. In that, he's always reminded me of John,' she said and laughed. But Joanna did not. 'Joanna . . . what is it? Is it Llewelyn?'

Joanna hesitated. 'Yes.' Rising, she moved restlessly to the window. 'It began this summer, when Reginald de Braose submitted to Henry. To the Welsh, that was a betrayal. Llewelyn was furious, made up his mind to teach Reginald a sharp lesson. But I . . . I could

580

not see it in the same light. I could think only of Gwladys – torn between husband and father. We quarrelled, and he departed with angry words between us. As it turned out, he brought Reginald to heel in short order. He swept into Brecknock, and as soon as he crossed the border into Gower, Reginald hastened to meet him at Llangiwg, humbled his pride and yielded up the castle of Swansea to Llewelyn. It was a quick and bloodless triumph for the Prince. But an utter failure for the father.'

'Was Gwladys very distraught?'

'No,' Joanna said reluctantly, and then managed a rueful smile. 'In truth, she was not. Llewelyn can do no wrong in her eyes, and she thinks he was perfectly justified. To Gwladys, there is but one side to any quarrel – the Welsh.'

'I see. Well then, do you not think you may have . . . overreacted somewhat?'

'You need not be so tactful. Say what you mean, that I was really reacting to past pain of my own. Of course I was. But that does not change the fact that Llewelyn put political aims above his daughter's welfare.'

'Darling, men do that all the time. At least ambitious men do . . . and is there any other kind?' Isabelle rose, too, followed Joanna to the window. 'I am sorry, though, Joanna. I've known a few women who were well and truly in love. But you were the only one in love with her own husband! I admit I never thought it would last, yet I hoped for your sake that it might.'

Joanna had been listening in surprise. 'I once told Llewelyn that I did not always like him, and this summer was for certès one of those times. But I still do love him, Isabelle . . . and fear for him. Over the past eleven years, I've learned to live with his wars, with the knowledge that a well-aimed spear or arrow could make me a widow at any moment. But now . . . now he is under sentence of excommunication, and that pushes my fear beyond endurance. I'll not deny I find it hard, knowing he is always going to put Gwynedd first. But he found it hard, too, being wed to John's daughter. And no matter how angry he makes me, I could not envision my life without him . . . even now, when our marriage is admittedly at low tide!'

'I am glad, Joanna,' Isabelle said and meant it, although she remained convinced that a love so intense was no gift of God. 'Now tell me,' she said, because she knew it would please Joanna, 'about

Elen and your Davydd. From your letters, I suspect that he is your favourite, no?'

'No!' Joanna protested swiftly, if not altogether convincingly. 'I love Elen dearly. But . . . I just cannot understand her as I would like. No matter how I try, there remains a barrier between us, one I've not been able to breach. With Davydd, it's different, mayhap because I see so much of myself in him. I know what he is thinking and feeling and dreaming; even without words, I know.'

'And what of the snake in your Eden? What of Gruffydd?'

Joanna's reaction was a revealing one. Her mouth tightened noticeably, and her eyes darkened; at that moment, she looked very like John. 'Davydd will be nine in November. Gruffydd is one-and-twenty . . . and has a large following amongst Llewelyn's people.'

'Not surprising. He's a handsome youth, and there's something utterly compelling about his sort of recklessness. It's rather like watching a rock slide; you do not want to get caught up in it, but for certès you cannot ignore it, either. You're saying, then, that the Welsh regard him as Llewelyn's rightful heir?'

Joanna nodded. 'If it were left to the Welsh, it would be no contest, would be Gruffydd by acclamation. And Llewelyn loves him very much, puts up with outrageous behaviour he'd not tolerate from another living soul because of that love. As for Gruffydd, I sometimes think his hatred of England borders upon madness, for it is so impassioned, so . . . so utterly implacable. He despises me, of course, and is wildly jealous of Davydd. You want the truth, Isabelle? I think I was not so much angry with Llewelyn over Gwladys as over Gruffydd. You see, when Llewelyn led his army into Reginald's lands and then against the Flemings in Rhos, he was not just risking his own life. He was risking Davydd's, too.'

'I do not know what to tell you, Joanna,' Isabelle said and sighed. 'I know what John would have said, though. He'd say this was one of God's more macabre jests. Your son's danger will not cease till the day Gruffydd draws his last breath. Yet Gruffydd lives because of you. John spared him for you, because he thought you wanted that. He'd have sent Gruffydd to the gallows in a trice if you'd only asked . . .' Isabelle sighed again. 'I so wish you'd come to him at Oxford, Joanna. It hurt him grievously that you did not.'

'I could not!' Joanna's face was flaming. 'I had no choice, had to put my husband and children first, and I'll not feel guilty about it!'

'Then why,' Isabelle said coldly, 'are you so angry?'

Joanna said nothing; her throat was suddenly too tight for speech. She turned abruptly away, back towards the window. She was still in profile; Isabelle could see how long it took for the colour to fade from her face and her own anger ebbed away. She reached out, touched Joanna's shoulder. Joanna spun around and they embraced, clung together in one of the most intense yet ephemeral of bonds, the solidarity of a shared loss.

'I'm sorry, Joanna. I never meant to hurt you.' Isabelle's cheek was wet with Joanna's tears; she wiped them away, gave the younger woman an apologetic hug. 'But I need to talk about John, and you're the only –'

'I cannot.' Joanna's voice was muffled, all but inaudible. 'Isabelle, I cannot . . .'

'I know you're grieving. But Joanna, so am I. These last months have been the most wretched of my life!'

Joanna had rarely heard Isabelle speak with such emotion, with such stark sincerity, and she felt shame for having assumed Isabelle's grief would be so easily assuaged.

Isabelle had begun to pace. 'John was a . . . a law unto himself, was not an easy man to understand . . . or to live with. Especially these last few years. But I think I made him happy, and I . . . I loved being his Queen, Joanna. As far back as I can remember, I could turn heads, attract attention, but that was only because men found me fair to look upon. As Queen, it was different; I truly mattered. People sought to please me, to court my goodwill – because they knew John loved me. And now . . . now I might as well be a deaf-mute for all the heed they pay me. Without John, I count for naught.'

'Surely you exaggerate,' Joanna said slowly, and Isabelle gave a vehement shake of her head.

'I know I'm no Eleanor of Aquitaine. It never occurred to me – or anyone else obviously – that I should act as regent. But I ought to have some say in my son's upbringing, and I have none at all. Nor will I as long as Chester and Pembroke have the government. They like me not, Joanna, think I'm frivolous and vain and foreign, a bad influence upon Henry. Yes, that is what I said – foreign. For suddenly my birthplace has become a liability. People now look at me askance because my mother is a first cousin to the French King, as if that somehow makes me suspect!'

583

'Isabelle . . . might you not be over-sensitive, seeing slights when none was meant?'

'Then why did the Pope feel the need to issue a stern warning last February, forbidding people to harass me or molest my property and goods?'

Joanna's emotions were too ambivalent to allow for dispassionate analysis. The realization that Isabelle grieved more for the privileges and prerogatives of queenship than for the man who'd made them possible had done much to sour her sympathy for the other woman. And yet she could not help but identify with Isabelle's isolation, her sense of alienation, for she, too, had suffered for the sin of foreign birth.

Isabelle had stopped before a small table. It was littered with jars, with belladonna and kohl and marigold balm, casting-bottles of jasmine and violet perfumes, vials of rose-water; Joanna had never seen such an assortment. Isabelle was picking up jars at random; she seemed suddenly – and uncharacteristically – uncertain. Jerking off her wimple and veil, she loosened her hair, shook it free about her shoulders. Although it was not as pure a shade as in her early youth, and owed something now to rinses with lemon-water, her hair was still soft and shimmering, evoking in Joanna an unexpected and nostalgic memory of her mother Clemence, so many years dead, Clemence with her swirling cloud of bright blonde hair.

'I might as well say this straight out, know no other way to tell you.' Isabelle leaned back against the table, as if bracing herself. 'I asked you to come to Windsor because I think of you as a sister, Joanna . . . and I wanted to bid you farewell.'

'Farewell? I do not understand.'

'I am more than the widow of a dead King, Joanna. I am Countess of Angoulême in my own right, and I have decided to go home, to go back to my own lands, my own people.'

Joanna was stunned, at a loss for words. It did not surprise her that Isabelle should, even after seventeen years, have so little loyalty to England, for she did not feel truly bound to her own husband's homeland. But Isabelle would never be allowed to take her children. In abandoning England, she was abandoning Henry, Dickon, Nell, and Isabella, and Joanna could conceive of no circumstances, however wretched, under which she would willingly forsake Davydd and Elen. Although she said nothing, her shock showed plainly in her face, and Isabelle frowned, said defensively:

584

'It is for the best, Joanna. It's not as if they'll want for anything. Moreover, I have another daughter. Joanna – your namesake – is seven now, and I've not seen her since she was four.'

'But the de Lusignans have custody of her. Will they let you see her?'

'I think so. Hugh is a reasonable man, after all. Why would he not agree?'

'Reasonable?' Joanna echoed incredulously. 'Hugh de Lusignan?'

Isabelle laughed. 'No, I was speaking of his son, of the younger Hugh.' She'd picked up a mirror, was gazing pensively at the image it reflected, at the beauty not even polished metal could distort. 'No,' she repeated softly, 'I do not think Hugh will refuse me.'

February, 1218
Dolbadarn, North Wales

Situated on a rocky knoll eighty feet above Llyn Padarn, Dolbadarn Castle commanded the route from Caer yn Arfon to the Conwy Valley. This was Joanna's first visit to Dolbadarn since Llewelyn had constructed the two-storey circular keep, and she was dazzled at sight of mountains mirrored in the deep blue depths of a snow-fed lake. She stood now at the window in the upper chamber, gazing out at the regal heights of Yr Wyddfa, a stark, snow-shrouded pinnacle framed against a cloudless winter sky.

'I wonder if I'm falling under the spell of Wales at long last. Or does it seem so spectacular merely because I'm so happy? Shall I tell you why? Last night I had a letter from my brother Richard, telling me that his wife has given birth to a daughter. And this morning Llewelyn gave me a gift of immeasurable value. He has agreed to make peace with Henry, which means no more war . . . for a time, anyway, and a chance to visit my brother's court, and most blessed mercy of all, the papal legate Guala will now restore Llewelyn to God's grace. Oh, indeed? Well, that might not mean much to you, but it means everything to me!'

Her audience, a small, amber-coloured spaniel, yawned again, and Joanna laughed, scooped up the puppy. 'I know I'm silly, but I feel like being silly this morn. What shall we do now? Go play in the snow?'

The castle bailey seemed carpeted in crystal, so brilliant was the sunlight upon the drifts of ice and snow. Joanna's puppy ran in circles, barking joyously, and Joanna wished suddenly that she was not twenty-six, that she was still young enough to make angels in the snow, to spin till she was dizzy, drunk on the utter purity of the icy mountain air.

'Topaz!' The puppy was barking at a woman crossing the bailey.

Joanna called again, hastened to retrieve her errant pet. The hood of the woman's mantle shadowed her face, and Joanna did not recognize her until they were several feet apart. When she did, her exuberance vanished as if it had never been. Grabbing for the dog, she politely greeted Gruffydd's bride.

'Good morrow, Madame.'

Joanna opened her mouth, shut it again. She'd twice suggested that Senena call her by her given name; what more could she do? It annoyed her that she should find conversation so difficult with this girl; she'd thought she'd long since prevailed over the anxieties and insecurities of her own girlhood.

Seeing Senena glance down at the dog, she said, 'Topaz is a gift from my husband. I'd had a dog for nigh on thirteen years, did not think I wanted another when Sugar died. But Llewelyn was right, and I find Topaz a joy.'

'I like dogs,' Senena said. Hers was a breathless, little-girl voice that made her seem even younger than seventeen. So, too, did her size; she was barely five feet tall, looked incredibly fragile and tiny when standing next to her husband. She was not a beauty, was too pale, with unfashionable freckles and thick eyebrows she refused to pluck. Her eyes were undeniably her best feature, wide-set and compelling, a dark sea-grey, but to Joanna, too watchful, too unrevealing.

Joanna had made one or two half-hearted attempts to befriend Gruffydd's young wife, but she was not altogether sorry when Senena did not respond to her overtures. She was a quiet girl who rarely spoke in company, and Joanna had assumed she was shy. She was no longer so certain that was the case, was slowly concluding that Senena's reticence was not so much timidity as it was wariness. More and more, she reminded Joanna of a cat put down in strange surroundings, cautiously learning the lie of the land.

Senena was still studying Topaz. 'I prefer a larger dog myself,' she said in the colourless little voice that made it so difficult to determine if she meant to give offence. 'I think dogs should be useful, not just decorative. If you'll excuse me now, Madame, Gruffydd awaits me in the great hall.'

'By all means.' Joanna stood watching as Senena walked away, not moving until Topaz pawed at her skirt. 'Well, Topaz, I'm afraid you've just been dismissed as a decadent Norman trinket. Like me, no doubt.' But she felt no real surprise. Senena was Gruffydd's

587

cousin. She was also his choice; their marriage had come about because he wanted it so. It was only to be expected, therefore, that he and Senena shared more than a bed, that they shared a common outlook, a common enemy.

Senena had a surprisingly lithe, athletic stride, was already passing the West Tower. As she did, a small figure darted out behind her. Senena did not notice. But Joanna did, sharply cried out her daughter's name.

Elen whirled. She flushed at sight of her mother, hid her hands behind her back, but not before Joanna caught a glimpse of the snowball in her daughter's fist.

By the time she reached Elen, Senena had disappeared into the hall, apparently oblivious of the thwarted ambush. Joanna took Elen's arm, drew her aside.

'Elen, what am I to do with you? If you must throw snowballs, at least pick your victims with greater care. Believe me, Senena would not have been amused.'

Elen shrugged. 'I do not like her.'

'Why ever not?'

'Because . . . because she's Gruffydd's wife.'

Joanna stared at her daughter. 'But you've always been very fond of Gruffydd, and he of you. Have you quarrelled?'

Elen looked down at the ground; her hair was loose, windblown, fell forward to hide her face. Joanna suddenly understood, drew a sharp dismayed breath.

'It's Davydd,' she said, and Elen nodded.

'Gruffydd hates him.' She no longer sounded sulky, looked up at Joanna, brown eyes full of bewilderment. 'The day ere we left Aber, I was playing at the waterfall. Gruffydd and Senena were walking by the river. When they did not see me, I hid in the rocks so I could surprise them. I did not mean to eavesdrop, Mama, not really. They were saying mostly silly things, the way grown people do. Laughing and kissing, you know. But then Gruffydd began to talk about you and Davydd. He was telling Senena that you meant to deprive him of his rightful inheritance. He was saying hateful things about Davydd. Mama, he . . . he even said Davydd should never have been born!'

Joanna bit her lip. It was so unfair, so unjust that Davydd – and now Elen – should be caught up in adult passions, in ambitions and antagonisms beyond their ken. They were too young, she thought, too young! But she had no comfort for her child, could not lie. 'I am so sorry, Elen,' she said, after a troubled silence. 'I truly wish you could love both Davydd and Gruffydd. But since you must choose, I'm very glad you chose Davydd.'

'I had to, Mama. Gruffydd has Gwladys and Marared and Gwenllian. But Davydd has only me.'

Never had Joanna felt so inadequate, so unequal to the task of motherhood. 'The hardest part of being a mother, Elen, is that we want so much to protect our children from all evil, all hurt. And we cannot . . .'

'I do not need to be protected, Mama,' Elen protested indignantly. But when Joanna put her arm around the girl's shoulders, Elen did not pull away, and she stayed by Joanna's side as they walked together towards the great hall.

They had not yet entered the hall when they heard the shouting and quickened their steps, for they recognized the voices as Gruffydd's and Llewelyn's.

'But you turned down the English last September, rightfully refused to take part in the peace between Henry and the French Prince. Why have you changed your mind, Papa? Why should you now be willing to submit to the English?'

'I do not consider it submission,' Llewelyn snapped. 'When they offered peace last autumn, it was conditioned upon our surrender of all the lands we'd taken from them in South Wales. Of course I refused, and then I waited. It was well worth the wait, Gruffydd. Yes, I have now agreed to do homage to Henry. But in return, Guala will absolve me of excommunication and lift the Interdict from Wales. Our past conquests will be recognized. I will be invested with custody of the royal castles they call Carmarthen and Cardigan, will hold them until Henry comes of age. The English have even agreed to acknowledge my authority in lower Powys until Gwenwynwyn's sons reach manhood. Moreover, they –'

'"Acknowledge"? Who are they to acknowledge or legitimize your rights? You're a Welsh Prince, are not dependent upon the whims, the indulgence of the English Crown!'

'For the love of Christ, Gruffydd, when will you –' Llewelyn stopped abruptly. This was not the way, and for certès not the place. 'Come outside where we can talk in private,' he said curtly and turned without waiting to see if Gruffydd was, in fact, following him. By the time he'd reached the bailey, he was once more in control of his temper and determined that this time it would be different, this time he would somehow make his son understand.

'Gruffydd, listen to me. I know how you feel. When I was your age, I felt just as you do, wanted what you want – an utterly independent Wales, free of all foreigners, united under my control.'

'Is that so foolish a dream?' Gruffydd challenged, and Llewelyn slowly shook his head.

'No, lad, it is not. But it's a dream beyond our reach. God has decreed otherwise. We're too sparsely populated, too contentious, and we dwell in the shadow of England, a country some twenty times the size of ours. We will always have to seek some sort of accommodation with the English. The realities of power dictate that, Gruffydd.'

When Gruffydd started to speak, he said, 'I am not done; hear me out. I fought against believing it, too, Gruffydd, refused to admit that my horizons could be limited, my dreams denied. I followed my heart and not my head, let my pride lure me into disaster, into a near-fatal confrontation with the King of England. It was only by the luck of the angels that I survived it, that I did not lose all, that Gwynedd did not become an English shire.' He paused, put his hand upon Gruffydd's arm.

'I see so much of myself in you, Gruffydd. But in just three days I shall be forty-and-five and you're not yet twenty-and-two. I want you to be able to benefit from my years, my experience. I do not want you to make the same mistakes I did.'

'Whatever mistakes you may have made in the past, Papa, they are nothing when compared to the one you're about to make now.' But the emotion in Gruffydd's voice was no longer anger, and as he looked at Llewelyn now, his green eyes were misted, almost pleading. 'England has a boy-King, Papa. This is a God-given opportunity for us, and you're throwing it away. You're throwing it away and I cannot understand why!'

Llewelyn's hand slipped from Gruffydd's arm. 'No,' he said at last, 'you truly cannot, can you?'

'Papa, you're not a coward. I'd kill any man who called you one. But why, then, must you make the craven choice, demean yourself before men not worthy of your piss? Why will you not –'

'This discussion is done, Gruffydd. I go to Worcester next month to meet with Henry. And this time you shall go with me.'

'No! Never!'

590

'You will have to live with the lords of Henry's court, have to deal with Pembroke and Chester and Peter des Roches. So it is time you met them, learned what manner of men they are.'

'No, Papa. I will not go.'

'Yes,' Llewelyn said, 'you will,' and Gruffydd's eyes were the first to waver. He swung about, all but fled across the bailey. Llewelyn let him go, for he knew he'd won. But it was not a victory to give him joy. He stood motionless, staring down at Gruffydd's footprints in the snow, and suddenly he was remembering a childhood mishap, remembering that long-ago encounter with Walter de Hodnet.

'God help you, Gruffydd,' he said softly, 'but you'd never have done what Walter demanded. You'd have forced him to break your arm, to leave you maimed for life.'

Llewelyn found Joanna by the river wall in the Bishop of Worcester's gardens. It had been a wet, chill March and nights of killing frost had wreaked havoc among the Bishop's early-blooming crocus plants. Joanna was bundled up in a fur-lined mantle, but as Llewelyn reached her, she exclaimed, 'Listen to that. A curlew, a sure harbinger of coming spring.'

'My teeth are chattering too much to hear it. Are you not ready to come back to the Bishop's palace?'

'Well . . .' Joanna hesitated. 'What I'd truly like to do now is to go into the church, to light a candle for my father.' Although she knew she did not have to ask permission, her voice rose questioningly, none the less. Seventeen months after his death, John was still a sensitive subject between them.

'That's probably a good idea,' Llewelyn said dryly, leaving unsaid the rest of his thought, that John's soul was in need of all the prayers he could get. 'Come on,' he said, sliding his arm around Joanna's waist. 'I'll walk over with you.'

Joanna was very pleased. 'Admit it,' she teased, 'it did bother you, all those months when you could not enter a church. It had to, for how could you be sure God was on your side?'

'Just between you and me, *breila*, I've always suspected that the Almighty was Welsh,' Llewelyn said and they both laughed. They were still laughing as they entered the north door of the church, moved into the nave. But their laughter stopped abruptly a moment later, for they were face to face with Joanna's uncle Will and his wife.

Joanna had known such a meeting was inevitable, but she'd been dreading it all the same. Her feelings for Will were hopelessly entangled. She could not reproach him for deserting her father, not when she felt herself to be guilty of the same sin. But she could not help remembering what Isabelle had told her, how devastated John had been by Will's betrayal, and that memory drained all warmth, all vivacity from her voice.

Her greeting was so lame, so unlike her that Will flushed. 'I see,' he said flatly. 'So, you, too, judge me.'

'No,' Joanna said, without much conviction.

'Isabelle and Richard blame me. But I expected you to be fairer than them, Joanna. After all, you made a choice, too, did you not? You disavowed John to please your husband, and if you ever cared about the grief that gave John, he never knew it!'

The words were no sooner out of his mouth than Will would have given anything to recall them. Joanna looked so stricken that he was swept with remorse. No matter how raw his nerves had grown, there was no excuse for taking out his pain upon the lass, and he started to tell her so, to offer his apologies. But Llewelyn forestalled him, saying scathingly:

'Joanna was estranged from John over a matter of conscience. She could not stomach the murder of children. You, however, seemed to have had no such qualms. For three full years after the Nottingham hangings, you continued to keep faith with John, to benefit from his favour. You did not abandon him until he seemed sure to be beaten, until you thought Louis likely to –'

'No!' Will had flushed even darker. 'That's not so,' he said in a choked voice. 'It was not self-interest. It was because of what John did to my wife, to Ela. It was only then that she told me . . . told me that whilst I was a prisoner in France, John sought to seduce her.'

It was suddenly very quiet in the church. Llewelyn and Joanna both appeared dumbfounded. Will swallowed. 'I'm sorry, Joanna,' he said miserably. 'I did not mean to tell you that . . .'

Joanna was staring, not at him, but at Ela. For a long moment their eyes held, and then she said, 'It's all right, Uncle Will. I know you did what you thought you had to do.'

There was an awkward pause, and then Ela stepped forward, kissed Joanna on the cheek. Will wanted to do likewise, but felt too discomfited. He patted his niece on the shoulder, then made haste to lead his wife from the nave.

Joanna moved on into the choir, towards her father's tomb. Llewelyn followed more slowly. The irony did not escape him, that he of all men should find himself cast as John's defender, but he did not have to strive for conviction; for once he thought John truly deserved the benefit of the doubt. '*Breila*, I do not believe Will. I'm sure your aunt Ela is a good, pious woman, but I cannot see her as a siren. John was no fool, would not risk so much for so little. From what you've told me, his women were invariably young and fair to look upon, and Will's Ela is no Eve.'

'You need not seek to persuade me, Llewelyn. I know it's not true. I saw it on Ela's face.' Joanna's smile was sad, tremulous, but still a smile of sorts. 'You're right; Ela is no Eve. But she is the mother of eight children. If she could salvage her family's future with a lie, I dare say she thought that a small price to pay. And how can I blame her? For loving her children? If my father had not earned himself such a vile reputation, men would not have been so quick to suspect the worst of him, and Will could never have convinced himself that Ela spoke true. What you said about Will was right; he is a weak man. But he's a decent man, too, and he deserves some peace of mind.'

She reached up, kissed him softly on the mouth. 'Thank you for speaking up for me, beloved. Now I want to light a candle for my father. If you do not mind, I'd rather do it alone.'

Llewelyn watched as she turned away. If you can forgive Will, *breila*, why can you not forgive yourself? But the question was a silent one. They could not talk about John; that was a terrain too fraught with pitfalls and remembered pain. It troubled him, though, that Joanna seemed unable to talk about her father with anyone at all, even Catrin or Richard. At first he'd thought she only needed time to be able to come to terms with John's death. But he was beginning to realize that her grieving was interwoven with guilt – guilt she would not even acknowledge – that the normal healing process was ineffectual. Her grief was still raw and he did not know how to help her.

He glanced down at John's coffin, and his mouth twisted in a bitter smile. John had been no easy foe to defeat, and as a ghost, he was even more formidable, defying all attempts at exorcism. In death, he was causing as much pain and turmoil as ever he had in his accursed lifetime. Joanna was not his only victim. Gruffydd, too, was one, Gruffydd who could not outrun his memories of English prisons.

*

The talk in Worcester was all of the coming crusade to capture the Egyptian city of Damietta. Both in England and France, an impressive roster of wellborn barons had taken the cross, among them Robert Fitz Walter, Saer de Quincy and his eldest son, John's illegitimate son Oliver Fitz Roy – even Hugh de Lusignan. But the plans of one crusader in particular interested Llewelyn, and he deliberately set about encountering the Earl of Chester alone on the east walk of the priory cloisters.

They greeted each other with the wary regard men reserve for adversaries worthy of respect. Llewelyn at once came to the point. 'I hear you mean to join the crusade. Is that true?'

Chester nodded. 'I took the cross with King John, received a dispensation until the French were defeated. Now that the realm is at peace, I can fulfil my vow.'

'Tell me,' Llewelyn said with a faint smile, 'have you no qualms about leaving your holdings in Cheshire? With you in the Holy Land, men might see your manors and estates as fruit ripe for the picking.'

Chester thought Llewelyn's jest a rather dubious one, but he made a polite attempt to reply in kind, saying wryly, 'It is good of you to be so concerned on my behalf. Of course if you truly want to ease my mind, you can always offer a truce for the length of my absence.'

As he expected, Llewelyn laughed and shook his head. But then he said, 'Actually, what I had in mind was not a truce, but an alliance.'

Chester stopped dead. 'Are you serious?'

'Very.'

'We've been enemies for most of our lives. Yet now, when you have an opportunity to raid into Cheshire with impunity, you are offering to make peace? Why?'

'I'll not deny that your absence would enable me to seize an advantage. But it would be short-lived. You're right, we have been enemies, but by geography, not by choice. We each wield a great deal of power. If we joined together, how much greater that power might be, great enough to protect our common interests, to give us a formidable say in the King's council.'

'Yes,' Chester said slowly, 'it would indeed.'

Although he was sure he already knew the answer, Llewelyn took care to observe the formalities, asking, 'Well? What do you think?'

594

'I think,' Chester said, 'that we ought to talk.'

Gruffydd was utterly wretched at Worcester. The suffocating sensations of confinement had come back to haunt his sleep. He awoke in an English bed, craving Senena's warmth, dreading the daylight hours when he must mingle with men he despised, speak their alien tongue, watch as his father humbled himself before John's son.

As he crossed from sun into shadow, he paused, blinking as his eyes adjusted to the loss of light. He was not sure what drew him so often to the priory church, but on three different occasions he'd found himself standing before the High Altar, before the tomb of the English King. It gave him a curious kind of comfort to touch the cold marble of John's coffin. Once he'd even spat on to it, knowing the gesture was childish and not caring in the least.

But as he moved now into the choir, he came to an abrupt halt, for he was not alone. Two young boys were standing by John's coffin, a lone wall sconce spilling light on to their bowed heads, one bright as flame, the other black as jet. His brother Davydd and the boy-King.

Having offered a prayer, Henry carefully crossed himself, then reached out, ran his hand over the smooth surface of the tomb. Davydd, too, started to touch the coffin, but so tentatively that Henry said encouragingly, 'Go ahead. Papa would not mind. You're his grandson, have the right.'

At that, Davydd drew back. My grandfather, he thought, and it did not seem real to him, not at all. 'Do you miss him?' he asked, and Henry nodded.

'I did not see him all that often, but I always knew I would sooner or later. Now when I think that I'll never, never see him again, sometimes it . . . it scares me.'

Davydd gave Henry a look of sharp pity. 'You must miss your mother, too. Why did she go?' He did not mean to be rude, but he found Isabelle's mysterious departure very disturbing; it made him wonder if his own mother might not one day go back to England, leave him as Isabelle had left Henry.

'I do not know,' Henry admitted. 'She –' His head came up. 'Davydd,' he whispered, 'someone is watching us. Over there, see?'

Davydd peered into the shadows. 'It's my brother,' he said, but the sudden tautness in his voice, his stance, communicated to Henry an inexplicable sense of unease.

'Let's go,' he urged, tugging at Davydd's sleeve.

Davydd wanted to go, too, but he did not want Gruffydd to think he was running away. He circled around to the far side of the coffin. 'Do you like your brothers, Henry?'

Henry smiled at the silliness of the question. 'Of course I do. I like Richard and Oliver best, and I love my little brother Dickon; he's nine, like you.'

'We Welsh have a saying about brothers,' Davydd said, so loudly that Henry flinched. '*Gwell ceiniog na brawd.*'

'What does that mean?'

'Better a penny than a brother.'

'I do not understand.'

'Gruffydd does.'

'Not so loud,' Henry cautioned, 'lest he hears you. I do not like being watched. Do you think that we can slip out without him seeing us?'

'No,' Davydd said, but then he sighed. 'It's all right. He's gone.'

One of the monks was moving sedately up the cloister walk, towards the south door of the church. He stumbled backward as Gruffydd burst through the doorway, his box of candles spilling on to the cloister tiles. Gruffydd did not offer assistance; he'd not even noticed the man. He continued rapidly up the path, not pausing until he neared the Chapter House. At this time of day it would be empty, would be a good place to be alone. He was reaching for the latch as the door swung open and his father and the Earl of Chester emerged on to the walk.

Llewelyn had often deplored his eldest son's sense of timing, but never more than now. 'Were you looking for me, Gruffydd?'

Gruffydd shook his head. They'd been laughing together; he even thought he'd heard his father call Chester by his Christian name, call him Ranulf as if he were a friend, a comrade in arms.

'You know my son, of course, Ranulf,' Llewelyn said, and Gruffydd stiffened. Ranulf. So he'd not imagined it. Ranulf.

'Indeed. I was present at Dover Castle the day he defied King John. I've never forgotten it, for that was one of the most courageous acts I've ever seen.' In Chester's considered opinion, it was also one of the most foolhardly, and he might have said that to Llewelyn. But not to Gruffydd; he knew instinctively that this was one young man who'd never learned to laugh at himself.

'You might as well be the first to know,' he said and smiled. 'Your lord father and I have pledged to forget past differences, to act as allies from this day forth.' He heard Llewelyn's indrawn breath, and knew at once that he'd blundered, even before he saw the shock on Gruffydd's face.

'Papa . . . Papa, tell me he's lying. Tell me you'd not do this, you'd not befriend this . . . this Norman butcher!'

'Hold your tongue! The man speaks our language!'

'And slaughters our people! How often has his sword been smeared with Welsh blood? What else does he want from you? Are you to stand guard over his lands whilst he's in the Holy Land, act as his lackey, his –'

Llewelyn grabbed Gruffydd's wrist, shoved him back against the door, into the Chapter House. 'Do not ever shame me like that before a stranger! You understand, Gruffydd? Not ever!'

Gruffydd had never seen Llewelyn so angry. Unnerved in spite of himself, he took a backward step. That there was some justification for his father's rage, he could not deny. 'I ought not to have spoken out in Chester's hearing. In that, I was in the wrong. But . . . but my God, Papa, think what you do! Ever since you took that Norman witch into your bed, you've –'

Llewelyn was incredulous. 'Have you lost your wits? Joanna is no witch!'

That was a very serious accusation to make, and Gruffydd realized he'd gone too far; he had no proof whatsoever that Joanna had ever used the Black Arts to ensorcell his father. 'Mayhap she's not,' he conceded, 'but she is still to blame. She's got you to betray your birth-right, to –'

'I've heard enough from you, more than enough. Go back to the guest hall, gather your belongings. I want you gone from here within the hour, want you back in Wales ere you bring further disgrace upon me.'

'Gladly!' Gruffydd spun around, strode towards the door. There he paused for the briefest of seconds. But whatever he'd meant to say, he thought better of it. He shoved the door back, let it slam defiantly behind him.

Llewelyn sat down upon the closest wooden bench. Leaning back against the wall, he closed his eyes, rubbed his fingers over his throbbing temples; his anger had turned inward, and he felt suddenly sick. He'd lost track of time when the creaking of the door jolted him upright; he'd hoped Chester would have the common sense to leave him alone. The door opened wider. Not Chester. Morgan.

597

Llewelyn's mouth twitched, in what was almost a smile. 'You always know when I have need of you. What have you – second sight?'

Morgan shook his head. 'Gruffydd has gone.'

Llewelyn closed his eyes again, then felt the priest's hand on his shoulder. 'What can I do, Morgan? He's my son. Christ Jesus, but what can I do?'

3

April, 1220
Dolwyddelan, North Wales

Joanna was accustomed to having her bedchamber appropriated whenever her husband required a particularly private meeting place. She was not accustomed, however, to being present at such times, and was attracting more than her share of curious, covert looks. When Ednyved sauntered over to her window seat, she murmured, 'If I tell them I'm here at Llewelyn's bidding, will they stop staring at me as if I'm a Norman spy in their midst?'

'Even after fourteen years in Wales, do you still know so little of our ways? They've never thought of you as a Norman spy – but rather as an English one.'

Joanna bit her lip, but once more he'd won; she was unable to suppress a smile. She gestured for him to join her in the window seat, marvelling – not for the first time – how unlikely and yet how dear a friend this man had become. Not that he'd changed any; he still had a sharp tongue, a sardonic eye, and spared none the cutting edge of his humour. But now she caught the glint of amusement behind the heavy eyelids, caught the echoes of affection. Now she knew that Ednyved was her ally, that he alone of her husband's friends did not want to see Gruffydd as Prince of North Wales.

'Did Llewelyn tell you why he wants us all here like this?'

'You know Llewelyn better than that, Ednyved. When he's truly troubled, he keeps his own counsel.' And Llewelyn was troubled, that Joanna knew. So did Ednyved. They shared that awareness with no need for words, then glanced expectantly towards the door.

But it was not Llewelyn. At sight of her son, Joanna half-rose. 'Davydd, you'd best come back later, after your father's council is done.'

'But Papa told me to come, Mama. He said I ought to be here.' Davydd glanced uncertainly about the chamber. He knew all in the room very well, but he was somewhat self-conscious, none the less,

599

and was grateful when his mother slid over, made room for him beside her in the window seat. As flattered as he was to be here, he was nervous, too, as nervous as the first time Llewelyn had taken him hunting. Gruffydd had spoiled that memory for him; Davydd still flushed sometimes, remembering Gruffydd's scorn when he missed his target, shot his arrow a full foot over the roebuck's withers. But Gruffydd was not here now to mar his pleasure in this, his first inclusion into the world of politics and statecraft, into the world of men.

'What does Papa want to tell us?' he whispered, and Joanna shook her head.

'I would that I knew!'

Llewelyn entered as she was speaking. He stood for an unusually lengthy time in the doorway, as if reluctant to enter, and once he was in the room, he seemed in no hurry to begin. He crossed to the table and picked up a wine cup, only to set it down untasted. The people in this chamber were those closest to him, those who'd celebrated his triumphs and endured his defeats, those who had the right to know what he meant to do. His eyes moved slowly from face to face. His brother Adda. Rhys. Morgan. Ednyved. Joanna. He could only hope they'd try to understand . . . and try to forgive.

His gaze lingered the longest upon his son. Davydd was now in his twelfth year, poised for entry into the uncharted terrain that lay between boyhood and manhood. A child and yet not a child, this youngest son of his. When he finally spoke, it was to Davydd.

'What can you tell me, Davydd, about the English laws of inheritance?'

Flustered to find himself suddenly the cynosure of all eyes, Davydd blurted out, 'The eldest son gets all,' only then to be seized with doubts, with the sinking sensation that he'd misfired another arrow. But his father nodded, as if satisfied.

'You're right, lad. That is the crux of it, the heart of the matter.' Llewelyn's eyes left the boy, shifted towards the others. 'I think we'd all agree that ours is a more just way. We do not leave younger sons to gain their bread as best they can; we divide a man's holdings equally amongst all his sons. But Scriptures say a kingdom divided against itself shall be made desolate. Is that not so, Morgan?'

He did not wait for confirmation. 'I've often spoken to you of my

600

grandfather, Joanna. But I've not said much of his brother. There was naught but envy and dissension between them, a sharp rivalry that lasted the whole of their lives. And when my grandfather died, his sons fought for Gwynedd, not against the English, but against each other. My father was slain by his own kindred.'

He turned away from the table, moved towards the centre of the room. 'Ours is a bloody past, but no bloodier than that of Powys and Deheubarth. There, too, a prince's death inevitably brought about the same slaughter, brother against brother. Verily, a man reading our history might well conclude that Cain and Abel, too, were Welsh. That is the ugliest of our legacies, that the sons of our princes must seize power over the bodies of their brothers. It is not a legacy I want to leave my sons.'

'What you say is true, Llewelyn. It is not in man's nature to share a kingdom. And because it is not, Welsh princes love their brothers not. Indeed, had I been born whole of body, the affections of our boyhood might not have survived the ambitions of our manhood. A disquieting thought, that, but who is to say? Yet there is nothing to be done about it. Our ways are not always easy, but they are ancient and revered, and above all, they are ours.'

'You're wrong, Adda. There is something I can do. Amongst God's Commandments, which one says that the laws of Hywel the Good cannot be changed?'

A shocked silence greeted so blasphemous a suggestion. Why were men so set upon clinging to the past at all costs? Why did the phrase 'as it's always been done' give them such false comfort? Llewelyn's was an old and familiar impatience, made all the sharper now by his anxiety, and he said abruptly, almost defiantly, 'I do not expect you to agree with me. But so be it. I summoned you here to tell you that I have decided to bequeath my realm to one son, as the English kings do.'

Davydd heard his mother whisper, 'Oh, dear God,' and there was so much fear in her voice that he was suddenly afraid, too, both of what his father would say next and of shaming himself before an audience of adults. He sat very still, scarcely breathing, thinking not of crowns and kingdoms but of Gruffydd, the firstborn son, the Welsh-born son, the best-loved.

'Our people love you well, Llewelyn. But in this, you ask too much. I do not think they'll willingly forsake a custom so deeply rooted in our past, accept in its stead the practice of our enemies.

To men reared on the concept of equality amongst sons, such a change would be both alien and offensive.'

Even before Morgan had finished speaking, both Rhys and Adda were nodding in vigorous agreement. Ednyved, too, looked exceedingly dubious. 'There's truth in that, Llewelyn. It will not be easy.'

'I know,' Llewelyn conceded. 'That is why it must be done in my lifetime. People will need time to come to terms with it, as with any new idea. But I think they can be made to see that it is for Gwynedd's good. Surely none amongst you can argue that it benefits a kingdom to have it split asunder by civil war.'

'The common sense of what you say cannot be denied,' Adda said and then smiled thinly. 'But men heed other voices than reason. I see, however, that your mind is set upon this, upon naming Gruffydd as your sole heir, and so –'

'No,' Llewelyn said. 'Not Gruffydd. Davydd.'

'Me?' Davydd gasped, sat suddenly upright, then flushed as he realized they were all staring at him. Joanna reached over, squeezed his arm, but her eyes never left Llewelyn's; he had seen such a look upon her face before, the very first time he'd kissed her. Ednyved was smiling, but Rhys and Adda looked appalled, and Morgan, who understood, looked neither surprised nor judgmental, just unutterably sad.

'Do not speak of this yet, not even to your wives,' Llewelyn said before either Adda or Rhys could recover, could burst out with impassioned arguments upon Gruffydd's behalf. As he'd hoped, they were constrained by Davydd's presence. Ednyved now prompted the others by rising; they reluctantly followed suit.

'Papa . . .' Davydd was still dazed. 'Papa, I'll make you proud, I will.'

'You'd better,' Llewelyn said, and the boy gave him a radiant smile. He looked slight, almost frail, when compared to Gruffydd at the same age. Although Davydd was still quite young yet, Llewelyn did not think it likely he'd ever approach Gruffydd's uncommon height, and he could never hope to match Gruffydd's strength. But he'd once punctured his hand upon a nail, and when his playmates panicked, he calmly walked a half-mile for help with the nail protruding from his palm. And Llewelyn had known for several years now that of his eight children, Davydd's was by far the best brain.

Davydd was the last to depart. Joanna stood for a moment with him upon the porch, not speaking, just sharing. Then she turned, went back into the chamber where Davydd had been born, where Llewelyn awaited her.

They both moved towards each other at once, came together in the middle of the room. 'Beloved, what can I say? I know that my joy is your pain, know, too, how very difficult a decision it was. In truth, Llewelyn, you are a remarkable man.'

Llewelyn tightened his arms around her. 'No,' he said, his voice muffled in her hair. 'No, I am a man who is going to lose his son.'

Llewelyn had dreaded nothing – not even his surrender to John at Aberconwy – as much as he dreaded telling his son. And it proved to be even more of an ordeal than he expected. Gruffydd listened in unnerving silence, never taking his eyes from Llewelyn's face, eyes filled with such stunned disbelief that Llewelyn found his throat tightening, his own eyes stinging.

'The cantref of Meirionydd has been mine since my cousin Hywel's death. I am giving it now to you, Gruffydd. Also, the lordship of Ardudwy. And in time, mayhap even –'

'Why?'

'As I told you, lad, Gwynedd has to be kept intact. It is the only way we can hope to resist English incursions, to –'

'Why Davydd? Why Davydd and not me?'

'Davydd is the nephew of the English King. That will afford him some degree of influence at the English court, for Henry gives great weight to blood-ties. And they are of an age, have taken a liking to one another. That, too, might one day work to our advantage.'

'I know you love her. But you loved my mother, too. I am your firstborn. And lest you forget, I was four years as an English prisoner – for you, Papa, for you!' Some of Gruffydd's control cracked. 'Does that now count for nothing?'

Llewelyn flinched, but he did not relent. 'I know you suffered on my account. But I cannot allow that to unbalance the scales, not when so much is at stake.'

'Do not do this to me, Papa. All my life I've sought to please you, to make you proud of me. And I . . . I thought you were!'

'I am proud of you. There is no man in Christendom I'd rather have by my side in battle.' Llewelyn drew a constricted breath. 'But I cannot let you rule in my stead. I cannot let you destroy yourself in a war you could never win.' His voice changed, steadied. 'And I

603

cannot let you destroy Gwynedd. I will not prove my love by the loss of Welsh independence.'

'What independence? You've turned Wales into an English fief and yourself into an English lackey!'

'I know what I've taken from you, do not begrudge you your anger. But your bitterness will change nothing, Gruffydd, and that is what you must try to understand, to accept.'

'Must I, indeed? I think not, my lord Prince, I think not! You're not just denying me my birthright. I have a son of my own now, or have you forgotten? What of Owain, what of his right?'

Gruffydd was blinded by tears, but they were tears now of rage. He turned away, and Llewelyn caught his arm.

'Gruffydd, wait!'

Gruffydd wrenched free. 'Tell your woman and her half-breed son to savour their victory whilst they can!'

Llewelyn made no further attempt to hold him. 'When your anger cools, I hope you will remember what I am about to say now – that you will always have a place at my court, in my life, in my heart.'

Gruffydd was already at the door. 'Rot in Hell,' he said and sobbed. 'Rot in Hell!'

As Joanna and Llewelyn left the abbey, crossed the stone bridge into Shrewsbury, Joanna felt uncomfortably conspicuous. It seemed strange to her that they should be riding so peacefully along a route Llewelyn had once followed in war. Llewelyn, however, did not share her self-consciousness. He was indifferent to the stares of the townspeople, had been amused that they should be staying in the very abbey guest-house once fired by Welsh arrows. As they turned on to the street called Altus Vicus, he nonchalantly pointed towards the High Cross, telling her that was where he'd accepted the surrender of Shrewsbury.

'Of course that wall was not there then,' he said, gesturing towards the structure in progress; stones were being mortared in horizontal layers under the supervision of masons while men hoisted buckets of rubble up on to the scaffolding to fill in the space between the inner and outer faces of the wall. 'The citizens of Shrewsbury can thank me for their new wall. In the past, the Crown was never willing to put up the money needed to wall the city in.'

'So you're saying you did the townspeople a favour by attacking them?' Joanna was delighted by Llewelyn's laughter, for she'd heard it so seldom in the past month, not since Gruffydd had left the court. 'I was so proud of Davydd yesterday,' she confided, seeing again in her mind's eye the ceremony in which Henry formally took his nephew under the protection of the English Crown, acknowledged Davydd as Llewelyn's heir. 'Henry seemed to enjoy it, too. He has quite a liking for pageantry, cannot wait till his coronation on the 17th. I think he felt cheated before, not being crowned at Westminster like our other kings.'

'Their other kings, if you please, Madame,' Llewelyn objected, but he was smiling. 'Should you like to attend the coronation, Joanna?'

'I would, indeed!' Joanna guided her mare closer to Llewelyn. 'May I take Davydd and Elen?' And when he nodded, she experienced a surge of heart-felt happiness. 'I'm very fond of Henry. There's a sweetness about him, a vulnerability that can be quite touching. I see in him Isabelle's extravagance and generosity, her love of surprises and compliments and secrets. But I can find in him nothing of my father. Tell me, Llewelyn, what sort of king do you think he'll make?'

'I agree with you that he's a likeable lad. But he has two traits that do not augur well for kingship. He is rather timid, and yet inflexible, too, loath to compromise. In truth, I do not think he'll make a good King for the English. He may well, however, prove to be a very good King, indeed, for Wales.'

Joanna joined in his laughter. 'I suspect,' she said, 'that you intrigue even in your sleep. I know you truly do like Henry, but you're deliberately cultivating his good will, too. Sometimes you look at him as if he were a fallow field, just waiting for your plough!'

Llewelyn grinned, did not deny it. They had just crossed through the arched gateway into the inner bailey of the castle, and Llewelyn himself helped Joanna to dismount. 'I do not tell you nearly as often as I ought,' he murmured, 'but you hold my heart.' She gave him so loving a look that he almost kissed her right then and there. 'Come on,' he said, taking her arm, 'lest these English think I'm besotted with my own wife!'

Davydd was waiting for them upon the steps of the great hall. He had spent the night with Henry at the castle, and Llewelyn's smile faded at sight of him, for he could not help thinking of his other son, the son who would have socialized with the English King only at swordpoint.

605

Davydd looked troubled. 'Something is wrong,' he said.

As they entered the great hall, Llewelyn paused to greet Pandulf, who'd recently replaced Guala as the papal legate, and Stephen Langton, restored to favour by the new Pope; as Archbishop of Canterbury, it was he who would crown Henry eleven days hence. Llewelyn addressed both prelates with marked respect, as genuine men of God. He did not hold the urbane, luxury-loving Bishop of Winchester in the same esteem, but Peter des Roches was deserving of notice, too, if for altogether different reasons. With Pembroke dead and Chester still on crusade, Peter des Roches was undeniably the most powerful man in England, the one with the most influence upon the young King.

Peter was flanked by Hubert de Burgh, the Justiciar, and William Marshal, who'd succeeded his father as Earl of Pembroke. His greeting to Llewelyn was noticeably cool; the Pembroke holdings in South Wales were extensive and it was inevitable that the young Earl, who was not the statesman his late father had been, should feel threatened by Llewelyn's growing power. Llewelyn was equally cool to him in return, before saying to Peter, 'My son tells me a disturbing letter has come from the Queen.'

Pembroke was affronted that Llewelyn should feel so free to meddle in affairs of the Crown. But he was not in high favour at Henry's court, for he'd been one of those lords who'd abandoned John for Louis, while Llewelyn was brother-in-law to the King. He was aggrieved but not surprised, therefore, when Peter des Roches responded as if Llewelyn had a right to know.

'It's my fault, in part. I should have read the letter ere I passed it on to Henry. The Queen's never been one for writing letters, but I just assumed it concerned Hugh de Lusignan's death. You did hear he died on crusade?'

Llewelyn nodded. The latest endeavour to free the Holy Land had taken a heavy toll of Christian lives, among them Saer de Quincy and his eldest son and Joanna's half-brother Oliver, although those who lost loved ones on crusade at least had the consolation of knowing the slain were admitted at once into Paradise.

'Prepare yourself for a startling piece of news,' Peter said. 'It seems Queen Isabelle has married Hugh de Lusignan's son, her daughter's betrothed!'

Joanna had joined them just in time to hear Peter's improbable announcement. 'She what?'

She sounded so amazed that Peter smiled; unlike Pembroke and de Burgh, who appeared genuinely shocked by Isabelle's wayward behaviour, he seemed more grimly amused than anything else. 'Here, my lady,' he said, infuriating Pembroke by handing the Queen's letter to Joanna. 'Read it yourself.'

Llewelyn followed Joanna to the window where the light was better. Although his outdoor sight was still eagle-keen, as he moved into his late forties he was becoming increasingly farsighted. Knowing that, and knowing, too, that he was somewhat sensitive about it, Joanna elected to read Isabelle's letter aloud.

'She says that after the deaths of Hugh de Lusignan and his brother, the young Hugh remained alone and without heirs in Poitou, and he felt he could not marry her daughter because of her tender age. His friends counselled him to take a French wife by whom he could beget an heir. She writes: "If he had done this, all your and our lands in Poitou and Gascony would have been lost. When we, however, saw the great peril which might arise should that marriage take place, we married the said Hugh, Count of La Marche, and let Heaven witness that we did this rather for your benefit than for our own. Wherefore we ask you, as our dear son, to be pleased with this, as it greatly profits you and yours."'

Joanna raised her eyes from the letter, saw her husband struggling not to laugh, and she smiled ruefully. 'She is not very convincing, is she? Isabelle, the martyred mother, bravely sacrificing herself for her son's sake. The rest of the letter asks Henry to give them her dower castles at Niort, Exeter, and Rockingham, and three thousand five hundred marks she says my father bequeathed to her.'

'Does she mention her daughter at all?'

Joanna scanned the letter again. 'At the end. She says she and Hugh will send Joanna back to England if Henry desires it. Llewelyn . . . I just remembered something very intriguing. When I last saw Isabelle, she spoke very kindly of this same Hugh de Lusignan, sounded as if he'd already made quite an impression upon her.'

'Mayhap he had,' Llewelyn said dryly, 'but she's been back in Angoulême for two years now, and you notice she did not marry him until his father died, until he became the new Count of La Marche. Our Isabelle might look like gossamer and gold dust, but when it comes to practicality, she'd put an English miller to shame.'

'None the less, I mean to cling to my romantic illusions,' Joanna said and laughed. 'What's more, I wish Isabelle well, hope she finds contentment in her new marriage.'

'I wonder what the Pope will make of it. Isabelle was plight-trothed to Hugh's father and Hugh to Isabelle's daughter. The truth, *breila* – does that not sound somewhat incestuous?'

But Joanna was no longer listening to his banter, for Henry had just entered the hall.

Henry turned as Joanna joined him in the window recess. He was an attractive youngster, with his mother's striking blue eyes; they were reddened now, suspiciously swollen. 'You heard?' he mumbled, and Joanna took a sister's liberty, kissed him sympathetically upon the cheek.

'I know it was a shock, dearest. But it was only to be expected that your mother would one day wed again. She's been a widow for more than three years, and although thirty-two doubtless seems ancient from your vantage point, she ought to have many years ahead of her. You'd not want those years to be lonely or empty, Henry, I know you would not.'

'You do not understand.' Henry had checked his tears, but his voice still quavered. 'Do you not see what this marriage means, Joanna? Now Mama will never come home.'

In the early years of the twelfth century, the English King had encouraged the settlement of large numbers of Flemings in South Wales. The settlements thrived, and in time Dyfed lost much of its Welsh character; Welsh was no longer spoken there, and the area came to be known as 'Little England beyond Wales'. There was much bitterness between the displaced native-born Welsh and the Flemings, and the Welsh had been complaining to Llewelyn that the Flemings were burning their churches and running off their cattle. Llewelyn was quite willing to intervene on behalf of his countrymen, to punish the Flemish intruders, for that was how he viewed them. That the Flemings were tenants of the new Earl of Pembroke had not escaped his attention, either.

On August 16, Llewelyn was waiting in the city of Chester to welcome the Earl of Chester home from the crusade. Just a few days later, Llewelyn led an army south into Dyfed. Accompanied by most of the Welsh Princes, he destroyed the castles of Narbeth and Wiston, burned the town of Haverford, and did extensive damage to the Earl of Pembroke's lands in Rhos.

Pembroke vowed vengeance, but for the time being, he was unable to act upon his anger, and the Welsh Prince's year closed in triumph.

But Gruffydd, his wife, and infant son had withdrawn from Llewelyn's court, and Gruffydd still spurned all Llewelyn's attempts at reconciliation.

July, 1221
Aber, North Wales

Rhys, Adda, and Morgan were seated at the high table in the great hall of Llewelyn's palace at Aber. Llewelyn had not yet returned from Shrewsbury where, meeting with the young English King and the papal legate Pandulf, he'd agreed to a truce with the Earl of Pembroke and Reginald de Braose. It was a truce none expected to last; the interests of the Welsh Prince and the Marcher lords were too antithetical to reconcile for long.

In Llewelyn's absence, Adda was accorded the place of honour, but he'd barely touched the food ladled on to his trencher. Neither Rhys nor Morgan had much appetite, either.

'Are you sure we ought to wait till Llewelyn returns from Shrewsbury?'

Adda nodded. 'We can be that merciful at least, can give him a few more days ere he has to know about Gruffydd.'

Rhys could not quarrel with that. Picking up a piece of bread, he occupied himself in cleaning his knife for the next course. 'I still do not understand why Llewelyn took his wife with him. A council chamber is no fit place for a woman.'

'Llewelyn thinks otherwise,' Morgan said composedly. 'He told me he felt certain he would benefit from her presence at Shrewsbury, even said – only half in jest – that he considers Joanna his ambassador to the English court.'

Rhys looked rather sceptical, but then he startled them by saying, 'I would that I'd gone to Shrewsbury, too, with Llewelyn and Ednyved.'

It had been more than six years since Llewelyn had chosen Ednyved to replace the ailing Gwyn ab Ednewain as his Seneschal, and Ednyved had made the most of the opportunity; he'd become Llewelyn's mainstay, wielding far more political power than his predecessor. But Rhys had never before given the slightest sign of jealousy, given any indication that he nurtured political ambitions of his own or begrudged Ednyved his ascending star, and Morgan and Adda were not sure now whether his remark was an oblique admission of envy for his cousin's privileged position.

Rhys was unmindful of their speculative looks. He swallowed a mouthful of gingered carp before concluding morosely, 'If I had, I'd not yet know about Gruffydd, would not be sitting here wondering how to tell Llewelyn that his son is in rebellion against him.'

'You're sure it was Gruffydd? There can be no mistake?'

Llewelyn's voice was quite even, but Morgan was not deceived; he found it very hard to continue, to take away Llewelyn's last shred of hope. 'A fortnight ago Gruffydd led an army for Ardudwy into Eifionydd. Our people took refuge in Cricieth Castle, and he swung south into Llŷn, burned your manor at Pwllheli. Before retreating into Meirionydd, he crossed into Arfon, harassed the monks at Beddgelert when they balked at emptying their larders for his men.'

Adda rarely laid his emotions open for others to see. But he'd loved Gruffydd too much to be dispassionate now. 'There is no mistake, Llewelyn. Gruffydd is known on sight throughout most of Gwynedd. Nor did he seek to conceal his identity. To the contrary, he flaunted his banners for all to see. He wanted you to know, Llewelyn, went to some pains to make sure you would.'

Llewelyn turned towards Ednyved. 'I want a courier to depart at dawn for Meirionydd. He is to tell Gruffydd that I command him to appear before my court to answer for his actions.'

Ednyved nodded, then gave Llewelyn the only comfort he had to offer – privacy. Adda and Morgan followed him from the chamber, leaving Joanna in a quandary. Her every instinct counselled her to remain, but she was at an utter loss for words. Gruffydd – no less than John – had always been an exceedingly dangerous subject, to be broached only with the utmost caution.

'Do you think Gruffydd will obey your summons?'

'No,' Llewelyn said, 'I do not.'

'Then–' Joanna paused–'what will you do, beloved?'

At first she thought Llewelyn did not intend to answer. He moved away from her, stood for some moments staring at her newest acquisition, a wall hanging of heavy linen embroidered in brilliant shades of worsted yarn.

'You look at that hanging and what do you see, Joanna? Unicorns and birds of paradise, Eden. But up close the pattern becomes thousands of individual threads. Pull just a few and the entire pattern can unravel.'

'I do not understand what you are saying, Llewelyn.'

'Authority is no different, unravels just as easily. Men obey me for a number of reasons, one of which is that they fear the consequences if they do not.'

'You're telling me that you cannot afford to let Gruffydd's raiding go unpunished. But can you do that, Llewelyn? Can you truly make war upon your own son?'

'I do not know,' he admitted. 'And that is what frightens me so, Joanna. I just do not know.'

Fording the River Mawddach at Cymmer Abbey, Llewelyn led his men south. They were deep in Meirionydd now, having reached the mile-long lake called Llyn Myngul. It was a beautiful valley, but narrow and deep, and although Llewelyn's scouts had been able to allay his fears of ambush, he was relieved, none the less, as they left the lake behind, moved on to more open ground.

'Did I ever tell you about the time I climbed Cader Idris?' Ednyved gestured towards the towering summit on their right. 'There's a lake hidden away up there as dark as ink, and local folk say it has no bottom, say that a creature of terrifying mien lurks in its depths. Mind you, I never saw it myself but . . .'

Llewelyn turned in the saddle. His eyes rested for a long moment upon the other man, a plain face made more so by a disfiguring scar, a familiar face showing little of the sharp, pragmatic intelligence that made his advice so valuable, his friendship so dear. Llewelyn knew that Ednyved's son Tudur was one of Gruffydd's most trusted companions. He knew, too, that Ednyved had been unable to track down Tudur's whereabouts, might well find him with Gruffydd. And yet he'd said nothing of his own anxiety, instead had been doing his utmost to keep Llewelyn from dwelling upon the coming confrontation.

You are indeed the friend lauded in Scriptures, he who sticketh closer than a brother. But Llewelyn dared not say it aloud lest his emotions break free. He had twenty-five years of memories he must somehow keep at bay, memories that stretched from Gruffydd's first spoken word to his last choked 'Rot in Hell.'

'Look!' Ednyved pointed, but Llewelyn already saw; one of their scouts was coming up from the south-west, coming fast.

'They've gathered near Craig Aderyn,' he gasped out as soon as he was within hearing range. 'I saw your son's banners, my lord. They're waiting for us, waiting to do battle.'

Craig Aderyn was a breeding ground for peregrine falcons, and they were circling overhead, airborne and uncaring witnesses to the human drama about to be enacted below them. From time to time a man would glance upward, as if wondering what the sleek birds of prey portended. Tudur suspected that to many, the falcons seemed suddenly as unlucky as ravens, feathered omens of ill fortune.

Warfare as they knew it usually consisted of raids and sieges. Pitched battles were a rarity, and as he moved among the men, Tudur could sense their unease. But it was more, he knew, than their lack of battlefield experience. Although Gruffydd was their lord, Llewelyn was their Prince. Most of them felt very strongly that Gruffydd had been grievously wronged. Few of them were eager, however, to take up arms against a man who was already becoming something of a legend in his own lifetime.

Moreover, this war had split families asunder. Tudur and Gruffydd were not the only ones facing blood kin across a battlefield, and Tudur was not alone in his dread of what was to come. He felt torn in two, and he was not here now in Gruffydd's encampment by choice. It was simply that he had not known how to tell Gruffydd that he wanted no part in Gruffydd's war.

'Amlyn, ought we not to say a prayer ere the battle begins, ask God's blessing upon us?'

The other man nodded. 'Tudur, I do not like this, not at all. I just tried to talk to Gruffydd, but I do not think he heard a word I said. He's acting right strange, Tudur. Not once did he take his eyes from Llewelyn's banner, not once.'

Gruffydd was astride his favourite destrier, a black stallion so temperamental that none but he could ride it. The horse bared its teeth now at Tudur's approach, and Tudur's mount shied away. 'Gruffydd? Gruffydd, we have to talk whilst there's time. Do you still want Amlyn to lead the vanguard?'

He waited, and then repeated, more urgently, 'Gruffydd, do you not hear me? Gruffydd, answer me!'

Even then, Gruffydd did not respond, not until Tudur reached out, grabbed his arm. Gruffydd's stallion reared up, and he reined it in a semi-circle until he'd got it back under control. His face was drained of all colour; Tudur had never seen him look so shaken.

'Gruffydd, what is it?'

'I cannot do this, Tudur.' Gruffydd's mouth twisted. 'God help me, but I cannot!' And with that, he suddenly spurred his horse forward, ignoring Tudur's shocked protest, the baffled cries of his men. As if racing his own regrets, he set the stallion at a dead run towards his father's camp.

'Llewelyn!'

Llewelyn was conferring with two of his captains, spun around at Ednyved's shout. All around him men were pointing, staring at the lone rider galloping towards them. Ednyved was now at Llewelyn's side; he, too, had recognized Gruffydd, and he said hastily, 'Do not do anything rash, Llewelyn. Make sure it is not a trick of some kind.'

But Llewelyn was not listening. He'd already turned, was swinging up into the saddle. 'Hold our men here,' he said, then gave his stallion its head, rode out to meet his son.

When Gruffydd was fifty yards away, Llewelyn reined in his mount, waited for his son to come to him. Gruffydd had some trouble in stopping his horse. He'd always had a heavy hand, in his agitation jerked too hard upon the reins and the stallion reared up again, sending sand and clods of grass flying.

'I assume you want to talk.' Llewelyn was startled at the sound of his own voice; it sounded so cold and unyielding, revealed nothing of his inner turmoil.

Gruffydd had acted on impulse, had not thought out what he wanted to say. He could only blurt out the truth. 'I thought I could fight you, Papa. I truly did.'

'And now you cannot?'

'No.' Gruffydd shook his head helplessly. 'I saw your banners and I knew . . .' Unsure what to do next, he slid from the saddle, waited as Llewelyn dismounted, too. Although they were now close enough to touch, still the words would not come. Gruffydd was well aware of the magnitude of his offence, but he was not able to humble himself, not even now with so much at stake. He slowly unsheathed his sword, held it out towards Llewelyn. 'I submit myself unto your will, Papa,' he said, in unconscious echo of Llewelyn's own submission to John at Aberconwy, adding tautly, 'What mean you to do?'

Llewelyn took the sword, and then handed it back. 'I mean,' he said, 'to forgive you,' and Gruffydd's pride dissolved in a surge of anguished emotion.

'Christ, Papa, I'm sorry. I never wanted it to come to this, I swear it.'

'Neither did I, Gruffydd.' And stepping forward, Llewelyn embraced his son, while hearing the distant shouts of both armies, the reprieved cheering of brothers and cousins spared a war none of them had truly wanted.

Llewelyn's encampment at Llyn Myngul was a scene of reunions and rejoicing. Camp fires flared like beacons in the dark, and the summer wind carried the sounds of singing for miles as the two armies mingled, celebrated far into the night.

Ednyved had been looking for Llewelyn for some time, at last found him walking alone by the lakeside. It was a night of rare beauty; the sky was filled with stars, and the placid waters of the lake reflected an infinity of shimmering pinpoint lights, the luminous sheen of a crescent moon. But Llewelyn appeared oblivious of his surroundings. He seemed deep in thought, started visibly as Ednyved came up beside him.

'Will Gruffydd come back with us to your court?'

Llewelyn nodded. 'Yes. We talked about it and he's agreed to return. I do not plan to leave Meirionydd yet, though. I want to do some further scouting in the Dysynni Valley, look for a suitable site for a castle.'

Ednyved was quick to comprehend. 'I see. You mean, then, to reclaim Meirionydd and Ardudwy.'

'Yes.' Llewelyn stopped, turned to face the other man. 'I have no choice, Ednyved,' he said bleakly. 'I love my son. But I can no longer trust him.'

5

October, 1222

Llanfaes, North Wales

'No! No, I'll not do it. I'll not marry him.'

'Elen, what are you saying?' Joanna rose, moved quickly towards her daughter. 'We thought you would be delighted. The Earl of Chester has no children; his sister's son John is his sole heir. Do you not realize what that means? Upon his father's death, John became Earl of Huntingdon, and he'll one day inherit the earldom of Chester, too. You'll be marrying into one of England's greatest families. Moreover, John is a first cousin of the Scots King. Your father and I could not hope to make a better match for you.'

'But I do not want him!'

'Elen, I am trying to understand, I truly am. But I do not see why you would balk at the marriage. John is not a stranger to you; you met him at Shrewsbury two years past. He's a personable youth, well mannered and agreeable. You're nigh on fifteen and he's almost seventeen, so your ages are quite suitable. And this marriage will make you Countess of Huntingdon, and eventually, Countess of Chester. So why then are you so reluctant?'

Elen said nothing, but her mouth was still set in mutinous lines, and Joanna reached out, turned the girl to face her. 'Elen, listen to me. I'll not deny that this marriage is very important to your father. But we want you to be happy, darling. If you have a valid reason for opposing the marriage, now is the time to tell me. Why do you not want to marry John the Scot?'

'I do not like him, Mama.'

Exasperation and bafflement – familiar emotions to Joanna where her daughter was concerned. 'But you do not know him well enough to make a judgment like that,' she pointed out, striving for patience.

Elen tossed her head. 'His eyes are too close together. And he has a weak chin.'

'Elen, for the love of God! What does that have to do with marriage?'

Elen knew her mother was right; marriages were based upon pragmatic considerations of property and political advantage. Unable to defend her position, she could only fall back upon accusation, upon raw emotion. 'I should have known you'd not understand! You never do!'

'As it happens, Elen, I understand more than you realize. It is only natural that you might feel qualms. When I married your father, I –'

'Oh, Mama, that was different! You love Papa!'

'I learned to love him, Elen. The truth is that I did not want to marry your father, to live in Wales, and I was utterly wretched when we were first wed.'

But Elen's image of Joanna was still circumscribed by childhood boundaries, and she found it impossible to identify her mother with a fearful fourteen-year-old bride. 'You're happy with Papa. But I'd not be happy with your John the Scot, and he can just look for a wife elsewhere.'

'Elen, it is not that simple. I do not think you understand how much this alliance means to your father. What are you going to tell him, that you do not like John the Scot's eyes?'

Elen flushed. 'Do not laugh at me!'

'Believe me, child,' Joanna said wearily, 'I find nothing remotely amusing about this.'

'I am not a child. In three weeks, I'll be –'

'Fifteen. I know; I was present at your birth, remember?' Joanna could hear her own sarcasm, but could not help herself. Her anger was rising, fuelled by insidious misgivings that defied all logic, all common sense. She knew this marriage was for her daughter's good; so why, then, was she suddenly plagued by doubts?

'I had good reason for reluctance – marriage to a man I'd never even seen, a man more than eighteen years older than I, from an utterly alien world, my father's enemy. None of that is true for you, Elen. I just cannot comprehend your attitude. Why must you always be so wilful? Your sisters were quite content to let your father choose their husbands, did not –'

'They would! Gwenllian and Marared have as much spirit as . . . as sheep,' Elen said scornfully, while prudently making no mention of Gwladys. 'But I'll not be wed against my will to a Scots-Norman

617

coxcomb. And you cannot make me, Mama. Welsh law states that "every woman is to go the way she willeth, freely". A Welshwoman has the right to pick her own husband, unlike the women of your blood, who pass with the land like serfs!'

'That is not precisely true, Elen,' Joanna snapped. Her daughter's taunt had stung, more than she wanted to admit. 'A Welsh widow may indeed marry again – or not – as she freely chooses. But a young girl, a maiden, is still in her family's care.'

'Mayhap if you spoke better Welsh, Mama, you'd have learned more of our ways. You're right; the family of a virgin maid can prevent her from marrying a man not of their choice. But they can do nothing whatsoever about it if she is no longer a virgin. So I need only lose my maidenhead and I will be utterly free to wed or not as I wish.'

Joanna's reaction was all Elen could have hoped for; she'd rarely managed to render her mother speechless. But her moment of satisfaction was fleeting – and costly. She spun around as the door slammed, gasped at sight of her father.

Llewelyn had always shunted the onus of discipline off on to Joanna, at least where his daughters were concerned; Elen had long ago learned which of her parents was more likely to laugh away a minor misdeed. But there was nothing of the familiar indulgent father about Llewelyn now. He looked no less incredulous than Joanna and a good deal angrier.

'I cannot believe what I just heard you say,' he said, and Elen blushed.

'I did not mean it, Papa, truly!'

'I would hope to God not. If I ever thought a daughter of mine would so shame herself –'

Joanna interrupted hastily. 'I'm afraid, Llewelyn, that Elen does not want to marry John the Scot.'

'I gathered as much. But what I do not understand is why. Suppose you tell me that, Elen. Tell me why you'd scorn an earldom.'

'I . . . I do not like him, Papa. He seemed so staid and proper; I thought him a bit of a prig. And he has no sense of humour, none!' Elen's eyes suddenly brimmed over. While her distress was real enough, her tears might not have flowed so readily had she not so many memories of times when she'd won her way by tears. Her father was frowning; she put a hand upon his arm, looked up entreatingly into his face. 'Please, Papa. Do not make me wed John the Scot. I'd be so unhappy, Papa, I just know I would.'

For a long moment Llewelyn studied his daughter. Joanna watched, holding her breath. And then, to her utter astonishment, he said, 'I'll not force you, Elen.'

Elen flung her arms around his neck, bestowing grateful, haphazard kisses. 'Thank you, Papa, thank you!'

'Llewelyn?' Joanna was staring at her husband in disbelief. He gave her an oblique glance, one she could not interpret at all, then turned back to Elen.

'I want what is best for you, Elen. Your mother and I would not see you hurt, not for all the political gains under God's sky. John the Scot is Chester's nephew and heir. But he is also a decent young man, would never use you ill. You could be content with him, Elen, I have no doubts of that.'

'But . . . but Papa, you said you'd not force me!'

'Nor will I. I am not ordering you to this, lass. I am asking it of you, asking you to trust my judgment. It is that important, Elen. I need not tell you, a Welshwoman, what is the most binding of all bonds, that of blood.'

Elen sensed that she was being outflanked. 'I know that, Papa. But there is no need for this marriage. You and Chester are already allies.'

'Yes, lass, we are. But I am forty-and-nine, and Chester even older. What happens when my power passes to Davydd and Chester's earldom to John the Scot? The alliance is too valuable to leave its survival to chance. If I no longer have to fight the Earl of Chester – whosoever he may be – I am then free to act in South Wales. The Welsh Princes will always have to defer to the English Crown. But we can prevent further Norman encroachments into our lands. We can make sure that there are no more Flemish settlers moving in to displace the Welsh, that men like Pembroke build no more Norman towns on Welsh soil. We can still safeguard the future, and this marriage will help to do that.'

Elen's breathing had quickened. 'You're not being fair, Papa,' she said, almost inaudibly. 'I do not want to marry him.'

'I know, lass.' Llewelyn's voice had softened, too. 'And I understand. How could I not? For much of my life, I've had to do things that I did not want to do. But they had to be done, none the less, because so much was at stake.'

Elen was silent. But the sudden droop of her shoulders was more expressive than any words she could have uttered. Llewelyn brushed the tears from her face. 'I trusted you to make the right decision, Elen. I knew I could. Can you not trust me as much? You'll have no regrets, lass, I promise you.'

John had once made the same promise to Joanna, under identical circumstances, and he'd been right. Joanna closed her eyes, said a silent, fervent prayer to the holiest and most merciful of mothers that Llewelyn, too, might be right.

'I'll do as you wish, Papa.' But it was a stranger's voice, did not sound like Elen at all, and suddenly Joanna found herself wishing passionately that her daughter could be a child again, with a child's choices and the easy comfort to be found within a mother's embrace. She moved forward, put her arm around Elen's shoulders. The girl stiffened at the touch; pulling away, she fled the chamber. She stumbled several times, bumped into the table as she turned, and that, too, was unlike Elen.

They let her go. Llewelyn sat down abruptly in the nearest chair. He was the first to break the silence. 'Was I wrong, Joanna?'

She shook her head. 'No, love, you were not. I do believe what I told Elen, that we could not make a better match for her than this.'

Crossing to his chair, Joanna put her arms around his neck, rested her cheek against his hair; although she teased him at times about going grey, it was still thick and dark, showed silver only under fullest sunlight. But he looked his age at the moment, looked so careworn that she leaned over, kissed the corner of his mouth. 'I'll talk to Elen,' she promised. 'I'll go and look for her right now.'

'I wish you would, *breila*. There's no logical reason for Elen to oppose this marriage, and once she's wed, finds herself the Countess of Huntingdon, she'll see it was for the best. I know that, Joanna. And yet . . . yet I still feel as if I'd been hunting for roebuck and instead, shot someone's tame fawn.'

Llanfaes was one of Joanna's favourite manors. She liked the relatively mild island climate, loved to walk along the shore, to gaze across the narrow strait towards the lofty range called Eryri by the Welsh and Snowdon by the English. She knew that Elen, too, loved the dramatic contrast of sea, sky, and mountains, and she headed for the beach. As she expected, there she found her daughter, standing alone by the water's edge.

Elen was clutching her veil; it was crumpled, wet with tears. But her eyes were dry as she turned to face Joanna; they held no tears, only anger. 'Go away, Mama,' she said. 'I do not want to talk to you.'

'Darling, I know you're hurting. But it will pass, I swear it will. Elen, I know.'

'You've felt like this, Mama? You've felt trapped? Trapped and helpless?'

'Yes, Elen, yes. God's truth, I did. You must believe me, darling.'

'I do, Mama. I believe you. And that is why I cannot forgive you.' Elen's voice was coldly accusing. But all the while she was twisting and knotting the veil with hands that shook.

'I know Papa loves me. But he is a man, cannot possibly understand how it feels, to be bartered to the highest bidder like a prized filly. You, though, Mama, you should have understood. You should have spoken up for me. But you did not, did you? And now you tell me you know how I feel. Well, that just makes your failure all the more unforgivable!'

'Elen, I could not argue against this marriage. I believe it is right for you. John can offer you a good life, can offer you all I've ever wanted for you and more. And he –'

'But what of me? What of what I want?'

'You're fourteen, Elen. You're not in a position to make a decision that will affect your entire life. Nor was I at your age. A young girl cannot choose her own husband. Darling, you know that. This is how marriages are made. This is how it's always been done.'

'Just because something has always been done a certain way does not make it right. But you cannot see that, can you, Mama? You'll not talk to Papa. You'll not try to change his mind.'

'No, Elen,' Joanna said softly. 'I cannot do that.'

Elen dropped her veil, watched as the wind carried it away, an incongruous splash of colour against the drifting sand. 'Then we have nothing more to say, do we? I'll marry your John the Scot, Mama. And you may be right: I may in time be reconciled to it, to him. But what if I'm not? Have you thought of that? What if you're wrong?'

Llewelyn and Chester selected Tuesday, November 22, as the date for the wedding, three weeks past Elen's fifteenth birthday, five days before the beginning of Advent when the marriage Mass would be prohibited. Elen and John the Scot were wed in the city of Chester, in the same abbey church in which Llewelyn and Joanna had been wed sixteen years earlier. The wedding was a social event of impressive proportions, attracting the highborn of Wales and England alike. Rhys Ieunac had died that past August, but his brother Owain was present, as were his uncles Maelgwn and Rhys Gryg. So, too, was Llewelyn's cousin Madog, lord of upper Powys. Henry could not attend, but he'd sent his younger brother Dickon and his seven-year-old sister Nell in his stead. And as Joanna glanced now around the great hall of the Earl's castle, she saw most of the Norman nobility.

'I was astonished when Hubert de Burgh accepted his invitation,' she confided to Richard. 'He and Chester have been at odds for months now, and I would not think he'd want to socialize with a man who likes him so little.'

'The English court thrives on such feuds,' Richard said dryly. 'The very fact that de Burgh mistrusts Chester would guarantee his presence here; he'd want to make sure Chester and Llewelyn are not conspiring against him. I dare say that if he were not in Ireland, even Pembroke would have attended the wedding.'

'I'm right glad he did not. The last thing I want is a brawl, thank you. Speaking of which, I was not heartbroken when Gruffydd refused to come. But he and Senena are the only ones absent. That's Tegwared, Llewelyn's other son, standing over there with my Davydd. You've never met Tegwared, have you? I do not know him that well myself, for he was with Cristyn till he was seven, and was then reared in Ednyved's household as a foster son, in accordance with custom. The lass with him is his betrothed, one of Ednyved's daughters.' Joanna's smile was fleeting. 'At least that is one marriage we need not worry about.'

Richard followed the path of her gaze, across the hall to where Elen and her new husband were standing, surrounded by well-wishers. 'Is it strange for you, Joanna, being back at the scene of your own wedding?'

'Somewhat strange, yes. Sixteen years does not seem so very long, but a surprising number of our wedding guests are now dead. Hugh Corbet. His brother Robert, just last month. Stephen de Hodnet; you did not know him, a friend of Llewelyn's.'

Fearing that she was going to name Maude de Braose next, Richard sought to distract her, saying hastily, 'And of course Isabelle is not here. I miss her, Joanna, more than I'd have expected. Does she write to you?'

'Isabelle? Not likely! But I did have news of her just a fortnight ago. Although it's less than a year since she gave Hugh a son, Henry says she is with child again.'

Joanna paused, looking about the hall. The feasting was now done, and the trestle tables were being dismantled to allow for dancing. 'I'm rather glad Thomas Corbet is not here; I remember him stirring up trouble at my wedding. So, too, did Fulk Fitz Warin; he kept going on about the bedding revels at the top of his voice! But he was not invited, either; he's siding with Pembroke these days. So, too, is Baldwin de Hodnet, even though Llewelyn once gave both men refuge at his court. They are just about the only Marcher lords not present, though. All the Fitz Alans are here, and more de Braoses than I can count.'

It surprised Richard that she sounded so nonchalant, almost flippant. 'Are you more comfortable now, Joanna? Being with the de Braoses?'

'The truth, Richard? No, I am not. But that is a problem I'm learning to live with. What other choice do I have, with three of my husband's daughters wed into the de Braose clan?'

'Three? Gwladys and Reginald de Braose, of course. And then – what is her name – Marared and Reginald's nephew Jack. Who else?'

'Last year Gwenllian was wed to William de Lacy, half-brother to Hugh de Lacy, Earl of Ulster, and Walter de Lacy, Lord of Meath. Walter is husband to Margaret de Braose, Maude's daughter.'

'Ah, Joanna, what a tangled coil.' But after a moment Richard started to see the perverse humour in Joanna's predicament. His mouth twitched, and he coughed, trying to camouflage a laugh.

Joanna gave him a look that was quizzical, half-resentful. But there was something contagious about his amusement, and she was soon laughing, too. 'I know; it's ludicrous,' she admitted. 'I'm utterly surrounded by de Braoses, any day now expect to find one under my bed!'

Their laughter had been a spontaneous, almost involuntary reaction to the absurd, and it ended as abruptly as it began. Much sobered, Joanna said quietly, 'It is not so bad with Reginald, for I do not see much of him any more; he and Llewelyn have not been on good terms for several years now. But Jack de Braose is often at our court. We're polite to each other, Richard, too polite. But I cannot look into his face without remembering that his father and grandmother died in a Windsor dungeon, that he spent eight years in confinement at Corfe Castle. And if it is so uncomfortable for me, how must it be for him?'

Richard knew it was not the place, but the opportunity might not arise again. 'Joanna, I hope you'll not take amiss what I'm about to say. Your problem is not with the de Braoses. It's Papa. Until you face the truth about him, about the manner of man he was and how you feel about that, about him, you're going to continue doing this to yourself, and I hate to see it. Jesu, we earn enough guilt and remorse of our own in this life without taking on the sins of others.'

'I have faced the truth! Do I deny the cruelties Papa committed, do I defend him? What more do you want of me?'

Joanna's voice had risen; several people were looking in their direction. Richard leaned over and, in a rare gesture of public affection, kissed his sister on the cheek. 'I'm sorry,' he said, and was. He had no answers for Joanna. What had worked for him – distancing himself from John – obviously did not work for her. 'I just want you to be happy, that's all.'

'I am happy, Richard, in truth I am,' Joanna said, and then she smiled. 'I think you are, too; I've rarely seen you look so relaxed. It must suit you, being Lord of Chilham, sheriff of Berkshire and Staffordshire.'

'It does indeed. Whatever else may be said of Papa, he did right by us in our marriages.'

'Yes,' Joanna said, 'he did. I only hope Llewelyn and I did as well for Elen.'

She was still thinking of that a few moments later as she made her way across the hall towards Gwladys. How could a parent ever know which marriage would flourish and which would fail? Marared seemed utterly content with Jack de Braose, had given him a son they both doted upon. But Gwladys and her husbad treated each other with the cool politeness of strangers, and after seven years, their marriage was still barren.

'I'm so glad you were able to come, Gwladys,' Joanna said warmly, for she'd not been at all sure that Reginald would agree to attend the wedding; he was rarely seen these days in the same company as his nephew. The feud between Reginald and Jack had been dragging on for several years now, ever since Jack regained his freedom and laid claim to the bulk of the de Braose lands, as the heir of Will and Maude's eldest son. Nor had Llewelyn eased the tension any by siding with Jack, allowing him to wed Marared.

Joanna had found it difficult to forgive Llewelyn for that, for putting additional strain upon his daughter's troubled marriage. But Gwladys kept her own counsel, and if she had regrets, none but she knew. She and Reginald seemed to find no lack of reasons for increasingly long absences apart, and now she said, quite composedly, 'I'd have come with or without Reginald. Surely you do not think I'd ever miss Elen's wedding?'

Both women turned, gazed across the hall. Elen was clad in a gown of Alexandrine velvet, a brilliant blue-green shade that set off to perfection her free-flowing black hair, gleaming like polished ebony against a gossamer gold veil.

'She makes a lovely bride,' Gwladys said, and Joanna nodded slowly.

'Yes . . . but not a happy one.'

'I do not think you need fret about Elen, Joanna. She's so volatile that she needs a steadying hand. I expect John will be good for her.'

Gwladys accepted a wine cup from a passing servant, clinked it against Joanna's. 'To Elen,' she said. 'And speaking of volatile spirits, my husband's wayward son has decided to put in an appearance after all.'

'Will? He's here?'

'Indeed he is. And how like Will; he misses the wedding entirely, but arrives in time for the celebration. I am sorry about this, Joanna, hope you do not mind too much.'

'No, I . . . I do not mind. You just caught me by surprise, for he turned down the invitation. Did he bring his wife?'

'No, thank God!' Gwladys said and laughed at Joanna's startled look. 'You do not know her, do you? Take it from me, the Lady Eva Marshal is a bitch, every bit as haughty and obdurate as her brother Pembroke.'

Joanna was only half-listening; she had no interest whatsoever in Will's wife. She'd not expected this, that she'd feel so flustered at the thought of seeing Will de Braose again. She did not truly know him; theirs had been a brief afternoon encounter more than twelve years past. But she'd thought of him often since learning of Maude's fate, and she knew suddenly that of all the de Braoses, it was Will she'd always most dreaded facing.

'You do not like Will, do you, Gwladys? Would you tell me why?'

'Well, he opposed my marriage to his father, so from the beginning there was tension betwixt us. But it's more than that, Joanna. I think he's a dangerous man, the sort that breaks hearts and heads with equal ease. Down in Deheubarth, the Welsh call him *Gwilym Ddu*.'

'Black Will?' Joanna echoed in surprise. 'That's passing strange, for I remember his hair as being very light, a flaxen colour.'

'It still is,' Gwladys said, very dryly.

'I see. He's not very well thought of then?'

'That depends upon whom you ask. Men do not like him much, women generally like him too much. There's been more than one scandal involving an angry husband, an errant wife. Will's not trustworthy, Joanna. Local legend has it that he once sold the same piece of land to three different buyers, and whilst I cannot vouch for the truth of that, I'd not put it past him. He cuts with a sharp blade, does our Will, leaves himself no margin for error.'

The dancing had begun; a circle was forming for the carole, and Elen and John the Scot were soon coaxed into the centre. They danced well together, won themselves a round of applause when the figure was completed. Elen then shook her head and John led her back towards the sidelines. He had a naturally ruddy complexion, even more flushed now from the dance, and the same unruly sandy hair as his cousin the Scots King, but he did have an engaging grin, which he flashed as he caught Joanna's eye.

Elen, however, had no smiles at all to offer. Although she was standing beside John, her hand in his, she seemed set upon acting as if their proximity were mere coincidence. She was watching the other dancers, looking so aloof that Joanna wanted to take her aside, to shake some sense into her. Remembering how she'd laboured to hide her own reluctance from Llewelyn, it seemed to her that Elen was behaving very badly, and she started towards them, intent upon having a brief word in private with her daughter. For better or worse, Elen was now John's wife, and she must be made to see how important it was that she make an effort to please him.

So engrossed was Joanna in her concern that she did not notice the man until he moved into her path, so suddenly they almost collided. She stepped back, looking up at a stranger, a very attractive stranger, with bright blond hair and beard, clear grey eyes, an unsmiling, sharply sculptured mouth. The fourteen-year-old boy Joanna had remembered was utterly gone. But she still recognized him and smiled, said not altogether truthfully, 'I am glad to see you again, Will.'

'Are you, Madame? Are you indeed?' he drawled, and while the words themselves were innocuous, he invested them with so much hostility that the blood surged up into her face.

Her reaction was instinctive, purely defensive. 'Of course I am, Will,' she heard herself say archly. 'We'll talk later, I hope?' She managed another smile, polite but dismissive, moved away before he could respond.

Joanna was more shaken by the encounter than she should have been; dimly she realized that. She did not doubt that Will was voicing what all the de Braoses thought; he just happened to be the only one who did not need her husband's favour, who could afford to be honest. So why, then, did it hurt so?

She sought without success to catch Elen alone, had no more luck in tracking down Llewelyn. She danced several times, but could find no pleasure in it, for by then she was aware again of Will. He made no approach, but he never took his eyes from her, a cool challenging stare that she could neither ignore nor acknowledge. She endured it as long as she could, and then her anger broke through. Draining her wine cup, she turned, walked directly towards Will.

'I think,' she said, 'that it is time we talked.'

She'd rarely seen eyes so compelling, or so cold. 'What do we have to say?'

'If you do not want to talk to me, why are you staring at me? Why are you following me about the hall?'

'Was I?'

'You know very well you were!' She heard her own voice, sharp-edged and shrill, and took several quick breaths. 'I do not want to quarrel with you. Surely we can talk without anger. You once told me that you did not believe in blood guilt for women, remember?'

Something flickered in those grey eyes, too elusive for analysis. 'Yes,' he said, 'I do remember. But your father taught me otherwise.'

Joanna waited until she was sure she could trust her voice. 'It seems I was mistaken. I have nothing to say to you after all.'

The porch of the great hall connected directly to the chapel in Cæsar's Tower; the chamber above it had been set aside for Joanna's little sister. But Nell had shown herself to be as strong-willed as the grandmother after whom she'd been named, resisting bedtime until she was half-asleep on her feet. Only then had she yielded, allowed Joanna and her nurse to put her to bed.

Joanna lingered longer than necessary, sitting on the bed and stroking Nell's hair, sunlit ringlets that curled around her fingers like finely spun silk. There had been no need for her to accompany Nell, just as there was no need for her to remain. But she was in no hurry to return to the hall. As miserable as her own wedding had been, her daughter's was proving to be no less of an ordeal.

She could delay only so long, though, for it was almost time for the bedding revels. Soon she would have to help put Elen to bed, as she'd just done with Nell. But unlike Nell, Elen would not be sleeping alone. She swallowed the last of her wine, moved reluctantly towards the door.

The spiral stairway was not lit; the cresset light had burned out, and she'd forgotten her candle. She'd had too much to drink, was feeling light-headed and had to stop repeatedly, groping her way blindly in the darkness, a few steps at a time.

She had no warning, nothing to alert her that she was no longer alone. She simply turned a bend in the stairwell and there he was, looming over her, barring her way. She recoiled against the wall, a scream starting in her throat, and he swiftly put his hand over her mouth.

'Jesu, but your nerves are on the raw,' he muttered, and Joanna sighed with relief, recognizing his voice.

'Of course you startled me, Will!' she said indignantly. 'How did I know who it was? What are you doing here? Did you follow me?'

'Would you believe me if I said I was looking for a privy chamber?'

'No, I would not.' Joanna was becoming aware now of the untoward aspects of this encounter, becoming acutely aware of Will. She was standing on the step above him, but he was still taller than she, and so close that she could smell the sugared wine on his breath. 'I think you'd best let me pass,' she said, her voice suddenly husky, and he laughed.

'You wanted to talk, did you not? Well, here I am.'

'You're drunk, Will. Let me by.'

'Suppose . . . suppose I do not want to do that,' he murmured, and when Joanna pushed against him, he did not move.

'What do you want from me?' she whispered, feeling behind her for the wall, seeking to orient herself in this eerie black well.

'I do not know.' He, too, was whispering now, his breath hot against her cheek. And then his hand was on her throat, and his mouth on hers. She'd been expecting violence, but he was surprisingly gentle with her, and the kiss was unhurried, almost tender. It was that which held her immobile for several seconds, which kept her from struggling at first. But the spell did not last. With a gasp, she tore her mouth from his, shoved against his chest.

Again he surprised her; when she pulled free, he let her go. She stumbled, nearly lost her balance on the stairs. Her head was spinning; she could not seem to catch her breath.

'Have you lost your wits? Jesus God, my husband would kill you if he knew!'

'Are you going to tell him?'

To her fury, he did not sound particularly impressed. But as much as she wanted to tell him Yes, she was going to tell Llewelyn, common sense prevailed. 'No,' she said as coldly as she could. 'No, I'd not do that to Elen, would not stain her wedding day with blood.'

Her words sounded hollow to her, even a little pompous. Will apparently thought so, too, for he laughed. He was above her now; the way below was clear, and she turned away, started down the stairs. He stopped laughing, for the first time called her by her name. She ignored him, lifted her skirts and plunged around the final bend in the stairwell, into the light. He caught up with her at the bottom of the stairs, reached for her arm, saying, 'Joanna, wait.'

She jerked away. 'Do not touch me,' she spat. 'Not ever again, do you understand?'

Some of the guests had overflowed from the hall, several couples seeking privacy in the empty chapel. They turned towards the stairwell at sound of voices, and Will faded back into the shadows. Joanna stood there alone for a moment, leaning against the wall. And then she scrubbed the back of her hand vigorously across her mouth, stepped out into the torchlit chapel. Will watched from the stairwell as she re-entered the hall.

The bedding revels were not as raucous as they might have been, due in large measure to Llewelyn's presence in the bedchamber. Even the most obstreperous of wedding guests tended to be somewhat circumspect, to curb their cruder jests in the hearing of the bride's father. But Joanna still found the experience exceedingly painful. The sight of her daughter naked in bed with an unwanted stranger tore at her heart. She no longer cared at that moment about the cogent, convincing arguments that could be made in favour of this marriage, not when she looked at Elen's face. Elen had lost her air of defiance; she clutched the sheet against her breasts, looking unbearably young to Joanna, utterly vulnerable. When she leaned over the bed to kiss her daughter, Elen clung to her, for the first time since agreeing to the marriage.

'It will be all right, darling,' Joanna whispered, but there was nothing more she could do. She and Llewelyn had made this bed, and now it was for Elen to lie in it.

The wedding party trooped back towards the great hall under a cloudless star-studded sky. Traces of the first snowfall still lay unmelted upon the bailey ground, and some of the younger men began to pelt one another with snowballs, to chase the women, who fled into the hall, shrieking with laughter. Joanna was enveloped in a fur-lined mantle of Lincoln wool, but she could not stop shivering, not even after reaching the huge centre hearth. She was soon joined by others, found herself in the midst of a boisterous, rowdy argument as to who felt the greater lust, men or women.

Joanna was in no mood for ribald jests, for jokes about bitches on heat and rutting stags, and she turned away, pushed towards the edge of the crowd, only to stop abruptly at sight of Will. She spun about, but not in time; she knew he'd seen her blush. She brought her hand up to her cheek, felt the heat burning her face and throat. She could still taste Will's kiss. It was a disconcertingly intense memory, even though she was sure she knew why – she had never been kissed before by any man but Llewelyn. Damn you, *Gwilym Ddu*, she thought, fighting the urge to cry the words aloud. Damn your arrogance and your audacity and your mocking eyes, damn you, damn you!

'There you are, Joanna.' Llewelyn was smiling at her. 'What are you doing so far from the hearth?' Catching her hand, he shoved his way through the crowd, into the coveted inner circle. There was some grumbling, stilled as men recognized him, grudgingly gave way. Joanna followed reluctantly in his wake. She'd seen very little of him all night. Where had he been when she truly needed him? If he'd been more attentive, Will would not have dared to follow her into the stairwell. Llewelyn knew how she felt about the de Braoses. Why in God's name could he not have found other husbands for his daughters? Why could he not have put her needs first, just once?

The sexual argument was still going strong. Hubert de Burgh had claimed centre stage, was insisting that it was not open to dispute; women were more lustful because they were imperfect. As the imperfect always yearned for union with the perfect, it only stood to reason that woman's desire was greater. Undaunted when the women in the audience hissed good-naturedly, he said complacently:

'You cannot deny what is set down in Scriptures. "All wickedness is but little to the wickedness of a woman," *Ecclesiasticus*. The noted theologian Tertullian put it even plainer. Woman, he said, is the gate of the Devil, the first deserter of Divine Law, responsible for the loss of Eden.'

Joanna had never liked de Burgh. But never had he seemed so odious to her as he did now. In truth, he looked like a sleek well-fed cat, insufferably well-pleased with himself. The braggart. And who in the world was Tertullian?

'But the final word ought to go to the great Aristotle. He proved conclusively through his writings that the female state is one of deformity, albeit a common one. When the man's seed is perfect, it produces a male child; when flawed or imperfect, a female. You might even say,' he quipped, 'that the female is merely a misbegotten male!'

Joanna had not meant to speak out. But with that, the same imp that had once beguiled her into defying Maude de Braose again took possession of her tongue. 'I do hope, my lord, that you will at least grant us poor "misbegotten males" one small virtue. You will admit that without women, your Aristotle and Tertullian would never have been born?'

There was laughter, and some of the women cheered; spirited debates were always a favoured form of entertainment.

Hubert de Burgh was smiling, quite unperturbed. 'Indeed I will, Madame. But even as a breeder, woman is of secondary importance in the divine order. All know that the child belongs more to the man than to the woman since the foetus forms from the male's seed. You need only think of a tree sending forth roots. The father is like the tree, the mother like the earth that nurtures it. Whilst it cannot exist without the two, it clearly belongs more to the tree whence it sprang than to the earth where it was planted.'

It may have been the smugness of his smile. It may have been the memory of a bloody birthing chamber, those endless hours of agony and fear. It may only have been the proverbial last straw in a day of emotional turmoil. Suddenly Joanna was trembling, as angry as she'd ever been in her life. But Llewelyn had been alerted by her first outburst, had known at once that this was no game. Now he saw how

631

her eyes narrowed, saw the pupils contract, like the eyes of a cat about to pounce, John's eyes in a blazing Angevin rage, and he said swiftly, with just enough sardonic inflection to be insulting,

'You surprise me, my lord de Burgh. Surely you have not forgotten the Lady Mary, mother of Our Saviour? If Our Lord Jesus was not ashamed to be born of woman, why should you?'

De Burgh's smile froze. 'I never said I was!'

'Mayhap you should learn to choose your words with greater care then,' the Earl of Chester observed coolly, 'for I, too, took that as your meaning.'

The crowd had fallen silent. Even the most politically naïve among them was aware that the conversation was heading for deep waters, pushed by currents that had nothing whatsoever to do with the Virgin Mary or the failings of women.

De Burgh had reddened, but he was too well mannered – and too intelligent – to provoke an open row while a guest under Chester's roof. He could wait. 'It grows late,' he said tersely.

He heard someone in the crowd, one of the Earl's partisans safely cloaked in anonymity, mutter, 'Later than you think,' and there was some scattered laughter. It was Joanna's uncle Will who acted to defuse the tension, to avert a confrontation. Will was not as friendly with Chester as he'd once been, and he had yet to forgive Llewelyn for that scene in Worcester Abbey. But Joanna was still his niece, and for her sake he raised his wine cup high, saying loudly:

'It is indeed late, and for certès we want this evening to conclude upon a cordial note. Let's drink, then, to the happiness of the bride and groom. To John the Scot and the Lady Helen!'

The ploy worked; others took it up, until John and Elen's names rang from the rafters. People began to make ready to depart, those who were not bedding down in the castle. Llewelyn and Chester were talking together; Joanna heard them laugh. So, too, did Hubert de Burgh.

'Mama, that was wonderful, the best part of the whole wedding!' Davydd was grinning. 'I was so proud of you.'

'You should not have been, Davydd. If not for your father, I'd have caused a scene that they'd have been talking about for the next twenty years.'

'Really? I wish you had! Hubert de Burgh went red as a radish; it was so hard not to laugh. Why do he and my lord Chester hate each other so much?'

632

'The usual cause, Davydd – power. Chester was on crusade when the old Earl of Pembroke died, and when he returned, it was to find de Burgh was now clinging closer to Henry than a limpet. Chester feels that he was shunted aside, that de Burgh usurped his rightful place as Henry's chief counsellor. And because de Burgh feels threatened by Chester, he is beginning to side with Llewelyn's foe, the Earl of Pembroke. Does any of this make sense to you?'

Davydd nodded. 'Oh yes, Mama. You have to counter your opponent's moves, try to guess what he'll do ere he does it. Just like chess!'

Llewelyn was coming towards them now, and Joanna moved to meet him. 'Ought I to thank you?' she murmured, and he shook his head.

'No need; I enjoyed myself thoroughly!'

'You do thrive on turmoil, I'll grant you that. Llewelyn, I want to go back to the abbey. If this night does not end soon –'

'No, not yet. I've a surprise for you.' Ignoring her protests, he put his arm around her waist, escorted her across the hall, into the solar towards a corner stairwell. As she followed him, still objecting half-heartedly, she found herself thinking of her stairwell encounter with Will de Braose, and she wondered how long it would take for that memory to fade.

As they reached the top of the stairs, the door swung open. 'Morgan?' Joanna was utterly baffled by now. 'What are you doing up here? What is –' She broke off, gazing about her in wonder. The chamber was ablaze with light, with scented wax candles. The floor rushes were freshly laid, and across the bed coverlets were scattered the last flowers of the season: marigolds, lilies of the field, even a few Christmas roses.

'It looks like a bridal chamber, Llewelyn,' Joanna exclaimed, and then, 'Good Lord, it is! This is the chamber in which we passed our wedding night!'

Llewelyn was laughing. 'I decided it was time to rectify a wrong. Sixteen years ago we neglected to get the nuptial blessing for our bed. But if you'll come over here with me, *breila*, Morgan is prepared to remedy that.'

Joanna took Llewelyn's hand, knelt with him by the bed as Morgan made the sign of the cross, rapidly intoning a brief prayer to God Eternal, seeking His blessings upon His servants, Llewelyn and Joanna, that they might live in good accord in His divine love, and

633

that their offspring might increase till the end of the ages. He then sprinkled holy water about, made a discreet departure.

Llewelyn rose, started to help Joanna to her feet. '*Breila?* Are you crying?'

Joanna gave a shaken laugh. 'Hold me,' she entreated, 'just hold me close. Your timing could not have been better. You'll never know how much this means to me, never . . .'

Llewelyn pulled off her veil, began to loosen her hair. 'It was not a good night for you, was it?'

'It was an absolutely wretched night . . . until now.'

'It gets better,' he said, and picking her up, he carried her to the bed, where they lay together midst the flowers, made love by candlelight in the bridal chamber where their marriage had begun.

The chamber was dark, utterly still. Through a parting of the bed hangings, Joanna watched the dying embers of the hearth burn lower and lower, at last flicker out.

'Joanna?' Llewelyn propped himself up on his elbow. 'Can you not sleep?'

'I was thinking of you, of our belated nuptial blessing. I do not know you as well as I thought I did, never suspected you had a romantic streak.'

'Just make sure no one else suspects,' he warned. 'There are some secrets to be shared only betwixt man and wife, and only in the dark, only in bed.'

Joanna laughed softly. 'Ah, Llewelyn, you do know how much I love you?'

'I might have an inkling or two.' Her hair was caught under his arm and he shifted so she could pull free. 'But you were not thinking of me, *breila*. You were worrying about Elen.'

'Yes . . . I was. How did you know?'

'Because,' he admitted, 'so was I.'

July, 1223
Ludlow Castle, England

The Earl of Pembroke had been attending to his Irish estates since November of 1222. Early in the new year, Llewelyn took advantage of Pembroke's absence and struck at the Earl's allies in Shropshire, capturing castles from Fulk Fitz Warin and Baldwin de Hodnet. Hubert de Burgh persuaded the young King to mount a punitive expedition into Wales, and by March 7, they were assembling an army at Shrewsbury. But the Earl of Chester now interceded upon Llewelyn's behalf, persuaded Henry that Llewelyn's dispute with Pembroke could be settled by peaceful means.

The Earl of Pembroke thought otherwise. Arriving back in South Wales in mid-April, he laid successful siege to the castles at Cardigan and Carmarthen, which Llewelyn had held since the winter campaign of 1215. Llewelyn was just as swift to retaliate, and in early May Gruffydd led an army south. After taking and burning the Norman town of Kidwelly, Gruffydd and his men clashed with Pembroke at Carmarthen Bridge. What followed was a bloody daylong battle in which many men died but neither side could gain the advantage.

At this point, Stephen Langton, Archbishop of Canterbury, intervened. Henry was now in his sixteenth year, and although not of a martial nature, he had his share of Angevin ambition. But his dreams of conquest centred upon the recovery of Normandy, not all-out war with his sister's husband, and he was quite willing to heed Langton, to act as peacemaker. While Llewelyn was sceptical, he yielded to Henry's request, agreed to attend a July council at the border castle of Ludlow.

In an upper chamber of the castle keep, Llewelyn was meeting with Henry, Stephen Langton, and Hubert de Burgh, while Joanna waited his return in the great hall. Although Henry had welcomed them with genuine warmth, Joanna was not comfortable at Ludlow. This was unfriendly territory, the great hall filled with hostile Marcher lords, men with extensive Welsh holdings, with very strong reasons for wishing Llewelyn ill.

But Joanna was not alone for long. Within moments her young son-in-law approached, holding out a wine cup. She smiled, touched that he should feel the need to look after her in Llewelyn's absence. 'Thank you, John. Did I tell – Oh no!'

John swung about, but could see no cause for alarm. 'What is amiss?'

'Across the hall. Ralph de Mortimer and Thomas Corbet just walked up to Gruffydd.' Seeing that he did not comprehend, Joanna added impatiently, 'I know Thomas Corbet. He's up to no good, means to bait Gruffydd into a fight. And believe me, it'll not take much!'

'You need not fret; I'll see to it,' John assured her, but then he smiled. 'It seems the Bishop of Winchester has the same idea,' and they watched as Peter des Roches adroitly herded the malcontent Marcher lords safely away from Llewelyn's son.

'Thank Heaven for Peter's sharp eye,' Joanna sighed. 'My father often joked that Peter might not be as innocent as the dove, but he was verily as guileful as the serpent! John, tell me. I could not help but notice how cordial Peter suddenly is towards your uncle Chester. The Welsh have a proverb: the enemy of my enemy is my friend. I was wondering if Peter might not be taking that to heart?'

There was surprise in the look John gave Joanna, a startled and reluctant reappraisal. It had baffled him that Llewelyn would make use of a woman for delicate diplomatic manoeuvrings, that Joanna so often acted as his envoy to the English court. But her questions showed a shrewd perception of political undercurrents, and suddenly Joanna's presence here at Ludlow did not seem so inexplicable after all. How much, he wondered, did she cull from careless male speech? How many men would think to guard their tongues, to be wary of a comely woman?

'Peter des Roches is not the only one with a sharp eye,' he conceded. 'You are quite right. Des Roches is a man quick to tend to his own pastures, and he suspects Hubert de Burgh of grazing on the wrong side of the fence. There is no love lost betwixt them these days. But de Burgh still holds the ear of the one who matters most, our young King.'

Joanna nodded. 'John . . . I do not mean to interfere between a man and his wife. But I've had a disturbing letter from Elen. She wrote that you forbade her to visit us –' She stopped in mid-sentence. 'You did not?'

'Indeed not,' he said indignantly. 'I would never act to cut Elen off from her family. I did tell her that I did not want her to go into Wales this summer, but only because war seems imminent. I know how homesick she is, but I had to put her safety first.'

'Yes,' Joanna agreed slowly. 'Of course.' If John the Scot was not speaking the truth, he was as skilled an actor as any she'd ever seen at Christmas mummeries. And Elen had ever been capricious and headstrong. But however Joanna sought to rationalize, one fact still stood out starkly, that some seven months after her marriage, Elen was not happy with the husband they'd chosen for her.

At that moment there was a sudden stir; Henry and Llewelyn were re-entering the hall. Joanna hastened towards her husband. Gruffydd and Ednyved were also converging upon Llewelyn. He met with all three of them in the centre of the hall, gave them the bad news they could already read in his face.

'Shall I tell you their terms for peace? I am to yield up the castles I took from Fitz Warin and de Hodnet. But Pembroke gives up nothing, gets to keep my castles of Cardigan and Carmarthen.'

Gruffydd swore under his breath. 'What did you tell them, Papa?'

'What do you think I said?' Llewelyn paused, looked directly at Joanna. 'You'd best go and bid your brother farewell. I told him we'd be leaving Ludlow within the hour.'

Joanna was dismayed, but she knew better than to argue, not when Llewelyn sounded like that. She nodded, did as he said.

Henry gave her no chance to speak, took her arm and led her towards the window recess. 'Joanna, you must talk to your husband, must get him to see reason.'

'Henry, there is nothing I can do.'

'I do not want war with the Welsh, you must know I do not. But I had no choice, Joanna. Cardigan and Carmarthen have too much strategic importance to leave them in the hands of a Welsh Prince. Surely you can see that?'

'Yes, of course I can. Why should a Welsh Prince have any right to castles on Welsh soil?'

Henry had vivid blue eyes, a drooping left eyelid that gave him

637

a drowsy, appealingly vulnerable look. But both eyes opened wide now, showed so much hurt that Joanna was at once remorseful.

'I am sorry, Henry. I do love you,' she said softly. 'But I love my husband, too, and I am so very tired of always having to choose . . .'

Henry watched as she moved away, back to Llewelyn. When Hubert de Burgh joined him, he said, 'I never meant to hurt my sister, Hubert. I was so sure I could make her understand. You said she would.'

'It cannot be helped, my liege. It is no easy thing to be a King, to find the courage to make difficult decisions. You must be strong, lad, must –'

'I am!' Henry cried, stung. 'I'll do what must be done. But that does not mean I have to like it.'

Gwenwynwyn's two young sons had been living in England as wards of the Crown. On the same day that Llewelyn rode away from Ludlow, Henry ordered the boys to be brought to his court at Gloucester in hopes of winning away from Llewelyn the allegiance of the men of Powys. He then sent the Earls of Pembroke and Salisbury into Wales.

While Llewelyn sought to cut off their supply lines, Gruffydd sprang a lethal ambush in a hilly pass of Carnwyllion. But Pembroke and Will were able to fight their way free, began to lay waste to the countryside of Dyfed. Once more Wales was at war.

Llewelyn's siege of Buellt Castle was in its second week. The Welsh had at last been able to cross the deep wet moat, to breach the outer curtain walls. But they'd been repulsed when they sought to assault the inner defences, had been driven back in disarray.

Llewelyn and his captains were conferring behind the shelter of the outer curtain wall, mapping out a new plan of attack. 'Do you want to try the battering ram again, Llewelyn?'

'Yes. But first I think I'll go up on the wall, see if I cannot find a weak spot in their defences, a section that seems undermanned.'

'May I go with you, Papa?'

'No, Davydd, you may not.' The boy's disappointment was all too obvious, and Llewelyn knew he was not being fair. But he had no intention of relenting. Although he'd gone cheerfully off to start a rebellion at fourteen, with nary a thought for his own mortality, he'd discovered that his views on fourteen year olds and warfare had moderated considerably over the years, at least when the fourteen year old in question was his son.

The fighting for the outer bailey had been fierce, and the dank, scum-covered moat had taken on a sinister reddish cast. Always fetid and foul-smelling, the water now hid decomposing bodies in its murky depths, even the partially submerged carcass of a horse, bloated and black with flies. The stench was overpowering, followed Llewelyn even after he'd crossed their makeshift bridge, climbed a thong ladder to the top of the wall. Here, too, bodies lay exposed to the sun, crumpled along the parapet, sprawled in the bailey.

Below Llewelyn, the bailey was a scene of disorder and commotion. His soldiers had put up sheds to shelter themselves from the English crossbows, and they scurried back and forth, readying the battering ram for another run at the barbican, while panicked animals – goats, sheep, cattle – milled about in their midst. But as chaotic as it was in the outer bailey, Llewelyn knew it must be infinitely worse within the cramped inner ward, for Reginald de Braose had to shelter not only his own people, but the villagers who'd fled to the castle at the outset of the attack.

Gruffydd and Ednyved had followed him up, were in a huddled colloquy with several Welsh bowmen. Llewelyn continued along the walkway, stepping over the body of an English soldier, a broken sword scant inches from his outstretched hand. The more Llewelyn studied the inner defences, the more dubious he became. Reginald de Braose had refortified Buellt in 1219, to impressive effect. Llewelyn knew he could eventually starve the garrison into submission, but he was not sure he'd have the time. Pembroke and Salisbury were already in Wales, and Henry was said to be gathering an army at Gloucester.

He happened to glance down, saw Davydd standing by the moat, staring up at him. Davydd looked so forlorn that Llewelyn felt a conscience qualm. It was one thing to make sure Davydd was kept well away from the fighting, quite another to try to shield him from any and all risks. Leaning over the embrasure, Llewelyn signalled to his son, beckoned for Davydd to join him on the wall. Davydd grinned, began to run.

Llewelyn would never know what prompted him to turn away from the embrasure at that precise moment. It may have been a sixth sense awareness of danger; it may have been sheer luck, of the sort he'd had all his life. He caught a blur of motion as the Englishman

639

lunged at him, stumbled backward under the impact. But the broken blade struck only a glancing blow, instead of burying itself in his back.

Llewelyn had no time to draw his own sword, grabbed for the man's arm as he raised the blade again, thrusting downward as if it were a dagger. They grappled desperately for control of the weapon. It was only inches from Llewelyn's throat when he managed to wrench the man's wrist down against the stone battlement. The man grunted in pain, but did not – would not – drop the sword. His face was very close to Llewelyn's, a young face, freckled and dirt-smeared, a face not to be forgotten. Dried blood had caked in his hair. His lashes were very fair, almost white, his lips peeled back from his teeth in a grimace of pain and hate. Llewelyn could smell his sweat, hear his rasping breath, a sound so loud as to blot out all else.

They struggled silently on the narrow walkway, each man seeking to kill, to survive. Llewelyn slammed the other man's hand on to the battlements again. This time he cried out and the blade slipped from fingers gone suddenly numb. Llewelyn reeled backward, fumbling for his sword. But the English soldier was staring past him, making no move to defend himself. His mouth contorted and he caught at the embrasure for support. His eyes were already glazing over by the time his knees buckled. As he fell forward, almost at Llewelyn's feet, Llewelyn saw the arrow protruding from his back.

During the timeless span of their struggle, it had seemed to Llewelyn that they were alone on the walkway, alone in the world. But now he saw men running towards them, swords drawn. Llewelyn slid his own sword back into its scabbard, leaned against the battlement. It hurt to breathe, and he winced as he ran his hand over his ribs. But the chain links of his hauberk had deflected the blow; although he'd be badly bruised, he was not bleeding.

Gruffydd and Ednyved came panting up. No one spoke; they stared down at the body, at that quivering arrow shaft. Hastening across the parapet from the opposite direction was a bowman as young as the man he'd shot. He was grinning, flushed with pride and excitement, utterly unprepared for what was to come. As soon as he reached them, Gruffydd grabbed his arm, shoved him roughly against the battlement.

'You stupid, foolhardy dolt! Of all the lunatic stunts I've ever seen . . .' Gruffydd was all but incoherent in his rage and the youngster shrank back, too flustered even to offer a defence.

Llewelyn tended to agree with Gruffydd. The young bowman had taken an enormous risk; it was not unheard of for an arrow to pin a rider to his horse. But he knew, too, that Gruffydd's anger was spurious, was actually fear masquerading as fury, and he said, still labouring for breath, 'Let it lie, Gruffydd.'

'Christ, Papa, he could have killed you! What if he'd missed, if he'd hit you instead?'

Llewelyn preferred not to dwell upon that. 'What's your name, lad?'

The bowman swallowed. 'Trefor, my lord,' he mumbled. 'Trefor ab Alun.'

'You're a good shot, Trefor. I'll remember.'

Trefor beamed, but dared not linger. Gruffydd's anger counted for more at that moment than Llewelyn's approval, and he hurried to rejoin his comrades.

Ednyved picked up the broken sword, flung it out into the moat. 'It seems to me, Llewelyn, that you're the one who needs the nursemaid, not your Davydd!'

Llewelyn's smile was wry, faintly discomfited. 'I should have known better,' he admitted. 'But it did prove one thing, that I was right about these Norman hauberks. Without it, I'd have been skewered through like a stuck pig.'

'Papa . . .' Davydd was standing several feet away. He'd lost all colour, was so shaken that Llewelyn knew at once he'd witnessed the fight.

As Llewelyn climbed down the scaling ladder, he began to appreciate the extent of his injuries; his muscles were already exceedingly sore and tender. But he knew how very lucky he had been, and as soon as he and Davydd were standing on firm ground, he said:

'I'm glad you saw that, lad. I hope to God you remember, for it might save your life one day. I did something very foolish up there. I saw a man lying on the wall, just took it for granted that he'd been killed in the morning's assault. But on the battlefield you can take nothing for granted, Davydd, nothing. Careless men do not make old bones, lad.'

'I was so scared for you, Papa. Were . . . were you scared, too?'

Llewelyn turned, looked into the hazel eyes upturned to his, Joanna's eyes. 'Not whilst we were fighting, Davydd. You do not have time to be afraid during a battle, are too busy trying to stay alive. But afterwards, when you think about it, about all the loathsome ways

641

there are to die, I suspect most men feel fear. I have, for certès.'

Davydd no longer met his eyes. 'I've heard men say that Gruffydd knows no fear.'

'Do not measure yourself against Gruffydd, lad. I chose you as my heir because I saw in you qualities of leadership.' Llewelyn hesitated, for it was not easy to say. 'I did not find those qualities in Gruffydd. I trust you not to repeat that to anyone else. But I trust you, too, to remember it.'

'Llewelyn!' Ednyved was leaning over the wall embrasure. 'De Braose wants to talk, says he'll send his son out if you'll warrant his safety.'

'Agreed.' Llewelyn looked at Davydd and then grinned. 'Tell him I'll even invite him to dinner!'

The tents of English kings were opulent, even sumptuous, spacious enough for privacy as well as comfort. Llewelyn's tent was of a more modest scale, for even if he'd had the resources to indulge himself, no Welshman could have respected a commander who went to war with feather mattresses and silver plate. Llewelyn contented himself with a pallet, and when dinner was served, he and his guests sat in a circle on the ground, just as his men did around their campfires.

If Will de Braose thought Llewelyn's accommodations spartan, it did not show in his face. The Marcher lords tended to be a hardy lot, as robust and tough-minded as the Welsh they fought and befriended, and Will ate with gusto, even knowing that he was being served one of his own beef cows. As much as it irked Gruffydd to hear Normans pervert his tongue, it offended him even more to hear one speak such fluent Welsh, and he was hard pressed to manage even a semblance of politeness. He would never understand how his father could bring himself to eat and drink with their enemies, never.

'It scarcely seems fair to repay your hospitality with what I have to tell you now.' Will reached for another piece of bread. 'But my father and I thought you had a right to know. Your daughter Gwladys is within the castle.'

There was a moment's silence. Then Llewelyn laughed derisively and Gruffydd spat, 'Liar!'

'My son speaks bluntly, but true . . . which is more than you do. Do you think I'd besiege Buellt without first making sure of my daughter's whereabouts, her safety? Gwladys is many miles to the north, at my court on the isle of Môn.'

Will did not seem at all abashed. He shrugged, said with an unrepentant grin, 'Well, you cannot blame a man for trying, can you?'

Llewelyn shifted his position with unwonted care; neither mutton fat nor a lanolin ointment had done much to ease his discomfort. 'You'd not be here unless you had an offer to make. What is it?'

'Seven hundred head of cattle if you ride away on the morrow.'

That was a fair offer. But there was more to consider than profit, more at stake than cattle. 'I'll think about it,' Llewelyn said noncommittedly. He'd noticed that Will kept glancing over at Davydd, had noticed, too, that it was making the boy uncomfortable. 'You do know my son Davydd?' he said pointedly, but Will did not take up the challenge.

'I suppose I was staring,' he conceded calmly. 'It's just that he looks so much like his mother. It's not often a blood kinship shows so plainly as that.'

Gruffydd set down his wineskin. 'I always thought Davydd looked verily like John, God rot him.'

Will's eyes cut towards Gruffydd. 'I'll drink to that, to John, King of England . . . and of Hell.'

Even in the subdued lantern light, Llewelyn could see the colour rising in Davydd's face. It did not surprise him; if Joanna at thirty-two could not resolve her relationship with John, how could Davydd at fourteen? For his son's sake, he acted to end the conversation. 'I'll give you my answer on the morrow.'

But Will did not move. 'You must have hated John, even as much as I did. Christ knows, he gave you reason enough!'

Llewelyn looked over at Davydd, then nodded slowly. 'Yes, I hated John.'

Will leaned forward. 'Then . . . then how could you live in contentment with John's daughter?'

Llewelyn was astonished. But as he studied Will's face, he saw that the younger man had not meant to offend. His grey eyes held Llewelyn's own; he seemed truly to want to know. Llewelyn had no intention, however, of answering a question so intensely personal. 'I fail to see,' he said coolly, 'how my marriage is of concern to you.'

Will's eyes flickered; he was the first to look away. 'You're right, of course; it is not my concern. If my curiosity has led me astray, I apologize.' His smile was self-mocking. 'If there is one thing we de

643

Braoses pride ourselves upon, it is that we never offer an unintentional insult!'

Llewelyn was not taken in by Will's nonchalant disclaimer. He did not know Reginald's son well at all, but one thing he did not doubt, that the mere mention of John had touched a very raw nerve indeed. It was Davydd who told Will what he wanted to know. Davydd could not bear to have his mother associated in any way with the cruelties of the English King, and he said abruptly, 'My lady mother and King John were estranged for the last four years of his life.'

Gruffydd opened his mouth, but for once discretion prevailed. Llewelyn had risen, and this time Will took the cue, rose, too. They were exchanging ironic courtesies when one of Llewelyn's men ducked under the tent flap.

'My lord, one of our scouts has just ridden in, says it is urgent that he speak with you.'

The man was unshaven, begrimed, had obviously passed a full day in the saddle. He knelt before Llewelyn, but wasted no further time on protocol. 'My lord, I bear evil tidings. The English King and the Justiciar marched out of Hereford at dawn this morn, heading towards the Gwy Valley – towards Buellt.'

'How large an army?'

'Too large, my lord. Mayhap twice the size of ours.'

Llewelyn turned aside. He heard Gruffydd cursing softly, damning the English to a particularly vile quarter of Hell; rarely had his son's sentiments so perfectly mirrored his own. It was at that moment that Will de Braose did something as provocative as it was impolitic: he laughed.

He at once regretted it, found himself the focus of icily measuring eyes. His hand dropped instinctively to his sword hilt, but he put greater faith in his privileged status, a guest at Llewelyn's hearth. 'Need I remind you that you swore to my safety?'

'No, you need not. Just be thankful a Welshman's word is not as worthless as you Normans claim.' Llewelyn turned to the closest man, said curtly, 'Escort de Braose back to the castle.'

Will did not press his luck, held his tongue. But no one objected. Not even Gruffydd had seriously considered harming him, for it was understood that there were promises that could be broken and promises that must be kept; John might not have been so hated had he not blithely broken both kinds.

Once Will had gone, they could give vent to their disappointment, their rage that their prize was to be so rudely snatched from their grasp. But they could not long afford to indulge their anger, not with an English army less than a day's march from Buellt. 'Give the order to break camp,' Llewelyn said grimly. 'We are done here. De Braose has won . . . this time.'

After raising the siege of Buellt, Henry and Hubert de Burgh continued north, feeding their troops with Welsh cattle, burning and pillaging. By September 30, they had reached the border castle of Montgomery. Soon thereafter, they made use of their ultimate weapon – the Church of Rome. Llewelyn was excommunicated again, and warned that if he did not capitulate, his subjects would be absolved of all oaths of allegiance.

But Llewelyn was not a man to repeat his mistakes; he'd learned when to fish and when to cut bait. He sent word to Henry that he and the other Welsh Princes would come to Montgomery on the 8th of October, submit themselves to the English Crown.

October 8 was a Sunday, God's day. An autumn sun shone upon the surrounding hills with a mellowed warmth, burning away the mists that had shrouded the valleys for days and revealing blazing oaks, maples dappled in russet and saffron. But the day's beauty only deepened Davydd's forebodings. His unease intensified with each mile that brought them closer to Montgomery. He could think of nothing but the tales he'd heard of his father's surrender at Aberconwy. How could he watch as Papa humbled himself to Henry? What would the English demand of Papa? Would men blame him, too, remembering he was Henry's kindred, half-Norman?

When the sun-silvered waters of the Severn came into view, Davydd could endure no more. Urging his mount forward, he reined in beside Llewelyn. 'Papa, do you have to do this? Is there no other way? Why can we not withdraw up to Gwynedd?'

Llewelyn signalled for his companions to drop back. 'Whilst it is true that my own domains are not endangered, that cannot be said of my allies. If we do not come to terms with the English, Maelgwn and Rhys Gryg and Owain risk losing all. And although Gwynedd is not yet threatened, my influence in Powys and Deheubarth is. By making peace now, we can still salvage something from this debacle.

645

Henry has agreed to restore to the other Princes the lands they'd lost to Pembroke, and to –'

'But what of you? You'll have to yield up those Shropshire castles, and Carmarthen and Cardigan, too! It's not fair, Papa, you know it's not!'

'I cannot pretend that I like losing those castles, Davydd. But I do not see that I have a choice . . . just the dubious consolation that we Welsh take as a tenet of faith, the understanding that no matter how grievous our troubles are, they can always get worse.'

'Jesu, Papa, how can you jest? You've told me how John sought to shame you, to –'

'Is that what you fear, another Aberconwy? Ah no, lad. This is no life-or-death struggle; we're talking about a couple of castles, a loss of face, no more than that. Most importantly, Henry is not John.'

Davydd was still dubious, but upon their arrival at Montgomery, he discovered that his father was right, an astute judge of men. While Henry would later reveal his fair share of human failings, vindictiveness was never among them. He was genuinely glad to accept Llewelyn's submission, had no intention of turning the occasion into an ugly object lesson for the Welsh. Llewelyn was his sister's husband and therefore entitled to err. Henry pardoned the Welsh with artless generosity, with an ingenuous simplicity that was both his strength and his weakness, that he would never entirely outgrow.

Nor did Llewelyn's foes gloat openly over their victory, Pembroke because his antagonism towards Llewelyn was impersonal and thus without rancour, and Hubert de Burgh because he was dangerously dependent upon Henry's good will.

The Archbishop of Canterbury had already restored Llewelyn to God's grace, lifted the Interdict from Wales. All that remained to be done was to acknowledge the supremacy of the English Crown, and this Llewelyn did, kneeling and pledging oaths of homage and fealty to the sixteen-year-old King. It was nowhere near as painful as Davydd had expected, and he watched with great relief, grateful that Henry had not his father's vengeful nature, that Llewelyn's English allies – Chester, John the Scot, Jack de Braose – were there to lend moral support.

As Maelgwn and Rhys Gryg came forward to swear fealty to Henry, Llewelyn crossed the hall, moved towards his son. 'You see?' he said. 'No lasting scars.'

Davydd nodded. 'I'm learning, Papa,' he said, and Llewelyn grinned.

'I'm counting upon that, Davydd.' But as he glanced about the great hall, his smile faded. 'Where's Gruffydd?'

'He walked out, Papa.'

Llewelyn said nothing, for what was there to say? How long, he wondered, would he keep expecting more than Gruffydd could deliver? How long ere it stopped hurting?

Henry and Hubert de Burgh were planning to erect another castle at Montgomery, and construction had already begun at the new site, a mile to the south of the existing motte and bailey. As he wandered aimlessly about the bailey, Gruffydd heard the boisterous sounds of returning workers, miners and carpenters coming back from their daylong labours. Already trees and underbrush had been burned away, scarring the land; the hill was being cleared, made ready to receive a new Norman fortress.

Gruffydd had walked out of the hall because he did not trust himself, did not think he'd be able to keep silent, to watch passively as his father shamed himself before their enemies. That was a harsh judgment to pass upon Llewelyn, upon a man he still loved, and it gave him no small measure of pain. But he could interpret Llewelyn's behaviour in no other way. They could have withdrawn into the mountain fastness of Eryri, fought the English on their own land, their own terms. Papa need not have yielded, need not have come to Montgomery. To Gruffydd, this was a dishonourable and indefensible surrender, one he could neither understand nor forgive.

He knew he could not remain indefinitely out here in the bailey, braced himself to go back into the hall. But his good intentions were forgotten as he approached the steps, saw his brother standing in the sun.

Gruffydd stopped abruptly, staring up at Davydd. 'Why are you not inside with your English kindred? You cannot tell me that you needed to get away as I did. Not you, Henry's nephew, John's grandson. Why should you care if Welsh pride is trampled into the dust?'

'I care.'

To Gruffydd's exasperation, that was all he got. No matter how he prodded Davydd, he could never break through the boy's defences. When Davydd felt threatened, he simply withdrew into him-

647

self, and that only strengthened Gruffydd's contempt, his conviction that Davydd was utterly unfit to rule in Llewelyn's stead.

He moved closer and Davydd stepped back. But the knowledge that Davydd feared him did not give him any satisfaction. Christ pity Gwynedd, he thought, and suddenly he could keep silent no longer, the truth was bursting forth of its own accord, in a scalding surge of bitterness.

'Prince Davydd. The heir apparent. The favourite. The usurper! Tell me, are you enough of a fool to believe that will ever come to pass?'

He saw Davydd's jaw muscles tighten. But the boy's voice was colourless, devoid of emotion. 'Papa will not change his mind.'

'I know,' Gruffydd admitted, and that was the hurt beyond healing. 'But Papa will not live forever,' he said roughly. 'And then we shall see. I could not fight Papa. But I shall take great pleasure in fighting you, in claiming what is rightfully mine!'

Davydd swung around, started back into the hall. He was cautious by nature, as deliberate of action as he was quick of thought. He'd learned to turn silence into a shield, understood Gruffydd far better than Gruffydd understood him. Gruffydd's were volatile and impassioned rages, outbursts of heat and elemental energy, summer lightning in a cloudless sky. Davydd's rages were rare, seldom seen and long smouldering; as slow as he was to anger, he was even slower to forgive. Now as he reached the door, he stopped, turned to face Gruffydd.

'You are right,' he said. 'Papa will not live forever. But neither will I be fourteen forever. And then, just as you said, we shall see.'

August, 1226
Shrewsbury, England

In January Henry fell gravely ill, and it was feared he might die. He did recover, but his uncle Will of Salisbury was not as fortunate. Sailing from Gascony back to England, Will was shipwrecked, for a time was presumed lost. Although he survived several harrowing weeks at sea, his health declined. He died on March 7, much mourned, and was buried with great honours in the partially constructed cathedral church at Salisbury.

Henry watched complacently as Joanna scanned the letter he'd just handed her. 'You see? Nell is quite content now with Pembroke. Did I not tell you that wedding was for the best?'

'And it seems you were right,' Joanna conceded. This buoyant, sprightly missive was a far cry from the tear-splotched forlorn letter she'd received from Nell two years ago, pleading with Joanna to intercede for her, to persuade Henry not to make her marry the Earl of Pembroke. But Pembroke had been very kind to his child-bride, indulging her every whim, and the little girl seemed to have found in her husband the father she could not remember.

'I've something else for you, too, an early birthday present. I'm giving you the manor of Condover in Shropshire.'

Joanna was delighted. Until Henry had given her an English manor the preceding year, she'd not realized what a secure feeling there was in being a property owner, in having land of her own. 'You spoil me as much as Pembroke spoils our Nell,' she said, and Henry laughed.

'I try. I just like to make people happy, to surprise them. And this ought to do both.' Henry was holding out a parchment scroll. But as Joanna reached for it, he snatched it back. 'How could I forget? You do not read Latin, do you? Ah well, mayhap I could be coaxed into reading it to you.'

'Please do,' Joanna said, utterly intrigued by now. Llewelyn and Davydd were no less curious. Only Elen did not join the circle, stayed where she was in the window seat.

Henry was thoroughly enjoying the suspense, took his time in unrolling the scroll. 'You'll observe the papal seal, no doubt. I had it in my hands two months ago, but I wanted to wait, wanted to see your face, Joanna. Are you ready? "Dispensation to Joanna, wife of Llewelyn, Prince of North Wales, daughter of King John, declaring her legitimate, but without prejudice to the King and realm of England."'

Their response was entirely satisfactory; they were staring at him in obvious astonishment. 'Henry, I . . . I do not understand,' Joanna said at last. 'How can this be?'

'Does it matter? Is it not enough that I asked and His Holiness the Pope obliged?'

'But there had to be more to it than that, Henry!'

'Ah, Joanna, it is not such a mystery. Papa's marriage to the Lady Avisa was dissolved, declared to have been void from its inception. That meant he was free to enter into another marriage or plight troth up to the time he wed my mother. Suppose he had pledged his troth with your mother. If that were so, you'd have a claim to legitimacy, would be entitled to recognition.'

'But Henry, he did not plight troth with my mother!'

'Since she's dead and Papa's dead, who is to say?' Henry grinned, held out his arms. 'Are you pleased, Joanna? I did surprise you?'

'That you did for certès!' Joanna moved into his embrace, while Llewelyn studied the papal dispensation.

'"Without prejudice to the King and realm of England,"' he quoted. 'I take it that means Joanna's legitimacy is qualified, bars her from any claim to the English Crown?'

'I knew you'd catch that straight off!' Henry laughed. 'It seemed for the best. No offence, Llewelyn, but you've shown yourself to be too adroit at taking a weak claim and making of it an irresistible one!'

They all laughed at that, and Joanna kissed Henry again. Henry was so delighted at the success of his stratagem that it was some time before Joanna was able to disengage herself, to join Elen in the window seat.

'Darling, are you all right? Why are you sitting over here by yourself?'

'I'm fine, Mama, truly.' Elen summoned up a smile. 'So . . . tell me. How does it feel to be legitimate after all these years?'

'I'm not sure. My father would likely have found this hilarious, but I doubt if my mother would have seen the joke. How could she?'

'Speaking of jokes, what did Papa say to make you laugh so?'

Joanna grinned. 'Oh, that. He asked me if conditional legitimacy was like being somewhat pregnant. He – Elen, what is it?' For Elen had not been able to turn away in time; Joanna had seen the sudden tears well in her daughter's eyes.

'Elen . . .' Rising, Joanna caught Elen's hand, drew her reluctant daughter to her feet. 'Let's go out into the gardens where we can talk.'

'I have nothing to say, Mama.'

'Well, I have,' Joanna said, propelled Elen towards the door.

The garden at Shrewsbury was enclosed by whitethorn hedges; within the flowery mead were several wooden benches and a small fountain. Joanna and Elen halted before the fountain, while Joanna searched for the right words.

'Elen . . . sometimes men act kindly towards their wives in public, seem to be loving husbands. But these same men then treat their wives very differently in private. Most women have no choice but to suffer in silence. But that is not true for you, darling. I know you are unhappy. If that is why, if John is abusive or cruel to you, for God's sake, tell me. We can help, Elen. But we can do nothing as long as you keep silent.'

Elen had plucked a briar rose, was dropping the petals, one by one, into the fountain. 'Oh, Mama, do you not know me better than that? Do you truly think I'd stay with a man who beat me?'

'Well, then, what is it? Is he openly unfaithful? Has he brought a mistress into the castle keep?'

'Are those your standards for sympathy, Mama? If he beats me or flaunts his sluts, I'm deserving of pity. If not, I bear my lot as best I can.'

'Elen, I did not say that!'

Elen picked up a daisy this time; it soon joined the shredded rose in the fountain. 'No,' she admitted, after a long pause, 'you did not, did you? To answer your question, I cannot say with certainty that John is faithful, but he is discreet. You and Papa were right about

651

him. He is indeed a good man: pious, courageous, steadfast, and honest.' She turned away from the fountain, began to pace. 'What woman could ask for more in a man? What woman would have the right to ask for more?'

Joanna followed her across the grassy mead. 'Yet you are not content.'

Elen shook her head. 'No. I feel . . . feel trapped. I expect that sounds right foolish, but it's true all the same. Do you remember that caged magpie I had as a child, how fond I was of it? I will not permit my maids to keep pet birds on any of our manors, cannot abide them now . . .'

Joanna caught her breath. 'Ah, child, why did you not confide in me ere this?'

Elen shrugged. 'I did once, Mama. I told you I did not want to marry John, and what did that avail me?' As always when she was distraught, she could not keep still, moved restlessly back and forth, heedlessly trampling flowers underfoot. 'John and I never quarrel. Would you believe me if I told you that in nigh on four years I've never seen him well and truly wroth? He believes in control, you see. He does not argue, he analyses. He even explains my own emotions to me, patiently shows me not only how I erred but why. So you need not fear, Mama. He hardly sounds like an abusive husband, does he?'

'No,' Joanna said slowly. 'Just an unloved one,' and Elen turned her head away, surreptitiously brushed the back of her hand against her cheek.

'At first I was glad when I did not get with child; that may be sinful, but I was. After a time, though, I could not help wondering why I did not become pregnant. And . . . and then I began to want a baby, my baby. For the first time in my life, I took an interest when other women talked of birthing and children and the marriage bed, of the ways a barren wife might conceive. So I put mistletoe over our bed. I drink feverfew and anise in wine. I pray to St Margaret. And each month I count the days, dread that first spotting of blood . . .'

'Darling, you must not give up hope. Isabelle was barren for six full years ere she finally conceived. But she then was able to give my father five healthy children, and four so far to Hugh de Lusignan. Nor is she the only –'

'Mama, I know you mean well. But that is no comfort. Better I should face the truth, that my marriage is barren.' Elen laughed suddenly, mirthlessly. 'Barren in every sense of the word!' Choking back a sob, she spun about, fled the garden.

Joanna reached out, caught the edge of the fountain for support. This was her fault, all her fault. When she'd wept upon being told she must wed a Welsh Prince, Isabelle had sought to comfort her, assuring her she'd learn in time to be content with Llewelyn. Isabelle had been right; most women did adjust, did find a measure of contentment in all but the most wretched marriages. But not Elen. And she should have realized that, should have known the marriage was doomed. When had Elen ever learned to compromise? Did it even matter that she brought so much of her unhappiness upon herself? How could she blame Elen for the nature God had given her? It was like blaming Elen for having brown eyes. But if anyone should have foreseen this, it was she. For who knew better than she how stubborn Elen could be, how passionate, and for all her bravado, how easily hurt?

And what was she to do now for her daughter? What could she do? Leaning over the fountain, Joanna splashed water upon her face, and a memory surfaced. St Winifred's Well – Gwenfrewi in Welsh – was a holy shrine in North Wales, close by Basingwerk Abbey. It was celebrated for its cures, and the ailing and infirm made painful pilgrimages to avail themselves of its restorative waters.

Joanna felt the faintest stirring of hope. There was something she could do. She and Elen would make a pilgrimage to St Winifred's Well, implore the saint to heed their prayers, to give Elen a child.

August, 1228
Cricieth, North Wales

Of all the diseases that ravaged the countries of Christendom, none was so feared as leprosy. The Church sought to ease the suffering of those afflicted by proclaiming it as a sacred malady, an admittedly agonizing means of achieving salvation. But Scriptures said otherwise. According to Leviticus, the leper was unclean and defiled, to be shunned by his fellow men, and people were only too willing to obey that harsh dictum, to banish the leper from their midst, stifling the voice of conscience with the comforting belief that the leper's fate was deserved, God's punishment for sins of the flesh, for lust and lechery and unholy pride.

In England, lepers fared better than in other countries; the English were generally more tolerant, more sympathetic to the leper's dreadful plight. An English leper was not taken to the cemetery and forced to stand in an open grave whilst a priest declared, 'Be thou dead to the world, but alive again unto God,' as was often done in France. But the English leper was still subject to banishment, was escorted to the church as if he were a dead man, where he knelt under a black cloth as the congregation chanted, *'Libera me, Domine.'*

For the leper, there would be no release but death. No longer could he enter churches, markets, inns. He must wear his distinctive leper garb, a dark hooded cloak, and carry clappers or bell in order to warn others of his approach. He must shun the company of all but his fellow lepers, and when he died, he would be buried as he'd lived, alone.

What befell him once he'd been stigmatized depended upon his own resources and the loyalty of family and friends. If he was wealthy and well loved, he could sequester himself in his own home. Or he could seek to enter a leper hospital, a lazar house. Life in a lazar house was not easy; the leper was compelled to bequeath his possessions to the hospital, to forswear such worldly amusements as chess and dicing, to take an oath of chastity, poverty, and obedience. But few balked, for the alternative was to be cast out upon one's own, to survive by begging, to face the hostility of people who shrank from the disfigurement, the ulcerated sores and, as the disease took its gruesome toll, eventually to starve.

There was deep mourning, therefore, at Llewelyn's court when Iorwerth, one of Ednyved's sons, was diagnosed as having the disease of Lazarus. For Iorwerth, of course, there would be no hut by the roadside, with alms-dish nailed to a pole. He had a manor at Abermarlais, had a father wealthy enough to provide for his needs, influential enough to soften the strictures of his exile. He would not want for food or comfort or medical care. Ednyved could provide him with ointments, juniper oil, viper potions, even so exotic a remedy as the blood of a turtle from the faraway Cape Verde Islands. He could aid Iorwerth in making pilgrimages to the shrine of St Davydd and the holy well at Harbledown near Canterbury. He could even coerce Iorwerth's reluctant wife into keeping faith with her marriage vows, for while the Church did not recognize leprosy as grounds for divorce, Welsh law did. But what Ednyved could not do was to command a miracle, and nothing less would save his son. Knowing that, he could only grieve for his doomed child. And his friends could only grieve with him.

They could not even offer the meagre comfort of forced cheer, could not seek to console Ednyved with false optimism, fabricated tales of wondrous cures, for he would not speak of his son. Even with Gwenllian, he refused to share his grief, for Iorwerth was not hers, was a son of Tangwystl, the mother who'd died giving him birth. And so the bleak lenten season dragged on under the heavy burden of Ednyved's frozen silence, and when it was spring, fate dealt another blow, no less cruel.

It was Easter, and Davydd Benfras, son of Llewelyn's court bard Llywarch, was entertaining the court at Aber. He was reciting a lively account of a long-ago battle when Rhys suddenly stumbled to his feet. Rhys looked quizzical, surprised rather than alarmed, but then he reeled backward, his clutching hands seeking support and finding only the edge of the tablecloth. He dragged it down with him, sent platters and dishes and tureens of soup clattering to the floor. Llewelyn was the first to reach him, cradled his head as Rhys fought for breath. But he was dead by the time Llewelyn's physician could be summoned.

Catherine was so bereft that they feared for her very sanity. Nothing could comfort her, not her children or her Church or her friends. At Joanna's insistence, she stayed for several weeks at Llewelyn's court, but then she went back to the manor house she'd shared for so many years with Rhys. In the months that followed, she withdrew into the past, into her memories and her regrets, until even to those who loved her, she seemed no more than a pale wraith, a wan, frail shadow trapped in a time no longer hers.

Llewelyn and Ednyved had been stunned by Rhys's sudden death, for they'd lost more than a cherished friend, companion of boyhood and manhood. Standing in the shadowed choir of Aberconwy Abbey before Rhys's coffin, the same thought was in each man's mind, that it could have been him.

That thought, too, had been Joanna's. Common sense told her that she was likely to outlive Llewelyn, but she'd never allowed herself to dwell upon that likelihood, upon that eighteen-year gap in their ages. She knew their life together was bound to change as he aged, but not yet. Merciful Lady Mary, not yet.

Llewelyn's hair had begun to silver. His sight was no longer as sharp, and he tired more easily, complained of slowing reflexes. But he could still put in a day's hard riding. His health was excellent. Like all the Welsh, he'd taken good care of his teeth, and he still had a handsome smile, a young man's smile. While he and Joanna no longer made love as frequently as in the early years of their marriage, Joanna had no complaints about their lovelife. She found it hard to believe that twenty-two years could have passed since the day of their wedding, and time seemed to be treating Llewelyn so kindly that it was surprisingly easy to pretend it was also standing still.

But then Rhys had died in seizure upon the floor of Aber's great hall, Rhys who was four-and-fifty, a year younger than Llewelyn. And a few weeks later, word reached Aber that Reginald de Braose had died at Abergavenny Castle. Like Rhys, Reginald had been in apparent good health, and he, too, was younger than Llewelyn. Joanna began to look upon her husband with new eyes, eyes haunted and full of fear.

Her anxiety was all the greater because the news from England was not good. After five years of peace, the Marches were once more in turmoil, and Joanna passed this, her thirty-sixth summer, in growing dread, for it was beginning to seem more and more likely that Llewelyn would be riding again to war.

Stephen Langton had died early in July, and with his death an irreplaceable voice for peace and conciliation was stilled, the last check upon Hubert de Burgh's growing ascendancy, for Peter des Roches had departed England the preceding year to fulfil a crusading vow, Chester had been thwarted, Will was dead, and Pembroke in uneasy alliance with de Burgh. Flourishing a new title, Earl of Kent, de Burgh now turned his eyes and ambitions west – towards Wales. In April, Henry agreed to give him the castle and lordship of Montgomery.

The local Welsh reacted with alarm, laying siege to the castle and pressing their attack with such vigour that Henry and de Burgh were compelled to lead a royal army to the rescue. So far Llewelyn had not taken up arms himself, but he was deeply mistrustful of de Burgh's motives, and Joanna feared he would eventually be drawn into the fray. She was to meet Henry later in the month at Shrewsbury in hopes of preserving their fragmenting peace, but she was not optimistic of success, for the interests of her husband and brother were at heart irreconcilable.

August found Llewelyn's court at his seaside castle of Cricieth. On Tuesday, the Assumption of the Blessed Mary, Joanna spent the afternoon dictating letters to Elen, Catherine, her young sister Nell. A brief letter was also dispatched to Gwladys, who'd returned to South Wales to settle a dispute over her late husband's lands; Reginald's son Will was contesting her dower rights. Joanna was just completing the last, and most important of the lot, informing Henry that she had received his safe-conduct and would be meeting him in a fortnight's time at Shrewsbury.

Branwen and Alison had long since departed Joanna's service, had been found husbands and were raising families of their own. Glynis, Joanna's latest maid, had grown bored and wandered to the window, where she stood gazing out to sea. 'The sun has just broken through, Madame. After nigh on a week of rains, I'd all but forgotten what it looked –' A loud blaring noise intruded over the sound of rolling surf, the raucous gulls. It blasted again and Glynis exclaimed, 'Did you hear that, my lady? A hunting horn; your lord is back from the hunt!'

By the time Joanna reached the bottom of the stairs, Llewelyn was already dismounting. The bailey was thronged with laughing men, lathered horses, and barking dogs; even before Joanna saw the deer carcasses strapped to the sumpter horses, she knew their hunt had been a rousing success.

Giving his reins to a groom, Llewelyn reached for Joanna as she came within range, bending her backward in a playful embrace. He was begrimed and sweaty and when he kissed her, she tasted mead on his breath; they'd apparently begun celebrating on the way back to the castle. That meant, she knew, dinner would likely be a rowdy, boisterous affair. But she did not mind in the least, for this was the first time since Rhys's death that she'd seen Llewelyn in such high spirits.

'What were you doing?' she chided. 'Chasing deer through a mud wallow?'

'Is that the thanks I get for putting venison on your table?' He gave her a sudden squeeze, laughing when she squealed. 'Come, I'll show you the prize kill of the day, a fine ten-point buck brought down by Davydd. Unfortunately, two of the brachet hounds were hurt –'

Llewelyn had stopped, was gazing across the bailey. Joanna turned, saw at once what had caught his eye. Several horsemen had just been ushered through the gateway. But it was the horse being led that was drawing such admiring glances. The destrier was always larger than the palfreys used for daily riding, but this particular stallion was one of the largest Joanna had ever seen, standing almost seventeen hands high. It was a magnificent animal: broad chest, lengthy flanks, a powerfully muscled body and small head, a sweeping silvery tail and a coat as white as the foaming breakers crashing down upon the beach. Joanna smiled at her husband, said indulgently, 'Go ahead, go and take a closer look.'

Llewelyn was not the only one to be captivated by the cream-coloured stallion. It had attracted a crowd of admirers, men who looked on enviously now as one of the riders handed over the reins to Gruffydd.

'I bought him in Powys last month,' Gruffydd said proudly as Llewelyn came up beside him. 'What do you think, Papa?'

'He's a beauty, in truth.' Llewelyn circled around to get a better look, taking care not to get too close. One reason the destrier was rarely ridden except to war was that its natural gait was a rather jarring trot. But the other reason was that it was notorious for its fiery nature, and the other men, too, were giving the horse respectful room.

'I had to pay nigh on forty pounds for him,' Gruffydd volunteered, and several men whistled. 'As soon as I saw him, though, I knew I had to have him. You know what he put me in mind of, Papa? That white stallion you gave me for my twelfth birthday, remember?'

'I remember. That was a well-bred palfrey, but I doubt if it could hold a candle to this one. I'd say he's cheap at twice the price.'

Gruffydd smiled. 'I'm glad you're so taken with him, Papa. You see, I bought him for you.'

'You're serious?' Llewelyn turned to stare at his son. 'What can I say, Gruffydd? I think you're too generous for your own good; a horse like this does not come along that often.'

'None the less, I want you to have him.' Gruffydd watched as Llewelyn reached out, lightly stroked the stallion's arched neck; it snorted, flung its head up. 'However, I'm afraid you cannot ride him just yet. The man I bought him from said he was somewhat skittish, no easy horse to ride. What I'd like to do is to school him myself, until I'm sure he's a safe mount for you.'

'A safe mount for me?' Llewelyn echoed incredulously. But his astonishment yielded almost at once to irritation. It was not just that he prided himself upon his horsemanship; it was also that he knew himself to be a much better rider than Gruffydd, who tight-reined his horses, seemed to take a perverse pride in high-strung, half-broken mounts. 'I hardly think that necessary, Gruffydd. I expect I've been riding long enough to know how to handle a skittish horse.'

Gruffydd was still smiling. 'I know you have in the past, Papa. But you were much younger then; the danger was less. I do not mean to offend you, but aging bones are brittle, break more easily. What you were once able to do might now be beyond you, might –'

'Lead the stallion over to the horse block,' Llewelyn cut in sharply. Men at once moved back, cleared space and took up positions to watch. Gruffydd shrugged, stepped aside. And Davydd felt a sudden chill.

Llewelyn did not mount right away; instead he stood quietly, letting the horse become accustomed to his scent, the sound of his voice. As he studied the stallion, his anger ebbed and his eyes grew wary. He was close enough now to see the knotted ridges on the horse's withers, the marks of abuse. When he ran his hand over the stallion's shoulder, it flinched. Somewhat skittish, Gruffydd had

659

said. More than that, he suspected, much more. The stallion's head and neck were held well down; the position of its tail told him that so was its croup, while its back was arching like a cat. Even more than the laid-back ears, these were the signs of a restive animal, a likely bolter.

'Papa.' Davydd had decided to trust his instincts. Following Llewelyn to the horse block, he said quietly, 'Papa, I wish you'd reconsider. I have a bad feeling about this horse.'

'So have I.'

'Then why risk it? You always told me that horses can best be tamed with patience, that in any contest of brute force, the horse is bound to win.'

'I know, lad. But if I back down now, I take an even greater risk, that men think me afraid to ride him.'

'Jesu, Papa, who could doubt your courage?'

Llewelyn gave the boy a twisted smile. 'Do not deceive yourself, Davydd. When a man reaches a point where he has nothing left to prove, he's either dead or dying.' Davydd looked so troubled that he added reassuringly, 'There's no great trick to handling a bolting horse. I need only get him turning in circles, let him tire himself out.'

Unbuckling his scabbard, Llewelyn handed Davydd his sword. Taking the reins, he waved Davydd and the groom back, then gripped the pommel and swung up into the saddle. He was expecting some sort of resistance, but what he got was bottled lightning. The stallion shot forward, but instead of bolting, it began to buck wildly, kicking out in a frenzy, coming down with such force that Llewelyn felt as if his spine would snap in two.

Men had scattered in all directions, were shouting encouragements. But Llewelyn knew there could be but one outcome, knew he could absorb only so much of this punishment. He was half-blinded by his own sweat, tasted blood where his teeth had torn his inner lip, and his legs were cramping in painful spasms; he was finding it harder and harder to throw his weight into his heels, to maintain his grip in the saddle. But the stallion had yet to show any signs of tiring, was twisting and plunging as if crazed, so desperate to free itself that at times all four feet were off the ground.

The castle dogs were going berserk, making excited dashes at the panicked horse, and they only frightened it all the more. When a large alaunt cut directly in front of it, the stallion reared up suddenly, and Llewelyn felt his first jolt of real fear. It was not that he expected the horse to throw itself backward. For all the folklore he'd heard of outlaw stallions that deliberately sought to crush their riders, he'd never encountered such a rogue killer, did not know a man who had. What he feared now was not so much the stallion's intentions as the muddy bailey; the ground had not had time to dry, was still slippery and rain-soaked. He slackened the reins, leaned forward, but the stallion was already scrambling, starting to slide. For several terrifying seconds the animal struggled to keep its balance, and then it was going over backward and Llewelyn kicked his feet free of the stirrups, flung himself sideways as the stallion fell.

The ground was soft, but Llewelyn landed at an awkward angle, his leg twisting under him. He lay stunned for several moments, conscious but dazed, aware at first only of pain. There was mud in his mouth; he spat it out, started to sit up. But the bailey began to spin, and he lay back, closed his eyes. When he opened them again, Joanna was kneeling beside him, cradling his head as he'd done for Rhys. He recognized other faces now, Davydd and Ednyved and Gruffydd, faces white and taut, the faces of men looking into an open coffin, and he swallowed, said, 'How is the horse?'

They stared at him and then burst into unsteady laughter. Joanna laughed, too, or perhaps she sobbed; he could not tell which, for she was leaning forward, had begun to cover his mud-streaked face with kisses. Llewelyn braced himself on his elbow, started to sit up again. Now that his head had cleared, he was concerned that he might have broken a bone, and it was with some trepidation that he ran his hand over his throbbing left leg. Once he concluded that he'd done no more than pull a muscle, he closed his eyes again, silently giving thanks to the Virgin for protecting him on this, the holiest of her days. As he turned his head, he saw the stallion had regained its feet. It, too, seemed to have been accorded a measure of divine mercy, for it had also escaped serious injury. It was standing quietly, sides heaving, head down, looking – for the moment at least – like the most docile of palfreys.

Llewelyn looked from the horse to his eldest son. 'Somewhat skittish, Gruffydd?' He said it with deliberate wryness, as if it were a jest, and a number of people laughed. But Gruffydd did not. Nor did Davydd.

'Before God, Papa, I did not know he was so wild. And I did try to discourage you from riding him . . .'

Llewelyn heard Davydd draw a sharp, hissing breath. But he kept his eyes upon Gruffydd, saw the colour mount in the younger man's face. At last he said abruptly, 'Help me up, Davydd.' It was painful to bear weight upon his left leg, but not enough for alarm. He glanced down at himself and grimaced, for his tunic was soaked with sweat and caked with mud. 'See to the stallion for me, Gruffydd. Right now I need a long, hot bath. And whilst I soak, I shall try to decide who best deserves to own such a remarkable beast. Pembroke's a possibility, but I'm more inclined to offer it to Hubert de Burgh.'

As he expected, that got a laugh, gave him the opportunity to make an unhurried graceful exit. But Joanna was not deceived; she knew him too well, knew he was playing to their audience, that only when they were alone would she find out the full extent of his injuries.

Entering their bedchamber, Joanna discovered that Llewelyn had not bothered to summon his squires; he had simply flung himself down upon the bed. She moved towards him, stopping several feet away. 'I have to tell you,' she said slowly. 'That was one of the most foolhardy things you've ever done.'

Llewelyn's mouth twitched. 'No, *breila*. That was the most foolhardy.'

He held out his hand and Joanna caught it between her own. 'Let me summon a doctor, Llewelyn. I'll not rest easy until I hear him say you are well and truly unhurt.'

'If you must. But not now, not yet.' He allowed Joanna to help him strip off his tunic, his muddy boots, then lay back against the pillows, his eyes closing again. She stroked his hair, pressed her lips to the pulse in his throat. He was drenched in perspiration; she could hear the rapid pounding of his heart and her own took up a quicker cadence. But he did not seem to be in great discomfort; she read exhaustion in his face more than pain.

'You look so . . . remote, so far away. What are you thinking of?'

'A day twenty years past, the day I gave Gruffydd that white palfrey.' His eyes remained closed, but he seemed to sigh. 'What a twisted road we've travelled since then . . .'

'Llewelyn . . . do you believe Gruffydd? That he truly did not know the stallion was so wild?'

'He knew.' Llewelyn turned his head on the pillow, met her eyes. 'He wanted to see me take a fall,' he said softly. 'To see me fail.'

Joanna's suspicions were uglier than his. But she said nothing, for she knew now that he'd not walked away unscathed, after all. Knowing that he'd insist upon eating in the great hall, she said, 'I'll go to the kitchens, instruct the cooks to delay dinner. Try to rest, beloved; I'll be back.'

Ednyved was waiting for her on the outer stairway of the Great Tower. 'How does he, in truth?'

'He has no hurts you can see. Where is Gruffydd?'

Usually, grooms had to resort to a lip twitch in order to handle the white stallion. But this time it had submitted meekly, too shaken by its fall to summon up a spirit of defiance.

Gruffydd was still shaken, too. He lingered in the stable long after the grooms had gone, slumping down on a large bale of hay. It was quiet, and the smells of horses and hay and manure were comforting in their very familiarity. He sat there for some time, alone in the semi-darkness, listening to the soft nickering of the animals, trying to make sense out of emotions that were as contradictory as they were compelling. His senses were normally acute, but he'd let himself be lulled into incaution, and he did not hear the footsteps in the straw, jumped when a voice spoke suddenly out of the shadows.

'How disappointed you must be.'

The voice was familiar and yet it was not. It sounded like Davydd, but it held none of Davydd's vaunted control, the icy indifference that Davydd had learned to wield like a whip. This voice was uneven, raw with rage, throbbing with hatred. Gruffydd got slowly to his feet and one of the shadows moved, revealed it was indeed his younger brother. But this was a Davydd he'd never seen before, and he instinctively dropped his hand to his sword hilt.

'I do not know what you mean.'

'Yes, you do. You deliberately goaded Papa into riding that stallion, knowing full well that the horse was not broken!'

'That is not true. I did not know.'

Davydd's lip curled back. 'Liar!' he jeered. 'No man buys a horse without riding it first. And you even claim you were warned it was skittish. You'd never have resisted a challenge like that, not you! You tried to ride that stallion, and if there were any justice, you'd have broken your worthless neck! Was that when you got the idea? When you found you could not master him yourself?'

Gruffydd took a swift, threatening step forward. He towered over the younger man, but Davydd stood his ground. Gruffydd had flushed. Lying did not come easily to him, and he made no more false denials, instead fell back upon the truth, as he perceived it to be. 'Even if I did know about the stallion, I had no evil intent in mind, never meant for Papa to be hurt.'

'I'll grant you that. You were more ambitious, were hoping for more than a broken leg. I think you've grown weary of waiting, think you wanted him dead!'

Gruffydd gasped, then lashed out. Davydd saw the blow coming and recoiled, but he was not fast enough. Had he not pulled away, it might have broken his jaw. As it was, it had enough force to snap his head back, to stagger him. He stumbled and Gruffydd swung again, buried his fist in Davydd's stomach. He doubled up, fell to the floor just as Joanna and Ednyved entered the stable.

'Jesus God, no!' Joanna gave Gruffydd one incredulous look of horror, knelt by her son. He was bleeding profusely, and she was afraid to touch him, afraid to find a wound that might be mortal.

Ednyved, too, had whitened at sight of Davydd's blood. 'Christ, what have you done?' he demanded, grabbing Gruffydd roughly by the arm.

Gruffydd jerked free. 'What do you think, that I stabbed him?' Outraged, he drew his sword half-way up the scabbard. 'Do you see any blood on the blade? I hit him, that's all.'

'He's lying, Ednyved, has to be. Jesu, look at all this blood!'

'Mama . . .' Davydd coughed, struggled to sit up. 'Mama, I'm not hurt.'

Gruffydd let his sword slide down the scabbard. 'Your precious nestling has a nosebleed, Madame,' he said scornfully, 'no more than that . . . this time.'

Joanna could see now that Gruffydd spoke the truth, that this frightening rush of bright red blood was indeed coming from Davydd's nose. Forcing him to lie flat, she sought to staunch the bleeding with her veil. Gruffydd stood watching for a moment longer, and then turned, stalked out.

As soon as the bleeding ceased, Davydd insisted upon sitting up. 'I need some water,' he muttered. 'I cannot go out there with blood all over me.' Ednyved found a drinking pail, but when Joanna tried to help, Davydd snapped, 'I am not a child, Mama, do not need to be coddled!'

'Davydd, that was not my intent!' But Gruffydd's taunt came back to Joanna then – 'your precious nestling' – and her hand slipped from Davydd's sleeve. She would have protested, though, when he turned to go. But Ednyved caught her eye, shook his head.

'It's best to let him be,' he advised once Davydd was out of hearing. 'His pride is sore, and that's not a hurt a mother can heal.'

Joanna did not agree, but she had not the energy to argue. Reaction had set in and she was trembling again. She looked about in vain for a stable work-bench, dropped down upon the bale of hay. 'Till the day I die,' she said numbly, 'I'll never be able to forget that sight, Davydd crumpled on the ground, drenched in blood, with Gruffydd standing over him, hand on sword hilt. Can you blame me, Ednyved, for thinking what I did?'

Ednyved sat beside her on the bale. 'No, for I thought it, too.'

'Llewelyn thinks Gruffydd wanted to see him take a fall. I would that I could believe he had nothing more in mind. Tell me the truth, Ednyved. Do you think Gruffydd was hoping Llewelyn would be badly hurt, mayhap even killed?'

He seemed in no hurry to respond. 'I saw his face when Llewelyn was thrown. If he was not fearful for Llewelyn, he's a rather remarkable actor, and acting has never been one of his talents.'

'But he had to know the risk!'

'Joanna, you're asking me what only Gruffydd can answer. It may be that even he does not know for certès. If you're asking whether Gruffydd hates Llewelyn, I think he has learned to hate him. But in a strange way, I think he still loves him, too.'

'How can he hate and love Llewelyn at the same time?'

Ednyved shrugged. 'Probably the same way you hate and love John,' he said, and Joanna jumped to her feet, began to pace.

'Gruffydd has no intention of honouring Llewelyn's wishes, of accepting Davydd as his liege lord. As soon as Llewelyn is dead, he means to lay claim to the crown.'

'I know that, and I know, too, what you fear. But you're seeing Davydd with a mother's eye. Do not underestimate the lad, Joanna. He is stronger than you think.'

'I am not saying Davydd is weak! I am saying he is young, too young. He's just nineteen, Ednyved, and Gruffydd is thirty-two, with years of battlefield experience. Can you honestly tell me you believe Davydd could hold his own against Gruffydd?'

'Not now,' he conceded. 'Not yet.' A silence fell between them. He watched Joanna pace, finally said, 'I can think of only one way

665

to solve the problem Gruffydd poses. But I doubt if you could bring yourself to do it, not even for Davydd. Hire men to arrange a killing.'

Joanna recoiled, and he said dryly, 'You see? I knew you could never do it.'

'Neither could you.' Joanna moved towards him. 'But you've given me an idea, Ednyved. What if Gruffydd were banished from Llewelyn's court, banished from Wales?'

He looked thoughtful, nodded slowly. 'Yes, that might well give Davydd the time he'd need. But you'd best think this through, Joanna. You're talking about causing Llewelyn a great deal of pain.'

'I know.' She shook out her crumpled veil, stared down at the bloodstains. 'Will you help me, Ednyved? If not for Davydd, for Gwynedd?'

'Yes,' he said. 'I'll help you. How?'

'I do not know yet,' she admitted. 'But I'll find a way. Somehow, I'll find a way.'

Joanna's mission to Shrewsbury met with surprising success. She was able to patch up another peace, to stave off a confrontation between Llewelyn and the English Crown. But she was not sanguine about the long-term prospects of this truce, suspected it would be of fleeting duration, for Hubert de Burgh was not content with his acquisition of Montgomery Castle, was casting covetous eyes upon the neighbouring Welsh commote of Ceri.

Gruffydd reacted with predictable fury to Llewelyn's announcement of a truce, and after quarrelling bitterly with Llewelyn, he withdrew from his father's court for several weeks. Joanna usually welcomed his absences, but for the first time she found herself waiting impatiently for Gruffydd's return. She had finally hit upon a plan, likely to be successful by its very simplicity. She meant to exploit Gruffydd's own weaknesses, to let his blazing temper be the instrument of his downfall.

A midday sun was stalking shadows across the rush-strewn floor of Aber's great hall. In one corner, a spirited dice game was in progress. Davydd Benfras was replacing a horsehair string on his favourite harp. All around him men were working at various chores, with differing degrees of enthusiasm, rubbing saddle leather with goose grease, mending harnesses, whittling wooden combs for wives, toys for children. Women were churning butter, spinning wool, while dogs wandered about, hunting for discarded bones midst the floor rushes.

The scene seemed to be one of perfect domestic tranquillity, but rarely had Joanna been so tense. She and Glynis spread a length of wool upon a trestle table, were cutting out a gown for Catherine. But she could not keep her mind on the task at hand, could not keep her eyes away from Gruffydd.

Gruffydd was putting a keener edge upon his sword, set the sharpening stone aside at Senena's approach. She brought him a brimming wine cup, then she lingered to talk, and Joanna's nerves grew more taut by the moment. First she'd had to wait for Gruffydd's son Owain to leave the hall, not wanting a child to witness the ugly scene to come. And now Senena was unwittingly acting as saboteur.

Gruffydd was laughing, reached out and tweaked one of Senena's long brown braids. Although many Welshwomen still cut their hair fairly short, more and more of them were following the Norman fashion, following the example set by their Prince's wife, and Joanna was grimly amused that Senena, too, had adopted the style of a people she so despised.

As she watched them bantering together, Joanna found herself thinking that they were a mismatched pair. They put her in mind of a brilliantly coloured linnet and its dowdy, drab-brown mate. Senena was not so much plain as overshadowed, an ordinary woman with an uncommonly handsome husband. Joanna felt sure that Gruffydd strayed from time to time, just as she knew Llewelyn had occasionally strayed. But if Gruffydd was like Llewelyn in that he could have his pick of very willing young women, he was like Llewelyn, too, in that he seemed to have no need of numerous, ever-changing bedmates. He was content with one woman, with the wife who obviously adored him, who was as fiercely protective of him as any lioness could be.

That was a better analogy, Joanna decided, Gruffydd as the tawny-maned male lion, awesome to behold but actually dependent upon his less flamboyant mate, the rangy lioness who did the hunting. Senena of the watchful cat eyes, Senena who was more calculating than her tempestuous husband, and thus more dangerous. But no, she was being unfair now, letting her dislike of Senena lead her astray. How could she blame the woman for being loyal to her husband, her children? They had three now, nine-year-old Owain, six-year-old Gwladys, and a second son born just that spring, named after Llewelyn.

Joanna frowned, brought her mental ramblings to an abrupt halt. Why was she going on like this? Yes, Gruffydd was a caring husband, a loving father. What of it? Why was she culling out his virtues from amongst his failings, searching for those few traits she might justifiably honour?

After some moments of conjecture, she thought she knew. It was as if she were seeking to reassure herself, to show that she was not acting out of malice, that her hatred of Gruffydd played no part in what she was about to do. Well, mayhap her motives were not as pure as she'd have liked, but she would not be lying when she answered to the Almighty for this, when she avowed that she could see no other way, no other choice.

At last Senena was moving away. Joanna laid her scissors down, stood up. Her eyes searched out Ednyved. He nodded almost imperceptibly, started towards the door. Joanna braced herself, then crossed the hall, sat down beside Gruffydd in the window seat.

Gruffydd could not hide his surprise. 'Yes, Madame?' he said coldly, warily.

'I thought you might want to congratulate me. I did avert a war, did I not?'

This was so unlike Joanna that Gruffydd's suspicions kindled like sun-dried straw, and he responded with uncommon caution. 'No, you did not. You did but delay it. You did my father no service by your meddling, for Hubert de Burgh will take our restraint as weakness. He'll be all the more likely now to move into Ceri, because we failed to halt him at Tre Faldwyn . . . or as you Normans call it, Montgomery.'

'I'm sorry you take that view. But I cannot say I'm surprised. After all, you have such a limited understanding of political matters. How fortunate for Gwynedd that Davydd and not you shall rule in Llewelyn's stead.'

Gruffydd caught his breath. 'Just what do you want from me?'

This was not going as she'd hoped it would. Gruffydd was furious, but so far he was keeping his voice as low as hers; they'd yet to attract attention. Moreover, she was finding it harder than she'd expected to provoke a quarrel in cold blood, to insult without the excuse of anger.

'There is no mystery, Gruffydd. You remember that day last month at Cricieth Castle, that day you deliberately baited Llewelyn into riding that crazed stallion? I knew that was not mischance, knew

668

what you had in mind, letting a poor dumb brute do your killing for you. I just could not prove it . . . until now.'

Gruffydd was on his feet before she could finish speaking. 'That's a lie, an accursed Norman lie!'

Joanna rose, too. Heads were turning now, swivelling in response to Gruffydd's shout. From the corner of her eye, she saw Llewelyn and Ednyved entering the hall. But she saw, too, that Senena was hastening towards them. She reached out, put a hand upon Gruffydd's arm, as if seeking to placate him, and said softly. 'As I said, I have proof. One of the grooms came to me, confessed he found a spiked burr under the stallion's saddle –'

She got no further. Gruffydd's outrage, his sense of injustice and injury overrode all else, swept aside the last shreds of his restraint. He'd always suspected Joanna of trying to poison Llewelyn's mind against him, but in his worst imaginings, he'd never expected her to concoct so blatant, so brazen a lie. Had she been a man, he'd have already exacted his vengeance. But his was a society in which women were not to be subjected to violence. Even now the ingrained discipline of a lifetime held, and he did the only thing he could do, flung the contents of his wine cup into Joanna's face.

Joanna gasped, no longer had to feign anger. 'You're a lunatic, an utter and absolute lunatic!' she cried, backing away, frightened by his fury. The hall was in pandemonium; through a roaring in her ears, she heard voices rising, saw a blur of shocked faces, most registering stunned disbelief of what they'd just seen. And then Llewelyn had reached her side, and she forgot the pretence, forgot she had sprung this trap herself, threw herself into his arms with a heartfelt, 'Thank God you're here!'

'You're not hurt?' Waiting only for her to shake her head before he swung around to confront his son. 'All your life I've made excuses for you, found reasons to explain away your deranged behaviour. I cannot even begin to count the times I've overlooked your tempers, your blunders. But no more. This time you'll answer for what you've done.'

'But it was not my fault!'

'It never is, is it? You're always the injured innocent, never accountable for your own actions. It's as if your entire history begins and ends with those years you spent in English prisons. Well, that was thirteen years ago, Gruffydd, and my patience has at last run out.'

Senena was tugging frantically at Gruffydd's arm. 'Do not argue with him, love, I beg you. Do not say what you may later regret!'

Gruffydd ignored her, did not even hear her. 'Your patience? What of mine? You talk of making excuses for me. What do you think I've had to do for you? I've watched for years as you shamed yourself, shamed us all, watched and could do nothing about it. I do not know why this last surrender surprised me so. You're so eager to stay in the good graces of the English King that nothing else matters to you . . . least of all, pride. I once accused her' – pointing towards Joanna – 'of bewitching you, and you denied it. But how else explain your actions? You demean yourself before the English King, allow de Burgh and Pembroke to humiliate you, to –'

'That is enough, Gruffydd!'

'What do you call it if not humiliation? You can posture all you want, boast that you're a brother sovereign of the Scots King, but the truth is that you've shackled us to the English throne, made us vassals of John's son. And yet we're likely to look back upon your reign as the Golden Age of Gwynedd in comparison with what would befall us under Davydd! Christ, Papa, you must see him for what he is, a craven weakling, a pampered milksop who'd panic at the first hint of trouble, and yet you'd have him over me! You'd forsake your firstborn, abandon our ancient laws of inheritance, and all to please a Norman-French bedmate!'

'I do see Davydd for what he is, and I see you for what you are, irresponsible and wilful and foolish beyond belief. You talk of governing Gwynedd and yet you cannot even govern your own temper. You're a child, Gruffydd, a child of two-and-thirty, and it is time you faced the truth. I would never have turned Gwynedd over to you. Should evil befall Davydd in my lifetime, I'll choose Tegwared then, or even Adda's son. But not you, never you, for you'd blunder into a war you could never win, destroy the work of a lifetime in less than a twelvemonth.'

Gruffydd was stunned. 'You'd do that? You'd truly choose Tegwared over me?'

'Yes.' Llewelyn's voice was very cold. 'If it came to that, I would.'

In the silence that followed, Gruffydd could hear the ragged, laboured sound of his own breathing; it seemed so loud to him that he feared others, too, might hear. Senena was plucking again at his sleeve; her eyes were wet with tears. 'Beloved, please. Come away now.'

'Not yet.' His voice sounded strange to him, as if coming from a distance. 'So you do not think I'm fit to rule? Well, go ahead, have Davydd acknowledged by the English, by the Pope, the Marcher lords. The Lord Jesus Himself can anoint him for all I care. For it will avail you naught, old man. Your power stops this side of the grave. Once you're dead, I'll take what is rightfully mine. I'll take Gwynedd and I'll take my vengeance.'

Llewelyn had gone very white. 'Do you think I'd let that happen?'

Gruffydd forced a laugh. 'How can you stop me? You'll be safely gone to God, remember?'

A muscle had begun to jerk in Llewelyn's cheek. 'Courage such as yours is not always a blessing, Gruffydd. Sometimes it can be a curse.' He no longer sounded angry, sounded oddly dispassionate and distant, and then, as Gruffydd puzzled over the cryptic meaning of his words, he raised his hand, said, 'Seize him.'

Llewelyn's household guards looked utterly appalled, but they did not hesitate, at once surrounded Gruffydd, drawing their swords. Gruffydd's reaction was as instinctive and as explosive as his white stallion's had been; he made a dive for the window seat, for his sword. But although the sharpening stone still lay untouched, the sword was gone, for Ednyved did not believe in taking undue risks and had quietly appropriated the weapon. Trapped in the window seat, Gruffydd drew his dagger, turned to face his pursuers. They advanced warily, nervously aware that Llewelyn's command had been 'Seize him,' not 'Slay him,' and they made no attempt to stop Senena when she darted between them.

'Gruffydd, you cannot fight them! Beloved, save yourself, I beg you!'

Gruffydd had friends in the hall, had men sworn to him. With a bitter sense of betrayal, he saw now that none of them were going to come to his aid, that they'd not go against Llewelyn. He knew Senena was right, but he knew, too, that he could not yield. 'Senena, I cannot . . .' he said huskily, and then, 'Christ, no! Owain, get back!'

His son had entered the hall unnoticed, had stood transfixed until the scene erupted in violence. The boy did not understand what was happening, saw only that his father was in danger, and he sprinted forward, crying, 'Papa!' Sobbing, he began to flail out at the men encircling Gruffydd, until Llewelyn grasped him by the arms, pulled him away. Even then, he continued to struggle. There was no sound

671

in the hall but that of his sobs. No one moved. And then Gruffydd's shoulders slumped; he dropped the knife into the rushes.

'You win, Papa. What now? Are you going to do Davydd's killing for him?' That was sheer bravado, though, for Gruffydd felt certain Llewelyn would never put him to death. 'I can only tell you what I told John, that I'll not beg.'

Llewelyn released his grandson, watched as Owain ran to his father. 'Alun,' he said, still sounding like a stranger to Gruffydd, one remote and unrelenting and beyond reach, 'you are to escort my son to Deganwy Castle. He is to be confined there until I personally give you orders to the contrary. He is to be well treated at all times, and his wife and children may join him there. But he cannot be trusted, and is to be closely watched. If you fail me, you'll long regret it. You understand?'

'Indeed, my lord.' Alun gestured, and Gruffydd found his arms being forced behind his back. He no longer resisted, for he had too much pride to let himself be dragged, bound and helpless, from the hall. But at the door he halted, his voice rising in a defiant shout. 'You've just bought Davydd some time, no more than that! You'll have to kill me, old man, and I doubt if you can do it, if you –' His guards shoved him forward; the rest of his words were cut off by the closing door.

Senena had stood very still. Now she turned, crossed to Llewelyn and dropped to her knees before him, a supplicant's posture belied by the blazing grey eyes. 'Gruffydd will not beg, my lord, but I will. You must not do this. Confinement will kill Gruffydd, you know it will. He's your son, your firstborn son. Let him go. We'll leave Wales, I swear it, will never return. Just let him go.'

'I cannot do that. He would never accept exile, and you know it, Senena.'

Senena rose to her feet. 'It would have been a greater mercy if you killed him then.' Reaching for her son, she said, 'Dry your tears, Owain. We go to Deganwy Castle to be with your lord father.'

A path cleared at once; no one seemed to want to touch her, even to meet her eyes. Head high, she started towards the door, leading her son by the hand. But she stopped as she reached Joanna, and then whirled, spun around to face Llewelyn.

'Do you want to know whose fine hand brought about my husband's downfall? She did it, your so innocent and right loving wife! She sought Gruffydd out in the window seat, deliberately goaded him to violence, to his ruin. None of this need have happened if not for her!'

After seeking Llewelyn in their private chamber and the chapel, Joanna was at a loss as to where to look next. But as she approached the stables, a young groom came hurrying out at sight of her.

'Madame, how thankful I am to see you! My lord Prince first told me to saddle his chestnut palfrey, then ordered me to go, saying he'd do it himself. And when I tried to tell him that I was right glad to serve him, he lashed out in a fury, told me to get out, to . . .' The groomed trailed off in despair. 'My lady, I did not mean to displease him, do not even know what I did. And now he's wroth with me . . .'

'No, he is not. You need not fret; you've done nothing wrong. Just go about your other duties. All will be well, I promise you.'

As she entered the stable, Joanna could feel inquisitive equine eyes upon her. Horses were poking their heads over their stall doors, and her favourite roan mare gave a welcoming nicker. But Llewelyn was nowhere to be seen. She paused uncertainly before the stall of his chestnut palfrey, and then moved towards the far door, out into the stable yard. He was not there, either, and she crossed to the shed where the stable gear was kept.

'Llewelyn?' The shed was dark; coming from sunlight, she could see no more than a man's silhouette. 'Llewelyn, I've been looking all over for you. You left the hall so suddenly . . .' She came closer, said hesitantly, 'Beloved, I was worried about you . . .'

'Did Senena speak the truth? Did you deliberately goad Gruffydd into that rage?'

When Senena had accused her in the great hall, she'd responded with an instinctive, heated denial, indignant enough to carry conviction. But alone now with Llewelyn in the darkened shed, Joanna found she could not lie to him.

'Yes . . . I did. I wanted him to show you his true nature, to show you how dangerous he is. I thought you might banish him from your court, into exile. But I never meant for this to happen, Llewelyn. I never thought you'd be forced to imprison him, I swear it.'

She waited, at last entreated, 'Are you not going to say anything? It is bad enough that I cannot see your face, but your silence is worse. I did it for Davydd, Llewelyn, for our son. Surely you can understand?'

He brushed past her, moved out into the yard. As he stepped

673

into the sunlight, Joanna was shocked at sight of him. His face looked ravaged, as if he were bleeding from an internal wound, one that could drain away a man's lifeblood before his physicians even diagnosed the danger. She ran to catch up with him, followed him back into the stable.

'Llewelyn, you must listen to me. I know your pain, know –'

'Do you?' But he turned away before she could answer, entered the chestnut's stall, where he took undue care in bridling the horse. Joanna watched helplessly as he laid a sweat pad across the animal's back, passed the crupper under its tail.

'Will you not talk to me? Llewelyn, this serves for naught!'

He positioned the saddle, began to adjust the girth buckles. 'Senena was right. Killing Gruffydd would be kinder than caging him.'

'Ah, Llewelyn . . . what else could you do? He forced you to it, gave you no choice.'

He swung around to face her, and she shrank back. Never had he looked at her like this, a look that went beyond anger, that came perilously close to denying a lifetime of love. 'You blame me for what happened? Llewelyn, that's not fair! I know how this hurt you. But I had no choice, either. I had to put Davydd's life above all else. I had to do whatever I could to protect him. How could you expect me to do less?'

'I would have expected you to come to me! Davydd is my son, too. Do you think I'd not have done what I could to safeguard his life, his inheritance?'

'But I knew you would not have banished Gruffydd! You yourself admitted you've always indulged him, forgiven him. I was sure talking would do no good, that you had to see for yourself just how untrustworthy he truly is. Be honest, Llewelyn. What would you have done had I come to you with my fears, my suspicions?'

'We'll never know, for you never gave us the chance. Had you trusted me enough to confide in me, mayhap I could have found another way. At the least, I'd not have had Gruffydd taken by force at high noon in the great hall, whilst his nine-year-old son looked on!'

'I am sorry about that, truly I am . . .' Joanna said haltingly. 'But I thought I was acting for the best.'

'By going behind my back? By lying and conniving? You said I had no choice. You're right, for you saw to that!'

'Why will you not try to understand? Jesus wept, I did it for Davydd!'

He shoved the stall door back, led the stallion out into the row. 'I do understand, more than you think. This is not the first time, after all, that you've lied to me. When you sent John that secret warning, you justified that just as easily, swore you'd done it for me. And now Davydd. Who are you to make my decisions for me, to decide what I ought to do?'

He was leading the stallion towards the door. Joanna hastened to keep pace, grabbed his arm. 'I did not believe you'd banish Gruffydd unless forced to it. I still believe that! How can I not, when you've forgiven him time and time again?'

He pulled free, swung up into the saddle. 'To give you credit where due, your scheme worked admirably. You duped me into doing exactly what you wanted, like a master puppeteer. My congratulations, Madame. I dare say John would be very proud of you!'

Joanna flinched as if from a physical blow. 'Damn you,' she cried. 'Damn you, damn you!'

Llewelyn spurred his stallion forward. Joanna did not try to stop him. Standing in the stable doorway, she watched as he cantered across the bailey.

9

Tregarnedd, North Wales

Joanna waited for Catherine's servant to move out of earshot before continuing. 'Davydd returned the next day from Bangor, and when he learned what had happened, he was furious. He accused me of having no faith in him, insisted he needed no help in thwarting Gruffydd's ambitions, and how could I argue?' She smiled, but without humour. 'At Davydd's age, a mother's fear is taken as a mortal insult.'

'And what of Llewelyn? You could not reconcile?'

'No. I've never seen him so angry. But by then I was no less angry myself. In the days that followed, we avoided one another whenever possible, no longer spoke unless absolutely necessary. It was dreadful, Catherine. And then on the fourth day came word that Henry and Hubert de Burgh had invaded Ceri.' Again that bleak, mirthless smile. 'For once, Gruffydd was actually in the right; he'd predicted as much. I was still angry, still hurt. But I did not want Llewelyn to ride to war with harsh words or unhealed wounds between us. I swallowed my pride, sought to make peace . . . to no avail. Llewelyn rebuffed me so sharply that he kindled our quarrel all over again.'

Joanna sighed, picked listlessly at the food set before her. 'And now it has been three weeks since he and Davydd rode south. They are waging war in Ceri, fighting Henry and de Burgh, but I know no more than that. Not a single message has Llewelyn sent me, nary a word.'

Putting the bread down, Joanna gave Catherine a speculative look. 'You've heard me out in virtual silence. Surely you understand why I acted as I did? We're talking about nothing less than Davydd's very life!'

'I am myself a mother. Of course I understand. But I can understand Llewelyn's anger, too. If only you'd have come to him first . . .'

Resentment flickered, failed to catch. Was Catherine's caution truly so surprising? Joanna doubted if, in all her married life, she'd ever acted independently of Rhys. Moreover, she looked ghastly, looked frail and thin and colourless, had aged shockingly in these months of widowhood. 'I did not mean to burden you with my troubles, Catherine. We'll talk of them no more,' Joanna promised, and kept to that resolve for the remainder of her stay.

When Joanna returned to Aber at dusk the following day, she was tired and dispirited. With each visit to Catherine, she could see the distance between them widening, could see in Catherine only a gentle ghost of the lively, loving woman she'd once been. But she did not know how to arrest the drift; her every lifeline seemed to fall short of Catherine's indifferent fingers.

Her mood did not improve on finding her bedchamber in disarray. Not only had Madlen taken advantage of her absence to sleep in Joanna's feather bed, she'd neglected to make it up afterwards. Moreover, several of Joanna's more expensive gowns were spread helter-skelter about the chamber, and Joanna doubted Madlen's glib explanation that she'd been sorting them out; trying them on was more likely. Joanna was annoyed, but Glynis was outraged, began to berate the younger girl for such unseemly behaviour.

Madlen was quite unperturbed by Glynis's ire. Nor was she apprehensive of losing her place in Joanna's household; she was comfortably confident that Joanna would overlook all but the most egregious of impudences, for she was a cousin once removed from Ednyved. But Madlen still had no liking for reprimands, and she sought to avoid one now with a tried and true tactic, diversion.

'Madame, I have wonderful news for you! A letter arrived this afternoon from your lord husband. He says the war is going very well for us. The English are running low on food, are sore beset by our men, and they're losing their will to fight, are squabbling amongst themselves. Lord Llewelyn has cut off their supply lines, even captured a great Norman lord when he ambushed a foraging party, one who'll bring a goodly ransom. He writes that he expects the war will soon be over, that Hubert de Burgh will have to abandon the castle he hoped to build at Pen y Castell and withdraw from Wales.'

'I am not going to ask how you know the contents of my husband's letter . . . not yet. Right now I just want you to fetch it for me, and be quick!'

677

'Madame, I would not pry into your letter! I cannot read! Lord Adda shared it with us in the great hall.'

Joanna could not hide her dismay. 'The letter was to Adda? Not to me?'

'No, Madame, not to you.' Not spiteful, just oblivious, Madlen added blithely, 'Oh, but Lord Llewelyn did include a message for you in the letter. He sent that captive Norman lord to us for safekeeping, but he says the lord is to be treated as a hostage of high rank, not as a common prisoner, and he is to be given the freedom of the court as he pledged his knight's honour he'd not try to escape. Yet our lord would as soon rely upon a more tangible barrier than an enemy's honour, and he thinks it best to put a swift current betwixt the lord and temptation. That was his message, that you should at once move the court to the isle of Môn.'

Joanna spun about, moved to the window so she'd not betray herself with burning colour. Almost immediately, though, she recoiled, having caught sight of Senena crossing the courtyard. 'What is she doing here, Madlen?'

'The Lady Senena? She came back yesterday, is making arrangements to send some of Lord Gruffydd's household goods to Deganwy: his favourite feather bed, wall hangings, and the like.' Madlen gave Joanna a look of avid curiosity, wishing that just once Joanna might confide in her, share those intimate details she could now only speculate about. But Joanna was silent, and she began to pick up the discarded dresses with a sigh of frustration. So much excitement, Lord Gruffydd's confinement, Lord Llewelyn's quarrel with her lady, war with the English, and she was at the very heart of it all; but what good did it do her when her lady hoarded her secrets like a miser?

Joanna's anger had not yet abated by the time she entered the great hall. In truth, she welcomed her resentment, her sense of injury, for it kept her fear at bay. Llewelyn's silence was becoming more and more ominous. For the first time she found herself thinking the unthinkable: what if Llewelyn could not forgive her?

Much to Joanna's relief, Senena was not in the hall. She started towards the dais, while Madlen chattered on cheerfully at her side. 'There is the Norman lord, Madame. I think he's very handsome, in truth. And I've never known a Norman to speak such perfect Welsh; he sounds verily like a Welshman. Not that I mean to say your Welsh is so faulty, but – Madame?' Madlen all but bumped into Joanna, so suddenly had she stopped. 'Madame, you look so queer of a sudden! Why, I'd almost think you'd seen a demon spirit of some sort. You know Lord de Braose?'

Joanna swallowed. 'Yes,' she said. 'I know him.'

As Llewelyn's daughter by marriage, the mother of his grandchildren, Senena had every right to be at his court, however unwelcome Joanna found her presence. Senena made no more accusations, managed a brittle, bitter courtesy in response to Joanna's strained civility. But she watched Joanna constantly, with narrowed grey eyes full of accusation and implacable hate.

Will de Braose's manners were less forced. To be taken captive in warfare was not an uncommon occurrence, and while costly, it was not shaming. Will accepted his plight with the fatalistic sangfroid of a man sure he'd eventually be able to purchase his freedom. If at Chester Castle he could see Joanna only as John's daughter, he took care to accord her now the public politeness due Llewelyn's wife. But like Senena, he, too, followed her with his eyes, eyes no less grey than Senena's, and although not as overtly hostile, somehow even more disquieting.

Joanna had always enjoyed their stays on Môn; she liked the island climate, loved the magnificent views of the mainland mountain ranges. But now she began to feel as if Môn was as much her prison as it was Will's. She came to dread the evening meal, when she could neither avoid nor ignore her unwelcome guests, and she did whatever she could to make the dinner hour her only point of contact with Will and Senena. She took to riding the eight miles to Tregarnedd, passing the mornings with Catherine. In the afternoons, she and Glynis went for long walks around Rhosyr, and when Glynis fretted that Llewelyn would not approve of them wandering about unescorted, Joanna then refused even Glynis's company, continued her walks in defiant solitude.

Ordinarily, she walked in the meadows near Rhosyr, taking care not to venture into the marshlands that lay off to the west, where the River Cefni wound its way to the sea. But on this particular afternoon she wandered down to the beach. The strait was rough, the winds coming not from the usual south-west, but from the east, what the Welsh called *gwynt coch Amythig*, the red wind of Shrewsbury. Joanna was just about to turn back when she rounded a sand dune, saw Will de Braose standing by the water's edge. She spun about,

679

but not in time. Topaz had begun to bark, and she heard Will calling her name.

He was panting slightly by the time he reached her. 'Why are you so set upon avoiding me?'

His smile was challenging enough to sting her into a rude rejoinder. 'Possibly because I do not like you much.'

Undisturbed, he laughed. 'Do you know what I think? I think you're afraid of me.'

Even after so many years in Wales, Joanna knew but one Welsh obscenity. She used it now, snapping, '*Twll dy dîn*,' and then turning on her heel. Will caught up with her in two strides and, still laughing, put his hand upon her arm.

Joanna gave him no chance to speak. She pulled free, faced him with such fury that his laughter stilled. 'If you ever touch me again, I will have you taken by force to Dolbadarn Castle and confined there till my husband's return.'

He arched a brow. 'I do not think your husband would like that. He gave orders that I was to be well treated.'

At this moment Joanna did not much care what Llewelyn liked or not, and she almost blurted that out, catching herself just in time. 'You've had one warning,' she said coldly. 'That is all you get.' And this time when she turned away, he made no attempt to stop her.

On one of her walks, Joanna had come upon an abandoned hut. A simple wattle-and-daub structure, circular in shape, it put Joanna in mind of the *hafods* she'd so often seen on the mainland, rudely built houses occupied only during those summer months when the Welsh drove their flocks to higher pastures. It surprised her to find a *hafod* here on the flatlands; she could only surmise that some unknown herdsman had once sought to fatten his sheep on the salty marsh grass. Whatever the reason for its existence, Joanna was grateful for the discovery, for October was a month of sudden rains and the hut provided welcome shelter, a solitary refuge from the antagonisms and tensions swirling about Rhosyr.

As the days drew closer to October 19, Joanna was caught up in a treacherous tide from her past, a backwash of painful memories. John always weighed heavier on her thoughts as the anniversary of his death approached, but never so oppressively as this. Suddenly she found herself yearning to make a pilgrimage to Worcester, to pray in the shadow of her father's tomb and have a Requiem Mass said for his tormented soul. So very strong was the urge that it invoked in her a sense of superstitious unease; what if John himself were struggling to reach her, beseeching her help in escaping the sufferings of Purgatory? But even if it were truly so, she was powerless, trapped in Wales by yet another of her husband's wars.

That was unfair to Llewelyn and she knew it, knew this latest war had been Hubert de Burgh's doing. But she was not particularly concerned about fairness, not on this grey October noon after yet another sleepless night, a night of tallying up grievances, marital debts long overdue. How fair was Llewelyn being to her? Was it fair to send Will de Braose to their court, knowing how she dreaded contact with any member of Maude's family? Was it fair to let a full month of silence go by? And when he returned, what then?

Would he expect her to beg his forgiveness, to disavow the action that might well have saved Davydd's life? Yet if he was still angry, what choice would she have? She'd have to placate him, to be properly remorseful and contrite if that was what it took to heal her marriage. And while she did not question the cost, for she loved her husband, she could muster up no eagerness for a reconciliation such as that.

Glynis had insisted upon packing a basket for her, and when it began to rain, Joanna spread a blanket upon the *hafod* floor, prepared to eat a picnic meal under Topaz's hopeful eye. The sun soon broke through the cloud cover, spangling the dripping trees with iridescent light and giving false promise of abiding summer warmth. However brief this respite from the rain, it was heralded in with a resurgence of meadowland music, the trills of thrush and wren, the raucous cawing of jackdaw. Joanna even thought she heard the nightjar's whistle and quickly crossed herself, for it was known to the Welsh as the *Aderyn Corff*, the Corpse Bird.

When Topaz bounded up, darted for the door, Joanna rose, too. Although she reached for her eating knife at sound of the dog's barking, hers was a gesture more of inbred caution than of alarm, for she knew there were neither wolves nor boars on the island and she did not fear men; it was inconceivable to her that any Welshman would dare to offer insult or injury to Llewelyn's wife. 'Topaz, come!' she called and the dog came frisking back into the *hafod*. A moment later a man's shadow fell across the doorway, blocking out the sun.

'Jesu, but you're a hard woman to track down,' Will complained, bending over to pat the spaniel, who was – to Joanna's intense annoyance – fawning upon him as if he were family.

'You admit it, then?' she demanded. 'You were following me?'

'Of course I was. I had no choice, what with you bound and determined to shun me at court. I thought if I could find you alone, mayhap you'd not be so quick to bolt.'

Joanna was infuriated by the imagery his words suggested, that she was a skittish, high-strung filly to be gentled with soft words and sugar lumps. She was also faintly afraid, instinctively sensing danger of some sort. 'I do not want you here. And if you do not leave, I shall.'

He shrugged, moved aside so he no longer blocked the doorway. Nor did he attempt to touch her as she brushed past him. But as she stepped out into the sunlight, he said softly, 'You truly are afraid of me, Joanna. Why?'

Joanna stopped, turned reluctantly back to face him. 'Just what do you want from me?'

'To talk. I think I owe you an apology.' He was standing in shadow and she moved cautiously back into the *hafod* so she could see his face. He did not seem to be mocking her, but she was still assailed by doubts; who knew the depths of those inscrutable grey eyes?

'You said you like me not. I expect I gave you cause, that night at Chester Castle. But you do not strike me as a woman who'd nurse a grudge. Can we not agree that I was in my cups and put it behind us?'

'Yes . . . if I could be sure you mean what you say.'

'I do.' He smiled, ever so slightly. 'I cannot say I regret kissing you; that would be both unchivalrous and untrue. But I do regret hurting you, and I regret lying to you.'

Joanna took a step closer. 'Lying to me? When?'

'When I told you I now believed in blood guilt for women. For I do not, Joanna, not for you.'

Joanna bit her lip, said nothing. Rarely had she been so torn, so pulled by ambivalent emotions. Will's words could not have been better calculated to disarm her defences; she wanted to believe him, to believe Maude's ghost could be exorcized at long last. But a second self stood apart and jeered; what was this if not the sugar lump? She wavered, and then chose to heed the voice of her heart. 'I would rather bury a grudge than nurture it. If you truly want that night forgotten, it is, then.'

Will smiled. 'Let us say, then, that we are friends reunited for the first time in many years, that we last met on that beach at Cricieth? Agreed?' And when she nodded, he gestured towards the basket. 'Have you enough for two? I'm famished.'

Taking her consent for granted, he sat down on the blanket, began to root in the basket. 'Glory to God, roast chicken!' he exclaimed, with such boyish exuberance, such irrepressible enthusiasm that Joanna could not help herself; she sat down, too.

Will pushed the basket towards her. 'Now that I think on it, I lied to you once before. You remember asking me why I'd come to your rescue that day on the beach? I told you it was because I wanted to do Gruffydd an ill turn, and that was true enough. But it was more than that. I was rather taken with you, Lady Joanna, thought you quite the most alluring, exotic creature I'd ever seen!' He grinned suddenly. 'Every lad should have a memory like that tucked away, remembrances of a beautiful older woman who helped to guide him along the way to manhood. Regrettably, we never reached that road, but –'

Joanna suspected she should be offended, but in all honesty, she was not. Instead, she felt a certain guilty pleasure in knowing Will found her desirable, even now at thirty-and-seven. But she did not think it wise to allow the conversation to take too intimate a turn, and she said hastily, 'Will, I think I'd best say this plain out. I know that for many wives the line between friendship and flirtation blurs, but not for me. I want a friend, not a lover.'

Will laughed. 'Who has been telling tales on me . . . Gwladys?' He was one of those men who talked with his hands and as he gestured now, he brought his drum stick too close to Topaz's nose. She took that as an invitation, snatched it as Will gave a startled yelp and Joanna cried:

'Stop her, Will! A chicken bone can choke her!'

It took several chaotic moments before they managed to retrieve the bone from the disgruntled dog. Will finally collapsed, laughing, on the blanket as Joanna stripped the bone of meat, hand fed it to Topaz. 'I cannot believe all this bother about a dog. Are you always so tender of those you love? If so, your husband is indeed a lucky man.'

'Yes,' Joanna said, very evenly, 'he is.' Will was sucking on a finger, claiming the dog had bitten him. His hair had tumbled down across his forehead; it shone like silver where the sun touched it, and she wondered how it would feel. 'I ought to be getting back,' she said abruptly, and he sat up at once, began to protest.

'Not yet. If you go, I'll have nothing to do but return to Rhosyr, brood about the exorbitant ransom your husband will demand for my release. Or try to coax a civil word from the sour-tongued Senena. On my first day here, I did but bid her good morrow and she drew back her skirts as if she'd just come across a pox-ridden beggar!'

Joanna had to laugh. 'You have not changed as much as I first thought,' she said and Will grinned.

'By all accounts, that holds true for Gruffydd, too. He was God's greatest fool at fourteen, is no less of one today. Tell me, Joanna, just how did he end up at Deganwy Castle? I've been indulging in some discreet eavesdropping, enough to gather you had a hand in it.'

Joanna's jaw muscles tensed. 'Yes,' she said defiantly. 'I did. I deliberately provoked Gruffydd into a heedless rage, hoping he'd force my husband into banishing him. Why? Are you going to stand in judgment upon me, too? I suppose you think a woman has no right to meddle in the concerns of men, that I ought to have done nothing, just let my son lose –'

'Do I get a chance to speak? I think you ought to be proud of yourself.'

'Truly?' Joanna said uncertainly. 'You mean that?'

'Indeed I do. I'll grant you I might feel differently if you were my wife and pulled such a trick on me. But since you are not, I am free to give credit where due. It was a deed well done, Joanna. Just think upon what befell Rhys Gryg last year. His own son lured him to Llanarthneu, took him prisoner and held him till he agreed to yield Llandovery Castle. Gruffydd may be half-mad; in truth, I think he is. But so is a wood-hound and if it bites you, you're like to die.'

'You do understand! I had to give Davydd time to reach manhood, Will, had to put him first.'

He nodded. 'Is this why you've been so unhappy, Joanna? Because your husband blames you for what happened?'

Joanna had no intention whatsoever of discussing either her unhappiness or Llewelyn's anger. 'My husband does not blame me, Will. If I've seemed disquieted, it is because of Senena.' Casting about for a safer topic of conversation, she said hurriedly, 'But I do not want to talk of her. I'd rather hear about you. I know you wed the Earl of Pembroke's sister. And I seem to remember Gwladys telling me you have daughters. How old are they? What are their names?'

'Daughters I have, indeed, in over-abundance,' he said ruefully. 'No less than four! My oldest is nigh on nine, the youngest still in her cradle. We christened them with the family names of de Braose and Marshal; Isabella, Eva, Eleanor . . . and Maude.'

Maude. Of course he'd have named a daughter after the grandmother he loved. Fool that she was, had she truly thought they could ever be friends? Joanna rose, sought to busy herself in brushing off her skirt. 'I have to go,' she said, not meeting his eyes.

He rose, too. 'Joanna, wait. There is something I must ask you. Your son Davydd told me that you and John were estranged during the last years of his life. Is that true?'

'I do not want to talk about it, Will.'

'Joanna, I want – nay, need to know.'

Joanna's throat had tightened. 'Why? What does it matter now?'

'It matters,' he said grimly. 'You could not have loved him, not a man like that. What sort of father could he have been? The Angevin temper was one with legend. The Devil's brood. And John . . . John was the worst of the lot. You had to have suffered at his hands, to have feared him.'

'No, Will. No, it . . . it was not like that. My father was always good to me.'

'I do not believe that, do not believe you. Why do you defend him to me? Christ, if any man knows the truth about John, I do!'

'I am not defending him! I am not denying what he has done. You have every reason to hate him. But I will not lie to you. Whatever evil he may have committed, he was still a kind father, even a loving one.'

'A loving father? God in Heaven, do you hear yourself? He was accursed, utterly evil and beyond redemption, and for you to –'

'No!' Joanna's voice was shaking. 'My father repented his sins, died in God's grace. His soul is in Purgatory, not in Hell. The Almighty says there is forgiveness for all, that –'

'Not for John. Never for John!'

'Do not say that!' Joanna was appalled. 'He did repent ere he

685

died and God will forgive him. He was not utterly evil, he was not! He was capable of kindness, too, and the Almighty will take that into account when judging him.'

'Kind? Because he gave you hair ribbons and sugared quince? Do you truly think such trifles can be balanced against the gallows, the rotting bodies?'

'I was not talking of trifles!' Joanna drew a laboured breath, sought to call to mind John's acts of charity, of compassion. 'My father truly loved England, as his father and brother did not. And he cared for his subjects' weal. He was the most accessible of kings, was hearing appeals even whilst fighting for his throne, that last fortnight of his life.'

When Will would have interrupted, she cried, 'No, hear me out! You asked for particulars and you shall have them. The son of a friend was recently stricken with leprosy. I know I need not tell you the horrors of such a fate. Yet as pitiful as the leper's plight is, it can be even more wretched if his king or lord lacks pity. Under such lords, lepers have oft-times been burnt, even buried alive. But my father did pity them, Will, and he did whatever he could to ease their travail. At Shrewsbury, he entitled the lepers to a portion of all flour sold at market. At Bristol, he granted lepers a settlement of their own, where they could dwell under the protection of the Crown. He even founded St Leonard's Hospital at Lancaster long ere he became King, when he was but two-and-twenty! Do such acts sound like trifles to you? Would a man utterly evil care for the least of his brethren?'

'You want to talk of John's pity? Let's begin then at Windsor Castle. I am sure my grandmother and uncle were fearful, for they knew John well. But I doubt even they could have guessed what he had in mind for them. They were dragged to an underground dungeon, thrust into the dark and left to die. They were given no candles, no water, no food but a basket of oats and an uncooked ham. For ten days they were left alone in that hellhole, with the door barred against their screams. On the eleventh day the guards entered the cell, found them both dead. There was no way of knowing just when they'd died, how long their suffering had lasted. The guards could tell, though, that my uncle had died first and that my grandmother had gone mad at the last. Shall I tell you why, Joanna? Shall I tell you how they knew that?'

'No,' she whispered. 'No, please . . .'

686

'Because my uncle's cheek was bitten and chewed, as if gnawed by a rat. But it was not a rat who'd eaten his flesh, it was his own mother. Those were her teeth marks in his face. That was what she'd been driven to in the final hours of her life, by your father, by the man you call kind!'

He'd grasped Joanna's wrist, forcing her to listen. When he released her, she stumbled backward, fled the hut. Her stomach was heaving and she fell to her knees on the grass, lay prone as the trees whirled above her head, spinning in sickening circles. She clutched tufts of grass, clung as if the earth itself were falling away from her. She was weeping as Will knelt beside her. Gathering her into his arms, he held her as if she were a child, and for a time there was no sound but that of her choked sobbing, the whimpering of her spaniel.

'I'm going to take you back inside now.' The voice was so gentle that she wondered if it was truly Will's, but she obediently put her arms around his neck, and he lifted her up, carried her back to the shelter of the *hafod*. 'Here,' he said, handing her his flask. 'Drink.' She did; the liquid was warm and so spiced that she choked anew. It burned her throat, set her head to spinning. She drank again, at his insistence, shook her head weakly when he offered the flask a third time.

The last of her tears squeezed through her lashes. 'Will, I'm sorry, so sorry . . .'

'So am I, Joanna. I ought never to have told you that. There've been times,' he confessed, 'when I'd have given up my chances of salvation if only I'd not known, if only I could forget . . .'

Joanna shuddered. 'How could your father have told you? Why did you have to know?'

He reached out, touched her tear-stained face. 'You were weeping for me? For that fourteen-year-old boy?'

Joanna shuddered again, and when he put his arm around her, she did not move away. 'There was no need for you to know, no need . . .' She turned so she could look up into his face, into eyes fringed with surprisingly long, fair lashes. 'You were so young. How could you live with pain like that?'

'By learning to hate. Not just John. The men he trusted, the men who waxed fat on his favour, men like Hubert de Burgh and Peter des Roches. Your uncle Salisbury.'

'And me?'

687

'I wanted to hate you, thought I did . . . until I saw you again at Chester Castle. But you know that, Joanna. You know how much I wanted you, how much I want you right now.'

'Will, I cannot . . .' But he was leaning towards her, covered her mouth with his. His breathing had quickened, but there was no urgency in his kiss, not yet. It was both unexpected and reassuring, this gentleness; he had about him such unsettling undertones of violence that it was startling, somehow, to find he could be so tender a lover. Joanna knew she had to protest now, while there was still time for protesting, for thinking. But when he kissed her again, she found herself responding, kissing him back.

He was too practised for awkward fumbling with clothing, slid his hand into the bodice of her gown. She gasped as he cupped her breast and he gave a low laugh. 'God, how I want you! It'll be so good, I promise you . . .' And for Joanna, there was only that moment, the feel of his hands on her bared skin, and an urgency to match his own. When he lowered her back on to the blanket, she reached up, drew him down into an impassioned embrace, and it was not long before he was murmuring, 'Now, love. Spread your thighs for me. Ah, yes, yes . . .' There was a tense moment in which they feared he was too ready, too eager. But he was able to keep control, moving slowly at first, deliberately, until Joanna moaned, dug her nails into his neck, and then he did lose control, but it no longer mattered; there was for them both a shattering release, convulsive and complete.

Will was the first to move, shifting his weight off Joanna and sitting up. She lay still, her head turned away until he tugged gently on her braid, compelling her towards him. Leaning over, he kissed her possessively on the mouth. 'You were worth waiting for,' he said, smiling, and Joanna flushed even darker.

'What have I done, Will?' Her voice was muffled, almost inaudible. 'My God, what have I done?'

He tilted her chin up, forcing her to meet his eyes. 'What you wanted to do. For you did want me, Joanna, just as much as I wanted you.'

Joanna's lashes swept down, shadowing her cheek. Sitting up, she pulled her skirt down, began relacing her bliaut. Her fingers were unsteady, but when Will reached over to help, she shook her head. She was on her feet now, retrieving her mantle from the floor. 'Will . . . I have to go.'

He rose without haste, draped her mantle about her shoulders.

'Give me a minute to make myself presentable and I'll walk back with you.'

'No!' She pulled away, staring at him with such wide, frightened eyes that he was both touched and amused.

'What do you fear, Joanna? That people need only glance at us now to know?' Laughing, he caught her by the shoulders, drew her back into his arms. 'My love, it does not show in your face. You look no different.'

'I feel different. I feel . . .' Joanna's mouth twisted. She turned away, moved rapidly to the door.

'Joanna.' She paused, with obvious reluctance, and he said, 'I shall be here at noon on the morrow.'

'No,' she said. 'No.'

'I'll be waiting for you.'

His words stayed with her as she walked back towards Rhosyr. 'I'll be waiting for you.' He'd smiled, as if her denial meant nothing, as if sure she'd come to him. Joanna stopped abruptly, stood motionless for so long that Topaz began to whine. Kneeling there on the path, Joanna put her arms around the dog. 'What am I to do?' she whispered. 'Lady Mary . . .' But she could not pray. Hers was a mortal sin. She had betrayed her marriage vows, betrayed her husband. And on the morrow, what then? For Will was right. She had wanted him, was as much to blame for what happened as he. She did not understand it, could not fully believe it even now, but she could not deny it. She did want Will.

Will reached the *hafod* well before noon. Joanna had been too distraught to think of the blanket and basket. The former lay as they'd left it, still rumpled from the weight of their bodies, but the basket had been overturned, emptied by scavenging animals. Will righted the basket, smoothed the blanket, and sat down to wait. At 12.30 he left the *hafod*, stood for some moments squinting up at the sun. He was turning to go back inside when he heard a dog bark. Several birds broke cover, went winging over the hut. The spaniel appeared first, with Joanna following much more slowly.

She was so tense, her approach so hesitant that Will instinctively stayed quite still. She reminded him of a woodland creature, one not tamed and poised for flight, and he said, very quietly, 'I was beginning to fear you were not coming.'

'I did not think I was.'

They regarded each other in rapt silence until Will deemed it safe to move. Stepping towards her, he took her hand. 'I thought about you half the night. I kept remembering how you wept, wept for my pain.' He smiled, his familiar smile of self-mockery, but to Joanna, it was unexpectedly suggestive of sadness. 'Over the years many women have wept because of me. But I honestly could recall nary a one weeping for me . . . just you.'

Joanna had wept again at night, lying alone in Llewelyn's bed. But she did not know if her tears were for the boy Will had been or for this madness that had so suddenly come upon her, that had brought her back to the *hafod*, to Will. She closed her eyes, but could still see him behind her lids: tousled hair, streaked by the sun, thin mobile mouth, golden lashes and beard, details she'd not even been aware of noticing, a small scar on his right temple, a shaving scratch on his throat. He was very close now; she could feel his breath on her cheek. Her lashes lifted and she saw his mouth soften, curve just before he kissed her.

In the days that followed, Joanna felt as if she were drifting farther and farther from shore, from the sureties of the world she knew, the world she was terrified of losing. She had no appetite at mealtimes, and sleep eluded her; she lay awake some nights till dawn, rose hollow-eyed and racked with guilt, unable to understand why she was jeopardizing her marriage, perhaps even her life, for a man she did not truly know, and yet unable to stay away from him. She knew she did not love him. The sexual attraction between them was undeniably intense and had been since that night at Chester Castle, for she could see that now, could acknowledge it had first flared on that darkened stairway in Cæsar's Tower. But could she be so foolish as to risk so much for that, for lust? Why, then, had she never been tempted ere this? Why had she never even fantasized about any man but Llewelyn?

Llewelyn. What would he do if her sin was found out? Joanna thought of the French Queen Ingeborg, held fast at Étampes Castle for no fault of her own. She thought of the innocent Lady Alys, confined by Richard in Rouen for six long years. And she thought of the look on Llewelyn's face should he ever learn of her infidelity. But each afternoon she found herself walking in the meadows, towards the *hafod* where Will awaited her.

They would make love on the blanket and for a brief while Joanna could forget her fears, even her guilt. Sometimes they would eat food Will smuggled from Rhosyr, and they would talk. Lying with his head in her lap, Will was relaxed enough to let down some of his defences, to trust her with an occasional truth. He spoke of his boyhood at Bramber and Buellt, of his exile in France, conceded he'd earned his reputation for reckless risk-taking. He was intelligent, ambitious, and could be very amusing. He was also cynical and not overly burdened with scruples, was quite candid in admitting that when he wanted something, he set out to get it, rarely counting the cost. But every now and then Joanna would catch glimpses of another Will, glimpses of the boy he'd been and the man he might have become, and at such moments she would feel the sadness of loss and yet at the same time, a curious sense of vindication.

She encouraged him to talk about Maude, and as painful as it was, forced herself to listen attentively, prompted by a hazy hope that dwelling upon happier memories might somehow help him to forget the other, the horror. He talked sometimes of John, with such venom that she suspected he was testing her. She listened in silence to these embittered outbursts, without protest. It shamed her to remember her yearning to visit Worcester, to pray at John's tomb. Each time she thought of what had happened in the darkness of that Windsor dungeon, she was overcome with revulsion and self-loathing. To love a man capable of such cruelty was to condone it, even to make herself an accomplice of sorts. And yet she had loved him, loved him and then grieved for him. Topaz rings and Maltese lapdogs and honeyed words. How cheaply she'd sold herself. How little it had taken to claim her heart.

'How could you have been so rash? Whatever were you thinking of, Will?'

At first Will had been amused by Joanna's anger, but he was beginning to lose patience. 'This is ridiculous, Joanna. All I did was to greet you when you entered the hall. I kissed your hand. Why should that give rise to gossip?'

'You kissed my palm, a lover's kiss! Jesus God, Will, what if someone had seen?'

He shrugged. 'But no one did, so why are you so fretful?'

'Because Senena was standing not five feet away! You know how she hates me. If she ever suspected –'

691

He stepped towards her, silenced her with a lingering kiss. 'Forget about Senena, love. Let's not waste time quarrelling.'

'I do not want to quarrel. But it frightens me, Will, that you would take such a risk, and it frightens me even more that you seem to find it amusing.' Will was not listening, though, had pulled her back against him, encircling her within his arms, kissing her throat. Joanna yielded, allowed him to draw her down on to the blanket. 'Promise me,' she said huskily. 'Promise me you'll not be so reckless.'

It may have been the quarrel, the fact that they'd resolved nothing. It may have been her realization that Will was excited by the dangers of discovery, by the very risks she found so frightening. But for the first time the magic failed to take. She could not shut off her thoughts, could not surrender unconditionally to her body's needs, was unable to reach climax. And afterwards she was caught up in despair, hers the panicked sensations of a swimmer swept far beyond her depth. She turned on her side so Will would not see she wept. Never had her sense of foreboding been so strong, a terrified certainty that this could only end in tragedy. The Lord God was a God of wrath, would punish her for so great a sin, would punish her and Will as they deserved. But what of Llewelyn? He would also suffer for her sin, and where was the fairness in that?

Will had been disappointed by their lovemaking; he was too experienced not to know when a woman's response was genuine and when it was feigned. He was irked now by her prolonged silence, and he wondered why women had to complicate things so unduly, why they had to bring so much baggage into bed with them, remorse and regrets and, inevitably, recriminations. Such qualms rarely stopped them from sinning, he thought, just from truly enjoying it. He'd hoped Joanna might be different, should have known what a frail hope that was. Knight's widow or king's daughter, there was not one of them who seemed capable of taking her pleasure as she found it, not even a woman like Joanna, as passionate as any he'd ever bedded.

'Are you still vexed about Senena? Or are you having conscience pangs?'

'Is that so surprising? Need I remind you that adultery is a sin?'

Will sighed, raised himself up on his elbow. 'What kind of sins are there, Joanna?'

'What kinds? Mortal and venial,' she said, sounding puzzled, and he shook his head.

'No, my love. There are secret sins and found-out sins, and it is foolish to worry about the first until it becomes the second. Think on it, Joanna. Who are we hurting as long as no one knows?' Leaning over, he nuzzled her neck. 'You're not the fool most women are, ought to have learned that lesson by now.'

He meant that as a compliment, for he truly did think she was more intelligent than most of her sex, and he was taken aback by her reaction. She sat up abruptly, gave him a look of utter outrage.

'And just how am I to have learned such a lesson? By practice? You think I've done this before?'

'You're saying you've never taken a lover? I'm the first?' Will was surprised and pleased, but somewhat sceptical, too, and it showed in his face. Joanna jumped to her feet, began tugging at her dishevelled clothing. He rose, too, put a hand upon her arm.

'I did not mean to offend you, love. I just did not expect it. You are a beautiful woman, after all, must have had more than your share of offers.'

'And you think that is what determines infidelity – opportunity?' Joanna was even angrier because she saw he was not taking her anger seriously. 'By your measure, the only wife to be trusted would be the one plain as homespun. How does your own wife figure in your calculations, Will? I hear she's a handsome woman; so am I to assume, then, that she takes lovers?'

'No.' His voice was suddenly sharp. 'No, she does not.'

'I see.' Joanna reached for her mantle, fumbled with the catch. He stepped in front of her, barring her way.

'Joanna, you do not understand.'

'You explain it to me then, Will. Explain why it is right for me to dishonour my marriage vows and wrong for your wife.'

'This is such an absurd argument, so utterly needless. Your pride is too tender, love; you see insults where none were intended. If you say I am your first lover, of course I believe you. And in truth, I'm very flattered.' He sought to unfasten the catch of her mantle. 'Do not go, not yet.' The mantle slipped from her shoulders, fell to the floor at her feet. 'Stay with me,' he said coaxingly. 'Do you not want to?'

'Yes,' Joanna confessed. 'I hate to quarrel. But can you not see why I was upset? I know what we are doing is wrong, cannot pretend otherwise. And for all your talk of secret sins, you know it, too, Will. If adultery is a sin for your wife, it is no less a sin for me. And if –'

693

'Will you forget about Eva? I was not saying that Eva is more virtuous than you. If her circumstances were like unto yours, she, too, might stray. That is all I meant, love, I swear.'

Joanna was not mollified, for he had inflicted a hurt no less painful for being unintentional. 'How are my circumstances so different from Eva's?'

Ignoring her challenging tone, he put his arms around her, drew her close. She stood irresolute for a moment, and then, as his hands slid up from her waist to her breasts, she sighed softly, rested her head against his chest.

'Well, to begin with, your blood runs much hotter than Eva's.' He laughed, and Joanna bit her lip to keep from laughing, too.

'You have a wicked tongue,' she chided. 'A man should not talk so of his wife.'

'Not even to his mistress? I do but speak the truth. You are more passionate than Eva. Fairer to look upon. Far more exciting in bed. I do not doubt Eva could have been quite content in a nunnery. Could you say the same, sweetheart?' he teased, and to his delighted amusement, Joanna actually blushed. 'No, my love, you could not. It's more than a waste, it's a crime against nature to fetter a woman like you to an aging husband.'

Joanna wrenched free. 'How dare you!' Her voice was low, but so full of rage that for a moment Will merely stared at her in surprise.

'Joanna?' He moved towards her, but she backed away, out of reach. He'd never seen eyes as green as hers, and he found himself thinking suddenly of the tales he'd heard of her fabled grandmother, the outrageous and autocratic Eleanor of Aquitaine. But he was rapidly tiring of these displays of Angevin temper. 'Now what's wrong? Jesu, but your nerves are on the raw today! I did but speak another truth, that you are wed to a man much older than you. Nigh on twenty years older. I am being blunt, but not unkind. A man cannot be blamed for growing old. But neither can a woman for wanting what he can no longer give. So what harm if we –'

'You fool!' Joanna all but spat the words. 'You vain, boastful fool. You talk so glibly about truths. Let me give you one, then. Yes, Llewelyn is five-and-fifty and you're but two-and-thirty. But for all that, he is twice the man you could ever hope to be, in bed or out!'

'Is he now?' Will had gone rigid, first incredulous and then infuriated. 'Then suppose you tell me this. If you're such a satisfied

694

wife, why have I been able to tumble you all week on the floor of this stinking *hafod*?'

Joanna had begun to tremble. 'I do not know,' she admitted, sounding not so much angry now as despairing. 'God help me, I do not know. But no more. May the Blessed Mary be my witness, no more!'

Snatching up her mantle, she whirled, ran from the *hafod*, ran until she was sobbing for breath, ran until the meadows were misted by a light, warming rain and she saw ahead the distant timbered walls of Llewelyn's manor.

Joanna left Rhosyr that same afternoon, was gone by the time Will returned to the manor. Catherine showed no surprise at her unexpected arrival, welcomed her as if hers was a visit planned long in advance. She found some comfort in Catherine's quiet company, but Catherine could not give her the advice she most needed, could not tell her what to do about Will. Joanna dared not confide in her, could not even risk confessing to her chaplain. Until she could find a way to confess in anonymity, she must live with a mortal sin upon her soul. As frightened as she was at being denied absolution, she was even more fearful of blaspheming her vow. She had sworn to the Blessed Virgin that she would not bed with Will again. And she had to keep that vow. She had betrayed Llewelyn, betrayed herself. She could not betray the Lady Mary, too. But could she trust herself? She must pray for strength, must find it in her to resist temptation. And she must somehow see to it that she and Will were never alone again.

Joanna passed three days at Tregarnedd, returned to Rhosyr with great reluctance. The sun had been elusive all morning, making weak forays through the clouds rolling in off the Irish Sea, and by the time Joanna dismounted in the manor bailey, she could no longer see her shadow.

'Have Madlen see to the unpacking, Glynis. I'm sure she's done not a stitch of work whilst we were gone.' Topaz was sprinting towards her and Joanna bent down, gathered the whimpering little animal into her arms, absurdly grateful for at least one heartfelt welcome.

'Mama!'

'Davydd?' She straightened up, watched wordlessly as her son

695

hastened towards her. As he'd grown into manhood, he'd become less and less given to public displays of affection. But he showed no such reticence now, embraced Joanna warmly.

'When did you get back? Davydd, why did you not send word to Tregarnedd?'

'We rode in last night, would have dispatched a messenger this morn.'

'But why are you back so soon? Your father . . . he's not hurt? Davydd, tell me if –'

'He's fine, Mama, truly. He's in the great hall, discussing ransom terms with Will de Braose. All is well, could not be better. We won, Mama. The war is over.'

'Llewelyn . . . Llewelyn is with Will?'

Davydd nodded. 'Have you no questions for me? Do you not want to hear how we triumphed over the English? We gave them no respite, harassed them day and night, finally forced them to make peace. We met with Henry and Hubert de Burgh and they agreed to dismantle Hubert's new castle, to withdraw at once from Ceri, whilst Papa agreed to assume the costs of the expedition. That was truly clever of him, Mama, for Henry is now grateful to Papa for helping him save face, and he's begun to blame de Burgh for the entire debacle.' Davydd grinned. 'Papa can put a fox to shame at times. And the best part of the jest is this. The three thousand marks Papa is to pay Henry – that is the amount he is demanding for Will's release!'

'And Will agreed to this? He is to be freed?'

'Well, there's more to it than that, but I'll let Papa tell you the rest. Come on, let's tell him you're here.' When Joanna did not move, Davydd turned back with a quizzical smile. 'Mama? Are you not coming?'

'No, I . . . I want to change my gown first. I was not expecting . . .' Joanna's voice trailed off in confusion, but Davydd just laughed.

'Mama, you look fine,' he insisted, as Glynis chimed in, assuring Joanna that the gown was quite becoming.

'But . . . but it's green,' Joanna said, very low, and both Davydd and Glynis looked at her in surprise.

'Mama, green is your favourite colour!'

Joanna said nothing. Green was her favourite and most flattering hue. It was also the symbolic shade of fidelity. Abandoning further protests, she allowed Davydd to lead her into the hall.

Davydd was still talking about their campaign, laughing as he told her de Burgh's half-built castle was now known as 'Hubert's Folly'. But Joanna was no longer listening. Llewelyn and Will were seated together by the open hearth; they seemed surprisingly at ease with one another, were talking with animation, and as she watched, they exchanged smiles. And then they were turning, getting to their feet as she walked towards them.

Joanna's mouth was suddenly parched; she sought to shape it into a smile, said as calmly as she could, 'Welcome home, Llewelyn.' Had they been alone, she would have waited for his rejoinder, taken her cue from that. But with Will's eyes upon her, she felt she had no choice but to step forward, to kiss Llewelyn lightly on the mouth. His response told her nothing; even if he were still furious with her, he'd never have been so churlish as to rebuff her in public. His face was impassive; as well as she knew him, she could not read his expression.

'You look pale,' he said. 'Have you been ailing?'

She shook her head, started visibly when Will chose that moment to interject himself into the conversation. 'I'm glad you're back, Madame. I confess it was rather lonely here the past few days, what with both you and the Lady Senena gone.' And then, before she could anticipate him, he caught her hand, brought it up to his mouth, with impeccable manners and laughing eyes.

Joanna's reaction was instinctive and vehement; she jerked her hand away. They were all staring at her now, Will with poorly concealed amusement, Davydd with surprise, and Llewelyn with a look that brought the blood up into her face, a look of curiosity . . . and conjecture. 'Actually, you were right, Llewelyn,' she said unsteadily. 'I do not feel well. If you'll excuse me, I think I shall go and lie down.' Not waiting, not daring to wait, she turned and walked swiftly from the hall, feeling their eyes upon her all the while.

Upon reaching her bedchamber, Joanna dismissed her maids. She'd decided she really would lie down, hoping in that way to avoid a discussion with Llewelyn should he seek her out. She stripped to her chemise, began to unbraid her hair. But her fingers had become infuriatingly clumsy; she kept dropping hairpins and brush, even a small glass bottle of her favourite scent. Glass was very much a luxury and this perfume vial was of a particularly delicate design, the handiwork of a Genoan master craftsman. With a cry of dismay,

697

Joanna knelt, began to search the rushes for the broken shards. But once she'd salvaged the fragments, she saw the bottle was beyond repair. She stared down at the glass splinters, and suddenly her eyes were brimming over with tears. Sitting on the floor in the middle of her bedchamber, she began to cry.

Llewelyn found himself hesitating before the door, not at all sure what sort of reception he would get. The memory came to him then of another quarrel with Joanna, another occasion when he'd stood before a bedchamber door, reluctant to go in. The memory was very vivid for being more than twenty years old; it had been their first true quarrel, but a memorable reconciliation, leading to the consummation of their marriage. He no longer hesitated, reached for the latch.

'Joanna?' He was beside her at once, brushing back the cascading dark hair that hid her face. At his touch, she fell forward into his arms, buried her face in his shoulder. Her sobbing was spasmodic, out of control, but he was more alarmed by her violent trembling, like one with the ague. He was baffled to discover that she was clutching several broken pieces of glass; he had to pry her fingers loose before she'd drop them. In all the years of their marriage, he'd never seen her weep like this, as a maltreated child might weep, helplessly, utterly without hope.

When he lifted her in his arms, she felt as light as a child, too, frighteningly fragile. After putting her down upon the bed, he started to rise, but she clung to him and he sat beside her, holding her as she wept.

At last her sobs began to subside. She no longer sounded so incoherent and he leaned over, put his lips to her forehead. Although she did not feel feverish, he was not yet reassured. 'Shall I summon my physician?'

Her head moved on the pillow, tossed emphatically from side to side. He rose, crossed to the washing laver and came back to the bed. Joanna stirred when he gently wiped her face with a wet cloth, lay looking up at him with tears silently trickling from the corners of her eyes. 'I'm sorry,' she whispered. 'I'm so sorry. I love you, I do. I never meant for it to happen, I swear it . . .'

'I know that, *breilia*.'

'You . . . you know?'

'Why should that surprise you so? You wanted to see Gruffydd banished, not imprisoned. That was no part of your plan. Did you think I doubted that?'

'Gruffydd.' Joanna closed her eyes. 'No,' she echoed faintly, 'that was no part of my plan . . .'

Llewelyn regarded her in silence for several moments. The signs of strain were much more apparent now than they'd been in the hall, the hollowed cheekbones, the smudges that lurked like bruises under her eyes, the way her fingers plucked aimlessly at the coverlets. 'I thought I knew you so well,' he said, saw her flinch. 'But I could not have misjudged your mood more. I knew you were angry with me, and upset. But I did not understand how truly troubled you were.' Their time apart had been for the best, or so he'd thought, for it had given him the opportunity to come to terms with his own anger, with resentments he alone could resolve. But Joanna's face told him a far different story, told him their estrangement had done much more damage than he'd realized.

Tears still seeped through Joanna's lashes. She had been angry with Llewelyn, very angry. She'd blamed him for his stubbornness, for his unwillingness to understand, for words spoken in anger, slights to her pride, and above all, for that last taunt flung at her as he'd ridden out of the stable. But how insignificant those complaints seemed now, how trivial when weighed against the enormity of her sin, her betrayal.

'Can you forgive me, Llewelyn? In all honesty, can you forgive me?'

'I'll not lie to you, Joanna. You were wrong. You should have come to me, and I'll never fully understand why you did not.' But he spoke without anger, for he'd concluded that he had no choice but to forgive her. If he did not, the grievance was likely to fester, an untreated wound dripping daily poison until, in time, the marriage itself would be infected.

'Yes,' he said, 'I do forgive you,' and it was easier than he'd thought it would be; her contrition was balm in and of itself.

Joanna struggled to sit up. 'Hold me,' she implored. 'Hold me so tightly that I can believe you'll never let me go.'

He obliged with a smile, held her close, listening to the shuddering sounds of her breath, smoothing her long, tangled hair. 'No more tears,' he murmured, 'lest we both become waterlogged.'

'I never wanted you to be hurt, Llewelyn, never. You must believe that, beloved.'

Llewelyn did not want to talk about Gruffydd, did not want to think about Deganwy Castle. 'Hush, *breila*, hush.' He pressed his mouth to her swollen eyelids, continued to stroke her hair. Her perfume was beguilingly familiar; he'd missed her scent, her softness, missed waking up beside her in the morning, reaching for her in the night.

'Are you feeling better now?' When she nodded, he ran his fingers caressingly along her throat. 'Then how would you like to give me a proper welcome home? I did win a war, after all.' He laughed, leaned over to kiss her, utterly taken aback when she recoiled, gasping, 'No!'

'We've played some intriguing games in bed, but I cannot say this one appeals to me, Joanna, would as soon we save it for another time.' He frowned. 'Unless you truly are ailing?'

'No, beloved, I am fine.' Joanna's reaction had been both involuntary and irrational. But for one panicked moment, she'd actually found herself thinking that Llewelyn had only to kiss her to know she'd been unfaithful. 'I did not mean to cry out like that. I am not ailing and it is not the time of my flux. Of course I want to make love with you; when do I not? It's just that . . . that I was expecting Glynis to come in at any moment. If you would but bar the door, my love, I'm sure we can find a game more to your liking.'

She lay back against the pillows. But by the time he returned to the bed, she was beset by a new fear. She felt frozen, numbed, emotionally drained. What if she could not respond to him?

At first she did find it difficult to relax, to blot out all but the feel of his hands and mouth on her body. Llewelyn was in no hurry, though. He'd long ago learned that pleasures could be all the sweeter for being prolonged, but as his body's slowing reflexes compelled him, of necessity, to pace himself more prudently, he'd discovered that delay could act upon a woman as an aphrodisiac; the more drawn-out and deliberate their lovemaking, the more excited his wife became, and he no longer regretted having lost the immediate and urgent arousals of early youth.

He took his time, and slowly, skilfully, he kindled a fire between them, one that burned hot and bright and eventually became all consuming. Joanna drifted back to reality with reluctance. Their lovemaking had been more than a physical bonding, a source of intensely intimate and perfect pleasure. For her, it had been a catharsis. For the first time, she dared hope that she need not lose her husband. She would never forgive herself, but mayhap it was not too late. If she were well and truly contrite, mayhap the Almighty might show mercy, let hers remain one of Will's secret sins. If so, she would devote the rest of her life to making Llewelyn happy. She would gratify his every whim, be the wife he deserved, bedmate, companion, confidante, whatever he wished.

'What are you thinking of, *breila*? You look very far away.'

'No farther than this,' she said, taking his hand and holding it against her heart. 'I'd tell you it beats just for you if I were not fearful you'd think me maudlin, hopelessly lovesick. See? You're laughing at me already.'

'Just a little.' Llewelyn settled himself more comfortably, propped pillows against his back as Joanna rose from the bed, padded barefoot across the chamber to fetch wine. He'd been utterly thankful that she'd been spared the travails of yearly pregnancies, having come so close to losing her in the birthing chamber of Dolwyddelan. But as he looked at her now, he was thinking that there were other benefits, as well, to her subsequent barrenness, for her body had retained the supple muscle tone, the lissome and willowy grace of her youth. His eyes followed the fall of her hair, from breast to hip, and up again to her face. Feeling his gaze upon her, she glanced over her shoulder, smiled radiantly, and he said, 'Joanna, what is there between you and Will de Braose?'

Joanna would never know how she managed to continue pouring wine, how she kept her hand steady. Very carefully, she set the flagon back on the table. 'What do you mean, Llewelyn?'

'The tension in the hall was hard to miss.' His voice was dry, his eyes unwavering upon her face. She gripped the wine cup between her palms, took one quick swallow, and then walked back to the bed. Why had she not foreseen this? Who knew better than she how keen his eye could be?

'You are right,' she said slowly. 'I suppose I was not very good at hiding my feelings. I'm sorry if I was rude. But I find it very difficult to be in Will de Braose's company. You know how I feel about his family. And with Will, it is more than I can bear, for he loved Maude well, and his hatred of John is still green, still very raw. He told me . . . told me that Maude died mad.'

Her shudder was not feigned, was all too real. It did not escape Llewelyn, nor did the sudden reversion back to 'John'. He slid over and she got into bed, handed him the wine cup. 'I thought it was something like that,' he said. 'Ah, lass, I am truly sorry.'

Joanna forced herself to lift her head, to look into his eyes, dark eyes full of intelligence and affection . . . and faith. He loved her, would never suspect her of so base a betrayal. He trusted her. She'd have to bear that to the end of her days, the burden of his trust.

Llewelyn put his arm around her shoulders, drew her down against his chest. 'Would it be easier for you if I moved the court back to Aber, whilst keeping Will here at Rhosyr till his ransom is paid?'

'Jesu, yes! Oh yes, please.' She kissed his throat, blinking back tears. She'd thought she'd reached the nadir of shame and self-loathing on that last day in the *hafod*, raging at Will, at her incredible folly. But it was infinitely worse now, having to lie to Llewelyn, to look into his eyes and take such despicable advantage of his love.

'Joanna, I do understand your feelings for the de Braose family. I know you've never been at ease with any of them. And I would that I could promise you need never set eyes upon Will again. But I cannot.'

'Llewelyn . . . what are you saying? What are you trying to tell me?'

She sounded suddenly so frightened that he frowned, bit his lip. 'I want Buellt Castle, *breila*. I've got to have it, for it commands the upper reaches of the Gwy Valley.'

'I . . . I do not understand. Davydd said Will had agreed to pay you three thousand marks. Surely he'd not yield up Buellt, too?'

'No, of course not. But he is willing to give it as his daughter's marriage portion. That is what I am trying to tell you, Joanna. Will and I have agreed upon an alliance, one secured by wedlock, the marriage of his eldest daughter and our son.'

'Davydd . . . Davydd is to wed Will's daughter?'

'In time. Isabella is but a little lass yet, so I expect they'll only plight troth for now.' Llewelyn leaned over, tenderly kissed Joanna's upturned face. 'I know this does not please you, love, and I am sorry. But it cannot be helped.'

Joanna turned her head into his shoulder, brought her hand up to her mouth, bit down on her fist. She must not laugh. If she did, she'd not be able to stop. Like her mother. So many years ago, but Joanna could still hear her, hear peal after peal of that shrill, hysterical laughter as her mother looked at her, at her bastard child, her 'mistake'. 'We pay and pay for our sins,' she'd gasped. 'We pay and pay.'

702

10

September, 1229

Deganwy, North Wales

Llewelyn's grandsons were standing on the stairs of the keep, watching as he rode through the gateway into the inner bailey. The younger boy, his namesake, was a dark, solemn child, a toddler clutching a bedraggled toy. But Owain could have been a ghost from Llewelyn's past. His hair was redder, brighter than Gruffydd's, and his eyes were grey, but for all that, he looked enough like his father at age ten to evoke memories better left buried.

Whether by inheritance or empathy, Owain had adopted his father's body language as his own; the squared shoulders, the jutting little chin were wrenchingly familiar. 'Why have you come?' he demanded. 'We do not want you here. Go away!'

'Owain, hold your tongue!' Hastening down the stairs, Senena grasped her son by the shoulders. 'How dare you speak to Lord Llewelyn like that? He is your Prince and your grandsire and you owe him respect!'

'But Mama . . .' The boy looked so bewildered that Senena felt a conscience pang; he was, after all, only parroting what he'd heard in their private chamber. She could not risk antagonizing Llewelyn, however, and she said sharply, 'See to your little brother. I shall expect you to apologize to your grandfather ere he leaves.' Moving forward then to greet Llewelyn, she mustered a taut smile. 'It was good of you to come.'

Llewelyn dismounted, tossed the reins to the nearest man. 'You sent word that Gruffydd was asking to see me. Did you think I'd refuse?' He signalled for his men to await him in the great hall, glanced towards Senena and then back again, much more searchingly. 'Senena? Gruffydd did ask for me?'

'No.' Reaching out, she clutched at his arm. 'I lied. I had to lie.

It was all I could think to do. Llewelyn, you must see him, talk to him. Please say you will!'

Llewelyn slowly shook his head. 'I think it better if I do not, Senena. If he does not want to see me, what would it serve?'

'Wait, please. At least hear me out. You want the truth? I'll tell you, tell you whatever you want to know. I've tried so hard to help Gruffydd, to raise his spirits, to keep him from despairing. But he of all men cannot abide confinement. Some days he'll not talk to me at all, and he spends hours standing at the window, never taking his eyes off the horizon, those soaring seagulls.' Llewelyn made an involuntary movement, and her hand tightened on his arm. 'If you could just see him, Llewelyn, if you could but talk together, mayhap then . . .'

Llewelyn knew better, knew talking would change nothing. But as he looked into his daughter-in-law's face, he could not refuse her. 'Your loyalty does you credit, lass. I'll talk to him. Just do not expect too much to come of it.'

Senena heard only the consent, not the qualification. 'Thank you,' she sighed, and he followed her up into the keep. Gruffydd's chamber was on the uppermost floor. Pausing on the threshold, she gave Llewelyn a look of anxious entreaty. 'It might be better if I speak to him first. If you'll wait . . .' He nodded and she slipped inside.

The door was ajar. Llewelyn could see a marble-top table, the sweep of velvet bed-hangings. Senena had not stinted in making Gruffydd's captivity as comfortable as possible, as if enough luxuries might somehow compensate for the guards at the bottom of the stairwell. The table was cluttered with the evidence of Gruffydd's struggle to fill empty hours, to vanquish the enemy time had become: a chess set, a draughts board, a stack of books. It was the books that Llewelyn found most poignant, for Gruffydd had never been a reader. He backed away from the door. A mistake. This was a grievous mistake.

'No! I'll not see him!' Gruffydd's voice carried clearly into the stairwell. Senena's response was softer, less distinct; she seemed to be pleading with him. Her importuning was in vain; Gruffydd's voice came again, raw with the rage of impotence. 'Would you have me grovel to him? And for what? He's not going to relent, and I'll be damned ere I'll give him absolution. Tell him if his conscience wants easing, he can seek it elsewhere. Let his Norman slut console him,

704

let her whelp –' Llewelyn heard no more; he turned, moved into the shadows of the stairwell.

The guards stepped aside respectfully, let him pass. His spurs clinked, struck sparks against the stones, and then he was emerging into the sun, into brilliant, blinding light. Owain had disappeared, but the younger boy was sitting on the outer stairs; when Llewelyn said his name, he smiled up at the man, with innocent camaraderie, heart-rending trust.

'Llewelyn, wait!' Senena was flushed, breathless. She ignored her son, caught up with Llewelyn at the foot of the stairs. 'Do not go, not like this. I know you heard Gruffydd, but . . . but can you blame him? I'll not apologize for his pride and I'll not make excuses for his bitterness. He is still your son, your firstborn. How can you turn your back on him like this? Do you hate him so much?'

'Hate him?' Llewelyn swung about, pointed towards the little boy. 'Do you think you could ever hate Llelo? Or Owain? How could you hate the man as long as you remembered the child?'

'You want to free him!' Senena cried, and it was both a challenge and a plea. 'I can see that now. You truly do. Why will you not do it, then? Llewelyn, I beg you. Let him go.'

'And then what? Can you honestly tell me he'd willingly go into exile? That he'd accept Davydd as my heir? You know he would not. Within hours of my death, Gwynedd would be at war. He'd never yield to Davydd, would die first. And if he won . . . if he won, Davydd would be the one to die. He'd put Davydd to death, disavow all allegiance to England, antagonize the other Welsh Princes, goad the Marcher lords and the Crown into an invasion, and as for Joanna . . . How do you think she would fare at his hands, Senena?'

'What are you saying, then? That you can never let him go?'

'No . . . I am not saying that. When I feel confident that Davydd can stave off any challenge to his authority, that he can safeguard what I've won, I'll give Gruffydd his freedom.'

'And you think that should give me comfort? That day will never come! Davydd will never be able to hold his own against Gruffydd!'

Llewelyn was not vulnerable from that quarter. 'You are wrong, Senena,' he said quietly, with such calm certitude that Senena's rage spilled over.

'This is Joanna's doing, all of it! She's set you against your own, scrupled at nothing to get what she wanted – the crown for her son! How could you be so taken in? My God, if you only knew –'

705

'If I only knew what, Senena?'

The coldness of the query brought her up short. What could she tell him? She had nothing but suspicions, needed more than afternoon disappearances, Joanna's obvious unease, and her own instincts. Not only would Llewelyn not believe her, he'd never forgive her.

'I do not mean to offend you, my lord. But I love your son and who will speak for him if I do not? If you do not free Gruffydd in your lifetime, he will never be freed. If he is still confined at your death, he will remain caged for the rest of his days. Davydd will never let him go. Can you do that to him? Can you condemn him to a life in shadow, away from the sun and the changing seasons? Can you –'

Llewelyn had no answer for her. He turned away in silence.

At Michaelmas Davydd and his sister Gwladys departed for London, where Davydd was to do homage to Henry. Joanna had decided not to accompany her son, in part because she did not want to take any attention away from Davydd's first diplomatic mission and in part because she did not want to leave Llewelyn for very long. He'd been sleeping badly since his return from Deganwy; all too frequently of late, she would awaken to find him staring into the dark, and she could offer only the most evanescent and ephemeral of comforts, winding her arms around him and holding him close, able to sympathize with his pain but not to share it.

She did agree to meet Davydd in Shrewsbury upon his return, and she arrived at the Benedictine abbey on a mild afternoon in October. Later that day a plainly dressed woman entered a Shrewsbury church, asked the priest to hear her confession. That she was a stranger did not surprise him, for there was a lamentable reluctance even among the truly devout to confess their more serious sins to their own parish priests. She followed him towards the chancel, seated herself on the shriving stool, where she could be seen by all yet not heard, and in a very low voice confessed to the sin of adultery. Afterwards, Joanna walked back to the abbey with a lighter step, for the first time in a year feeling at peace with herself.

Davydd and Gwladys rode into the abbey precincts the following morning, laden with gifts and London news. Joanna was delighted to discover they were accompanied by Elen and John the Scot. But her smile froze at sight of the man riding at Elen's side, at sight of Will de Braose.

In accordance with Norman custom, dinner was served in the forenoon. The meal was less stressful, however, than Joanna had expected, for Will was on his best behaviour; even Gwladys thawed towards him, enough to laugh heartily at his maliciously accurate imitation of Hubert de Burgh at his most pompous. Not surprisingly, the London visit was the focal point of conversation and the talk was easy, often amusing, the dinner passing without incident.

Afterwards, Davydd took Joanna to the stables, where he proudly displayed his London purchase, a superb red-gold stallion. 'I remembered those stories Papa would tell me of Sul, his first horse, so I named this one Sulwyn. You think Papa will like him?'

Joanna was not deceived by Davydd's offhand manner, knew he'd gone to great pains to find this particular look-alike for Sul, to give his father this substitute solace. 'Nothing could please him more, darling,' she said, and Davydd smiled. Linking her arm in his, he led her towards a beckoning sheen of blue, towards the placid waters of the abbey fishpond.

'Does Will plan to return with us to Aber?' Joanna asked as nonchalantly as she could, felt a dizzying rush of relief when Davydd shook his head. 'Davydd . . . I'd like to talk to you about Will and the plight troth. How do you feel . . . truly . . . about taking his daughter to wife? Darling, if you'd rather not, it's still not too late. Your father and I made a mistake with Elen, would not –'

'Mama, I appreciate your concern, but there's no need. I've no objections to this match. Why should I? How many brides bring their husbands a prize like Buellt Castle?'

'You are sure, Davydd? The girl's youth does not matter?'

Davydd picked up a pebble, sent it skipping across the surface of the pool. 'I know it'll be years ere Isabella can be a true wife to me, but in all honesty, Mama, I see that as no disadvantage.' He gave her a sideways glance, a self-conscious smile. 'There is a girl, you see . . .'

Joanna did see. 'Do you love this girl, Davydd?'

'I think so,' he admitted. 'But you need not fret. I've always known mine must be a marriage of state. Mari knows it, too, never expected more of me than I could give. But I'd not see her hurt if I could help it. A marriage like this would be easier for her, would give her no cause for jealousy.'

It came as something of a shock to Joanna, to realize Davydd could be so pragmatic, so dispassionate even about passion. How unalike her children were! She yearned to know more about this mysterious Mari, but knew she'd never ask; this was not a part of a man's life that he'd share with his mother. She wondered suddenly if it had been like this for Llewelyn, too, if he'd felt the same uneasy blend of pride and loss upon seeing his son for the first time as a man grown.

'But what of Isabella's lineage? You have no objections to wedding a girl of Norman blood?'

'I think of myself as Welsh, Mama. For certès, my loyalties are to Wales, to Papa's people. But I am no less your son than Papa's, and to disavow my Norman blood would be to disavow you. When I was but a lad, Papa told me I was luckier than most, having two heritages to draw upon. I came to see that he was right, that a man who can claim descent from Owain Fawr and Eleanor of Aquitaine, too, is indeed blessed with a remarkable family tree!'

Joanna was deeply touched, but too wise in the ways of motherhood to embarass her son by letting him know. She contented herself with a smile, a kiss upon his cheek, and a necessary lie. 'Now that I know it is truly your wish to wed Isabella de Braose, my mind is greatly eased.'

'Mama, I must talk to you about Henry. I wanted to be the one to tell you, made the others agree to that, for I know how fond you are of him. He has been forced to delay his expedition against the French, for when he arrived at Portsmouth, he found less than half the expected ships in the harbour. I had remained in London, but Elen's husband was at Portsmouth, and his account can be trusted, however unlikely it first sounds to you; John could not embellish a tale in the telling to save his very soul. He says Henry flew into a wild rage, blamed Hubert de Burgh for failing to assemble enough ships. He lost all control, cursed de Burgh as a traitor, as a pawn of the French, even went so far as to draw his sword.'

'He did what?'

Davydd nodded. 'John says it was a right ugly scene, says his uncle Chester had to step between them, intercede for de Burgh; Chester of all men! When they were at last able to calm Henry, the rupture was somehow patched over. De Burgh is to continue as Justiciar, but I doubt that he'll forget. Nor will the men who witnessed it. It showed Henry in no favourable light, Mama, made him look unsteady of purpose, unreliable of temper . . . and not a little ridiculous.'

708

'This sounds so unlike him. His is a gentle spirit, Davydd, not given to violence . . .'

'It seems he has more of the Angevin temper than men thought.'

Joanna frowned. 'You mean his father's temper. But you're wrong in that, Davydd. John would never have thrown such a tantrum. He once put a sword to Llewelyn's throat, but that was very deliberately done. He'd not have drawn a sword upon one of his own councillors, not unless he fully meant to use it. Whatever men may say of John, he was never inept.'

Davydd had developed a morbid fascination with the Angevin King, the grandfather he'd never known. Even now, in his twenty-first year, he found it impossible to identify with John in any sense, to acknowledge a blood bond with a mortal enemy of the Welsh. He found it equally hard to associate his mother with such a man, and he loved Joanna too much to indulge his curiosity at her expense. He wanted to take advantage of this sudden breach in her defences, to ask those questions only she could answer. But he did not want to hurt her, and he hesitated.

'They sound as unlike as chalk and cheese, Mama. Henry is well-meaning but weak, and John . . .' He paused, watching her intently. But she was already pulling back; the moment had passed.

'And John was neither,' she said, with forced flippancy. 'Well-meaning or weak, I mean. Let's go back, Davydd. I want to talk to Elen, see if I cannot coax her into returning to Aber with us for a time.'

'I think she – Will? What are you doing out here? Were you seeking us?'

Joanna spun around, saw Will ambling towards them. 'Yes, I was,' he said, favouring them with a lazy smile. 'I need to talk to your mother, Davydd. Would you mind if I borrowed her for a few moments?'

Davydd felt some reluctance, knowing Joanna was never fully at ease with a de Braose. But he could not refuse without rudeness, without offending the man who was to be his father-in-law. 'Of course, Will. I'll go and find Elen, Mama, shall await you back at the guest hall.'

As Davydd moved away, Joanna began to walk rapidly along the water's edge, not waiting for Will. But he had no difficulty in keeping stride, fell into step beside her. 'Come now, Joanna, surely you cannot object to us meeting like this, in a monastery garden in the

709

middle of the afternoon? What could be more innocent? Moreover, the plight troth did make us kin of sorts. Of course we were already linked by an earlier marriage, that of my father and Gwladys. I once sought to figure our relationship out, did only give myself a right sharp headache! It's a tangled coil in truth; see what you can make of it. Gwladys is your stepdaughter and was, for nigh on thirteen years, my stepmother. Now my question is this. As the stepmother of my stepmother, does that make you my step-grandmother?'

Joanna gave an involuntary splutter of laughter. 'Jesu forfend!'

Will was grinning. 'I thought I could coax a smile if I truly tried. Am I forgiven, then?'

Joanna stopped, for the first time looked him full in the face. 'I am not angry with you, Will. I do not blame you for what happened. I want only to forget.'

'I'd rather remember,' he said, plucked a sprig of honeysuckle from the closest vine, and handed it to her. She took it, but then began to walk again.

'I would like to thank you, Will, for your kindness at the time of Catherine's death. I know I never answered your letter, but it did help.' Not at first, though; she'd been terrified when Will's messenger was ushered into the great hall, handed her the letter in full view of all. She'd broken the seal with unsteady fingers, but her fears were unrealized; the contents did not compromise her in any way. Will had written a graceful letter of condolence, explaining that he'd only recently heard of Catherine's death, and expressing his sympathies to Joanna and Catherine's family. She'd been able to pass the letter over to Llewelyn without the slightest qualm. 'It was a kind thought,' she repeated, bringing the honeysuckle up to breathe in its fragrance.

'I knew you were very fond of her. Was she ill for long?'

'I loved her,' Joanna said softly. 'And no, not long at all . . .'

'Did you ever tell her about us?'

'No.'

'Just as well. But what of your maid . . . Glenna? Can you trust her?'

'Glynis? Yes, I believe so. Why?'

'No . . . it was a foolish whim, much too risky. However trustworthy she seems, it would be madness to put yourself into her power like that. A pity, though; to have had an entire night together . . .' He shook his head regretfully. 'Well, we'll just have to make do with what we can. At least we'll have an afternoon. What about tomorrow?

I know an inn not far from Shrewsbury, a bit on the shabby side but no hovel. It can provide what we most need, clean sheets, decent wine, and privacy.'

'No, Will. No.'

'Think on it, love; just us and a soft bed.' Will's smile was wry. 'I might as well confess; I'm past the age where I enjoy rolling about on dirt floors, like my comforts with my pleasures. I want to be able to take my time, to undress you myself . . . very slowly. I want you to unbind your hair so I can feel it against my chest as I kiss you, and then –'

'Will, stop, please stop! I cannot, not ever again!'

'Why not?' He sounded truly surprised. 'You need not fear discovery, love. I'll take care of it, arrange everything –'

'No. I love my husband.' To Joanna's dismay, her voice was unsteady. 'I do, Will, I do!'

'I no longer doubt that,' he said hastily. 'You made that quite clear the last time we were together in the *hafod*. You love him, well and good. But you still want me, Joanna.' She was shaking her head and he stepped closer. 'Look me in the eye then and say you do not. Tell me you do not want to go to that inn, do not want to be in my arms right now, do not want me to make love to you.'

Joanna's face was burning. But she raised her chin, met his eyes. 'I do not want to go to an inn with you. I do not want to bed with you. It's over, Will. It's done.'

His eyes shifted from her face, followed the rapid rise and fall of her breasts. 'Now why,' he murmured, 'do I not believe you?'

Joanna backed away. 'You act as if this were some sort of game! Have you never thought what would happen should my husband find out about us?'

He shrugged and she began to understand. 'I once told you that you could not trade upon being fourteen forever. But that's what you're still doing. Only now it's your name, your family's power.'

He was no longer smiling. 'And what does that mean?'

'Tell me the truth, Will. How many unhappy husbands have suspected you of cuckolding them and yet looked the other way? How many of your vassals were unwilling or unable to act upon their suspicions?'

He shrugged again. 'What does it matter? That has naught to do with us.'

'But it does matter! Can you not see that? Do you truly think

711

Llewelyn, too, would turn a blind eye? That being a de Braose, a highborn Norman lord, would save you? It would not, Will; believe me in this, it would not. Llewelyn would kill you if he knew. As simple as that. He would kill you.'

'He need never have to know, Joanna. Why can I not convince you of that?' He glanced about, saw no one in sight, and caught her hand, brought it up to his mouth. 'If you do not want me, darling, why does your pulse jump so when I touch you? Why does your breath come so quick?'

Joanna jerked free. 'Yes,' she gasped, 'yes, I do want you. Is that what you would have me say? But it will avail you naught, for I will never act upon it. I will not destroy my marriage for you!'

She'd dropped the honeysuckle on the path and Will picked it up, crushed it between his fingers as he watched her move away. She was all but running in her haste to put distance between them, did not look back.

April, 1230

Aber, North Wales

Joanna and Gwladys were seated at a table in the great hall, making up the guest list for Gwladys's forthcoming marriage to Ralph de Mortimer. This was no less political a match than the other marital alliances Llewelyn had forged with his Norman-French neighbours. Ralph de Mortimer was an influential Marcher lord, baron of Wigmore, his a family that had long been hostile to Llewelyn. But antagonism had yielded to expediency, and he'd shown himself eager to ally with the Welsh Prince, to wed Llewelyn's eldest daughter. Joanna was not all that impressed with Mortimer, a brash, forceful man, noted both for his candour and his quick temper. Gwladys, however, obviously saw something in him that Joanna did not; she had suggested the match to Llewelyn, after meeting Mortimer during her London visit, and now, with the wedding but weeks away, she gave every indication of looking forward to her new life as Ralph de Mortimer's lady.

'Shall we begin with the Marshals, Gwladys? My sister Nell will attend, of course, but Pembroke will have sailed with Henry for Brittany by then. I think we ought to invite Pembroke's younger brothers, though; they are –'

'Joanna . . . I'd rather we wait. I asked Senena to join us.'

Although Joanna said nothing, hers was an expressive face. Gwladys leaned across the table. 'Let us speak plainly. I do not blame Papa for keeping Gruffydd at Deganwy, for Gruffydd gave him no choice. Nor do I blame you. It is only natural that you should try to safeguard Davydd's rights. Gruffydd has a man's courage, a man's will, but a child's grasp of the world we live in. Yet I still love him, I still feel his pain, and I would never forsake him. When he asks me for something, I try to oblige, and he asked me to include Senena in my wedding plans. She needs this, Joanna, needs some pleasure in her life. I want to do this for Gruffydd, want you to do it for me. Will you?'

Such a question could have but one answer. Joanna nodded. 'I'll try,' she said grudgingly. 'In all honesty, I cannot promise that she'll not provoke me, but I will try.'

'That's more than fair.' Gwladys half-rose, beckoned to her sister-in-law. 'Ah, there you are, Senena. Joanna and I were just discussing those who cannot attend. Chester, too, will be sailing with the English King and Pembroke. I doubt that Gwenllian and her husband will come from Ireland. But at least Marared and her husband will be present. What of Elen and John the Scot, Joanna?'

'I think not,' Joanna said regretfully. 'They're visiting the court of John's cousin, the Scots King, will not be back in time. But my brother Richard and his wife will come for certès, and mayhap my aunt, the Countess of Salisbury.'

'May I assume you do mean to squeeze in a few Welsh midst all these Normans?'

Joanna dropped her pen, splattering the parchment with ink. Gwladys said hastily, 'The Welsh will be well represented, Senena. Here is our list. Have you any suggestions to make?'

Senena gave the list only a perfunctory glance. 'What of Will de Braose and his wife? Surely you do not mean to overlook them. Or have you already given Will an invitation, Madame?'

'No, I have not!' Joanna drew a deliberate breath. She could not do this to herself, could not allow her suspicions and her guilt to colour the most innocent of utterances; in that way lay madness. 'Of course I mean to invite Will and Eva de Braose; they are Davydd's kin now.' And picking up the pen, she inked in the names of her lover and his wife.

Gwladys laughed suddenly, none too happily. 'That man always did have a diabolic sense of timing,' she said, as Joanna turned with foreboding, saw Will de Braose being ushered into the hall.

He greeted the three women in turn, and then smiled at Joanna. 'I suppose I ought to have sent word ahead, but I took it for granted that you could accommodate me.'

How long, Joanna wondered in sudden despair, was it to be like this? How long ere she could talk to this man and not feel a shamed sense of intimacy? 'You are ever welcome at my husband's court,' she said reluctantly, stressing the words 'my husband' in the vain hope that Will would understand the emphasis, abandon the chase.

'But neither Llewelyn nor Davydd are here. They are meeting in Bangor with the Bishop, and I do not expect them to return until the morrow. Mayhap you would rather continue on to Bangor, join them there?'

'Bangor is but six miles,' Gwladys chimed in, no more eager than Joanna to have Will at Aber. But he was shaking his head, saying only a churl would give up an opportunity to pass an evening with three charming women, and Joanna could only pray that neither Gwladys nor Senena caught the mockery beneath the good manners, that none but she could read the message in those amused grey eyes.

Dinner should have been a festive occasion, freed as they were of the monotonous menus of Lent; the table was bountifully set and afterwards, there was music and dancing. But for Joanna, the evening was an ordeal. Will was in recklessly high spirits; he insisted upon dancing with Joanna and Gwladys, even attempted to coax Senena into joining the carole, and he flirted outrageously with Glynis, who seemed both flustered and flattered by his attentions. And all the while, Joanna could feel Senena's eyes upon them, upon her and Will.

Joanna was standing alone, watching the dancers. When Will materialized unexpectedly at her side, her nerves betrayed her and she splashed half her wine into the floor rushes. 'Shall I fetch you another cup, Lady Joanna?' Will asked, so solicitously that she yearned to slap him.

'No. You've had enough wine tonight for both of us. You can do something for me, though. You can stop trying to bedazzle Glynis. Let her be, Will. There's no sport in seducing such an innocent.'

Will laughed so loudly that he turned several heads in their direction. '"Jealousy is cruel as the grave,"' he quoted softly. 'Do you recognize that, Joanna? *The Song of Solomon*. Who'd ever expect to find so erotic a love poem in Scriptures? Shall I recite it for you? "Behold, thou art fair, my love. Thy lips are like a thread of scarlet. Thy breasts are like two —"'

'Will, hush!' Joanna was truly frightened now. 'When the stakes have become life or death, it is no longer a game. Have you not noticed how Senena keeps watching us? She puts me in mind of a stalking cat, makes me feel like a bird with a broken wing.'

'The cat eyes are yours, love, not Senena's.'

'Will, stop! Listen to me . . . please. You must leave me alone.

715

If you do not, I'll have no choice but to denounce you, accuse you of making unwelcome advances. Do not make me do that, Will. I do not want you to come to harm!'

Will grinned. 'Nor do I, darling!' But as he studied her face, his smile changed, became softer, more sympathetic. 'I wish I could convince you, Joanna, that you're distressing yourself for naught. Why should you care what Senena suspects as long as you have Llewelyn's trust? But if it will ease your mind, I'll strive for discretion. Now . . . tell me quickly whilst we're still alone. Where can we meet . . . and when?'

Joanna gave a strained, shaken laugh. 'You never hear me, do you? I do not know what else to say to you, how to convince you . . .' Shoving her wine cup into his hand, she said, 'I do want more wine, after all, Will. Would you mind?' And as soon as he moved away, she turned, crossed the hall to Gwladys.

'I know you like Will's company no more than I do, but I need you to act in my stead for the rest of the evening. Will you do that for me?'

Gwladys gave a mock grimace. 'I cannot pretend I'm thrilled at the prospect. But I owe you a favour. Go along then; I'll see to the hall and our guests.'

As Joanna hurriedly departed the hall, Senena came to stand at Gwladys's side. 'It is rather early for bed, is it not?'

Gwladys shrugged. 'Joanna does not find it easy, being with a de Braose.' Senena laughed; Gwladys did not like the sound of it, and she said, with far less friendliness, 'I am not asking you to sympathize with her predicament, Senena, merely to understand it.'

'But I do.' Senena was smiling. 'I do understand, Gwladys. I understand very well, indeed.'

One of the windows in Joanna's bedchamber was unshuttered, and the sounds of laughter and music carried on the quiet April air. Glynis was dutifully brushing out Joanna's hair, but she kept casting such wistful glances towards the window that Joanna at last relented.

'Never mind,' she said. 'You need not braid my hair into a night plait. Would you like to return to the hall?'

'Oh yes, Madame, thank you!'

'But Glynis . . . do take care. Do not pay too much heed to Will de Braose's honeyed words. His promises are counterfeit coins; they look genuine until you seek to spend them.'

Glynis blushed and then grinned impishly. 'I know that, Madame, I do. But it's like our trips to the Shrewsbury market; I can enjoy looking without necessarily meaning to buy!'

Joanna smiled, waved the girl out. Alone now in the bedchamber, she felt calmer, safe both from temptation and exposure. Talking to Will would do no good whatsoever. The more she said 'no', the more intrigued he became. She could not trust him, and in all honesty, she was still not sure she could trust herself. She and Will must never be alone. She must avoid him whenever possible, and if that meant open rudeness, so be it. She could only hope Davydd would understand. But even if he could not, that changed nothing.

She took several books and a candle with her to bed . . . and Topaz, for the spaniel always took shameful advantage of Llewelyn's absences, abandoning its sleeping basket for its mistress's feather bed. Joanna removed her bedrobe, gave the dog an indulgent pat, and reached for the books.

The first she discarded at once, a romance of the ill-fated love of Tristan for his uncle's wife, the beguiling Iseult. There was a perverse comfort in attributing adulterous passion to a love potion; Joanna wryly wished she could so easily explain away her own infidelity. But she was in no mood for an object lesson – however lyrical – in the inevitable wages of sin, and she chose instead a French translation of a lengthy English poem, *The Owl and the Nightingale*.

Even this selection was not as innocuous as it first seemed. A cynical couplet could have served as John's epitaph: 'The dark way he so fully knows, that in the bright he never goes.' Other lines struck too close to home. 'A woman may sport beneath the sheet, in wedded love or lustful heat.' 'For sure it is a better thing, for wife to love her husband pure, than wanton with a paramour.' Joanna dropped the book into the rushes, blew out the candle.

She was almost asleep when Topaz began to whine. The door creaked; she heard the bolt slide into place. Glynis. She pulled the pillow closer. But Topaz continued to whimper. She was rolling over, a drowsy reprimand forming on her lips, when the bed hangings were drawn back. A candle still burned on the table; framed in flickering light, a man was standing by the bed. Llewelyn? Joanna sat up, blinking sleepily. But then he moved, and the candle caught the sheen of flaxen hair. Joanna gasped, grabbed for the sheet. 'Will?'

'Did you think I was not coming? I did not want to be too obvious, love, waited nigh on an hour.' He grinned. 'And I know what you're going to ask now. But no one saw me; it's full dark.' As he was speaking, he was unfastening his mantle. Tossing it on to a coffer, he began unbuckling his scabbard and sword.

'Will, no! My God, you're mad! Someone could come in at any moment!'

'Who'd dare enter your private chamber at such an hour? Only Glynis, love, and she's over in the great hall, dallying with my squire. Sometimes the more unlikely a trysting place, the safer it actually is.'

Unbelting his tunic, he pulled it over his head, and Joanna's fear suddenly gave way to outrage. 'You truly think I'd do this to Llewelyn, that I'd lay with you in my husband's own bed? Get out, get out ere I start to scream!'

He dropped the tunic on to the floor, stared at her in surprise. 'What game are you playing now, Joanna? You know you want me. Why did you depart the hall like that if you did not expect me to follow –'

'I expected nothing! I'll take no blame for your mistakes, for your accursed, overweening pride. For months now, I've told you that it was over. And even if I were utterly besotted with you, I'd never have invited you into Llewelyn's bedchamber, never!'

Will gave a half-angry laugh. 'You make it sound as if we're about to defile a sacred shrine!' Yet he was not as irked as he might otherwise have been; she was clutching the sheet up to her breasts, but the material was soft, clinging, adhered to the curves of hip and thigh, and her hair spilled over her breasts, on to the pillow in a midnight cloud. 'Mayhap I did misread you, Joanna,' he conceded. 'But I'm here now, and I cannot believe you truly want me to leave. You admitted it yourself at Shrewsbury, how much you still wanted me. You remember how it was between us . . .' He leaned over the bed, his mouth seeking hers, and Joanna screamed.

Will never had more reason to bless his quick reflexes. As stunned as he was, he reacted instinctively, swiftly clasping his hand over her mouth, choking back her cry. He'd encountered resistance from women before, but it was usually playfully offered, a lover's game. Joanna was struggling in earnest, in panic, trying to bite his hand, to scratch, to roll off the bed. He realized at once that he could not restrain her without truly hurting her, and when he loosened his grip on her mouth, she succeeded in giving another muffled scream.

Never had Will's desire diminished so rapidly; never had he lost an erection with such speed. He was no longer aware of the soft

718

female body thrashing under his, was aware only of that unshuttered window, her hysterically barking dog.

'Joanna, calm yourself. I do not want to hurt you. Joanna, listen to me! Do you know what will happen to me if anyone heard your scream? Christ Jesus, I'll be gelded with a dull knife! I'll not force you, I swear. If I take my hand away, let you up, do you promise not to scream?'

She nodded, after an unnervingly long pause. He released her then, very cautiously. She was gasping for breath, but she did not cry out, and he relaxed somewhat, enough for anger. 'Whatever possessed you? Good Christ, woman, you almost got me killed!'

Joanna was too shaken for speech, half-blinded by her own hair. She pulled the sheet up, panting, rubbing her wrists. But when Will took a step towards the bed, she cried, 'If you dare to touch me again . . .'

Her voice had risen and he hastily backed away. 'What do you think, that I had rape in mind? At your own court, in your own bedchamber? What kind of a bloody fool do you think I am?'

They glared at each other, but his protest had the ring of truth. Joanna acknowledged that by reaching for the spaniel, seeking to quiet it. Will moved to the table, poured himself a double measure of mead. 'I cannot remember when I've felt death so damned close,' he confessed. 'Between you and that wretched dog, I expected half the court to come bursting in at any moment.'

'You're luckier than you deserve. I want you out of here . . . now!'

'You do want me to dress first? I'd look somewhat conspicuous wandering about the bailey in my shirt and chausses.' Will set the cup down, studied Joanna with baffled, angry eyes. He still could not believe he'd not have been able to bring her around, if only he had enough privacy and time. But not here, not now, not when a single scream could bring a dozen men on the run.

'Here,' he said, moving warily towards the bed. 'Take the rest of this mead. If your nerves are half as frayed as mine, you need it.'

Joanna did, but she shook her head. 'Just put it down and get out.'

She was still rubbing her wrist, and he said, 'Are you hurt? In truth, Joanna, I did think you were expecting me, that I was welcome in your bed. I suppose every man has coerced a consent at one time or another. But I would never in this lifetime or the next force a

719

woman like you. A Prince's wife, the King of England's sister? That mad I am not! I frightened you, I know. But you gave me a turn, too. Let's call it check and mate, and –'

'I do not want to talk. I just want you to go.'

'All right. I'll go.' It was for the best; she was too distraught to be trusted. But on the morrow, he'd have to find a way to talk privately with her, to mollify her somehow. Women could be vindictive, unforgiving, and she was in a unique position to do him harm, to poison the King's mind against him. 'I'll go,' he repeated, but instead he turned, moved swiftly towards the window.

Joanna sat up in alarm. 'Now what are you about? Get back lest you be seen!'

'Something is amiss.' Very cautiously, he peered around the shutter edge. 'People are coming out of the hall. I cannot be sure, but I think I hear your name, hear "Siwan".'

Joanna heard it, too, now, a confused babble of voices, barking dogs. 'What is it, Will?'

'I do not know, mayhap a fire . . .' He risked another look, and then drew back hastily. 'Christ, it's Llewelyn!'

Even then, Will kept his wits about him. Llewelyn was dismounting in front of his lodgings, but if the door was thus eliminated as a means of escape, that still left the side window. Will darted towards it, began jerking at the shutter latches. 'Joanna, hide my clothing and sword!' But Joanna was incapable of moving. She sat frozen, staring at the door.

'Joanna? Joanna, are you all right? Unbar the door!' The voice was Llewelyn's. She heard other voices, too; someone was pounding on the door, and Llewelyn was shouting for the key. Will had the latches up by now; he jerked the shutters open, and then recoiled.

'Jesu, there are men outside! Quick, Joanna, where can I hide?' But Joanna did not reply, and as he swung about, he saw the latch begin to move. As they watched, it was slowly, inexorably, pushed upward, and then the door was thrust open.

Llewelyn was not alone, and the chamber was cast into eerie brightness by the sudden flare of torches. But Joanna saw none of the men. No one existed for her but Llewelyn. She watched, stunned, as he strode into the room, watched as he came to an abrupt halt, watched as his face changed, watched as her world fell apart.

Llewelyn looked from Will to Joanna, and despite the irrefutable evidence of infidelity, there was still a moment in which he half-

720

expected Joanna to offer a rational, convincing explanation for Will's presence, half-dressed, in their bedchamber. But she had yet to utter a word, and all the colour had drained from her face. She looked up at him in stricken silence, silence more damning than any confession could have been, and he could read in her eyes only horror, despairing entreaty, and an admission of a betrayal beyond forgiving.

Will stood very still. He'd talked his way out of awkard corners before, but none like this. He'd seen the disbelief on Llewelyn's face give way to a far more frightening emotion, and he thought, Christ, he loves her! He'd always prided himself upon his glibness of tongue, but as he looked at Llewelyn, he knew suddenly that it would not avail him now, that nothing would.

He no longer had enough saliva for swallowing, had to try twice before he could get the words out. 'I know this looks bad, but –' He got no further; Llewelyn's sword was already clearing its scabbard. He had nowhere to run, felt the wall at his back, and knew the last sight he'd ever see was the light reflecting off that gleaming steel blade.

Joanna was petrified, averted her eyes. But she made no sound. Her throat had closed up; even if Llewelyn turned the sword upon her next, she'd not have been able to cry out.

'Llewelyn, wait!'

Joanna opened her eyes, saw that Ednyved had stepped between Llewelyn and Will. 'No,' he said grimly, 'not like that. It's too easy. Give him the death he deserves. Hang him.'

Will drew an audible breath. No one else spoke. And then Llewelyn slowly lowered his sword. 'Yes,' he said, in a voice Joanna had never heard before. 'You're right. It is too quick this way. Take him.'

For the first and only time in his life, Will panicked, made a sudden lunge for the window. But Llewelyn's sword came up with eye-blurring speed, and Will froze, his stomach muscles contracting, anticipating that first thrust into the belly or groin. There'd be nothing easy or quick about such a death, not with Llewelyn wielding the blade. Better to take his chances with the hanging, for there was a hope – however slight – that enough political pressure might reprieve him.

He no longer resisted, therefore, when Llewelyn's men laid hands upon him, but they treated him roughly all the same, jerking his arms behind his back and shoving him towards the door. He did not

721

struggle, realizing that Llewelyn had only to say the word and they'd gladly hang him then and there, over the bed. He stumbled, nearly fell, and for a moment his eyes found Joanna.

'I ought to be gallant and say you were worth it, darling,' he said huskily, 'but no woman is worth hanging for.'

His words meant nothing to Joanna; she never even heard them. 'Llewelyn . . .' She had yet to take her eyes from her husband's face. 'Llewelyn, I'm sorry . . .'

Llewelyn moved towards the bed. When he brought the sword up, he heard gasps. Joanna's lips parted; her breath quickened. Tears had begun to streak her face. He knew suddenly this was the way he would always remember her, clutching a sheet to hide her nakedness, dark hair falling about her face in wanton disarray, kneeling in the middle of the bed, the bed in which she'd betrayed him. Her death-bed. One downward stroke of his sword and the sheets would be soaked with blood. His hand tightened on the hilt, and then he thrust the sword back into its scabbard, turned to face the others.

'I want de Braose's men taken prisoner, too. See to it.'

Men hastened to obey. Llewelyn became aware now of their audience, of the people crowding into the antechamber. 'Get them out of here,' he snarled, and the antechamber cleared as if by magic, while through the open window he could see Will de Braose being dragged across the bailey.

'Llewelyn . . . Llewelyn, I did not ask him to come to me. It was over between us. Beloved, I swear it, swear I never would have brought him here, into your bed . . .'

If her words had registered with him, Joanna could see no indication of it in his face. He turned away from her, and as he moved through the doorway, Joanna sobbed, begged him to wait, to listen, but he did neither.

'Llewelyn . . .' Joanna sobbed again, collapsed upon the bed. He was gone and he would not be back. She'd lost him, lost all, all . . . She did not think it was possible to feel pain greater than this. But then she heard her son's voice, heard Davydd say:

'Why, Mama, why?'

'Davydd?' Her voice broke. 'Davydd . . . you saw? My God, oh, my God, no . . .'

He moved from the shadows of the antechamber, stood there staring at her as if he no longer recognized her. 'Glynis sent word that you'd been taken ill, that the doctors feared a rupture . . .' He sounded dazed, his words laboured, coming as uncertainly as if he were speaking a language not his own. 'She said . . . said you might be dying. Papa, he . . .' He shook his head, as if to clear it. 'We half-killed the horses, and when we rode into the bailey, no one knew, no one . . .' The words trailed off raggedly, his mouth contorting.

'What have you done, Mama? Jesus God, what have you done?'

Davydd had gone. Joanna was alone. She would never know how long she lay there in the darkness. Upon the table a solitary candle still sputtered, burning down towards the wick. When it at last flickered out, Joanna rose from the bed, groped her way across the chamber. She did not bother with stockings or chemise; finding a gown in one of her coffers, she pulled it over her head, began to search for her shoes. She did not braid her hair, merely brushed it back over her shoulders. She had to see Llewelyn. She had to tell him that she'd not lain with Will in his bed. Nothing else mattered. He could never forgive her. She knew that. But let his grieving be for those October afternoons in the *hafod*. Not for this, not for a betrayal in his own bedchamber. She could at least do that for him. She could give him the truth about tonight and hope it might in time help to heal some of his pain.

Once she was dressed, though, she found herself standing motionless by the door. How could she find Llewelyn? The thought of entering the great hall in search of him was terrifying. She wanted only to stay here in the dark, never to have to face others again. But she must somehow find the courage to do this, for Llewelyn's sake if not her own. She braced herself and then opened the door, only to find her way barred by armed guards.

12

April, 1230

Aber, North Wales

The men came for Joanna the following morning. She had no warning; they entered without knocking, announced brusquely that she was to accompany them. 'Where are you taking me?' she asked, the composure of her question utterly belied by the tremor in her voice, and one of the men laughed.

'Did you not hear the hammering? Carpenters have been labouring since dawn to erect a gallows . . . for two.'

Even before she saw the startled looks on the other faces, Joanna was sure the man lied. If Llewelyn meant her to die, she'd have died last night in her own bed. He would never hang her; she knew that with such certainty that she found the assurance now to challenge their authority. 'I want to know where I am to be taken.'

'Do you, indeed? Well, I'd not give a fig for what you want,' he jeered, and Joanna stiffened, for that expression had long since taken on obscene connotations. 'You've no right to ask questions. You forfeited all rights the day you chose to play the whore for a Norman lord.'

No one had ever dared to speak to her with such contempt, and Joanna felt as if she'd been torn, naked and defenceless, from a cocoon of privilege and power, with no skills for survival in this harsh new world. But indignation was an indulgence no longer available to her. All she could do was to salvage what dignity she could. 'Very well. I will come with you as soon as I braid my hair.'

Her tormentor stepped towards her, took the brush out of her hand. 'No, you will come now,' he said, and she had no choice but to obey. When Topaz sought to follow, he thrust the dog aside impatiently, and Joanna had no choice but to accept that, too.

Just as they reached the door, a terrifying thought came to her. What if he were not lying about the gallows? What if she were being brought out to watch as Will was hanged? Merciful Jesus, let it not be so, she was praying wordlessly, desperately, as they opened the antechamber door.

As early as it was, the bailey was thronged with men and women. They watched in unnerving silence as Joanna emerged into the sunlight, but as she was led forward, they began to murmur among themselves. Several spat deliberately upon the ground; one bolder than the rest called out loudly, 'Norman slut!' Joanna flushed, suddenly seeing herself through other eyes, hostile eyes. How she regretted dressing last night in such haste; without stockings or chemise, she felt half-naked, slatternly, and with her hair loose, tumbling down her back, blowing untidily about her face, she must look as if she'd just been roused from a man's bed, a lover's embrace.

There was a sudden stir; Glynis broke through the crowd, ran towards Joanna. 'I did not do it, Madame,' she cried. 'I sent no message, I swear by Our Lady I did not!'

'I know, Glynis, I know.' Joanna's eyes swept the crowd. 'Where is Senena?'

'Gone, my lady. She left nigh on an hour ago for Deganwy Castle.'

That came as no surprise to Joanna. Senena would want to tell Gruffydd with no delay. Glynis was gazing at her in sudden comprehension. 'Madame, you think it was she . . .?'

'Who else? But you must go back now, Glynis, lest the others think you too sympathetic, lest they suspect you of aiding and abetting me in a liaison with Will.'

Glynis looked frightened, but she stayed resolutely by Joanna's side for several strides. 'Go with God, my lady.'

The crowd's anger was growing, and as Joanna feared, some of it was now directed at Glynis. But most of the abuse was reserved for Joanna, and as she heard herself called 'whore' and 'harlot', she began to comprehend at last the political implications of her adultery. Their outrage was in fact rooted in fear, the fear that she'd made Llewelyn ridiculous in the eyes of his English enemies. Nor was the fear ill-founded. The aging husband with a wanton young wife was a stock figure of fun, found in innumerable comic tales and guild mummeries, and for a prince, nothing could be more injurious to authority than laughter, the mockery of other men. As Joanna came to this appalled understanding, she realized, too, that her sin was

725

twofold in the eyes of Llewelyn's countrymen, for not only had she betrayed her husband, she had betrayed him with a Norman, with one of her own.

She faltered, and the heckling increased. She knew she must not weep, must not show fear. For Davydd's sake, she must be strong enough to endure their scorn. As a child in London, she'd once seen a harlot doing public penance through the city streets; the hapless woman had been followed by a jeering crowd, pelted with mud and rotten apples, and that memory came treacherously back to haunt Joanna now. The insults were getting uglier. Would they dare to subject her to the same harsh treatment?

Another memory came to her then, this one more merciful, for it enabled her to find the courage she so needed, the memory of a woman more than twenty years dead, the memory of a woman who'd also been an unfaithful wife, a woman who would have faced down such a hostile crowd with haughty indifference, her father's mother, her grandmother, Eleanor of Aquitaine.

Joanna squared her shoulders, nerved herself to get through this ordeal with what grace she could. But her resolve carried her no farther than the great hall, for there Gwladys awaited her.

Gwladys had passed a sleepless night; her shock was only now yielding to a raw and very bitter rage. 'You made a fool of my father, made fools of us all. You even turned me into an accomplice of sorts, taking care of your duties in the hall whilst you took care of Will de Braose, and in my father's own bed!'

'Gwladys, no! That's not so, I swear it!'

'And upon what do you swear, your honour as a faithful wife, a devoted mother? Gruffydd and Senena were right about you, right all along. What grief we might have been spared had we only heeded them!'

Gwladys no longer trusted herself, whirled and plunged back into the hall. Joanna forgot all else; intent only upon telling Gwladys the truth about Will's presence in her bedchamber, she started after her stepdaughter, and the most hostile of her guards grabbed her by the arm, swung her about so roughly that she cried out, as much in shock as pain.

'Get your hands off her . . . now!' At sight of Davydd, the crowd fell silent. To many, he was an object of sincere if embarrassed sympathy. But to others, he was still the *alltud* – the foreigner – who had usurped the rightful place of Llewelyn's more deserving son, his

Welsh son. The guard was one of these, and although he obeyed Davydd's command, released Joanna, he did so grudgingly.

'I am but following orders,' he said, with a belligerence he'd never have dared to show if not for Joanna's disgrace.

'Not any longer. You have just been relieved of your duty.'

The man's eyes flickered. 'My lord Ednyved told me I was to take the woman from Aber,' he said stubbornly, and Davydd stared at him, incredulous.

'Are you defying me?'

There was in Davydd's voice the arrogance of one accustomed to unquestioning obedience, the arrogance of a Prince's son. But was he? How could they ever be sure now? The taunt never left the man's lips, though, checked in great measure by fear of Llewelyn, but in part, too, by what he saw now in Davydd's eyes.

He had not misread Davydd; for a moment, he'd truly found himself hoping the guard was defying him, giving him justification for what he'd wanted to do since first walking into his mother's bedchamber, seek to ease his pain and disbelief in a killing rage. It unnerved him now to realize how precarious was his self-control, for after that stable confrontation with Gruffydd, he'd vowed never to allow his emotions such free rein again.

The guard yielded, turning away in sullen, resentful silence, and Davydd raised his voice. 'Bran!' A man at once detached himself from the crowd of onlookers. The other guards were shifting uneasily, no longer sure what was expected of them. 'You are to answer to Bran, to take your orders from him.' Davydd paused, and then said, deliberately, speaking for the benefit of all within hearing, 'The Lady Joanna is to be treated with the respect due her as the King of England's sister . . . and my lady mother. Bear that well in mind, for the man who forgets it will have cause to regret it.'

Davydd paused again, to make sure that his warning had taken effect. And then Joanna stepped forward, touched his arm.

'Madame?' Said with such cold, remote formality that to Joanna, it was as much of a rebuff as a physical recoil. Her hand slipped from his sleeve; he heard her indrawn breath.

'Davydd . . . where am I to be taken?'

'My father has commanded that you be ferried across the strait to Llanfaes, held there until he decides what should be done.'

Llanfaes! Joanna had not dared admit until now just how truly frightened she was, how much she dreaded the thought of incarcera-

727

tion in a darkened castle dungeon. But Llanfaes held no dungeons; it was a seacoast manor. She deliberately dug her nails into the palm of her hand, for Llewelyn's unlooked-for leniency threatened to shred her composure as even the crowd's hostility could not. 'Davydd, I must speak with your father. I must see him, if only for a few moments.'

But Davydd was already shaking his head. 'He is gone. He rode out at first light.'

'Can I not wait till he returns?'

'It would serve for naught. He'll not see you.' Davydd gestured abruptly and Bran touched Joanna's arm, politely but firmly indicating she was to follow. She did, but gave Davydd one last despairing look over her shoulder, and Davydd cried out, 'Wait!'

Beckoning to the nearest man, he gave a terse, low-voiced order, one that earned him a look of surprise. But the man obeyed, hastened across the bailey towards Joanna's lodgings, re-emerging a moment later with Topaz straining upon a leather leash.

Davydd stood motionless, watching as Joanna moved to claim her dog, as she was then escorted towards the gateway. He ignored the stares, the whispers. Even the most probing eyes could read nothing in his face and many marvelled that he could be so impassive a witness to his mother's banishment from his father's court, his father's life. None were close enough to see the tears welling in his eyes.

As Joanna's guards carried the coffer chests into her bedchamber, Glynis said apologetically, 'They would not allow me to take your jewellery, Madame. But I was permitted to pack your clothing and your harp and your bath vials and –'

'That is more than I expected, Glynis.' And more than she deserved. During Ingeborg's years of confinement at Étampes Castle, it was said that Philip had denied her warm blankets, a physician's care. But I, Joanna thought bleakly, I am to do penance in my own bedchamber, with silver brushes and bath oils, and her guilt suddenly seemed more than she could bear. For the first time, she could understand why repentant sinners sought to expiate their wrongdoing with hair shirts, with sackcloth and ashes. Such gestures no longer seemed extravagant or suspect; theirs was actually the easier way, mortifying the flesh in order to mend the spirit.

As the men withdrew, Joanna moved towards the younger

woman. 'It was kind of you to come, Glynis. But you need not stay with me.'

'I know that, Madame. Lord Davydd said that if I did not want to come to Llanfaes, he'd find another to serve you. But I told him it was my wish to be with you.'

Joanna felt tears prick her eyes, but she blinked them back, fearing that if she started to cry, she'd not be able to stop. She hugged Glynis wordlessly, and the girl said shyly, 'Madame, will you tell me how this came to be? I do not understand, for I know you love Lord Llewelyn.'

'Yes . . . I do. And I will try to answer you, Glynis. But there is something I must do first. Did you bring parchment, pen and ink?'

Glynis nodded sadly. 'They were the very first items I packed, my lady.'

It took Joanna most of the afternoon to compose the letter to her husband. Again and again she had to scrape the parchment clean, but at last the words began to come. She did not try to make Llewelyn understand her infidelity; she knew that was hopeless. She gave him, instead, a factual account of the chronology of her brief liaison, swore that it was over long before Will's foolhardy intrusion into her bedchamber. She told him she loved him, would always love him, and she begged him to do what he could for Davydd, and to find the right words when telling Elen. And then she sent Glynis in search of Bran.

'Will you take this letter back to Aber, to Lord Llewelyn?' Seeing him about to refuse, Joanna hastily pulled a ring from her finger. 'I would like you to accept this garnet ring as a token of my gratitude.'

He eyed the ring with longing, but still he hesitated, and Joanna realized that he feared to face Llewelyn, to be the bearer of an unfaithful wife's plea. 'Take the letter to Lord Davydd. Tell him I ask that he give it to his father.'

He reached for the ring, and then the letter, and after that, Joanna could do nothing but wait. He was back sooner than she expected, shortly after dusk. At sight of the letter, she felt a sudden throb of hope, for she'd not thought Llewelyn would answer her. What mattered was that he would read her letter, learn the truth. But as she turned it over, she saw her own seal, unbroken, intact.

Bran averted his eyes, made uncomfortable by what he saw now in her face. 'As you see, Lord Llewelyn would not open it, and Lord

Davydd said . . . he said it will avail you naught to write again. He said his lord father will not read your letters.'

Joanna was standing at the window, gazing up at a spring sky as brightly blue as the Irish Sea; clouds drifted by like floating islands, trailing fleece in their wake. The meadows would be ablaze in gorse, a brilliant yellow flower she'd picked by the armful in springs gone by. How strange that something so simple as a walk on the beach could suddenly mean so much.

'Glynis, is this a Thursday or a Friday? When I awoke this morn, I could be sure neither of the day nor the date.'

'This is a Friday, Madame, the 3rd of May.'

'May 3rd,' Joanna echoed, and then, 'eighteen days.' She turned abruptly from the window. A week from the morrow would be the anniversary of her wedding. Twenty-four years since that fourteen-year-old girl had shyly clasped Llewelyn's hand upon the steps of St Werburgh's abbey church, twenty-four years. She almost spoke her thoughts aloud to Glynis, caught herself just in time. She was learning that to yield to memories was to embrace pain beyond endurance, was the surest route to madness.

There was a knock upon the bedchamber door. Bran opened the door but did not enter; instead, he stepped aside, allowed Ednyved to stride into the room.

Ednyved was brutally blunt. 'I've come to tell you that Will de Braose was hanged yesterday at Aber.' He was watching Joanna intently, but whatever reaction he might have expected, it was not this; she merely looked at him, showing no emotion at all, and he said curtly, 'You did hear me?'

'Yes.' He seemed to be waiting, and Joanna wondered what he wanted her to say. Was she supposed to show surprise? She'd known from the moment Llewelyn walked into her bedchamber that Will was a dead man. Was she supposed to grieve for Will? Mayhap one day she might, that he should have died at four-and-thirty, died so needlessly. But she would have to forgive him first, and she could find no forgiveness in her heart.

Ednyved moved farther into the chamber. 'I think he did not truly believe it, up to the last expected Llewelyn to relent. But when he realized there was to be no reprieve, he died well, with courage.'

'Yes,' Joanna said again. Will had never lacked courage. If only he had, he'd still be alive, and she'd be at Aber with her husband

730

and son. She swallowed, said softly, 'Ednyved . . . tell me. How is Llewelyn?'

'Bleeding.'

His answer was so graphic, so unexpectedly expressive that Joanna shuddered. Turning her back upon Ednyved, she moved blindly towards the window. He followed, grasping her shoulders and compelling her to face him.

'What would you have me do, sugar the truth for you? Nay, no tears. The time for tears is past. Ere I go, I want you to tell me why. You weep for Llewelyn and not for de Braose. You did not love him?'

He was hurting her, his fingers digging into her flesh, but she neither protested nor pulled away. She shook her head and he released her, stepped back, staring at her in baffled bitterness.

'That only makes your betrayal all the more unforgivable. Sweet Jesus, woman, why? I've watched as you struggled and schemed and fought to secure the succession for Davydd. Only then to play into Gruffydd's hands like this! And for what? A tumble in bed with a swaggering cock, a rakehell not worthy of Llewelyn's spit!'

'What . . . what do you mean, that I've played into Gruffydd's hands? Whilst I dare say he is taking great satisfaction in my fall, the shame is mine, not Davydd's.'

'You think not? When you've given Gruffydd's supporters a weapon they'd never dreamed within their grasp, an opportunity to cast doubts upon Davydd's paternity?'

Joanna gasped. 'But . . . but that is the most outrageous of lies! And utterly impossible. Will was just a lad when Davydd was born, could not possibly –'

'You truly do not see, do you? A woman's honour is verily like her maidenhead in that, once gone, it cannot be regained. Now that you've been taken in adultery with one man, there will be those who'll think de Braose was not the first, that there must have been others.'

'My God . . .' No more than a whisper. 'My God, what have I done?'

'Madame . . . Madame, sit down.' Glynis was beside her, putting a protective arm around her shoulders. 'Just sit there and I'll fetch some wine.'

A cup was hastily thrust into Joanna's hand; the stem felt cool to her fingers, wet and sticky with wine. She drank deeply, without

731

tasting, holding the cup with both hands. 'Llewelyn . . . Llewelyn does not believe this? Tell me he does not, Ednyved,' she pleaded, 'tell me he knows Davydd is his!'

'No . . . he does not believe it. I am sure of that.' Answering her unspoken question then, he added, 'Nor do I. Nor would most people, I'd wager. Given your extreme youth at the time of Davydd's birth, I think it unlikely that such a suspicion would gain widespread belief.' His voice hardened. 'But do not deceive yourself. There will be some who'll give it credence, if only because they want to believe it. Davydd's enemies – and he does have them – will seek to use it against him, as they'd use any weapon at hand.'

'And I . . . I gave it to them,' Joanna said, sounding so dazed, so devastated that Ednyved felt a flicker of unwelcome pity. But he did not contradict her.

'Well, I've had my say,' he said, thinking Llewelyn was wise in refusing to see her, to spare himself yet more pain. For as easy as it was to hate what she had done, it was not as easy to hate her, not as easy as it should have been.

'Ednyved, wait. There is something you must know. I did allow myself to enter into an intrigue with Will de Braose, in a moment of weakness, of madness if you will, during that time Llewelyn and I were estranged, whilst he was waging war in Ceri. But I ended the affair almost ere it began. I did not ask Will to my chamber that night, and nothing happened between us, nothing.'

When he did not reply, she fumbled for her crucifix chain. 'You do not believe me? I'll swear it then, swear it upon the lives of my children, upon their very –'

'That is not necessary. I think I do believe you, if only because your version makes more sense. I've known men like de Braose; they scorn the merlin hawk nesting free in the heather, must have the one under guard in another man's mews. But women rarely share that lust for risk-taking, and I could not see you bringing a lover into Llewelyn's bed, not unless you were love-blinded . . . or bewitched.'

'Will you tell Llewelyn, then? Will you tell Davydd?'

'I will tell Davydd. I cannot tell Llewelyn.'

'But why? I am not asking this for my sake; I know he cannot forgive me. But if he knew the truth, his grieving might not be so great. Can you not see that?'

'It is you who do not see, Joanna. Llewelyn is not about to believe anything you say, not now. Yours was the one betrayal he never expected. I truly think he'd have killed any man who'd have dared to come to him with suspicions, would never have believed it of you. And now . . . now he will not allow your name to be spoken in his hearing. Only once has he mentioned you, saying you were dead to him . . . and the measure of his bitterness is the measure of the love he once bore you.'

13

May, 1230

Dolwyddelan, North Wales

Leaving Aber soon after Will de Braose's hanging, Llewelyn began a wide circuit of his domains, maintaining a highly visible presence to discourage speculation and sct gossip at rest. He was at Dinbych Castle by mid-May, where he was overtaken by a Cistercian Abbot who'd often served as an emissary of the Crown; the Abbot was bearing letters from the English King and his Chancellor, and Llewelyn agreed to meet the Chancellor at Shrewsbury in June. From Dinbych, Llewelyn moved south into Powys, and then on to the Cistercian abbey of Strata Florida. He did not linger, however, and the last days of May found him back in Gwynedd, in the heartland of his realm, the mountain citadel he most loved, his castle at Dolwyddelan.

He'd been travelling so rapidly, spending so many hours in the saddle that he'd outdistanced most couriers, and the table in his bedchamber was strewn with letters that had only recently caught up with him. He was sorting through them, dictating responses to a scribe as Davydd entered the chamber.

'Papa . . .' Davydd was unsure how to identify Richard, but after a moment's reflection, he realized it was immaterial; announcing him as Richard Fitz Roy would not make him any the less Joanna's brother. 'Papa, my uncle Richard has just ridden in. Are you willing to see him?'

Llewelyn was not, but he was even less willing to admit it, and he nodded.

The exchange of greetings was awkward for them all. Richard looked fatigued, and not a little embarrassed. 'It is good of you to make me welcome.'

'You are Davydd's uncle,' Llewelyn said dispassionately, but Richard was not deceived, saw Llewelyn's courtesy for what it was, an icy exercise in self-control.

Richard had given much thought to what he would say to Llewelyn, but he realized that was time misspent. To offer this man sympathy would be to offer a mortal insult. Although he'd never lacked for courage, he did not find it easy now to make mention of his sister's name. 'Davydd tells me that Joanna is at Llanfaes. Have I your permission to see her?'

'Yes,' Llewelyn said, still in those dangerously soft tones, and Richard thanked him, thinking all the while that Will de Braose must have been one of God's great fools . . . second only to his sister.

'I'll see that my uncle and his men are fed and bedded down in the great hall,' Davydd offered, and when Llewelyn nodded, he ushered Richard towards the door. But within moments, he was back, glancing first at the stacked parchments and then at Llewelyn's scribe.

'It grows late, Papa, and Celyn looks tired. Can the letters not wait till the morrow?'

'Your concern for Celyn's well-being is commendable,' Llewelyn said dryly, but then he smiled at his son. 'Very well, lad. That will be all, Celyn.'

'Shall I summon your squires, Papa?'

Llewelyn resisted the temptation to ask if Davydd wanted to keep vigil by his bedside till he slept. 'No, Davydd, that's not necessary. Go back to the hall now, make sure that our guests are looked after.'

Gathering up the correspondence, the scribe made a discreet departure; those who served Llewelyn this spring had, of necessity, learned to be as prescient as soothsayers, as unobtrusive as shadows. Davydd paused in the doorway. 'God grant you a restful night, Papa,' he said, and Llewelyn thought it might be for the best, after all, that Richard had come to his court. Mayhap Richard might be able to do what he could not, talk to the lad about Joanna. That Davydd had such a need, he well knew. A man might disavow a wanton, cheating wife. But a son could not be expected to disavow his mother.

Reaching for a flagon, Llewelyn poured himself a cup of malmsey. He drank slowly, rationing himself, for he was not such a fool as to think he could drown his dreams in wine. Picking up the cup, he crossed to the bed, lay down upon it fully clothed. The dreams had a numbing sameness, differing only in detail. Most often the dream did but reflect reality; he would walk into his bedchamber, unsuspect-

735

ing, and find his wife with her young lover. More than once, though, the dream took an even uglier turn, and he would enter the chamber while they were making love, naked bodies entwined together in his bed, so lost in their lust they did not perceive their danger until it was too late, until he had sword in hand. Sometimes he heeded Ednyved, took a more calculating, cold-blooded vengeance; sometimes Will died at once, there in the bedchamber. But not Joanna, for even in his dreams he could never bring himself to thrust the sword into her breast.

As harrowing as these dreams were, they were not as rending as the others, the dreams of days gone by, those that recreated his world before his discovery of Joanna's infidelity. Like most dreams, they were an incongruous blend of the fanciful and the commonplace, dreams in which a man might get saddle sores from riding a unicorn. But in them all, Joanna was the one constant. Taking a bath, she'd splash him with soapy water, giggling like a little girl. Or she'd look up at him over a Welsh grammar lesson, grimace and vow she'd master his tongue if it took her a lifetime. She was there to welcome him home from war, and there beside him in the night, and the seductive lure of memory was such that he would awaken in drowsy arousal, reaching for her. And then he would remember.

Llewelyn took a deep swallow of malmsey. Upon his first night at Dolwyddelan, he'd been crossing the bailey, had come upon some of his soldiers, squatting by the door of the great hall, passing a flask back and forth as they discussed his wife's betrayal, her lover's death. They tempered their abuse of Will de Braose with a grudging acknowledgment of his gallows courage, but they spared Joanna nothing, damned her in language as coarse as it was colourful. When Llewelyn stepped out of the darkness, they scrambled to their feet, staring at him in stricken silence. All save one youngster, drunker than the rest, who blurted out:

'I do not understand your forbearance, my lord. You must hate her now, you must! So why have you not punished her as she deserves?'

Appalled, his more sober comrades made haste to intervene, sought to turn aside Llewelyn's anger with a babble of apology and excuse. Llewelyn looked at the boy, younger even than Davydd, trying in his muddled way to empathize with his lord's pain. How easy it would be to make a scapegoat of this imprudent youth. Easy and understandable and unjust. 'I do not suffer fools gladly,' he said

736

curtly, 'but luckily for you, lad, I have more patience with drunkards. Go sleep it off.' The soldiers did not press their luck; they scattered.

But the boy's question stayed with Llewelyn in the days to come. Why had he not punished Joanna as she deserved? Why had he sent her to Llanfaes? Why had he made hers such a comfortable confinement? He'd done it for Davydd's sake. That was the obvious answer, the easy answer. But was it the only answer?

His last memory of Joanna had yet to fade; he had only to close his eyes to bring it into sudden, sharp focus, to see the tangled dark hair, the rumpled sheets, even the sweat trickling down her throat, into the hollow between her breasts. That woman he could hate, and did, the woman who'd taken a Norman lover, made him a laughing-stock, betrayed his trust, jeopardized Davydd's succession. Blood will tell, the soldiers had jeered; who should be surprised that John's daughter showed herself to be a shameless wanton? Harlot. Whore. Harsh, ugly names. The woman who'd taken Will into his bed deserved them all.

But what of the seventeen-year-old girl who'd almost died giving birth to Davydd? Or the woman who'd stood in this chamber, pleaded with him to let her intercede with John? What of the woman who'd curtseyed to him that day at Aberconwy, salvaging his pride, defying her father for his sake? Did she, too, deserve to be called slut?

Llewelyn drained the last of the wine, threw the cup across the room, watched it shatter against the wall. It was an act of impulse, one he at once regretted. Come morning, the servants would find the broken clay shards upon the floor; they would make no comment, would clean up the wreckage with impassive faces. And they would not understand.

No one did. Morgan had come the closest to comprehending; in his one attempt at consolation, he'd counselled endurance. 'Give yourself time, Llewelyn, time to grieve. Try to remember that pain does pass. Think upon Tangwystl and how you mourned her. But the hurt did eventually heal . . . and so will this.'

At least Morgan could understand that it was possible to grieve for an unfaithful wife; few others did. But he was wrong to equate Tangwystl's death with Joanna's betrayal. This was a different sort of loss, and in its own way, more painful, for he'd lost more than Joanna, he'd lost their life together, too. In destroying their future, Joanna had also poisoned their past.

Closing his eyes, Llewelyn lay back against the pillow. But no man could ever fully master memory. The tides ran higher at night, and he found himself engulfed without warning, carried back in time to an October afternoon, to the cloistered silence of the White Ladies Priory. Joanna was standing again before him, dishevelled, breathless, a russet leaf clinging to her hair, turning up to him a face streaked with tears. And Llewelyn gave a sudden, bitter laugh, for what greater irony could there be than this, that the one person able to understand exactly how he now felt should be Joanna, Joanna who'd cried out in such despair:

'If he'd died, I'd still have had memories. But now even my memories are false. They do not comfort, they only torment . . .'

'Richard!' Joanna's book thudded to the floor; in three strides she was across the room, in her brother's arms. 'How glad I am to see you, how very glad!' He did not return her embrace, merely patted her awkwardly on the shoulder, but he'd always been sparing with physical demonstrations of affection, and she reached up, kissed him on the cheek before stepping back to smile at him.

'I'm not sure what I expected, Joanna. But not this,' he said, glancing about the bedchamber. 'One might think you were still Princess of Gwynedd.'

Joanna's smile vanished; his voice was very cold. 'Would you rather have found me in a dungeon at Cricieth, Richard?'

'Of course not,' he said impatiently. 'But I cannot help marvelling at Llewelyn's leniency.'

'You've seen him, talked to him? Tell me how he is, Richard. How does he?'

'How do you think he does? The man loved you, Joanna.'

'I know,' she whispered. 'I know . . .'

'How could you do it? How could you shame yourself, shame your family like this? At first I thought it had to be some sort of macabre hoax! And if I could not believe it, I would not even attempt to imagine what Llewelyn –'

'Richard, enough! I do not need you to tell me of the pain I've caused those I love. I was there, I saw, and those are memories I'll have to live with for the rest of my life. I do not deny that I have committed a grievous sin, and I'll willingly answer for it to my husband, to my children, to the King, and to God. But not to you, Richard. Least of all to you!'

'You do not think I've a right to be angry? Disappointed?'

738

'I do not think you've the right to pass judgment upon me. I think you forfeited that right when you refused to pass judgment upon John.'

'What mean you by that, Joanna?'

'You knew, Richard. You knew about Arthur, about Maude de Braose and her son. You saw the hangings. But you stood by John even then, even after watching those Welsh children die at Nottingham. So I do not think it is for you to judge me. Unless you can explain why adultery is a greater sin in your eyes than murder.'

'I see it was a mistake for me to come.'

'Mayhap it was,' Joanna agreed, and he turned, walked out.

But no sooner had he gone than Joanna's anger was gone, too. She sat down upon the closest coffer, feeling weak, empty, and alone, utterly alone. Why had she sent Richard away? Who else did she have? Henry would be no less shocked than Richard, no less judgmental. An unfaithful wife was a creature utterly beyond her aunt Ela's ken. She was not close to her other brothers. Two of her three sisters were strangers to her, and Nell was but fourteen.

Even her dead would not have understood. Catherine had been her dearest friend, but Catherine had been Llewelyn's friend, too. Her grandmother? Eleanor would have been indifferent to the immorality of her adultery, but would never have forgiven the stupidity of it. Her mother would have been horrified, with the peculiar intolerance of the onetime sinner. Her father? Hating Llewelyn as he did, how could he not have been delighted by her infidelity? But her mockery went awry, for she knew better. John would not have forsaken her. The man who had murdered Maude de Braose was the same man who had loved her enough to forgive her any sin.

She had sent Glynis to gather gorse and wood sorrel, and she was grateful now to hear footsteps in the antechamber, grateful for Glynis's opportune return; hers were not thoughts she cared to dwell upon. She rose, moved towards the door. But it was not Glynis, it was Richard.

His smile was tentative, almost but not quite apologetic. 'I would not have become so angry if there were not some truth in what you said. But I was half-way to the ferry ere I would admit it to myself.'

'You came back, Richard. That is what matters,' Joanna said, and this time their embrace was mutual, comforting and conciliatory. Drawing him down beside her upon the settle, Joanna entwined her fingers in his. 'I will answer your questions as best I can. But first you must tell me if you spoke to Davydd, if he gave you any message for me.'

He shook his head. 'He's not yet able to talk about you, Joanna. Mayhap in time . . .' He tightcncd his grip upon her hand. 'How much have you been told? You do know Will de Braose has been hanged?'

'Yes,' she said, startling him by her matter-of-fact tone. If she could sound so indifferent to Will's fate, then all his assumptions had to be in error.

'I can offer no excuses, no explanations for my conduct, Richard. But there is this you must know. My liaison with Will was a brief one, and long over. But Will was not accustomed to a woman telling him "no" and meaning it, thought he would be welcome in my chambers. He was not.' Richard was looking at her so strangely that she felt sudden dismay. 'You do not believe me?'

'How could I have been so stupid? I actually believed you must have been beguiled by this man, had become so infatuated you'd lost all common sense. Knowing you as I do, how could I have been so blind?' He rose to his feet, began to pace. 'Why did I not see the truth ere this?'

'What are you talking about?'

'I think you know, Joanna. But if you'd have me elaborate upon the obvious, I am willing. Where shall we begin? With Llewelyn? You love your husband, you truly do. You have a marriage that was tested in fire and found true, a marriage that by rights ought to have foundered years ago, and yet it not only survived, it somehow flourished. You're no fool; you well knew the consequences of a wife's infidelity, knew you risked divorce and disgrace, mayhap even death. You knew, too, that adultery is a mortal sin. Yet despite all that, you still decided to take the risk, to take a lover. And of all the men in Christendom, whom did you happen to choose? None other than Maude de Braose's grandson! Need I say more?'

Joanna's protest was immediate . . . and indignant. 'What are you saying, that John's sins led me to sin in atonement? That is ridiculous, Richard. I am not responsible for my father's cruelties!'

'I know,' he said. 'And I've been seeking to convince you of that for nigh on twenty years.'

Joanna opened her mouth to argue, to insist he was wrong. Instead, she surprised herself by saying, 'I do think it was important to Will, that I was John's daughter. I think he found a perverse satisfaction in that. He learned to hate too young. But he had cause, Richard, more cause than you know . . .' She did not finish the sentence, said abruptly, 'What of Henry? Does he know?'

Richard nodded. 'He got word ere he sailed for St Malo.' He sat down beside her again. 'I'll not lie to you, Joanna; better that you know. Sentiment is very much on Llewelyn's side, even in England. Men feel he was justified in acting as he did, that Will de Braose well deserved to die. More than eight hundred people gathered to witness his execution, and not all of them Welsh. Will was too familiar with too many bedchambers; even amongst his own family, he does not seem to have been much mourned.'

Joanna linked her fingers in her lap. She found herself thinking now, not of the man who'd brought disaster upon them both, not even of the man who'd been her lover, but of the youngster who'd come to her aid with boyish, good-natured gallantry, who'd put her in mind of Llewelyn at fourteen. 'To die alone and unloved,' she said softly. 'What a sad fate . . .'

Richard shrugged. 'It is your fate that concerns me now. I'll admit I was none too sanguine ere today . . . ere seeing this,' he said, gesturing about the bedchamber. 'But I am beginning to believe all is not as bleak as I first thought.'

Joanna bowed her head. 'Llewelyn says . . . he says I am dead to him, Richard.'

'Yes, I know. But have you not noticed the startling discrepancy between what Llewelyn has said and what he has done? I do not mean to inflict further hurt, Joanna, but few men would treat an unfaithful wife as indulgently as he has so far treated you. I think his forbearance bodes well for the future. Whilst it is true that the Church does not formally recognize adultery as grounds for divorce, Llewelyn will have no trouble in –'

'Welsh law does provide for dissolving a marriage upon a wife or a husband's infidelity,' Joanna interrupted, and despite herself, she could not help remembering the night Llewelyn had told her that, the night they'd first shared a bed as man and wife.

'A husband's infidelity, too?' Richard echoed, so surprised he almost allowed himself to be sidetracked. But the oddities of the Welsh legal system would have to wait. 'Joanna, listen. I've been giving it much thought. As I see it, Llewelyn has three choices open to him. He can continue to keep you here, at Llanfaes. He can compel you to enter a nunnery. Or he can banish you from his

741

domains. I expected him to select the second alternative. You're something of an embarrassment, you know . . . both to the Welsh and to the English, and a cloistered embarrassment would fade more quickly from men's memories. But now that I've seen your confinement, I think we might reasonably hope for the best, that he might agree to your return to England.'

'Mayhap he might. I do not know, Richard. Nor do I much care,' Joanna confessed, and Richard smiled.

'Not now, no. But even the most benign captivity is still that, captivity. You need only think of our cousin, Eleanor of Brittany, comfortably kept at Bristol and Corfe castles for nigh on thirty years. In time, you will care, Joanna, you'll care passionately.'

Joanna said nothing, and he reached out, patted her hand. 'You must be patient, though. It would be disastrous to pressure Llewelyn now. We can only wait, first for the divorce and then for his decision. But Henry will not forsake you. You're family, and that matters more to Henry than scandal. I do believe that eventually you will be set at liberty, and once that happens, you'll have a home with my wife and me, a home at Chilham Castle.'

'Thank you, Richard,' Joanna said, because it was expected of her. But his offer seemed no more real than did the future he envisioned for her. Rising, she moved to the table, opened a small casket.

'I've written letters to Elen and Davydd, to Henry, and to Nell. Will you take them, Richard? Will you engage couriers for me?'

'Of course. And I shall write to Llewelyn on your behalf, ask him if you cannot be allowed to leave these rooms occasionally. I think he might agree, if only for Davydd's sake.'

'I would like that,' Joanna admitted, 'being able to walk on the beach.' She hesitated, reluctant to make a request that might be misconstrued. 'There is one thing more you can do for me, Richard. I would like to have Masses said for Will, for the repose of his soul.' And when he made no comment, merely nodded, she sighed, said quietly:

'I cannot mourn him. I'm not even sure I can forgive him. But at least I can pray for him.'

14

June, 1230
Llanfaes, North Wales

Richard read Llewelyn correctly, and an order did arrive in due course, allowing Joanna the freedom of the manor compound and the nearby beach. Her guards objected to this new duty in vain, protesting that they felt foolish trailing after a lone woman and an aging spaniel. Lady Joanna could not swim; did Bran fear she could walk on water? But Bran remained adamant. Would any of them want to face their lord if she disappeared? Or if harm befell her? For so baffled were they about what their duties were, uncertain whether they were gaolers . . . or bodyguards.

It was a warm Sunday in late June, too warm for walking, and when Joanna came upon the debris of an ancient wreck, she sat down upon a salt-encrusted spar. The guard following at a discreet distance stretched out on the sand, began to doze. So, too, did Joanna's spaniel.

Joanna spent many hours like this, gazing across the strait towards Aber. She knew Llewelyn was no longer there, so even this last tenuous link had been sundered, but she found herself drawn to the beach, none the less. It was an uncommonly clear day; the wind was still and the Eryri Mountains had shed their cloud haloes. She was able to recognize individual peaks, Llewelyn's lessons in geography having at last taken effect, and she realized suddenly how much she would miss these familiar soaring silhouettes, miss the stark splendours of her husband's realm. 'You were right, love,' she whispered. 'You always said I'd come in time to see the grandeur of your homeland . . .'

Topaz had begun to bark. From the corner of her eye, Joanna glimpsed a woman crossing the sand. 'Hush, girl,' she soothed. ''Tis only Glynis.' But the dog knew better, was already capering about in eager welcome. Joanna turned and her heart skipped a beat, then began to race. Flustered and not a little fearful, she stood

743

very still, watching as her daughter walked towards her. This was the confrontation she'd most dreaded. Davydd might in time forgive her, but Elen? They'd been too often at odds, never quite connecting, theirs an erratic sort of intimacy, one with boundaries, self-imposed constraints, vast areas left uncharted, unexplored by mutual consent. What could she say to Elen now? How could she expect Elen to understand?

'Well, I will say this for you, Mama. No half measures; when you decide to come down off your pedestal, you do so with a vengeance.'

The words were tart, but surprisingly, the tone was not; it was more rueful than reproachful, almost whimsical. Joanna stared at her unpredictable daughter, saying at last, 'I am glad you've come, Elen.'

'I would have come sooner, but John and I had gone north from Edinburgh, were doubtlessly the last to know.' Elen glanced over at the sleeping soldier before sitting down upon the sea-warped driftwood. 'Your guard is out of hearing range. Sit with me, Mama, so we can talk.'

'Did you get my letter?' Joanna asked, sighing with relief when Elen nodded.

'Yes, it finally caught up with me, and just in time. Papa's letter had been sparing of details, and I was well nigh going mad, trying to envision circumstances under which you'd have taken a lover into Papa's bedchamber. I could only conclude you were sore crazed with love, and yet you'd showed no symptoms of it at Shrewsbury. When your letter came, I could only wonder why I'd not guessed the truth. That was so very like Will, after all.'

Elen finally paused for breath. 'All this did clear up one mystery for me, though. Will was notorious for his roving eye, and yet with me he was always quite circumspect, could not have been more respectful had I been a nun. At least now I know why!'

'Elen . . . I will never understand you. How can you jest?'

'I suppose . . . suppose because I'm nervous. I just did not know what to say to you.' Elen mustered a wan smile. 'You will admit, Mama, that my lessons in the social graces never covered a situation quite like ours.'

She did not wait for Joanna's response, leaned forward and touched her mother's hand. 'I do have some good news for you. I asked Papa if the priest from St Catherine's could say weekly Mass at the manor, and he agreed. Mama . . . does that not please you? Why do you look at me so strangely?'

'I . . . I never expected sympathy, Elen.'

Elen withdrew her hand. 'Why not? Why should you think I'd be less understanding than Davydd?'

'Davydd does not understand, darling. I can only hope that he will in time, as I'd hoped you might. But I would not have blamed you for being bitter. We've so often been at cross-purposes, and I know . . . I know how much you love your father.'

'Yes, I do. I love Papa dearly. But what would you have me do, Mama? Disavow you because you made a mistake? Would that change anything? Would it make Papa's hurt any the less?'

'A mistake,' Joanna echoed, dismayed. Had Elen so misconstrued her letter? 'Elen, I thought you understood. I was unfaithful to your father.'

'Yes, Mama, I know. You broke your marriage vows. But a few afternoons in an abandoned *hafod* do not make you the whore of Babylon. You sinned and then were sorry. I dare say the same can be said of Papa. Papa is a remarkable man, in truth, but he wears a crown, not a halo. Surely you know he has been unfaithful to you?'

Joanna was both disconcerted and defensive. 'Yes . . . I know. But when I compared my lot with that of most wives, I had no cause for complaint. Llewelyn never kept a mistress at court; he even put aside Cristyn for me. Whilst we never discussed it, I knew he did bed with other women, but only when I was not available, only when we'd been long apart.'

'As when he was waging war in Ceri?'

'Elen, I do not see the point of this. What would you have me say? Of course I would rather Llewelyn shared no bed but mine. But I could not realistically expect him to abstain for weeks at a time.'

'You did.'

'Why are you being so perverse? You cannot equate Llewelyn's occasional lapses with my adultery. Infidelity is a greater sin for a woman; so it has always been.'

'Yes, so men keep telling us,' Elen said dryly, and Joanna found herself staring at her daughter as if at a stranger.

'I once told my father that blood breeds true,' she said slowly. 'I spoke greater truth than I knew, for none could ever doubt you are Eleanor of Aquitaine's great-granddaughter. It frightens me to hear you talk like this, for I do not think you realize the danger in it. Elen

. . . Elen, you've never . . .' She let the sentence trail off, and Elen gave her a smile of gentle mockery.

'You ought not to ask a question, Mama, unless you are sure you truly want to know the answer.'

'Oh, Elen, no . . .' Joanna whispered, sounding so horrified that Elen flushed, sprang to her feet.

'What are you going to do, Mama? Lecture me on morality? I should think that would be rather droll, coming from you!'

Joanna, too, was on her feet now. 'Elen, you must listen to me. I am not passing judgment upon you, ask only that you hear me out. Walk towards the water with me, so we may be sure we cannot be overheard. Please, darling, you do not know what you risk!'

Elen hesitated. 'Very well, Mama. But I'll hear no sermons from you!'

'I said I was not judging you. I want only to ask you a question. Mine could have been a far different fate. But your father has shown me remarkable leniency. Why do you think that is, Elen?'

This was not the question Elen was expecting. 'I . . . I suppose he did it for us, for Davydd and me. And then, he did love you. Mayhap he finds it hard to hurt you, even now . . .'

Joanna flinched, but then she nodded. 'You are right. But I think there is yet another reason for his restraint. I think his response might have been different had he not been Welsh.'

Elen came to an abrupt halt. 'I do not understand. Welsh law holds adultery to be a grave sin, indeed. So why . . .'

'Because the Welsh look upon women in a different light. A Welshman does not think of his wife as his property; she has rights of her own. But a Norman wife does not, and that makes her betrayal all the more unforgivable in her husband's eyes. Elen, I know of what I speak, for I am Norman-French born and bred; their ways are mine. I know no Norman lord capable of treating an unfaithful wife as Llewelyn has so far treated me, not even the men of my own family. My darling, your husband is a good man, but he does not share your heritage, and you must ever bear that in mind. Promise me that, Elen, promise me you'll not forget.'

Elen's resentment had ebbed away as Joanna spoke. 'You've no cause for fear, Mama. That question you almost asked? The answer is no, I have not.'

Joanna looked into her daughter's beautiful brown eyes, eyes that held hers quite candidly, and realized she had no way of knowing if

Elen spoke the truth. Even if she had, what of tomorrow? Elen was entrapped in an unhappy marriage, a barren marriage. How long would it be ere she sought satisfaction elsewhere, ere that rebellious spirit led her astray?

'Ah, Elen . . .' Her voice wavered. 'How could we have meant so well and done so wrong? I truly thought you could learn to love John the Scot, but I should have known, should have seen . . .'

'I no longer blame you, Mama.' Elen stooped to pick up a cockle shell. 'None of us are given a warranty of happiness, not in this life. Even if I'd wed another man, who's to say we'd have found contentment together? Sometimes even love is not enough. After all, you loved Papa, and where did it get you?'

'To Llanfaes,' Joanna said tonelessly, and Elen dropped the shell, moved to close the space between them.

'Mama, I'm sorry! I do not know why I said that. Why must my accursed tongue inflict wounds I never mean?'

'It does not matter, Elen . . . truly.'

'But it does! I swore to myself that this time I would not do it, that I'd say nothing hurtful or harsh.' Elen turned her back, stood staring out over the water. When she spoke again, her voice was indistinct, pitched very low. 'But I've sworn that before, only to hear myself provoking yet another quarrel with you, stirring up strife betwixt us . . .'

'Why?' Joanna reached out, touched her daughter's arm. 'Why, Elen?'

'I would that I knew! Frustration, resentment, mayhap sheer perversity. You do not bring out the best in me, Mama. But then I hardly need tell you that, do I? I've always been a disappointment to you, as far back as I can remember –'

'Darling, that's not so! Elen, I love you, I do!'

Elen kept her eyes stubbornly set upon the distant mountains, but her lashes were wet, tangled. 'That may be so, Mama, but you do not approve of me. I used to wonder how Davydd did it, how he knew unerringly just how to please you, for I . . . I never did, you see. I did try, though. You may not believe that, but I did.

'I was about seven the first time I realized you were not like the mothers of my friends. Your father had freed some of Papa's hostages, merely because you asked it of him. People were so joyful, so grateful, and I was so proud of you. I wanted to be a great lady, too . . . just like you. And as I grew older, I watched as you acted for

747

Papa at the English court, I saw how much Papa loved you, and I tried to be what you wanted, to be like you. But you were so controlled, so serene, so sure of yourself, and I . . . I was none of those things, Mama. In truth, I was not in the least like you, at best could only hope to become an imperfect copy of a perfect original, and that seemed rather pointless to me, even at fourteen. And so I stopped trying to gain your approval. Only I . . . I could not stop wanting it.'

Elen had not intended to reveal so much and she forced an abrupt, self-conscious laugh. 'I did not mean to babble on like this. I suppose I've been like a bottle corked too long. One inadvertent touch and the contents spew out in a great gush. Let that be a lesson to you, Mama. There are few questions so full of risk as a seemingly simple "why".'

Joanna had been listening to her daughter's outpouring in astonishment. 'Is that how you truly saw me, Elen? As controlled, serene, sure of myself? God in Heaven!' She caught Elen's arm, turned the younger woman to face her. 'Elen, look at me. Truly look at me. I was a King's bastard. Under our law, I had no claims to anything, least of all to my father's name. My father loved me, but he could not legitimize my position at his court; I was there on sufferance and all knew it. And then at fourteen, I became a foreign wife, the English bride, the outsider once more.'

Elen's eyes had widened. 'I never knew you felt like that, Mama. You always seemed at home in Wales.'

'That is what I am trying to tell you, Elen. I learned at a very early age to hide my fears, to appear what I was not. Pride, no less than charity, covers a multitude of sins. I was very fortunate, found with your father what had been denied me in John's world, and in time, I did gain greater assurance; the poise was not entirely pretence. But scrape away the surface gloss, dig through the glaze to the raw clay, and you'll find a little girl forbidden to play with the other village children, a little girl who'd lie for hours in the heather above Middleham Castle, wanting only to belong.

'And that is what I wanted to give you, a sense of belonging. You were so impulsive, Elen, so . . . so rash. I did try to curb your spirits, to teach you to adapt to the world you'd one day have to live in, as the wife of a Norman lord. I did want you to conform; I cannot deny it. And I was disappointed when you would not. But only because I loved you so much, because I feared for you. My darling, you seemed

748

so heart-rendingly vulnerable, so open to hurt. I wanted to spare you that if I could, to show you how to construct a woman's defences, how to make castle walls out of courtesy, to distance yourself whilst still preserving the inner keep, the secret self that is Elen.'

Elen was blinking back tears. 'I dare say you're right, Mama.' She gestured towards a tiny bird skittering along the water's edge. 'Life probably would be easier for me if I had protective colouring, if I could blend into my background like that little sandling.' She smiled tremulously. 'But I'm not a sandling, Mama, am more akin to the magpie, I fear, curious and conspicuous and too venturesome for my own good!'

Joanna stepped forward, touched her hand to Elen's cheek. 'As it happens,' she said, 'magpies have ever been one of my favourite birds,' and Elen came into her arms, clung tightly.

Joanna was reluctant to end their embrace, kept her arm around Elen's waist. 'Passing strange, that you should have drawn that analogy to the sandling, for your father once made a surprisingly similar comparison. He, too, talked of protective colouring, told me I cloaked myself in the muted earth tones of a wellborn Norman lady. But he knew it was a camouflage, knew me so well . . .'

He'd never been taken in by her act. Right from the first he'd seen through it, had seen the frightened little girl behind the bridal silk, the brittle smile. Joanna's eyes filled with tears. 'Elen . . . Elen, I've made such a botch of things. Tell me the truth. How badly have I hurt Llewelyn? I do not mean the man; that I know. But what of the Prince? How much damage have I done?'

'Not as much damage as you fear, Mama. I'll not deny the potential was there for disaster, that you threw a burning brand into a sun-dried field. But Papa acted to contain the fire, seems to have quenched it in time. Not so surprising, at least not to anyone who knows Papa. He holds all Wales in the palm of his hand, has for nigh on fifteen years now. It would take a brave man to challenge him, an even braver one to mock him. Mayhap if he'd showed weakness . . . But he hanged Will de Braose at high noon before eight hundred witnesses. Men will remember that, Mama.'

'And Davydd?'

Elen did not pretend to misunderstand. 'Again, the answer is not as much damage as you think . . . or as there could have been. Papa has made a point of keeping Davydd close by his side – conspicuously so. When he met the English Chancellor in Shrewsbury last week,

749

Davydd was with him, and will be with him again when he meets with Maelgwn next month. It is an effective strategy, Mama, will do much to discourage speculation, to still all but the most vicious tongues.'

'I would to God I could believe that . . .'

'I'm not offering false comfort, Mama. Papa is a man well able to take care of himself, to look to his own interests. He was never a defensive battle commander, preferred to take the war into enemy territory. And that is what he has done. He is no longer calling himself Prince of Gwynedd, has begun to make use of a new title – Prince of Aberffraw and Lord of Eryri.'

After more than twenty years in Wales, Joanna at once grasped the significance of the change. Aberffraw was the ancient capital of Gwynedd and in Welsh lore, the Prince of Aberffraw held a position of dominance. Although he was shrewd enough to do it by indirection, with a subtlety to allay the suspicions of his English neighbours and the jealousies of his Welsh allies, Llewelyn was in effect claiming for himself the title Prince of Wales.

Joanna bit her lip. 'How very like him that is,' she said, and there was in her voice such a poignant blend of pride and pain that Elen felt as if their roles had suddenly been reversed; she found herself yearning to comfort Joanna as a mother might comfort a hurt and helpless child.

'Let's go back to the manor, Mama. You look so careworn; you've not been sleeping, have you?'

'Not much,' Joanna admitted. She whistled for Topaz and they began to walk along the shore. 'We'd best wake Ifan up ere we go; I think he might be discomfited if we just went off and left him. Tell me about Gwladys and Ralph de Mortimer. Were they wed as planned?'

'No, the wedding was delayed. But it has been rescheduled for next month.' Elen's eyes rested pensively upon her mother's face. She'd not exaggerated; the strain was telling upon Joanna. She sighed, knowing what she had now to say would only lacerate an over-burdened conscience even more.

'I know no other way than to say this straight out, Mama. Papa and the de Braose family have decided to honour the plight troth.'

Joanna stared at her daughter in disbelief. 'Davydd . . . Davydd is still going to wed Will's daughter?'

Elen nodded. 'Papa wrote to Eva de Braose and her brother

Pembroke, told them that whilst he'd had no choice but to put Will to death, he was still willing to consider a marital alliance. Will's widow and Pembroke showed themselves to be no less pragmatic than Papa. Not only did they want the marriage to take place, they wanted it to be celebrated as soon as possible, despite Isabella's tender years. The wedding is to be held at Cricieth in Michaelmas week.'

Joanna closed her eyes, but the sun still burned against her lids, dried the tears on her cheeks. How could Llewelyn bear to do this? How could he look at Isabella de Braose and not think of Will? 'And Davydd . . . he's willing?'

'Yes, Mama, it seems he is. In part, I think, because he wants so to please Papa. If Papa were to suggest he wed with a mermaid, I dare say Davydd would start scouring the beaches for one. But there's more to it than that. People often misjudge Davydd. He's more like Papa than men realize; theirs are differences more of style than substance. Davydd knows his own mind, Mama, knows what he wants – and obviously that is Buellt Castle.'

Elen, like Llewelyn and Davydd, spoke French with Joanna, partly from habit, partly for the greater privacy it accorded their conversations, and partly because their French was more fluent than Joanna's Welsh. She was surprised now to hear her mother murmur, as if to herself, '*Un pechod a lusg gant ar ei ol.*'

'One sin draws a hundred after it? Ah, Mama, you're too hard on yourself.'

'Am I? I think not, Elen.' Joanna turned away, stared blindly out to sea. 'That poor little lass,' she said softly. 'How bewildered she must be, how fearful . . .'

15

September, 1230

Cricieth, North Wales

Will de Braose was not entirely unmourned. There was one who grieved for him, his ten-year-old daughter. Isabella's was a world of restrictive boundaries, hers a life of absolutes and order, subject at all times to the astringent, exacting disciplines laid down by Eva de Braose. A timid child, Isabella had learned obedience at an early age, but she had also learned to fear her mother. Eva was the bedrock to which their family clung, anchor and mainstay, and she ruled her small domain with a tight rein – in Will's absences. For into this cloistered citadel of enforced serenity, Will would burst like a flaming comet, trailing the real world in his wake like celestial vapours. He invariably disrupted daily routine, unsettled the servants, and took a malicious pleasure in disobliging his coolly competent wife. Isabella – quite simply and unknowingly – he bedazzled.

To a child nurtured upon reprimands, starved for affection, it was not difficult to unearth evidence of love in Will's benign neglect, to magnify his careless kindnesses to epic proportions. Isabella treasured his smiles, the small gifts he would occasionally bestow, kept a lock of his bright blond hair in her birthday locket. His death had devastated her, and her grieving was all the greater for its secret, unsanctioned nature. That her mother did not mourn Will, the child well knew, and fear made her mute, for she could not risk Eva's disapproval. Now that Will was dead, Eva's favour was all the more precious, was all she had.

Eva had spared her eldest daughter none of the sordid circum-stances of Will's death, but that account was too brutal, too degrading for the child to accept. In self-defence, she set about weaving Eva's ugly facts into a softer pattern, one that reflected the colours of romance and high tragedy. All the minstrel tales that so enthralled her celebrated the splendours of illicit passions, celebrated star-crossed

752

lovers like Arthur's Queen and the brave Lancelot, Tristan and the fair Iseult. So it must have been for Papa and the Lady Joanna, she decided, and she found comfort in casting Will as the gallant knight who died for love, Joanna as the tragic beauty who'd loved him as Eva did not. And then her mother called her into the solar at Abergavenny Castle, told her that the plight troth still held, that she must wed Llewelyn's son at summer's end.

Although Eva de Braose had no qualms about marrying her daughter to a son of the man responsible for her husband's death, she did feel it would not be seemly for her to attend the wedding. As the Earl of Pembroke was in Brittany, it fell upon his young wife Nell, and Gilbert, another of Eva's brothers, to escort Isabelle to Cricieth.

Nell slowed her mare, dropped back to ride at Isabella's side. 'We're but a few miles from Cricieth Castle, will be there by noon.' Isabella's was by nature a pale, delicate complexion, but it showed now such a waxy whiteness that Nell grew alarmed. Poor little bird, she thought, and sought for words of cheer. 'I shall be your aunt twice over come the morrow, for not only is my lord husband brother to your lady mother, the Lord Davydd is my nephew. Passing strange, I know, for he is a full seven years older than I! But he is a good man, Isabella, will treat you kindly.' Would he, though? How could she be sure? In truth, she did not know Davydd well at all, could only wonder what had motivated him to make such a marriage as this.

Isabella swallowed. 'Cricieth . . . is this where my father died?'

'No, lass. That was at Aber.'

'He's buried there . . . at Aber?'

'Yes,' Nell said, all the while heaping mental curses upon the head of her sister-in-law. Whatever ailed Eva? Had she told the child nothing?

'Aunt Nell . . . will they let me visit Papa's grave?'

'Jesu!' Nell turned sharply in the saddle, stared at the child. Merciful Christ, the lass loved her father! Damn Eva de Braose for this. How could she not know? Or was it that she did not care? 'Yes, sweeting, I am sure they will,' she said hastily, making a silent vow that she'd somehow see to it.

'I dared not ask Mama about her . . . about the Lady Joanna. Aunt Nell, will you tell me what befell her? Will she . . . will she be at Cricieth?'

Nell was getting in over her depth. She ought never to have

753

agreed to this. She might be the child's aunt, but she was also Joanna's sister. At least, though, she could reassure the lass on this one point. 'No, dearest, Joanna is not at Cricieth. You need not see her, not ever, for she has been sent away in disgrace.'

'Oh . . .' An involuntary sound, a quavering sigh that communicated to Nell the unlikeliest of emotions, disappointment. Nell subsided into a baffled silence. She pitied Isabella, but was perplexed by her, too. She'd never known her own father, for John had died before her first birthday. But she had tried to imagine how she'd feel if she were being forced to marry into a family responsible for her brother Henry's death, and that only showed her how deep and divergent were the differences between her and Isabella de Braose, for she would never have agreed to the wedding, would have had to be dragged kicking and screaming to the altar.

She glanced reflectively at Isabella's profile. A pity the lass did not have more pluck. A lamb to the slaughter, in truth, and what could she do to help? 'Isabella, I'm going to speak right plainly. As you're to be Davydd's wife, all you can do now is seek to make the best of it.'

'Will they . . .' Isabella's voice was tremulous, faltering. 'Will they hate me?'

'No, of course not,' Nell said, somewhat impatiently, for that was a question she'd never have asked. The hatred would have been hers. But she could sense in Isabella only fear.

As they entered the great hall, Isabella balked suddenly, and Nell slipped a supportive arm around her waist. 'When we reach the dais, remember to make your curtsy. Lord Davydd is the one at Lord Llewelyn's right, and those are Davydd's sisters, the Lady Elen, Countess of Huntingdon, and the Lady Gwladys de Mortimer. Come forward now, Isabella, and greet them.' Still Isabella did not move; she was trembling so violently that Nell could only hope she'd not shame them by fainting. She murmured soothing words of reassurance, and when they had no effect, she hissed, 'Isabella, show some spirit!' And that worked; Isabella had been taught unquestioning obedience. She followed Nell towards the dais, clinging to Nell's arm.

It did not surprise Llewelyn that Isabella was so fair, for both Will and Eva de Braose had flaxen hair. Still, the sight of the child's blonde braids triggered a sudden, sharp memory. He could see again her father standing on the gallows, the sun gilding his hair with a silvery sheen. He'd never looked so young, so vital and alive as he did then, in his last moments of life. And as Llewelyn had watched, all he could see was that blond head cradled in Joanna's lap. He shook off the past with difficulty, moved down the steps of the dais.

'Look at me, child,' he said quietly. Isabella did as he bade. To his relief, she did not have Will's smoke-grey eyes; hers were a soft misty blue. 'You are very welcome at my court, Isabella. I hope in time you'll come to feel at home with us.' Seeing that his words sank like stones into the depths of the child's fear, left no impression, not even a ripple.

Davydd had no better luck. He was not particularly at ease with children, and found himself at a loss now. Feeling rather foolish, he murmured conventional words of welcome, handed Isabella her bride's gift, an opal pendant set in silver; it might better, he thought, have been a doll. Isabella mumbled an all but inaudible 'thank you'. She did not even unfasten the velvet wrapping until prompted by Nell.

'Look, Isabella, how lovely it is. Here, let me clasp it about your neck.'

Llewelyn was faintly amused by Nell's purposeful, take-charge manner, so at variance with her ethereal blonde beauty. For she was a beauty, as young as she was, was very much Isabelle d'Angoulême's daughter. But he could see nothing in her of John or Joanna. Never had he been so aware how fleeting time was, how unfairly and heart-rendingly finite, looking now at Nell and realizing she was the same age as Joanna at the time of their wedding.

'Should you like to see the chamber made ready for you, Isabella?' he suggested, and Isabella nodded quickly. She was, he suspected, so anxious to escape their company that she'd have acquiesced no less eagerly had he offered a tour of the stables. But when Gwladys volunteered to take her, she hung back, blue eyes imploring Nell not to desert her, not to forsake her so soon.

'I'll be along shortly, Isabella. I promise,' Nell said, and the adults watched in troubled silence as Gwladys led the girl away. Nell's eyes, no less blue than Isabella's but a good deal more vivid, flicked from face to face. A deal struck in theory could prove to be quite different in fact, in the flesh and blood embodiment of a terrified ten year old. Did they, she wondered, still think Buellt Castle was worth the price of purchase?

Gilbert Marshal cleared his throat, said with overly hearty assurance, 'I dare say she just needs a little time. She's a gentle, biddable lass, and it's not as if she had a particular attachment to her father –'

'That's simply not so,' Nell interrupted. 'The girl thought the world of Will. And you need not glower at me like that, Gilbert. It's better they know the truth. Davydd, you will bear that in mind? Watch what you say to her?'

Her tone was a shade too peremptory for Davydd's liking. 'Yes . . . Aunt Nell,' he said dryly, but Nell was heedless of the sarcasm, so single-minded was she in the pursuit of her own ends.

'Llewelyn, I must talk with you . . . about Joanna.'

She at once felt the change in atmosphere, the sudden chill. Llewelyn's eyes grew guarded, gave away nothing of his thoughts, at once remote and utterly aloof. Davydd looked no less distant. Elen, too, had tensed. Gilbert hastened into the breach, said sharply, 'Nell, you have no right –'

Nell refused to retreat. 'Yes, I do. Who will speak for my sister if I do not? Llewelyn, it has been more than five months now. How much longer do you mean to hold Joanna at Llanfaes?'

Nell was the first one to put that question to Llewelyn; until now, no one else had dared. It may have been the challenging thrust of her query, as if he had to defend what he'd done. It may have been that he was unaccustomed to being interrogated by a fourteen-year-old girl. Or that he had no answer for her. But whatever the reasons, the result was a sudden flare of anger, intense enough to prevail over the constraints of courtesy, and he said curtly, 'As long as I choose.'

No one spoke. Nell flushed, lost some of her aplomb, showed herself vulnerable, after all, to the insecurities and misgivings of adolescence. 'I'll . . . I'll go and see to Isabella now,' she said, sounding so subdued that Elen, too, excused herself, followed Nell from the hall.

They walked in silence for some moments. Nell at last gave Elen a look that was both apologetic and embarrassed. 'I did not help Joanna much, did I?'

'No,' Elen said tartly. 'For certès, you did not.'

'I meant well, truly I did,' Nell said, and sighed. 'Henry says I'm too forthright for my own good. I suspect that's a polite way of saying I talk too much. But Elen, do you not think it strange? That your father has not yet divorced Joanna?'

'Yes,' Elen admitted, and she, too, sighed. 'Yes . . . I do.'

*

Elen had persuaded her husband to come back to Wales for Llewelyn's Christmas court at Aber. She understood the political considerations behind Llewelyn's choice; he could not let his subjects think him reluctant to return to his chief residence. But it was a political decision undertaken at great personal cost; never had Elen seen her father look so haggard, so bone-weary, so suddenly aged. Aber's atmosphere was proving oppressive to them all. An aura of gloom overhung the court, and the Christmas revelries were muted, lacking spontaneity, any genuine sense of joy.

Elen was standing with her husband John, and Gwladys and Ralph de Mortimer, for Gwladys, too, had felt the need to be with her father on this particular Christmas Eve. As Elen watched, Isabella bade Davydd goodnight, made an unheralded, unnoticed departure from the hall. 'That poor little lass,' she said sadly, unconsciously echoing Joanna's prophetic judgment. As difficult as it was for Papa and Davydd to be back at Aber, might it not be hardest of all upon Will's daughter? 'That child flits about like a wraith, does not even seem to cast a shadow. John, shall we have her with us for a time?'

'Another bird with a broken wing, Elen?' John's smile was indulgent. 'Mayhap in the spring,' he temporized. But then Isabella was forgotten. A few feet away a woman in blue velvet was holding forth to a small but attentive audience; John recognized her as the Lady Gwenllian, wife to Ednyved. She had a loud, carrying voice, a distinctive laugh, and her words came clearly now to John's ear, words of venomous contempt, words that brought a rush of hot colour into his wife's face, and he said hastily, 'Let it lie, Elen. You do not want to cause a scene.'

'No? Just watch me.' Elen evaded his restraining hand, pushed her way through those encircling Gwenllian. An embarrassed silence fell at sight of her; few had realized she was within hearing range. Even Gwenllian was slightly discomfited, but too proud to show it. She smiled archly, said, 'Lady Elen?' and Elen very deliberately tilted her wine cup, poured the contents on to Gwenllian's velvet gown.

Gwenllian screamed loudly enough to turn heads, stared at her wine-stained skirt as if she could not believe the evidence of her own eyes. Shock gave way almost at once to outrage, and she cried, 'You've ruined my gown, you spoiled, wilful –'

Gwenllian choked off further utterance so abruptly that Elen

757

knew there could be but one reason why, and she turned, found Llewelyn was close enough to touch. She felt no surprise that he should have materialized with a suddenness a sorcerer might envy; she was too familiar with his uncanny sense of timing. He took in the situation at a glance, said without emotion, 'How careless of you, Elen.'

Gwenllian opened her mouth, closed it again. She saw her husband standing at the edge of the crowd, but he did not contradict Llewelyn; his face was impassive, and Gwenllian yearned to rake her nails across that dark, weathered skin, to damn Elen as she deserved, to spit and scratch and call down the wrath of the Almighty upon the lot of them. She did nothing, though, for greater than her fury was her fear of public humiliation. She bit down until her jaw muscles ached, until she could trust herself to say, 'No matter. Who amongst us has never spilled a little wine?' She even managed a grimacing smile of sorts, but dared not let her eyes meet Elen's. Or Ednyved's. She'd saved face. But she would not forget, would not forgive.

'Elen.' Llewelyn's voice was very low. As people drifted away, began to disperse, his hand closed on Elen's wrist. 'I would like to talk with you,' he said, and Elen could gauge the full extent of his anger by the unremitting pressure of those hard, bruising fingers. She followed him to a far corner of the hall, with Ednyved but a step behind. 'Well?' Llewelyn said coldly. 'You owe me an explanation.'

'I think I'm entitled to one, too,' Ednyved interjected, no less coldly.

'I could not help it, Papa. She . . . she called Mama a slut.'

Llewelyn's mouth thinned, twisted down. He glanced towards Ednyved. The other man nodded, said, 'I'll see to it.'

Llewelyn looked at his daughter, and then he did something he'd not done since she was a child; he tilted her face up to his, kissed her upon the forehead, with enough tenderness to bring tears to her eyes. But when she started to speak, he shook his head, then turned and walked away.

Across the hall, Elen caught her husband's eye. John slowly shook his head. He was too well-bred to berate her before witnesses, but she knew she'd earned herself a long lecture on decorum and propriety. Gwladys and Davydd were making their way towards her; they, too, looked judgmental.

758

'When,' Davydd said, 'will you learn not to act upon your emotions?'

'Never, I hope,' Elen said, and saw that her brother was not as disapproving as he'd have her think.

'Elen, do not mistake what I am about to say.' Gwladys paused, intent upon choosing just the right words, for Joanna was a sensitive subject between them. 'I am not defending Gwenllian, not at all. But there's more to her bad manners than sheer malice. Gwenllian and Ednyved's youngest son made up a bawdy, satiric song about Joanna and Will de Braose, and then he was foolhardy enough to boast of the authorship. As you'd expect, Papa was enraged; so, too, was Ednyved. Gwenllian thought it prudent to pack her son off to Ireland for a stay, to give Papa's anger time to cool. But the incident put some noticeable cracks in her marriage, and she finds it easier to blame Joanna than to blame her son.'

Ednyved had nine sons in all. Most of them were comparative strangers to Elen, and when she asked Gwladys for the rash poet's name, it meant nothing to her. But it would from now on. Gruffudd ab Ednyved. She would remember him. She would make a point of it.

Gwladys soon wandered away. Elen and Davydd stood alone for a time, watching the dancers circle back and forth. Elen loved to dance, but she could find in herself now not the slightest desire to join the carole. 'I would have expected Papa to be wroth with Gwenllian; his pride would demand as much. But I saw more than anger in his face. Davydd, he still loves her.'

'I know,' Davydd said. 'And how much easier it would be for him if he did not. I would that there were some strange alchemy to change love into hate, to blot out memories, to banish yesterdays . . .'

'Are you speaking for Papa? Or for yourself?'

'For Papa, Elen.' Davydd sounded annoyed, and a silence fell between them. But then he said, very softly, 'I could never hate Mama.'

'Papa looks so tired. I worry about him so much, Davydd . . .' Elen's eyes searched the hall, seeking her father. 'Who is that woman with him? The one in green?'

'You mean . . . Hunydd?'

'If that be her name. Who is she, Davydd? I've never seen her before.' She looked at Davydd expectantly, was surprised to see colour mount in his face.

'It has been over eight months, Elen.' But even then she did not

759

understand, not until he added defensively, 'What did you expect Papa to do, take holy vows?'

Elen's eyes narrowed, focusing upon Hunydd with sudden, probing intensity, subjecting the older woman to an exacting scrutiny, one that was far from friendly. Hunydd's were quiet attractions, a smile of singular sweetness, a tranquil composure. There was nothing gaudy or obvious about her appearance, nothing garish in her dress. She was listening attentively to Llewelyn, but she was not clinging to him, was not giving herself proprietary airs. That mattered little to Elen; she still found herself seething with resentment, with a child's sense of betrayal and loss.

Davydd was watching her. 'The marriage is dead, Elen,' he said quietly.

'I know.' Elen tore her gaze from Hunydd. 'But tell me the truth, Davydd. Tell me it does not bother you to see that woman in Mama's place.'

Davydd beckoned to a passing servant, claimed a cup of mead. He drank, glanced at his sister, and drank again. 'It bothers me,' he said, and passed the cup to Elen.

They looked at one another. All around them swirled the sounds of music, of harp and crwth. The hall was bedecked with evergreen boughs and Christmas holly, lit by blazing torches, flickering rush lights, gilded candelabras. But to Elen, it was as festive as a wake. 'Davydd . . . is it always like this?'

'No,' he said, giving her a bleak smile. 'Sometimes it is not nearly as cheerful.'

At low tide, the white sands known to the Welsh as Traeth Lafan lay exposed and men could venture out upon them with little risk. Davydd stood at the water's edge, watching as his sister was ferried across the strait, and as the boat touched bottom, he strode forward, held out his hand to help her alight upon the sand.

'Dismiss your men,' he said, 'and I'll escort you back to Aber.' Elen linked her arm in his, and they began to walk up the beach. 'Tell me,' he said, after a few moments. 'How is Mama?'

'The truth? Wretchedly unhappy.'

'Did you give her my letter?'

'You know I did.' Elen stopped, put her hand imploringly upon his arm. 'Summon the boatmen back, Davydd. Go and see her. It would mean so much to her if you –'

'No,' he said hastily. 'No . . . I cannot.'

She stepped back, stared at him. 'How can you be so self-righteous, so unwilling to forgive? Jesu, Davydd, Mama would have forgiven you any sin under God's sky!'

'I know,' he admitted. 'Do you not think I want to see her? But I cannot, Elen. I cannot do that to Papa.'

'But Davydd, Papa knows I go to Llanfaes. I've made no secret of it; nor has he ever attempted to dissuade me.'

'You're not his son.'

'Davydd, he would not –'

'You just do not understand. You do not see Papa every day as I do. All his life, Papa has been the most decisive of men. Yet now he does nothing. Men expected him to divorce Mama months ago. But he has not. He cannot bring himself to do it . . . not yet. The wound is still too raw. It's not healing as it ought, Elen, and till it does, I'll do nothing that might add to his pain.'

'Ah, Davydd . . .' But she did not know what to say, and they walked the rest of the way in silence.

'Am I intruding, Papa?'

Llewelyn shoved his chair back, smiled at his daughter. 'An opportune intrusion, lass. As you can see,' he said, gesturing towards the chessboard, 'Ednyved has manoeuvred me into a right perilous position.'

Elen closed the door, came forward into the bedchamber. As she did, she could not help envisioning the desperate drama that had been played out in this chamber at Eastertide, and she thought, How can Papa bear to sleep here? 'Papa, we do need to talk . . . about Mama.'

Llewelyn's smile froze, and when Ednyved started to rise, he said, 'There is no need to go. Elen, I've told you this before. There is nothing to say.'

'But there is, Papa, and I beg you to hear me out. Not only for your sake, for Davydd's.'

Llewelyn pushed his chair back still farther, got to his feet. 'Davydd?'

'Papa, he is being torn in two. He thinks he cannot be loyal to you unless he disavows Mama.'

Llewelyn frowned. 'I never wanted that, would never have asked it of him.'

'I know, Papa. But until you act, Davydd is not free to act, either. He cannot be reconciled with Mama, will not even go to Llanfaes. Papa, do you not see? To go on like this, month after month, with nothing resolved . . . it only causes greater pain. It is not fair to you, to Davydd, to me . . . or to Mama.'

'Fair to Joanna?' Llewelyn's voice had taken on a cutting edge, and Elen's resolve began to waver; she'd never found it easy to gainsay her father.

'Please, Papa, hear me out. I'm not defending what Mama has done, but I do not think she's forfeited all claims to fairness. She was your wife for nigh on twenty-four years. All the love and loyalty she gave you cannot be blotted out as if it never were, not for one wretched mistake.'

'Mistake?' he echoed incredulously. 'That is rather a quaint way to describe adultery, Elen.'

Elen was too deeply committed now to recant. 'A mistake, Papa. She let herself be seduced at a vulnerable time in her life, at a time when you and she were estranged. She erred. But she repented of it, she –'

'Indeed?' he said scathingly. 'Was that what she was doing with Will de Braose in my bed – penance?'

'Nothing happened that night, Papa – nothing. They were together, yes. But it was Will's doing, not Mama's. She did not lay with him.'

Llewelyn's face was very still, suddenly unreadable. Elen took a step closer, and then he said, 'Do you expect me to believe that?'

'I believe it, Papa.'

They'd all but forgotten Ednyved. He spoke up unexpectedly, laconically. 'For what it's worth, Llewelyn, so do I.'

Llewelyn glanced towards Ednyved, and then away. Could there be any truth to Elen's claim? Could it be that Joanna had not brought de Braose into this chamber, into her marriage bed? But why did he care? Why did he want so to believe it?

He swung back towards his daughter, said roughly, 'That changes nothing. She has never denied laying with de Braose. Does it matter when . . . or where? She was unfaithful. She betrayed me. Do you think I could forget that? Forgive?'

'No,' Elen admitted. 'No, I do not. Nor does Mama. Even though she always forgave you.'

'Just what do you mean by that?'

Elen had never meant to go so far. But she could no longer control her tongue, heard herself say, 'I mean, Papa, that you were not always faithful to Mama. She knew that, too . . . and yet loved you no less.'

Llewelyn's anger was tempered by disbelief. 'What are you saying, Elen? Are you truly likening my occasional lapses to Joanna's adultery with de Braose?'

Elen smiled wanly, sadly. 'Those were Mama's very words . . . occasional lapses. She agrees with you, Papa, sees her sin as unforgivable. But I . . . I find myself wondering why marriage vows are only for women. Why is it so one-sided, Papa? Why is it so damnably unfair?'

'Because,' Llewelyn said bluntly, 'if it were not, how would a man ever know if a child were his?' He saw at once, though, that his daughter had given his words a meaning he'd never intended. Elen paled, then held out her hand in instinctive entreaty.

'You do not doubt that, do you, Papa? You do believe that Davydd and I are yours?'

Llewelyn drew a sharp breath. 'Ah, Elen . . .' He swiftly closed the space between them, took her in his arms. 'I know you are, lass. I've never doubted that, not even for a moment.'

'Papa, I want only for you to be happy again. I think I understand why you've not yet divorced Mama. It's . . . it's like repudiating your past, like an amputation of the soul. But sometimes amputation is the only way. You've seen enough battlefield injuries to know that.'

Elen had rehearsed her plea often enough so that it came readily to her lips now, but she could not altogether stifle a sense of guilt at what she was doing, urging her father to forsake Joanna. Yet what else could she do? If Papa could not forgive Mama, he had somehow to forget her. But however much she told herself that, she still felt that hers was at once an act of healing . . . and betrayal. Raising up, she kissed Llewelyn on the cheek, then all but ran from the chamber.

Ednyved rose without apparent haste. 'Let's leave the rest of the game till the morrow.'

He had almost reached the door when Llewelyn said, 'What would you or Rhys . . .'

He regretted the impulse in mid-sentence, let the words trail off into oblivion. Ednyved stopped, gave him a pensive, searching look. 'I've thought about that,' he conceded. 'I dare say there's not a man at your court who has not. I suspect Rhys would have slain them

763

both, Catrin and her lover. I'd have hanged the man, divorced Gwenllian.' He paused. 'But then Rhys loved Catrin too much, and I love Gwenllian too little.'

Llewelyn said nothing. Ednyved reached for the door latch, glanced back over his shoulder. 'I'd not presume to advise you, Llewelyn. But whatever you decide, my friend, do it soon. One way or another, lay your ghosts to rest.'

Llewelyn stood motionless in the centre of the room, staring at the bed, the bed in which Joanna had lain with Will de Braose. Or had she? He swore under his breath. The silence was illusory; so, too, was his solitude. He swore again. 'Lay my ghosts to rest. Christ, if only I could . . .'

January, 1231
Llanfaes, North Wales

Joanna drew the shutter back, gazed up at a sky opaque and dark. Clouds had begun to drift over the island shortly after dusk. It was unseasonably mild for late January and the air was damp and drizzly. She caught muffled echoes of thunder, a sound as ominous as it was uncommon; winter thunderstorms were ill-omened occurrences, often portents of coming grief, untimely death. Joanna crossed herself, pulled the shutters into place, closing out the sounds of night and sea, but not those forebodings born of superstition . . . and solitude.

Loneliness was an unrelenting foe, one Joanna had come to know well in the past nine months, thirteen days. It could never be conclusively defeated; at best, she could hope for a stalemate, but in the last week it had gained hard-fought ground, for Glynis had departed for a fortnight's visit with her family.

If loneliness was the enemy, time was its ally. Never had the hours in a day seemed so interminable to Joanna. For more than twenty years, hers had been a life of constant activity, unremitting responsibilities. In learning Welsh, she'd taken up the obligations of a woman of rank, and from dawn till dusk she'd been occupied in the management of her husband's vast household, acting as consort, wife, mother. Hers were supervisory skills; she was not expected to turn her own hand to domestic chores. But it was for her to see that those chores were performed, that soap was made and candles were dipped and bread baked, that salt was hauled in from Cheshire brine springs and Spanish cottons from the great fairs at Winchester and Smithfield, that meat was salted for winter and linen woven from flax, that no man be turned away hungry from Llewelyn's hearth, be he highborn lord or lowborn beggar. Any free time was given over to the universal female pastime, sewing, for not even queens were exempt from the demands of needle-work.

There was an embroidery frame in one corner of the bedchamber, but it collected only cobwebs; Joanna had no one to sew for. Now she filled her days with vain regrets, played listless games of chess, merels, and tables with Glynis, read and re-read her meagre library, and yearned for her freedom. For Richard had been right; jewelled fetters were no less onerous for being gilded, and she was no longer indifferent to what her future might hold. But she had decided not to accept her brother's offer, did not want to dwell at Chilham Castle upon his charity. Llewelyn could banish her from Wales, but not from the Marches. She had a Shropshire manor at Condover, a hunting lodge near Ellesmere, and she meant to put down roots in the shadow of her husband's realm, as close as she could get to her son.

There was a Welsh proverb that Joanna put great store by these days: For every wound, the ointment of time. She fervently hoped it would prove true for Davydd, that eventually the breach between them could be mended. But until she was free, she could do nothing to effect a reconciliation, and it was this aspect of her confinement she found most crippling. How much longer did Llewelyn mean to hold her here? Why had he not divorced her ere now? She was baffled by his failure to act, for by rights he ought to have repudiated her months ago. He had ever been a man to cut his losses, to jettison useless cargo and, for a Prince, what greater encumbrance could there be than an unfaithful wife?

There was an hourglass on the table, but the sands seemed to have frozen. No matter how often Joanna glanced at it, she could detect not the faintest trickle of time. After unbraiding and brushing out her hair, she wandered aimlessly about the chamber, at last settling down with her harp. The one benefit she'd gained from these months of enforced leisure was that her harp-playing had improved dramatically since her first halting efforts under Llewelyn's tutelage. Striking a chord, she began to sing softly.

'In orchard where the leaves of hawthorn hide, the lady holds a lover to her side. Until the watcher in the dawning cried, "Ah God, ah God, the dawn! It comes how soon."' The song had five additional verses, but she did not continue; the melody was too plaintive, the lyrics too easy to identify with.

Next to the hourglass was her most cherished possession, a small ivory casket of letters, her only link with the world beyond Llanfaes. Lifting the casket lid, she took inventory of these much-handled keepsakes: four letters from Elen, two from Richard, one from Nell and one – heartbreakingly brief and stilted – from Davydd. Sliding the candelabra towards her, she picked a letter at random, one of Elen's, began to read aloud passages long since memorized.

Her head jerked up at sound of Bran's footsteps in the ante-chamber; she knew he would not come to her at such an hour unless he had news of grave import. Her breathing quickened, for these months in isolation had honed her nerves to the breaking-point. All too often, she tormented herself with morbid visions of Llewelyn lying ill and feverish, refusing to send for her, damning her with his dying breath, never knowing that she loved him still. She'd become obsessed with this fear, that death would end their estrangement, that as it had happened with John, so, too, would it happen with Llewelyn, and she rose hastily to her feet as the door opened.

Bran's sombre face did nothing to reassure her. 'Madame,' he said, 'my lord is here to see you.'

Joanna stared at him, doubt giving way to dawning joy, for Bran was Davydd's man and it did not occur to her that he could mean anyone but her son. When Bran stepped back, she was stunned, therefore, at sight of her husband.

Llewelyn closed the door with deliberation, but he did not slide the bolt into place. There was a part of Joanna's mind that noted this, for she seemed suddenly able to focus only upon irrelevancies, and she found herself noting, too, that the wool of his mantle was dry. The storm must still be nigh, she thought, and then, How tired he looks, and thinner; he's not eating as he ought.

'Well?' Llewelyn said, and the challenging, hostile tone of his voice brought her abruptly back to the realities of their respective positions. 'Have you nothing to say to me?'

Joanna swallowed. 'These months past,' she said huskily, 'I've begged the Almighty for but one favour, that I might see you once more, have the chance to explain. Now . . . now you are here and suddenly I do not know where to begin.'

'I want the truth from you. Not what you think I'd rather hear, or what you'd have me believe. Can I trust you for that much, for the truth?'

He'd turned words into weapons, each one inflicting a wound of its own. Joanna nodded. 'Yes,' she whispered. 'I will tell you the truth.' But what was it? If only she could think coherently, calmly. Why had he not forewarned her of his coming, given her time to prepare? She knew why, though. His was first and foremost a military mind, trained to take advantage of surprise. He'd removed his mantle, flung it carelessly across a coffer, but she read tension in his stance, in every line of his body, and she changed her mind as she watched him. There'd been nothing premeditated about this visit; his was the taut wariness of a man acting on impulse, acting against his better instincts.

He had yet to unbuckle his scabbard, had yet to move away from the door. Over the years, she'd seen his moods range across the emotional spectrum, had seen him enraged, jubilant, disheartened, sardonic, playful, calculating, and occasionally frightened. But never had she seen him so obviously ill at ease.

'Elen told me that you did not bring de Braose to our bedchamber that night. Is that true?'

'Yes,' Joanna said. 'I swear it.' But how could she make him believe that? Her eyes strayed from his face, to the open casket, and then she was rummaging through the letters, scattering them about the table in her heedless haste. 'This letter explains it better than I could. Will you read it, Llewelyn? Please?' She held out the sealed parchment to him; their fingers brushed as he took it, and she was jolted by even so brief and casual a contact as that. Did he feel it, too? She could not tell, for he was turning away, shifting so that she could not watch his face as he read.

The few moments it took him to scan her letter encompassed an eternity for Joanna. 'I tried to tell you,' she said. 'And when I could not see you, I wrote that letter. But you sent it back unread . . .'

Llewelyn glanced again at the letter and then dropped it on to the table. 'It would not have mattered. I'd not have believed you.'

'Do you believe me now?' she asked, but he did not answer her. Moving to the far side of the table, he reached for the flagon, splashed wine into an earthenware cup. Joanna watched, bracing herself for whatever was to come. His first question, though, was utterly unexpected.

'Do you blame me for his death?'

She gave a startled shake of her head. 'No, of course not. You had the right.'

His eyes had narrowed. 'You did not mourn him?'

She shook her head again, and he took a step towards her. 'And what you said in your letter, it was true? You did not love him?'

'No, never.' She drew a sharp, shuddering breath. 'In all honesty, I am not sure if I even liked him . . .'

His mouth twisted. Striding forward, he grasped her by the wrist and jerked her towards him. 'Then why did you do it? If you did not love him, why did you lay with him? What did you get in his bed that you could not get in mine?'

She gasped and he loosened his grip. But although she'd later find bruises upon her wrist, now she did not even feel the pain. Was there no limit to the damage she'd done? That Llewelyn of all men, Llewelyn who was so confident, so secure in his sense of self, secure in his manhood, that he should have succumbed to doubts of this dark nature . . . Jesu, if only she had those October afternoons to live over! Her infidelity could not have been better calculated to penetrate her husband's armour, to strike with devastating effect at his one vulnerability, that he was a man wed to a much younger wife. A wife who'd then taken a lover of thirty-two.

'Beloved, no, it was not like that! No great passion burned between us. I swear it, Llewelyn, swear upon all the saints,' she cried, for at that moment she was willing to perjure herself even to the Almighty if only that would give Llewelyn a measure of comfort. 'You must believe me. Will was never able to pleasure me as you did,' she said, and realized that she was not lying after all; those feverish urgent couplings with Will had never been more than flesh unto flesh, lacking utterly the deep and abiding intimacy of her lovemaking with Llewelyn.

'You must believe me,' she repeated. 'Think back upon our lovemaking in the months after your return from Ceri. Did I want you any the less? You know the answer to that, know how hot my blood ran for you. Ah, Llewelyn . . . we've shared so much, overcome so much. What man could hope to compete with memories such as mine? What man could hope to compete with you?'

'Will de Braose.'

'He meant nothing to me! Why do you find that so hard to believe? What of the women you've bedded with? I always told myself that yours were infidelities of the flesh, never of the heart. Was I wrong? What happened between Will and me did not touch upon the love I have for you. It . . . it was . . .' She faltered and he said sharply:

'Was what? If it was not for love and not for lust, just why did

769

you do it, then? Christ, Joanna, why would you risk so much for so little?'

'I . . . I do not know if I can make you understand. I am not sure if I fully understand it myself . . . even now. But this I can tell you, that it would never have happened if he had not been Maude de Braose's grandson.'

She had so often rehearsed this very speech, as an act of faith. But she found herself fumbling for words, so fearful was she that he'd not hear her out. 'There . . . there was a strange sort of bond between Will and me. No – not carnal, not like that!' She could no longer meet his eyes, for she was now getting into an area of half-truths and equivocation, denying a sexual attraction that had been magnetic, fateful . . . and mutual. But that was a secret she would take to her grave, and she said hastily, wretchedly:

'I never meant it to happen, Llewelyn. I was seeking only to comfort him, to –'

'I see. And in offering your sympathy, it seemed only natural to offer yourself as well? A veritable angel of mercy. Tell me, Joanna, what of Will's cousin? Jack de Braose suffered, too, at John's hands, even more than Will, for he lost both father and grandmother in that Windsor dungeon. What of his grieving? What did you feel obliged to do for him?'

Patches of hectic colour stood out suddenly along Joanna's cheek-bones. 'Do you truly believe that, Llewelyn, believe I had other lovers? That Will was not the first? Or did you say that just to hurt me?'

Llewelyn stepped back, gave her a long, measuring look. 'No,' he said softly. 'No, I do not believe there were others.' And then he slowly unbuckled his scabbard, sat down at the table.

For Joanna, that simple act was fraught with significance. She took a seat across from him, knowing now that he would listen to her . . . truly listen, and she'd never asked for more than that.

'Richard thinks it was an . . . an act of atonement. I told him that was lunacy, of course, but now I am not so sure. I've never pitied anyone in my life as I pitied Will that day. He told me, you see, told me just how his grandmother and uncle died. Maude went mad at the last. Will told me she . . . Oh God, Llewelyn, they found her teeth marks in her son's face! And Will was not spared that. He was but fourteen, and still they told him . . .'

Llewelyn had not known the gruesome details of Maude's death.

770

But it stirred in him no pity for Will, only outrage that he should have shared so grisly a secret with Joanna, the one woman least able to bear such a burden. He reached for the wine cup but did not drink, pushed it, instead, across the table towards Joanna. He was beginning to understand. A clever man, de Braose. God rot him, too clever by half. Starvation and seduction . . . and John again. Always John.

Joanna drank deeply, gratefully. She was perilously close to tears. 'I sometimes dream of Maude, that Windsor dungeon. Once or twice I've even awakened screaming. And I keep wondering if John knew, or if he would have cared.'

'You cannot blame yourself for John's cruelties, Joanna.'

'I know. And I do not. But I can blame myself for loving him. For I did love him, Llewelyn. There's a part of me that still does . . . even now. I think that's what I find hardest to admit, or to understand, that I could still love him . . .'

Llewelyn found himself responding to the pain in her voice. Reclaiming the cup, he, too, drank deeply. Joanna reached out; her fingers stopped just short of his. But then she drew back, said quietly:

'I am not making excuses, Llewelyn, truly I am not. But I wanted you to understand that mine was not a betrayal of the heart. In some ways it was almost adultery by mischance, for it would never have happened had even one of the circumstances been different. If Will had not been sent to Rhosyr. If we had not quarrelled so bitterly over Gruffydd. If I had not known Will as a lad, had not been able to identify so readily with his pain. If you had not –'

Llewelyn set the cup down with a thud. 'What?' When she hesitated, he said, 'Tell me, Joanna. We agreed this would be a night of truths. Tell me.'

'I am afraid to tell you, afraid you'll think I am blaming you.'

'What are you talking about?'

'About the de Braose marriages.' She saw him stiffen and she leaned across the table towards him. 'You can so easily misconstrue what I'm about to say. I shall risk it, though, ask only that you hear me out. Llewelyn, I understand why you sought those alliances, I truly do. You did not act lightly, had compelling reasons for wanting the marriages. But that did not make it any easier for me. Four times I had to stand by as you married your children into the de Braose clan, four times I –'

'You said you understood why, understood I was acting for Gwynedd's good.'

She nodded. 'And I did understand. But . . . but I think I needed – just once – for you to put me first. When you did not, I was hurt . . . and aggrieved. More than I knew. I truly thought my anger was over, quenched. But there were embers still smouldering, and I can see now that they fuelled our quarrels. Unacknowledged anger acts like flint to tinder, can spark fires where we least expect them.'

Llewelyn shoved his chair back. 'What are you saying? That your anger led you into adultery?'

Joanna rose as he did, hastened around the table towards him. 'No, that is not what I am saying. I did not take a lover to spite you. Does that sound like me?'

Her eyes were riveted upon his face, eyes full of entreaty. As he looked into those eyes, his mouth softened. 'No,' he admitted. 'No . . . it does not.'

'I did not knowingly act upon that anger, Llewelyn. That I swear to you upon the surety of my soul. Nor did I ever seek to justify my infidelity by tallying up grievances of my own. I knew from the beginning that there was no justification for what I was doing. But I am trying to be honest with you, honest with myself . . . and I'll never be sure if I did not unwittingly let that resentment taint my judgment, my –'

She stopped abruptly, for he was shaking his head. 'Since that is not a question you can ever answer, Joanna, what point is there in dwelling upon it? Can you not see the folly in holding yourself accountable for thoughts you are not even sure you had?'

The corner of his mouth quirked; it was only a phantom, fleeting shadow of the smile that could invariably catch at her heart, but it was still a smile, and she responded to it. It seemed almost miraculous to her that they could be talking together like this, without rancour or recriminations, and she hesitated to say or do anything to jeopardize this fragile, astonishing accord. But she had to know.

'Llewelyn . . . why have you not yet divorced me?' He looked at her, saying nothing. She reached out; her hands brushed his sleeve. 'Will you tell me this, then? Will you tell me what you mean to do?'

'Until tonight,' he said, 'I did not know.'

'And now?'

But even as she spoke, the storm broke. A sudden gust of wind blew the shutter back, quenching candles and scattering her letters about the floor. Rain was slanting in through the window, and they both flinched as thunder cracked directly overhead.

They exchanged startled looks, and then, sheepish smiles. 'Christ, but that one was close,' Llewelyn said, and moved hastily to relatch the shutter, while Joanna gathered up her letters, sought to comfort her cowering spaniel.

'Llewelyn, stay here tonight. Please do not attempt a crossing of the strait in weather this vile.'

'All right.'

'You mean it? You'll stay?'

He shrugged, gestured towards the window. 'What choice do I have?'

Joanna nodded slowly. 'Yes,' she echoed, 'what choice?' More fool she, to read so much into his ready assent; what else could he do, in truth? 'Llewelyn, there is something I must say to you. I'd not blame you if you do not believe me, but I must say it all the same. I love you. I've loved you since the summer of my fifteenth year, and divorce will not change that. Nothing will.'

He stood very still, for one of the few times in his life at a loss for words, troubled in no small measure to realize how much he wanted to believe her.

Joanna awoke sometime before dawn. The chamber was dark, but the hearth log still burned. Taking care not to disturb Llewelyn, she rose from the bed. He did not stir, not even when she settled down beside him again, having placed a candle in one of the headboard niches. His breathing was even, deep. He seemed to have shed years in his sleep, looked so peaceful that she found herself blinking back tears.

If not for the fact that they were still clothed, this could have been one of a thousand nights she and Llewelyn had passed in this bedchamber, in this bed. But it would be the last. Come morning, he would awaken, arise and walk out of the bed-chamber, out of her life. She had two, mayhap three hours at most.

Leaning over, she drew the coverlets up around his shoulders. How had he been able to fall asleep so easily? She'd lain awake for hours. That was not an uncommon experience for her; there'd been many a night in these past months when her body's cravings had banished sleep, when memories of their lovemaking would set her to trembling. The needs of the flesh were not always easy to subordinate to enforced, involuntary chastity, and she was finding it increasingly difficult to be so tantalizingly close to Llewelyn now, to be sharing his bed but not his embrace.

His lashes flickered; opening his eyes, he looked up at her. As always, she marvelled at his ability to shift so smoothly from sleep to wakeful alertness; his dark eyes showed no disorientation, no surprise at sight of her. 'Is it dawn?' he asked and she shook her head.

'No, not yet. Go back to sleep.'

He raised up on his elbow, glanced upward. 'Why the candle?'

Colour crept into her cheeks, but she gave him an honest answer. 'I wanted to watch you.'

His mouth curved. 'It is not sporting to watch a man whilst he sleeps.' Pushing the pillow back against the headboard, he regarded her in silence for several moments. 'It ought to feel strange, waking up beside you after so many months. But it does not feel strange at all, feels very natural.'

'I'm glad,' she said, rather breathlessly, 'so glad you came.' He had yet to take his eyes from her face, and her colour was deepening. 'Do you know now what you will do . . . about me?'

'I've always known what I ought to do.' He reached for a strand of her hair, entwined it about his fingers. 'But now . . . now I know what I want to do.'

'What?' she whispered, not daring to move, to risk breaking the spell.

'This,' he said, and leaned towards her. The kiss was very gentle, almost tentative. But then her arms went up around his neck, and he felt her tears on his face. When he kissed her again, her mouth clung to his, and it was as if they'd never been apart. Theirs was suddenly a world bounded by bed hangings of Tripoli silk, a world without yesterdays or tomorrows, just the here and now and two halves made whole – all too briefly.

Joanna's breathing had yet to slow; it still came in loud, uneven gasps. She heard Llewelyn panting, knew his climax had been no less intense, no less overwhelming than her own. When he started to withdraw, she tightened her arms around him. 'No,' she entreated, 'no, not yet.' He shifted so that his weight no longer bore down upon her, and then he laughed, a sound Joanna had never thought to hear again.

'I was just thinking,' he said, 'that there's more to be said for laying one's ghosts to rest than most people realize.'

She kissed the corner of his mouth. 'Llewelyn . . .'

Their eyes met, held. 'No, *breila*,' he said. 'Not now.'

She nodded, disappointed but not surprised. She was afraid to attach too much significance to their lovemaking. It was too easy to explain it away as a onetime occurrence, a natural male response to intimacy and opportunity. Common sense warned there was no place in a Prince's life for a discredited, sullied wife. But lying now in Llewelyn's arms, his breath upon her cheek, his hand upon her hip, she could not help but hope, and she settled back against him, closing her eyes. After a time, the change in his breathing told her he slept. She watched the hearth log burn down, listened to the lulling rhythm of rain upon the slate roof. Shortly before dawn, she fell asleep, too.

When she awoke, the rain had stopped, the room showed the shadowy half-light of early morning, and she was alone. She sat up, pushing her hair out of her eyes, her brain clouded with sleep. 'Llewelyn?' Reaching over, she jerked the bed hangings all the way back; the chamber was empty. If not for the sight of her discarded clothing scattered about the floor, she might almost have believed she'd dreamed it all. The fire had gone out and the air was chill; she shivered, fumbled for her bedrobe, and began numbly to follow her routine upon rising, as she'd done every morning for the past nine months.

Five minutes later, she halted her brushing in mid-stroke, sat down in the closest seat. She'd known that what happened between a man and woman in bed was not a reliable indication of intent. But however acute his morning-after regrets, how could he have left her like this, without even a word of farewell?

A knock sounded at the door and a young man entered, carrying a tray. 'Where shall I put this, my lady?'

Joanna had never seen him before. 'Who are you?'

He was staring past her at the bed, at its telltale dishevelment, his eyes wide and wondering. When he turned back to Joanna, his expression made it clear he thought her a practitioner of sexual sorcery, a Norman-French Circe. 'I am Phylip, Madame,' he mumbled. 'I came over last night with my lord; he ordered me to fetch this from the kitchen.' And only then, as he set the tray upon the table, did Joanna see that it held food for two.

Although she caught the enticing aroma of hot baked bread, Joanna did not stir. She was still sitting there, the tray untouched before her, when Llewelyn returned. One glance at her face and he crossed swiftly to her side. 'Joanna?'

'I thought . . . thought you'd gone,' she said, and he drew her to her feet, his hands tightening on her shoulders.

'Gone? What did you think that was for?' With a jerk of his head towards the canopied bed, the rumpled sheets. 'Old time's sake? *Hiraeth?*'

'I did not know what to think,' she confessed. 'I was afraid to expect too much.'

'I told you once that you held yourself too cheaply, *breila*. It seems you still do,' he said, and slipped his arm around her waist. 'Let's eat first, and then you can finish dressing. Do not bother about packing; we'll send for your belongings later.'

'You . . . you want me back, Llewelyn?'

She sounded so dumbfounded that he smiled and shrugged. 'After twenty-four years, you're a hard habit to break, Joanna.'

She did not return his smile. Her eyes searched his face intently, incredulously. 'Can you do that, Llewelyn? Can you truly forgive me? Could you live with the shadow Will would cast?'

He tilted her face up to his, touched her cheek. 'In all honesty, I do not know, Joanna. I can make you no promises, can only say I am willing to try. I do know this, that after living without you for nigh on ten months, I think it's worth the risk.'

The Llanfaes ferry had suffered storm damage, and they had to ride west, to cross at Abermenai. The sun shone with a lucent, incandescent brilliance for Joanna; never had she been so dazzled by the sapphire of the sky, the turquoise of the strait, the snow-glazed summits of Eryri. The wind was brisk, the road mired in mud, and her mantle was soon splattered, but she did not care in the least. Her only regret was that she could not ride pillion behind Llewelyn, for her sense of reality seemed dependent upon physical contact with her husband; only he could dispel her disbelief, and she kept her mount so close to his that once his spur even caught in the skirt of her gown.

She was still in a state of dazed euphoria as they approached Bangor. Ahead, a herdsman and his dogs were seeking to corral several stray cows. The cattle were milling about, blocking the road, and their master's impatience changed to chagrin at sight of his sovereign.

'Good morrow to you, my lord. God blight these contrary beasts, but I'll have them clear in a trice, will –' His jaw dropped; his words choked off into an unintelligible splutter.

Llewclyn appeared indifferent to this peculiar behaviour. Glancing over his shoulder, he beckoned to one of his men. 'Seth, give this fellow a hand.'

The herdsman did not even acknowledge his lord's kindness, for he could not take his eyes from his lord's wife. He was gaping at Joanna as if she were an apparition, one to be warded off with incantations and henbane. Only then did Joanna comprehend the true magnitude of what Llewelyn meant to do.

'Llewelyn, wait!' She urged her horse forward, caught at his sleeve. 'Llewelyn, this is madness. Your people scorn me as an adulteress, feel I betrayed you both as wife and consort. They'll never understand, never accept me.'

'They may not understand, but they will accept you,' he said, and his voice was suddenly grim.

Joanna bit her lip, stared at him in despair. 'But . . . but what if they will not? They hate me now, Llewelyn, and that hatred might well spill over on to you if you take me back. There will be those who'll say I've bewitched you, and . . . and others who'll think you've grown soft, weak . . .' There was no need to continue; she saw that. She was warning him of dangers he knew far better than she. When had he ever acted without considering the consequences? She'd been the blind one, the selfish one.

'How can I let you do this? How can I let you risk so much on my behalf?' She saw his face – dark, haggard, but still handsome – through a haze of tears. 'I know . . . know what I ought to do. But I am not strong enough, beloved, cannot give you up . . .

'The decision is mine, Joanna, not yours. You bear no responsibility for it.' He held up his hand, halting his men upon the pathway, and taking the reins of Joanna's mount, he led her off the road into the woods.

He drew rein in the shadow of a silver birch, stripped naked by winter winds. The ground was covered by decaying leaves, broken branches. Joanna inhaled the scent of spruce, the scent of the sea. 'You said our reconciliation was worth the risk. But is it, Llewelyn? Is it truly worth what you might lose?'

He did not answer at once; his eyes swept the horizon, tracked a cormorant's shooting dive into the sea. 'When I came to you last night, it was not – knowingly – with thoughts of reconciliation. I was seeking answers only you could give me, Joanna, seeking to cauterize a wound that would not heal. But as I listened to you, I found myself able to understand why it had happened. It was not my wife who lay with Will de Braose; it was John's daughter. Once I realized that, I could balance the scales without bitterness, balance a marriage against a mistake – albeit a monumental one.' His last words were sardonic; his smile was not. 'I want you by my side again, in my bed, at my table, as my lady, lover, wife.'

'They will never understand,' she said unsteadily, and he nodded.

'Probably not. I dare say I'll forfeit a great measure of good will. There will be men who'll think I've lost my wits, am in my dotage. I know that. But they'll govern their tongues in my hearing. That,' he said coolly, "I can damned well guarantee.'

'Llewelyn . . . are you sure? Am I truly worth it?'

'Do you remember what you said last night about the de Braose marriages?' He leaned over, dried her tears with the back of his hand. 'This time, Joanna, this time I do mean to put you first.'

Neither Welsh culture nor Welsh topography had been conducive to the development of English-style towns and villages. Small settlements had sprung up, however, around Llewelyn's manors at Aber, Llanfaes, and Trefriw, and monasteries often served, too, as beacons for community life. So it was for the cathedral church of St Deiniol at Bangor Fawr yn Arfon, episcopal see for the diocese of Bangor.

Although official fairs and markets were unknown in Llewelyn's domains, informal markets thrived wherever people tended to congregate, and this was such a market day in Bangor. Stalls had been set up in the churchyard, and the market-place and street were crowded with those who'd come to barter, to browse, and to gossip with their neighbours. Vendors sold hot pies and rolled out kegs of ale for the thirsty; itinerant pedlars loudly hawked their wares; animals offered for trade added to the clamour. It was the sort of chaotic market scene Joanna had often seen in England, but with a distinctly Welsh flavour, boisterous bedlam that ceased within moments of her arrival in their midst.

Llewelyn was known on sight to all in Bangor; to many, he was the only Prince they'd ever known. He'd first gained political power at twenty-one, and now, in his fifty-eighth year, he was well enshrined in local legend, eclipsing even his famous grandfather in the folklore of his people, the uncrowned Prince of Wales. As word circulated that he'd just ridden into the town, men and women deserted the market stalls and the wrestling and archery bouts; some even abandoned a bloody cock fight, those with no money on the outcome.

But the cheering stopped abruptly as the people recognized Joanna. She heard shocked murmurings spreading through the crowd, heard the name Siwan repeated in growing wonder. As men doffed their caps, Llewelyn held his stallion to a stately canter, and then slowed to a walk. Joanna paced her mount with his, but her mouth was dry, her heart pounding. She knew men often drew false courage from crowd companionship, knew, too, that the Welsh were more outspoken, less awed by rank than the English, and she waited now for the jeers, the shouts of derision.

None came. Llewelyn reined in before one of the vendors. 'My throat is right parched. What have you for such a thirst?'

'Wine, my lord. But it is poor stuff, not fit for Your Grace,' the man protested, while fumbling for a clean, uncracked cup.

'It will do,' Llewelyn said and smiled at the man. He drank slowly, keeping his eyes upon the crowd; he found none willing to meet his gaze. 'Here, love, drink,' he said, in Welsh, not French, and held the cup out to Joanna.

She could not swallow, but she obediently put the cup to her mouth. Llewelyn never carried money himself, but he gestured now and one of his men tossed a coin to the vendor. It was eerily still. Llewelyn urged his mount forward; Joanna followed. The crowd fell back, watching in stunned silence.

The road to Aber wound its way along the sea coast, offering a superb view of the strait, but Joanna had eyes only for her husband. She was still astonished at their reprieve, so sure had she been that men would rail at her, call her slut or harlot. She glanced again at Llewelyn's profile. 'Not in my hearing,' he'd said, and it was not bravado. What had happened in Bangor was as much a testament to his personality as to his power. But then, she thought, the two were one and the same.

'I only hope you can cast such a spell upon the folk at Aber,' she said, mustering a strained smile; Aber was now less than five miles distant. She slowed her mount, earning herself a quizzical look from Llewelyn. But then he, too, eased his chestnut. Joanna stared at the road ahead; did Llewelyn ever think of that desperate midnight ride in answer to Senena's false summons? Davydd's words seemed to echo on the wind: 'We half killed our horses . . .' Only to arrive at Aber and discover –

'Joanna, that serves for naught.'

She gasped, then gave a weak laugh. 'Jesu, what are you, a warlock?'

'I know you,' he said simply.

She hesitated, then realized the folly in that; silence could cripple no less effectively than suspicion. They had to be able to talk about it. 'It was not Glynis, Llewelyn. It was Senena who sent you that message.'

'I know. She later admitted it.'

'I can well imagine her satisfaction,' Joanna said bitterly. Senena had guessed, gambled, and been lucky beyond belief, and all it had cost was a man's life.

'At first, mayhap. But her satisfaction soon turned sour. She'd somehow convinced herself that I would then free Gruffydd. As if I'd been holding him just for your pleasure . . .' Llewelyn shook his head. 'I ought to warn you though, *breila*. Senena is at Aber.' He heard her sharp intake of breath, said dryly, 'It should be a memorable homecoming.'

Within moments of their arrival at Aber, the bailey was packed with people. Joanna was gripping the saddle pommel so tightly that it was digging painfully into her palm. Never had she seen a crowd assemble so fast. Many of the faces were familiar to her; all shared a common expression, one of utter disbelief.

Llewelyn had dismounted, was reaching up to help her from the saddle. Setting her down, he tilted her face up to his. The kiss was lingering, very deliberate. And then he turned to face his countrymen.

No one spoke. The silence was even more absolute than in Bangor. Llewelyn had known there would be no overt defiance, not at his own court. The sheer audacity of his act would paralyse dissent. There was a sudden stir; people were stepping aside. Ednyved had his wife's arm in an inexorable grip; Gwenllian's body was stiff, resistant, but she followed him as he moved towards Llewelyn and Joanna.

Reaching for Joanna's hand, Ednyved brought it to his mouth. 'Welcome home, Madame.'

Gwenllian's face was a study in frustrated fury. 'Yes,' she said tonelessly, while her eyes bored like gimlets into Joanna's.

There was nothing for the others to do then but to follow the example of Llewelyn's Seneschal. One by one they came forward, mumbled grudging words of welcome, made awkward obeisances. Joanna had retreated into her public persona; her answers were automatic and, to many, she appeared aloof, unrepentant. She saw Senena standing some distance apart, but it was the hostility of the others that she felt most keenly. Adda's greeting had been edged in ice. How can I bear it? she thought; how can I live surrounded by so much hatred? But then Llewelyn touched her arm, and she turned, saw her son.

Joanna forgot all else. She started towards Davydd; he quickened his step and they met in the middle of the bailey. 'Your father has forgiven me,' she said softly. 'Do you think you can forgive me, too, Davydd?'

'Yes,' he said, 'oh yes.'

Ednyved had remained at Llewelyn's side, and he seized this opportunity now to say, very low, 'Well, you've just set tongues wagging from Cricieth to Colchester. They'll be gossiping about naught else for the next six months, on both sides of the border. Are you sure, Llewelyn . . . truly sure?'

Llewelyn's eyes were fastened upon his wife and son. As he watched, they embraced. He glanced back to Ednyved. 'Yes,' he said, 'I am sure.'

'Are you certain she'll be at the waterfall, Davydd?'

'Not really. But she does play there sometimes, and I know not where else to look.' Davydd gave Joanna an oblique, inquiring glance. 'Are you positive you want to do this now, Mama?'

'I do not want to do it at all,' Joanna admitted. 'In truth, I dread facing the child. Does she blame me, Davydd, for her father's death?'

'I could not say. Isabella is a timid little lass, keeps very much to herself. I confess I know naught of what goes on in her head. I think she fears Papa. I suspect she fears me, too.'

'Does she look . . .'

'Like Will? No, she favours her mother.'

They were within sight of the cataract; it had been known to freeze during exceptionally bitter winters, but now it shimmered in the January sun, patterned the mossy rocks below with lacy foam and spray. Davydd pointed. 'There she is. Isabella!'

The girl whirled, and even at that distance Joanna could see how she flushed, as if caught in some flagrant misdeed. Davydd moved towards the rocks, beckoned to her. 'Isabella, come here. I want you to meet my mother.'

'The Lady Joanna?' Isabella lifted her skirts, scrambled up the rocks. 'You've come back!' The change in her was startling; her face was eager, expectant. 'I prayed you would, I prayed so hard, and the Almighty heeded me, He brought you back!'

Joanna reached out, took Isabella's hands between her own. Her heart went out to this lonely little girl, but the last thing she'd expected was to be hailed as Isabella's saviour. She smiled at the child, and then Isabella gave her the poignant answer to the puzzle.

'You're so pretty,' she breathed, and raised up to whisper shyly, 'No wonder Papa loved you so.'

Over the girl's head, Joanna's eyes met her son's in mutual dismay, if for different reasons. Davydd was thinking that Isabella's attachment to his mother might prove politically embarrassing, only fuelling gossip all the more. Joanna was thinking that to keep faith with Isabella, she'd be obliged to live a lie. It seemed the ultimate irony to her that she should be given the responsibility of rearing Will's child, but it was both a penance and a privilege. Putting her arm around Isabella's shoulders, she said gently, 'Let's go home, darling.'

Joanna was standing in the antechamber, staring at her bedroom door. Hours after her arrival at Aber, she had yet to cross that threshold. During her months at Llanfaes, Will's ghost had mercifully kept his distance. But if she were to encounter him at all, surely it would be here, and she reached reluctantly for the door latch, dreading that first onslaught of memory.

Within this bedchamber she'd passed much of her married life. It looked as she'd remembered it, and yet it did not, familiar but somehow foreign, too. It took a moment for her to realize why; all traces of her had been erased. Gone were her favourite silver candlesticks, her carefully tended violets and gillyflowers, even the wall hangings embroidered with unicorns.

Joanna's eyes filled with tears. It was not Will who'd haunt her peace; it was the memory of her husband's face as he walked into this chamber, found her with Will. How could she ever forget that moment of horror? How could she forgive herself?

'Joanna.'

She spun around, saw Llewelyn standing in the doorway. 'I'm afraid, beloved,' she whispered. 'Suddenly I am so afraid. Not just of the hostility I know I must face, not even of my memories. I'm afraid, too, of tomorrow. No matter how expertly a thing is mended, Llewelyn, the break is ever visible thereafter . . .'

'Yes,' he said, 'I know. A scar signifies past pain, a wound that did not heal as it ought. But it testifies, too, to survival, *breila*.'

Joanna looked at him, and then she held out her arms. He closed the door, moved towards her.

July, 1234
Aber, North Wales

Joanna stared down at the parchment, daunted by its blankness. Letters to her cousin Eleanor were never easy; she kept up the contact partly from habit and partly from pity. But this letter was particularly difficult to compose, for so much time had elapsed since she'd last written. The days when Eleanor had been welcomed at John's Christmas court were long gone; for some years now, her horizons had extended no farther than the outer bailey walls of Bristol Castle. Joanna could not be sure what, if anything, Eleanor knew of the momentous events of the past three years.

Had Eleanor heard of Hubert de Burgh's fall from power? Did she know that Llewelyn had fought two bloody and successful wars against the English? Did she know of the Peace of Middle concluded just three weeks ago? Did she know of all the deaths?

Joanna glanced towards the window seat where her sister Nell was plucking a harp; she played badly but with characteristic concentration. Her husband's sudden death in April, 1231 had devastated Nell; so impassioned had her grieving been that she'd even taken a holy oath of chastity, an emotional extravagance Joanna had argued against in vain. And just as she had feared, Nell's mourning ran its course in time, but the oath endured, locking Nell into a lifelong widowhood.

The political consequences of Pembroke's death were no less far-reaching, for he'd held the wardship of Will de Braose's daughters, and with the wardship went control of the de Braose estates. When Henry imprudently bestowed the wardship and lands upon Hubert de Burgh, Llewelyn reacted with alarm, for de Burgh already held the lordships of Cardigan, Carmarthen, Gower and Glamorgan. The igniting spark flared at Montgomery Castle, where de Burgh's garrison beheaded Welsh prisoners, and in June Llewelyn swept south, levelled Montgomery to the ground. He then pressed on into the de Braose lands, burning and pillaging on such a scale that the English bishops excoriated him as a 'despoiler of churches'.

This was the third time that Llewelyn had been excommunicated for what he saw as political sins, and he would later joke about installing a turnstile for his private chapel. But Joanna had never seen any humour in it, and her relief was inexpressible when Llewelyn was restored to God's grace in December, after a botched campaign by Henry and de Burgh.

The following year was one of uneasy truce along the Marches. Peter des Roches, Bishop of Winchester, was back from his Holy Land pilgrimage, and he was so successful in blaming Hubert de Burgh for the Welsh fiasco that in July Henry stripped de Burgh of his high office, demanded an accounting; by November, he was being held at the Tower. But 1232 was also the year in which death claimed the man who'd shown himself to be Llewelyn's most steadfast ally; in October, Ranulf, Earl of Chester, died at his manor of Wallingford in his sixty-third year.

The precarious peace of 1232 did not long endure into 1233. As Nell and William Marshal had been childless, the earldom of Pembroke passed to his brother Richard. But the relationship between Henry and Richard Marshal had gone sour from the start, fraught with suspicion and mutual mistrust. After months of misunderstanding and strife, Henry yielded to Peter des Roches's urgings, proclaimed Marshal a traitor, thus making of the man a reluctant rebel, a rallying point for dissent. A civil war erupted and Llewelyn was not long in entering the fray upon Richard Marshal's behalf, even though Marshal was a partisan of the disgraced Hubert de Burgh. Llewelyn's objective was always the same, to weaken the power of the English Crown in Wales, and he saw in Richard Marshal's rebellion an opportunity that would not come again.

Once again the Marches took fire, and once again Joanna had to watch helplessly as her husband and son rode to war. But the outcome was not long in doubt. Henry was no general, found himself facing two of the most experienced battle commanders in his realm. In November, 1233, he fled in disarray as the royal encampment at Grosmont was overrun by Marshal's Welsh and English allies. In January, 1234, Llewelyn and Richard Marshal ravaged Shropshire to the very gates of Shrewsbury, and Henry found himself under increasing political pressure to come to terms. In March he agreed

785

to a truce, and in April he capitulated to Marshal's demands, dismissed Peter des Roches and his other Poitevin advisers, vowed to keep faith with the Runnymede charter.

But Richard Marshal never knew he'd won. He'd crossed over to Ireland to see to his estates there, and in early April he was wounded in a skirmish with Henry's supporters, taken prisoner and treated so harshly that he died within days. It was left to Llewelyn to gain reparations for the followers of his fallen ally. On June 21, the Archbishop of Canterbury met Llewelyn at the Shropshire village of Middle and peace returned to Henry's realm.

The Pact of Middle was the crowning achievement of Llewelyn's reign, the culmination of a lifetime's struggle against the English Kings. But on this, the eve of the festivities planned to honour her husband's triumph, Joanna was thinking, not of Llewelyn's victory celebration but of their dead. So many deaths. William and Richard Marshal. Llewelyn's sons by marriage, Jack de Braose and William de Lacy. Chester. Maelgwn. His brother Rhys Gryg, slain at the siege of Carmarthen Castle. Morgan, dead nigh on a twelvemonth now. Llewelyn rarely talked of him; he could not. She gazed down at the parchment. So many deaths. And each time she looked into Llewelyn's face, she could not but wonder how much time remained to them. How precious days and hours became with the realization of how few they were.

'You look so solemn, Joanna. What are you thinking of?'

'That Llewelyn and I have been wed twenty-eight years. That sounds so long, Nell, but in truth it passed in a blur of light, days into months into years . . .'

'Your mind takes the most morbid turns,' Nell admonished. 'Fretting about time's passing will not slow it down one whit. Let's talk instead of tomorrow's revelries. Have all the guests arrived? I hope none of the Marshals will be coming; I did tell you, did I not, how disagreeable they've been since William's death, begrudging me my dower rights?'

'Repeatedly,' Joanna said, and smiled to soften the sting. 'I ought to find Isabella; I promised her I'd help her decide what to wear tomorrow.'

'Come to my chamber first. I want to show you the gown I bought in London at Whitsuntide, a samite silk of willow green.'

'I'd love to see it,' Joanna said, remembering in spite of herself the ceremony in which Nell placed a gold band upon her finger to symbolize her marriage to Christ, adopted a nun's habit of homespun. She still wore the ring, but she'd long since put aside the homespun, resumed her rightful place at her brother's court.

As if reading her thoughts, Nell said suddenly, 'I know people were quick to judge me when I began wearing bright colours again. But I've not abjured my oath and that should be what matters to the Almighty, should it not? It vexed me beyond bearing to think of others gossiping behind my back, poking their noses into my life. And when I think how it must have been for you . . . How did you endure it, Joanna? Were you not enraged at their impudence, their effrontery?'

As always, Joanna was amused by Nell's uncalculating candour. It was, Joanna thought wryly, not a trait she'd inherited from either of her parents. 'I think I felt not so much resentful as uncomfortable. But you speak as if the disapproval was all in the past. I would that it were.'

'Even after three years . . .'

'Oh, it gets easier, Nell, with each passing year. But for some, three lifetimes would not be enough time for me to expiate my sins. They've accepted me because Llewelyn gave them no choice, but they will never truly forgive me. I've had to face that, to learn to live with it, even though that includes some of my husband's own family. His daughter Gwladys, his brother Adda. My family, too. Our aunt Ela for one. Elen's husband for another. John will never understand how Llewelyn could take me back.'

Joanna had been sketching aimlessly as she spoke; the letter to Eleanor was covered with interlocking circles. She looked down at her handiwork, put the pen aside. 'Nor do I think I'll fare well at the hands of Welsh historians. I ought not to mind what's said about me once I'm safely dead, but I'm afraid I do.' Her smile was rueful. 'I never hungered for fame, much less notoriety, but I seem fated to be remembered as Llewelyn's wanton foreign wife.'

Nell did not dispute her; she knew how swiftly gossip became enshrined as gospel. 'What matters, Joanna, is that you and Llewelyn have been able to salvage your marriage. In all honesty, I was not so sure you could.'

'In all honesty, neither was I,' Joanna confessed. 'At first we were so wary with one another, so painstakingly polite we'd have put a couple of saints to shame! And God pity us, but we went on like that for weeks, so anxious not to tread amiss that we could scarce move

787

at all. Luckily a day came when I had a right sharp headache, a day when I walked in and found Llewelyn ransacking our bedchamber for his privy seal. The room looked as if a whirlwind had struck: I regret to say neatness has never been one of Llewelyn's virtues. And as I stood there surveying the wreckage, Llewelyn demanded to know where the seal was – as if I stored it under my pillow. I lost my temper, snapped at him; he snapped back, and as quickly as that, we found ourselves in a flaming row . . . like any husband and wife on a bad day. That realization hit us both at once, in mid-shout. We stopped, looked at each other, and then, as if on cue, we burst out laughing.' And in remembering, Joanna laughed again. 'It was then,' she said, 'that I truly began to believe we might make it, after all.'

Joanna was standing beside her brother, bringing him up to date on the happenings at her husband's court. 'Llewelyn's cousin Madog is here, as is Maelgwn's son. Gwenllian is still in Ireland, but Llewelyn's other daughters are present, and Tegwared and his wife; they've given Llewelyn and Ednyved four grandchildren so far. Gwladys, too; did you know? After thirteen barren years with Reginald de Braose, she found herself with child within a twelvemonth of marrying Ralph de Mortimer, has two sons by him now. There's Glynis; you remember her from Llanfaes? Llewelyn and I made a most advantageous marriage for her, and I stood godmother to her firstborn. That is Marared over to your right; did I tell you she's to marry Walter Clifford?'

Richard had been listening indulgently, having no real interest in Welsh weddings and birthings. But an alliance with a Marcher lord like Clifford was of no small significance, and he said admiringly, 'So Llewelyn has entangled another Norman fish in his nuptial nets. He's pulled in quite a catch over the years: Chester, de Braose, de Mortimer, de Lacy . . . and now Clifford. Had he only a few more daughters and a sister or two, he might have won over the Marches by marriage!'

'Strange you should say that. Morgan, may God assoil him, once told Llewelyn the same thing, almost word for word.'

'I heard he'd died?'

She nodded. 'Last year. No great surprise, for he'd been ailing, and he'd reached a venerable age. But Llewelyn took his death hard, still misses him sorely.'

A sudden burst of laughter drew their attention. They turned to discover that Nell was displaying the same magnetic allure for males her mother had so often demonstrated; she was surrounded by bedazzled admirers, a vision in willow green, and Richard murmured, 'Jesu, how like Isabelle she is. The man on her left, the one gazing at her as if bewitched, damn me if he does not look remarkably like the Earl of Winchester.'

'That's because he is. And the man laughing is his younger brother, Robert de Quincy.' Richard did not comment, but Joanna felt a need to elaborate further, to explain why the sons of one of their father's bitterest enemies were guests at her hearth. 'Saer de Quincy,' she said. 'How Papa hated him. And how long ago it all seems. Roger and Robert de Quincy came with John the Scot and Elen. They are kin to John; his aunt was wed to their uncle.'

'You owe me no explanations, Joanna. As you say, it was a long time ago. Seeing Nell brings it back, though, for she could be Isabelle at eighteen, in truth she could. Do you ever hear from her . . . Isabelle?'

'Not for years. What with Hugh de Lusignan's intrigues and Isabelle's yearly pregnancies, when would she find the time to write?'

Richard grinned. 'I've lost count; how many children has she borne de Lusignan . . . seven? Eight? For certès we know what they do when they're not plotting against Henry or the French King.' Nell's laughter came to them again and he shook his head. 'That chastity oath of hers was an act of arrant lunacy, Joanna. She'll never hold to it. How can she? Look at her; she's the most beautiful woman in the hall.'

'Not so.' Neither had heard Llewelyn's approach; they turned as he said, 'Elen is the most beautiful woman at Aber . . . and that's because she so resembles her mother.'

Fair colouring was prized no less by the Welsh than by the English, was valued even more for its rarity, and that awareness made Llewelyn's gallantry all the more endearing to Joanna. She touched her lips to the rim of her wine cup, then handed it to him. He smiled, put his mouth to the imprint of her kiss, and drank.

Watching their byplay, Richard felt both amusement and awe. He'd not been sanguine about their chances of reconciliation; Llewelyn's bloody rending of the de Braose lands in 1231 had given incontrovertible evidence of the sort of wound infidelity could inflict. But there was such intimacy in the look that now passed

789

between them that he no longer doubted, and he could only marvel at what he could not understand.

There was a lull in the dancing; John the Scot was calling for silence. As conversation hushed and heads turned, he strode up on to the dais. 'I hope our Welsh brethren will not take it amiss if I speak French; my father's Gaelic enabled me to understand your tongue, but I speak it too poorly for public utterance.' Glancing towards Llewelyn, he said, 'In the recent strife betwixt King Henry and your Prince, I was sorely tried. I had to hold with my King, but I am bound to Lord Llewelyn, too, both by choice and wedlock. I can say, therefore, in all certitude that few welcomed the Treaty of Middle more wholeheartedly than I.'

He raised his wine cup high. 'I drink to peace between our peoples . . . and to your Prince. Wales has had its share of strong-willed, able rulers, men like Hywel the Good and Owain the Great. It is my pleasure now to honour a man whose feats equal if not eclipse theirs. A man who is my ally, friend, father by marriage, a man whose memory will burn brightly for generations to come amongst the Welsh, a man who well deserves to be remembered by history as Llewelyn the Great.'

It was a memorable tribute, one Llewelyn had not been expecting. 'Llewelyn Fawr?' he echoed, then shook his head and grinned. 'I do not know, John. Although I can say for certès that no one will ever call me Llewelyn the Good!'

Midst the ensuing laughing, his eyes met Joanna's. She saw how deeply he'd been pleased, put her hand upon his arm, her happiness spilling over in full and intoxicating measure. But it was then that her gaze happened to fall upon her daughter. Elen was watching her father and husband, and there was on her face an expression of unutterable sadness, a look of yearning and of despair.

'Lady Joanna? I saw you leave the hall, feared something might be wrong.'

'Not at all, Isabella. I am but returning to my bedchamber to tighten a garter.'

'Shall I fetch your maid? Or mayhap I could help you myself?'

At times Isabella's emotional dependence could be cloying, but Joanna's fondness for the girl was genuine, and she smiled, shook her head. 'No, darling, there's no need; you go back to the hall,' she said, and she would ever after thank God fasting for that casually made decision to go unaccompanied to her bedchamber.

The night was warm, starlit and scented with honeysuckle, Joanna's favourite fragrance, but she was too preoccupied to notice. Ere the evening was over, she'd have to find time alone with Elen. But would Elen confide in her?

Entering the antechamber, she was reaching for the door latch when she heard it, a sound so unexpected, so chilling that her fingers froze on the ring – the sound of a man's laughter. She stared at the door, disbelieving, caught up in a surge of superstitious fear, for what man would dare intrude into Llewelyn's private chamber? There was but one answer to that question, an answer that raised gooseflesh on her arms, sweat on her forehead. No mortal man.

'Will?' she whispered as the laughter came again. All knew ghosts walked at night, evil spirits come to tempt the unwary, incubi to lay with women whilst they slept. But as she stood there, she suddenly remembered a night when she'd awakened Llewelyn with kisses, and he'd pretended to believe she was a succubus, intent upon stealing his seed. It was an incongruous, bawdy memory, but it stiffened her spine, gave her the courage to do what she knew Llewelyn would have done, confront the unknown. She groped for her crucifix, gripped the latch and thrust the door open.

They sprang apart, turned startled faces towards her, faces that mirrored her own fear. Her daughter and Robert de Quincy. 'Mama!' Elen's voice was uneven, breathless. 'What are you doing here?'

Joanna moved forward into the room. 'I might well ask you the same question, Elen. '

Robert de Quincy stepped into the light cast by Joanna's lantern; she had not paid him much mind in the hall, had noted only that he had a ready laugh. She saw now a thatch of dark hair, high hollowed cheekbones, full mouth and intensely blue eyes, full of anxiety. 'Do not blame Elen, Madame. I lured her here, told her –'

'That's not so. This was my doing, Mama, not Rob's.' Elen put her hand upon his arm. 'Go back to the hall, Rob, ere you be missed. I'll talk to my mother.'

'You're sure?' he asked, and the intimacy of that brief exchange was enough to confirm Joanna's worst fears. She looked from her daughter to de Quincy, with a sinking certainty that they were lovers.

'Yes,' Elen said, 'I'm sure.' But before he reached the door, she cried, 'Rob!' He stopped and she flung her arms around his neck, kissed him full on the mouth. And then she turned defiantly back to face her mother.

The door closed; Joanna put her lantern down. 'Well?' Elen said. 'Go ahead, Mama. Say what you will. But ere you do, you might remember what Scriptures say about sins and casting the first stone.'

'What can I say?' Joanna sat down upon the bed. Never had a headache come upon her so suddenly; her temples were throbbing, her vision blurring. 'You must love him. I cannot believe you'd take such a risk if you did not. But to bring him here . . . Jesus wept, Elen, what were you thinking of?'

Colour rose in Elen's face. 'It was folly, I know,' she admitted. 'But I had to be alone with him, if only for a few moments, and I dared not bring him to my own chamber . . .' She moved towards the bed. 'I love him, Mama,' she said softly, 'and he loves me.'

Elen had not dared to light candles and the only illumination came from Joanna's lantern; she stared at it, a weak, flickering flame in a sea of shadows. 'What do you mean to do, Elen?'

Elen shrugged. 'What can I do? Even if John would agree to a divorce, we have no grounds the Church would recognize. Till death us do part; was that not what the vows said, Mama?'

She was back at the table, like Joanna, drawn by the light. 'You remember how often you berated me for my impulsiveness, my lack of caution? Well, Rob is like me, too quick to act, heeding his heart, not his head. He'd run away with me tomorrow if I agreed.'

Joanna caught her breath. 'Elen . . . you would not?'

'How could I?' Elen had begun to pace. 'That would make John a laughing-stock. I could not do that to him, not when I remember how Papa –' She broke off abruptly; a silence fell.

'I would not hurt John if I could help it.' Defiance had crept back into Elen's voice, as if she expected disbelief. 'Nor would I ever willingly hurt Papa. If I ran away with Rob, Papa's alliance with John would come apart like cobwebs. And you'd be hurt, too, Mama. Men would say "Like mother, like daughter", would rake up all the old gossip about you and Will de Braose. We'd all be splattered with the mud, Mama, not just Rob and John and me, but you, too, and Papa, even Davydd.'

She came back to the bed, sat down beside Joanna. 'I might be willing to risk all that, might be selfish enough to put my happiness first; I'll never know. But I could never risk Rob's life. John is not a vindictive man, but he is a prideful one. If I ran away with his cousin, he'd not rest until he'd avenged himself upon Rob, avenged his honour.'

Joanna reached over, took Elen's hand. 'If you love him, Elen, let him go.'

'I cannot,' Elen said, 'I cannot.' And after that, there was nothing left to say.

Llewelyn raised himself up on his elbow, watching as Joanna brushed her hair. 'Are you sure nothing is troubling you, *breila*?'

'Very sure, Llewelyn.' What would it serve to tell him? She'd only be burdening him for naught; there was nothing he could do. To forestall further questioning, she hastily slipped off her bedrobe, climbed into the bed. He put his arm around her shoulders, drew her close. She was relieved when he seemed content only to hold her; after her scene with Elen, she was not in the mood for lovemaking. She pillowed her head against his chest, felt his hand on her hair, gently stroking.

'Joanna, we do need to talk.'

She shifted so she could see his face. He sounded so grave; could he possibly have guessed about Elen and Robert de Quincy? 'Talk about what?'

'On the morrow I am going to Deganwy Castle.' The body he held was suddenly rigid; the muscles in her back contracted, stiffened under his hand. He kissed her on the forehead. 'If Gruffydd can give me the assurances I must have, I mean to set him free.'

'Llewelyn, no!'

'Joanna . . . Joanna, you must try to understand. When I confined Gruffydd at Deganwy, Davydd was nineteen and untried. He is now twenty-and-five, has fought at my side in three wars. I've secured for him the recognition of the Pope, the English King, my Welsh allies, and when I die, he will inherit a united realm, a legacy no other Welsh Prince has been able to leave his son. But I've done all I can. What I bequeath him, he – and he alone – will have to hold. I have every confidence that he can.'

'I have faith in Davydd, too. But why risk civil war?'

'Because,' he said slowly, 'I cannot condemn Gruffydd to a lifetime shut away from the sun.'

And that she could understand. She reached out, touched his cheek. Would there ever be a time when she was not being torn between those she loved? For so many years, her father and husband.

793

And now . . . now husband and son. How could she blame Llewelyn for wanting to set his son free? But Davydd's right to the succession could be guaranteed only by Gruffydd's continuing captivity.

'Joanna . . . can you accept my decision?'

'I shall have to accept it.' She lay back beside him, closed her eyes. What else could she do? The last time she'd intervened on Davydd's behalf, she'd come close, Jesu, so close to destroying her marriage. He was a man grown, no less ambitious than Gruffydd, and twice as clever. He would prevail. But the words rang hollow. She could not stave off a sense of dread, of coming calamity. Lady Mary be merciful, it was beginning all over again.

Llewelyn returned to Aber at dusk the following day, and Gruffydd rode by his side. Joanna had not expected Llewelyn to act so swiftly, had thought she'd have more time to prepare herself for Gruffydd's return. As people surged out into the bailey, she followed slowly, her mind echoing to the refrain of a French chanson, one that warned against allowing the wolf into the fold.

Had so much not been at stake, she might have been able to summon up sympathy, for Gruffydd showed the rigours of long confinement. He had a pronounced pallor, the beginnings of a double chin, and hair cut so carelessly that it was obvious he'd long since become indifferent to appearance, while the deep grooves around his mouth told Joanna more than she wanted to know of his years in Deganwy's great keep.

Senena, however, looked radiant; an uninformed bystander might well have identified her as the released prisoner. Their son Owain rode beside her, and the sight of him was a shock to Joanna. The younger children had often stayed at Llewelyn's court, but Owain, never. The nine-year-old boy she remembered was a gangling youth of fifteen, awkward in his newfound manhood, a flesh and blood ghost from Gruffydd's troubled past.

Llewelyn had dismounted. His smile was dazzling, and Joanna yearned to be able to rejoice with him, to be truly and wholeheartedly happy that his son was free.

'Madame.' Gruffydd was bending over her hand. His demeanour was scrupulously correct; captivity had taught him caution, if nothing else, Joanna thought, and she, too, took refuge in courtesy, in the most formal of Welsh greetings, a hollow 'May God prosper you.'

Gruffydd's eyes shifted to her face; deep in their depths she saw a raw flame flicker. 'I wish no less for you, Madame.'

Almost at once Gruffydd was surrounded by family and friends, well-wishers, embraced by his sisters, his uncle. He was greeted far more coolly by Elen and Tegwared, but enough people were clustering about him to give his return the aura of a hero's homecoming. Joanna turned, walked away.

Elen soon joined her. 'Nothing has changed,' Joanna said tonelessly, 'nothing,' and Elen shook her head.

'You think not? Watch,' she said, and Joanna followed her daughter's gaze, saw her son had just ridden into the bailey.

If Davydd was surprised by Gruffydd's early arrival, it did not show in his face. He reined his stallion in, waited for Gruffydd to come to him. After a conspicuously long pause, Gruffydd did. They exchanged but a few terse words before Gruffydd swung about, stalked back to his wife and sisters. Llewelyn moved swiftly towards his youngest son. Davydd slid from the saddle. They spoke softly together for several minutes and then Davydd smiled, nodded. But he kept his eyes upon Gruffydd all the while.

As Joanna watched, a memory stirred, elusive, perplexing. She frowned, seeking to bring it into focus. There was something so tantalizingly familiar about this scene, about Davydd's cool composure, his detachment, the way his hazel eyes narrowed as they took the light, took Gruffydd's measure . . . and then the memory broke through, with such vivid clarity that time blurred, the years fell away, and she exclaimed, 'Mirebeau!' in startled revelation.

'Mama?'

'Do you see how Davydd is watching Gruffydd? So distant and yet so deliberate. I knew I'd seen that look before, and now I remember. I once saw my father watch Arthur in that very same way.'

The little church of St Rhychwyn was cool and still. Not even the parish priest was there to disturb Joanna. Kneeling before the altar, she was alone with God, alone with her dead. She prayed first for her father, for his need was greatest. And then she prayed for the others: Clemence, Eleanor of Aquitaine, Will of Salisbury, Catherine, Rhys, Morgan, Chester, Maude de Braose, Arthur, Will. She concluded with prayers for those who'd died in Llewelyn's compulsive

795

war against a ghost, the war that had wrought such devastation to the de Braose lands.

The sun was beginning its slow descent towards the west by the time Joanna emerged from the church, started back to Llewelyn's hillside manor at Trefriw. She'd stopped to gather bell heather when she heard Elen's voice; a moment later her daughter came around a bend in the path.

'They told me you'd gone up to Llanrhychwyn, Mama, so I thought I'd walk up and meet you. But why did you not go to St Mary's? Papa had it built for you, after all, to spare you this walk.'

'I do attend St Mary's for morning Mass. But now and then I need the solitude of Llanrhychwyn, need that time alone to pray for loved ones . . . and to remember.'

They walked in silence for a time; it was too hot for haste. Pine woods rose up on both sides of the path, dark and shadowy and primeval. 'Look,' Elen said, stooping to pick a daisy. 'Did you ever play that game, Mama, plucking the petals to see if love will last?' Her eyes shifted from the flower, up to Joanna's face. 'Were you praying for your father?'

Joanna nodded. 'Elen . . . we can talk about him if you like. You have the right, darling; he was your blood kin, too.'

'Can you talk about him, Mama . . . truly? You pray for him. Does that mean you've forgiven him?'

Joanna was quiet. 'No,' she said at last. 'That is for the Almighty to do. But I have forgiven myself for loving him, am no longer ashamed of that love, and mayhap that's as much as I can hope for.'

They'd almost reached Trefriw. Joanna stopped, touched Elen on the arm. 'Elen, I am so glad you agreed to stay for a time with us. But I want you to promise me that you'll turn to us if ever you need help, if ever –'

'Mama, I will. But you need not fear.' Elen smiled impishly, held out the daisy. 'See,' she said. 'I just pulled the last petal, and it promises love will prevail!'

Dismounting in a clearing within sight and sound of Rhaeadr Ewynnol, Llewelyn walked to the edge of the cliff, stood gazing down at the cataract, a surging spillover of foam and flying spray. Joanna had remained a prudent distance from the precipice, and at last he heeded her entreaties, joined her on the grass under an ancient oak.

Joanna and Elen had returned to Trefriw just as Llewelyn and

Davydd rode in after a day's hawking, and when Llewelyn suggested they ride over to Rhaeadr Ewynnol to see the results of recent heavy rains, Joanna had accepted with alacrity; except in bed at night, they'd had little time alone this summer. Now she leaned back against the tree and Llewelyn stretched out beside her, pillowing his head in her lap.

'I had another talk with Ednyved,' he said. 'He's still set upon making that pilgrimage to the Holy Land, says he can begin laying plans now that Gwynedd is at peace.'

That would be a strenuous, dangerous undertaking for a man of any age, and Ednyved was past sixty. Joanna frowned, stopped stroking Llewelyn's hair. 'Do you not think you can dissuade him?'

'No,' he said regretfully, 'I do not.' A comfortable silence settled over the glen. When Llewelyn spoke again, he sounded lazily content. 'John the Scot gave me a remarkable book Chester picked up in France, written by a man who'd gone on pilgrimage to the Holy Land. It's an account of his adventures, interspersed with suggestions for his fellow pilgrims. I think Ednyved might find it right useful, for he tells the reader how to deal with Venetian money-changers, which ports are best for engaging passage to Palestine, that syrup of ginger helps to ease seasickness. He even includes a vocabulary of foreign words and sentences, those phrases a man would be most likely to need, like "Where is the inn?" "How much?" And one so utterly essential I thought it best to commit it to memory: "*Marrat nyco.*"'

When Joanna gave him a quizzical, curious look, he laughed. 'That is Arabic for "Maiden, wilt thou sleep with me?"'

Joanna laughed, too. 'You've just convinced me how fortunate I am that you're not going on pilgrimage with him!' But a pilgrimage was more than a propitious opportunity for spiritual salvation; it offered, too, a rare chance for great adventure. 'Llewelyn . . . you would not want to accompany Ednyved?'

'No, *breila*. I've thought of pilgrimage; what Christian has not? But I do not think I'd transplant well, need to keep my roots in Welsh soil.' His eyes began to gleam; he added, 'Furthermore, as much as I would like to see the Holy City wrested away from the Saracens, even more would I like to see Wales free of you English.'

Joanna tugged at his hair. 'If you must be insulting, at least be accurate. Norman-French, if you please.'

'I stand corrected. Although I think English will win out, if not in Davydd's lifetime, mayhap in his children's. Now that you've lost

Normandy, the day might well come when English, not French, will be the language even of the court.'

'Be serious,' Joanna said, and tossed an acorn to a small red squirrel. 'I only wish the crusaders had been as successful in their quest as you've been in yours; there'd not be a mosque left intact in all Jerusalem.'

'You make it sound as if I've won my war, Joanna.'

'Beloved, you have! You've outwitted or outfought two English Kings, unified your people, secured the succession for Davydd, and engendered a sense of shared identity amongst the Welsh, an awareness of their common destiny. Llewelyn, those are remarkable achievements.'

'Yes,' he said, 'but will it last?'

Joanna had been able to find a curious sort of comfort in that courtyard scene at Aber, in that sudden glimpse of Davydd in a new and unnerving guise, as a man utterly intent upon claiming a crown. She opened her mouth now, ready to reassure Llewelyn that Davydd would triumph, and then realized he was not speaking of Davydd's succession, but rather of Wales. Her smile was both wry and resigned; whilst she worried about people, his concern would ever be for empires.

She very much wished she could foretell for him the future of Gwynedd, assure him the Welsh would continue to thrive in the shadow of a stronger neighbour. Since she could not, she leaned over, kissed him tenderly, then made him laugh by calling him Llewelyn Fawr, for they'd turned John the Scot's lavish praise into a private bedtime joke.

The sun was very low in the sky, the river reflecting the red-gold of a summer sunset. Joanna sat up reluctantly. 'We ought to be getting back,' she said, but Llewelyn shook his head.

'No,' he said, 'not yet. We have time.' And so they lingered awhile longer in the clearing, watched together the passing of day.

EPILOGUE

Joanna died in 1237 and was buried, at her own request, at Llanfaes. Llewelyn established a Franciscan monastery there in honour of her memory. He died three years later and was succeeded by their son Davydd. But Llewelyn's triumph was ephemeral, for it was personal, and his dream of a united, independent Wales was not destined to be.

AUTHOR'S NOTE

In seeking to resurrect a time more than seven centuries distant from ours, I often found research would take me only so far. It was necessary to rely upon imagination to a greater extent than in my earlier novel of fifteenth-century England, for Llewelyn's world was not as well chronicled as that of the Yorkist Kings. But the structure of *Here Be Dragons* is grounded in fact; even the more unlikely occurrences are validated by medieval chroniclers. Joanna's secret warning to John did reach him at Nottingham as Llewelyn's hostages were being hanged. Llewelyn and Gruffydd did reconcile on the battlefield. And Llewelyn did indeed return unexpectedly to Aber on an April night in 1230, only to discover Joanna and Will de Braose alone in his bedchamber. I took but one factual liberty; Llewelyn captured Mold Castle in January of 1199, but I placed the siege in April, the better to integrate the Welsh and Norman story lines.

All of my major characters in *Dragons* actually lived, with the exception of Morgan, Rhys and his wife Catherine; whenever possible, I also cast my secondary characters from real-life moulds. While history has preserved for us the identity of Tangwystl, the mother of Llewelyn's son Gruffydd, other female figures remain in shadow. Llewelyn's concubine lived, but 'Cristyn' is a name of my choosing. Little is known of Joanna's mother, other than her Christian name; I gave her a surname and a family background to reflect the skeletal known facts and the most common circumstances of illegitimacy.

Llewelyn's third son Tegwared has been utterly eclipsed by the embittered rivalry between his brothers Gruffydd and Davydd; most historians make no mention of him whatsoever. I discovered him in the remarkable *Welsh Genealogies*, a life's work by Peter C. Bartrum. From *Welsh Genealogies*, I was able, too, to determine the name of Llewelyn's brother Adda. Like Tegwared, Adda has been relegated to the outer reaches of historical obscurity. I knew Llewelyn had a sibling, as a letter of his refers to his nephews, but until I consulted Mr Bartrum's work, I had no luck in tracking down this elusive sibling. As I sought to dramatize in *Dragons*, the Welsh system of inheritance all too often fostered fratricide. Adda, therefore, is an anomaly, neither Llewelyn's rival nor his active ally. So unusual was his absence from the political arena that I could only explain it in terms of a disability of some sort.

Little is known of Llewelyn's early years. It is believed he passed his childhood in Powys and England; by his fifteenth year, he was challenging his uncles for control of Gwynedd. Historians have long been cognizant of his kinship to the Corbet family; he often stayed his hand, spared Corbet lands, and a letter of his addresses William Corbet as 'uncle'. In the nineteenth century, historians speculated that Llewelyn's mother might be a hitherto unknown Corbet daughter, but Marared ferch Meredydd's identity has since been established beyond any doubt. Marared must therefore have made a second marriage after Iorwerth's death in 1174. In researching the Corbet family, I was able to eliminate Robert Corbet without difficulty. His brother William was the 'uncle' of Llewelyn's letter. Walter Corbet was a monk. By the process of elimination, Hugh Corbet had to be Marared's second husband, Llewelyn's stepfather.

I made use of Welsh spellings and place names wherever possible (e.g., Cricieth, not Criccieth), except when referring to the Norman towns and castles in South Wales. While 'Llywelyn' is the purest Welsh form of the name, I chose a slightly Anglicized version, knowing that most readers would be unfamiliar with Welsh. The same reasoning governed my spelling of Davydd; although the modern Welsh alphabet contains no letter v, it was in use in the Middle Ages, and I thought a phonetic spelling might aid in pronunciation. For consistency, I called Llewelyn's Seneschal and friend by his family name – ap Cynwrig – but he is more commonly known as Ednyfed Fychan; readers of *The Sunne in Splendour* might be interested to know he is the ancestor of Henry Tudor.

Lastly, I made use of 'Norman' as an inclusive term for all of French descent, e.g., Normans, Angevins, Poitevins, et cetera. To have referred to them as 'French' would have created endless confusion, and it seemed the lesser sin to opt for clarity. In the same way, I referred to those of Anglo-Saxon descent as Saxons, not as English, the term they would have used, thus enabling me to stress the divisions still so prevalent in King John's England. Certain words and phrases, which may sound incongruous or discordant to modern ears, such as lay or Scriptures, follow valid medieval usage. And for those readers curious about Joanna's knowledge of such countries as Ethiopia and India, I wholeheartedly recommend *Medieval Lore From Bartholomew Anglicus*; he was a thirteenth-century English Franciscan monk who wrote a marvellous book that now serves as an invaluable encyclopedia of medieval knowledge, offering an irresistible blend of the factual and the fanciful.

As a point of interest, the title of this book has its roots in the common practice of medieval cartographers; when a mapmaker had drawn upon all of his geographical knowledge, he would neatly letter across the void beyond: Here be dragons. I found the symbolism hard to resist, given how very little the English of the thirteenth century knew of Wales and the Welsh. Then, too, the national emblem of Wales is a winged red dragon, much like those heraldic dragons once emblazoned upon the banners of her princes.

John was much maligned in the lurid tales told of him after his death, and a compelling, colourful legend gradually took root – John, Nature's Enemy, John of the Devil's Brood. Only in the twentieth century have the myths been stripped away, permitting historians to judge John's reign without passion or prejudice, to judge John – as a king, as a man – a judgment I sought to convey in *Dragons*. History's judgment upon Llewelyn echoes that of his contemporaries, to whom he was Llewelyn Fawr – Llewelyn the Great.

S.K.P.
October 1984

LANARK

Alasdair Gray was born in Glasgow in 1934. He was educated at Whitehill Senior Secondary School and studied drawing and painting at the Glasgow School of Art from 1952–7. After Art School he worked as a part-time art teacher and on commissions for portraits and murals. During this time he was also writing short stories and a semi-autobiographical novel which changed and developed through several drafts over the course of twenty years, to become *Lanark*. After training at Jordanhill in 1960 he taught art in Glasgow schools for the next two years before going on to make a difficult living as an artist, a writer, a scene painter and part-time lecturer. Gray married Inge Sørensen in 1962 and the couple had a son in 1964 but were divorced in 1970. In 1968 his play *The Fall of Kelvin Walker* was broadcast on BBC TV. In the 1970s Gray was attending Glasgow University lecturer Philip Hobsbaum's creative writing sessions, in a group which included Tom Leonard, Liz Lochhead and James Kelman. During this period he wrote several plays for radio and television, some of which were done on stage, while he continued to paint and to work on murals. (Some of his murals can still be seen at Palace Rigg Nature Reserve in Cumbernauld, in Abbots House local history museum in Dunfermline, and in the Ubiquitous Chip restaurant in Glasgow.) Gray's first novel, *Lanark*, was published by Canongate in 1981 to widespread critical acclaim, followed by short stories in *Unlikely Stories, Mostly* (1983), a second major novel *1982 Janine* (1984), *The Fall of Kelvin Walker* as a novel (1985), and *Lean Tales* (with Agnes Owens and James Kelman) in the same year.

Gray's work is characterised by an exuberant imaginative energy, which uses fantasy and fabulation to good-humoured effect, while never losing sight of his darker and more critical sense of the effects of personal, cultural, and political alienation in the modern world. Technically his books make free use of meta-narrative games, typographical effects, mock scholarly addenda and his own fine and complex illustrations.

Gray produced a brief *Saltire Self Portrait* in 1988 and a collection of poems, *Old Negatives*, appeared in 1989, with *McGrotty and Ludmilla* (the novel version of a play written in 1975) and the novel *Something Leather* in 1990. A wholly original revision of the Frankenstein theme featured in the novel *Poor Things* (1992) and further short stories were published as *Ten Tales True and Tall* (1993), with two further books *A History Maker* (1994) and *Mavis Belfrage* (1996). A polemical essay *Why Scots Should Rule Scotland* was published in 1992 and revised in 1997. His most recent works are *An Anthology of Prefaces* (2000) and *A Short Survey of Classic Scottish Writing* (2001). Gray's fiction has been translated into more than a dozen languages throughout the world, including Lithuanian, Polish, Czech, Japanese, Swedish and Serbo-Croatian.

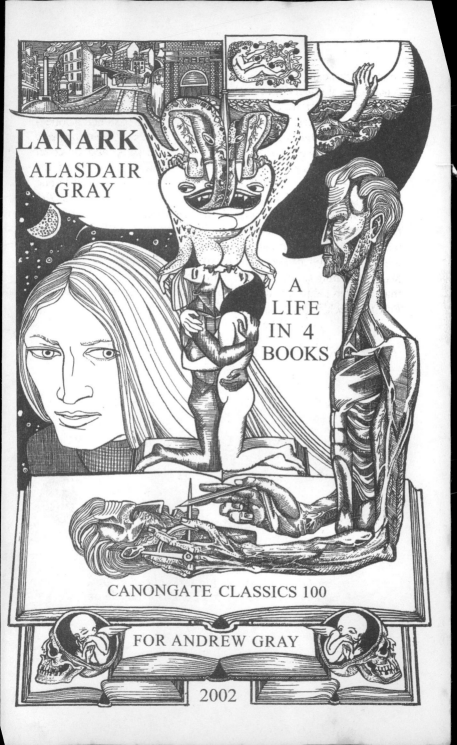

LANARK

ALASDAIR
GRAY

A
LIFE
IN 4
BOOKS

CANONGATE CLASSICS 100

FOR ANDREW GRAY

2002

First published in Great Britain in 1981 by Canongate
Publishing Ltd. This edition published as a Canongate
Classic in 2002 by Canongate Books Ltd, 14 High
Street, Edinburgh EH1 1TE.

Portions of this work originally appeared in *Scottish
International Review, Glasgow University Magazine*,
and *Words Magazine*.

The publishers gratefully acknowledge general
subsidy from the Scottish Arts Council towards the
Canongate Classics series and a specific grant towards
the publication of this volume.

Typeset by Hewertext Ltd, Edinburgh. Printed by
Nørhaven Paperback A/S, Denmark.

10 9 8 7 6 5 4

British Library Cataloguing-in-Publication Data
A catalogue record for this book is available on
request from the British Library.

ISBN 1 84195 183 8

www.canongate.net

Creatures shall be seen on the earth who will always be fighting one another, with the greatest losses and frequent deaths on either side. There will be no bounds to their malice; by their strong limbs the vast forests of the world shall be laid low; and when they are filled with food they shall gratify their desires by dealing out death, affliction, labour, terror, and banishment to every living thing; and from their boundless pride they will desire to rise towards heaven, but the excessive weight of their limbs will hold them down. Nothing shall remain on the earth or under the earth or in the waters that shall not be pursued, disturbed, or spoiled, and that which is in one country removed into another. And their bodies shall be made the tomb and the means of transit of all the living bodies they have slain.

O earth, why do you not open and hurl them into the deep fissures of thy vast abysses and caverns, and no longer display in the sight of heaven so cruel and horrible a monster?

—From Leonardo da Vinci's Notebooks

VLADIMIR: Suppose we repented.
ESTRAGON: Repented what?
VLADIMIR: Oh . . . *(he reflects)* We wouldn't have to go into the details.

—From Beckett's *Waiting for Godot*

TABLE OF

CONTENTS

Introduction

SOMETHING TO SAY

'Someone told me everything would end in a deluge;
he was very definite about it. Yes, we must go as high
as possible, if only for the view.'

Trying to get my thinking done for me before writing this piece, I
asked a friend what his thoughts were, these twenty years after its
first publication, of Alasdair Gray's first novel, *Lanark*. *Lanark*? he
said. *Lanark* eh? His expression changed from interest to puzzlement to concern. Is there anything to say about *Lanark* that hasn't
been said? I didn't flinch, exactly, but I knew what he meant. He
meant that this book, much trumpeted on its first appearance in the
manner then deemed appropriate to Scottish novels (viz, trumpeted
somewhat contextlessly and with the breathy excitement of permitting a heathen into the Vatican), had been harrowed enough by the
processes of academic and/or journalistic analysis and that he, at
least, was not keen to add more. *Lanark*, eh? The Scotland Question
playful blend of genres fusion of real and surreal towering imagination precursor of efflorescence of contemporary Scottish literature politics sex painting Armageddon – *that* Lanark. Well, no.

No. In common with all Great Books, the critical mythology
that *Lanark* has acquired over its twenty years is no more than a
handy ready-reckoner, not real currency. The book itself says so. A
novel full of voice and voices, of Art concealing and revealing Art
at one and the same time, it makes multiple invitations to its reader
to reject distanced analysis and enter, "headfirst and naked," into
the story itself. And *Lanark* is certainly a story, dear me yes, there

is always a story. It is also a fine compendium of information, asides, satirical and not-so-satirical advice and further supplies its own introduction, summary and critical appraisal. When Nastler, the author caricature of Mr Gray himself, appears near the end and blusters: "What the Aeneid had been to the Roman Empire, my epic would be to the Scottish Co-Operative Wholesale Republic" – it's not only to allow the reader to enjoy a joke at Gray's expense, but to provoke the reader to read more critically *for herself alone*.

ADVERTISING OVERSTIMULATES, MISINFORMS, CORRUPTS.

If you feel this, send your name and address to the council Advertising Commission and receive your free booklet explaining why we can't do without it.

This needlesome book is in no mood for subservience, not even toward its own author. From the beginning, it demands its reader be an active participant in the imaginative process, not a passive recipient of others' ideas. This is advice you should certainly take, here and now, by making a start on Chapter I without delay. For those, however, who feel value for money is not addressed by such a course of action, here are a few pages of further preparation. They claim no expertise, no academic thrust, no authority and, given the timely reminder from a friend, no novelty: they are merely a few of this reader's observations and remembrances of her first encounter with A Book that Made a Difference.

Oh I know you, Thaw, I know all about you, the hysterical child, the eager adolescent, the mad rapist, the wise old daddy, oh I've suffered all your tricks and know how hollow they are so don't weep. Grief is the rottenest trick of all.

I tripped over *Lanark*, literally, on the floor of friend's house and recall quite clearly being struck by the (then) cover as I picked it up. A cheeky echo of the engraved title page of the first edition of Hobbes' *Leviathan*, it showed an enormous man, his corporate body and clothing made of faceless folk, wielding a sword and a crook over the city he hoped to rule by fear. The city stretched beneath his arms was a cluster of skyscrapers and factories, pylons and gasworks and clocktowers, its coastline fraught with crested waves, its hills rising through the urban sprawl like naked limbs. A closer look found the monster-humps of the Forth Bridge bounding over black, nameless water; what was surely the paddle steamer *Waverley* chugged a narrower channel further south. And there, no mistake, were Glasgow Cathedral and the Necropolis overlooking Dennistoun. At the foot, sitting on the rim of the picture frame and almost missable, was a tiny man with glasses; someone, in the later words of the book itself, "whose bewildered face looked straight out at the viewers, making them feel part of the multitude too". And he was looking, it seemed, at me.

That the solid black lines of the cover encompassed a text chunky as a doorstop is another authorial joke, for *Lanark* is a novel built on shifting sands, defying solidity at a number of levels. Opening it reveals not one, but four books arranged slightly out of synch on a vaguely epic canvas stitched about with literary allusion and quotations, aphorisms, illustrations, and sermons. Within these books, the stories of Duncan Thaw and Lanark, men who inhabit cities called Glasgow and Unthank, interlace and reflect upon each other. Thaw, who is revealed from the age of five or so, inhabits more the "naturalistic" books; Lanark, ageing by the page, the more surreal, but that the cities are the same city, both men the same man is never in question. There is nothing particularly complicated in that. Indeed, the story as shown in the author's own honed to the bone précis is, on one level, simple enough:

> First he had been a child, then a school boy, then his mother died. He became a student, tried to work as a painter and became very ill. He hung uselessly around cafés for a time, then took a job in an institute. He got mixed up with a woman there, lost the job, then went to live in a badly governed place where his son was born. The woman and child left him, and for no very clear reason he had been sent on a mission to some sort of assembly . . .

Stories, however, are only stories: *Lanark*, at 560 odd pages, is much more than that. At first reading, as now, it was not the story so much as the voice in which the tale unfolded, the eyes through which it was seen that compelled. Gray's clarity, brinksmanship and near-childlike sincerity of tone were more than surprising, they demanded a reaction. This author asked questions, he played games. He spoke aloud from the page in an at times exuberant, at times despairing, always vivid voice – a voice, moreover, that sounded surprisingly, almost shockingly, familiar. As though whispering aloud what I had always assumed a local secret, Gray spoke using the words, syntax and places of home, yet he did it without the tang of apology or rude-mechanical humour, the Brigadoon tartanry or long-dead warrior chieftain stuff I had grown used to thinking were the options for how my nation appeared in print. Neither had he chosen the heather-strewn hills, the dank glens, the isles or the fishing communities as his location. With its Royal Infirmary cupolas and Victorian Great Western road, its Blackhill kids and the Clyde widening out to the sea, the place in which this epic would reveal itself was Glasgow, a breathing, many-layered Glasgow that was not just an industrial warehouse for ships, but a resonant and fully-claimed city that could stand for the nation entire.

> "Glasgow is a magnificent city," said McAlpin. "Why do we hardly ever notice that?" "Because nobody imagines living here," said Thaw . . . "Think of Florence, Paris, London, New York. Nobody visiting them for the first time is a stranger because he's already visited them in paintings, novels, history books and films. But if a city hasn't been used by an artist, not even the inhabitants live there imaginatively."

A city imagined at length into *being itself.* I had fleetingly encountered so-called "magic realism" in translated Spanish, swallowed whole some oddball 19th-century Russians, a few American books that contained depictions of very "ordinary" lives told with grandeur and depth, but nothing of the kind about, well, *home.* I had barely encountered any of my country's writers at all, let alone one this engaged with the present tense, this bravely *alive.* Scotland, my schooling had at times implied, at times openly professed, was a small, cold, bitter place that had no political clout, not much cultural heritage, joyless people and writers who were all male and all dead. As modern Scots, we were unfit to offer Art, politics or philosophy to the world, we were fit only for losing at football games.[1] Not so, this book said: on a number of levels, not so.

Not that the voice was naïve. It too had been subjected to the unspoken Scottish catechism, but the familiar panoply of self-hatreds and jealously internalised repressions were present in the text, *outed*, as it were, that they might be moved beyond. "I do not love Glasgow much," Thaw admits gloomily. "I sometimes actively hate it, but I am at home there." And who can blame him? His city is sick and repressive, lacking light, hope and love. It breeds asthmas and illness, dependencies and unhealthy sexual stupors, threatens dragon-hide and twittering rigor – all versions of emotional and intellectual hope-lessness. Yet how he strives. Peering up at the slate-grey slab over-head from the balcony of the Elite Café, squinting at his never-to-be-finished mural on the doomed kirk wall, struggling to walk an impossibly-tilting, poorly-signposted road, he is driven mad, to tears, to hysteria and despair, but he persists. True, Thaw's efforts to paint his city imaginatively lead to possible suicide and Lanark, charged with the task of imagining the city into words of such force they will save the place from total destruction, cocks up the whole show following a night of booze and easy sex. Even Nastler, the self-mocking projection of the author, only invents an ending (judged by the characters to whom that ending must apply) no better than "bloody rotten". But their efforts remain a constant, and something, at least something. Reward, even the effectiveness of the characters in living up to their own high expectations, is not the point, after all: the point and their – our – greatest justification is the striving itself.

To a reader in a country where resignation is a national pastime, a country where the standard childhood training lists "showing off" as the worst sin of all, a country whose church, family and educa-tion systems used once to ring with the hurled accusation "Who do

[1] There is a recurring strain of thought in my country that football is Scotland's "true" culture, and that for adults to obsess about an agreeable boys' game is "democ-ratising". In some ways this recalls Scotland's past attraction to restrictive religions, possibly fostered by our nation's history of lousy leaders, failed political hopes and subsequent belief in itself as only a small, even childish, nation that should cherish only the smallest of ambitions lest it seem presumptuous and in need of a damn good thrashing.

you think you are – someone special?" this encouragement *to strive nonetheless* was powerful stuff. And how much, how very much, it touched the heart.

"Perhaps the best thing I could do is write a story in which adjectives like commonplace and ordinary have the significance which glorious and divine carried in earlier comedies. What do you think?"

Indeed what *did* I think? As I recall, a great deal. Stimulated not only by the story and its scraps and lists, headings and maxims and authorial notes (triumphant among which were the delightfully silly, hair-splitting list of "plagiarisms" and typographical liberty-taking that existed within the text, not as "post-modern devices" – surely no writer worth their salt writes through anything as tawdry and manipulative as *devices*? – but as means through which the author spoke to the reader in a direct and deliciously subversive way), I found myself *thinking* a great deal indeed. The voice of the story would not allow anything else. Curious and informed, angry and rational, this voice was not afraid of fun or of confessing its vanities or of having Big Ideas. It was urban and wholly contemporary, yet suffused with the past. More daringly still, it hinted at the possibility of a future. It was willing to share its power, to make me a partner in the enterprise, capable of creative insights of my own. Even more, however, it was a voice that took for granted it wasn't the only voice. It knew the whole truth didn't belong to one sex either. Gray's, it seemed, was a man's voice that knew that's all it was – a man's. As he named his characters' repressions to move beyond them, so he named their selfishnesses, paranoias, spites and incomprehensions in their dealings with women.

"If it's woman trouble," said the man, "I can advise you because I was married once. I had a wife who did terrible things, things I cannae mention in the presence of a wean. You see, woman are different from us. They're seventy-five per cent water. You can read that in Pavlov."

And how different! Every time a woman appeared, it seemed, she disappointed, or caused pain, or inflamed resentment – and resented it herself. At the same time, Thaw/Lanark's wish for female companionship rises chokingly from between the pages, as heady as aftershave. Whatever bitterness he falls into, a masculine need to cling, to seek protection and communion, recurs with near-pathetic regularity. Gray's hero expects the wrong things from his women, confesses his stupidities, does it all over again. And how he *yearns*. The drenching sadness of his blighted need to bond more fully with the unknowable other sex is powerful, poignant and, to this woman at least, an undeniable admission that another story is waiting to be told, imagined, confessed. And the women of the text knew it too.

> He said, "That was very unsatisfying. Why did the oracle not make clear which of these things happened?"
> Rima said, "What are you talking about?"
> "The oracle's account of my life before Unthank. He's just finished it."
> Rima said firmly, "In the first place, that oracle was a woman, not a man. In the second place, her story was about me. You . . . fell asleep and obviously dreamed something else."

Alasdair Gray's writing offered me something freeing. He made me feel acknowledged, spoken to, listened for. Twenty years after the initial gratitude for this book's having been written at all, that alone is worth re-saying. These days, Scottish confidence – a regained parliament of sorts, a more admissible literary, musical and artistic culture – is in notionally better shape, and that partly in direct response to this book. But the daily corruption of language that is *Lanark*'s political dialogue, Unthank's carefully controlled broadcast media and press diet of dead and deadly, trivia-laden, celebrity and soap-opera twaddle, the Institute's reduction of real lives into impoverished "lifestyle choices" and bland words covering gross actions, seem if anything more recognisable than they were those twenty years ago.

What's worth saying, these decades on, is that *Lanark*, in common with all Great Books, is still, and always will be, an act of resistance. It is part of the system of whispers and sedition and direct communion, one voice to another, we call literature. Its bravery in finding voice, in encouraging the enormous power of public, national, artistic, sexual and political imagination, is not something to take for granted. Alasdair Gray's big book about Glasgow is also a big book about everywhere. Its insistence on the literal if mistrusted truth – that Glasgow and Scotland and every small nation and individual within it are part of the whole wide world – is something worth saying indeed. Dear reader, delay no longer. Engage with the text. Imagine. Admire the view.

Janice Galloway

CHAPTER 1. The Elite

The Elite Café was entered by a staircase from the foyer of a cinema. A landing two thirds of the way up had a door into the cinema itself, but people going to the Elite climbed farther and came to a large dingy-looking room full of chairs and low coffee tables. The room seemed dingy, not because it was unclean but because of the lighting. A crimson carpet covered the floor, the chairs were upholstered in scarlet, the low ceiling was patterned with whorled pink plaster, but dim green wall lights turned these colours into varieties of brown and made the skins of the customers look greyish and dead. The entrance was in a corner of the room, and the opposite corner held a curved chromium and plastic counter where a bald fat smiling man stood behind the glittering handles of a coffee machine. He wore black trousers, white shirt and black bow tie and was either dumb or unusually reticent. He never spoke; the customers only addressed him to order coffee or cigarettes, and when not serving these he stood so still that the counter seemed an extension of him, like the ring round Saturn. A door by the bar opened onto a narrow outdoor balcony above the cinema entrance. This had room for three crowded-together metal-topped tables with parasols through the middle. Coffee was not drunk here because the sky was often dark with strong wind and frequent rain. The tabletops had little puddles on them, the collapsed cloth of the parasols flapped soddenly against the poles, the seats were dank, yet a man of about twenty-four usually sat here, huddled in a black raincoat with the collar turned up. Sometimes he gazed in a puzzled way at the black sky, sometimes he bit thoughtfully on the knuckle of his thumb. Nobody else used the balcony.

When the Elite was full most languages and dialects could be heard there. The customers were under thirty and sat in cliques of five or six. There were political cliques, religious cliques, artistic cliques, homosexual cliques and criminal cliques. Some cliques talked about athletics, others about motor cars, others about jazz. Some cliques were centred on particular people, the biggest being dominated by Sludden. His clique usually occupied a sofa by the balcony door. An adjacent clique contained people who had belonged to Sludden's clique but grown tired of it (as they claimed) or been expelled from it (as Sludden claimed). The cliques disliked each other and none liked the café much. It was common for a customer to put down his coffee cup and say, "The Elite is a hellish place. I don't know why we come here. The coffee's bad, the lighting's bad, the whole dump teems with poofs and wogs and Jews. Let's start a fashion for going somewhere else." And someone would answer, "There is nowhere else. Galloway's Tearoom is too bourgeois, all businessmen and umbrella stands and stuffed stags' heads. The Shangri-la has a jukebox that half deafens you, and anyway it's full of hardmen. Armstrong had his face slashed there. There are pubs, of course, but we can't always be drinking. No, this may be a hellish place but it's all we have. It's central, it's handy for the cinema and at least it's a change from home."

The café was often crowded and never completely empty, but on one occasion it nearly emptied. The man in the black raincoat came in from the balcony and saw nobody but the waiter and Sludden, who sat on his usual sofa. The man hung his coat on a hook and ordered a coffee. When he left the counter he saw Sludden watching him with amusement. Sludden said, "Did you find it, Lanark?"
"Find what? What do you mean?"
"Find what you were looking for on the balcony? Or do you go there to avoid us? I'd like to know. You interest me."
"How do you know my name?"
"Oh, we all know your name. One of us is usually in the queue when they shout it at the security place. Sit down."
Sludden patted the sofa beside him. Lanark hesitated, then put his cup on the table and sat. Sludden said, "Tell me why you use the balcony."
"I'm looking for daylight."
Sludden pursed his mouth as if tasting sourness. "This is hardly a season for *daylight*."

"You're wrong. I saw some not long ago and it lasted while I counted over four hundred, and it used to last longer. Do you mind my talking about this?"

"Go on! You couldn't discuss it with many people, but I've thought things out. Now you are trying to think things out and that interests me. Say what you like."

Lanark was pleased and annoyed. He was lonely enough to feel flattered when people spoke to him but he disliked condescension. He said coldly, "There's not much to say."

"But why do you like daylight? We're well lit by the usual means."

"I can measure time with it. I've counted thirty days since coming here, maybe I've missed a few by sleeping or drinking coffee, but when I remember something I can say, 'It happened two days ago,' or ten, or twenty. This gives my life a feeling of order."

"And how do you spend your . . . *days?*"

"I walk and visit libraries and cinemas. When short of money I go to the security place. But most of the time I watch the sky from the balcony."

"And are you happy?"

"No, but I'm content. There are nastier ways of living."

Sludden laughed. "No wonder you've a morbid obsession with daylight. Instead of visiting ten parties since you came here, laying ten women and getting drunk ten times, you've watched thirty days go by. Instead of making life a continual feast you chop it into days and swallow them regularly, like pills."

Lanark looked sideways at Sludden. "Is your life a continual feast?"

"I enjoy myself. Do you?"

"No. But I'm content."

"Why are you content with so little?"

"What else can I have?"

Customers had been arriving and the café was nearly full. Sludden was more casual than when the conversation started. He said carelessly, "Moments of vivid excitement are what make life worth living, moments when a man feels exalted and masterful. We can get them from drugs, crime and gambling, but the price is rather high. We can get them from a special interest, like sports, music or religion. Have you a special interest?"

"No."

"And we get them from work and love. By work I don't mean

shovelling coal or teaching children, I mean work which gives
you a conspicuous place in the world. And by love I don't
mean marriage or friendship, I mean independent love which
stops when the excitement stops. Perhaps I've surprised you
by putting work and love in the same category, but both are
ways of mastering other people."
Lanark brooded on this. It seemed logical. He said abruptly,
"What work could I do?"
"Have you visited Galloway's Tearoom?"
"Yes."
"Did you speak to anyone there?"
"No."
"Then you can't be a businessman. I'm afraid you'll have to
take up art. Art is the only work open to people who can't
get along with others and still want to be special."
"I could never be an artist. I've nothing to tell people."
Sludden started laughing. "You haven't understood a word
I've spoken."
Lanark had an inner restraint which stopped him displaying
much resentment or anger. He pressed his lips together
and frowned at the coffee cup. Sludden said, "An artist doesn't
tell people things, he expresses himself. If the self is unusual
his work shocks or excites people. Anyway, it forces his personality on them. Here comes Gay at last. Would you mind making
room for her?"

A thin, tired-looking, pretty girl approached them between
the crowded tables. She smiled shyly at Lanark and sat beside
Sludden, saying anxiously, "Am I late? I came as soon as—"
He said coldly, "You kept me waiting."
"Oh, I'm sorry, I really am sorry. I came as fast as I could. I
didn't mean to—"
"Get me cigarettes."
Lanark looked embarrassedly at the tabletop. When Gay had
gone to the counter he said, "What do you do?"
"Eh?"
"Are you a businessman? Or an artist?"
"Oh, I do nothing, with fantastic ability."
Lanark looked hard at Sludden's face for some trace of a smile.
Sludden said, "Occupations are ways of imposing yourself on
others. I can impose myself without doing a thing. I'm not
boasting. It just happens to be the truth."
"It's modest of you to say so," said Lanark, "but you're wrong
to say you do nothing. You talk very well."

Sludden smiled and received a cigarette from Gay, who had
returned meekly to his side. He said, "I don't often talk as
frankly as this; my ideas would be wasted on most people.
But I think I can help you. Do you know any women here?"
"None."
"I'll introduce you to some."
Sludden turned to Gay and lightly pinched the lobe of her
ear, asking amiably, "Who will we give to him? Frankie?"
Gay laughed and at once looked happy. She said, "Oh no Slud-
den, Frankie's noisy and vulgar and Lanark's the thoughtful
type. Not Frankie."
"What about Nan, then? She's quiet, in a will-'oo-be-my-daddy
sort of way."
"But Nan's crazy about you!"
"I know, and it's a nuisance. I'm tired of seeing her weep in
the corner whenever you touch my knee. Let's give her to
Lanark. No. I've a better idea. I'll take Nan and Lanark can
have you. How would you like that?"
Gay leaned toward Sludden and kissed him daintily on the
cheek. He said, "No. We'll give him Rima."
Gay frowned and said, "I don't like Rima. She's sly."
"Not sly. Self-contained."
"But Toal is keen on her. They go around together."
"That means nothing. He has a sister fixation on her and she
has a brother fixation on him. Their relationship is purely incestuous. Anyway, she despises him. We'll give her to Lanark."
Lanark smiled and said, "You're very kind."
He had heard somewhere that Gay and Sludden were engaged.
A fur gauntlet on Gay's left hand stopped him seeing if she
wore a ring, but she and Sludden exhibited the sort of public
intimacy proper to an engaged couple. Lanark had been impressed unwillingly by Sludden but now Gay had come he
felt comfortable with him. In spite of the talk about "independent love" he seemed to practise a firmer sort than was usual
in the Elite.

Sludden's clique arrived from the cinema. Frankie was
plump and vivacious and wore a tight pale-blue skirt and had
pale-blue hair bunched round her head. Nan was a small shy
uncombed blonde of about sixteen. Rima had an interesting,
not pretty face with black hair drawn smoothly from her brow
and fixed in a ponytail at the back. Toal was small, haggard,
and pleasant, with a young pointed red beard, and there was
a large stout pale boy called McPake in the uniform of a first

lieutenant. Sludden, an arm round Gay's waist, neither paused
nor glanced at his friends but continued talking to Lanark as
they sat down on each side of him. Frankie was the only one
who paid Lanark special attention. She stood staring at him
with feet apart and hands on hips and when Sludden stopped
talking she said loudly, "It's the mystery man! We've been
joined by the mystery man!" She stuck her stomach forward
and said, "What do you think of my belly, mystery man?"
"It probably does its work," said Lanark.
Sludden smiled slightly and the others looked amused.
"Oh! He makes little jokes!" said Frankie. "Good. I'll sit beside
him and make McPake jealous."
She sat beside Lanark and rested her hand on his thigh. He
tried not to look embarrassed and managed to look confused.
Frankie said, "God! He's gone as tense as . . . hm. I'd better
not say. Relax, son, can't you? No, he can't relax. Rima, I'll
change seats with you. I want to sit with McPake after all.
He's fat, but he responds."
She changed seats with Rima. Lanark felt relieved and insulted.

    Two or three conversations began around him but he
lacked the confidence to join one. Rima offered a cigarette.
He said, "Thank you. Is your friend drunk?"
"Frankie? No, she's usually like that. She's not really my friend.
Did she upset you?"
"Yes."
"You'll get used to her. She's amusing if you don't take her
seriously."
Rima spoke in an odd, mewing, monotonous voice, as if no
words were worth emphasis. Lanark looked sideways at her
profile. He saw black glossy hair drawn back from a white
brow, a large perfect eye slightly emphasized by mascara, a
big straightish nose, a small straight mouth without lipstick, a
small firm chin, a neat little bust under a black sweater. If
she felt his glance she pretended not to but tilted her head
back to breathe smoke from her nostrils. This so reminded
him of a little girl trying to smoke like a woman that he felt
an ache of unexpected tenderness. He said, "What was the
film about?"
"It was about people who undressed soon after the beginning
and then did everything they could think of in the circumstances."
"Do you enjoy those films?"
"No, but they don't bore me. Do they bore you?"

"I've never seen one."

"Why not?"

"I'm afraid of enjoying them."

"I enjoy them," said Sludden. "I get genuine pleasure from imagining how the actors would look wearing flannel underwear and thick tweed skirts."

Nan said, "I enjoy them too. Except the best bits. I can't help closing my eyes during those, aren't I silly?"

Frankie said, "I find them all very disappointing. I keep hoping to see a really surprising perversion but there don't seem to be any."

A discussion began about the forms a surprising perversion might take. Frankie, Toal and McPake made suggestions. Gay and Nan punctuated these with little screaming protests of horror and amusement. Sludden sometimes contributed a remark, and Lanark and Rima remained silent. Lanark was embarrassed by the conversation and thought Rima disliked it too. This made him feel nearer her.

Later Sludden whispered to Gay and stood up. He said, "Gay and I are leaving. We'll see you all later."

Nan, who had been watching him anxiously, suddenly folded her arms upon her knees and hid her face in them. Toal, who was seated beside her, put a comforting arm around her shoulders and smiled at the company in a humorous mournful way. Sludden looked at Lanark and said casually, "You'll consider what I said?"

"Oh, yes. You gave me a lot to think about."

"We'll discuss it later. Come on, Gay."

They went out between the crowded tables. Frankie said mockingly, "The mystery man seems to be replacing you as court favourite, Toal. I hope not, for your sake. You'd have to take up your old job of court jester. Rima never sleeps with the court jester."

Without taking his arm from Nan's trembling shoulders Toal grinned and said, "Shut up, Frankie. You're the court jester and always will be." He said apologetically to Lanark, "Pay no attention to what *she* says."

Rima took her handbag from the seat beside her and said, "I'm going."

Lanark said, "Wait a bit, so am I."

He edged round the table to where his coat hung and put it on. The others said they would see him later and as he and Rima went out Frankie shouted after them, "Have fun!"

CHAPTER 2.
Dawn and Lodgings

The foyer downstairs was empty apart from the girl at the cash desk. Through the glass doors Lanark saw lamplight reflected in a rain-wet street. Sometimes the wind dunted the doors extra hard and made them swing inward and admit a hissing draught. Rima took a plastic raincoat from her handbag. He helped her put it on and said, "Where do you get your tram?"

"At the cross."

"Good. So do I."

Outside they had to struggle against the wind. He took her hand and forced himself to go fast enough to feel he was dragging her. The cross was not far away and the tram stop was near the mouth of a close. Laughing breathlessly they stepped into this and sheltered from the wind. Rima's hair had unloosed from its clasps and her composed, large-eyed face glanced at him between two falls of moist hair. She combed it back with her fingers, grimacing and saying, "A bother."

"I like your hair that way."

They were silent for a while, standing against opposite walls and looking out into the street. At last Lanark cleared his throat. "That Frankie is a *bitch*."

Rima smiled.

He said, "She was very nasty to Toal."

Rima said, "She was under a strain, you know."

"Why?"

"She feels the same about Sludden as Nan does. Whenever Sludden and Gay go off together, Nan weeps and Frankie is rude to people. Sludden says it's because Nan has a negative ego and Frankie a positive one."

"My God!" said Lanark. "Do all of Sludden's girlfriends love
him?"
"I don't."
"I'm glad to hear it. Oh, look! Look!"
"Look at what?"
"*Look*!"

The cross was a place where several broad streets met
and they could see down two of them, though the dark had
made it difficult to see far. And now, about a mile away, where
the streets reached the crest of a wide shallow hill, each was
silhouetted against a pearly paleness. Most of the sky was still
black for the paleness did not reach above the tenement roofs,
so it seemed that two little days were starting, one at the end
of each street. Rima said again, "Look at what?"
"Can't you see it? Can't you see that . . . what's the word?
There was once a special word for it. . . ."
Rima looked in the direction of his forefinger and said coldly,
"Are you talking about the light in the sky?"
"Dawn. That's what it was called. Dawn."
"Isn't that a rather sentimental word? It's fading already."
The wind had fallen. Lanark stepped onto the pavement and
stood leaning forward and staring along each street in turn,
as if wanting to jump to the end of one but unable to decide
which. Rima's indifference to his excitement had made him
forget her for the moment. She said with slight distaste, "I
didn't know you were keen on that kind of thing," then, after
a pause, "Good, here's my tram."
She went past him into the road. An antique-looking almost-
empty tramcar came groaning along the track and stopped between Lanark and the view. It would have taken him to his
lodgings. Rima boarded it. He took a step to follow her, then
hesitated and said, "Look, I'll see you again, won't I?"
As the tram started moving Rima waved offhandedly from
the platform. He watched her settle in an upstairs seat, hoping
she would turn and wave again. She didn't. He looked along
the two streets. The wan watery light was perceptibly fading
from the ends of them. He abruptly crossed over to the broadest
and started running up the middle of it.

He ran with his gaze on the skyline, having an obscure
idea that the day would last longer if he reached it before
the light completely faded. The wind rose. Great gusts shoved
at his back making it easier to run than walk. This race with
the wind toward a fading dawn was the finest thing he had

done since coming to that city. When the sky had grown altogether black he stopped, rested up a close mouth to recover his breath, then trudged back to the tramstop at the cross.

    The next tram took him along a succession of similar tenement-lined streets. The stop where he got off had tenements on one side and a blank factory wall on the other. He entered a close, climbed ill-lit steps to a top landing and let himself quietly into the lobby of his lodgings. This was a bare room with six doors leading from it. One led to Lanark's bedroom, one to the lavatory and one to the kitchen where the landlady lived. The other doors led to empty rooms where bits of the ceiling had fallen in opening them to the huge draughty loft under the roof. As Lanark opened his bedroom door the landlady shouted from the kitchen, "Is that you, Lanark?"
"Yes, Mrs. Fleck."
"Come here and see this."
The kitchen was a clean, very cluttered room. It contained armchairs, a sideboard, a scrubbed white table, a clumsy gas cooker with shelves of pots above it. An iron range filled most of one wall and there was a sink and draining board under the window. All horizontal surfaces were covered with brass and china ornaments and bottles and jam-jars of artificial flowers, some made of plastic, some of coloured wax, some of paper. One wall had a bed recess and Mrs. Fleck, a small middle-aged lady, stood beside it. She beckoned Lanark over and said grimly, "Look at this!"

    Three children with serious wide-open mouths and eyes lay in a row under the quilt. There was a thin boy and girl of about eight years and a plump wee girl of four or five. Lanark recognized them as children from the house across the landing. He said, "Hullo you lot."
The older ones grinned, the young one giggled and spread her hands on her face as if hiding behind them. Mrs. Fleck said morosely, "Their bloody mother's disappeared."
"Disappeared? Where to?"
"How do I know where folk disappear to? One minute she was there, the next she had gone. Well, what could I do? I couldn't leave them to look after themselves. Look at the size of them! But I'm too old, Lanark, to be pestered by bloody weans."

"But surely she'll come back?"

"Her? She won't come back. Nobody comes back who disappears when the lights go out."

"What do you mean?"

"I was standing at the sink washing dishes when the lights went out. I knew it wasn't a power cut because I could see the streetlights through the window, and right away I thought, 'Somebody's disappearing,' and then I thought, 'Oh, what if it's me?' My heart was thumping like a drum, though I don't know why I should be scared. I get so tired and my back is so sore that I often feel I'd be glad to disappear. Anyway, the lights went on again, so I went and had a look in your bedroom. I *thought* you were out but you might have come back without letting me know and it might have happened to you."

Lanark said uneasily, "Why should I disappear?"

"I've told you already I don't know why folk disappear."

"If I had been in the bedroom and . . . and disappeared, how would you have known?"

"Oh, there's usually a sign. My last lodger left a hell of a mess, bedclothes all over the room, the wardrobe on its side, half the plaster out of the ceiling—I haven't been able to let that room since. And his screams! They were awful. But I knew you wouldn't go like that, Lanark. You're the quiet type. Anyway, you hadn't been in so I crossed the landing. The door was open so I stuck my head in and shouted 'Susy!' I was always friendly with her even if she was a tart and didn't look after the kids. Sweets, sweets, sweets, that was all she fed them on, and look at the result. Open your mouth!" she commanded the smallest girl, who obediently opened her mouth to show, on the top and bottom gums, a row of little brown points with gaps between them.

"Look at that! Hardly older than a baby and without a sound tooth in her head."

"What happened then?" said Lanark.

"I shouted 'Susy!' and the kids yelled to me that their mammy had disappeared. Isn't that so?"

She glared at the children, who nodded vigorously.

"Well, Lanark, that house is a bloody midden. It's like a pigsty. I couldn't leave them in it, could I? I brought them here and washed them and put them to bed and now I'm washing their clothes. But you'd better look out if I'm going to see to you!" she told the children fiercely. "I'm not soft like your mammy!"

They grinned at her and the youngest giggled.

Mrs. Fleck leaned over the bed and groaned as she tucked the blankets round them. She said, "Oh Lanark I hate bloody kids."
Lanark shook his fist at the children and pulled such grotesquely threatening faces that they shouted with laughter, then he went back to his bedroom.

It was a high-ceilinged corridor of a room with the door at one end and a curtainless window at the other. A chair, camp bed and wardrobe stood against one wall, the wallpaper and linoleum were brown, there was no carpet, and only a small rucksack on top of the wardrobe suggested the place was used. Lanark took off his jacket and coat together, hung them on a hook behind the door, then lay on the bed with his hands behind his head. Weariness would eventually make him undress and get between the sheets, but he had a disease which made sleep unpleasant and he usually tried to postpone it by thinking of recent events.

There were the disappearances. The lights had gone out and the mother of three children had vanished. Lanark knew the woman well. She had been a friendly dirty attractive woman who often brought strange men to her house. He could think of no reason why she should vanish. He dismissed that matter and thought of the Elite. He would never again go there to sit on the balcony for now he had acquaintances who expected his company. This was not a wholly pleasant thought. The Sludden clique lacked dignity. Surely it was nobler to sit outside it, watching the sky and waiting for the light? Then he recalled how often he had sat on the balcony pretending to watch the sky but really wishing to sit in the warmth talking to the sexual-looking well-dressed women. "Admit!" he told himself, "You watched the sky because you were too cowardly to know people."
He remembered Rima, who sat with the group but seemed aloof from it. He thought, 'I must get to know her. Ach, why did the damned dawn come when I might have arranged to take her home?'
He thought of Sludden. Like Rima, Sludden seemed aloof from the emotions around him. Though loved by three women he was faithful to one, and Lanark thought this rather fine. Furthermore, Sludden had ideas about life and had suggested something to do. Lanark did not wish to be an artist but he felt increasingly the need to do some kind of work, and a writer needed only pen and paper to begin. Also he knew something

about writing, for when wandering the city he had visited public libraries and read enough stories to know there were two kinds. One kind was a sort of written cinema, with plenty of action and hardly any thought. The other kind was about clever unhappy people, often authors themselves, who thought a lot but didn't do very much. Lanark supposed a good author was more likely to write the second kind of book. He thought, 'Sludden said I should write to express myself. I suppose I could do it in a story about who I am and why I have decided to write a story. But there's a difficulty.'

He became restless and started walking up and down the room.

This restlessness happened whenever his thoughts blundered on the question of who he was. "What does it matter who I am?" he asked aloud. "Why should I care why I came here?" He went to the window and pressed his brow to the glass, hoping the cold pressure would banish that problem. It did the opposite. The window overlooked a district of empty tenements, and he saw nothing through it but the black silhouette of his face and the bedroom reflected dimly behind. He remembered another window with only a reflection in it. Distaste and annoyance flooded him and some sexual fantasies about Rima.

Suddenly he went to the wardrobe and opened the single deep drawer at the foot. It was empty but for brown paper lining the bottom. He took the paper, folded it into neat rectangles and by careful tearing along the creases produced a sheaf of about twenty sheets. Removing the drawer he stood it on end beside the chair and laid the paper on top, then took a pen from the jacket pocket, sat down and wrote in small precise letters on the first page:

The first thing I remember is

After a few more words he scored out what he had written and started again. He did this four times, each time remembering an earlier event than the one he described. At last he found a beginning and wrote steadily until he had filled thirteen pages, but rereading them he noticed half the words had no definite meanings, having been added to make the sentences sound better than they were. He scored these words out and copied the rest onto the remaining pages with whatever improvements occurred to him. And then, completely tired for the first time since he came to that place, he undressed to his underwear, slid between the sheets and fell into a profound sleep.

CHAPTER 3. Manuscript

The first thing I remember is a thumping sound, then either I opened my eyes or the light went on for I saw I was in the corner of an old railway compartment. The sound and the blackness outside the window suggested the train was going through a tunnel. My legs were cramped but I felt very careless and happy. I stood up and walked about and was shocked to see my reflection in the carriage window. My head was big and clumsy with thick hair and eyebrows and an ordinary face, but I could not remember seeing it before. I decided to find what other people were on this train.

A cold wind blew along the corridor from the direction of the engine. I walked into it, looking through the windows of the compartments. They were empty. The wind at the end of the corridor was so strong that I had to grip the loose rubbery stuff on the walls of the doorway which usually leads to the next carriage. I could not go farther, for the entrance opened on a dark surface of wooden planks rocking from side to side. It was the back of a goods truck. I returned along the corridor with the wind at my back and recognized my own compartment by the open door. The compartments beyond were empty and the far entrance opened onto a metal tank of the kind used for transporting oil. So I returned to my compartment and noticed, as I shut the door behind me, a small rucksack on the rack above the corner seat. This made me wary. Since waking up I had felt wonderfully free and comfortable. I had been pleased to see I was alone and amused to find the carriage coupled in a goods train, but the knapsack frightened me. I knew it was mine and held something nasty but I was reluctant to throw it through the window. So I took it cautiously down, telling myself there was nobody looking and I need not be bound by what I discovered.

I first looked in the two outside pockets and found safe things, a shaving kit in a plastic envelope, some socks and a magnetic compass which didn't work. I opened the top of the knapsack and found a rolled-up black raincoat, dirty underwear and a suit of pyjamas. Underneath was a folded map and a wallet stuffed with papers so I opened the window, dropped them out and pulled the window shut. Feeling safe again, I repacked the knapsack and returned it to the rack and then (for the rucksack business suggested this) searched my pockets. They all held some grit and tiny seashells. I also found a handkerchief, pen, key and pocket diary. I threw the key and diary after the wallet and map. After that the train tooted its whistle and came out of the tunnel.

It ran along a viaduct among the roofs of a city. Rainclouds covered the sky and the day was so dull that lamps were lit in the streets. They were broad streets, and crossed at right angles, and were lined with big stone buildings. I saw very few people and no traffic. Beyond the rooftops were rows of cranes with metal hulls among them. The train travelled toward these and crossed a bridge over the river. It was a broad river with stone embankments, cracked khaki-coloured mud on the bottom and a narrow black stream trickling zigzag down the middle. This worried me. I felt, and still feel, that a river should be more than this. I looked down into a yard where two hulls stood. They were metal cylinders with rusty domes on top, and a rattle of machinery inside suggested they were being worked on. The train entered another tunnel, slowed down, came out into a marshalling yard and stopped. Through the windows on either side I saw lines of goods trucks with railway signals sticking out of them. The sky was darker now.

I sat for a while in my warm corner, not wanting to leave it for the bad weather outside. Then the light went out, so I shouldered the knapsack, went into the corridor, opened a door and jumped to the ground. I stood between two lines of trucks. Thin rain was falling, so I put down the knapsack and unpacked my coat. As I put it on I saw a man in black overalls and peaked cap come toward me looking closely at the trucks of the train and pencilling in a notebook as he passed each one. He stopped beside me, marked his book and asked if I had

just arrived. I said I had. He said, "They needn't have provided
a whole carriage for one passenger. They could have brought
you in the guard's van."
I asked what time it was. He said, "We don't bother much
with time now. The sky is lighter than normal but that sort
of light is too chancy to be useful."
I asked if he knew where I could go. He said someone was
coming who usually helped with that sort of thing then went
on along the train.

A small figure ran toward us and passed the railwayman
without a look. He stopped beside me and stared up with a
feeble ingratiating smile. He had a weak-chinned handsome
face and greasy hair sloping wavily back to a paltry wisp of
curl on the nape of his neck. He wore a maroon bow tie, a
jacket with maroon lapels which came down to his knees, tight
black trousers and maroon suède shoes. His accent was soft
and whined on the vowels. He said, "You're new here, aren't
you?"
I said yes.
"I've come to help you. You can call me Gloopy. You don't
have a name yet, I suppose. Is anybody with you?"
I said no.
"I'll take a look, just to be on the safe side. Give me a hitch
up, will you?"
He insisted on entering every compartment and looking under
the seats. And he giggled when I helped him down and said
I was very strong. Then he offered to carry my knapsack but
I shouldered it and asked if he would tell me where I could
spend the night. He said, "Of course! That's why I'm here!
I'll take you to my boardinghouse, we've got a spare room."
I said a boardinghouse was no use, I had no money.
"Of course you've no money! We'll leave your knapsack in
my boardinghouse and then we'll go to the security place and
they'll *give* you money."
We emerged from among the trucks and crossed some railway
lines. The city lights glittered between a pair of black hills
ahead of us. It was dark now and raining heavily and my guide
turned up the sodden collar of his fancy jacket. He was far
worse dressed for this weather than I was. I asked who paid
him to meet people and he said in a hurt voice, "Nobody
pays me. I do this job because I like people. I believe in friendship. People ought to be nice to one another."
I pitied him. I knew it was wrong to dislike people for their

appearance and way of speaking but I disliked him very much.
I explained that I wanted to collect the money before I did
anything else. He said slyly, "If I take you to the security place
first, will you promise to come to my boardinghouse after?"
I told him I promised nothing and walked fast to get away.
He trotted behind shouting, "All right! All right! I never said
I wouldn't take you to the security place, did I?"

We continued side by side till the way grew narrow then
he walked in front. The path went down a steep embankment
between the two hills which seemed to be rubbish dumps.
Where it twisted sharply I sometimes walked forward and found
myself wading in what felt like ashes and rotten cloth. We
crossed the dry bed of an old canal and reached the end of a
street. The city did not seem a thriving place. Groups of adolescents or old men stood in occasional close mouths, but many
closes were empty and unlit. The only shops not boarded up
were small stores selling newspapers, sweets, cigarettes and
contraceptives. After a while we came to a large square with
tramcars clanging around it. The street lamps only lit the lowest
storeys of the surrounding buildings but these looked very big
and ornamental, and people sheltered between pillars on their
façades. Some soot-black statues were arranged round a central
pillar whose top I couldn't see in the black sky. In spite of
the wet a man stood on a high part of the pillar's pedestal
and spoke to an angry crowd. We passed through the edge
of the crowd and I saw the speaker was an anxiously smiling
man with a clergyman's collar and bruised brow. His words
were drowned by jeering.

A street leaving the square was blocked with long wooden
huts joined by covered passageways. The lit windows of these
huts had a cheery look when compared with the black windows
in the solider buildings. Gloopy brought me onto a porch with
a sign over it saying **SOCIAL SECURITY—WELFARE DIVISION.**
He said, "Here it is, then."
I thanked him. He kicked his heels and said, "What I want
to know is, are you even going to *try* and be friendly? I don't
mind coming in and waiting for you, but it's a hell of a long
wait and if you're going to be nasty I don't think I'll bother."
I said he shouldn't wait. He said sorrowfully, "All right, all
right. I was only trying to help. You don't know what it feels
like to have no friends in a big city. And I could have introduced
you to some very interesting people—businessmen, and artists,

and girls. I've some lovely high-class girls in my boardinghouse."
He eyed me coyly. I said goodnight and turned but he grabbed
my arm and gabbled into my ear. "You're right, girls are no
use, girls are cows, and even if you don't like me I've got
men friends, military gentlemen—"
I pulled myself free and stepped into the hut. He didn't follow.

It was not a big hut but it was very long and most of
the floor was covered by people crowded together on benches.
There was a counter partitioned into cubicles along one wall,
and the cubicle near the door had a seat in it and a sign saying
ENQUIRIES. I stepped in and sat down. After a very long time
an old man with bristling eyebrows arrived behind the counter
and said, "Yes?"
I explained that I had just arrived and had no money.
"Have you means of identifying yourself?"
I said I had none.
"Are you sure? Have you searched your pockets thoroughly?"
I said I had.
"What are your professional qualifications and experience?"
I could not remember. He sighed and brought from below
the counter a yellow card and a worn, coverless telephone
directory saying, "We can't give you a number before you've
been medically examined, but we can give you a name."
He flicked through the directory pages in a random way, and
I saw each page had many names scored out in red ink. He
said, "Agerimzoo? Ardeer? How about Blenheim. Or Brown."
I was shocked at this and told him that I knew my name. He
stared at me, not believing. My tongue felt for a word or syllable
from a time earlier than the train compartment, and for a moment I thought I remembered a short word starting with *Th*
or *Gr* but it escaped me. The earliest name I could remember
had been printed under a brown photograph of spires and trees
on a hilltop on the compartment wall. I had seen it as I took
down the knapsack. I told him my name was Lanark. He wrote
on the card and handed it over saying, "Take that to the medical
room and give it to the examining doctor."
I asked the purpose of the examination. He was not used to
being questioned and said, "We need records to identify you.
If you don't want to cooperate there's nothing we can do."

The medical room was in a hut reached by a passageway.
I undressed behind a screen and was examined by a casual

young doctor who whistled between his teeth as he wrote the results on my card. I was 5 feet 7¾ inches high and weighed 9 stone 12 pounds 3½ ounces. My eyes were brown, hair black, blood group B (111). My only bodily markings were corns on the small toes and a patch of hard black skin on the right elbow. The doctor measured this with a pocket ruler and made a note saying, "Nothing exceptional there."
I asked what the hard patch was. He said, "We call it dragonhide, a name more picturesque than scientific, perhaps, but the science of these things is in its infancy. You can dress now."
I asked how I could get it treated. He said, "There are several so-called medical practitioners in this city who claim to have cures for dragonhide. They advertise by small notices in tobacconists' windows. Don't waste money on them. It's a common illness, as common as mouths or softs or twittering rigor. What you have there is very slight. If I were you I'd ignore it."
I asked why he had not ignored it. He said cheerfully, "Descriptive purposes. Diseases identify people more accurately than variable factors like height, weight, and hair colour."
He gave me the card and told me to take it back to the enquiry counter. And at the enquiry counter I was told to wait with the others.

The people waiting were of most ages, none well dressed and all (except some children playing between the benches) stupid with boredom. Sometimes a voice cried out, "Will Jones"—or another name—"go to box forty-nine," and one of us would go to a cubicle, but this happened so rarely that I stopped expecting it. My eye kept seeking a circular patch of paler paintwork on the wall behind the counter. A clock had been fixed there once and been removed, I felt sure, because people would not have borne such waiting had they been able to measure it. My impatient thoughts kept returning to their own uselessness until they stopped altogether and I grew as unconscious as possible without actually sleeping. I could have endured eternity in this state, but I was roused by a woman who sat down beside me, a new arrival still in the restless stage. Her legs were encased in tight discoloured jeans and she kept crossing and recrossing them. She wore an army tunic over a plain shirt, and glittery earrings, necklaces, brooches, bangles and rings. Thick black hair lay tangled down her back, she smelled of powder, scent and sweat and she brought several of my senses to life again, including the sense of time, for she kept smoking cigarettes from a handbag which seemed to

hold several packets. When she lit the twenty-third I asked
how long they would keep us waiting. She said, "As long as
they feel like it. It's a damned scandal."
She stared at me a moment then asked kindly if I was new
here. I said I was.
"You'll get used to it. It's a deliberate system. They think
that by putting us through a purgatory of boredom every time
we ask for money we'll come as seldom as we can. And by
God they're right! I've three weans to feed, one of them almost
a baby, and I work to keep them. When I can get work, that
is. But not everyone pays up the way they should, so here I
am again. A mug, that's what I am, a real mug."
I asked what work she did. She said she did things for different
people on a part-time basis and gave me a cigarette. Then she
said, "Are you looking for a place to stay?"
I said I was.
"I could put you up. Just for a wee while, I mean. If you're
stuck, I mean."
She looked at me in a friendly sideways assessing way which
I found stirring. I liked her, she was pleasant to be with, yet
she was the first woman I had met and I knew most of my
lust came from loneliness. I thanked her and said I wanted
something permanent. After a moment she said, "Anyway, a
neighbour of mine, Mrs. Fleck, has just lost a lodger. You
could get a room with her. She's old but she's not too fussy.
I mean she's very respectable, but she's nice."
I thought this a good idea, so she wrote the address and how
to reach it on a used cigarette packet.

Someone shouted that I should go to box fifteen. I went
there and was received by the bristling old clerk who returned
the card saying, "Your claim is being allowed. Report to the
cash desk for the money."
I asked how long the money was meant to last. He said, "It
should last until you find work, but if you spend it before
then this card entitles you to present another claim, which we
shall be obliged, in due course, to honour. Eventually. Have
you any other questions?"
After considering I asked if he could tell me the name of the
city. He said, "Mr. Lanark, I am a clerk, not a geographer."
The cash desk was a small shuttered hatch in the wall of a
room full of benches, but few people were sitting on them.
The shutter was soon raised. We queued and were swiftly paid
by a woman who asked our names in turn, then shoved out

between the bars a heap of notes and coin. I was surprised by the size of these heaps and the careless way the clerk handled them. The notes were creased and dirty and drawn from several currencies. The coins were thick copper pennies, worn silver with milled edges, frail nickel counters and plain brass discs with holes through the centre. I distributed this money into several pockets but I've never learned to use it for everyone has a different notion of its value. When buying anything I hold out a handful and let the waiter or shopman or conductor take what he thinks right.

The directions on the cigarette packet led me to the house where I write this, thirty-one days later. I have not looked for work in that time or made friends, and I count the days only to enjoy their emptiness. Sludden thinks I am content with too little. I believe there are cities where work is a prison and time a goad and love a burden, and this makes my freedom feel worthwhile. My one worry is the scab on my arm. There is no feeling in it, but when I grow tired the healthy skin round the edge starts itching and when I scratch this the scab spreads. I must scratch in my sleep, for when I waken the hard patch is always bigger. So I take the doctor's advice and try to forget it.

CHAPTER 4. A Party

Lanark was wakened by someone bumping up and down on his chest. It was the small girl from next door. Her brother and sister stood astride his legs, holding his coat aloft on the head of a floor brush and swaying from side to side so that the struts of the frail bed creaked. "The sea! The sea!" they chanted. "We're sailing into the sea!"
Lanark sat up rubbing his eyes. He said, "Get away! What do you know about the sea?"
They jumped to the floor where the boy shouted, "We know all about the sea! Your pockets are full of seashells, hahaha! We searched them!"
They ran out giggling and slammed the door. Lanark arose feeling unusually fresh and relaxed. The hard skin on his elbow had spread no farther. He dressed, rolled up the manuscript and went outside.

There was a surprising change in the weather. The dreary rain, the buffeting winds had given way to an air so piercingly still and cold that he had to walk quickly, flapping his arms to keep warm, the breath snorting from his nostrils in jets of mist. His toes and ears were painfully chilled aboard the tram and after climbing the cinema stairs the crowded Elite seemed wonderfully warm and homelike. In the usual corner sat Sludden with Gay, McPake with Frankie, Toal with Nan, and Rima reading a fashion magazine. Rima nodded to him and continued reading but the rest looked surprised and said, "Where have you been?" "What have you been doing?" "We thought you'd disappeared."
Lanark dropped the manuscript on the table beside Sludden who raised an eyebrow and asked what it was.

"Something I've written. I took your advice."
There was no room near Rima so Lanark squeezed onto the
sofa between Sludden and Frankie. Sludden read a couple of
pages, flicked through the rest, then handed it back saying,
"It's dead. Perhaps you're more naturally a painter. I mean,
it's good that you've tried to do something, I'm pleased about
that, but what you've written there is dead."
Lanark blushed with anger. He could think of nothing to say
which wouldn't show injured vanity so he pressed his lips into
a smile. Sludden said, "I'm afraid I've hurt you."
"No no. But I wish you had read it carefully before judging."
"No need. Two pages showed me that your prose is totally
flat, never departing an inch from your dull experiences. If a
writer doesn't enjoy words for their own sake how can the
reader enjoy them?"
"But I do enjoy words—some words—for their own sake!
Words like river, and dawn, and daylight, and time. These
words seem much richer than our experiences of the things
they represent—"
Frankie cried out, "Sludden, you're a sadist, leave the mystery
man alone! Don't bother about Sludden, mystery man. He
thinks he's God but he can only prove it by torturing people.
Isn't that true, Sludden?"
Sludden raised an imaginary hat from his head and bowed,
but her wrath was too impressive to seem a joke. She stood
up saying, "Anyway, McPake's taking us to this party, so come
on, everybody. Rima, you don't care about fashion, give up
pretending to read that magazine and look after Lanark. Try
to stop rotten things happening to him. I can't do it."
She walked off toward the stairs. Toal, McPake and Sludden
grinned at each other and pretended to wipe sweat from their
brows. Everybody stood up. Sludden said to Lanark, "Come
along, it might be fun."
"Who's giving this party?"
"Gay and I. It's our engagement party. But the house belongs
to a friend and the army is providing the booze."
"Why?"
"Prestige reasons. The army likes to be liked."

Outside the cinema a steel-grey truck was parked beside
the pavement and they scrambled through the sliding door
into the narrow seats. Only McPake, in gauntlets and fleece-
lined jacket, was dressed for the intense cold. He gripped the
wheel and the truck charged smoothly forward. Sludden hugged

Gay to his side with one arm and Frankie with the other. Frankie resisted fretfully until he said, "I need you both, girls. This frost is killing me."
Toal and Nan embraced in the seat behind but Rima sat so forbiddingly erect that Lanark (who was beside her) folded arms on chest and clenched his teeth to stop their chattering. Gradually the heater raised a comfortable temperature. The truck nearly had the streets to itself but when passing a tramcar or pedestrian McPake sounded a clanging blast on the horn. Lanark said, "Rima, will there be dancing at this party?"
"I suppose so."
"Will you dance with me?"
"I suppose so. I'm not selective."
Lanark clenched his fist and bit hard on the thumb knuckle. After a moment he felt his arm touched. She said quietly, "I'm sorry I said that—I didn't mean to be nasty. I'm more nervous than I seem."
He almost laughed with relief and drew her gently against him saying, "I'm glad you told me. I was deciding to leave the truck and walk home."
"You're too serious."

The truck travelled down broad streets between over-grown gardens, then entered a drive which curved through a shubbery. The headlights made points of frost glisten among the dark leaves. McPake sounded his horn and stopped before a large mansion and everyone got out. The mansion was a square three-storey building with outhouses and a conservatory at the sides. The enclosing larches, hollies and rhododendrons gave it a secret look, although the windows were lit, music resounded and many cars were parked on the gravel near the porch. The front door was open, but Sludden pressed the bell before leading his party into the hall. This was heavily magnificent, terrazzo tiled and oak panelled, with a pair of black marble columns separating a space where the staircase began. A small figure looked out of a door on the right. It was Gloopy. He was shorter and fatter than Lanark remembered, his hair was streaked with grey and he wore a silver lamé jacket. He said, "There you are, Sludden. Leave the coats in here, will you?" The room was hung with paintings of fruit and lobsters in gilded frames. There was an oval table in the centre nearly covered by coats and scarves. As Lanark helped Rima remove her coat Gloopy gazed at him with a grin and said, "Hello, hello! So you've arrived after all. You'd have been here sooner if you'd come with me."

"Is *this* your boardinghouse?"

"It's not mine in the sense of owning it. I suppose you could call me the concierge."

"What's a concierge?"

"Why must you be nasty to me? I haven't hurt you."

"You don't understand our mystery man, Gloopy," said Sludden, who was straightening his tie at a mirror. "He's never nasty. He's just very very serious all the time. Where's the revelry tonight?"

"We're in the downstairs drawing room."

The interior walls and doors of the house seemed soundproof, for nothing could be heard in the hall but the click of their feet on the tiles, yet the opposite door opened into a crowded room where couples were dancing to loud jazz. The people were the kind who visited the Elite, though the girls were more exotically dressed and Lanark noticed a few elderly men in dark business suits. He took Rima's hand and led her onto the floor.

He couldn't remember enjoying music before but the rhythm excited him and his body moved to it easily. He kept his eyes on Rima. Her movements were abrupt yet graceful. Her dark hair lay loosely about her shoulders, she was smiling absentmindedly. The record came to an end and each stood with an arm round the other's waist. Lanark said, "Will we do that again?"

"Yes, why not?"

Suddenly he stared across the room, his mouth open. A table laden with food and drink stood in the curve of a bay window and a girl sat on the edge chatting to a stout spectacled man. Lanark muttered, "Who is the girl—the big blonde there in the white dress?"

"I don't know. One of the camp followers, I suppose. Why has your face gone that colour?"

"I've met her before."

"Oh?"

"Before I came here—before I came to this city. I know her face but I can't remember anything else."

"Does it matter?"

"How can I speak to her?"

"Ask her to dance."

"Do you mind, Rima?"

"Why should I?"

He hurried through the crowd to the table and reached it as

the music started. The girl was sipping from a glass while the
stout man laughed heartily at something she had said. Lanark
touched her shoulder. She set the glass down and let him lead
her onto the floor. She was a vivacious girl with gaudy makeup
and a rich brown tan. Lanark held her urgently and said,
"Where have I seen you before?"
She smiled and shook her head. "I couldn't say."
"I think I know you well."
"I doubt it."
"I killed you, didn't I?"
She stepped violently back from him and said, "Oh my God!"
People stopped and looked. She pointed at Lanark and said
loudly, "How's this for party conversation? We've just met
and he asks if he killed me once. How's that for small talk?"
She turned to an onlooker (it was McPake) and said, "Take
me away from that bastard."
They joined the dance, McPake winking at Lanark as they
passed him. Lanark looked desperately round for Rima, then
pushed to the door, stepped outside and closed it behind him.

    The hall was completely empty and silent. It was also rather
cold. Lanark strolled up and down wondering what to do. He
could not think why he had blurted such words to the blond
girl, but he would go far to avoid anyone who had been in
the room at that time, excepting Rima. Yet he had no wish
to leave. His elbow itched and he wondered if a wash would
cool it. There was sure to be a bathroom in the house, a tiled
bathroom with clean towels warming on heated towel rails,
and soap crystals, and sponges, and all the hot water he could
use. There was no bathroom in his own lodgings, he had not
bathed since arriving there, and now (feeling dirty inside and
out) he thought a bath would be beautifully soothing. He
walked to the end of the hall and climbed the softly carpeted
stairs. The upper floors were in darkness and he found his
way by light from the hall below. At the second landing a
corridor began. Halfway along it a triangle of light was cast
on the floor from an ajar door. He moved toward this, his
steps silent in the thick carpet, then stopped and peeked through
the narrow door-slit. A vertical ribbon of wallpaper was visible,
the light on it flickering slightly. Lanark pushed the door wide
and stepped through.

    The room was a library illuminated by a vivid fire burning
beneath a carved mantelpiece. Above surrounding bookcases

hung massive portraits with antique weapons crossed on the
walls between them. There were many high-backed leather armchairs, and a standard lamp with a red silk shade shone beside
one with a man getting up from it. He smiled at Lanark and
said, "Why, it's the writer! Come on in."
He was nearly seven feet high and wore a polo-necked sweater
and well-cut khaki trousers and, though perhaps fifty, gave an
impression of youthful fitness. He had a bronzed bald head
with tufts of white hair behind the ears, a clipped white moustache and good-humoured, boyishly alert features. Lanark said
awkwardly, "I'm afraid I don't know you."
"Quite so. Not many of your crowd know me. Yet the whole
place belongs to me. Funny, isn't it? I often have a laugh about
that."
"Does Sludden know you?"
"Oh yes, Sludden and I are great buddies. What would you
like to drink?"
He turned to a sideboard with bottles and glasses on it.
"Nothing."
"Nothing? Well, sit down anyway, I want you to tell me some-
thing. Meanwhile I will pour myself . . . a drop . . . of Smith's
Glenlivet Malt. Here's health."
The warm fire, the mild light, the host's calm manner made
Lanark feel this a pleasant place to relax. He sat in one of
the chairs.

The tall man returned with a glass in his hand, sat down
and crossed his legs. He said, "What makes you chaps tick?
What satisfaction do you, personally, get from being a writer?"
Lanark tried to remember. He said, "It's the only disciplined
work I remember trying. I sleep better after it."
"Really? But wouldn't you sleep better after other kinds of
discipline?"
"I don't know. I suppose it's possible."
"And you've never thought of joining the army?"
"Why should I?"
"Because in a couple of terse, commonplace sentences you
connected the ideas of work, discipline and health. So I suspect
that, in spite of your association with sponges and leeches, you
are still a vertebrate. Am I wrong?"
Lanark thought about this for a while, then asked, "What use
is the army?"
"What use to society, you mean? Defence and employment.
We defend and we employ. I believe you lodge with a woman

called Fleck in a tenement beside Turk's Head Forge."

"How do you know?"

"Aha! There's not much we don't know. The point is that
the Turk's Head Forge produces components for our Q39.
Industry is slack just now, as you may have noticed. If it wasn't
for the Q39 programme the Forge would have to close, thousands would be unemployed and they'd have to cut the social
security allowance. Think of that next time you feel like knocking the army."

"What is the Q39?"

"You've seen them. They're being assembled in the yards near
the river."

"Do you mean these big metal constructions like bombs or
bullets?"

"You think they look like bombs, do you? Good! Good! That
cheers me greatly. Actually they're shelters to protect the civil-
ian population. Each one is capable of housing five hundred
souls when the balloon goes up."

"What do you mean?"

"About the balloon? It's a figure of speech derived from an
outmoded combat system. It means, when the sign goes out
that the big show is starting."

"What show?"

"I can't tell you precisely, because it could take several different
forms. We could be on the receiving end of any one of sixty-
eight different types of attack, and I don't mind telling you
that we're only capable of defending ourselves against three
of them. 'Hopeless! Why bother?' you say, and miss the point
entirely. The other side is as badly placed as we are. These
preparations for the big show may be pretty inadequate, but
if we stop them the balloon will go up. Am I depressing you?"

"No, but I'm confused."

The tall man nodded sympathetically. "I know, it's difficult.
Metaphor is one of thought's most essential tools. It illuminates
what would otherwise be totally obscure. But the illumination
is sometimes so bright that it dazzles instead of revealing."

It struck Lanark that in spite of his smooth flow of words
the tall man was drunk. Somebody grunted nearby. Lanark
turned and saw a stout elderly man sitting immobile in one
of the chairs. He wore a dark blue suit and waistcoat. His
eyes were shut but he was not asleep, for his hands were grasping his knees. Lanark gasped and said, "Who is that?"

"That is one of our city fathers. That is Baillie Dodd."

The man in the chair said, "No."

"Well, actually he's more than just Baillie Dodd. He's Provost Dodd." The tall man began to laugh. "Yes!" he said between gasps, "that's the Lord Provost of this whole, fucking big metropopolis."

He silenced his chuckles by drinking what was left in the glass, then went to the sideboard to refill. The Provost said, "What does he want?"

The tall man looked over his shoulder. "Yes, Lanark, what do you want?"

"Nothing."

"He said he wants nothing, Dodd."

After a moment the Provost said flatly, "Then he's no use to us."

The tall man returned to his seat saying, "I begin to fear you're right." He smiled at Lanark and sat down. "I suppose in the end you'll join the protest people."

"Who are they?"

"Oh, they're very nice people. No bother, really. My daughter is one. We have great arguments about it all. I had hoped you were a vertebrate, but I see you're a crustacean. You'll be at home with the protest people because most of them are crustaceans. Now you're going to ask what crustaceans are, so I'll tell you. The crustacean isn't a mere mass of sentient acquisitiveness, like your leech or your sponge. It has a distinct shape. But the shape is not based on a backbone, it derives from the insensitive shell which *contains* the beast. In the crustacean class you will find the scorpion, the lobster and the louse."

He smiled into his whisky. Lanark knew he had been insulted and stood up, saying sharply, "Could you tell me where the bathroom is?"

"Third on the left as you go out."

Lanark went to the door but turned before reaching it. He said, "Perhaps the Provost could tell me what his city is called?"

"Certainly he could. So could I. But for security reasons we're not going to."

Lanark opened the door to step through but was arrested by a cry of "Lanark!"

He turned and saw the man standing up gazing at him intently. "Lanark, if you ever come to feel you would like (how can I put it?) like to strike a blow for the good old vertebrate Divine Image, get in touch with me will you?"

There were tears in his eyes. Lanark went quickly out, feeling embarrassed.

The corridor was still in darkness. He turned left and moved toward the staircase, counting doors. The third one did not open into a bathroom but into a luxurious, brilliantly lit bedroom. On the quilt of the double bed moved a huge knot of limbs with the heads of Frankie, Toal and Sludden sticking out. Lanark slammed the door and clapped his hands over his eyes but the image of what he had seen stayed inside the lids: a knot of limbs with three crazily vacant faces, and Sludden's mouth opening and shutting as if eating something. He hurried to the stairs and ran down them to the cloakroom. He was looking for his coat among the heap on the table when a slurred voice said, "I feel we've never really understood each other."
Gloopy stood grinning emptily in the doorway. His legs were together and his arms pressed to his sides, his oiled grey hair and silver jacket glistened wetly. He took a few steps nearer, walking as if his thighs were glued together, then fell forward onto the floor with a sodden slap. He lay in the posture in which he had stood, except that his face was tilted so far back that it grinned blindly at the ceiling. Without moving his limbs he suddenly slid an inch or two toward Lanark along the polished floorboards, and then the light went out.

The darkness and silence were so complete that for a moment Lanark was deafened by the noise of his own breathing. Then he heard Gloopy say, "People ought to be nice to one another. Why can't you and I—"
The words were cut short by a chilling draught which blew up suddenly from the floor bringing with it a salt stench like rotting weeds. Lanark felt he was on the lip of a horrible pit. He grew dizzy and crouched to the floor, afraid to move his feet and terrified of falling down. He squatted in the darkness like this for a very long time.

At last he saw light from the hall shining through the doorway. A bulky figure appeared in it, grunted and switched the light on. It was Provost Dodd. Lanark stood up, feeling sick and foolish, and said, "Gloopy. He's disappeared. Gloopy's disappeared!"
The Provost stared about the room as if Lanark were not in it and muttered, "No great loss, I would have thought."
Lanark was filled with the conviction that every footstep in that room might land in an invisible trap. He managed to move

to the door without running. The Provost said, "Wait."
Lanark stepped into the hall before turning to him. The Provost
pushed out his lower lip, frowned down at his shoes, then
said, "You came with a girl. She had black hair and wore a
black sweater and her skirt was . . . I forget the colour."
"Black."
"Quite so. Do you know where she is?"
"No."
The Provost stared at him for a while then turned away, saying
heavily, "Anyway, it's all the same. It's all the same."
Lanark hurried out, slamming the door hard behind him.

CHAPTER 5. Rima

There was fog outside. The light from the windows saturated
it so that the mansion seemed wrapped in a cocoon of milky
light, but outside the cocoon Lanark walked in total obscurity
and only found his way down the drive by the crunch of gravel
underfoot and the touch of rimy leaves on his hands and face.

On the pavement it was possible to steer through the murk
by the glow of the street lamp ahead. The clammy air made
his footsteps resound loudly but after five minutes he decided
that what seemed like echoes were the footsteps of someone
behind. His back prickled apprehensively. He stood against a
hedge and waited. The other footsteps hesitated, then came
boldly on. In the fog's cloudy dimness a shadow appeared and
developed an unusual density of black, then the slim black
figure of Rima passed by giving him only the flicker of a glance.
He hurried after her crying gladly, "Rima! It's me!"
"So I see."
"Provost Dodd was looking for you."
"Who's Provost Dodd?"
The question seemed meant to stop conversation rather than
aid it. He walked beside her, thinking of what he had seen
of her friends in the bedroom. This memory no longer horrified.
It combined with his words to the blond girl, with Gloopy's
disappearance and with the fog; it cast around her an odour
of exciting malign sexual possibility. He asked abruptly, "Did
you enjoy the party?"
"No."
"What did you do?"
"If you must know I spent most of the time in the bathroom
with Gay. She was very sick."

"Why?"

"I don't want to talk about it."

"Do you want to talk to me at all?"

"No."

His heart and penis hardened in angry amazement. He gripped her arms and pulled her round to face him saying softly, "Why?" She glared into his eyes and yelled, "Because I'm afraid of you!"

He was hit by a feeling of shame and weariness. He let her go, shrugging his shoulders and muttering, "Well, maybe that's wise of you."

Half a minute later he was surprised to find her walking beside him. She said, "I'm sorry."

"Don't be. Maybe I am a dangerous man."

She began laughing but quickly smothered this and slipped a hand through his arm. The light pressure made him calmer and stronger.

They came to a street corner. The fog was very thick. A tramcar clanged past a few feet in front of them, but nothing could be seen of it. Rima said, "Where's your coat? You're shivering."

"So are you. I'd take you for a coffee but I don't know where we are."

"You'd better come with me. I live nearby and I stole a bottle of brandy from the party."

"You shouldn't have done that."

Rima withdrew her hand sharply and said, "You, are a very, big, wet, drip!"

Lanark was stung by this. He said, "Rima, I am not clever or imaginative. I have only a few rules to live by. These rules may annoy folk who are clever enough to live without them, but I can't help that and you ought not to blame me."

"All right, I'm sorry, I'm sorry, I'm sorry. You can make me apologize by breathing on me, it seems."

They turned the corner. Lanark said, "But I can frighten you too."

She was silent.

"And I can make you laugh."

She laughed slightly and took his arm again.

They seemed to enter a lane between low buildings like private garages. Rima unlocked a door, led him up a steep narrow wooden stair and switched a light on. Her austere man-

ner and clothing had made Lanark expect a stark room. This room was small, with a sloping ceiling and not much furniture, but there were many sad little personal touches. Childish crayon sketches of unconvincing green fields and blue seas were fixed to the walls. There was the only clock Lanark remembered seeing, carved and painted like a log cabin, with a pendulum below and a gilt weight shaped like a fir cone. The hands were missing. A stringless guitar lay on a chest of drawers and a teddy bear sat on the bed, which was a mattress on the floor against the wall. Rima clicked the switch of the electric radiator, removed her coat and became busy with a kettle and gas ring in a cupboard-sized scullery. There were no chairs, so Lanark sat on the floor and leaned on the bed. The radiator heated the small place so quickly that he was soon able to remove his fog-sodden jacket and jersey, yet though his skin was warm he was still shaken from inside by spasms of shivering. Rima carried in two large mugs of black coffee. She sat on the bed with her legs folded under her and handed a mug to Lanark saying, "You probably won't refuse to drink it."
The coffee flavour was drowned by the taste of sugar and brandy.

Later Lanark lay back on the bed, feeling comfortable and slightly drunk. Rima, her eyes closed, rested her shoulders against the wall and cradled the teddy bear in her lap. Lanark said, "You've been kind to me."
She stroked the old toy's head. Lanark tried to think of other words. He said, "Did you come to this town long ago?"
"What does 'long' mean?"
"Were you very small when you came?"
She shrugged.
"Do you remember a time when days were long and bright?"
Tears slid from under her closed lids. He touched her shoulders.
"Let me undress you?"
She allowed this. As he unfastened her brassière his hands met a familiar roughness.
"You've got dragonhide! Your shoulderblades are covered!"
"Does that excite you?"
"I have it too!"
She cried out harshly, "Do you think that makes a bond between us?"
He shook his head urgently and placed a finger on her lips, feeling that words would move them farther apart. His anxiety to be tender to someone who needed and rejected tenderness

made his caresses clumsy, until genital eagerness sucked thought out of him.

He felt relieved afterward and would have liked to sleep. He heard her rise briskly from his side and start dressing. She said curtly, "Well? Was it fun?"

He tried to think then said defiantly, "Yes. Great fun."

"How nice for you."

A nightmare feeling began to rise around him. He heard her say, "You're not good at sex, are you? I suppose Sludden is the best I'll ever get."

"You told me that you didn't . . . . love . . . . Sludden."

"I don't, but I use him sometimes. Just as he uses me. He and I are very cold people."

"Why did you let me come here?"

"You wanted so much to be warm that I thought perhaps you were. You're as cold as the rest of us, really, and even more worried about it. I suppose that makes you clumsy."

He was drowned in nightmare now, lying on the bottom of it as on an ocean bed, yet he could breathe. He said, "You're trying to kill me."

"Yes, but I won't manage. You're *terribly* solid."

She finished dressing and slapped his cheek briskly saying, "Come on. I can't apologize to you again. Get up and get dressed."

She stood with her back against the chest of drawers, watching while he slowly dressed, and when he finished she said inexorably, "Goodbye, Lanark."

All his feelings were numbed but he stood a moment, staring stupidly at her feet. She said, "Goodbye, Lanark!" and gripped his arm and led him to the door, and pushed him out and slammed it.

He groped his way downstairs. Near the bottom he heard her open the door and shout "Lanark!" He looked back. Something dark and whirling came down on his head, heavily enfolding it, and again the door slammed. He dragged the thing off and found it was a sheepskin jacket with the fleece turned inward. He hung this on the inside knob of the bottom door and stepped into the lane and walked away.

After a time the dense freezing fog and his arctic brain and body blended. He moved along streets in them, a numb kernel of soul kept going by feet somewhere underneath. The only thing he felt very conscious of was his itching right arm, and several times he stopped and rubbed it backward and forward against corners of walls to scratch it through the sleeve. The sounds and lights of tramcars passed him frequently now, and after crossing a street he was puzzled by a complicated shape between himself and the flow of a high lamp. Going nearer he discerned a queen with a long train riding side-saddle on a rearing horse. It was a statue in the great square. He considered going for warmth to the security office but decided he needed something to drink. He crossed other streets till he saw red neon shining above the pavement. He opened the tinkling door of a small aromatic tobacconist shop, crossed to a staircase and went down into Galloway's Tearoom. This was a low-ceilinged place much bigger than the shop upstairs. Most of it was alcoves, some opening from others, each with a sofa, table and chairs in it and a stag's head on a plaque. Lanark ordered lemon tea, sat in the corner of a sofa and fell asleep.

He awoke long afterward. The glass of tea was cold on the table before him and he was listening to a conversation between two businessmen. His ear was an inch from a thick brown curtain separating his sofa from where they sat and clearly they had no sense of being overheard.
". . . Dodd is on our side. After all, the Corporation has nothing to do but light the streets and keep the trams running, and these services don't pay for themselves. They have to be subsidized by the sale of municipal property, so Dodd is selling and I'm buying."
"But what will you do with it?"
"Sublet. The smallest of these rooms could contain sixteen single apartments if we divided them up with matchboard partitions. I've measured."
"Don't be mad! Why should anyone want a tiny apartment just because it's on the square? There's no profit in being a landlord with a third of the city standing empty."
"No profit at the moment. I mean to sublet these eventually."
"Don't be mysterious, Aitcheson. You can trust me."
"All right. You know the population is smaller than it used to be. Have you faced the fact that it gets smaller all the time?"
"Why?"
"You know why."
There was a silence. "What about the new arrivals?"
"Not enough of them. You live in a hotel, don't you?"
"Of course."

"Of course. So do I. Nobody notices disappearances in a hotel. In the normal way you expect the man in the next room to disappear after a while. Life is different in a tenement. Suddenly the house across the landing is empty. A little later the one upstairs goes empty too. Then you notice there are no lights in half the windows across the street. It's disturbing! Mind you, people are still pretending not to notice. Wait till they have no neighbours left. Wait till they're lonely and the panic starts! They'll crowd to the city centre like drowning men onto a raft. If the city chambers are still empty they'll break in and squat. But they won't be empty because I'll be subletting them."

After a pause, the other voice said grudgingly, "Very clever. But aren't you being a bit optimistic? You're gambling on a trend that may not continue."

"What is there to stop it?"

Lanark stood up, feeling terribly afraid. A short while ago he had told Sludden he was content. Now everything he heard or saw or remembered was pushing him toward panic. He desperately wanted Rima beside him, a Rima who would smile and be sad with him, a Rima whose fears he could soothe and who would not fling words at him like stones. He paid for the tea and went back to his own room and undressed. When jacket and jersey were removed he saw the right shirt-sleeve was stiff with dried blood, and on taking off the shirt he found the arm was dragonhide from shoulder to wrist, with spots of it on the back of his hand. He put on his pyjamas, got into bed and fell asleep. There seemed nothing else to do.

CHAPTER 6. Mouths

With no will to see anyone or do anything he immersed himself in sleep as much as possible, only waking to stare at the wall until sleep returned. It was a sullen pleasure to remember that the disease spread fastest in sleep. Let it spread! he thought. What else can I cultivate? But when the dragonhide had covered the arm and hand it spread no further, though the length of the limb as a whole increased by six inches. The fingers grew stouter, with a slight web between them, and the nails got longer and more curving. A red point like a rose-thorn formed on each knuckle. A similar point, an inch and a half long, grew on the elbow and kept catching the sheets, so he slept with his right arm hanging outside the cover onto the floor. This was no hardship as there was no feeling in it, though it did all he wanted with perfect promptness and sometimes obeyed wishes before he consciously formed them. He would find it holding a glass of water to his lips and only then notice he was thirsty, and on three occasions it hammered the floor until he waked up and Mrs. Fleck came running with a cup of tea. He felt embarrassed and told her to ignore it. She said, "No, no, Lanark, my husband had that before he disappeared. You must never ignore it."

He thanked her. She rubbed her hands on her apron as if drying them and said abruptly, "Do you mind if I ask you something?"

"No."

"Why don't you get up, Lanark, and look for work? I've lost a husband by that"—she nodded to the arm—"and a couple of lodgers, and all of them, before the end, just lay in bed, and all of them were decent quiet fellows like yourself."

"Why should I get up?"

"I don't like talking about it, but I've an illness of my own—
not what you have, a different one—and it's never spread very
far because I've had work to do. First it was a husband, then
lodgers, now it's these bloody weans. I'm sure if you get up
and work your arm will improve."
"What work can I get?"
"The Forge over the road is wanting men."
Lanark laughed harshly and said, "You want me to make components for the Q39."
"I know nothing about factory work, but if a man gets pay
and exercise by it I don't see why he should complain."
"How can I go for work with an arm like this?"
"I'll tell you how. My husband had the same trouble on exactly
the same arm. So I knitted him a thick woollen glove and
lined it with wash leather. He never used it. But if you wear
it along with your jacket nobody will notice, and if they do,
why bother? There are plenty of men with crabby hands."
Lanark said, "I'll think about it."
He was prevented from saying more by the hand's raising the
teacup to his lips and holding it there.

Sometimes the children played on the floor of the room.
He liked this. They were quarrelsome but they never explained
what life was or persuaded him to do something, their selfishness did not make him feel wicked. At these times he felt
ashamed of his great arm and kept it below the covers, but
once he awoke to find it lying outside with the children squatting round it staring. The boy said admiringly, "You could
murder someone with that."
Lanark was ashamed because the thought had occurred to himself. He drew the arm out of sight and muttered without much
conviction that two human hands would be better. The boy
said, "Yes, but not in a fight."
Lanark found the limb beginning to fascinate him. The colour
was not really black but an intensely dark green. It looked
diseased because it grew on a man, but considered by itself
the glossy cold hide, the thorny red knuckles and elbow, the
curving steel-blade claws looked very healthy indeed. He began
to have fantasies about the damage it could do. He imagined
entering the Elite and walking across to the Sludden clique
with the hand inside the bosom of his jacket. He would smile
at them with one side of his mouth, then expose the hand
suddenly. As Sludden, Toal and McPake leapt to their feet
he would knock them down with a sweeping sideways blow,

then drive the squealing girls into a corner and rake the clothes off them. Then the image grew confused, for each of his fantasies tended to dissolve into another one before reaching a climax. After these dreams he would become dismally cold and depressed. Once he discovered himself stroking the cold right hand with the fingertips of the left and murmuring, "When I am all like this. . . ." But if he was all like that he would have no feeling at all, so he thought of Rima and her moments of kindness: the time in the truck when she touched him and said she was sorry, the dance and how they held each other, the moment in the fog when she laughed at him and slid her hand round his arm, the coffee she had made and even the jacket she had flung. But these memories were too feeble to restore human feeling, and he would return to admiring the feelingless strength of the dragonish limb until he fell asleep.

At last he wakened in pain which made him scream aloud. Mrs. Fleck ran in. A ragged wound had been torn in his side through the pyjama jacket, blood from it flooded the blankets. Lanark bit the thumb knuckle of his left hand to prevent further screaming and glared at the bloodstained claws of the right. Mrs. Fleck ran to get bandages and water but when she returned dragonhide had crystalized over the wound and Lanark sat on the bed pulling his clothes on. He said, "You spoke about a glove. Can I have it?"
She went to a lobby cupboard and took out her husband's glove and an old waterproof coat. She helped Lanark put them on and he left the house.

Snow had fallen but thin rain was reducing it to slush. He had gone to bed because the alternatives were detestable and now he walked the streets because sleep was dangerous, choosing streets where the slush lay thinnest. Once again he came to the square. The ground-floor windows were alight in a building along one side of it, and hammering and sawing resounded within. Arched doors stood open, showing a marble-floored entrance hall with a red wooden hut in the middle. It was covered with posters saying YOU HAVEN'T MUCH TIME—PROTEST NOW. The words seemed meant for him, so he crossed the marble to the hut and stepped inside.

A thin, bearded man wearing a clerical collar and an old woman with wild white hair sat behind a counter putting pamphlets into envelopes. A young man with bushy hair typed

rapidly at a table behind them, and an attractive girl sat on
the table plucking idly at a guitar. As Lanark approached the
counter the woman clasped her hands below her chin and
looked at him with an encouraging smile. After hesitating
awhile he said in a low voice, "I'm frightened of what's happening to me."
She nodded vigorously. "Yes! No wonder. If you've been looking around you'll see we haven't much time."
"What can I do?"
"The primary need is to persuade others of the danger. When
we have a majority we can act. Would you care to distribute
some pamphlets for us?"
"That wouldn't help. You see my arm is all—"
"Oh, we understand that! And we're glad you came, even so.
Please, please don't believe we don't care. We have launched
this campaign because we care deeply. But for troubles of that
personal kind hard work is the only answer, hard work for a
decent cause. I'm sure if you sit down calmly and address those
envelopes it will help more than you believe."
Lanark pulled the glove off and showed her the right hand.
Her round, pleasant face grew red but she smiled determinedly
into his eyes and said, "You see, the only cure for these—
personal—diseases is sunlight. Which our party is trying to restore. The artificially inflated land values at the centre have
produced such overbuilding on the horizon that the sun is barely
able to rise above it. As soon as we have a majority we can
persuade the authorities to act."
The bushy-haired young man had stopped typing to roll a cigarette. He said, "Ballocks. If we had a majority tomorrow the
situation would be the same. A city is ruled by its owners.
Nine tenths of our factories and houses are owned by a few
financiers and landlords, with a bureaucracy and a legal system
to defend them and collect the money. They are a minority
and they are in power. Why should we wait until there are
more of us before we seize it? Numerically there are more
of us already."
The girl looked up from the guitar and said, "I think you're
being too hard on the boss class. They feel in their bones that
the system is unfair and unwieldy, so the intelligent ones get
terribly bored and join us. That's what I did. My daddy's a
brigadier."
"We contain all shades of opinion," said the white-haired
woman, becoming flustered, "but we are agreed upon one
thing: the need for sunlight. You need that too, so why not
join us?"

Lanark stared at her and she smiled bravely back but eventually shrugged her shoulders and resumed work with the envelopes. The clergyman beside her leaned forward toward Lanark and said in a low voice, "You're on the edge of a pit, aren't you?" In spite of the beard his face looked childish and eager, with a blue mark like a bruise above the right eyebrow. He said quietly, "People in this organization see the pit a long way ahead, so put your glove on, we can't help you." Lanark bit his underlip and pulled on the glove. The man said, "If you get out of the pit I hope you'll join us all the same. You won't need us then but we will certainly need you." Lanark said heavily, "I don't know what you're talking about," and walked away.

He crossed the square and walked to the Elite because it was the only other place he could think of and Rima might be there. Her kindly moments had become radiant in the coldness he moved through, and she had dragonhide too, and what had it made of her? He leaped flooded gutters and plunged through ridges of slush; he pushed open the glass doors of the foyer and rushed upstairs, and the café was empty. He stood in the entrance and stared unbelievingly around but nobody was there, not even the man who had stood so fixedly behind the counter. Lanark turned and went downstairs.

Crossing the halfway landing he saw a girl below in the foyer buying cigarettes at the cash desk. It was Gay. He called her name and hurried down. She looked whiter and thinner but greeted him with surprising vivacity, bobbing lightly up to kiss his lips. She said, "Where have you been, Lanark? Why those mysterious disappearances?"

"I've been in bed. Come upstairs with me."

"Upstairs? Nobody goes upstairs nowadays. It's so horrible. We use the downstairs café now, the light is more soothing." She pointed to a thick red curtain which Lanark had thought covered a door to the cinema. She pulled it slightly aside, saying, "Come and join us. All the old gang are here."

Beyond the curtain was perfect blackness. Lanark said, "There's no light here at all."

"Yes there is, but your eyes take a while to get used to it."

"And is Rima in there?"

Gay let the curtain go and said uneasily, "I don't think I've seen Rima since my . . . my engagement party."

"Then she's at home?"

"I suppose so."

"Could you tell me how to get to it? I went there in the fog
and I couldn't find it now."

Gay's face seemed suddenly ancient. She folded her arms,
bowed her head and shoulders, looked at him sideways and
said faintly, "I could take you there. But Sludden wouldn't
like it."

"Take me there, Gay! She helped you when you were sick at
the party. I'm afraid something is happening to her too."

She gave him a sly, frightened look and said. "Sludden sent
me to buy cigarettes and he hates waiting for anything."

Lanark saw that his dragon hand was clenching to strike her.
He thrust it into his pocket where it squirmed like a crab.
Gay did not notice. She said wistfully, "You're very solid, Lanark. I can go with you if you hold me, I think. But Sludden
never lets go."

She held out a hand to him. He seized it gladly and they went
into the street.

Gay's footsteps were so feeble that he put his good arm
round her waist to help her onward. At first they went quickly,
then the pressure on his arm began to increase. Her feet were
not engaging the slippery pavement, and though her body was
light it felt as if an elastic cord fixed to her back were making
forward movement more difficult with each step. He paused
for a moment under a lamppost, breathing hard from exertion.
Gay put an arm round the pole to steady herself but seemed
wholly placid. With a coy sideways look she said, "You're wearing a glove on your right hand. I've got one on my left!"

"What about it?"

"I'll show you my disease if you show me yours!"

He began to say he was not interested in her disease but she
pulled off her fur gauntlet. Surprise gagged him. He had expected dragon claws like his own, but all he could see was a
perfectly shaped white little hand, the fingers lightly clenched,
until she unclenched them to show the palm. He took a moment
to recognize what lay on it. A mouth lay on it, grinning sarcastically. It opened and said in a tiny voice, "You're trying to
understand things, and that interests me."

It was Sludden's voice. Lanark whispered, "Oh, this is hell!"

Gay's hand sank to her side. He saw that the soles of her
feet were an inch above the pavement. Her body dangled before him as if from a hook in her brain, her smile was vacant
and silly, her jaw fell and the voice which came from the mouth

was not formed by movement of tongue or lip. Though it had a slightly cavernous echo it was Sludden's voice, which said glibly, "It's time we got together again, Lanark," while a tiny identical voice from her left hand cried shrilly, "You worry too much about the wrong things."

"Oh! Oh!" Lanark gabbled. "This is hell!"

He pressed gloved and ungloved hands to his mouth and without ceasing to stare at Gay's dangling image stepped backward away from her. Like something sliding on a wire she quivered and moved backward too, slowly at first, then accelerating till he saw her emptily grinning face recede and dwindle to a point in the direction of the café.

He turned and ran.

He ran blindly till his foot slipped and he fell on the slushy pavement, bruising hip and shoulder and soaking his trousers. When he stood up the panic had been replaced by desperation. His wish to leave this city was powerful and complete and equalled by a certainty that streets and buildings and diseased people stretched infinitely in every direction. He was standing near railings with a bank of snow beyond them which the rain had not dissolved. Some naked trees grew out of it. The trees and snow had such a fresh look that he climbed the railings and waded upward between the trunks. The lamps in the street behind showed a dim hillside laid out as a cemetery. Black gravestones stood on the snowy paleness and he climbed between them, amazed that the ground of this place had once swallowed men in a natural way. He reached a path with a bench on it, brushed snow from the seat with his sleeve, then knelt and banged his brow hard there three times, crying from the centre of his soul, "Let me out! Let me out! Let me out!" After a moment he stood up, dazed by the blows but indifferent to sodden clothes and aching body. He felt strangely buoyant. There was a yellow radiance among some obelisks on the hilltop, lighting the base of a few and silhouetting others, so he ran uphill.

The slope below the summit was unusually steep, and Lanark kept rushing up and slithering back until he gained the momentum to reach the top and stumble between two monuments onto flat ground. The summit was a circular plot with a ring of obelisks round the edge and a cluster of them in the middle. They were old and tall with memorials carved on the pedestals. He was puzzled by the light. It was a glow like the light from a steady fire, it lit nothing over five feet from the ground and cast no shadows, and Lanark walked round the central monuments without discovering a source. The glow was brightest on a pedestal near the place where he had entered the ring, so he examined it for a clue. It was a marble block erected by the workers and management of the Turks Road Forge in gratitude to a doctor who had rendered them skilled and faithful service between 1833 and 1879. Lanark was reading the inscription for a second time when he noticed a dim shadow across the centre of the stone. He glanced over his shoulder to see what cast it and saw nothing, though when he glanced back it looked like the shadow of a bird with outspread wings. But the colour deepened and he saw that the shape forming there was a mouth three feet wide, the lips meeting in a serene, level line. His heart beat now with an excitement which was certainly not fear. When the lips had fully formed they parted and spoke, and just as a single intense ray can dazzle an eye without lighting a room, so this voice pierced the ear without sounding loud. It pierced so painfully that he could not understand the syllables as they were spoken, but had to remember them when they stopped. The mouth had said, "I am the way out."

Lanark said, "What do you mean?"

The lips pressed together in a line which seemed ruled on the stone and moved swiftly to the ground, crossing the projections of the base as simply as the shadow of a gull passes over a waterfall. It sped over the snow, then stopped and opened into an oval pit in front of his feet. The edges of the lips were shaded lightly on the snow but curved steeply down to the projecting tips of the perfect teeth. From the blackness between these rose a cold wind with the salty odour of rotting seaweed, then a hot one with an odour like roasting meat. Lanark shuddered with dread and giddiness. He remembered the mouth in Gay's hand which had nothing behind it but a cold man being nasty to people in a dark room. He said, "Where will you take me?"

The mouth closed and became dim at the corners. He saw it was fading and would leave him on a hilltop in a city more sterile and lonely than anything a pit could hold. He shouted, "Stop! I'll come!"

The mouth grew distinct again. He asked humbly, "How should I come?"

It replied. When the sound stopped hurting his ears he found it had said "Naked, and head first."

It was hard to remove the coat and jacket because his side had grown thorns which pierced the cloth. He ripped them free and threw them down, then looked at the mouth which lay patiently open. He rubbed his face with the good hand and said, "I'm afraid to go head first. I'm going to lower myself backwards and hang by the hands, and if I'm too scared to let go I will consider it a kindness if you let me hang till I drop."
He stared at the mouth but no part of it moved. He sat on the rags of the coat and removed his shoes. Fear was making him slow, he grew terrified of its stopping him altogether so he went to the mouth without undressing further. The hot breath alternating with the cold one had melted the surrounding snow into a margin of firm moist gravel. Moving fast to avoid thinking, he sat with his legs in the mouth, gripped the teeth opposite and slid down until he hung from them. Since the right arm was longer than the left he hung by that alone, buffeted by hot roast and cold rot blasts and waiting for the hand to weary and loosen. It didn't. His claws gripped a big incisor as if screwed to it, and when he tried to loosen them the muscles of the whole limb began to contract and lift him toward the oval of dark sky between the teeth. In a moment his head and shoulders would have come through them, but he yelled, "Shut! Bite shut!"
Blackness closed over him with a clash and he fell.

But not far. The cavity below the mouth narrowed to a gullet down which he slithered and bumped at decreasing speed as his clothing and thorny arm began catching on the sides. The sides began to tighten and loosen, heating as they tightened, cooling as they loosened, and the descent became a series of freezing drops from one scalding grip to another. The pressure and heat grew greater and gripped him longer until he punched and kicked against it. He was dropped at once but only fell a few feet, and the next hold was so sickeningly tight that he could not move his arms and legs at all. He opened his mouth to scream and a mixture of wool and cloth squeezed into it, for the pressure had dragged vest, shirt and jersey over his face. He was suffocating. He urinated. The great grip stopped, he slid downward, the garments slid upward, freeing mouth and nose, and then the sides contracted and crushed him harder than ever. Most senses abandoned him now. Thought and memory, stench, heat and direction dissolved and he knew nothing but pressure and duration. Cities seemed piled on him with a weight which doubled every second; nothing but movement could lessen this pressure; all time, space and mind would end unless he moved but it had been aeons since he could have stirred toe or eyelid. And then he felt like an infinite worm in infinite darkness, straining and straining and failing to disgorge a lump which was choking him to death.

After a while nothing seemed very important. Hands were touching his sides, softly sponging and softly drying. The light was too strong to let him open his eyes. Some words were whispered and someone softly laughed. At last he opened his eyelids the narrowest possible slit. He lay naked on a bed with a clean towel across his genitals. Two girls in white dresses stood at his feet, clipping the toenails with tiny silvery scissors. Between their bowed heads he saw the dial of a clock on the wall beyond, a large white dial with a slender scarlet second hand travelling round it. He glanced toward his right side. Growing down from the shoulder was a decent, commonplace, human limb.

CHAPTER 7. The Institute

The food was always a lax white meat like fish, or a stronger one like breast of chicken, or pale yellow like steamed egg. It was completely tasteless, but though Lanark never ate more than half the small portion on his plate the meals left him unusually comfortable and alert. The room had milk-coloured walls and a floor of polished wood. Five beds with blue coverlets stood against one wall, and Lanark, in the middle bed, faced a wall pierced by five arches. He could see a corridor behind them with a big window covered by a white Venetian blind. The clock was over the middle arch, its circumference divided into twenty-five hours. At half past five the light went on and two nurses carried in hot water and shaving things and made the bed. At six, twelve and eighteen o'clock they brought meals in a wheeled cabinet. At nine, fifteen and twenty-two o'clock a cup of tea was given him by a nurse who measured his temperature and felt his pulse in a slightly offhand manner. At half past twenty-two the neon tubes in the ceiling faded and the only light filtered in through the corridor blind. This was a pearly mobile light from several sources, all moving and growing or dimming as they moved, yet the movement was too stately and suggestive of distances to be cast by traffic. Lanark was soothed by it. Each pillar between the arches threw several shadows into the room, every one a different degree of greyness and all sweeping at different slow rates in one direction or another. The dim, rhythmical, yet irregular movement of these shadows was reassuringly different from the horrifying black pressure which the pressure of the pillow on his cheek still brought to mind. One morning he said to the nurses making the bed, "What's outside the window?"

"Just scenery. Miles and miles of scenery."
"Why are the blinds never raised?"
"You couldn't stand the view, Bushybrows. We can't stand it and we're perfectly fit."
They had begun calling him Bushybrows. He examined his face in two square inches of shaving mirror and noticed that his eyebrows had white hairs in them. He lay back thoughtfully and asked, "How old do I look?"
One said, "A bit over thirty."
The other said, "No chicken, anyway."
He nodded glumly and said, "A short while ago I seemed ten years younger."
"Well, Bushybrows, that's life, isn't it?"

He was visited that morning by a bald professional man wearing a white coat and half-moon-shaped rimless glasses. He stood by the bed surveying Lanark with a grave look which did not completely hide amusement. He said, "Do you remember me?"
"No."
The doctor fingered a piece of sticking plaster on his chin and said, "Three days ago you punched me, just here. Oh yes, you came out fighting. I'm sorry I haven't had time to see you since. We have hardly enough staff to deal with the serious cases, so the totally hopeless and the nearly fit are left much to themselves. Can you go to the lavatory yet?"
"Yes, if I hold onto the beds and walls."
"I suppose your sleep is still pretty troubled?"
"Not very."
"You're recovering fast. You would be running around already if you'd undressed properly and come head first. At present you are convalescing from severe shock, so take things easily. Is there anything special you would like?"
"Could you get me something to read?"
The doctor slid each hand up the opposite sleeve and stood for a moment with his lips pursed, looking like a mandarin. He said, "I'll try, but I can't promise much. Our institute has been isolated since the outbreak of the second world war. There is only one way of coming here and you've seen yourself how impossible it is to bring luggage."
"But the nurses are young girls!"
"Well?"
"You said the place was isolated."

"It is. We recruit our staff from among the patients. I expect
you'll be joining us soon."

"When I get better I intend to leave."

"Easier said than done. We'll discuss it in a day or two, when
you're able to walk. Meanwhile I'll hunt out some reading
material."

The nurses who brought the midday meal also brought
a children's cartoon book called *Oor Wullie's Annual for 1938*,
a crime novel with the covers missing called *No Orchids for
Miss Blandish*, and a fat squat little book in good condition,
The Holy War, in which the *s* was usually printed *f* and half
the pages were uncut. Lanark began reading *Oor Wullie*. It made
him smile in places but many pages had been spoiled by someone's colouring them with a blunt brown crayon. He began
No Orchids and was halfway through it that evening when the
nurses hurried in and set screens around the bed beside him.
They brought metal cylinders and trolleys of medical equipment
and went out saying, "Here comes a friend for you, Bushybrows."

A male nurse wheeled in a stretcher and the room was
filled with the sound of hoarse guttural breathing. The figure
on the stretcher was hidden by two doctors walking alongside,
one of them Lanark's doctor. They went behind the screens
and the stretcher was taken away. Lanark could read no longer.
He lay listening to the tinkle of instruments, the murmur of
professional voices, the huge harsh breathing. His evening cup
of tea was brought and the lights went out. Except for a lamp
behind the screens the room was bathed in moving shadows
cast by the corridor windows. The breathing became a couple
of quietly repeated vocal sighs and then grew inaudible.
Screens, trolley and instruments were wheeled out and everyone left except the doctor with the rimless glasses, who came
to Lanark's bed and sat heavily on the edge wiping his brow
with a piece of tissue. He said, "He's cured of his disease,
poor sod. God knows how he'll recover from the journey here."
Under the bed lamp, propped against a bank of pillows, was
a face so shockingly like a yellow skull that the only indication
of age and sex was a white moustache with drooping corners.
The sockets were so deep that it was impossible to see the
eyes. A skeletal arm lay on the coverlet, and a rubber tube
carried fluid from a suspended bottle to a bandage round the
biceps.

The doctor sighed and said, "We did what we could, and he

should be comfortable for eight hours at least. I wish you would
do us a favour. You still sleep pretty lightly, I suppose?"
"Yes."
"He may gain consciousness and feel like talking. I could leave
a nurse here but their damned professional cheerfulness depresses introspective men. Talk to him, if he feels like it, and
if he wants a doctor call me on this."
He took from his pocket a white plastic radio the size of a
cigarette packet. There was a circular mesh on one surface
and a red switch at the side. The doctor pressed the switch,
and a small clear frantic voice asked Dr. Bannerjee to come
to delivery room Q. The doctor switched it off and slid it under
Lanark's pillow. He said, "It works two ways. If you speak
into it and ask for me they'll pass the message on; I'm called
Munro. But don't try to stay awake, he'll waken you if he
needs you."

Lanark could not sleep. He lay at the edge of the glow
surrounding the sick man, turned his back to the bony head
and played the radio under the pillow. Munro had said his
institute was understaffed but the staff was still very large. In
ten minutes he heard forty different doctors summoned in tones
indicating an emergency to places and tasks he was wholly
unable to picture. One call said, "Will Dr. Gibson go to the
sink? There is resistance on the north rim." Another said,
"Ward R-sixty requires an osteopath. There is twittering. Will
any free osteopath go at once to deterioration ward R-sixty."
He was greatly puzzled by a call which said, "Here is a warning
for the engineers from Professor Ozenfant. A salamander will
discharge in chamber eleven at approximately fifteen-fifteen."
At last he switched the clamour off and dozed uneasily.

He was wakened by a low cry and sat up. The sick man
was craning forward from his pillows, moving his head from
side to side as if seeking something, yet Lanark was still unable
to see eyes in the black sockets. The man said loudly, "Is any-
body there? Who are you?"
"I'm here. I'm a patient, like yourself. Should I call a doctor?"
"How tall am I?"
Lanark stared at the thin figure beneath the blue coverlet. He
said "Quite tall."
The man was sweating. He gave a dreadful shriek. *"How tall?"*
"Nearly six feet."
The man lay back on the pillow and his thin mouth curled in

a surprisingly sweet smile. After a moment he said languidly,
"And I don't glitter."

"What do you mean?"

"I'm not covered with . . . you know, red, white, blue, green
sparkles."

"Certainly not. Should I call a doctor?"

"No no. I expect these fellows have done what they can."

The man's skull was no longer a reminder of death. Feeling
had softened it and now it seemed a daringly austere work
of art commemorating human consciousness. The thin lips still
curved in a faint smile. They opened and said, "What brought
you here?"

Lanark considered several answers and decided to use the shortest. "Dragonhide."

The man seemed not to hear. At last Lanark asked, "What
brought you?"

The man cleared his throat. "Crystalline hypertrophy of the
connective tissue. That's the medical name. Laymen like you
or I call it rigor."

"Twittering rigor?"

"I did not twitter. All the same, it came as a shock."

He seemed to become thoughtful and Lanark fell asleep. He
was wakened by the man crying out, "Are you there? Am I
boring you?"

"I'm here. Please go on."

"You see, I loved the human image and I hated the way people
degraded it, overdeveloping some bits to gain temporary advantage and breaking others off to get relief from very ordinary
pain. I seemed surrounded by leeches, using their vitality to
steal vitality from others, and by sponges, hiding behind too
many mouths, and by crustaceans, swapping their feelings for
armour. I saw that a decent human life should contain discipline,
and exertion, and adventure, and be unselfish. So I joined the
army. Can you tell me what other organization I could have
joined? Yet in spite of five dangerous missions behind enemy
lines, and in spite of launching the Q39 programme, I grew
to be nine feet tall and as brittle as glass. I could exert fantastic
pressure vertically, upward or downward, but the slightest sideways blow would have cracked me open. We do crack, you
know, in the army."

Indignation had entered his voice and exhausted it. He lay
breathing deeply for a while; then his lips curved in the surprising smile. He said, "Can you guess what I did?"

"No."

"I did something rather unusual. Instead of waiting till I cracked and leaving the pit to eat up the pieces I *invoked* the pit. I asked for a way out, and the pit came to me, and I entered it in a perfectly decorous and manly fashion."

"So did I."

For a moment the man looked indignant again, then he asked in a low voice, "How many of us are there in this room?"

"Just you and I."

"Good. Good. That means we are exceptional cases. Depend on it, not many pray for that way out. The majority spend their lives dreading it. Did you lose consciousness coming down?"

"Yes, after a while."

"I lost consciousness almost at once. The trouble was, I kept coming back to it, again and again and again. I wish I had taken their advice and removed my uniform."

"You came down in a uniform!" cried Lanark, horrified.

"Yes. Belt, boots, braid, brass buttons, the lot. I even had my pistol, in a holster."

"Why?"

"I meant to surrender it to the commander here: a symbolic gesture, you know. But there isn't a commander. That pistol made a trench as deep as itself across my right hip, which is why I am dying, I suppose. I could have survived the uniform but not the revolver."

"You're not dying!"

"I feel I am."

"But why, why, why should we suffer that pit and blackness and pressure, why should we even try to be human if we are going to die? If you die your pain and struggle have been useless!"

"I take a less gloomy view. A good life means fighting to be human under growing difficulties. A lot of young folk know this and fight very hard, but after a few years life gets easier for them and they think they've become completely human when they've only stopped trying. I stopped trying, but my life was so full of strenuous routines that I wouldn't have noticed had it not been for my disease. My whole professional life was a diseased and grandiose attack on my humanity. It is an achievement to know now that I am simply a wounded and dying man. Who can be more regal than a dying man?"

His languid voice had become a very faint murmur.

"Sir!" said Lanark fervently. "I hope you will not die!"

The man smiled and murmured, "Thank you, my boy."
A moment later sweat suddenly glittered on the visible parts
of him. He clawed the coverlet with both hands and sat upright
saying in a harsh commanding voice, "And now I feel very
cold and more than a little afraid!"
The lamp went out. Lanark leaped onto the polished floor,
slipped, fell and scrambled to the man's side. Some pearly light
from the window passed over the body half sprawling from
the covers, the head and neck hanging off the mattress and
an arm trailing on the floor. A dark stain was spreading on
the bandage where the rubber tube had been wrenched out.
Lanark ran to his bed, grabbed the radio and flicked the switch;
he said, "Get Dr. Munro! Get me Dr. Munro!"
A small clear voice said, "Who is speaking, please?"
"I'm called Lanark."
"Dr. Lanark?"
"No! No! I'm a patient, but a man is dying!"
"Dying naturally?"
"Yes, dying, dying!"
He heard the voice say, "Will Dr. Munro report quickly to
Dr. Lanark, a man is dying naturally; I repeat, a man is dying
naturally."
A minute later the ward lights went on.

Lanark sat on the bed staring at his neighbour, who looked
crudely and insultingly dead. His mouth hung open and it was
now obvious that his sockets were eyeless. By the hand on
the floor a tiny puddle was spreading from the nozzle of the
rubber tube. Dr. Munro came in and walked briskly to the
bedside. He lifted the arm, felt the pulse, hoisted the body
farther onto the mattress, then turned off a tap on the suspended
bottle. He looked at Lanark sitting on the edge of his bed in
a white nightshirt and said, "Shouldn't you cover yourself up?"
"No. I shouldn't."
"Did he speak to you?"
"Yes."
"Did he recognize himself?"
"Yes. What are you going to do with him?"
"Bury him. Strange, isn't it. We can find a practical use for
any number of dead monsters, but a mere man can only be
burned or shovelled into the ground."
"I don't know what you're talking about."
"Get into bed, Lanark."
"I want to see out the window."

"Why?"

"I feel enclosed."

"Can you walk there?"

"Of course I can walk there."

The doctor opened a locker beside the bed, took out dressing gown and slippers and handed them to Lanark, who put them on and walked to the window, ignoring a feeling of floating above the floor. He was surprised to find the corridor hardly longer than the room he had left: to right and left it ended in a blank wall with a circular door closed by a red curtain. Lanark hesitated before the slats of the blind until Dr. Munro appeared at his side and placed a hand on a green cord hanging from the top. He said, "I'll raise the blind, Lanark, but first I want you to repeat certain words."

"What words?"

"If I lose my way I will shut my eyes and turn my head."

"If I lose my way I will shut my eyes and turn my head."

Munro raised the blind.

It was a view of mistily moving distances with the sun shining through them. Snowy ranges of cloud divided snowy ranges of mountain and silvery skies lay so near to sparkling oceans that they were hard to tell apart. The institute seemed drifting toward the sun between the precipices of a canyon and he peered forward and down, trying to catch sight of the bottom, but when the mist below the window thinned and parted he saw a dark violet space containing stars and a sickle moon. Feeling dizzy he looked back at the sun for reassurance, for though dimmed by haze it shone solidly in the centre of the scene, illuminating and uniting it; but now he wondered if the sun was maybe far overhead and this a reflection in the sea, or perhaps it was behind him and he was seeing it mirrored in a glacier among the mountains in front. Nothing was visible now but sunlight and milky cloud with a single peak rising from it. Streams like silver threads poured through gullies in the lower slopes and white lines of waterfalls fell from cliff tops into the clouds. He saw this peak was not a simple cone but a cluster of summits with valleys between them. One valley was full of lakes and pasture, another was shaggy with forests, through a third lay a golden-green ocean with a sun setting behind it. The act of seeing became an act of flight. He raised his eyes to the horizon but above the level lines of every sea and plain lay islands, mountains, storm clouds, cities, and setting or ascending suns. He tried to escape this recession by staring at a village on a little hill in a shaft of morning light. A cloud passed overhead and he only saw the village by the light sparkling on windows and roofs, then the sparkles shifted and drifted sideways like snowflakes into silvery blueness where they circled like gulls above a steamship, then changed colour and became black specks circling like aeroplanes in a flashing red glow above a bombed city. So Lanark clapped a hand over his eyes, turned round and returned soberly to the room.

The body of his neighbour, swathed in blankets, was wheeled past on a stretcher by a male nurse. Lanark put the slippers and gown in the locker, climbed into bed and pulled the covers to his chin. Dr. Munro had lowered the blind and gone to the locker beside the dead man's bed. He took out a pistol and stood examining it thoughtfully. He said, "This is why he died, you know. He wore it on the way down."
"Yes, he told me."
"Still, he came head first, which not many do."
"Where is this institute?"
"We occupy a system of galleries under a mountain with several peaks and several cities on top. I believe you come from one of these cities."
"Under a mountain?"
"Yes. That screen isn't a window. It shows images caught by a reflector on one of the peaks. This ward has one because patients of your kind sometimes do feel enclosed. If I showed that view to other patients they would curl up like watchsprings."
"How deep down are we?"
"I don't know. I'm a doctor, not a geologist."

Lanark had received more than he could consciously absorb. He fell asleep.

CHAPTER 8. Doctors

He wakened next morning feeling tired and sick, but the nurses brought a bland omelette which restored vitality. On a chair by the bed they laid clothes with the same soft glazed texture as the food: underwear, socks, shirt, dark trousers, a pullover and a white coat. They said, "You're joining us today, Bushybrows."

"What do you mean?"

"You're a doctor now. I hope you aren't going to bully us poor nurses."

"I am not a doctor!"

"Oh, don't refuse! The ones who refuse at first always bully us worst."

When they left Lanark arose and dressed in all but the coat. He found shoes of suède-like stuff below the bed. He put them on, entered the corridor, lifted the blind and saw a white flagpole in the middle of a warm, sunlit terrace of level grass. Children ran about playing anarchic ballgames and on the far edge two older boys sat on a bench gazing across a great valley, the valley-floor covered by roofs made prickly by smokestacks. On the right a river meandered among fields and slag bings, then the city hid it though the course was marked by skeletal cranes marching to the left. Beyond the city was a bleak ridge of land, heather-green and creased by watercourses, and the summits of mountains appeared behind that like a line of broken teeth. This view filled Lanark with such unexpected delight that his eyes moistened. He returned and lay down on the bed, wondering why.

"Anyway," he told himself, "I'll go there."

Munro came through an arch and Lanark sat up to face
him saying, "Before you speak, I want to assure you I will
not be a doctor."
"I see. How do you intend to pass the time while you stay
here?"
"I don't want to stay. I want to leave."
Munro flushed suddenly red and pointed to the window. Outside it grey waves were rising and falling against a great cliff
with mist on the summit.
"Yes, leave! Leave!" he said in a controlled voice, "I'll take
you to an emergency exit. It will let you out at the mountain
foot, and after that you can find your own way through the
world. Men used to find homes like that, leaving the safe oasis
or familiar cave and crossing wildernesses to make houses in
unknown lands. Of course these men knew things you don't.
They could plant crops, kill animals, endure pains that would
deprive you of your wits. But you can read and write and
argue, and if you go far enough you may find people who
appreciate that, if they talk the same language."
"But a minute ago I saw a habitable city out there!"
"And have you never heard how fast and far light travels?
And how masses warp it and surfaces reflect it and atmospheres
refract it? You have seen a city and think it in the future, a
place to reach by travelling an hour or day or year, but existence
is helical and that city could be centuries ahead. And what if
it lies in the past? History is full of men who saw cities, and
went to them, and found them shrunk to villages or destroyed
centuries before or not built yet. And the last sort were the
luckiest."
"But I recognized this city! I've been there!"
"Ah, then it lies in the past. You'll never find it now."
Lanark looked miserably at the floor. The view had given him
dreams of a gracious, sunlit life. He said, "Are there no civilized
places I can reach from here?"
Munro had regained his mandarin calm and sat down beside
the bed. "Yes, several. But they won't take you without a
companion."
"Why?"
"Health regulations. When people leave without a companion
their diseases return after a while."
"Am I the only healthy individual who wants to leave this
place?"
"One woman doctor hates her work so much that she'll leave

with anyone, but take care. Entering another world with someone is a form of wedding, and this woman will hate any world
she lands in."

Lanark groaned and said, "What can I do, Dr. Munro?"

Munro said cheerfully, "That is your first sensible question
Lanark, so stop worrying and listen. You can look for a companion among three classes of people: the doctors, the nurses and
the patients. Not many doctors want to leave, but when they
do, it is with a colleague. Nurses leave more often, with men
they thoroughly trust, and doctors have proverbial advantages
where they are concerned. But the biggest class are the patients,
and you can only know them by working on them."

"I'm not qualified to work on anybody."

"And were you not nearly a dragon? And are you not cured?
The only qualification for treating a disease is to survive it,
and right now seventeen patients are crushing themselves under
belligerent armour without one reasonable soul to care for
them. Don't be afraid! You need see nobody whose problem
is not a form of your own."

They sat in silence until Lanark stood up and put the white
coat on. Munro smiled and produced a hospital radio saying,
"This is yours. You know how to make contact through it,
so I'll show how it contacts you."

He flicked the switch and said to the mesh, "Send a signal to
Dr. Lanark in ten seconds, please. There's no message, so don't
repeat it."

He dropped the radio into Lanark's pocket. A moment later
two resonant chords from there said *plin-plong*.

"When you hear that, your patient is near a crisis or a colleague
needs help. If you need help yourself, or lose your way in
the corridors, or want a lullaby to soothe you to sleep, speak
to the operator and you'll be connected to someone suitable.
Now get your books and we'll go to your new apartment."

Lanark hesitated. He said, "Has it a window?"

"As far as I know this is the only room with a viewing screen
of that kind."

"I prefer to sleep here, Dr. Munro."

Munro sighed slightly. "Doctors don't usually sleep in a patients' ward, but certainly this is the smallest and least required.
All right, leave the books. I'll show you something of the institute's scope then we'll visit Ozenfant, your head of department."

They went through an arch to one of the circular doorways. The curtain of red pleated plastic slid apart for them and closed behind.

The corridors of the institute were very different from the rooms they connected. Lanark followed Munro down a low curving tunnel with hot gusts of wind shoving at his back, his ears numbed by a clamour of voices, footsteps, bells going *plin-plong* and a dull rhythmic roaring. The tunnel was six feet high and circular in section with a flat track at the bottom just wide enough for the wheels of a stretcher. The light kept brightening and dulling in a way that hurt the eyes; dazzling golden brightness slid along the walls with each warm blast and was followed by fading orange dimness in the ensuing cold. The tunnel slanted into another tunnel and grew twice as large, then into another and grew twice as large again. The noise, brightness and windpower increased. Lanark and Munro travelled swiftly but doctors and nurses with trolleys and stretchers kept overtaking and whizzing past them on either side. Nobody was moving against the wind. With an effort Lanark came beside Munro and asked about this, but though he yelled aloud his voice reached his ears as a remote squeaking and the reply was inaudible; yet amid the roaring and gongings he could hear distinct fragments of speech spoken by nobody in the vicinity:
". . . is the pie that bakes and eats itself . . ."
". . . . . is that which has no dimensions . . . . ."
". . . is the study of the best . . ."
". . . . . an exacting game and requires patience . . . . ."
They entered a great hall where the voices were drowned in a roaring which swelled and ebbed like waves of cheering in a football stadium. Crowds poured over the circular floor from tunnels on every side and disappeared through square doors between the tunnel entrances. Among white-coated nurses and doctors Lanark saw people in green dustcoats, brown overalls, blue uniforms and charcoal-grey business suits. He looked upward and staggered giddily. He was staring up a vast perpendicular shaft with gold and orange light flowing continually up the walls in diminishing rings like the rings of a target. Munro gripped his arm and led him to a door which opened, then slid shut behind them.

They were in a lift with the still air of a small ward. Munro looked up at a circular mesh in the middle of the ceiling and said, "The sink, please. Any entrance."

There was a faint hum but no sense of movement. Munro said, "Our corridors have confusing acoustics. Did you ask something?"

"Why do people only walk in one direction?"

"Each ward has two corridors, one leading in and the other out. This allows the air to circulate, and nobody goes against the current."

"Who were the people in the big hall?"

"Doctors, like you and me."

"But doctors were a tiny minority."

"Do you think so? I suppose it's possible. We need engineers and clerks and chemists to supervise lighting and synthesize food and so on, but we only see those in the halls; they have their own corridors. They're a strange lot. Every one of them, even the plumbers and wireless operators, think their own profession *is* the institute, and everyone else exists to serve them. I suppose it makes their work seem more worthwhile, but if they reflected seriously they would see that the institute lives by purging the intake."

"Purging the intake?"

"Doctoring the patients."

The lift door opened and Lanark's nostrils were hit by a powerful stink, the foul odour he had first noticed when Gloopy vanished in the dark. Munro crossed a platform to a railing and stood with his hands on it, looking down. To right and left the platform curved into distance as though enclosing an enormous basin, but though searchlights in the black ceiling cast slanting beams into the basin itself Lanark was unable to see the other side. From high overhead came huge dismal sounds like a dance record played loudly at an unusually low speed, and from the depths beyond the railing came a multitudinous slithering hiss. Lanark stood at the door of the lift and said shakily, "Why did we come here?"

Munro looked round.

"This is our largest deterioration ward. We keep the hopeless softs here. They're quite happy. Come and look."

"You said I need see nobody whose problem is not a form of my own!"

"Problems take different forms but they're all caused by the same error. Come and see."

"If I look over that railing I think I will be sick."

Munro stared at him, then shrugged and re-entered the lift.

He said to the mesh, "Professor Ozenfant," and the door closed and the air softly hummed. Munro leaned against the wall with his hands tucked into the opposite sleeves. He frowned at his shoes for a moment then looked up with sudden brightness saying, "Tell me, Dr. Lanark, is there a connection between your love of vast panorama and your distaste for human problems?"
Lanark said nothing.

The door opened and they entered another huge roaring ceilingless hall. Pulses of sound and bright air beat down from above and flowed out into the surrounding tunnels with crowds of people from the surrounding lifts. Munro led the way to a tunnel with a block of names on the wall by the entrance:

McADAM	McIVOR	McQUAT	McWHAM
McCAIG	McKEAN	McSHEA	MURRAY
McEVOY	McMATH	McUSKY	NOAKES
McGILL	McOWEN	McVARE	OZENFANT

They sped along it hearing bodiless voices conversing among the clamour:
". . . glad to see the light in the sky . . ."
". . . . . frames were shining on the walls . . . . ."
". . . you need certificates . . ."
". . . . . camels in Arabia . . . . ."
". . . annihilating sweetness . . ."
They reached a place where half the names were printed on one wall and half on the other, and here the tunnel forked and diminished. It forked and diminished three more times until they entered a single low tunnel labelled OZENFANT. The red glossy curtain at the end opened on a surface of heavy brown cloth. Munro pulled that aside and they stepped into a large and lofty apartment. Tapestries worked in red, green and gold thread hung from an elaborate cornice to a chequered floor of black and white marble. Antique stools, chairs and sofas stood about in no kind of order with stringed instruments of the lute and fiddle sort scattered between them. A grand piano stood in a corner beside a cumbersome, old-fashioned X-ray machine, and in the middle Lanark saw, from behind, a figure in black trousers and waistcoat leaning over a carpenter's bench and sandpapering the edge of a half-constructed guitar. This figure stood up and turned toward them, smiling and wiping hands on a richly patterned silk handkerchief. It was a stout young man with a small blond triangular beard.

His sleeves were rolled well above his elbows exposing robust hairy forearms, but collar and tie were perfectly neat, the waistcoat unwrinkled, the trousers exactly creased, the shoes splendidly polished. He came forward saying, "Ah, Munro, you bring my new assistant. Sit down both of you and talk to me." Munro said, "I'm afraid I must leave. Dr. Lanark has tired of my company and I have work to do."

"No, my friend, you must stay some minutes longer! A patient is about to turn salamander, an always impressive spectacle. Sit down and I'll show you."

He gestured to a divan and stood facing them and dabbing his brows with the handkerchief. He said, "Tell me, Lanark, what instrument do you play?"

"None."

"But you are musical?"

"No."

"But perhaps you know about ragtime, jazz, boogie-woogie, rock-and-roll?"

"No."

Ozenfant sighed. "I feared as much. No matter, there are other ways of speaking to patients. I will show you a patient."

He went to the nearest tapestry and dragged it sideways, uncovering a circular glass screen in the wall behind. A slender microphone hung under it. He brought this to the divan pulling a fine cable after it, and sat down and said, "Ozenfant speaking. Show me chamber twelve."

The neon lights in the ceiling went out and a blurred image shone inside the screen, seemingly a knight in gothic armour lying on the slab of a tomb. The image grew distinct and more like a prehistoric lizard on a steel table. The hide was black, the knobbly joints had pink and purple quills on them, a bush of purple spines hid the genitals and a double row of spikes down the back supported the body about nine inches above the table. The head was neckless, chinless, and grew up from the collarbone into a gaping beak like the beak of a vast cuckoo. The face had no other real features, though a couple of blank domes stuck out like parodies of eyeballs. Munro said, "The mouth is open."

Ozenfant said, "Yes, but the air trembles above it. Soon it shuts, and then *boom!*"

"When was he delivered?"

"Nine months, nine days, twenty-two hours ago. He arrived nearly as you see him, nothing human but the hands, throat and sternum mastoid. He seemed to like jazz, for he clutched the remnant of a saxophone, so I said, 'He is musical, I will treat him myself.' Unluckily I know nothing of jazz. I tried him with Debussy (who sometimes works in these cases) then I tried the nineteenth-century romantics. I pounded him with Wagner, overwhelmed him with Brahms, beguiled him with Mendelssohn. Results: negative. In despair I recede further and further, and who works in the end? Scarlatti. Each time I played *The Cortege* his human parts blushed as pink and soft as a baby's bottom."

Ozenfant closed his eyes and kissed his fingertips to the ceiling. "Well, matters remain thus till six hours ago when he goes wholly dragon in five minutes. Perhaps I do not play the clavichord well? Who else in this wretched institute would have tried?"

Munro said, "You assume he blushed pink with pleasure. It may have been rage. Maybe he disliked Scarlatti. You should have asked."

"I distrust speech therapy. Words are the language of lies and evasions. Music cannot lie. Music talks to the heart."

Lanark moved impatiently. Light from the screen showed Ozenfant's mouth so fixed in a smile that it seemed expressionless, while the eyebrows kept moving in exaggerated expressions of thoughtfulness, astonishment or woe. Ozenfant said, "Lanark is bored by these technicalities. I will show him more patients."

He spoke to the microphone and a sequence of dragons on steel tables appeared on the screen. Some had glossy hides, some were plated like tortoises, some were scaled like fish and crocodiles. Most had quills, spines or spikes and some were hugely horned and antlered, but all were made monstrous by a detail, a human foot or ear or breast sticking through the dinosaur armour. A doctor sat on the edge of one table and studied a chessboard balanced on a dragonish stomach.

Ozenfant said, "That is McWham, who is also unmusical. He treats the dryly rational cases; he teaches them chess and plays interminable games. He thinks that if anyone defeats him their armour will fall off, but so far he has been too clever for them. Do you play any games, Lanark?"

"No."

In another chamber a thin priest with intensely miserable eyes sat with his ear close to a dragonish beak.

"That is Monsignor Noakes, our only faith healer. We used

to have lots of them: Lutherans, Jews, Atheists, Muslims, and others with names I forget. Nowdays all the hardened religious cases have to be treated by poor Noakes. Luckily we don't get many."

"He looks unhappy."

"Yes, he takes his work too seriously. He is Roman Catholic and the only people he cures are Quakers and Anglicans. Have you a religion, Lanark?"

"No."

"You see a cure is more likely when doctor and patient have something in common. How would you describe yourself?"

"I can't."

Ozenfant laughed. "Of course you can't! I asked foolishly. The lemon cannot taste bitterness, it only drinks the rain. Munro, describe Lanark to me."

"Obstinate and suspicious," said Munro. "He has intelligence, but keeps it narrow."

"Good. I have a patient for him. Also obstinate, also suspicious, with a cleverness which only reinforces a deep, deep, immeasurably deep despair."

Ozenfant said to the microphone, "Show chamber one, and let us see the patient from above."

A gleaming silver dragon appeared between a folded pair of brazen wings. A stout arm ending in seven brazen claws lay along one wing, a slender soft human arm along the other. "You see the wings? Only unusually desperate cases have wings, though they cannot use them. Yet this one brings such reckless energy to her despair that I have sometimes hoped. She is unmusical, but I, a musician, have stooped to speech therapy and spoken to her like a vulgar critic, and she exasperated me so much that I decided to give her to the catalyst. We will give her to Lanark instead."

A radio said *plin-plong*. Ozenfant took one from a waistcoat pocket and turned the switch. A voice announced that patient twelve was turning salamander.

Ozenfant said to the microphone, "Quick! Chamber twelve."

Chamber twelve was obscured by white vapours streaming and whirling from the dragon's beak, which suddenly snapped shut. Radiant beams shot from the domes in the head, the figure seemed to be writhing. Ozenfrant cried, "No light, please! We will observe by heat alone."

There was immediate blackness on which Lanark's dazzled eyes projected stars and circles before adjusting to it. He could hear

Munro's quick dry breathing on one side and Ozenfant breathing through his mouth on the other. He said, "What's happening?"

Ozenfant said, "Brilliant light pours from all his organs—it would blind us. Soon you will see him by his heat."

A moment later Lanark was startled to feel Ozenfant murmuring into his ear.

"The heat made by a body should move easily through it, overflowing the pores, penis, anus, eyes, lips, limbs and fingertips in acts of generosity and self-preservation. But many people are afraid of the cold and try to keep more heat than they give, they stop the heat from leaving though an organ or limb, and the stopped heat forges the surface into hard insulating armour. What part of you went dragon?"

"A hand and arm."

"Did you ever touch them with your proper hand?"

"Yes. They felt cold."

"Quite. No heat was getting out. But no heat was getting in! And since men feel the heat they receive more than the heat they create the armour makes the remaining human parts feel colder. So do they strip it off? Seldom. Like nations losing unjust wars they convert more and more of themselves into armour when they should surrender or retreat. So someone may start by limiting only his affections or lust or intelligence, and eventually heart, genitals, brain, hands and skin are crusted over. He does nothing but talk and feed, giving and taking through a single hole; then the mouth shuts, the heat has no outlet, it increases inside him until. . . watch, you will see."

The blackness they sat in had been dense and total but a crooked thread of scarlet light appeared on it. This twitched and grew at both ends until it outlined the erect shape of a dragon with legs astride, arms outstretched, the hands thrusting against darkness, the great head moving from side to side. Lanark had a weird feeling that the beast stood before him in the room. There was nothing but blackness to compare it with, and it seemed vast. Its gestures may have been caused by pain but they looked threatening and triumphant. Inside the black head two stars appeared where eyes should be, then the whole body was covered with white and golden stars. Lanark felt the great gothic shape towering miles above him, a galaxy shaped like a man. Then the figure became one blot of gold which expanded into a blinding globe. There was a crash of thunder and for a moment the room became very hot. The floor heaved and the lights went on.

It took a while to see things clearly. The thunder had ended, but throughout the apartment instruments were jangling and thrumming in sympathy. Lanark noticed Munro still sitting beside him. There was sweat on his brow and he was industriously polishing his spectacles with a handkerchief. The blank screen was cracked from side to side but the microphone hung neatly under it. Ozenfant stood at a distance examining a fiddle. "See!" he cried. "The A-string has snapped. Yet some assert that a Stradivarius is without a soul."

Munro said, "I am no judge of salamanders, but that vibration seemed abnormally strong."

"Indeed yes. There were over a million megatherms in that small blast."

"Surely not!"

"Certainly. I will prove it."

Ozenfant produced his radio and said, "Ozenfant will speak with engineer Johnson. . . . Johnson, hello, you have received our salamander; what is he worth? . . . Oh, I see. Anyway, he cracked my viewing lens, so replace it soon, please."

Ozenfant pocketed the radio and said briskly, "Not quite a million megatherms, but it will suffice for a month or two." He bent and hoisted up a harp which had fallen on its side.

Lanark said sharply, "That heat is used?"

"Of course. Somehow we must warm ourselves."

"That is atrocious!"

"Why?"

Lanark started stammering then forced himself to speak slowly. "I knew people deteriorate. That is dismal but not surprising. But for cheerful healthy folk to profit by it is atrocious!"

"What would you prefer? A world with a cesspool under it where the helplessly corrupt would fall and fester eternally? That is a very old-fashioned model of the universe."

"And very poor housekeeping," said Munro, standing up. "We could cure nobody if we did not utilize our failures. I must go now. Lanark, your department and mine have different staff clubs but if you ever leave the institute we will meet again. Professor Ozenfant is your adviser now, so good luck, and try not to be violent."

Lanark was so keen to learn if the last remark was a joke that he stared hard into Munro's calm benign face and let his hand be gravely shaken without saying a word. Ozenfant murmured, "Excellent advice."

He uncovered a door and Munro went through it.

Ozenfant returned to the centre of the room chuckling and rubbing his hands. He said, "You noticed the sweat on his brow? He did not like what he saw; he is a rigorist, Lanark. He cannot sympathize with our disease."

"What is a rigorist?"

"One who bargains with his heat. Rigorists do not hold their heat in, they give it away, but only in exchange for fresh supplies. They are very dependable people, and when they go bad they crumble into crystals essential for making communication circuits, but when you and I went bad we took a different path. That is why an exploding salamander exalts us. We feel in our bowels the rightness of such nemesis. You were exalted, were you not?"

"I was excited, and I regret it."

"Your regret serves no purpose. And now perhaps you wish to meet your patient."

Ozenfant lifted the corner of another tapestry, uncovered a low circular door and said, "Her chamber is through here."

"But what have I to do?"

"Since you are only able to talk, you must talk."

"What about?"

"I cannot say. A good doctor does not carry a remedy to his patient, he lets the patient teach him what the remedy is. I drove someone salamander today because I understood my cure better than my invalid. I often make these mistakes because I know I am very wise. You know you are ignorant, which should be an advantage."

Lanark stood with his hands in his pockets, biting his lower lip and tapping the floor with one foot. Ozenfant said, "If you do not go to her I will certainly send the catalyst."

"What is the catalyst?"

"A very important specialist who comes to lingering cases when other treatments have failed. The catalyst provokes very rapid deterioration. Why are you reluctant?"

"Because I am afraid!" cried Lanark passionately, "You want to mix me with someone else's despair, and I hate despair! I want to be free, and freedom is freedom from other people!"

Ozenfant smiled and nodded. He said "A very dragonish sentiment! But you are no longer a dragon. It is time you learned a different sentiment."

After a while the smile left Ozenfant's face, leaving it startlingly impassive. He let go the tapestry, went to the carpenter's bench and picked up a fretsaw.

He said sharply, "You feel I am pressing you and you dislike it. Do what you please. But since I myself have work to do I will be glad if you waste no more of my time."

He bent over the guitar. Lanark stared frustratedly at the corner of the tapestry. It depicted a stately woman labelled *Correctio Conversio* standing on a crowned and sprawling young man labelled *Tarquinius*. At last he pulled this aside, stepped through the door and went down the corridor beyond.

CHAPTER 9. A Dragon

Lanark was not a tall man but he had to bend knees and neck to pass comfortably down the corridor. The differences between bright and dull, warm and cool were slight here and the voices were like whispers in a seashell: "Lilac and laburnum . . . . marble and honey . . . . the recipe is separation . . . ."
The corridor ended in a steel surface with a mesh in the centre. He said glumly, "Please open. I'm called Lanark."
The door said, "Dr. Lanark?"
"Yes yes, Dr. Lanark."
A circular section swung inward on a hinge. He climbed through, raised his head, banged it on the ceiling and sat down suddenly on a stool beside the table. The door closed silently leaving no mark in the wall.

For more than a minute he sat biting his thumb knuckle and trying not to yell to be let out, for the observation lens had not prepared him for the cramped smallness of the chamber and the solid vastness of the monster. The tabletop was a few inches above the floor and from the crest on the silver head to the bronze hooves on the silver feet the patient was nearly eight feet long. The chamber was a perfect hemisphere nine feet across and half as high, and though he pressed his shoulders against the curve of the ceiling it forced him to lean forward over the gleaming stomach, from which icy air beat upward into his face. Soft light came from the milk-coloured floor and walls and there were no shadows. Lanark felt he was crouching in a tiny arctic igloo, but here the warmth came from the walls and the cold from the body of his companion. The hand at the end of the human arm was clenching and unclenching, and this was a comfort, and he liked the wings folded along the dragon's sides, each long bronze feather tipped with the spectrum of rich colour that is got by heating copper. He leaned over and looked into the gaping beak and was hit in the face by a welcome gush of warmth, but he saw only darkness. A voice said, "What have you brought this time? Bagpipes?" The question had a hollow, impersonal tone as if transmitted through a machine too clumsy for the music of ordinary speech, yet he seemed to recognize the fierce energy beating through it.

"I'm not a musician. I'm called Lanark."

"What filthy tricks do you play on the sick?"

"I've been told to talk to you. I don't know what to say."

He was no longer afraid and sat with elbows on knees, holding his head between his hands. After a while he cleared his throat and said, "Talk, I suppose, is a way of defending and attacking, but I don't need to defend myself. I don't want to attack you."

"How kind!"

"Are you Rima?"

"I'm done with names. Names are nothing but collars men tie round your neck to drag you where they like."

Again he could think of nothing to say. A remote faint thudding noise occupied the silence until the voice said, "Who was Rima?"

"A girl I used to like. She tried to like me too, a little."

"Then she wasn't me."

"You have beautiful wings."

"I wish they were spikes, then I wouldn't need to talk jaggedly to bastards like you."

"Why do you say that?"

"Don't pretend you're not like the others. Your technique will be different but you'll hurt me too. I'm helpless in this freezing coffin so why not begin?"

"Ozenfant didn't hurt you."

"Do you think these noises made me happy? Ballet music! Sounds of women flying and floating in moonlight like swans and clouds, women leaping from men's hands like flames from candles, women disdaining whole glittering audiences of czars and emperors. Yes, the liar talked, he left nothing to my imagination. He said *I* could have done these things once. 'Open your heart to my music,' he said. 'Weep passionately.' He could not reach my skin so he raped my ears, like you."

"I haven't raped your ears."

"Then why shout?"

"I haven't shouted!"

"Don't get hysterical."

"I'm *not* hysterical."

"You certainly aren't calm."

Lanark bellowed, "How can I be calm when . . ." and was deafened by the reverberation around the narrow dome. He folded his arms and waited grimly. The uproar faded out as a faint ringing with perhaps (he wasn't sure) an echo of laughter in it. Eventually he said in a low voice, "Should I leave?"

She murmured something.

"I didn't hear that."

"You could tell me who you are."

"I'm over five and half feet tall and weigh about ten stone. My eyes are brown, hair black, and I forget the blood group. I used to be older than twenty but now I'm older than thirty. I've been called a crustacean, and too serious, but recently I was described by a dependable man as shrewd, obstinate and adequately intelligent. I was a writer once and now I'm a doctor, but I was advised to become these, I never wanted it. I've never wanted anything long. Except freedom."

There was a metallic rattle of laughter. Lanark said, "Yes, it's a comic word. We're all forced to define it in ways that make no sense to other people. But for me freedom is . . ."

He thought for a while.

". . . life in a city near the sea or near the mountains where the sun shines for an average of half the day. My house would have a living room, big kitchen, bathroom and one bedroom for each of the family, and my work would be so engrossing that while I did it I would neither notice nor care if I was happy or sad. Perhaps I would be an official who kept useful services working properly. Or a designer of houses and roads for the city where I lived. When I grew old I would buy a cottage on an island or among the mountains—"

"Dirty! Dirty! Dirty! Dirty!" said the voice on a low throb of rage. "Dirty bastards giving me a killer for a doctor!"

The blood boomed in Lanark's eardrums and his scalp prickled. A wave of terror passed over him in which he struggled to get up, then a wave of rage in which he sat, leaned forward and whispered, "You have no right to despise my bad actions without liking my better ones."

"Tell me about these, were they many? Were they pretty?"

He cried, "Dr. Lanark is ready to leave!"

A circular panel opened on the other side of the chamber. He stepped carefully across the body and paused with one

foot on each side of it, his shoulders against the height of the
dome.

"Goodbye!" he said with a conscious cruelty which startled
him. He stared down at the clenching and unclenching hand
for a while, then asked humbly, "Are you very sore?"

"I'm freezing. I knew you would leave."

"Talking doesn't help. What can I say that won't annoy you?"
After a moment she spoke in a voice he just managed to hear.

"You could read to me."

"Then I will. Next time I'll bring books."

"You won't come back."

Lanark climbed out through the opening into a tunnel where
he could stand erect. He leaned into the chamber and said
cheerfully, "I'll surprise you. I'll be quicker than you think."
The panel closed as he turned away.

At the end of the corridor a red curtain admitted him to
a passage between a large window and a row of arches. Through
the arches he recognized, with a sense of homecoming, the
five beds of his own ward. It seemed strange that the silver
dragon had been so near him since his arrival. He went to
his locker, lifted the books and hurried back to the curtain.
From the other side it had slid open at the touch of a finger,
he knew it was a paper-thin membrane with no locking device,
and yet he couldn't open it; and though he stood back and
ran his shoulder into it several times it only quivered and rumbled like a struck drum. He was about to kick it in a fit of
bad temper when he noticed the view from the window. He
was looking down on a quiet street with a skin of frost over
it and a three-storey red sandstone tenement on the far side.
The windows glinted cleanly in early morning sunlight; smoke
from a few chimney-pots flowed upward into a pale winter
sky. A boy of six or seven with a dark blue raincoat, woollen
helmet and schoolbag came down some steps from a close and
turned left along the pavement. Directly opposite Lanark a
thin woman with a tired face appeared between the curtains
of a bay window. She stood watching the boy, who turned
and waved to her as he reached the street corner and banged
the side of his head into a lamppost. Lanark felt inside himself
the shock, then amusement, which showed on the mother's
face. The boy went round the corner, rubbing his ear mournfully. The woman turned and looked straight across at Lanark,
then lifted a hand to her mouth in a startled puzzled way.
He wanted to wave to her as the boy had waved, to open

the window and shout something comforting, but a milk cart pulled by a brown horse came along the street, and when he looked back from it the bay window was empty.

This vision hit Lanark poignantly. He lowered the blind to prevent a new scene from replacing it and wandered into the ward feeling very tired. It seemed many days since he had been there, though the clock showed it was not three hours. He put the books and white coat on the chair, slid his shoes off and lay on the bed, intending to rest for ten or fifteen minutes.

He was wakened by the radio saying *plin-plong, plin-plong, pin-plong.* He reached across, took it from the coat pocket and switched it on. Ozenfant said, "My dear fellow, sleep is not enough, sometimes you must eat. Come to the staff club. Leave the white coat behind. Evening is a time for mirth and gaiety."
"How do I reach the staff club?"
"Go to the nearest hall and enter any lift. If you ask it nicely it will bring you direct. Mention my name."
Lanark put on the shoes, took the books under his arm and passed through the curtain into the noise of the exit corridors. This time he ignored the voices and studied how to move as swiftly as those around him. The usual laws governing the motion of bodies seemed not to apply here. If you leaned backward against the force of the current you were certain to fall, but the farther you bowed before it the faster it carried you with no danger of falling whatsoever. Most people were content to move rapidly at an angle of forty-five degrees, but one or two flashed past Lanark's knees like rockets, and these were bent so far forward that they appeared to be crawling. The great hall was less crowded than last time. Lanark entered a lift which seemed waiting to be filled before ascending. Two men carrying a surveyor's pole and tripod were chatting in a corner.
"It's a big job, the biggest we've handled."
"The Noble Lord wants it ready in twelve days."
"He's off his rocker."
"The creature is sending tungtanium suction delvers through the Algolagnics group."
"Where will we get power to drive those?"
"From Ozenfant. Ozenfant and his tiny catalyst."
"Has he said he'll give it?"
"No, but he can't oppose the president of the council."

"I doubt if the president of the council could oppose Ozenfant."
The lift filled and the door closed. Voices said: "The drawing
rooms." "Leech-dormitory Q." "The sponge-sump club."
Lanark said, "The staff club."
The lift said, "Whose staff club?"
"Professor Ozenfant's."
The lift hummed. The people near Lanark were silent but the
farthest away whispered and glanced at him. The door opened
and sounds of Viennese dance music floated in. The lift said,
"Here you are, Dr. Lanark."

He entered a softly lit restaurant with a low blue ceiling
and thick blue carpet. The tables were empty with their cloths
removed, except for one on the far side where Ozenfant sat.
He wore a light grey suit with yellow waistcoat and tie; the
corner of a white napkin was tucked between two buttons of
the waistcoat. He was cutting a small morsel on his plate with
obvious pleasure, but he looked up and beckoned Lanark over.
The light came from two candles on his table and from low
arches in the walls, arches of a moorish pattern which seemed
to open into bright rooms at a lower level. Through the nearest,
Lanark saw a section of dance floor with black trouser legs
and long skirts waltzing over it. Ozenfant said, "Come, join
me. The others have long finished, but I am somewhat addicted
to the joys of the feeding trough."
A waitress came from among the shadowy tables, pulled out
a chair and handed Lanark a menu. The dishes were named
in a language he didn't understand. He returned the menu
and said to Ozenfant, "Could you order for me?"
"Certainly. Try Enigma de Filets Congalés. After the slops of
the invalid ward you will appreciate stronger meat."
Ozenfant gulped from a tulip-shaped glass and pulled his mouth
down at the corners.
"Unluckily I cannot recommend the wine. Synthetic chemistry
has much to learn in that direction."

The waitress placed before Lanark a plate with a cube of
grey jelly on it. He cut a thin slice from a surface and found
it tasted like elastic ice. He swallowed quickly and the back
of his nose was filled by a smell of burning rubber, but he
was surprised by a sense of friendly warmth. He felt relaxed,
yet capable of powerful action. He ate another slice and the
smell was worse. He laid down the knife and fork and said,
"I can't eat more than that."
Ozenfant dabbed his lips with the napkin. "No matter. A mouth-

ful gives all the nourishment one needs. As you learn to like
the flavour you will come to take more, and in a few years
you will be overeating like the rest of us."
"I won't be here in a few years."
"Oh?"
"I'm leaving when I find a suitable companion."
"Why?"
"I want the sun."
Ozenfant began laughing heartily then said, "I beg your pardon,
but to hear such a sober fellow declare such a strange passion
was a little unexpected. Why the *sun?*"
Lanark was irritated beyond normal reticence. He said, "I want
to love, and meet friends, and work in it."
"But you are no Athenian, no Florentine, you are a modern
man! In modern civilizations those who work in the sunlight
are a despised and dwindling minority. Even farmers are moving indoors. As for lovemaking and friendship, humanity has
always preferred to enjoy these at night. If you wanted the
moon I could sympathize, but Apollo is quite discredited."
"You talk like Sludden."
"Who is he?"
"A man who lives in the city I came from. The sun shines
there for two or three minutes a day and he thinks it doesn't
matter."
Ozenfant covered his eyes with a hand and said dreamily, "A
city on the banks of a shrunk river. A city with a nineteenth-
century square full of ugly statues. Am I right?"
"Yes."
"Excuse me but the temptation is too great."
Ozenfant reached for Lanark's plate, placed it on his own empty
plate and ate slowly, talking as he did so.
"That city is called Unthank. The calendar in Unthank is based
on sunlight, but only administrators use it. The majority have
forgotten the sun; moreover, they have rejected the clock. They
do not measure or plan, their lives are regulated by simple
appetite varied by the occasional impulse. Not surprisingly nobody is well there. Politically, too, they are corrupt and would
collapse without subsidies from healthier continents. But do
not blame its condition upon lack of sunlight. The institute
has none, yet it supports itself and supplies the staff with plenty
of healthy food and exercise. The clock keeps us regular."
"Have you a library?"
"We have two: one for film and one for music. I am in charge
of the latter."

"What about books?"

"Books?"

"I want to read to my patient and I have only these three."

"Read! How Victorian. Let me see them. Hm. That seems a well-balanced selection. I don't know how you could add to it unless you borrowed from poor Monsignor Noakes. He always has a fat little book with him. It might be a Bible. Bibles are full of funny stories."

Lanark said, "Where could I find him?"

"Don't be in such a hurry—I want to dissuade you from leaving us. Think of the time you could lose by it."

"What do you mean?"

"In this universe every continent measures time by different calendars, so there is no means of measuring the time between them. A traveller going from the institute to a neighbouring continent—Unthank, perhaps, or Provan—must cross a zone where time is a purely subjective experience. Some make the transition and hardly notice it, but how many years did you lose when you came here?"

Lanark was troubled by a feeling of dread which he hid by standing up and saying abruptly, "Thank you for the warning, but a patient is expecting me. Where is Monsignor Noakes?"

"At this hour he is usually in the smoking room watching the bathers. Go through the arches behind me and walk straight ahead. Turn left when you enter the third room, he will be behind the arch facing you."

Lanark walked from the restaurant into a brilliant room where older people were playing bridge. The room beyond was dim and full of billiard tables with low lights over them. The next room contained a swimming bath. Amid raucous echoes some men and women with the even brown tan that comes from exposure to ultraviolet light were diving or racing or chatting on the edge. Lanark turned left along the tiled slippery platform until he reached a wall pierced by the usual arches. He climbed a few steps into a softly lit, thick-carpeted room full of leather armchairs. Noakes sat near the steps smoking a slim cigar and glancing furtively at the brown bodies refracted by the blue-green water. Lanark sat opposite him and said, "I am Dr. Lanark."

"Oh yes."

"A patient of mine needs reading material and I'm collecting books. Professor Ozenfant suggested you could lend me one."

Noakes gave no sign of noticing Lanark was there. He glanced from the bathers to his cigar and spoke quietly and listlessly. "Professor Ozenfant is a noted humorist. He knows I have only my breviary. If your patient had been interested in prayer she would have been my patient."

"He thought you had a bible."

"Another joke. I have a Greek testament, and I suppose your patient understands Greek as little as you do. What have you gathered so far?"

He looked at the books Lanark held out and waved wearily toward *The Holy War*.

"The other two are trash, but that one is good in parts. The main message, I mean, is true. I knew the author slightly. He wrote me as a character into one of his books—not that book, another. His description was malicious but insignificant. He described Ozenfant too, but more truthfully and at greater length. Ignore what I say. Ozenfant has warned you against me."

"Ozenfant has said nothing against you."

Noakes stared at the floor and whispered, "Then he has come to despise me as much as that."

He raised his chin and spoke almost loudly.

"He owes his position to me, you know. It was I who cured him. Ozenfant was a very difficult case, half leech, half dragon. (Nowadays he pretends he was pure dragon. I know otherwise.) I believed that the Mass had cured him, and my prayers and sermons, but it was the music. Ah, what music we had in those days! When I discovered that he had no sense of holiness apart from music I made him our organist. He has risen since then, and I—I have declined. You notice, I suppose, a fretful querulous note in my voice?"

"Yes."

"Then try to understand why. All these professors and artists and heads of department have become powerful by tearing tiny bits off the religion which cured them and developing these bits into religions of their own. No God unites them now, only mutual assistance pacts based upon greed. Where we had Christ's vicar upon earth we have now"—he spat the words at Lanark accusingly—"Lord Monboddo, president of the council!"

Lanark said defensively, "I'm new here. I don't understand you."

Noakes bowed his head and murmured, "You like your work?"

"No."

"Then you will come to like it."

"No. When I've cured this patient I'm going to leave with her, if she wants me."

Noakes jerked upright and shouted, "What nonsense!" then leaned forward and grabbed Lanark's hands, speaking in a low quick gabble of words. "No, no, no, no, my child, forgive me, forgive me, it is *not* nonsense! You *must* cure your patient, you *must* leave with her, and if—forgive me, I mean *when*— you leave, you will do something for me, will you not? You promise to do this one thing?"

Lanark pulled his hands free and asked irritably, "What thing?"

"Tell people not to come here. Tell them they must not enter this institute. A little more faith, and hope, and charity, and they can cure their own diseases. Charity alone will save them, if it is possible without the others."

"Why should I warn folk against coming here when coming here cured me?"

"Then tell them to come willingly, in thousands! Let them enter like an army of men, not wait to be swallowed like a herd of victims. Think of the institute with twenty staff to every patient! We will have no excuse for not curing people then! We will be like"—his voice grew wistful—"a cathedral with a congregation of priests. It would burst the institute open to the heavens."

Lanark said, "I don't think telling people things helps them much. And if you are still working here after so many years, you can't think it much worse than it was."

"You are wrong. In all the corridors there are sounds of increased urgency and potency, and behind it all a sound like the breathing of a hungry beast. I assure you, the institute is preparing to swallow a world. I am not trying to frighten you."

Lanark was more embarrassed than frightened. He stood up and said, "Is there a lift near here?"

"I see you will not try to save others. Pray God you can save yourself. There is one in the far corner."

Lanark passed between the chairs and found an open lift in a wall between two arches. He entered and said, "Ignition chamber one."

"Whose department?"

"Professor Ozenfant's."

The door opened on a familiar surface of brown cloth. He thrust it aside and stepped into the high-ceilinged tapestry-hung studio, almost expecting to find it in darkness. It was lit as before, and in the middle Lanark saw from behind a familiar figure in black trousers and waistcoat leaning over the carpenter's bench. Lanark tiptoed uneasily round the walls looking for the figure of *Correctio Conversio* and sometimes glancing sideways at Ozenfant. The Professor was fixing the bridge on his guitar with a delicacy and concentration it would have been wrong to disturb. Lanark was relieved to lift the tapestry and, stooping, enter the low tunnel.

He sat in the tiny chamber pressing his back against the warm curve of the wall. The only movement was the silver creature's clenching and unclenching hand, the only sound the remote and regular thumping. Lanark cleared his throat and said, "I'm sorry I'm late, but I have a book here which someone who knew the author tells me is very good."
There was no answer so he began reading.

"**A RELATION OF THE HOLY WAR. In** my travels, as I walked through many regions and countries, it was my chance to happen into that famous continent of Universe. A very large and spacious continent it is; it lieth between the heavens. It is a place well watered, and richly adorned with hills and valleys, bravely situate, and for the most part, at least where I was, very fruitful, also well peopled, and a very sweet air."

"I refuse to listen to lies!" cried the voice, making a ringing echo. "Do you think *I* don't live in the universe? Do you think I don't know what a stinking trap it is?"
"My own experience supports your view rather than the author's," said Lanark cautiously, "but remember he says 'for the most part, at least where I was.' Frankly, if I felt there were no such places and we could never reach them, I wouldn't be reading to you."
"Then read something else."
"Here is a story about a small boy called Oor Wullie, and it is told in pictures. The first picture shows him coming with his father out of the front door, which is separated from the pavement by a single step. His hair is brushed and his boots are shining. His mother looks after them and says, 'Since it's Sunday, ye can tak Wullie a walk before dinner, but see he doesnae dirty his good claes, Paw.' His father, who is tall and thin with a flat cap, says, 'Leave it tae me, Maw!' Wullie is thinking, 'Crivens! Some fun this walk is going to be!' In the next picture they're walking beside a fence made of upright

pieces of timber joined edge to edge. I can't read what Wullie is saying because the words have been scored out with crayon, but his father—"

"Is this meant to be entertaining?"

"I wish you could see the pictures. They have a humorous, homely look which is very comforting."

"Have you no *other* book?"

"Only one."

He opened *No Orchids for Miss Blandish* and read:

"It began on a summer morning in July. The sun up early in the morning mist, and the pavements already steaming a little from the heavy dew. The air in the streets was stale and lifeless. It had been an exhausting month of intense heat, rainless skies, and warm, dust-laden winds.

Bailey walked into Minny's hash-house, leaving Old Sam asleep in the Packard. Bailey was feeling lousy. Hard liquor and heat don't mix. His mouth felt like a birdcage and his eyes were gritty. . . ."

He read for a long time. Once or twice he asked, "Are you enjoying this?" and she said, "Go on."

At last she interrupted with a harsh rattle of laughter. "Oh, yes, I like this book! Crazy hopes of a glamorous, rich, colourful life and then abduction, rape, slavery. That book, at least, is true."

"It is not true. It is a male sex fantasy."

"And life for most women is just that, a performance in a male sex fantasy. The stupid ones don't notice, they've been trained for it since they were babies, so they're happy. And of course the writer of that book made things obvious by speeding them up. What happens to the Blandish girl in a few weeks takes a lifetime for the rest of us."

"I deny that," said Lanark fiercely. "I deny that life is more of a trap for women than men. I know that most women have to work at home because people grow in them, but working at home is more like freedom than working in offices and factories; furthermore—"

His voice raised an echo which competed with the words. To end the sentence audibly he began shouting and caused a deafening explosion which took minutes to fade. Afterward he sat scowling at the air before him until the voice said, "Just go on reading."

CHAPTER 10. Explosions

He visited her chamber twice a day and read aloud there, only stopping when he was hoarse. He soon lost count of the times he had read *No Orchids for Miss Blandish*. Once, to have a different story to tell his patient, he watched a cowboy film in the staff club cinema, but mention of it threw her into a cold violent rage. She only believed in repetitious accounts of brutal men and humiliated women and thought anything else was deliberate mockery. Lanark left her chamber each time with a sore throat and a determination not to return, and had there been anywhere to go but the staff club he might have stayed away. The soft, brightly lit rooms with their warm air and comfortable furniture made him feel oppressively enclosed. The members were polite and friendly but talked as if there was nothing important outside the club, and Lanark was afraid of coming to believe them. At other times he suspected that his own ungraciousness made him dislike gracious people. He spent most of his free time on his bed in the ward. The window was no longer enjoyable for it had begun giving views of small rooms with worried people in them. Once he thought he glimpsed Mrs. Fleck, his old landlady, tucking the children into the kitchen bed. After that he preferred watching the lights move mysteriously between the slats of the half-shut blind and listening idly to the radio. He noticed that the requests for doctors were increasingly varied by a different kind of message.

"Attention, please note! Attention, please note! The expansion committee announces that after the hundred and eightieth all twittering is to be treated as a sign of hopelessness."

"Attention, please note! Attention, please note! The expansion committee announces that after the hundred and eightieth the sink will take no more softs. All helpless softs will be funnelled

into the compression sluices under the main wards."
But none of this urgency showed in the staff club unless it
was displayed through increased jollity at mealtimes. People
sat at tables smiling and talking loudly in groups of four. Ozenfant's booming laughter sounded among them; he was always
to be seen there wearing a light suit, talking hard and eating
hugely. Only three people sat quiet and alone: himself, Monsignor Noakes, and a big, strikingly sullen girl wearing khaki
overalls who ate almost as much as Ozenfant.

One evening Lanark had entered the restaurant and seated
himself when Ozenfant sat down beside him saying cheerfully,
"Twice today, at breakfast and at lunch, I beckon you to my
table and you do not notice. And so"—he passed a hand down
the yellow curve of his waistcoat—"the mountain comes to
Mahomet. I want to tell you I am pleased, very pleased indeed."
"Why?"
"I am a busy man, even at mealtimes I am working, so I have
only had time to observe closely two of your sessions, but
believe me, you do well."
"You're wrong, I do badly. She's freezing, I don't warm her
and everything I talk about increases her pain."
"Well, of course you are treating an impossible case, a case I
would have judged hopeless had you not needed someone to
practise on. But you have employed a tact, a tolerance, a patience which I never expected from a novice. So now I want
you to withdraw from this case and start on someone more
important."
Lanark leaned forward over the table and said, "You mean
those hours of reading that bloody book were *for nothing?*"
"No, no, no, my dear fellow, they have been very valuable;
they have shown me the sort of doctor you are and the kind
of patient you should treat. There are layers of stolid endurance
in you which make you a perfect buffer for these tragic intelligent females whose imagination exceeds their strength. We
have just such a patient in chamber thirty-nine who would, if
cured, be a delightful addition to our staff, and her head and
limbs are unarmoured. If you still wish to visit chamber one
you can do so, but I want you to spend most of your time in
chamber thirty-nine."
"What if my first patient gets well and wants to leave with
me? Do I simply abandon the second?"
Ozenfant made an impatient gesture. "Those are the scruples
of a novice. Patient one will not get well, and you have no

reason to leave. Suppose you did leave, and reached (which is unlikely) a more sunlit continent, how would you earn your bread? By picking up litter in the public parks?"

Lanark said in a low voice, "I shall visit my first patient, and nobody else, until she doesn't want me."

Ozenfant drummed his fingers on the tablecloth. His expression was blank. He said, "Dr. Lanark, what will you do when you have failed to reclaim your Eurydice?"

"I am too ignorant to understand your jokes, Professor Ozenfant," said Lanark, rising and walking away.

He was angry and upset and felt that his patient's rage against life would be a consolation. Instead of going to bed he entered the lift and said, "Ozenfant's studio."

"Professor Ozenfant is recording just now. If I were you I wouldn't disturb him."

Lanark seemed to recognize the voice. He said, "Is it you, Gloopy?"

The lift said, "No. Only part of me."

"Which part?"

"The voice and feelings and sense of responsibility. I don't know what they've done with the rest."

This was said with a stoical dignity which filled Lanark with pity. He laid his hand against the lukewarm wall and said humbly, "I'm sorry!"

"Why? People need me now. I'm never alone and I hear all kinds of interesting things. You'd be amazed at what happens in a lift between floors. Why, yesterday—"

Lanark said quickly, "I'm very glad. Will you take me to Ozenfant's studio?"

"But he's recording."

"He can't be, I've just left him in the restaurant."

"Don't you know that heads of departments can feed and work at the same time? And he gets really poisonous when his music's interrupted."

"Take me to the studio, Gloopy."

"All right, but I warned you."

The door slid open and Lanark heard the complicated squealing of a string quartet playing very badly. He pulled the tapestry aside, went in and struck a hanging microphone with his shoulder. He was confronted by four music stands with people behind them. A gaunt woman in a red velvet gown was grappling a cello. Three men in tailcoats, white waistcoats and bow ties scraped on a viola and fiddles. One of them was Ozenfant.

He silenced the others with a hoarse cry and marched toward Lanark, fiddle under elbow and bow clutched in the right hand like a riding crop. When his face was an inch from Lanark's he stopped and whispered, "Of course you knew I was recording?"

"Yes."

Ozenfant began speaking in a quiet voice which grew steadily to a deafening yell: "Dr. Lanark, you have been allowed very special privileges. You use a public ward as a private apartment. You employ my name in lifts and they take you everywhere direct. You ignore my advice, disdain my friendship, sneer at my food and now! Now you deliberately ruin the recording of an immortal harmony which might save the souls of thousands! What other insults do you plan to heap on me?"

Lanark said, "Your anger is misplaced. You have bullied me into trying to cure a difficult patient and now you try to stop me reaching her. If you don't want to see me you should contact the engineers. Get them to fix that door in my ward so I can go back through it, and we need never meet again."

Ozenfant's rage-swollen features relaxed into astonishment. He said faintly, "You want the current of the whole institute thrown into reverse for *that?*"

He wiped his face with his handkerchief and turned away, saying wearily, "Get out of here."

Lanark quickly lifted the tapestry and stooped into the corridor.

He crouched in the ignition chamber feeling too discouraged to pick up the book where he had left it. He stared at the slim human arm, noticing silver freckles above the elbow and wondering if they had been there before. He tried to hold the moving hand but it clenched into a fist.

The voice said, "Yes I'm unprotected there. Why not use force?"

"Rima!"

"I'm not your Rima. Go on reading."

"I'm sick of that book. Couldn't you talk to me? You must be lonely. I know I am."

There was no answer. He said, "Tell me about the world before you came here."

"It was like this."

"It was not."

"Take care! You're afraid of the past. If I told what I know you would go mad."

"Sinister hints don't frighten me now. I don't care about the past and future, I want nothing but some ordinary friendly words."

"Oh, I know you, Thaw, I know all about you, the hysterical child, the eager adolescent, the mad rapist, the wise old daddy, oh, I've suffered all your tricks and know how hollow they are so don't weep! Don't dare to weep. Grief is the rottenest trick of all."

Lanark was too disturbed to feel the tears on his face. He said, "You don't know me. I'm not called Thaw. I've been none of these things. I'm something commonplace that keeps getting hurt."

"So am I but I have courage, the courage not to care and clutch. Go away! *Can't you see what's happening?*"

From shoulder to wrist her arm was spotted with silver blots and stars. Lanark had a horrible feeling that each of his words had caused one. He whispered, "Dr. Lanark wants out." The panel swung open and he climbed through.

Someone had raised the blind in the ward and he looked out on a dingy plaster wall with brickwork showing through big cracks in it. For a moment he turned giddy and almost fell, then remembered he had left the staff club without eating. It seemed the one comfort he could get was the institute's nasty, invigorating food, so he returned to the restaurant. It was nearly empty but Ozenfant sat at his usual table talking intensely with two other professors. Lanark went to a table in the farthest corner and was approached by a waitress. He said, "Have you anything brown, dry and crumbly?"

"No sir, but we've something pink, moist and crumbly."

"I'll have a quarter of a plateful, please."

He had begun to eat when a hard, slightly hesitant voice said, "Can I sit here?"

He looked up and saw the big girl in the khaki overalls. She stood with hands in pockets staring at him fiercely. With a sense of relief he said, "Oh, yes."

She sat opposite. Her face had straight clear handsome lines like a Greek statue, though the chin was heavy and forward-jutting. She did not hold her fine shoulders erect but slumped and hunched them forward. Her brown hair was twisted loosely into a thick plait which hung over her left breast. Her fingers stroked it with short quick movements. She said abruptly, "Do you hate this place too?"

"Yes."

"What do you hate most?"

Lanark considered. "The manners of the staff. I know they
have to be professional to keep things clean and orderly, but
even their jokes and smiles seem to have professional reasons.
What do you dislike?"
"The hypocrisy. The way they pretend to care while using
the patients up."
"But they could help nobody if they didn't use their failures."
The girl bent her head so that he only saw the top of it and
muttered, "You don't hate this place if you can say that."
"I do hate it. I'm leaving, when I find a companion."
She looked up.
"I'll go with you. I want to leave too."
Lanark was confused. He said, "Well, thank you, but—but—
I have a patient, not a very hopeful case, but I can't leave
until I've definitely cured her or failed."
She said disgustedly, "You *know* nobody is ever cured, that
the treatment only keeps the bodies fresh until we need fuel
or clothes or food."
Lanark looked at her, said "Foooo?" and dropped his spoon
in the plate.
"Of course! What do you think you've been eating? Have
you never looked into the sink? Has nobody shown you the
drains under the sponge-wards?"
Lanark rubbed his clenched fists into his eye sockets. He wanted
to be sick but the pink stuff had nourished him well: he had
never felt stronger or more stable. He told himself wildly,
"I'll never eat here again!"
"Then you'll leave with me?"
He looked at her blindly, not thinking of her at all. She said,
"I frighten you, I frighten most men. But I can be very sweet
for short times. Look."
He looked vaguely round the room for a way out until there
was nowhere to look but in front, and the expression on her
face made him lean forward to see it clearly. She had a slight,
disdainful smile but within her defiant eyes he saw discontent,
and beyond that a vast humility and willingness to become,
for a while, anything he wanted. Looking into her eyes became
like a rapid flight across shifting worlds, all of them sexual,
and when he returned from the flight he saw that her fierceness
was pleading and the smile timid. He began trembling with
feelings of dizzy power. She said anxiously, "I can be very
sweet?"
He nodded and whispered, "Where can we go?"
"Come to my room."

They stood together and she led the way out, Lanark walking
awkwardly because of the pressure of his penis against his trousers. As they passed Ozenfant's table the Professor cried in
mock alarm, "Oh, Dr. Lanark, you must not deprive us of
our little catalyst!"

　　　In the lift she said, "The specialist apartments."
The lift vibrated. They embraced and the feel of her strongly
female body made him mutter, "Let's stop the lift between
floors."
"That would be silly."
"Give me that contemptuous smile you're good at."
She gave it and he kissed her fiercely. She pulled her mouth
away and said, "Open your eyes, you must look at me while
we kiss."
"Why?"
"I'll do anything but you must keep looking."
The door slid open and she led him by the hand into one of
the halls. It was circular and gigantic like the others but seemed
deserted and silent until Lanark recognized the silence listening
makes. A number of men and women in overalls stood against
the walls gazing upward. Lanark looked up and saw the perspective of gold and orange rings sliding toward him, and in the
centre a black triangular shape swaying and growing bigger.
It seemed to be the base of a piece of machinery lowered
from above. It was only slightly narrower than the shaft, for
a grinding hum came briefly from the walls as if a metallic
corner had scraped them, but it must have been more than a
mile overhead for it looked very small. He squeezed the girl's
hand.
"What is that?"
"A suction delver. The creature's lending some to the expansion
project."
They were speaking in whispers. Lanark said, "Where do you
get power to drive things like that?"
"From the current, of course."
"What drives the current?"
"Please don't be technical. Come to my room. You'll like it,
I decorated it myself."
As she led him over the floor he tried not to picture what
would happen if the immense machine fell. No corridors led
out of this hall. The lift doors had smaller doors between them,
and she whispered to one of these, "I'm home," and it opened
inward.

The room was a cube and walls, ceiling and floor were sheets of pure mirror. A low double bed in the centre was covered with velvet cushions, a spot lamp on one wall cast a beam of light on it, and that was all the furniture. Lanark stood stupefied; he seemed to be standing among a hundred gleaming glass boxes, each holding a bed, girl and himself. Looking down he saw his feet resting on the soles of a dangling self looking up. He stepped to the bed making figures advance on each side of him toward a row approaching in front. He knelt on the quilt and tried to see only the girl, who lay against a bank of pillows, watching. She said shyly, "Do you like it?"
He shook his head.
"Then you think I'm hard and brazen?"
He thought of the silver dragon and felt a gush of affection for this girl who had nothing to protect her but abrupt manners and a few defiant expressions. He said, "I know you aren't. Tell me your name."
"Let's not be personal until afterward."
He undressed quickly. Sympathy for the girl, and the many movements his actions caused all round, made his lust less greedy. He gently opened her overalls and drew them down to her hips. She whispered, "How should I look?"
"Smile as if you were seeing me after waiting a long time."
She smiled so sweetly that he leaned forward to kiss her shoulders. With her thumbs she pulled his eyes open, saying, "You must look at me, I go blank when I'm not watched."
A radio sounded: *plin-plong, plin-plong, plin-plong, plin-plong!*
She murmured, "Ignore it."
"Let me turn it off."
"You can't, you can only turn it on."
The musical braying continued until he stretched and grabbed the radio from his coat pocket. He turned the switch and Ozenfant said cheerfully, "Forgive if I interrupt but I thought you would like to hear that your patient is about to go salamander."
"What?"
"There is nothing to be done, of course, but hurry along if you wish to enjoy the spectacle. Bring your friend."
Lanark dropped the radio and sat biting his thumb, then stood up and started automatically dressing. The girl stared from the bed. She moaned, "You're leaving me to watch *that?*"
"Watch what?" He glanced at her hauntedly and added "I'm sorry" and pulled the shirt over his head. He hurriedly finished dressing, muttering at intervals, "I'm really sorry." He grabbed the radio from the bed and looked about for the door, but

the gleaming glass was perfectly smooth. He said, "Dr. Lanark
wants to leave."
Nothing happened so he shouted it. She said, "This is *my*
home."
"Please let me out."
She stared at him stonily. He knelt on the bed, gripped her
shoulders and said pleadingly, "You see a friend is—is—is going to burn up; you must let me go."
She hit him hard on the side of the face. He shook his head
impatiently and said, "Yes, yes, that's all right, but you must
let me go."
She cried out, "Oh, open for him! And slam behind him as
hard as you can!"
A door opened and he ran out shouting, "I'm sorry! I'm sorry!"

    If the exit slammed behind he did not hear for the noise
outside was too great. This hall had a pit in the centre and
two vast cables running into it from above and vibrating thun-
derously. Lanark rushed round the walls looking for a lift, but
all the doors had **OUT OF ORDER** signs on them. At last
he found a little tunnel with pulses of warmth and brightness
flowing out and forced his way in against the current. This
was almost impossible until he lay on the floor and drove forward by shoving with hands and feet against the narrow walls.
After several minutes of struggling he advanced about three
yards. "Oh, Rima!" he cried and had begun banging his head
on the floor and weeping with frustration when the pressure
against him stopped. He sat up. Before and behind the tunnel
had gone a dim orange which suddenly went completely black.
It was cold, and the noise had stopped, though there was a
distant twittering and occasional voices called forlornly:
"Dloc ma I ho."
"Sthgil! Teah dna sthgil!"
"Redloc ylnellus worg I won."
He got up and ran gladly forward through the dark until prevented by a surface which rumbled at the impact of his body.
It was one of the curtains. He drew back to fling himself on
it again when it opened and out poured a deafening noise
like many flocks of starlings crashing through plate-glass win-
dows. In the door's bright circle he saw three white-faced men
staring at him, two in overalls and one a doctor. They shouted,
"You were going against the current!"
Lanark said, "There was no other way through."

"But you've blacked out the staff clubs! You've jammed the suction delvers!"

The doctor said, "I don't give a damn about those but you've caused an epidemic of twittering and God knows how many fractures. If it had happened after the hundred and eightieth you'd have been a murderer! A mass murderer!"

"I'm sorry, but I have to reach Ozenfant's studio."

The men in overalls glanced at each other. The doctor said, "Ozenfant may be a big man but if he starts letting his staff block the current he's in trouble."

The doctor turned and walked away and Lanark was about to follow when one of the men put a hand on his sleeve and said, "No, no, Mac, you've done enough damage. We'll go the way you came."

The normal movements of light and air resumed in the tunnel as they went down it, one of the men in front of Lanark, the other behind. When they reached the hall even the noise was normal. The leader opened one of the lifts with a key, led them inside and said, "Professor Ozenfant's place, then the sink." He looked accusingly at Lanark and said, "The sink is iced over."

"I'm sorry."

The door opened. Lanark was pushed into the studio but the men did not follow.

The quartet sat on chairs before the observation lens chatting and sipping from glasses. Ozenfant looked round smiling and cried, "Aha, so you are in time! There was a temporary power cut which we feared might delay you. But my dear fellow, your brow is bleeding!"

A silver figure glowed in the lens, air faintly trembling above the gaping beak. Looking back from it to the cosy social group, Lanark was gripped by rage. He quickly crossed the studio, passed between Ozenfant and the lady cellist, raised his right leg and struck his heel into the centre of the lens. It cracked and went black. The room was completely silent as he crossed to the wall, lifted the tapestry and entered the tunnel behind.

He leaned into the chamber through the open panel. All her limbs were metal now and she was bigger, head pressing the wall on one side and hooves on the other, the wings spread so that the tips of the plumes touched the walls all round and

not an inch of floor was visible. The air was chokingly hot
and a white line like cigarette smoke rose from the beak. He
said, "Rima."
The voice answered with a throb of delight. "Is that you, little
Thaw? Have you come to say goodbye? I'm not cold now,
Thaw, I'm warm and soon I'll be shining."
"I am not little and I have not come to say goodbye."
He climbed in, crawled across the rigidly quivering copper
wings, sat astride the silver thorax and gasped breathlessly.
The chamber was getting dim with whirling steam. She laughed
exultingly and said, "Are you still there? I'm glad you came.
I like you now I'm leaving but you mustn't stay any longer."
"Listen! listen to me!" he shouted and could think of nothing
to add. He lay flat and shoved his head desperately into her
jaws. The heat scorched his face and made his hair stream upward. There was a crackling sound and Ozenfant's voice said
sharply, "You have ten seconds to leave, the dome must soon
be sealed, it should have been sealed already, you have seven
seconds to leave."
She laughed again and her voice rang directly in his ears. "Are
you angry that you'll have nobody to read to, Thaw? But I've
spread my wings, I'll fly everywhere and you can't come, I
will rise with my flaming hair and eat men like air."
"Soon her jaws will shut," said Ozenfant. "Listen, you dislike
me but I give you five more seconds, five unofficial seconds
to leave starting *now.*"
A moment later there was a faint hiss and such a blast of steam
from the mouth that Lanark jerked his head back with a yell.
She said, "You're not here?"
"Yes, I'm here."
"But I'll kill you."
"I don't care."
"I don't want to kill you."
He felt a wave of heat go through the cool metal under him
then the beak shut with a crack like a gunshot. There was a
second crack then a clang. The clouds of steam began clearing,
yet he was unable for a moment to see the great beak, for
the head had fallen off. There was a black hole between the
shoulders from which poured a pale shining stream. It was
hair. There was another clang as the thorax split. He fell sideways onto a wing and lay listening to sounds like buckets and
kettles falling downstairs. The silver body and limbs cracked
and fell apart until they covered the floor like ornate scrap
metal.

A naked girl crouched weeping in the middle, rubbing her cheeks with her hands. She was blond and tall but she was Rima for she shook her head at him and said, "You should have taken that coat. I didn't want you to be cold."

There was a crackling and Ozenfant said, "What is happening? What is happening? I can see nothing without the screen."

Lanark was too stunned to think or feel but he could not stop gazing at her with open mouth and eyes. Her skin looked drenched and she curled her knees up and hugged them, trembling. Lanark took his coat and jersey off, pushed away some cracked armour and crawled to her side saying, "You'd better put these on."

"Lay them round me please."

Ozenfant said, "Stop whispering! I demand to know what has happened!"

Lanark said, "I think we're all right."

After a moment Ozenfant said, without expression, "I wash my hands of the pair of you."

Lanark put the clothes round her shoulders and sat by her side with his arm about her waist. She leaned her head on him and said drowsily, "You look as if you've been in a fight, Lanark."

"I'll be better soon."

"I wonder if I can forgive you for breaking my wings. It's nice to be human again but they were beautiful wings."

She seemed to fall asleep and he passed into a kind of stupor.

Later she kissed his ear and murmured, "Should we try to leave?"

He roused himself and said, "Dr. Lanark is ready to leave."

The ignition chamber said sternly, "You are allowed to leave but you are no longer a doctor."

A line appeared dividing the milky dome in two and each half sunk into the floor and left them squatting in a small room with an entrance on each side. Down the low tunnel from the studio ran, stooping, a nurse with a broom, followed by a stretcher pushed by another nurse. The first swept the metal shards to one side while the second brought a plain white nightshirt to Rima and helped her on with it, and all the time they laughed and chattered excitedly.

"Poor Bushybrows looks stunned."

"He's found a girlfriend but he needs a wash."

"Can you stand up, dear? Lie on the stretcher and we'll take you gently to a lovely, lonely ward together."

"The Professor is cross with you, Bushybrows. He says you've been sabotaging the expansion project."

They wheeled Rima down the corridor to the ward and Lanark followed. The blind was raised. There was a deep green sky outside with a couple of stars in it and some feathery bloody clouds. The nurses fetched towels and basins and washed Rima in bed. Lanark took his dressing gown and undressed and bathed in the ward lavatory. When he returned the nurses were putting screens round the bed. He said, "Leave an opening so that we can see the window, please."

They did that, then one patted his cheek, the other said, "Have fun, Bushybrows," and both pressed fingers to their lips and tiptoed out with exaggerated stealth. Lanark went to the bed. Rima seemed to be sleeping. He slid gently in beside her and fell asleep himself.

Someone seemed to be shining a torch on his eyes so he opened them. The ward was dark but the window through the arches was filled with stars. A nearly full moon had risen, and its clear wan light shone upon the bed and Rima, who leaned on an elbow watching him with a grave small smile, nibbling the tip of a lock of silvery-gold hair. She said, "Were you the only one who could help me, Lanark? Nobody special? Nobody splendid?"

"Have you known many special men?"

"None who weren't pretenders. But I used to have fantastic dreams."

"I can imagine nobody more splendid than you."

"Take care, that makes me stronger. I may not find a better man but I'll always be able to imagine one."

"But that makes me stronger."

"Don't talk."

They did not sleep again until he had explored with his body all the sweet crevices of her body.

CHAPTER 11. Diet and Oracle

They lay in bed for three days for she was weak and he liked to be near her. The window showed azure skies with distant birds in them or sunlit or sullen cloudscapes changing before a wind. Lanark read *The Holy War* and looked at Rima, who slept a lot. He had been near beauty before but had never expected to touch and hold it, and being held and caressed by it was so luxurious that it made his insides feel golden. That she, delighting him, delighted in him was a reflection multiplying delight until it shone round them like a halo. Her clear lovely body glowed, even in sweat, as if the silver once containing her was softly breathing under the skin. When he told her this she smiled sadly and said, "Yes, I suppose good looks and money are alike. They make us confident but we distrust folk who want us for them."

"Don't you trust me? I said that as a compliment."

She stroked his cheek with a fingertip and said absently, "I like making you happy, but how can I trust someone I don't understand?"

He stared, astonished, and cried, "We love each other! What could understanding add to that? We can't understand ourselves, how can we understand others? Only maps and mathematics exist to be understood and we're solider than those, I hope."

"Take care! You're getting clever."

"Rima, which of us came out when that shell cracked? My thoughts are bigger than they used to be, I'm afraid of them. Hold me."

"I like big men. Hold me instead."

He refused all food on the first day, saying he had overeaten the day before. When the nurse brought breakfast next

morning he cut his pale sausage into thin slices while Rima
ate, then tried to hide them by laying her empty plate on his.
She said, "Why are you doing that? Are you sick?"
"I'll be all right in a day or two."
"We'd better get a doctor."
"I don't need one. I'll be fine when we leave the institute."
"You're being mysterious about something. What are you hid-
ing?"
She interrogated him for an hour and a half, pleading, threaten-
ing, and at last tugging his hair in exasperation. He fought
back and the tussle grew amorous. Later, as he lay quiet and
unthinking, she murmured, "Still, you'd better tell me."
He saw the argument like a ponderous boulder about to roll
over him again. He said, "I'll tell you if you promise to keep
eating."
"Of course I'll keep eating."
"You know that the institute gets light and heat from people
with our kind of sickness. Well, the food is made from people
with a different sickness."
He watched her anxiously, dreading an outcry. She looked
thoughtful and said, "These people aren't deliberately killed,
are they?"
He remembered the catalyst but decided not to mention her.
"No, but the staff don't cure people as often as they pretend."
"But without the staff they would go bad anyway."
"Perhaps. I suppose so."
"Anyway, if I stop eating I'll die, and nobody extra is going
to be cured. Why shouldn't I eat?"
"I want you to eat! I made you promise to eat."
"Why won't you eat?"
"No logical reason. I have instincts, prejudices, that stop me.
But don't worry, I'm fit enough to go without food for two
or three days."
She glared at him and cried, "I'm not!"
"But I want you to eat."
"And then you'll despise me."
Lanark grew confused and uneasy. He said, "No, I won't exactly
despise you. . . ."
She turned her back to him and said coldly, "Right. I won't
eat either."
She neither moved nor spoke for many hours, and when the
nurse brought lunch she ordered it away.

That afternoon the window showed pearly fog and a tiny
hard white sun. He could sense that Rima wasn't sleeping.

He tried to embrace her but she shook him off. He said abruptly, "You know that if I eat this food you'll have defeated me in a way I'll always remember?"

She said nothing. He took the radio and said to it "Dr. Lanark needs to speak to Dr. Munro."

"I'm sorry. There is no doctor called Lanark on the staff register."

"But Dr. Munro delivered me. I desperately need his advice."

"I'm sorry Mr. Lanark, the doctor is off duty just now, but we'll give him your message first thing after breakfast tomorrow."

Lanark put down the radio and bit his thumb knuckle. When the nurse brought the evening meal he tried to persuade Rima to eat without him, but again she told the nurse to remove it. He rose and walked up and down the ward for a long time, then returned to bed, lay down wearily with his back to her and said, "Don't worry. I'll eat."

A little later her arm slid round his waist. She kissed him comfortingly between the shoulderblades, pressed her breasts to his back, stomach to his bum, and knees to the backs of his knees. They lay like that till morning, fitted together like a couple of spoons in a drawer.

They were wakened by the nurse, who tidied the bed and helped Rima wash. Lanark shaved and washed in the lavatory, feeling relieved and happy. He had been foodless for two days and ached with hunger and was glad to have a reason for breaking his promise to himself, especially as Rima was not triumphant about it but gentle and grateful. When he returned to the freshly made bed the nurse brought in breakfast and placed on his knees a plate holding a small transparent pink dome. He stared at it, gripped the knife and fork, then looked at Rima, who waited, watching steadily. Feeling cold and lonely he handed the plate back, saying, "I can't. I meant to eat, I want to, but I can't."

Rima handed back her own plate, then turned away from him and started weeping. The nurse said, "You're nothing but a couple of babies. How can you get well if you won't eat?"

She pushed the trolley out and the radio *plin-plonged*. Lanark switched it on. Munro said briskly, "Are you there, Lanark?"

"Yes. When can we leave, Dr. Munro?"

"As soon as your partner is strong enough to walk. Four days of rest and proper feeding will put her on her feet. Do I hear someone sobbing?"

"Yes, you see we can't eat the food. Or I can't and she won't."

"That's unfortunate. What are you going to do?"
"Is there no way of getting decent food?"
Munro sounded angry.
"Why should you demand a superior diet to the rest of us?
The Lord Director eats nothing better. As I told you, the institute is isolated."
"Yet a certain creature is sending in tons of expensive machinery."
"That's different, that is for the expansion project. Stop talking
about what you don't understand. If you and your partner want
to leave you must eat what you're given and not fight the
current."
The radio went dead. The craving in Lanark's stomach had
vanished while he surveyed the food but now it came back
harder and stronger. It mixed with the woe of Rima's weeping
and filled him with dense, concrete misery. He folded his arms
on his chest and said loudly, "We must stay like this until
things improve or deteriorate further."
Rima turned on him, shouting, "Oh, what a fool you are!"
and scratched at his face with her hands. He slipped out of
bed and said fiercely, "I'd better leave, you'll be able to eat
then! Just say the word and I'll clear out for good!"
She pulled the coverlet over her head. He put on his dressing
gown, went out through the screens and walked aimlessly up
and down the ward. At last he returned and said soberly, "Rima,
I'm sorry I yelled. I was being selfish and brutal. All the same,
you would probably eat if I wasn't here. Should I go away
for a couple of days? I promise I'll come back."
She lay below the cover, giving no sign of hearing. He slipped
in beside her and dozed.

He was wakened by having a shin kicked. Her head was
still covered but a tall figure in a black cassock sat stiffly by
the bed. Lanark sat up. It was Monsignor Noakes, who sucked
his lower lip and said, "I apologize if I intrude, but I believe
the matter is urgent."
His voice was listless and quiet and he seemed to be talking
to a brown suitcase on his knees. Lanark was wondering what
to say when Noakes went on.
"A certain person (I name no names) has certainly told you
of the very considerable powers I once wielded here. I was
director of this institute once, though not called that, for in
those days the titles were different. Never mind. The only
relic of my ancient status is the privilege of attending ecclesiasti-

cal conferences in continents where the connection between feeding and killing folk is less obvious. This has enabled me to stock a small larder of delicacies which you may find useful. I hear you are refusing our meals."

Rima sat up and leaned on Lanark's shoulder and they stared while Noakes unpacked his case and laid upon the coverlet:

a carton of cheese with red cows and green fields on the label
a big block of chocolate wrapped in gilt foil   a date-pack
a salami sausage over two feet long   a tin of ravioli
four squat black bottles of stout   a tin of sliced apricots
a small bottle of cherry brandy   a tin of condensed milk
a tin of smoked oysters   a big paper poke of dried figs
cutlery,   plates,   a tin-opener

Rima cried, "Oh how kind you are!" and began eating figs. Lanark said passionately, "You are a decent man," and opened the carton of cheese. Noakes sat watching them with a faint wistful smile. He said, "Cannibalism has always been the main human problem. When the Church was a power we tried to discourage the voracious classes by feeding everyone regularly on the blood and body of God. I won't pretend the clergy were never gluttons, but many of us did, for a while, eat only what was willingly given. Since the institute joined with the council it seems that half the continents are feeding on the other half. Man is the pie that bakes and eats himself and the recipe is separation."

Lanark said, "You're very good to us. I wish I could do something in return."

"You can. I asked you, once, and you weren't interested."

"You wanted me to warn people against the institute."

"I want you to warn everyone against the institute."

"But Monsignor Noakes, I can't, I'm too weak. When I leave the institute I'll certainly denounce it in conversation and I'll certainly vote for parties opposing it, but I won't have time to work against it. I'll be working to earn a living. I'm sorry."

Noakes said drearily, "Don't apologize. A priest must always urge people to be better than himself."

Rima stopped munching and asked, "What's wrong with the institute? I got better here, don't others?"

Lanark said abruptly, "You were cured against the instructions of my department. The institute is a murder machine."

Noakes shook his head and sighed.

"Ah, it could be easily destroyed if it was a simple murder

machine. But it is like all machines, it profits those who own it, and nowadays many sections are owned by gentle, powerless people who don't know they are cannibals and wouldn't believe if you told them. It is also amazingly tolerant of anyone it considers human, and cures more people than you realize. Even the societies who denounce it would (most of them) collapse if it vanished, for it is an important source of knowledge and energy. That is why the director of the institute is also president of the council, though two thirds of the council detest him."

"A specialist told me nobody is ever cured."

Noakes glanced furtively at Rima and said in a low voice, "That specialist is employed to do what others try to prevent. Her view of our curative functions is necessarily pessimistic."

"If all that is true, why warn folk against it at all?"

Noakes sat upright and said strongly, "Because it is mad with greed and spreading like cancer, because it is fouling the continents and destroying the handiwork of God! It is horrible for a priest to confess this, but sometimes I care less for those the institute eats than for the plants, beasts, pure air and water it destroys. I have nightmares of a world where nothing exists outside our corridors and everyone is a member of the staff. We eat worms grown in bottles. Between meals we perform Beethoven's Choral Symphony for hours on end with Ozenfant conducting, while the viewing screens show ancient colour films of naked adolescents dancing through flowers and sunlight that no longer exist."

Rima stopped eating and Lanark stared fearfully at the window. A dazzling sun rested on the horizon of a sea of clouds with an eagle speeding across it. Lanark pointed and said, "That is not? That is not a . . . ?"

Noakes wiped his brow and said, "That is not a film. What I dread has not yet happened."

He shut his suitcase and stood up, saying, "My health is poor. I embarrass you and embarrass myself. God bless you, my children."

With thumb and forefinger he sketched a cross in the air above their heads and hurried out in a posture so like someone escaping that it would have been brutal to shout thank you or goodbye. Rima said, "Do you think he's mad?"

"No. He's been too decent."

"Yes, he's sweet, but I bet *he* never cures anyone."

The nurses brought lunch and were told to take it away and not bring food again. Lanark and Rima ate a quarter of the salami, a little cheese and a few figs; then he helped her walk to the lavatory, where she bathed and he washed her back. They returned to bed and drank cherry brandy and kissed drowsily. The silver was starting to glow under her skin when he thought of something and said, "Rima, in the ignition chamber you sometimes called me Thaw."

She pondered and said finally, "Yes, I dreamed a lot of strange things in that armour. You were called Thaw, or Coulter, and we stood on a bridge at night with the moon above us and an old man watching from among some trees. You wanted to kill me. I don't remember the rest."

"I wonder how I could discover more."

"Why bother? Aren't we happy, when we don't quarrel?"

"Yes, but I'll have to work soon and I've forgotten what I'm able to do. I should have asked Noakes if there was a way of learning about life before Unthank."

"Call him on the radio."

"No, I'll call Munro. I've more confidence in Munro."

He was linked to Munro with surprising speed and said, "I called to tell you we're all right: we've our own supply of food."

"Quite so. Is that your only reason for calling?"

"No. I'm wondering about the past, you see I can't remember it. . . ."

There was crackling and a smooth voice said, "These are the archives. May I help?"

"I'm trying to find out about my past. My name is Lanark. . . ."

There was a loud whirring then the voice spoke in a quick monotone: "You reached Unthank on the 3rd day of the 10th month of the 1956th solar year of the Nazarene calendar. Calling yourself Lanark you attended the central social security office, were registered as a dragon and awarded 8 pounds, 19 shillings, and 6 pence. You lodged with Bella Fleck, 738 Ashfield Street, Unthank N. 2 for 30 days and then applied for admission to the institute. You were delivered in human form on the 75th day of the 4999th decimal year from the foundation and on the 80th became a junior assistant to Professor Ozenfant in the energy division. Your talent was vitiated by acts of aimless violence. On the 85th you interrupted a recording session, insulted the catalyst, blocked the current and shattered a viewing lens. Your relocation is scheduled for the 88th subject to confirmation by Lord Monboddo, director of the institute, moderator of the expansion project and president of the council."

There was a brief, unexpectedly noisy fanfare of trumpets.

Lanark said irritably, "I know that. I want to learn what I did *before* I came to Unthank."

"You reached Unthank through water, which is outwith the jurisdiction of the council. Do you wish to consult an oracle?"

"Of course, if that will help."

The cool white plastic of the little radio went red hot. Lanark dropped it on the coverlet, Rima screamed, he brushed it with his sleeve to the floor, it exploded with a loud bang.

The space round the bed was dim with blue smoke which hurt the eyes. Rima lay staring at him. He pulled his scorched fingers from his mouth and asked if she was all right, but the detonation had numbed his eardrums. Her reply was remote and interrupted by a distant voice saying Help help, can nobody hear me?

Rima asked who was there and a moment after the voice spoke directly into his ear. It was sexless and eager but on an odd unemphatic note, as if its words could never be printed between quotation marks.

It said I am glad you called.

Lanark shook his head very hard then said firmly, "Could you tell me about my past, please? Starting with childhood?"

The voice said I'm very keen on this kind of work but you'll have to give me a clue. Have you anything belonging to that past?

"Nothing."

No clothes, for instance?

"My clothes were dissolved on the way here."

Had you nothing insoluble in the pockets?

"There was only . . . wait a minute."

Lanark remembered Munro's taking the pistol from the drawer in his dead neighbour's locker. He opened his own drawer and looked in. Most of the space was filled with food but in a corner he found a tiny fluted cockle and a quartz pebble with grey and cream veins through it. He said, "I've found a seashell and a stone."

Hold one in each hand. Yes, I can see the way backward now. You were called Thaw. Will I start the story when you're five or fifteen or ten?

"Five, please."

Lanark lay down comfortably and the oracle, in the voice of a precocious child, said Duncan Thaw made a blue line along the top of a paper and a brown line at the bottom. He drew a giant running along the brown line with a captured princess, but as he couldn't draw the princess beautiful enough he made the giant carry a sack. The princess was inside it. His father— "Excuse me," said Lanark. "That's a very abrupt beginning. Could you not start by telling me something of the geographical and social surroundings?"

After a moment of silence the voice said in a dry academic voice The river Clyde enters the Irish Sea low down among Britain's back hair of islands and peninsula. Before widening to a firth it flows through Glasgow, the sort of industrial city where most people live nowadays but nobody imagines living. Apart from the cathedral, the university gatehouse and a gawky medieval clocktower it was almost all put up in this and the last century—

"I'm sorry to interrupt again," said Lanark, "but how do you know this? Who are you anyway?"

A voice to help you see yourself.

"But I've heard too many of these voices. None of them belonged to liars, even Sludden and Ozenfant told a lot of truth, but only the truth which suited their plans. What plans have you? What bits will you leave out?"

The voice said mournfully I've no plans at all. The only things I'll try to leave out are the repetitions, and I'll probably fail. I've grown obsessed with detail since I faded into nothing.

"I don't understand."

Then I'll tell you my history before I go on to yours. It's less amusing but the lack of detail makes it shorter, and since I once lived in your country it will tell you something about the economics of the place.

The oracle began speaking in a male, pompous elderly voice and Lanark settled comfortably to listen. Rima yawned and snuggled against his back. Five minutes later he noticed she was asleep.

PROLOGUE

From an early age I only wanted to deal with what I was sure of, and like all thinkers I soon came to distrust what could only be seen and touched. The majority believe that floors, ceilings, each other's bodies, the sun, etc. are the surest things in the world, but soon after going to school I saw that everything was untrustworthy when compared with numbers. Take the simplest kind of number, a telephone number, 339-6286 for example. It exists outside us for we find it in a directory, but we can carry it in our heads precisely as it is, for the number and our idea of it are identical. Compared with his phone number our closest friend is shifty and treacherous. He certainly exists outside us, and since we remember him he also, in a feeble way, exists in our heads, but experience shows that our idea of the man is only slightly like him. No matter how well we know him, how often we meet him, how conservative his habits, he will constantly insult our notion of him by wearing new clothes, changing his mind, growing old or sick or even dying. Moreover, my idea of a man is never the same as someone else's. Most quarrels come from conflicting ideas of a man's character but nobody fights over his phone number, and if we were content to describe each other numerically, giving height, weight, date of birth, size of family, home address, business address and (most informative of all) annual income, we would see that below the jangling opinions was no disagreement on the main realities.

On leaving school my teachers suggested a career in physics, but I rejected the idea. Science certainly controls the physical world by describing it mathematically, but I have already mentioned my distrust of physical things. They are too remote from the mind. I chose to live by those numbers which are most purely a product of the mind and therefore influence it most strongly: in a word, money. I became an accountant, and later a stockbroker. It puzzles me that people who live by owning or managing big sums of money are commonly called materialistic, for finance is the most purely intellectual, the most sheerly spiritual of activities, being concerned less with material objects than with values. Of course finance needs objects, since money is the value of objects and could no more exist without them than mind can exist without body, but the objects come second. If you doubt this, think which you would rather own: fifty thousand pounds or a piece of land valued at fifty thousand pounds. The only people likely to prefer the land are financiers who know how to increase its value by renting or reselling, so either answer proves that money is preferable to things. Perhaps you will say that in some circumstances a millionaire would give his wealth for a cup of water, but these circumstances happen more in arguments than in life, and a better indication of how folk regard money is the instinctive reverence which all but ignorant savages feel toward the rich. Many deny this, but introduce them to a really wealthy man and see how unable they are to treat him casually.

I was thirty-five when I became really wealthy, but long before then I was living in a service flat, driving a Humber, playing golf at weekends and bridge in the evenings. People who did not understand financial reports thought my life a dull one: they could not see the steep determined climb from one level of prosperity to the next, the excitement of the barely avoided loss, the triumph of the suddenly realized profit. This adventure was purely emotional, for I was physically secure. I feared the greed of the working classes and the incompetence of governments, but only because they threatened some of the numbers in my accounts; I did not feel in danger of hunger or cold. My acquaintances lived like myself in the world of numbers rather than the muddle of seeable, touchable things which used to be called reality, but they had wives, which meant that as they grew richer they had to move into bigger houses and buy new cars and reproduction antique cocktail cabinets. These things naturally occurred in their conversation, but I also heard them gloat on other objects with an enthusiasm which seemed greater the more useless the object was. "I see the daffodils are with us again," they would say, or "My God! Harrison has shaved his moustache off." Where I saw a leaf they saw a "lovely green" leaf. Where I saw a new power station they saw "technological progress" or "industry ravaging the countryside." Once at a party a couple started fighting. I was explaining something to a client and the noise made me raise my voice, but the other guests were greatly excited and began whispering and spitting adjectives: "disgraceful," "pathetic," "ludicrous," "distressing," "inconsiderate." I saw that most people had excessive funds of emotion which they got rid of by investing in objects they could not use. I had no excess emotion, my work absorbed it all, but now I know that these casual investments showed a profit. Like vain women, the objects postured before their admirers in light and colours

I was never allowed to see. They showed me just enough of
themselves to let me know they existed. And one day they
began to stop doing even that.

I was studying a document when my attention was nagged
by some difference outside the printed paper. I examined the
top of my desk. It had been polished wood with a slightly
rippled grain, but now the grain had vanished and the surface
was as blank as a sheet of plastic. I looked round the office,
which was furnished in the modern manner for I detested fussy
details. The white walls and plain carpet were as usual but
the view through the window had altered. What had been a
typical street in the business centre of an old-fashioned industrial
city, a street of elaborately carved and pillared façades, was
now bordered by blank surfaces punctured by rectangular holes.
I saw at once what was happening. Not content with showing
itself in poorer materials than it kept for others, reality was
economizing further. Where I had once seen irrelevant details
and colours I saw none at all. Stone, wood and patterned
surfaces became plain surfaces. The weaves of cloths were
indistinguishable, and all doors looked flush-panelled.

Yet I did not feel ill-treated, for there was still enough
outer reality for me to work with and in some ways I could
work better. On entering a room of employees before this I
usually had to look at several before recognizing the one I
wanted, which wasted time, especially if I felt obliged to smile
or nod at the men I noticed first. Now, when I entered a
room, everyone but the man I wanted was as faceless as an
egg, so I knew him at once. And later I only saw the man I
wanted—nobody else was visible, unless they were slacking
or wanted to speak to me, in which case they displayed enough
substance to let me deal with them. You may wonder why I
never collided with those surrounding me. Well, in my office
it was other people's business to keep out of my way, and
when driving there I noticed traffic signs and adjacent vehicles,
though pedestrians and scenery were invisible. But one day I
parked the car in the usual side street, opened the door to
walk to the office and could see neither street nor pavement,
just a clear general greyness, and leading through it to the
dim silhouette of my office (there were no other buildings) a
line of solid, pavement-coloured stepping stones, each the size
and shape of the sole of my shoe. I could only leave the car
by walking along these; each vanished as I took my weight

from it; I had spasms of vertigo and was in terror of what
would happen if I stepped *between* the stones. On reaching the
office doorstep (which was completely visible) I squatted and
moved the palm of my hand experimentally down into the
emptiness. A piece of pavement the shape of the hand appeared
underneath it. Simultaneously three clerks solidified round me,
asking if I felt unwell. I pretended, not convincingly, to tie a
shoelace.

Later I sat on a swivel chair above fathoms of emptiness,
grey emptiness all around except where, six feet to the right,
a pencil moving on its point across an angled notepad showed
where my secretary was taking down the words I dictated to
her. My right hand felt as if it rested on my knee, but I could
see nothing but the dial of the wristwatch. At half-past five a
line of carpet-coloured stepping stones appeared which released
me from the chair, but walking on them was hard for I could
no longer see my feet, and when I reached the end, instead
of the linoleum-coloured stepping stones of the lift floor I saw
nothing: the emptiness before and behind was total and
complete. I saw nothing, heard nothing and felt nothing but
the soles of my feet pressing the floor under them. Suddenly
I was too tired and angry to continue. I stepped forward and
nothing happened, except that the pressure on my feet vanished.
I neither fell nor floated. I had become bodiless in a bodiless
world. I existed as a series of thoughts amidst infinite greyness.

At first I was greatly relieved. I have never been afraid
of loneliness, and the previous days had been more of a strain
than I had let myself believe. I slept almost at once, which
means that I stopped thinking and the surrounding greyness
went black. After a while it grew light again and for the first
time in my life I was idle. Every life has blank moments when
we stand waiting for a bus or a friend and there's nothing to
do but think. In the past I had filled these moments by
calculating how an unexpected war or election would affect
the wealth entrusted to me, but I had no zest for calculation
now. Money, even imaginary money, needs the future to give
it force. Without future it is not even ink in a ledger, paper
in a purse. The future had gone with my body. There was
nothing to do but remember, and I was depressed to find that
the work which had given my life a goal and a decent order
now looked like an arithmetical brain disease, a profit-and-loss
calculation lasting years and proving nothing. My memory

was a catalogue of things I had ignored and devalued. I had enjoyed no definite friendship or love, no intense hatred or desire; my life had been stony soil in which only numbers grew, and now I could do nothing but sift the stones and hope one or two would turn out to be jewels. I was the loneliest and most impotent man in the world. I was about to turn desperate when a lovely thing appeared in the air before me.

It was a cream-coloured wall patterned with brownish-pink roses. A beam of early morning summer sunlight shone on it and on me. I was sitting in bed with the wall on one side and two chairs on the other. It seemed a very big bed, though it was an ordinary single one, and two chairs had been placed to stop my falling out. My legs were covered by a quilt on which lay a tobacco pipe with a broken stem, a small slipper and a book with bright cloth pages. I was perfectly happy and singing a song on one note: *ooloolooloo*. When tired of that I sang *dadadadada* for I had discovered the difference between *loo* and *da* and was interested in it. Later still, having tired of singing, I took the slipper and thumped the wall until my mother came. Each morning she lay in bed with a thin solemn young man on the other side of the roses. Her warmth reached me through the wall so I was never cold or lonely. I don't suppose my mother was unnaturally tall but she seemed twice the size of anyone else, and brown-haired, and regally slender above the hips. Below the hips she changed a lot, being often pregnant. I remember seeing her upper body rising behind the curve of her stomach like a giantess half-hidden by the horizon of a calm sea. I remember sitting on that curve with the back of my head between her breasts, knowing her face was somewhere above and feeling very sure of myself. I can't remember her features at all. Light or darkness came from them according to her mood, and I am certain this was more than the fantasy of a small child. I remember her sitting very still in a room of chattering strangers and steadily reducing them to whispers by the sullen silent fury she radiated. Her good moods were equally radiant and made the dullest company feel gallant and glamorous. She was never happy or depressed, she was glorious or sombre, and very attractive to modest dependable men. The men I called father were all of that kind. Apart from loving her they had no peculiarities. She must have attracted them like an extravagant vice for she was a poor housekeeper; on coming to live with a man she tried to prepare meals and keep things tidy, but the effort soon waned. I think the first house

I remember was the happiest because it had only two small rooms and my first father was not fastidious. I believe he was a garage mechanic, for there was a car engine beside my bed and some huge tyres under the recess bed in the kitchen. As I grew older my mother was less ready to come when I thumped the wall, so I learned to crawl or stagger to the bed next door and be pulled in. She would lie reading newspapers and smoking cigarettes while my father made a hill under the blankets with his knees and suddenly flattened it when I had climbed on top. Later he would rise and bring us a breakfast of tea and fried bread and eggs.

The house was in a tenement with a narrow, busy street in front and a cracked asphalt yard at the back. Behind the yard was the embankment of a canal, and on sunny days my mother dragged me up this by straps fastened to a harness round my chest and we made a nest in the long grass beside the mossy towpath. The canal was choked with rushes and leafy weeds; nobody passed by but an old man with a greyhound or boys who should have been at school. I played with the tobacco pipe and my slipper, pretending I was my mother and the pipe me and the slipper my bed, or pretending the slipper was a car with the pipe driving. She read or daydreamed as she did at home, and I know now that her power came from these dreams, for where else could an almost silent woman without abilities learn the glamour of an enslaved princess, the authority of an exiled queen? The place where we lay was level with our kitchen window, and when my father returned from work he would prepare a meal and call us in to eat it. He seemed a contented man, and I am sure the quarrels were not his fault. One night I was wakened by noise from the dark wall at my ear, my mother's voice beating like high waves over protesting mutters. The noise stopped and she entered the room and lay with me and hugged me hungrily. This happened several times, filling the nights with anticipation and delight and leaving me stupefied all day, for her thundering kisses exploded like fireworks in my ears and for long spells annihilated thought entirely. So I hardly noticed when she dressed me, and packed a suitcase, and took me away from that house. I don't remember if we travelled by train or bus, I only remember that as night fell we walked along a track between trees whose high branches crashed together in the wind, and the track brought us to a farmhouse where we lived for over a year. My sister was born soon after we arrived.

My mother's ominous attraction is shown by the fact that even in a visible state of pregnancy, with a two-year-old son, she was employed as a housekeeper by a thrifty farmer whose wife had died. For the first few weeks I was happy. We slept together in a small low-ceilinged room at the back of the house and ate by ourselves. I remember us sitting furtively in a corner of the cosy parlour while the farmer and his children dined before the fire. My mother was singing softly in my ear:

> "Wee chooky birdy, tol-lol-lol
> laid an egg on the window sol.
> The window sol
> began to crack,
> Wee chooky bird roared and grat."

Soon afterward we all began eating together and I slept in the little low room by myself. My mother spent most of the time in an upstairs room I could never visit and an old woman came each day to do the housework. I believe the old woman was first employed as temporary help while the baby was born, but she was still cleaning the house and making meals many months later, and carrying eggs and toast upstairs on a tray while the farmer, his children, and I breakfasted on porridge at the kitchen table. All my memories of the farm have eggs in them. When exploring the barnyard one day I found a great cluster of brown eggs in a clump of nettles behind an old cart. It was a surprising sight, for our eggs usually came from wooden henhouses in a nearby field. I trotted into the kitchen to tell someone. The farmer was there, and he explained that hens sometimes laid astray in an effort to get their eggs hatched instead of eaten. I led him to the eggs; he gathered them in his cap, praised me and gave me a peppermint. Whenever I felt lonely after that I would crawl into a henhouse through one of the tiny doors the hens used, steal an egg from under a sitting fowl and go to the stackyard or byre and pretend to find it under hay or among the cowcake. Then I took it to the farmer, who always patted my head and gave me a peppermint. I think he must have known where I got the other eggs, but it was friendly of him to pretend otherwise. He probably liked me.

His children did not. There was a garden of tangled grass and stunted fruit trees behind the house, and on warm summer evenings I played there, building nests in the ivy round my

bedroom window. One evening the farmer's daughter came
and said, "What do you think you're doing?"
She may have been less than twelve but she seemed a grown
woman to me. I said I was making a nest for a bird to lay an
egg in. She said, "A wee chooky birdy? That's daft. And where
did you get the straw?"
I said, "On the ground in the yard."
"Then it belongs to my daddy and you stole it so put it back
there."
Since I continued building she gripped and twisted my wrists
until I kicked her ankle, then she went off screaming she would
tell my mother and I would be sent away. I ran crying to the
henhouse field, squeezed through a hen door on hands and
knees and squatted in a corner of the grain-sprinkled floor till
it grew dark. I meant to starve to death there but I heard my
mother distantly calling, sometimes nearer and sometimes farther, and at last I felt that the misery in her breast and the
misery in mine were the same thing. I squeezed through the
door and moved among the black henhouses under a high
ceiling of stars. An owl was hooting. Suddenly I found her
and wrapped my arms round her big stomach and she was
kind to me. A few nights later I was wakened by a great uproar
and she entered the room and climbed into bed. This was less
pleasant than it had been in town, for she brought my sister
and the bed was overcrowded. The loving heat she baked me
in was still deliriously exciting, but my mind was now too strong
to be unmade by it. I was worried, because I liked the farm
in some ways. A week later the farmer took us in his ponycart
to a railway station, gave me a bag of peppermints and left
us on the platform without saying a word.

I understand my mother now. She expected splendour.
Most of us expect it sometime or other, and growing old is
mainly a way of learning to do without. My mother could never
learn to do without so she kept altering her life in the only
way she knew, by shifting to other men. She shifted when
pregnant because pregnancy made her more hopeful than usual,
or because she feared that bearing a child when living with
the father would fix her to one man forever. If this is so then
I never saw my real father. The third substitute was a bank
manager who lived with his widowed sister in a mansion in a
small fishing port. He was a gentle, dismal, kindly man; she
was an abrupt, unhappy, slightly acid woman, and my mother

(with a four-year-old son, one-year-old daughter, five-month-old embryo) charmed and dominated both of them. But three is the smallest number that can make a series, and she no longer dominated me. Perhaps she no longer wanted to. At any rate, when she moved on I was left with the bank manager. My life became calm and dependable. I went to school, was good at lessons, and every evening the manager and his sister developed my powers of concentration by playing three-handed bridge with me, for small stakes, from half-past six till bedtime. That was how I learned to dread the body and love numbers.

Having relived these memories I saw that the path from the sunlit roses to the grey void had been inevitable, yet I was not content. I was appalled at having nothing to do but remember a life like that. I wanted madness to blot out the memories with the strong tones and colours of a delusion, however monstrous. I had a romantic notion that madness was an exit from unbearable existence. But madness is like cancer or bronchitis, not everyone is capable of it, and when most of us say, "I can't bear this," we are proving we can. Death is the only dependable exit, but death depends on the body and I had rejected the body. I was condemned to a future of replaying and replaying the tedious past and past and past and past. I was in hell. Without eyes I tried to weep, without lips to scream, and with all the force of my neglected heart I cried for help.

I was answered. A sullen, determined voice—your voice— asked me to describe *his* past. My experience of void had made me able to visualize things from very slight cues, and that voice let me see you as you were. From the pebble and shell in your hands I deduced the shore where you grasped them, and from the shore I saw a path stretching back through mountains and cities to the house where you were born. You know now why I am an oracle. By describing your life I will escape from the trap of my own. From my station in nonentity everything existent, everything *not me*, looks worthwhile and splendid: even things which most folk consider commonplace or dreadful. Your past is safe with me. I can promise to be accurate.

Lanark thought for a while, then said, "Your story contains a contradiction."
Oh?

"You said money can no more exist without objects than mind without body. Yet you exist without body."

That puzzles me too. Sometimes I think my body is in the world where I abandoned it, lying in bed in some hospital, kept going by infusions into my veins. If so, I have hope of coming alive one day or dying utterly. And now I'll tell you about Duncan Thaw.

Rima stirred slightly and murmured, "Yes, go on."

The oracle began speaking. His voice sounded so far inside the head that the story seemed less narrated than remembered. It was not delayed by eating, or going to the lavatory, or sleeping: at night Lanark dreamed what he could not hear and woke with no sense of interruption. All the time they saw through the window people moving in the rooms and streets of a city, though sometimes there were glimpses of mountains and sea, and at last huge waves moving slowly at the foot of a cliff.

CHAPTER 12. The War Begins

Duncan Thaw drew a blue line along the top of a sheet of paper and a brown line along the bottom. He drew a giant with a captured princess running along the brown line, and since he couldn't draw the princess lovely enough he showed the giant holding a sack. The princess was in the sack. His father looked over his shoulder and said, "What's that you're drawing?"

Thaw said uneasily, "A miller running to the mill with a bag of corn."

"What's the blue line supposed to be?"

"The sky."

"Do you mean the horizon?"

Thaw stared dumbly at his picture.

"The horizon is the line where the sky and land seem to touch. Is it the horizon?"

"It's the sky."

"But the sky isnae a straight line, Duncan!"

"It would be if you saw it sideways."

Mr. Thaw got a golf ball and a table lamp and explained that the earth was like the ball and the sun like the lamp. Thaw was bored and puzzled. He said, "Do people fall off the sides?"

"No. They're kept on by gravity."

"What's ga . . . gavty?"

"*Grrrrrr*avity is what keeps us on the earth. Without it we would fly up into the air."

"And then we would reach the sky?"

"No. No. The sky is just the space above our heads. Without gravity we would fly up into it forever."

"But wouldn't we come to a . . . a thing on the other side?"

"There *is* no other side, Duncan. None at all."

Thaw leaned over his drawing and drew a blue crayon along the line of the sky, pressing hard. He dreamed that night of flying up through empty air till he reached a flat blue cardboard sky. He rested against it like a balloon against a ceiling until worried by the thought of what was on the other side; then he broke a hole and rose through more empty air till he grew afraid of floating forever. Then he came to another cardboard sky and rested there till worried by the thought of the other side. And so on.

Thaw lived in the middle storey of a corporation tenement that was red sandstone in front and brick behind. The tenement backs enclosed a grassy area divided into greens by spiked railings, and each green had a midden. Gangs of midden-rakers from Blackhill crossed the canal to steal from the middens. He was told that Blackhill people were Catholics with beasts in their hair. One day two men came to the back greens with a machine that squirted blue flame and clouds of sparks. They cut the spikes from the railings with the flame, put them in a bag and took them away to use in the war. Mrs. Gilchrist downstairs said angrily, "Now even the youngest of these Blackhill kids will be able to rake our middens." Other workmen build air-raid shelters in the back greens and a very big one in the school playground, and if Thaw heard the air-raid warning on the way to school he must run to the nearest shelter. Going up to school by the steep back lane one morning he heard the siren wailing in the blue sky. He was almost at school but turned and ran home to where his mother waited in the back-green shelter with the neighbours. At night dark green blinds were pulled down over the windows. Then Mr. Thaw put on an armband and steel hat and went into the street to search for houses showing illegal chinks of light.

Someone told Mrs. Thaw that the former tenants of her flat had killed themselves by putting their heads in the oven and turning the gas on. She wrote at once to the corporation asking that her gas cooker be changed for an electric one, but as Mr. Thaw would still need food when he returned from work she baked him a shepherd's pie, but with her lips more tightly pursed than usual.

Her son always refused shepherd's pie or any other food whose appearance disgusted him: spongy white tripe, soft penis-like sausages, stuffed sheep's hearts with their valves and little arteries. When one of these came before him he poked it uncertainly with his fork and said, "I don't want it."

"Why not?"

"It looks queer."

"But you havnae tasted it! Taste just a wee bit. For my sake."

"No."

"Children in China are starving for food like that."

"Send it to them."

After more discussion his mother would say in a high-pitched voice, "You'll sit at this table till you eat every bit" or "Just you wait till I tell your father about this, my dear." Then he would put a piece of food in his mouth, gulp without tasting and vomit it back onto the plate. After that he would be shut in the back bedroom. Sometimes his mother came to the door and said, "Will you not eat just a wee bit of it? For my sake?" then Thaw, feeling cruel, shouted "No!" and went to the window and looked down into the back green. He would see friends playing there, or the midden-rakers, or neighbours hanging out washing, and feel so lonely and magnificent that he considered opening the window and jumping out. It was a bitter glee to imagine his corpse thudding to the ground among them. At last, with terror, he would hear his father coming *clomp-clomp* upstairs, carrying his bicycle. Usually Thaw ran to meet him. Now he heard his mother open the door, the mutter of voices in conspiracy, then footsteps coming to the bedroom and his mother whispering, "Don't hurt him too much."

Mr. Thaw would enter with a grim look and say, "Duncan! You've behaved badly to your mother again. She goes to the bother and expense of making a good dinner and ye won't eat it. Aren't ye ashamed of yourself?"

Thaw would hang his head.

"I want you to apologize to her."

"Don't know what 'polgize means."

"Tell her you're sorry and you'll eat what you're given."

Then Thaw would snarl "No, I won't!" and be thrashed. During the thrashing he screamed a lot and afterward stamped, yelled, tore his hair and banged his head against the wall until his parents grew frightened and Mr. Thaw shouted, "Stop that or I'll draw my hand off yer jaw!"

Then Thaw beat his own face with his fists, screaming, "Like this like this like *this?*"

It was hard to silence him without undoing the justice of the punishment. On the advice of a neighbour they one day undressed the furiously kicking boy, filled a bath with cold water

and plunged him in. The sudden chilling scald destroyed all
his protest, and this treatment was used on later occasions with
equal success. Shivering slightly he would be dried with soft
towels before the living-room fire, then put to bed with his
doll. Before sleep came he lay stunned and emotionless while
his mother tucked him in. Sometimes he considered withhold-
ing the goodnight kiss but could never quite manage it.

When he had been punished for not eating a particular
food he was not given that food again but a boiled egg instead.
Yet after hearing how the former tenants had misused their
oven he looked very thoughtfully at the shepherd's pie when
it was brought to table that evening. At length he pointed
and said, "Can I have some?"
Mrs. Thaw looked at her husband then took her spoon and
plonked a dollop onto Thaw's plate. He stared at the mushy
potato with particles of carrot, cabbage and mince in it and
wondered if brains really looked like that. Fearfully he put
some in his mouth and churned it with his tongue. It tasted
good so he ate what was on the plate and asked for more.
When the meal was over his mother said, "There. You like
it. Aren't ye ashamed of kicking up all that din about nothing?"
"Can I go down to the back green?"
"All right, but come when I call you, it's getting late."
He hurried through the lobby, banged the front door behind
him and ran downstairs, the weight of food in his stomach
making him feel excited and powerful. In the warm evening
sunlight he put his brow to the grass and somersaulted down
a green slope till he fell flat from dizziness and lay with the
tenements and blue sky spinning and tilting round and round
his head. He keeked between the stems of sorrel and daisies
at the midden, a three-sided brick shed where bins were kept.
The sound of voices came indistinctly through the grass blades
to his ears, and the scratchings of a steel-tipped boot on an
iron railing, and the rumble of a bin being shifted. He sat
up.

Two boys slightly older than himself were bent over the
bins and throwing out worn clothes, empty bottles, some pram
wheels and a doormat, while a big boy of ten or eleven put
them in a sack. One of the smaller boys found a hat with a
bird's wing on it. Mimicking the strut of a proud woman he
put it on and said, "Look at me, Boab, am I no' the big cheese?

The older boy said, "Stop that. You'll get the auld wife after us."

He dumped the sack over the railings into the next green and the three of them climbed over to it. Thaw followed by squeezing between the railings then lay down again on the grass. He heard them whisper together and the big boy said, "Never mind about him."

He realized he was frightening them and followed more boldly into the next green, though keeping a distance. He was slightly appalled when the big boy turned and said, "What d'ye want, ye wee bugger?"

Thaw said, "I'm coming with you."

His scalp tightened, his heart knocked on his ribs but this boy had never eaten what he had eaten. The boy with the hat said, "Thump him, Boab!"

Boab said, "Why d'ye want tae come with us?"

"Because."

"Because of what?"

"Nothing. Just because."

"Ye'll have tae carry things if ye come with us. Will ye collect the books?"

"Aye."

"All right then."

After this all magazines and comic papers were left to Thaw, who soon learned which were worth picking from the garbage. They visited every back green in the block, leaving some refuse scattered across each, and were chased from the last by a woman who followed them through her close shouting breathless promises to call the police.

A girl of twelve waited in the street outside holding the handle of a pram with three wheels. She pointed at Thaw and said, "Where did ye pick that up?"

Boab said, "Never mind him," and loaded his sack onto the pram which bulged with rubbish already. The two wee boys harnessed themselves to it with strings tied to the front axle, then with Boab and the girl pushing and Thaw running alongside they went quickly down the street. They passed semi-detached villas with privet hedges, a small power station humming behind aspen trees, allotments with beds of lettuce like green roses and glasshouses glittering in the late sunshine. They went through a gate in a rusty fence and climbed a blue cinder path through a jungle of nettles. The air was thick with vegetable stink, the wee boys groaned with the effort of pulling, a low thundering vibrated the ground under them and at the top they reached the brink of a deep ravine. One end was shut by double doors of huge rotting timber. A glossy arch of water slipped over this, crashed to the bottom, then poured along the ravine and flowed through open doors at the end into a small loch fringed with reeds and paved with lily leaves. Thaw knew this must be the canal, a dangerous forbidden place where children were drowned. He followed his companions uphill among structures where water spilled over ledges, trickled through cracks, or lay in rushy half-stagnant ponds with swans paddling on clear spaces in the middle. They crossed a plank bridge under the shadow of so high a waterfall that the din of it was deafening. They crossed stony ground and then another bridge and heard dimly a distant bugle blown in a caricature of a battle call.

"Peely Wally," said Boab.

They went quickly down a cinder path, through a gate and into a street.

Thaw found it a foreign kind of street. The tenements were faced with grey stone instead of red, landing windows had broken glass in them, or no glass, or even no window frames, being oblong holes half bricked up to stop children falling out. The men who had taken the spikes away to the war from Riddrie (where Thaw lived) had removed all the railings here, and the spaces between pavement and tenement (neat gardens in Riddrie) were spaces of flattened earth where children too young to walk scratched the ground with bent spoons or floated bits of wood in puddles left from last week's rain. In the middle of the street a pale lipless smiling young man sat on a donkey cart with a bugle on his knees. His cart held boxes of coloured toys which could be bought with rags, bottles and jam jars, and already a crowd of children surrounded him wearing cardboard sombreros, whooping on whistles or waving bright flags and windmills. When he noticed Boab and the pram he shouted, "Make way! Make way! Let the man through!"

While these two haggled Thaw and the smaller boys stood round the donkey and admired the mildness of its face, the hardness of its forehead and the white hair inside the trumpet-shaped ears. Thaw argued about the donkey's age with the boy wearing the hat.

"I bet ye a pound he's older than you onyway," said the boy.
"And I bet ye a pound he isnae."
"Why d'ye think he isnae?"
"Why d'ye think he is?"
"Peely!" shouted the boy. "How old is your donkey?"
"A hundred!" shouted Peely.
"There ye are—I wiz right!" said the boy. "Now you've tae give me a pound." He held his hand out, saying, "Come on now. Pay up!"
The children who had heard the argument whispered and giggled, and some beckoned friends who were standing at a distance. Thaw, frightened, said, "I havenae a pound."
"But ye promised! Didn't he promise?"
"Aye, he promised," said several voices. "He bet a pound."
"He's got to pay."
"I don't believe the donkey is a hundred," said Thaw.
"Ye think ye're awful clever, don't ye?" a thin girl shouted venomously and sarcastic voices cried, "Oh, Mammy, Mammy, I'm an awful smart wee boy."
"Why does the smart wee boy no' believe the donkey's a hundred?"
"Because I read it in an ENCYCLOPAEDIA," said Thaw, for though he was still unable to read he had once pleased his parents by saying encyclopaedia without being specially taught and the word had peculiar qualities for him. Pronounced in the service of his lie it had an immediate effect. Someone at the edge of the crowd jumped into the air, clapped hands above head and cried, "Oh, the big word! The big word!" and the mob exploded into laughter and mockery. Waving flags and blowing whistles, they raved and stamped around the frightened stone-still Thaw until his lips trembled and a drop of water spilled from his left eye.
"Look!" they yelled. "He's greeting!" "Crybaby! Crybaby!" "Cowardy custard, stick yer nose in the mustard!" "Riddrie pup with yer tail tied up!" "Awa' hame and tell yer mammy!" Thaw was blinded by red rage and screamed, "Buggers! Ye damned buggers!" and started running down the darkening street. He heard the clattering feet of pursuers and Peely Wally laugh like a cock-crow and Boab roar, "Let him go! Leave him alone!"
He turned a corner and ran down a street past staring children and men who paid no attention, through a small park with a pond and the sound of splashing water, then down a rutted lane, going slower because they weren't following now, with

longer intervals between his sobs. He sat down on a chunk of masonry and swallowed air until his heart beat more calmly.

There was empty ground in front of him with the shadows of tenements stretching a long way across it. Colours had become distinctions of grey and close-mouths' black rectangles in tenement walls. The sky was covered with blue-grey cloud, but currents of wind had opened channels through this and he could see through the channels into a green sunset air above. Down the broadest of these flew five swans on their way to a lower stretch of the canal or to a pond in the city parks.

Thaw started back the way he had come, sniffing and wiping tears from his nose. In the small dim park only the splashing of water was distinct. It was night in the streets. He was glad to see no children or grown people or any of the adolescent groups who usually gather by street corners at nightfall. Black lampposts stood at wide intervals on either kerb. The tenement windows were black like holes in a face. Twice he saw wardens cross the end of some street ahead, silent helmeted men examining blinded windows for illegal chinks of light. The dark, similar streets seemed endlessly to open out of each other until he despaired of getting home and sat on the kerb with his face in his hands and girned aloud. He fell into a dwam in which he felt only the hard kerb under his backside and awoke suddenly with a hushing sound in his ears. For a second this seemed like his mother singing to him then he recognized the noise of waterfalls. The sky had cleared and a startling moon had risen. Though not full there was enough of it to light the canal embankment across the road, and the gate, and the cinder path. He went gladly and fearfully to the gate and climbed the path with the hushing growing in his ears to the full thunder of the falling stream. Several trembling stars were reflected in the dark water below.

As he stepped off the bridge Thaw seemed to hear the moon yell at him. It was the siren. Its ululations came eerily across the rooftops to menace him, the only life. He ran down the path between the nettles and through the gate and past the dark allotments. The siren swooned into silence and a little later (Thaw had never heard this before) there was a dull iron noise, *gron-gron-gron-gron,* and dark shapes passed above him. Later there were abrupt thuddings as if giant fists were battering a metal ceiling over the city. Beams of light widened, narrowed and groped above the rooftops, and between two tenements he saw the horizon lit orange and red with irregular flashing lights. Black flies seemed to be circling in the glow. Beyond the power station he ran his head into the stomach of a warden running the other way. "Duncan!" shouted the man.

Thaw was picked into the air and shaken.

"Where have ye been? Where have ye been? Where have ye been?" shouted the man senselessly, and Thaw, full of love and gratitude, shouted, "Daddy!"

Mr. Thaw tucked his son under one arm and ran back home. Between the jolts of his father's strides Thaw heard the iron noise again. They went up steps into the close-mouth and Thaw was put down. They stood together in the dark, breathing hard; then Mr. Thaw said in a weak voice Thaw hardly recognized, "I suppose you know the worry you've given your mother and me?"

There was a shriek and bang and pieces of dirt hit Thaw on the cheek.

From the living-room window next morning he saw a hole in the pavement across the street. The blast had shaken soot down the chimney onto the living-room floor, and Mrs. Thaw cleaned it up, stopping sometimes to talk with neighbours who called to discuss the raid. They agreed that it might have been worse, but Thaw was very uneasy. His adventure with the midden-rakers was a horrider crime than not eating dinner so he expected punishment on an unusually large scale. After closely watching his mother that day—noticing the way she hummed to herself when dusting, her small thoughtful pauses in the middle of work, her way of scolding when he was stupid during a lesson on clock reading—he became sure that punishment was not in her mind, and this worried him. He feared pain, but deserved to be hurt, and was not going to be hurt. He had not returned to exactly the same house.

CHAPTER 13. A Hostel

The house was changing. Obscure urgency filled it and in bed at night he heard rumours of preparation and debate. Coming home from a friend's back green he stuck with his head on one side of the railings and his body on the other. Mr. and Mrs. Thaw released him by greasing his ears with butter and pulling a leg each, laughing all the time. When free he flung himself howling on the grass but they tickled his armpits and sang "Stop Yer Ticklin', Jock" until he couldn't help laughing. Then one day they all came out onto the landing and the house was locked behind them. His father and mother carried his sister Ruth and some luggage; Thaw had a gas mask in a cardboard box hanging from his shoulder by a string loop; they all went up to his school by the sunlit bird-twittering back lanes. Murmuring groups of mothers stood in the playground with small children at their side. The fathers spoke in noisier groups and older children played halfheartedly between.

Thaw felt bored and walked to the railings. He was sure he was going on holiday and that holidays meant the sea. From the edge of the playground's high platform he looked across the canal and the Blackhill tenements to remote hills with a dip in the middle. Looking the opposite way he saw a wide valley of roofs and smokestacks with more hills beyond. These hills were nearer and greener and so distinct that along a gently curved summit a line of treetops joined like a hedge and he saw the sky between the trunks underneath. It struck him that the sea was behind these hills; if he stood among the trees he would look down on a grey sea sparkling with waves. His mother shouted his name and he strolled toward her slowly, pretending he had not heard but was returning anyway. She adjusted the string of the gas mask which had got across his coat collar and was cutting the side of his neck, then made the coat sit better on his shoulders with tugs and pats which shook his head from side to side. He said, "Is the sea behind there?"

"Behind where?"

"Behind where those trees are."

"Who told you that? Those are the Cathkin Braes. There's nothing behind there but farms and fields. And England, eventually."

The sparkling grey sea was too vivid for him to disbelieve. It fought in his head with a picture of farms and fields until it seemed to be flooding them. He pointed to the hills behind Blackhill and asked, "Is the sea over there?"

"No, but there's Loch Lomond and the highlands."

Mrs. Thaw stopped tidying him, lifted Ruth on her left arm and stared straight-backed at the Cathkin Braes. She said thoughtfully, "When I was a girl those trees reminded me of a caravan on the skyline."

"What's a caravan?"

"A procession of camels. In Arabia."

"What's a procession?"

Red single-decker buses suddenly came into the playground and everyone but the fathers climbed on board. Mr. and Mrs. Thaw said goodbye through the window and after a long wait the buses drove out of the playground and down to the Cumbernauld Road.

A dim broken time followed when Thaw and his mother, with Ruth on her lap, sat in buses at night hurling through unseen country. The buses were always badly lit with windows blinded by blue-black oilcloth so that nobody saw out. There must have been many such journeys, but later he remembered a single night journey lasting many months in a cabin full of hungry tired people, though the movement of the bus was interrupted by confused adventures in dim places: a wooden church hall, a room over a tailor's shop, a stone-floored kitchen with beetles crawling over it. He slept in strange beds where breathing became difficult and he woke up screaming he was dead. Sores appeared on his scrotum and the bus brought them to the Royal Infirmary where old professors looked between his legs and applied brown ointment which stung the sores and smelled of tar. The bus was always crowded, Ruth crying, his mother weary and Thaw bored, though once a drunk man stood up and embarrassed everyone by trying to get them to sing. Then one evening the bus stopped and they got out and met his father, who led them onto the deck of a ship. They stood in the dusk near the funnel which gave out comfortable heat. The air was cold between slate-dark clouds and a heaving slate-blue sea. A reef lay among the lapping water like a long black log, and at one end an iron tripod upheld a lit yellow globe. The ship moved out to sea.

They came to live in a bungalow among low concrete buildings called the hostel. This stood between sea and moorland. Munition workers slept there and it held a canteen, cinema and hospital and had a high wire fence all round with gates that were locked at night. Each morning Thaw and Ruth were taken in a car along the coast road to the village school. This had two classrooms and a kitchen where a wife from the village made flavourless meals. A headmaster called Macrae taught the older pupils and a woman called Ingram the small ones. The pupils were all children of crofters excepting some evacuees from Glasgow who lodged in farms on the moors.

On his first day in the new school the other boys rushed to be Thaw's neighbour in the queue to go out to play, and in the playfield they gathered round to ask where he came from and what his father did. Thaw answered truthfully at first but later told lies to keep their interest. He said he spoke several languages and when asked to prove this could only say that "wee" was French for "yes." Most of the group went away after that, and next day in the playfield he had an audience of two. To stop it getting smaller he offered to show them round the hostel, then other boys approached him in threes and fours and asked if they could come too. Instead of going home that night in the car with Ruth, Thaw trudged along the coast road at the head of a mob of thirty or forty who talked and joked with each other and, apart from an occasional question, totally ignored him. He was not sorry about this. He wanted to seem mysterious to these boys, someone ageless with strange powers, but his feet were sore, he was late for tea and afraid he would be blamed for arriving with so many friends. He was right. The hostel gateman refused to allow the other boys in. They had walked two miles and missed their

tea to accompany him and though he walked back with them
a little way apologizing they were still very angry and the evacuees began to throw stones. He ran back to the hostel where
he was given a cold meal and a row for "showing off."

Next morning he pretended to be ill but unluckily the
asthma and the disease between his legs weren't troublesome
and he had to go to school. Nobody spoke to him there and
at playtime he kept nervously to the field's quietest corner.
On queuing to re-enter the classroom he stood beside an evacuee called Coulter who pushed him in the side. Thaw pushed
back. Coulter punched him in the side, Thaw punched back
and Coulter muttered, "A'll see you after school."
Thaw said, "A've to go straight home after school tonight;
my dad said so."
"Right. I'll see ye the morra."
At home that night he refused to eat anything. He said, "I've
a pain."
"You don't *look* sick," said Mrs. Thaw. "Where *is* the pain?"
"All over."
"What kind of pain is it?"
"I don't know, but I'm not going to school tomorrow."
Mrs. Thaw said to her husband, "You deal with this, Duncan,
it's beyond me."
Mr. Thaw took his son into the bedroom and said, "Duncan,
there's something you haven't told us."
Thaw started crying and said what the matter was. His father
held him to his chest and asked, "Is he bigger than you?"
"Yes." (This was untrue.)
"Much bigger?"
"No," said Thaw after a fight with his conscience.
"Do you want me to ask Mr. Macrae to tell the other pupils
not to hit you?"
"No," said Thaw, who only wanted not to go to school.
"I knew you would say that, Duncan. Duncan, you'll have to
fight this boy. If ye start running away now you'll never learn
to face up to life. I'll teach ye how to fight—it's easy—all ye
have to do is use your left hand to protect your face. . . ."
Mr. Thaw talked like this until Thaw's head was full of images
of defeating Coulter. He spent that evening practising for the
fight. First he sparred with his father, but the opposition of a
real human being left no scope for fantasy, so he practised
on a cushion and went confidently to bed after a good supper.

He was less confident next morning and ate breakfast very quietly. Mrs. Thaw kissed him goodbye and said, "Don't worry. *You*'ll knock his block off."
She waved encouragingly as the car drove away.

That morning Thaw stood in a lonely corner of the playfield and waited fearfully for the approach of Coulter, who was playing football with friends. Rain started falling and gradually the pupils collected in a shelter at the end of the building. Thaw was last to enter. In an agony of dread he walked up to Coulter, stuck his tongue out at him and struck him on the shoulder. At once they started fighting as unskilfully as small boys always fight, with flailing arms and a tendency to kick each other's ankles; then they grappled and fell. Thaw was beneath but Coulter's nose flattened on his brow, the resulting blood smeared both equally, each thought it his own and, appalled by the suspected wound, rolled apart and stood up. After that, in spite of encouragement from their allies (Thaw was surprised to find a cheering mob of allies at his back) they were content to stand swearing at each other until Miss Ingram came up and took them to the headmaster. Mr. Macrae was a stout pig-coloured man. He said, "Right. What's the cause of all this?"
Thaw started talking rapidly, his explanation punctuated by gulps and stutters, and only stopped when he found himself starting to sob. Coulter said nothing. Mr. Macrae took a leather tawse from his desk and said, "Hold your hands out."
Each held his hand out and got a hellish stinging wallop on it. Mr. Macrae said, "Again!" "Again!" and "Again!" Then he said, "If I hear of you two fighting another time you'll get the same treatment but more of it, a lot more of it. Go to your class."
Each bent his head to hide his distorted face and went to the next room sucking a crippled hand. Miss Ingram didn't ask them to do anything for the rest of the morning.

After the fight Thaw found playtimes more boring than frightening. He would stand in the lonely corner of the field with a boy called McLusky who didn't play with the other boys because he was feebleminded. Thaw told long stories with himself as hero and McLusky helped him mime the actable bits. The vivid part of his life became imaginary. Thaw and his sister slept in adjacent rooms, and at night he told her stories through the doorway between, stories with the adventures and landscapes of books he had read by day. Sometimes he stopped and asked, "Are you asleep yet? Will I go on?" and Ruth answered, "No, Duncan, please go on," but at last she would fall asleep. Next night she would say, "Go on with the story, Duncan."

"All right. Where did I stop last night?"

"They . . . they had landed on Venus."

"No, no. They had left Venus and gone to Mercury."

"I . . . don't remember that, Duncan."

"Of course you don't. Ye fell asleep. Well, I'm not going to tell *you* stories if you don't want to listen."

"But I couldnae help falling asleep, Duncan."

"Then why didn't ye tell me you were falling asleep instead of letting me go on talking to myself?"

After bullying her some more he would continue the story, for he spent a lot of time each day preparing it.

He bullied Ruth in other ways. She was forbidden to stott her ball indoors. He saw her do it once, and terrified her for weeks by threatening to tell their mother. One day Mrs. Thaw accused her children of stealing sugar from the livingroom sideboard. Both denied it. Later Ruth told him, "you stole that sugar."

He said "yes. But if you tell Mum I said so I'll call you a liar and she won't know who to believe." Ruth at once told their mother, Thaw called Ruth a liar, and Mrs. Thaw didn't know who to believe.

During the first few weeks at school he had looked carefully among the girls for one to adventure with in his imagination, but they were all too obviously the same vulgar clay as himself. For almost a year he resigned himself to loving Miss Ingram, who was moderately attractive and whose authority gave her a sort of grandeur. Then one day when visiting the village store he saw a placard in the window advertising Amazon Adhesive Shoe Soles. It showed a blond girl in brief Greek armour with spear and shield and a helmet on her head. Above her were the words **BEAUTY PLUS STAMINA,** and her face had a plaintive loveliness which made Miss Ingram seem commonplace. During the dinner intervals Thaw walked to the store and looked at the girl for the length of time it took to count ten. He knew that by looking too hard and often even she might come to seem commonplace.

CHAPTER 14. Ben Rua

Mr. Thaw wanted a keener intimacy with his son and liked open-air activities. There were fine mountains near the hostel, the nearest of them, Ben Rua, less than sixteen hundred feet high; he decided to take Thaw on some easy excursions and bought him stout climbing boots. Unluckily Thaw wanted to wear sandals.

"I like to move my toes," he said.

"What are ye blethering about?"

"I don't like shutting my feet in these hard solid leather cases. It makes them feel dead. I can't bend my ankles."

"But you arenae supposed to bend your ankles! It's the easiest thing in the world to break an ankle if you slip in an awkward place. These boots are made especially to give the ankle support—once a single nail gets a grip it can uphold your ankle, your leg, your whole body even."

"What I lose in firmness I'll make up in quickness."

"I see. I see. For a century mountaineers have gone up the Alps and Himalayas and Grampians in nailed climbing boots. You might think they knew about climbing. Oh, no, Duncan Thaw knows better. They should have worn *sandals.*"

"What's wrong for them might be right for me."

"My God!" cried Mr. Thaw. "What's this I've brought into the world? What did I do to deserve this? If we could only live by our own experience we would have no science, no civilization, no progress! Man has advanced by his capacity to learn from others, and these boots cost me four pounds eight."

"There would be no science and civilization and all that if everybody did things the way everybody else does," said Thaw. The discussion continued until Mr. Thaw lost his temper and Thaw had hysterics and was given a cold bath. The climbing boots lay in a cupboard until Ruth was old enough to use them. Meanwhile Thaw was not taken climbing by his father.

One summer day Thaw walked briskly along the coast road until the hostel was hidden by a green headland. It was a sunny afternoon. A few clouds lay about the sky like shirts scattered on a blue floor. He left the road and ran down a slope toward the sea, his feet crashing almost to the ankles among pebbles and shells. He felt confident and resolute, for he had been reading a book called *The Young Naturalist* and meant to make notes of anything interesting. The shingle gave onto shelving rocks with boulders and pools among them. He squatted by a pool the size of a soup plate and peered in, frowning. Below the crystalline water lay three pebbles, a small anemone the colour of raw liver, a wisp of green weed and several winkles. The winkles were olive and dull purple, and he thought he saw a tendency for the pale ones to be at the edges of the pool and the dark ones in the middle. Taking out a notebook and pencil he drew a map on the blank first page, showing the position of the winkles; then he wrote the date on the opposite page and added after some thought the letters:

SELKNIW ELPRUP NI ECIDRAWOC

for he wished to hide his discoveries under a code until he was ready to publish. Then he pocketed the notebook and strolled onto a beach of smooth white sand lapped by the sparkling sea. Tired of being a naturalist he found a stick of driftwood and began engraving the plans of a castle on the firm surface. It was a very elaborate castle full of secret entrances, dungeons and torture chambers.

Someone behind him said, "What's that supposed to be?" Thaw turned and saw Coulter. He gripped the stick tightly and muttered, "It's some plans."
Coulter walked round the plans saying, "What are they plans of?"
"Oh, they're just plans."
"Well, mibby you're wise no' to tell me what they're plans of. For all you know I'm mibby a German spy."
"*You* couldnae be a German spy."
"Yes I could."
"You're just a boy!"
"But mibby the Germans have a secret chemical that stops

folk growing so they look like boys though they're mibby twenty or thirty, and mibby they've landed me here off a submarine and I'm just pretending to be an evacuee but all the time I'm spying on the hostel your dad is managing."

Thaw stared at Coulter who stood with feet apart and hands in trouser pockets and stared back. Thaw said, *"Are* you a German spy?"

"Yes," said Coulter.

His face was so expressionless that Thaw became convinced that he was a German spy. At the same time, without noticing it, he had stopped being afraid of Coulter. He said, "Well I'm a British spy."

"You are not."

"I am so."

"Prove it."

"Prove you're a German spy."

"I don't want to. If I did you could get me arrested and hung."

Thaw could think of no answer to this. He was wondering how to make Coulter think he was a British spy when Coulter said, "Do you come from Glasgow?"

"Yes!"

"So do I."

"What bit of Glasgow?"

"Garngad. What bit do you come from?"

"Riddrie."

"Hm! Riddrie is quite near Garngad. They're both on the canal."

Coulter looked at the plans again and said, "Is it a plan of a den?"

"Well . . . a sort of den."

"I know some smashing dens."

"So do I!" said Thaw eagerly. "I've got a den inside a—"

"I've got a den that's a real secret cave!" said Coulter triumphantly.

Thaw was impressed. After a suitable silence he said, *"My* den is inside a bush. It looks like an ordinary bush outside but it's all hollow inside and it stands beside this road in the hostel so you can sit in it and watch these daft munition girls passing and they don't know you're there. The bother is"—truth made him reluctantly add—"it doesnae keep out the rain."

"That's the bother with dens," said Coulter. "Either they're secret and let in rain or they don't let in rain and arenae secret. My cave keeps the rain out fine, but last time I went there the floor was all covered with dirty straw. I think the tinkers had been using it. But I could make a great den if I had somebody to help me."

"How?"

"Will ye promise no' to tell anyone?"

"Aye, sure."

"It's up a place near the hotel."

They crossed the beach to the road and walked along it chatting amiably.

Before reaching the village they turned up a track which ascended to the tall iron gates and yew trees of the Kinlochrua Hotel. Past this the track became a path half covered by bracken. It led them precariously higher and higher between boulders and bushes until Coulter halted and said triumphantly, "There!"

They were on the lip of a gully sloping down to the waters of the burn. It had been used as a rubbish dump and was half filled by an avalanche of tins, broken crockery, cinders and decaying cloth. Thaw looked at it with pleasure and said, "Aye, there's plenty of stuff here for a den."

"Let's get out the big cans first," said Coulter.

They waded among the rubbish, collecting materials, then carried them to a flat place beneath two big rocks. They used petrol drums for the walls of the den and roofed it with linoleum laid across wooden spars. They were finishing by stuffing odd holes with sacking when Thaw heard a footstep and looked around. A shepherd was passing downhill waist deep in the bracken to their left. "Good afternoon, lads," he said.

Thaw began working more and more slowly. Until then he had been chatting enthusiastically, now he became silent and answered questions as shortly as possible. At last Coulter threw down a piece of pipe he had been trying to make into a chimney and said, "What's wrong with ye?"

"This den's no use. It's too near the path. Everybody can see it. It's not secret at all."

Coulter glared at Thaw then gripped the linoleum roof, wrenched it off and threw it down the gully.

"What are ye doing?" shouted Thaw.

"It's no use! Ye said so yourself! I'm taking it down!"

Coulter pushed down the walls and kicked the drums into the gulley. Thaw watched sullenly until nothing was left but a few spars of wood and a distant clanking sound. He said, "Ye neednae have done that. We might have camouflaged it with branches and stuff and hidden it that way."

Coulter shoved through the bracken to the path and started walking down it. After a few yards he turned and shouted, "Ye bugger! Ye damned bugger!"

"Ye bloody damned bugger!" shouted Thaw.

"Ye *fuckin'* bloody damned bugger!" yelled Coulter, and disappeared from sight among the trees. Brooding blackly on the den, which had been a good one, Thaw walked up the track in the opposite direction.

The glen had taken all the streams of the moor into its gorge where they tumbled and clattered among boulders, leaves and the songs of blackbirds, but Thaw paid little attention to the surroundings. His thoughts took on a pleasant flavour. Expressions of grimness, mockery and excitement crossed his face and sometimes he waved an arm imperiously. Once he said with a bleak smile, "I'm sorry, madam, but you fail to understand your position. You are my prisoner."

It was a while before he noticed he had left the glen behind but there was an uneasiness in the quiet of the open moor which daydreams couldn't shut out. The main sound was the water flowing clear and brown, golden brown where the sun caught it, along runnels which could have been bridged by a hand. In places the heather had knotted its twigs and roots across these and it was possible to follow their course by a melodious gurgling under the purple-green carpet which sloped and dipped upward to the humps and boulders of Ben Rua. Thaw suddenly saw himself as if from the sky, a small figure starting across the moor like a louse up a quilt. He stood still and gazed at the ben. On the grey-green tip of the summit he seemed just able to see a figure, a vertical white speck that moved and gestured, though the movement might have been caused by a flickering of warm air between the mountaintop and his eye. To Thaw the movement suggested a woman in a white dress waving and beckoning. He could even imagine her face: it was the face of the girl in the adhesive shoe-sole advertisement. This remote beckoning woman struck him with the force of a belief, though it was not quite a belief. He did not decide to climb the mountain, he thought, 'I'll follow this bit of stream,' or, 'I'll go to the rock over there.' And he would reach the top of a slope to find a higher one beyond and the ben looking nearer each time. Sometimes he climbed on a boulder and stood for minutes listening to small noises which might have been the distant scrape of a sheep's hoof on a stone, or the scutter of a rabbit's paw, or the fluttering of blood in his eardrum. From these pedestals the summit of Rua sometimes looked vacant, but later, with a pang, he would see on it the flickering white point. He advanced onto the mountain slope and the summit passed out of sight.

The lower slopes were mostly widths of granite tilted at the angle of the mountainside, level with the heather and cracked like the pavements of a ruined city. Higher up the heather gave way to fine turf, where grasshoppers chirped and flowerets grew with stalks less than an inch high and blossoms hardly bigger than pinheads. Becoming thirsty he found a shallow pool collected from last week's rain in the hollow of a rock. Stopping to drink he felt rough granite under his lips and warm sour water on the tongue. The mountain steepened into nearly vertical blocks with ledges of turf between. For half an hour he used his hands as much as his feet, squirming and wriggling up crooked funnels, pulling himself over small precipices, then lying flat on his back on a ledge under the shadow of the summit to let the sweat dry out of his damp shirt. At this height he heard noises that had been shut off from him on the moor: a barking dog on one of the farms, a door slamming in the hostel, a lark above a field behind the village, children shouting on the shore and the murmuring sea. He contained two equal sorts of knowledge: the warm lazy knowledge that above on the mountain a blond girl in a white dress waited for him, shy and eager; and the cooler knowledge that this was unlikely and the good of climbing was the exercise and view from the top. There was no conflict between those knowledges, his mind passed easily from one to the other, but when he stood up to begin the last of the climb the thought of the girl was stronger.

He was at the foot of a granite cliff about four times his height with a ledge sloping up it made by a lower stratum projecting beyond the one above. As he climbed his fear of height made the excitement keener. The ledge was decayed and gravelly, each step sent a shower of little lumps rattling and bouncing down into the sky beyond the edge. Gradually it narrowed to a few inches. Thaw pressed his chest against the granite, stood on tiptoe and, reaching up, brought his fingertips within an inch of the top. "Hell, hell, hell, hell, hell," he muttered sadly, gazing at the dark rock where it cut against a white smudge of cloud. A face suddenly stuck over this edge

and looked down at him. It was a small, round, wrinkled almost
sexless face, and the shock of it nearly made Thaw lose balance.
It took him a moment to recognize Mr. McPhedron, the minister from the village. The minister said, "Are you stuck?"
"No, I can go back."
"Aye. The right way up is round the other side. But bide
there a minute."
The face was withdrawn and Thaw saw something black and
straight with a curled end poke over the edge and slide toward
him. It was the handle of an umbrella. Swallowing the fear
that slid up his gullet Thaw gripped the handle with his left
hand and tugged. It stayed firm. He put the toe of his sandal
against a bump in the rock face, gripped the handle tighter,
heaved himself at the edge and got an arm across. The arm
was grabbed and he was pulled onto the summit. He sat up
and said, "Thank you."

The summit was a rock platform as big as the floor of a
room and tilted so that one side was higher than the others.
On the highest corner stood a squat concrete pillar like a steep
pyramid with the top cut off. With a sad pang he saw that
this had seemed the beckoning white woman. The minister,
a bald dry little man in crumpled black clothes, sat nearby
with his legs over the edge, fists resting on thighs and back
as upright as if sitting in a chair. The rolled umbrella lay behind
him. He turned and said, "Now you have your breath back,
give me your opinion of the view."
Thaw stood up. The moor lay below with dots of sheep grazing
on it, some shrub-filled glens and the green coastal strip beyond.
The village was hidden by the trees of the largest glen but
its position was shown by the hotel roof among its conifers
and by the end of a pier sticking into the Atlantic. To the
left of this, between the beach and the white road, the hostel
stood in neat rectangular blocks like a chess game, human specks
moving on the straight paths between. Farther off still, the
road—a bus moving down it like an insect—turned from the
coast into a district of moorland with small lochs and blue-
grey bens paling into the distance like waves of a stone sea.
The ocean in front, however, was as shining-smooth as slightly
wrinkled silk. It stretched to the dark mountains of the Isle
of Skye on the horizon, and the sun hung above these at the
height of Thaw himself. It was dimmed and oranged by haze
but firing golden wires of light from the centre. Thaw stared

at it miserably. The minister was someone he tried to avoid. On coming to the hostel his mother, who went to church, sent him to a Sunday school held by Dr. McPhedron after the morning service. He had expected to sing little hymns and draw little pictures of Bible stories; instead he was given a book of questions and answers to learn by heart so that when Dr. McPhedron asked a question like "Why did God make man?" Thaw could give an answer like "God made man to glorify his name and enjoy his works for ever." After the first day of Sunday school he didn't want to go back and his father, who was an atheist, said he needn't if he didn't enjoy it. Since then Thaw had heard his parents discuss the minister several times. His mother said there was too much Hell in his sermons. She thought churches were good because they gave people something to look up to and hope for, but she didn't believe in Hell and it was wrong to frighten children with it. Mr. Thaw said he saw no reason why people shouldn't believe what pleased them but McPhedron was a type found too often in the highlands and islands, a bigot who damned to Hell whoever rejected his narrow opinions.

To hide embarrassment Thaw turned and examined the pillar.
"Do you wonder what that is, now?" asked the minister. His voice was soft and precise.
"Yes."
"It is a triangulation point. Your name is still on my Sunday school enrolment book. Would you have me remove it?"
Thaw frowned and rubbed his fingers round an odd depression in the pillar's top.
The minister said, *"That* is to hold the base of an instrument used by government mapmakers. I notice you don't come to kirk with your mother any more. Why?"
"Dad says I needn't go to something I don't like if it isn't educational," muttered Thaw. The minister gave a slight friendly laugh.
"I admire your father. His notion of education embraces everything but the purpose of life and the fate of man. Do you believe in the Almighty?"
Thaw said boldly, "I don't know, but I don't believe in Hell."
The minister laughed again. "When you have more knowledge of life you will mibby find Hell more believable. You are from Glasgow?"

"Yes."

"I was six years a student of divinity in that city. It made Hell very real to me."

A muffled blast came to their ears from a distance. A white cloud drifted up from a dip in the moorlands to the south, shredding and vanishing as it rose. The sound was batted back and forth between the mountains, then trickled into echoes among far off glens.

"Yes," said the minister. "They are testing at the munition factory down there. The country must be preserved with all the Hell we can muster."

Thaw was filled with baffled anger. He had bitten into the splendid fruit of the afternoon and found a core of harsh dull words. He muttered that he'd better be getting home.

"Aye," said the minister. "It is late for a wee lad to be far from bed."

He got up and led Thaw from the summit by a fall of granite blocks which presented so many horizontal surfaces that he went down it like a flight of giant steps, hopping nimbly from one to another, using the umbrella to balance him in awkward places. Thaw jumped and scrambled sullenly after him. When they reached the more grassy slopes Thaw let the distance between them increase until the minister vanished behind a boulder; then he turned left and scrambled round the mountainside until a sufficient girth of it was between them and then set off toward the hostel.

The sun had set by the time he reached the road but it was still the gloaming, a protracted summer gloaming with the land dim but the sky lively with colours. He limped in at the hostel gate, the hard tarmac hurting his feet, and went by two straight paths to the manager's bungalow. His mother sat knitting on a deck chair on the lawn. Nearby his father stabbed casually with a hoe at weeds in a small rockery. As Thaw approached Mrs. Thaw called reprovingly, "We were beginning to worry about you!"

He had meant to keep quiet about the climb as he had made it wearing sandals, but standing between his parents he said, "I bet you don't know where I've been!"

"Well, where have you been?"

"There!"

Behind the hostel's low straight roofs Rua showed like a black wedge cut out of the green rotund-looking sky. Soft stars were beginning to shine between a few feathery bloody clouds.

"You were up Ben Rua?"

"Aye."

"Alone?"

"Aye."

His mother said gently, "That could have been dangerous, Duncan."

His father looked at his sandalled feet and said, "If you do it again you must tell someone you're going first, so we know where to look if there's an accident. But I don't think we'll complain this time; no, we won't complain, we won't complain."

CHAPTER 15. Normal

The Thaw family came home to Glasgow the year the war ended.
They arrived late at night as thin rain fell, took a taxi at the
station and sat numbly inside. Thaw looked out at a succession
of desolate streets lit by lights that seemed both dim and harsh.
Once Glasgow had been a tenement block, a school and a
stretch of canal; now it was a gloomy huge labyrinth he would
take years to find a way through. The flat was cold and disordered. During the war it had been let to strangers and the
bedding and ornaments locked in the back bedroom. While
his father and mother unpacked and shifted things he looked
at his old books and found them dull and childish. He asked
his mother, who was dusting, "How long will it be before
we get back to normal?"
"What do you mean, normal?"
"You know, settled down."
"I suppose in a week or two."
He went to the living room where his father was looking
through letters and said, "How long will it be before we get
back to normal?"
"Maybe in two or three months, if we're lucky."

Mr. Thaw spent the next months typing letters at his bureau
in the living room. With each post he got back letters with
printed headings which he gave to Thaw, who drew on the
blank backs. Thaw sat drawing and writing for hours at a tiny
desk in the back bedroom, wearing a dressing gown and an
embroidered smoking cap which had been his grandfather's.
He seldom looked at the letters whose backs he used, but once
his eye was caught by the heading of the factory where his
father had worked before the war. He read:

Dear Mr Thaw,

It would seem that a prophet is not without honour save in the city of his birth! I congratulate you on having done so well with the now defunct Ministry of Munitions.

Unfortunately we have no vacancy for a personnel officer at present. However, I am sure your manifest abilities will have no difficulty in finding employment elsewhere. Our hearty good wishes to you.

Yours faithfully,

John Blair

Managing Director

One day at dinner Mr. Thaw said to his wife, "I took a walk out Hogganfield way this morning. They're building a reservoir to serve the new housing scheme." He swallowed a mouthful and said, "I went in and got a job. I start tomorrow."

"What doing?"

"The walls of the reservoir are made by pouring concrete between metal shuttering. I'll be bolting the shutters into place and taking them down when the stuff has hardened."

Mrs. Thaw said grimly, "It's better than nothing."

"That's what I thought."

After this Mr. Thaw cycled to work each morning wearing an old jacket and corduroy trousers tucked into his stocking tops, and now when Thaw was not at school he scribbled at Mr. Thaw's bureau or lay reading on the hearth rug, enjoying his mother's proximity as she went about the housework.

One day Mr. Thaw said, "Duncan, you sit your qualifying exam in six weeks, don't you?"

"Yes."

"You realize how important this exam is? If you pass you'll go to a senior secondary school where, if you work well at your lessons and homework and pass the proper exams, you'll be able to take your Higher Leaving Certificates and work at anything you like. You can even do another four years at university. If you fail the qualifying exam you'll have to go to a junior secondary school and leave at fourteen and take any job you can get. Look at me. I went to a senior secondary school but I had to leave at fourteen to support my mother and sister. I think I had the ability to do well in life, but to do well you need certificates, certificates, and I had no certificates. The best I could become was a machine minder in Laird's box-making factory. During the war of course there was a short-

age of men with certificates, and I got a job purely on my
abilities. But look what I'm doing now. Have you any notion
of what you would like to be?"
Thaw considered. In the past he had wanted to be a king,
magician, explorer, archaeologist, astronomer, inventor and pilot of spaceships. More recently, while scribbling in the back
bedroom, he had thought of writing stories or painting pictures.
He hesitated and said, "A doctor."
"A doctor! Yes, that's a good thing to be. A doctor gives his
life to helping others. A doctor is always, and will always be,
respected and needed by the community, no matter what social
changes take place. Well, your first step is the qualifying exam.
Don't worry about anything but that first step. You're good
at English and General Knowledge but bad at Arithmetic, so
what you must do is stick in at Arithmetic." Mr. Thaw patted
his son's back. "Go to it!" he said. Thaw went to his bedroom,
shut the door, lay on the bed and started crying. The future
his father indicated seemed absolutely repulsive.

Whitehill Senior Secondary School was a tall gloomy red
sandstone building with a playing field at the back and on each
side a square playground, one for each sex, enclosed and mini-
mized by walls with spiked railings on top. It had been built
like this in the eighteen-eighties but the growth of Glasgow
had imposed additions. A structure, outwardly uniform with
the old building but a warren of crooked stairs and small classrooms within, was stuck to the side at the turn of the century.
After the first world war a long wooden annexe was added
as temporary accommodation until a new school could be built,
and after the second world war, as a further temporary measure,
seven prefabricated huts holding two classrooms each were put
up on the playing field. On a grey morning some new boys
stood in a lost-looking crowd near the entrance gate. In primary
school they had been the playground giants. Now they were
dwarfs among a mob of people up to eighteen inches taller
than themselves. A furtive knot from Riddrie huddled together
trying to seem blasé. One said to Thaw, "What are ye taking,
Latin or French?"
"French."
"I'm taking Latin. Ye need it tae get to university."
"But Latin's a dead language!" said Thaw. "My mother wants
me to take Latin but I tell her there are more good books in
French. And ye can use French tae travel."
"Aye, mibby, but ye need Latin tae get to university."

An electric bell screeched and a fat bald man in a black gown appeared on the steps of the main entrance. He stood with hands deep in his trouser pockets and feet apart, contemplating the buttons of his waistcoat while the older pupils hurried into lines before several entrances. One or two lines kept up a vague chatter and shuffle; he looked sternly at these and they fell silent. He motioned each class to the entrances one after another with a finger of his right hand. Then he beckoned the little group by the gate to the foot of the steps, lined them up, read their names from a list and led them into the building. The gloom of the entrance steeped them, then the dim light of echoing hall, then the cold light of a classroom.

Thaw entered last and found the only seat left was the undesirable one in the front row in front of the teacher, who sat behind a tall desk with his hands clasped on the lid. When everyone was seated he looked from left to right along the rows of faces before him, as if memorizing each one, then leaned back and said casually, "Now we'll divide you into classes. In the first year, of course, the only real division is between those who take Latin and those whos take . . . a modern language. At the end of the third year you will have to choose between other subjects: Geography or History, for instance; Science or Art; for by then you will be specializing for your future career. Hands up those who don't know what specializing means. No hands? Good. Your choice today is a simpler one, but its effects reach further. You all know Latin is needed for entrance to university. A number of benevolent people think this unfair and are trying to change it. As far as Glasgow University is concerned they haven't succeeded *yet.*" He smiled an inward-looking smile and leaned back until he seemed to be staring at the ceiling. He said, "My name's Walkenshaw. I'm senior Classics master. Classics. That's what we call the study of Latin and Greek. Perhaps you've heard the word before? Who hasn't heard of classical music? Put your hand up if you haven't heard of classical music. No hands? Good. Classical music, you see, is the *best* sort of music, music by the best composers. In the same way the study of Classics is the study of the *best.* Are you chewing something?"
Thaw, who had been swallowing nervously, was appalled to find this question fired at himself. Not daring to take his gaze from the teacher's face he stood slowly up and shook his head.
"Answer me."
"No sir."

"Open your mouth. Open it wide. Stick your tongue out."
Thaw did as he was told. Mr. Walkenshaw leaned forward,
stared, then said mildly, "Your name?"
"Thaw, sir."
"That's all right, Thaw. You can sit down. And always tell
the truth, Thaw."
Mr. Walkenshaw leaned back and said, "Classics. Or, as we
call it at university, the Humanities. I say nothing against the
study of modern languages. Naturally half of you will choose
French. But Whitehall Senior Secondary School has a tradition,
a fine tradition of Classical scholarship, and I hope many of
you will continue that tradition. To those without enough ambition to go to university and who can't see the use of Latin, I
can only repeat the words of Robert Burns: 'Man cannot live
by bread alone.' No, and you would be wise to remember it.
Now I'm going to read your names again and I want you to
shout Modern and Classics according to choice."
He read the list of names again. Thaw was depressed to hear
all the people he knew choose Latin. He chose Latin.

The Latin students queued at the door of another classroom
opening out of the hall. The girls who had chosen Latin were
already there, giggling and whispering. It took Thaw a second
to notice and fall in love with the loveliest of them. She was
blond and wore a light dress, so he looked loftily round the
hall with an absent-minded frown hoping she would notice
his superior indifference. The hall was like an aquarium tank,
the light slanted into it from windows in the roof. On a wall
at one end a marble tablet showed a knight in Roman armour
and the names of pupils killed in the first world war. Photographs of headmasters hung between surrounding doors:
shaggy bearded early ones and neatly moustached recent ones,
but all with stern brows and clenched mouths. From a balcony
above came the horrible detonation of a leather belt striking
a hand. Somewhere a door opened and a voice said querulously,
"*Marcellus animadvertit,* Marcellus noticed this thing, and at once
into battle line formed the forces, and did not reluctantly, er
reluctantly take the opportunity of recalling to them how often
in the past they had borne themselves, er, nobly. . . ."

A lank young teacher led them into the classroom. The
girls sat in desks to his right, the boys to the left, and he faced
them with hands on hips leaning forward from the waist. He
said, "My name is Maxwell. I'm your form teacher. You come

to me first period each day to have the class register called
and to bring reasons for having been absent or late. They'd
better be good reasons. I'm also your Latin teacher."
He stared at them a while, then said, "I'm new to teaching.
Just as I'm your first senior secondary school teacher, you are
my first senior secondary school class. We're starting together,
you see, and I think we'd better decide here and now to start
well. You do right by me and I'll do right by you. But if we
quarrel about anything *you're* going to suffer. Not me."
He stared at them brightly and the frightened class stared back.
He had a craggy face with a rugged nose, trimmed red moustache and broad lips. Thaw noticed the undersurface of the
moustache was clipped to exactly continue the flat surface of
the upper lip. This detail frightened him even more than the
grim, nervous little speech.

Through the morning depression gathered in his brain
and chest like a physical weight. Each forty minutes the bell
screeched and the class moved to a different room and were
welcomed by a few unfriendly words. The Mathematics teacher
was a small brisk woman who said if they tried hard she would
help them all she could, but one thing she could not and would
not stand was dreaming. There was no room for dreamers in
her class. She gave out algebra and geometry books in which
Thaw saw a land without colour, furniture or action where
thought negotiated symbolically with itself. The science room
had a pungent chemical smell and shelves of strange objects
which excited his appetite for magic, but the teacher was a
big bullying man with hair like a beast's fur and Thaw knew
nothing *he* taught would bring an increase of power or freedom.
The art teacher was mild and middle-aged. He talked about
the laws of perspective, and how these laws had to be learned
before true art became possible. He gave out pencils and got
them to copy a wooden block onto a small sheet of paper. In
each class Thaw sat in the front row and stared at the teacher's
face. He was in a world where he could not do well, and he
wanted to give an impression of obedience that would make
the authorities treat him leniently. All the time he felt the pale
blaze of the blond girl somewhere behind him on the left.
Twice he dropped a book as an excuse for looking at her while
he picked it up. She seemed an unstill flickering girl, always
moving her shoulders, shaking her head and hair, smiling and
glancing from side to side. He noticed with surprise that her
oval face had a thrust-forward, slightly clumsy jaw. Her beauty

lay more in the movement of her parts than the parts themselves, which was maybe why she was never still.

The boys from Riddrie stood chattering in a queue for the tram which would take them home at noontime. One said, "That big Maxwell—I hate him. He looks mad enough to murder ye."

"Ach, naw, he'll be all right if ye do as he says. It's the science man I'm feart from. He's the sort that'll hammer ye jist because he's in a bad mood."

"Ach, they're all out to terrorize us today. The theory is that if they scare us enough at the start we'll give them nae trouble later. They've got a hope."

There was a reflective silence; then somebody said, "What dae ye think of the talent?"

"I care for that wee blond bird."

"Aye, did ye see her? She couldnae keep still. I wouldnae mind feeling *her* belly in a dark room."

Everyone but Thaw sniggered. Someone nudged him and said, "What do you think of her, moon-man?"

"Her jaw's too ape-like for me."

"Is it? All right. But I wouldnae give her back if I got her in a present. Does anyone know her name?

"I do. It's Kate Caldwell."

Things improved in the afternoon for they had English and the teacher was a young man with a comforting likeness to the film comedian Bob Hope. Without any introductory speech he said, "Today is the last day for handing in contributions for the school magazine. I'll give you paper and you can try to write something for it. It can be prose or poetry, serious or comic, an invented story or something that really happened. It doesn't matter if the result isn't up to much, but maybe one or two of you will get something accepted."

Thaw leaned over the paper, elated thoughts flowing through his head. His heart began to beat faster and he started writing. He quickly filled two sheets of foolscap then copied the result out carefully, checking the hard words with a dictionary. The teacher collected the papers and the bell rang for the next lesson.

Next day the class had geometry. The Maths teacher talked lucidly and drew clear diagrams on the blackboard, and Thaw gazed at her, trying by intensity of expression to make up for

inability to understand. A girl came in and said, "Please, miss,
Mister Meikle wants tae see Duncan Thaw in room fifty-four."
As she led him across the playground to the wooden annexe,
Thaw said, "Who's Mr. Meikle?"
"Head English teacher."
"What does he want me for?"
"How should I know?"
In room fifty-four a saturnine man in an academic gown leaned
on a desk overlooking empty rows of desks. He turned toward
Thaw a face that was long, lined and triangular under the oval
of a balding skull. He had a small black moustache and ironical
eyebrows. Lifting two sheets of foolscap from his desk he said,
"You wrote this?"
"Yes sir."
"What gave you the idea?"
"Nothing, sir."
"Hm. I suppose you read a lot?"
"Quite a lot."
"What are you reading just now?"
"A play called *The Dynasts.*"
"Hardy's *Dynasts?*"
"I forget who wrote it. I got it out of the library."
"What do you think of it?"
"I think the choruses are a bit boring but I like the scenic
directions. I like the retreat from Moscow, with the bodies
of the soldiers baked by fire in front and frozen stiff behind.
And I like the view of Europe down through the clouds, looking
like a sick man with the Alps for his backbone."
"Do you do any writing at home?"
"Oh yes, sir."
"Are you at work on anything just now?"
"Yes. I'm trying to write about this boy who can hear colours."
"Hear colours?"
"Yes sir. When he sees a fire burning each flame makes a
noise like a fiddle playing a jig, and some nights he's kept
awake by the full moon screaming, and he hears the sun rise
through an orange dawn like trumpets blowing. The bother
is that most colours round about him make horrible noises—
orange and green buses, for instance, traffic lights and advertise-
ments and things."
"You don't hear colours yourself, do you?" said the teacher,
looking at Thaw peculiarly.
"Oh no," said Thaw, smiling. "I got the idea from a note
Edgar Allan Poe wrote to one of his poems. He said he some-

times thought he could hear the dusk creeping over the land
like the tolling of a bell."
"I see. Well, Duncan, the school magazine is rather short of
worthwhile contributions this year. Do you think you could
write something more for us? Along slightly different lines?"
"Oh yes."
"Don't write about the boy who hears colours. It's a good idea—
perhaps too good for a school magazine. Write about something
more commonplace. How soon could you manage it?"
"Tomorrow, sir."
"The day after will do."
"I'll bring it in tomorrow."
Mr. Meikle tapped his teeth with a pencil end, then said, "We
have a debating society in the school every second Wednesday
evening. You should come to it. You may have something to
say."

Thaw ran leaping back across the empty playground. Outside the maths room he paused, took the grin from his face,
frowned with his brows, smiled faintly with his mouth, opened
the door and went to his seat with the eyes of the class on
him. Kate Caldwell, who sat across the passage from his desk,
smiled and flickered questioningly. He bent over a page of
axioms, pretending to concentrate but working inwardly on a
new story. The elation in his chest recalled the summit of Rua.
He remembered the sunlit moor and the beckoning white speck
and wondered if these things could be used in a story and if
Kate Caldwell would read it and be impressed. Taking a pencil
he began to sketch furtively a steep mountain on the cover
of a book.
"What is a point?"
He looked up and blinked.
"Stand up, Thaw! Now tell me what a point is."
The question seemed meaningless.
"A point is that which has no dimensions. You didn't know that,
did you, yet it's the first axiom in the book. And—what's this?
You've been drawing on the cover!"
He stared at the teacher's mouth opening and shutting and
wondered why the words coming out could hurt like stones.
His ear tried to get free by attending to the purr of a car
moving slowly up the street outside and the faint shuffle of
Kate Caldwell's feet. The teacher's mouth stopped moving.
He muttered "Yes miss" and sat down, blushing hotly.

He took four nights to finish the new story properly. He gave it to Mr. Meikle with many apologies for the delay and Mr. Meikle read it and rejected it, explaining that Thaw had tried a blend of realism and fantasy which even an adult would have found difficult. Thaw was stunned and resentful. Though not satisfied with the story he knew it was the best he had written; the words "even an adult" hurt his pride by suggesting his work was only interesting because he was a child; moreover he had quietly told a few classmates of Mr. Meikle's request, hoping word of it would reach Kate Caldwell.

CHAPTER 16. Underworlds

Partly for pleasure, partly to save money, he walked to school each morning through Alexandra Park, mistakenly thinking a twisting path through flowerbeds was shorter than the straight traffic-laden road. The path crossed a hillside with a golf course above and football pitches below. The sky was usually pallid neutral and beyond the pitches a grey pragmatic light illuminated ridges of tenements and factories without obscuring or enriching them. Past the hill a boating pond lay among hawthorn and chestnuts. Often a film of soot had settled overnight on the level water and a duck, newly launched from an island, left a track like the track a finger makes on dusty glass. Crossing the flood of trucks and trams clanging and rumbling on the main road, he picked his way through a grid of small streets by a route which passed two cinemas with still photographs outside and three shops with vividly coloured magazines in the window. The women in these gave his daydreams a more erotic twist.

He had crossed the main road one morning and was descending a short street when Kate Caldwell came out of a close mouth in front of him and walked toward school, her schoolbag (a wartime gas-mask container) bumping at her hip. He followed excitedly, meaning to overtake but lacking the courage. What could he say to her? He imagined his stammering voice saying dull, awkward things about lessons and the weather and could only imagine her saying conventional things in response. Why didn't she turn and smile and beckon? Surely she knew he was behind? If she beckoned he would smile faintly and approach with eyebrows questioningly raised. She would say, "Don't you like my company?" or "I'm glad you come this way, these morning walks are a bit dull," or "I liked your story in the school magazine; tell me about yourself." He glared furiously at her dancing shoulders, willing her to turn and beckon, but she didn't, and they reached school without getting nearer together or farther apart. After this he hoped each day she would come from the close at the exact moment he passed it so he could speak to her without lowering himself, but either he didn't see her at all or she emerged ahead and he had to follow as if towed by an invisible rope. One morning he had just passed the close when he heard light quick footsteps overtaking from behind. A confusion of hope and distress hit him, and a nervous prickling in the skin of his face. Before the steps reached him he abruptly crossed the road to the opposite pavement, defiance and self-pity mingling in a sense of tragic isolation. Then he saw pass him, across the road, not the contemptuous dance of Kate Caldwell's shoulderblades but a small, vigorous old lady with a shopping bag. He reached the playground feeling baffled and disappointed, and afterward went to school by a route which bothered him with fewer emotional complications.

Doing well in some subjects, learning to do badly in others without offending the teachers, he came to accept school as a sort of bad weather, making only the conventional complaints. He was friendly with other boys but had no friends and rarely tried to make them. Apparent life was a succession of dull habits in which he did what was asked automatically, only resenting demands to show interest. His energy had withdrawn into imaginary worlds and he had none to waste on reality.

A small fertile land lay hidden in a crater made by an atomic explosion. Thaw was Prime Minister of it. He lived in an old mansion among lawns and clumps of forest on the shore of a loch ornamented with islands. The mansion was spacious, dim and peaceful. The halls were hung with his paintings, the library full of his novels and poems, there were studios and laboratories where the best minds of the day worked whenever they cared to visit him. Outside the sun was warm, bees hummed among flowers and fountains, the season was midway between summer and autumn when the trees showed their matured green and only the maples were crimson. Political work took little of his time, for the people of that country had such confidence in him that he had only to suggest a reform for it to be practised. Indeed, his main problem was to keep the

land democratic, for he would have been crowned king long
before if his socialist principles had not forbidden it. He looked
young for a Prime Minister, being a boy in early adolescence;
at the same time he had ruled that land for centuries. He was
a survivor of the third world war. The poisonous radiations
which had killed most of his contemporaries had, by a fluke,
given him eternal youth. In two or three centuries of wandering
about the shattered earth he had become leader of a small
group of people who had come to trust his gentleness and wisdom. He had brought them to the crater, protected by its walls
from the envy of unhappier lands, to build a republic where
nobody was sick, poor or forced to live by work they hated.
Unluckily his country was surrounded by barbaric lands ruled
by queens and tyrants who kept plotting to conquer it and
were only kept out by his courage and ingenuity. As a result
he was often involved in battles, rescues, escapes, fights with
monsters in the middle of arenas, and triumphal processions
of shocking vulgarity which he only took part in to avoid hurting
the feelings of the queens and princesses whose lives and countries he had saved. When these adventures were over he invited
the main characters home to stay with him, and since he annexed
the plot of every book and film which impressed him the house
by the loch was always crowded with the celebrities of many
different races, nations and historical phases. In the simplicity
of his spacious rooms they were amazed by the quiet friendliness
of a way of life more civilized than their own, and they learned
the true duties of a ruler by seeing him spend an afternoon
drawing the plans of a new reservoir or university. The women
guests usually fell in love with him, though some of the more
barbaric came to hate him for his friendly indifference, an indifference which clothed a deep shyness. He could only feel near
to women when rescuing them, and often envied the villains
who could humiliate or torture them. His position made it
impossible to imagine doing such things himself. Yet when
walking home from school or public library, these adventures
filled his head and chest with such intoxicating emotions that
he had to run hard to be relieved of them and often found
he had come through several streets without remembering anything of the people, houses or traffic.

His other imaginary world was enjoyed in the genitals.
It was a secret gold mine in Arizona which a gang of bandits
worked by slave labour. Thaw was bandit chief and spent his
time inventing and practising tortures for the slaves. The mine

got outside stimulus, not from the shelves of the library but, cryptically, from American comics. He never bought these, and had courage to look at their enticing covers only when the shop contained something else he could pretend to examine, but he sometimes borrowed one at school and in the privacy of the back bedroom copied out pictures of men being whipped and branded. He kept these pictures between pages of Carlyle's *French Revolution,* a book no one else was likely to open.

One evening he knelt by his bed with the pictures on the quilt before him. There was a familiar tension in his genitals but tonight, by a coincidence of positions, his stiffened penis touched a girder upholding the mattress. The contact fired a bolt of white-cold nervous electricity into him in a shock so poignant that he had to press harder and harder against the source of it until something gushed and squirted, the kicking mechanism broke down, shrunk and went limp and he was left feeling horribly flat and emptied out. All the while his mind had sat feebly aghast, wondering what was happening with the slight energy left to it. Now he looked disgustedly at the drawings, took them to the lavatory, flushed them down the pan and opened his trousers.
A grey slug-shaped blob of jelly lay on his stomach just under the navel. It was transparent, tiny milky wisps and galaxies hung in it and it smelled like fish. He wiped himself clean and went back to the bedroom, not knowing what had happened but sure it had to do with the sniggers, hints and sudden silences which instinctive distaste made him ignore among his classmates. He felt numb and disgusted and swore not to think again the thoughts that led to this condition. Two days later they came back and he gave way to them without much resistance.

And now the flow of his imaginative life was broken by three or four orgasms a week. His pleasure in the mine had once lasted indefinitely, for it never reached a climax. After drawing or brooding awhile he would be called to a meal, or to homework, or would go for a walk and return from it the humane triumphant Prime Minister of his republic. Now after brooding on the mine a few minutes his penis would yearn to touch something, and if denied this help often exploded by itself, leaving a sodden stain in his trousers and a self-contempt so great that it included all his imaginary worlds. He was as much estranged from imagination as from reality.

The asthma returned with increasing weight, by day lying on his chest like a stone, at night pouncing like a beast. One night he woke with the beast's paw so hard on his throat that he moved in a moment from fear to utter panic and leaped from bed with a cawing scream, stumbled to the window and clutched back the curtain. A gold flake of moon, a dim wisp of cloud hung above the opposite chimneys. He glared at them like words he could not read and tried to scream again. His father and mother came beside him and gently pressed him back to bed. Mr. Thaw held him tightly while his mother gave an ephedrine pill and brought first hot milk, then hot whisky, and held the cups to his mouth as he drank. His frightened grunting got less. They left him wrapped in a dressing gown, sitting cross-legged against a pile of pillows.

At the height of the panic, while glaring at the irrelevant moon, his one thought had been a certainty that Hell was worse than this. He had not been religiously educated and though he had a tentative faith in God (saying at the end of prayers "If you exist" instead of "Amen") he had none in Hell. Now he saw that Hell was the one truth and pain the one fact which nullified all others. Sufficient health was like thin ice on an infinite sea of pain. Love, work, art, science and law were dangerous games played on the ice; all homes and cities were built on it. The ice was frail. A tiny shrinkage of the bronchial tubes could put him under it and a single split atom could sink a city. All religions existed to justify Hell and all clergymen were ministers of it. How could they walk about with such bland social faces pretending to belong to the surface of life? Their skulls should be furnaces with the fire of Hell burning in them and the skin of their faces dried and thin like scorched leaves. The face of Dr. McPhedron came to him as abruptly as when it was thrust over the edge of the rock. He turned for help to a bookcase beside the bed. It held books got secondhand for sixpence or a shilling, mostly legends and fantasies with some adult fiction and nonfiction. But now the fantasies were imbecile frivolity, and poetry was whistling in the dark, and novels showed life fighting its own agony, and biographies were accounts of struggles toward violent or senile ends, and history was an infinitely diseased worm without head or tail, beginning or end. A shelf held his father's books, works by Lenin and the Webbs, *The History of the Working Classes in Scotland, Humanities Gain from Unbelief, The Harmsworth Encyclo-*

paedia and books about mountaineering. Putting out a desperate hand he took from among these a general history of philosophy, opened at random and read:

All the perceptions of the human mind resolve themselves into two distinct kinds, which I shall call IMPRESSIONS and IDEAS. The difference between these consists of the degrees of force and liveliness with which they strike upon the mind, and make their way into our thought or consciousness. These perceptions, which enter with the most force or violence, we may name *impressions;* and under the name I may comprehend all our sensations, passions and emotions, as they make their first appearance in the soul. By *ideas* I mean the faint image of these in thinking and reasoning. . . .

He read on with increasing relief, brought more and more into a world which, though made of words instead of numbers, was almost mathematical in its cleanness and lack of emotion. Looking up from the book much later he saw between the disordered curtains that the sky was pale and heard a faint distant music, a melodious thrumming which grew louder and louder until it seemed above his head, then faded into the distance. It was too rhythmical for birdsong, too harmonious for aircraft. He was puzzled but oddly comforted and fell into a smooth sleep.

   At seven an alarm rang in the living room where his parents slept in the bed settee. Mr. Thaw had breakfast and carried his bicycle downstairs to the street. Mrs. Thaw brought to the bedroom a tray set with porridge, fried egg, sausage, brown bread with marmalade and a cup of tea. She watched as he ate and said, "Is it any better, son?"
"A bit better."
"Ach, you'll be all right when ye get to school."
"Mibby."
"Take another pill."
"I have taken another. It's not doing much good."
"You've made up your mind it's not doing good! If you wanted it to work it *would* work!"
"Mibby."
After a while he said, "Anyway, I don't want to go to school today."
"But, Duncan, the exams are two weeks away."
"I'm tired. I didn't sleep well."
Mrs. Thaw said coldly, "Are you trying to tell me you *can't*

go to school? You weren't very well yesterday but you were
well enough to go to the library. You've always enough breath
for what you want to do; none for what's important."
Thaw laboriously dressed and washed. Mrs. Thaw helped him
on with his coat and said, "Now take your time going down
the road. It's church first period so it won't matter if you're
a bit late. The teachers understand. And straighten your back.
Stop walking about like a half-shut penknife. Look the world
in the face as if you owned it."
"I own none of it."
"You own as much of it as anyone! You can own *more* of it
if you use your brain and learn to do well in the exams. You
have a good brain. Your teachers say so. They want to help
you. Why don't you want to be helped?"

There was no special position for praying in. People sat
with legs apart or crossed, arms folded, hands clasped or
clenched as they pleased, but all shut their eyes to suggest
concentration and bowed their heads as a mark of respect. For
a long time Thaw had stopped shutting his eyes but lacked
the courage to lift his head. Today, arriving late and breathing
uneasily, a great carelessness filled him and he impatiently raised
his head during a lengthy prayer. He was seated on one side
of the gallery with a clear view down on the bent heads of
the congregation, the choir, the minister in the octagonal tower
of his pulpit and the headmaster at the foot of it. The minister
was a fat-faced man whose head wagged and nodded with every
phrase while his raptly shut eyes gave it a blind empty look,
like a balloon blown about in a draught. Thaw felt suddenly
that he was being watched. Among the rows of bowed heads
in the gallery opposite was an erect, slightly clumsy, almost
expressionless face which, if it noticed him (and he was not
sure it did) did so with a faint sarcastic smile. Something in
the face made him feel he knew it. Later that day the stranger
was introduced into the class as Robert Coulter, who had been
promoted to Whitehill Secondary School from Garngad Junior
Secondary School. He fitted into the class easily, making friends
without effort and doing fairly well at the things Thaw did
badly. He and Thaw exchanged embarrassed nods when accident brought them face to face and otherwise ignored each
other. Once, in the science room, the pupils stood talking by
their benches before the teacher arrived. Coulter approached
Thaw and said, "Hullo."
"Hullo."

"How are you getting on?"

"Not too bad. How are you?"

"Ach, not too bad."

After a pause Coulter said, "Would you mind swopping seats?"

"Why?"

"Well, I'd like a closer view. . . ." Coulter pointed at Kate Caldwell. "After all, you're not interested in that sort of thing."

Thaw took his books to Coulter's bench filled with black rage and depression. Nothing could have made him admit his interest in Kate Caldwell.

One day after the exams the teachers sat at their desks correcting papers while the pupils read comics, played chess or cards or talked quietly in groups. Coulter, at a desk in front of Thaw, turned round and said, "What are ye reading?"

Thaw showed a book of critical essays on art and literature. Coulter said accusingly, "You don't read that for fun."

"Yes, I read it for fun."

"People our age don't read that sort of book for fun. They read it to show they're superior."

"But I read this sort of book even when there's nobody to see me."

"That shows you arenae trying to make *us* think you're superior, you're trying to make *yourself* think you're superior."

Thaw scratched his head and said, "That's clever, but not very true. What are you reading?"

Coulter showed him a magazine called *Astounding Science Fiction,* with a picture on the cover of tentacled creatures manipulating a piece of machinery in a jungle clearing. Green lightning leaped from the machine into the sky where it split open a planet which seemed to be the earth. Thaw shook his head and said, "I don't like science fiction much. It's pessimistic."

Coulter grinned and said, "That's what I like about it. I was reading a great story the other day called *Colonel Johnson Does His Duty.* This American colonel is in a hideout miles underground. He's one of those in charge of fighting the third world war, which is all done by pressing switches. Everybody aboveground has been killed, of course, and even a lot of the army folk have had their hideouts blasted by special rockets that bore into the ground. Well, this Colonel Johnson, see, has been out of touch for months with the folks on his own side, because if you use the radio these special rockets can work out where your hideout is and come down and blast you. Anyway, this Colonel Johnson invents a machine that can find out

where people are by detecting their thought waves. He starts
using the machine on America. No good. Everyone in America's dead. He tries Europe, Africa, Australia. Everybody's dead
there too. Then he tries Asia and here there's only one other
man left alive in the world, and he's in a city in Russia. So
he gets into this plane and flies to Russia. Everything he passes
over is dead—no plants or animals or anything. He lands in
this Russian city and gets out. Everything's wreckage, of course,
but he creeps through it till he hears this other man moving
inside this building. It's eight years since he's seen another
human being, he's going mad with loneliness, see, and he's
been hoping to talk tae another man before he dies. The Russian
comes out of the building and Colonel Johnson shoots him."
"But *why?*" said Thaw.
"Because he's been trained tae kill Russians. Don't you like
that story?"
"I think it's a rotten story."
"Mibby. But it's true tae life. What do you do after school?"
"I go to the library, or mibby a walk."
"I go intae town with Murdoch Muir and big Sam Lang. We
stage riots."
"How?"
"D'ye know the West End Park?"
"The park near the Art Galleries?"
"Aye. Well, they don't lock it up at night like other parks
and folk can walk through it. There's a few lights in it but
no' many. Well, big Sam'll stand near some bushes and light
a fag, and when someone comes we charge out from the bushes
and pretend to kick big Sam in the guts and he lashes out
with his fists and we all fall down and roll about swearing.
We don't touch each other, but in the dark it's hellish convincing. You get lassies running away screaming for the police."
"Don't the police come?"
"We run away before they come. Murdoch Muir's dad is a
policeman. When we tell him about it he roars and laughs
and tells us whit he would dae tae us if he caught us."
Thaw said, "That's anti-social."
"Mibby, but it's natural. More natural than going walks by
yourself. Come on, admit you'd like tae come with us one
night."
"But I wouldnae."
"Admit you'd sooner look at that comic than read your art
criticism."
Coulter pointed at the cover of a neighbour's comic. It showed

a blonde in a bathing costume being entwined by a huge
serpent. Thaw opened his mouth to deny this, then frowned
and shut it. Coulter said, "Come on, that picture makes your
cock prick, doesn't it? Admit you're like the rest of us."
Thaw went to the next classroom alarmed and confused. "That
picture makes your cock prick. Admit you're like the rest of
us." He remembered other words heard long before but carefully ignored: "I wouldnae mind feeling *her* belly in a dark
room."

He had known from the age of four that babies hatched
from their mothers' stomachs. Mr. Thaw had described the
growth of the embryo in detail, and Thaw had assumed this
process occurred spontaneously in most women above a certain
age. He accepted this as he accepted his father's account of
the origin of species and the solar system: it was an interesting,
mechanical, not very mysterious business which men could
know about but not influence. Nothing he heard or read later
had mentioned inevitable links between love, sex and birth,
so he never thought there were any. Sex was something he
had discovered squatting on the bedroom floor. It was so disgusting that it had to be indulged secretly and not mentioned
to others. It fed on dreams of cruelty, had its climax in a jet
of jelly and left him feeling weak and lonely. It had nothing
to do with love. Love was what he felt for Kate Caldwell, a
wish to be near her and do things that would make her admire
him. He hid this love because public knowledge of it would
put him in an inferior position with other people and with
Kate herself. He was ashamed of it, but not disgusted. And
now, jerkily, under the influence of Coulter's remark, his separate pictures of love, sex and birth started to become one.

He was crossing the hill in the park when he heard musical
throbbing come from the sky. Five swans flew over his head
in V formation, their thrumming wings and honking throats
blending in one music. Lowering their feet they dropped out
of sight behind the trees which screened the boating pond.
During the next days he collected spare bits of bread and threw
them in the pond on his way to school. One morning he saw
something that kept him on the shore longer than usual. Beside
the island two swans faced each other in such an intent way
that he thought they were going to fight. Spreading their wings
they rose from the water almost to the tail, pressed their breasts
together, then their brows, then their beaks. Pointing their

faces skyward they twined necks, then untwisted and coiled them backward, each reflecting the other like a mirror. Together they made and unmade with their bodies the shapes of Greek lyres and renaissance silverware. Suddenly one of them broke the pattern, slipped adroitly behind the other, mounted her tail and thrust his body up and down it while she plunged across the water in a thresh of wings and waves. As they passed Thaw he saw the male push the female's head under water with his beak, perhaps to make her more docile. At the end of the loch they separated, straightened necks and sailed indifferently apart. The female, being more dishevelled, was readjusting her feathers when the male, in a remote bay, started probing unenthusiastically for minnows.

Ten minutes later Thaw joined the lines in the playground full of grey depression. In class he looked coldly on the pupils, the teacher, and Kate Caldwell most of all. They were part of a deceptive surface, horrifying this time not because it was weak and could not keep out Hell but because it was transparent and could not hide the underlying filth. That evening he walked with Coulter along the canal bank and told him about the swans. Coulter said, "Have you seen slugs do it?"
"Slugs?"
"Aye, slugs. When I was on MacTaggart's farm in Kinlochrua I came out one morning after some rain and here were all these slugs lying in the grass in couples. I took them apart and put them together again tae see how they did it. They seemed so human. Much more human than your swans."
Thaw stood still for a moment and then cried aloud, "I wish to God I would never want another human being in my whole life! I wish to God I was . . ."
He paused. A word from a recent botany lesson entered his head. ". . . self-fertilizing! Oh, Lord God Maker and Sustainer of Heaven and Hell make me self-fertilizing! If you exist."
Coulter looked at him, slightly awestruck, then said, "You scare me sometimes, Duncan. The things you say arenae altogether sane. It all comes of wanting to be superior to ordinary life."

CHAPTER 17. The Key

Mr. Thaw worked as a labourer and then as a wages clerk for a firm building housing estates round the city edge. The Korean war began, the cost of living rose and Mrs. Thaw got a job as a shop assistant in the afternoons. She came to feel very tired and suffered depressions which her doctor thought were caused by the change of life. When the tea things had been cleared away in the evenings she would sew or knit, glancing occasionally at Thaw, who sat frowning at the pages of a textbook and fingering his brow or cheek. His inattention drew comments from her.

"You're not working."

"I know."

"You ought to be working. The exams are coming off soon. You've made up your mind not to pass and you won't."

"I know."

"And you could pass if you tried. Your teachers all say you could. And you sit there doing nothing and you'll make us all ashamed of you."

"I'm afraid so."

"Well, do something! And don't scratch! You sit there clot-clot-clotting at your face till it's like a lump of raw meat. Think of your sister Ruth if you won't think of yourself or me. She's ashamed enough as it is of a brother who creeps about the school like a hunchback."

"I can't help my asthma."

"No, but if you did the exercises the physiotherapist at the Royal told you to do you could walk about like a human being. You were told to do five-minutes exercise each morning and evening. How often did you do them? Once."

"Twice."

"Twice. And why? Why don't you want to improve yourself?"
"Laziness, I suppose."
"Hm!"
Thaw pretended once more to study a page of mathematics but found himself brooding on a talk with the head English teacher about the school curriculum. Thaw said much of it was neither interesting in itself nor useful in a practical way. Mr. Meikle had looked thoughtfully across the bent backs and heads of his class and said, "Remember, Duncan, when most people leave school they have to live by work which can't be liked for its own sake and whose practical application is outside their grasp. Unless they learn to work obediently because they're told to, and for no other reason, they'll be unfit for human society."
Thaw sighed, picked up a textbook and read:

> A man and his wife clean their teeth from the same cylindrical tube of toothpaste on alternate days. The interior diameter of the nozzle through which the paste is squeezed is .08 of the interior diameter of the tube, which is 3.4 cms. If the man squeezes out a cylinder of toothpaste 1.82 cms in length each time he uses it, and his wife a cylinder 3.13 cms in length, find the length of the tube to the nearest mm. if it lasts from the 3rd of January to the 8th of March inclusive and the man is the first to use it.

A hysterical rage gripped him. Dropping the book, he clutched at his head and rubbed and scratched and towzled it until his mother shouted "Stop!"
"But this is absurd! This is ludicrous! This is unb-unb-unb-unb-unb-unb"—he choked—"unbearable! I don't understand it, I can't learn it, what good will it do me?"
"It'll get you through your exams! That's all the good it needs to do! You can forget it when you've got your Higher Leaving Certificate!"
"Why can't they examine me in standing on my head balancing chairs on my feet? Homework for that might improve my health."
"And do you really think you know what's good for you better than the teachers and headmasters who've studied the subject all their lives?"
"Yes. Yes. Where my own needs are concerned I do know better."
Mrs. Thaw put a hand to her side and said in a strange voice, "Oh, bloody hell!" Then she said, "Why did I bring

children into the world?" and began weeping.

Thaw was alarmed. It was the first time he had heard her curse or seen her weep and he tried to sound reasonable and calm. "Mummy, it doesnae matter if I fail those exams. If I leave school and get a job you won't need to work so hard."

Mrs. Thaw dabbed her eyes and resumed sewing, her lips pressed tight together. After a pause she said, "And what job will you get? An errand boy's?"

"There must be other jobs."

"Such as?"

"I don't know, but there must be!"

"Hm!"

Thaw shut his books and said, "I'm going for a walk."

"That's right, run away. Men can always run away from work. Women never can."

There was daylight in the sky but none in the streets and the lamps were lit. Boys of his own age strolled on the pavements in crowds of three and four, girls walked in couples, groups of both sexes gossiped and giggled by café doors. Thaw felt inferior and conspicuous. Overheard whispers seemed to mock the absent look he wore to disarm criticism, overheard laughter seemed caused by the upright hair he never brushed or combed. He walked quickly into streets with fewer shops where people moved in enigmatic units. His confidence grew with the darkness. His face took on a resolute, slightly wolfish look, his feet hit the pavement firmly, he strode past couples embracing in close mouths feeling isolated by a stern purpose which put him outside merely human satisfactions. This purpose was hardly one he could have explained (after all he was just walking, not walking to anywhere) but sometimes he thought he was searching for the key.

The key was small and precise, yet in its use completely general and completely particular. Once found it would solve every problem: asthma, homework, shyness before Kate Caldwell, fear of atomic war; the key would make everything painful, useless and wrong become pleasant, harmonious and good. Since he thought of it as something that could be contained in one or two sentences, he had looked for it in the public libraries but seldom on the science or philosophy shelves. The key had to be recognized at once and by heart, not led up to and proved by reasoning. Nor could it be an article of religion, since its discovery would make churches and clergy unnecessary.

Nor was it poetry, for poems were too finished and perfect to finish and perfect anything themselves. The key was so simple and obvious that it had been continually overlooked and was less likely to be a specialist's triumphant conclusion than to be mentioned casually by someone innocent and dull; so he had searched among biographies and autobiographies, correspondences, histories and travel books, in footnotes to outdated medical works and the indexes of Victorian natural histories. Recently he had thought the key more likely to be found on a night walk through the streets, printed on a scrap of paper blown out of the rubble of a bombed factory, or whispered in a dark street by someone leaning suddenly out of a window.

Tonight he came to a piece of waste ground, a hill among tenements that had been suburban twenty years earlier. The black shape of it curved against the lesser blackness of the sky and the yellow spark of a bonfire flickered just under the summit. He left the pallid gaslit street and climbed upward, feeling coarse grass against his shoes and occasional broken bricks. When he reached the fire it had sunk to a few small flames among a heap of charred sticks and rags. He groped on the ground till he found some scraps of cardboard and paper and added them to the fire with a torn-up handful of withered grass. A tall flame shot up and he watched it from outside the brightness it cast. He imagined other people arriving one at a time and standing in a ring round the firelight. When ten or twelve had assembled they would hear a heavy thudding of wings; a black shape would pass overhead and land on the dark hilltop, and the messenger would walk down to them bringing the key. The fire burned out and he turned and looked down on Glasgow. Nothing solid could be seen, only lights— streetlamps like broken necklaces and bracelets of light, neon cinema signs like silver and ruby brooches, the ruby, emerald and amber twinkle of traffic regulators—all glowing like treasure spilled on the blackness.

He went back down to the dingy streets and entered a close in one of the dingiest. The stair was narrow, ill lit and smelling of cat piss. Before a lavatory door on a half landing he stepped over two children who knelt on a rug, playing with a clockwork toy. The top landing had three doors, one with FORBES COULTER on it in Gothic script among gold vine leaves, framed behind glass which the passage of years had blotched

with mildew on the inside. The door was opened by a small
woman with an angry cloud of curly grey hair. She said plaintively, "Robert's down in the lavatory Duncan, you'll just have
to come in and wait."
Thaw stepped across a cupboard-sized lobby into a tidy comfortable crowded room. Wardrobe, sideboard, table and chairs left
narrow spaces between them. A tall window had a sink in front
and a gas cooker beside it. A shadow was cast over the fireplace
by drying clothes on a pulley in the ceiling, and the table held
the remains of a meal.

Mrs. Coulter began moving plates to the sink and Thaw
sat by the fire and stared into a bed-recess near the door. Coulter's father lay there, his shoulders supported by pillows, his
massive sternly lined blind enduring face turned slightly toward
the room.
Thaw said, "Are you any better, Mr. Coulter?"
"In a way, yes, Duncan; but then again, in a way, no. How's
the school doing?"
"I'm all right at art and English."
"Art is your subject isn't it? I used to paint a bit myself. During
the thirties a few of us—we were unemployed, you know—
we got together on Thursday evenings in a room near Brigton
Cross and we'd get a teacher or a model along from the art
school. We called ourselves the Brigton Socialist Art Club.
Have you heard of Ewan Kennedy? The sculptor?"
"I'm not sure, Mr. Coulter. Mibby. I mean the name's familiar
but I'm no' sure."
"He was one of us. He went to London and did quite well
for himself. A year ago. . . . No. Wait."
Thaw looked at Mr. Coulter's big gnarled hand lying quietly
on the quilt, a cigarette with a charred tip between two fingers.
"It was three years ago. His name was in the *Bulletin*. He
was making a bust of Winston Churchill for some town in
England. I thought when I read it, I used to know you."
Mr. Coulter hummed a quiet tune then said, "My father was
a picture framer to trade. He did everything in those days,
carving the wood, gilding it, even hanging the picture sometimes. Some of his work must be in the Art Galleries to the
present day. I used to help him with the hanging. Hanging a
picture is an art in itself. What I meant to tell you was this: I
was hanging these pictures in a house in Menteith Row on
the Green. It's a slum now but the wealthiest folk in Glasgow
once lived in those houses, and in my time some of them still

did, and this house belonged to Jardine of Jardine and Beattie, the shipbuilders. Young Jardine was a lawyer and became Lord Provost, and *his* son proved tae be a bit of a rogue, but never mind. I was hanging these pictures in the entrance hall: marble floor, oak-panelled walls. The frames were carved walnut covered with gold leaf, but the hall was dark because there were no windows opening into it, apart from a wee skylight window that was no use at all because it was stained glass. When I had finished I opened the front door and went down the steps onto the pavement outside and stood looking in through the open door. It was a morning in the early spring, cold, but the sun quite bright. A girl came along and said, 'What are ye staring at?' I pointed through the door and said 'Look at that. It looks like a million dollars.' The sun was shining intae the hall and the gold frames were shining on the walls. It really did look like a million dollars.''

Mr. Coulter smiled a little.

Coulter entered and said, "Hullo, Duncan. Hullo, Forbes. Forbes, your cigarette's out. Will I light it for you?"

"Ye can light it if you like."

Coulter got a match and lit the cigarette, then went to the sink, put an arm round his mother's waist, and said, "My ain wee mammy, how about a fag? You've given my daddy a fag, give me a fag."

Mrs. Coulter took a cigarette packet from her apron pocket and handed it over, grumbling, "You're no' old enough tae smoke but.''

"True, but my wee mammy can refuse me nothing. Have these two been discussing art?"

"Aye, they've been talking about their art."

"Well, Thaw, my intellectual friend, what's it to be? A game of chess or a dauner along the canal bank?"

"I wouldnae mind a dauner."

They walked on the towpath talking about women. Coulter had dropped the hard cheerful manner he wore at home. Thaw said, "The only time I reach them is when I speak at the debating society. Even Kate Caldwell notices me then. She was in the front row of desks last night, staring at my face with her mouth and eyes wide open. I felt dead witty and intellectual. I felt like a king or something. She sits behind me at maths now. I've made a poem about it."

He paused, hoping that Coulter would ask him to recite. Coulter said, "Everybody writes poems about girls at our age. It's what

they call a phase. Even big Sam Lang writes poems about girls.
Even I occasionally—"

"Never mind. I like my wee poem. Bob, if I ask you a question
will ye promise to answer truthfully?"

"Ask away."

"Is Kate Caldwell keen on me?"

"Her? On you? No."

"I think she's mibby a bit keen on me."

"She's a wee grope," said Coulter.

"What?"

"A grope. A feel. Lyle Craig in the fifth year is supposed to
be winching her steady, and last Friday I saw her being lumbered by a hardman up a close near the Denistoun Palais."

"Lumbered?"

"Groped. Felt. She's nothing but a wee—"

"Don't use that word!" cried Thaw.

They walked in silence until at last Coulter said, "I shouldnae
have told you that, Duncan."

"But I'm glad. Thank you."

"I'm sorry I told you."

"I'm not. I want to know every obstacle, every obstacle there
is. There's the obstacles of not being attractive, not having
money to take her out, not knowing how to talk to her, and
now it seems she's a flirt. If I ever reach her she'll shift elsewhere
and keep on shifting."

"Mibby it's a mistake to start with Kate Caldwell. You should
practise on someone else first. Practise on my girl, big June
Haig."

"Your girl?"

"Well, I've only been out with her once. There's a big demand
for her."

"What's she like?"

"She's got a back like an all-in wrestler. Her arms are as thick
as my thighs and her thighs as thick as your waist. Cuddling
her is like sinking intae a big sofa."

"You hardly make her sound attractive."

"Big June is the most attractive girl I know. She's exciting
and she's comfortable. Ask her to the third-year dance."

Thaw remembered June Haig. She was a sulky-looking girl
and not as large as Coulter pretended, but she had failed to
get out of the second year and was called Big June to distinguish
her from the less developed girls she sat among. Thaw felt a
pang of interest. He said, "Big June wouldnae come to a dance
with me."

"She might. She doesnae like you but she's intrigued by your reputation."

"Have I a reputation?"

"You've two reputations. Some say you're an absentminded professor with no sex life at all; others say that's just a disguise and you've the dirtiest sex life in the whole school."

Thaw stood still and held his head. He cried, "I see no way out, no way out. I want to be close to Kate, I want to be valued by her, I suppose I want to marry her. What bloody good is this useless wanting, wanting, wanting?"

"Don't think your problems would be solved by marrying her."

"Why not?"

"Fornication isnae just sticking it in and wagging it around. You've tae time things so that when you're pushing hardest she's exactly ready to take it. If ye don't get this exactly right she feels angry and disappointed with you. It needs a lot of practice tae get right."

"Examinations!" cried Thaw. "It's all examinations! Must everything we do satisfy someone *else* before it's worthwhile? Is everything we do because we enjoy it selfish and useless? Primary school, secondary school, university, they've got the first twenty-four years of our lives numbered off for us and to get into the year above we've to pass an exam. Everything is done to please the examiner, never for fun. The one pleasure they allow is anticipation: 'Things will be better after the exam.' It's a lie. Things are never better after the exam. You'd think love was something different. Oh, no. It has to be studied, practised, learnt, and you can get it wrong."

"You're eloquent tonight," said Coulter. "You've got me almost as mixed up as yourself. But not quite. You see there's really no connection between—"

"*What's that?*"

"That? A kid singing."

They were beside a fence of old railway sleepers planted upright at the towpath edge. From the other side a clear tuneless little voice sang:

> "Ah've a laddie in Ame-e-e-rica,
> Ah've a laddie ower the sea;
> Ah've a laddie in Ame-e-e-rica,
> And he's goantae marry me."

They looked through a gap in the sleepers onto a road with the canal embankment on one side and the black barred windows of a warehouse on the other. A small girl was skipping with a rope and singing to herself in a circle of light under a lamp. Coulter said, "That kid's too young to be up at this hour. What are ye grinning at?"

"I thought for a moment her words might be the key."

"What key?"

Thaw explained about the key, expecting it would send Coulter into a fit of annoyance, as most of his less practical concepts did. Coulter frowned and said, "Has this key to be words?"

"What else could it be?"

"When I was staying with auld MacTaggart in Kinlochrua during the war I remember two or three nights when I got a good view of the stars. Ye can always see more stars when you're in the country, especially if there's a nip of frost in the air, and these nights the sky was just hotching with stars. I felt this . . . this coming nearer and nearer me till I almost had it, but when I tried tae think what it was, it had gone. And this happened more than once."

"I don't know what you mean. What sort of thing was it? Did it tie up everything you believed? Could ye test things with it?"

"You could test nothing with it. It was a feeling, I suppose. It was gentle, and permanent, and more like a friend than anything else."

Thaw was unable to think of a similar experience and felt envious. He said, "It sounds a bit sentimental. Did you only feel it when you were seeing stars?"

"That was the only time."

Thaw looked at the sky. Though at first sight it was merely dark his eyes gradually resolved it into brownish-purple, turning dull orange on the horizon toward the city centre. Thaw said, "Why is it that colour?"

"I suppose it's the electric light reflected back from the gas and soot in the air."

They reached a point halfway between their homes and said goodbye. After Thaw had gone forward a few yards by himself he heard a cry from behind. He turned and saw Coulter wave and shout, "Don't worry! Don't worry! Tae hell with Kate Caldwell!"

Thaw walked onward with a small perfect image of Kate Caldwell smiling and beckoning inside him. Such a fog of desperate emotions was wrapped round it that at last he had to halt and gasp for breath. On the far bank of the canal stood the vast sheds of the Blochairn ironworks. Dull bangs and clangs came from these, an orange glare flickered on the sky above them, the canal water bubbled blackly and wisps of steam waltzed on the surface and flew in a cloud over the towpath. A high railing divided the path from the Alexandra park. Taking a great breath he rushed at this, gripped two spikes on top, pulled himself up and jumped down onto the golf course. He ran along the fairways feeling exalted and criminal and came to a place where trees grew from smooth turf around the pagoda of an ornamental fountain. The grey lawns with dim galaxies of daisies on them, the silhouettes of the trees and fountain, were excitingly unlike themselves as he had seen them on the way from school a few hours before. Stepping over a "Keep Off the Grass" sign he went to a tree he had often wished to climb. It had no branches for the first twelve feet but it was craggy and crooked and he climbed high into it before the impetus which had driven him over the railing ran out and left him astride a high bough with his arms round the trunk. He recalled Greek stories about female spirits who lived inside trees. It was possible to imagine that the trunk between his arms contained the body of a woman. He hugged it, pressed his face against it and whispered, "I'm here. I'm here. Will you come out?" He imagined the woman's body pressing the other side of the bark, her lips wrestling to meet his lips, but he felt nothing but roughness so he let go and climbed higher until the branches swung under his feet. Overhead the purple-brown sky had been pricked by a star or two. He tried to feel something gentle, permanent and friendly in them until he felt absurd, then climbed down and went home.

Mrs. Thaw opened the door to him. She said, "Duncan, how did you get in that mess?"
"What mess?"
"Your face is pot black, pot black all over!"
He went to the bathroom and looked in the mirror. His face was smeared with sooty grime, especially round the mouth.

CHAPTER 18. Nature

The manageress of the Kinlochrua Hotel was a friend of Mrs. Thaw and invited her children north for the summer holidays. They boarded a bus one morning in a garage on the Broomielaw and it took them through shadows of warehouses and tenements into bright sunlight on the broad, tree-lined Great Western Road. They hurled past Victorian terraces and gardens and hotels, past merchants' villas and municipal housing schemes into a region which (though open to the sky) could not be called country. New factories stood among tracts of weed and thistle, pylons grouped on hillsides and wire fences protected rows of grassy domes joined by metal tubes. The Clyde on their left widened to a firth, the central channel marked by buoys and tiny lighthouses. A long oil tanker moved procession-ally seaward between tugboats and was passed by a cargo ship going the other way. The hills on the right got steeper and nearer, the road was pinched between the river and a wooded crag, then they saw ahead of them the great rock of Dumbarton upholding the ancient fort above the roofs of the town. The bus turned north up the Vale of Leven, sometimes travelling between fields and sometimes through the crooked streets of industrial villages, then it reached the broad glittering water of Loch Lomond and ran along the western shore. Islands lay with trees, fields and cottages on them like broken-off pieces of the surrounding land, and on the far side arose the great head and shoulders of Ben Lomond. Fields gave way to heather and the islands grew small and rocky. The Loch became a corri-dor of water between high-sided bens, with the road twisting through trees and boulders at the feet of them.

The bus was full of folk going north for the holidays. Climbers sat at the back singing bawdy mountaineering songs

and Thaw pressed his brow to the cool window and felt desperate. On leaving home he had taken a grain of effedrine and boarded the bus feeling fairly well, but beyond Dumbarton his breathing worsened and now he tried to forget it by concentrating on the ache the vibrating glass made in the bones of his skull. In the passing land outside the colours were raw green or dead grey: grey road, crags and tree trunks, green leaves, grass, bracken and heather. His eyes were sick of dead grey and raw green. The yellow or purple spots of occasional roadside flowers shrieked like tiny discords in an orchestra where every instrument played over and over again the same two notes. Ruth said, "Feeling cheesed off, brother mine?"
"A bit. It's getting worse."
"Cheer up! You'll be fine when we arrive."
"It's not easy."
"Ach, you're too pessimistic. I'm sure you wouldnae get so bad if you were less pessimistic."

The bus stopped on a hillside in Glencoe to let climbers off and the passengers were told they could stretch their legs for five minutes. Thaw got laboriously out and sat on a sun-warmed bank of turf at the roadside. Ruth stood with climbers taking their rucksacks from the boot and talked to someone she had met when climbing with her father. The other passengers gossiped and glanced at the surrounding peaks with expressions of satisfaction or puzzled resentment. An elderly man said to his neighbour, "Aye, a remarkable vista, a remarkable vista."
"You're right. If these stones could talk they would tell us some stories, eh? I bet they could tell us some stories."
"Aye, from scenes like these Auld Scotia's grandeur springs."
Thaw looked upward and saw huge chunks of raw material hacked about by time and weather. From cracks in the highest a rocky rubble spilled over heathery slopes like stuff poured down slag-bings. A boy and girl in shorts and climbing boots strode past him down the road, the boy with a small rucksack bumping between his shoulders. The climbers by the bus cheered and whistled after them: they joined hands and grinned without embarrassment. The assurance of the boy, the ordinary beauty of the girl, the happy ease of both struck a pang of rage and envy into Thaw which almost made him choke. He glared at a granite slab on the turf beside him. It carried patches of lichen the shape, colour and thickness of scabs he had scratched from his thigh the night before. He imagined the

lichen's microscopic roots poking into imperceptible pores in what seemed a solid surface, making them wider and deeper. 'A disease of the rock,' he thought, 'A disease of matter like the rest of us.'

Back in the bus Ruth said, "That was Harry Logan and Sheila. They're going to do the Buchail and spend the night in Cameron's bothy. I wouldnae mind being Sheila for today. Not for tonight, but for today." She laughed and said, "Are you very bad, Duncan? Why not take another pill?"

"I've done that."

Ten minutes later he knew the asthma had grown too strong for pills and he began fighting it with his only other weapon. Withdrawing to the centre of his mind he recalled images from bookshop windows and American comics: a nearly naked blonde smiling as if her body was a joke she wanted to share, a cowering dishevelled girl with eyes and mouth apprehensively open, a big-breasted woman with legs astride and hands on hips and a sullen selfish stare which seemed to invite the most selfish kind of assault. His penis stiffened and he breathed easily. He fixed on the last of these women and her face became the face of big June Haig. He imagined meeting her in the precipitous waste landscapes through which the bus was rushing. She wore white shorts and shirt but high-heeled shoes instead of climbing boots, and he raped her at great length with complicated mental and physical humiliations. To stop these thoughts from coming to a climax of masturbation he sometimes wrenched his mind from them and sat amazed that thought could make such strong bodily changes. As his penis shrank the asthma got hard and heavy in chest and throat; then his mind gripped the image of the woman once more and a tingling chemical excitement spread again through his blood, widening all its channels and swelling the penis below and the air passages above. And behind it all suffocation waited like an unfulfilled threat.

The bus stopped in a street of uninteresting houses on the shore of a loch. Thaw and Ruth got out and found their mother's friend awaiting them in a car. Ruth sat in front beside her. She was a small lady with a tight mouth and an abrupt way with the gear lever. Thaw, dumb with sexual broodings, sat in the back seat hardly listening to the conversation.

"Is Mary still working in that drapery?"

"Yes, Miss Maclaglan."

"A pity. A pity your father can't get a better job. Won't these
open-air organizations he does so much for *pay* him anything?"
"I don't think so. He only works for them in his spare time."
"Hm. Well, I hope you're very helpful to your mother around
the house. She isn't at all well, you know."
Ruth and Thaw gazed out of the window in embarrassment.
The road undulated in slanting sunlight over a great boggy
moor with small irregular lochans in the folds of it. The summit
of a conical peak arose beyond the curve of the moor's horizon,
and Thaw saw, with distaste, it was Ben Rua. To keep sexually
excited he had been forced to imagine increasingly perverse
things and now whatever in the outer world recalled other
experiences upset him by its irrelevance. They came to the
height of the moor and descended toward an arm of the sea
with Kinlochrua on the other side, a strip of cottage-flecked
lands beneath a grey and grey-green mountain. The tide was
out and the clear shallow brine, reflecting blue sky over yellow
sands, made a colour like emeralds. A sudden muffled clattering
hurt their eardrums. Miss Maclaglan said, "They're testing
something at the munition factory. Let's hope it isn't atomic."
"Wasn't the munition factory shut down when the war stopped?"
said Ruth.
"Yes, it was shut for almost a year; then the Admiralty took
it over. They've taken over the hostel too but they haven't
opened it yet, more's the pity. The hostel was the best thing
that ever happened here, it shook up their ideas a bit. Kinlochrua was dead before and it's been dead since. Do you know
that Mary Thaw is the only real friend I've made in the place?
How can you be friendly with women who're afraid to knit
on Sundays because of what the minister will say? What has
nosey old McPhedron to do with their knitting? Your brother
isn't too well, is he?"
Ruth turned and gave Thaw a glance which meant, Pull yourself
together. She said, "He's having one of his wheezy spells, but
he's got pills for it."
"Well, I think he should go straight to bed the moment we
get to the hotel."

At the hotel Miss Maclaglan showed him upstairs to a small
clean flower-patterned bedroom. He undressed slowly, removing a shoe and staring for ten minutes through the window,
postponing from moment to moment the effort of removing
the next. Outside lay a mossy ill-kept garden hidden by a wing
of the building from the well-kept gardens in front. It was

hemmed in by dark green cypresses and pines. Small paths and hedges were arranged round a square half-stagnant pond with a broken sundial in the middle. The whole place fascinated him with a sense of sluggish malignant life. The hedges were half withered by the grasses pushing up among them; the grasses grew lank and unhealthy in the shadows of the hedges. With more fibrous limbs than the millipede has legs various plants struggled in the poor soil, fighting with blind deliberation to suffocate or strangle each other. Between the roots moved insects, maggots and tiny crustaceans: jointed things with stings and pincers, soft pursy things with hard voracious mouths, hard-backed leggy things with multiple eyes and feelers, all gnawing holes and laying eggs and squirting poisons in the plants and each other. In the corruption of the garden he sensed something friendly to his own malign fantasies. Convulsively, he wrenched off the other shoe, undressed and got into bed. Miss Maclaglan brought in a hot-water bottle and asked if he would like anything to read. He said no, he had his own books. Ruth brought up a meal on a tray. He ate, then lay and masturbated. Ten minutes later he masturbated again. After that he had no weapons to use against the asthma at all.

The garden behind the hotel was overlooked by a dusty porch containing a massive table and some chairs too worn for use inside. Next day he sat there with books and painting tools. Breathing heavily, he made pencil drawings, emphasized the best ones with India ink and tinted the result with watercolours. While he worked the asthma came to bother him less, and as he had hardly slept the night before he shut his eyes, leaned over the table and rested his brow upon clenched fists. He could hear the air lightly stirring the branches of the trees, the infrequent call of a bird and a wasp buzzing in the corner of the porch, but he listened most intently to a murmuring in his own head, a vague remote sound like the conversation of two people in an adjacent room. One speaker was excited and raised his voice so much above the steady drone of the other that Thaw almost heard the words: ". . . ferns and grass what's wonderful about grass . . ."

An external sound made him look up. The minister stood on the sunlit path beyond the shadow of the porch watching him in an interested way. His buttoned-up black figure was as Thaw remembered, but smaller, and the face more kindly. He said, "They tell me you are not well."

"I'm a lot better this morning, thanks."

The minister stepped into the porch and looked at a drawing. "And who is this fellow?"

"Moses on Sinai."

"What a wild wee man he looks among all that rock and thunder. So you are illustrating the bible."

Thaw spoke tonelessly to keep the note of pride out of his voice. "No. I'm illustrating a lecture I'm to give to the school debating society. It's called 'A Personal View of History.' The pictures will be enlarged onto a screen by epedaiescope."

"And what place has Moses in your view of history?"

"He's the first lawyer."

The minister laughed and said, "In a sense, yes, no doubt, Duncan; but then again, in a sense, no. What's this you are reading?" He picked up a thin book with a glossy cover.

"Professor Hoyle's lectures on continuous creation."

The minister sat down on a chair with his hands on the umbrella handle and his chin resting on his hands. "And what does Professor Hoyle tell us about the creation?"

"Well, most astronomers think all the material in the universe was once compressed in a single gigantic atom, which exploded, and all the stars and galaxies in the universe are bits of that old atom. You know that all the galaxies in the universe are rushing away from each other, don't you?"

"I have heard rumours to that effect."

"It's more than rumour, Dr. McPhedron, it's proved fact. Well, Professor Hoyle thinks all the material of the universe is made out of hydrogen, because the hydrogen atom is the simplest form of atom, and he thinks hydrogen atoms are continually coming into existence in the increasing spaces between the stars and forming new stars and galaxies and things."

"Dear me, is that not miraculous! And you believe it?"

"Well, it isn't definitely proved yet, but I like it better than the other theory. It's more optimistic."

"Why?"

"Well, if the first theory is true then one day the stars will burn out and the universe will be nothing but empty space and cold black lumps of rock. But if Professor Hoyle is right there will always be new stars to replace the dead ones."

The minister said politely, "I am fortunate to be rescued from a dying universe at the moment of finding myself menaced by it."

When Thaw had worked out what the minister meant he felt oppressed and angry. He said "Dr. McPhedron, you talk and—

and smile as if everything I say is stupid. What do you believe in that makes you superior? Is it God?"

The minister said gravely, "I believe in God."

"And that he's good? And made everything? And loves what he made?"

"I believe those things too."

"Well, why did he make baby cuckoos so that they can only live by killing baby thrushes? Where's the love in that? Why did he make beasts that can only live by killing other beasts? Why did he give us appetites that we can only satisfy by hurting each other?"

The minister grinned and said, "Dear me. God himself might be afraid to sit an examination like this. However, I'll do my best. You talk, Duncan, as if I believed that the world as it is is the work of God. That is not true. The world was made by God, and made beautiful. God gave it to man to look after and keep beautiful, and man gave it to the Devil. Since then the world has been the Devil's province, and an annexe of Hell, and everyone born into it is damned. We have either to earn our bread by the sweat of our brow or steal it from our neighbours. In either case we live in a state of anxiety, and the more intelligent we are the more we feel our damnation and the more anxious we become. You, Duncan, are intelligent. Mibby you've been searching the world for a sign of God's existence. If so, you have found nothing but evidence of his absence, or less, for the spirit ruling the material world is callous and malignant. The only proof that our Creator is good lies in our dissatisfaction with the world (for if the God of nature had made us the life of nature would suit us) and in the works and words of Jesus Christ, someone you may have read of. Has Christ a place in your view of history?"

"Yes," said Thaw boldly. "I regard him as the first man to make a religion of the equal worth of each individual."

"I'm glad you present him as something so respectable, but he's more than that. He is the way, the truth and the life. To find God you must believe Christ *was* God and discard every other knowledge as useless and vain. Then you must pray for grace."

Thaw shifted several times uncomfortably during this speech, for it embarrassed him; also, he was finding it hard to keep his eyes open. After a half minute of silence he realized a question was expected and said, "What's grace?"

"The Kingdom of Heaven in your own heart. The sure knowledge that you are no longer damned. Freedom from anxiety.

God does not send it to all believers, and to few believers for very long."

"Do you mean that even if I become a Christian I can never be sure of . . . of . . ."

"Salvation. Dear me, no. God is not a reasonable man like your grocer or bank manager, giving an ounce of salvation for an ounce of belief. You can't bargain with him. He offers no guarantee. I see I am boring you, Duncan, and I'm sorry for it, though I've said nothing that almost every Scotsman did not take for granted from the time of John Knox till two or three generations back, when folk started believing the world could be improved."

Thaw held his head between his hands feeling depressed and dull. The minister's answer was more thorough than he had expected and he felt trapped by it. Though certain there were many sound counter arguments, the only one he could think of was "What about the cuckoos?"

The minister looked puzzled.

"Why did God make cuckoos so that they have to live by killing thrushes? Did they give the world to the Devil too? Or did the thrushes?"

The minister got up and said, "The life of brute beasts, Duncan, is so different from ours that strong feelings for them are bound to be vanity and self-deception. Even your father the atheist would agree with me in that. I understand you will be here a week or two. Mibby we can discuss these matters another time. Meanwhile, I hope you have better health."

"Thank you," said Thaw. He pretended to scribble on a piece of paper till the minister had gone then folded his arms on the edge of the table and laid his head on them. He was very tired but if he lost consciousness for a moment the beast of suffocation might pounce on his chest, so he tried to rest without actually sleeping. This was difficult. He got up, collected his things and went slowly to bed.

That afternoon his memory of what is was like to be well faded and hope of improvement faded with it. The only imaginable future was a repetition of a present which had shrunk to a tiny painful act, a painful breath drawn again and again from an ocean of breath. No longer companioning erotic fancies (which, like the pills, had got useless through overuse) the sluggish resolute life of the garden grated on him as it grated on the soil feeding it. He felt the natural world stretching out from each wall of the hotel in great tracts of lumpy earth and rock coated thickly with *life,* a stuff whose parts renewed themselves by eating each other. Two or three hundred miles to the south was a groove in the earth with a gathering of stone and metal in it—Glasgow. In Glasgow he had been aided a little by a feeling that among many people someone might hear and help if he screamed loudly enough. But among these mountains screaming was useless; his pain was as irrelevant as the pain of the thrush starved out by the cuckoo, the snail crushed by the thrush. He started screaming but stopped at once. He tried to think but his thoughts were trapped by the minister's speech. How could the world be justified except as punishment? Punishment for what?

That evening Miss Maclaglan phoned for a doctor. He entered Thaw's room and sat by the bed, a not quite middle-aged man in plus fours with a black moustache and squarish head sunk so far into his shoulders that he seemed unable to move it independently of his body. He took Thaw's pulse and temperature, asked how long he had been like this and grunted sombrely. Miss Maclaglan brought a pan of boiling water with a small metal cage clipped inside it. He took glass and metal parts from the cage, fitted them together into a hypodermic syringe, filled this from a rubber-capped bottle then asked Thaw to pull up his pyjama sleeve. Thaw stared at a corner of the ceiling, trying to think of nothing but a crack in it. He felt the muscle of his upper arm wiped with something cold and then the needle running in. The steel point breaking through layers of tissue set his teeth on edge. There was a faint ache as the muscle swelled with pumped-in fluid, then the needle was withdrawn and an amazing thing started to happen. There spread through his body from the arm, but this time unsustained by thought, the tingling liberating flood he had only been able to make erotically. Each nerve, muscle, joint and limb relaxed, his lungs expanded with sufficient air, he sneezed twice and lay back feeling altogether comfortable and well. There was no sense of asthma waiting to return. He could not believe he would ever be unwell again. He looked out into the sun-warm garden. An overgrown rosebush beside the pond had put out white blossoms, and the black dot of a bee moved over one. Surely the bee was enjoying itself? Surely the bush grew because it liked to grow? Everything in the garden seemed to have grown to its appropriate height and now rested a moment, preserved in the amber light of the evening sun. The garden looked *healthy.* Thaw turned with servile gratitude to

the ordinary depressed-looking man who had made this change in things. The doctor was examining books and drawings on the bedside table and frowning slightly. He said, "Any better?"
"Yes, thanks. Thanks a lot. I'm a lot better. I can sleep now."
"Mm. I suppose you know that your kind of asthma is partly a psychological illness."
"Yes."
"You do a lot of reading, don't you?"
"Yes."
"Do you abuse yourself?"
"Certainly, if I've been stupid in public."
"No no. I mean, do you masturbate?"
Thaw's face went red. He stared down at the quilt.
"Yes."
"How often?"
"Four or five times a week."
"Mm. That's quite often. It's not widely agreed upon yet, but there is evidence that nervous diseases are aggravated by masturbation. The inmates of lunatic asylums, for instance, masturbate very often indeed. I would try to cut it out if I were you."
"Yes. Yes, I will."
"Here's a bottle of isoprenaline tablets. If you get bad again, break one in two and let half dissolve under your tongue. I think you'll find it'll help."
Thaw was left feeling faintly worried, but fell asleep almost at once.

He woke late at night and worse than ever. The isoprenaline tablets had no effect and the image of June Haig occurred to him, potent and burning like a hot poker in the blood of his stomach. He thought, 'If only I think things about her it will be all right. I don't need to masturbate.' He thought things about her and masturbated ten minutes later. The beast of suffocation pounced at once. He clenched his fists against his chest and dragged breath into it with a gargling sound. Fear became panic and broke his mind into a string of gibbering half-thoughts that would not form: I can't you are I won't it does it will drowning no no no no drowning in no no no no air I can't you are it does. . . .
A thundering hum filled his brain. He was about to faint when a sudden thought formed complete—*If I deserve this it is good*—and around the thought his mind began exultingly to reassemble. He grinned into the bulb of the bedside lamp. He was

in pain, but not afraid. Breathing hoarsely, he took a notebook
and pen from the bedside table and wrote in big shapeless
words:

> *Lord God you exist you exist my punishment proves it. My
> punishment is not more than I can bear what I suffer is
> just already the pain is less because I know it is just I
> won't ever do that thing again, it will be a hard fight but
> with your help I am able for it I won't ever do that thing
> again.*

Next day he did it three times. Miss Maclaglan sent a
telegram to his mother, who came north by bus the day after.
She stood by the bed and smiled sadly down at him. "So you're
not too well, son."
He smiled back.
"Ach," she said, "You're a poor auld man. Get a bit better
and I'll stay on with you awhile. It'll be an excuse for me to
have a holiday too."
He was moved to a big low-ceilinged room with two beds in
it. One was his, and Ruth and his mother shared the other.
That night when the lights were out Ruth said, "Sing to us,
Mummy. It's a long time since you sang to us."
Mrs. Thaw sang some lullabies and sentimental lowland songs:
Ca' the Yowes, Hush-a-baw Birdie, This is No' My Plaid. She
had once won certificates at musical festivals with her singing,
but now she only managed the high notes by singing
them very softly, almost in a whisper. She tried to sing *Bonnie
George Campbell,* which starts with a loud wild lamenting note,
but her voice cracked and went tuneless and she stopped and
laughed: "Ach, it's beyond me now. I'm getting an auld
woman."
"No! you're not!" Thaw and Ruth shouted together. Her words
alarmed them. She said, "I think we should try to sleep."
He lay against his pillows breathing heavily. When he coughed
Mrs. Thaw said hopefully, "That's right son, bring it up," and
afterward, "There now, that's better, isn't it?"
But he had brought up hardly anything, and nothing was better,
and the sense of her lying awake attending to the pains in
his chest made them harder to bear. He tried to be as still as
possible, keeping the small lumps in his gullet until the silence
from the other bed made him think she was asleep, but as
soon as he coughed, however stealthily, the creak of a mattress
told him she was awake and listening.

Suddenly he was sitting up and laughing in the darkness. He had been thinking about the key, or perhaps dreaming of it, and now he saw the universe and the meaning of things. It was hard to put his vision into words but he wanted to share it. "Everything is hate," he gabbled dreamily. "We are all hate, big balloons of hate. Tied together by Ruth's hair ribbons."

The two women screamed. Mrs. Thaw said in a high-pitched voice, "That settles it. We're going back. We're going back tomorrow. There must be *somebody* who knows how to cure him."

Ruth yelled, "You're selfish, utterly selfish! You just don't care about anyone but yourself!" and started crying. Thaw felt puzzled, knowing the words had not conveyed what he meant to convey. He tried again.

"Men are pies that bake and eat themselves, and the recipe is hate. I seem to be buried in this rockery . . ." for though he could dimly see the bedroom, and knew where his mother and sister lay, he also felt buried up to the armpits in a heap of earth and rocks. Mrs. Thaw shouted, "Shut up! Shut up!"

Next morning Thaw and his mother returned to Glasgow. Ruth was allowed to stay behind. That day a boat called at Kinlochrua and Miss Maclaglan drove them to the pier and waved from it as they put to sea. The sun shone as bright as when he had arrived five days before, and for the first time since arriving he saw the great green side of Ben Rua. A clean hard wind was blowing. A member of the crew, a thin boy of Thaw's age, leaned against the funnel playing a concertina. Gulls with spread wings hung above in the rushing air. Thaw sat on a ventilator which stuck out of the deck like an aluminium toadstool, and nearby his mother waved to the figure on the receding pier. On the mountaintop he could make out the white dot of the triangulation point. He thought of the previous night and tried to recover from the muddle of darkness and crying his vision of the key. He seemed to have thought that, just as hydrogen was the basic stuff of the universe, so hatred was the basic material of the mind. In the fresh sunlight it was not a convincing idea. He felt amazingly weak, yet liberated, and while sitting still was not conscious of asthma at all.

Two days later Thaw walked jauntily into town with Coulter to visit the Art Galleries. He talked about the visit to Kinlochrua and what the doctor said. Coulter became angry. "That's daft!" he said. "Everybody masturbates at our age. It's natural. We produce the stuff; how else can we get rid of it? Five times a week sounds about normal to me."

"But that doctor said that in lunatic asylums they do it all the time."

"I believe him. Lunatics are like us. They arenae allowed to have sex in other ways. And what else can they do with their time?"

"But whenever I do it nowadays I have another attack."

"I can believe it. That doctor made you think you would have asthma when you masturbate so you have asthma. Anybody can make you believe anything if they try hard enough. I remember once making you think I was a German spy."

Thaw started grinning. "The funny thing is," he said, "that doctor had me believing in God as well."

"How? No, don't tell me, I see how," said Coulter with disgust, "I bet you felt very special and superior, being punished by God for something he doesnae give a damn for in other folk. Well, I hate to disappoint you, but ye may as well leave God and masturbation out of it and go back to having asthma in the normal way."

CHAPTER 19.
Mrs. Thaw Disappears

Thaw opened his diary and wrote:

"Love seeketh not itself to please Nor for itself hath any care But for another gives its ease and builds a Heaven in Hell's despair." So sung a little Clod of Clay trodden by the cattle's feet, but a Pebble of the brook warbled out these metres meet. "Love seeketh only Self to please, to bind another to Its delight, Joys in another's loss of ease, and builds a Hell in Heaven's despite."

Blake doesn't choose, he shows both sorts of love, and life would be easy if women were clods and men were pebbles. Maybe most of them are but I'm a gravelly mixture. My pebble feelings are all for June Haig, no, not real June Haig, an imaginary June Haig in a world without sympathy or conscience. My feelings for Kate Caldwell are cloddish, I want to please and delight her, I want her to think me clever and fascinating. I love her in such a servile way that I'm afraid to go near her. This afternoon Mum was operated on for something to do with her liver. It seems that for the past year or two old Doctor Poole has been treating her for the wrong illness. I'm ashamed to notice that yesterday I forgot to record that she'd been taken into hospital. I must be a very cold selfish kind of person. If Mum died I honestly don't think I'd feel much about it. I can't think of anyone, Dad, Ruth, Robert Coulter, whose death would much upset or change me. Yet when reading a poem by Poe last week, Thou wast that all to me, love, for which my soul did pine, etc., I felt a very poignant strong sense of loss and wept six tears, four with the left eye, two with the right. Mum isn't going to die of course but this coldness of mine is a bit alarming.

They entered a vast ward in the Royal Infirmary flooded, through tall windows, with grey light from the sky outside. Mrs. Thaw leaned on her pillows looking sick and gaunt yet oddly young. Many lines of strain had been washed from her face by the anaesthetic. She looked more mournful than usual but less worried. Thaw got behind the bed and carefully combed the hair which lay matted around her head and neck. He took a strand at a time in his left hand and combed with the right, noticing how its darkness had been given a dusty look by the grey threads in it. He could think of nothing to say and the combing gave a feeling of closeness without the strain of words. Mr. Thaw said, holding his wife's hand and looking through a nearby window, "You've quite a view from here."

Below them stood the old soot-eaten Gothic cathedral in a field of flat black gravestones. Beyond rose the hill of the Necropolis, its sides cut into by the porches of elaborate mausoleums, the summit prickly with monuments and obelisks. The topmost monument was a pillar carrying a large stone figure of John Knox, hatted, bearded, gowned and upholding in his right hand an open granite book. The trees between the tombs were leafless, for it was late autumn. Mrs. Thaw smiled and whispered wanly, "I saw a funeral go in there this morning."
"No, it's not a very cheery outlook."

Mr. Thaw explained to his children that it would be weeks before their mother was well enough to come home and some months after that before she was able to leave her bed. The household would need to be reorganized, its duties distributed between the three of them. This reorganization was never effectively managed. Thaw and Ruth quarrelled too much about who should do what; moreover, Thaw was sometimes prevented by illness from working at all and Ruth thought this a trick to make her work harder and called him a lazy hypocrite. Eventually nearly all the housework was done by Mr. Thaw, who washed and ironed the clothes at the weekend, made breakfast in the morning and kept things vaguely tidy. Meanwhile, the surfaces of linoleum, furniture and windows became dirtier and dirtier.

At Whitehill School the pressure of work seemed to slacken for Thaw. The Higher Leaving Examination, the culmination of five years of schooling, was a few months away, and all around him his schoolmates crouched over desks and burrowed like moles into their studies. He watched them with the passion-less regret with which he saw them play football or go to dances: the activity itself did not interest, but the power to share it would have made him less apart. The teachers had stopped attending to pupils who would certainly pass or certainly fail and were concentrating on the borderline cases, so he was al-lowed to study the subjects he liked (art, english, history) ac-cording to his pleasure, and in Latin or mathematics classes sat writing or sketching in a notebook as far from the teacher as possible. After Christmas he was told he would not be put forward for his leaving certificate in Latin, and this gave an extra six hours a week to use as he pleased. He used them for art. The art department was in whitewashed low-ceilinged rooms at the top of the building, and nowadays he spent most of his time there making an illuminated version of the Book of Jonah. Sometimes the art teacher, a friendly old man, looked over his shoulder to ask a question.

"Er . . . is this meant to be humorous, Duncan?"

"No sir."

"Why have you given him a bowler hat and umbrella?"

"What's humorous about bowler hats and umbrellas?"

"Nothing! I use an umbrella myself, in wet weather. . . . Do you mean to do anything special with this when you have com-pleted it?"

Thaw meant to give it to Kate Caldwell. He mumbled, "I don't know."

"Well, I think you should make it less elaborate and finish it as soon as possible. No doubt it will impress the examiner, but he's more likely to be impressed by another still life or a drawing of a plaster cast."

Occasionally at playtime he went onto the balcony outside the art room and looked into the hall below where the captain of the football team, the school swimming champion and several prefects usually stood laughing and chatting with Kate Caldwell, who sat with a girlfriend on the edge of a table under the war memorial. Her laughter and hushed breathless voice floated up to him; he thought of going down and joining them, but his arrival would produce an expectant silence and revive the rumour that he loved her.

One day he came from the art room and saw her walk along the balcony on the other side of the hall. She smiled and waved and on an impulse he glared back timidly, opened the door behind him and beckoned. She came round, smiling with her mouth open. He said, "Would you like to see what I'm doing? In art, I mean?"

"Oh, that would be lovely, Duncan."

The only other student in the art room was a prefect called MacGregor Ross who was copying a sheet of Roman lettering. Thaw brought a folder of work from a locker and laid the pictures one after another on a desk in front of her.

"Christ arguing with the doctors in the temple," he said. "The mouth of Hell. This is a fantastic landscape. Mad flowers. These are illustrations I did for a debating society lecture. . . ."

She greeted each picture with small gasps of admiration and surprise. He showed her the unfinished Book of Jonah. She said, "That's wonderful, Duncan, but why have you given him a bowler hat and an umbrella?"

"Because he was that kind of man. Jonah is the only prophet who didn't want to be a prophet. God forced it on him. I see him as a fat middle-aged man with a job in an insurance office, someone naturally quiet and mediocre whom God has to goad into courage and greatness."

Kate nodded dubiously.

"I see. And what will you do with it when it's finished?"

Duncan's heart started thumping against his ribs. He said, "I'll mibby give it to you. If you'd like it."

She smiled flashingly and said, "Oh, thank you, Duncan, I'd love to have it. That's wonderful of you. It really is. . . . And what are *you* so busy with?" she asked, going over to MacGregor Ross. She pulled a stool up to MacGregor Ross's desk and spent twenty minutes with her head close beside his while he showed her how to use a lettering pen.

Mrs. Thaw left the Infirmary early in the new year. Mrs. Gilchrist downstairs and one or two other neighbours came into the house to prepare it for her, and dusted, washed and polished into the obscurest corner of every room.

"You'll have to be specially nice to your mother and help her all you can now," they said severely. "Remember, she won't be able to leave bed for a long time."

"Interfering old bitches," said Ruth.

"They mean well," said Thaw tolerantly. "They just have an unfortunate way of putting things."

Mrs. Thaw came home by ambulance and was tucked into the big bed in the front bedroom. She was allowed to sit by the fire in the evenings and soon gained enough strength for her children to quarrel with her without feeling very guilty. Thaw

brought home the completed "Book of Jonah." She took it
on her knee, looked thoughtfully through, asked him to explain
certain details then said seriously, "You know, Duncan, you
would make a good minister."

"A minister? Why a minister?"

"You have a minister's way of talking about things. What are
you going to do with this?"

"I'm giving it to Kate Caldwell."

"Kate Caldwell! Why? *Why?*"

"Because I love her."

"Don't be stupid, Duncan. What do you know about love?
And she certainly won't appreciate it. Ruth tells me she's nothing but a wee flirt."

"I'm not giving it to her because she'll appreciate it. I'm giving
it because I love her."

"That's stupid. Totally stupid. You'll have the whole school
laughing at you."

"The school's laughter is no concern of mine."

"Then you're a bigger fool than I thought. You've no sense
or pride or backbone at all and you'll marry and be made
miserable by the first silly girl who takes a fancy to ye."

"You're probably right."

"But I shouldn't be right! You ought not to let me be right!
Why can't you . . . oh, I give up. I give up. I give up."

The skin disease returned and his throat looked as if he
had made an incompetent effort to cut it. Each morning he
went to his mother's bedside and she wound a silk scarf tightly
round up to his chin and fixed it with small safety pins, giving
his head and shoulders a rigid look. One morning he entered
a classroom and found Kate Caldwell's eyes upon him. Perhaps
she had expected someone else to come in, or perhaps she
had looked to the door in a moment of unfocused reverie,
but her face took on a soft look of involuntary pity, and seeing
it he was filled by pure hatred. It stamped his face with an
implacable glare which stayed for a second after the emotion
faded. Kate looked puzzled, then turned with a toss of the
head to some gossiping friends. That night, without any sense
of elation, Thaw gave the "Book of Jonah" to Ruth and afterward sat glumly by his mother's bed.

"Do you know something, Duncan?" said Mrs. Thaw. "Ruth
will appreciate that a thousand times more than Kate Caldwell."

"I know. I know," he said. There was an ache between his
heart and stomach as if something had been removed.

"Ach, son, son," said Mrs. Thaw, holding out her arms to him, "never mind about Kate Caldwell. Ye've always your auld mither."
He laughed and embraced her saying, "Yes, mither, I know, but it's not the same thing, it's not the same thing at all."

The Higher Leaving Examination arrived and he sat it with no sense of special occasion. In the invigilated silence of the examination room he glanced through the mathematics paper and grinned, knowing he would fail. It would be too conspicuous to get up and walk out at once so he amused himself by trying to solve two or three problems using words instead of numbers and writing out the equations like dialectical arguments, but he was soon bored with this, and confronting the supervising teacher's raised and condemning eyebrows with an absentminded stare he handed in his papers and went upstairs to the art room. The other examinations were as easy as he had expected.

Mrs. Thaw had grown gradually stronger but at the time of the exams she caught a slight cold and this caused a setback. She only got up now to go to the lavatory. Mr. Thaw said, "Don't you think you should use the bedpan?"
She laughed and said, "When I can't go to the lavatory myself I'll know I'm done for."
One evening when Thaw was alone with her in the house she said, "Duncan, what's the living room like?"
"It's quite warm. There's a good fire on. It's not too untidy."
"I think I'll get up and sit by the fire for a bit."
She pulled the bedclothes back and put her legs down over the edge of the bed. Thaw was disturbed to see how thin they were. The thick woollen stockings he pulled on for her would not stay up but hung in folds round her ankles.
"Just like two sticks," she said, smiling. "I've turned into a Belsen horror."
"Don't be *daft!*" said Thaw. "There's nothing wrong that another month won't cure."
"I know, son, I know. It's a long, slow process."
At this time Thaw slept with his father in the bed settee. He did not sleep well, for the mattress had a hollow in the middle which Mr. Thaw, being heavier, naturally filled, and Thaw found it hard not to roll down on top of him. One night after the lights were out he remarked how pleasant it would be to get back to the usual sleeping arrangements when his

mother was better. After a pause, Mr. Thaw said strangely, "Duncan, I hope you're not . . . hoping too much that your mother will get better." Thaw said lightly, "Oh, where there's life there's hope."

"Duncan, there's no hope. You see, the operation was too late. She's been recovering from the effects of the operation, but it's a recovery that can't last. Her liver is too badly damaged."

Thaw said, "When will she die then?"

"In a month. Mibby in two months. It depends on the strength of her heart. You see, the liver isn't cleaning the blood, so her body is getting less and less nourishment."

"Does she know?"

"No. Not yet."

Thaw turned his face away and wept a little in the darkness. His tears were not particularly passionate, just a weak bleeding of water at the eyes.

He was wakened by a crash and a great cry. They found his mother struggling on the lobby floor. She had been trying to go to the lavatory. "Ach, Daddy, I'm done. I'm done. Finished," she said as Mr. Thaw helped her back to bed. Thaw stood transfixed at the living-room door, his brain ringing with echoes of the cry. At the moment of waking to it he had felt it was not an unexpected thing, but something heard ages ago which he had waited all his life to hear again.

Two days later Thaw and Ruth came home from school together and had the door opened to them by Mr. Thaw. He said, "Your mother has something to tell you."

They entered the bedroom. Mr. Thaw stood by the door watching. The bed had been moved to the window to give her a view of the street, and she lay with her face toward them and said timidly, "Ruth, Duncan, I think that one day soon I'll just . . . just sleep away and not wake up."

Ruth gasped and ran from the room and Mr. Thaw followed her. Thaw went to the bed and lay on it between his mother and the window. He felt below the covers for her hand and held it. After a while she said, "Duncan, do you think there's anything afterwards?"

He said, "No, I don't think so. It's just sleep."

Something wistful in the tone of the question made him add, "Mind you, many wiser folk than me have believed there's a new life afterwards. If there is, it won't be worse than this one."

For several days on returning from school he took his shoes off and lay beside his mother holding her hand. It would have been untrue to say he felt unhappy. At these times he hardly thought or felt at all, and did not talk, for Mrs. Thaw was becoming unable to talk. Usually he looked out at the street. Although joining a main road it was a quiet street and usually lit by cold spring sunshine. The houses opposite were semi-detached villas with lilacs and a yellow laburnum tree in the gardens. If he felt anything it was a quietness and closeness amounting to contentment. During this time Ruth, who had never taken much interest in household things, became very busy at cleaning and cooking and made her mother many light sorts of foods and pastries, but soon Mrs. Thaw had to be nourished on nothing but fluids and was too weak to speak clearly or open her eyes. Nobody in the household talked much, but once Thaw made a remark to his sister beginning. "When Mummy's dead . . ."

"She's not going to die."

"But Ruth . . ."

"She's not *going* to die. She's going to get better," said Ruth, staring at him brightly.

At school oral examinations were held to corroborate the results of the written exams. The English teacher told his students to learn by heart some passages of prose, preferably from the bible, since they might be asked to recite aloud. Thaw decided to shock the examiner by learning the erotic verses from the Song of Solomon which begin, "Behold thou art fair, my love, behold thou art very fair." On the morning of the English oral he went after breakfast to say cheerio to his mother. Mr. Thaw was sitting by the bed holding one of her hands between both of his. She lay back on the pillows, a line of white showing below her almost closed eyelids. She was mumbling desperately, "I aw ie, I aw ie."

"All right, all right, Mary," said Mr. Thaw. "You won't die. You won't die."

"Uh I *aw* ie, I *aw* ie."

"Don't worry, you're not going to die, you're not going to die."

For the first time in two weeks Mrs. Thaw shuddered and sat up. Her eyes opened to the full, she pulled her lips back from her teeth and shrieked, "I want to die! I want to die!" and fell back. Thaw collapsed on a chair, holding his head between his hands and sobbing loudly. Ten minutes later he ran to

school across the sunlit slope of the park, loudly chanting verses from the Song of Solomon. When he got home that afternoon Mrs. Thaw lay more quiet and still than ever and breathed with a faint wheezy sound. He put his lips to her ear and whispered urgently, "Mum! Mum! I've passed in English. I've got Higher English."
A faint smile moved her mouth, then sank into her blind face like water into sand. Next morning when Mrs. Gilchrist downstairs came in to wash her and pulled the curtain behind the bed she heard a very faint whisper: "Another day," but in the afternoon word that Thaw had passed in Art and History did not reach the living part of her brain, or else she had grown indifferent.

She died three days later, very early on a Saturday morning. The previous night Mrs. Gilchrist downstairs and Mrs. Wishaw from across the landing sat waiting in the living room and did not move out when Thaw went to bed there. Mr. Thaw sat in the bedroom holding his wife's hand. When Thaw awoke the light was filtering through the curtains and the neighbours had left and he knew his mother was dead. He got up, dressed, ate a bowl of cornflakes and switched the wireless on to a comedy programme. Mr. Thaw came in and said, slightly embarrassed, "Would you mind turning it down a bit, Duncan? The neighbours might be offended if they heard."
Thaw switched off the wireless and went for a walk to the canal. He stood at the edge of a deep stone channel and watched without thought or feeling the foam-flecked water swirl between rotting timbers.

In the afternoon he called on Coulter as he had arranged to do some while before. Mrs. Coulter had taken her husband for a walk, and Thaw sat by the fire while Coulter, in vest and trousers, washed at the sink. Thaw said awkwardly, "By the way, Bob, my mother died last night."
Coulter turned slowly round. He said "You're joking, Duncan."
"No."
"But I saw her two weeks ago. She was talking to me. She seemed all right."
"Aye."
Coulter towelled his hands, looking at Thaw closely. He said, "You shouldn't hold it in, Duncan. It'll be worse for you later."
"I don't think I'm holding anything in."

Coulter pulled a shirt and pullover on and said in a worried way, "The bother is, I arranged tae meet Sam Lang at Tollcross playing fields at three. We were going to do some running practice. I thought you wouldnae mind coming along."

"I don't mind coming along."

When he got home the undertaker had called. A coffin lay on a pair of trestles on the rug before the bedroom fireplace. The lid was placed to leave a square hole at the top and Mrs. Thaw's face stuck up through the hole. Thaw looked at it with puzzled distaste. The features had been his mother's but though he saw no difference in the shape all resemblance had vanished. The thing was without even the superficial life of a work of art and its material lacked the integrity of bronze or clay. He touched the brow with a fingertip and felt cold bone under the cold skin. This dense pack of dead tissues was not his mother's face. It was nobody's face.

In the days before the funeral the bedroom was pervaded by a sweet fusty odour which spread to other parts of the house. Air fresheners of the kind used in lavatories were placed under the coffin but made little difference. On Tuesday the minister of Mrs. Thaw's church conducted a short service in the living room while the coffin was screwed tight and taken deftly downstairs to the hearse. The living room was crowded with neighbours and old friends and relatives whom Thaw had heard his parents speak of but hardly ever met. Twice or thrice during the service the door was furtively opened and those beside it shifted to admit a stealthily breathing old man or woman. Thaw stood by the sideboard wearing his newest suit. It struck him that the minister had not visited his mother during the last weeks, and this not through failure of duty (he was a young earnest nervous man) but because his presence would have been an intrusion. To Mrs. Thaw and her friends the church had been a gathering place. They went to a service on Sunday, and on Thursday to a social club in the church hall, but none could have been accused of piety. Mrs. Thaw had been shocked when, some years before, Thaw called himself an atheist, but no more shocked than when, shortly afterward, he called himself a Christian and started turning the other cheek in his fights with Ruth. A phrase came into his head: "The consolations of religion." As far as he could see, his mother had lived and died without consolations of any kind at all.

The service ended and he went down to the cars with his father, the minister and a few others. The cars were shining black Rolls-Royces with silent engines and as they sped through the streets of the northern suburbs he looked out of the window feeling comfortable and privileged. It was a grey day, a lid of grey sky had shut down on Glasgow and thin smirr fell from it. They came to a municipal cemetery so precisely on the edge of the city that on three sides it was surrounded by open fields. There was a delay at the gate. The cars halted in a line behind the cars of a funeral party ahead. After a while the cars in front disappeared and they went up a curving drive between dripping rhododendrons and stopped outside a minia-ture Victorian-gothic church with a smokestack behind. More neighbours and relatives were waiting at the porch and followed Thaw and his father inside. They stood in the front row of pews and everyone else crowded into the pews behind. Just before them was a tall pulpit, and to the right of it a low platform with the coffin on top. Coffin and platform were cov-ered by a heavy red cloth. After a moment of silence Thaw began to wonder why nobody sat down. The same thought must have struck his father, for he sat down and everyone followed his example. The minister, in the black gown and white bands of a doctor of divinity, climbed into the pulpit, said a prayer and announced a hymn. Everyone stood and sang and sat down again. The minister produced a sheet of paper and said, "Before we proceed with the service I have been asked—er, to read this to you:

"During the last few months of her illness Mary Thaw was completely confined to her bed. I would like to thank those many good friends and neighbours who made these months as pleasant for her as they could. They brought gifts of fruit and of cake, and the even more precious gift of their company. I would like to tell them on her behalf how very much she appreciated their attentions, and to extend to them the thanks that she herself is unable to extend today."

In the pews behind somebody sniffed and blew their nose. Thaw looked sideways at his father and whispered, "That was very good." The service continued. At the words "Dust to dust and ashes to ashes," there began a lumbering rumbling sound and the red cloth began to sag as the coffin was drawn down under it. For a second it bulged up again with a rush of air from below, then flopped so that a rectangular depression

appeared where the coffin had been. Thaw was struck by a
poignant sense of loss neutralized at once by a memory of a
conjuror who had made a scone disappear from under a handkerchief.

Outside the church people squared their shoulders and
began talking in loud cheerful voices.
"Well, that didn't go too badly, did it?"
"A beautiful service, beautiful."
"Hullo, hullo! There's a voice I've not heard in many a long
day. How are ye, Jim?"
"No' too bad. A beautiful service, wasn't it?"
"Aye, beautiful. I liked that bit the minister read out in the
middle."
"Ye cannae beat good neighbours."
"Aye, but she deserved good neighbours. She was one hersel'."
"Who's that waiting by the gate? Don't tell me it's auld Neil
Bannerman?"
"Aye, it's Neil Bannerman."
"My God, he looks done. Really done. Fancy auld Neil Banner-
man surviving Mary Thaw. Last time I saw him was at her
father's funeral ten years back."
"Is it true, er, there's a quantity of refreshment, er, available
somewhere?"
"Aye, man, there's a tea laid on at the Grand Hotel at Charing
Cross. Come in my car."
The male relations gathered in a private room of a hotel in
Sauchiehall Street and ate a high tea of cold ham and warm
vegetables. They chattered about old acquaintances and football
and the days when the local churches had their own football
teams. Thaw sat silent among them. At one point Bernard Shaw
was mentioned and he was asked to tell an anecdote about
him. It was well received. Afterward he returned with his father
in someone's car. The rain was falling heavily now. He thought
how pleasant it would be to get home and sit by the bedroom
fire drinking tea with his mother, then remembered this was
impossible.

Mr. Thaw wanted his wife's ashes scattered on a hillside
overlooking Loch Lomond where they had walked together
in their courting days. One windy and sunny spring morning
he journeyed with his children to Loch Lomond by train. Thaw
held the oblong deal box with the ashes in it upon his knee.

The lid lacked hinge or fastening, and he raised it once or twice and looked curiously at the soft grey stuff inside. It was exactly like cigarette ash. Mr. Thaw said, "Be careful, Duncan." Duncan said, "Yes, we don't want to spill her before we get there."

He was surprised to see his father look shocked. They climbed the hillside by a stony lane sunk among bracken and budding hedges. Higher up this became a cart track over a green field, then they went through a gap in a dry-stone dyke and it became a sandy path among heather with curlews crying around it. Near the path lay a flat rock with a hole in the middle where the Colquhoun clan once stuck their banner pole when gathering to fight.

"I suppose this place is as good as any," said Mr. Thaw.

They sat and rested, looking down on the loch and the green islands in it. Northward the jagged wall of the highland bens looked distinct and solid enough to bang the knuckles against. They waited till a young couple who had paused to see the view passed out of sight, then opened the box and flung handfuls of ash into the air. The wind whisked it away like smoke into the heather.

A fortnight after Mr. Thaw sat at his desk in the living room and said, "Duncan, come here. I want ye to look at this. It's the bill for your mother's funeral. A fantastic figure, isn't it? You'd think cremation would be a lot cheaper than burial, but no. The costs are practically the same."

Thaw looked at the bill and said, "Aye, it does look a bit extravagant."

"Well, I'm not going to have that sum of money wasted on me, so I'm arranging to give my body to science. Would ye sign this paper? It's to prove that as next of kin you have no objection."

Thaw signed.

"Good. The arrangement is that when I die you inform the medical faculty of the university and they call and collect me with an iron coffin. If you do that within twenty-four hours, you and Ruth will be given ten pounds to divide between you, so you see it's not only cheaper, it's profitable."

"I'll spend the money drinking to the health of your memory," said Thaw.

"If you've sense you'll spend it otherwise."

Almost a year later Thaw was looking through a drawer when he found a letter in his mother's handwriting. It was written very faintly in pencil and was a rough draft of a letter she probably never got round to sending. It was superscribed to the correspondence page of a cheap woman's magazine.

> *I have enjoyed very much the letters from your readers telling about the funny mistakes some children make. I wonder if you would like to print an experience of mine. When my wee son was six or seven, we left the house one night quite late and were looking up at the stars. Suddenly Duncan said, "Where's the tractor?" His father had been teaching him the names of the stars, and he had got mixed up with the plough. I have not been very well recently and have had to spend most of the time in bed. I find my main pleasure nowadays in memories like these.*

Thaw stood awhile with the letter in his hand. He remembered the night she spoke of. It had been at the hostel in Kinlochrua at Christmas. The family had been going to a concert in the main building, and the question had been asked by Ruth. Mrs. Thaw had always preferred him to Ruth and had unconsciously transferred the incident. He put back the letter and shut the drawer. Grief pulled at an almost unconscious corner of his mind like a puppy trying to attract its master's attention by tugging the hem of his coat.

CHAPTER 20. Employers

The Higher Leaving Examination results were not yet published, but almost everyone knew how well or badly they had done and the school was full of excited discussions about maximum salaries and minimum qualifications. Employment officers came and lectured on careers in accountancy, banking and the civil service. A lawyer talked about law, an engineer about engineering, a doctor about medicine and a major about the army. A Scottish Canadian lectured on the advantages of emigration. Students argued in groups about whether it was best to stay a sixth year at school and win more certificates or leave at once for university or commercial or technical colleges. Mr. Thaw said, "So what are you going to do?"

"I don't know."

"What do you want to do?"

"That's irrelevant, isn't it?"

"Face facts, Duncan. If you can't live by doing what you want, you must take the nearest thing to it you can get."

"I want to write a modern Divine Comedy with illustrations in the style of William Blake."

"Well, surely the sensible thing to try for is work as a commercial artist?"

"For that I need four years at art school and you cannae afford to send me."

Mr. Thaw looked thoughtful. He said, "When I worked for Laird's, the box-makers, I was fairly friendly with Archie Tulloch, who was head of the art department. They used to take in boys of sixteen or seventeen then. They designed labels for packages and cartons, you know, and patterns for wrapping paper. That might not gratify your bohemian soul, but it would be a start. If I wrote to Archie Tulloch he would likely look your work over."

Thaw got an afternoon off school and walked down into Bridgeton wearing a newly cleaned overcoat and with a folder of work under his arm. The factory was near the river and he descended to it by narrow streets where many small factories stood between tenements and scrapyards. The sky was grey and beyond the rooftops the Cathkin Braes looked flat and dark like a wall shutting the city in, though he could make out the silhouettes of trees on the skyline. He remembered his mother talking about these trees when he was very small. They had reminded her of a line of camels in the desert. The ceiling of cloud pressed lower and released a thin smirr like a falling mist. It glazed the streets until they reflected the pale sky, a seagull skimming above the street appeared as far below it. The city seemed hung among distances of grey air, and windows were raised from the bottom and hands placed potted ferns on the sills to be watered. The rain soothed Thaw's misery. He started to feel confident, and to imagine coming often this way to Laird's. Even when very rich he would walk through these streets with such regularity that folk who lived there would set their clocks by him. He would be part of their lives. He came to a factory which was a huge brick cube at the junction of two streets. He straightened his tie, ran a hand through his hair, gripped the folder tightly and pushed through a revolving door of brass, glass and carved mahogany.

The entrance hall was a bare place with a small door marked INQUIRIES. He turned the knob and entered a wedge-shaped room with a switchboard and an elderly lady shut in a corner by a counter of polished yellow wood. The lady said, "Yes?"
"I've an appointment; that's to say I'm expected. Mr. Tulloch expects me."
"What is your name, please?"
He said shyly, "I am Duncan Thaw."
The lady moved her fingers among clicking plugs and said, "Mr. Tulloch? A Mr. Thaw to see you. He says he has an appointment. . . . Very well."
She deftly fingered more switches.
"Would you send down a junior? To take a Mr. Thaw to the waiting room? . . . Very well. . . . Would you wait here a little while, sir?"
"Yes, please," said Thaw, humbled at being called sir. He went to a low table with magazines arranged neatly on top in overlapping rows. Lacking the courage to disturb their order, he was content to look at the covers:

The Executive—A MAGAZINE FOR THE MODERN BUSINESSMAN.

Modern Business—A MAGAZINE FOR THE EXECUTIVE.

Ingot—THE THUNDERHAUGH STEEL GROUP MONTHLY BULLETIN.

Automobile—THE CAR DEALERS' MONTHLY BULLETIN.

They had the thin glossy covers of obscene novelettes and were mostly pictures of people in expensive clothes sitting behind desks.

A small neat pretty girl came in and said, "Mr. Thaw? Will you come this way, please?"
He walked behind her across the bare hall and climbed some wide metallic stairs. She hurried ahead of him through corridors of glass and cream-coloured metal, smiling downward as if sharing a tender secret with her bosom, and left him at a door labelled WAITING ROOM. Inside four men sat round a table, one of them saying in an English Midland dialect, "Yes, but what I don't understand is—"
"Will you excuse us?" said another man swiftly to Thaw. Thaw sat down in a comfortable chair and said, "Certainly. Please go on. I'm only here to wait."
"Then would you wait outside?" said the swift man, rising and opening the door. Thaw sat feeling insulted on a sofa against the corridor wall. It occurred to him that the men inside were capitalists plotting something. This floor of the factory was cut up into offices by glass screens supported by metal walls. The glass was rippled so that only shadows could be seen through it, and the bleakness, coldness, metallicness of the place gave a resounding quality to footsteps, clattering typewriters, ringing telephones, and the mutter of administrative voices. Two long spectacled men paused at a corner.
"I think I'd better check that teller."
"No no. No need for that at all."
"Still, if the figures aren't exact—"
"No no. Even if his figures are a hundred percent out, that's enough for my purpose."

Thaw realized Mr. Tulloch was beside him. He was a weary, paunchy man who said, "Duncan Thaw? . . . Yes . . ." and sat down.

"I haven't much time. Show me your stuff."

Thaw suddenly felt competent and businesslike. He opened his folder and said "Here is a series of watercolours, a series dealing with acts of God. The Deluge. The Tower of Babel. The Walls of Jericho Falling Flat."

"Um. Mmm. Next?"

"Penelope unweaving. Circe. Scylla and Charybdis. The last is least successful because at the time I was equally influenced by Blake and Beardsley and the two sorts of outline—"

"Yes. And this?"

"The Cave Artist. Moses on Sinai. Greek Civilization. Roman Imperialism. The Sermon on the Mount. Vandals. The Cathedral City. John Knox preaching to Mary Queen of Scots. The Factory City. The—"

Mr. Tulloch suddenly sat back and Thaw grinned at the air before him and shuffled the pictures back into the half-emptied folder. Mr. Tulloch was saying, ". . . take them at intervals of five years, so you see we really have no room for you. Your work, however, is very promising. Yes. Perhaps something in the illustrative line. Have you tried McLellan the publisher?"

"Yes, but—"

"Oh, yes, ha, ha, well of course the business is overcrowded just now. . . . Have you tried Blockcrafts, Bath Street? Well, try them. Ask for Mr. Grant and say I sent you. . . ." They stood up together. "Apart from that, you see, there's nothing I can do."

"Yes," said Thaw. "Thankyou very much."

He smiled and wondered if the smile looked bitter. It felt bitter. Mr. Tulloch conducted him to the head of the staircase and gave him a tired smile and an unexpectedly firm handshake. "Goodbye. I'm sorry," he said.

Thaw hurried into the drab street, feeling cheapened and defeated. He remembered with an odd pang that Mr. Tulloch had not once asked about his father.

A week later Thaw and his father saw the headmaster of Whitehill School, a white-moustached man who regarded them kindly from behind his desk. He said "Duncan, Mr. Thaw, has very strong imaginative powers. And undoubted talent. And his own way of seeing things, unfortunately." He smiled. "I say unfortunately because this makes it hard for plodding mediocrities like you and me to help him. You agree?"

Mr. Thaw laughed and said, "Oh, I agree all right. However, we must do our best."

"However, we must do our best. Now I think Duncan would be happiest in some job without too much responsibility, a job that would leave him plenty of spare time to develop his talents as he pleases. I see him as a librarian. He's good with books. I see him as a librarian in some small highland town like Oban or Fort William. What do you think, Mr. Thaw?"

"I think, Mr. McEwan, it is a very satisfactory *idea*. But is it a *possibility?*"

"I think so. To enter the library service two higher and two lower certificates are required. Duncan's higher art and english and lower history are guaranteed.The maths results aren't out yet. How do you think he did?"

Mr. Thaw said, "Well, Duncan?"

As the firm responsible voices passed his future gravely backward and forward between them Thaw sank into a fatalistic doze. It took him a moment to notice he was expected to speak. He said, "I've failed in maths."

"Why are you sure?"

"To pass I need full marks for everything I wrote, and what I wrote was mostly nonsense."

"Why does someone of your intelligence write nonsense after four years of study?"

"Laziness, I suppose."

The headmaster raised his eyebrows. "Indeed? The problem is, would you continue to be so lazy if your father was prepared to allow you another year at school?"

Mr. Thaw said, "In other words, Duncan, will you study for a certificate in lower maths if Mr. McEwan allows you another year at school?"

As Thaw considered this a grin began upon his face. He tried to suppress it and failed. The headmaster smiled and said to Mr. Thaw, "He's thinking of all the reading and painting he'll be able to do with practically no supervision at all. Is that not so, Duncan?"

Thaw said, "And mibby I'll be able to go to evening classes at the art school."

The headmaster struck the desk with his hand and leaned over it. "Yes!" he said seriously. "A year of freedom! But it has to be bought. The price is not high, but are you prepared to pay it? Do you faithfully promise your father to study and

master your trigonometry and algebra and geometry? Do you
promise to attend your mathematic lessons, not only in body
but in spirit?"
Thaw hung his head and muttered, "Yes, sir."
"Good, good. Mr. Thaw, I think you have an assurance you
can depend upon."

Next day Thaw met the mathematics teacher as he crossed
the hall. She looked at him brightly and said, "What happened
to you, Thaw?"
He was puzzled. She smiled and said, "Haven't you been going
around telling people you'd failed in maths?"
"Yes, Miss."
"Well, the official results have just been published. You've
passed. Congratulations."
Thaw stared at her in horror.

Later that week he walked into the white marble entrance
of the Mitchell Library. He had often come to this place to
see facsimiles of Blake's prophetic books, and as a plump man
in a brass-buttoned coat led him upstairs the air of scholastic
calm and polite attention produced a lightening of the spirit.
It might not be a bad thing to work in this place. He was
conducted to a door at the end of a corridor with chequered
marble floor and low white vaulted ceiling. The room within
was thickly carpeted, with a vase of flowers on the marble
mantelpiece and another on a desk at the window. A small
old man behind the desk was reading a document. He said
in a clogged voice, "Mr. Thaw? Pleaze take a zeat. I'll be
able to attend to you in a minute."
Thaw sat uneasily. The man had a hole in the right side of
his face where the cheek should have been and most of the
face was twisted toward it. His right eye had been pulled out
of line with the left and the eyeball was so exposed that when
he blinked, which was often, the eyelid could not cover it.
He laid the document down and said, "Zo you want to become
a librarian."
The muscles working his tongue moved awkwardly and beads
of saliva kept bouncing from it onto the desk. Thaw watched
them in fascination, nodding and making quiescent sounds when
these seemed appropriate.
". . . . . . hourz nezezzarily ztaggered. You will work two
eveningz per week till half pazt eight, but theze will be compen-

zated for by morningz off. You will be eczpected to attend night glazzez on two other eveningz."

"To learn what?" said Thaw, with effort.

"Bookkeeping and cataloguing. There are zeveral zyztems of cataloguing, each a world in itzelf. Each year you will zit an eczamination and be promoted accordingly, and within five yearz you zhould qualify for a zertificate qualifying you to aczept the pozt of zenior librarian anywhere in the United Kingdom."

"Oh. Oh, good," said Thaw feebly.

"Yez, it *iz* good. *Very* good. But I'm afraid you can't ztart for another zicz weeks. Only the head librarian can employ you and he's viziting the You Ezz Ay juzt now. But he'll be back in zicz weekz, and you'll zertainly be able to ztart then."

　As Thaw left the building a change came upon him. It was as if several pounds had been added to his weight, and his heart had begun beating more sluggishly, and the air had thickened in his lungs. His thoughts also became heavy and thick. At home over tea he told his father about the interview. Mr. Thaw sighed with relief.

"Thank God for that!" he said.

"Yes. Yes, thank *God*. Thank *God*. Yes, indeed, let us give thanks to *God*."

"Duncan, what's wrong? What's the matter?"

"Nothing. Nothing. Things are as finely arranged as they can be in a world of this sort. Praise be to the Maker and Upholder of all things. Yes! Yes! Yes! Yes! Yes! Yes! Ye—"

"Stop! You're talking like a madman! If you won't state the matter honestly then keep your mouth shut!"

Duncan shut his mouth. After a few minutes Mr. Thaw said on a note of pleading, "Tell me the matter, Duncan."

"I had a wish to be an artist. Was that not mad of me? I had this work of art I wanted to make, don't ask me what it was, I don't know; something epic, mibby, with the variety of facts and the clarity of fancies and all of it seen in pictures with a queer morbid intense colour of their own, mibby a gigantic mural or illustrated book or even a film. I didn't know *what* it would have been, but I knew how to get ready to make it. I had to read poetry and hear music and study philosophy and write and draw and paint. I had to learn how things and people felt and were made and behaved and how the human body worked and its appearance and proportions in different situations. In fact, I had to eat the bloody moon!"

"Duncan, remember what your headmaster said! In four years

you can be head librarian in some small country town and
then you can make yourself an artist. Surely a *real* artist could
wait four years?"

"I don't know if he could. I know that none ever did. People
in Scotland have a queer idea of the arts. They think you can
be an artist in your *spare* time, though nobody expects you to
be a spare-time dustman, engineer, lawyer or brain surgeon.
As for this library in a quiet country place, it sounds hellishly
like Heaven, or a thousand pounds in the bank, or a cottage
with roses round the door, or the other imaginary carrots that
human donkeys are shown to entice them into all kinds of
nasty muck."

Mr. Thaw rested his elbows on the table and held his head
in his hands. After a while he said, "Duncan, what do you
want me to do? I want to help you. I'm your father, even
though you've been haranguing me as if I was a social system.
If I was a millionaire I'd gladly support ye in idleness while
you developed your talents, but I'm a costing and bonus clerk,
and fifty-seven years old, and my duty is to make you self-
supporting. Show me an alternative to the library service and
I'll help you toward it."

Tears slid down Thaw's immobile face. He said harshly, "I
can't. There's no alternative. I have no choice but to cooperate
with my damnation."

"Stop being melodramatic."

"Am I melodramatic? I'm saying what I believe as succinctly
as I can."

They finished the meal in silence. Then Mr. Thaw said, "Duncan, go to the art school tonight. Join the evening classes."

"Why?"

"You've six weeks before you start work for the libraries. Use
them for what you like doing most."

"I see. Get a taste of that life before I give it up for good.
No thanks."

"Duncan, join the evening classes."

"No thanks."

That evening he waited in a corridor of the art school
outside the registrar's office in a queue of other applicants.
When his turn came he entered a spacious room and started
walking toward a desk at the far end, conscious of pictorial
and statuesque objects on either side. The man at the desk
looked up as he approached. He had a large, spectacled face
and a wide mouth with amused corners. He spoke drawlingly,

with an expensive English dialect. "Good evening. What can I do for you?"

Thaw sat down and pushed onto the desk a filled in application form. The registrar looked at it and said, "I see you want to go to life classes, ah, Thaw. How old are you?"

"Seventeen."

"Still at school?"

"I've just left it."

"I'm afraid you're rather young for life drawing. You'll have to convince us that your studies are sufficiently advanced to fit you for it."

"I've some work here."

Thaw pushed his folder onto the desk. The registrar looked through it examining each picture carefully. He said, "Are the mounted ones part of a series?"

"They illustrate a lecture I once gave."

The registrar put a few pictures aside and looked at them again. He said, "Don't you think you should join us as a day student?"

"My father can't afford it."

"We could arrange a grant from the Corporation, you know. What are you intending to do?"

"Join the library service."

"Do you like the idea?"

"It seems the only thing possible."

"Honestly, I think you would be wasted in the library service. This is remarkable work. Quite remarkable. I take it you would *prefer* to come to the art school as a full-time day student?"

"Yes."

"Your address is on this form, of course. . . . What school did you go to?"

"Whitehill Senior Secondary."

"Have you a telephone?"

"No."

"Has your father's place of work a telephone?"

"Yes. Garngash nine-three-one-three."

"Well, Thaw, I'll be seeing you again. I'll keep this work if I may. I want to show it to the director."

Thaw shut the door behind him. He had entered the building in an exhausted mood and had maintained through the interview a colourless, almost listless manner. Now he eyed the corridor outside with an excited speculation. It was lined with salt-white casts of renaissance nobility and nude and broken gods and goddesses. A door among these opened and a hectic little group of girls marched out and surrounded him for a moment with swinging skirts and hair, scent, chatter, thighs in coloured slacks and the sweet alien abundances of breasts. ". . . . . . charcoal charcoal charcoal always charcoal. . . . ." ". . . Did you see the way he posed the model? . . ." ". . . . . Wee Davie gives me the horrors. . . ." He ran down a staircase, through the entrance hall and into the street. Too elated to wait for the tram he walked home by a route which took in Sauchiehall Street, Cathedral Square and the canal bank. He saw himself at the school of art, a respected artist among artists: prominent, admired, desired. He entered corridors of glamorous girls who fell silent, gazing at him and whispering together behind their hands. He pretended not to notice but if his look fell upon one she blushed or turned pale. He soared into dreams of elaborate adventure all dimly associated with art but culminating in a fancy that culminated all his daydreams. There was a great hall lit by chandeliers and floored with marble and with a vast staircase at the end rising into the dark of a starless sky. On each side of the hall stood all the women he had loved or who had loved him, all the men they had loved and married, everyone superbly evil, virtuous, wise, famous and beautiful and all magnificently dressed. Then he himself, alone and in ordinary clothes, walked down the centre of the hall and started unhurriedly climbing the staircase toward some huge and ultimate menace at the top. This menace overhung all humanity but only he was fit to encounter it, although it was an encounter from which he would not return. He climbed to a tragic crescendo in which organs, solo voices and orchestras blended in a lament which combined the most impressive effects of Beethoven, Berlioz, Wagner and Puccini.

He got home after dark. Mr. Thaw said, "What kept you?" "I walked back."
"Did they let you join the life class?"
"I'm not sure. The registrar asked me a lot of questions. He thought I should join the day school. I told him it was impossible. He asked for your office telephone number."
Thaw spoke expressionlessly. Mr. Thaw said, "Well, well." They ate supper in silence.

Mr. Thaw came home next day slightly earlier than usual and slightly breathless. He sat facing Thaw across the living-room hearth rug and said, "He phoned me this morning—

Peel, the registrar, I mean. He asked me if I could call and
see him. I'd been talking over this business with Joe McVean,
and Joe said, 'Duncan, you take the afternoon off. I'll manage
fine here myself.' So I went and saw Peel there and then."
Mr. Thaw brought out his pipe and pouch and began filling
one from the other.
"You seem to have made an impression on that man. He said
your work was unusually good. He said it was rare for the
art school authorities to *persuade* someone to join. It had only
happened once in the last ten years. He said the director agreed
with him that you would be wasted as a librarian, and that
you could get a grant from the Corporation of a hundred and
fifty pounds a year. I said to him, 'Mr. Peel, I know nothing
about art. I do not appreciate my son's work. However, I can
vouch for his sincerity, and I accept your opinion as an expert
when you vouch for his ability. But tell me one thing: what
prospects has he when he finishes this four-year course of yours?'
"Well, he hummed and hawed a bit at that, then told me that
for someone of your talent there might well be a chance of
teaching in the art school when you had qualified. 'However,'
he said, 'the boy will be unhappy anywhere else, Mr. Thaw.
Let him decide himself what to do when the four years are
up. Don't rush him into a job he'll hate at this stage.' I said
I would think it over and tell him tomorrow. I went straight
from the art school to Whitehill and saw your headmaster.
Do you know what I found? Peel had phoned him and had a
talk with him. McEwan said to me, 'Mr. Thaw, that man is
better equipped to decide Duncan's future than you or I.' So
I phoned the art school and said you could join."
"Thanks," said Thaw, and left the room. A minute later Mr.
Thaw came to him in the front bedroom, kneeling by the bed
with his face pushed into the coverlet. Indrawn moans came
from his muffled face and his back shuddered spasmodically.
Mr. Thaw said in a puzzled voice, "What's wrong, Duncan?
Don't you want to go to the art school? Aren't you glad?"
"Yes. Very glad."
"Then why are ye greeting?"
Thaw stood up and dried his face with a handkerchief.
"I don't know. Relief, mibby."
Mr. Thaw patted his son affectionately under the chin with
his clenched fist. "Cheer up!" he said. "And if you don't make
another Picasso of yourself, I'll—I'll—I'll knock your block
off so I will."

One hot afternoon Thaw and Coulter came down a woodland path veined by tree roots and freckled with sunlight. Birds called in the green shadows above them. Coulter was talking about work. "At first the novelty made it not too bad. It was different from school, and you were getting paid, and you felt a *man;* you know, getting up and intae your clothes at seven, pulling at the day's first fag while your mother fried your breakfast, then down the road to the tram with your wee packet of sandwiches and sitting in your overalls with the other workers, crowding in at the gate and clocking on and then intae the machine shop—'Hullo,' 'Hullo, here it goes again,' 'You're fuckin' right it does'—and then the thumping and banging and feeling of danger—"
"Danger?" said Thaw.
"There's a bit of danger. You'll be battering away at something when the folk nearby start shouting. You wonder who they're yelling at this time, and they yell louder and it strikes you, 'Christ, what if it's me?' and you turn and there's a ten-ton girder swinging toward you on the overhead crane."
"That's hellish! Are there no rules against that sort of thing?"
"There's meant tae be a lane kept clear up the middle of the shed, but in a work like McHargs it's not easy."
Coulter chuckled.
"A weird thing happened the other day. This bloke was directing the lowering of a girder from the crane; you know, he was standing underneath directing the lowering with his hands (you cannae hear a word in that din); you know—lower, lower, a bit to the left; all right, let it go now. The funny thing was, he was looking up at the bloke at the controls most of the time and he didnae notice that at the last moment he directed the girder to be lowered ontae his foot. He gave a scream like a soprano hitting a top note. We all looked to see what the matter was, but it took a while tae find out. He was standing up like the rest of us, only his foot was crushed under this girder. He couldnae even fall down!"
Thaw gave an appalled laugh and said, "You know that's very funny but—"
"Aye. Well, anyway, this business of being a *man* keeps you happy for mibby a week, then on your second Monday it hits you. To be honest the thought's been growing on you all through Sunday, but it really hits you on Monday: I've tae go on doing this, getting up at this hour, sitting in this tram in these overalls dragging on this fag, clocking on in this queue at the gate. 'Hullo, here we go again!' 'You're fuckin' right

we go!' and back intae the machine shop. You realize you'll
be spending more of your life in this place than anywhere,
excepting mibby bed. It's worse than school. School was compulsory—you were just a boy, you neednae take it seriously,
you could miss a day if your mammy was agreeable and wrote
a note. But engineering isnae compulsory. I chose it. And I'm
a man now. I have tae take it seriously, I *have* tae keep shoving
my face against this grindstone."
Coulter was silent for a while.
"Mind you, this feeling doesnae last. You stop thinking. Life
becomes a habit. You get up, dress, eat, go tae work, clock
in etcetera etcetera automatically, and think about nothing but
the pay packet on Friday and the booze-up last Saturday. Life's
easy when you're a robot. Then accidents happen that start
you *thinking* again. You know the Royal visit last week?"
"Aye."
"Well, there's a railway line at the back of the works, and
the Royal train was to go along it at three in the afternoon,
so the whole work got time off tae see it. So when the train
comes along there are four or five hundred of us at the edge
of the line in our greasy overalls. The Queen's in the first
carriage looking dead cool and gracious and waving; and in
the middle are a lot of old men like Lord Provosts with chains
round their necks, all waving like mad; and in a sort of observation car at the end sits the Duke in his wee yachting cap. He's
sitting at a table with a glass of something on it, and he gives
us a wave, but more offhand. And we all just stand there,
glowering."
Thaw laughed. "Did nobody wave? I think I'd have waved.
Just out of politeness."
"With the whole Union there? They'd have hanged ye. You
can laugh, Duncan, but the sight of the Duke set me back a
good three weeks. I havenae recovered from it yet. Why should
he be enjoying a dram in a comfortable train while I . . .
ach!" said Coulter disgustedly. "It's enough to make you rob
a bank. I've thought a lot about bank robbery recently. If I'd
even a remote chance of succeeding I'd try it too. I've no
faith in football pools."
Thaw said, "You're an apprentice. You won't be in the machine
shop for good."
"No. Six months in the machine shop, six months in the drawing
office, two nights a week at the technical college, and if I pass
the exams I'll be a qualified engineering draughtsman in three
years."

"And then things won't be too bad."
"Won't they? How did you feel about becoming a librarian?"

They crossed a stream by a plank bridge and came to an acre or two of level turf with a white flagpole in the middle. Lovers and picnic parties sat in the shade at the edge of the wood and children charged about playing anarchic ball games. A few benches on the other side of this green space overlooked the sky and had one or two elderly couples on them. Thaw and Coulter crossed to the benches and sat on one. They were on the edge of a plateau near the top of the Cathkin Braes, and a small rocky cliff went down from their feet to another level space noisy with child play and fringed by trees. From there the land sank in steep wooded terraces to a valley floor carpeted with rooftops and prickly with factory chimneys. To the east the Clyde could be seen meandering among farms, fields, pitheads and slag-bings, then Glasgow hid it till the course was marked by a skeletal procession of cranes marching into the west. Behind the city stood the long northern ridge of the Campsie Fells, bare and heather-green and creased by watercourses, and at this height they could see the Highland bens beyond them like a line of broken teeth. Everything looked unusually distinct, for it was Fair fortnight when big foundries stopped production and the smoke was allowed to clear.
"D'ye see Riddrie?" asked Thaw. "That reddish patch? Look, there's my old primary school on one side and Alexandra Park on the other. Where's your house?"
"Garngad's too low to be seen from here. I'm trying to see McHargs. It should be near those cranes behind Ibrox. Aye, there! There! The top of the machine shop is showing above those tenements."
"I should be able to see the art school, it's on top of a hill behind Sauchiehall Street—Glasgow seems all built on hills. Why don't we notice them when we're in it?"
"Because none of the main roads touch them. The main roads run east and west and the hills are all between."
On the grass at the foot of the cliff a big strong-bodied girl of about fourteen stood with legs apart and hands on hips between two piles of jackets. She wore a blue dress and grumbled impatiently as her younger brothers placed a football some distance in front of her and prepared to kick it at the goal mouth. Thaw stared at her in admiration. He said, "She's great. I'd like to draw her."

"Nude?"

"Anyhow."

"She's not exactly an oil painting. She's no Kate Caldwell."

"Damn Kate Caldwell."

They got up and walked on.

"Yes," said Coulter glumly. "You know what you want and you're in a place where they'll help you get it."

"It was an accident," said Thaw defensively. "If the head librarian hadnae been in America, and my Dad hadnae insisted I go to night classes, and the registrar hadnae been English and liked my work—"

"Aye, but it was an accident that *could* happen to you. Not to me. No accident but an atom bomb can get me out of engineering. I've no ambitions, Duncan. I'm like the man in Hemingway's story, I don't want to be special, I just want to feel good. And I'm in work that's only bearable if I feel as little as I can."

"In four months you'll be in the drawing office and learning something creative."

"Creative? What's creative about designing casings for machine units? I'll be better off, but because it's better wearing a clean suit than dirty overalls. And I'll get more money. But I won't *feel* good."

"It'll be years before I earn money."

"Mibby. But ye'll be doing what you want."

"True," said Thaw. "I'll be doing what I want. I suppose"— he turned and waved toward the city—"I'm nearly the luckiest man living here."

They re-entered the wood and came to a clearing with the iron structure of a child's swing in it. Thaw ran and jumped onto the wooden seat, grabbed the chains on each side and swung violently backward and forward in greater and greater arcs.

"Yah—yip—yeaaaaaaaaaaah!" he shouted. "I'll be doing what I want, won't I?"

Coulter leaned against the trunk of a tree and watched with a slight ironical grin.

INTERLUDE

The swing with Thaw on it flew high and stopped, leaving him in an absurd position with his knees higher than his back-flung head. The tree no longer rustled. Each branch and leaf was locked photographically in a single moment and as in old photographs the colour faded out, leaving the scene mono-chrome and brownish. Lanark stared at it through the ward window and said thoughtfully, "Thaw was not good at being happy."

The oracle said He was bad at it.

"Yet that is almost a happy ending."

A story can always end happily by stopping at a cheerful mo-ment. Of course in nature the only end is death, but death hardly ever happens when people are at their best. That is why we like tragedies. They show men ending energetically with their wits about them and deserving to do it.

"Did Thaw die tragically?"

No. He botched his end. It set no example, not even a bad one. He was unacceptable to the infinite bright blankness, the clarity without edge which only selfishness fears. It flung him back into a second-class railway carriage, creating you.

Lanark spread cheese on a slice of rye bread and said, "I don't understand that."

Rima's head stirred among the waves of blond hair on the pillow. Without opening her eyes she murmured, "Go on with the story."

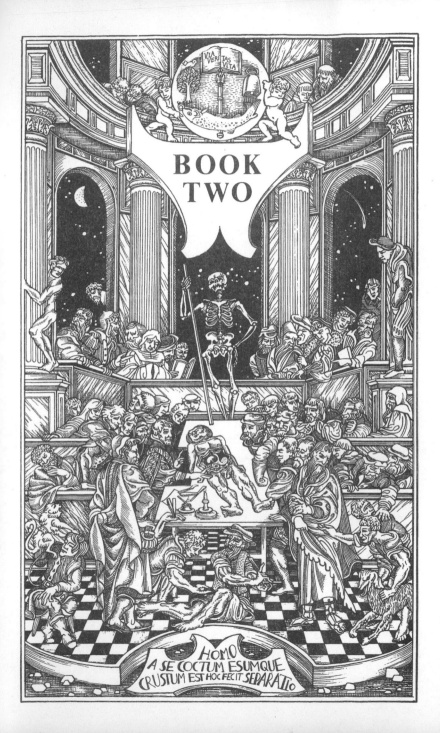

VIA VERITAS VITA

BOOK
TWO

HOMO
A SE COCTUM ESUMQUE
CRUSTUM EST HOC FECIT SEPARATIO

CHAPTER 21. The Tree

The front bedroom was dusty, the curtains unclean, books and papers overlapped the tortoise-shell combs and pin trays on the dressing table. On the wall near the bed a black-bordered photograph of the late king was stuck beside the only picture by Thaw his mother much liked: a childish one of a tree shedding leaves in an autumn gale. These remained because their presence brought Mrs. Thaw less to mind than their removal would have done.

On the first day of art school he woke to the sweet rotten odour which had come when the corpse lay coffined on the hearth-rug. It had taken two or three weeks to vanish and he still sometimes found it on entering the room unexpectedly, though he knew by now it must be altogether ghostly and subjective. Through a gap in the curtains he saw a slice of colourless sky with dark rags of cloud moving across like the shadows of smoke. The ten-to-eight factory horns mourned over the city roofs and he curled more tightly into the nest of warmth his body made in the mattress, for like all bad sleepers he enjoyed bed most in the minutes before leaving it. Faint sounds came from the kitchen where his father prepared breakfast. Hundreds of thousands of men in dirty coats and heavy boots were tramping along grey streets to the gates of forges and machine shops. He thought with awe of the energy needed to keep up a civilization, of the implacable routines which started drawing it from the factory worker daily at eight, from the clerk and shopkeeper at nine. Why didn't everyone decide to stay in bed one morning? It would mean the end of civilization, but in spite of two world wars the end of civilization was still an idea, while bed was a warm immediate fact. He heard his father approach the door and shut his eyes. Mr. Thaw entered quietly, pulled back the curtains, came to the bed and laid a hand on Thaw's brow. Thaw smiled and opened his eyes. His father smiled and said, "Were you really asleep?" "Not really."

Over breakfast they talked about money.
"How much will you need for materials?"
"I don't know. I don't yet know what materials I'll need. But I can get them on account at the school shop."
"That's a very bad idea. It's too easy. I can see you buying something, losing it and buying another."
Thaw said stiffly, "Have you reasons for doubting my honesty?"
"I don't doubt your honesty but I distrust your memory. If you get goods on account be sure to keep the invoices as a reminder. How much will you need for the midday meal?"
"Two shillings."
"Ten bob a week for food. Your tram fares won't come to more than five shillings, so here's a pound."
"That's too much."
"Regard the extra as pocket money. No doubt you'll want a coffee with a friend sometime."
Thaw had hoped for more pocket money. He said in no particular tone of voice, "Thanks very much."
"And Duncan, five shillings a week isn't much pocket money for a boy who'll soon be eighteen. If you ever want to take a lassie out, let me know and I'll give you more."

Garnethill was one of several whale-shaped hills lying parallel to the Clyde and the school was on a quiet street along the spine of it. The main part was an elegant building designed by Mackintosh in the eighteen-eighties but Thaw entered the annexe across the road: a terrace of old houses with new additions among them. He walked down a twisting corridor with so many unexpected descents that it seemed underground. The studio at the end was filled with clear grey morning light from windows in the girder-supported roof. Among tall easels, plaster statues and draught screens some girls crowded loosely in a space like a forest clearing, and boys sat on stools talking nonchalantly in couples. Some smoked and Thaw envied them, for a cigarette would have employed his hands. He could have opened a book and sat behind something reading it, but he was tired of being thought a bookish hermit and meant to forge a new, confident, sardonic, mysterious character for himself; so frowning and leaning against the wall he pretended to see nobody, though glancing furtively at one of the girls. She sat cross-kneed on the pedestal of the discus thrower, sometimes talking to the girls nearby, sometimes tilting her head back to exhale smoke from her nostrils. She wore a suède jacket and tight skirt, and a blond curl curved down to half hide her left eye. Thaw covered his own eyes with his hands as if shielding them from light and stared between the fingers at the other girls. Altogether they gave an impression of bright mirthful sexuality, but separately their attraction was lessened by something schoolgirlish in the dress or markedly individual in the face. From the babble of their conversation only the voice of the blond girl reached him distinctly. Her low notes impressed his ear as velvet impresses fingertips. "I'm glad they couldn't send me to university, actually, 'cause actually art school is more relaxing. . . ."

A brisk white-haired little lady entered and softly called their names from a register. She told them their curriculum, dictated a list of materials and gave the numbers of lockers to store them in.

"Each month you will paint a picture in your own time to be exhibited in the assembly hall. We on the staff look forward to these exhibitions with great interest and even excitement, for they show how well you have grasped what we teach you in class. The theme of your first painting is"—she took a slip of paper from her register and examined it—"the subject is *Washing Day* and must contain a minimum of three figures." Then she ordered them to get paper and a drawing board from the school shop, made them sit in twos before high-legged narrow tables, and went round with a basket of burned-out light bulbs, placing one on each table to be drawn in careful outline. Later she moved among them, giving quiet words of correction and encouragement and making feathery little sketches on the sides of papers to show how the bulbs should be represented. Thaw worked stolidly, his face sometimes expressionless, sometimes bewildered as he fought a gathering rage and disgust. Once he muttered to his neighbour, a square-faced, fair-moustached, well-dressed student, "This is incredible."

"What is?"

"Art from a dead light bulb."

"Not exciting, I admit, but perhaps we should learn to walk before we run."

He had a bland fee-paying school dialect and Thaw detested him.

Halfway through the morning the bell rang and they strag-
gled through the corridor to the refectory, a large low-ceilinged
place packed with students who seemed at home there. Thaw
stood for ten minutes at the end of an untidy queue. People
kept leaving the head of it with coffee and biscuits while others
kept joining friends in the middle, so he returned to the studio.
Two boys sat in a corner drinking tea from thermos flasks and
discussing landladies in a severe border dialect whose words
seemed cut in coarse granite. They fell silent as Thaw approached. He nodded at the flasks and said, "That's a good
idea. The refectory's too crowded for comfort."
"Aye, and too dear. On a grant like ours we've to economize."
The other said accusingly, "Judging by your face you don't
think much of the lesson."
"No. It's rotten, isn't it?"
"Is it? Have we not to master the techniques before practising
them?"
"But technique and practice are the same thing! We can draw
nothing well unless it interests us, and we only learn to draw
it well by first drawing it badly, not by drawing what bores
us stiff. Learning to draw from dead bulbs and boxes is like
learning to make love with corpses."
One student grinned and muttered that that depended on the
corpses. The other said sternly, "Are you a Communist?"
"No."
"Are you a Bevanite?"
"I agree with Bevan that Britain should not make atomic
bombs."
"I thought so."
The teacher entered and Thaw returned to his seat feeling
that he had somehow betrayed himself.

At noon he put the new materials in his locker, left the
building and went down to Sauchiehall Street where the pavement was busy with a crowd he could feel anonymous among.
He bought a pie from a dairy and wandered, eating thoughtfully, into Sauchiehall Lane, which was quiet except for pigeons
cooing and pecking casually between the cobbles. The morning
had been like the first morning at any school. It had left a
feeling of anxiety, overcrowding and dry curriculums, of minds
herded into grooves. Nothing had enriched or warmed except
the sight of a certain girl, and that had less warmed than
scorched him into a different kind of unease. But now he began
to relax, feeling (in that obscure channel between tenement

backs) a comfort he sometimes found in graveyards, the canal
and other neglected parts of the city. The stone walls, stapled
over with iron pipes, seemed to hold something grander and
stranger than the builders knew. He looked through a doorway
and saw a huge unhealthy tree. It grew in a patch of bare
earth among pale-green rhubarb-shaped weeds; it divided at
the roots into two scaly limbs, one twisting along the ground,
the other shooting up to the height of the third-storey windows;
each limb, almost naked of branches, supported at the end a
bush of withered leaves. Thaw stared and munched for several
minutes then moved away feeling triumphant. It was not a
feeling he understood. It might have come from identifying
with the tree, with the confining walls or with both.

The afternoon was spent in the modelling department making a clay copy of a plaster lip. At four-thirty he went to his
locker and found it empty. He stared dispassionately at the
vacant space, knowing the shock of it would break on him in
three or four minutes. To prepare for this he said aloud, "I
have done a stupid thing."
A student at a nearby locker said smoothly, "We all do, from
time to time."
"I have let myself be robbed of three pounds' worth of goods."
The student came over and looked at the empty locker. He
said, "You should have got a padlock before leaving anything
valuable there. You can get a fairly good one for two or three
shillings in Woolworth's."
Thaw recognized his fair-moustached neighbour of the morning
who had wanted to walk before running. A flash of intuition
separate from logic or evidence made him sure this man was
the thief. He said harshly, "You are right," and left the building.

At home over the teatable Mr. Thaw said cheerfully,
"Well? How did it go?"
"All right."
"You don't sound very sure."
"I'm tired."
"Did you get much in the way of materials?"
"A drawing board, a folder, cartridge paper, a metal-edged
ruler. I . . . . I had them stolen."
"My God! How? How?"
Thaw told him how.
"And how much did they cost?"

Thaw put a hand in his pocket and grasped the crumpled invoice tight. "Nearly a pound."

"*Nearly* a pound? *Nearly* a pound? How much did they cost?"

"Fifteen shillings."

Mr. Shaw stared at him disgustedly then said, "Never mind. Just get another lot on account tomorrow."

In bed that night Thaw realized his father would expect the stolen goods to be replaced for fifteen shillings, so to keep his lie a secret he would need to save three pounds minus fifteen shillings multiplied by two. It struck him that if he had a key in the side of his head and could die by turning it, he would gladly turn it now.

Next morning he rose at seven, walked to school to save tram fares and dined on a cheap pie. This left him hungry but came to seem sufficient in two or three days, then he lost appetite for it and drank a cup of milk instead. Daily his stomach grew content with less. His mind was clenched, his surface reinforced against surrounding life. Normal hesitancies of voice and manner vanished. Often a line of words sounded in his head: *clean bleak exact austere rigorous implacable.* Sometimes he whispered these words as though they were a tune his body moved to. Walking down streets and corridors his feet hit the ground with unusual force and regularity. All sounds, even words spoken nearby, seemed dulled by intervening glass. People behind the glass looked distinct and peculiar. He wondered what they saw in gargoyles, masks and antique door knockers that they couldn't see in each other. Everyone carried on their necks a grotesque art object, originally inherited, which they never tired of altering and adding to. Yet while he looked on people with the cold interest usually felt for things, the world of things began to cause surprising emotions. A haulage vehicle carrying a huge piece of bright yellow machinery swelled his heart with tenderness and stiffened his penis with lust. A section of tenement, the surface a dirty yellow plaster with oval holes through which brickwork showed, gave the eerie conviction he was beholding a kind of flesh. Walls and pavements, especially if they were slightly decayed, made him feel he was walking beside or over a body. His feet did not hit the ground less firmly, but something in him winced as they did so.

He could only rest when working properly. After sketching bulbs and boxes the class was given plants, fossils and small stuffed tropical birds. Thaw let his eyes explore like an insect the spiral architecture of a tiny seashell while his pencil point marked some paper with the eye's discoveries. The teacher tried to correct him by rational argument. She said, "Are you trying to make a pattern out of this, Duncan? I wish you wouldn't. Just draw what you see."

"I'm doing that, Miss Mackenzie."

"Then stop drawing everything with the same black harsh line. Hold the pencil lightly; don't grip it like a spanner. That shell is a simple, delicate, rather lovely thing. Your drawing is like the diagram of a machine."

"But surely, Miss Mackenzie, the shell only seems delicate and simple because it's smaller than we are. To the fish inside it was a suit of armour, a house, a moving fortress."

"Duncan, if I were a marine biologist I might care how the shell was used. As an artist my sole interest is in the appearance. I insist that it appears beautiful and delicate and should be drawn beautifully and delicately. There's no need to show these little cracks. They're accidental. Ignore them."

"But Miss Mackenzie, the cracks show the shell's nature—only this shell could crack in this way. It's like the wart on Cromwell's lip. Leave it out and it's no longer a picture of Cromwell."

"All right, but please don't make the wart as important as the lip. You've drawn these cracks as clearly as the edges of the shell itself."

Behind the teacher's back several classmates made gestures like spectators at a boxing match, and later Thaw was approached by Macbeth who said, "Where do you go after school these days?"

"Home, usually."

"Why not come to Brown's? A few of us meet there. It's a change from the concentration camp."

Thaw felt excited. Macbeth was the only first-year student who looked like an artist. He walked with a defiant slouch, wore a beret, rolled his own cigarettes and smelled of whisky in the afternoon. He was often seen on the edge of older groups of students: elegant tight-trousered girls and tall bearded men who laughed freely in public places. In class he did what the teachers wanted with an ease which looked contemptuous, but he impressed Thaw most by keeping company with Molly Tierney, the velvet-voiced girl with blond curls. He sat beside her in class, gave her cigarettes and carried her drawing board from place to place. His face usually had an anxious, babyish look.

Brown's cakeshop in Sauchiehall Street had a narrow staircase going down to a wide low-ceilinged room. The tobacco
smoke and faded luxury were so dense here that Thaw, like
a diver in the saloon of a sunk liner, felt them press against
his eardrums. In an alcove to his right Molly Tierney reclined
on a sofa, smiling and lightly fingering the curl overhanging
her brow. Others from Thaw's class sat at a table beside her
sipping coffee and looking bored. Thaw slid into a chair next
to Macbeth without being specially noticed. Sounds of people
moving and conversing at other tables blurred and receded,
but tiny noises nearby (Macbeth's breathing, a spoon striking
a saucer) were magnified and distinct. Molly Tierney came
into sharp focus. The colours of her hair, skin, mouth and
dress grew clearer like a stained-glass figure with light increasing
behind it. Second by second her body was infused with the
significance of mermaids on rocks and Cleopatra in her barge.
He heard someone say, "Has anyone started their monthly
painting yet? I haven't even thought of it."
Molly said, "I began mine last night. At least I meant to, only
my mother wanted me to watch television and we had a fight.
It ended with me being pushed out of doors into the co-o-ld
bla-a-a-ck night." She giggled. "Me! In my high-heeled shoes."
A voice said venomously, "Parents just won't allow you a life
of your own."
Other voices supported this.
"My father won't let me . . ."
"My mother keeps saying . . ."
"Last week my mother . . ."
"Last year my father . . ."
He thought of entering the conversation by recalling fights
with his mother but the details had grown dim; all he remem-
bered was their inevitability. Molly Tierney sighed and said,
"I think I'll become a nun."
Thaw said, "I think I'll become a lighthouse keeper."
There was silence, and then someone asked why.
"So I'll be able to walk in spirals."
Molly giggled and Thaw leaned toward her. He criticized the
theme of the monthly painting, quoting Blake and Shaw and
describing shapes in the air with his hands. People raised objections and he quoted folk tales from many lands to show how
fact and fancy, geography and legend were linked. Molly was
clearly listening. She put her feet on the floor and leaned toward
him saying, "You know a lot of fairy stories."

"Yes. They used to be my favourite reading."

"Mine too." She chuckled huskily. "In fact they still are. I like Russian tales best. Have you noticed how many of them are about children?"

They talked of ugly and beautiful witches, enchanted mountains, magic gifts, monsters, princesses and lucky younger sons. With feelings of wonder and freedom he found she loved and remembered much that he loved himself. Suddenly she curled her legs back on the sofa and said to Macbeth, "Give me a cigarette, Jimmy."

Macbeth rolled a cigarette and held a match to the tip while she inhaled it.

"And Jimmy, would you do me a favour? Please, Jimmy, a very special favour?"

"What is it?"

Her voice became a mixture of babyish and whorish. "Jimmy, it's my architecture homework. This model cathedral we've to make. I've tried to make it but I can't, I don't know how to begin, it's too complicated for my tiny mind and I've to hand it on Friday. Will you make it for me? I'll pay for the materials, of course."

No one else at the table looked at each other. A voice in Thaw's head raved at Macbeth, "Spit in her face! Go on, spit in her face!"

Macbeth looked down at his cigarette with a faint smile and said, "All right."

"Oh Jimmy, you're a pet."

Thaw got up and walked home. The sun had set. He felt cold and light-bodied and the streets semed to flow through him on a current of dark air. Clock dials glowed like fake moons on invisible towers. On Alexandra Parade by the Necropolis a drunk man lurched past muttering, "Useless."

"Right," said Thaw. "Useless."

He woke often that night to find his legs grinding against each other and his fingernails tearing healthy parts of his skin. In the morning the sheets were bloodstained and his body felt so heavy he had trouble bringing it out of bed. At school he went through the routines like a sleepwalker. At noon he went to the refectory and drank a cup of black coffee at a crowded table. A girl nearby shouted, "Hullo Thaw!"

He smiled feebly.

"Enjoying yourself, Thaw?"

"Well enough."

"You like the life here, do you, Thaw?"

"Well enough."

A boy leaned against her laughing, and whispered in her ear. She said, "Thaw, this man is saying rude things about you." The boy said quickly, "No, I'm not." Thaw said flatly, "I'm sure you're not." He looked at them and saw their faces did not fit. The skin on the skulls crawled and twitched like half-solid paste. All the heads in his angle of vision seemed irregular lumps, like potatoes but without a potato's repose: potatoes with crawling surfaces punctured by holes which opened and shut, holes blocked with coloured jelly or fringed with bone stumps, elastic holes through which air was sucked or squirted, holes secreting salt, wax, spittle and snot. He grasped a pencil in his trouser pocket, wishing it were a knife he could thrust through his cheek and use to carve his face down to the clean bone. But that was foolish. Nothing clean lay under the face. He thought of sectioned brains, palettes, eyeballs and ears seen in medical diagrams and butcher's shops. He thought of elastic muscle, pulsing tubes, gland sacks full of lukewarm fluid, the layers of cellular and fibrous and granular tissues inside a head. What was felt as tastes, caresses, dreams and thoughts could be seen as a cleverly articulated mass of garbage. He got quickly out of the tearoom trying to see nothing but the floor he walked on.

At home he stood in the kitchen after the evening meal, sometimes putting dishes away but mostly standing stock-still, his face open-mouthed and aghast. Mr. Thaw entered and said impatiently, "Haven't you finished yet? You've been here over an hour. Is my company so disagreeable that you can't share a room with me?"

"No, but I'm thinking things I don't like to think about and I can't stop."

"What sort of things?"

"Diseases, mostly. Skin diseases and cancers and insects that live in people's bodies. Some of them are real but I've been inventing new ones. I can't stop."

"For God's sake do your homework or go for a walk. Do *something,* at any rate."

"How can I, with my mind full of these things?"

"Then go to bed."

"But when I shut my eyes I see them. They're so active. They gnaw and gnaw. Surely this is how people go mad."

Mr. Thaw stared at his son with mingled impatience and worry.
"Will I call the doctor then?"

"How would that help? 'Doctor Tannahill, I'm having thoughts I don't like to think!' How would that help?"

"He might send you to a psychiatrist."

"When? I'm thinking these things now."

"But what makes you think them?"

"That's easy. I don't need a psychiatrist to tell me that. Frustration. If a man hath these two, honesty and intelligence, and hath not sex appeal, then he is as sounding brass and tinkling cymbal."

"You're talking hysterically."

"Yes. That's unlucky, isn't it?"

"Get to bed, Duncan, and I'll bring you a toddy."

He sat in bed propped up with pillows to make sleep difficult. He invented a maggot called the Flealouse. It was white and featureless except on the underside, which was all mouths. It bred in connective tissues and moved by eating a trench in the surfaces it travelled among. It spread through bodies without upsetting them at first, for it sweated a juice which worked on the nerves like a drug, making diseased people plumper and rosier, more cheerful and active. Then it started feeding on the brain. The victims felt no less happy but their actions became mechanical and frenzied, their words repetitive and trite. Then the lice, whose movement so far had been sluggish and gradual, suddenly attacked the main bodily organs, growing hugely as they did so. Infected people turned white, collapsed in the street, swelled and burst like rotten sacks of rice, each grain of which was a squirming louse. Then the lice themselves split open releasing from their guts swarms of winged insects so tiny that they could enter anybody through pores in the skin. In less than a century the Flealouse infected and ate every other sort of life on the globe. The earth became nothing but rock under a heaving coat of lice of every size, from a few inches up to five hundred feet. Then they began to eat each other. In the end only one was left, a titan curled round the equator like a grub round a pebble. The body of the last Flealouse contained the flesh of everything that had ever lived. It was content.

While elaborating this fantasy he fell asleep several times and continued it in dreams, sometimes being a victim of the Flealouse, sometimes a Flealouse himself. The dreams were

so detailed that horror made him recoil into wakefulness and
fix wide-open eyes on the electric light, hoping the pain of
the dazzle would keep him conscious. Meanwhile part of his
mind tried to get free with the desperation of a rat roasting
in a revolving cage.
"Stop! Stop! Stop!"
"You can't."
"Why? Why? Why?"
"Your mind is rotting. Minds without love always breed these
worms."
"How can I get love?"
"You can't. You can't."
Something happened shortly after five in the morning. He was
struggling against thoughts of the lice and against the sleep which
made them seem solid when the image of Molly Tierney came
like coolness to a heated brow. He lay down filling slowly
with relief. He would go to her the next day and explain calmly,
without pathos, that only she could stop him going mad. If
she refused to love him what happened after that would be
her responsibility, not his. And she might help. This was not
a world of certainties but of likelihoods, so the glorious lovely
accident must happen *sometimes*. The Flealouse vanished from
his mind. He fell into a smooth, wholly dreamless sleep.

He woke as his father was drawing the curtains.
"How's your mind this morning?"
"It's all right now. It's fine."
"But will it last?"
"I think so."
"And you don't want a doctor?"
"Certainly not."
"Good. Three weeks ago, Duncan, you told me you had been
robbed of goods worth fifteen shillings. That was a lie. Now
I want the truth."
"The goods cost three pounds."
"I know. I was looking in your pocket for handkerchiefs to
wash when I found the invoice. I was shifting it to its proper
place on the spike in the scullery when I noticed the true
amount."
Mr. Thaw went to the window and stood, hands in pockets,
looking down the street. There was a small distinct frenzied
sound in the room like a mouse gnawing wood or a steel nib
scribbling on paper.

"For God's sake stop scratching!" said Mr. Thaw. "Aren't there
enough bloodstains on the sheets?"

"Sorry."

"I don't understand why you had to lie about it, unless from
a love of lying for its own sake. You could have hidden the
truth just by keeping your mouth shut."

"I came as near truth as I dared."

"Dared? What were you afraid of? Did you think I'd thrash
you?"

"I deserve to be thrashed."

"But Duncan, I've not thrashed you since you were a wee
boy!"

Thaw considered this and said, "True."

"Furthermore, how could you keep hiding the right amount
from me? Sooner or later I'd have had to pay the bill."

"I'm paying that myself. I've already saved thirty-five shillings."

"Thirty-five shillings in three weeks! You've saved it out of
food money. No wonder you're sick. How can you expect to
be well if you starve yourself? *How? How?*"

"Please don't attack me."

"What else can I do?" said Mr. Thaw piteously. "When you
were wee you could be beaten, but you're a man now. How
else can I bring home your wrongdoing but by driving at you
and driving at you with words?"

After a moment he added quietly, "I would be glad in future
if you would trust me with the facts of your condition, however
disastrous they may be."

"I'll try to."

"Then get up for your breakfast, son."

"I want to stay in bed. I feel feeble."

His father stared at him then left the room saying, "I'll bring
your breakfast in."

Thaw lay and remembered the night before. Asking for Molly
Tierney's love seemed foolish and unnecessary now, but the
decision to do it had cured his fear of decay and disease. When
such thoughts came in future he would entertain them calmly,
and move on to other thoughts.

For two days his father, before going to work, brought
him breakfast in bed. At noon Mrs. Colquhoun downstairs
brought up a tray of dinner. Between meals his body basked
in unhurried time: time to scribble in notebooks or read or
lie thoughtfully dreaming. It was good to be free from the

tensions of art school, yet the place haunted him. He had been part of the life of the students there, a voice among voices heard by attractive girls, a face among the faces surrounding them. He wrote:

From under loose sweaters and tight blouses their breasts threaten my independence like the nosecaps of atomic missiles. Cannibal queens carnivorous nightingales why should I feel my value depends on being valued by women, what makes them the bestowers of value? Oh I want to grip them somehow and show them the universe is bigger, stranger, more sombre, colourful and distinct than they know. And how can I do this in a picture called "Washing Day" with a minimum of three figures? Yah what grandeur can be shown in that? I want to make a series of paintings called Acts of God showing the deluge, the confusion of Babel, the walls of Jericho falling flat, the destruction of Sodom. Yes, yes, yes, a hymn to the Old Testament Catastropher who makes things well but hurts and smashes them just as well. Or I would make a set of city scapes with the canal through them. Or

His pen paused above the page then descended and sketched the tree on Sauchiehall Lane, making it larger, and leafless, and among the tenements and back greens of Riddrie. Around it three dwarfish housewives were stretching ropes between iron clothes-poles, and he drew them from a memory of a home help who had looked after the house while his mother was dying. They wore headscarves, men's boots, and big aprons covered their chests and skirts giving them a sexless, surgical look. At the top of the picture the tree's highest branch stuck into a strip of sky among the tenement chimneys. He remembered a Blake engraving of a grey ocean with an arm sticking out of a wave, the hand clutching at the empty sky. Another Blake engraving showed a tiny pair of lovers watching a small frenzied figure set foot on a ladder so thin and high that the top rested in the sickle of a moon. A caption said, "I want! I want!" Thaw drew a moon in the sky above the treetop.

Next day he rose after breakfast and sat in a thick dressing gown before the living-room fire turning the sketch into a picture. In the evening Ruth called from the kitchen, where she was making the tea, "It seems to me if you're well enough to paint you're well enough to help with the housework."
"True," said Thaw.
"Then will you kindly set the table?"
"I'm too busy."
"For Pete's sake! It won't take ten minutes."

"If I stop now I won't work so well when I start again."

"I suppose you think your old picture is more important than anything else?"

Ruth stood in the kitchen doorway with a milk jug in her hand. Thaw looked at her and said coldly, "Yes. What I'm doing just now is more important than anything else happening in this whole city."

"You're mad!"

"Mibby."

He turned back to the picture. Ruth came over and held the full milk jug above it.

"How would you like a dirty big puddle in the middle of your important picture?"

"Your actions aren't on my conscience," said Thaw, working.

Ruth tipped the jug slowly forward until a trickle of milk spattered onto the centre of the paper, leaving a small puddle. Thaw rose and went into the kitchen saying, "That was a wrong and childish thing to do."

He brought back a clean cloth, wiped up the milk and continued working. Ruth watched him ominously, jug in hand, then said, in a low vibrating voice, "God, how I hate you! How I hate you!"

"At present, yes, but you'll soon stop. It's a tiring emotion."

"Oh, I'll keep it going! Don't you *worry.*"

She flung the jug to smash in the hearth and ran from the room, slamming the door after her. Four minutes later she returned with homework notebooks and sat studying them by the fire, her lips pressed tightly together.

Suddenly Thaw jumped up, crying out on a rising note, "Oh! Oh! *Oh!*"

He had been drawing with waterproof ink on stiff paper. He had thought the milk had fallen on a dry part of the picture, but it was not completely dry, and now that the damp had evaporated a grey smear stained the centre. He had not expected this. He turned to Ruth, his head craning toward her and swaying a little at the end of the neck. With fists clenched he advanced on her whispering, "By God I'll hurt you for this, my dear."

She retreated into the bay window. In former fights she was usually the aggressor and he coldly or hysterically defensive. Now she sank to the floor, protecting her head with her hands, and he stooped and twice drove his fist hard into her stomach, then went back and glowered at the picture. A new wave of rage rose in him and he turned vengefully to her again. She lay curled on herself with her eyes shut, drawing choking breaths and looking very white. He went to the front bedroom and lay on the bed, feeling nothing now but listlessness and defeat, and the fading daylight in the room, and the occasional shout of children playing in the street. After a while he heard Ruth go to the lavatory and taps rushing and the cistern flushing. She looked into the bedroom for a moment and said sobbingly, "Duncan, you've hurt me. You don't know how you've hurt me."

He said coldly, "I'm sorry."

He could only think of the grey smear on the picture. Coldness and indifference spread through him like a stain. Later he heard his father come in and murmurs of conversation from the living room. Mr. Thaw opened the bedroom door abruptly saying, "Duncan! Did you punch Ruth in the stomach?"

"Yes. We were fighting."

"Look, Duncan, I'm glad you're prepared to defend yourself but you should *never* punch a *woman* in the *stomach.*"

"I'm sorry. I don't know how to hurt women properly yet." His father left and he lay inert, thinking of the picture. 'I can't do it all again' he thought, then sat up, shaken by a new idea. For an hour before Ruth spoiled the picture his pleasure in it had vanished and now he knew why. The moon was wrong. It did not belong to such a picture; it was a piece of sentimental overemphasis, like a serenader with a guitar. The picture should be made bigger with no sky showing at all.

Mr. Thaw made tea that evening and the family ate in silence. Inside himself Thaw was very cheerful indeed but hid the feeling because the others could not share it. Afterward he began the picture again and finished it three days later.

He brought it to art school and it hung in the assembly hall, where he moved about among the other thoughtful or chattering students. He was sick of it now, it seemed overworked and dull, but he had still expected it to eclipse the work of everyone else and was depressed to see two other pictures equally good. They showed ordinary kitchen interiors. Their paint was carefully used to represent solid figures and the space between, and their common depth of light and air was finer and saner than the unique sombreness of his own rigid composition. Other pictures interested by their oddity.

Molly Tierney showed a tropical landscape where twenty or thirty blondes like herself washed their hair in a waterfall. Macbeth's picture looked like a forgery of a painting by Van Gogh. A plump white-haired white-moustached teacher entered and walked up and down before the pictures talking in a lordly way about the aims of art and indicating with a plump white hand those paintings whose qualities or flaws illustrated his ideas. Once or twice he paused and regarded the tree picture thoughtfully, then moved on leaving Thaw's nerves jangling with colliding messages of anticipation and resentment. The criticism ended without his picture being mentioned and for several hours disappointment worked in him like a speck of acid.

CHAPTER 22.
Kenneth McAlpin

Once a week they queued outside the lecture theatre for a talk on the history of art. Everyone seemed friendly; lightly chattering currents of emotion flowed easily between them and Thaw stood in the flow feeling as dense and conspicuous as a lump of rock. One day he arrived when the queue had gone in but before the lecturer came. Pausing outside the door he made his face expressionless, softened it with a thoughtful frown and entered. There was an explosion of laughter and someone shouted, "This was the noblest Roman of them all!" The theatre confronted him with a collection of grinning, glaring and roaring heads. The mirth crashed like a wave into his shell of loneliness and gravity. He grinned and said, "Is my nose green or something?" sitting down beside the fair-moustached student he had once instinctively hated.
"No, but you looked like Caesar pondering over the head of Pompey."

After the lecture they walked to the refectory together. The moustached student was called Kenneth McAlpin. Thaw said, "It's queer to be enjoying a coffee here."
"I've noticed you hardly ever use the place."
"I never know where to sit. The world sometimes seems a chessboard where the pieces move themselves. I'm never sure what square to go to. Yet it can't be a difficult game, most folk play it instinctively."
"The rules are fairly simple," said McAlpin. "You stick near pieces like yourself and move along with them. The people at that table are in the school choir. The clan over there are

highlanders. These four in the corner are serious Catholics. After the second year your group is usually decided by the subject you specialize in."

"Have you a group?"

McAlpin pursed his lips then said, "Yes. I suppose I'm a snob. My family used to be rather well off so I've grown up feeling a bit grander than the majority, and I'm slightly uncomfortable when I'm in a group who don't feel the same. I suppose the people I sit with are snobs too. They'll be here soon, so you can judge for yourself."

Thaw smiled and said, "I'll leave when they come. I don't want to embarrass you."

"Actually I'd be glad if you stayed. I enjoy your conversation more than theirs. With the exception of Judy, of course."

"Judy?"

"My girlfriend. Don't mistake me, they're nice people, you know some of them already. But it's snobbery which keeps us together, I sometimes think."

Judy and Rushford arrived. Judy was a handsome, sturdy girl with a vaguely displeased expression. Rushford wore an embroidered waistcoat copied from one worn by Benjamin Disraeli. "The Victorians were far from being the stuffy monsters we used to assume," he said in a fluting, meticulous voice. Molly Tierney arrived followed by Macbeth and some others, and the group was complete. Macbeth looked lost and unhappy because Molly ignored him but Thaw felt perfectly comfortable. The conversation was about people he never met and parties he never visited but his occasional remarks were heard politely.

After this Thaw and McAlpin worked side by side in the studio, drank coffee together, brought to school books they enjoyed and read the best parts aloud to each other. Thaw preferred poetry and drama, McAlpin music and philosophy. They discussed these but avoided politics in case their opinions divided them. Once or twice they had tea in each other's homes. McAlpin lived in the small posh suburban town of Bearsden. The house had a garden round it and warm well-carpeted rooms. The furniture was large and beautifully kept with Indian cabinets and Chinese ornaments. Mrs. McAlpin was small, brisk and cheerful. "This is the tiniest of the houses we owned when Kenneth's father died," she said with a faint sigh, pouring tea into thin cups. "Not that I wanted the others, even if I could have afforded to keep them. We really were rather prosperous once. Kenneth, for instance, had a nanny when he was small . . ."

"We keep it, stuffed, in a cupboard under the stairs," murmured McAlpin.

". . . we had a chauffeur too, Stroud, a delightful character, a real Cockney. I do miss the car. Still, if I had it I would probably use it all the time because I'm naturally terribly lazy. I suppose running up and down to the shops helps keep me young. Another thing we don't do much nowadays is entertain. Still, I want Kenneth's twenty-first birthday party to be one he'll really enjoy. You'll come to it, Duncan, I hope? Kenneth often talks of you."

"I'd like to," said Thaw. He sat on a sofa so deep that it supported the whole length of his legs, and he sipped tea and wondered why he felt so much at home. Perhaps when he was small his own house had seemed as spacious and secure.

At the refectory table he often heard parties and excursions planned. McAlpin took little share in the plans for in that group practical details were left to the girls, but Judy brought him in by asking, "What do you think, Kenneth?" or "Have you any ideas about that?" while Thaw sat hoping to be invited and wondering why Aitken Drummond was always invited. Aitken Drummond was not a member of the group. He was over six feet tall and usually wore green tram conductor's trousers, a red muffler and an army greatcoat. His dark skin, great arched nose, small glittering eyes, curling black hair and pointed beard were so like the popular notion of the Devil that on first sight everyone felt they had known him intimately for years. Drummond was always asked to parties and next day stories were told of him amid mocking, slightly horrified laughter. Thaw envied him, but the question "Can I come to the party, Kenneth?" though often in his mind, was never asked. He was sure McAlpin would answer "Yes, why not?" with hurtful coolness. Yet coolness was the quality in McAlpin he most admired. It showed in his polished solidity, his relaxed confidence which nothing, nobody, seemed to perturb. It showed in his calm robust body, his good manners and good clothes, in the finely rolled umbrella he carried with careless ease when the weather was cloudy. It showed most of all on the few occasions he spoke of his private life, as if that life were entertainment he watched, with ironical sympathy, from a distance. One day he said to Thaw, "I behaved badly last night."

"How?"

"I took Judy to a party. I got rather drunk and started kissing the host's daughter on the floor behind the sofa. She was drunk too. Then Judy found us and was furious. The trouble is I was enjoying myself so much I couldn't even pretend to be sorry."

He frowned and said, "That was bad, wasn't it?"

"If Judy loves you, yes, of course it was bad."

McAlpin looked gravely at Thaw for a moment, then flung his head back and roared with laughter.

One morning Thaw and McAlpin went into the Cowcaddens, a poor district behind the ridge where the art school stood. They sketched in an asphalt playpark till small persistent boys ("Whit are ye writing, mister? Are ye writing a photo of that building, mister? Will ye write *my* photo, mister?") drove them up a cobbled street to the canal. They crossed the shallow arch of a wooden bridge and climbed past some warehouses to the top of a threadbare green hill. They stood under an electric pylon and looked across the city centre. The wind which stirred the skirts of their coats was shifting mounds of grey cloud eastward along the valley. Travelling patches of sunlight went from ridge to ridge, making a hump of tenements gleam against the dark towers of the city chambers, silhouetting the cupolas of the Royal infirmary against the tomb-glittering spine of the Necropolis. "Glasgow is a magnificent city," said McAlpin. "Why do we hardly ever notice that?"

"Because nobody imagines living here," said Thaw. McAlpin lit a cigarette and said, "If you want to explain that I'll certainly listen."

"Then think of Florence, Paris, London, New York. Nobody visiting them for the first time is a stranger because he's already visited them in paintings, novels, history books and films. But if a city hasn't been used by an artist not even the inhabitants live there imaginatively. What is Glasgow to most of us? A house, the place we work, a football park or golf course, some pubs and connecting streets. That's all. No, I'm wrong, there's also the cinema and library. And when our imagination needs exercise we use these to visit London, Paris, Rome under the Caesars, the American West at the turn of the century, anywhere but here and now. Imaginatively Glasgow exists as a music-hall song and a few bad novels. That's all we've given to the world outside. It's all we've given to ourselves."

"I thought we had exported other things—ships and machinery, for instance."

"Oh, yes, we were once the world's foremost makers of several useful things. When this century began we had the best organized labour force in the United States of Britain. And we had John McLean, the only Scottish schoolteacher to tell his students what was being done to them. He organized the housewives' rent strike, here, on Clydeside, which made the government stop the landlords getting extra money for the duration of World War One. That's more than most prime ministers have managed to do. Lenin thought the British revolution would start in Glasgow. It didn't. During the general strike a red flag flew on the city chambers over there, a crowd derailed a tramcar, the army sent tanks into George Square; but nobody was hurt much. Nobody was killed, except by bad pay, bad housing, bad feeding. McLean was killed by bad housing and feeding, in Barlinnie Jail. So in the thirties, with a quarter of the male workforce unemployed here, the only violent men were Protestant and Catholic gangs who slashed each other with razors. Well, it is easier to fight your neighbours than fight a bad government. And it gave excitement to hopeless lives, before World War Two started. So Glasgow never got into the history books, except as a statistic, and if it vanished tomorrow our output of ships and carpets and lavatory pans would be replaced in months by grateful men working overtime in England, Germany and Japan. Of course our industries still keep nearly half of Scotland living round here. They let us exist. But who, nowadays, is glad just to exist?"

"I am. At the moment," said McAlpin, watching the sunlight move among rooftops.

"So am I," said Thaw, wondering what had happened to his argument. After a moment McAlpin said, "So you paint to give Glasgow a more imaginative life."

"No. That's my excuse. I paint because I feel cheap and purposeless when I don't."

"I envy your purpose."

"I envy your self-confidence."

"Why?"

"It makes you welcome at parties. It lets you kiss the host's daughter behind the sofa when you're drunk."

"That means nothing, Duncan."

"Only if you can do it."

"Ten weeks is a long, long holiday," said Mr. Thaw that summer. "What's your friend Kenneth doing?"

"Working on the trams. Almost everyone I know is taking some kind of job."

"And what are you going to do?"

"Paint, if you let me. There's an exhibition when we go back with a competition for a picture of the Last Supper. The prize is thirty pounds. I think I can win it."

He walked the streets looking at people. He used the underground railway where passengers faced each other in rows and could be examined without seeming to stare. Folk near the river were usually gaunter, half a head shorter and had cheaper clothes than folk in the suburbs. He had not seen the connection between physical work, poverty and bad feeding before because he came from Riddrie, an in-between district where tradesmen and petty clerks like his father lived. He noticed too that the sleek office faces and roughened workshop ones had the same tight mouths. Nearly everyone looked anxious, smug or grimly determined. Such faces would suit the disciples, who had been chosen from labourers and clerks, but they wouldn't suit Jesus. He began looking for harmonious faces whose mouths closed serenely. Most children had these when they sat still, but the people who kept them after adolescence were usually women with a mild, mysterious, knowing look. For a while he thought this might be the incarnate God's expression, for Leonardo and the carvers of oriental Buddhas had thought so. One morning he found it on the face of a three-inch embryo in the university medical museum. The huge little head nodding over the bent-up knees, the great closed eyes and subtly smiling mouth seemed dreaming of a satisfying secret as big as the universe. And he saw such an expression could not belong to Christ, who had looked steadily at the people around him. He needed the face of a mature, sane, outward-looking man whose love abolished all advantage over whom he beheld, a face without triumph or blame in it because triumph is smug and condemnation is Devil's work. He raked for a Christian expression among old drawings. A sketch of Coulter showed a calm unafraid friendly face but was far too wistful, and one of McAlpin was calm and strong but had disdainful eyelids. He decided to steal a face from a masterpiece, but in Glasgow Art Gallery the only good Christs were infants, apart from Giorgione's "Christ and the Adulteress," where the painter's modesty or restorer's cowardice had kept the holy face in shadow. He took a day trip to the National Gallery in Edinburgh and at last found the face in a trinity by Hugo Van der Goes. It came from the fifteenth century when the Flemish masters discovered oil paint and made brown the subtlest colour of all while keeping the crisp brightness of tempera. God sat on a clumsy gold and crystal throne floating among gaudy turbulent clouds. He wore a plain red robe with green lining and was preventing, by a hand under each armpit, a pained, thin, dead, nearly nude Christ from sliding off the seat beside him. A white pigeon hovered between their heads. God had the same ordinary thin brown face as his son and a look of pure sorrow without bitterness or blame. In spite of the golden seat neither he nor his son looked like well-paid men. They had the thin faces of providers, not owners or directors. And the suffering father, not the dead son, had Thaw's sympathy. This was the face of his Christ, and he knew he could never paint it. Nobody can paint an expression that is not potentially their own, and this face was beyond him.

In the end he decided to imagine the supper as Jesus would see it from the head of the table. On each side of the board the disciples, anxious, hopeful, doubting, delighted, hungry, replete, were craning and leaning for a glimpse of the viewer's face. The only visible part of Jesus was his hands on the tablecloth. They entered the picture from the bottom margin, and Thaw copied them from his father. He took so long preparing this picture that there was no time to paint it so he submitted the black and white cartoon.

The picture won no prize but was easy to photograph, and *The Bulletin* showed Molly Tierney and Aitken Drummond in front of it. A caption said, "Art students discuss Douglas Shaw's interpretation of the Last Supper at the opening of Glasgow Art School's summer exhibition." Thaw took a copy of the paper into a lavatory cubicle to gloat over it. Though sick of the picture the published photograph gave him a moment's pleasure of almost sexual potency. He went over to the refectory in a mood of unusual confidence and sat by Judy, who asked in a friendly way, "Duncan, did you enjoy drawing those unpleasant people? Or does your picture shock you as much as us?"
Her interest delighted him. He said, "No, I didn't try to paint unpleasant people. After all, Christ picked his disciples at random, like a jury, so they must have been an ordinary representative lot. I may have drawn them grotesque. Not many of us are as we should be, even in our own estimations, so how can we help being grotesque? But we aren't often unpleasant."
Judy said, "Draw a portrait of me Duncan, here, on the tabletop." She kept her head still while Thaw scribbled on the formica surface. He said, "I've finished, but it's not a success."

Judy said, "You see, you've made me look evil. You've shown my bad qualities."

Thaw looked at the drawing. He thought he had only shown the shape of her face, and not well. She said, "I know I have more bad qualities than good. . . ." He started to protest but she said, "Look at Kenneth!"

Thaw looked across at McAlpin who had put his head back to laugh at a joke. He had grown a beard over the holidays and the gold spire of it wagged at the ceiling. Judy said, "Kenneth has no bad qualities. If he hurt anyone it would be from stupidity, not deliberately."

"He's a gentleman," said Thaw. "It's civilizing to know him."

In the tramcar that evening he felt unusually conscious of his appearance: the paint-stained trousers like a labourer's below the waist, the collar and tie like an office worker above. Passing the park someone plucked at his sleeve. He turned and saw a plump pretty girl who said, "Hullo there. How are you doing?"

"Fine thanks. And yourself?"

"Not too bad. D'ye live out here?"

"Aye. Opposite the chapel."

"I'm visiting my auntie. I'll be seeing you."

She went downstairs and Thaw wondered who she could be. Suddenly he realized she was Big June Haig who had been to Whitehill School. He went downstairs and stood beside her on the platform. She said, "Oh, there you are."

"I usually get off farther up the hill," said Thaw, as if explaining something.

"Your house faces the Chapel?"

The tram halted and they got off.

"No, it's in the street which runs into the road just opposite the Chapel."

He stood still, describing this geography with his hands. She gripped his lapel and drew him onto the pavement out of the path of a lorry, saying, "I don't want to be held as a witness to a road accident."

"Where are you working just now?"

"Brown's. I'm a waitress in the dining room."

"Oh I go there sometimes, but downstairs to the smokeroom."

Thaw described his eating habits in detail and she seemed to listen intently. He showed her the photograph in the paper and she was less impressed than he expected. There were gaps in the conversation in which he expected her to say cheerio, but she stayed quiet until he thought of something new to say. He said, "I'll walk you to your auntie's house," and they set off side by side. June moved with chin held up and vivid mouth set haughtily as if disdaining herds of admirers, and Thaw's heart thumped hard against his ribs. They turned some corners and stopped at a close. June explained that she visited her aunt twice a week; the aunt was an old lady who had recently had an operation. Thaw made an unsubtle reference to her unselfishness. There was another silence. He said desperately, "Look, could I meet you sometime?"

"Oh sure."

"Where do you live nowadays?"

"Langside, near the monument."

"Hm . . . Where will we meet?"

After a pause she suggested Paisley's corner near Jamaica Street Bridge.

"Good!" said Thaw firmly, then added, "But we haven't fixed the night or the hour have we?"

June said, "No. We haven't."

After some silence she suggested Thursday night at seven o'clock.

"Good!" said Thaw firmly again. "I'll see you then."

"Yes."

"Well . . . cheerio."

"Cheerio, Duncan."

That night Thaw kept stopping work to walk up and down the living room, chuckling and singing. Mr. Thaw said, "What's got into ye? Did a lassie look at ye sideways?"

"My painting aroused a certain interest."

Next morning Thaw told McAlpin about June as they sat in the school library. McAlpin studied the page of a glossy magazine, then said, "Does she smell of the bakery, the brewery, or the brothel?"

Thaw felt shocked and cheapened and cursed himself for speaking. McAlpin glanced at him and said, "All women have an odour, you know. The deodorant adverts pretend it's a bad thing, which is all balls. If the girl is clean it's a very attractive thing. Judy has an odour."

"Good."

"What you need, Duncan, is a friendly, experienced older woman, not a silly wee girl."

"But I don't like being condescended to."

"I admit she'd have to handle you cleverly. I'm sure there

are many women in continental brothels who could do it. Of
course there are no brothels deserving the name in Scotland.
This is such a bloody *poor* country."
Thaw said, "Your mind is full of brothels this morning."
"Yes. . . . What do you think will happen to you when you
leave art school?"
"I don't know. But I can't teach children and I won't go to
London."
McAlpin said, "I don't want to teach but I probably will. I
would like to travel and have freedom before I settled down,
visit Paris, Vienna, Florence. There are a lot of quiet little
cities in Italy with frescoes by minor masters in the churches
and their own wine served under awnings in the squares outside.
I'd like to wander around exploring these with a girl, not necessarily a girl I'd marry. Think! After sunset the air is as warm
as a fine summer afternoon here . . . but I can't leave my
mother for long. At least when I do leave her it will be to
marry Judy, which—as far as freedom is concerned—will
be leaving the frying pan for the fire. Meanwhile I'm getting
older."
"Blethers."
"Does time never worry you?"
"No. Only feelings worry me, and time isn't a feeling."
"I feel it."
After a moment McAlpin said on a baffled note, "I suspect
that if I started living in a slum, and consorting with a prostitute,
and wore nothing but a leopard skin, Judy and my mother
would visit me four days a week with baskets of food."
"I envy you."
"Don't."

That afternoon in the lecture theatre Thaw's body came
to an uneasy compromise with the wooden bench and he dozed.
Later he heard the lecturer say ". . . something of a thug. In
fact he broke Michelangelo's nose once, in a brawl, when they
were young. It is consoling to remember that he died, most
unhappily, a raving lunatic in a Spanish prison, ha-ha. However,
that will do for today."
The lights went on and people crowded to the exits. Thaw
noticed McAlpin and Judy ahead of him; they ran hand in
hand across the street to the annexe and he followed slowly.
They were not in the refectory. He sat down at a table near
Drummond and Macbeth. Drummond was saying, "I can't understand why I've been asked. I hardly know Kenneth."

"When is it?" said Macbeth.
"Tomorrow night. We go to his house for a meal and a booze-up, then to a fancy-dress party at a hotel."
"How old is he?" said Macbeth.
"Twenty-one."
A sad kind of shock flowed through Thaw like water. He sat still, not saying much, then went to the counter and brought food back to the table. Drummond left and Macbeth sat in a way which told Thaw he was depressed at not being asked to the party. Macbeth said, "You're quiet tonight, Duncan."
"I'm sorry. I was thinking."
"I suppose you've been asked to Kenneth's party tomorrow?"
"No."
Macbeth became cheerful. "No? That's queer. You and Kenneth are always about together. I thought you were friends."
"I thought that."

He walked a lot around the streets that evening and let himself into the house after midnight.
"Is that you, Duncan?" said his father from the bed settee in the living room.
"I think so."
"Is anything wrong?"
Thaw explained what had happened. He said, "I can't get used to this. An acquaintance becomes a friend in a gradual, genial way. The reverse is . . . shocking."
"What's that noise?"
"I'm fiddling with ornaments on the lobby table. In God's name how can I face him tomorrow? What can I say?"
"Don't say much, Duncan. Quietly and politely wish him many happy returns of the day."
"That's a good idea, Dad. Goodnight."
"And go straight to sleep. No writing."
He went to bed, grew breathless, took two grains of ephedrine, slept for an hour and woke feeling excited. He opened his notebook and wrote, *The future demands our participation. To participate willingly is freedom, unwillingly is slavery.*
He scored this out and wrote:
The universe compels cooperation. To cooperate consciously is freedom, unconsciously is. . . .
Nature always has our assistance. To assist eagerly is freedom, resistingly is. . . .
God needs our help. Giving it joyfully is freedom, resentfully is. . . .
We have God's help. To know this is freedom, not to notice is . . . .
He snarled and threw the notebook at the ceiling where it

rebounded onto the top of the wardrobe, dislodging an avalanche of books and papers. He lay feeling happy about the
changes in life, then masturbated and fell asleep. His happiness
had gone when he awoke.

McAlpin was not at school that day. At tea break Judy,
Molly Tierney and Rushford discussed the costumes they would
wear at the fancy-dress dance. Thaw was unsure how to behave.
He drew on the tabletop and grinned with the left side of
his mouth.
"You should see my costume!" said Molly gleefully. "It's terrible. All pink and nineteen-twentyish, with a cigarette holder
three feet long. Here, give me a pencil."
She seized the pencil from Thaw's fingers and drew the costume
on the tabletop. That evening he went into town to meet June
and stood in an entry to a clothes shop looking at suave dummies
in evening dress and sportswear. Grey dusk became black night.
The entrance was a common place for appointments, and he
often had the company of people waiting for boy or girlfriends.
None waited longer than fifteen minutes. When it was not
possible to pretend June would come he walked home feeling
horribly insulted.

McAlpin entered the classroom briskly next day with a
new book in one hand. He hooked his neatly rolled umbrella
on a radiator, laid his coat and bag on a pedestal and came
briskly to Thaw. He said, "Listen to this!" and read out the
first paragraph of *Oblomov*.
Thaw heard him with embarrassment then said, "Very good"
and went into a corner to sharpen a pencil. That morning he
and McAlpin worked apart from each other. At lunchtime Thaw
went to the main building and obtained an interview with the
registrar. In a careful voice he said he thought the school's
anatomy course inadequate, that he was going to ask permission
to sketch in the dissection room of the university, that he would
be grateful for a letter from the registrar saying that such permission would be useful to his art. The registrar swung reflectively
from side to side in his swivel chair. He said, "Well, I'm not
sure, Thaw. Morbid anatomy certainly was in our curriculum
till shortly after the fourteen-eighteen war. I was trained in it
myself. I don't think I benefitted from it, but of course I was
not so dedicated an artist as you. But would such training do
you good psychologically? I honestly think it would do harm."
"I am not—" Thaw said, then cleared his throat and knelt
before the electric fire near Mr. Peel's desk. He stared into

the red-hot coil and plucked fibres out of the coconut matting.
"I am not a complete person. A good painter one day, mibby,
but always an inadequate man. So my work is important to
me. If that work is to develop I must see how people are made."
"Your 'Last Supper' showed a detailed grasp of anatomy,
gained, I assume, by the usual methods?"
"Yah. That detail was bluff. I padded out the definite things
I knew with imagination and pictures in books. But now my
imagination needs more detailed knowledge to work on."
"I am not convinced that morbid anatomy will be good for
you, Thaw, but I suppose you must convince yourself of that.
I'm remotely acquainted with the head of the university medical
faculty. I'll get in touch with him."
"Thank you, sir," said Thaw, standing up. "Some sketching
in the vivisection room is really necessary at this stage."
"Dissection room."
"Pardon?"
"You said vivisection room."
"Did I? I'm sorry," said Thaw, confused.

He ran back to the classroom to work off his exhiliration.
McAlpin stood at an easel near the door. Thaw stopped and
muttered to him, "Peel's getting me permission to sketch in
the university dissection room."
"Good! Good!"
"I've not felt so happy since I invented the bactro-chlorine
bomb."
McAlpin bent over and emitted muffled bellowing laughter.
Thaw went to his seat thinking what a waste of time unfriendli-
ness was. Later on their way to the refectory he said to McAlpin,
"Why didn't you ask me to your party?"
"We had only a few tickets for the fancy-dress ball and had
to give them to people who had asked Judy and me to their
parties. I wanted to invite you but—er, it just wasn't possible.
I thought you wouldn't mind because you were taking out
that girl you picked up. How did you get on with her?"

CHAPTER 23. Meetings

One evening Thaw came down to Sauchiehall Street when the air was mild and the lamps not yet lit. So fine a lake of yellow sky lay behind the western rooftops that he walked toward them in a direction opposite home and was overtaken by Aitken Drummond at Charing Cross.

"This isn't your usual territory, Duncan."

"I'm just walking."

"I suppose you're waiting for the ball to start?"

"Is there a ball tonight? No, I cannae afford a ticket."

"I admit money is useful but don't bother about a ticket. Come with me."

They walked past the Grand Hotel then turned down a stunted unlit lane into a cluttered little yard. Thaw made out heaps of coke and coal, bins overflowing with garbage, stacks of milk, beer and fish crates. Drummond opened a door.

They entered so hot an air that Thaw felt stifled for a minute or two. Below a weak electric bulb an old man in a boiler suit sat smoking a pipe beside the furnace door. Drummond said, "This is Duncan Thaw, Dad. We're going to the art school ball."

Mr. Drummond took the pipe from his mouth and directed Thaw to an empty chair with the stem. His amused sunken mouth indicated a lack of teeth; his nose was almost as big as his son's but more craggy; spectacles were pushed up on his brow, the legs mended with insulating tape. He said, "So you're going dancing? It's a waste of time, Douglas, a damned waste of time."

"He's called Duncan!" shouted Drummond.

"That doesn't matter, it's still a waste of time."

"Who's in the kitchen tonight?"

"Eh? Luigi."

"Why not get Duncan and me something to eat? He's hungry."

"No, I'm not," said Thaw.

Mr. Drummond left the room. Drummond pulled his father's chair to the furnace door and opened it, showing a red-hot gullet of flame-roaring coal. He sat and spread his palms to the blaze saying, "It's only a coincidence that I look like the Devil but I do enjoy heat. Pull your chair nearer, Duncan."

Mr. Drummond returned with a big plate of sandwiches and placed it on the floor between Thaw and Drummond. He said, "There's cheese, there's egg, there's salmon, there's meat paste. Help yourselves."

He brought another chair from a corner, sat down and lifted a library book from the floor. "Do you read this man, Duncan?" he asked, showing the title of a novel by Aldous Huxley.

"Yes, but he annoys me. He shows a world with too little in it to believe or enjoy."

"Too little?" said Mr. Drummond with a cackle of anarchic glee. "He leaves you with *nothing,* Duncan. Nothing whatsoever. Nothing at all. And he's right."

He turned a page and read while Thaw and Drummond ate.

"Tonight's pay night!" said Drummond suddenly in a loud voice. Mr. Drummond looked up.

"I said you got paid tonight. Can I have some money?"

"The Glasgow Corporation, Duncan, gives this man one hundred and twenty pounds a year. He spends it on nothing but clothes and pocket money. He lives—"

"And materials," said Drummond.

"And painting materials. He lives at home—he's twenty-four— he pays nothing toward his rent or rates or fuel or light or food—"

"Food!" cried Drummond triumphantly. "I'm glad you mentioned food! Do you know what my father gave me for dinner today, Duncan? Fried kippers. Kippers, mind you, and fried with their heads and tails on."

"Well, if you don't like it you know what to do," said Mr. Drummond mildly, returning the pipe to his mouth.

"Give me ten shillings," said Drummond. His father fished four half crowns from his overalls pocket, handed them over, saw the plate was empty and stood up.

"Have some more sandwiches," he told Duncan.

"No thanks, Mr. Drummond. That was good, but more would be too much."

"Well, the cook's a friend of mine. I'm not buying them and I'm not stealing them. You wouldn't like some more?"

"No thanks, Mr. Drummond."

"Duncan has to go now, Dad. We've an appointment. Would you like more coal?"

"If you can spare the time from your *urgent appointment.*"

A wooden hatch opened upon the coal heap outside. Thaw and Drummond pulled lumps onto the boiler-room floor with clumsy wooden rakes. Drummond shovelled them into the furnace and they left after washing their hands below a tap in the darkened yard.

They walked into the Cowcaddens and entered a close where the narrow stairs were worn to such a slant that the foot trod them uneasily. Thaw grew breathless and leaned a moment on a windowsill. He could see the flat back of a dingy church across a window box in which the soot-freckled crests of three stunted cauliflowers rose above a clump of weeds. On the top landing, Drummond pushed open a bright yellow door (the lock was broken), stuck his head inside and shouted, "Ma!" After a moment he said, "Come in, Duncan. I have to be careful in case my mother's at home. If she dislikes someone she's liable to retire to her bedroom and burn a pheasant's tail feather."

"What does that do?"

"I shudder to think."

Thaw entered the queerest house he had ever seen. Parts of it were very like a home but these lay like valleys between piled furniture and objects salvaged from scrap heaps, middens and junk shops. As he edged into the kitchen he felt threatened by empty picture frames, stringless instruments and old wireless sets. The ceilings were loftier than in his own home but there was no open space and no planning.

"Excuse the mess," said Drummond. "I haven't had time to tidy up. I'm hoping to get a studio nearer the art school soon. What can we use?"

He began shifting things from in front of a cupboard. Thaw bent to help but Drummond said, "Leave it to me, Duncan. If you shift these I won't know precisely where to find them." When the cupboard door could be opened about twelve inches

Drummond thrust his arm into the crevice and brought out, one at a time, a top hat, a Roman helmet, a pith helmet, a deerstalker, a mortarboard and an Indian feathered headdress, all with labels saying they belonged to the Acme Costume Hiring Agency.

"I used to work there," said Drummond. "They stored their best things with an almost criminal carelessness."

Drummond put on the top hat, a tail coat and spats. He cut himself a gleaming shirtfront, collar and cuffs from a sheet of glossy cardboard and fixed these in place with pins and drops of glue, then took a long pair of green rubber fangs from a drawer and inserted them carefully between his teeth and upper lip. He rubbed green greasepaint into his cheeks and, glaring balefully, asked with difficulty, "Dracula?"

"Oh yes," said Thaw, nodding.

Drummond slipped the rubber teeth into his pocket and said, "Who do you want to be?"

"A sorcerer. But I'll settle for an academic."

He put on the mortarboard.

"Not enough," said Drummond. "Go in there."

He moved a tailor's dummy and opened another door. Thaw entered a neat little room which clearly belonged to a woman. There were flowered curtains, striped wallpaper and a pink satin quilt on the bed. There was a scrolled and gilded bird cage, an ashtray shaped like a skull, and sweet peas blooming in a window box.

"Open the wardrobe," commanded Drummond from outside.

"I don't think I should be here."

"You should do exactly what I tell you."

The wardrobe door was ajar and as Thaw opened it a ginger cat strolled out.

"Is there a black silk dressing gown among the coats to the right?" called Drummond.

"Yes."

"Bring it here. Touch nothing else."

Thaw returned to the chaotic kitchen. Drummond said, "Sorry, I would have fetched it myself but my mother made me promise not to go into her bedroom. Put it on. It'll work rather well as an academic robe."

"Won't she find out?"

"No no. She's managing a tearoom in Largs and her visits home are erratic, to say the least."

Drummond took a knobbed cane in one hand and they set off for the ball.

Outside the lamps were lit and tramcars clanged and sparkled. A cryptic drama seemed unfolding throughout the city. An old woman and man argued quietly at a street corner watched by two little girls keeking round the corner of a lighted fruit shop. In a firelit room, seen through a ground-floor window, a man stood with a towel round his neck, shaving perhaps. Near the school they stepped into a room full of smoke, noise and people. Drummond forced a way to the bar and Thaw slid after him between backs and shoulders. Drummond handed him a large whisky and told him to knock it back in one. A blonde and a brunette leaned smiling toward Thaw and the blonde said, "Does your mother know you're here?"

He said, "Mibby. She's dead," and turned away, pleased by his harshness. Drummond bought two cigars. They lit them, went out and marched up Sauchiehall Street issuing smoke like chimneys. Thaw was surprised to find the stares of the bypassers amusing. He began laughing violently but coughed violently instead.

"For God's sake don't inhale, Duncan!" said Drummond, slapping his back.

"There's prestige in looking ridiculous with you, Aitken."

The door of the annexe was thronged with people trying to buy tickets or bribe an entrance from the doorkeepers. Drummond and Thaw mounted the steps side by side, Drummond cleaving a path with his great axe-blade-edged nose, Thaw opening one with the pallid inclined carapace of his brow. Officials in exotic costumes shouted "It's the Drummond!" "It's the Thaw!" and cheerily ushered them in. The janitor gripped Thaw's sleeve, drew him aside and indicated Drummond, saying, "Beware of that lad. When drunk he's fit company for neither man nor brute."

The triumph of arrival faded. He sat at the edge of the dance hall grinning unhappily at the revolving carnival of couples brushing past his knees, his eyes sucking visions of thighs and hips, fluttering breasts, throats and glances. Molly Tierney, dressed like an oriental dancing girl, spun gleefully in the arms of a white-robed Arab who was McAlpin and saluted Thaw with a raised forefinger. Suddenly two girls said "Hullo!" and sat on each side of him. "Don't you recognize us?" asked the smaller girl on the left.

"I'm sorry, I've a poor memory for people."

"You met us in the pub, don't you remember?"

"Are you the girls who asked that question? No, I don't remember your faces."

"Why?" asked the girl on his right. "Did we look awfully hard and experienced?"

"Not at all," said Thaw hurriedly. "Are you at the university?"

"No, the art school."

"Are you in the first year?"

They laughed.

"No, the fourth."

The pale girl said to the dark, "It makes you feel terribly ageing," and then, to Thaw, "Why aren't you dancing?"

"I've no sense of bodily rhythm."

"Oh, we'll soon teach you *that*," said the dark girl, rising to her feet. She led him to a corner and showed him how to move his feet; then she took him onto the floor where he partnered her, feeling clumsy and apologetic and desperately wishing she was the pale girl; then she took him back and gave him to her friend. He felt the difference at once. Her body was firmer, supple without fragility, her hair was pale gold, drawn smoothly back from pale brows to the back of her head. She wore earrings made from small stones hung on thin chains, her dress was black with a square-cut neckline. Sometimes she spoke words directing his steps, sometimes words of congratulation. He looked straight into her eyes, imagined being married to her, thought of Molly Tierney and felt no regret at all. He thought, I'm being ridiculous, and kept looking in her eyes; the dark pupils grew very clear and her face and head became a dim white and gold shape around them. He thought, She's like marble and honey, and shaped the words with his lips. The music stopped and he had to dance with the smaller girl again. He looked straight across her shoulder and talked about painting and the art school. She said, "Is your father a minister?"

"No, my father's a pious atheist. Do I look like a minister's son?"

"You look like a kid of twelve. But you sound like an old highland minister."

He danced again with the pale girl in a silence which grew desperate, for he knew it must end. So he said, "You're like marble and honey."

"What?"

"You're like marble and honey."

"Oh. Am I? Thank you."

She looked at him without smiling and said, "You should dance more often."

"No, really, I can't."

"If you come to more balls I'll dance with you."

He grew more worried, feeling she could not dance with him all evening, wondering when and how she would break from him. When the music stopped he excused himself and hurried from the hall.

He went upstairs thinking, 'I love her,' and, 'You're daft.' He wondered if she had a boyfriend and why he wasn't around. Anyway, she had danced with him from kindness; their connection had no equality in it. He imagined her friends mocking the lost look on his face when he danced with her. She would laugh and say, "He's just a kid!" He looked for a place to hide. Intimate whispers came from all the dark corridors so he opened a door onto the dance hall balcony, a small place used as a store for chairs. A man was slumped there with arms on the balustrade and head on arms. It was Drummond. Thaw had never seen him alone or depressed before. Drummond smiled faintly and pointed to a chair.

"How are you, Duncan? Why aren't you dancing?"

"I can't."

From up here the dancers seemed blind caps of hair with projecting hands and feet like the limbs of starfish. The linked couples twitched and turned as if the music was a fluid vibrating them. When it stopped they hurried to the side of the hall like corpuscles into a clot. Drummond sighed and said, "They're villainous, Duncan, downright villainous, absolutely villainous."

"Who are?"

"Women."

Drummond gazed down on the dancers and said, "One kept following me around tonight and looking at me . . . she went off with someone else ten minutes ago. I think I could have had her if I'd wanted. But I saw Molly dancing, and I'd no heart for anything of that kind. I don't know why. She's past her best and engaged to an Irish vet and flirting away. . . ."

"Molly Tierney?"

"I used to go about with her. You must admit she's good-looking. She avoids me now."

"Why?"

"I suppose because her parents are nice and mine aren't. My mother told her she wasn't fit to sleep with a pig. Which forced me into the unenviable position of declaring she *was* fit to sleep with a pig."

They were silent again, gazing on the dancers. Then Drummond said, "I tried to cure myself by imagining her pissing and excreting and menstruating, but the connection made these acts beautiful to me."

"How do women menstruate? At regular times on regular days?"

"When they reach Molly's age they can do it running for a tram, or standing before an easel, or at dinner or talking quietly to a friend, as we are. She let me watch her sometimes."

"What?"

"We shared many little secrets of that kind," said Drummond gloomily. This aspect of love had never entered Thaw's fantasies. He rubbed his face in frustration. Drummond said, "You'll be happier with women when you're better known—prestige makes a lot of them randy. Janet Weir used to go around with the president of the students' representative council, but when Jimmy Macbeth grew famous for drinking himself to death she kept company with him for a day or two. Then the film *Cyrano de Bergerac* popularized long noses and she turned to me. A lot of girls like me because I'm supposed to be a symbol of something. It's humiliating in some ways but lucky in others. What do you think of Janet?"

"I don't know her."

"She looks like the Mona Lisa but has nicer legs. She invited me into her room last night and told me she loved me."

"Oh, *God,"* said Thaw, beating his brow. It felt like a gate which had been locked and soldered shut. Drummond stretched his arms and yawned. "Yes, I was embarrassed too. Girls who say they love you expect all sorts of irrational things, like sincerity, in exchange. Still, we passed a pleasant night. She's a virgin, you know. I'd seen her with so many men that I hadn't expected that. I was careful not to destroy it. I like virginity; it seems a pity to destroy it for fun. But I suppose she'll get me doing it eventually. Virgins are terribly single-minded."

"I'm going to the lavatory."

Two hours later Thaw leaned despondently on the railings by the entrance watching the last dancers leave in ones and twos. He had stowed the mortarboard and gown in a locker. Drummond, still dressed like Dracula, capered on the pavement among laughing friends.

"I must get a woman to take home," he was saying. "I must take *some* woman home. Lorna, Lorna, Lorna!"

He tried to embrace a girl who slipped under his arm, laughing and saying, "Not tonight, Aitken, not tonight!"

A girl in a blue coat came out and paused, looking vaguely from side to side. Drummond took her hand politely and said, "Let us walk you home, Marjory."

The girl's face crinkled in a shy amused smile. She said, "I'm sorry, Aitken. My father is coming for me in the car."

"Phone him up, he may not even have left yet. Tell him we're walking you home. I'll hold one hand and Duncan the other. Two is a perfectly safe escort."

The girl hesitated.

"It's only half past eleven. And a warm night," said Drummond with soft urgency.

"All right," said the girl. She smiled quickly at Thaw and went indoors to phone.

"Marjory is a nice girl, a really nice girl," said Drummond musically. "I don't know why people think I'm incapable of liking nice girls."

Thaw yawned at the sky. One or two stars were visible. He said, "Goodnight, Aitken."

"Don't go," said Drummond quickly. "Don't you *like* Marjory?"

"That's not the point," said Thaw; yet when Marjory came out Drummond took her right hand and Thaw her left, holding it lightly and carefully. It was small, faintly warm, neither dry nor quite moist, and he was very conscious of it.

They walked, talking about ordinary things, across the arch of the hill and followed the lamp-reflecting steel of the tramlines over the River Kelvin into a district of trees and terraces. Somewhere beyond the university they heard some sharp barks and a black dog ran toward them round a curving pavement.

"It's Gibbie!" said Marjory, and squatting down on her haunches received the dog's head in her lap. "How are you, Gibbie? Eh, Gibbie? Good dog, Gibbie," she whispered, rubbing its cheeks with her hands. The dog panted and lolled its tongue out, grinning up at her with shut ecstatic eyes. She stood up and it shot back the way it had come. They followed until they reached a tall, slightly gawky woman standing by a gate in a hedge. She smiled amiably and gave her hand to the students in turn.

"Oh, I've met you before, Aitken, of course. So this is Duncan. How are you, Duncan? Thank you both for seeing our little daughter so safely home. My husband is just bringing the car round to drive you back to the city centre. Neither of you live near here, do you?"

A car drove slowly toward them along the edge of the kerb. It stopped and the back door was pushed open. They said goodbye to Marjory and her mother and climbed in.

Though Marjory had given him no more than some friendly glances and a squeeze of the hand he spent the weekend cleaning paint stains from his clothes and started brushing his teeth before going to bed. On Monday he stood with friends on the staircase of the main building when she went swiftly by. He followed her down to the entrance hall, across the street and into the annexe, where, singing, she turned unexpected corners. Her voice echoed along an unseen corridor until silenced by the remote slam of a door. He stood for a while as if still listening. The song had been tuneful but without definite tune, a line of melodious notes as casual as bird notes. On the staircase he had glimpsed her throat in silhouette, the outline pulsing like a plucked string. He felt baffled and wondered whether to feel insulted. She must have known he was following; why hadn't she stopped? But then he could have reached her side by walking faster; why hadn't he walked faster?

At noontime she was several places ahead of him in the refectory queue and smiled and raised her hand in greeting. He nodded, looked casually elsewhere, and three minutes later arrived beside her in a way that seemed accidental. He waited until she noticed him before smiling. She said, "Hullo, Duncan. How are you?"
"Well. How are you?"
"Oh! Well."
A pleasant little giggle suggested, not that he amused her, but that it was amusing for them to be talking there. He said, "I enjoyed our walk on Friday."
"I enjoyed it a lot too."
"Aitken is good company."
"You were not bad company yourself, Duncan."
A dangerous silence widened between them. He drew breath and plunged over it.
"Can I . . . eat at your table?"
"Of course, Duncan."
She smiled so kindly that he felt he had said nothing difficult or strange. They took their plates to a table and ate beside Janet Weir and a couple of other girls who were attractive and welcoming. He enjoyed the meal for it was easier talking to several girls than one, but when Janet left to get cigarettes

he leaned towards Marjory and his face went red.
"Would you . . . let me take you to the pictures some night?"
"Of course, Duncan."
"Will tomorrow night do?"
"Yes. . . . yes, I think so."
"I'll call about seven, will I?"
She frowned vaguely. "I . . . think so, Duncan. Yes."

After tea next evening he took from his wardrobe a blue
pin-striped double-breasted suit, a gift of a neighbour whose
son had outgrown it. Thaw had enraged his mother by saying
he would never wear it because it was the kind of suit businessmen and American gangsters wore. Tonight he put it on, slid
a clean white folded handkerchief into the breast pocket and
set off for Marjory's home, buying a box of chocolates on the
way. Aboard the bus his heart beat loudly and his knees trembled, but entering the district where she lived he was unable
to find the house. It had been at the end of a curving terrace
but there were many of these. He searched for a phone box
to look up her address in the directory and found one near
the docks, but with the book in hand he discovered he didn't
know her second name. He punched his brow violently for a
while, then phoned McAlpin who said, "Her father's Professor
Laidlaw, who does biochemistry at Gilmorehill. I'll look up
the address for you. You sound rather . . . distraught."

Half an hour later Thaw rang a doorbell and Mrs. Laidlaw
opened to him, saying, "Come in, Duncan."
Having despaired of getting there he felt his arrival was insub-
stantial. He said, "I'm sorry I'm late. I lost my way."
"Are you late? Marjory's still upstairs getting ready."
The lobby had shining dark furniture and dark landscapes in
guilt frames. A golf club and umbrella lay in a huge blue earthenware vase, and on the polished floor nearby a golf ball
was tethered by a cord to a rubber mat. Mrs. Laidlaw led him
into a room with a bright fire in the hearth and switched on
the light. A massive man hoisted himself out of an armchair
and said in a gentle voice, "How do you do?"
Thaw said, "How do you do?"
"This is Marjory's father—oh, but you met last Friday. Now
sit down, both of you, and I'll see if I can hurry up my daughter
a little."
Thaw sat down and tried to seem at ease. The professor had
sounded small and clerkly in the car but here the quiet voice

emphasized his suave bulk. He was leaning forward and tickling with one finger the ear of the dog, Gibbie, who sprawled on the hearth rug.

"Do you play golf?" he asked gently.

"No. But my father does—did, I mean, during the war. He's mainly a climber, though."

"Ah."

Thaw cleared his throat and said, "I received some golfing lessons at my secondary school, but the game required more care, concentration and precision than I was prepared to bring to it." The professor said, "Yes. It is an exacting game and requires . . . . . patience."

They were silent until a small yellow budgerigar landed with a thump on Thaw's shoulder and said "Hurry up, Marjory! Good old Mr. Churchill! Hurry up, Marjory!"

Thaw said, "Ah. A budgerigar."

"Yes indeed. We call him Joey. I'm sure I've seen you around the university."

"I sometimes sketch in the medical building."

"Why?"

"To see the insides of people. And death too, of course."

"Why?"

"Because it's stupid to share the world with something you're afraid to look at. You see I want to like the world, life, God, nature, et cetera, but I can't because of pain."

"Pain poses no problem. It warns individuals that they're defective."

"Oh, I know pain is usually good for us," said Thaw, "but what good is it to a woman who bears a limbless baby with a face on top of its head? What good is it to the baby?"

"I deal with life at a cellular level," said the professor.

A little later he and Thaw said simultaneously, "How is Marjory—" "Tell me about golf—"

"I beg your pardon," said Thaw. "How is Marjory?"

"Getting on at school."

"I . . . I don't know. What year is she in?"

"The second, I think."

"Then she's probably doing quite well," said Thaw. "Hardly anyone fails their second year," he added.

"I thought you were in her class," said the professor, faintly hostile.

"Indeed no," said Thaw coldly.

Marjory came in with her mother. She wore a flower-patterned dress and long earrings and her breasts seemed more prominent than usual. The budgerigar fluttered to her shoulder twittering, "Hurry, hurry up, Marjory! Good old Mr. Churchill!"

She blushed and smiled.

"Naughty Joey's giving away secrets," said Mrs. Laidlaw.

"I'm sorry I kept you waiting, Duncan."

"I was very late myself," said Thaw.

"Off the pair of you go now," said Mrs. Laidlaw kindly. She stood in the doorway watching them go down the path. Thaw felt like a child going to school with his sister. On the pavement Marjory hesitated and said nervously, "Duncan—I hope you won't be annoyed about this—when I said I could go out with you tonight I'd forgotten I'd arranged to see a friend. . . . She's very nice. . . . Would it be all right if she came with us? She lives quite near."

"Of course!" said Thaw, and talked heartily to cover the stoical adjustments happening inside him. They reached a gate in a thick hedge and Marjory whispered that she wouldn't be long and left him outside. The night was chilly and glints of frost shone in the pavement under the street lamp. He heard a door open and the light murmur of Marjory's voice, then the darker tones of someone else. Eventually the door shut and Marjory joined him with a slight vertical crease between her eyebrows. "I'm sorry, Duncan—she wasn't able to come. I think maybe she has a cold."

"Don't worry about it."

She gave a quick polite smile. He was disturbed by the strained lines it made near the corners of her mouth. If she often smiled like that a wrinkle would come there in ten or twelve years.

They were late for the film. It had love scenes which made him very conscious of Marjory beside him. He leaned toward her but she sat so upright and stared so straight ahead that he dispiritedly brought out the chocolates and resignedly popped one at intervals into her mouth. After the film the nearby cafés had queues outside so they boarded the bus home. He sat on the upper deck watching the pure line of her face and throat against the black window. They filled him with delight and terror for he would need to cross over to them and he hadn't much time. He stared desperately, trying to learn what to do by intensity of vision. Her eyes were downcast under a

brown feathery brow, her mouth had a lost remote look but
the chin was strong, her brown hair was drawn into a flat coil
at the back of her skull and the tip of an ear peeped through
like a delicate section of seashell. The head turned and faced
him enquiringly. Sweat trickled down his brow.
"Can I . . . hold your hand?"
"Of course, Duncan."
"It's queer. When I ask for something I'm usually sure you'll
give it, but I sweat as if I'd no chance at all."
Her throat was shaken by a note of bitten-back laughter.
"Do you, Duncan?"
The handhold was mainly pleasing for symbolic reasons, but
where their shoulders touched so soft a silence and relaxation
flowed into him that his mind bathed in vacancy for a while,
untroubled by thoughts of what to do when they reached her
house.

     They paused at the garden gate. She shut her eyes suddenly
and tilted her blind face upward. He put his mouth on hers.
After a moment she slipped away, saying "Goodnight, Duncan."
"Goodnight—I'll see you tomorrow, won't I?"
"Yes, tomorrow. Goodnight."
He walked thoughtfully home, for the last tram had gone. Frost
stiffened the substance of the pavement so that his feet hit
the glittering surface with a tweeting note. Crossing the hill
by the university he was struck by the clarity of the stars. They
were not like lights stippling the inner surface of a dome but
like galactic chandeliers hung at different levels in black air.
He felt vaguely happy, yet vaguely puzzled and flat, and very
cold. The kiss had meant nothing, nothing books, films and
gossip had made him expect. Was it his fault? Or Marjory's?
Did it matter? He reached home, went to bed and slept.

     He was standing on the golf course of Alexandra Park
shortly after dawn, listening to a lark in the grey air overhead.
The song stopped and the bird's corpse thumped onto the turf
at his feet. He walked downhill through a litter of sparrows
and blackbirds on the paths to the gate. On Alexandra Parade
a worker's tram, apparently empty, groaned past the traffic
lights. He watched the lights change from red and amber to
green, then to green and amber, and then go out. The tramcar
came to a halt.

Not everything died at once for the lowlier plants put on final spurts of abnormal growth. Ivy sprouted up the Scott monument in George Square and reached the lightning conductor on the poet's head; then the leaves fell off and the column was encased in a net of bone-white bone-hard fibre. Moss carpeted the pavements, then crumbled to powder under his feet as he walked alone through the city. He was happy. He looked in the windows of pornography shops without wondering if anyone saw him, and rode a bicycle through the halls of the art galleries and bumped down the front steps, singing. He set up easels in public places and painted huge canvases of buildings and dead trees. When a painting was completed he left it confronting the reality it depicted. The weather had also died. There was no rain or wind. The sky was always grey and warm and the time mid-afternoon.

He sat in the courtyard of Holyrood Palace in Edinburgh painting a view of Arthur's Seat. A harsh beak whispered gratingly in his left ear, "This is all much as Queen Mary remembered it."
A white speck appeared high on the crags and moved down the path toward the courtyard's southern gate. A load of depression settled in his heart. He leaned toward the canvas and worked with his face against it, determined to see nobody. A chilling shock went through him and he knew she had laid her hand on the back of his neck. He tried to ignore her but work was intolerable under her suffering eyes, so he motioned her to stand before the easel. She did so, thinking he meant to put her in the picture. He took a rifle and shot her. She stared at him reproachfully, then broke, crumpled, crumbled into a turd.

Great beetles emerged. The city was full of them. They were five feet long and shaped like rowing boats with antennae and had mouths in their stomachs. They were in every building throwing furniture and the bodies of the dead out of the windows. They feared open spaces and crossed these at a quick scuttling run. In the angle between a wall and pavement Thaw crouched between two who flickered their antennae incuriously over him. Since they had no eyes they thought him one of themselves as he squatted down and moved as they did.

He awoke with a chill that kept him in bed for a week.

CHAPTER 24. Marjory Laidlaw

Convalescence was sweetened by the thought of Marjory and he returned to school full of anxious hope. Once again he was standing on the staircase talking to McAlpin and Drummond when she passed without noticing him wave and call. He gaped after her, wondering if he should chase and strike her. Surely she must have seen him! Why did she pretend not to? Or was the fault his? Perhaps on their night out together he had bored or disappointed her beyond any hope of forgiveness. An hour later in the school shop she said "Hello, Duncan!" and stood looking at him with a shy gay open amused smile.

"Hullo!" he said, gazing joyfully back.

"Have you been ill, Duncan?"

"Just a bit."

"What a shame."

She still smiled, but her voice sympathized.

In the following weeks she brought him increasing splendour and discontent. He told her of a studio he was sharing near Kelvingrove Park.

"It's a great big attic and by clubbing together it only costs a few shillings a week each. On Friday nights we go there from school and take turns at making a big meal. Most of the others get help from their girlfriends but Kenneth is a great chef. Last week he made Spanish onion soup with toast on top. Next week it's my turn and I'm going to boil a haggis. A shop in Argyle Street has good big cheap ones and they're nice with tatties and turnip. Afterwards we put off the lights and play records by the fire, jazz and classical. You should come."

"It sounds marvellous." She sighed. "I wish I could come."

"Why can't you?"

"Well . . . there's a friend I always have to see on Fridays."

At tea breaks and lunch time they sat in the refectory or went to a café and returned holding hands and talking. He joined the school choir because she sang there, and after late practices they walked to her home. At the garden gate conversation suddenly failed, their mouths met in a ritual pressure and she slipped away with a soft "Goodnight," leaving him as baffled as the first time they kissed. When they left the school together she always murmured "Excuse me a minute," slipped into the ladies' lavatory and left him outside for a quarter of an hour. She never recognized him if he was with friends. These insults filled reservoirs of rage which evaporated whenever she smiled at him. And when their bodies accidentally touched a current of stillness and silence flowed in from her and he felt that before touching Marjory he had never known rest. His calmest moods had been full of fear, hope, lust and memory, all clashing to make a discord of ideas and words. Her touch silenced these, letting him know nothing for a while but the pressure of hand or knee, and Marjory beside him, and sunlight on rooftops or a cloud seen through a window. That didn't happen often. His frequentest pleasure was waking in the morning, hearing pigeons among the chimneypots and being warmed by the thought of soon seeing her. When words came at these times the memory of Marjory orchestrated them into phrases. He wrote poems and slid copies into her hands as they passed in the school corridors. He started combing his hair, brushing his teeth, polishing his shoes, changing underwear twice a week and (to the annoyance of Mr. Thaw, who laundered them) shirts four times a week. He wore the pinstriped suit to school and cleaned off the stains with turpentine, though this made temporary rashes on the skin. His manner with other girls grew more playful. He thought they were interested in him.

After school one evening he saw her on the edge of a group outside the annexe. She smiled and raised her hand and he said, "Remember tonight, Marjory?"

She grew agitated and distressed. "No, Duncan. . . . Duncan I think I . . . I'm sure I've something to do tonight. . . . This isn't an excuse; I really have too much work to do."

"Never mind," said Thaw amiably. He entered the refectory and found McAlpin alone at a table. Thaw sat down, folded arms on the tabletop and hid his face in them. "Damn her," he said muffledly. *"Damn* her. *Damn* her. *Damn* her."

"What happened this time?"

Thaw explained. McAlpin said, "She's afraid of you."

"That's impossible. I'm not aggressive. Even in masturbation fantasies I never dream of being cruel to *real* girls."

After a pause, McAlpin said, "Imagine you are quiet, timid, rather conventional, and not long out of a middle-class fee-paying school which prides itself on producing genteel young ladies. You are chased by a clever peculiar boy. He's polite but his clothes and hair have paint on them, he breathes heavily and his skin is often . . . mmmm . . . medically interesting. How would you react? Remember, you've been brought up not to hurt people."

Thaw said, "I've thought of that. And next time we meet I'll nod to her distantly and she'll be specially inquiring and charming. She'll suggest we have coffee together. Oh, she wants me. Slightly. Sometimes."

"Maybe she's frigid."

"Of course she's frigid. So am I. But nobody stays the same forever and even lumps of ice, surely, will melt if they rub together long enough. Perhaps she's not frigid. Perhaps she loves someone else."

"She's honest, Duncan—I doubt if there's anyone else."

"Do you? I would doubt but . . . she's so much more bonny each time I see her that I feel she must love somebody."

McAlpin said, "Hm!" and glanced sideways at Thaw beneath lethargic eyelids.

He sat on the top deck of the homeward tramcar and his rage at her increased with the distance between them. A voice said, "Hullo, Duncan."

It took a moment to recognize June Haig, who was going downstairs. He rose and followed, saying, "Hullo, June. You are a bad girl."

"Oh? Why that?"

"Last year you kept me waiting for nothing for a whole hour at Paisley's corner."

She gave him a quick startled smile. "Did I? Oh, yes. Something happened."

He saw that she didn't remember. He grinned and said "Don't worry. The point is . . ." —the tramcar stopped and they crossed to the pavement—"the point is, will you forget again if we arrange to meet again?"

"Oh no."

"Yes you will, if we don't meet soon. What about Paisley's corner tomorrow night? About seven?"
"Yes, all right, then."
"Good. I'll be there."

He turned and walked quickly home. June had aroused him like an erotic fantasy, yet he hadn't once blushed or stammered. He wondered why this arousal made him her equal when his feeling for Marjory made him subordinate. In the living room he walked up and down for a while, then said, "Dad, tomorrow night I'm taking out a girl. I want you to give me five pounds."
Mr. Thaw turned slowly and stared at him.
"What kind of girl is this?"
"Her kind is no business of yours. I want to be free and openhanded. A few shillings will keep me mean and cautious and I'll get no pleasure at all. I need pleasure."
"And how often do you intend to have it?"
"I don't care. I don't know. I'm only thinking of tomorrow night."
Mr. Thaw scratched his head. "Your grant is a hundred and twenty a year. With that I'm to clothe, house, feed you and pay for materials and pocket money. You won't work in the holidays because it interferes with your artistic self-expression—"
"Don't talk to me about self-expression!" cried Thaw fiercely. "Do you think I'd paint if I'd nothing better to express than this rotten *self*? If my self was made of decent material I could relax with it, but self-*disgust* keeps forcing me out after the truth, the truth, the truth!"
"I can make neither head nor tail of that," said Mr. Thaw, "but I know the result. The result is that I toil so that you can paint. And now you want over a quarter of my weekly salary to spend on pleasure. What kind of fool do you think I am?"
After a moment Thaw said, "In future I'll handle my grant money myself. I know you don't mind me sleeping here, but I'll try not to ask for other favours."
"You'll try and you'll fail because you're so damned impractical. But all right, all right. Try anyway."
"Thank you. It'll be two months before the next grant comes through. Please give me five pounds, Dad."
His father looked hard at him, then brought out a wallet and handed over the money.

In Paisley's shop door next night he knew after ten minutes that June would not come, yet numbness in his limbs and heart kept him waiting an hour longer. A lame old man in a dirty coat approached and asked for money. Thaw stared resentfully into bloodshot eyes, a twisted helpless mouth and a tangled beard slimy with spittle. He could not think why he should own a five-pound note and this man not, so he handed it over and walked quickly away. He felt his soul was being deliberately crushed, yet there was nobody to blame. He could not bear to face his father. He walked to the Cowcaddens, climbed the stair to Drummond's house, pushed the door open and went into the kitchen.

Drummond and Janet Weir sat on each side of the kitchen range looking at a crate on the hearth rug. The ginger cat sprawled on a sheet of glass covering this and stared down at two white mice among cheese rinds at the bottom. Drummond said, "Hullo, Duncan. Ginger's at his television set."
"How did this happen?" said Thaw.
"My mother visited us yesterday. She brought the mice as a present for the cat, since it was his ninth birthday. My father and I took them away from her."
"And now Ginger sits there, foiled of his rightful prey," said Mr. Drummond. He lay in the recess bed with spectacles on his craggy nose, a flat cap on his head, an open library book propped on the quilt over his knees. Janet shivered and said, "Surely it's cruel, having him on top of them like that."
Drummond said, "What? Make the tea, Duncan looks tired. These mice are nearly blind, Duncan. If anyone is suffering it's Ginger."

Drummond left the room and came back with a picture of himself chalking a cue beside a snooker table. He propped the painting on the sideboard, took paint and brushes and began altering the position and number of the balls. The air was permeated by the pleasant smell of linseed oil and turpentine. At intervals Drummond stood back and said, "How's that, Duncan?"
Janet handed Thaw a cup of tea and a bacon sandwich, and when he had drunk and eaten he began to draw her. She crouched near the fire with the cat on her lap, copious hair overhanging and surrounding her subtle face. She looked rather like Marjory, but Marjory moved with childish carelessness and Janet seemed to feel eyes watching the secretest parts of her.

"What o'clock is it?" said Thaw.

"I don't know," said Drummond. "None of the clocks in this house can be relied on, least of all the ones that go. It's a pity Ma isn't here. She could estimate the time by things like passing aeroplanes. Couldn't she, Dad?"

"What?"

"I said Ma could always tell the time."

"Oh, aye. She would shake my shoulders in bed in the morning. 'Hector! Hector! It's ten past four. There's Mrs. Stewart going to her work in the bakery—I'd know her step anywhere.' Or it would be 'It's a quarter to eight—I can hear the horse of Eliot's milk cart two streets away.'"

"Do you know the time, Mr. Drummond?" said Thaw.

Mr. Drummond lifted an alarm clock which lay face down on a pile of books by the bed. He held it to his ear, shook it and put it carefully down saying, "The hands have ceased to go round and round, and no trust whatever can be placed in it." He closed his eyes, opened his mouth, lay back on the pillow and at last said definitely, "We are in the region of midnight."

"Then the trams have stopped, you'll have to stay here tonight," said Drummond.

"The trams haven't stopped. I can hear them," said Janet.

"Can't you keep your mouth shut?" cried Drummond savagely. "I don't know why I tolerate you! You're the epitome of all . . . of all . . . Duncan! You aren't going to let this woman drive you out of my house?"

"No. I'm going home to bed. Goodnight."

Drummond followed Thaw into the lobby. "Let's be sensible about this, Duncan. Why should you go to bed?"

"To sleep."

Drummond stood erect, folded his arms, drew his black eyebrows together at the bridge of his nose and said in a firm quiet voice, "I'm telling you not to go out of that door, Duncan."

"Heech! You're in a bad way when you have to resort to commanding," said Thaw, but lingered. "Why should I *not* go out that door?" he asked plaintively.

"Because you'd rather not," said Drummond, ushering him back into the kitchen.

"I'm being weak," said Thaw, settling into a chair by the fire. *"No, damn me!"* he cried, jumping up. "Why should I be commanded by you or by any man? Goodnight!"

"Janet, ask him to stay!" said Drummond. "Tell him it's stupid going back to Riddrie at this hour of night."

"I think you should stay, Duncan," said Janet.

"Well, if you're convinced of that . . ." said Thaw, sitting down. For the first time since waiting for June he felt relaxed and cheerful.

Thaw drew, Drummond painted, they gossiped and improvised jokes and sometimes chuckled continuously for many minutes. They had spells of listlessness when Janet made the tea. Each time he drew her his hand moved more easily and depicted more of the surrounding room. It was as if Janet's body gave out light which clarified nearby things and turned the cluttered furniture, Drummond working at the sideboard, Mr. Drummond reading or dozing, even stale breadcrusts on the table, into parts of a cunning harmony. She sat still easily under his concentrated stare. Sometimes her eyes returned it for a second, then glanced slyly sideways at Drummond. Thaw said, "You're a flower beneath the foot, Janet."

"What do you mean, Duncan?"

"You're beautiful and neglected and dishevelled."

"Don't encourage her," said Drummond grimly. "Don't you know it's deliberate? She probably wants the girls at school to think I beat her."

"Why have you always to be offensive?" said Janet.

"Why have I . . .? Why have you always to be offensive? Stupid!" said Drummond, almost kindly, for he was staring at his painting. He had taken out all but one white ball and said, "How's that, Duncan?"

"Good. But I preferred it with more balls."

Drummond frowned at the picture, took a saw from a drawer and cut off the part with the snooker table on it. He placed the self-portrait on the mantelpiece and said "How about that, Duncan?"

"More perfect but less worthwhile."

Drummond said, "Make the tea, Janet."

He took a small gilt frame from under the sideboard, measured it, sawed the head off the portrait and fitted it into the frame. He hung it on the wall and stood back regarding it with arms folded and head on one side. He said, "More perfect? You're right, Duncan, it is more perfect. Yes, I'm pleased with my night's work."

"All sheer bloody nonsense!" snorted Mr. Drummond from his bed.

"Yes, I'm pleased with my night's work," said Drummond, accepting a cup of tea from Janet.

The darkness outside the window paled and soft pink came into the sky behind the pinnacles of the dingy little church. Drummond shot up the window to let in a cool draught. From grey rooftops on the left rose the mock Gothic spire of the university, then the Kilpatrick hills, patched with woodlands and with the clear distant top of Ben Lomond behind the eastward slope. Thaw thought it queer that a man on that summit, surrounded by the highlands and overlooking deep lochs, might see with a telescope this kitchen window, a speck of light in a low haze to the south. The dim sky broke into cloudbergs with dazzling silver between. Mr. Drummond lay back on his pillow snoring wheezily through open mouth.
"The dairy will be open now," said Drummond. "Janet, here's half a crown. Go and buy something nice for breakfast. Duncan and I will get ready for bed."

Thaw and Drummond went into a room with an open bed settee in the middle. They undressed to their underwear, removed their socks and got between rough blankets. They heard Janet return and do something in the kitchen, then she entered with three plates of stewed pears and cream. She ate on the edge of the bed and when Thaw and Drummond lay down she wrapped herself in a khaki greatcoat and lay across their ankles with the cat curled against her stomach. Thaw said sleepily, "I would now be getting out of my bed at home if—"
Suddenly he was struck by an image, not of June Haig but of Marjory. He imagined her breasts trembling under skilful hands and sat up, saying, "Janet! You're Marjory's friend. Is she carrying on with somebody else?"
"I don't think so, Duncan."
"Then what is wrong with her? What is wrong with her?"
"I think she's too contented at home, Duncan. She's very happy with her father and mother."
"I see. She's in love with her parents. Instead of learning to be adult by teaching me to be adult she basks idly at home. Oh, God, if you exist, *hurt* her, *hurt* her, God, let her find no comfort but in me, make life afflict her as it afflicts me. Oh, Aitken! Aitken! How *dare* she be happy without me?"
Thaw lay back glaring at the ceiling. After a pause Drummond

said bitterly, "I understand your feelings."

Janet sneered and said, "In case you don't know, Duncan, he's thinking about Molly—*oh!*"

Drummond's foot below the blankets had struck her chin. She put her hands to her face and wept quietly. They stewed in their separate miseries and gradually fell asleep.

Thaw dreamed he was fornicating awkwardly with Marjory, who stood naked and erect like a caryatid. He rode astride her hips, holding himself off the ground by gripping her sides with knees and arms. The cold rigid body stayed inert at first, then gradually began to vibrate. He had a thin, lonely sensation of triumph.

He awoke late in the afternoon. Slowly drawing his feet from below Janet without disturbing her he carried his clothes into the kitchen, washed at the sink, dressed, gave water and cheese to the mice in the crate and rolled up the drawings he had made the night before. On the way to the front door he glanced into the bedroom. Janet no longer lay on the bed foot and there was movement under the blankets. In the close he met Mr. Drummond returning from the hotel, tall, spectacled, flat-capped, raincoat open over boiler suit.

"Hullo, Duncan. You're not leaving? I'm just going to make dinner. I've some cod roe here."

He indicated a paper parcel under his armpit.

"No thanks, Mr. Drummond."

"Well, it's a present from the chef. I neither pinched it nor paid for it. You're sure you won't have some?"

"No thanks. If I go back to your house I'm afraid I'll never get away."

Mr. Drummond laughed and started filling a short-stemmed pipe. "You're a reader, aren't you?"

"I read books, yes."

"I'm inclined that way myself. I tried to make Aitken a reader, but I failed. Do you know how he passed his English exams?"

"No."

"I read his schoolbooks, Scott, Jane Austen, and so on, and told him the stories. He can remember anything he hears, you see, but he's never read a book from start to finish in his life, unless it was about art. Consequently his mind is cramped, narrow and lacking in sympathy for his fellow man. He'll never prosper. But you'll prosper, Duncan."

"I hope so, Mr. Drummond."
"Oh, yes, you'll prosper, Duncan."

Cheered by this prophecy Thaw walked quickly uphill to the school and passed Marjory in the entrance hall. He nodded coldly but she stopped him, smiled and said, "Where have you been, Duncan?"
"I've been sleeping."
"Are you coming for a coffee?"
He was filled with relief and delight. She gave him her hand to hold on the way to the refectory. He thought, 'This is an interesting world.'

CHAPTER 25. Breaking

He took the 1875 *Imperial Gazetteer of Scotland* from his father's bookcase and read:

MONKLAND CANAL, an artificial navigable communication between the city of Glasgow and the district of Monkland in Lanarkshire. The project of the canal was suggested in 1769 as a measure for securing to the inhabitants of Glasgow, at all times, a plentiful supply of coals. The Corporation of the city immediately employed the celebrated James Watt to survey the ground, obtained an act of parliament for carrying out the measure, and subscribed a number of shares to the stock. The work was begun in 1771. Previous to its formation the lands in the neighbourhood were comparatively shut up, the mineral fields unproductive, and only a thatched cottage was seen here and there to dot the surface. But once the canal was in operation a change, as if effected by magic, came over the face and feelings of the district, a change accelerated by the establishment of ironworks in the district of Monkland. Public works were erected, population gathered in masses by thousands, splendid edifices were called into existence, a property once considered valueless, except for the scanty returns of its tillage or hortage, became a mine of wealth which may enrich many succeeding generations.

When the project of opening the district by railways was first mooted it created much alarm in the canal company, lest traffic be wholly diverted from their navigation. The alarm was not unfounded, but it only induced the company to reduce their dues by two thirds and expend large sums on improvements to facilitate traffic. New locks were made at Blackhill, of a character excelling all works of their class in Great Britain. They comprised two entire sets of four double locks each, either set being worked independently of the other; and were formed at the expense of upward of £30,000. In 1846, when the Monkland Canal became one concern with the Forth and Clyde Canal, the purchase price was £3,400 per share.

The canal had closed to traffic before he was born. From a channel carrying trade into the depth of the country it had become a ribbon of wilderness allowing reeds and willows, swans and waterhens into the heart of the city. He was puzzled by the phrase "splendid edifices were called into existence." The only splendid building he knew east of the city was the canal itself, a ten-mile-long artwork shaped in stone, timber, earth and water. He went to sketch the Blackhill locks.

This was difficult. He knew how the two great water staircases curved round and down the hill, but from any one level the rest were invisible. Moreover, the weight of the architecture was seen best from the base, the spaciousness from on top; yet he wanted to show both equally so that eyes would climb his landscape as freely as a good athlete exploring the place. He invented a perspective showing the locks from below when looked at from left to right and from above when seen from right to left; he painted them as they would appear to a giant lying on his side, with eyes more than a hundred feet apart and tilted at an angle of 45 degrees. Working from maps, photographs, sketches and memory his favourite views had nearly all been combined into one when a new problem arose.

He had meant to people the canvas with Sunday afternoon activity: children fishing for minnows with jam-jars, a woman clipping a hedge round an old lockkeeper's cottage, a pensioner exercising a dog on the towpath. But the locks now looked so solid that he wanted them to frame something vaster. He opened the last book of the bible and read of ultimatums and proclamations, of war, starvation, profiteering and death, of flaming bodies hurled through the sky to poison whole nations. The politics of the book seemed as modern as in the days of St. John and Albrecht Dürer. The final splitting of people into good and bad and the survival of the good into a luxurious new world was unconvincing, but politicians usually talk like that in a crisis. He changed the time of day from afternoon to gloaming and made a black descending dart high up between the moon and the roof of his old primary school. Being painted on the sky it could not fall, nor could the crowds under it escape. They fled along towpaths, over bridges, and collected on heights, yet there was no brutality in their fearful rush: mothers still clung to children, fathers shielded both, on open spaces single figures pointed to doors in the hillside. To show the crowds properly he made great changes in the landscape and these were nearly complete when a new need arose. In that huge multitude only *types* were visible, and he suddenly wanted a life-size figure in the foreground, someone whose bewildered face looked straight at the viewers, making them feel part of the multitude too.

Thaw stopped to think, for the whole composition would have to be rearranged again if the new figure was to fit it and not be just stuck on top. His painting teacher, a conscientious man, approached and said, "How much longer will you be on this? It's all you've done this term. The others have finished three or four paintings by now."
"Mine is bigger than theirs, sir."
"Bigger, yes. Ridiculously big. When will you finish it?"
"Mibby next week, Mr. Watt. It looks nearly finished."
"Quite. It looked nearly finished three weeks ago. It looked finished a fortnight before that. Each time you suddenly painted most of it out and began what seemed a different picture."
"I got ideas for improvement."
"Quite so. If you get any more ideas, ignore them. I want that picture finished next week."
Thaw stared uneasily at his feet and said in a low voice, "I'll try to finish it next week, sir, but if I get a good idea I can't promise to reject it."—He was filled with sudden gaiety and tried hard not to grin.—"If I did that, God might not give me others."
After a pause Mr. Watt said, "Show me your folder of work."
Thaw brought over a folder of drawings and the teacher looked slowly through them.
"Why all the ugly distortions?"
"I may have over-emphasized some shapes to make them clearer, but surely you don't think all my work distorted, sir?"
Mr. Watt looked through the folder again, frowning slightly, and set aside a sheet of hands drawn in pencil. He said, "I like these. They're well observed and carefully described."
Thaw hunted through the folder and brought out a foreshortened drawing of a woman seen from the feet. He said, "Don't you think she is beautiful?"
"No. I honestly think you've made her ugly and tortured-looking."
Thaw shuffled the drawings back into the folder and said embarrassedly, "I'm sorry. I can't agree."

"We're going to discuss this later," said the teacher in a muffled voice, and left the room. McAlpin, who was working nearby, looked up and said, "I enjoyed that. I kept wondering which of you would burst into tears first."

"It was nearly me."

"It's a good thing the registrar likes your work."

"Why?"

"It would take too long to explain."

They worked in silence, then Thaw asked in a pleading voice, "Kenneth, am I impudent?"

"Oh, no. You obviously dislike having to hurt their feelings."

On the way to the classroom next morning Thaw met Mr. Watt who said, "One moment, Thaw! I'd like a word with you."

They stepped into a window recess and sat on a bench. Mr. Watt sucked grimly at his lower lip, then said, "I've just been talking about you to Mr. Peel. I told him that you rejected my advice, were a disturbing influence on other students, and that I didn't want you in my class."

Thaw's heart began beating hard and heavily. He said, "I like you to advise me, sir, I like advice from anyone, but advice which can't be rejected doesn't deserve the name. Moreover—"

"Let's not discuss it. McAlpin tells me you share a studio near the park."

"Yes."

"I have asked Mr. Peel to let you paint there. You'll come to school as usual for lectures, but the rest of the time you'll work by yourself. At the end of the term we'll see what you have to show."

Thaw took a moment to digest this, then gave his teacher a look of such delight, affection, and pity that Mr. Watt stirred impatiently and said, "I'd be grateful for an answer to a strictly unofficial question, Thaw. Do you have the faintest notion what you're trying to do?"

"No sir, but this new arrangement will help me find out. Can I start shifting my things today?"

"Start when you like."

At home that evening Thaw packed books and papers he had not yet taken to the studio. To Mr. Thaw, who was helping, he said, "Could I take the spare mattress from the single bed?"

"So I'm to see even less of you than usual?"

"It helps to be in the same room as my work when I wake in the morning."

"All right. Take the mattress. And sheets. And blankets. And why not the bed when you're about it?"

"No. A mattress and sleeping bag are easily rolled out of the way. A real bed would be a waste of space."

"All right, all right. But I'll consider it a favour if you come home to see me sometimes, and not only when you need money."

These words held such humility and bitterness that Thaw felt an unfamiliar pang. He said sadly, "I respect and admire you, Dad. I even like you. But I'm afraid of you, I don't know why."

"Perhaps we chastised you too much when you were wee."

"Chastised . . . ?"

"Thrashed."

"Did you do it often?"

"Quite often. You took it badly. We had to give you cold baths to stop your hysterics."

This struck Thaw as an odd way to treat a small child. He hid his embarrassment by saying heartily, "I'm sure I deserved it."

On Saturday morning he waited for Marjory in Central Station, for she had agreed to lunch with him, then help clean the studio. He felt lively and excited though he knew she was coming because he had asked for help, not pleasure. This would be their first time alone in a private place, and if they ever considered marriage her work in the studio would give him a notion of her domestic stamina. She was an hour and five minutes late and he could not look at her grimly, for the nearly hopeless wait gave her the appearance of a splendid surprise. She explained that she had worked hard the night before, her mother thought it best not to wake her, and the alarm clock had failed to ring. The waitress serving them in the restaurant they visited was June Haig.

"It's a while since I saw you, June," he said while Marjory considered the menu.

"Hello, Duncan. And er you still et the ert school?" she said, tapping her ruby underlip with a pencil end. She spoke drawlingly, for her accent had turned Anglo-Scottish.

"I've been twice jilted by that girl," said Thaw when June left with the order.

"When was that, Duncan?" said Marjory, looking interested.

"I'll tell you one day. It's a sordid wee story," said Thaw jovially. He enjoyed a vision of himself as a worldly man who could joke about being jilted by a waitress. While they ate Marjory looked up once or twice and saw his face intent on hers and smiled a small strained smile. He remembered when that smile had seemed ugly. Now it seemed lovely, and he was sure that after twelve years the wrinkle it caused would seem lovely too.

"Duncan," said Marjory, "you won't mind if I . . . well, I may have to leave you early this afternoon."

After a pause Thaw said dryly, "If that's so it can't be helped."

"Well anyway, we'll see," said Marjory vaguely.

The studio was a long whitewashed attic. Two windows allowed a view of trees, paths and lawns sloping up to the mansions of Park Terrace. A gas cooker, table, sofa and some chairs stood round a fireplace at one end. The other end was filled by a canvas stretched on the wall which bore the first strokes of a bigger version of the Blackhill locks landscape. The middle of the floor held the grime and rubbish which comes when a few young men use a room carelessly. Among it were easels, Thaw's bedding and a heavy old sideboard loaded with paint material. There was a figurine of a dancing faun on the mantelpiece and several sentences drawn on the sloping ceiling.

IF MORE THAN 5% OF THE PEOPLE LIKE A PAINTING
THEN BURN IT FOR IT MUST BE BAD

James McNeil Whistler

I DO NOT PRETEND TO UNDERSTAND ART BUT I BE-
LIEVE MOST SO-CALLED MODERN ART IS THE WORK
OF LAZY, HALF-BAKED PEOPLE   President Truman

GOING DOWN TO HELL IS EASY: THE GLOOMY DOOR
IS OPEN NIGHT AND DAY. TURNING AROUND AND
GETTING BACK TO SUNLIGHT IS THE TASK, THE HARD
THING   Vergil

HUMANITY SETS ITSELF NO PROBLEM WHICH CANNOT
EVENTUALLY BE SOLVED   Marx

Thaw lit the fire, folded back the carpet, swept the floor, carried boxes of rubbish down to the midden, shook mats out of the window and washed the panes. Marjory cleaned the rusty stove, then washed pans and utensils and scrubbed the floor. It was six o'clock when they finished. The room looked wonderfully neat and clean.

"Wash yourself and we'll have tea," said Thaw. He brought parcels out of a cupboard. "Chops," he said. "Onions. Cakes. Bread. Real butter. Jam."

"Oh, Duncan! How lovely! But . . . Mummy expects me for tea. . . ."

"Run down to the phone box at the corner and tell her you're having it here. Here's three pennies for the call."

When Marjory returned the meal was almost ready. They ate hungrily and washed up, then Marjory sat on the sofa by the fire. Thaw occasionally went to the other end of the room and returned with folders. He opened them and spread the contents on the rug at her feet: paintings, drawings and sketches, reproductions and photographs clipped from newspapers and magazines.

"Goodness, Duncan. What a lot of good work. You make me feel very lazy."

He put the work away and returned to the hearth. It was nearly dark outside and most of the light came flickering from a sheaf of vivid flames in the grate. Marjory looked up at him and smiled. Her hands were folded in her lap. Thaw stood by the table and felt a silence like the silence in the mathematics room when the teacher had asked a question he couldn't answer.

"You know I'm afraid of you, Marjory," he blurted.

"Why, Duncan?"

"I suppose because I . . . I like you very much."

"I like you too, Duncan."

There was more silence. He thought to break it with a joke. He said derisively, "Do you know that a while ago I actually believed you were going out with another man—"

She interrupted at once. "Oh, Duncan, I meant to tell you about that. I know a boy at the university, he . . . takes me sometimes to dances and things, but I—I don't know how to say this without seeming vain—I think he . . . likes me more than I like him."

"That's all right," said Thaw abstractedly. He sat on the hearth rug by her feet and laid his head against her knee.

"I . . . oh, I . . ." he murmured.

His intellect had dissolved. He shaped words with his lips but only one or two became sound: "mother" he said once, and shortly after that "world," but he was unconscious of thoughts and later could not remember thinking.

"And yet you . . ." he murmured, reaching up and touching

her cheek curiously. She stirred a little. "I think I'll have to
be going home now," she said.
"Of course," he said, standing up. "I was dreaming. I'll see
you home."
He helped her on with her coat and they went downstairs.

He stopped outside the close mouth and pointed across
at the sighing silhouette of the park trees. "Let's go through
the park."
"But Duncan, the gates are locked."
"There's a railing missing here. Come on. It'll be a shortcut."
He helped her through the narrow gap and down an embankment on the other side. Their feet rustled dead leaves. They
crossed dark smooth lawns and walked round a splashing fountain among the dumpy bodies of holly trees. Two glimmering
swans paddled drowsily in the black water of the ornamental
pond and they heard the somnolent squawk of a goose from
the island in the middle. There was a wide bridge over the
Kelvin with lightless iron candelabra on plinths at each end.
Thaw rested his elbows on the parapet and said, "Listen."
Nearby an almost full moon was freckled by the top leaves
of an elm. The river gurgled faintly against its clay bank, the
distant fountain tinkled. Marjory said, "Lovely."
He said, "I've once or twice felt moments when calmness,
unity and . . . and glory seemed the core of things. Have
you ever felt that?"
"I think so, Duncan. I once went with friends onto the Campsies
and I got separated from them. It was a lovely warm day. I
think I felt it a little then."
"But must these moments always be lonely? Won't love let
us enjoy them with somebody else?"
"I don't know, Duncan."
Thaw looked at her. "Yah. Come on," he said genially. "And
please put your arm through mine."
Beyond the bridge the road divided and a monument to Carlyle
stood in the fork. It was a rough granite pillar with the top
cut in the shape of the prophet's upper body. Moonlight lay
like white frost on brow, beard and shoulders and left the
hollow cheeks and concave eye sockets in gloom. Thaw shook
his free fist and shouted, "Go home, ye spy! Go home, ye
traitor to democracy! . . . He follows me everywhere," he
explained to Marjory, and helped her over a locked gate into
the lighted street.

As they passed the university Marjory said, "Duncan, have you had much experience of girls?"

"Not much, and all of one sort."

He told her about Kate Caldwell, Molly Tierney and June Haig, speaking lightly and jokingly. She punctuated the story with murmurs of "Oh, Duncan."

"And there you have my experience of girls," he ended.

"Oh, Duncan."

The phrase was so loaded with affectionate pity that he began to think he had done a stupid thing. She said, "You see, Duncan, I think you're too afraid. Do you remember in the bus back from the pictures when you asked if you could hold my hand?"

"Yes."

"You needn't have asked. I knew you wanted to. Any girl would have known and let you do it."

"I see."

"And to a certain extent it's the same with kissing. When a girl feels you're worried and frightened she gets upset too."

"Like life models who only feel embarrassed when an embarrassed student draws them."

"Yes, it's like that."

He stopped and gripped her arm. "Marjory, can I draw you? Naked, I mean?"

She stared. He said eagerly, "I won't be embarrassed—my picture needs you. The professional models are good to practise on but they come out like film actresses. I need someone who's beautiful but not fashionable."

"But Duncan . . . I'm not beautiful."

"Oh, you are. If I paint you I'll show you you are."

"But Duncan, I . . . I . . . I have an ugly birthmark down my side."

He shook his head impatiently. "Surface discolourations aren't important." He gave a slight, helpless laugh and added, "You ought to do it, to make us equal again. I stripped naked in front of you just now, in words."

"Oh, Duncan!"

She gave him an affectionate pitying smile and sighed.

"All right, Duncan."

They walked on.

"Good. When? Next week?"

"No, the week after. I'm very busy just now."

"Monday?"

"No. Well . . . Friday."

"Good. About seven?"

"Yes."

"And should I keep reminding you till then?"

"No, I . . . I really will remember, Duncan."

"Good."

At the garden gate she tilted up her mouth. He brushed his cheek on hers and murmured, "We're not mature enough for mouths. Mine hardens when I touch you with it. Please hold me."

They clasped, and her ear against his cheek made a point of tingling excitement. He began breathing deeply. She whispered, "Are you happy, Duncan?"

"Aye."

A car stopped at the kerb. Glancing sideways they saw the profile of the professor sitting immobile behind the wheel. They broke apart, laughing.

The enlarged landscape would show Blackhill, Riddrie, the Campsie Fells, the Cathkin Braes and crowds from both sides mixing around the locks in the middle. Over 105 square feet of canvas he wove, unwove and rewove a net of blue, grey and brown guidelines. He was contemplating them glumly one night when McAlpin entered and said, "What's wrong?"

"I wish the shapes weren't so restless."

"A landscape seen simultaneously from above and below and containing north, east and south can hardly be peaceful. Especially if there's a war in it."

"True, but I'm making a point of rest in the middle foreground: Marjory, looking at us."

"What expression will she have?"

"Her usual expression. I hope you remember she's posing tomorrow. I don't want interruptions."

"Don't worry, you'll be left to yourselves. What exactly do you expect from tomorrow evening? You seem to be building a lot on it."

"I expect an evening of good sound work. I'll be glad to get more but I'm not hoping for it so I can't be disappointed. I love the slight gawkiness in her. She doesn't seem to feel she has breasts and that emphasizes them. She's pretty, isn't she?"

"Yes. Mind you, she could dress to show it more."

"What do you mean?"

"Her clothes are a bit schoolgirlish, don't you think?"

"No, I don't think that."

"You don't? I see."

"My grapes are not sour, you foxy plutocrat."
"Sour gra—? Why, you shabby socialist!"
They laughed at each other.

Next morning he prepared his drawing board, brought
in a bottle of wine and carefully set the fire so that it would
flare at the touch of a match; but he was restless and went to
school for the coffee break. In the refectory he met Janet Weir
and asked if she had seen Marjory.
"No, Duncan. She's not at school today."
"Did she—yesterday, I mean—look a bit tired and ill?"
"I don't think so, Duncan."
He returned to the studio and at half-past six lit the fire and
sat by it trying to read. The doorbell rang at ten to eight.
Making an effort not to run he strolled down and casually
turned the knob. It took him two or three seconds to see that
the girl on the mat was Janet. She said, "Duncan, Marjory
sent me to say she's terribly sorry. She was working very hard
last night and isn't feeling very well."
After a moment Thaw said heavily, "Tell her I'm not surprised,"
and closed the door. He went upstairs and uncorked the wine,
intending to drink himself silly, but after one glass he felt so
dull that he spread his mattress and slept.

There was a sound of wind and of seagulls squabbling
above the park. He woke in a square of sunlight and saw blue
air and white clouds through the window. Turning his back
to it he curled tightly into the mattress and deliberately remembered his friendship with Marjory from the time she first passed
him on the stairs to the evening before. It seemed such a history
of insult that he bit his fingers with rage and at the end his
eyes were warm with tears. He grew calmer by moving onto
the dais of the lecture theatre and talking in a quiet, distinct
voice.
". . . an art school without classes or examinations where life
drawing, morbid anatomy, tools, material and information are
free to whoever wants them. I am ready to lay these plans
before the director and the board of governors, but without
your loyalty I can do nothing."
Her face was in the cheering crowd which parted to let him
through. He noticed her with a slight nod, having more important things to think about. A Labour administration made him
Secretary of State for Scotland, and arising in the House of
Commons he announced his plan for a separate Scottish parlia-

ment: "It is plain that the vaster the social unit, the less possible is true democracy."

A stunned silence was broken by the Prime Minister denouncing him as a renegade. Thaw strode from the chamber and an amazing thing happened. All seventy-one Scottish MPs—Labour, Liberal and Tory—rose and followed him. On the terrace above the Thames he was turning to address them when McAlpin came in and said, "Hullo. Having a long lie?"

"She didn't come."

"The bitch! Listen, it's a glorious day, come out sketching with me."

"I don't feel like moving."

"Make yourself. You'll be better for it."

"I can't."

McAlpin stretched paper on a drawing board. Thaw said abruptly, "I've finished with her."

"Very wise."

"But I haven't worked out how to say 'Goodbye.' "

"Don't bother. Just don't say 'Hello' again."

"No. I must be definite."

"It's useless brooding, Duncan. The light will have gone in three or four hours. Come out sketching."

"No."

McAlpin left, and after the civil war Thaw became head of the reconstruction committee. Fountains splashed and trees grew where the demolished banks had stood. Backcourts were given benches and open-air draughtboards for the old, paddling ponds and sand pits for infants, communal non-profitmaking launderettes for housewives. Pleasure boats with small orchestras sailed down the canal from Riddrie to the Clyde islands. Marjory read his name in newspapers, heard his voice on the wireless, saw his face in cinemas; he surrounded her, he was shaping her world, yet she could not touch him. Then he dozed and dreamed of a fearful twilit country dripping with rain. He was trying to escape from it with a little girl who insulted and betrayed him. She grew tall and sat wearing jewellery on a throne in a dark ancient house. She had sent her club-footed butler to catch him. Tiny Thaw fled from room to room, slamming doors behind him, but the slow limping sound drew nearer all the time. He came at last to a cupboard with no way out and clutched the doorknob, trying to hold it shut. Freezing water swirled up his legs.

He woke in darkness with half the bedding on the floor.
Three stars shone through the window and geese sang discor-
dantly from the pond. Pulling the blankets round him, he eased
his breathing with an ephedrine pill and imagined her a slave
in a luxurious brothel where he tortured her into making shameless love to him. The second time he masturbated she changed
into June Haig, the third time became a boy. Disgusted with
himself he stared at the ceiling till dawn, then fell asleep again.
It was Sunday, and that afternoon other students came and
made coffee, painted and gossiped. Thaw lay pretending to
read but actually composing farewell speeches for Marjory,
speeches amused, pathetic, stoical, coldly insulting and madly
violent. In the evening Macbeth arrived. The art school had
expelled him for drunkenness and he sagged into a chair saying,
"Wha's wrong wi' Duncan? Why's he curled up like that?"
"Shh. He's breaking with Marjory," murmured McAlpin.
"Why're you breaking, Duncan? Can you not get your hole,
is 'at it! Will she not give you your hole?"
"No. Partly, mibby. I don't know."
"Listen to me, Duncan. Listen. Listen. Holes don't matter. I've
had my hole regular since I was seventeen, just because Molly
wouldnae look at me don't think I've gone without my hole.
I go to Bath Street. I get it twice, three times, four times a
week and it doesnae matter *that* much."
He snapped his fingers. "Marjory is a nice girl. You stick to
her, hole or no hole."
"She isn't kind to me," said Thaw from under the blankets.
"I admit that is depressing. I admit that no hole, with no kindness on top of it, can be depressing."

On Monday he went to art school and met Marjory on
the steps. His mind had split with her so completely that the
pretty smiling girl before him was as confusing as a resurrection.
"Hello, Duncan! I'm sorry about Friday. Janet told you why,
didn't she?"
"She told me, yes."
"There's a choir practice after lunch today. Are you going to
the refectory?"
"I suppose so."
Her smile was so direct and bright that his face had to reflect
it, but in the refectory he sat beside her and Janet Weir without
talking and drew on the tabletop. Marjory said, "Janet and I
are going to the opera tonight, Duncan."
"Good."

"We haven't booked seats, we're going to queue for the balcony."

"Good."

Janet went to get cigarettes. Marjory said, "Aitken isn't coming—he hates opera. But you like it, Duncan, don't you?"

"Yes."

She moved nearer. "Duncan, you know I'll pose for you whenever you like."

"Marjory, we must stop this." He drew a dark shadow under an eye, pressing hard on the pencil and saying, "We'll be better rid of each other."

He glanced sideways. Her quiet profile seemed to examine the drawing. Janet returned saying, "No Gauloise! I wish they'd sell us Gauloise."

Thaw said, "There's no satisfaction in the present way of things."

"Shall we go over to the choir, Duncan?" Marjory asked.

As they crossed the street she said, "I'm sorry, Duncan."

"It doesn't matter. I spent the weekend getting used to leaving you and now I'm used to it."

They paused at the door of the theatre where the choir rehearsed. He said, "So there's nothing to be done."

"I see. Oh, Duncan, I'm sorry you've liked me so much. And Duncan, I'm sorry I haven't—"

"Oh, don't be sorry," he said, taking her hands and leaning his brow on hers. "Don't be sorry! You gave me friendship, and for a long time I was grateful."

"But Duncan, can't we still be friends? Not now, perhaps, but later?"

They put their cheeks together and he murmured, "Later, mibby, when I have a real girlfriend I can . . . perhaps. . . ."

"Yes. Then."

She clasped his waist and he caressed her easily, moving his mouth into the soft nook between her neck and shoulder. Janet and two friends went past saying, "Oho!" "Aha!" "Hurry up, you're late."

He wondered why his mouth and hands had never done these things before. More footsteps sounded along the corridor and they separated.

"I'm leaving the choir," he said. "So go through that door, and goodbye."

She smiled and went quickly through the door. He set out briskly for the studio, meaning to start work at once. Their parting had been so kind that for three minutes he was almost happy, but as time and space widened between them resentment developed. Along Sauchiehall Street the glances of passers-by made him notice he was chanting aloud, "If you *exist* let me kill her, if you *exist* let me kill her."

At the studio he saw nothing in his picture but a tangle of ugly lines. He sat and stared at them till it was dark.

CHAPTER 26. Chaos

He waited a long time next morning for an impulse to get
out of bed, and at last crawled to the larder, and to the lavatory,
and back to bed again. He lay like a corpse, his brain rotten
with resentful dreams. He tortured her in sexual fantasies, and
revised and enlarged the farewell speeches he had failed to
make when parting, and minutely remembered and resented
every moment they had passed together. He wondered why
his thoughts were so full of a girl who had given him so little.
The aching emotions gradually became muscular tightness, his
limited movement a way of saving breath. He kept wanting
her to enter the dark, dusty, muddled room, switch on the
light and glance round it, smiling. His own face would stay
hard and immobile but she would remove her coat, give a
small pat to the back of her hair and start to clean up. She
would make a warm drink, sit by the mattress and hold the
cup for him to sip like a child. With a sardonic smile he would
submit to this but at last he would take her hands and press
them to where she could feel the heart knocking on his ribs.
They would lean against each other. The sweat would go from
his brow, the tension from his body and he would sleep. He
was afraid of sleep now and sat as rigid as possible to keep it
away.

One day during the summer holidays McAlpin, who was
painting in a corner, said, "I know advice is always useless
but wouldn't you feel better if you got up and tackled your
picture?"
"It's ludicrous to think anyone in Glasgow will ever paint a
good picture."
"You should go home, Duncan."

"Afraid to move."

Later McAlpin went out and returned with Ruth. Thaw stared at her fearfully for she often called his illness a disgusting way of grabbing attention. She asked kindly, "How are you, old Duncan?" and gently helped him to dress and led him downstairs to a taxi. As they sped homeward she spoke of her training college in Aberdeen. She had been a year there, her intelligent bright bounciness had no aggression in it and he sensed he need never fear her again. Mr. Thaw had laid the table for tea. As they sat round it Ruth said "I like Aberdeen, I've got so many boyfriends! I go swimming with Harry Docherty, who was the Scottish Junior Breaststroke Champion, and I go dancing with Joe Stewart, and I go to parties with anybody—anybody I like, I mean. The girls at college think I'm a scarlet woman but I think they're daft. Most of them have only one boyfriend and talk about nothing but marriage. I'm not going to marry for four or five years, and there's safety in numbers, I say."

"Quite right," said Mr. Thaw. "Don't commit yourself to another human being until you're able to be independent. You're young, enjoy yourself."

"On Sunday I go for walks with Tony Gow, who's a medical student. You'd like him, Duncan. He knows all about animals and flowers and folk songs. He's not much use in the back row of a cinema but he's really interesting. Our walks haven't been much fun lately because of this new rabbit disease the farmers are spreading. All along the country roads you find these poor dying rabbits, gasping for breath with their eyes bulging out. Tony takes them by the hind legs and brains them on the ground. I can't do it. I know it's the kind thing to do but I can't even look. Tony—"

Thaw screamed, "Stop!"

After a moment Mr. Thaw said, "Go to bed son. I'll get the doctor."

The doctor ordered rest and new kinds of pill. Thaw sat in bed, unable to concentrate on reading but willing to argue. "I wish I was a duck."

"What?"

"I wish I was a duck on Alexandra Park pond. I could swim, and fly, and walk, and have three wives, and everything I wanted. But I'm a man. I have a mind, and three library tickets, and everything I want is impossible."

"My God, what are you saying? What's this I've fathered? Look at penicillin and the national health service, look at all these books and pictures you're so keen on! And you want to be a bird!"

"Look at Belsen!" cried Thaw. "And Nagasaki, and the Russians in Hungary and Yanks in South America and French in Algeria and the British bombing Egypt without declaring war on her! Half the folk on this planet die of malnutrition before they're thirty, we'll be twice as many before the century ends, and the only governments with the skill and power to make a decent home of the world are plundering their neighbours and planning to atom bomb each other. We cooperate in millions when it comes to killing, but when it comes to generous, beautiful actions we work in tens and hundreds."

Mr. Thaw rubbed the side of his face and said, "You've read more books than me. How long have there been men in the world?"

"About three hundred thousand years."

"How long have we had cities?"

"About six thousand years."

"And how long have there been governments with worldwide powers? I know the answer to that one. Hardly more than a century."

"Well?"

"Duncan, modern history is just beginning. Give us another couple of centuries and we'll build a *real* civilization! Don't worry, son, others want it beside yourself. There's not a country in the world where folk aren't striving and searching. Don't be fooled by the politicians. It isn't the loud men on platforms but the obscure toilers who change things. And if a few damned power cliques start an atomic war in the next ten or twenty years, humanity will survive. We may take centuries to breed out the effects of radiation, but ordinary folk will do it and start the steep upward climb once more."

"Yah, I'm *sick* of ordinary people's ability to eat muck and survive. Animals are nobler. A fierce animal will die fighting against insults to its nature, and a meek one will starve to death under them. Only human beings have the hideous versatility to adapt to lovelessness and live and live and live while being exploited and abused by their own kind. I read an essay by a little girl in a book about children in wartime. Her house had been bombed. She wrote, 'I am nothing and nobody. My cat was stuck to the wall. I tried to pull her off but they threw my cat away.' Worse things have happened to children every day for the last quarter million years. No kindly future will ever repair a past as vile as ours, and even if we do achieve a worldwide democratic socialist state it won't last. Nothing decent lasts. All that lasts is this mess of fighting and pain and I object to it! I object! I object!"

"Stop pitying yourself."

Thaw opened his mouth to protest, noticed he was pitying himself and shut it again. Mr. Thaw sighed and said, "Let's agree the world is one helluva mess. What do you think will improve it?"

"A memory and a conscience. I hate the heedless way it puts on life without noticing or caring, like a rotten fruit putting on mould."

"But Duncan, memory and conscience are human things!"

"Unluckily."

"Is it a God you want?"

"Yes. Yes, it's a big continual loving man I want who shares the pain of his people. It's an impossibility I want."

Mr. Thaw pushed flat some wisps of hair on his head and said, "My father was elder in a Congregationalist church in Bridgeton: a poor place now but a worse one then. One time the well-off members subscribed to give the building a new communion table, an organ and coloured windows. But he was an industrial blacksmith with a big family. He couldnae afford to give money, so he gave ten years of unpaid work as church officer, sweeping and dusting, polishing the brasses and ringing the bell for services. At the foundry he was paid less the more he aged, but my mother helped the family by embroidering tablecloths and napkins. Her ambition was to save a hundred pounds. She was a good needlewoman, but she never saved her hundred pounds. A neighbour would fall sick and need a holiday or a friend's son would need a new suit to apply for a job, and she handed over the money with no fuss or remark, as if it were an ordinary thing to do. She got a lot of comfort from praying. Every night we all kneeled to pray in the living room before going to bed. There was nothing dramatic in these prayers. My father and mother clearly felt they were talking to a friend in the room with them. I never felt that, so I believed there was something wrong with me. Then the 1914 war started and I joined the army and heard a different kind of prayer. The clergy on all sides were praying for victory. They told us God wanted our government to win and was right there behind us, with the generals, shoving us forward. A lot of us in the trenches let God go at that time. But Duncan, all these airy-fairy pie-in-the-sky notions are nothing but aids to doing what we want anyway. My parents used Christianity to help

them behave decently in a difficult life. Other folk used it to
justify war and property. But Duncan, what men believe isn't
important—it's our actions which make us right or wrong. So
if a God can comfort you, adopt one. He won't hurt you."
"Will he not?" said Thaw sullenly. "The only God I can imagine
is too like Stalin to be comforting."
"I don't condone Stalin's methods, of course, but I firmly believe anyone else ruling Russia in the thirties would have had
to behave like him."

The new pills stopped working and the doctor prescribed
others which didn't work either. On the worst nights Mr. Thaw
sat by the bed wiping trickles of sweat from Thaw's face with
a towel and holding out a basin to take the thick yellow phlegm.
Thaw was wholly occupied by the disease now. He felt it in
him like civil war sabotaging his breathing and allowing only
enough oxygen to feel pain, helplessness and self-disgust. Once
after midnight he said, "Doctor thinks . . . this illness . . .
mental."
"Aye, son. He's hinted at it."
"Fill bath."
"What?"
"Fill bath. Cold water."
With difficulty he explained that maybe (like a land forgetting
inner differences when attacked by another) the clenched air
tubes might relax if his whole skin was insulted by cold water.
Mr. Thaw reluctantly filled the bath and helped Thaw to the
edge. Thaw dropped his pyjamas, placed one foot in the water
and stood, breathing heavily. After a while he brought in the
other foot and with a spasmodic effort knelt on one knee.
"Hurry up, Duncan. Put yourself under!" said Mr. Thaw and
moved to thrust him down.
"No!" screamed Thaw, and five minutes later managed to lie
on his back with nose and lips above the surface. Breathing
was as hard as ever. Mr. Thaw dried him and helped him back
to bed. "You should have lain down at once, Duncan. If shock
treatment *can* work, it has to come as a shock."
Thaw sat for a while, then said, "You're right. Hit me."
"What?"
"Hit me. On face."
"Duncan! . . . I *cannae.*"
After more minutes of sore breathing, Thaw cried, "Please!"
"But Duncan—"
"Can't stand . . . more this. Can't stand."

Mr. Thaw struck his face with his open palm.

"No good. Could hit . . . *myself* . . . harder. Again!"

Mr. Thaw struck harder. Thaw reeled, recovered, compared the painful cheek to the pain in his chest and muttered, "No bloody good."

Mr. Thaw bowed his head and wept. He was sitting on the edge of the bed and Thaw embraced him, saying, "Sorry, Dad. Sorry."

He felt his father's body shake with the sobs erupting inside. It did not feel a large body, and looking down at the thin white hair strands on the freckled scalp he sensed it was an ageing body, and was puzzled to find his own, for a moment, the stronger.

"Go to bed, Dad," he said. "I'm better now."

The tension in his chest had eased.

"My God, Duncan, if I could take your damned illness myself I would! I would!"

"What good would that do? Who would support us then? No, this is the best arrangement."

Mr. Thaw went to bed and the breathing worsened again. When he tried to ignore it by staring at things in the surrounding room they became unstable, as if walls, furniture and ornaments were pieces of a destructive force gripped into shape by a hostile force which could only just hold them. A glazed jug before the window seemed about to explode. Its shiny green hardness threatened him across the room. Everything he saw seemed made of panic. He stared at the ceiling and gathered his thoughts into an intense, silent cry: 'You exist. I surrender. I believe. Help me please.'

The asthma worsened. He gave a fearful moan, then controlled himself enough to make an amused sound and say, "Nobody. There. At all."

He said it again, louder, but it sounded like a lie. Without comfort he found himself condemned to a faith which would never again let him end a prayer by saying, 'If you exist.'

Again he fired his thoughts through the ceiling.

'This belief comes from my cowardice, not from your glory. You won it by a torturer's trick. But you are far from winning my approval. And I will never, never, never, never pray to you again.'

Next day the doctor said, "This has gone on far too long. He should be in hospital. Have you a neighbour with a telephone?"

Ruth and his father helped him dress. The neighbours stood at their doors as the ambulance men carried him downstairs. Mrs. Gilchrist called out glumly, "A fine way to go your holidays, Duncan."

It was a fresh July morning. He sat clutching the edge of the ambulance bench while Mr. Thaw on the bench opposite grunted and prized at the lock of a suitcase with a propelling pencil. Thaw said, "What's wrong?"

"The bloody lock's stuck."

"I won't need a case in hospital."

"Of course you won't. This is to take away your clothes."

The frosted glass window was slightly open at the top and he watched the streets of Blackhill through the slit. The sun shone and children shouted. He said, "That was quick."

"Yes," said his father, putting the case down. "I can't help feeling relieved. When Ruth and I are climbing in Zermatt we'll know you're being better cared for than you could be at home."

"I don't suppose I'll be in long."

"If I were you, Duncan, I wouldn't be too anxious to get out. It might be wise to tell the doctor in charge that there's nobody to look after you outside. Give them time to discover the fundamental root cause of the trouble."

"It doesn't have a fundamental root cause."

"Don't make up your mind about that. Modern hospitals have all kinds of resources, and Stobhill is the biggest in Britain. I was in it myself in 1918: a shrapnel wound in the abdomen. Don't worry, I'll make sure you've plenty of books. I read a lot in Stobhill, authors I couldnae face now, Carlyle, Darwin, Marx. . . . Of course I was on my back for five months."

Mr. Thaw looked out of the window a while, then said, "There's a railway cutting in the grounds which goes to a kind of underground station below the clock tower. The army sent us there in trains. Would you like me to bring you Lenin's *Introduction to Dialectical Materialism?*"

"No."

"That's shortsighted of you, Duncan. Half the world is governed by that philosophy."

The ward was so long that the professor and his company took over an hour to inspect the beds on one side and come down the other to where Thaw lay, near the door. The professor was robust and bald. He stood with folded arms and tilted head as if studying a corner of the ceiling. His quiet speech reached patient, staff doctor, sister, staff nurse and medical students equally, though a bright glance at one of them sometimes underlined a remark or question.

"Here we have a pronounced bronchial infection based on a chronic weakness which may be hereditary, since the father's sister died of it. . . . *You* won't die of it. Nobody dies of asthma unless they've a weak heart, and your ticker should keep you running another half century, with ordinary care. There may be a psychological factor—the illness first appeared at the age of six, when the family was split by war."

"My mother was with us," said Thaw defensively.

"But the father wasn't. Note the eczema on scrotum and behind knee and elbow joints. Typical."

"Has he had skin tests?" asked a student.

"Yes. He reacts violently to all pollens, all hair, fur, feather, meat, fish, milk and every kind of dust. So these can only be irritations. If they were causes he'd have spent his whole life in bed and he frequently gets by without asthma. . . . Don't you?"

"Yes," said Thaw.

"As to treatment: penicillin to reduce the infection, a course of aminophylline suppositories for long-term relief and isoprenaline for temporary relief. Physiotherapy to encourage breath control, that's quite important if they're young, and later a course of de-allergizing injections to cope with the irritation. Coal tar for the skin. It's messy, it's old-fashioned, but the best we can do till we get our hands on this new American cortisone cream. And a sedative to help him relax. . . . Are you a nervous type?"

"I don't know," said Thaw.

"Do you lose yourself in daydreams, then jump violently at ordinary noises?"

"Sometimes."

The professor lifted a drawing of a winged woman from Thaw's locker. "Artistic, too. Would you mind chatting to a psychiatrist?"

"No."

"Good. I know you're not bonkers, but a few talks about family, sex, money and so on can cut down feelings which might interfere with the more straightforward treatments. Your teeth need attention too. You don't brush them often enough, do you?"

"No," said Thaw.

The ward was murmurous with conversations which coalesced, once or twice a week, into political arguments in which lumps of language were hurled backward and forward across great distances. Sometimes in the morning a distant clanking drew near and a huge man toiled past, bowing low over a tiny complicated crutch. His face was shrunk to a bright animal eye, a lump of nose and a mouth twisted over toothless gums. He kept muttering, "God knows how I got this way." "I've been a hard worker all my life." "I've earned every penny I owned" and "I do *nut* like hospitals."

The men in the beds on each side were more self-absorbed. On the left Mr. Clark frowned thoughtfully, moving his hands in slow descriptive gestures or lifting and letting fall the bed-clothes in different folds. In the afternoon he made croaking sounds which the nurses interpreted as requests for a urine bottle, bedpan or cigarette; he was allowed to smoke if someone was there to see he didn't burn himself. His face and neck were leathery and corded like a turtle's, his nose high-bridged and imperious. Propped up by pillows he sometimes dozed, his head dithering in space a fraction away from them, then lurched awake with a faint cry of "Agnes!" Nobody visited him. Mr. McDade on Thaw's left was a small man whose chest bulged like a fat stomach against his chin. He had wiry red hair and a severe face made clerkly by steel spectacles without lenses. These held up each nostril a rubber tube from an oxygen cylinder behind the bed. He removed them to sleep, and sometimes at night rose up in bed on all fours like a dog, making an orchestral noise as if forcing breath through hundreds of tiny flutes and whistles. The nurses would turn him over and restore the spectacles for a while. A small brisk wife and some very tall sons came to see him regularly and before visiting hour he was given an injection which let him talk knowledgeably about grandchildren and prizefighting in a low, clogged voice. He and Thaw often exchanged a slight, negative headshake, and one day when his relatives were late he said, "Some business this, eh?"

"Aye."

"A bad bugger, thon."

"Who?"

"Clark."

Thaw glanced the other way and saw Mr. Clark holding up the top edge of his sheet and studying it like a newspaper. Mr. McDade muttered, "Have you noticed? When the nurses have tucked him in he untucks himself and croaks for a bottle. Outside he'd get six months for it. Outside they call that indecent exposure."

"He's old."

"Aye, he's old. When old men reach that state there's a place for them."

Twice a week Thaw put on slippers and dressing gown and was pushed in a wheelchair to the psychiatric block, or walked there if he was well enough. The psychiatrist was a well-dressed man of about forty with no special characteristics. He said, "During our conversations you may experience several unexpected emotions toward me. Please don't be ashamed to mention them, however bizarre they seem. I won't be at all offended. They'll be part of the treatment."

Thaw talked about parents, childhood, work, sexual fantasies and Marjory. The words poured from him, and once or twice he burst into tears. The psychiatrist said, "In spite of your blinding resentment of women I suspect you are basically heterosexual," and, later, "The truth, you know, isn't black *or* white, it's black *and* white. I keep a ceramic zebra on my mantelpiece to remind me of that," but usually he said "Why?" or "Tell me more about that," and Thaw felt no emotions toward him at all. He enjoyed the visits but returned to the ward feeling slightly anxious and flat, like an actor whose performance has been neither applauded nor booed. When able to walk he prolonged his return through the hospital grounds. The long low red-brick wards lay on the slopes of an airy hill. Seagulls were always circling overhead or perched on gables, perhaps because of stale bread flung out by the kitchens. There was a high red clock tower with a tinny chime, and all was gardened around with shrubberies, gravel paths and beds of bee-humming, dazzling, blue and scarlet flowers. It was a summer of extraordinary heat. Patients in dressing gowns walked carefully on the lawns or brooded on benches. Most of them were aging and solitary, and when white-clad nurses passed briskly in chattering couples and threes, Thaw was startled by the mercy of these bright young women caring for so many made lonely, feeble and repulsive by disease.

Each week his breathing improved for a few days, then worsened. Mr. Clark stopped smoking and calling for Agnes and lay perfectly still. The deep lines cut by experience were fading from his face; each day he was more like a young man though his eyes looked different ways and one side of his mouth opened in a grin while the other was firmly shut. Mr. McDade in the right-hand bed was aging. The hollows between the cords of his cheeks and neck grew deeper. He stared at passing doctors and nurses with unusually wide red-rimmed eyes. He spoke less to his wife and sons but often glanced toward Thaw, muttering, "Some . . . business . . . this . . . *eh?*"

He plainly wanted companionship in pain, but Thaw muttered "Aye" without looking up from scribbling. The notebook had become a neutral surface between the pain of the ward and the pain of breathing. He hated leaving it to feed or to sleep. At night, when a lamp shone on the nurses' table far down the ward, enough gloaming filtered in from the summer sky to make a pale tablet of his page, and his hand continued shading enigmatic female heads, and grotesque male ones, and monsters that were part bird, part machinery, and huge cities mingling every style and century of architecture. After midnight he put the books aside and sat erect, clinging so tightly to consciousness that for many nights he thought himself sleepless. Then he noticed that though he heard the remote melancholy *ding-dong* of the clock tower sounding the quarters, they never seemed to sound the hour, and once he saw the two night nurses whispering near a corner bed, and then, without crossing the floor, one was reading a book at the central table and the other sat crocheting nearby. All night he was dipping in and out of sleep, but at such a shallow angle he never noticed. Sometimes he slept soundly and then waking was difficult, for it was hard at first to recognize the shapes and sounds of the ward and breathing was a vile science to be relearned by a lot of choking.

Late one night the nurse in charge led round a sister he had never seen before. They stopped at Mr. McDade's bed. He was sleeping in the oxygen spectacles, his mouth continually gulping air and a sound like distant bagpipes coming from his chest. Below her stiff, white, sphinx-like cap the sister's face looked keen and fiftyish. She said, "Poor McDade! God help him!" on a low note of such stern pity that warmth gushed in Thaw's chest and he gazed at her lovingly. She moved to his bed-foot, smiled and said, "And how are you tonight, Duncan?"

He whispered, "Fine, thanks."

"Would you like a cup of cocoa?"

"Very much, thanks."

"You'll see to it, nurse?"

They moved on and later the nurse brought sweet warm cocoa and two pink pills on a teaspoon.

He awoke in sunlight breathing easily amid the bright clangour of washbasins being passed round. For the first time since entering hospital he felt well enough to shave, but after fondling the shrub of hair on his chin he merely freshened his face and hands and lay basking in the kind light and air. Mr. Clark looked much better. His face was old and thoughtful again and he appeared to be conducting a tiny orchestra with his right forefinger. Mr. McDade's bed was empty and stripped down to the wire mattress. Thaw imagined the small pigeon-chested body being carried away by the quiet, black-suited young man who replaced the oxygen cylinders but he was too happy to feel anything but relief. He wanted to talk to people and make them laugh. When the nurse brought breakfast he tasted and said, "Nurse! I refuse to eat this porridge without proper anesthetic!"

He said it again, louder. Nobody noticed, so he wrote it down to tell Drummond or McAlpin and went on eating.

CHAPTER 27. Genesis

Slanting sunshine lit a cut-glass vase of cowslips and canterbury bells on Mr. Clark's table. Thaw sat in an armchair admiring the butter-yellow cowslips with pale green drooping stems, the dark spear-leaved stalks with transparent blue-purple bells. He whispered, "Purple, purple," and the word felt as purple to his lips as the colour to his eyes. A nurse making Mr. McDade's old bed said, "You'll have to be on your best behaviour today, Duncan. You're getting a new neighbour. A minister."

"I hope he isn't talkative."

"Oh, he'll be talkative. Ministers are paid to be talkative."

She placed screens round the bed and someone with a suitcase went behind them. The screens were removed and a small grey-haired man in pyjamas sat against his pillow receiving elderly lady visitors. These talked in quick, low, consoling voices while the minister smiled and nodded absentmindedly. When they left he put on spectacles with lenses like half-moons and read a library book.

After dinner that day Thaw sat in bed sketching when a voice said, "Excuse me, but are you an artist?"

"No. An art student."

"I'm sorry. I was misled by your beard. Would you mind showing me that drawing? I'm fond of flowers."

Thaw handed over the notebook, saying, "It's not very good. I'd need more time and materials to make it good."

The minister held up the book before his face and after nodding once or twice began turning the earlier pages. Thaw felt worried but not annoyed. The minister had the quality of a mildly shining, useful, grey, neglected metal; his accent was the one Thaw liked best, the accent of shopkeepers, schoolteachers, and working men with an interest in politics and religion. He said, "Your flowers are beautiful, really beautiful, but—I hope you're not offended—the earlier drawings confuse me a little. Of course I can see they're very clever and modern."

"They're doodles, not drawings. I haven't been fit enough to draw properly."

"How long have you been here?"

"Six weeks."

"Six weeks?" said the minister respectfully. "That's a long time. I expect to be only a few days myself. They want to make certain tests and see how I react. The heart, you know, but nothing serious. Now tell me, because I've often wondered, what makes people artists? Is it an inborn talent?"

"Certainly. It's born into everyone. All infants like playing with pencils and paints."

"But not many of us take it further than that. I, for instance, would like nothing better than to sketch a nice view, or the face of a friend, but I couldnae draw a straight line to save my life."

"There are very few good jobs for handworkers nowadays," said Thaw, "so most parents and teachers discourage that kind of talent."

"Did your parents encourage you?"

"No. They allowed me paper and pencil when I was an infant, but apart from that they wanted me to do well in life. My father only let me go to art school because he heard I might get a job there."

"So your talent *must* be inborn!"

After pondering awhile, Thaw said, "Someone might work and work at a thing, not because they were encouraged, but because they never learned to enjoy anything else."

"Dear me, that sounds very bleak! Tell me, just to change the subject, why are modern paintings so hard to understand?"

"As nobody employs us nowadays we've to invent our own reasons for painting. I admit art is in a bad way. Never mind, we've some good films. So much money has been put into the film industry that a few worthwhile talents have got work there."

The minister said slyly, "I thought artists didn't work for money."

Thaw said nothing. The minister said, "I thought they toiled in garrets till they starved or went mad, then their work was discovered and sold for thousands of pounds."

"There was once a building boom," said Thaw, growing excited, "In north Italy. The local governments and bankers of three or four towns, towns the size of Paisley, put so much wealth and thought into decorating public buildings that half Europe's greatest painters were bred there in a single century. These bosses weren't unselfish men, no, no. They knew they could only win votes and stay popular by giving spare wealth to their neighbours in the form of fine streets, halls, towers and cathedrals. So the towns became beautiful and famous and have been a joy to visit ever since. But today our bosses don't live among the 'folk they employ. They invest surplus profits in scientific research. Public buildings have became straight engineering jobs, our cities get uglier and uglier and our best paintings look like screams of pain. No wonder! The few who buy them, buy them like diamonds or rare postage stamps, as a form of non-taxable banking."

His voice had grown shrill and he gulped rapidly from a glass of water. The minister said, "That sounds rather communistic, but in Russia I believe—"

"Russia," cried Thaw, "has a more rigid ruling class than ours, so while western art is allowed to be hysterical, eastern art is allowed to be merely dull. No wonder! Strong, lovely, harmonious art has only appeared in small republics, republics where the people and their bosses shared common assemblies and a common—"

He coughed violently.

"Well, well," said the minister soothingly. "You've given me a lot to think about."

He began reading again. Thaw stared back at the flowers, but delight and freshness had leaked out of them.

Next morning Thaw sat in the armchair while the minister, hands clasped on chest, lay gazing at the ceiling. He said suddenly, "I've been thinking that maybe you should talk to Arthur Smail."

"Who?"

"He's our session clerk, a young man, very enterprising and full of modernistic ideas. Would you open the drawer of my locker, please? I'm not supposed to move. Do you see a wallet? Take it out and look inside and you'll find some snapshots. No, put that one back, that's my sister. It's my church I want you to see."

Thaw looked at two photographs showing the inside and outside of an ordinary Scottish church.

"Cowlairs Parish Church. Not grand maybe, but I've been there thirty-two years so I like it. I like it. Since the engine works closed the district has gone sadly downhill, I'm afraid. And the Presbytery have decided that next year our congregation and the congregation of St. Rollox must combine, for there aren't enough members to justify the upkeep of two establishments. St. Rollox is a church round the corner from us. Do you follow me?"

"Yes."

"Now the two congregations are nearly equal size, so Arthur Smail thought that if we cleaned and rewired our fabric, the Presbytery would send the congregation of St. Rollox to us instead of we to them. Am I boring you?"

"No."

"Mr. Smail belongs to a firm of shopfitters and we have Mr. Rennie, a painter and decorator, and two electricians, so we had the necessary skill and any number of willing helpers. The church is cleaner and brighter than I've known it for years. Unluckily, however (though quite understandably), St. Rollox have done the same thing and done it better. A member of theirs who did well in Canada sent a donation which let them clean the outside stonework, a thing we can't afford. So Mr. Smail came up with a new idea. . . . Have you ever attended a church of Scotland?"

"When I was at school."

"Then you may have observed that in the last century a lot of features were brought back which our ancestors had cast out. Nothing harmful, of course, like prayer books and bishops, just small embellishments: side pulpits, organs, stained-glass windows and even, in a few cases, crucifxes on the communion table. But a modern mural painting would be a complete novelty; newspapers, wireless and even television might take note, which would put an extra card up our sleeve in dealing with the Presbytery. So Mr. Smail wrote to the director of the art school asking if he could recommend a student who would like to take on the job. Because, you see, we couldn't pay him. The director wrote back saying it would be a shame to spoil an old building with the work of inexperienced hands. Mr. Smail was much annoyed. Excuse me telling you this, I have very little to do with it."

Thaw stared into the photographs. From in front the church looked like a blackened stone dog kennel with a squat little tower, a tower no taller than the tenements on each side. The interior was surprisingly spacious, the exact pattern of the church used by Thaw's old school. A balcony surrounded three sides and the fourth was pierced by a high arched chancel with three lancet windows in the back wall and an organ in the left. Intuitively he stood under the arch appraising the flat plaster surfaces. A sudden dread filled him that he wouldn't be allowed to decorate this building. He returned the snapshots, muttered "Excuse me," and hurried off down the ward.

He crossed bright lawns between vivid flowerbeds and sank, wrestling for breath, upon a bench. He shut his eyes and saw the inside of the church. Images were flowing up the walls like trees and mingling their colours like branches on the ceiling. He opened his eyes and stared across fields and woodland at the dip in the heat-dimmed Campsies. Self-pitying tears sprung on his cheeks and he whispered at the blue sky, *"Bastard,* giving me ideas without the strength to use them." He punched the side of his head, muttering, "Take that for having ideas. And that."
He broke into a fit of giggling, got up and returned to the ward.

"I must explain something," he said, sitting down by the minister. "I am not a Christian. I have a sort of faith in God but I can't believe he came down and made wheelbarrows in a shop. I like most of what Christ taught and I prefer him to Buddha, but only because Buddha started life with exceptional social privileges. I also want very, very much to paint this mural."
Thaw wondered if the minister was smiling, for he had hidden his face by a hand adjusting the spectacles, but when he lowered it he said gravely, "If you are willing to help and your design satisfies the kirk session we'll be perfectly content. There are no inquisitors among us."
"Good. The chancel ceiling is divided by plaster ribs into six panels. The most suitable theme for them is surely the six days of creation: Genesis, chapter one."
"The ceiling? . . . Mr. Smail thought the wall facing the organ would be the best place."
"The wall facing the organ will show the world on the seventh day, when God looks at it and likes it."
"That sounds acceptable."
"Good. I'll make sketches."

The ideas he scribbled in the notebook grew so fast that they burned up energy needed for breathing and he had to stop twice for injections. God was the easiest part of the design. He came out strong and omniscient, like Mr. Thaw, but with

an unexpected expression of reckless gaiety got from Aitken
Drummond. Next evening he showed sketches to the minister.
"I've decided to begin with the universe before creation starts,
when the spirit of God moves on the face of the deep. I'll
paint it on the back wall round the three windows."
"Dear me, that's a very large area."
"Yes, but I'll make it a simple deep, dark blue with silver
ripples. Modern science thinks the primordial chaos was hydrogen. I can't paint hydrogen so I'll stick to the old Jewish notion
of a universe filled with water. The Greeks believed everything
was made of water too."
"I thought they believed the original chaos was a mixture of
atoms and strife, with love outside it. Then love worked its
way in, driving strife out and linking the atoms."
"You refer to Empedocles. I refer to Thales, who was earlier."
"You're very erudite."
"We have to be. Nowadays we cannae depend on the education
of our patrons. Traditionally, in the chaos stage, the spirit of
God is shown as a bird. I'm making him a man above the
point of the middle window. He's small, and shaped like a
falling diver, and in black silhouette so we can't see if he's
swooping toward us or away. He is the seed fertilizing chaos,
the word that will order it into worlds."
"Perfectly orthodox."
"Here is the ceiling. The first panel shows Monday's work,
the making of light. A golden egg with God inside floats on
the dark water. He's naked and fully visible and represented
conventionally as a middle-aged vigorous man."
"His expression is rather alarming."
"I can soften it. On Tuesday we have the making of space. A
firmament is set up dividing the waters above it from the waters
below. God wades waist deep in the lower waters, raising a
tent-shaped sky above his head. The light fills the tent. On
Wednesday the lower waters are drawn back and the dry land
fixed in the middle and clothed with grass, flowers, herbs and
trees. The early Jews seemed obsessed with water, they have
God grappling with it for one and a half working days."
"They lived in the Euphrates delta," said the minister. "Where
water not only fell from the sky but in seasons of flood actually
bubbled out of the soil. It nourished their crops and flocks
and often drowned them too."
"I see. Thursday: night and day, sun, moon, stars. Friday: fishes
and birds. With each addition to his universe God is more
hidden behind it, till on Saturday all we see are his nostrils

in a cloud, breathing life into Adam who is wakening among the creatures below. Adam is shaped like God but more pensive. Lastly, here is the wall facing the organ. Adam and Eve kneel cuddling beside the river which springs from under the tree of life. The bird in the tree is a phoenix. I've several other details to work out yet."

After a long pause the minister said, "I admire, of course, the skill and thought you have put into this and so, I'm sure, will the kirk session. But I'm afraid they won't allow your depiction of God. No. You see, he'll frighten the children. Everything else is just fine however: light, space, oceans, mountains, all these birds and animals—but not God. Oh, no."

"But without God we have a purely evolutionary picture of creation!" cried Thaw.

"There is a lot to be said for the Mosaic notion that the Almighty is most present when least imagined. And it would be a pity to frighten the children," said the minister, closing his eyes.

"Very well," said Thaw, after a pause. "I'll take him off the ceiling. But I *must* show him diving through chaos. That is essential."

"Hardly anyone will notice him there. I'm sure that Arthur Smail will raise no objection."

At medical inspection next morning the professor paused by Thaw's bed and said, "Mr. Clark and Mr. Thaw here are our oldest inhabitants. Everyone else in the ward when they were admitted has cleared out or kicked the bucket but these two have got into a repetitive cycle of improvement and deterioration. Mr. Clark is seventy-four, there's some excuse for him. There's none for you, Duncan. Why do you do it?"

"I don't know," said Duncan.

"Then I'll tell you," said the professor cheerfully. "And don't get angry. You're intelligent and tough enough to understand me, which is why I'm not whispering behind your back. This patient, gentlemen, is suffering from adaption. Let me give you an example of adaption. A hardworking man of thirty loses his job through no fault of his own. For two or three months he hunts for work but can't find any. His national insurance money runs out and he goes on the dole. In these circumstances his energy and initiative are a burden to him. They make him want to break things and punch people. So instinctively his metabolism lowers itself. He grows slovenly and depressed. A year or two passes, he's offered a job at last and refuses it. Unemployment has become his way of life. He's adapted to

it. In the same way some people come here with commonplace
illnesses which, after an initial improvement, stop responding
to treatment. Why? In the absence of other factors we must
assume that the patient has adapted to the *hospital itself.* He
has reverted to an infantile state in which suffering and being
regularly fed feel actually safer than health. And mind you,
he's not a malingerer. The adaption has occurred in a region
where mind and body are indistinguishable. So what do we
do? In your case, Duncan, we're going to do this. No more
ephedrine, isoprenaline, aminophylline suppositories, sedatives
or sleeping pills. From now on we give you nothing: nothing
but an injection if the attacks are really bad. And if you aren't
well by next Friday we'll give you a hypodermic needle, a
bottle of adrenalin and sling you out. Of course if this were
America, and your father were rich, we could make a packet
by hanging on to you till you croaked. So think yourself lucky.
And now we will look at the heart of the minister of Cowlairs
Parish Church. Screens, please."

Thaw lay trembling with indignation. When the professor
left the ward he scrambled up, put on his dressing gown and
hurried outside. He found himself running through the grounds
muttering, "All right, I'll leave. I'll leave now. I'll demand a
taxi and leave now."
He leaned on the parapet of a bridge across a cutting near
the clock tower. Rails at the bottom were hidden by lank grass
and a litter of broken wicker baskets. The banks were overhung
by elders and brambles, but he glimpsed through them a station
platform, cracked, mossy and strewn with rubbish. He returned
thoughtfully to the ward.

A spruce fresh-faced man of about thirty sat by the minister,
who said, "Duncan, this is Mr. Smail, our session clerk. I've
been showing him your new designs and he's quite pleased
with them."
"Very impressive," said Mr. Smail, "though, of course, I'm
no judge of painting. My concern is with the practical side,
and I'm heartily glad we've got it moving at last. With your
permission I'll show these sketches to the kirk session next
Sunday."
He patted a glossy briefcase on his lap.
"I can make more elaborate designs if you like," said Thaw.
"Oh, no need at all. If the minister's pleased nobody else will

complain—not openly, at any rate. You know, of course, that we're a poorly endowed church and can't pay you. However, I think I've enough contacts to ensure a fair bit of publicity when the work's complete. No, we won't hide your light under a bushel. Now, how long will you take?"

Thaw pondered. He had no idea at all. He said cautiously, "Perhaps three months."

"And when can you start?"

"As soon as I'm well again," said Thaw, suddenly feeling well, "In fact I'm getting out on Friday."

"So you'll be finished by Christmas. Good. That will give us time to clear the scaffolding out for the Watch Night service. Perhaps the dedication ceremony and the Christmas service might be combined?"

"I don't think so," said the minister. "No. But it could be combined with the service at Hogmanay."

"Good. A newly decorated church by the new year. That will give the Presbytery something to think about."

Thaw felt a hidden alarm within him. He said, "It's a huge area. I'll need a lot of help. Not skilled help—just folk who can lay a colour inside the shapes I chalk for them."

"Oh, I'll help you myself. I've been practising on the kitchen ceiling. And Mr. Rennie, who's going to lend the scaffolding, I'm sure will lend a hand as well. We'll have no shortage of helpers."

Thaw took nail scissors from the minister's locker and snipped a corner from his dressing gown. He said, "First of all the plaster surfaces in the chancel must be painted this colour, a dark blue inclining to violet, in good-quality oil paint, eggshell finish, at least two coats."

Mr. Smail made a note in a pocket diary and shut the half-inch of cloth between the pages saying, "Leave it to me. And mibby sometime next week you'll give me a list of your materials. With my contacts I'm sure I can get them at a discount."

Thaw lay down on his bed with a sensation of Napoleonic power.

On Friday he was ill again. The night before, the ward sister had given him a hypodermic needle, cotton wool, surgical spirit and a rubber-capped adrenalin bottle. She had shown him how to use them and later his father arrived with clothes and money. Now he laboriously dressed, glanced unhappily at Mr. Clark (who was smoking again) and said goodbye to the minister. In the reception hall he phoned for a taxi, then huddled on the back seat, soothed by the sizzling of the tyres on the wet roads, for at last the weather had broken.

He got out at the art school and slowly climbed to the hall called "the museum" where several students were writing at tables. He filled the registration form for his final year and carried it down a corridor, noticing that the dark panelled walls, white plaster gods and tight-trousered girls no longer seemed excitingly solid but shallow, like a photograph of a once-familiar street. There was a queue outside the registrar's door so he stepped into an empty studio and squirted six minims of adrenalin into his calf muscle. He entered the registrar's office shortly after, feeling businesslike on the outside but relaxed and dreamy within. He handed over the form and was asked to sit down.
"Well, Thaw, how are you getting on?"
"Not badly, sir. I've been offered a really big job." He explained about the mural and said, "Do you think I could work on it till Christmas?"
"I see no reason why not. When your diploma exam comes along next June the school could take the assessors to the church to see what you've done. Talk it over with Mr. Watt."
"Can I tell him you approve of the idea?"
"No. I neither approve or disapprove; it has nothing to do with me. Mr. Watt is your head of department."
"He may not want to give me permission."
"Oh? Why not?"
"He has already allowed me a great deal of freedom—freedom to paint in my own studio, I mean."
"Well?"
"I have nothing to show for it; no finished work, I mean."
"Why?"
"Ill health. But I've recovered now. If you like I can prove it with doctors' certificates."
The registrar sighed, rubbed his brow and said, "Go away, Thaw, go away. I'll speak to Mr. Watt."
"Thank you, Mr. Peel," said Thaw, briskly standing. "That is abnormally decent of you."

In the tram home he sat beside a lady with a shopping bag who eyed him for a while out of a sharp profile and at last said, "You're Duncan Thaw, of course."
"Yes."

"You don't remember me."

"Were you a friend of my mother?"

"A friend of your mother? I was the best friend Mary Needham had. I worked beside her in Copland and Lyes long, long, long before your father appeared on the scene. Mind you," she added musingly, "a lot of folk thought they were Mary's best friend. She knew so many and they all trusted her. Neighbours would confide in her who hated each other like poison. But there, she's gone. And so has your grampa, that good old man."

Her tone irritated Thaw. He could hardly remember his mother's father, a tall man with a white moustache who lived in a semi-detached villa a block away. The woman sighed and said, "Of course, your granny was the first to go. You were very fond of your granny."

"Was I?" said Thaw, startled, because he couldn't remember having a granny.

"Oh, yes. Whenever you quarrelled with your mother (you were always a difficult lad) you ran to your granny's house and she petted and spoiled you and gave you everything you liked. You were very upset when she died. You would go to her back door and lie there crying for her."

"Aren't you mixing me with someone else?"

"Who else? Surely not your sister. She was barely two at the time. A wild girl, your sister."

A moment later the woman chuckled and said, "Mind you, Mary was a wild one too in her day. Oh, she shocked me all right. I was one of the mousey kind. I remember two lads from haberdashery arranged to meet us at the Scott monument one Saturday. It was my first date and I was there punctual to the minute, dolled up to the nines. So were the lads. We waited half an hour and then by strolls Mary, arm in arm with a six-foot Australian soldier. Glasgow was full of them that summer. She strolled past without a word, just a sort of sideways wink at me. Wee Archie Campbell was heartbroken. Next day I asked her, 'How can you be so cruel?' She said, 'Ach, how else can you treat men who wear spats?' Another time she was out three nights running with three different boys. 'How can you?' I asked. She said, 'It's the opera this week. I cannae afford to go three nights running by myself.' One of these boys was your father. Nobody was more surprised than me when Mary Needham married Duncan Thaw. Well, she learned."

"Learned what?"

"Nothing, but it was surprising. He was the last man I'd have thought she'd marry. Four years passed before you appeared on the scene."

Thaw got home three hours before his father returned from work. The fire was set. He lit it then took a pile of sheet music from the piano stool and spread it on the hearth rug: cheap adaptations from Rossini and Verdi, the songs of Burns and sentimental translations from the Gaelic: *Ca' the Yowes* and *By the Light of the Peat-Fire-Flame*. His mother's unfamiliar maiden name was written in neat copperplate in faded brown ink on the inside cover, and his grandparents' address on the Cumbernauld Road, and the dates of purchase: none earlier than 1917 or later than 1929, when she married.

With sudden curiosity he looked at a wedding photograph on the mantelpiece. His father (shy, pleased, silly and young-looking) stood arm in arm with a slender laughing woman in one of the knee-length bridal dresses fashionable in the twenties. Her high-heeled shoes made her look the taller of the two. Thaw could think of no connection between this lively shop girl full of songs and sexual daring and the stern gaunt woman he remembered. How could one become the other? Or were they like different sides of a globe with time turning the gaunt face into the light while the merry one slid round into shadow? But only a few old people remembered her youth nowadays and soon both her youth and her age would be wholly forgotten. He thought, 'Oh no! No!' and felt for the only time in his life a pang of pure sorrow without rage or self-pity in it. He could not weep, but a berg of frozen tears floated near his surface, and he knew that berg floated in everyone, and wondered if they felt it as seldom as he did.

He fell asleep with his head on the heap of music and woke an hour later feeling so fit that he flung the syringe and adrenalin into the rubbish bin and drank a mouthful of the surgical spirit. It affected him like a glass of whisky taken in good company but the taste was so abominable that he poured the rest onto the packet of cotton wool and flung it on the fire. It boomed up the chimney in a satisfying flame.

CHAPTER 28. Work

Two and a half weeks later he stood with chalk and measuring rod on a plank platform forty feet above the chancel floor. As he scribbled on the blue vault he sang aloud:

> "Immortal, invisible, God only wise,
> In light inaccessible hid from our eyes,
> Most blessed, most glorious, the Ancient of Days,
> Almighty, victorious, you knew what you were about
> when you created me."

There was laughter from the helpers on the lower levels of scaffolding and on the ladders against the walls. They came two evenings a week: Mr. Smail, Mr. Rennie the decorator, a young electrician and a girl of sixteen who wanted to go to art school. Mr. Rennie was the most useful, a robust man of sixty who had attended evening classes in sign writing. With a skilled hand and loving patience he covered the tall arched deep-blue window wall with a fluid pattern of silver scrolling ripples. The others worked less finely but just as hard, excepting the girl, who had no head for heights. Most of the time she sat in the front row of the pews sketching the others at work. They liked her because she was good-looking and made tea and sandwiches.

At the start of November the ceiling was so full of different shapes that the delicately patterned window wall looked insipid, so Thaw chalked boulders, flames and clouds on it and prepared new cans of colour to paint them. When his helpers came that evening Mr. Smail climbed to the platform and said, "I'm afraid you've hurt Mr. Rennie's feelings."
"Why?"

"He put a lot of hard work into that wall. He was proud of it."

"No wonder. It was beautiful. I was only able to think of this better idea because he carried out my first one so well. And a quarter of his water will still be visible when the fire, clouds and rock are painted in. I'll go down and explain."

But when Thaw got down Mr. Rennie had left, and he didn't return. After that the other helpers stopped coming. Thaw missed them, for he liked working with people and enjoyed chatting over tea and sandwiches. But the main areas had been filled so he could now starting changing and refining by himself.

Each morning his palette, cleaned and laid out with new paint, looked prettier than any picture. While climbing to the platform he almost regretted that these tear-shaped pats of intense colour (Naples and marigold yellow, Indian red and crimson lake, emerald green and the two blues) could not be spread on the walls in their tropical vividness. To show distance and weight they had to be mixed with each other and white, black or umber. Yet it was magical that pig bristles fastened to a stick, spreading oily brown mud on a pale grey surface, could make a line of hills appear against a dawn sky. As he applied the paint his mind became a mere link between hand, colour, eye and ceiling. On descending to see the work from the church floor he had sometimes moments of selfish excitement, but his mind was sick of domineering over something as ramshackle as himself and glad to climb up again to where sight, thought, limbs, paint, feelings and brushes were a kit of tools the picture needed to complete itself. When busiest in this pure kind of work he was often visited by bizarre sexual fantasies. He got rid of them by quickly masturbating a few times, which left him free for a couple of days afterward.

When he paused to listen the usual sounds were from traffic outside and the *clicklick . . . clicklick* of the clock in the tower. Sometimes steps resounded from a warren of meeting rooms, kitchens and corridors at the back of the building and around noon on weekdays came a muffled clangour from a hall used as a dining centre by a local school. The only regular visitor was the old minister, who came in the evening after seeing people in his vestry. He sat so still in the front pew, staring so quiet and open-mouthed at the ceiling, that he was usually forgotten until Thaw, finding some flaw in a cloud, wave, or animal, yelled, "That's not how you should be!" then looked down and added, "I'm sorry," but the minister only smiled and nodded. One evening when Thaw descended to wash brushes he said, "You won't have it finished for the Watch Night service, will you?"

"I'm sorry. Probably not."

"Oh, that's a pity. You see, people are starting to complain. When do you think it *will* be finished?"

Thaw winced and said, "When will the Presbytery need to see it?"

"June, I suppose, at the latest. But surely you can finish before then? How about Easter Sunday? That gives you at least four extra months."

Thaw said cautiously, "Oh, I'll probably have it done by then."

"Now is that a promise? Can I tell the kirk session that?"

"Yes. A promise," said Thaw gloomily.

Shortly before Christmas he was eating lunch at the communion table when a middle-aged lady came in. Her hair was a cloud of angry grey curls. She wore a white smock, and stared at him, glanced once at the mural and stared back. He hurried over saying "Mrs. Coulter!"

"Well, Duncan?"

"What are you doing here? Are you working on the school dinners?"

"It brings in the pennies."

"How are you? How's Robert?"

"Not bad, I suppose. Of course, he's not very pleased with you. You could at least have come to the wedding."

"Robert married? I never knew."

"You were sent an invitation three weeks ago."

"But I've not been home. I'm sleeping here just now."

"Here?"

"I've a mattress behind that pew over there. How's the engineering?"

"Oh, he gave that up a year ago. He's in Dundee writing the sports page for the *North East Courier*."

"Robert a journalist?"

"Aye. He was always keen on the writing."

"He never told me that!"

"He didn't want to. When you get onto your high horse, Duncan, nobody else gets a word in edgeways. Well, the Thomson press was advertising for journalists, and he sent them a story he'd written. I don't know why, he was doing all right at engineering. Anyway, they took him on, and now he's married a girl in one of their offices."

"I must write to him."

"Oh, you'll never write to him. You're too full of yourself.
But I suppose that's how people get on in the world . . . not
that you seem to have got very far."
She stared at the paint-stained dressing gown he wore on top
of his overalls. His mother had made it from a thick grey army
blanket and it was warm and draught-proof. He said awkwardly,
"Tell Robert I'm sorry I missed the wedding."

    The pulpit was draught-proof with an electric foot warmer.
In frosty weather he found it cosier sleeping curled on its octagonal floor than extended on the mattress, and grew so used
to this that he continued there when spring came. Small corns
embossed the palms of his hands from climbing the tubular
steel. The ceiling was finished and the scaffolding removed
before Easter, and now he worked from ladders upon the great
wall facing the organ. One day Mr. Smail came and asked
crisply, "When will you finish this, Duncan?"
"I don't know."
"But good heavens, you asked for three months and have taken
seven! And the Presbytery are coming to inspect this in June
and we should be arranging favourable publicity as soon as
possible!"
After a pause Thaw said, "You can show it to journalists in a
fortnight. It won't be finished then, but it will look as if it
is."
"I have your solemn word on that?"
"Oh, yes, my solemn word, if you want it."

    When Mr. Smail left he climbed down and glumly consid-
ered the tall arched panel. At the top a phoenix sank into flames
among the leaves and yellow fruit of the tree of life, whose
branches sheltered crows, pigeons, wrens and squirrels. The
straight dark trunk divided the wall in half and grew from a
lawn in the foreground. Rabbits nibbled cowslips, a mole delved
and a roe deer nursed her fawn. There was enough killing to
keep predators alive and the herbivores jumpy: a fox brought
a pheasant to its cubs, a tawny owl in the tree of knowledge
held a vole in a claw while other voles played among dead
leaves between the roots. The naked man and woman embracing under the great tree of knowledge were clearly reflected
in a pool of rushes and irises. This pool, the source of a river,
contained a salmon rising to a gnat and mosaic turrets of caddis
larvae on weedy pebbles. So far he was satisfied. His trouble
began in the background where history was acted in the loops
and delta of the river on its way to the ocean. The more he

worked the more the furious figure of God kept popping in
and having to be removed: God driving out Adam and Eve
for learning to tell right from wrong, God preferring meat
to vegetables and making the first planter hate the first herdsman, God wiping the slate of the world clean with water and
leaving only enough numbers to start multiplying again, God
fouling up language to prevent the united nations reaching
him at Babel, God telling a people to invade, exterminate and
enslave for him, then letting other people do the same back.
Disaster followed disaster to the horizon until Thaw wanted
to block it with the hill and gibbet where God, sick to death
of his own violent nature, tried to let divine mercy into the
world by getting hung as the criminal he was. It was comical
to think he achieved that by telling folk to love and not hurt
each other. Thaw groaned aloud and said, "I don't enjoy hound-
ing you like this, but I refuse to gloss the facts. I admire most
of your work. I don't even resent the ice ages, even if they
did make my ancestors carnivorous. I'm astonished by your
way of leading fertility into disaster, then repairing the disaster
with more fertility. If you were a busy dung beetle pushing
the sun above the skyline, if you had the head of a hawk or
the horns and legs of a goat I would understand and sympathize.
If you headed a squabbling committee of Greek departmental
chiefs I would sympathize. But your book claims you are a
man, the one perfect man of whom we are imperfect copies.
And then you have the bad taste to put yourself in it as a
character and show that you're socially repulsive. You've never
been house-trained. Very few men are as nasty to their children
as you are to yours. Why didn't you give me a railway station
to decorate? It would have been easy painting to the glory of
Stevenson, Telford, Brunel and a quarter million Irish navvies.
But here I am, illustrating your discredited first chapter through
an obsolete art form on a threatened building in a poor province
of a collapsing empire. Only the miracle of my genius stops
me feeling depressed about this, and even so my brushes are
clogged by theology, that bastard of the sciences. Let me remember that a painting, before it is anything else, is a surface
on which colours are arranged in a certain order. There is
too much blue in this picture and I'd better not cover it with
more birds. There could be no harm in another cloud, a thun-
dercloud over Sinai, shaped like a chariot with you standing
in it, very black-coated and Presbyterian. If I make you small
enough Mr. Smail might not notice you and the composition
doesn't need a big man there."

Two days later a telegram was handed to him which said, RETURN TO ART SCHOOL AT ONCE. DIPLOMA EXAM STARTED YESTERDAY. PETER WATT. The art school looked flimsier than ever and as he entered the old studio the other students gave an ironical cheer. Mr. Watt muttered, "Better late than never, Thaw," and handed him a paper which required him to design a decorative panel for the dining room of a luxury liner. He took a sheet of hardboard and spent the morning filling it with a merman and a mermaid chasing each other's tails with a knife and fork, then he said, "That's the best I can do, Mr. Watt. I'll go back to the church now."

"Wait a minute! You're allowed six weeks for this examination. Half the diploma assessment is based on it."

"I know, sir. I'm sorry, but I must return to Cowlairs. You see—"

"You will not return to Cowlairs. You will come with me, now, to the registrar."

Thaw was left outside the office door for ten or fifteen minutes and ushered in by the registrar's secretary, an unusual formality. Mr. Peel and Mr. Watt were seated on the same side of a long table, a single chair facing them at a distance. Thaw sat on it and some seconds of tribunal silence ensued. The two men looked so solidly forbidding that he instinctively blurred them by unfocusing his eyes. At last the registrar said, "Have you any complaint about your treatment in this school, Thaw?"

"None. I have been treated very well."

"Correct. Yet you have ignored our advice, flouted our authority and not only obliged us to bend our rules but actually to improvise new ones to avoid expelling you. Of course we have been influenced by consideration of your health: and I don't mean merely your physical health."

There was more silence, so Thaw said, "Thank you, sir."

"When you started here you signed an application form. That form was a contract, a contract you have renewed at the start of each school year. Society is upheld by contracts, Thaw. All government, all business, all industry is the result of people making promises and working to keep them. In return for a steady grant of money you promised to qualify for the Scottish Education Department Diploma of Painting. This school exists to award that diploma. Mr. Watt tells me you refuse to sit the examination."

"But I've finished it."

Mr. Watt said, "What will the other students think of the exam if you are allowed to pass on half a day's work?"

Thaw said, "Mr. Watt, I realize that schools need examinations, and admit that many students wouldn't work at all if they weren't rewarded with paper rolls printed by the government. And, Mr. Peel, I've been thrilled to hear you defending contracts and promises, because if these weren't defended we'd have mere anarchy. I cannot deny your truths, I can only oppose them with mine. This exam is endangering an important painting. It would be blasphemy to waste my talent making frivolous decorations for a non-existent liner. But I see your difficulty. You must uphold the art school, while I am upholding art. The solution is simple. Don't award me this diploma. I promise not to feel offended. The diploma is useless, except to folk who want to be teachers."

Thaw leaned forward to see the pleased light of agreement on the registrar's face, but it was so compressed and wrinkled that he sank back feeling lonely. The registrar said, "I have never in my life heard such a display of intellectual arrogance. You've made me more miserable than I've felt for many years. You have sat smugly declaiming that black is white and evidently expecting me to agree. I have no advice to give, but I tell you this: If you do not return at once to the examination your connection with the art school ends today, and for good."

Thaw nodded and left the office feeling dazed. He went upstairs to the studio trying to think of entertaining nonsense to add to the background of the examination panel. He climbed slower and slower, then stopped and turned. On the way down he passed Mr. Watt coming up. They pretended not to see each other.

The following evening his father entered the church and cried, "Come down and read this, Duncan!"

Thaw wiped his brush and descended the ladder.

"Read this!" commanded Mr. Thaw, stiffly holding out a letter.

"No need."

"Damn you, read it!"

"No. It's from Mr. Peel explaining why I've been expelled."

"My God, you've made a mess of your life."

"It's too early to judge."

"How do you intend to eat in future?"

"I've still some of my grant money. And the minister says the congregation may hold a collection for me when the mural's done."

"What will that bring you? Twenty pounds? Fourteen? Eight?"

"There's going to be a lot of good publicity, Dad. I may get other mural jobs, paying ones, in cafés and pubs. The ceiling's finished. What do you think of it?"

"I don't appreciate painting, Duncan! I take my opinion from the experts. And you've quarrelled with your experts."

"The experts who matter are you and me, the only people here. Please look at my ceiling! Don't you enjoy it? Look at the hedgehog! I copied her from a cigarette card you stuck in an album for me when I was five. Don't you remember? Will's *Wild Animals of Britain?* She fits that corner perfectly. Don't you like her?"

Mr. Thaw sat on a corner of the communion table and said, "Son, when will I be footloose?"

Thaw was puzzled by the word. He said, "Footloose?"

"Yes. When can I live as I want? I don't enjoy working as a costing clerk in a city. This summer I meant to get a job with the Scottish Youth Hostels or the Camping Club. The money's poor but I'd be among hills and able to walk and climb and mix with the sort of folk I like. I'm nearly sixty, but thank God I have my health. I expected you to get a job at the art school. Peel told me it was a probability four years ago. Instead you've chosen to become a social cripple. Not like Ruth! She's independent."

"I'm independent too. If I've recently eaten your food or slept under your roof it's because I was sick," said Thaw sullenly. He was disconcerted, for he had never expected his father to become a man who lived by doing what he liked. Mr. Thaw said mildly, "Son, I don't hate helping you. Listen, I'm prepared to pay the rent of the house for at least another year, even if I'm not living there. We can both use it as a base, a point of departure. Of course, I'd prefer you to pay for the electricity you burn."

"That's fair enough."

"Another thing. Since you were wee I've put a few bob a month into a couple of insurance policies for you. It's time you did that yourself. Keep up the payments, and you'll get five pounds a week from the time you're sixty. Of course, if you realize it right away you'll get less than fifty pounds. That's up to you."

"Thank you, Dad," said Thaw and nearly smiled. He had not lied in saying he still had some grant money left, but it was only a few shillings.

A week later a group containing Mr. Smail and the minister entered. Mr. Smail said jovially, "Here's a young lady who wants to speak to you, Duncan."

Thaw came down from the ladder. The lady was dwarfed by a tall man with an expensive camera. The details of her person and dress were slightly sloppy, but she moved with such smiling confidence that this wasn't seen at first. She held out her hand, saying, "Peggy Byres of the *Evening News.*"

Thaw laughed and said, "Are you going to make me famous?" He talked for six or seven minutes about the ceiling. She glanced at it, scribbled in a note pad and said, "Is your family very religious, Duncan?"

"Oh, no. I've never been christened."

"Then why are you so religious?"

"I'm not. I never go to church services. Sunday is my day of rest."

"Then what makes you paint a religious work without payment?"

"Ambition. The Old Testament has everything that can be painted in it: universal landscapes and characters and dreams and adventures and histories. The New Testament is more single-minded. I don't enjoy it so much."

"Look at these rabbits beside the pool, Miss Byres," said Mr. Smail. "You can almost hear them nibbling."

The reporter looked at the Eden wall and said, "Who's that behind the bramble bush with a lizard at his feet?"

"God," said Thaw, glancing uneasily at the minister and Mr. Smail. "The lizard is the serpent before his legs were removed. God has his back to us—you can hardly see his face."

"But what we can see looks very . . . looks rather . . ."

"Enigmatic," said Thaw. "He's not just watching Adam and Eve make love, he can see the expulsion afterward and the river of bloody history down to the wars of the apocalypse. We've had a lot of these wars recently. He can even see past them to the just city predicted by St. John, Dante and Marx. I haven't read Marx but—"

"These birds in the tree of life are miracles of delicacy, aren't they, Miss Byres?" said Mr. Smail from a distance.

"But why is Adam a Negro?"

"He's actually more red than black," the minister murmured, "and the name 'Adam' derives from a Hebrew word meaning 'red earth.'"

"But Eve is white!"

"Pearly pink," said Thaw. "I'm told that for a few moments

love makes different people feel like one. My outline shows the oneness, my colours emphasize the difference. It's an old trick. Rubens used it."

"Did you draw Eve from a model?"

"Yes."

"A girlfriend?" asked the reporter, with an arch smile.

"No, a friend of a friend," said Thaw, who had drawn Janet Weir. He added glumly, "Most girls will pose naked for an artist if he only wants to draw them."

The reporter tapped her lip with the pencil, then said, "Do you find life a tragedy or really more of a joke?"

Thaw laughed and said, "That depends on the part of it I'm looking at."

"And what will you do when you've finished here?"

"I hope to paint some commercial murals. I'll need the money."

"Do you like the mural, Miss Byres?" said Mr. Smail.

"I'm afraid I'm not an art critic. The *Evening News* doesn't have a regular art critic. Duncan, would you go up your ladder and pretend to paint Adam and Eve for a minute? We'll take a photograph, anyway."

He bought the paper on Saturday and carried it eagerly into the pulpit. The article began:

ATHEIST PAINTS
FACE OF GOD

Most people think artists are mad. The wild-bearded figure in the paint-stained dressing gown who haunts Cowlairs Parish Church will hardly reassure them on that point. And Duncan Thaw, a self-proclaimed atheist and Marxist, freely admits he is painting a large mural there with nothing in mind but the lust for fame.

His eyes clenched shut in horror. Eventually he opened them and skimmed quickly through the rest.

He has a terrifying laugh, like the bark of an asthmatic sea lion, and produces it unexpectedly for no reason at all. I sometimes wondered if it was caused by something I had said, but on reflection I saw this was impossible. . . .

> Was Adam a Negro? Duncan Thaw
> thinks so. . . .
>
> "I have no trouble finding nude
> models," he remarks, with some-
> thing suspiciously like a wink. . . .
>
> He hopes this will be the first of
> many murals. He hopes to make a
> lot of money this way. He says he
> needs it.

He felt as if there was poison in his chest, as if half his blood
had been removed. He sat still until the old minister wandered
in and asked, "Have you read . . . ?"
"Yes."
"It's unfortunate. Unfortunate."
"Surely she was trying to be cruel!"
"No, I don't think so. I met many reporters when I was chaplain
at Barlinnie Jail and on average they're no more wicked than
other people. But their job depends on being entertaining,
so they make everything look as clownish or as monstrous as
they can. If any more reporters come, Duncan, my advice is
to tell them nothing you really feel or believe."

A reporter came that evening, took Thaw for a drink in
a pub and explained that he too would have been an artist if
his uncle hadn't opposed the idea. Thaw said, "Please tell your
readers I am not an atheist. I may have my own conception
of God, but it doesn't clash with the opinions of the church,
my employer."
This appeared two days later under the heading:

NOT AN
ATHEIST

> The Cowlairs "mad muralist," Dun-
> can Thaw, has denied he is an athe-
> ist. He says he has his own concep-
> tion of good but it doesn't clash.

After this Thaw noticed that journalists weren't interested in
his thoughts, though they asked him what it felt like to sleep
alone in a big building and kept photographing Adam and
Eve. An exception was a tall man in a beautifully cut grey
suit from the *Glasgow Herald*. He sat for half an hour in the

front pew staring at the ceiling, then sat on the organ stool and gazed at the Eden wall. At last he said, "I like this."

"I'm glad."

"Of course it will be almost impossible for me to criticize it. It isn't cubist or expressionist or surrealist, it isn't academic or kitchen sink or even naive. It's a bit like Puvis de Chavannes, but who nowadays knows Puvis de Chavannes? I'm afraid you're going to pay the penalty of being outside the main streams of development."

"The best British painters are that."

"Eh?"

"Hogarth. Blake. Turner. Spencer. Burra."

"Oh, you like these? Turner *is* good, of course. His handling of colour anticipates Odilon Redon and Jackson Pollock. Well, I'll do my best for you, though this is one of my busy weeks. The Glasgow and Edinburgh schools are having their diploma shows, so I haven't much space."

At the end of an article about other people the *Herald* said this:

> It isn't easy to discover Cowlairs Parish Church in the depths of northeast Glasgow, but hardy souls who make the effort will find Duncan Thaw's (unfinished) Genesis mural worth a great deal more than a passing glance.

The newspapers sickened him of the mural. He had taken months to make every shape as clear and harmonious as possible, putting in nothing he didn't feel lovely or exciting. He knew that reports must always simplify and twist, but he also felt that the most twisted report gives some idea of its cause, and his work had caused nothing but useless gossip. He lay curled on the pulpit floor, dozing and waking till afternoon, then rose and stared, biting his thumb knuckle, at the unfinished wall. All he could see in it now were complicated shapes. With a slam and clattering McAlpin and Drummond came in followed by Macbeth. Thaw gazed at them astonished and relieved.

"We are here," said Drummond, "because we read in the papers that you are holding weekday services in which Negroes are raped by white women."

"You will gather that we are slightly puggled," said McAlpin.

"Stotious," said Drummond.

"Miraculous," said McAlpin.

"Full," said Drummond.

They starting running round the church along the backs of pews, zigzagging through the nave and up into the gallery, pausing for new views of the mural and shouting to each other: "I can see the whole window wall from here."

"Good God, there's a diver in it."

"The tree looks best from above."

"But I see a dung beetle you can't see."

Macbeth sat heavily beside Thaw saying, "They've got their diplomas. They can laugh."

They came down at last and Drummond said soberly "It's all right, Duncan, you've nothing to worry about."

"You like it?"

"We're envious," said McAlpin. "At least I am. Come for a drink."

"Gladly! Where to?"

"Remember I've only half a crown," said Drummond.

"I've twenty-six pounds," said Thaw. "But it has to last till my next mural."

Drummond said, "This is clearly a Wine 64 night."

"What is Wine 64?"

"Not a drop of it is drunk before it's sixty-four days old, yet a tumblerful costs only fourpence. It's so strong I only drink it once a year. Twice would damage the health. The only pub selling it is in Grove Street, but we'll be safe because there's three of us."

"Four," said Macbeth, standing up firmly.

Sliding patches of evening sunshine mingled with flurries of so warm a rain that nobody thought of sheltering from it. Drummond led them round Sighthill cemetery, across some football pitches and up a wilderness of slag bings called Jack's Mountain. From the top they saw the yellow-scummed lake called the Stinky Ocean, then came down near a slaughterhouse behind Pinkston power station, along the canal towpath, between bonded warehouses, across Garscube Road and into a public house. The customers sat on benches against the wall, staring at each other across the narrow floor like passengers in a train. They were all older than forty with very creased faces and clothes. An old lady sitting beside Thaw said quietly, "All God's people, sonny."

He nodded.

"And he loves every one of us."

Thaw frowned. She said, "You neednae be afraid to speak to a granny, son."

"I'm not afraid. I was wondering about what you said."

She took his hand. "Listen, son, God was the humblest man who ever walked the earth. He didn't care who you were or what you did, he still sat with you and drank with you and loved you."

Thaw was astonished. He imagined the creator as an erratically generous host, not as a friendly fellow guest, but the old woman's faith had been tested by more life than his so he said gently, "He drank with you?"

She nodded and smiled at a sherry on the table before her and squeezed his hand, saying, "Yes, he did, because it lifts the heart. I was reading the *Sunday Post,* and a doctor writing in it said a lot of people died of drink but more died of worry. Now I can come in here on a Saturday night and have a half or two, and I hear folk talking and I feel I love everyone in the room."

Macbeth leaned toward her. "If God loves us why are we in such a mess?"

He smiled at her as if she was a joke, but she was not offended and not only reached out to squeeze his hand but stroked his hair.

"Because we don't love God, we mock and despise him. But he still loves us, no matter what we do."

"Even if we kill someone?"

"Even if we kill someone."

"Even if you're a Communist?"

"It doesn't matter who you are. When God meets you at the gates of pearl and asks who you are and you say to him, 'God forgive me,' then it's 'Come in. You're welcome.'"

Thaw had never before met a religious person who thought God's love an easy thing. He said abruptly, "What if we can't forgive ourselves?"

She didn't understand the question and he repeated it. She said, "Of course you can't forgive yourself! Only God can forgive you."

"Tell me this," said Macbeth. "Are you a Catholic?"

"I come from Ireland—I'm Irish through and through."

"But are you a Catholic?"

"It doesn't matter who you are. . . ."

Thaw sipped Wine 64 which tasted like watered strawberry jam. In leaning forward to speak Macbeth left a gap through which McAlpin was visible. Thaw told him quietly, "I left the church tonight for a complete change of air and the first stranger I meet is a friend of God."

"Ah!" said McAlpin cheerfully, setting down his glass. "Shall I tell you about God? I'm unusually lucid tonight."

Beyond him a haggard man was discussing with Drummond the chances of selling one's body for medical research while still alive. Thaw said, "Will you take long?"

"Certainly not. God, you see, is a word. It is the word for everything not speaking when someone says 'I think.' And by Propper's Law of Inverse Exclusion (which enables a flea in a matchbox to declare itself jailor of the universe) every single 'I think' has intimate knowledge of the surface of what it is not. But as every thinker reflects a different surface of what he isn't, and as God is our word for the whole, it follows that all agreement about God is based on misunderstanding."

"You're a liar," cried Macbeth, who had caught some of this, "The old woman is right. God is not a word, God is a man! I crucified him with these hands!"

McAlpin said soothingly, "Since competitive capitalism split us off from the collective unconscious we've all been more or less crucified."

"Don't talk to me about crucifixion," snarled Macbeth. "How can a man with a diploma understand crucifixion? A year ago a friend said to me, 'Jimmy, if you go on like this you'll end in the gutter, the madhouse or the Clyde.' Since then I have been in all three."

McAlpin raised a forefinger and said, "To a sensitively poised intelligence like me a wrong note in a Beethoven quartet is as excruciating as a boot up the backside or a fall from Clyde Street suspension bridge is to you."

"You think you're fucking clever, don't you?" said Macbeth. Meanwhile the old lady had jumped up and was shaking everyone by the hand. When she came to Drummond he grinned at her and sang with surprising sweetness:

> "The Lord's my shepherd: I'll not want.
> He makes me down to lie
> In pastures green. He leadeth me
> The quiet waters by."

Several people joined in, others laughed and a few frowned and muttered. The old lady caressed Drummond's hair and said he looked like Christ, then said her name was Molly O'Malley and danced a jig on the narrow floor, calling out to Thaw

from the middle of it, "God love you, my boy! God love you,
my bonny boy!"
"You're after the auld woman, eh?" asked an old man nearby.
"Me?" said Thaw. "No!"
"Blethers. I'd have ridden a cat at your age."
A stout bartender arrived and said firmly, "Right, lads, you've
had your fun."
"Fun?" cried Macbeth querulously. "What fun have I had?"
But they were forced to leave.

There was a chill wind outside and a sky bright with the
green and gold of a slow summer sunset. Drummond said he
knew of a party and led them up Lynedoch Street, a normally
shallow hill which tonight seemed perpendicular. They avoided
falling off by clinging to each other, except Macbeth who drifted
away down a sidestreet. The party was in a large, well-furnished
house and Thaw found the other guests daunting. They were
his own age but had the clothes and conversation of adults
with monthly salaries. He found a corner in a dim room where
couples clung and turned to the sound of a gramophone. Suddenly a woman in a black dress said loudly, "Good heavens,
is that you, Duncan? Won't you dance with me?"
They danced and he gazed fascinated at her blond hair and
naked shoulders. She giggled and said, "You don't remember
me, but you should. I was the first girl you ever danced with.
Ever, ever, ever."
He grinned thankfully and said, "I'm very glad."
"Do you remember what you thought I was like?"
"Marble and honey."
"Am I still like that?"
"Yes."
"What a relief. You see, I'm marrying a solicitor next month.
He's very rich and sexy and what more can a woman want?"
Her manner was strained and cheerful and he didn't understand
it. She said, "I'm a terrible woman, Duncan. I've still four or
five boyfriends and I play them against each other, and at the
moment I rather fancy that woman talking to Aitken. Have
you ever fancied a man?"
"Not in the cuddling way," said Thaw.
His head lay on her shoulder and his hands clasped the halves
of her bottom. She said, "Stop touching me, Duncan."
He said, "I'm sorry," and went over to a table of drinks, filled
a tumbler of whisky and forced it quickly down him like
medicine. It tasted horrible. The words "Stop touching me,

Duncan" were sounding in the centre of him. He couldn't
bear them, but they were in his centre. He filled and drank a
tumbler of sherry, which tasted better; then one of gin, which
tasted much worse; then he went upstairs to the lavatory.

When he got inside the room was visibly whirling. He
closed his eyes and felt it drop like a crashing aeroplane. He
fell to the wall, then to the floor. He embraced the narrow
part of the lavatory pan and lay shivering and wishing he was
unconscious. Whenever he opened his eyes he saw the room
whirl: when he closed them he felt it fall. There were hammer-
ings and voices shouting, "Open the door," but he said, "Go
away, I'm cold," and after a while they went away. Later he
heard such an odd scratching and tapping that he sat up. The
tapping was mingled with faint cries of "Let me in!" and the
bluster of strong wind. There was a white mouthing face behind
the black glass of the window and he felt a pang of superstitious
terror, for he remembered the lavatory was on the second or
third floor. At last he crawled over, reached up a hand and
raised a catch. The window swung in and Drummond jumped
through with a gust of rain. He said, "Don't worry, Duncan,"
and wiped Thaw's face and shirt with a sponge. Thaw said,
"I'm cold, leave me alone."
Two people helped him downstairs through an empty house.
A door was opened and he was taken into a dark shed with
a concrete floor. He screamed, "This is a cold place, I don't
want to be here."
He was laid on the skin of a cold sofa, some doors slammed
and a voice said, "Where do you live?"
"Cowlairs Parish Church."
"For Christ's sake where does he live?"
A voice gave an address on the Cumbernauld Road and the
sofa throbbed and swung forward. It was clearly part of a car,
and when it stopped outside the close in Riddrie he was able
to get out and walk upstairs alone. Luckily his father no longer
lived there.

A week later he recovered enough self-esteem to return
to the church. The mural broke upon him in an altogether
fresh way. He chuckled and skipped about, looking at it from
different angles, his mind brightening with new ideas. He was
laying paint on his palette when the minister came in. He said,
"You took a holiday, Duncan. Good. You needed a rest. . . .
I'm afraid I have bad news. The Glasgow Presbytery have been

here and . . . they've seen it and they're not very happy. Of
course, our publicity was bad and the colour of Adam was
rather a shock. I told them you could change that, but it was
the *principle* of the thing they disliked. I'm afraid we're going
to lose our church."
Anger flooded Thaw's veins with adrenalin. He laid his ladder
against the wall and said, "When?"
"In another six or seven months. Sometime early in the coming
year."
"At least it gives me time to finish the mural," said Thaw,
mounting the ladder.
"I'm sorry, but you'll have to stop."
"Why?" said Thaw, staring.
"We've had complaints from the congregation. They'd like
to worship without this mess of ladders and pots and drips
on the chancel floor. The session say you must stop. Even Mr.
Smail says so, and he was a great supporter of yours."
"When?"
"Next Sunday."

On Sunday the minister came an hour before the service
and said, "Well, Duncan."
Thaw climbed wearily down the ladder for he'd been working
all night. He said, "That's the best I can do in the time."
"It looks just fine."
"If anyone wonders about these marks tell them they would
have become a herd of cattle."
"Oh, no one will ask. It looks fine."
"And if they say the sky is cluttered, tell them I meant to
simplify it."
"It's beautiful, Duncan, but you could be an eternity on it.
An eternity."
"And if they say the events on the horizon distract from the
big simple foreground shapes, tell them I'd begun to notice
that, but this was my first mural, I'd seen nobody else paint
one, and I'd to teach myself as I went along. Tell them I couldn't
afford assistants."
The minister hesitated, then said firmly, "Finish the mural when
you like, Duncan. Pay no attention to them. Work on it as
much as you like."
"Oh!" said Thaw, and wept with relief. The minister patted
his shoulder and said kindly, "Just you go ahead and pay no
attention to them."

CHAPTER 29. The Way Out

He could no longer ask the church to pay for materials. When only ten pounds remained he knew he would be a desperate man when it was spent; on the other hand if he survived without touching it he could probably last forever. A smell of boiled cabbage from the depths of the building suggested an idea. In the early afternoon he went to a lane behind the church where rubbish bins stood and found scraps from the school dinners tipped there. He started bringing a plate round and picking out slices of bread and mutton, lumps of macaroni and dumpling. One day he heard someone cry "Duncan Thaw!" and looked into the accusing eyes of Mrs. Coulter. He said defensively, "I'm not stealing this. Nobody wants it."
"You should be ashamed, a well-brought-up boy like you!" He walked past her with the heaped plate, but around noon the next day she brought a large covered bowl into the church and set it on the end of a pew saying, "Your dinner."
He said irritably, "You don't need to do that Mrs. Coulter."
She snorted and went out and did the same every following weekday except Friday, when she left two bowls. And the decorator, Mr. Rennie, arrived one evening and said abruptly, "Do you still want help?"
"More than ever."
"Right. I'll give you a couple of nights a week."
He began changing into overalls and Thaw, who wept easily nowadays, hurried to a quiet corner of the church. Then he returned and said, "You see my tree of life, Mr. Rennie? It's big and beautiful and in the wrong place. Far too central. It must be shifted two and a quarter inches to the left, fruit, birds, squirrels and all. Do you see why?"

"Don't ask me why, just show me how to do it."

"I will, Mr. Rennie. Excuse me if I chatter nervously, I'm afraid of you vanishing. And could you lend me scaffolding again for a few days? I want to get back to the ceiling."

"That won't please the minister."

"Just for a few days."

The help of Mr. Rennie, though only six hours a week, was so welcome that Thaw found comfort in addressing him when he wasn't there.

"We aren't working on the rim of the universe, are we, Mr. Rennie? No, no, Cowlairs is a historic region. A cinema down the road has a granite slab set in the wall above a bunged-up drinking fountain. It must have lain flat once, for the inscription says James Nisbet lies under it who suffered martyrdom there in 1684. I suppose the district was wild moorland then. He was shot by government troops for worshipping God without a prayerbook, just making up the words as he went along. . . . A bad business? No, a question of law and order. Men who refused to pray out of a properly licensed book might undermine the government by asking God to change it. So *bang-bang,* cheerio, Jimmy Nisbet. But four years later came a different lot of politicians who found it easy to govern Scotland without prayerbooks. So the troops stopped chasing Presbyterians, who wouldnae pray out of books, and returned to chasing Catholics, who prayed out of Latin ones. And a slab was laid over Nisbet's bones on the site of the Casino picture house (they're turning it into a bingo hall next year) and a slipshod verse was carved on it which ends with the rousing words:

As Britain lyes in guilt, you see,
'Tis asked o reader, art thou free?

Are we free, Mr. Rennie? Of course we are. We're making our own model of the universe and nobody gives a damn for us. . . ."

"Yes, a great ground for martyrs, Mr. Rennie. Overby in the cemetery is a monument to Baird, Hardie and Wilson, some weavers who nearly overturned the British government around 1820. The government was very insecure in those days. It had just won a large war and there was widespread unemployment. Mechanization was making the owning classes richer and the working classes poorer—especially the weavers. A secret organization grew up in the weaving towns which planned to call a general strike, assassinate the cabinet, attack the barracks and give everybody the vote. Cunning, eh? The details of the revolt were mostly worked out by government agents, and when the great day dawned they had trouble getting anyone to move. However, in the villages of Strathaven and Bellshill some enthusiasts set out with red flags. Four of them actually hoisted one on Cathkin Braes and then went home to their teas, for clearly nothing was happening. So Baird, Hardie and Wilson were arrested, tried and hung, and the bloody tide of revolution receded. Then one day the government noticed it could give the vote to almost everyone without losing power. The unemployed got assisted passages to Canada, Australia, Asia and Africa, where they prospered by grabbing land from the natives. Britain became an empire, everyone lived happily ever after, and a monument was erected to Baird and Hardie and Wilson who had died to make us free. But don't think this red-hot radicalism made us less religious, Mr. Rennie. Glasgow is still full of churches built in the last century. Half of them have been turned into warehouses. Perhaps you and I are painting what will become the best decorated motorcycle and television accessories depot in the United Kingdom."

Later he said, "I apologize, Mr. Rennie, I don't believe that. I believe this church will be knocked down, but first the mural must be made perfect. When a thing is perfect it is eternal. It can be destroyed afterward, or slowly decay, but its perfection is safe in the past, which is the only inevitable part of the universe. No government, no force, no God can make what has been not have been. The past is eternal and every day our abortions fall into it: love affairs we bungled, homes we damaged, children we couldn't be kind to. Let you and I, Mr. Rennie, make eternity a present of a complete, perfect, harmonious, utterly harmless thing; something whose every part is the result of intelligent, loving care; something which isn't a destructive weapon and can't be sold at a profit by public-spirited businessmen. And remember, Mr. Rennie, we're doing nothing novel. For five or six thousand years Egyptian and Etruscan and Chinese artists put their best work into graves which were never opened. The old Greeks and Romans had as many Leonardos, Rembrandts and Cézannes as we have, all painting on plaster that's turned to powder now, apart from a few square yards in Pompeii. I'm not sorry. There are too many colour photographs of the Great Art of the Past. If it didn't have colour reproduction, the mid-twentieth century would have no

reason to think itself artistic at all . . . and if it didn't have
you and me, Mr. Rennie."
"Stop condescending to me," said a voice.
Thaw started and dropped his brush, for it was three o'clock
in the morning. He laughed shakily and climbed down the
ladder, saying, "I will never condescend to you again, Mr.
Rennie, if you promise not to speak to me when you aren't
here. Excuse me, I'm a little tired."

Sleeping had become as easy as work, for he dreamed
he was in the mural. "Here it is: land, sky and sunlight," he
said to God his father as they strolled round the bramble bush,
the serpent wagging its tail behind them. It was a clear day
and anemones were singing in the tidal pools. "You'll get it
back when I've put it in decent order. I don't like being in
debt. As you see I've had no trouble with rational pain and
death." They looked up at a hawk with a young rabbit hanging
from its claws, then paused on the summit of a cliff. On the
river below two swans twined their necks and the first lovers
knelt to each other on the far shore. On the western horizon
arose the great stump of the Babylonian tower, tiny figures
waved flags on the summit; to the east, on Ben Sinai, in a
patch of bad weather, the minister was carving the triangulation
tables of the law. "Sex and history are problems I can't solve,
so I'm returning them in the form you gave them, though
stated a little more clearly. I'll finish by the new year and then
I'll owe you nothing. Though I'll be grateful if you give me
some paying customers after that, I'll need the money. Excuse
me a moment." He went up and moved the lightning over
Sinai two and a quarter inches to the right, making it echo
the rift in the tree of knowledge. He had no sensation of waking.
As he lay with closed eyes his mind circled the chancel walls
with lazy power, pausing in the vault to choose the area he
would work upon that day. He even had a plan view of his
body, curled in the pulpit like a grub in a nut, and knew it
would soon bring his working weight up the ladder to join
his thoughts. Body and mind so completely served the mural
that sexual fancies never came to him now and he only knew
he needed food when the brush felt too heavy to hold. His
strangest, most dreamlike times happened away from the mural.
He sat at the communion table eating lumps of custard from
Mrs. Coulter's bowl while the old minister stared at him murmuring, "Oh yes, you're a real artist. A real artist."
Later he was in a crowded art shop in the city centre stealing

tubes of paint without haste or panic. Later still he stood on
a pavement arranging to meet June Haig.

"You won't come!" he said, laughing in her face. "I know
you won't come."

"Oh, don't worry, I'll be there. Paisley's corner by the bridge.
I'll be there."

"So will I, but you won't come."

He laughed again because he felt he was not talking to her
in the present but two or three years earlier.

The afternoon darkened early and he was working peer-
ingly in the semi-dusk when someone coughed behind him.
A man and a woman stood in the aisle, and when his eyes
were used to the better light on the church floor he noticed
the woman was Marjory. The man said heartily, "Hullo, Duncan," and Marjory raised her hand and smiled. Thaw said
"Hullo" and looked down on them, smiling slightly. The man
said, "We were visiting friends in Lenzie and we thought, old
times and so forth, why not run in and see Duncan? So here
we are."

The man peered up through the ladders.

"You must have cat's eyes to work in this light."

"The switches are behind the door."

"No no. No no. I quite like it in this dimness, more mysterious,
if you know what I mean. . . . Very impressive. Very impressive."

Marjory said something he couldn't hear. He said, "What?"

"This isn't your usual style of work, Duncan."

After a short silence Thaw said, "I'm trying to show more
air and light."

The man said, "So you are. So you are." He moved back
into the body of the church, looking at the mural and quietly
humming. He said, "You're nearly finished."

"Far from it."

"It looks finished to my untutored eye."

Thaw indicated bits to be repainted.

"How much longer will you be on it?"

"A few weeks."

"Then what will you do. Teach?"

"I don't know."

He turned round and pretended to work. After a moment
he heard the man cough and say, "Well, Marjory," and, "I
think we'll be getting along now, Duncan."

Thaw looked round and said goodbye. The two people had

moved back into the middle of the church. The man said, "By
the way, did you know Marjory and I are thinking of getting
married?"
"No."
"Yes, we're thinking about it."
"Good."
There was silence then the man said, "Well, goodbye, Duncan.
When we're married you must look in on us. We still think
of you now and again."
Thaw shouted, "Good."
The syllable clattered upon the ceiling and walls. At the door
he saw Marjory look back and raise her hand, but couldn't
see if she was smiling or not.

It was too dark to work now. He lay on the planks, his
thoughts returning to Marjory in a puzzled way, like a tongue
tip returning to a hole from which a tooth has been pulled.
He was sure he had just seen a girl without special beauty or
intelligence. He wondered why she had been all he wanted
in a woman. She was as unlike Marjory as Mrs. Thaw's corpse
had been unlike his mother. He wished he had said something
ironic and memorable but she had given him no chance.
"This isn't your usual style of work, Duncan."
He shivered and climbed slowly down. His body felt unusually
heavy. He switched on the lights and stared at the mural. It
looked horrible. He went up into the gallery where he kept
a large mirror for such emergencies. Reflected in it, the left
and right sides transposed, the mural sometimes looked new
and exciting when he had been working too close to it for
too long. Now it appeared even worse than his naked eyes
had seen. He flung the mirror onto the pews beneath shouting,
"Not beauty! Not beauty! Nothing but hunger!"
He tried to cram all his knuckles into his mouth, then went
downstairs and picked the biggest mirror fragment from among
the pews and hurried about trying to catch a fresh new glimpse
of the work. He had wanted to make a harmony of soft blue,
brown and gold livened here and there by sparks of pure colour,
but he could see only clumsy black and grey, glaring reds and
greens. He had tried to show bodies in a depth of tender light,
sharing space with clouds, hills, plants and creatures, but his
space was hardly a foot deep and his people were crushed in
it as if into a narrow cupboard. His mural showed the warped
rat-trap world of a neurotic virgin. He hurled the mirror fragment into the chancel.

"That is not art," he shouted, bending his head and wildly scratching. "Not art, just hungry howling. Oh, why did she hunt me out? Why didn't she stay? How can I make her a beautiful world if she refuses to please me? Oh, God, God, God, let me kill her, kill her! I must get out of here."

He went into the lavatory beside the vestry, stripped off dressing gown and overalls and started washing. From upstairs the voices of Cowlairs Women's Social Club were bawling a chorus of "Who's Sorry Now?" As he rubbed a paint stain from his knee with newspaper soaked in turpentine he noticed an advertisement for a film called *Test Pilot*. A strong, slightly pained male head looked skyward out of a padded husk hung with microphones, cables and dials. A woman stood nearby in profile, her back to the pilot but glancing at him with a sidelong inviting provocative smile. She had short dark hair and lips like June Haig. She was barefoot and wore bangles and black gauze trousers with a slit from ankle to waist. A sleeveless black gauze shirt covered her breasts but left bare the valley between them and her throat and midriff. Stealthily arising, his sexual imagination began slowly to rip and toy with her, but he crumpled the paper and flung it aside, thinking, "Women are never like that. Or they seem to be and then, 'Stop touching me, Duncan.' But that's my fault. I've seen them with other men at bus stops, leaning toward them, looking into their faces, nakedly wanting to be liked or happy because they see they're wanted. But I'm unattractive. Never mind. Prostitutes make a living from men like me. I must go to Bath Street."

He put on his suit, noticing the two five-pound notes still in the jacket pocket. Returning to the church to switch the lights off he noticed the place was stinking, stinking so powerfully he thought for a moment it was on fire. Then he recognized the corrupt sweet odour that had come after his mother's death. He laughed mournfully and said, "Still there, auld woman? And bigger than ever, if my nose is any judge. I must see if I can get rid of you in Bath Street."

It was ten o'clock and the tram into town was nearly empty. He sat chewing a knuckle and staring out of the window. Visions of viciously exciting intercourse were blurred by thoughts of peaceful sleep in the arms of someone pretending to like him. He left the tram and walked up West Regent Street. Two women stood at opposite corners of Blythswood Square. He quickened as he passed them, then slowed up, cursing his cowardice. It occurred to him that he hadn't eaten for two or three days. He bought a poke of chips in a shop near Charing Cross and walked, eating them, up Bath Street. A woman stood at a corner wearing a red coat and carrying a big black handbag. She looked too old and dignified to be a prostitute but though on the far side of the road she seemed to be noticing him sideways. He stood against some railings, finishing the chips while the heart hammered in his chest. He crumpled and dropped the cardboard container and was about to cross the road when he saw someone coming. A small man walked lurchingly toward the woman along the opposite pavement. She turned to look at him. He slowed down, fumbled in several pockets and brought out a cigarette case. For a moment they stood talking then she took a cigarette, the man lit it and they set off toward Sauchiehall Street. Thaw walked on full of anger and relief and entered a café near Green's Playhouse. He ordered a coffee and sat till the Italian behind the counter started to stand chairs on tables and sweep the floor. The idea of prostitution was wholly depressing now but there was nowhere to retreat. Church and home were places he never wanted to visit again. He went out into Renfield Street.

It was midnight but there were people about: one or two smart-suited men walking briskly, a lounger in a dirty coat reading a newspaper at a street corner. Two women halted across the road from him. They were young, tall and wore fur-trimmed black coats open over their dresses. One of them put a leg forward, pulled the hem of her dress halfway up her thigh and did something for a while to the top of her stocking. The woman at her side glanced around disdainfully. Thaw stopped, his stomach transbarbed by a shaft of nervous excitement. He raised his hand and crossed over, trying to smile. He said to the woman, who was now pulling down the hem of her dress, "Hullo. I think we know each other."
The other woman said, "You're wrong. It's me ye know," and stared at him. He said, "All right."
The bending woman stood up and said, "I'll be seeing ye, Greta."
"Aye, all right. Wait, come here a minute."
They moved aside and whispered together. Both had bright bronze hair permed exactly alike. Greta wore a tight dress which showed the urn-like curves of her thighs and hips. It was fastened down the front with buttons from which creases

ran round her body like lines of latitude. Thaw was excited
and puzzled that things were going so easily. The smaller girl
said, "Goodnight, Greta. Goodnight, big boy," and walked
away. The other took his arm. His nostrils were buffeted by
cheap sweet perfume. He said, "Have you a place of your
own?"
"Sure I've a place."
"Will we take a taxi?"
"Aye. Let's be stylish."
He waved to an approaching taxi and with a feeling of compe-
tence saw it come to the kerb. They entered and the woman
gave an address. He leaned back, feeling cared for. The woman
said, "Is it a short time you're after?"
"All night, please. I'm a bit tired."
"It'll cost ye."
"How much?"
"Oh, ten pounds, easy."
Thaw was slightly shocked. "As much as that? . . . I've only
nine pounds sixteen and tenpence. Less, when I've paid for
the taxi."
"I suppose that'll have to do."
He hesitated, then said, "You'll have trouble warming me up.
I'm as cold as a fish."
She patted his knee. "Oh, I'll warm you up. I'm good."
The taxi stopped at the white portico of a church. He paid
the driver and joined the woman on the pavement saying, "Are
we getting married?"
"I live just round the corner."

They entered a close in the block of buildings which held
his old studio. He had difficulty climbing the stairs. She said,
"You aren't well, are you?"
"Just a bit tired."
A frosted glass window beside the door had a black triangular
hole in it. She put her hand through the hole and took out a
key. She opened the door, carefully closed it behind them,
and whispered to Thaw to be quiet. She led him in darkness
up narrow creaking stairs, opened another door, closed it behind them, touched a switch and he saw the rosy light of a
table lamp in a pink satin shade. They were in a cosy attic
bedroom with a sloping ceiling. The woman switched on an
electric fire, took off her coat and sat down on the bed looking
at him. He started to undress.

Sometime later she said in a sudden suspicious voice, "What's that?"

Thaw was breathing hard and didn't answer. She said, "Stop! What's that?"

"Nothing."

"You call that nothing?"

"It's eczema, it isn't infectious, look—"

"No you don't! Stop! Stop it!"

She got up and started to dress, saying, "I cannae afford to take chances."

Thaw watched her, his mouth hanging stupidly open. He couldn't quite believe what was happening. She buttoned up her dress.

"Get up!" she said roughly.

He sat up slowly and started dressing. His mouth still hung open. Once or twice he stopped and stared hard at the floor and she told him to hurry up. He felt dizzy and said, "Let me sit for a bit."

He heard her say in a kindlier voice, "I cannae afford to take chances."

"It wasn't what you thought. Not contagious or infectious."

He took three pound notes from his hip pocket and laid them on the table.

"What's that for?"

"Your time."

"Take it back."

He stared at the money without moving. She seized it and shoved it into the pocket of his jacket. He stood up and put the jacket on. She led him downstairs.

He went slowly by back streets to Drummond's house, opened the broken-locked door and moved stealthily into a room off the lobby. Light, reflected from a street lamp, showed a leatherette armchair with china ornaments on the seat. He moved these and sat, elbows on knees, chin on knuckles, until cold sunlight dawned on the roofs outside the window and his teeth were chattering. In occasional waking dreams he seemed another object in the room, like the clock on the mantelpiece, the ornaments at his feet. The sound of conversation from the kitchen struck him as it struck the objects. Once Mr. Drummond passed the door muttering loudly, "Sheer bloody nonsense . . . " then came noises of the lavatory being used. Thaw wrapped a small carpet round himself as protection from the cold. He began to dream he was a carpet himself, a mat of flesh with a hole in it. Something dreadful was going to emerge from that hole, he could smell its cold breath. He heard quick footsteps and a voice shouted, "Sponger and scrounger!"

He opened his eyes and saw a brisk, erect, fairly old woman staring at him accusingly. One hand was on her hip; the other held a bird cage with a stuffed canary on the perch. She glanced down at it and tears came to her eyes.

"Poor wee Joey," she whispered softly. "Poor wee Joey. That bloody cat. Sponger and scoundrel!" she yelled again. "I won't stand it!"

Drummond strode in saying, "Pull yourself together Ma. Oh, hullo Duncan. Ma, for God's sake make yourself a cup of strong black coffee."

"I won't stand any more! You fill the house with Mollys and Janets till I'm driven out by the stink of bloody women, then your lazy friends come crawling in and shift all my good sister's china, I won't stand it!"

"Sorry about this, Duncan," said Drummond grimly. He picked up his mother and wrestled her out of the room. Thaw went away.

It was a bright morning and the city stank of cheap perfume. He wandered eerily round to Brown's tearoom and sat an hour or two in the teaspoon-tinkling warmth. His head ached. A small girl sat by him and said, "Hullo, Duncan, you look very well dressed today. Crumpled, perhaps, but quite smart really."

He stared at her. She said, "Do you remember you once said illness was useful sometimes?"

He stared at her.

"Well, my doctor's told me the same thing. You see, my mother committed suicide when I was three which probably . . . and then I lived with an aunt and the doctor thinks I made myself ill to . . . to be attended to. He said first I gave myself pleurisy and then anæmia and then colds, so now I'm going to a psychiatrist. Are you all right?"

Thaw stared at her. He heard the words but they seemed meaningless.

"Did you know that somebody, I forget his name, said you were a genius? Do you know who said that?"

Thaw stared at her.

"I forget his name but he's a painter. . . . I think his first name begins with B. He's quite well known. Anyway, that should make you feel . . . rather . . . I'm expecting Peter here soon. Did you know I was married?"

Thaw stood up awkwardly and climbed to the street. A Riddrie tram stopped at nearby traffic lights and he boarded with an effort. His seat in the downstairs cabin seemed to be a dog. When he looked at it or stroked it with his hand it was clearly a seat, but when he closed his eyes against the glare it seemed a huge dog. Getting up to the house was difficult. Inside he squatted on the hearth rug and pressed his fists to his aching brow. After a while he felt the rug get up, walk to the bedroom and tip him onto the bed. He got his clothes and shoes off and pulled the blankets over him. Oblivion seemed to fall on him from the ceiling like a ton of bricks.

He wakened in the air above his body which lay with open mouth and eyes, the head lolling sideways off the pillow. He wondered whether to leave it but it moved, groaned, and at once he became part of it and sat up. He was full of dull peace. No noise came from the main road outside, not the faintest sound from upstairs or down. Air flowed in and out of his lungs so easily that he would have imagined himself dead if he hadn't felt hungry. He pulled the heavy bedclothes aside, lowered his feet to the floor, tried carefully to stand and fell down. He lay awhile with his head under a chair, shuddering with laughter, and later drew his clothes on without standing and crawled into the kitchen, shaking his head from side to side and muttering, "All for a bit of skin, all for a bit of dried skin." Pulling himself upright with difficulty he ate two oatcakes, washed and ate a shrivelled carrot, and that was all his stomach could hold. He sat on a chair and tried to arrange the thoughts in his head like pieces on a chessboard, but the thoughts were few and small and kept slipping between his fingers, so he stared at a spider which sat on the electric stove twitching far too many legs. He loathed it and brought the weight of his clenched fist down on it, yet when he withdrew the hand the insect sat there, twitching and unhurt. He struck many times in a fit of rage but the blows did not flatten it, and he stopped when the metal-topped stove had bruised his fist.

Suddenly words came to him out of the air, whispered by an invisible beak. He became tense, said "Yes," walked upright out of the house, shut the door behind him and started fingering his pockets to learn if he had the key.
"Too many pockets," he mumbled. "Must sew some up. Oh." Mrs. Colquhoun's cat sat in the opposite doorway looking at him. Part of her head and throat was missing. The right side was cut away and he saw the brain in section, white and pink

and pleated like the underneath of a mushroom. The cat yawned, opening her half-mouth wide and unrolling her tongue across the white needle teeth. Thaw could see the tongue down to its root in the thin corridor of her throat. His lips moved, speaking indistinct words about his terror. His fingers shut upon the key's cold steel. Clutching it for comfort he went down to the street. The air was warm and the sky as black as tar. A red planet in the middle put out rings of dark air like ripples from a stone dropped in a pond. Thaw obeyed the whisper and turned left. The whisperer was a black crow which flew behind his head. In the great silence its orders were very distinct. He was himself that black bird looking down on Duncan Thaw and the streets he walked through. Sometimes he soared to the end of a street, leaving the small walking figure behind, or he would drop back and follow at a distance. At corners he came up, bringing his beak close to an ear to whisper: *turn this way, turn that.* At the end of one street a rusty gate was chained shut and twined with convolvulus, but he squeezed between some bent railings. He saw the crimson planet between pagoda-shaped growths whose brittle fleshy stalks sweated white syrup. The crow flapped up the cinder path in front of his feet, chattering wildly:

> *"Eenty teenty haligalum*
> *the head is hatched, the sky is crackit*
> *and John Knox boozed up a kee-kark lum*
> *and all the Gods are humpy-kee-kark, kee-kark, kee-kark."*

Thaw staggered, slipped and was flying. The crow soared a hundred feet below him. His position and speed depended on it. They passed above the dull ribbon of the weedy canal and he saw into rooms where women ironed beneath pulleys hung with washing, men in shirtsleeves read newspapers, children and lovers lay under quilts in dim bedrooms. He swung as if on trapezes across the city's cut honeycomb. The intricate compact life fascinated, then appalled him. He covered his eyes. His feet touched ground at once.

He leaned his stomach on a baluster of the bridge and folded his arms on the parapet. He felt sick. The river had shrunk to a narrow trickle among cracked mudflats. A thin cloud of gulls screamed above something dead under the suspension bridge to the east. A subterranean murmuring began as a vibration in the soles of the feet, increased until it thrummed on his eardrums and welled over the horizon like the thunder of a gong. He raised his head and saw the warehouses on the left bank. The city beyond them was growing into the sky. First the towers of the municipal building ascended, and beyond them the hump of Rotten Row with all the tenement windows lit, and then the squat cathedral spire with tower and nave and a nearby cluster of Royal infirmary domes and beyond those, like the last section of a telescope, the tomb-rotten pile of the Necropolis slid up with the John Knox column overtopping the rest. The book in the hand of the stone man struck across the throbbing planet and a blue shadow sped from the book to Thaw's heart, chilling it. The city was forcing itself into the sky on every side. Factory, university, gasometer, slagbing, ridges of tenements, parks loaded with trees ascended until he looked up at a horizon like the rim of a bowl with himself at the bottom. The rim was crowded with watchers. He felt a rage of self-pity that so many were focussing on as few as he and saluted them with two fingers. One of the watchers left the rim and passed down out of sight behind rooftops. Thaw shut his eyes and imagined her descending the streets like a water drop sliding down the side of a basin, then he walked over the bridge and met her at Paisley's corner.

She smiled and took his arm and he was competent. He grinned to see himself shift his arm to her waist as they walked and how his remarks made her giggle. He flapped and tumbled in the air above their heads, helpless and screeching with laughter, then brought his beak close to an ear and made suggestions. They climbed a narrow road between staring crowds. Sometimes he recognized a face to the left or right, but he had to keep his whole attention on Marjory, feeding her with the talk which made her smile and being careful not to laugh. She did not notice that the hand holding hers was as senseless as granite and prevented by an effort from crushing her fingerbones. They crossed the rocking planks of the canal bridge, passed some warehouses and climbed a grassy slope. Thaw went first, pulling her behind. She was laughing when he forced her down and rubbed her body and neck with his stone hands. She struggled.
"Quick quick quick!" screamed the crow. "Cut her off quick."
He moved his stone mouth across her throat into the angle of the jaw near the ear and cut her off quick.

He woke in drizzling rain with a crust on his lips and something beside him he did not want to see. He attempted to fly home but was too breathless to do it for more than short distances, otherwise he crawled on the slimy towpath. Coming upstairs he kept falling from side to side and inside the house he lay on the lobby floor and started grunting, mainly for breath but partly for attention. He grunted louder and louder until a policeman broke the lock of the door. He expected to go to prison, but a doctor was there and they lifted and laid him in bed. The doctor gave a morphine injection and he fell into a sweet sleep. He woke in the Southern General Hospital and was nearly a fortnight there.

CHAPTER 30. Surrender

Lanark stared through the ward window at a bed which seemed a reflection of his own except that the figure in it was under the sheets. He said, "Did Thaw really kill someone or was that another hallucination?"

I'm only able to tell the story as he saw it.

"But did the police arrest him?"

No. In hospital he kept vaguely expecting them to, but they didn't come, which worried him. He wanted to get away from everything he knew, and arrest would have made that easy.

"Then it was a hallucination."

Not necessarily. In 1956 there were a hundred and fifty officially recognized murders in Britain, a third of them unsolved. Thaw certainly felt he had done something foul but denouncing himself to the police needed effort, so he thought as little and slept as much as possible. He didn't dream nowadays. His mind was under a cold bandage of dullness.

He had a bruised hand, malnutrition and bronchial asthma, and received cortisone steroids, a new drug which healed the asthma in two days. The other things took longer. The hospital almoner wanted to contact his father but Thaw withheld the address. He said he would visit Mr. Thaw when he got out, not really meaning to.

He was released, went home, and packed a small canvas knapsack with some clothes and a shaving kit.

"You said he had given up shaving."

He resumed it after the *Evening News* article in order not to look like his newspaper photograph. The knapsack contained one of Mr. Thaw's old compasses. With over nine pounds in his pocket he went to the bus station at the end of Parliamentary Road. He thought of going to London, of sliding down the globe into the cluttered and peopled south, but at the station the needle of his mental compass swung completely and pointed to the northern firths and mountains. He decided to visit his father after all.

Consider him passing along the route described at the start of Book One, Chapter 18 only he dozes most of the way and gets out at Glencoe village. He walks up a narrow road to the youth hostel, a road through a tunnel of branches. It is autumn, when the highlands are rich with purples, oranges and greeny-golds which would look gaudy if the grey light didn't soften them.
"Leave out the local colour."
All right.

It isn't yet five o'clock and some climbers are waiting on the hostel steps. Thaw walks round the side of the building to the warden's quarters at the back, but before knocking at the door he looks through a window. The room is a neat one with small watercolours of Loch Lomond on the walls which used to hang in the living room at Riddrie. He recognizes also a bookcase, writing desk and wooden tobacco jar carved in the shape of an owl. His father sits reading in an easy chair by a warm stove. There is a teapot under a cosy on a low table at his elbow, some cups, a cut-glass sugar bowl, milk jug and plate of biscuits. Two women sit on a sofa opposite. One is grey-haired and sixtyish; the other might be her daughter and is dark-haired and fortyish. The older woman knits, the younger reads. The quiet interior has a completeness, a calm contented polish, which Thaw feels should not be touched. He can break it, not add to it, so he finds a gap in the hedge leading to the road and returns to the village.

He has tea in a restaurant for tourists and wonders what to do. Going back to Glasgow feels impossible so he goes toward Fort William.

The lochside road is a dull one and at the dreary slate-bings by Ballachulish his breathing worsens and later makes him sit on a low wall beside a line of cars queuing for the ferry. An American lady stands by her car staring up the hill at a whitish stone thing like an old-fashioned petrol pump in

the woods above. She asks, "Do you know what that is?"
He tells her he thinks it marks the spot where Colin Campbell,
nicknamed the Red Fox, was murdered. She smiles slowly and
says, "Did I read about that in Robert Stevenson's *Kidnapped?*"
Thaw says it is possible. She says, "You don't look too well.
Can I do anything to help?"
He mentions the illness and says it will pass. She says, "My
husband is also a sufferer," and gets back into the car. Then
she comes out and hands him a paper tissue with some blue
and pink torpedo-shaped pellets in it. She says, "Try one of
these, they're new."
He swallows one and a moment later a happy warmth spreads
through him. He looks at her lovingly. She says, "Don't take
more than four a day, they can make you high. We're going
to Mallaig, can we give you a lift?"

He steps into a detached part of America. The seats seem
upholstered in soft buffalo hide, the climate is five degrees
above skin heat, somewhere a tiny orchestra is playing. The
engine is inaudible and, once over the ferry, the lochs and
mountains, like films projected onto the windows, pass backward at great speed. The driver, a taciturn man with a thick
neck, asks Thaw where he's heading. After a while Thaw says
he's going to Stirr. The lady says, "You may find Henry a
little taciturn. There's a blood clot in President Eisenhower's
brain and the market's responding badly."

Thaw shuts his eyes and dimly sees his father and sister
in a grey field. Mr. Thaw holds out a skein of wool which
his sister winds into a ball. When he opens his eyes it is dark
and the car climbs a long winding drive to a building like
Balmoral Castle but with a neon hotel sign on the front. He
is breathless again. The lady says, "We've looked up Stirr on
the map and you'll never make it tonight. We're going to stay
here and we suggest you do the same. It's a little expensive
but—"
She is clearly going to make a generous suggestion so Thaw
interrupts by saying that a good night's rest is worth any expense. They all get out of the car and enter the hotel. At the
reception desk he says he isn't hungry and will go straight to
bed. They bid him goodnight.

The hotel is vast and he is surprised by the smallness of
his room. He is very breathless but gets into bed, takes two
torpedo pills and sinks into sleep at once.

Twice or thrice next morning he dimly hears someone knocking and calling the time and he rises at last about eleven. He breathes easily but his mind is stupid, his body heavy. He has missed breakfast and takes coffee and toast uneasily in the corner of a huge lounge. He pays his bill at the reception desk and goes outside. The day is windy and overcast. A dislike of returning makes him unwilling to face the long drive-way; besides, the wind is pushing him the other way. He walks round the hotel and over some lawns, fingering the last half-crowns and coppers in his pocket. Passing a rectangular pool of waterlilies he flings them in. A path leads through a rhododendron shrubbery to a gate onto a moor. He goes through.

The moor rises to a ridge between two rocky hills. There is no path, and sometimes the heather gives way to mossy patches where his feet sink and squelch. He takes two or three hours to reach the ridge and rests on the leeward side of an untidy heap of stones. The heather before him slopes down to the ocean, but a hump of it hides the shore. He sees arms of land dividing the grey water, some patched with fields, others rocky and sloping up into mountains. He thinks one might be Ben Rua. He notices that a nearby stone in the heap has a surface carved with words:

Upon
THIS SPOT
King Edward
had lunch after stalking
28th August, 1902

For some reason this seems funny and he laughs a lot but isn't really happy. He takes another pill which makes him slightly happy, but not much, so he throws the rest away. The wind feels colder. He stands and idly consults the compass. The needle directs him downhill.

After walking for a while he sees the ground sloping away on each side as well as in front. He seems to be on a promontory, but the wind and the slope and his instinct make it easier to go on. The promontory ends in many little cliffs with slopes of heather and tumbled rocks between. Descent is easy at first, then he comes to steeper rocks and must scramble down gullies of loose stones that collapse and slide. He falls the last few yards and lies under boulders among withered bracken, thinking, I'm sore and don't like it. There is a bleeding scratch along one leg and a shoulder aches. He feels sticky and sweating, his heart hammers and he thinks, I need a bath. He pulls off knapsack, coat, jacket, jersey, and then feels the cold and walks down a steep beach of big pebbles like stone eggs and potatoes. They slide awkwardly. He stumbles across them.

The first wave is no shock but the beach shelves steeply and the next, which is large and sudden, slaps his chest, floats him off his legs and knocks him backward onto the sliding pebbles in two or three feet of water. He rises spluttering, the shirt sticking and rasping on his skin. Laughing with rage he pulls it off and wades out against the sea shouting, *"You can't get rid of me!"* He bows his head into the slapping waves, struggles through them with his arms and finds he is rising higher and higher out of the water. His feet are on a submerged ridge, he is waist deep when he reaches the end and steps forward onto fluid. He wallows under, gasping and tumbling over and over in salt sting, knowing nothing but the need not to breathe. A humming drumming fills his brain, in panic he opens eyes and glimpses green glimmers through salt sting. And when at last, like fingernails losing clutch on too narrow a ledge, he, tumbling, yells out last dregs of breath and has to breathe, there flows in upon him, not pain, but annihilating sweetness.

By Arts is formed that great Mechanical Man called a State, foremost of the Beasts of the Earth for Pride

FORCE

BOOK
FOUR

THE MATTER,
FORM AND POWER of
a COMMONWEALTH

CHAPTER 31. Nan

Lanark opened his eyes and looked thoughtfully round the ward. The window was covered again by the Venetian blind and a bed in one corner was hidden by screens. Rima sat beside him eating figs from a brown paper bag. He said, "That was very unsatisfying. I can respect a man who commits suicide after killing someone (it's clearly the right thing to do) but not a man who drowns himself for a fantasy. Why did the oracle not make clear which of these happened?"

Rima said, "What are you talking about?"

"The oracle's account of my life before Unthank. He's just finished it."

Rima said firmly, "In the first place that oracle was a woman, not a man. In the second place her story was about me. You were so bored that you fell asleep and obviously dreamed something else."

He opened his mouth to argue but she popped a fig in, saying, "It's a pity you didn't stay awake because she told me a lot about you. You were a funny, embarrassing, not very sexy boy who kept chasing me when I was nineteen. I had the sense to marry someone else."

"And you!" cried Lanark, angrily swallowing, "were a frigid cock-teasing virgin who kept shoving me off with one hand and dragging me back with the other. I killed someone because I couldn't get you."

"We must have been listening to different oracles. I'm sure you imagined all that. Is there anything else to eat?"

"No. We used it all up."

With a clattering of purposeful feet a stretcher was pushed into the ward among a crowd of doctors and nurses. Munro

marched in front; technicians followed dragging cylinders and
apparatus. They went behind the screens in the corner and
nothing could be heard but low hissing and some phrases which
seemed to have drifted from the corridors.

". . . the conceived conceiving in mid conception . . ."

". . . . . inglorious Milton, guiltless Cromwell . . . . ."

"Why inglorious? Why not guilty?"

"She came naked. That helped."

Munro came over and stood at the bed's foot regarding them
gravely. He said, "I've arranged a meeting with Lord Monboddo three hours from now to authorize your departure from
the institute. I had meant you to wait here till then but we've
had an unexpected delivery of human beings. They're in good
condition, but feeble, and will die if someone puts them off
their food. A nurse is bringing your clothes. You can dress
and wait in the staff club."

"No need," said Lanark. "We wouldn't spread our opinions
in a case like this."

Munro asked Rima, "Do you agree?"

"Of course, but I'd like to see the staff club."

"If I can trust you I'd like you to stay here. This is a lonely
ward and company would help the woman feel at home."

Rima said brightly, "I'll be delighted to help you, Dr. Munro,
but will you do something for us? Get Monsignor Noakes to
send more of his lovely food. It will be easy to not mention
food when we have some."

Munro walked away saying grimly, "I promise nothing, but
I'll do what I can."

Lanark stared at her and said, "You are unscrupulous!"

She asked in a hurt voice, "Aren't you glad I'm not like
you?"

"Very glad."

"Then show it, please."

They heard the technicians and their apparatus leave the
ward. Only a few doctors were busy behind the screens when
a nurse came to Rima and Lanark with an armful of clothes
and a couple of fat rucksacks and said, "Dr. Munro wants you
to dress now. He says the rucksacks are full of food for your
journey and you can start eating it when you like."

Rima seized the female garments and stroked them with her
fingertips. They were blond and velvety. A small excited smile
curved her lips. She sprang naked from bed, saying, "I'll dress
in the bathroom." She ran to the door at the end of the ward

and Lanark examined the rucksacks. Each contained a rolled-up leather overcoat and hard little blocks of compressed fruit and meat wrapped in rice paper. One held a red thermos flask of coffee and a flat steel flask of brandy, the other a first-aid kit and an electric torch. Departure from this far too warm, too insulated place seemed disturbingly near. Lanark got up and carried his clothes to the bathroom.

Rima stood before a mirror, brushing her hair downward over a shoulder with slow, even strokes. She wore a short, amber-coloured, long-sleeved dress, and sandals of yellow leather, and Lanark stood half-hypnotized by her cool golden elegant figure. She murmured, "Well?"
He said, "Not bad," and started washing at a basin.
"Why don't you say I'm beautiful?"
"When I do you disparage me."
"Yes, but I feel lonely when you don't."
"All right. You're beautiful."
He dried himself and began putting on a grey tweed suit and pullover. She tied her hair carefully with a dark yellow ribbon, looking sad and thoughtful. He kissed her and said, "Cheer up! You're the light and I'm the shadow. Aren't you glad we're different?"
She pulled a face and went out, saying, "It's hard to shine without encouragement."

When he re-entered the ward, the doctors, nurses and screens had gone and Rima was talking to a woman in the corner bed. He joined them, noticing a small bald wrinkled head sticking from under a coverlet. The mother lay half sunk in a bank of pillows. Her body was slight, there were grey glints in her brown hair and youth and age were equally mingled in her gaunt little face. She smiled wanly and said, "It's strange seeing you again, mystery man."
He stared blankly. Rima said, "It's Nancy. Don't you remember Nan?"
He sat by the bed almost laughing with surprise. He said, "I'm glad you escaped from the Elite."
He could not stop grinning. Since entering the institute he had forgotten Sludden and his harem, and now these tangled love-lives seemed wonderfully funny. He pointed at the cot. "You've a nice-looking baby."
"Yes! Isn't she like her father?"
"Don't be silly," said Rima gently. "Babies aren't like people.

Who is the father anyway? Toal?"
"Of course not."
"Then who is he?"
"Sludden."
Rima peered at what was visible of the baby's face.
"Are you sure?"
Nan smiled sadly. "Oh, yes. I wasn't his fiancée, like Gay, or
his vulgar mistress, like Frankie, or his clever mistress, like
you. I was the poor little girl he had been kind to, but he
loved me most, though I had to keep that a secret. Whenever
I was tired of being neglected and tried to escape he would
come to my lodgings and climb drainpipes and break in through
windows. Sludden was tremendously athletic. He would hold
me tight and tell me that though we'd slept together so often
our lovemaking was still fresh and adventurous and it would
be stupid to give it up because of the other girls. He said he
needed all of you so that he could be lively with me. He was
the first man I ever loved and I never really wanted anyone
else, though I was always planning to leave him, before my
illness got bad."
"What illness?"
"I began to grow mouths, not just in my face but in other
places, and when I was alone they argued and shouted and
screamed at me. Sludden was very good with them. He could
always get them singing in tune, and when we slept together
he even made me glad of them. He said he'd never known a
girl who could be pierced in so many places."
Nan smiled in an almost motherly way and Lanark, with a
pang of jealousy, saw the same soft, remembering look on Rima's face. Nan sighed and said, "But they drove even Sludden
away in the end (the mouths did), because as I grew worse I
needed him more and he didn't like that. He was going into
politics and he had a lot to do."
Lanark and Rima cried out together, "Politics?" and Rima said,
"He always made fun of people who went into politics."
"I know, but when you disappeared he replaced you with a
protest girl, a big brassy blonde who played the guitar and
kept telling us her father was a brigadier. I didn't like her at
all. She said we should prepare to seize the reins of the economy,
and it was very important to care for people, but she always
talked too much to listen to anyone. While she was speaking
Sludden would wink at us behind her back. A lot of the Elite
crowd went protestant then. Hundreds of new cliques appeared
with names and badges I can't even remember. Even criminals

wore badges. Suddenly Sludden came in wearing a badge
and laughing his head off. He'd gone with the blonde to a
protest meeting and been elected to a committee. He said we
should all become protestants because nobody had confidence
nowadays in Provost Dodd and we had a real chance of seizing
the city. None of that made sense to me. You see I was pregnant
and Sludden wouldn't allow me near enough to tell him. When
I managed it at last he grew very serious. He said it was a
crime to bring children into the world before it had been redeemed by revolution. He wanted the baby killed before it
was born but I wouldn't allow that. Pass her to me, please."
Rima lifted the baby into Nan's arms. It opened its eyes, gave
a small mew of complaint and returned to sleep against her
breast. She said, "He called me selfish, and he was right, I
suppose. I had never known anyone who wanted me before
I met Sludden, and now he didn't want me at all, and I needed
someone else, though the thought of the coming baby often
made me quite mad and sick. I felt I was being crushed under
a whole pile of women with Sludden jumping up and down
on top, wearing a crown and laughing. Then the baby would
move inside me and I would suddenly feel calm and complete.
I was sorry for Sludden then. He seemed a frantic greedy child
running everywhere looking for breasts to grab and mothers
to feed him and who would never, never have enough. Did
you feel that, Rima?"
Rima said shortly, "No."
"Why did you like him so much?"
"He was clever and amusing and kind. He was the only man
among us who hadn't a disease."
Lanark said, "He had no disease because he *was* a disease.
He was a cancer afflicting everyone who knew him."
Rima snorted. "Huh, you don't know who you're talking about.
Sludden liked you. He tried to help you, but you wouldn't
let him."
Nan smiled. "You're making Lanark jealous."
"Oh yes, she's making me jealous. But I can be jealous and
correct."
Rima said, "How did you get here, Nancy?"
"Well, I was in my lodgings when the pains began and I knew
my baby was coming. I asked the landlord to help but he was
frightened and ordered me out of the house, so I shut myself
in my room and managed (I can't remember how) to drag a
heavy wardrobe in front of the door. That nearly killed me.
The pains were so bad I fell down and couldn't move. I was

sure the baby had died after all. I felt I was nothing then, nothing and nobody, a nobody feeling nothing but horror, a piece of dirt as evil as the world. I suppose I screamed to get out because an opening appeared in the floor beside me."

Lanark shuddered and said, "Going through *that* nearly killed me. I knew a soldier who jumped in with his revolver and was gored to death by it. I don't see how a pregnant woman could survive at all."

"But it was easy. It was like sinking through warm dark water that could be breathed. Every bit of me was supported. I still felt the labour pains but they weren't sore, they were like bursts of music. I felt my little girl break free and float up to my breast and cling there. No, she must have drifted down for I was coming head first. I felt all kinds of muck flow out of me and vanish in the darkness. That darkness loved me. It was only when the light returned that the music became pain again and I fainted. That was a long time ago, and here I am, talking to you, in a lovely clean room."

Lanark said abruptly, "You'll be well cared for here."

He rose and walked through the nearest archway. Nan's story had recalled his own crushing descent in a way which made him long for sunlit landscapes of hill and water. Hopefully he raised the great Venetian blind, but the screen he had once thought a window was no longer there. In the centre of the wall, from floor to ceiling, was a double door of dark wood with panels of ornamental bronze. He pressed it but it was immovable, without handles or keyhole. He returned to the ward.

Nan breast-fed the baby and gossiped quietly to Rima. Lanark sat on his bed and tried to finish *The Holy War* but found it irritating. The writer was unable to imagine an honest enemy, and his only notion of virtue was total obedience to his strongest character. A nurse brought Nancy's lunch. She only ate part and a moment later Lanark was startled to see Rima eat the rest, glancing at him defiantly between forkfuls. He pretended not to notice and nibbled a block of dense black chocolate from the rucksack. The sour taste was so unwelcome that he lay down and tried to sleep, but his imagination projected cityscapes on the insides of his eyelids: sliding views of stadiums, factories, prisons, palaces, squares, boulevards and bridges. Nancy and Rima's conversation seemed like the murmur of distant crowds with fanfares sounding through it. He opened his eyes. The noise was not imaginary. An increasing

din of trumpets shook the air. Lanark stood up and so did
Rima. The trumpets grew deafening, then silent as a black
and silver figure entered and stood under the central arch. It
was a man in a black silver-buttoned coat, black knee breeches
and white stockings. He wore white lace at the throat and
wrists, silver-buckled shoes and a snowy periwig with a three-
cornered black hat on top. He held a portfolio in his left hand
and in his right an ebony staff tipped with a silver knob. His
face was the most surprising thing about him for it was Munro's.
Lanark said, "Dr. Munro!"
"At the moment I am not a doctor, I am a chamberlain. Bring
your rucksacks."
Lanark slung a rucksack on his shoulder and carried the other
in his hand. Rima said goodbye to Nan, who was comforting
her crying baby. Munro turned and rapped his staff against
the great doors, which clanged and swung inward. Munro led
them through, Rima pressing against Lanark's side. The doors
closed.

CHAPTER 32.
Council Corridors

They were in a wood-panelled, low-ceilinged, circular room, thickly carpeted and smelling like an old railway carriage. An upholstered bench went round the wall and a mahogany pillar in the centre supported a bald bronze head wearing a laurel wreath. Munro said loudly, "The northern lobby."

The head nodded and a faint rumbling began. Lanark realized they were in a carriage travelling sideways. Munro said, "The machinery joining the institute to the council chambers is rather antiquated. Take a seat, we'll be some minutes here."

They sat and Rima murmured, "Isn't this exciting?"

Lanark nodded. He felt strong and sure of himself and thought that a lord president director could have frightened him once, but not now. He was too old. Munro was pacing round the pedestal and Lanark called out, "Where do we go when we've seen Lord Monboddo?"

"We'll see what he says first."

"But these rucksacks have been packed for a particular kind of journey!"

"You're leaving at your own request, so you'll have to travel on foot. It's too late to discuss it now."

The doors opened and someone dressed like Munro led in two plump men in evening dress. Soon after the lift stopped again and another chamberlain brought in a group of worried men in crumpled suits. The three chamberlains talked quietly by the pedestal while the rest babbled in clusters on the bench.

". . . not honouring us, it's the creature he's honouring . . ."

"His secretary is an algolagnics man."

". . . . . but he'll maintain the differential. . . . ."

"If he doesn't he's opening the floodgates to a free-for-all."
Munro approached Lanark and said grimly, "Bad luck! I expected to have the director to ourselves but he's receiving a deputation and conferring a couple of titles. He's available for ten minutes, I'll have to settle our business in three, so when we leave the lift stay close to me and say as little as possible."
"But this meeting will shape our whole future!"
"Don't worry, I won't let you down."
The doors opened and the chamberlains led them out onto such a bright floor that Lanark's heart lurched, thinking he was in open daylight.

It was a floor of coloured marble inlaid in geometrical patterns. It was nearly a quarter of a mile across, but as the eye took in the height of the ceiling the width seemed insignificant. It was an octagonal hall where eight great corridors met below a dome, and looking down them was like looking down streets of renaissance palaces. The place seemed empty at first, but when his eyes got used to the scale Lanark noticed a great many people moving like insects about the corridor floors. The air was cool and, except for the remote sonorous echoes of distant footfalls, refreshingly quiet. Lanark looked around with open mouth. Rima sighed, slid her fingers out of his and stepped elegantly away across the marble floor. She seemed to grow taller and more graceful as she receded. Her figure and colouring blended perfectly with her surroundings. Lanark followed, saying, "This place suits you."
"I know."
She turned and walked past him, smoothing the amber velvet over her hips, her chin raised and face dreamy. Feeling excluded he stared around once more. Some benches upholstered in red leather lay about the floor and Munro sat on the nearest looking intently along a corridor, the staff and portfolio across his knees. Some distance behind stood a wooden medieval throne on top of three marble steps. The other chamberlains had brought their parties to it, and now the plump men in evening dress knelt side by side on the lowest step in an attitude of prayer. Close by, with folded arms, the deputation stood in a tight cluster. Their chamberlain was photographing them. Rima continued walking past Lanark in an aimless dreamy way till he said sharply, "It's impressive, of course, but not beautiful. Look, at those chandeliers! Hundreds of tons of brass and glass pretending to be gold and diamonds and they don't even light

the place. The real light comes from behind the columns round the walls. I bet it's neon."

"You're jealous because you don't belong here."

He was hurt by the truth of this and said in a low voice, "Quite right."

She laid a hand on his chest and stared excitedly into his eyes. "But Lanark, we could live here if you wanted to! I'm sure they'd give you a job, you can be very clever when you try! Tell Munro you want to stay. I'm sure it's not too late!"

"You've forgotten there's no sunlight here and we don't like the food."

Rima said wistfully, "Yes, I had forgotten that."

She walked away from him again.

He sat beside Munro and tried to keep calm by looking up into the deep blue dome. It was painted with angels blowing trumpets and scattering blossoms around figures on clouds. He specially noted four ponderous horsemen on some puffs of cumulus. They wore Roman armour, curly wigs and laurel wreaths and managed the horses with their knees, for each held a sword in the left hand and a mason's trowel in the right. On similar clouds facing them stood four venerable men in togas holding scrolls and queerly shaped walking sticks. Both groups were gazing at the height of the dome where a massive man sat upon a throne. His strong face looked benevolent, but something peering in it suggested he was shortsighted or deaf. The painter had tried to distract from this by loading him with impressive instruments. A globe lay in his lap and a sword across his knees. He held scales in one hand and a trowel in the other. An eagle with a thunderbolt in its beak hovered over his head and an owl looked out from under the hem of his robe. A turbaned Indian, a Red Indian, a Negro and a Chinaman knelt before him with gifts of spice, tobacco, ivory and silk. Lanark heard Munro ask, "Do you like it?"

"Not much. Who are these horsemen?"

"Nimrod, Imhotep, Tsin-Shi Hwang and Augustus, early presidents of the council. Of course the titles were different then."

"Why the wigs and armour?"

"An eighteenth-century convention—the mural was painted then. The men facing them are former directors of the institute: Prometheus, Pythagoras, Aquinas and Descartes. The figure on the throne is the first Lord Monboddo. He was an insignificant legislator and an unimportant philosopher, but when council and institute combined he was a member of both, which made him symbolically useful. He knew Adam Smith."

"But what is the institute? What is the council?

"The council is a political structure to lift men nearer Heaven. The institute is a conspiracy of thinkers to bring the light of Heaven down to mankind. They've sometimes been distinct organizations and have even quarrelled, though never for long. The last great reconciliation happened during the Age of Reason, and two world wars have only united us more firmly."

"But what is this heavenly light? If you mean the sun, why doesn't it shine here?"

"Oh, in recent years the heavenly light has never been confused with an actual *sun*. It is a metaphor, a symbol we no longer need. Since the collapse of feudalism we've left long-term goals to our enemies. They're misleading. Society develops faster without them. If you look closely into the dome, you'll see that though the artist painted a sun in the centre it's almost hidden by the first Monboddo's crown. Stand up, here comes the twenty-ninth."

A tall man in a pale grey suit was crossing the smooth marble floor accompanied by three men in dark suits. A herald in medieval tabard marched in front with a sword on a velvet cushion; another came behind carrying a coloured silk robe. The whole party was advancing briskly to the throne when Munro stepped into the path and bowed saying, "Hector Munro, my lord."

Monboddo had a long narrow face with a thin, high-bridged nose. His hair was pale yellow and his eyes grey behind gold-rimmed spectacles, yet his voice was richly, resonantly masculine. He said, "Yes, I know. I never forget a face. Well?"

"This man and woman have applied for relocation."

Munro handed his portfolio to someone at Monboddo's side, who pulled out a document and read it. Monboddo glanced from Lanark to Rima.

"Relocation? Extraordinary. Who's going to take them?"

"Unthank is keen."

"Well, if they understand the dangers, let them go. Let them go. Is that paper in order, Wilkins?"

"In perfect order, sir."

Wilkins held out the document at an angle supported by the portfolio. Monboddo glanced at it and made snatching movements with his right hand until Munro placed a pen between the fingers. He was going to sign when Lanark shouted, "Stop!"

Monboddo looked at him with raised eyebrows. Lanark turned on Munro and cried, "You know we don't want to return to Unthank! There's no sunlight in Unthank! I asked for a town with sunlight!"

"A man with your reputation can't be allowed to pick and choose."

Monboddo said, "Has his chief given him a poor report?"

"A very poor report."

There was a silence in which Lanark felt something vital being filched from him. He said fiercely, "If that report was written by Ozenfant it ought not to count. We dislike each other."

Munro murmured, "It is written by Ozenfant."

Monboddo touched his brow with a fingertip. Wilkins murmured, "The dragonmaster. A strong energy man."

"I know, I know. I never forget a name. An abominable musician but an excellent administrator. Here's your pen, Munro. Uxbridge, give me that cape, will you?"

A herald placed a heavy green cloak lined with crimson silk round Monboddo's shoulders and helped him adjust the folds. Monboddo said, "No, we won't go against Ozenfant. Look, Wilkins, sort this out while I attend to these other chaps. We haven't much time, you know."

Monboddo strode onward to the throne, the cape billowing behind him. Most of his retinue followed.

Wilkins was a dark, short, compact man. He said, "What seems to be the problem?"

Munro said crisply, "Mr. Lanark does not know what relocation involves. He has asked to leave. I have found a city whose government will take him in spite of his poor record. He refuses to go because of the climate."

Lanark said obstinately, "I want sunlight."

"Would Provan suit you?" asked Wilkins.

"I know nothing of Provan."

"It is an industrial centre surrounded by farming country but in easy distance of highlands and sea. The climate is mild and damp with a yearly average of twelve hours' sunlight per day. The inhabitants speak a kind of English."

"Yes, we'll go there gladly."

Munro said, "Provan won't take him. Provan was the first place I asked."

Wilkins said, "Provan will have to take him if he goes to Unthank first."

Munro rubbed his chin and began to smile. "Of course. I had forgotten."

Wilkins turned to Lanark and said smoothly, "Industrially speaking, you see, Unthank is no longer profitable, so it is going to be scrapped and swallowed. In a piecemeal way we've been doing that for years, but now we can take it *en bloc* and I don't mind telling you we're rather excited. We're used to eating towns and villages but this will be the first big city since Carthage and the energy gain will be enormous. Of course people like you who've joined us already won't need to go through that messy business again. You'll be moved to Provan, which has a lively expanding economy. So visit Unthank with a clear mind. Think of it as a stepping stone to the sun."

"But how long will we have to live there?"

Wilkins glanced at his wristwatch.

"In eight days a full meeting of council delegates will give the go-ahead. We start work two days after."

"Then Rima and I will be in Unthank for twelve days?"

"No longer. Only a revolution can change our programme now."

"But I've heard Unthank is a more political place nowadays. Are you sure a revolution can't happen?"

Wilkins smiled.

"I meant that only a revolution *here* can change our programme."

"But have I no other choices?"

"Stay with us if you like. We can find work for you. Or leave and just wander about. Space is infinite to men without destinations."

Lanark groaned and said, "Rima, what should we do?"

She shrugged impatiently.

"Oh, don't ask me! You know I like it here and that hasn't influenced you so far. But I refuse to wander about in space. If you want to do that you can do it alone."

Lanark said in a subdued voice, "Right. We'll return to Unthank."

Wilkins and Munro straightened their backs and spoke in louder voices. Wilkins slid the paper into the portfolio and said, "Leave this with me, Hector. Monboddo will sign it."

Munro said, "They'd better not go without visas."

"Give me the ink, I'll stamp them."

Munro unscrewed the silver knob from his staff (it was shaped like a pair of spread wings) and held it upside down. Wilkins stuck his thumb in the socket and drew it out with a glistening blue tip. Rima was leaning forward to watch and Wilkins dabbed his thumb at her forehead, making a mark between the brows

like a small blue bruise. She gave a little shriek of surprise.
Wilkins said, "That didn't hurt, did it? Now you, Lanark."
Lanark, too depressed to ask for explanations, received a similar
mark; then Wilkins put his thumb in the knob a second time
and brought it out clean. He said, "It's not a conspicuous sign
but it tells educated people that you've worked for the institute
and are protected by the council. They won't all like you for
that but they'll treat you with respect, and when Unthank falls
you'll have no trouble getting transport to Provan."
Rima said, "Will it wash off?"
"No, only strong sunlight can erase it, and you won't find
that till you reach Provan. Goodbye."
He walked away across the floor, diminishing toward the tiny
distant throne where Monboddo, like a green and scarlet doll,
was graciously receiving a paper from the leader of the pygmy
deputation. Munro screwed the knob onto his staff and beckoned Rima and Lanark in the opposite direction.

Beyond the northern lobby the corridor was crossed by
a wrought-iron screen ten feet high. A gate in the middle was
guarded by a policeman who saluted as Munro led them
through. The corridor grew busier. Black and silver chamberlains led past small groups of people, some of them negro and
oriental. From windows overhead came the applause of distant
assemblies, faint orchestras and fanfares, the rumble and hum
of machinery. Brisk, well-dressed men and women came and
went through doorways on either side, and Lanark's rucksacks
made him feel unnatural among so many people carrying brief-
cases and portfolios. If Rima had offered to carry hers he would
have felt he had an ally, but she moved along the corridor
like a swan down a stream. Even Munro seemed a servant
clearing the way for her, and Lanark felt he would be unkind
not to trudge alongside like a porter. After twenty minutes
they came to another high octagonal hall where corridors met.
The blue dome here was patterned with stars and a lamp in
the height cast a white beam down on a granite monument
in the centre of the floor, a rough block carved with giant
figures and with water trickling from it into ornamental pools.
Girls and boys lounged smoking and chatting on steps surrounding this, and on the smooth tiled floor older people ate and
drank at tables among orange-trees in tubs. Soft laughter and
music sounded from windows overhead and blended with the
conversation, clinking cutlery, splashing fountains and whistling
of canaries from cages in the little trees.

Munro halted and said, "What do you think of it?"

Lanark no longer trusted Munro. He said, "It's better than the staff club," but the leisurely air of the place made his heart swell and eyes water. He thought, 'Everyone should be allowed to enjoy this. In sunlight it would be perfect.'

Munro said, "Since we're beside the exit we may as well rest while I give you advice on your journey."

He stuck his staff into the soil of a tub, sat at a table and beckoned a waiter. Rima and Lanark sat down too. Munro said, "I suppose you won't refuse a light refreshment?"

Rima said, "I'd love it."

Lanark looked round for the exit. Munro said, "Lanark appears to be angry with me."

Rima laughed. "No wonder! I liked hearing him argue with you and Monboddo and that secretary. I thought 'Good! I'm being defended by a strong man!' But you were too clever for him, weren't you?"

"He won't lose by it."

As Munro ordered from the waiter Lanark had the feeling of being watched. At nearby tables sat a mother, her twelve-year-old son and an old couple playing chess. None of these seemed specially attentive, so he gazed up at the rows of windows above the doors where waiters ran in and out. They were curtained with white gauze and seemed empty, but overhead, not far below the dome, a balcony projected and a group of men and women in evening dress were leaning over the parapet. The distance was too great to distinguish faces but a stout man in the centre dominated the party with wide gestures of the hands and arms, and appeared to point in Lanark's direction. Something like a pair of binoculars was produced and clapped to the face of a woman at the stout man's side. Feeling exasperated Lanark seized a newspaper on a nearby chair, opened it and started reading, presenting the back of his head to the watchers above. The paper was called *The Western Lobby* and was soberly printed in neat columns without spreading headlines or large photographs. Lanark read:

ALABAMA JOINS THE COUNCIL

By accepting the creature's help in constructing the continent's largest neuron energy bank, New Alabama becomes the fifth black state to be fully represented on the council. Inevitably this will strengthen the hand of Multan of Zimbabwe, leader of the council's black bloc. Asked last night if this would not lead to increased friction in the council's already unwieldy conferences, the president, Lord Monboddo, said, "All movement creates friction if it doesn't happen in a vacuum."

Farther down the page his eye was caught by a name he knew.

OZENFANT RAMPANT

When presenting the energy department's quinquennial audit yesterday, Professor Ozenfant roundly condemned the council's adoption of decimal time. The old duodecimal time scale (declared the fiery Professor) had been more than an arbitrary subdivision of the erratic and unstable solar day. The duodecimal second had allowed more accurate readings of the human heartbeat than decimal seconds. Predictions of deterioration on the decimal scale had a 1.063 greater liability to error, which accounted for the recent reduction in the energy surplus. Sabotage by a rogue element in the intake had also been responsible, but the main culprit was the new time scale. Professor Ozenfant insisted that his words must not be taken as a criticism of Lord Monboddo. In committing us to decimal time the lord president director had simply ratified the findings of the expansion project committee. It was unfortunate that nobody in that committee had first-hand experience of the lonely, difficult and dangerous work of sublimating dragons. The whole business was one more example of a council rule undermining an institute process.

Lanark folded the paper into his pocket and peered upward again. The party still leaned upon the balcony wall, and the gestures of the man in the centre had a familiar, mocking, flamboyant quality. Rima had accepted a cigarette from Munro who was holding a lighter to the tip. Lanark said sharply, "Is that Ozenfant watching us? There, on the balcony?"

Munro looked upward.

"Ozenfant? I don't know. It's hardly likely; he isn't popular on the eighth floor. It might be one of his imitators."

"Why do people imitate him if he isn't popular?"

"He's successful."

The waiter placed a full glass of wine before each of them and a plate of something like an omelette. Rima took her fork and began eating. After a gloomy pause Lanark was about to follow her example when there came a sound of booing, laughter and ironical cheers. Along the space between the tables and the monument marched a procession of shaggy young men and women holding placards with slogans:

EAT RICE, NOT PEOPLE

EATING PEOPLE IS WRONG

FUCK MONBODDO

MONBODDO CAN'T FUCK

A policeman marched on either side and behind them slid a platform loaded with men and filming equipment.

"Protestants," said Munro without looking up. "They march every day to the barrier about this time."

"Who are they?"

"Council employees or children of council employees."

"What do *they* eat?"

"The same as everyone else, though that doesn't stop their denouncing us. Their arguments are ludicrous, of course. We don't eat people. We eat the processed parts of certain life forms which can no longer claim to be people."

Lanark saw Rima push her plate away. There was a tearful look on her face, and when he reached out and grasped her hand she grasped his in turn. He said sternly, "You were going to give us advice about our journey."

Munro looked at them, sighed and laid down his fork. "Very well. You will walk to Unthank across the intercalendrical zone. This means the time you take is unpredictable. The road is fairly distinct, so keep to it and trust nothing you can't test

with your own feet or hands. The light in this zone travels at
different speeds, so all sizes and distances are deceptive. Even
the gravity varies."
"Then the journey could take months?"
"I repeat, you will cross an intercalendrical zone. A month is
as meaningless there as a minute or a century. The journey
will simply be easy or strenuous or a combination of both."
"What if our supplies give out?"
"Some reports suggest that people who find the journey difficult
reach the other side in the moment of final despair."
Rima said faintly, "Thank you. That's very encouraging."
"Better put your coats on. It's cold down there."

The coats were ankle-length with hoods and a thick fleecy
lining. They pulled on their rucksacks, smiled anxiously at each
other, kissed quickly, then followed Munro across the floor
and up the steps to the monument. The giant rock overhung
the steps like a boulder balanced on a pyramid. Shadows cast
by the light defined figures brooding in crevices, declaiming
from ledges and emerging from a cave in the centre. A figure
on top seemed to represent the sculptor. His face looked up
at the light but his fists drove a chisel with a mallet into the
stone between his knees. Lanark touched Munro's shoulder
and asked what this represented.
"The Hebrew pantheon: Moses, Isaiah, Christ, Marx, Freud
and Einstein."
They passed through a group of young people who stared and
murmured, "Where are they going?" "The emergency exit?"
"Look at those crazy coats!" Surely not the emergency exit!"
Someone shouted, "What's the emergency, Granddad?"
Munro said, "No emergency, just relocation. A simple case
of relocation."
There was silence then a voice said, "They're insane."
They reached the summit where water trickled down into gold-
fish ponds. The great boulder was supported by a surprisingly
small pedestal with an iron door in it. Munro struck the door
with his staff. It opened. They stooped and passed through.

CHAPTER 33. A Zone

In watery green light, between narrow cement walls, they descended a metal staircase for many minutes. The air grew chilly and at length they came into a cavernous low-ceilinged place which gave a sense of width without spaciousness, for the floor was covered by pipes and tubes of every size from the height of a man to the thickness of a finger, while the ceiling was hidden by cables and ventilation ducts. They emerged from a door in a brick pillar onto a metal walkway leading across the pipes. Munro moved down this and Lanark and Rima followed, sometimes clambering over an unusually large pipe by an arched metal ladder. For a long time the only sound was a distant pulsing hum mingled with gurgles and clanking and their echoing footsteps. Rima said, "This bending hurts my back."

"I see a wall in the distance. We'll soon be out of here."

"Oh, Lanark, how dreary this is! I was excited when we went up to Monboddo. I expected a glamorous new life. Now I don't know what to expect, except horror and dullness."

Lanark felt that too. He said, "It's just a zone we've got to cross. Tomorrow, or the next day, we'll be in Unthank."

"I hope so. At least we've friends there."

"What friends?"

"Our friends at the Elite."

"I hope we can make better friends than those."

"You're a snob, Lanark. I knew you were insensitive, but I never thought you were a snob."

They forgot their misery in the heat of a small quarrel until the walkway reached a platform before an iron door in a wall of damp-streaked cement. It was the first door they had

seen for many days with hinges and a key in the lock. It was
stencilled with large red letters:

EMERGENCY EXIT 3124
DANGER! DANGER! DANGER! DANGER!
YOU ARE ABOUT TO ENTER
AN INTERCALENDRICAL
ZONE

Munro turned the key and opened the door. Lanark expected
darkness but his eyes were dazzled by an amazingly bright white
mist. A road began at the threshold with a yellow stripe down
the middle, but it was only visible for five or six feet ahead.
He stepped outside and a wave of coldness hit his face
and hands making him draw deep breaths of freezing air. They
exalted him. He cried, "It's good to be in the open at last!
Surely the sun is up there!"
"Several suns are up there."
"There's only one sun, Munro."
"It's been shining a long time. The light of many days keeps
returning to zones like this."
"Then it ought to be even brighter."
"No. When light rays meet at certain speeds and angles they
negate each other."
"I'm not a scientist, that means nothing to me. Come on, Rima."
"Goodbye Lanark. Maybe you'll trust me when you're a little
older."
Lanark didn't answer. The door slammed behind him.

       They walked into the mist guided by the yellow line on
the road between them. Lanark said, "I feel like singing. Do
you know any marching songs?"
"No. This rucksack hurts my back and my hands are freezing."
Lanark peered into the thick whiteness and sniffed the breeze.
The landscape was invisible but he could smell sea air and
hear waves in the distance. The road seemed to rise steeply
for it became difficult to walk fast, so he was surprised to see
Rima vanishing into the mist a few paces ahead. With an effort
he came beside her. She didn't seem to be running, but her
strides covered great distances. He caught her elbow and
gasped, "How can . . . you go . . . so quickly?"
She stopped and stared.
"It's easy, downhill."
"We're going uphill."
"You're mad."

Each stared at the other's face for a sign that they were joking until Rima backed away saying fearfully, "Keep off! You're mad!"

He stepped after her and felt acutely dizzy. At the same time something shoved him sideways. He staggered but kept his feet and stood swaying a little. He said weakly, "Rima. The road slopes downhill on this side of the line and uphill on the other."

"That's impossible!"

"I know. But it does. Try it."

She came near, put a foot hesitantly across, then withdrew it saying, "All right, I believe you."

"But why not test it? Hold my hand."

"Since we're both on the downhill side we may as well keep to it. We'll travel faster."

She began walking and he followed.

He now had sensations of descending steeply. Each stride covered more and more ground until he shouted, "Rima! Stop! Stop!"

"I'll fall if I try to stop!"

"We'll fall if we don't. It's getting too steep. Give me your hand."

They grabbed hands, dug heels in, slithered to a standstill and stood precariously swaying. He said, "We'll have to take this slowly and carefully. I'll go first."

He released her hand, stepped slowly and carefully forward, his feet slid from under him, he grabbed her for support and pulled her heavily down. They rolled over each other then he was tumbling sideways with a rhythmical bumping each time the rucksack passed under his body. When he came to rest and managed to stand up the ground seemed level and he was alone in the mist. Not even the yellow line was visible. He yelled "Rima! Rima! Rima!" and listened, and heard the distant sea. For a moment he felt utterly lost. He took the torch from his rucksack, switched it on and found the yellow line a yard away from him; then he remembered that if Rima had fallen over the line she would have rolled the opposite way. This was a cheering thought for it made events seem logical. He turned and climbed the hill, torch in hand, and after a lot of effort reached a summit where he heard a sound of weeping. Ten steps farther he found her squatting on the far side of the line, her hands covering her face. He sat down and put an arm round her shoulders.

After a while she looked up and said, "I'm glad it's you."
"Who else could it have been?"
"I don't know."
Her knuckles were bleeding. He brought out the first-aid kit,
cleaned the grazes and put on sticking plaster. Then they sat
side by side, tired out and waiting for the other to suggest a
move. At last Rima said, "What if we walked on different sides
of the line but held hands across it? Then when one of us
went downhill we'd be steadied by the one going up."
Lanark stared at her and cried, "What a clever idea!"
She smiled and stood up. "Let's try it. Which way do we go?"
"To the left."
"Are you sure?"
"Yes. You slid over the line without noticing."
The new way of walking was a strain on the linking arm but
worked very well. Eventually the road grew level on both sides
and part of a huge rocky wall could be seen through the mists
ahead. The yellow line ran up to an iron door painted with
these words:

**EMERGENCY EXIT 3124
NO ADMITTANCE**

Lanark kicked the door moodily. It was like kicking rock. He
said "It was me who slid over the yellow line, not you."
They turned round and set off again.

They had not gone far when they heard a strange wavering
sound, a sound Lanark seemed to recognize. Rima said, "Someone's crying."
He took the torch from his pocket and shone it ahead and
Rima drew a sudden breath. A tall blond girl, wearing a black
coat and a knapsack, squatted on the road with her hands over
her face. Rima whispered, "Is it me?"
Lanark nodded, went to the girl and knelt beside her. Rima
gave a little hysterical giggle. "Aren't you forgetting? You've
done that already."
But the grief of the girl before him made him ignore the one
behind. He held her shoulders and said urgently, "I'm here,
Rima! It's all right. I'm here!"
She paid no attention. The upright Rima walked past him, saying coldly, "Stop living in the past."
"But I can't leave a bit of you sitting on the road like this."
"All right, drag her along. I suppose helpless women make

you feel strong and superior, but you'll find her a bore eventually."

Her voice throbbed with such scorn, helplessness and humour that it drew him to his feet. Since the crouching Rima seemed unable to notice him he followed the moving one.

They joined hands and silently travelled a great distance. Nothing was visible but the pallor of the mist, nothing audible but the sighing sea. The cold air stung their faces; shoulder, elbow and fingers grew sorely cramped and burning, especially in mid-gradient when one was straining downhill to drag the other steeply up. They passed into a stupor in which they knew nothing but the pain in their arms and the ache of their feet on the road. Sometimes they entered a real sleep from which they were wakened by a pang of vertigo as one or the other wandered onto the line. These pangs, as strong as electric shocks, at last conditioned them into sleepwalking straight forward because Lanark had been unconscious for a long time when something cut him hard on the knee. He blinked and saw a huge tilted shape in the whiteness ahead. He brought out the torch and shone it down. His knee had struck the rim of a rusty iron wheel, flat on its side and blocking the roadway. He helped Rima onto it, led the way along one of the spokes, climbed over the hub and shone the torch at the shape overhanging them. He expected to see something heavily industrial, like the tower above a derelict mine shaft, so the object confused him. It was made of timber bound with iron into a shape like a tub cut away on one side. Rima said, "It's a chariot."

"But there's room inside for twenty or thirty men! What beasts could ever pull it? The head of that bolt is bigger than *my* head."

"Maybe you've shrunk."

"And it's ancient—look at the rust! Yet it's lying on top of a modern road. We'll have to walk round."

He jumped down between the chariot and the severed wheel and sank to his knees in dry sand. Rima landed near him, dropped her rucksack and flopped beside it, saying, "Goodnight."

"You can't sleep here."

"Tell me when you find somewhere better."

He hesitated but the narrow space shielded them from the cold air and the sand was very soft. He dropped his own rucksack and lay beside Rima, saying, "Rest your head on my arm."

"Thanks. I will."

They wriggled to make the sand fit their bodies and lay still
for a while. Lanark said, "Last night I lay on a goosefeather
bed with the sheets turned down so bravely. Tonight I'll sleep
in a cold open field along with the raggle-taggle gypsy."
"What's that?"
"A song I remember. Are you sorry we left the institute?"
"I'm too exhausted to feel sorry about anything."
A little later her voice seemed to reach him from a distance.
"I'm glad I'm exhausted. I couldn't sleep here if I wasn't ex-
hausted."

He was wakened by musical whirring which came from
far away, passed overhead and faded into silence. Rima stirred
and sat up, spilling sand from her shoulders, then stretched
her arms and yawned. "Ooyah, how fat and sticky and stale I
feel."
"Fat?"
"Yes, my stomach's swollen."
"It must be wind. You'd better eat."
"I'm not hungry."
"Could you drink hot coffee? There's a flask of it in your rucksack."
"Oh, I could drink that, yes."
She unbuckled the rucksack, put her hand in and drew out,
with a disgusted look, the red thermos flask which tinkled and
shed a stream of brown droplets. She tossed it away and began
brushing sand from her hair with her hands. Lanark said, "You
must have smashed it when you fell. You'd better take your
food out, the damp will spoil it."
Nothing he said would persuade her to touch the food so he
removed it himself, peeled off the sodden wrappings and repacked it in his own rucksack along with the brandy flask. Then
they rose, walked around the chariot and saw the shadowy
prow of another chariot. The road was hidden by a wilderness
of broken chariots which loomed in the mist like a fleet of
sunk battleships, the shafts, axles, broken rims and naked spokes
sticking up between sand-logged hulls like masts, anchors and
titanic paddlewheels. It was impossible to climb through so
they trudged round, often stopping at first to pour sand from
their shoes but soon tiring of this and plodding uncomfortably
on. Many hours seemed to pass before they stepped onto asphalt
again. They sat and had a nip of brandy before emptying their
shoes for the last time, then they joined hands over the yellow
line and resumed walking.

New freshness filled them. There was little or no strain
on their arms, the mist grew warm as if the sun was about to
come through and they were soothed by pleasant sounds: first
larksong overhead, then the crooning of pigeons and a swishing
as if heavy rain were falling in a forest. Once they heard such
a loud gurgling and creaking of oars that Lanark groped with
his torch to the roadside, expecting to see the bank of a wide
river, but though the water noise grew louder he saw nothing
but sand. Farther on they were passed by footsteps and voices
going the opposite way. The voices travelled in clusters of two
and three and spoke quietly and indistinctly except for a couple
who seemed to be arguing.
". . . a form of life like you or me."
". . . here's ferns and grass. . . ."
"What's wonderful about grass?"
As they passed through an invisible crowd of chattering children
some real raindrops dashed in their faces and the mist turned
golden and lifted. The straight road, embanked in places, ran
without undulation across undulating sand to a mountain on
the horizon. Tiny farms, fields and woodlands covered foothills
which glittered in the rain as though dusted with silver: the
summit was split into many snowy peaks with clouds drifting
down between them, and all this was seen under a rainbow,
a three-quarter violet blue green yellow orange red arc shining
sweetly in a shining sky. Rima smiled at the distance and gripped
both his hands. She said, "It was good of you to bring me
out of that place. You're very wise sometimes."
They kissed and walked onward. The mist descended and the
strange gravities of the road strained their arms once more.
Again they avoided the strain by walking in a half-conscious
daze. At last Rima said, "We're nearly there."
Lanark jerked awake and saw a rocky wall above them in the
mist. He switched on the torch and an iron door appeared
with these words on it:

EMERGENCY EXIT 3124
NO ADMITTANCE

Rima sat down with her back to the door and folded her arms.
Lanark stood staring at the words, trying not to believe what
he saw. Rima said, "Give me something to eat."
"But—but—but this is impossible! Impossible!"
"You led us right round these chariots and back along the
road."
"I'm sure it's a different door. It's rustier."
"The same number's on it. Give me that rucksack."

"But Munro said the road was clearly marked!"

"Are you deaf? I'm starving! Pass the bloody rucksack!"

He sat down and laid the rucksack between them. She opened it and began eating with tears flowing down her cheeks. He laid a hand on her shoulder. She shook it off so he started eating too. Hunger and thirst hadn't troubled him much since entering the zone and now he found the food so tasteless that he returned it to the rucksack, but Rima chewed as fast and savagely as if eating were a sort of revenge. She devoured dates, figs, beef, oatmeal and chocolate and all the time the tears poured down her cheeks. Lanark stared in awe and at last said timidly, "You've eaten more than half the food."

"Well?"

"We've still a long way to travel."

She made a noise between a howl and a laugh and went on eating till nothing was left, then she uncorked the brandy flask, drank two mouthfuls and got up and staggered into the mist. He dimly saw her kneel at the roadside and heard vomiting sounds. She returned looking pale, lay down with her head in his lap and fell asleep at once.

The weight on his lap was comforting at first. Her face, childish in sleep, filled him with the tender, sad superiority we usually feel for the sleeping; but the road was hard, his position uncomfortable and he began to feel trapped. His thoughts kept exploring the road ahead, wondering how to escape from it. His muscles ached with the effort of keeping still. At last he kissed her eyelids until she raised them and asked "What's wrong?"

"Rima, we must get away from here."

She sat up and pressed her hair back with her hands.

"If you don't mind I'll just stay and wait for you to come wandering back."

"You may wait a long time. I refuse to die at the door of a place where I've acted wickedly."

"Wickedly? Wickedly? You use more meaningless words than anyone I've ever met."

He wondered how to be soothing and said experimentally, "I love you."

"Shut up."

His anger rose to the surface. "I love the reckless way you abandon courage and intelligence whenever things get really difficult."

"Shut up! Shut up!"

"Since we're determined to behave badly, please pass the brandy."

"No, I need it."

He got to his feet and said, "Are you coming, then?"

She folded her arms. He said sharply, "If you need the first-aid box, you'll find it in the rucksack."

She didn't move. He said humbly, "Please come with me."

She didn't move.

"If you knock the door hard enough, somebody might open it."

She didn't move. He laid the torch beside her, said quickly, "Goodbye," and walked away. He was descending the first hill in great strides when something punched his back. He turned and saw her, tearstained and breathless. She cried, "You'd have left me! You'd have left me alone in the fog!"

"I thought you wanted that."

"You're a cruel nasty idiot."

He said awkwardly, "Anyway, give me your hand."

They joined hands and all at once his body felt aching-feeble. He even lacked strength to hold her fingers. It was Rima who kept them together and moving along the road. He loathed her. He wanted to lie down and sleep so he disguised his staggers as a carefree way of walking and thought malignantly, 'She'll soon tire of dragging me along,' but Rima continued for a great distance without complaining. At last, feeling lightheaded, he pretended to hum a tune to himself. She stopped and cried, "Oh, Lanark, let's be friends! Please, please, why can't we be friends?"

"I'm too tired to be friendly. I want to sleep."

She stared at him, then her face relaxed into a smile. "I thought you hated me and wanted to get away."

"At the moment that is perfectly true."

She said cheerfully, "Let's sit down. I'm tired too," and sat on the road. He would have preferred the sand at the roadside but was too tired to say so. He lay beside her. She stroked his hair and he was almost sleeping when he felt something strange and sat up.

"Rima! This asphalt is cracked! It's covered with moss!"

"I thought it was more comfortable than usual."

He looked uneasily around and saw through the mist a thing which shocked him out of tiredness. A dark humped headless creature, about four feet high with many legs, stood perfectly

still in front of them. The feet were gathered together and
the legs bent as if to jump. Lanark felt Rima grip his shoulder
and whisper, "A spider."
His scalp tightened. There was a thudding in his ears. He stood
up and whispered, "Give me the torch."
"I haven't a torch. Come away."
"I'm going nowhere with that behind me."
He took a breath and stepped forward. The dark body became
a cluster of bodies, each with its own leg. He called happily,
"Rima, it's toadstools!"
A clump of big toadstools grew on the yellow line so that
half the domed heads tilted left and the other half to the right.
Lanark bent down and stared between the stems. They were
rooted in a heap of rotten cloth with rusty buckles and a blis-
tered blue cylinder in it. He pointed: "Look, the thermos flask!
That pile of old clothing must be your rucksack!"
"Don't touch! It's horrible!"
"How did they come here? We left them beside the chariots.
They can't have crawled along the road to meet us."
"Can any dreadful thing not happen here?"
"Be sensible, Rima. Strange things have happened here but
nothing dreadful. This fungus is a form of life, like you and
me."
"Like you, perhaps. Not like me."
Lanark was fascinated. Peering closely he moved round the
cluster and felt his ankles brushed by something light.
"And, Rima, here's ferns and grass."
"What's wonderful about grass?"
"It's better than a desert full of rusty wheels. Come on, there's
a slope. Let's climb it."
"Why? My back's sore, and you're supposed to be tired."
Beyond the toadstools the road vanished under an overgrown
embankment. Lanark scrambled upward and Rima, grumbling,
came after.

They climbed through gorse, brambles and bracken, feeling glad of the protective coats. The white mist faded until
they emerged into luminous darkness under an immense sky
of stars. They stood beside a ten-lane motorway which lay across
the mist like a causeway across an ocean of foam. Vehicles
were whizzing along too quickly to be recognized: tiny stars
in the distance would suddenly expand, pass in a blast of wind,

shrink to stars on the opposite horizon, and vanish. There was a thirty-feet-high road sign on the grassy verge:

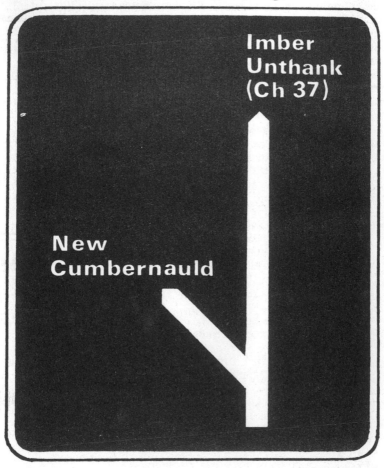

:"Good," said Lanark happily. "We're on the right road at last. Come on."
"It seems a general rule that when I'm able to walk you feel exhausted and when I need a rest you keep dragging me along."
"Are you really tired, Rima?"
"Oh, no. Not at all. Me tired? What a strange idea."
"Good. Come along, then."

As they started walking a glow appeared on the misty horizon to their left and a globe of yellow light slid up into the sky from behind a jagged black mountain. Rima said, "The moon!"
"It can't be the moon. It's going too fast."
The globe was certainly marked like the moon. It swung upward across Orion, passed near the Pole Star and sunk down below the horizon on the far side of the road. A little later, with a piece of rim missing from one side, it rose again behind the mountain on the left. Rima stood still and said desperately "I can't go on. My back hurts, my stomach's swollen, and this coat is far too tight."
She unbuttoned it frantically and Lanark stared in surprise. The dress had hung loose from her shoulders, but now her stomach was swollen almost to her breasts and the amber velvet was as tight as the skin of a balloon. She gazed down as if struck by something and said faintly, "Give me your hand."
She pressed his hand against the lower side of her belly, staring wildly at his face. He had begun to say, "I feel nothing," when his palm received, through the tense stomach wall, a queer little pat. He said, "Somebody is in there."
She said hysterically, "I'm going to have a baby!"
He gaped at her and she glared accusingly back. He struggled to keep serious and failed. His face was stretched by a huge happy grin. She bared her teeth and shrieked, "You're *glad!* You're *glad!*"
"I'm sorry, I can't help it."
In a low intense voice she said, "How you must hate me. . . ."
"I love you!"
". . . grinning when I'm going to have horrible pains and will split open and maybe die . . ."
"You won't die!"
". . . beside a fucking motorway without a fucking doctor in fucking sight."
"We'll get to Unthank before then."
"How do you know?"
"And if we don't I'll take care of you. Births are natural things, usually."
She knelt on the grass, covered her face and wept hysterically while Lanark started helplessly laughing, for he felt a burden lifted from him, a burden he had carried all his life without noticing. Then he grew ashamed and knelt and embraced her, and she allowed him. They squatted a long time like that.

CHAPTER 34. Intersections

When he next looked at the sky a half-moon was sailing over
it. He said, "Rima, I think we should try to keep moving."
She got to her feet and they started walking arm in arm. She
said miserably, "It was wrong of you to be glad."
"There's nothing to worry about, Rima. Listen, when Nan was
pregnant she had nobody to help her, but she still wanted a
baby and had one without any bother."
"Stop comparing me with other women. Nan's a fool. Anyway,
she loved Sludden. That makes a difference."
Lanark stood still, stunned, and said, "Don't you love me?"
She said impatiently, "I like you, Lanark, and of course I depend
on you, but you aren't very inspiring, are you?"
He stared at the air, pressing a clenched fist to his chest and
feeling utterly weak and hollow. An excited expression came
on her face. She pointed past him and whispered, "Look!"

Fifty yards ahead a tanker stood on the verge with a man
beside it, apparently pissing on the grass between the wheels.
Rima said, "Ask him for a lift."
Lanark felt too feeble to move. He said, "I don't like begging
favours from strangers."
"Don't you? Then I will."
She hurried past him, shouting, "Excuse me a minute!"
The driver turned and faced them, buttoning his fly. He wore
jeans and a leather jacket. He was a young man with spiky
red hair who regarded them blankly. Rima said, "Excuse me,
could you give me a lift? I'm terribly tired."
Lanark said, "We're trying to get to Unthank."
The driver said, "I'm going to Imber."
He was staring at Rima. Her hood had fallen back and the

pale golden hair hung to her shoulders, partly curtaining her
ardently smiling face. The coat hung open and the bulging
stomach raised the short dress far above her knees. The driver
said, "Imber isn't all that far from Unthank, though."
Rima said, "Then you'll let us come?"
"Sure, if you like."
He walked to the cab, opened the door, climbed in and reached
down his hand. Lanark muttered, "I'll help you up," but she
took the driver's hand, set her foot on the hub of the front
wheel and was pulled inside before Lanark could touch her.
So he scrambled in after and shut the door behind him. The
cabin was hot, oil-smelling, dimly lit and divided in two by a
throbbing engine as thick as the body of a horse. A tartan
rug lay over this and the driver sat on the far side. Lanark
said, "I'll sit in the middle, Rima."
She settled astride the rug saying, "No, I'm supposed to sit
here."
"But won't the vibration . . . do something?"
She laughed.
"I'm sure it will do nothing nasty. It's a nice vibration."
The driver said, "I always sit the birds on the engine. It warms
them up."
He put two cigarettes in his mouth, lit them and gave one to
Rima. Lanark settled gloomily into the other seat. The driver
said, "Are you happy then?"
Rima said "Oh, yes. It's very kind of you."
The driver turned out the light and drove on.

    The noise of the engine made it hard to talk without shout-
ing. Lanark heard the driver yell, "In the pudding club, eh?"
"You're very observant."
"Queer how some birds can carry a stomach like that without
getting less sexy. Why you going to Unthank?"
"My boyfriend wants to work there."
"What does he do?"
"He's a painter—an artist."
Lanark yelled, "I'm not a painter!"
"An artist, eh? Does he paint nudes?"
"I'm *not* an artist!"
Rima laughed and said, "Oh, yes. He's very keen on nudes."
"I bet I know who his favourite model is."
Lanark stared glumly out of the window. Rima's hysterical de-
spair had changed to a gaiety he found even more disturbing
because he couldn't understand it. On the other hand, it was

good to feel that each moment saw them nearer Unthank. The
speed of the lorry had changed his view of the moon; its thin
crescent stood just above the horizon, apparently motionless,
and gave a comforting sense that time was passing more slowly.
He heard the driver say, "Go on, give it to him," and Rima
pushed something plump into his hands. The driver shouted,
"Count what's in it—go on count what's in it!"
The object was a wallet. Lanark thrust it violently back across
Rima's thighs. The driver took it with one hand and yelled,
"Two hundred quid. Four days' work. The overtime's chronic
but the creature pays well for it. Half of it yours for a drawing
of your girl here in the buff, right?"
"I'm not an artist and we're going to Unthank."
"No. Nothing much in Unthank. Imber's the place. Bright
lights, strip clubs, Swedish massage, plenty of overtime for art-
ists in Imber. Something for everybody. I'll show you round."
"I'm not an artist!"
"Have another fag, ducks, and light one for me."
Rima took the cigarette packet, crying, "Can you really afford
it?"
"You saw the wallet. I can afford anything, right?"
"I wish my boyfriend were more like you!"
"Thing about me, if I want a thing, I don't care how much I
pay. To heck with consequences. You only live once, right?
You come to Imber."
Rima laughed and shouted, "I'm a bit like that too."
Lanark shouted, *"We're going to Unthank!"* but the others didn't
seem to hear. He bit his knuckles and looked out again. They
were deep among lanes of vast speeding vehicles and container
trucks stencilled with cryptic names: QUANTUM, VOLSTAT,
CORTEXIN, ALGOLAGNICS. The driver seemed keen to show
his skill in overtaking them. Lanark wondered how soon they
would reach the road leading off to Unthank, and how he
could make the lorry stop there. Moreover, if the lorry did
stop, he (being near the door) must get out before Rima. What
if the driver drove off with her? Perhaps she would like that.
She seemed perfectly happy. Lanark wondered if pregnancy
and exhaustion had driven her mad. He felt exhausted himself.
His last clear thought before falling asleep was that whatever
happened he must not fall asleep.

He woke to a perplexing stillness and took a while understanding where he was. They were parked at the roadside and
an argument was happening in the cabin to his right. The driver

was saying angrily, "In that case you can clear out."
Rima said, "But why?"
"You changed your mind pretty sudden, didn't you?"
"Changed my mind about what?"
"Get out! I know a bitch when I see one."
Lanark quickly opened the door saying, "Yes, we'll leave now.
Thanks for the lift."
"Take care of yourself, mate. You'll land in trouble if you
stick with her."
Lanark climbed on the verge and helped Rima down after him.
The door slammed and the tanker rumbled forward, becom-
ing a light among other lights whizzing into the distance.
Rima giggled and said, "What a funny man. He seemed really
upset."
"No wonder."
"What do you mean?"
"You were flirting with him and he took it seriously."
"I wasn't flirting. I was being polite. He was a terrible driver."
"How does the baby feel?"
Rima flushed and said, "You'll never let me forget that, will
you?"
She started rapidly walking.

    The road ran between broad shallow embankments. Rima
said suddenly, "Lanark, have you noticed something different
about the traffic? There's none going the opposite way."
"Was there before?"
"Of course. It only stopped a minute ago. And what's that
noise?"
They listened. Lanark said, "Thunder, I think. Or an aero-
plane."
"No, it's a crowd cheering."
"If we walk on we may find out."

    It became plain that something strange was happening
ahead, for lights had begun clustering on the horizon. The
embankment grew steeper until the road passed into a cutting.
The verge was now a grassy strip below a dark black cliff with
thick ivy on it. Wailing sirens sounded behind them and police
cars sped past toward the light and thunder. The cutting ahead
seemed blocked by glare, and vehicles slowed down as they
neared it. Soon Rima and Lanark reached a great queue of
trucks and tankers. The drivers stood on the verge talking in

shouts and gestures, for the din increased with every step. They passed another road sign:

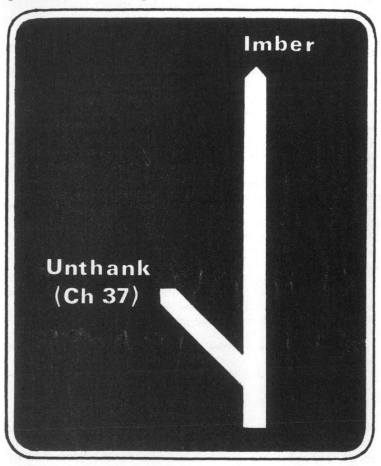

:and eventually Rima halted, pressed her hands over her ears, and by mouthings and headshakings made it clear she would go no farther. Lanark frowned angrily but the noise made thought impossible. There was something animal and even human in it, but only machinery could have sustained such a huge screeching, shrieking, yowl-ing, growling, grinding, whining, yammering, stammering, trilling, chirping and yacacawing. It passed into the earth and jarred painfully on the soles of the feet. Still holding her ears Rima turned and hurried back and Lanark, after a moment of hesitation, was glad to follow.

Many more vehicles had joined the queue and drivers were standing on the road between them, for the backs of the trucks gave shelter from the sound. A young policeman with a torch was speaking to a group and Lanark gripped Rima's sleeve and drew her over to listen. He was saying, "A tanker hit an Algolagnics transporter at the Unthank intersection. I've never seen anything like it—nerve circuits spread across all the lanes like bloody burst footballs and screaming enough to crumble the road surface. The council's been alerted but God knows how long they'll take to deal with a mess like that. Days—weeks, perhaps. If you're going to Imber you'll need to go round by New Cumbernauld. If you're for Unthank, well, forget it."

Someone asked him about the drivers.

"How should I know? If they're lucky they were killed on impact. Without protective clothes you can't get within sixty metres of the place."

The policeman left the group and Lanark touched his shoulder saying, "Can I speak to you?"

He flashed his torch on their faces and said sharply, "What's that on your brows?"

"A thumb print."

"Well, how can I help you, sir? Be quick, we're busy at the moment."

"This lady and I are travelling to Unthank—"

"Out of the question sir. The road's impassable."

"But we're walking. We needn't keep to the road."

"Walking!"

The policeman rubbed his chin. At length he said, "There's the old pedestrian subway. It hasn't been used for years, but as far as I know it isn't *officially* derelict. I mean, it isn't boarded up."

He led them across the grass to a dark shape on the cutting wall. It was a square entrance, eight feet high and half hidden by a heavy swag of ivy. The policeman flashed his torch into it. A floor, under a drift of withered leaves, sloped down into blackness. Rima said firmly, "I'm not going in there."

Lanark said, "Do you know how long it is?"

"Can't say, sir. Wait a minute. . . ."

The policeman probed the wall near the entrance with his torch beam and revealed a faded inscription:

EDESTRIAN UNDER ASS
UNTHAN   00   ETRES

The policeman said, "A subway with an entrance like this can't be very long. A pity the lights are broken."

"Could you possibly lend me your torch? We mislaid ours and Rima—this lady—is pregnant, as you see."

"I'm sorry sir. No."

Rima said, "It's no use discussing it. I refuse to go in there."

The policeman said, "Then you'll have to hitch a lift back to New Cumbernauld."

He turned and walked away. Lanark said patiently, "Now listen, we must be sensible. If we use this tunnel we'll reach Unthank in fifteen minutes, perhaps less. It's unlit but there's a handrail on the wall so we can't lose our way. New Cumbernauld may be hours from here, and I want to get you into hospital as quickly as possible."

"I hate the dark, I hate hospitals and I'm not going!"

"There's nothing wrong with darkness. I've met several dreadful things in my life, and every one was in sunshine or a well-lit room."

"Yet you pretend to *want* sunshine!"

"I do, but not because I'm afraid of the opposite."

"How wise you are. How strong. How noble. How useless."

Bickering fiercely they had moved into the tunnel mouth to escape the blast of the din outside. Lanark abruptly paused, pointed into the dark and whispered, "Look, the end!"

Their eyes had grown used to the black and now they could see, in the greatest depth of it, a tiny, pale, glimmering square. Rima suddenly gripped the handrail and walked down the slope. He hurried after her and silently took her arm, afraid a wrong word would overturn her courage.

The roaring behind them sank into silence and the withered leaves stopped whispering under their feet. The ground levelled out. The air grew cold, then freezing. Lanark had kept his eyes fixed on the glimmering little square. He said, "Rima, have you let go the handrail?"

"Of course not."

"That's funny. When we entered the tunnel the light was straight ahead. Now it's on our left."

They halted. He said, "I think we're moving along the side of an open space, a hall of some kind."

She whispered, "What should we do?"

"Walk straight toward the light. Can't you button your coat?"

"No."

"We must get out of this cold as fast as we can. Come on. We'll go straight across the middle."

"What if . . . what if there's a pit?"

"People don't build pedestrian subways with pits in the middle. Let go of the rail."

They faced the light and stepped cautiously out, then Lanark felt himself slipping downward and released Rima's arm with a yell. Head and shoulder met a dense, metal-like surface with such stunning force that he lay on it for several seconds. The hurts of the fall were far less than the intense freezing cold. The chill on his hands and face actually had him weeping.

"Rima," he moaned, "Rima, I'm sorry . . . I'm sorry. Where are you, please?"

"Here."

He crawled in a circle, patting at the ground until his hand touched a foot. "Rima . . . ?"

"Yes."

"You're wearing thin sandals and you're standing on ice. I'm sorry, Rima, I've led you onto a frozen lake."

"I don't care."

He stood up, his teeth chattering, and peered about, saying, "Where's the light?"

"I don't know."

"I can't see it . . . I can't see it anywhere. We must find our way back to the handrail."

"You won't manage it. We're lost." Her body was beside him but her voice, low and dull, seemed to come from a distance. She said, "I'm a witch. I deserve this for killing him."

Lanark thought she had gone mad and felt terribly weary. He said patiently, "What are you talking about, Rima?"

After a moment she said, "Pregnant, silent, freezing, all dark, lost with you, feet that might fall off, an aching back, I deserve all this. He was driving badly to impress me. He wanted me, you see, and at first I found that fun; then I got tired of him, he was so smug and sure of himself. When he made us get out I wanted him to die, so he went on driving badly and crashed. No wonder you mean to lock me in a hospital. I'm a witch."

He realized she was weeping desperately and tried to embrace her, saying, "In the first place, the tanker that crashed may not be the one that gave us the lift. In the second place, a man's bad driving is nobody's fault but his own. And I'm not going to lock you up anywhere."

"Don't touch me."

"But I love you."

"Then promise not to leave when the baby comes. Promise you won't give me to other people and then run away."

"I promise. Don't worry."

"You're only saying that because we're freezing to death. If we get away from here you'll hand me over to a gang of bloody nurses."

"I won't! I won't!"

"You say that now, but you'll run away when the real pains begin. You won't be able to stand them."

"Why shouldn't I stand them? They'll be your pains, not mine." She gasped and shrieked, "You're glad! You're glad! You evil beast, you're glad!"

He shouted, "Everything I say makes you think I'm evil!"

"You are evil! You can't make me happy. You *must* be evil!"

Lanark stood gasping dumbly. Every comforting phrase which struck him was accompanied by a knowledge of how she would twist it into a hurt. He raised a hand to hit her but she was with child; he turned to run away, but she needed him; he dropped down on his hands and knees and bellowed out a snarling yell which became a howl and then a roar. He heard her say in a cold little voice, "You won't frighten me that way."

He yelled out again and heard a distant voice shout, "Coming! Coming!"

He stood up, drawing breath with effort and feeling the chill of the ice on his hands and knees. A light was moving toward them over the ice and a voice could be heard saying, "Sorry I'm late."

As the light neared they saw it was carried by a dark figure with a strip of whiteness dividing head from shoulders. At last a clergyman stood before them. He may have been middle-aged but had an eager, smooth, young-looking face. He held up the lamp and seemed to peer less at Lanark's face than at the mark on his brow. There was a similar mark on his own. He said, "Lanark, is it? Excellent. I'm Ritchie-Smollet."

They shook hands. The clergyman looked down on Rima, who
had sunk down on her heels with her arms resting wearily
on her stomach. He said, "So this is your good lady."
"*Lady,*" snarled Rima contemptuously.
Lanark said, "She's tired and a bit unwell. In fact she'll be
having a baby quite soon."
The clergyman smiled enthusiastically.
"Splendid. That's really glorious. We must get her into hospi-
tal."
Rima said violently, "No!"
"She doesn't want to go into hospital," explained Lanark.
"You must persuade her."
"But I think she ought to do what she likes."
The clergyman moved his feet and said, "It's rather chilly here.
Isn't it time we put our noses above ground?"
Lanark helped Rima to her feet and they followed Ritchie-
Smollet across the black ice.

It was hard to see anything of the cavern except that the
ceiling was a foot or two above their heads. Ritchie-Smollet
said, "What tremendous energy these Victorian chaps had. They
hollowed this place out as a burial vault when the ground upstairs was filled up. A later age put it to a more pedestrian
use, and it still is a remarkably handy short cut. . . . Please
ask any questions you like."
"Who are you?"
"A Christian. Or I try to be. I suppose you'd like to know
my precise church, but I don't think the sect is all that important,
do you? Christ, Buddha, Amon-Ra and Confucius had a great
deal in common. Actually I'm a Presbyterian but I work with
believers of every continent and colour."
Lanark felt too tired to speak. They had left the ice and were
climbing a flagged passage under an arching roof. Ritchie-Smollet said, "Mind you, I'm opposed to human sacrifice: unless
it's voluntary, as in the case of Christ. Did you have a nice
journey?"
"No."
"Never mind. You're still sound in wind and limb and you
can be sure of a hearty welcome. You'll be offered a seat on
the committee, of course. Sludden was definite about that and
so was I. My experience of institute and council affairs is rather
out of date—things were less tense in my time. We were delighted when we heard you had chosen to join us."

"I've chosen to join nobody. I know nothing about committee work and Sludden is no friend of mine."
"Now, now, don't get impatient. A wash and a clean bed will work wonders. I suspect you're more exhausted than you think."

The pale square of light appeared ahead and enlarged to a doorway. It opened into the foot of a metal staircase. Lanark and Rima climbed slowly and painfully in watery green light. Ritchie-Smollet 'came patiently behind, humming to himself. After many minutes they emerged into a narrow, dark, stone-built chamber with marble plaques on three walls and large wrought-iron gates in the fourth. These swung easily outward, and they stepped onto a gravel path beneath a huge black sky. Lanark saw he was on a hilltop among the obelisks of a familiar cemetery.

CHAPTER 35. Cathedral

After they had gone a little way Lanark stopped and declared,
"This isn't Unthank!"
"You are mistaken. It is."
They looked down a slope of pinnacled monuments onto a
squat black cathedral. The floodlit spire held a gilt weathercock
above the level of their eyes, but Lanark was more perplexed
by the view beyond. He remembered a stone-built city of dark
tenements and ornate public buildings, a city with a square
street plan and electric tramcars. Rumours from the council
corridors had made him expect much the same place, only
darker and more derelict, but below a starless sky this city
was coldly blazing. Slim poles as tall as the spire cast white
light upon the lanes and looping bridges of another vast motorway. On each side shone glass and concrete towers over twenty
floors high with lights on top to warn off aeroplanes. Yet this
was Unthank, though the old streets between towers and motor-
lanes had a half-erased look, and blank gables stood behind
spaces cleared for carparks. After a pause Lanark said, "And
Unthank is dying?"
"Dying? Oh I doubt it. The population has shrunk since they
scrapped the Q39 project, but there's been a tremendous building boom."
"But if a place is losing people and industry how can it afford
new buildings?"
"Ah, I know too little about chronology to say. I feel that
what happens between *hearts* matters more than these big public
ways of swapping energy. You tell me, no doubt, that this is
a conservative attitude. On the other hand, radicals are the
only people who'll work with me. Odd, isn't it?"

Lanark said irritably, "You seem to understand my questions, but your answers make no sense to me."

"That's typical of life, isn't it? But as long as you've a good heart and keep trying there's no need to despair. *Wer immer streband sich bemüht, den können wir erlösen.* Oh, you'll be a great deal of use to us."

Rima suddenly leaned on a stone and said quietly, without bitterness, "I can't go on."

Lanark, alarmed, clasped her waist though it worried him to be clasping two people instead of one.

Ritchie-Smollet said softly, "A giddy spell?" "No, my back hurts and I . . . I can hardly think."

"In my missionary phase I took a medical degree. Give me your pulse."

He held her wrist in one hand, beat time with the other, then said, "Eighty-two. Considering your condition that's quite good. Could you manage down to that building? A sleep is what you need most, but I'd better examine you first to make sure everything's in order."

He pointed to the cathedral. Rima stared at it. Lanark murmured, "Could we join hands and carry her?"

Rima pushed herself upright and said, "No, give me your arm. I'll walk."

The clergyman led them down dim weedy paths past the porticoes of mausoleums cut into the hillside. Gleams of light from below lit corners of inscriptions to the splendid dead:

". . . His victorious campaign . . ."
". . . . . whose unselfish devotion . . . . ."
". . . revered by his students . . ."
". . . . . esteemed by his colleagues . . . . ."
". . . beloved by all . . ."

They crossed a flat space and walked along a cobbled lane. Ritchie-Smollet said, "A tributary of the river once flowed under here."

Lanark saw that a low wall beside him was the parapet of a bridge and looked over onto a steeply embanked road. Cars sped up this to the motorway but there seemed to be a barrier: after slowing and stopping they turned and came back again. A tiny distinct throbbing in the air worked on the eardrum like the point of a drill on a tooth.

"What's that noise?"

"There appears to be a pile-up at the intersection: a burst trans-porter, one of these huge dangerous God-the-Father jobs. The council ought to ban them. The city looks like being sealed off for quite a while. However, we've adequate food stocks. Come through here, it's a short cut."

The parapet had given way to a wall screened by bushes. Ritchie-Smollet parted two of these uncovering a hole into brighter air. Lanark helped Rima through. They were in the grounds of the cathedral where gravestones lay flat like a pave-ment. Vans and private cars stood on them against the surround-ing wall, and Rima sank down on the step of a mobile crane. Ritchie-Smollet thrust hands into trouser pockets and stared ahead with a small satisfied smile.

"There she stands!" he said. "Our centre of government once again."

Lanark looked at the cathedral. At first the floodlit spire seemed too solid for the flat black shape upholding it, a shape cut through by rows of dim yellow windows; then his eye made out the tower, roofs and buttresses of a sturdy Gothic ark, the sculpted waterspouts broken and rubbed by weather and the hammers of old iconoclasts.

"What do you mean, centre of government? Unthank has a city chambers."

"Ah, yes, we use it nowadays for property deals. Quite a lot of work is done there, but the *real* legislators come here. I know you're keen to meet them but first you'll have to sleep. I speak as a doctor now, not as a minister of the gospel, so you mustn't argue with me."

They walked over inscriptions more laconic than in the higher cemetery.

"William Skinner: 5½ feet North × 2¼ West."

"Harry Fleming, his wife Minnie, their son George, their daughter Amy: 6 feet West × 2½ North."

They reached a side entrance and crossed a shallow porch into the cathedral.

A long-haired young man wearing blue overalls sat reading a book on a lidded stone font near the door. He glanced up and said, "Where have you been, Arthur? Polyphemus is going berserk. He thinks he's discovered something."

"I'm in a hurry, Jack," said Ritchie-Smollet crisply. "These people need rest and attention. Will anywhere be clear for a while? I mean really clear?"

"Nothing scheduled for the arts lab."

"Then get blankets and pillows into it and clean sheets, really clean sheets, and make up a bed."

"Yes but" —the youth laid down his book and slid to the floor—"what will I tell Polyphemus?"

"Tell him politics is not man's chief end."

The youth hurried off between rows of rush-bottomed chairs covering the great flagged floor. The cathedral seemed vaster inside than out. The central pillars upholding the tower hid what lay beyond, but organ tones and blurred hymnal voices indicated a service there. At the same time the hard beat of wilder music sounded from somewhere below. Ritchie-Smollet said, "Not a bad God kennel, is it? The October Terminus are having a gig in the crypt. Some people don't approve of that, but I tell them that at the Reformation the building was used by three congregations simultaneously and in my father's house are many mansions. Do you need the lavatory?"

"No," muttered Rima, who had sunk into a chair. "No, no, no, no."

"Come on, then. Not far now."

They moved slowly down a side aisle and Lanark had time to notice that the cathedral had clearly been used in several ways since its foundation. Torn flags hung overhead; against the walls stood ornate memorials to soldiers killed while invading remote continents. Before the arches under the tower they turned left and went down some steps, then right and descended others into a small chapel. An orange light hung in the stone-ribbed ceiling but the stone was whitewashed and the effect was restful. The air was warmed and scented by paraffin heaters in the corners; a stack of plastic mattresses against a wall nearly touched the ceiling. Three of these were laid edge to edge and Jack was making a bed on the middle one. Rima lay down on it when he finished and Lanark helped remove her coat. "Don't go to sleep yet—I'll be back in a jiff," said Ritchie-Smollet and went out. Jack adjusted the wicks of the heaters and followed him. Lanark shed his own coat and sat with Rima's head on his lap. He was weary but couldn't relax because his clothes felt sticky and foul. He fingered the matted beard on his cheeks and chin and touched the thinning hair on his scalp. Clearly he had grown older. He looked down at Rima, whose eyes were closed. Her hair was black once more, and apart from the big belly her whole figure seemed slighter than in the council corridors. A small insulted frown between the brows suggested an angry little girl, but her lips had the beautiful repose of a mature, contented woman of thirty or forty. He gazed and gazed but couldn't decide her age at all. She sighed and murmured, "Where's Sludden?"

He overcame a pang of anger and said gently, "I don't know, Rima."

"You're nice to me, Lanark. I'll always trust you."

Ritchie-Smollet and Jack brought basins of hot water, towels, clean nightshirts, and went out again. Rima lay on the towels while Lanark sponged and dried her, taking special care of the great belly, which looked more normal naked than clothed. She slid between the sheets and Ritchie-Smollet returned with a black leather case. He knelt by the bed and took out thermometer, stethoscope and sterilized gloves in a transparent envelope. He slipped the thermometer below Rima's armpit and was tearing the envelope when she opened her eyes and said sharply, "Turn round Lanark."

"Why?"

"If you don't turn round I won't let him touch me."

Lanark turned round and walked to the far side of a pillar, his feet cold on the bare stone. He stopped and stared at the ceiling. The arching ribs came together in carved knops, and one showed a pair of tiny snakes twining across the brow of a very cheerful skull in the middle of a wreath of roses. Nearby on the vault someone had scribbled in pencil:

GOD = LOVE = MONEY = SHIT.

"Well, that seems all right," said Ritchie-Smollet loudly. Lanark turned and saw him repacking the case. "The little fellow seems the correct way up and round and so forth. If she insists on having it here I suppose we can manage."

"*Here?*" said Lanark, startled.

"Not in hospital, I mean. Anyway, I'll leave you to some well-earned rest."

He went out, pulling a red curtain across the door. Rima murmured, "Get in behind me."

He obeyed and she pressed her freezing soles greedily to his shins, but her back was familiar and cosy and soon they grew warm and slept.

He wakened among whispering and rustling. Chains of bright spots flowed zigzag over the dark vault and pillars and crowded floor. They were cast by a silver-faceted globe revolving where the orange lamp had hung, and now the only steady light shone on the steps to the entrance. These were the breadth of the wall. Young men in overalls were arranging electrical machines on them which sometimes filled the chapel with huge hoarse sighs. Three older men sat on the lower steps holding instruments joined by wires to the machinery, and a fourth was setting up a percussion kit with BROWN'S LUGWORM CASANOVAS printed on the big drum. Lanark saw he was part of an audience: the whole floor was paved with mattresses and covered with people squatting shoulder to shoulder. Beside him a delicate girl in a silver sari was leaning on a hairy, bare-chested man in a sheepskin waistcoat. Just in front a girl in the tartan trews and scarlet mess jacket of a highland regiment was whispering to a man with the braided hair, headband and fringed buckskin of an Indian squaw. People from every culture and century seemed gathered here in silk, canvas, fur, feathers, wool, gauze, nylon and leather. Hair was frizzed out like the African, crewcut like the Roman, piled high like Pompadour, straightened like the Sphinx or rippled over the shoulders like periwigs. There was every kind of ornament and an amount of nakedness. Lanark looked unsuccessfully for his clothes. He felt he had rested a long time but Rima was still sleeping, so he decided not to move. Other couples were reclining at length and even caressing in the shelter of sleeping bags.

There was applause and a small gloomy man with a heavy moustache stood with a microphone on the steps. He said, "Glad to be back, folks, in legendary Unthank where I've had so many legendary experiences. I'm going to lead off with a new thing, it bombed them in Troy and Trebizond, it sank like stone-cold turkey in Atlantis, let's see what happens here. 'Domestic Man.' "
He threw his head back and shouted:

"The cake she baked me bit me till I cried!"

The instruments and machines said BAWAM so loudly that hearing and thought were destroyed for a second.

"The bed she made me was so hard I nearly died!"
(BAWAM)

"The shirt she washed me folded its arms and tied
me up inside!"

(BAWAM)

"She's going domestic, she's got a great big domestic
plan, But *please* baby believe me lady I am
not a domestic man
not a domestic man
not a domestic man."

(BAWAM BAWAM BAWAM BAWAM BAWAM BAWAM
BAWAM BAWAM BAWAM)

Rima was sitting up, hands pressed over ears and tears pouring
down her cheeks. She spoke but the words were inaudible.
Lanark saw Ritchie-Smollet beckoning violently from the doorway behind the singer. He pulled Rima up and they stumbled
through the audience. The singer shouted:

"She cleans windows till they shine so I can't see!"

(BAWAM)

"She polishes floors till they suck my foot in up to
the knee!"

(BAWAM)

"She papers rooms till the walls start squeezing in on
me!"

(BAWAM)

As they passed the singer Rima waved so threateningly at a
bank of loudspeakers that someone grabbed her arm. Lanark
pulled him off and clumsy punches were exchanged on the
way to the door. Ritchie-Smollet separated them, his voice coming through the BAWAMing like a far-off whisper: ". . . entirely
my fault . . . delicate condition . . . failure of liaison. . . ."

It was quieter outside the door where Jack waited with
dressing-gown and slippers. Rima kept muttering "Bastards"
as she was helped into these.
"They dislike space, you see, and noise fills that up," said Ritchie-Smollet, leading them across the nave. "The fault is really
mine. I went out with a man who thought I could save his
marriage because I'd performed the ceremony. Illogical, really.
Didn't know him from Adam. I hadn't expected you to sleep
so long—if we had a clock it would be safe to say you snoozed
right round the bally thing. Contractions started yet?"
"No," said Rima.
"Good. In a brace of shakes you'll have a bed and a bite in

the triforium. I'd have put you there when you came but I
feared you were too feeble to face the stairs."
He opened a little door and they saw a stair hardly two feet
wide spiralling upward in the thickness of the wall. Lanark
said, "Excuse me, but can't we get a decent room in a decent
house?"
"Rooms are hard to find just now. The house of God is the
best I can offer."
"When I was last here a quarter of the city stood empty."
"Ah, that was before the new building programme started.
Someone on the committee may offer you a spare room eventually. Anyway, we can wait for them in the triforium—your
clothes are there."
Ritchie-Smollet ducked through the doorway and climbed.
Rima followed and Lanark came after. The stairs were laboriously steep. After several turns they passed through another
door onto the inner sill of a huge window. Rima gasped and
clutched a handrail. Far below a man moved like a beetle over
the flagged floor and the echoing throbs of "Domestic Man"
added to the insecurity. Ritchie-Smollet said, "That's Polyphemus on his way to the chapterhouse. My word, but the Lugworms are going it some."
A few steps took them onto a walkway between rows of organ
pipes, and a few more into the end of a very long low attic.
The ceiling slanted from the floor to a wall of arches overlooking the nave. As they walked down it Lanark saw partitions
dividing the loft on his left into cubicles, each containing a
little furniture. In one a man in a dirty coat sat trying to mend
an old boot. In another a haggard woman lay drinking from
a flat-sided bottle. Ritchie-Smollet said, "Here we are," stepped
into one and squatted on the carpet.

The cubicle had a homely look mitigated by a smell of
disinfectant. It was lit by a pink silk-shaded lamp above a low
bed that covered a third of the floor. The seats were stools
and cushions but there was a low table, a chest of drawers
and a tiny sink. The boards between the ceiling joists were
covered by forget-me-not patterned paper, and on one of the
two walls a hanger on a hook held Lanark's clothes, newly
cleaned and pressed.
"Small but snug," said Ritchie-Smollet. "A regrettable lack of
headroom but nobody will disturb us. I suggest Rima slip into
bed (she'll find a hot-water bottle there) and you get dressed.
Then Jack will bring us a meal, a companion will arrive for

your good lady, and we two can attend the meeting in the chapterhouse. The provost should be there by now."

Lanark sank on a stool with elbows on knees and chin on hands. He said, "You keep moving me about and I don't know why."

"Yes, it's difficult. In the present state of chronological confusion it's impossible to state things clearly. As secretary I can only arrange meetings by keeping members here till the rest arrive. But Gow's come, and poor Scougal and Mrs. Schtzngrm and the ubiquitous Polyphemus. And chairman Sludden, praise God."

Lanark looked at Rima. The sight soothed him. She lay smiling against the pillows, a hand touching her full breast. There was a soft calmness about her; the dimples at the corners of her mouth were unusually deep. She said fondly, "It's all right, Lanark. Don't worry."

He sighed and started dressing.

Jack entered with a loaded tray and Ritchie-Smollet poured coffee into cups and passed plates around, chatting as he did so.

"All out of tins, of course, but good of its kind. Easy to serve, too, which is handy because there's only room for a very tiny kitchen. There was amazing opposition when we set up this little refuge—even more than to the arts lab in the lady chapel. Yet these lofts have lain empty since the old monks marched round them telling their beads. And what could better conform to the wishes of the founder? You know the poem, of course:

> "If at the church they would give us some ale,
> and a pleasant fire our souls to regale,
> we'd sing and we'd pray all the livelong day,
> nor ever once wish from the church to stray,
>
> "And God, like a father, rejoicing to see,
> His children as pleasant and happy as He,
> would have no more quarrel with Devil or barrel,
> But kiss him and give him both drink and—"

"What the hell am I eating?" shouted Lanark.

"Enigma de Filets Congalés. Is it underdone? Try this pink moist crumbly stuff. I can heartily recommend it."

Lanark groaned. A stink of burning rubber was fading from his nostrils and his limbs were invaded by a familiar invigorating warmth. He said, "This is institute food."

"Yes. The Quantum group delivers nothing else to us nowadays."

"We left the institute because we hate this food."

"I admire you for it!" cried Ritchie-Smollet enthusiastically. "And you've moved in the right direction! We have two or three millennialists on the committee and who's to blame them? Has not the prayer of humanity in all ages been for innocent and abundant food? Impossible, of course, but *wer immer strebend sich bemüht* et cetera. And one has to eat, unless one feels with Miss Weil that anorexia nervosa is a sacred duty."

"Yes I will eat!" cried Lanark savagely. "But please stop bombarding me with funny names and meaningless quotations!" He finished all the plates that Rima and Ritchie-Smollet left untouched and in the end felt bloated, drugged and horribly tricked. A voice cried, "Rima!" A plump woman of about forty wearing tarty clothes came in. Rima laughed and said, "Frankie!"

Frankie dropped a huge embroidered handbag on the floor, sat on the bed and said, "Sludden told me you were here—he's coming later. So the mystery man has put a bun in your oven, has he? Actually you don't look too bad—quite surprisingly winsome, really. Hullo, mystery man, I'm glad you've grown a beard. You look less vulnerable."

"Hullo," said Lanark ungraciously. He was not pleased to see Frankie.

CHAPTER 36. Chapterhouse

Ritchie-Smollet led them to the far end of the attic, through a small kitchen where Jack was washing dishes, and down another spiral stair in the thickness of the wall. They came into a square room with vaulted ceiling upheld by a great central pillar. A row of stone chairs with wooden backs were built into the length of each wall. Lanark thought this an awkward arrangement: if all the seats were occupied everyone would find the central pillar hiding three or four people opposite. A small, fit-looking man stood with feet apart and hands in pockets warming his back at an electric fire. Ritchie-Smollet spoke with less than usual enthusiasm.

"Ah, Grant. This is Lanark, who has news for us."

"Council news, no doubt," said Grant with a sarcastic emphasis, "I've been waiting over an hour."

"Remember the rest of us haven't got your knack of timing things. The provost may be in the crypt; I'll go and look."

Ritchie-Smollet left by a door in a corner. Grant and Lanark stared at each other. Grant seemed about thirty though there were some deep vertical wrinkles on his cheeks and brow. His short crisp hair was carefully combed and he wore a neat blue suit and red necktie. He said, "I know you. When I was a lad you used to hang around the old Elite with Sludden's mob."

"Not for long," said Lanark. "How do you time things? Have you a watch?"

"I've a pulse."

"You count your heartbeats?"

"I estimate them. We all developed that talent in the shops when the old timekeeping collapsed."

"You keep a shop?"
"I'm talking abut workshops. Machine shops. I'm a maker, not a salesman."

Lanark sat on a seat near the fire. Grant's voice offended him. It was loud, penetrating and clearly used to addressing crowds without help from the equipment which lets a man talk softly to millions. Lanark said, "Where's Polyphemus?"
"Eh?"
"I heard that someone called Polyphemus was here."
Grant grinned and said, "I'm here all right. Smollet calls me that."
"Why?"
"Polyphemus was a one-eyed ogre in an old story. I keep reminding the committee of a fact they want to forget, so they say I have only one way of seeing things."
"What fact is that?"
"None of them are makers."
"Do you mean workers?"
"No, I mean makers. Many hard workers make nothing but wealth. They don't produce food, fuel, shelter or helpful ideas; their work is just a way of tightening their grip on folk who do."
"What do you make?"
"Homes. I'm a shop steward with the Volstat Mohome group."
Lanark said thoughtfully, "These groups—Volstat, Algolagnics and so on—are they what people call the creature?"
"Some of us call it that. The council is financed by it. So is the institute. So it likes to call itself the foundation."
"I'm sick of these big vague names that power keeps hiding behind," said Lanark impatiently.
"So you prefer not to think of them," said Grant, nodding amiably. "That's typical of intellectuals. The institute has bought and sold you so often that you're ashamed to name your masters."
"I have no masters. I hate the institute. I don't even like the council."
"But it helped you come here, so it still has a use for you."
"Blethers!" cried Lanark. "People usually help each other if they can do it without troubling themselves much."
"Try a cigarette," said Grant, offering a packet. He had grown friendlier as Lanark grew angrier.
"Thank you, I don't smoke," said Lanark, cooling a little.

A while later Lanark said, "Would you tell me exactly what the creature is?"

"A conspiracy which owns and manipulates everything for profit."

"Are you talking about the wealthy?"

"Yes, but not the wealthy in coins and banknotes—that sort of wealth is only coloured beads to keep the makers servile. The owners and manipulators have smarter ways of banking energy. They pay themselves with time: time to think and plan, time to examine necessity from a distance."

An old man leaning on a stick and a dark young man with a turban entered and stood talking quietly by the pillar. Grant's loud voice had been even and passionless, but suddenly he said, "What I hate most is their conceit. Their institute breaks whole populations into winners and losers and calls itself *culture*. Their council destroys every way of life which doesn't bring them a profit and calls itself government. They pretend culture and government are supremely independent powers when they are nothing but gloves on the hands of Volstat and Quantum, Cortexin and Algolagnics. And they really think they are the foundation. They believe their greed holds up the continents. They don't call it greed, of course, they call it profit, or (among themselves, where they don't need to fool anyone) *killings*. They're sure that only their profit allows people to make and eat things."

"Maybe that's true."

"Yes, because they make it true. But it isn't necessary. Old men remember when the makers unexpectedly produced enough for everyone. No crop failed, no mine was exhausted, no machinery broke down, but the creature dumped mountains of food in the ocean because the hungry couldn't pay a *profitable* price for it, and the shoemaker's children went shoeless because their father had made too many shoes. And the makers accepted this as though it was an earthquake! They refused to see they could make what they needed for each other and to hell with profit. They would have seen in the end, they would have had to see, if the council had not gone to war."

"How did that help?"

"As the creature couldn't stay rich by selling necessary things to the folk who made them it sold destructive things to the council. Then the war started and the destructive things were used to wreck the necessary things. The creature profited by replacing both."

"Who did the council fight?"

"It split in two and fought itself."

"That's suicide!"

"No, ordinary behaviour. The efficient half eats the less efficient half and grows stronger. War is just a violent way of doing what half the people do calmly in peacetime: using the other half for food, heat, machinery and sexual pleasure. Man is the pie that bakes and eats himself, and the recipe is separation."

"I refuse to believe men kill each other just to make their enemies rich."

"How can men recognize their real enemies when their family, schools and work teach them to struggle with each other and to believe law and decency come from the teachers?"

"My son won't be taught that," said Lanark firmly.

"You have a son?"

"Not yet."

The chapterhouse had filled with chattering groups and Ritchie-Smollet moved among them collecting signatures in a book. There were many young people in bright clothing, old eccentric men in tweeds and a large confusion of in-between people. Lanark decided that if this was the new government of Unthank he was not impressed. Their manners were shrill and vehement or languid and bored. Some had the mark of the council on their brow but nobody displayed the calm, well-contained strength of men like Monboddo, Ozenfant and Munro. Lanark said, "Could you tell me about this committee?"

"I'm getting round to it. The war ended with the creature and its organs more dominant than ever. Naturally there was a lot of damage to repair, but that only took half our time and energy. If industry and government had been commanding us for the common good (as they pretend to do), the continents would have become gardens, gardens of space and light where everyone had time to care for their lovers, children and neighbours without crowding and tormenting them. But these vast bodies only cooperate to kill or crush. Once again the council began feeding the creature by splitting the world in two and preparing a war. But it ran into unexpected trouble—"

"Stop! You're simplifying," said Lanark. "You talk as if all government was one thing, but there are many kinds of government, and some are crueller than others."

"Oh, yes," said Grant, nodding. "An organization which encloses a globe must split into departments. But you're a very

ordinary victim of council advertising if you think the world
is neatly split between good governments and bad."

"What was the council's unexpected trouble?"

"The creature supplied it with such vast new weapons that a
few of them could poison the world. Most folk are dour and
uncomplaining about their own deaths, but the death of their
children depresses them. The council tried to pretend the new
weapons weren't weapons at all but homes where everyone
could live safely, but for all that an air of protest spread even
to the council corridors. Many who had never dreamed of governing themselves began complaining loudly. This committee
is made of complainers."

"Has complaint done any good?"

"Some, perhaps. The creature still puts time and energy into
vast weapons and sells them to the council, but recent wars
have been fought with smaller weapons and kept to the less
industrial continents. Meanwhile the creature has invented
peaceful ways of taking our time and energy. It employs us to
make essential things badly, so they decay fast and have to be replaced. It bribes the council to destroy cheap things which don't
bring it a profit and replaces them with new expensive things
which do. It pays us to make useless things and employs scien-
tists, doctors and artists to persuade us that these are essential."

"Can you give me examples?"

"Yes, but our provost wants to speak to you."

Lanark stood up. A lean, well-dressed man with bushy
grey hair came through the crowd and shook his hand, saying
briskly, "Sorry I missed you upstairs, Lanark—you were too
quick for me. Don't worry—she's all right."

The voice was familiar. Lanark stared into the strange, haggard,
bright-eyed face. The provost said reassuringly, "It's all right—
she's in excellent spirits. I'm glad there was someone dependable like you with her. Frankie will tell us when the contractions
start."

Lanark said, "Sludden."

"You didn't recognize me?" asked the provost, chuckling.

"Well, none of us are the men we were."

Lanark said harshly, "How's your fiancée?"

"Gay?" said Sludden ruefully. "I hoped *you* could tell me about
Gay. The marriage didn't work. My fault, I'm afraid; politics
puts strain on a marriage. She joined the institute. The last I
heard of her was that she had gone to work for the council.
If you didn't see her in the corridors she's probably with a

foundation group, Cortexin perhaps. She had a talent for communications."
Lanark felt baffled and feeble. He wanted to hate Sludden but couldn't think of a reason for doing it. He said accusingly, "I saw Nan and her baby."
"Rima told me. I'm glad they're well," said Sludden, smiling and nodding.
"The committee is convened," said Ritchie-Smollet. "Please be seated."

People moved to the walls and sat down. Sludden took a chair with a high carved back and armrests; Ritchie-Smollet led Lanark to a seat on Sludden's right and himself sat on his left. Grant sat beside Lanark. Ritchie-Smollet said, "Silence, please. The internal secretary has failed to make an appearance, so once again we must take the minutes of the last meeting as read. Never mind. The reason for the present meeting is . . . but I call on our chairman, provost Sludden, to explain that."
"We are privileged to have among us," said Sludden, "a former citizen of Unthank who till recently worked for the institute under the famous—perhaps I should say infamous—Ozenfant. Lanark—here he is beside me—has elected to return here of his own free will, which is no doubt a testimonial to the charm and friendliness of Unthank but proves also the strength of his own patriotic spirit."
Sludden paused. Ritchie-Smollet cried, "Oh, jolly good!" and clapped his hands. Sludden said, "I understand he has had personal consultations with Monboddo."
A voice behind the pillar shouted, "Shame!"
"Monboddo certainly has no friends here, but information about where Unthank stands in the council is hard to obtain, so we welcome any source of light on the subject. Also with me is Grant, sufficiently known to us all."
A voice behind the pillar shouted, "Up the makers, Poly!"
"Grant feels he has important news for us. I don't know what it is, but I suppose it will keep till we have heard our guest speaker?"
Sludden looked at Grant, who shrugged.
"So I will call on Lanark to take the floor."

Lanark rose confusedly to his feet. He said, "I'm not sure what to say. I'm not patriotic. I don't like Unthank, I like sunshine. I came here because I was told Unthank would be scrapped and swallowed in a few days, and anybody here with a council passport would be transferred to a sunnier city." He sat down. There was silence, then Ritchie-Smollet said, "Monboddo told you this?"

"No, one of his secretaries did. A man called Wilkins."

"I strongly object to the tone of the last speaker's remarks," cried a bulky, thick-necked man in a voice twice as penetrating as Grant's.

"Though he openly boasts of being no friend to Unthank, our provost has introduced him as if he was some sort of ambassador, and what news does the ambassador bring? Gossip. Nothing but gossip. The mountain has laboured and given birth to a small obnoxious rodent. But what is the *tendency* of the speech by this self-proclaimed enemy of the city which nurtured him? He tells us that after some vague but imminent doomsday those who carry a council passport will be transferred to a happier land while the majority are *swallowed,* whatever that means. I will, however, say this. *I* have a council passport, like several others on the committee, and like the speaker himself. His statements are clearly devised to spread distrust among our brothers and dismay and dissension in our rank and file. Let me assure this messianic double agent that he will not succeed. Nobody is better able to fight the council than men like Scougal and me. We love our people. We will sink or swim with Unthank. Meanwhile I propose that the committee combat the demoralizing tendency of the guest speaker's tirade by pretending we never heard it."

"Oh, not a tirade, Gow!" said Ritchie-Smollet mildly. "Lanark spoke four short sentences. I counted them. We ought to hear a little more before dismissing him totally. Wilkins said Unthank would be scrapped and swallowed. Did he indicate why?"

"Yes," said Lanark. "He said you were no longer profitable, and scrapping you would bring some kind of energy gain. He said his people were used to eating towns and villages, but Unthank would be their first city since Carthage."

A howl of laughter went up from different parts of the room. A voice behind the pillar cried, "Carthage? What about Coventry?" and others shouted "Leningrad!" "Berlin!" "Warsaw!" "Dresden!" "Hiroshima!"

"I would like also to menshun," said a slow-voiced, white-haired lady, "Münster in 1535, Gonstantinoble in 1453 and 1204, ant Hierusalem more vrequently than vun cares to rememper."

"Please, please! A little more moderation!" cried Ritchie-Smollet. "These unhappy rationalizations took place when the council was split in two or menaced by sectarian extremists. I am sure Lanark is not lying when he tells us what he heard. I do suggest his informant misled him."

"The peaceful destruction of a modern city would be something new," said Sludden thoughtfully. "It would have to be a city with no effective government. And the creature would have to provide a lot of powerful new machinery. And the destruction would have to be approved by a full meeting of the council, a meeting where Unthank was represented."

"Wilkins said a meeting of council delegates would approve the action in eight days," said Lanark. "That was a while ago. The creature has delivered large suction delvers to something called the expansion project. I saw one. As for your government, you know it better than I do."

"Utter nonsense!" cried Gow. "The council has no heartier opponent in Unthank than myself. As the oldest and most active member of the committee I have wrestled with it since the last world war, and never till recently have we obtained from it such enormous concessions. A short while ago our roads and buildings were a century out of date. Now look at them! Modern motorways. High-rise housing. A city centre full of towering office blocks. We could have done none of this without council aid. Yet you suggest the council plans to smash us!"

"These new developments do not greatly veigh with me," said the slow-voiced lady. "The profits of this building vork haf gone to the creature. A city lives by its industry ant ours still declines. But ve cannot, on the vort of von man, assume the vorst. Ve neet documentary corroboration."

Gow said, "I have no wish to stoop to personal invective but—"

"Excuse me, Gow, Jack would like a chance to speak," said Sludden, indicating Ritchie-Smoller's helper who was waving from a corner.

"I was cleaning the guest speaker's suit," said Jack, "and I noticed a council paper in the pocket. Maybe that could tell us something."

Lanark pulled out the newspaper he had lifted in the council café. Sludden took it and started reading. Gow said, "I don't like using insulting language, but the welfare of the community drives me to it. This guest speaker of ours, this would-be plenipotentiary, is no stranger to *me*. On a recent delegation to the council *I* saw this so-called Lanark sniffing around Monboddo's throne with his long-haired girlfriend and his shabby little rucksack. He made no very creditable impression on the powers that be, I don't mind telling you. Is it likely, if there *was* a plot to dismantle this city, that they would trust the details to someone like *this?*"

"Give him laldy, Gow!" yelled a voice behind the pillar. Lanark gaped and stood up. He heard Grant at his side murmuring, "Careful now!" but a growing unease in his stomach had nothing to do with the debate. He said sharply, "Nobody trusted me with details. Wilkins would have told anybody these plans; he said only a revolution could change them. I don't care if you believe me or not."

He walked toward the door he had entered by.

Before he reached it Sludden cried, "Wait, everyone should hear this!" so he paused by the pillar. Sludden said, "This is from the chronology section of the *Western Lobby*:

Nobody but a fanatic would suggest that the material of time is moral, but on occasions like the present, when the boundaries of the most stable continents seem melting into intercalendrical mist, it appears probable that a working timescale needs a higher proportion of common decency than the science of chronology has hitherto assumed. Decency is a vague term, and at present we suggest no more by it than a little more brotherhood between colleagues of equal or nearly equal standing.

The authority of the council has always depended on the support of the creature, and until recently it was widely felt that Monboddo's connections with the Algolagnics–Cortexin group merely ratified his standing as a strong president. Recent disclosures, however, by the fiery energy chief Ozenfant show that recent loans of creature energy have been absorbed by the lord president's office to the almost total exclusion of the normal power corridor network.

Although respect for the president director and respect for the decimal hour are not connected in logic, they seem to feed irrationally on each other in a state of collapsing

confidence. There is deep alarm in
council corridors that speculation
against the new timescale has now
exceeded the boundaries of reason
and may no longer be susceptible
to rational remedy. Only one thing
is certain. The swift dismantling of
a certain darkened district, which
once seemed a daring and debatable
act of rationalization, has become
a matter of urgent necessity."

"What's that supposed to mean?" asked Gow. "There are hundreds of darkened districts. What conceivable reason have you for thinking they've chosen Unthank?"

"I came here to tell you that," said Grant. "Nearly two days ago a Cortexin tanker and an Algolagnics transporter collided at the intersection. All incoming traffic is diverted to Imber. We have food supplies for three more days. By 'day' I mean the old fashioned solar day of twenty-four hours, with roughly seventeen hundred heartbeats an hour."

"Pull yourself together, Grant!" said Ritchie-Smollet. "Do you suggest these vehicles were smashed in a criminal plot between Algolagnics and the council? That is pure paranoia. The council is sending experts to deal with the damage."

"You don't need a plot to cause crashes on a motorway," said Grant. "They happen all the time. When they happen on the council's doorstep they're cleared at once. Why the delay with us?"

"Because we are not on the council's doorstep. From the council's viewpoint we are a remote and unimportant province, but that does not mean they are out for our blood. The council traffic commissioner has talked to me on the phone. His clearance teams are fighting an imbalance at the Cortexin cloning plant. Half West Atlantis will sink if that isn't stabilized first. But he's moving heaven and earth to get the right men quickly here too. He said so. I know him. He is an honest man."

"Haven't you seen how the council works in peacetime?" asked Grant. "It never behaves badly. It never destroys a country of peasant villages, for example, but it lets the creature turn whole forests into paper so there are no roots to hold the water back. And when an accidental storm arises (as they always will), half a million people drown or die in the following famine, and the council helps the survivors, and the helpers organize the country's industry in ways the creature finds profitable. I'm sure your traffic commissioner honestly wants to clear the intersection. I'm sure his honest experts have more urgent work to do. And I'm sure that three days from now, when our administration crumbles and the city is a horde of starving rioters, the council will introduce an honest emergency-aid programme and honestly evacuate Unthank down whatever gullet the creature offers."

There was a long silence.

"It is true," said the slow-voiced lady softly, "that with efery passing moment a broken nerf circuit of the new Algolagnics model becomes a more dangerous object. Virst ve haf only the fibrations, but after two days, on the old timescale, sublimation produces radioactive fumes of an unusually lethal ant videspreading type."

"Why not clear up the mess yourselves?" said Lanark impatiently.

"We lack protective clothing. Vithout it nothing is able to lif vithin sixty metres of these objects."

"Are they heavy?" asked Lanark. "Could you flood the road and float them off it?"

"Powerhoses," said Grant to Sludden. "Open a storm drain and order the fire brigade to flush the mess down it with powerhoses."

"Impossible!" bellowed Gow. "Even if Unthank *is* menaced in the way you suggest, which I do *not* for one moment admit, the forcing of unqualified firemen to do the dangerous work of trained nerve-circuit experts is in flagrant defiance of all normal and democratic procedure. I am sure our provost is not going to be led astray by the jeremiads of the guest speaker and the rantings of brother Grant. Once again we see extremists of the right and left combining in an unholy alliance against all that is most stable in—"

"Blood will have to flow," said a loud dull voice behind the pillar. "I'm sorry, I see no other way."

"Whose blood will have to flow, Scougal?" asked Ritchie-Smollet gently, "and when, and where, and why will it flow, Scougal?"

"I'm sorry if my remarks upset people" said the dull voice, "I apologize. But blood will have to flow, I see no other way."

Lanark walked over to the little door, opened it, ducked under the lintel and closed it behind him.

CHAPTER 37.
Alexander Comes

Finding no light-switch he climbed the narrow steep spiral in
blackness, patting the wall as he neared the level of the attic.
At last his hand touched a clumsy wooden bolt. He slid it
back, shoved hard and stepped out into fresh air with a few
stars overhead. Either he had left the chapterhouse by the wrong
stairs or the stairs by the wrong door for he now stood in a
gutter between two dim slopes of roof. He could hear muffled
kitchen noises of water and clinking dishes, so the attic was
nearby. The gutter was clearly a walkway too, so he moved
along it toward the noise and came to a stone parapet overlooking a city square. It was a quiet square with a couple of tiny
figures walking across. The houses on the far side were the
old tenement kind with shops on the ground floor and some
upper windows curtained and lit from inside. These seemed
so pleasantly familiar that he stared, perplexed. Unthank was
the only city he remembered, but he had always wanted a
brighter place: why should he like the look of it now? The
yattering noise from the intersection was very audible. So were
the kitchen sounds which came from a door in a gable behind
him. He knocked on this, and a moment later Frankie opened
it. He was so delighted that he seized her waist and kissed
her surprised mouth. She pushed him away after a while, laughing and saying, "Passionate, eh?"
"How is she?"
"She was sleeping when I left, but I sent for the nurse to be
on the safe side."
"Thanks, Frankie, you're a good girl."

He walked beside the arches along the attic and softly entered the bright little cubicle. Rima smiled at him softly from her pillow. He said "Hullo" and squatted on a cushion by the bed. She whispered, "The contractions have begun."
"Good. A nurse is coming."
He held her hand under the bedclothes. A stout lady came busily in and frowned at him, then bent over Rima with a very wide smile.
"So you're going to have a wee baby!" she said in the loud slow voice some people use when speaking to idiots. "A wee baby just like your *mummy* had when *you* were born! Isn't that nice?"
"I'm not going to speak to her," said Rima to Lanark, then drew a sharp breath and seemed to concentrate on something.
"That's right!" said the nurse consolingly. "It doesn't *really* hurt now, does it?"
"Tell her my back's sore!" said Rima sharply.
"Her back's sore," said Lanark.
"And do you really want your husband to stay here? Some men find it very, very difficult to take."
"Tell her to shut up!" said Rima and a moment later added bitterly, "Tell her I've wet the bed."
"It isn't what you think," said the nurse. "It's perfectly natural." She turned the mattress and changed the sheets while Rima sat on a cushion wrapped in a blanket. Rima said, "I'm having a girl."
"Oh," said Lanark.
"I don't want a boy."
"Then I do."
"Why?"
"So that one of us will welcome it, whoever comes."
"You must always put me in the wrong, mustn't you?"
"Sorry."
She returned to bed, scowled, ground her teeth and worked hard for a while, holding his hand tight; then she relaxed and cried desperately, "Tell her to stop this pain in my back!"
"Things must get worse before they get better," said the nurse soothingly. She was drinking tea from a thermos flask.
"Ha!" snarled Rima. She thrust Lanark's hand away, clenched her fists outside the covers and started working again, sweating hard. For a long time spells of fretful repose were followed by spells of silent, urgent, determined labour.

At last she raised her knees high, spread them wide and said sharply, "What's happening?"

The nurse folded back the covers. Lanark leaned against the wall by the bed foot and stared into the red widening gash between Rima's thighs. She gasped and cried, "My back! My back! What's happening?"

"He's coming. I can see the face," said Lanark, for in the depth of the gash he seemed to see a squeezed-thin face emerging, six inches high and less than half an inch wide, the nose thin as a string and ending in an absurd little flap, the eyes on each side sunk in vertical creases. The mouth was a tight-pursed hole and the nurse kept sticking her finger in it, presumably to help it breathe. Then the mouth opened into an oval with something flat inside, and the oval grew and filled the whole gash, and the flatness was a dome coming out, and the dome was a head gripped by the nurse's hand. Then the universe seemed to go slow and silent. In slow silence a small, pale-lavender, enraged little person was lifted up, dragging after him a meaty cable. He had a penis, and his elbows and knees were bent, and his fists and eyes clenched tight, and his aghast mouth was yelling a soundless scream of fury. Rima, whose face seemed to have been scrubbed by a storm, turned on him a slow smile of loving recognition. The small person flushed red, opened an eye, then another, and after some hiccups his scream wavered out into angry sound. The universe returned to the usual speed. The nurse gave the baby to Rima and told Lanark sternly, "Go and get two soup plates from the kitchen."

"Why?"

"Do what you're told."

He ran along by the arches hearing sounds of a service from the cathedral floor. A remote ministerial voice was chanting, "My buird thou hast hanselled in face o' my faes; thou drookest my heid wi' ile, my bicker is fou an' skailin. . . ." Jack sat in the kitchen listening to Ritchie-Smollet, who was leaning on a table. "I would have advised more caution, but we've burned our boats and must abide the issue. Ah, Lanark! How are things with you?"

"Fine. Can I have two soup plates, please?"

"Congratulations! Boy or girl? How's the mother?" asked Ritchie-Smollet, handing over plates from a pile.

"Thank you. A boy. She seems all right."

"One has become two: the first and best miracle of all, eh? I hope you'll allow me the privilege of christening the little chap."

"I'll mention it to his mother but she isn't religious," said Lanark going to the door.

"Are you sure of that? Never mind. Come back when you can and we'll drink their health. I believe we've some cooking sherry in the larder."

The cubicle seemed full of women. Rima suckled the baby, Frankie poured water from a kettle into a basin, the nurse seized the plates and said, "That's fine, you can go now."
"But—"
"We can hardly move as it is, there's no room for you."
He watched his son enviously for a moment then went slowly away, but not toward the kitchen, for he didn't want company. He suddenly wanted to use himself vigorously, to run fast or climb high. He found a spiral stair near the organ loft and climbed quickly to another open walkway under the stars. It led through a chilling wind to another little door. He opened this and entered a large, dim, square, dusty room lit by hurricane lamps on the floor. A steep iron ladder slanted upward near the centre, and six Lugworm Casanovas lay smoking in sleeping bags along a wall. One of them said, "Shut it, man, nobody's too hot in here."
Lanark said, "Sorry," closed the door and crossed to the ladder. Its rungs were cold and gritty with rust, it shuddered at each step. When the upper shadows hid him from the eyes below he climbed more slowly, not lifting a foot until both hands gripped a rung, not raising a hand till both feet were firmly placed. He came to a floor of narrow planks set an inch apart. Light shining up between them showed the foot of a steeper ladder. He climbed this more slowly than ever. In the wall before, to each side, and behind him, were huge windows barred by horizontal stone slats. He looked down through them onto the black cathedral roof edged with city lights. He stood on thin rungs high up in an old stone cage and listened to the faintly whistling breeze. With each extra step he tried to remember that the ladder was solid, and braced by an occasional rod against a wall that had stood for many centuries, and would probably not collapse suddenly without warning. At last he reached, not a floor, but a narrow metal bridge. Black machinery overhung it. He made out timber beams, a big wheel and a bell whose rim, when he stepped underneath, came down to his shoulders. He raised a hand to the massive clapper and carefully pushed it forward, meaning gently to touch the side, but the weight increased with the angle, he had to use unexpected force and the shock of contact bathed him in a sudden sonorous *Dong*. Half deafened, half intoxicated by the sound,

he laughed aloud, let the clapper fall back and shoved it at the rim with both hands, ducked as it swung back again and then reached up again to hurl it forward. The detonation of the strokes grew inaudible. He felt only a great droning reverberating the bell, the bridge, his bones, the tower, the air. His arms were tired. He ducked out from under the bell and gripped a handrail for support, though at first the sound in it hurt his palms like an electric current.

The droning faded. He seemed to hear protesting cries from below and, ashamed of the noise he had made, climbed a ladder away from them. He came to a higher floor of wooden slats where the blackness was total, except for a chink of light below a door. He groped toward it, slid the bolt and went out onto a windy platform at the foot of the floodlit steeple. The racket from the intersection was audible again, sometimes louder, sometimes fainter. He wondered if this was caused by the blustering wind and stepped to the parapet facing the Necropolis, for the din seemed to come from behind it. The highest monuments were silhouetted against a pulsing glow in the sky. Wedges of shadow moved over this like the arms of a windmill. The yattering noise sank to a dull stutter, hesitated, coughed and stopped. The majestic beams of shadow swept the sky in silence for a while, then suddenly widened as the glow faded. The main light now was cast by the great lamp standards on the motorway. A remote mechanical braying began and came swiftly nearer. A line of red fire engines with braying sirens appeared round a curving bridge from the intersection and sped down the gorge between Necropolis and cathedral. The air began filling with traffic sounds. Lanark walked round the platform to the far side of the tower and looked down onto the square. A couple of trucks rumbled across it pulling trailers with metal wreckage on them; then a trickle of cars began flowing in the opposite direction. A mobile crane drove through a gateway to the cathedral grounds, crossed the stones of the old graveyard and parked against a wall. Lanark suddenly felt his chilled ears, hands and body and returned to the door in the spire.

Coming down on the ladders he found the light from below much stronger than before. The room where the Lugworms had lain was lit by bulbs hung from improvised brackets. Two electricians were working near the door and one of them said, "A bloke was looking for you, Jimmy."

"Who was he?"

"A young bloke. Long hair."

"What did he want?"

"He didnae say."

Near the cubicle he heard a strange, steady little song. Sludden lay on the bed singing "Dadadada" and dandling a robust little boy in a blue woollen suit. Rima, in a blouse and skirt, sat knitting beside them. The sight filled Lanark with a large cold rage. Rima gave him an unfriendly glance and Sludden said brightly, "The wanderer returns!"

Lanark went to the tiny sink, washed his hands, then turned to Sludden and said, "Give him to me."

He took the child, who started wailing. "Oh, put him down!" said Rima impatiently. "He needs a rest and so do I."

Lanark sat on the bed foot and sang quietly, "Dadadada." The boy stopped complaining and settled in his arms. The small compact body was warm and comforting and gave such a pleasant feeling of peace that Lanark wondered uneasily if this was a right thing for a father to feel. He laid the boy in a pram by the bed and tucked a soft blanket round him.

Sludden stood up and stretched his arms, saying, "Great! That's really great. I came here for several reasons, of course, but one is to congratulate you on your performance. Don't sneer at him, Rima, he's a good committee man when he accepts discipline. He jostled Gow, and that allowed us to act. The committee is in permanent session now. I don't mean we're all in the chapterhouse all the time, but some of us are in the chapterhouse all the time."

Lanark said, "Listen, Sludden, I want the company of my wife and child. Do you understand me?"

"Of course!" said Sludden cheerily. "I'm just leaving. I'll come back for you all later."

"What do you mean?"

"Sludden has offered us room in his house," said Rima.

"We're not taking it."

"I don't want to force anything on you," said Sludden. "But this seems a strange place to bring up a child."

"Unthank is dead and done for, don't you realize that?" cried Lanark. "The boy and Rima and I are leaving for a much brighter city. Wilkins promised us."

"Don't trust your council friends too far," said Sludden gravely. "We've cleared the motorway, the food trucks are rolling in again. And even if Wilkins did tell the truth, you're forgetting differences in timescale. The decimal calendar hasn't been introduced here and what the council calls days can be months—years, where we're concerned. And remember, Alexander was born here. You have a council passport. He hasn't."

"Who is Alexander?"

Sludden pointed to the pram. Rima said, "Ritchie-Smollet christened him that."

Lanark jumped up shouting, *"Christened?"*

Alexander started crying. "Shushush," whispered Rima, reaching for the pram handle and gently rocking it. "Shushushush."

"Why Alexander?" whispered Lanark furiously. "Why couldn't you wait for me? Why the bloody hurry?"

"We waited as long as we could—why didn't you come when we called?"

"You never called me!"

"We did. Jack went to the tower when you started your row and shouted up the ladder, but you wouldn't come down."

"I didn't know that was Jack shouting," said Lanark, confused.

"Were you drunk?" asked Rima.

"Of course not. You've never seen me drunk."

"Perhaps, but you often act that way. And Ritchie-Smollet says a bottle of cooking sherry has vanished from the kitchen."

"I'm leaving," said Sludden with a chuckle. "Outsiders should never mix in a lovers' quarrel. I'll see you later."

"Thank you," said Lanark. "We'll manage by ourselves."

Sludden shrugged and left. Alexander gradually fell asleep.

Rima sat with tight-shut lips, knitting hard. Lanark lay on the bed with hands behind his head and said gloomily, "I didn't want to leave you. And I didn't think I was long."

"You were away for hours—ages, it seemed to me. You've no sense of time. None at all."

"Alexander is quite a good name. We can shorten it to Alex. Or Sandy."

"He's called *Alexander.*"

"What are you knitting?"

"Clothes. Children need clothes, hadn't you noticed? We can't always live on Ritchie-Smollet's charity."

"If Sludden is right about calendars," Lanark mused, "we'll be a long time in this place. I'll have to look for work."

"So you're going to leave me alone again. I see. Why did you ring that bell? Are you sure you weren't drunk?"

"I rang it because I was happy then. Why are you attacking me?"

"To defend myself."

"I'm sorry I shouted at you, Rima. I was surprised and angry. I'm very glad to be back with you."

"Yes, it's easy for you to live in a box, you can run off to your towers and committee meetings whenever you like. When will I get some freedom?"

"Whenever you need it."

"And you'll stay here and look after Alex?"

"Of course. That's only fair."

Rima sighed and then smiled and rolled up her knitting. She came to the bed, kissed him quickly on the brow, then went to the chest of drawers and peered at her face in a mirror.

Lanark said, "Are you leaving already?"

"Yes, Lanark. I really do need a change."

She made up her mouth with lipstick. Lanark said, "Who gave you that?"

"Frankie. We're going dancing. We're going to get ourselves picked up by a couple of young young young boys. You don't mind, do you?"

"Not if you only dance with them."

"Oh, but we'll flirt with them too. We'll madden them with desire. Middle-aged women need to madden somebody some times."

"You aren't middle-aged."

"I'm no chicken, anyway. When Alex wakens you can change his nappy—there's a clean one in the top drawer. Put the dirty one in the plastic bag under the bed. If he cries you must heat some milk in the kitchen—not too hot, mind. Test it with your finger."

"Aren't you breastfeeding him?"

"Yes, but he has to learn to drink like an ordinary human being. But I'll probably be back before he wakens. How do I look?"

She posed before him, hands on hips. He said, "Very young. Very beautiful."

She kissed him warmly and left. He lay back on the bed, missing her, and fell asleep.

He was wakened by Alexander crying so he changed his nappy and carried him to the kitchen. Jack and Frankie were eating a meal at a table there. Frankie said, "Hullo, passionate man. How's Rima?"

He stared at her, confused, and blushed hotly. He muttered, "Gone for a walk. The boy needs milk."

"I'll make him a bottle."

Lanark strayed round the kitchen murmuring nonsense to Alexander, for there was a strange appalling pain in his chest and he didn't want to talk to adults. Frankie handed him a warm bottle with teat folded in a white napkin. He muttered some thanks and went back to the cubicle. He sat on the bed and held the teat to Alexander's mouth but Alexander twisted aside, screaming, "NononononoMumumumum!"

"She'll be back soon, Sandy."

"NononononononononononoMumumumumumumumumum!"

Alexander kept screaming and Lanark walked the floor with him. He felt he was carrying a dwarf who kept hitting him on the head with a stick, a dwarf he could neither disarm nor put down. People in neighbouring cubicles began banging their walls, then a man came in and said, "There are folk trying to sleep in this building, Jimmy."

"I can't help that, and I'm not called Jimmy."

The man was tall and bald with white stubble on his cheeks, a single black tooth in his upper jaw, and wore a dirty grey raincoat. He stared at Lanark for a while then pulled a brown bottle from his pocket and said, "Milk's no use. Give him a slug of this—it's a great quietener."

"No."

"Then take a slug yourself."

"No."

The man sighed, squatted on a stool and said, "Tell me your woes."

"I have no woes!" yelled Lanark who was too plagued to think. Alexander was screaming "Mumumumumumumumumum!"

"If it's woman trouble," said the man, "I can advise you because I was married once. I had a wife who did terrible things, things I cannae mention in the presence of a wean. You see, women are different from us. They're seventy-five percent water. You can read that in Pavlov."

Alexander fastened his gums on the teat and started sucking. Lanark sighed with relief. After a moment he said, "Men are mostly water too."

"Yes, but only seventy percent. The extra five percent makes the difference. Women have notions and feelings like us but they've got tides too, tides that keep floating the bits of a human being together inside them and washing it apart again. They're governed by lunar gravity; you can read that in Newton. How can they follow ordinary notions of decency when they're driven by the moon?"

Lanark laid Alexander in the pram with the bottle beside him and gently rocked the handle.

The man said, "I was ignorant when I was married. I hadnae read Newton, I hadnae read Pavlov, so I kicked the bitch out—pardon the language, I am referring to my wife. I wish now that I'd cut my throat instead. Do me a favour, pal. Give yourself a holiday. Have a drink."

Lanark glanced at the brown bottle held toward him, then took it and swigged. The taste was horrible. He passed it back, trying to say thank you, but there were tears in his eyes and he could only gulp and pull faces. A warm stupidity began to spread softly through him. He heard the man say, "You have to like women but not care for them: not care what they do, I mean. Nobody can help what they do. We do as things do with us."

"What is for us," said Lanark, with a feeling of profound understanding, "will not go past us."

"A hundred years from now," said the man, "it'll all be the same."

Lanark heard Alexander asking sadly, "When will she come?"

"Soon, son. Very soon."

"When is soon?"

"Near to now but not now."

"I need her now."

"Then you need her badly. You must try to need her properly."

"What is proply?"

"Silently. Silence is always proper. When I understand this better I'll stop talking. You won't be able to hear me for miles. I will radiate silence like a dark star shining in the gaps between syllables and conversation."

"You're ignoring politics," said the man aggressively. "Politics depend on noise. All parties subscribe to *that* opinion, if to no other."

Alexander screamed, "They're biting me!"

"Who's biting you?" said Lanark leaning unsteadily over the pram.

"My teeth."

Lanark put a finger in the small mouth and felt a tiny bone edge coming through the gum. He said uneasily, "We age quickly in this world."

"You must remember one important thing," said the man, "You've emptied the bottle. I'm not complaining. I know where to get another, but it costs a coupla dollars. A dollar a skull. Right?"

"I'm sorry. I've no money."

"What's happening here?" asked Rima, coming angrily in.
"Sandy is teething," said Lanark.
"I'm just leaving, missus," said the man, and left.

Rima changed Alexander's nappy, saying grimly, "I can't
trust you to do a thing."
"But I've fed him. I've cared for him."
"Huh!"
Lanark lay on the bed watching her. He was sober now and
some of the ache had returned to his chest, but he was also
thankful and relieved. After a while he said, "Did you enjoy
the dancing?"
"Dancing?"
"You said you were going dancing with Frankie."
"Did I? Maybe I did. Anyway I missed Frankie and went house-
hunting with what's-his-name. The fat soldier. McPake."
"McPake?"
"He used to hang around the old Elite with us. The Elite
has vanished under a motorway now. Nothing there but a great
concrete trench. They really are making a mess of this place."
"Did you find any houses?"
"Hundreds of them, all furnished and all beautiful. But we've
no money so I was wasting my time. Is that what you're going
to say?"
"Of course not!"
She had settled Alexander in the pram and was sitting despondently with drooping head and arms folded under breasts. He
was pricked by tenderness and desire and went to her with
arms outstretched, whispering, "Oh, Rima dear, let's love each
other a little. . . ."
She smiled, jumped up and danced toward him with hands
outstretched and nipping. "Oh, Rima dear!" she moaned
through pursed-out lips. "Oh, lovey-dovey earie-dearie Rima,
let's lovey-dovey an itsy-bitsy little. . . ."
Her nips were painful and he fended them off, laughing until
they both fell side by side and breathless on the bed. A moment
later he asked sadly, "Do I really seem like that?"
"I'm afraid you do. You're too nervous and pathetic."
She sighed, then unfastened her blouse, saying, "However,
since you want it, let's love each other a little."
He stared, astonished, and said, "I can't make love when you've
made me feel small and absurd."
"I've made you fell absurd, have I? I'm glad. I'm delighted.
You make me feel small all the time. You've never paid

attention to my feelings, never once. You dragged us here from a perfectly comfortable place because you disliked the food, and what good did it do? We still eat the same food. You laughed when I gave you a son and you can't even give him a home. You use use use me all the time, and you're so smugly sure you're right all the time. You're heavy and dismal and humourless, yet you want me to pet you and make you feel big and important. I'm sorry, I can't do it. I'm too tired." She went to the seat by the pram and resumed knitting.

Lanark sat on the bed with his face in his hands. He said, "This is Hell."
"Yes. I know."
"I wish you could love me."
"You take me for granted, so I can't. You don't know how to make me love you. Some men can do it."
He looked up and said, "Which men?"
She continued to knit. He stood up and cried, *"Which men?"*
"I might tell you if you wouldn't get hysterical."
Alexander sat up and asked in an interested voice, "Is Dad going to get hysterical?"
Lanark shook his head dumbly then whispered, "I must get out of here."
"Yes, I think you should," said Rima. "Look for a job. You need one."
He went to the entrance and turned, hoping for a look of friendship or recognition, but her face was so full of stony pain that he could only shake his head.
"Goodbye Dad," said Alexander casually. Lanark waved to him, hesitated, then left.

CHAPTER 38.
Greater Unthank

The shadowy nave seemed vast and empty till he neared the door and saw Jack sitting on the font. Lanark meant to pass him with a slight nod but Jack was watching with such a frank stare that he stopped and said tensely, "Could you please direct me to a labour exchange?"

"They're not called labour exchanges now, they're called job centres," said Jack, springing down. "I'll take you to one."

"Can Ritchie-Smollet spare you?"

"Maybe not, but I can spare him. I change bosses when I like."

Jack led him through the cathedral grounds to a bus stop on the edge of the square. Lanark said, "I can't afford a bus fare."

"Don't worry, I've got cash. What do you want at a job centre?"

"An unskilled job doing something useful exactly the way I'm told."

"Not many jobs like that in Unthank nowadays. Except in cleansing, perhaps. And cleansing workers have to be young and healthy."

"How old do you think I am?"

"Past the halfway mark, at least."

Lanark looked down at the prominent veins on the back of his hands and muttered after a while, "No dragonhide, any-way."

"What did you say?"

"I may not be young but I don't have dragonhide."

"Of course you don't. We aren't living in the dark ages."

Lanark felt like the victim of a sudden horrible accident. He

thought, 'Over halfway through life and what have I achieved?
What have I made? Only a son, and he was mostly his mother's
work. Who have I ever helped? Nobody but Rima, and I've
only helped her out of messes she'd have missed if she had
been with someone else. All I have is a wife and child. I must
make them a home, a secure comfortable home.'
As if answering the thought a bus crossed a corner of the square
with a painting on the side of a mother and child. Printed
over it were the words A HOME IS MONEY. MONEY IS
TIME. BUY TIME FOR YOUR FAMILY FROM THE
QUANTUM CHRONOLOGICAL. (THEY'LL LOVE YOU
FOR IT.)
"I need a lot of money," said Lanark. "If I can't get work
I'll have to beg from the security people."
"The name's changed," said Jack. "They're called social stability
now. And they don't give money, they give three-in-one."
"What's that?"
"A special kind of bread. It nourishes and tranquillizes and
stops your feeling cold, which is useful if you're homeless.
But I don't think you should eat any."
"Why?"
"A little does no harm, but after a while it damages the intelli-
gence. Of course the unemployment problem would be a catas-
trophe without it. Here comes our bus."
"This *is* Hell," said Lanark.
"There are worse hells," said Jack.

The bus was painted to look like a block of Enigma de
Filets Congalés. On the side it said NOW EVERYONE CAN
TASTE THE RICH HUMAN GOODNESS IN FROZEN
SECRETS, THE FOOD OF PRESIDENTS.
Jack led Lanark to a seat on the top deck and brought out a
cigarette packet labelled POISON. He said, "Like one?"
"No thanks," said Lanark and stared as Jack lit a white cylinder
with DON'T SMOKE THIS printed along it.
"Yes, they're dangerous," said Jack, inhaling. "That's why the
council insisted on the warning."
"Why doesn't it stop them being made?"
"Half the population is hooked on them," said Jack. "And
the council gets half the money spent on them. They're an
Algolagnics product. There are less dangerous drugs, of course,
but they wouldn't be so profitable if they were legalized."
A bus going the other way carried a sentence past the window:
QUICK MONEY IS TIME IN YOUR POCKET—BUY

MONEY FASTER FROM THE QUANTUM EXPONENTIAL.

Jack said, "You were being sarcastic—weren't you?—when you asked if Ritchie-Smollet could spare me?"

"I'm sorry."

"I don't mind. Yes, he depends on me, does old Smollet. So does Sludden. I choose my bosses carefully. *That* bloke was my boss once."

Jack pointed through the window at a tattered poster covering the end of a derelict tenement. It showed a friendly-looking man behind a desk with telephones on it. The words below said **ARE YOU LOOKING FOR A FACTORY SITE, A FACTORY OR A LABOUR FORCE? PHONE 777-7777 AND SPEAK TO TOM TALLENTYRE, CHAIRMAN OF THE WORK FOR UNTHANK BOARD.**

"Tallentyre was a very big man after they scrapped the Q39 project," said Jack. "In fact he was provost for a while. But Sludden did for him in the end. Sludden pointed out that the posters were put up in parts of Unthank where the unemployed lived, and folk with power to start new factories didn't live in Unthank anyway. So the action shifted to Sludden and Smollet, and so did I. I enjoy being where the action is. That's why I'm with you, just now."

"Why are you with me?"

"You aren't what you pretend, are you? I agree with Gow. You're some sort of agent or investigator. Why ask about cleansing and social stability when you work for Ozenfant and carry a council passport?"

"I don't work for Ozenfant. And what use is a council passport to me?"

"It could get you a very well-paid job."

"I want that!" said Lanark excitedly. "How do I get one? I want that!"

"Ask the employment centre to put you on the professional register," said Jack sulkily. He seemed disappointed.

Lanark looked out of the window, feeling more hopeful. The bus was passing busy new shops whose fronts spread along whole blocks and showed brightly packaged food and drugs and records and clothes. He noticed many restaurants with oriental names and many kinds of gambling shops. In some he glimpsed people sitting with bags and baskets at counters, apparently gambling for food. The gaps left by demolished buildings were crammed with parked cars and surrounded by

fences with wild threats scrawled on them in bright paint.
CRAZY MAC KILLS, they said and **MAD TOAD RULES**,
and **THE WEE MALCIES ARE COMING**, but they didn't
distract from the larger message of the posters. These showed
pictures of family life, sex, food and money, and their words
were more puzzling.
**BOOST YOUR THERMS WITH NULLITY GREEN—BAG
HER IN YOUR BLOCKAL BLOOPER-MARKET.
GRIND YOUR SPECTACLES WITH METAL TEA, THE
SEX CHAMP ON THE CHILIASM.
THE SWEETEST DREAMERS INHALE BLUE FUME,
THE POISON WITH THE WARNING.
WISE BUYERS ARE THE BEST SEXERS—BUY HER A
LONG LIFE, AN EASY DEATH FROM QUANTUM
PROVIDENTIAL. (SHE'LL LOVE YOU FOR IT.)**
Lanark said, "What a lot of instructions."
"Don't you like advertisements?"
"No."
"The city would look pretty dead without them—they add to
the action. Read that."
Jack pointed to a small poster on the bus window which said:

ADVERTISING OVERSTIMULATES,
MISINFORMS,
CORRUPTS.

If *you* feel this, send your name and address
to the Council Advertising Commission and
receive your free booklet explaining why we
can't do without it.

They got off the bus in a large square Lanark knew well,
though it was brighter and busier than he remembered. He
gazed at the statues on their massive Victorian pedestals and
reflected that he had seen them before he saw Rima. The square
was still enclosed by ornate stone buildings except where he
and Jack stood before a glass wall of shining doors. Above
this great horizontal strips of concrete and glass alternated to
a height of twenty or thirty floors. Jack said, "The job centre."
"It's big."
"All the central job centres are housed here, and it's the central
centre of stability and surroundings too. I'll leave you now,
right?"
Lanark felt he was reliving something which had happened
once before, perhaps with Gloopy. He said awkwardly, "I'm

sorry I'm not what you thought—not a man of action, I mean."
Jack shrugged and said, "Not your fault. I'll give you a bit
of advice—"
He was interrupted by sudden siren blasts and a rattling like
thin thunder. The traffic halted round the square. Pedestrians
stood staring as an open truck sped past full of khaki-clad men
wearing black berets and holding guns. It had caterpillar treads
of a sort Lanark had seen rolling slowly over rough ground
in films, but on the smooth road it raced so swiftly that it
was past as soon as recognized.
"The army!" cried Jack with a smile of pure appetite. "Now
we'll see some action. Hoi! Hoi! Hoi!"
He ran along the pavement shouting and waving to a taxi in
the resuming traffic. It came to the kerb and he leaped in.
Lanark watched it turn a corner, then stood awhile feeling sickened and uneasy. He was thinking about Alex, Rima and the
soldiers. He had never seen armed soldiers in a street before.
At last he turned and entered the building.

To a uniformed man in the entrance hall he said, "I'm
looking for work."
"Where do you live?"
"The cathedral."
"The cathedral's in the fifth district. Take lift eleven to floor
twenty."
The lift was like a metal wardrobe and packed with poorly
dressed people. When Lanark got out he had another feeling
of entering the past. He saw a dingy expanse tiled with grey
rubber and covered by men of all ages crowded together on
benches. A counter divided into cubicles by partitions ran along
one wall, and the cubicle facing the lift contained a chair and
a sign saying INQUIRIES. As Lanark walked toward this he felt
the air of the place resisting him like transparent jelly. The
men on the benches had a statuesque, entranced look as though
congealed there. All movement was exhausting—it would have
been equally tiring to go back. He reached the chair, slumped
onto it and sat, upright but dozing, until someone seemed to
be shouting at him. He opened his eyes and said thickly, "I
. . . am not . . . an animal."
An old clerk with bristling eyebrows behind the counter said,
"Then you ought to be on the professional register."
"Eh? . . . How?"
"Go down to the second floor."

Lanark got back to the lift and only wakened properly inside it. He wondered if all offices in that building had the same deadening influence.

But the second floor was different. It was covered by a soft green carpet. Low easy chairs clustered round glass tables with magazines on them, but nobody was waiting. There were no counters. Men and women too elegant to be thought of as clerks chatted to clients across widely spaced desks divided from each other by stands of potted plants. A girl receptionist showed him to the desk of a slightly older woman. She pushed a packet labelled BLUE FUME toward him, saying, "Please sit down. Do you inhale this particular poison?"

"No thank you."

"How very wise. Tell me about yourself."

He talked for a while. She opened her eyes wide and said, "You've actually worked with Ozenfant? How exciting! Tell me, what kind of man is he? In private life, I mean."

"He overeats and he's a bad musician."

The woman chuckled as if he had said something clever and shocking, then said, "I'm going to leave you for a moment. I've just had rather a good idea."

She came back saying, "We're in luck—Mr. Gilchrist can see you right away."

As they walked between the other desks she murmured, "Strictly between ourselves, I think Mr. Gilchrist is very keen to meet you. So is Mr. Pettigrew, though he doesn't show it, of course. You'll enjoy Mr. Pettigrew, he's a *tremendous* cynic." She led him to a door but didn't follow him through.

Lanark entered an office with two desks and a secretary typing at a table in the corner. A tall bald man sat telephoning on the edge of the nearest desk. He smiled at Lanark and pointed to an easy chair, saying, "He must be suffering from *folie de grandeur*. Provosts are buffers between us and the voters; they aren't supposed to *do* things. But nobody wants a riot, of course."

At the desk behind him a stout man leaned back smoking a pipe. Lanark sat looking through the window at the floodlit roof of a building across the square. A dome at one end had a glittering wind-vane shaped like a galleon. The tall man put the receiver down, saying, "That's that. My name is Gilchrist— I'm very pleased to meet you."

They shook hands and Lanark saw the council mark on Gilchrist's brow. They sat down in chairs beside a coffee table and Gilchrist said, "We want coffee, I think. Black or white, Lanark? See to that, Miss Maheen. I hear you are looking for professional employment, Lanark."

"Yes."

"But you've no definite idea of the kind of work you want."

"Correct. I'm more concerned about the salary."

"Would you like to work here?"

Lanark looked round the room. The secretary was attending to an electric percolator on top of a filing cabinet. The man behind the other desk had a large, dolorous, clownish face and winked at Lanark with no change of expression. Lanark said, "I'm very willing to consider it."

"Good. You mentioned salary. Unluckily salaries are a vexed question with us. It's impossible to pay a monthly or yearly sum when we can't even measure the minutes and hours. Until the council sends us the decimal clocks it's been promising for so long Unthank is virtually part of the intercalendrical zone. At present the city is kept going by force of habit. Not by rules, not by plans, but by habit. Nobody can rule with an elastic tape measure, can they?"

Lanark shook his head impatiently and said, "I've a family to feed. What can you offer me?"

"Credit. Members of our staff receive a Quantum credit card. That's much more useful than money."

"Will it let me rent a comfortable home for three people?"

"Easily. You could even buy a home. The energy to pay for it would be deducted from your future."

"Then I'll be glad to work here."

"I should explain the range of our activities."

"No need. I'll do whatever I'm told."

Gilchrist smiled and shook his head, saying "Social ignorance is only a virtue in the manufacturing classes. We professionals must understand the organism as a whole. That is our burden and our pride. It justifies our bigger incomes."

"Blethers!" said the stout man at the other desk. "Who in this building understands the organism as a whole? You and me and an old woman upstairs, perhaps, but the rest have forgotten. They were told, but they've forgotten."

"Pettigrew is a cynic," said Gilchrist, laughing.

"A *lovable* cynic," muttered Pettigrew. "Remember that. Pettigrew is everybody's lovable cynic."

The secretary laid a tray of coffee things on the table. Gilchrist carried his cup to the window, sat on the ledge and said oracularly, "Employment. Stability. Surroundings. Three offices, yet properly understood they are the same. Employment ensures stability. Stability lets us reshape our surroundings. The improved surroundings become a new condition of employment. The snake eats its tail. Nothing has precedence. This great building—this centre of all centres, this tower of welfare— exists to maintain full employment, reasonable stability and decent surroundings."

"Animals," said Pettigrew. "We deal with animals here. The scruff. The scum. The lowest of the low."

"Pettigrew is referring to the fact that there are not enough jobs and houses for everyone. Naturally—as in all freely competing societies—the unemployed and homeless tend to be less clever, or less healthy, or less energetic than the rest of us."

"They're a horde of stupid, dirty layabouts," said Pettigrew. "I know them, I grew up among them. You middle-class liberals like to pet them, but I wouldn't even let them breed. What we need is an X-ray device under the turnstiles at the football stadiums. Each man going through gets a blast of 900 roentgens right on the testicles. It would be perfectly painless. They wouldn't know what had happened till they got a wee printed card along with their entrance ticket. 'Dear Sir,' it would say. 'You may now ride your wife in perfect safety.' "

Gilchrist laughed until his coffee spilled into the saucer. "Pettigrew, you're incorrigible!" he said. "You talk as if a man's misery was all his own fault. You must admit that poverty, insanity and crime have multiplied since our major industry shut down. That isn't coincidence."

"Blame the unions!" said Pettigrew. "Prosperity is made by the bosses struggling with each other for more wealth. If they have to struggle with their workers too, then everybody loses. No wonder the big groups are shifting their factories to the coolie continents. I'm only thankful that the folk who lose most in the end are the envious sods who own the least. Greed isn't a pretty thing but envy is far, far worse."

"You're talking politics. It's time you shut up for a while," said Gilchrist amicably. He put down his cup on the window ledge, sat beside Lanark and said quietly, "Don't let his rough tongue upset you. Pettigrew is something of a saint. He's helped more widows and orphans than we've had good breakfasts."

"There's no need for excuses," said Lanark. "I realize now that nobody does well in this world if they don't belong to a big strong group. Your group handles the people who don't have one. I want to be with you, not under you, so tell me what to do."

"You're very abrupt," said Gilchrist. "Please remember we are here to help the unfortunate, and we *do* help them, as far as we can. Our problem is lack of funds. The recent Greater Unthank reorganization has given us a much larger staff to deal with the increasing number of unfortunates, so we have thousands of experts—planners, architects, engineers, artists, renovators, conservers, blood doctors, bowel doctors, brain doctors—all sitting on their bottoms praying for funds to start working with."

"So what can *I* do?"

"You can start as a grade D inquiry clerk. You will sit behind a desk hearing people complain. You must note their names and addresses and tell them they'll hear from us through the post."

"That's easy."

"It's the hardest job we have. You must give an appearance of listening closely. You must prod them with questions to keep the words flowing if they look like drying up. You must keep each one talking till they're exhausted—longer, if possible."

"And I write a report on what they tell me?"

"No. Just note their name and address and tell them they'll hear from us through the post."

"Why?"

"I was afraid you would ask that," said Gilchrist, sighing slightly. "As I already indicated, there are many whom we cannot help through lack of funds. A lot of these are still strong and vigorous, and it is a dangerous thing to suddenly deprive a man of hope—he can turn violent. It is important to kill hope *slowly,* so that the loser has time to adjust unconsciously to the loss. We try to keep hope alive till it has burned out the vitality feeding it. Only then is the man allowed to face the truth."

"So a grade D inquiry clerk does nothing but postpone."

"Yes."

Lanark said loudly, "I don't want—" then hesitated. He thought of the credit card, and a home with three or four rooms, perhaps in walking distance of this great building. Perhaps he would be able to go home for lunch and eat it with Sandy and Rima.

He said feebly, "I don't *want* this job."

"Nobody wants it. As I said, it's the hardest job we have. But will you take it?"

After a moment Lanark said, "Yes."

"Excellent. Miss Maheen, come over here. I want you to smile at our new colleague. He's called Lanark."

The secretary sat down facing Lanark and looked into his eyes. She had a smooth, vacant, fashionably pretty face and her hair was so golden and perfectly brushed that it looked like a nylon wig. For a split second her mouth widened in a smile, and Lanark was disconcerted by a click inside her head. Gilchrist said, "Show her your profile." Lanark stared at him and heard another click. Miss Maheen slid two fingers inside a pocket of her crisp white blouse above her left breast and drew out a plastic strip. She handed it to Lanark. There were two clear little pictures of him at one end, a disconcerted full face and a perplexed profile. The rest was covered by fine blue parallel lines with LANARK printed on top and a long number with about twelve digits.

"She's a reliable piece," said Gilchrist, patting Miss Maheen's bottom as she returned to her table. "She issues credit cards, makes coffee, types, looks pretty and her hobby is oriental martial arts. She's a Quantum-Cortexin product."

Lanark said bitterly, "Can't Quantum-Cortexin make something to work as a grade D inquiry clerk?"

"Oh, yes, they can. They did. We tried it out at a stability sub-centre and it provoked a riot. The clients found its responses too mechanical. Most people have a quite irrational faith in human beings."

"Roll on, Provan," said Pettigrew.

"Amen, Pettigrew. Roll on, Provan," said Gilchrist.

"What do you mean?" said Lanark.

"*Roll on* is a colloquialism whereby an anticipated event is conjured to occur more quickly. We're looking forward to our transfer to Provan. You know about that, of course?"

"I was told I could go there because I'd a council passport."

"Yes indeed. We'll manage things much better from Provan. I'm afraid this big expensive building has been a great big expensive mistake. Even the air conditioning doesn't work very well. But let's go to the twentieth floor."

They went through the desks of the outer office to a large and quiet lift. It brought them to a long narrow office containing about thirty desks. Half were occupied by people typing or phoning; many were empty, and the rest surrounded by talkative groups. Gilchrist led Lanark to one of these and said, "Here is our new inquiry clerk."

"Thank God!" said a man who was carefully folding a paper form into a dart. "I've just faced six of the animals, six in a row. I'm not going out there again for a long, long time." He launched the dart which drifted sweetly down the length of the office. There was scattered applause.

"Good luck!" said Gilchrist, shaking Lanark's hand. "I promise you'll be promoted out of here as soon as we find a replacement for you. Pettigrew and I drink in the Vascular Cavity. It's a vulgar pub but handy for the office and one always gets a good eyeful." (He winked.) "So if you call there later we'll have a jar together."

He went out quickly. The dart thrower led Lanark to the last of a long row of doors in one wall. He softly opened it a little way, peeked through the crack and whispered, "He seems quiet. I don't think there's anything to worry about. You know what to do?"

"Yes."

Lanark stepped through the door into a cubicle behind a counter with an inquiries sign on it.

A thin, youngish man sat facing him. He had short ruffled hair, a clean suit of cheap cloth, his eyes were closed and he seemed barely able to avoid falling sideways. Lanark took the knob of the door he had just come through, slammed it hard and sat down. The man opened his eyes and said, "No no no no . . . no no, you've got me wrong."

As his eyes focused on Lanark's face his own face began to change. Vitality flooded into it. He smiled and whispered, "Lanark!"

"Yes," said Lanark, wondering.

The man almost laughed with relief. "Thank Christ it's you!" He leaned over the counter and shook Lanark's hand, saying, "Don't you know me? Of course not, I was a kid at the time. I'm Jimmy Macfee. Granny Fleck's wee Macfee. You remember the old Ashfield Street days when me and my sisters played at sailing ships on your bed? My, but you've put on the beef. You were thin then. You had pockets full of seashells and pebbles, remember?"

"Were you that boy?" said Lanark, shaking his head. "How's Mrs. Fleck? Have you seen her lately?"

"Not lately, no. She hardly goes out these days. Arthritis. It's her age. But thank Christ it's you. I've seen six of these clerks, and every one of them has tried to put me off by sending me to another. The problem is, see, that I'm married, see, and me and the wife have a mohome. *And* we've two weans, six years and seven years, boy and girl. Now I'm not criticizing mohomes—I *make* the bloody things—but there's not much room in them, right? And when we took this one the housing department definitely said that if I paid my rent prompt and kept my nose clean we'd get a proper house when we needed it. Well we've had an accident. The wife's pregnant again. So what can we do? Four of us and a screaming wean in a mohome? And having to use a public lavatory when we need a wash or a you-know-what? So what can we do?"

Lanark stared down at a pen and a heap of forms on the counter. He picked up the pen and said hesitantly, "What's your address?" Then he dropped the pen and said firmly, "Don't tell me. It's no use. This place isn't going to help you at all."

"What?"

"You'll get no help here. If you need a new house you'll have to find a way of getting it yourself."

"But that needs money. Are you advising me . . . to steal?"

"Perhaps. I don't know. But whatever you do please be careful. I haven't met the police yet, but I imagine they're fairly efficient when dealing with lonely criminals. If you decide to do something, do it with a lot of other people who feel the same way. Perhaps you should organize a strike, but don't go on strike for more money. Your enemies understand money better than you do. Go on strike for things. Strike for bigger houses."

Macfee screwed his face up incredulously and shouted, "Me? Organize a . . . ? Thanks for bloody nothing!"

He sprang up, turned and went toward the lift.

"Wait!" cried Lanark, climbing over the counter. "Wait! I've another idea!"

He forced his way through the dead air of the floor and managed to press into the lift before the doors shut. He was pushed against Macfee's shoulder in a mass of older men and younger women.

"Listen, Macfee," he whispered. "My family and I are shifting into a new place soon—you could get the old one."

"Where is it?"

"In the cathedral."

"I'm not a bloody squatter!"

"But this is legal—it's run by a very helpful minister of religion."

"How big is it?"

"About six feet by nine. The ceiling slopes a bit."

"Christ, my mohome's nearly that size. *And* it has a flat roof and two rooms."

"But it would suit us fine, mister!" said a haggard woman holding a baby. "Six feet by nine? My man and his brother and me *need* a place like that."

"Tell me one thing," said Macfee belligerently. "What do they pay you for working here?"

"Enough to buy my own house."

"Why do they pay you anything?"

"I think they employ a lot of well-educated people to keep us comfortable," said Lanark. "And because they're afraid we'd be dangerous if we had no work at all."

"Fucking wonderful!" said Macfee.

"Honest, mister, that room you're leaving sounds very, very nice. Where did you say it was?"

The door opened and they hurried across the entrance hall, Lanark keeping close to Macfee's shoulder. As they came onto the pavement three armoured trucks full of soldiers thundered past. "What's happening?" cried Lanark. "Why all these soldiers?"

"How do I know?" shouted Macfee. "I'm pig-ignorant, all I hear is the news on television and funny noises in the street. They were ringing the cathedral bell like madmen a short while back. How do I know what's going on?"

They walked in silence till they reached a corner where a sign projected above a door. It was a fat red heart with pink neon tubes running into it and *The Vascular Cavity* underneath. Lanark said, "At least let me buy you a drink."

"Can you afford it?" said Macfee sarcastically. Lanark fingered the credit card in his pocket, nodded and pushed the door open.

The room was lit by a dim red glow with some zones of gaudy brightness. Most of the tables and chairs were partitioned off by luminous grilles shaped and coloured like pink veins and purple arteries. A revolving ball cast a flow of red and white corpuscular spots across the ceiling, and the music was a low, steady, protracted throbbing like a lame giant limping up a thickly carpeted stair.

"What kind of boozer is this?" said Macfee.

Lanark stood and stared. He would have turned and walked out if it hadn't been for women. They filled the place with laughing, alert, indifferent young faces and throats, breasts, midriffs and legs in all kinds of clothing. He felt he had never seen so many girls in his life. Looking closely he saw there were as many men but they made a less distinct impression. For all he cared they were duplicates of the same confident long-haired youth and Lanark hated him. He stood transfixed between fascination and envy until someone shouted his name from a corner. He looked across and saw Gilchrist, Pettigrew and Miss Maheen standing at a bar quilted with red plastic. "Listen," he told Macfee. "That tall man is my boss. If anyone can help you it's him. Let's try anyway."

He led the way to the bar, and said "Mr. Gilchrist, this is an old friend of mine—Jimmy Macfee—I knew him as a boy. He's a client of mine, a really deserving case, and—"

"Now, now, now!" said Gilchrist cheerfully. "We're here on pleasure, not business. What would you both like?"

"A whisky as big as yours," said Macfee.

"The same, please," said Lanark.

Gilchrist gave the order. Macfee was clearly attracted by Miss Maheen who turned her head at regular intervals, smiling at each of them in turn.

"Why are you not drinking?" he asked when her split-second smile reached him.

"She doesn't drink," said Pettigrew dourly.

"Can't she speak for herself?" said Macfee.

"She doesn't need to."

"Are you her husband or something?" said Macfee.

Pettigrew coolly emptied his whisky glass and said, "What do you do?"

"I'm a maker. I make mohomes," said Macfee boldly. *"And I live in one."*

"Mohome makers aren't real makers," said Pettigrew. "My father was a real maker. I respect real makers. You're in the luxury trade."

"So you think a mohome is a luxury?"

"Yes. I bet yours has colour television."

"Why shouldn't it have?"

"I suppose you came to us because you wanted a house you could stand up in, with an inside lavatory, and separate bedrooms, and wooden window frames, and maybe a fireplace?"

"Why shouldn't I have a house like that?"

"I'll tell you. When mohome users get a house like that they crowd into one room and sublet the others, and rip out the plumbing to sell as scrap metal, and rip out the window frames and chop up the doors and burn them. A mohome user isn't fit for a decent house."

"I'm not that sort! You know nothing about me!" cried Macfee.

"I knew all about you as soon as I clapped eyes on you," said Pettigrew softly. *"You,* are an obnoxious, little, bastard."

Macfee stared at him, clenching his fists and inhaling loudly. His shoulders swelled and he seemed to grow taller.

"Miss Maheen!" said Pettigrew loudly. "If he threatens me, chop him."

Miss Maheen stepped between Macfee and Pettigrew and raised her right hand to throat level, holding it flat and horizontal with the small finger outward. Her smile widened and remained. Gilchrist said hastily, "Oh, there's no need for violence, Miss Maheen. Just *look* at him."

Lanark heard a snapping sound inside Miss Maheen's head. He couldn't see her face but he saw Macfee's. His mouth fell open, the lower lip trembled, he clapped his hands over his eyes. Gilchrist said quietly, "Lead him out, Lanark. This isn't his kind of pub."

Lanark gripped Macfee's arm and led him through the crowd.

Outside the door Macfee leaned against the wall, dropped his hands and shuddered. "Wee black holes," he whispered. "Her eyes turned into wee black holes."

"She's not a real woman, you see," said Lanark. "She's a tool, an instrument *shaped* like a woman."

Macfee bent forward and was sick on the pavement; then he said, "I'm going home."

"I'll take you there."

"Better not. I'm going to hit someone tonight. I *need* to hit someone tonight. If you don't keep away it'll probably be you."

He sounded so feeble that Lanark took his arm and walked with him along several busy streets, then several quiet ones. They passed a parked truck beside three workmen cementing a concrete block over a sewer grating. A soldier with a gun stood smoking nearby. Lanark asked the foreman, "What are you doing?"

"Cementing a block over this stank."

"Why?"

"Just don't interfere," said the soldier.

"I'm not interfering, but couldn't you tell us what's happening?"

"There's going to be an announcement. Just go to your homes and wait for the announcement."

Lanark noticed that every drain they passed was blocked up. A hollow shouting began in the distance and drew nearer. It came from a loudspeaker on top of a slow-moving van. It said, "SPECIAL EMERGENCY ANNOUNCEMENT. IN FIFTEEN MINUTES NORMAL HEARTBEAT TIME, PROVOST SLUDDEN WILL MAKE A SPECIAL EMERGENCY ANNOUNCEMENT. IF YOU HAVE NEIGHBOURS WITHOUT TELEVISION OR WIRELESS, CALL THEM IN TO HEAR PROVOST SLUDDEN'S SPECIAL EMERGENCY ANNOUNCEMENT IN FIFTEEN MINUTES NORMAL HEARTBEAT TIME. ALL SHOPS, OFFICES, FACTORIES, DANCEHALLS, CINEMAS, RESTAURANTS, CAFÉS, SPORT CENTRES, SCHOOLS AND PUBLIC HOUSES ARE ASKED TO RELAY PROVOST SLUDDEN'S EMERGENCY ANNOUNCEMENT OVER THEIR LOUDSPEAKER SYSTEMS IN FOURTEEN AND A HALF MINUTES NORMAL HEARTBEAT TIME. THIS IS URGENT. . . ."

"What's *happening* to this city?" asked Macfee, shaking his arm free. They passed a long queue of people outside a public lavatory, then a wall of gigantic posters. Macfee said "Here" and they stepped through a gap between two posters onto a great area of gravel covered by rows of parked cars. He stopped beside one and opened the door. Lanark opened the door on the other side.

The front seat of the car extended the whole width and a plump young woman with a thin face sat in the middle. She said, "Come in. Sit down. Shut the door and shut up, both of you. Excuse my manners. I'll make tea in a minute but I don't want to miss my garden."
Lanark shut the door and leaned back with a feeling of relief. Sunlight streamed in through the windows and the car seemed to be thrusting slowly forward through a shrubbery of rosebushes. Green leaves and heavy white blossoms brushed across the windscreen and past the windows of the doors. He saw golden-brown bees working in the hearts of the roses and heard their drowsy humming, the rustle of leaves, some distant bird calls. Mrs. Macfee took a small can from a shelf and pressed the top. A fine mist smelling like roses came out. She sighed and leaned back with closed eyes saying, "I don't need to see it. The sound and scent are good enough for me."
The car had no clutch or steering column, and the seat was the sort that could slide forward while the back flattened to form a bed. A glass panel and a blind shut out the back seat where the children were probably sleeping. Under the wind-

screen was a set of drawers, shelves and compartments. One compartment held an electric plate, another a plastic basin with a small tap above it. Macfee opened a tiny refrigerator door, took out two cans of beer and passed one to Lanark.

The roses parted before the windscreen and the car, with a sound of gurgling water, floated like a yacht onto a circular lake surrounded by hills sloping up from the water's edge and clothed from base to summit in a drapery of the most gorgeous flower blossoms, scarcely a green leaf visible among the sea of odorous and fluctuating colour. The lake was of great depth but so transparent that the bottom, which seemed to be a mass of small round pearly pebbles, was distinctly visible whenever the eye allowed itself *not* to see, far down in the inverted heaven, the duplicate blooming of the hills. The whole impression was of richness, warmth, colour, quietness, softness and delicacy, and as the eye traced upward the myriad-tinted slope, from its sharp junction with the water to its vague termination in the cloudless blue, it was difficult not to fancy a wide cataract of rubies, sapphires, opals and golden onyxes rolling silently out of the sky. Mrs. Macfee took another little can and sprayed the interior with a scent of pansies. Macfee shouted "Sentimental rot!" and violently twisted a switch.

The interior became part of a sharp red convertible speeding down a multi-lane freeway under a dazzling sun. A swarm of dots grew visible in the heat haze ahead. The dots became a pack of motorcyclists. The car accelerated, moving in sideways toward the bikes.

"Jimmy!" said Mrs. Macfee. "You know I don't like this."

"You're unlucky, aren't you?" said Macfee. She pressed her lips together, pulled open a drawer in the dashboard, took out a sock and needle and started darning. Looking past her profile Lanark saw the car drawing level with the leader of the pack. He wore leather clothes with skull and swastika badges. A girl like Miss Maheen dressed in leather clung behind him. Then *froom!*—a glittering barbed dart shot out from Macfee's side of the car and entered the cyclist's body under the armpit. With a great screech the car swung round sideways and ploughed into the pack. The scene outside went suddenly slow. Slowly crashing and screaming cyclists were tossed into the air or fell and clung in agony to the car bonnet until they slid slowly off. Lanark shoved open the door beside him and stared with relief at the dingy gravel park and a row of quiet mohomes.

"Shut the door, we're freezing," yelled Macfee. Lanark reluctantly closed it. Bodies still spun ballet-like through swirling clouds of dust. Two bikes crashed with a tremendous explosion; then the scene was replaced by the head and shoulders of a man with a vividly patterned necktie. He said, "We are sorry to interrupt this programme but here is an emergency announcement by Provost Sludden, the chief executive officer of Greater Unthank. As this announcement contains a warning of serious health hazards for inhabitants of the Greater Unthank region, it is vital that everyone—especially those with children—gives it very special attention. Provost Sludden."

Sludden appeared, sitting on a leather sofa under a huge map of the city. His hands were clasped between his knees, and he looked gravely at the camera a while before speaking.

"Hullo. Not many of you have seen me face to face like this, and I promise you I regret having to appear. A provost is a public servant, and a good servant should never march into the living room when the family is enjoying an evening of television and complain about the difficulties of his job. Good servants work quietly behind the scenes, providing their employers with what the employers need. But sometimes an unforeseen accident occurs. Perhaps a bath falls through the kitchen ceiling, and then no matter how competent a servant is, he must tell the boss and the boss's wife what has happened, because the household routine is going to be upset and everyone has a right to know why. Something unexpected has happened to the plumbing of the Unthank region, and as chief executive officer I am going to take you into my confidence and explain why.

"But first I must tell you how your elected servants recently defeated a much greater problem: starvation. Yes. Starvation. The council was allowing a heap of poisonous muck from a burst transporter to isolate the city. Our foodstocks were nearly exhausted. We might have introduced severe rationing in the hope that the council would intervene to save us at the last minute, but we decided not to risk that. We decided to act ourselves. We told our heroic fire brigade to sweep the poison into the sewers—there was nowhere else for it to go. They did. Unthank was saved. We didn't publicize this triumph. It was enough reward for us that nobody would go hungry.

"Now for the bad news. The poison from the motorway is creeping backward through the sewage system in the form of a very lethal and corrosive gas. It is undermining our streets, our public buildings and our houses."

Sludden stood up and pointed to an area of the map outlined in red.

"Here is the danger area: central Unthank inside the ring road and the district east of the cathedral."

"That's us, all right," said Macfee.

"To prevent loss of life we must stop the gas from spreading. Every drain and sewer-opening in the danger area must be blocked. This work is proceeding in the streets and will soon start in houses and other buildings. Sanitary workers will call in to seal up every sink, urinal and lavatory pan. Naturally this takes time, so we invite your cooperation. Tubes of plastic cement will soon be obtainable, on demand, from your local police station and post office. The homes of householders who block their own drains will receive nothing more than a routine inspection. Meanwhile everyone should immediately plug their sinks and fill them with water. Lavatory pans will also stay safe for a while if they are not actually employed. I will now pause for three minutes to let everyone attend to their sink."

Three sentences appeared on the screen:

PLUG YOUR SINK.
FILL IT WITH WATER.
DON'T FLUSH YOUR LAVATORY PAN.

"Have another beer," said Macfee, passing a can across. "You too, Helen,"
She said, "I'm frightened, Jimmy."
"Frightened? Why? We're in luck at last. Mohomes don't have lavatories. Our sink isn't connected to the sewage system."
"But what will we do if we cannae use the public toilet?"
"I think the provost will announce plans for that," said Lanark. The speech had greatly impressed him. He thought, 'I'm glad Rima and Sandy are in the cathedral. Ritchie-Smollet will have taken the necessary precautions by now.' He sipped from the can. The inscription vanished and Sludden appeared once more.

> "There is one question I am sure you are all asking yourselves: How are we to get rid of our bodily waste? Well, you know, that question is as old as humanity itself. We tend to forget that interior flush lavatories are comparatively recent inventions, and three quarters of the world doesn't have them. For a while we must be content to use one of these, as our great-grandparents did."

He held up a chamberpot.

> "Those of you with small children probably have one already. New stocks are being rushed to the shops from the Cortexin Adhoc Sanitation plant at New Cumbernauld. Large orders have been placed with a small factory in Unthank which still makes the old-fashioned earthernware article, thus giving a much-needed boost to a neglected part of the city's economy. And though many will have to manage without one for a short period, I am sure they will be able to improvise with some other domestic utensil. As to the removal of the waste, you will receive through the post, if you have not received it already, a packet of these."

He held up a black plastic bag.

"This is large enough to comfortably hold the contents of one full chamberpot. When tied at the neck it is both damp proof and odour proof. These should be stacked *beside,* not *inside,* your usual midden or dustbin. To speed collection, the cleansing workers will be helped by the army. That is why you have seen so many soldiers on the street lately."

"Soldiers don't need guns to shift shit," said Macfee.

"Washing, if kept to a minimum, will present no problem. Once your sink is blocked it can be used in the usual way, except that the dirty water (which should be employed more than once) should be ladled into a pail and emptied into a gutter or convenient piece of ground. The same goes for urine. Fortunately a spell of mild weather is forecast, and our liquid waste will either evaporate or flow into districts where the drains still work."

"What if it rains?" said Macfee.

"But we must also tackle the *causes* of this dangerous annoyance. We have already demanded action from the council, whose slowness caused this disaster in the first place. We have appealed to the Cortexin Group, who manufactured the poison. Both reply that experts are being consulted, the matter will be considered, that in due course we will hear from them. This is not good enough. So Professor Eva Schtżngrm has been made leader of a team who are working to gain the technology to clear the gas themselves, and we are choosing a delegate to speak up boldly for Unthank at the general assembly of council states soon to be held in Provan. The fact is that the council has treated Unthank badly. It is a long time since they introduced their decimal calendar based on the twenty-five-hour day. They promised us new clocks, so we rashly scrapped the old ones, and the new clocks failed to arrive. I was a young man then and I confess that, like most people, I didn't care. Everyone likes to feel they have plenty of time; nobody likes seeing how fast it passes. But we can't cope with a public emergency without clocks, so we have created a new department, our own department of chronometry. This department has commandeered a television channel—this television channel—and I will show you what it is going to transmit."

Sludden walked over to a clock hanging on a wall, a pendulum clock with a case shaped like a small log cabin.
"Fucking miraculous," said Macfee, opening another beer can.
Helen said, "Don't you think you've had enough?"

"This is one of many clocks recently unearthed from museums, lumber-rooms and antique shops. It may not look very impressive, but it is the first to be restored to perfect working order. When the others have been repaired they will be installed in the head offices of our essential services, and each one of them will be synchronized with this."

Sludden pointed to a weight shaped like a fir cone.

"Notice that the weight has been wound up and placed on a small shelf immediately under the case. At the end of this announcement, I will suspend it, and the clock will strike the hours of midnight: the time when an old day dies and a new day begins. The sound will be reinforced by a long blast upon police and factory sirens, who will repeat the noise at noon tomorrow. Employees of the chronometry department have also taken over ninety-two church towers with bells in them, and from now on they too will broadcast the message of this little clock.

"I know that quiet-minded people
will find this a rude intrusion on their privacy; that intellectuals will say that a return
to a solar timescale, when we don't have
sunlight, is putting clocks backward, not
forward; and that manual workers, who
time themselves by their pulses, will find
the whole business irrelevant. Never
mind. This clock allows me to make definite promises. By eight o'clock tomorrow
every house, mohome, office and factory
will have received an envelope of plastic
wastebags. By ten o'clock the first free
tubes of plastic cement will be available
at your local post office. And at every hour
I or some other corporation representative
will appear on this channel to tell you how
things are going. And now—"

Said Sludden taking the weight in his hand—

"I wish you all a very good night.
Eternity, for Greater Unthank, is drawing
to an end. *Time* is about to begin."

He suspended the weight. The pendulum swung left with
a tick, then right with a tock. The clock face grew till it nearly
filled the windscreen. Both hands pointed straight upright to
a small door above the dial, which flapped open. A fat wooden
bird popped out and in shouting "Cuckoo! Cuckoo! Cuck—"
Macfee turned a switch and the windscreen went transparent. The three of them sat in a row and stared through it at
the darkened carpark. Sirens, hooters and distant clanging could
be heard outside. Helen switched on a light.
"A maniac!" said Macfee. "The man's a maniac."
"Oh no," said Lanark. "I've known him a long time, and
he's not a maniac. As a private person I don't trust him, but
he seems to have thoroughly grasped the political situation.
And that speech sounded honest to me."
"He's a friend of yours?"
"No, a friend of my wife."
Macfee leaned over and grabbed Lanark's lapels and said,
"What's the score?"
"Jimmy!" cried Helen.
Lanark cried, "What's wrong?"
"That's what I'm asking you! You've a council passport, right?

And you work for social stability, right? You know Sludden, right? So just tell me what you folk are trying to do!"

Lanark had been half dragged across Helen's lap, his ear was pressed against her thigh and comforting warmth began flowing through it. He said dreamily, "We're trying to kill Unthank. Some of us."

"Christ, that isn't news. We've known that for ages in the shops! 'All right,' I said. 'Let the place die as long as my weans are spared.' But you bastards are really putting the boot in now, aren't you? *Aren't you?*"

Macfee shifted a hand to grip Lanark's nostrils and cover his mouth. Lanark found he was watching a bulging reflection of his face and Macfee's hand on the side of a shiny kettle on a shelf a few inches away. The reflection flickered and grew dim and he supposed that when it went black he would be unconscious. He felt no pain so he was not much worried. Then he heard slapping sounds and Helen panting, "Let *go,* let him *go.*" he was released and heard much louder slapping sounds. Helen moaned, then yelled, "Clear out, mister! Leave us! Leave us alone!"

He found and pulled a handle and scrambled sideways out the door and slammed it shut. He hesitated beside the mohome, which was rocking slightly. Muffled noises came from the front seat and a frail childish wailing from the back. His eye was distracted by a lit poster on a gable showing an athletic couple in bathing costume playing beach ball with two laughing children. The message above said **MONEY IS TIME. TIME IS LIFE. BUY MORE LIFE FOR YOUR FAMILY FROM THE QUANTUM INTERMINABLE. (THEY'LL LOVE YOU FOR IT.)**

CHAPTER 39. Divorce

"Let the place die as long as my weans are spared." Jimmy's words had brought Sandy alarmingly to mind. Lanark ran from the park and along some empty streets, trying to retrace his steps. A warm heavy rain began falling and the gutters filled rapidly. The surrounding houses were unfamiliar. He turned a corner, came to a railing and looked down over several levels of motorway at the dark tower and bright spire of the cathedral. He sighed with relief, climbed the rail and scrambled down a slope of slippery wet grass. The water was nearly two feet deep at the edge of the road and flowing swiftly sideways like a stream. He waded through to the drier lanes. The only vehicle he saw was a military jeep which whizzed round a curve sending out sizzling arcs of spray, then slowed down and stopped beside him.

"Come here!" cried a gruff voice. "I've a gun, so no funny business."

Lanark went closer. A fat man in a colonel's uniform sat beside the driver. The fat man said, "How many of you are there?"

"One."

"Do you expect me to believe that? Where are you going?"

"The cathedral."

"Don't you know you're trespassing?"

"I'm just crossing a road."

"Oh, no! You are crossing a freeway. Freeways are for the exclusive use of wheeled carriages propelled by engines burning refined forms of fossilized fuel, and don't forget it. . . . Good heavens, it's Lanark, isn't it?"

"Yes. Are you McPake?"

"Of course. Get inside. Where did you say you were going?"

Lanark explained. McPake said, "Take us there, Cameron," then he leaned back, chuckling. "I thought we had a riot on our hands when we saw you. We're on the watch for them, you know, at times like these."
The jeep turned down toward the cathedral square. Lanark said, "I suppose Rima told you about Alexander?"
McPake shook his head. "Sorry, I only know one Rima. She used to hang about with Sludden in the old Elite days. Had her myself once. What a woman! I thought she took off for the institute when you did."
"Sorry, I'm getting confused," said Lanark.

He sat in a state of miserable excitement until the jeep put him down at the cathedral gates. In the doorway he heard organ strains, and the floor inside held a scattering of elderly and middle-aged people (But *I'm* middle-aged, he thought), standing between the rows of chairs and singing that time, like an ever-rolling stream, bears all her sons away, they fly, forgotten, as the dream dies at the opening day. He hurried past them with his mouth shaping denunciations, opened the small door, and rushed up the spiral stair, and along the window ledge, through the organ loft and past the cubicles of the attic. Rima and Alex were in none of them. He rushed to the kitchen and stared at Frankie and Jack, who looked up, startled, from a card game. He said, "Where are they?" There was an embarrassed silence; then Frankie said in a small voice, "She said she left a note for you."
He hurried back and found the empty cubicle. A note lay on the carefully made bed.

Dear Lanark,
I expect you won't be surprised to find us gone. Things haven't been very good lately, have they. Alexander and I will be living with Sludden, as we arranged, and on the whole it's better that you aren't coming too. Please don't try to find us—Alex is naturally a bit upset by all this and I don't want you to make him worse.
You probably think I've gone with Sludden because he has a big house, and is famous, and is a better lover than you in most ways, but that isn't the real reason. It may surprise you to hear that Sludden needs me more than you do. I don't think you need anybody. No matter how bad things get, you will always plod on without caring what other people think or feel. You're the most selfish man I know.
Dear Lanark, I don't hate you but whenever I try to write something friendly it turns out nasty, perhaps because if you give the devil

your little finger he bites off the whole arm. But you've often been nice to me, you aren't really a devil.

Love

Rima

P.S. I'm coming back to collect some clothes and things. I may see you then.

He undressed slowly, got into bed, switched off the light and fell asleep at once. He woke several times feeling that something horrible had happened which he must tell Rima about, then he remembered what it was. Lying drearily awake he sometimes heard the cathedral bell tolling the hours. Once it struck five o'clock and when he awoke later it was striking three, which suggested that the regular marking of time had not slowed it down much.

At last he opened his eyes to the electric light. She stood by the bed quietly taking clothes from the chest of drawers. He said, "Hullo."

"I didn't mean to wake you."

"How's Sandy?"

"Very quiet but quite happy, I think. He has plenty of room to run about and Sludden lives outside the danger zone so there's no stink, of course."

"There's no stink here."

"In another twenty-four hours I'm sure even you will begin to notice it."

She snapped the suitcase shut and said, "I wanted to pack this before I left but I was afraid you would suddenly come in and get hysterical."

"When have you seen me hysterical?" he asked peevishly.

"I don't remember. Of course that's partly your trouble, isn't it? Sludden and I often discuss you, and he thinks you would be a very valuable man if you knew how to release your emotions."

He lay rigid, clenching his fists and teeth in order not to scream. She placed the suitcase by the bed foot and sat on it, twisting a handkerchief. She said, "Oh, Lanark, I don't like hurting you but I must explain why I'm leaving. You think I'm greedy and ungrateful and prefer Sludden because he's a far better lover, but that's not why. Women can live quite comfortably with a clumsy lover if he makes them happy in other ways. But you're too serious all the time. You make my ordinary little feelings seem as fluffy and useless as bits of dust. You make life a duty, something to be examined and corrected.

Do you remember when I was pregnant, and said I wanted a girl, and you said you wanted a boy so that someone would like the baby? You've always tried to *balance* me as if I were a badly floating boat. You've brought no joy to my happiness or sorrow to my misery, you've made me the loneliest woman in the world. I don't love Sludden *more* than you, but life with him seems open and free. I'm sure Alex will benefit too. Sludden plays with him. You would only explain things to him."
Lanark said nothing. She said, "But we enjoyed ourselves sometimes, didn't we? You've been a friend to me—I'm not sorry I met you."
"When can I visit Sandy?"
"I thought you were going away to Provan soon."
"Not if Sandy isn't going."
"If you phone us first you can come anytime. Frankie has the number and the address. We'll be needing a babysitter."
"Tell Sandy I'll see him soon and I'll visit him often. Goodbye."
She stood, lifted the case, hesitated and said, "I'm sure you would be happier if you complained more about things."
"Would complaining make you like me and want to stay? No, it would make it easier for you to leave. So don't think—"
He stopped with open mouth, for heavy grief came swelling up his throat till it broke out in loud, dry choking sobs like big hiccups or the slow ticking of a wooden clock. Wetness flooded his eyes and cheeks. He stretched a hand toward her and she said softly, "Poor Lanark! You really are suffering," and went softly out and softly closed the door behind her. Eventually the sobbing stopped. He lay flat with a leaden weight in his chest. He thought wistfully of getting drunk or smashing furniture, but all activity seemed too tiring. The leaden weight kept him flat on his back till he fell asleep.

Later someone laid a hand on his shoulder and he opened his eyes sharply saying, "Rima?"
Frankie stood by the bed with food on a tray. He sighed and thanked her and she watched him eat. She said, "I've taken your clothes away—they were terribly dirty. But there's a new suit and underthings laid out for you downstairs in the vestry."
"Oh."
"I think you need a shave and a haircut. Jack was a barber, once. Will I ask him to see to it?"
"No."
"Can Sludden speak to you?"
He stared at her.

She flushed and said, "I mean, if he comes to see you, you won't lose your temper or attack him, will you?"

"I certainly won't lose my dignity because I'm faced by someone with none of his own."

She giggled and said, "Good. I'll tell him that."

She removed the tray and later Sludden entered and sat by the bed, saying, "How do you feel?"

"I don't like you, Sludden, but the only people I do like depend on you. Tell me what you want."

"Yes, in a minute. I'm glad you agreed to see me, but of course I knew you would. What Rima and I admire in you is your instinctive self-control. That makes you a very, very valuable man."

"Tell me what you want, Sludden."

"We're sensible modern men, after all, not knights who've been jousting for the love of a fair lady. I dare say the fair lady picked you up somewhere, but you were too weighty for her so she dropped you and picked me up instead. I'm a lightweight. Women enjoy lifting me. But you're made of sterner stuff, which is why I'm here."

"Please tell me what you want."

"I want you to stop pitying yourself and get out of bed. I want you to do a difficult, important job. The committee sent me here. They ask you to go to Provan and speak for Unthank in the general assembly of council states."

"You're joking!" said Lanark, sitting up. Sludden said nothing. "Why should they ask me?"

"We want someone who's been through the institute and knows the council corridors. You've worked for Ozenfant. You've spoken to Monboddo."

"I've quarrelled with the first and I don't like the second."

"Good. Stand up in Provan and denounce them for us. We don't want to be represented by a diplomat now, we want someone tactless, someone who will tell delegates from other states exactly what is happening here. Use your nose and take back some of our stink to its source."

Lanark sniffed. The air had an unpleasant familiar smell. He said, "Send Grant. He understands politics."

"Nobody trusts Grant. He understands politics, yes, but he wants to change them."

"Ritchie-Smollet."

"He doesn't understand politics at all. He believes everyone he meets is honestly doing their best."

"Gow."

"Gow owns shares in Cortexin, the company that fouled us up. He makes belligerent noises but he would only pretend to fight the council."

"And you?"

"If I left the city for more than a week our administration would collapse. There would be nobody in control but a lot of civil servants who want to clear out as soon as they can. We're under very strong attack, inside and out."

"So I've been chosen because nobody else trusts one another," said Lanark. An intoxicating excitement began to fill him and he frowned to hide it. He saw himself on a platform, or maybe a pedestal, casting awe over a vast assembly with a few simple, forceful words about truth, justice and brotherhood. He said suddenly, "How would I get to Provan?"

"By air."

"But do I cross a zone, I mean an incaldrical zone, I mean—"

"An intercalendrical zone? Yes, you do."

"Won't that age me a lot?"

"Probably."

"I'm not going. I want to stay near Sandy. I want to help him grow up."

"I understand that," said Sludden gravely. "But if you love your son—if you love Rima—you'll work for them in Provan."

"My family isn't in the danger area now. It's living with you."

Sludden smiled painfully, stood up and walked the floor of the cubicle. He said, "I will tell you something only one other person knows. You'll have to be quiet about it till you reach Provan, but then you must tell the world. The whole of the Greater Unthank region is in danger, and not just from a typhoid epidemic, though that is probable too. Mrs. Schtzngrm has analyzed a sample of the poison—two firemen died getting it for her—and she says it has begun filtering down through the Permian layer. As you probably know, the continents, though not continuous with it, are floating on a superdense mass of molten—"

"Don't blind me with science, Sludden."

"If the pollution isn't cleared up we're going to have tremors and subsidences in the earth's crust."

"Something must be done!" cried Lanark, aghast.

"Yes. The knowledge of what to do belongs to the institute. The machinery to do it belongs to the creature. Only the council can force them to act together."

"I'll go," said Lanark quietly, and mainly to himself. "But first I must see the boy."

"Get dressed in the vestry and I'll take you to him," said Sludden briskly. "And by the way, if you've no objection we'll have you declared provost: Lord Provost of Greater Unthank. It doesn't mean anything—I'll still be senior executive officer—but you'll be going among people with titles, and a title of your own helps to impress that kind."

Lanark pulled on the old greatcoat like a dressing gown, thrust his bare feet into the mud-caked shoes and followed Sludden downstairs to the vestry. His feelings were pulled between a piercing sad love for Sandy and an excited love of his own importance as a provost and delegate. Nothing interrupted the colloquy between these two loves. A warm bath was ready for him, and afterward he sat in a bathrobe while Jack shaved and trimmed him and Frankie manicured his fingernails. He put on clean new underwear, socks, shirt, a dark blue necktie, and a three-piece suit of light grey tweed, and beautifully polished black shoes; then he withdrew to the lavatory, excreted into a plastic chamberpot fitted inside the lavatory pan and had the comfortable feeling that someone else was expected to empty it. There was a mirror above the blocked lavatory sink; a medicine cabinet with a mirror for a door hung on the wall facing it. By moving the door to an angle he managed to see himself in profile. Jack had removed the beard and trimmed the moustache. His greying hair, receding from the brow, swept into a bush behind the ears: the effect was impressive and statesmanlike. He placed his hands on his hips and said quietly, "When Lord Monboddo says that the council has done its best for Unthank he is lying to us—or has been lied to by others."

He returned to the vestry and Sludden escorted him out to a long black car by the cathedral door. They climbed into the back seat and Sludden said, "Home, Angus," to the chauffeur.

They sped swiftly through the city and Lanark was too occupied with himself to notice much, except when the pervading stink grew unusually strong as the car crossed the riverbed by a splendid new concrete bridge. Heaps of bloated black plastic bags were scattered across the cracked mud. Sludden said glumly, "Nowhere else to dump them."

"On television you said these bags were odour-proof."

"They are, but they burst easily."
They came to a private housing scheme of neat little identical
bungalows, each with a small garden in front and a garage
alongside. The car stopped at one with a couple of old-fashioned
ornamental iron lampposts outside the gate. Sludden led the
way to the front door and fumbled awhile for his key. Lanark's
heart beat hard thinking he would meet Rima again. Through
an uncurtained plate-glass window on one side he saw into a
firelit sitting room where four people sat sipping coffee at a
low table before the hearth. Lanark recognized one of them.
He said, "Gilchrist is in there!"
"Good. I invited him."
"But Gilchrist is on the side of the council!"
"Not on the sanitary question. He's on our side on that, and
it's important to present a broad front when dealing with journalists. Don't worry, he's a great fan of yours."
They entered a small lobby. Sludden took a note from a tele-
phone stand, read it and frowned. He said, "Rima's gone out.
Alex will be upstairs in the television room. I suppose you'd
prefer to see him first."
"Yes."
"Go through the first door on your right at the top."

He climbed a narrow, thick-carpeted stair and quietly
opened a door. The room he entered was small and had three
armchairs facing a television set in the corner. Two dolls wearing different kinds of soldier uniform lay on the floor among
a litter of plastic toy weapons. A table had a monopoly game
spread on it and some drawings on sheets of paper. Alexander
sat on the arm of the middle chair, stroking a cat curled on
the seat and watching the television screen. Without turning
he said, "Hullo, Rima," and then, glancing round, "Hullo."
"Hullo, Sandy."
Lanark went to the table and looked at the drawings. He said,
"What are these?"
"A walking flower, a crane lifting a spider over a wall, and a
space invasion by a lot of different aliens. Would you like to
sit down and watch television with me?"
"Yes."
Alexander shoved the cat off the seat and Lanark sat down.
Alexander leaned against him and they watched a film like
the film Lanark had seen in Macfee's mohome, but the people
killing each other in it were soldiers, not road users. Alexander

said, "Don't you like films about killing?"

"No, I don't."

"Films about killing are my favourites. They're very real, aren't they?"

"Sandy. I'm going to leave this city for a long time."

"Oh."

"I wish I could stay."

"Mum said you would come and see me often. She doesn't mind us being friends."

"I know. When I told her I would visit you often I didn't know I would have to go away."

"Oh."

Lanark felt tears behind his eyes and realized his mouth was straining to girn aloud. He felt it would be horrible for a boy to remember a pitiable father and turned his face away and hardened the muscles of it to keep the grief inside. Alexander had turned his face to the television set. Lanark got up and moved clumsily to the door. He said, "Goodbye."

"Goodbye."

"I've always liked you. I always will like you."

"Good," said Alexander, staring at the screen. Lanark went outside, sat on the stairs and rubbed his face hard with both hands. Sludden appeared at the foot and said, "I'm sorry but the press are in a hurry."

"Sludden, will you look after him properly?"

Sludden climbed some steps toward him and said, "Don't worry! I know I played around a lot when I was younger but I've always liked Rima and I'm past wanting a change. Alex will be safe with me. I *need* a home life nowadays."

Lanark looked hard into Sludden's face. The shape seemed the same but the substance had changed. This was the eager, slightly desperate face of a burdened and caring man. With a pang of pity Lanark knew Sludden would have very little domestic peace with Rima. Lanark said, "I don't want to talk to journalists."

"Don't worry. Just appearing to them is the main thing."

A shaded lamp on the mantelpiece cast an oval of soft light on the small group before the hearth. Sludden, Gilchrist, a quiet-looking man and a reckless-looking man sat on a long leather sofa facing the fire. A grey-haired lady Lanark had seen in the chapterhouse sat on an armchair with a briefcase on her lap. Lanark pushed his own chair as far back into the shadow

as possible. Sludden said, "These two gentlemen fully understand the situation. They're on our side, so there's no need
to worry."
The quiet man said quietly, "We aren't interested in the detailed
character stuff. We just want to convey that the right man has
been found for the right job."
"A new figure strides into the political arena," said the reckless
man. "Where does he come from?"
"From Unthank," said Sludden. "He and I were close friends
in our early days. We hung about sowing our wild oats with
the same bohemian crowd, measuring out our life with coffee
spoons and trying to find a meaning. I did nothing at all in
those days but Lanark, to his credit, produced one of the finest
fragments of autobiographical prose *and* social commentary it
has been my privilege to criticize."
"No use to our readers," said the reckless man. The quiet
man said, "We can use it. What happened then?"
"He entered the institute and worked with Ozenfant. Although
a mainstay of the energy division, his qualities were *not*
appreciated and eventually, sickened by bureaucratic ineptitude,
he returned to Unthank: but not before registering a strong
personal protest to the lord president director."
"Room for a bit of dramatic detail here," said the reckless
man. "Exactly why did you quarrel with Ozenfant?"
Lanark tried to remember. At last he said, "I didn't quarrel
with him. He quarrelled with me, about a woman."
"Better leave that out," said Sludden.
"All right," said the quiet man. "He returned to Unthank.
And then?"
"I can tell you what happened then," said Gilchrist amiably.
"He devoted himself to public service by working in the Central
Centre for Employment, Stability and Surroundings. I was his
boss and I soon realized he was something of a saint. When
confronted by human suffering he had absolutely no patience
with red tape. To be frank, he often went too fast for me,
and that is why he is exactly the lord provost the region needs.
I can imagine no better politician to represent Greater Unthank
at the forthcoming general assembly."
"Good!" said the reckless man. "I wonder if Provost Lanark
would care to say something quotable about what he is going
to *do* at the Provan assembly?"
After thinking for a while Lanark said boldly, "I will try to
tell the truth."
"Couldn't you make it more emphatic?" said the reckless man.

"Couldn't you say, 'Come hell or high water, I will tell the world the TRUTH'?"

"Certainly not!" said Lanark crossly. "Water has nothing to do with my visit to Provan."

"Come what may, the world will hear the truth," murmured the quiet man. "We'll quote you as saying that."

"Very good, gentlemen!" said Sludden, standing up. "Our provost is leaving now. It's a very ordinary departure so you needn't watch. If you want a photograph Mr. Gilchrist's secretary can provide one. I'm sorry my wife was not here to offer you stronger refreshment, but you will find a bottle of sherry and a half bottle of whisky on the telephone-stand outside. Consume them at your leisure. Mr. Gilchrist will drive you back into town."

Everybody stood up.

Sludden showed Gilchrist and the journalists out. The grey-haired lady sighed and said, "Communicating with the press is a science I will nefer understand. This briefcase, Mr. Lanark, holts passcart, identification paper and three reports relating to the Unthank region. Before you speak in Provan I advise you to master them. There is a seismological report on the effect of pollution upon the Merovicnic discontinuity. There is a sanitary report on the probability of typhoid and related epidemics. There is a social report cuffering all the olt ground—no region our size has so much unemployment, uses so much corporal punishment in schools, has so many children cared for by the state, so much alcoholism, so many adults in prison or such a shortage of housing. It is all very olt stuff but people should be reminded. The seismological report is the only von whose language is at all technical because it contains an analysis of certain deep Permian samples vich *may* haf a commercial value. I haf put in a dictionary of scientific terms to help you out."

"Thank you," said Lanark, taking the case. "Are you Mrs. Schtzngrm?"

"Eva Schtzngrm, yes. There is von other matter personal to your*self,*" she said, lowering her voice. "In crossing the intercalendrical zone by air I think you vill pass very rapidly through the menopause barrier."

"What?" said Lanark, alarmed.

"No neet to worry. You are not a voman and so vill not be greatly changed. But you may haf very odd experiences of contraction and expansion which neet not be referred to aftervards. Don't vorry about them. Don't vorry."

Sludden looked round the door and said, "Angus has set up
the lights. Let's go to the airfield."

They went through a kitchen to a back door and followed
an electric cable which snaked up a path between seedy cabbage
stumps.

"Remember," said Sludden, "your best tactic is open denuncia-
tion. It's pointless complaining to the council chiefs when the
other delegates aren't present, and vice versa. The leaders must
be shamed into making concrete promises in the hearing of
the rest."

"I wish you were going instead," said Lanark. They reached
an overgrown privet hedge whose top leaves were black against
a low glowing light. Sludden, then Lanark, then Mrs. Schtzngrm
pushed through a gap onto the airfield. This was almost too
narrow to be called a field, being a grassy triangular space
on the summit of a hill completely surrounded by back gardens.
A square tarpaulin was spread on the grass with three electric
lights placed round it, and in the centre of the tarpaulin, upon
very broad feet and short bowed legs, stood something like a
bird. Though too large for an eagle it had the same shape
and brownish gold feathers. The figures U-1 were stencilled
on the breast. In the back between the folded wings was an
opening about eighteen inches wide, though overlapping feathers made it seem narrower. As far as Lanark could see the
interior was quilted with blue satin. He said, "Is this a bird
or a machine?"

"A bit of both," said Sludden, taking the briefcase from Lanark's
hand and tossing it into the cavity.

"But how can it fly when it's hollow inside?"

"It draws vital energy from the passenger," said Mrs.
Schtzngrm.

"I haven't enough energy to fly that to another city."

"A credit cart vill allow the vehicle to draw energy from your
future. You haf a cart?"

"Here," said Sludden. "I took it from his other suit. Angus,
the chair, please."

The chauffeur brought a kitchen chair from the darkness and
placed it beside the bird; Lanark, feebly protesting, was helped
onto it by Sludden.

"I don't like doing this."

"Just step inside, Mr. Delegate."

Lanark put one foot in the cavity, then the other. The bird
rocked and settled as he slid down inside; then the head came

up and turned completely round so that he was faced by the down-curving dagger point of the great beak. "Give it this," said Sludden, handing him the credit card. Lanark held it by an extreme corner and thrust it shyly toward the beak, which snapped it up. A yellow light went on in the glassy eyes. The head turned away and lowered out of sight. Mrs. Schtzngrm said, "He cannot fly till you haf put yourself mostly inside. Remember, the less you think the faster he vill go. Do not fear for your goot clothing, the interior is sanitizing and vill launder and trim you while you sleep."

The smooth strong satin inside the bird supported Lanark as though he sat in a chair, but when he pulled his arms in it stretched him out and the rear end sank until his feet inside the neck felt higher than his face. This looked out of the cleft between two brown wings, which started rising higher and higher on each side. Squinting forward he could see a bungalow roof with a yellow square of window. The black shape of someone's head and shoulders looked out of this, and if the window belonged to Sludden's house the watcher was surely Sandy and at once the grotesque flimsy aircraft and being a delegate and a provost seemed stupid evasions of the realest thing in the world and he shouted "No!" and began struggling to get out but at that moment the arching wings on each side thrashed down and with a thunderous *wump-wump-wump* he was flung upward feet first like a javelin and a sore blast of cold air on the brow knocked him out of his senses.

CHAPTER 40. Provan

He wakened cradled in stillness and looking at a bright full moon. The surrounding sky held a few big stars. His eyes were so dazzled that he rested them on the deep spaces between, but other stars started glittering there, and then whole constellations; he could not watch a space, however tiny, without the silver dust of a galaxy coming to glimmer in it. With outspread wings his aircraft seemed hanging, slightly tilted, between the ceiling of stars and a floor of smooth clouds which spread, like them, from horizon to horizon, and was that most mysteriously splendid of all colours, whiteness seen by a dim light. This thinned and opened under him and for a moment the craft seemed to overturn, for the bright moon shone through the opening. He was looking down into the sky reflected in a circular lake, reflected and magnified, for a black speck in the centre of the lower moon was clearly a reflection of his bird-machine. The lake, though sombre, had colour of its own. A jet black halo surrounded the reflected moon, and a ring of deep blue water flecked with stars surrounded that. To left and right was a beach of pure sand as pearly-pale as the clouds, and the round lake and its beaches were enclosed by two curving shores which made the shape of an eye. And Lanark saw that it was an eye, and the feeling which came to him then was too new to have a name. His mouth and mind opened wide and the only thought left was a wonder if he—a speck of a speck floating before that large pupil—was seen by it. In an effort to think something else he looked up at the stars but looked down again almost at once, and the eye was nearer now, he could only see the stars reflected in the depth. There was a sound like remote thunder or the breathings of wind in the ear. *"Is . . . is . . . is . . . ."* it said. *"Is . . . if . . . is. . . ."* He knew that half the stars were seeing the other half and smiled slightly, not knowing up from down or caring which was which. Then, dazed by infinity, he did not fall asleep but seemed to float out into it.

He wakened next in pale cold azure. He was above a plain of snowy clouds with a blue bird-like shadow skimming over them on one side and on the other, not far above the horizon, a small piercing sun which seemed to shoot golden wires at his eyes when he glimpsed it. Sometimes he passed through fountains of birdsong squirting up through rifts in the clouds and looked down for a moment on grass or rocks a mile or so beneath, but the only steady sound was the quietly thudding wings of the eagle-machine muted by the thin air. His body lay relaxed and warm on the firm satin. His face lay in a pool of cold air as refreshing as a rinse of cold water. On the horizon ahead he saw a mountain of white cloud as single as a milk jug on the edge of a bare table. A bird-shaped black dot, casting a fleck of shadow, seemed to cross the side of it. Later, when the peak and precipices of the mountain floated above him, creamy and dazzling toward the sun and toning into blue shadow away from it, he saw that the cloudy plain ended here and a real mountain stood under the cloud one. It had a sharp summit and granite precipices and was highest of a jagged range rising from heathery purple moors. It combined the massiveness of great sculptures with the most delicately imagined detail. A drifting movement on the shadowy side of a glen resolved into a herd of deer. A small loch on the moor had a waterfall spilling out of it and an angler, knee deep, near the edge. He saw differently coloured fields with white farmhouses along a shore, and a bay where the sand under shallow water was lemon-yellow with reddish gardens of weed. Farther out the water was ribbed by sea swells and ruffled all over by little waves that sparkled where the sunlight caught them. He passed over a pale green, slow-foaming triangle of wake with a long tanker moving onward at the tip. Then conversational sounds came from inside his eagle-machine, and he pulled his head in out of the sunlight.

A small voice near his toes was saying ". . . identify self. This is Provan Air Authority addressing the U-1 flight from Unthank. Repeat: will passenger please identify self. Over." "I am the Lord Provost of the Greater Unthank region," said Lanark firmly, yet with elation, "and delegate to the general assembly of council states." "Please rep—please rep—please repeat. Over."

Lanark said it again.

"The U-1 flight from Unthank may proceed to Hampden as planned on beam co—beam co—beam coordinate zero flux zero parahelion 43 minutes 19 point nought 7 seconds epihelion ditto neg—ditto neg—ditto negating impetus reversal flow 22 point nought 2—nought 2—nought 2—nought 2—nought 2 beyond the equinoctial of Quebus on the international nerve—national nerve—national nerve-circuit-decimal-calendar-cortexin-quantum-clock. Message understood? Over."

"It sounds like gibberish to me," said Lanark.

"Proceed as planned. Repeat: as planned. Repeat: as planned. Out."

There was a click and silence. He lay thinking of how he kept being pushed into certain actions, and how people kept talking to him as though he had planned them. But perhaps the message had not been for him but for his aircraft. It had sounded very like a machine talking to a machine. He pushed his head out into sunlight again.

He was flying up a wide and winding firth with very different coasts. To the right lay green farmland with clumps of trees and reservoirs in hollows linked by quick streams. On the left were mountain ridges and high bens silvered with snow, the sun striking gold sparkles off bits of sea loch between them. On both shores he saw summer resorts with shops, church spires and crowded esplanades, and clanging ports with harbours full of shipping. Tankers moved on the water, and freighters and white-sailed yachts. A long curving feather of smoke pointed up at him from a paddle steamer churning with audible chunking sounds toward an island big enough to hold a grouse moor, two woods, three farms, a golf course and a town fringing a bay. This island looked like a bright toy he could lift up off the smoothly ribbed, rippling sea, and he seemed to recognize it. He thought, 'Did I have a sister once? And did we play together on the grassy top of that cliff among the yellow gorsebushes? Yes, on that cliff behind the marine observatory, on a day like this in the summer holidays. Did we bury a tin box under a gorse root in a rabbit hole? There was a halfcrown piece in it and a silver sixpence dated from that year, and a piece of our mother's jewellery, and a cheap little notebook with a message to ourselves when we grew up. Did we promise to dig it up in twenty-five years? And dug it up two days later to make sure it hadn't been stolen? And were we not children then? And was I not happy?'

The shores grew steeper, more wooded and close together; the firth was pinched between them to a water-lane marked by buoys and light-towers. In places docks embanked it and vessels were being built or unloaded beneath the arms of cranes. Then the high land sloped away left and right and he came to a valley, a broad basin of land filled by a city with the river gleaming toward a centre of spires, towers and high white blocks. The eagle-machine left the river and soared in a long curve over sloping hills to the south, then to the east, then to the north. It crossed tenements of clean stone enclosing gardens where children played and lines of washing flapped in a slow breeze. There was a holiday in this city for the air was transparent and the bowling greens and tennis courts busy with players. The width and beauty of the view, its clearness under the sun seemed not only splendid but familiar. He thought, 'All my life, yes, all my life I've wanted this, yet I seem to know it well. Not the names, no, the names have gone, but I recognize the places. And if I really lived here once, and was happy, how did I lose it? Why am I only returning now?'

Sometimes he heard a sound like a slow explosion, a huge soft roaring from the city centre, and looking over there he saw tiny bird shapes moving to and fro. A shadow touched him and looking upward he saw, overhead toward the east, a great eagle crossing his course with the sign Z-1 on the underside of the breast. He realized his own craft was following a spiral path aimed at the city centre and getting lower all the time. It soared down the tree-filled gorge of another river, a small one linking parks full of strollers and sunbathers. Children on a grassy slope waved handkerchiefs at him and he thought, 'Soon I'll see the university.' A moment later he looked down on twin quadrangles framed by pinnacled rooftops. He thought, 'Soon we'll reach the river with the big dock basin and cranes and warehouses', but this time he was wrong. The small river entered a mainstream which spread out into arms of quiet water, but these lay among paths and trees surrounding a gigantic sports stadium. Figures were racing and vaulting round the tracks, on the rich green grass of the centre rested athletes in variously coloured suits, from the crowded terraces a dull hubbub of applause welled into a roar. Lanark's aircraft joined five or six others circling overhead. At intervals one would drop toward a white canvas square spread before the main grandstand with red, blue and black target rings painted on

it. A voice over a loudspeaker was saying ". . . and now Posky, Podgorny, Paleologue and Norn are entering the last lap; and just descending, bang on target, is Premier Kostoglotov of the Scythian People's Republic; and Norn and Paleologue are passing, yes, passing Podgorny into second place, almost neck and neck, and the gap between them and Posky is closing fast"— here a great roar went up—
"and the Toltec of Tiahuanaco dips toward the target just as Posky falls into third place and now Norn leads, then Paleologue, then Posky with Podgorny a very poor fourth; and here comes the Provost of Unthank—I'm sorry the *Lord* Provost of *Greater* Unthank—dropping toward the target just as Norn, yes, Norn, yes, Norn of Thule breaks the tape, closely followed by Paleologue of Trebizond and Posky of Crim Tartary."

Lanark's eagle-machine thumped down on the canvas and stood rocking slightly. Six men in dust coats seized it and carried it a few yards to a row of similar machines standing against a long narrow platform. Lanark gripped his briefcase and was helped onto the platform by a girl in a scarlet skirt and blouse who said hurriedly, "The Unthank delegate, yes?"
"Yes."
"This way, please, you're half a minute behind schedule."
She led him down some steps, through groups of relaxing athletes, across a momentarily bare cinder track and into a doorway under the terracing of the main grandstand. After the wide spaces of the sky it was perplexing to trot up a narrow passage in artificial light. He decided that whatever happened he would remain dour, sceptical and unimpressed. They came to a hall with open lifts along the walls. The girl ushered him into one, saying, "Go up to the executive gallery, they're expecting you. Leave your luggage with me; I'll make sure it reaches your room in the delegates' repose village."
"No, I'm sorry, these documents are vital," said Lanark. He saw a row of buttons in a polished metal panel and touched one beside the words EXECUTIVE GALLERY. The lift ascended and he watched his reflection in the polished panel with satisfaction. Though older he was even more dignified than in the vestry lavatory. He had grown a pointed, compact, captainish little white beard, his cheeks were smooth and rosy, the effect was of well-groomed efficiency. The lift door opened and Wilkins, looking exactly as Lanark remembered him, shook his hand, saying, "Provost Sludden! Am I right?"
"No, Wilkins. My name is Lanark. We've met before."

Wilkins peered closely and said, "Lanark! My God, so you are. What's happened to Sludden?"

"He is coping at present with a very dangerous sanitary problem. The Greater Unthank regional committee have judged it wiser for me to represent the city."

Wilkins smiled crookedly and said, "That man is a fox: a ninth-generation ecological fox. Never mind. Join the queue, join the queue."

"Wilkins, our sanitary problem is assuming catastrophic dimensions. I have more than one report in this briefcase which shows that people will start dying soon and—"

"This is a social reception, Lanark, public health will be debated on Monday. Just join the queue and say hello to your hosts."

"Hosts?"

"The Provan executive officer and Lord and Lady Monboddo. Join the queue, join the queue."

They were in a broad curving corridor with glass double-doors on one side and a queue moving steadily through. Lanark noticed a woman in a silver sari and a brown man in a white toga but most people wore sober uniforms or business suits and had the wary look of important people who, without showing friendship, are prepared to respond judiciously to it in others. They were an easy crowd to join. At the glass door a loud voice announced the arrivals to a company beyond: "Senator Sennacherib of New Alabama. Brian de Bois Guilbert, Grand Templar of Languedoc and Apulia. Governor Vonnegut of West Atlantis. . . ."

He reached the door and heard the satisfying cry, "Lord Provost Lanark of Greater Unthank," and shook hands with a hollow-cheeked man who said, "Trevor Weems of Provan. Glad you could come."

A stately woman in a blue tweed gown shook his hand and said, "Had you a nice trip?"

Lanark stared at her and said, "Catalyst."

"Call her Lady Monboddo," said Ozenfant, who was standing beside her. He shook Lanark's hand briskly. "Time changes all the labels, as you yourself are proving also."

A girl in a scarlet skirt and blouse took Lanark's arm and led him down some steps saying, "Hello, I'm called Libby. I expect you need some refreshment. Shall I get you a snack from the buffet? Pâté de something? Breast of something? Locusts and honey?"

"Was Ozenfant . . . ? Is Ozenfant . . . ?"

"The new lord president director, yes hadn't you heard?
Doesn't he look tremendously fit? I wonder why his wife is
wearing that hairy frock? Perhaps you aren't hungry. Neither
am I. Let's tuck into the booze instead, there's heaps of it.
Just sit there a minute."
He sat down at the end of a long leather sofa and looked
perplexedly around.

He was on the highest and largest of four floors which
descended like steps to a wall of window overlooking the stadium. Half the people standing around seemed to be delegates
and stood talking in quiet little groups. Girls in scarlet lent
some liveliness to the company by carrying trays between the
groups with flirtatious quickness, but they were balanced by
silent, robust men who stood watchfully by the walls wearing
black suits and holding glasses of whisky which they did not
sip. On a glass-topped table near the sofa lay a sheaf of pamphlets
entitled **ASSEMBLY PROGRAMME.** Lanark lifted and
opened one. He read a printed letter from Trevor Weems
welcoming the delegates on behalf of the people of Provan
and trusting their stay would be a happy one. There was no
possibility of danger to life or limb, as the newest sort of security
staff had been rented from the Quantum-Cortexin group; the
Red Girls, however, were human and anxious to help with
any difficulty the delegates could bring to them. Then came
six pages of region names listed alphabetically from Armorica
to Zimbabwe. Lanark saw that the Greater Unthank delegate
was given as Provost Sludden. Then came a page headed:

FIRST DAY

HOUR 11. Arrival and reception of delegates by Lord
    and Lady Monboddo

After this a press conference was listed, a lunch, an "opportunity
for social and informal lobbying," a sheepdog trial, a pipe band
contest, a dinner with speeches, a performance by the Erse
Opera Company of Purser's *Misfortunes of Elphin,* a firework
display and a party. Lanark turned a page impatiently and found
something less frivolous.

SECOND DAY

HOUR 8.50.   Breakfast. Lobbying.

HOUR 10.   **World Education Debate.**
                                  Chairman, Lord Monboddo.
Opening speech: "Logos into Chaos." The Erse delegate and sociosophist Odin MacTok analyzes the disastrous impact of literacy on the undereducated.
Speeches.   Motions.   Voting.
HOUR 15.   **Lunch. Lobbying.**
HOUR 17.   **World Food Debate.**
                                  Chairman, Lord Monboddo.
Opening speech: "Excrement into Aliment." The Bohemian delegate and Volstat research scholar Dick Otoman explains how organic pollutions can be pre-processed to revitalize each other within the human body.
Speeches.   Motions.   Voting.
HOUR 22.   **Dinner. Lobbying.**

THIRD DAY

HOUR 8.50.   **Breakfast. Lobbying.**
HOUR 10.   **Public Order Debate.**
                                  Chairman, Lord Monboddo.
Opening speech: "Revolutionary Stasis." Kado Motnic, sociometrist and delegate of the People's Republic of Paphlogonia describes the application of short-nerve-circuitry to libido-canalization in the infra-supra-25-40 spectrum.
Speeches.   Motions.   Voting.
HOUR 15.   **Lunch. Lobbying.**
HOUR 17.   **World Energy Debate.**
                                  Chairman, Lord Monboddo.
Opening speech: "Biowarp." South Atlantis delegate and Algolagnics director Timon Kodac presents gene-warping as the solution to the fossil-fuel failure.
Speeches.   Motions.   Voting.
HOUR 22.   **Dinner. Lobbying.**

FOURTH DAY

HOUR 8.50.   **Breakfast. Lobbying.**

HOUR 10.   **World Health Debate.**
                              Chairman, Lord Monboddo.
     Opening speech: "Kindness, Kin and Capacity."
     Hanseatic delegate and sociopathist Moo Dackin
     explains why healthy norms must be preserved
     by destroying other healthy norms.
     Speeches.   Motions.   Voting.

HOUR 15.   **Lunch, social and informal.**
HOUR 17.   **The Subcommittees report. Voting.**
HOUR 21.   **Press conference.**
HOUR 22.   **Dinner. Speeches.**
                              Master of Ceremonies, Trevor Weems.
     Opening speech: "Then, Now and Tomorrow." Six
     millennia of achievement will be outlined by the
     Chairman of the Assembly, Moderator of the Ex-
     pansion Project, Director of the Institute and Presi-
     dent of the Council, the Lord Monboddo. Trevor
     Weems, Chief Executive Officer of the Provan Ba-
     sin, will propose a vote of thanks. Toadi Monk,
     Satrap of Troy and Trebizond, will move the vote
     of thanks to the hosts.

HOUR 25.   **The delegates depart.**

Before reading all this Lanark had been gripped by a large undirected excitement. Since wakening to sunlight in his aircraft that morning he had felt himself nearing the centre of a great event, approaching a place where he would utter, publicly, a word that would change the world. The sight of Wilkins, the catalyst and Ozenfant-Monboddo had not damaged this feeling. He had been startled, but so had they, which was satisfying. But the assembly programme disconcerted him. It was like seeing the plans of a vast engine he meant to drive and finding he knew nothing about engineering. What did "Speeches. Motions. Voting" mean? What was "Lobbying" and why did it happen at mealtimes? Did the other delegates understand these things?

The gallery was very crowded now and two men sat at the other end of the sofa sipping pint glasses of black beer and gazing at the active little figures on the sunlit sports field below. One of them said cheerfully, "It's great to see all this happening in Provan."

"Is it?"

"Oh, come now, Odin, you've worked as hard as anyone to bring the assembly here."

The other said morosely, "Bread and circuses. Bread and circuses. A short spell of reasonable wages and long holidays while they plunder us and then *wham!* The chopper. Provan will be turned into another Greater Unmentionable Region."

Lanark said eagerly, "Excuse me, are you complaining about the condition of this city?"

The morose man had thick white hair, a body like a wrestler's and a pinkish battered face like a boxer's. He looked at Lanark balefully for a moment, then said, "I think I've a right to do that. I live here."

"Then you don't know how lucky you are! I'm from a region with an unusually dangerous sanitary problem, and Provan strikes me as the most splendidly situated—"

"Are you a delegate?"

"Yes."

"So you've just arrived by air."

"Yes."

"Then don't talk to me about Provan. You're in the early stages of a Gulliver complex."

Lanark said coldly, "I don't understand you."

"The first recorded aerial survey happened when Lemuel Gulliver, a plain, reasonable man, was allowed to stand on his feet beside the capital of Lilliput. He saw well-cultivated farms surrounding the homes, streets, and public buildings of a very busy little people. He was struck by the obvious ingenuity and enterprise of the rulers, the officials and the workmen. It took him two or three months to discover their stupidity, greed, corruption, envy, cruelty."

"You pessimists always fall into the disillusion trap," said the cheerful man cheerfully. "From one distance a thing looks bright. From another it looks dark. You think you've found the truth when you've replaced the cheerful view by the opposite, but true profundity blends all possible views, bright as well as dark."

The morose man grinned and said, "Since nearly everyone clings to the cloud-cuckoo view it's lucky one or two of us aren't afraid to look at the state of the sewers."

"Sorry I took so long," said the Red Girl, placing a tray on the table. "I thought it might be fun to try a gaelic coffee."

"I'm glad you mentioned sewers," said Lanark eagerly, "I come from Unthank, which is having trouble with its sewers. In fact the future of the whole region is being menaced—I mean, decided—by this assembly, and I've been sent here as advocate for the defence. But the programme"—he waved it—"tells me nothing about where and when to speak. Can you advise me?"

"There's no need to be so serious on the first day," said the Red Girl.

"The future of a crippled region," said the morose man slowly, "is usually hammered out by one of the subcommittees."

"Which subcommittee? When and where does it meet?"

"This is a friendly social reception!" said the Red Girl, looking distressed. "Can't we keep all this heavy stuff till later? There's going to be *such* a lot of it."

"Shut up, dear," said the morose man. "Wilkins knows all the ropes. You'd better ask him."

"Listen," said the Red Girl. "I'll take you to Nastler. He knows everything about everything, and he's expecting to see you soon in the Epilogue room. He told me so."

"Who is Nastler?"

"Our king. In a way. But he's not at all grand," said the Red Girl evasively. "It's hard to explain."

The morose man guffawed and said, "He's a joker. You'll get nothing out of him."

Lanark opened his briefcase, locked the assembly programme inside and stood up.

"I understand that you are employed to help me with my difficulties," he told the Red Girl. "I will speak to both Wilkins and this Nastler person. Which can I see first?"

"Oh Nastler, definitely," said the red girl, looking relieved. "He's an invalid, anyone can see him anytime. But won't you drink your coffee first?"

"No," said Lanark, and thanked the morose man, and followed the Red Girl into the crowd.

Weems and the Monboddos were still shaking hands with the queue by the door, which was a short one now. As Lanark passed them the announcer was saying, "Chairman Fu of Xanadu. Proto-Presbyter Griffith-Powys of Ynyswitrin. Premier Multan of Zimbabwe."

The Red Girl led him along the outer corridor till they came to a white panel without hinges or handle. She said, "It's a door. Go through it."

"Aren't you coming?"

"If you're going to talk politics, I'm going to wait outside."

As Lanark pressed the surface he noticed a big word on it:

EPILOGUE

He entered a room with no architectural similarity to the building he had left. The door on this side had deeply moulded
panels and a knob, the ceiling was bordered by an elaborate
cornice of acanthus sprays, there was a tall bay window with
the upper foliage of a chestnut tree outside and an old stone
tenement beyond. The rest of the room was hidden by easels
holding large paintings of the room. The pictures seemed
brighter and cleaner than the reality and a tall beautiful girl
with long blond hair reclined in them, sometimes nude and
sometimes clothed. The girl herself, more worried and untidy
than her portraits, stood near the door wearing a paint-stained
butcher's apron. With a very small brush she was adding leaves
to a view of the tree outside the window, but she paused,
pointed round the edge of the picture and told Lanark, "He's
there."

A voice said, "Yes, come round, come round."

Lanark went behind the picture and found a stout man leaning
against a pile of pillows on a low bed. His face, framed by
wings and horns of uncombed hair, looked statuesque and noble
apart from an apprehensive, rather cowardly expression. He
wore a woollen jersey over a pyjama jacket, neither of them
clean, the coverlet over his knees was littered with books and
papers, and there was a pen in his hand. Glancing at Lanark
in a sly sideways fashion he indicated a chair with the pen
and said, "Please sit down."

"Are you the king of this place?"

"The king of Provan, yes. And Unthank too. And that suite
of rooms you call the institute and the council."

"Then perhaps you could help me. I am here—"

"Yes, I know roughly what you want and I would like to help.
I would even offer you a drink, but there's too much intoxication in this book."

"Book?"

"This world, I meant to say. You see I'm the king, not the
government. I have laid out landscapes, and stocked them with
people, and I still work an occasional miracle, but governing
is left to folk like Monboddo and Sludden."

"Why?"

The king closed his eyes, smiled and said, "I brought you here
to ask that question."

"Will you answer it?"

"Not yet."

Lanark felt very angry. He stood up and said, "Then talking
to you is a waste of time."

"Waste of time!" said the king, opening his eyes. "You clearly don't realize who I am. I have called myself a king—that's a purely symbolic name, I'm far more important. Read this and you'll understand. The critics will accuse me of self-indulgence but I don't care."[1]

With a reckless gesture he handed Lanark a paper from the bed. It was covered with childish handwriting and many words were scored out or inserted with little arrows. Much of it seemed to be dialogue but Lanark's eye was caught by a sentence in italics which said: *Much of it seemed to be dialogue but Lanark's eye was caught by a sentence in italics which said:*

Lanark gave the paper back asking, "What's that supposed to prove?"

"I am your author."

Lanark stared at him. The author said, "Please don't feel embarrassed. This isn't an unprecedented situation. Vonnegut has it in *Breakfast of Champions* and Jehovah in the books of Job and Jonah."

"Are you pretending to be God?"

"Not nowadays. I used to be part of him, though. Yes, I am part of a part which was once the whole. But I went bad and was excreted. If I can get well I may be allowed home before I die, so I continually plunge my beak into my rotten liver and swallow and excrete it. But it grows again. Creation festers in me. I am excreting you and your world at the present moment. This arse-wipe"—he stirred the papers on the bed—"is part of the process."

"I am not religious," said Lanark, "but I don't like you mixing religion with excrement. Last night I saw part of the person you are referring to and it was not at all nasty."

"You saw part of God?" cried the author. "How did that happen?"

Lanark explained. The author was greatly excited. He said, "Say those words again."

"*Is . . . , is . . . is . . .* , then a pause, then *Is . . . if . . . is. . . .*"

"If?" shouted the author sitting upright. "He actually said if? He wasn't simply snarling 'Is, is, is, is, is,' all the time?"

Lanark said, "I don't like you saying 'he' like that. What I saw may not have been masculine. It may not have been human. But it certainly wasn't snarling. What's wrong with you?"

The author had covered his mouth with his hands, apparently

1. To have an objection anticipated is no reason for failing to raise it.

to stifle laughter, but his eyes were wet. He gulped and said,
"One *if* to five *is*es! That's an incredible amount of freedom.
But can I believe you? I've created you honest, but can I trust
your senses? At a great altitude *is* and *if* must sound very much
alike."

"You seem to take words very seriously," said Lanark with a
touch of contempt.

"Yes. You don't like me, but that can't be helped. I'm pri*ma*rily
a literary man," said the author with a faintly nasal accent,
and started chuckling to himself.

The tall blond girl came round the edge of the painting
wiping her brush on her apron. She said defiantly, "I've finished
the tree. Can I leave now?"

The author leaned back on his pillows and said sweetly, "Of
course, Marion. Leave when you like."

"I need money. I'm hungry."

"Why don't you go to the kitchen? I believe there's some
cold chicken in the fridge, and I'm sure Pat won't mind you
making yourself a snack."

"I don't want a snack, I want a meal with a friend in a restaurant.
And I want to go to a film afterward, or to a pub, or to a
hairdresser if I feel like it. I'm sorry, but I want money."

"Of course you do, and you've earned it. How much do I
owe?"

"Five hours today at fifty pence an hour is two pounds fifty.
With yesterday and the day before and the day before is ten
pounds, isn't it?"

"I've a poor head for arithmetic but you're probably right,"
said the author, taking coins from under a pillow and giving
them to her. "This is all I have just now, nearly two pounds.
Come back tomorrow and I'll see if I can manage a little extra."

The girl scowled at the coins in her hand and then at the author.
He was puffing medicinal spray into his mouth from a tiny
hand-pump. She went abruptly behind the painting again and
they heard the door slam.

"A strange girl," murmured the author, sighing. "I do my
best to help her but it isn't easy."

Lanark had been sitting with his head propped on his hands.
He said, "You say you are creating me."

"I am."

"Then how can I have experiences you don't know about?

You were surprised when I told you what I saw from the aircraft."

"The answer to that is unusually interesting; please attend closely. When *Lanark* is finished (I am calling the work after you) it will be roughly two hundred thousand words and forty chapters long, and divided into books three, one, two and four."

"Why not one, two, three and four?"

"I want *Lanark* to be read in one order but eventually thought of in another. It's an old device. Homer, Vergil, Milton and Scott Fitzgerald used it.[2] There will also be a prologue before book one, an interlude in the centre, and an epilogue two or three chapters before the end."

"I thought epilogues came after the end."

"Usually, but mine is too important to go there. Though not essential to the plot it provides some comic distraction at a moment when the narrative sorely needs it. And it lets me utter some fine sentiments which I could hardly trust to a mere character. And it contains critical notes which will save research scholars years of toil. In fact my epilogue is so essential that I am working on it with nearly a quarter of the book still unwritten. I am working on it here, just now, in this conversation. But you have had to reach this room by passing through several chapters I haven't clearly imagined yet, so you know details of the story which I don't. Of course I know the broad general outline. That was planned years ago and mustn't be changed. You have come here from my city of destruction, which is rather like Glasgow, to plead before some sort of world parliament in an ideal city based on Edinburgh, or London, or perhaps Paris if I can wangle a grant from the Scottish Arts Council[3] to go there. Tell me, when you were landing this morning, did you see the Eiffel Tower? Or Big Ben? Or a rock with a castle on it?"

"No. Provan is very like—"

"Stop! Don't tell me. My fictions often anticipate the experiences they're based upon, but no author should rely on that sort of thing."

Lanark was so agitated that he stood and walked to the window

2. Each of the four authors mentioned above began a large work *in medias res*, but none of them numbered their divisions out of logical sequence.
3. In 1973, as a result of sponsorship by the poet Edwin Morgan, the author received a grant of £300 from the Scottish Arts Council for the purpose of helping him write his book, but it was never assumed that he would use the money to seek out exotic local colour.

to sort out his thoughts. The author struck him as a slippery person but too vain and garrulous to be impressive. He went back to the bed and said, "How will my story end?"

"Catastrophically. The Thaw narrative shows a man dying because he is bad at loving. It is enclosed by your narrative which shows civilization collapsing for the same reason."

"Listen," said Lanark. "I never tried to be a delegate. I never wanted anything but some sunlight, some love, some very ordinary happiness. And every moment I have been thwarted by organizations and things pushing in a different direction, and now I'm nearly an old man and my reasons for living have shrunk to standing up in public and saying a good word for the only people I know. And you tell me that word will be useless! That you have *planned* it to be useless."

"Yes," said the author, nodding eagerly. "Yes, that's right." Lanark gaped down at the foolishly nodding face and suddenly felt it belonged to a horrible ventriloquist's doll. He raised a clenched fist but could not bring himself to strike. He swung round and punched a painting on an easel and both clattered to the floor. He pushed down the other painting beside the door, went to a tall bookcase in a corner and heaved it over. Books cascaded from the upper shelves and it hit the floor with a crash which shook the room. There were long low shelves around the walls holding books, folders, bottles and tubes of paint. With sweeps of his arm he shoved these to the floor, then turned, breathing deeply, and stared at the bed. The author sat there looking distressed, but the paintings and easels were back in their old places, and glancing around Lanark saw the bookcases had returned quietly to the corner and books, folders, bottles and paint were on the shelves again.

"A conjuror!" said Lanark with loathing. "A damned conjuror!"

"Yes," said the conjuror humbly, "I'm sorry. Please sit down and let me explain why the story has to go like this. You can eat while I talk (I'm sure you're hungry) and afterward you can tell me how you think I could be better. Please sit down." The bedside chair was small but comfortably upholstered. A table had appeared beside it with covered dishes on a tray. Lanark felt more exhausted than hungry, but after sitting for a while he removed a cover out of curiosity. There was a bowl beneath of dark red oxtail soup, so taking a spoon he began to eat.

"I will start," said the conjuror, "by explaining the physics of the world you live in. Everything you have experienced and are experiencing, from your first glimpse of the Elite café to the metal of that spoon in your fingers, the taste of the soup in your mouth, is made of one thing."

"Atoms," said Lanark.

"No. Print. Some worlds are made of atoms but yours is made of tiny marks[4] marching in neat lines, like armies of insects, across pages and pages and pages of white paper. I say these lines are marching, but that is a metaphor. They are perfectly still. They are lifeless. How can *they* reproduce the movement and noises of the battle of Borodino, the white whale ramming the ship, the fallen angels on the flaming lake?"

"By being read," said Lanark impatiently.

"Exactly. Your survival as a character and mine as an author depend on us seducing a living soul into our printed world and trapping it here long enough for us to steal the imaginative energy which gives us life. To cast a spell over this stranger I am doing abominable things. I am prostituting my most sacred memories into the commonest possible words and sentences. When I need more striking sentences or ideas I steal them from other writers, usually twisting them to blend with my own. Worst of all I am using the great world given at birth— the world of atoms—as a ragbag of shapes and colours to make this second-hand entertainment look more amusing."

"You seem to be complaining," said Lanark. "I don't know why. Nobody is forcing you to work with print, and all work involves some degradation. I want to know why your readers in their world should be entertained by the sight of me failing to do any good in mine."

"Because failures are popular. Frankly, Lanark, you are too stolid and commonplace to be entertaining as a successful man. But don't be offended; most heroes end up like you. Consider the Greek book about Troy. To repair a marriage broken by adultery, a civilization spends ten years smashing another one. The heroes on both sides know the quarrel is futile, but they continue

4. This is a false antithesis. Printed paper has an atomic structure like anything else. "Words" would have been a better term than "print," being less definably concrete.

INDEX OF PLAGIARISMS

There are three kinds of literary theft in this book:
BLOCK PLAGIARISM, where someone else's work is printed as a distinct typographical unit, IMBEDDED PLAGIARISM, where stolen words are concealed within the body of the narrative, and DIFFUSE PLAGIARISM, where scenery, characters, actions or novel ideas have been stolen without the original words describing them. To save space these will be referred to hereafter as Blockplag, Implag, and Difplag.
ANON.
Chap. 29, para. 2. The couplet ends a verse on a monument now standing beside a pedestrian lane under a flyover of an intersection of the Monkland Motorway and Cathedral Street, Glasgow.
ANON.
Chap. 30, para. 12. Blockplag of inscription on cairn on moor

beside the String Road near Black-waterfoot on Isle of Arran, Firth of Clyde.
ANON.
Chap. 43. Ozenfant's speech. Blockplag of first stanza of Middle English epic poem *Gawain and the Green Knight*, omitting 3rd and 4th lines, "The tyke that the trammels of treason there wrought/Was tried for his treachery, the truest on earth" (the translation is also anonymous).
BLACK ANGUS
See Macneacail, Aonghas.
BLAKE, WILLIAM
Chap. 19, para. 1. Implag of poem "The Clod and the Pebble" from *Songs of Experience*. Chap. 35, last paragraph. Implag. Ritchie-Smollet quotes "The Little Vagabond" from *Songs of Experience*.
BORGES, JORGE LUIS
Chap. 43, Ozenfant's speech. Blockplag from short essay "The Barbarian and the City."
BOYCE, CHRISTOPHER
Chap. 38, para. 16. The encounter between the "sharp red convertible" and the motorcyclists is an Implag from the short story "Shooting Script."
BROWN, GEORGE DOUGLAS
Books 1 and 2 owe much to the novel *The House with the Green Shutters* in which heavy paternalism forces a weak-minded youth into dread of existence, hallucination, and crime.
BUNYAN, JOHN
Chap. 9, para. 10. Blockplag of first paragraph of the *Relation of the Holy War Made by Shaddai Upon Diabolus for the Regaining of the Metropolis of the World; or the losing and taking again of the town of Mansoul*.
BURNS, ROBERT
Robert Burns' humane and lyrical rationalism has had no impact upon the formation of this book, a fact more sinister than any exposed by mere attribution of sources. See also Emerson.
CARLYLE, THOMAS
Chap. 27, para. 5. "I can't believe," etc., is an Implag of the youthful sage of Ecclefechan's query of his mother, "Did God

it because they think willingness to die in a fight is proof of human greatness. There is no suggestion that the war does anything but damage the people who survive it.

"Then there is the Roman book about Aeneas. He leads a group of refugees in search of a peaceful home and spreads agony and warfare along both coasts of the Mediterranean. He also visits Hell but gets out again. The writer of this story is tender toward peaceful homes, he wants Roman success in warfare and government to make the world a peaceful home for everyone, but his last words describe Aeneas, in the heat of battle, killing a helpless enemy for revenge.

"There is the Jewish book about Moses. It's very like the Roman one about Aeneas, so I'll go on to the Jewish book about Jesus. He is a poor man without home or wife. He says he is God's son and calls all men his brothers. He teaches that love is the one great good, and is spoiled by fighting for things. He is crucified, goes to Hell, then to Heaven which (like Aeneas's peaceful world) is outside the scope of the book. Jesus taught that love is the greatest good, and that love is damaged by fighting for things; but if (as the song says) "he died to make us good" he too was a failure. The nations who worshipped him became the greediest conquerors in the world.

"Only the Italian book shows a living man in Heaven. He gets there by following Aeneas and Jesus through Hell, but first loses the woman and the home he loves and sees the ruin of all his political hopes.

"There is the French book about the giant babies. Pleasing themselves is their only law so they drink and excrete in a jolly male family which laughs at everything adults call civilization. Women exist for them, but only as rubbers and ticklers.

"There is the Spanish book about the Knight of the Dolorous Countenance. A poor old bachelor is driven mad by reading the sort of books *you* want to be in, with heroes who triumph here and now. He leaves home and fights peasants and innkeepers for the beauty which is *never* here and now, and is mocked and wounded. On his deathbed he grows sane and warns his friends against intoxicating literature.

"There is the English book about Adam and Eve. This describes a heroic empire-building Satan, an amoral, ironical, boundlessly creative God, a lot of warfare (but no killing) and all centered on a married couple and the state of their house and garden. They disobey the landlord and are evicted, but he promises them accommodation in his own house if they live and die penitently. Once again success is left outside the scope of the book. We are last shown them setting out into a world to raise children they know will murder each other.

"There is the German book about Faust, an old doctor who grows young by witchcraft. He loves, then neglects, a girl who goes mad and kills his baby

Almighty come down and make wheelbarrows in a shop?" The device of giving a ponderous index to a work of ponderous fiction is taken from *Sartor Resartus.*

CARROLL, LEWIS
Chap. 41, para. 3. The taste of the white rainbow is a Difplag of the taste in the bottle marked "drink me" in *Alice in Wonderland.*

CARY, JOYCE
Chaps. 28 and 29. Difplags of the novel *The Horse's Mouth.* Here and elsewhere Duncan Thaw is a hybrid formed by uniting Gulley Jimson (the Blake-quoting penniless painter of a mural illustrating the biblical Genesis in a derelict church) with his untalented working-class disciple, Nosey Barbon.

CHASE, JAMES HADLEY
Chap. 9, para. 1. Blockplag of first two paragraphs of *No Orchids for Miss Blandish.*

COLERIDGE, SAMUEL TAYLOR
Chap. 41, para. 12. This reference to God, orphans and Hell is a debased Implag of "An orphan's curse would drag to hell/A spirit from on high," from *The Rime of the Ancient Mariner.*
Chap. 26, para. 10. The warmth which gushes in Thaw's chest at the kind sister's words, freeing him from the constriction which came when he prayed God that Marjory be killed, is a difplag of that "spring of love" the Ancient Mariner felt for the watersnakes, and which freed him from the Nightmare Life-in-Death caused by killing the albatross.

CONRAD, JOSEPH
Chap. 41, para. 6. Kodac's speech contains a dispersed Implag of names and nouns from the novel *Nostromo.*

DISNEY, WALT
In Book 3, the transforming of Lanark's arm and the turning of people into dragons is a Difplag of the transformed hero's nose and turning of bad boys into donkeys from the film *Pinocchio.* So is the process of purification by swallowing in the last paragraphs of Chap. 6. (*See also* GOD and JUNG.)

ELIOT, T. S.
Chap. 10, para. 4. "I'm something commonplace that keeps getting hurt" is a drab Difplag of the "notion of some infinitely gentle,/Infinitely suffering thing" in *Preludes*.

EMERSON,
RALPH WALDO
Ralph Waldo Emerson has not been plagiarized.

EVARISTI, MARCELLA
Chap. 45, para. 3. "Dont knife the leaf" is from the song *Lettuce Bleeds*.

FITZGERALD, F. SCOTT
Epilogue, para. 1. The sentence "You don't like me" etc. is from McKisco's bedroom dialogue with Rosemary Hoyte in Book 1 of *Tender Is the Night*. Chap. 10, para. 6. "We think a lot of new friends" etc. echoes Dick Diver's remark to Rosemary on the beach.

FREUD, SIGMUND
Difplags in every chapter. Only a writer unhealthily obsessed by all of Dr. Freud's psycho-sexual treatises would stuff a novel with more oral, anal and respiratory symbols, more Oedipal encounters with pleasure-reality/Eros-thanatos substitutes, more recapitulations of the birth-trauma than I have space to summarize. (*See also* DISNEY, GOD and JUNG.)

GLASHAN, JOHN
Chap. 38, para. 13. The snapping noise in Miss Maheen's head is an Implag from the "Snapping Song" from "Earwigs Over the Mountains" sung by the Social Security choir in *The Great Meths Festival*.

GOD
Chap. 6, paras. 11, 12, 13, 14. The purification by swallowing is a Difplag from the verse drama *Jonah*. (*See also* DISNEY and JUNG.)

GOETHE,   JOHANN
WOLFGANG VON
Chap. 35, para. 1. "*Wer immer strebend*" etc. is from the verse drama *Faust*, angel chorus Act V, Scene VII. Bayard Taylor translates this as "Whoe'er aspires unweariedly is not beyond redeeming"; John Anster as "Him who, unwearied, still strives on/We have the power to save" and Hopton Upcraft as "It's a great life/If you don't weaken."

son. He becomes banker to the emperor, abducts Helen of Troy and has another, symbolic son who explodes. He steals land from peasants to create an empire of his own and finances it by piracy. He abandons everything he tires of, grabs everything he wants and dies believing himself a public benefactor. He is received into a Heaven like the Italian one because 'man must strive and striving he must err' and because 'he who continually strives can be saved.' Yah! The only person in the book who strives is the poor devil, who does all the work and is tricked out of his wages by the angelic choir showing him their bums.[5] The writer of this book was depraved by too much luck. He shows the sort of successful man who captains the modern world, but doesn't show how vilely incompetent these people are. *You* don't need that sort of success.

"It is a relief to turn to the honest American book about the whale. A captain wants to kill it because the last time he tried to do that it bit off his leg while escaping. He embarks with a cosmopolitan crew who don't like home life and prefer this way of earning money. They are brave, skilful and obedient, they chase the whale round the world and get themselves all drowned together: all but the storyteller. He describes the world flowing on as if they had never

---

5. "*Von hinten anzusehen—Die Racker sind doch gar zu appetitlich*" is little more than a line. Louis MacNeice omits it from his translation as inessential because it reduces the devil's dignity. The author's amazing virulence against Goethe is perhaps a smokescreen to distract attention from what he owes him. *See* GOETHE and WELLS in the Index of Plagiarisms.

existed. There are no women or children in this book, apart from a little black boy whom they accidentally drive mad.

"Then there is the Russian book about war and peace. That has fighting in it, but fighting which fills us with astonishment that men can so recklessly, so resolutely, pester themselves to death. The writer, you see, has fought in real battles and believed some things Jesus taught. This book also contains"— the conjuror's face took on an amazed expression—"several believable happy marriages with children who are well cared for. But I have said enough to show that, while men and women would die out if they didn't usually love each other and keep their homes, most of the world's great stories[6] show them failing spectacularly to do either."

6. The index proves that *Lanark* is erected upon an infantile foundation of Victorian nursery tales, though the final shape derives from English language fiction printed between the 40's and 60's of the present century. The hero's biography after death occurs in Wyndham-Lewis's trilogy *The Human Age*, Flann O'Brien's *The Third Policeman* and Golding's *Pincher Martin*. Modern afterworlds are always infernos, never paradisos, presumably because the modern secular imagination is more capable of debasement than exaltation. In almost every chapter of the book there is a dialogue between the hero (Thaw or Lanark) and a social superior (parent, more experienced friend or prospective employer) about morality, society or art. This is mainly a device to let a self-educated Scot (to whom "the dominie" is the highest form of social life) tell the world what he thinks of it: but the glum flavour of these episodes recalls three books by disappointed socialists which appeared after the second world war and centred upon what I will call dialogue under threat: *Darkness at Noon* by Arthur Koestler, *1984* by George Orwell, and *Barbary Shore* by Norman Mailer. Having said this, one is compelled to

Epilogue, para. 1. "I am part of that part which was once the whole" is an Implag from Mephistopheles' speech in *Faust* Act I, Scene III: *"Ich bin ein Theu des Theus, der Angango alles war."*

GOLDING, WILLIAM
See footnote 6.

GOODMAN, LORD
Chap. 38, para. 9. "Greed isn't a pretty thing but envy is far, far worse" is a slightly diffuse Implag from the speech in which the great company lawyer compared those who fight for dividends with those who fight for wages and declared his moral preference for the former.

GUARDIAN
Chap. 36, para. 8. The newspaper extract is a distorted Blockplag of the financial report from Washington, July 9, 1973.

HEINE, HEINRICH
Chap. 34, para. 5. "screeching, shrieking, yowling, growling, grinding, whining, yammering, skammering, trilling, chirping" etc. contains Implag from the Hellnoise described in Chap. 1 of *Reisebilder* in Leland's translation.

HIND, ARCHIE
Epilogue, para. 14. The disciplines of cattle slaughter and accountancy are dramatized in the novel *The Dear Green Place*.

HOBBES, THOMAS
Books 3 and 4 are Difplags of Hobbes's daemonic metaphor *Leviathan*, which starts with the words "By art is created that great Leviathan called a Commonwealth or State (in Latin, *Civitas*), which is but an artificial man." Describing a state or tribe as a single man is as old as society—Plutarch does it in his life of Coriolanus—but Hobbes deliberately makes the metaphor a monstrous one. His state is the sort of creature Frankenstein made: mechanical yet lively; lacking ideas, yet directed by cunning brains; morally and physically clumsy, but full of strength got from people forced to supply its belly, the market. In a famous title page this state is shown threatening a whole earth with the symbols of warfare and religion. Hobbes named it from the verse drama Job, in which God

describes it as a huge water beast he is specially proud to have made because it is "king of all the children of pride." The author of *The Whale* thought it a relation of his hero. (*See* MELVILLE.)
HOBSBAUM, DR. PHILIP
Chap. 45, paras. 6, 7, 8. The battle between the cloth and wire monkeys is a Difplag of *Monkey Puzzle:*
Wire monkeys are all
    elbows, knees and teeth.
Cloth monkeys can be leant
    upon.
Wire monkeys endure,
    repel invaders.
Cloth monkeys welcome all
    comers.
They set up wire monkeys to test the youngsters' hunger, Cloth monkeys their loneliness.
Wire monkeys suckle, give food.
Cloth monkeys are barren.

You will see the youngster
    turn to the wire monkey
For sustenance merely
Then go back and embrace
    the cloth monkey
Who affords nothing.
When frightened the youngster
    will bury its head in
    the soft
Warm protruding bosom of the
    cloth.
The wire monkey stands
    against the blast.
Everyone prefers cloth monkeys.
HUME, DAVID
Chap. 16, para. 9. Blockplag from treatise: *An Enquiry Concerning Human Understanding.*
IBSEN, HENRIK
Books 3 and 4. These owe much to the verse drama *Peer Gynt,* which presents an interplay between a petit-bourgeois universe and supernatural regions which parody and criticise it. (*See also* KAFKA.)
IMPERIAL GAZETTEER OF SCOTLAND, 1871
Chap. 25, para. 1. This is not the simple Blockplag it seems. It unites extracts from the *Monkland Canal* entry and the *Monkland and Kirkintilloch Railway* entry which preceeds that.
JOYCE, JAMES
Chap. 22, para. 5. This monologue by a would-be artist to a

"Which proves," said Lanark, who was eating a salad, "that the world's great stories are mostly a pack of lies." The conjuror sighed and rubbed the side of his face. He said, "Shall I tell you the ending you want? Imagine that when you leave this room and return to the grand salon, you find that the sun has set and outside the great windows a firework display is in progress above the Tuileries garden."
"It's a sports stadium," said Lanark.
"Don't interrupt. A party is in progress, and a lot of informal lobbying is going on among the delegates."
"What is lobbying?"
"Please don't interrupt. You move about discussing the woes of Unthank with whoever will listen. Your untutored eloquence has an effect beyond your expectations, first on women, then on men. Many delegates see that their own lands are threatened by the multinational companies and realize that if something isn't quickly done the council won't be able to help them either. So

ask why the "conjuror" introduces an apology for his work with a tedious and brief history of world literature, as though summarizing a great tradition which culminates in himself! Of the eleven great epics mentioned, only one has influenced *Lanark.* Monboddo's speech in the last part of *Lanark* is a dreary parody of the Archangel Michael's history lecture in the last book of *Paradise Lost* and fails for the same reason. A property is not always valuable because it is stolen from a rich man. And for this single device thieved (without acknowledgement) from Milton we find a confrontation of fictional character by fictional author from Flann O'Brien; a hero, ignorant of his past, in a subfuse modern Hell, also from Flann O'Brien; and, from T. S. Eliot, Nabokov and Flann O'Brien, a parade of irrelevant erudition through grotesquely inflated footnotes.

tomorrow when you stand up in the great assembly hall to speak for your land or city (I haven't worked out which yet), you are speaking for a majority of lands and cities everywhere. The great corporations, you say, are wasting the earth. They have turned the wealth of nations into weapons and poison, while ignoring mankind's most essential needs. The time has come etcetera etcetera. You sit down amid a silence more significant than the wildest applause and the lord president director himself arises to answer you. He expresses the most full-hearted agreement. He explains that the heads of the council have already prepared plans to curb and harness the power of the creature but dared not announce them before they were sure they had the support of a majority. He announces them now. All work which merely transfers wealth will be abolished, all work which damages or kills people will be stopped. All profits will belong to the state, no state will be bigger than a Swiss canton, no politician will draw a larger wage than an agricultural labourer. In fact, all wages will be lowered or raised to the national average, and later to the international average, thus letting people transfer to the jobs they do best without artificial feelings of prestige or humiliation. Stockbrokers, bankers, accountants, property developers, advertisers, company lawyers and detectives will become schoolteachers if they can find no other useful work, and no teacher will have more than six pupils per class. The navy and air forces will be set to providing children everywhere with free meals. The armies will dig irrigation ditches and plant trees. All human excrement will be returned to the land.

tolerant student friend is a crude Difplag of similar monologues in *A Portrait of the Artist as a Young Man.*

JUNG, CARL

Nearly every chapter of the book is a Difplag of the mythic "Night Journey of the Hero" described in that charming but practically useless treatise *Psychology and Alchemy.* This is most obvious in the purification by swallowing at the end of chapter 6. (*See also* DISNEY, GOD and FREUD.) But the hero, Lanark, gains an unJungian political dimension by being swallowed by Hobbes's Leviathan. (*See* HOBBES.)

KAFKA, FRANZ

Chap. 39, last paragraph. The silhouette in the window is from the last paragraph of *The Trial.*

KELMAN, JIM

Chap 47. God's conduct and apology for it is an extended Difplag of the short story *Acid:*

In this factory in the north of England acid was essential. It was contained in large vats.

Gangways were laid above them. Before these gangways were made completely safe a young man fell into a vat feet first. His screams of agony were heard all over the department. Except for one old fellow the large body of men was so horrified that for a time not one of them could move. In an instant this old fellow who was also the young man's father had clambered up and along the gangway carrying a big pole. Sorry Hughie, he said. And then ducked the young man below the surface. Obviously the old fellow had had to do this because only the head and shoulders . . . in fact, that which had been seen above the acid was all that remained of the young man.

KINGSLEY, REVEREND CHARLES

Most of *Lanark* is an extended Difplag of *The Water Babies,* a Victorian children's novel thought unreadable nowadays except in abridged versions. *The Water Babies* is a dual book. The first half is a semi-realistic, highly sentimental account of an encounter between a young chimney sweep from an indus-

trial slum and an upper-class girl who makes him aware of his inadequacies. Emotionally shattered, in a semi-delirious condition, he climbs a moorland, descends a cliff and drowns himself, in a chapter which recalls the conclusion of Book 2. He is then reborn with no memory of the past in a vaguely Darwinian purgatory with Buddhist undertones. At one point the hero, having stolen sweets, grows suspicious, sulky and prickly all over like a seaurchin! The connection with dragonhide is obvious. He is morally redeemed by another encounter with the upper-class girl, who has died of a bad cold, and then sets out on a pilgrimage through a grotesque region filled with the social villainies of Victorian Britain. (*See also* MacDONALD.)
KOESTLER, ARTHUR
See footnote 6.
LAWRENCE, D. H.
See footnote 12.
LEONARD, TOM
Chap. 50, para. 3. "In a wee while, dearie" is an Implag of the poem "The Voyeur."
Chap. 49. General Alexander's requiem for Rima is a Blockplag of the poem "Placenta."
LOCHHEAD, LIZ
Chap. 48, para. 25. The android's discovery by the Goddess is a Difplag of *The Hickie.*
I mouth
sorry in the mirror when I see the mark I must have
　　　　　made just now
loving you.
Easy to say it's alright
adultery
like blasphemy is for
　　　　believers but
even in our
situation simple etiquette
　　　　　　says
love should leave us
　　　　both unmarked.
You are on loan to me
　　　　like a library book
and we both know it.
Fine if you love both of us
but neither of us
　　　　must too much show it.

In my misted mirror
you trace two toothprints
on the skin of your
　　　　shoulder and sure
you're almost quick enough

I don't know how Monboddo would propose to start this new system, but I could drown the practical details in storms of cheering. At any rate, bliss it is in this dawn to be alive, and massive sums of wealth and technical aid are voted to restore Unthank to healthy working order. You board your aircraft to return home, for you now think of Unthank as home. The sun also rises. It precedes you across the sky; you appear with it at noon above the city centre. You descend and are reunited with Rima, who has tired of Sludden. Happy ending. Well?"

Lanark had laid down his knife and fork. He said in a low voice, "If you give me an ending like that I will think you a very great man."
"If I give you an ending like that I will be like ten thousand other cheap illusionists! I would be as bad as the late H. G. Wells! I would be worse than Goethe.[7] Nobody who knows a thing about life or politics will believe me for a minute."
Lanark said nothing. The conjuror scratched his hair furiously with both hands and said querulously, "I understand your resentment. When I was sixteen or seventeen *I* wanted an ending like that. You see, I found Tillyard's study of the epic in Dennistoun public library, and he said an epic was only written when a new society was giving men a greater chance of liberty. I decided that what the *Aeneid* had been to the Roman Empire my epic would be to the Scottish Cooperative Wholesale Republic, one of the many hundreds of

7. This remark is too ludicrous to require comment here.

small peaceful socialist republics which would emerge (I thought) when all the big empires and corporations crumbled. That was about 1950. Well, I soon abandoned the idea. A conjuror's best trick is to show his audience a moving model of the world as it is with themselves inside it, and the world is not moving toward greater liberty, equality and fraternity. So I faced the fact that my world model would be a hopeless one. I also knew it would be an industrial-west-of-Scotland-petitbourgeois one, but I didn't think that a disadvantage. If the maker's mind is prepared, the immediate materials are always suitable.

"During my first art school summer holiday I wrote chapter 12 and the mad-vision-and-murder part of chapter 29. My first hero was based on myself. I'd have preferred someone less specialized but mine were the only entrails I could lay hands upon. I worked poor Thaw to death, quite cold-bloodedly, because though based on me he was tougher and more honest, so I hated him. Also, his death gave me a chance to shift him into a wider social context. You are Thaw with the neurotic imagination trimmed off and built into the furniture of the world you occupy.[8] This makes you much more capable of action and slightly more capable of love.

"The time is now"—the conjuror glanced at his wristwatch, yawned and lay back on the pillows—"the time is

8. But the fact remains that the plots of the Thaw and Lanark sections are independent of each other and cemented by typographical contrivances rather than formal necessity. A possible explanation is that the author thinks a heavy book will make a bigger splash than two light ones.

to smile out bright and
                    clear for me
as if it was O.K.

Friends again, together in
                    this bathroom
we finish washing love away.

McCABE, BRIAN
Chap. 48, para. 2. The Martian headmaster is from the short story *Feathered Choristers*.
MacCAIG, NORMAN
Chap. 48, para. 22. The cursive adder is from the poem *Movements*.
MacDIARMID, HUGH
Chap. 47, para. 22. Major Alexander's remark that "Inadequate maps are better than no maps; at least they show that the land exists" is stolen from *The Kind of Poetry I Want*.
MacDONALD, REVEREND GEORGE
Chap. 17, *The Key*, is a Difplag of the Victorian children's story *The Golden Key*. The journey of Lanark and Rima across the misty plain of Chap. 33 also comes from this story, as does the death and rebirth of the hero halfway through (*see also* KINGSLEY) and the device of casually ageing people with spectacular rapidity in a short space of print.
MacDOUGALL, CARL
Chap. 41, para. 1. *Poxy nungs* is the favourite expletive of the oakumteaser in the colloquial verse drama *A View from the Rooftops*.
McGRATH, TOM
Chap. 48, para. 22. The android's circuitous seduction of God is from the play, *The Android Circuit*.
MacNEACAIL, AONGHAS
See Nicolson, Angus.
MANN, THOMAS
Chap. 34, para. 5. "Screeching, shrieking, yowling, growling, grinding, whining, yammering, stammering, trilling, chirping" etc. contains Implag of the devil's account of Hellnoise in the novel. *Doktor Faustus*, translated by H. T. Lowe-Porter.
MAILER, NORMAN
See footnote 6.
MARX, KARL
Chap. 36, paras. 3 and 4. Grant's long harangue is a Difplag of the pernicious theory of history as class warfare embodied in *Das Kapital*.

MELVILLE, HERMAN
See footnote 12.
MILTON, JOHN
See footnote 6.
MONBODDO, LORD
Chap. 32, para. 3. The reference to James Burnett, Lord Monboddo, demonstrates the weakness of the fabulous and allegorical part of *Lanark*. The "institute" seems to represent that official body of learning which began with the ancient priesthoods and Athenian academies, was monopolized by the Catholic Church and later dispersed among universities and research foundations. But if the "council" represents government, then the most striking union of "council" and "institute" occurred in 1662 when Charles II chartered the Royal Society for the Advancement of the Arts and Sciences. James Burnett of Monboddo belonged to an Edinburgh Corresponding Society which advanced the cause of science quite unofficially until granted a royal charter in 1782. He was a court of session judge, a friend of King George and an erudite metaphysician with a faith in satyrs and mermaids, but has only been saved from oblivion by the animadversions against his theory of human descent from the ape in Boswell's *Life of Johnson*. By plagiarizing and annexing his name to a dynasty of scientific Caesars the author can only be motivated by Scottish chauvinism or a penchant for resounding nomenclature. A more fitting embodiment of government, science, trade and religion would have been Robert Boyle, son of the Earl of Cork and father of modern chemistry. He was founder of the Royal Society, and his strong religious principles also led him to procure a charter for the East India Company, which he expected to propagate Christianity in the Orient.
NicGUMARAID, CATRIONA
Like all lowland Scottish literateurs, the "conjuror" lacks all understanding of his native Gaelic culture. The character and surroundings of the Rev. McPhedron in Chap. 13, the least convincing chapter in the

1970, and although the work is far from finished I see it will be disappointing in several ways. It has too many conversations and clergymen, too much asthma, frustration, shadow; not enough countryside, kind women, honest toil. Of course not many writers describe honest toil, apart from Tolstoy and Lawrence on haymaking, Tressel on housebuilding and Archie Hind on clerking and slaughtering. I fear that the men of a healthier age will think my story a gafuffle of grotesquely frivolous parasites, like the creatures of Mrs. Radcliffe, Tolkien and Mervyn Peake. Perhaps my model world is too compressed and lacks the quiet moments of unconsidered ease which are the sustaining part of the most troubled world. Perhaps I began the work when I was too young. In those days I thought light existed to show things, that space was simply a gap between me and the bodies I feared or desired; now it seems that bodies are the stations from which we travel into space and light itself. Perhaps an illusionist's main job is to exhaust his restless audience by a show of marvellously convincing squabbles until they see the simple things we really depend upon: the movement of shadow round a globe turning in space, the corruption of life on its way to death and the spurt of love by which it throws a new life clear. Perhaps the best thing I could do is write a story in which adjectives like *commonplace* and *ordinary* have the significance which *glorious* and *divine* carried in earlier comedies. What do you think?"

"I think you're trying to make the readers admire your fine way of talking."

"I'm sorry. But yes. Of course," said the conjuror huffily. "You should know by now that I have to butter them up[9] a bit. I'm like God the Father, you see, and you are my sacrificial Son, and a reader is a Holy Ghost who keeps everything joined together and moving along. It doesn't matter how much you detest this book I am writing, you can't escape it before I let you go. But if the readers detest it they can shut it and forget it; you'll simply vanish and I'll turn into an ordinary man. We mustn't let that happen. So I'm taking this opportunity to get all of us agreeing about the end so that we stay together right up to it."

"You know the end I want and you're not allowing it," said Lanark grimly.

"Since you and the readers are the absolute powers in this world you need only persuade them. My wishes don't count."

"That *ought* to be the case," said the conjuror, "but unluckily the readers identify with your feelings, not with mine, and if you resent my end too much I am likely to be blamed instead of revered, as I should be. Hence this interview.

"And first I want us all to admit that a long life story cannot end happily. Yes, I know that William Blake sang on his deathbed, and that a president of the French Republic died of heart-failure while fornicating on the office sofa,[10] and that in 1909 a dental patient in Wumbijee, New South Wales, was struck by lightning after receiving a

---

9. In this context to butter up means to flatter. The expression is based upon the pathetic fallacy that because bread tastes sweeter when it is buttered, bread enjoys being buttered.

10. The president in question was Felix Fauré, who died in 1909 upon the conservatory sofa, not office sofa, of the Elysée Palace.

---

book, seem to be an effort to supply that lack. As a touchstone of his failure I print these verses by a real Gael. See also MacNeacail, Aonghas.

Nan robh agam sgian
ghearrainn ás an ubhal
an grodadh donn a th'ann
a leòn's a shàraich mise.

Ach mo chreach-s' mar thà
chan eil mo sgian-sa biorach
's cha dheoghail mi ás nas mò
an loibht' a sgapas annad.

NICOLSON, ANGUS
See Black Angus.

O'BRIEN, FLANN
See footnote 6.

ORWELL, GEORGE
Chap. 38. The poster slogans and the social stability centre are Difplags of the Ingsoc posters and Ministry of Love in *1984*.

PENG, LI
Books 3 and 4. These owe much to *Monkey*, the Chinese comic classic eclectic novel, first Englished by Arthur Waley, which shows the interplay between an earthly pilgrimage and heavenly and hellish supernatural worlds which parody it. (*See also* KAFKA.)

PLATH, SYLVIA
Chap. 10, para. 10. "I will rise with my flaming hair and eat men like air" is an Implag of the last couplet of "Lady Lazarus," with "flaming" substituted for "red."

POE, EDGAR ALLAN
Chap. 8, para. 7. The "large and lofty apartment" is an Implag from the story *The Fall of the House of Usher*. Chap. 38, para. 16. The three long first sentences are Implag from *The Domain of Arnheim*. The substitution of "pearly" pebbles for "alabaster" pebbles comes from Poe's other description of water with *c.* pebbly bottom in *Eleonora*.

POPE, ALEXANDER
Chap. 41, para. 6. Timon Kodac's statement "Order is heaven's first law" is from the poetic *Essay on Man*.

PRINCE, REV. HENRY JAMES
Chap. 43, Monboddo's speech. "Stand with me on the sun" is from *Letters addressed by H. J. Prince to his Christian Brethren at St. David's College, Lampeter.*

PROPPER, DAN

Chap. 28, para. 7. McAlpin's statement of Propper's law is a distorted Implag from *The Fable of the Final Hour:* "In the 34th minute of the final hour the Law of Inverse Enclosure was rediscovered and a matchbox was declared the prison of the universe, with two fleas placed inside as warders."
QUINTILIANUS
MARCUS FABRICIUS
Chap. 45, para. 5. Grant's "form of self-expression second only to the sneeze" is an Implag from Book 11 of the *Institutio Oratoria* translated by John Bulwer in his Chironomia.
REICH, WILHELM
Book 3. The dragonhide which infects the first six chapters is a Difplag of the muscular constriction Reich calls "armouring."
REID, TINA
Chap. 48, para. 15. The android's method of cleaning the bed is a Difplag of *Jill the Gripper* from *Licking the Bed Clean.*
SARTRE, JEAN-PAUL
Chap. 18, para. 6. Chap. 21, para. 12. These are Difplags of the negative epiphanies experienced by the hero of *Nausea.*
SAUNDERS,
DONALD GOODBRAND
Chap. 46. The peace-force led by Sergeant Alexander is blocked by God in a land whose shapes and colours come from *Ascent:*

The white shape is Loch Fionn,
Intimate with corners.
From here, the foothills
    of Suilven,
The white shape is Loch Fionn.

The green shape is Glencanisp,
Detailed with rocks,
From here, the shoulder
    of Suilven,
The green shape is Glencanisp.

The blue shape is the seas.
The blue shape is the skies.
From here, the summit
    of Suilven,
My net returns glittering.
SHAKESPEARE, WILLIAM
Books 1 and 2 owe much to the play *Hamlet* in which heavy paternalism forces a weak-minded youth into dread of existence, hallucinations and crime.
SITWELL, EDITH
Chap. 41, para. 12. "Speaking

dose of laughing gas.[11] The God of the real world can be believed when such things happen, but no serious entertainer dare conjure them up in print. We can fool people in all kinds of elaborate ways, but our most important things must seem likely and the likeliest death is still to depart this earth in a 'fiery-pain-chariot' (as Carlyle put it), or to drift out in a stupefied daze if there's a good doctor handy. But since the dismaying thing about death is loneliness, let us thrill the readers with a description of you ending *in company.* Let the ending be worldwide, for such a calamity is likely nowadays. Indeed, my main fear is that humanity will perish before it has a chance to enjoy my forecast of the event. It will be a metaphorical account, like Saint John's, but nobody will doubt what's happening. Attend!

"When you leave this room you will utterly fail to contact any helpful officials or committees. Tomorrow, when you speak to the assembly, you will be applauded but ignored. You will learn that most other regions are as bad or even worse than your own, but that does not make the leaders want to cooperate: moreover, the council itself is maintaining its existence with great difficulty. Monboddo can offer you nothing but a personal invitation to stay in

11. The township of Wumbijee is in southern Queensland, not new South Wales, and even at the present moment in time (1976) is too small to support a local dentist. In 1909 it did not exist. The laughing gas incident is therefore probably apocryphal but, even if true, gives a facetious slant to a serious statement of principle. It will leave the readers (whom the author pretends to cherish) uncertain of what to think about his work as a whole.

Provan. You refuse and return to Unthank, where the landscape is tilted at a peculiar angle, rioters are attacking the clock towers and much of the city is in flame. Members of the committee are being lynched, Sludden has fled, you stand with Rima on the height of the Necropolis watching flocks of mouths sweep the streets like the shadows of huge birds, devouring the population as they go. Suddenly there is an earthquake. Suddenly the sea floods the city, pouring down through the mouths into the corridors of council and institute and short-circuiting everything. (That sounds confusing; I haven't worked out the details yet.) Anyway, your eyes finally close upon the sight of John Knox's statue—symbol of the tyranny of the mind, symbol of that protracted male erection which can yield to death but not to tenderness—toppling with its column into the waves, which then roll on as they have rolled for . . . a very great period. How's that for an ending?"

"Bloody rotten," said Lanark. "I haven't read as much as you have, I never had the time, but when I visited public libraries in my twenties *half* the science-fiction stories had scenes like that in them,[12] usually at the end. These banal world destructions prove nothing but the impoverished minds of those who can think of nothing better."

The conjuror's mouth and eyes opened wide and his face grew red. He began speaking in a shrill whisper which swelled to a bellow: *"I am not writing*

---

12. Had Lanark's cultural equipment been wider, he would have seen that this conclusion owed more to *Moby Dick* than to science fiction, and more to Lawrence's essay on *Moby Dick* than to either.

purely as a private person," and much of the religious sentiment, are Im- and Difplag from the section of *Facade* which starts "Don't go bathing in the Jordan, Gordon."

SMITH, W. C.
Chap. 28. Blockplag from hymn "Immortal, Invisible, God Only Wise" with distorted final line.

SPENCE, ALAN
Chap. 45, para. 9. The fine colours are taken from the anthology *Its Colours They Are Fine.*

THACKERAY, WILLIAM MAKEPEACE
Chap. 11, para. 5. The bag and listed contents are a Plag, Block- and Dif-, from the Fairy Blackstick's bag in *The Rose and the Ring.*

THOMAS, DYLAN
Chap. 29, para. 5. Contains small Implag and Difplag from the prose poem "The Map of Love." Chap. 42, para. 5. Lanark's words when urinating are a distorted Implag of the poem "Said the Old Ramrod."

TOTUOLA, AMOS
Books 3 and 4. These owe much to *The Palm Wine Drinkard,* another story whose hero's quest brings him among dead or supernatural beings living in the same plane as the earthly. (*See also* KAFKA.)

TURNER, BILL PRICE
Chap. 46, para. 1. "The sliding architecture of the waves" is from *Rudiment of an Eye.*

URE, JOAN
Chap. 48, para. 8. The batman's wife is singing her own version of the song in the review *Something may come of it:* "Nothing to sing about/getting along/ very pedestrianly./People in aeroplanes/singing their song/ continue to fly over me./Something they've got that I've not?/ Something I've got that they've not?/Nothing to sing about./ Nothing to sing about."

VONNEGUT, KURT
Chap. 43, Monboddo's speech. The description of the earth as a "moist blue-green ball" is from the novel *Breakfast of Champions.*

WADDEL, REVEREND P. HATELY
Chap. 37, para. 4. The overheard prayer is from Rev. Waddel's lowland Scottish translation of Psalm 23.

science fiction! Science-fiction stories have no real people in them, and all my characters are real, real, real people! I may astound my public by a dazzling deployment of dramatic metaphors designed to compress and accelerate the action, but that is not science, it is magic! Magic! As for my ending's being banal, wait till you're inside it. I warn you, my whole imagination has a carefully reined-back catastrophist tendency; you have no conception of the damage my descriptive powers will wreak when I loose them on a theme like THE END."

"What happens to Sandy?" said Lanark coldly.

"Who's Sandy?"

"My son."

The conjuror stared and said, "You have no son."

"I have a son called Alexander who was born in the cathedral."

The conjuror, looking confused, grubbed among the papers on his bed and at last held one up, saying, "Impossible, look here. This is a summary of the nine or ten chapters I haven't written yet. If you read it you'll see there's no time for Rima to have a baby in the cathedral. She goes away too quickly with Sludden."

"When you reach the cathedral," said Lanark coldly, "you'll describe her having a son more quickly still."

The conjuror looked unhappy. He said, "I'm sorry. Yes, I see the ending becomes unusually bitter for you. A child. How old is he?"

"I don't know. Your time goes too fast for me to estimate."

After a silence the conjuror said querulously, "I can't change my overall plan now. Why should I be kinder than my century? The millions of children who've been vilely murdered this century is—*don't hit me!"*

Lanark had only tensed his muscles but the conjuror slid down the bed and pulled the covers over his head; they subsided until they lay perfectly flat on the mattress. Lanark sighed and dropped his face into his hand. A little voice in the air said, "Promise not to be violent."

Katrina Veronica Margaret Inge Inge Inge Inge Inge Inge Inge Inge Inge Inge Inge Inge Inge Inge Inge Inge Inge Marian Beth Liz Betty Daniele Angel TinaJanetKate; the final descent to healthy commonplace and finding a silk smooth you inside that husk are Blockplags, Implags, Difplags of *The Marriage of Heaven and Hell* translated into clear images and sublime distances by William Blake and William Turner for the benefit of all makers of useful and lovely things.

Lanark snorted contemptuously. The bedclothes swelled up in a man-shaped lump but the conjuror did not emerge. A muffled voice under the clothes said, "I didn't need to play that trick. In a single sentence I could have made you my most obsequious admirer, but the reader would have turned against both of us. . . . I wish I could make you like death a little more. It's a great preserver. Without it the loveliest things change slowly into farce, as you will discover if you insist on having much more life. But I refuse to discuss family matters with you. Take them to Monboddo. Please go away."

"Soon after I came here," said Lanark, lifting the briefcase and standing up, "I said talking to you was a waste of time. Was I wrong?"

He walked to the door and heard mumbling under the bedclothes. He said, "What?"

". . . know a black man called Multan . . ."

"I've heard his name. Why?"

". . . might be useful. Sudden idea. Probably not."

Lanark walked round the painting of the chestnut tree, opened the door and went out.[13]

13. As this "Epilogue" has performed the office of an introduction to the work as a whole (the so-called "Prologue" being no prologue at all, but a separate short story), it is saddening to find the "conjuror" omitting the courtesies appropriate to such an addendum. Mrs. Florence Allan typed and retyped his manuscripts, and often waited many months without payment and without complaining. Professor Andrew Sykes gave him free access to copying equipment and secretarial help. He received from James Kelman critical advice which enabled him to make smoother prose of the crucial first chapter. Charles Wild, Peter Chiene, Jim Hutcheson, Stephanie Wolf Murray engaged in extensive lexical activity to ensure that the resulting volume had a surface consistency. And what of the compositors employed by Kingsport Press of Kingsport, Tennessee, to typeset this bloody book? Yet these are only a few out of thousands whose help has not been acknowledged and whose names have not been mentioned.

CHAPTER 41. Climax

He looked down, startled, at Libby, who lay curled with her legs under her in the angle between wall and carpet looking unconscious. She was a gracefully plump, dark-haired girl. Her skirt was shorter and blouse silkier than he remembered, and her sulky slumbering face looked far more childish than the clothes. She opened her eyes saying "What?" and sat up and glanced at her wristwatch. Without blame she said, "You've been hours in there. Hours and hours. We've missed the opera."

She held out a hand and he helped her up. She said, "Did he feed you?"

"He did. Now I would like to speak to Wilkins."

"Wilkins?"

"Or Monboddo. On second thought, I would prefer to see Monboddo. Is that possible?"

She stared at him and said, "Do you never relax? Don't you ever enjoy yourself?"

"I did not come here to relax."

"Sorry I asked."

She walked down the corridor. He followed, saying, "Listen, if I'm being rude I apologize, but I'm very worried just now. And anyway, I've always been bad at enjoying myself."

"Poor old you."

"I'm not complaining," said Lanark defensively. "Some very nice things have happened to me, even so."

"When, for instance?"

Lanark remembered when Sandy was born. He knew he must have been happy then or he wouldn't have rung the cathedral bell, but he couldn't remember what happiness felt like. His past suddenly seemed a very large, very dreary place. He said tiredly, "Not long ago."

In the hall beside the lift doors she halted, faced him and said firmly, "I don't know where Monboddo and Wilkins are just now. I expect they'll drop in later when the party starts, so I'll give you some advice. Play it gelid. I see you've got it bad, Dad, but the hard sell is no go on day one when everybody's casing each other. The real hot lobbyists start cashing their therms halfway through countdown on day two. And there's something else I'd like to tell you. The Provan executive pays my salary whether I stay with you or not. If you want me to vanish say 'vanish' and I'll vanish. Or else come for a quiet drink with me and talk about *anything* but this general bloody awful assembly. Even their language gives me the poxy nungs."

Lanark stared at her, seeing how attractive she was. The sight was a great pain. He knew that if she let him kiss her petulant mouth he would feel no warmth or excitement. He looked inside himself and found only a hungry ungenerous cold, a pained emptiness which could neither give nor take. He thought, 'I am mostly a dead man. How did this happen?'

He muttered, "Please don't vanish."

She took his arm and led him toward the gallery saying slyly, "I bet I know one thing you enjoy."

"What?"

"Bet you enjoy being famous."

"I'm not."

"Modest, eh?"

"No, but I'm not famous either."

"Think I'd have waited all these hours outside Nastler's door if you'd been an ordinary delegate?"

Lanark was too confused to answer. He pointed to a silent crowd of black-suited security men on each side of the glass door and said, "What are they doing here?"

"They're staying outside to make the party less spooky."

Though nearly empty the gallery throbbed with light rhythmical music. In the night sky outside the window the pink-tipped petals of several great chrysanthemums were spreading out from golden centres among the stars and dipping down toward the floodlit stadium where tiny figures thronged the terraces and crowded upon dance floors, one at each end of the central field. The chrysanthemums faded and a scarlet spark shot through them, drawing a long tail of white and green

with piles of huge coloured cushions. The floor above that
had a twelve-man orchestra at one end, though at present the
only player was a clarinettist blowing a humorous little tune
and a drummer softly stroking the cymbals with wire brushes.
The floor above that had four well-laden buffets along it, and
the top floor had many empty little chairs and tables, and a
bar at each end, and four girls sitting on stools by one of the
bars. Libby led Lanark over to them and said, "Martha, Solveig,
Joy and the other Joy, this is you-know-who from Unthank."
Martha said, "It can't be."
Solveig said, "You look far too respectable."
Joy said, "Shall I put your briefcase behind the bar? It'll be
safe there."
The other Joy said, "My mother is a friend of yours, or says
she used to be."
"Is she called Nancy?" said Lanark glumly, handing over the
briefcase and sitting down. "Because if she is I met you when
you were a baby."
"No, she's called Gay."
"Don't remind him of his age," said Libby. "Be a mother
yourself and mix us two white rainbows. (She's good at white
rainbows.)"

Solveig was the largest of the girls and the other Joy was
the smallest. They were all about the same age and had the
same casually friendly manners. Lanark was not very conscious
of them as distinct people but he was soothed by being the
only man among them. Libby said, "We've got to persuade
Lanark that he's famous."
They all laughed and the other Joy, who was measuring drops
of liquor into a silver canister, said, "But he knows. He must
know."
"What am I famous for?" said Lanark.
"You're the man who does these weird, weird things for no
reason at all," said Martha. "You smashed Monboddo's tele-
screen when he was conducting a string quartet."
"You fought with him over a dragon-bitch and blocked the
whole current of the institute," said Solveig.
"You told him exactly what you thought of him and walked
straight out of the council corridors into an intercalendrical
zone. On foot!" said Joy.
"We're mad keen to see what you do tonight," said the other
Joy. "Monboddo's terrified of you."

Lanark started explaining how things had really happened, but the corners of his mouth had risen and were squeezing out his cheeks and narrowing his eyes; he could not help his face being contorted, his tongue gagged by a huge silly grin, and at last he shook his head and laughed. Libby laughed too. She was leaning on the bar, her hip brushing his thigh. Martha told him, "Libby's using you to make her boyfriend jealous."
"No I'm not. Well, just a bit, I am."
"Who's your boyfriend?" asked Lanark, smiling.
"The man with the glasses down there. The drummer. He's horrible. When his music isn't going right for him nothing goes right for him."
"Make him as jealous of me as you like," said Lanark, patting her hand. The other Joy gave him a tall glass of clear drink and they all watched him closely as he sipped. The first sip tasted soft and furry, then cool and milky, then thin and piercing like peppermint, then bitter like gin, then thick and warm like chocolate, then sharp like lemon but sweetening like lemonade. He sipped again and the flow of tastes over his tongue was wholly different, for the tip tasted black currant, blending into a pleasant kind of children's cough mixture in the centre and becoming like clear beef gravy as it entered the throat, with a faint aftertaste of smoked oysters. He said, "The taste of this makes no sense."
"Don't you like it?"
"Yes, it's delicious."
They laughed as if he'd said something clever. Solveig said, "Will you dance with me when the music starts?"
"Of course."
"What about me?" said Martha.
"I intend to dance once with everybody—except the other Joy. I'm going to dance twice with the other Joy."
"Why?"
"Because being unusually kind to someone will give me a feeling of power."
Everyone laughed again and he sipped the drink feeling worldly and witty. A small man with a large nose arrived and said, "You all seem to be having a good time, do you mind if I join in? I'm Griffith-Powys, Arthur Griffith-Powys of Ynyswitrin. Lanark of Unthank, aren't you? I only just missed you this morning, but I heard you'd been hard at it. It was good to know somebody was knocking the gelid lark. We've had too much of that. You'll be sounding off loud and clear tomorrow, I hope?"

The gallery was filling with older people who were clearly delegates or delegates' wives, and others in their thirties who seemed to be secretaries and journalists. There were more red girls too, though few of them now wore the whole red uniform. Groups were forming but the group round Lanark was the largest. Odin, the pink-faced morose man, came over and asked, "Any luck with His Royal Highness?"

"None. In fact he said he wasn't a king at all but a conjuror."

"Young people must find the modern world very confusing," said Powys, patting Martha's arm paternally. "So many single people have different names and so many different people have the same name. Look at Monboddo. We've all known at least two Monboddos and the next one will likely be a woman. Look at me! Last year I was Arch Druid of Camelot and Cadbury. This year, what with ecumenical pressure and regionalization, I'm Proto-Presbyter of Ynyswitrin, yet I'm the same man doing the same job."

Odin said in a low voice, "Here comes the enemy."

Five black men of different heights entered, two in business suits, two in military uniform and the tallest in caftan and fez. Martha shivered and said, "I hate the black bloc—they drink nothing stronger than lemonade."

"Well, I *love* them," said Libby stoutly. "I think they're charming. And Senator Sennacherib drinks whisky by the quart."

"What I can't take is bloody Multan's air of superiority," said Odin. "I know we sold and flogged his ancestors, which proves we're vicious; but it doesn't prove he's much good."

"Is that Multan?" said Lanark. The blacks had descended to the next floor and were standing at one of the buffets. "Excuse me a minute," said Lanark. He passed quickly through the other groups, descended three or four steps and approached the black bloc. "Please," he said to the tall man in the fez, "are you Multan of Zimbabwe?"

"Here is General Multan," said the tall man, indicating a small man in military uniform. Lanark said, "May I speak to you, General Multan? I've been told you . . . we might be able to help each other."

Multan regarded Lanark with an expression of polite amusement. He said, "Who told you that, man?"

"Nastler."

"Don't know this Nastler. How does he say we be useful?"

"He didn't, but my own region—Greater Unthank—is having trouble with—well, many things. Almost everything. Is yours?"

"Oh, sure. Our plains are overgrazed, our bush is undercultivated, our minerals are owned by foreigners, the council sends us airplanes, tanks and bulldozers and our revenues go to Algolagnics and Volstat to buy fuel and spare parts to work them. Oh, yes, we got problems."

"Oh."

"I don't expect help from your sort, man, but I listen hard to anything you say."

Multan held a plate of sweet corn and chopped meat in one hand and ate delicately with the other for a minute or two, closely watching Lanark, who could now hear the dance orchestra playing very loudly, for the nearest groups had fallen silent and an attentive and furtive murmuring came from the rest of the gallery. Lanark felt his face blush hotter and hotter.

Multan said, "Why you go on standing there if you got nothing to say?"

"Embarrassment," said Lanark in a low voice. "I started this conversation and I don't know how to end it."

"Let me help you off the hook, man. Come here, Omphale." A tall elegant black woman approached. Multan said, "Omphale, this delegate needs to talk to a white woman."

"But I'm black. As black as you are," said the woman in a clear, hooting voice.

"Sure, but you got a white voice," said Multan, moving away. Lanark and the woman stared at each other then Lanark said, "Would you care to dance?"

"No," said the woman and followed Multan.

Suddenly, on a note of laughter, all the conversations started loudly again. Lanark turned, blushing, and saw the two Joys laughing at him openly. They said "Poor Lanark!" and "Why did he leave the friends who love him?" Each linked an arm with him and led him down steps to a side of the dance floor where Odin, Powys, the other girls and some new arrivals had gathered. They received him so genially that it was easy to smile again.

"I could have told you it was useless talking to that bastard," said Odin. "Have a cigar."

"But wasn't it exciting?" said Libby. "Everybody expected something gigantic to happen. I don't know what."

"The opening of a new intercontinental viaduct, perhaps," said Powys jocularly. "The unrolling across the ocean of a fraternal carpet on which all the human races could meet and sink into one human race and get Utopia delivered by parachute with their morning milk, no?"

"Congratulations! You've done something rather fine," said

Wilkins, shaking his hand. "The rebuff doesn't matter. What counts is that you put the ball fair and square into their arena *and* they know it. One of you girls should get this man a drink."

"Wilkins, I want to talk to you," said Lanark.

"Yes, the sooner the better. There are one or two unexpected developments we must discuss. Shall we breakfast together first thing tomorrow at the delegates' repose village?"

"Certainly."

"You don't mind rising early?"

"Not at all."

"Good. I'll buzz your room before seven, then."

"Please, sir," said Solveig very meekly, "please can I have the dance you promised me earlier, please, please?"

"In a wee while, dearie. Let me finish my drink first," said Lanark kindly.

As he sipped a second white rainbow he looked out at the starry field of the sky where rockets bloomed, tinting thousands of upturned faces in the stadium beneath with purple, white, orange and greenish-gold. He was leaning on a rail guarding the drop to the lowest and narrowest floor and he also saw in the window a dark distinct reflection of himself, the captainish centre of a company standing easily in midair under the flashing fireworks and above the crowd. He nodded down at the people below and thought, 'Tomorrow I will defend you all.' He brought the cigar to his lips, turned round and carefully surveyed the gallery. His group was still the largest, though Wilkins had left it and was moving among the others. Lanark even saw him pause for a word with Multan. He thought tolerantly, 'I must keep my eye on that fellow; he's a fox, an ecological fox of the first water. . . . Fox? Ecological? First water? I don't usually think in words like these but they seem appropriate here. Yes, tomorrow I will talk to Wilkins. There will be some shrewd bargaining but no compromise. No compromise. I'll play it by ear. I'll play it hot, gelid, dirty, depending on how he deals the deck. I'll cash every therm in my suit, and then some, but no compromise! If a region's to be thrown to the crocodiles it won't be Unthank; upon that I am resolved. Monboddo is afraid of me: understandably. The hell with the standings, the top rung is up for grabs! All bets are off, the odds are cancelled, it's anybody's ballgame! The horses are all drugged, the track is glass . . . what is happening to my vocabulary? This cigar is intoxicating. Good thing I noticed: stub it out, stay calm, sip your drink. . . . I know why this is called a white rainbow. It's clear like water, yet on the tongue it spreads out into all the tastes on an artist's peacock palette (badly put). It contains as many tastes as there are colours in the mother of pearly stuff lining an abalone seashell. Poetry. Shall I tell the other Joy? She mixed this drink, she's standing over there, what a clever attractive little . . . I used to prefer big women but . . . oh, if my hand were between her small . . .'

"I am pleased to encounter you, sir," said a quiet, bald man with rimless spectacles, shaking Lanark's hand. "Kodac, Timon Kodac of South Atlantis. God knows why they chose me as a delegate. My true field is research, for Algolagnics. But it's nice to visit other continents. My mother's people hailed from Unthank."

Lanark nodded and thought, 'She is smiling at me just as Libby smiled. I thought Libby meant to seduce me but she had a boyfriend. All young attractive healthy girls have young attractive healthy boyfriends. I've heard that young girls prefer older men, but I've never seen it.'

"That's a very good woman you've got," said Kodac.

Lanark stared at him. Kodac said, "That little old professor. What's her name? Schtzngrm. That was quite a report she sent to the council. You know, the preliminary report with the Permian deep pollution samples. It made us sit up, in Algolagnics, when we got word of it. Oh, yes, we have our sources."

Lanark smiled, nodded and sipped. He thought, 'Surely her face is making me smile at her? It's so merry and intelligent, so quick to be surprised and amused. I will smile, but not much. A leader should be an audience, not a performer. His crowd should feel he is noticing, assessing, appreciating them, but from a position of strength.'

Kodac said, "Of course what interests us is her *final* report, giving the locations. I believe you are seeing Wilkins tomorrow. He's a very, very shrewd man, best man the council owns. We have a lot of respect for Wilkins at Algolagnics. So far we've always been one or two paces ahead of him, but it's been a hassle. By the way, a lot of us in Algolagnics feel Unthank has had a pretty raw deal from the council. It doesn't surprise us that you and Sludden are taking an independent line. More power to you! And speaking unofficially, I know these are also the sentiments of the Tunc-Quidative and Quantum-Cortexin clusters. But I suppose they've told you that?"

Lanark nodded gravely and thought, 'If she knew what her odd, thoroughly alive young face makes me feel, and how I envy the seam in her jeans which goes down over her stomach and over the little mound between the thighs and through and up between behind . . . if she knew how much less than a leader I am, I would bore her. I must give her the same smile I am giving this bald man who is hinting something: the knowing smile which tells them I know more than they know I know.'

"Hey!" said Kodac chuckling. "See that little tulip watching you over there? Bet you she would go like a bomb. Yes, I'm sure Wilkins is just wild to get his hands on that final report of yours. If he knows it exists. Does he?"

Lanark stared at him. Kodac laughed, patted Lanark's shoulder and said, "A straight question at last, eh? I'm sorry, but though government and industry are interlocking we ain't *fully* interlocking. Not yet. We support each other because order is Heaven's first law, but remember Costaguana? Remember when the Occidental Republic split off from it? That could never have happened without our support. Of course we weren't called Algolagnics then; that was in the time of the old Material Interests Corporation. Boy, what a gang of pirates *they* were! And the mineral was silver, which doesn't thrust as hard as a certain other mineral, you follow?"

Lanark smiled bitterly and thought, 'The only feeling she gives me is stony pain, the pain of being slightly alive in a pot-bellied old body with thinning hair. But leaders need to be mostly dead. People want solid monuments to cling to, not confused men like themselves. Sludden was wise to send me. *I* can never melt.'

"Your glass is empty," said Kodac, taking it. "I'll find a girl to fill it; I need a drink myself."

"Don't be nasty to me, Lanark," said the other Joy, smiling in front of him. "You promised me two dances, remember? Surely you can give me one?"

Without waiting for a reply she drew him out among the dancers.

Bitterness fell from him. The firm bracelet of her fingers round his wrist gave lightness and freedom. He laughed and held her waist, saying, "And Gay is your mother? Has the wound in her hand healed?"

"Was she ever wounded? She never tells me anything."

"What does she do nowadays?"

"She's a journalist. Let's not talk about her; surely I'm enough for you?"

Holding her was hard, at first, for the music was so quick and jerky that the other men and women danced without touching each other. Lanark danced to the slower sound of the whole room, whose main noise was conversation. Heard all together the conversations sounded like a waterfall blattering into a pool and made the orchestra seem the chirping of excited insects. At first the other dancers collided with him but later they moved to the side of the floor and stood cheering and clapping. The orchestra lapsed raggedly into silence and the other Joy broke away and ran into the crowd. He followed her through laughter to his group and found her talking vigorously to the other girls. She faced him and asked, "Was that not nearly incest?"

He stared at her. She said, "You are my father, aren't you?"

"Oh, no! Sludden is. Probably."

"Sludden? My mother never tells me anything. Who is Sludden? Is he successful? Is he good-looking?"

Lanark said gently, "Sludden is a very successful man, and women find him very attractive. Or used to. But I don't want to talk about him tonight."

He turned sadly away and looked at the crowded gallery where the dancing had resumed. On the faces of all these strangers he saw such familiar expressions of worry, courage, happiness, resignation, hope and failure that he felt he had known them all his life, yet they had surprising variety. Each seemed a world with its own age, climate and landscape. One was fresh and springlike, another rich, hot and summery. Some were mildly or stormily autumnal, some tragically bleak and frozen. Someone was standing by his side and her company let him admire these worlds peacefully, without wanting to conquer or enter them. He heard her sigh and say, "I wish you were more careful," and he turned and saw Lady Monboddo. Her face looked younger, more solemn and lonely than he remembered. Her breasts were bigger and a floor-length gown of stiff tapestry patterned with lions and unicorns gave her a pillar-like look. Lanark said gladly, "Catalyst!"

"That was my job, not my name. I think you should leave this place and go to bed, Lanark."

"I would, if I could go with you," said Lanark, placing an arm round her waist. She frowned at him as though his face was a page she was trying to read. He withdrew his arm awkwardly and said, "I'm sorry if I'm greedy, but I don't think these little girls like me much. And you and I were nearly very good friends once."

"Yes. We could have done anything we liked together. But you ran away to a dragon-bitch."

"But good came of it!" said Lanark eagerly. "She didn't stay a dragon long and we have a son now. He's very tall and healthy for his age, and seems intelligent too, and may be quite a kind person when he grows up."

She still stared at his face as if trying to read it. He looked away, saying uncomfortably, "Don't worry about me. I'm not drunk, if that's what you're thinking."

When he looked back she had gone and Martha stood there offering a glass and saying, "I mixed this one. It doesn't taste very nice but it's strong. Please, sir, will it soon be time for me to dance with you?"

"Why do you girls keep replacing each other?" said Lanark moodily, "I've had no time to know any of you yet."

"We think a lot of new friends can have more fun together than a pair of old friends."

"So when will you leave me?"

"Maybe I'll stay with you. Tonight," said Martha, looking at him unsmilingly.

"Maybe!" said Lanark sceptically, and drank.

At first the taste was sickly sweet and then so appallingly bitter that he gulped it hastily. Somewhere he could hear Powys saying ". . . wants the council to ban the manufacture of footwear, because the earth, you see, is like the body of a mother, and direct contact with her keeps us healthy and sane. He says the recent increase in warfare and crime is caused by composition rubber shoe soles which insulate us from the cthonic current and leave us a prey to the lunar current. Once I would have laughed, of course, but modern science is reinstating so much that we regarded as superstition. It seems that hedgehogs really *do* suck the teats of cows. . . ."

Lanark was lying outspread on cushions upon the lowest floor of all. Someone had removed his shoes and his feet gently explored the softer parts of a silk-clad body. His cheek lay on another one, each hand was snug between a pair of canvas-covered thighs and someone caressed his neck. The sounds of the gallery and orchestra were subdued and distant but he could hear two people talking high above his head.

"It's nice to see women combining to make a man feel famous."

"Drivel. They're making him a sot."

"I believe he comes from a region where coitus is often reached through stupefaction."

"And just as often missed."

"I hate these voices," said Lanark. There was whispering and he was gently raised and helped forward. A door closed somewhere and all noises stopped.

He said loudly, "I am walking . . . along a corridor."

Someone whispered, "Open your eyes."

"No. Touch tells me you are near me but eyes talk about the space between."

Another door closed and he lay down among whispers like falling leaves and felt his clothes removed. Someone whispered "Look!" and he opened his eyes long enough to meet a thin-lipped small smiling mouth in a glade of dark hair. Softly, sadly, he revisited the hills and hollows of a familiar landscape, the sides of his limbs brushing sweet abundances with surprisingly hard tips, his endings paddling in the pleats of a wet wound which opened into a boggy cave where little moans bloomed like violets in the blackness. There were dank odours and even a whiff of dung. Losing his way he lay on his back feeling that he too was a landscape, a dull flat one surrounding a tower sticking up into a dark and heavy sky. In the darkness above he felt people climbing off and onto his tower and swinging there with rhythmical gasps or shrieks. He hoped they were enjoying themselves and was glad of the company, and he kissed and caressed to show this; then everything turned over and he was the heavy sky pressing the tower into the land below, yet he felt increasingly lost, knowing the tower could stand for hours and never fire a gun. Someone whispered, "Won't you give yourself?"

"I can't. Half my strength is locked in fear and hatred."

"Why?"

"I don't remember."

"How would you like to show it?"

"I would like to . . . I can't say. You'd be disgusted."

"Tell us."

"I would like . . . I can't tell you. You would laugh."

"Risk it."

"I want you to hate and fear me too, but be unable to escape. I want you captured and bound, and waiting helplessly in perfect dread for the slash of my whip, the touch of my branding iron. And then, at the climax of your terror, what enters you is simply naked me—ah! You would have . . . to . . . be . . . de . . . lighted. Then."

The land and foundation melted and he was thrusting, biting, grunting and clutching among squealing jelly meats like a carnivorous pig with fingers. Later on, feeling expended, he lay again in kindness gently rooting in soft clefts, rocking and drifting on smoothness, afloat and basking in softness. He clasped a waist, his penis nestled between two gentle mounds and he was filled with kind nowhere.

He was knee-deep in a cold quick little burn gurgling over big rounded stones, some black, some grey, some speckled like oatmeal. He was tugging some of the stones out and carefully flinging them onto the bank a yard or two upstream where Alexander, about ten years old, very brown, and wearing red underpants, was building a dam with them. The hot sun on Lanark's neck, the chill water round his legs, the ache in his back and shoulders suggested he had been doing this for a long time. He hauled out an extra large black and dripping boulder, heaved it into the heather, then climbed up and lay flat on his back beside it, breathing hard. He closed his eyes against the profound blue and the dazzle came hot dark red through his lids. He could hear the water and the click of stones. Alexander said, "This water keeps getting through."
"Plug the holes with moss and gravelly stuff."
"I don't believe in God, you know," said Alexander.
Lanark blinked sideways and watched him wrenching clods from the bank. He said, "Oh?"
"He doesn't exist. Grampa told me."
"Which Grampa? Everyone has two."
"The one who fought in France in the first war. Give me a lot of that moss."
Without sitting up Lanark plucked handfuls from a dank mossy cushion nearby and chucked them lazily over. Alexander said, "The first war was the most interesting, I think, even though it had no Hitler or atomic bombs. You see, it mostly happened in one place, and it killed more soldiers than the second war."
"Wars are only interesting because they show how stupid we can be."
"Say that sort of thing as much as you like," said Alexander amiably, "but it won't change me. Anyway, Grampa says there isn't a God. People invented him."
"They invented motorcars too, and there are motorcars."
"That's nothing but words. . . . Shall we go for a walk? I can show you Rima, if you like."
Lanark sighed and said, "All right, Sandy."
He stood up while Alexander climbed out of the burn. Their clothes lay on a flat rock and they had to shake small red ants

off them before dressing. Alexander said, "Of course my real
name is Alexander."
"What does Rima call you?"
"Alex, but my *real* name is Alexander."
"I'll try to remember that."
"Good."

They walked down the burn to a place where it vanished
into a dip in the moor. Lanark saw it fall from his feet down
a reddish rock into a pool at the head of a deep glen full of
bushes and trees, mostly birch, rowan and small oaks. A couple,
partly screened by the roots of a fallen mountain ash, lay on
some grass beside the pool. The woman seemed asleep and
Lanark saw more of the man, who was reading a newspaper.
He said, "That isn't Sludden."
"No, that's Kirkwood. We don't see Sludden nowadays."
"Why not?"
"Sludden became too dependent."
"Kirkwood isn't?"
"Not yet."
"Sandy, do you think Rima would like to see me?"
Alexander looked uncertainly into the glen, then pointed the
other way saying, "Wouldn't you like to walk with me to the
top of that hill?"
"Yes. I would."

They turned and walked uphill toward a distant green
summit. Alexander flung himself down for a rest at the top
of the first slope and did the same thing halfway up the next.
Soon he was resting for two minutes every minute or two.
Lanark said irritably, "You don't need as much rest as this."
"I know how much rest I need."
"The sun won't hang around the sky forever, Sandy. And it
bores me, sitting still so often."
"It bores me walking all the time."
"Well, I'll go on at a slow steady pace and you catch up with
me when you like," said Lanark, standing up.
"Yah!" cried Alexander on a strong whining note. "You must
be right all the time, mustn't you? You won't leave anyone
in peace, will you? You have to spoil everything, haven't you?"
Lanark lost his temper, thrust his face toward Alexander's and
hissed, "You hate visiting the country, don't you?"
"Have I been howling and whining like this all the time? If
I hated the country I would have been, wouldn't I?"

"Stand up."
"No. You'll hit me."
"I certainly will *not*. Stand up!"
Alexander stood up, looking worried. Lanark went behind him, gripped his body under the armpits and with a strong heave managed to sit him on his shoulders. Staggering slightly he set off through a plantation of tiny fir trees. A minute later Alexander said, "You can put me down now."
Lanark plodded on up the slope.
"I said you can put me down. I can walk now."
"Not till . . . we leave . . . these trees."
The weight at first had been so heavy that Lanark told himself he would only walk ten paces, but after that he went another ten, and then another, and now he thought happily, 'I could carry him forever by taking ten steps at a time.' But he put him down at the far side of the plantation and rested on the heather while Alexander hurried ahead. Eventually Lanark followed and overtook him on a ridge where heather and coarse brown grass gave place to a carpet of turf. The land here dipped into a hollow then rose to the steep cone of the summit. Alexander said, "You see that white thing on top?"
"Yes."
"It's a triangle point."
"A triangulation point."
"That's right, a triangule point. Come on."
Alexander started straight toward the summit. Lanark said, "Stop Sandy, that's the difficult way. We'll take this path to the right."
"The straight way in the shortest, I can *see* it is."
"But it's the steepest too. This path keeps to the high ground, it will save a lot of effort."
"You go that way then."
"I will, and I'll reach the top before you do. This path was made by sensible people who knew which way was the quickest."
"You go that way then," said Alexander and rushed straight down into the hollow.

Lanark walked up the path at an easy pace. The air was fresh and the sun warm. He thought how good it was to have a holiday. The only sound was the *Wheep! Wheep!* of a distant moorbird, the only cloud a faint white smudge in the blueness over the hilltop. In the hollow on his left he sometimes saw Alexander scrambling over a ridge and thought tolerantly, 'Silly of him, but he'll learn from experience.' He was wondering sadly about Alexander's life with Rima when the path became a ladder of sandy toeholes kicked in the steepening turf. From here the summit seemed a great green dome, and staring up at it Lanark saw an amazing sight. Up the left-hand curve, silhouetted against the sky, a small human figure was quickly climbing. Lanark sighed with pleasure, halted and looked away into the blue. He said, "Thank you!" and for a moment glimpsed the ghost of a man scribbling in a bed littered with papers. Lanark smiled and said, "No, old Nastler, it isn't you I thank, but the cause of the ground which grew us all. I have never given you much thought, Mr. cause, for you don't repay that kind of effort, and on the whole I have found your world bearable rather than good. But in spite of me and the sensible path, Sandy is reaching the summit all by himself in the sunlight; he is up there enjoying the whole great globe that you gave him, so I love you now. I am so content that I don't care when contentment ends. I don't care what absurdity, failure, death I am moving toward. Even when your world has lapsed into black nothing, it will have made sense because Sandy once enjoyed it in the sunlight. I am not speaking for mankind. If the poorest orphan in creation has reason to curse you, then everything high and decent in you should go to Hell. Yes! Go to Hell, go to Hell, go to Hell as often as there are vicitms in your universe. But I am not a victim. This is my best moment. Speaking purely as a private person, I admit you to the kingdom of Heaven, and this admission is final, and I will not revoke it."

Near the top of the slope he began to grow breathless. The turf of the summit was broken by low gnarls of rock. The concrete triangulation pillar stood on one and Alexander was using it as a backrest. He had the air of man sprawling on a comfortable sofa in his own house and seemed not to see Lanark at first, then patted invitingly the rock beside him, and when Lanark sat down he leaned against him and they looked a long time at the view. In spite of their height the sea was only a soft dark line on the horizon. The land up to it was wide low hills given over to pasture, and there were strips of windbreak wood with half-reaped fields of grain in the valleys between. Lanark and Alexander faced a steep side of the hill which sloped straight down to a red-roofed town with crooked streets and a small ancient palace. This had round towers with conical roofs and a walled garden open to the public. Many figures were moving between the bright bushes and flowerbeds, and there was a full car-park outside. Alexander said, "It would be nice to go down there."

"Yes."

"But Mum might worry."

"Yes, we must go back."

They sat a little longer and when the sun was three-quarters across the sky they arose and descended to the moor by a path which led round a small loch. Two men with thick moustaches, one carrying a rifle, came up the path and nodded to Lanark as they passed. The rifle man said, "Will I shoot the delegate?" and the other laughed and said, "No, no, we mustn't kill our delegate."

Shortly after, Alexander said, "Some jokes make me tremble with fear."

"I'm sorry."

"It can't be helped. Are you really a delegate?"

Lanark had been pleased by the recognition but said firmly, "Not now. I'm on holiday just now."

The loch was embanked as a reservoir on one side and on the grass of the embankment a dead seagull lay with outspread wings. Alexander was fascinated and Lanark picked it up. They looked at the yellow beak with the raspberry spot under the tip, the pure grey back and snowy breast which seemed unmarked. Alexander said, "Should we bury it?"

"That would be difficult without tools. We could build a cairn over it."

They collected stones from the shingle of the lochside and heaped them over the glossy feathers of the unmarked body. Alexander said, "What happens to it now?"

"It rots and insects eat it. There are a lot of red ants around here; they'll pick it to a skeleton quite fast. Skeletons are interesting things."

"Could we come back for it tomorrow?"

"No, it probably needs several weeks to reach the skeleton stage."

"Then say a prayer."

"You told me you didn't believe in God."

"I don't, but a prayer must be said. Put your hands like this and shut your eyes."

They stood on each side of the knee-high cairn and Lanark shut his eyes.

"You begin by saying *Dear God.*"

"Dear God," said Lanark, "we are sorry this gull died, especially as it looks young and healthy (apart from being dead). Let there be many young, living gulls to enjoy the speed and freshness this one missed; and give us all enough happiness and courage to die without feeling cheated; moreover . . ." He hesitated. A voice whispered, "Say amen."
"Amen."

Something cold stung his cheeks. He opened his eyes and saw the sky dark with torn, onrushing clouds. He was alone with nothing at his feet but a scatter of stones with old bones and feathers between them. He said "Sandy?" and looked around. There was nothing human on the moor. The light was fading from two or three sunset streaks in the clouds to the west. The heather was crested with sleet; the wind whipped more of it into his face.
"Sandy!" he screamed, starting to run. "Sandy! Sandy! *Alexander!*"
He plunged across the heather, tripped and fell into darkness. He wrestled awhile with something entangling, then realized it was blankets and sat up.

He was in a square room with cement floor and tiled walls like a public lavatory. It seemed large, perhaps because the only furniture was a lavatory pan in one corner without seat or handle to flush it. He lay in the diagonally opposite corner on part of the floor raised a foot above the rest and covered with red linoleum. The door of the place had a metal surface, and he knew it was locked. He had a headache and felt filthy and was sure something dreadful had happened. He pulled the blankets around him and huddled up, biting the thumb knuckle and trying to think. His main feeling was of filth, disorder and loss. He had lost someone or something, a secret document, a parent, or his self-respect. The past seemed a muddle of memories without sequence, like a confused pile of old photographs. To sort them out he tried recalling his life from the start.

First he had been a child, then a schoolboy, then his mother died. He became a student, tried to work as a painter and became very ill. He hung uselessly round cafés for a time, then took a job in an institute. He got mixed up with a woman there, lost the job, then went to live in a badly governed place where his son was born. The woman and child left him, and for no very clear reason he had been sent on a mission to some sort of assembly. This had been hard at first, then easy, because he was suddenly a famous man with important papers in his briefcase. Women loved him. He had been granted an unexpected holiday with Sandy, then something cold had stung his cheek—

His thoughts recoiled from that point like fingers from a scalding plate, but he forced them back to it and gradually more recent, more depressing memories came to him.

CHAPTER 42. Catastrophe

There had been a sky dark with onrushing clouds. He had been alone with some scattered rocks, old bones and feathers at his feet and had looked round saying "Sandy?" but there was nobody else on the moor and the light was fading from two or three sunset streaks in the clouds to the west. He had run across the heather screaming Alexander's name and tripped and fallen into darkness. He had wrestled a while with something entangling, then realized it was a downy quilt, flung it aside and sat up.

He was in bed in a darkened room with a headache and a feeling of terrible loss. He was sure he had come here with people who had been kind to him, but who were they? Where had they gone? His hand found and flicked the switch of a bedlight. The room was a dormitory with a pair of beds to each wall and dressing tables between them loaded with female cosmetics. The walls had coloured posters of male singers on them and notices saying things like JUST BECAUSE YOU'RE PARANOID DON'T THINK THEY AREN'T PLOTTING AGAINST YOU. His clothes were scattered about the floor. He groaned, rubbed his head, got up and quickly dressed. He felt that something very good had happened recently. It may not have been love, but it had left him ready for love. Delight had opened him, prepared him for someone who wasn't there. He was anguished by the absence of someone to hold and whisper to affectionately, someone to hold him and speak lovingly back. He left the room and hurried along a dark corridor toward a sound of music and voices behind a door. He pushed the door open and stood blinking in the light. The voices stopped then someone shouted, "Look out! Here he comes again!" and a huge explosion of laughter went up.

The gallery was emptier than he remembered. Most people lay on cushions on the lowest floor and he hurried through them looking left and right. He remembered meeting a thin-lipped smiling little mouth in a glade of dark hair and cried to a laughing mouth among dark hair, "Is it you? Were you with me?"

"When?"

"In the bedroom?"

"Oh, no, not me! Wasn't it Helga? The woman dancing up there?"

He rushed onto the dance floor, crying, "Are you Helga? Were you with me in the bedroom?"

"Sir," said Timon Kodac, who was dancing with her, "this lady is my wife."

Laughter came from every side though nobody else was dancing and the only player was a saxophonist. The rest of the orchestra sat with girls on cushions round the floor and he suddenly saw Libby very clearly. She leaned against the drummer, a middle-aged man with horn-rimmed glasses. Her gracefully plump young body yearned toward him, little ripples flowed up it, thrusting her shoulder into his armpit, a breast against his side. Lanark hurried over and said, "Libby, please, was it—was it you, please?"

"Nyuck!" she said with a disgusted grimace. "Certainly not!"

"It's all sliding away from me," wept Lanark, covering his eyes. "Sliding into the past, further and further. It was lovely, and now it has turned to jeering."

A hand seized his arm and a voice said, "Take a grip of yourself."

"Don't let go," said Lanark opening his eyes. He saw a small, lean, young-looking man with crew-cut hair, black sweater, slacks and sandshoes.

The man said, "You're being bloody embarrassing. I know what you need. Come with me."

Lanark let himself be led up to the top floor, which was completely empty. He said, "Who are you?"

"Think a bit."

The voice sounded familiar. Lanark peered closely and saw deep little creases at the corners of the eyes and mouth which showed that this smooth, pale, ironical face belonged to quite an old man.

He said, "You can't be Gloopy."
"Why not?"
"Gloopy, you've changed. You've improved."
"Can't say the same for you."
"Gloopy, I'm lonely. Lost and lonely."
"I'll help you out. Sit there."

Lanark sat at a table. Gloopy went to the nearest bar and returned with a tall glass. He said, "There you are. A rainbow." Lanark gulped it and said, "I thought you were operating as a lift, Gloopy."
"Doesn't do to stay too long at the same thing. What is it you want? Sex, is it?"
"No, no, not just sex, something more gentle and ordinary." Gloopy frowned and drummed his fingers on the tabletop. He said, "You'll have to spell it out more definite than that. Think carefully. Male or female? How old? What posture?"
"I want a woman who knew and liked me a long time ago and still likes me. I want her to take me in her arms easily, casually, as if it was a simple thing to do. She'll find me cold and unresponsive at first, I've lived too long alone, you see, but she mustn't be put off by that. We'll sleep together calmly all night, and then I'll lose my fear of her and toward morning I'll wake with an erection and she'll caress me and we'll make love without worry or fuss. And spend all day in bed, eating, reading and cuddling happily, making love if we feel like it and not *bothered* by each other."
"I see. You want a mother figure."
"No!" yelled Lanark. "I don't want a mother figure, or a sister figure, or a wife figure, I want a woman, an attractive woman who likes me more than any other man in the world yet doesn't pester me!"
"I can probably fix you up with something like that," said Gloopy. "So stop shouting. I'll give you one more drink, and then we visit your rooms in Olympia. All types of attractive bints in Olympia."
"My rooms? Olympia?"
"Olympia is the delegates' repose village. Didn't they tell you?"
"Are you a pimp, Gloopy?" said Lanark, gulping another white rainbow.
"Yeah. One of the best in the business. There's a great need for us in times like these."
"Times like what, Gloopy?"
"Don't you read the glossies? Don't you watch the talk shows?

Ours is an era of crumbling social values. This is the age of
alienation and non-communication. The old morals and manners are passing away and the new lot haven't come in yet.
Result is, men and women can't talk about what they want
from each other. In an old-fashioned flower culture like Tahiti
a girl would wear a pink hibiscus blossom behind her left ear,
which meant, I got a good boyfriend but I'd like to have two.
So the boys understood her, see? The European aristocracy
used to have a very sophisticated sex language using fans, snuff-
boxes and monocles. But nowdays people are so desperate for
lack of a language that they've taken to advertising in newspapers. You know the kind of thing! *Forty-three-year-old wealthy
but balding accountant whose hobby is astronomy would like to meet
one-legged attractive not necessarily intelligent girl who wouldn't mind
spanking him with a view to forming a lifelong attachment.* That's
just not good enough. Too much room for accident. What
society needs is me, a sensitive trustworthy middleman with
wide connections and access to a good Tunc-Quidative-Cor-
texin-Cluster-Computer."

"Smattera fact, Gloop," said Lanark shyly, "sometimes I am
a . . . a . . . a . . ."

"Yeah?"

"a . . . a . . . an imaginary sadist."

"Yeah?"

"Not a damaging sadist. Namaginary one. So from standpoint
of occasional perverse frolic it would help matters if lady nques-
tion, along with the other points numerated, which *are* the
'sential points, make no mistake about that, these other points
I numerated are the 'sential ones . . . where was?"

"Perverse frolic."

"Good. I'd like her *not* to be namaginary masochist, because
I want to give her imaginary pain, not imaginary pleasure."

"Yeah. Defeat whole purpose."

"So I require namaginary *weaker* sadist than myself."

"Yeah, difficult, but I might just manage to swing it. Come
on, then."

Gloopy steered him through the dozen Quantum-Cortexin
security men who remained outside the gallery and opened a
door beside the doors of the lifts. They walked down a paved
path between lawns and trees with Chinese lanterns in them.
Lanark said, "I thought we were very high up, Gloop."

"Only on the inside. The stadium is built in an old dock basin,
you see. The river's down here, Narky boy."

They passed a wharf where small pleasure boats were gently rocking and came to a smooth sheet of water with lamps along the far shore. Lanark stopped and pointed dramatically to the long reflections of the lights in the dark water.

"Gloop!" he cried. "Poem. Listen. 'Magine these lights stars, right? Here goes. Twilit lake, sleek as clean steel—"

"This is a river and it's nearly dawn, Narky boy."

"Doninerrupt. You're not a cricit, Gloop, you're a chamberlain, like Munro. Know Munro, no? Nindividual who delivers folk from one chambèr to nother. Listen. Twilit lake, sleek as clean steel, each star a shining spear in your deep. Pottery. I have been twitted, in my time, with solidity, Gloop. Dull solid man of few words, me. But *pottery* is lukring in these dethps, Gloop!" said Lanark, thumping his chest. He thumped too hard and started coughing.

"Lean on me, Nark," said Gloopy.

Lanark leaned on him and they came to a footbridge which crossed the water in one slender white span to a shining arrangement of glass cubes and lantern-hung trees on the other shore.

"Olympia," said Gloopy.

"Nice," said Lanark. In the middle of the bridge he stopped again saying, "No fireworks now, so we have waterworks, yes? It's urgent that I piss."

He did so between two railings and was disappointed to see his urine jet two feet forward and then fall straight down.

"When I was a small-bellied boy!" he cried, "tumbling ninepin over the dolly mixture daisies, my piss had an arc of thirteen feet. A greybeard now, belly flabby from abuse of drink, I cannot squirt past my reflection. Piss. A word which sounds like what it means. A rare word."

"Police," muttered Gloopy.

"No, Gloop, you are wrong. Police does not sound like what it means. It is too like polite, please and nice."

Gloopy was running down the slope of the bridge toward the village. When he reached the shore he turned his head for a moment and yelled, "All right, officers! Just a perverse frolic!"

Lanark saw two policemen advancing toward him. He zipped up his trousers and hurried after Gloopy. As he reached the shore two men stepped onto the bridge and stood blocking the way. They wore black suits. One held out a hand and said in a dull voice, "Pass please."

"I can't, you're blocking the way."

"Show your pass, please."

"I don't have one. Or if I do it's in my briefcase—I've left that somewhere. Do I need a pass? I'm a delegate, I have rooms here, please let me through."

"Identify self."

"Provost Lanark of Greater Unthank."

"There is no Provost Lanark of Greater Unthank."

Lanark noticed that the man's eyes and mouth were shut and the voice came from a neatly folded white handkerchief in his breast pocket. His companion was staring at Lanark with eyes and mouth wide open. A metal ring with a black centre poked out between his teeth. With great relief Lanark heard the voice of an ordinary human policeman behind him: "Just what's happening here?"

"There is no Provost Lanark of Greater Unthank," said the security man again.

"There is!" said Lanark querulously, "I know the programme says the Unthank delegate is Sludden but it's wrong, there was an unexpected last-minute change. *I* am the delegate!"

"Identify self."

"How *can* I without my briefcase? Where's Gloopy? He'll vouch for me, he's a very important pimp, you've just let him through. Or Wilkins, send for Wilkins. Or Monboddo! Yes, contact the bloody Lord Monboddo, he knows me better than anyone."

In his own ears the words seemed shrill and unconvincing. The voice from the security man's pocket sounded like a record slowing to a stop: "Proof-burden property of putative prover."

"What the hell does that mean?"

"It means, Jimmy, that you'd better come quietly with us," said a policeman, and Lanark felt a hand grip each shoulder. He said feebly, "My name is Lanark."

"Don't let it worry you, Jimmy."

The security men stepped back. The policemen pushed Lanark forward, then sideways and down to a landing stage. Lanark said, "Aren't you taking me to the repose village?"

They pushed him onto the deck of a motor launch, then down into a cabin. He said, "What about Nastler? He's your king, isn't he? *He* knows me."

They pushed him down on a bench and sat on a bench opposite. He felt the launch move out into the river and was suddenly so tired that he had to concentrate to keep from falling down.

Later he saw the planks of another landing stage, and a pavement which continued for a long time, then a few stone steps, a doormat and some square rubber tiles fitted edge to edge. He was allowed to lean on a flat surface. A voice said, "Name?"

"Lanark."

"Christian or surname?"

"Both."

"Are you telling me your name is Lanark Lanark?"

"If you like. I mean yes yes yes yes yes."

"Age?"

"Ndtermate. I mean indeterminate. Past halfway."

Someone sighed and said "Address?"

"Nthank cathedral. No, 'Lympia. Olympia."

There was some muttering. He noticed the words "bridge" and "security" and "six fifty." That jerked him awake. He stared across a counter at a police sergeant with a grey moustache who was writing in a ledger. He saw a room full of desks where two policewomen were typing and the number 6.94 very big and black was framed upon the wall. With a click it charged to 6.95. He realized that a decimal clock had a hundred minutes an hour and licked his lips and tried to talk quickly and clearly.

"Sergeant, this is urgent! An important phone call is probably going through just now to my rooms in the delegates' repose village; can it be diverted here? It's from Wilkins, Monboddo's secretary. I've been drunk and foolish, I'm sorry, but there may be a public disaster if I can't speak to Wilkins!"

The sergeant stared at him hard. Lanark had flung out his hands appealingly and now saw they were filthy. His waistcoat was unbuttoned, his suit crumpled. There was a bad smell in the room and he noticed, with a shudder, that it came from a brown crusted stain on his trouser leg. He said, "I know I look detestable but politicians can't always be wise! Please! I'm not asking for myself but for the people I represent. Put me on to Wilkins!"

The sergeant sighed. He took an assembly programme from under the counter and studied a back page printed in small type. He said, "Is Wilkins a surname or a Christian name?"

"Surname, I think. Does it matter?"

The sergeant pushed the programme over the counter saying, "Which?"

A list of names headed COUNCIL STAFF filled ten pages. In the first four Lanark found Wilkins Staple-Stewart, the Acting Secretary for Internal-External Liaison, Peleus Wilkins, Procurator Designate for Surroundings and Places, and Wendel Q.

Wilkins, Senior Adviser on Population Energy Transfer.
"Listen!" said Lanark. "I'll phone every Wilkins in the list till
I get the—no! No, I'll phone Monboddo and get the full name
from him; he knows me even if his damned robots don't. I'm
sorry the hour is so early, but . . ."
He hesitated, for his voice sounded unconvincing again and
the sergeant was slowly shaking his head. "Let me prove who
I am!" said Lanark wildly. "My briefcase is in Nastler's room
in the stadium—no, I gave it to Joy, a Red Girl, a hostess in
the executive gallery; she put it behind the bar for me I must
get it back it contains a vitally important document please this
is vital—"
The sergeant, who was writing in the ledger, said "All right,
lads."
Lanark felt a hand clapped on each shoulder and cried, "But
what am I charged with? I've hurt nobody, molested nobody,
insulted nobody. What am I charged with?"
"With being a pisser," said a policeman holding him.
"All men are pissers!"
"I am charging you," said the sergeant, writing, "under the
General Powers (Consolidation) Order, and what you need
is a nice long rest."
And as he was led away Lanark found himself yawning hugely.
The hands on his shoulder grew strangly comforting. Surely
he had often been pushed forward by strong people who
thought he was wicked? The feeling was less dreamlike than
childlike.

He was led into a small narrow room with what looked
like bunks piled with folded blankets along one wall. He climbed at once to the top bunk and lay down, but they laughed
and said, "No, no, Jimmy!"
He climbed down and they gave him two blankets to carry
and led him to another door. He went through and it was
slammed and locked behind him. He wrapped the blankets
round him, lay on a platform in a corner and slept.

And now he was awake and wildly miserable. He sprang
up and walked in a circle round the floor, crying, "Oh! I have
been wicked, *stupid*, evil, *stupid*, daft daft daft *daft* and stupid,
stupid! And it happened exactly when I thought myself a fine
great special splendid man! How did it happen? I meant to
find Wilkins and talk to him sensibly, but the women made
me feel famous. Did they want to destroy me? No, no, they

treated me like something special because it made *them* feel special but all the time nothing good was being made, nothing useful was done. I was drunk, yes, with white rainbows, yes, but mostly with vanity; nobody is as crazy as a man who thinks he is important. People tried to tell me things and I ignored them. What was Kodac hinting at? Valuable minerals, special reports, government ignorance, it sounded like dirty trickery but I should have listened carefully. And . . . Catalyst . . . why didn't I ask her name? She tried to warn me and I thought she wanted to sleep with me. Yah! Greed and idiocy. *I forgot the reports!* I lost the reports without even reading them, I was seduced by people I can't even remember (but it was lovely). And how did I come to be paddling in that burn with Sandy? What was that but a useless bit of happiness put in to make my fall more dreadful? (But it was wonderful.) Oh, Sandy, what kind of father have you been cursed with? I left you to defend you and have turned into a ludicrous lecherous discredited stinking goat!"

He stopped and stared at some things he had not noticed beside the platform: three plastic mugs of cold tea and three paper plates of rolls with cold fried sausages in them. He grabbed the rolls and with tears trickling down his cheeks gulped and swallowed between sentences, saying, "Three mugs, three plates, three meals: I've been a whole day in here, the first day of the assembly is over. . . . When will I be let out? . . . I was fooled by false love because I never knew the true kind, not even with Rima. Why? I was faithful to her not because I loved her but because I *wanted* love, it is *right* that she left me it is *right* that I'm locked up here, I deserve much worse. . . . But who will speak for Unthank? . . . Who will cry out against that second-hand second-rate creator who thinks a cheap stupid *disaster* is the best ending for mankind? O, heavens, heavens fall and crush me! . . . ."

He noticed that self-denunciation was becoming a pleasure and sprang up and beat his head hard against the door; then stopped because it hurt too much. Then he noticed someone else was shouting and banging too. The door had a slit like a small letterbox at eye level. He looked through and saw another door with a slit immediately opposite. A voice from there said, "Have you a cigarette Jimmy?"

"I don't smoke. Do you know the time?"

"It was two in the morning when they brought me in and that was a while ago. What did they get you for?"

"I pissed off a bridge."

"The police," said the voice bitterly, "are a shower of bastards. Are you sure you don't have a cigarette?"

"No, I don't smoke. What did they get you for?"

"I hammered a man up a close and called the police a shower of bastards. Listen, they can't treat us like this. Let's batter our doors and yell till they give us some fags."

"But I don't smoke," said Lanark, turning away.

His main feeling now was of physical filth. The lavatory pan suddenly flushed and he examined it. The water looked and smelled pure. He undressed, wet a corner of a blanket and scrubbed himself hard all over. He draped a dry blanket round him like a toga, rinsed his underclothes several times in the pan and hung them on the rim to dry. He scraped with his nails the crust of vomit from the trouser leg and rubbed the place with the wettened blanket. The creased cloth offended him. Though thirsty he had only been able to empty one mug of cold tea. He spread the trousers on the platform and rubbed them steadily in small circles with the mug base, pressing down hard. He did this a long time without seeing an improvement, but whenever he stopped there was nothing else to do. The door opened and a policeman entered with a mug and a plate of rolls. He said, "What are you doing?"

"Pressing my trousers."

The man collected the other mugs and plates. Lanark said, "When will I get out, please?"

"That's up to the magistrate."

"When will I see the magistrate?"

The policeman went outside, slamming the door. Lanark ate, drank the hot tea and thought, 'The assembly has begun the work of the second day.' He began pressing again. Whenever he stopped he felt so evil and useless, evil and trivial that he bit his hands till the pain was an excuse for screaming, though he did it quietly and undramatically. Another policeman brought lunch and Lanark said, "When will I see the magistrate?"

"The court sits tomorrow morning."

"Could you take my underclothes please and hang them somewhere to dry?"

The policeman went out, laughing heartily. Lanark ate, drank, then walked in a circle, flapping the underpants in one hand, the vest in the other. He thought, 'I suppose the assembly is discussing world order just now.' A feeling of hatred grew in him, hatred of the assembly, the police and everyone who wasn't in the cell with him. He decided that when he was released he would immediately piss on the police station steps, or smash a window, or set fire to a car. He bit his hands some more, then worked at pressing trousers and drying underclothes till long after the evening tea and rolls. He felt too restless to lie down, and when the underwear was only slightly damp he dressed, polished his shoes with the blanket and sat waiting for breakfast and the magistrates' court. He thought drearily, 'Perhaps I'll be in time for the pollution debate.'

And then he wakened with a headache, feeling filthy again. Three mugs of cold tea, three plates of rolls lay beside the platform. He thought, 'My life is moving in circles. Will I always come back to this point?' He didn't feel wicked any more, only trivial and useless. Another policeman opened the door and said, "Outside. Come on. Outside."
Lanark said feebly, "I would like to stay here a little longer."
"Outside, come on. This isn't a hotel we're running."

He was led to the office. A different sergeant stood behind the counter and an old lady wearing jeans and a fur coat stood in front. Her face was sharp and unpleasant; her thin hair, dyed blond, was pulled into an untidy bun on top of her head and the scalp showed between the strands. She said, "Hullo, Lanark."
The sergeant said, "You have this lady to thank for bailing you out."
She said, "Why didn't he appear in the magistrates court this morning?"
"Pressure of business."
"The court didn't look busy to me. Come on Lanark."
Her voice was harsh and grating. He followed her to the station steps and was slightly blinded by the honey-coloured light of an evening sun sparkling on the river beyond a busy roadway. He stopped and said, "I'm sorry. I don't know who you are."
She pulled off a fur gauntlet and with a queer, vulnerable gesture held out her hand, palm upward. One of the lines across it was deep, like a scar.
He said "Gay!" with immense regret, for though she had been ill when he last saw her she had also been attractive and young. He gazed into her lean old face, shaking his head, and her expression showed she had the same feeling about himself.

She pulled on the glove and slipped her arm round his, saying quietly, "Come on, old man. We can do something better than stand round regretting our age. My car is over there."

As they went toward it she said with sudden violence, "The whole business stinks! Everyone knew you disappeared two days ago; there were plenty of rumours but nothing was done. Twice daily I phoned every police station in the Provan region and they pretended they hadn't heard of you till an hour ago; then the marine police station admitted they had a prisoner who *might* be you. An hour ago! After the subcommittee reports had been read and voted on and all the smiling statements made to the press. Did you know I was a journalist? I write for one of those venomous little newspapers that decent people think should be banned: the sort that print nasty stories about rich, famous, highly respected citizens."

She opened the car door. He sat beside her and she drove off. He said, "Where are we going?"

"To the banquet. We'll be in time for the speeches at the end."

"I don't want to go to a banquet. I don't want the other delegates or anybody to see me or be reminded of me ever again."

"You're demoralized. It'll wear off. My daughter is a stupid, gelid little nung. If she'd looked after you none of this would have happened. Have you guessed who caused all this?"

"I blame nobody but myself."

She laughed almost merrily and said, "That's a splendid excuse for letting bastards walk all over you. . . . Do you really not know who pushed you into that trap?"

"Gloopy?"

"Sludden."

He looked at her. She frowned and said, "Perhaps Monboddo is in it too, but no, I don't think so. The big chief prefers not to know certain details. Wilkins and Weems are more likely, but if so Sludden has been too smart for them. Instead of neatly carving up Greater Unthank for the council my bloody ex-husband has handed it over to Cortexin lock, stock and ballocks."

"Sludden?"

"Sludden, Gow and all the other merry men. Except Grant. Grant objected. Grant may manage to start something."

"I don't understand you," said Lanark drearily. "Sludden sent me here to argue against Unthank's being destroyed. Will it be destroyed?"

"Yes, but not in the way they first planned. The council and creature-clusters meant to use it as a cheap supply of *human* energy, but they won't do that now till they've sucked out these lovely rich juices discovered by your friend Mrs. Schtzngrm."

"What of the pollution?"

"Cortexin will handle that. For the moment, at any rate."

"So Unthank is safe?"

"Of course not. Bits of it have become valuable property again, but only to a few people and for a short time. Sludden has sold your resources to an organization with worldwide power run by a clique for the benefit of a clique. That isn't safety. Why do you think were you sent here as a delegate?"

"Sludden said I was the best man available."

"Ha! Politically speaking you don't know your arse from your elbow. You don't even know what the word 'lobbying' means. You were fucking well *certain* to pox up everything, that's why Sludden made *you* delegate. And while people here got excited about you, and plotted against you, and passed big resolutions about world order and energy and pollution, Sludden and Cortexin were doing with Unthank exactly what they wanted. You aren't very intelligent, Lanark."

"I have begun to notice that recently," said Lanark, after a pause.

"I'm sorry old man, it isn't your fault. Anyway, I'm trying to make you angry."

"Why?"

"I want you to raise hell at this banquet."

"Why? I won't do it, but why?"

"Because this has been the smoothest, politest, most docile assembly in history. The delegates have handled each other as gently as unexploded bombs. All the dirty deals and greedy devices have been worked out in secret committees with nobody watching, nobody complaining, nobody reporting. We need somebody, just once, to embarrass these bastards with a bit of the truth."

"Sludden told me to do that."

"His reasons are not my reasons."

"Yes. He was a politician, you are a journalist, and I like neither of you. I like nobody except my son, and I'm afraid I'll never see him again. So I care for nothing."

The car was passing down a quiet street. Gay parked it suddenly by a vast brick wall and folded her arms on the wheel.

She said quietly, "This is terrible. In the days of the old Elite you were a definite, independent sort of man in your limited way. I was slightly afraid of you. I envied you. I was a silly weakling then, the mouthpiece of someone who despised me. And now that I've lost my looks and gained some sense and self-confidence you've gone as feeble as putty. Did Rima chew your balls off?"

"Please don't talk like that."

Gay sighed and said, "Where will we go?"

"I don't know."

"You're my passenger. Where do you want me to drive you?"

"Nowhere."

"All right," she said, reaching into the back seat. "Here's your briefcase. My daughter found it somewhere. It was empty, apart from a scientific dictionary and this pass with your name on it." She stuck a long strip of plastic into his breast pocket. "Get out."

He got out and stood on the kerb, trying to find comfort in the familiar smoothness of the briefcase handle. He expected the car to drive away but Gay got out too. She took his arm and led him to a double door, the only feature in a wilderness of wall. He said, "What place is this?" but she hummed softly to herself and touched a bell button. Each wing of the door suddenly swung inward and Lanark was appalled by the sight of two tight-mouthed security men. They spoke sharply and simultaneously, the voices springing from their shirtfronts: "Pass, please."

"You can see it in his pocket," said Gay.

"Identify self."

"He's the Unthank delegate, slightly late, and I'm from the press."

"Delegate may enter. No press may enter without the red card. No press may enter without the red card. Delegate may enter."

They moved apart, leaving a narrow space between them. Gay said, "Well, goodbye, Lanark. I'm sorry I won't be able to twist your arm when the right moment comes. But if you manage to improvise some guts, old man, I'll certainly hear about it."

She turned and walked away.

"Delegate may enter. Or Not," said the security men. "Delegate may enter. Or not. Invite expression of intention by progression or retrogression. Request expression of intention. Demand expression of intention. Command expression of intention!"

Lanark stood and pondered.

"Think hard!" said the security men. "In default of expression of intention, delegate demoted to condition of obstruction. Think hard! In def of exp of int del dem to con of ob think, conofobthink, conofobthink."

And although it made him shudder, he stepped through the narrow space between them because he could think of nowhere else to go.

CHAPTER 43. Explanation

A concrete floor, dusty and stained by pigeon droppings, lay under a high roof upheld by iron girders. From the doorway a long blue carpet ran into the shadowy distance. He walked down this till it touched a similar carpet at right angles. He turned the corner round a little gurgling fountain in a glass bowl and heard a hubbub of voices. A dozen security guards stood before the door of a circus tent. He went forward, holding out his pass and saying loudly, "Unthank delegate!"

A displeased-looking girl in red shirt and jeans appeared between the black-clad men and said, "I'm surprised to see *you* here, Lanark. I mean, everything's finished. Even the food." It was Libby. He muttered that he had come for the speeches. "Why? They'll be horribly boring, and you look as if you hadn't washed for a week. Why do you want to hear speeches?"

He stared at her. She sighed and said, "Come inside, but you'll have to hurry."

He followed her through the door. The hubbub grew deafening as she led him along between the inner wall of the tent and a line of waiters carrying out trays laden with used dishes. He glimpsed the backs of people sitting at a table which curved away to the left and right. Libby pointed to an empty chair saying, "That was yours."

He slunk into it as quietly as possible. A neighbor stared at him, said "Good God, a ghost!" and started chuckling. It was Odin. "It's very, very, very good to see you," said Powys, the other neighbour. "What happened? We've been terribly alarmed about you."

The table formed a white-clothed circle filling most of the tent. There was a wineglass to each chair and a sign with

the guest's name and title facing outward. Red girls carried
bottles about inside the circle, filling glasses. Lanark explained
what had happened to him.

"I'm glad it was only that," said Powys. "Some people whispered you'd been shot or abducted by the security guards.
Of course we didn't really believe it. If we had we'd have
complained."

"That rumour did the assembly a power of good," said Odin
cheerfully. "A lot of cowardly loudmouths were afraid to say
a word during the big energy debate. Bloody idiots!"

"Well, you know," said Powys, "I don't mind admitting I was
worried too. These guards are ugly customers, and nobody
seems to know what their precise instructions are. Yes, the
business of the last few days has been settled with unusual
promptness, so you did not piss in vain. But it was reckless
of you to pollute their river. They're very fond of it."

Solveig came along the table filling wineglasses. He stared down
at the tablecloth, hoping not to be noticed. There was a sound
like a colossal soft cough then a perfectly amplified voice said,
"Ladies and gentlemen, you will be glad to hear that after an
absence of three days one of our most popular delegates has
returned. The witty, the venerable, the *not always perfectly sober*
Lord Provost Lanark of Greater Unthank is in his place at last."
Lanark's mouth opened. Though total silence had fallen he
seemed to hear a great roar go up. The multitude of glances
on him—mocking, he was sure, condescending, contemptuous,
amused—seemed to pierce and press him down. Someone
yelled, "Give the man a drink!"

He sobbed and laid his head on the tablecloth. The hubbub
of voices began again, but with more speculation than laughter
in it. He heard Odin murmur, "That wasn't necessary," and
Powys said, "No, they didn't need to rub it in like that."

There was another soft cough and the voice said, "My lords,
ladies and gentlemen, pray silence for Sir Trevor Weems,
Knight of the Golden Snail, Privy Councillor of Dalriada, Chief
Executive Officer of the Greater Provan Basin and Outer Erse
Confederacy."

There was some applause then Lanark heard the voice of
Weems.

"This is a strange occasion for me. The man sitting on
my left is the twenty-ninth Lord Monboddo. He has been many
things in his time: musician, healer, dragon-master, scourge
of the decimal clock, *enfant terrible* of the old expansion project,

stupor mundi of the institute and council debates. I have known him as all these things and opposed him as every one of them. A rash, rampant, raving intellectual, that's what I called him in the old days. Everyone remembers the unhappy circumstances in which his predecessor retired. I won't tell you what I thought when I heard the name of the new Monboddo. If I spoke too plainly our excellent Quantum-Cortexin security guards might be obliged to lead me away under the Special Powers (Consolidation) Order and lock me in a very small room for a very long time. The fact is, I was appalled. Our whole Provan executive was flung into profound gloom when we realized we would be hosts to a general assembly chaired by the dreadful *Ozenfant*. But what has been the outcome?" There was a pause. Weems said fervently, "Ladies and gentlemen, this has been the most smoothly run, clear-sighted, coherent assembly the council has ever convened! There are many reasons for this, but I believe future historians will mainly ascribe it to the tact, tolerance and intelligence of the man sitting on my left. He need not shake his head! If he is a rebel we need more of them. Indeed, I might even be persuaded to vote for a revolution—if the twenty-ninth Lord Monboddo undertook to lead it!"
There was some loud laughter.

By slow degrees Lanark had come to sit upright again. The centre of the circle was empty. Far to the right Weems stood beside Lord and Lady Monboddo. Microphones protruded from a low bank of roses on the tablecloth before him. All the guests on that side of the circle were pink. On the other side they were sallow or brown, with the five members of the black bloc directly facing Monboddo. Several dark delegates talked quietly among themselves, not attending to the speech. Weems was saying, ". . . will be far too deep for me, I'm afraid, and what I do understand I'll almost certainly disagree with. But he has heard so much from us in the past three days that it is only fair to allow him his revenge. And so, Lord Monboddo, I call on you to summarize the work of the council, Then, Now and Tomorrow."
Weems sat down amid applause. Monboddo had been smiling down at the table with half-shut eyes. He arose and stood with one hand resting on the table, the other in his pocket, the smiling head tilted a little to one side. He waited until applause, faint conversation, coughs and stirrings sank into silence. As the silence continued his figure, casual yet unmoving, gained

power and authority until the whole great ring of guests was like an audience of carved statues. Lanark was amazed that so many could make so complete a silence. It weighed on him like a crystal bubble filling the top of the tent and pressing down on his skull: he could shatter it any time by yelling a single obscenity, but bit his lips hard to stop that happening. Monboddo began to speak.

> "Some men are born modest. Some achieve modesty. Some have modesty thrust upon them. I fear that Sir Trevor has firmly placed me in the last of these categories."

Laughter went up, especially from Weems.

> "Once I was an ambitious young department chief. I launched policies and had flashes of creative brilliance which, believe me, my friends, verged, I thought, upon genius! Well, ambition has met its nemesis. I now stand on the top tip of our vast pyramid and create nothing. I can only receive the brilliant proposals of younger, more actively placed colleagues and find ways to reconcile and promote them. I examine the options and discard, without emotions, those which do not fit our system. Such work uses a very *small* part of human intelligence."

"Oh, nonsense!" shouted Weems cheerfully.

> "Not nonsense, no, my friend. I promise you that in three years all the limited skills of a council supremo will be embodied in the circuits of a Quantum-Cortexin humanoid, just as the skills of secretaries and special policemen are embodied. It may be my privilege to be the last of the fully human Lords Monboddo. The idea would flatter my very considerable vanity, were it not for the great improvement people will see in government business when the change takes place. Everything will suddenly go much faster.

Yes, today human government stands at a very delicate point of balance. But before opening the path ahead I must describe the steps which brought us here.

"So stand with me on the sun some six thousand years ago and consider, with sharper eyes than the eagle, the moist blue-green ball of the third planet. The deserts are smaller than now, the forest jungles much bigger, for where soil is thick, shrubberies clog the rivers and spread them out into swampland. There are no broad tracts of fenced field, no roads or towns. The only sign of men is where the globe's western edge is rolling into the shadow of night. Some far-apart gleams are beginning on that dim curve, the fires of hunters in forest clearings, of fishers at river mouths, of wandering herdsmen and planters on the thin soil between desert and jungle, for we are too few to take good land from the trees. Our tiny tribal democracies have spread all over this world, yet we influence it less than our near relation the squirrel, who is important to the survival of certain hardwoods. We have been living here for half a million years, yet history, with its noisy collisions and divisions of code and property, has not yet started. No wonder the first historians thought men had been created a few centuries before themselves. No wonder later theorists called prehistoric men *childlike, savage, rude,* and thought they had wasted time in fighting and couplings even more ferocious than those of today.

"But big killings, like big buildings, need large populations to support them, and fewer people were born in 500,000 years of the stick-and-stone age than in the first 50 years of the twentieth century. Prehistoric men were too busy cooperating against famine, flood and frost to hate each other very much; yet they tamed fire and animals, mastered joinery, cooking, tailoring, painting, pottery and planting. These skills still keep most of us alive. Compared with the sowing and reaping of the first grain crop, our own biggest achievement (sending three men to and from a dead world in a self-firing bullet) is a marvellously extravagant baroque curlicue on the recentest page of human history."

"That's crap, Monboddo! And you know it!" yelled someone across the circle from Lanark. There was laughter from the darker-skinned delegates. Monboddo smirked at them before continuing:

"I still represent modern government, Mr. Kodac, do not worry. But the tools for harpooning other planets are still in the primitive phase, and it does no harm to admit that clever fellows like ourselves need not be ashamed of our ancestors. All the same, this petit-bourgeois world of gamekeepers and peasant craftmen bores me. Yes, it bores me. I thirst for the overweening exuberance of the Ziggurats and Zimbabwes, the Great Walls and Cathedrals. What is lacking from this prehistoric nature-park where sapient men have lived so long with such little effect? Surplus is lacking: that surplus of food, time and energy, that surplus of *men* we call wealth.

"So let a handful of centuries pass and look at the globe again. The biggest land mass is split into three continents by a complicated central sea. East of it, a wide river no longer meanders through swamps but flows in a distinct channel across a fertile geometry of fields and ditches. On the glittering surface boats and barges move upstream and down to unload their cargoes beside the cubes, cones and cylinders of the first city. A great house with a tower stands in the city centre. On the summit, high above the hazes of the river, the secretaries of the sky use the turning dome of heaven as a clock of light where sun, moon and galaxies tell the time to dig, reap and store. Under the tower the wealth of the state, the sacred grain surplus, is banked: sacred because a sack of it can keep a family alive for a month. This grain is stored life. Those who own it can command others. The great house belongs to modern men like ourselves, men, not skilful in growing and making things, but in managing those who do. There is a market beside the great house from which tracks radiate far across plain and forest. These tracks are beaten by tribesmen bringing fleeces, hides and whatever else can be exchanged for the life-giving grain. In time of famine they will sell their children for it. In time of war they can sell enemies captured in battle. The wealth of the city makes warfare profitable because the city managers know how to use cheap labour. More trees are felled, new canals widen the cultivated land. The city is growing.

"It grows because it is a living body, its arteries are the rivers and canals, its limbs are the trade routes grappling goods and men into its stomach, the market. We, whose state is an organization linking the cities of many lands, cannot know what sacred places the first cities seemed. Luckily the librarian of Babylon has described how they looked to a visiting tribesman:

He sees something he has never seen, or has not seen . . . in such plenitude. He sees the day and cypresses and marble. He sees a whole that is complex and yet without disorder; he sees a city, an organism composed of statues, temples, gardens, dwellings, stairways, urns, capitals, of regular and open spaces. None of these artifacts impresses him (I know) as beautiful; they move him as we might be moved today by a complex machine of whose purpose we are ignorant but in whose design we intuit an immortal intelligence.

"Immortal intelligence, yes. That undying intelligence lives in the great house which is the brain of the city, which is the first home of institutional knowledge and modern government. In a few centuries it will divide into law court, university, temple, treasury, stock exchange and arsenal."

"Here here!" shouted Weems unexpectedly, and there was some scattered applause.
"Bugger this," muttered Odin. "He's talked for ten minutes and only just reached the topic."
"I find these large vague statements very soothing," said Powys. "Like being in school again."

"But all tribesmen are not servile adorers of wealth [said Monboddo]. Many have skill and greed of their own. The lords of the first cities may have fallen before nomads driving the first wheeled chariots. No matter! The new masters of the grain may only keep it with help from the clever ones who rule land and time by rod and calendar, and can count and tax what others make. The great riverine cultures (soon there are five of them) absorb wave after wave of conquerors, who add to the power of the managers by giving them horsemen for companions. So the growth of cities speeds up. Their trade routes interlock and grapple, they compete with each other. Iron swords and ploughshares are forged, metals command the wealth of the grain. The seaside cities arise with their merchant and pirate navies."

"He's getting faster," whispered Powys. "He's covered twelve civilizations in six sentences."

"Men increase. Wealth increases. War increases. Nowadays, when strong governments agree *there must not be* another big war, we can still applaud the old battles and invasions which blended the skills of conquerors and conquered. The are no villains in history. Pessimists point to Attila and Tamerlane, but these active men liquidated unprofitable states which *needed* a destroyer to release their assets. Wherever wealth has been used for mere self-maintenance it has always inspired vigorous people to grasp and fling it into the service of that onrushing history which the modern state commands. Pale pink people like myself have least reason to point the scorning finger. Poets tell us that for two millennia Europe was boisterous with energies released by the liquidation of Asiatic Troy. I quote the famous Lancastrian epic:

"Since the siege and assault was ceaséd
                                    at Troy,
The burgh broken and burned to
                            brands and ashes,
It was Aeneas the Able and his high
                                        kind
That since despoiled provinces and
                            patrons became
Wellnigh of all the wealth in the West
                                        Isles;
For rich Romulus to Rome riches he
                                    swipes,
With great bobbaunce that burgh he
                            builds upon first,
And names with his own name as now
                                    it hath;
Ticius in Tuscany townships founds,
Langbeard in Lombardy lifts up homes,
And far over the French flood Felix
                                        Brutus,
On many banks full broad Britain he
                    builds with his winnings,

Where war and wreck and wonder
By turns have waxed therein,
And oft both bliss and blunder
Have had their innings.

"Bliss and blunder. The flow of
wealth around the globe has involved
much of both, but wealth itself has continued to grow because it is always served
by the winners."

"Pale pink people," muttered Odin broodingly. "Pale pink
people."
"I don't think the blackies and brownies are much amused,"
said Powys. "Are you all right, Lanark?"
Monboddo's strong quiet voice purred on like a stupefying
wind.

". . . so north Africa becomes a desert, with several useful consequences. . . ."
"After the clean camaraderie of the
steam bath-house, the new recruits notice
that their parents stink. . . ."
". . . but machinists only work effi-
ciently in a climate of hope, so slavery is
replaced by debt and money becomes a
promise to pay printed by the government. . . ."
". . . by the twentieth century,
wealth has engrossed the whole globe,
which now revolves in a tightening net
of thought and transport woven round it
by trade and science. The world is enclosed in a single living city, but its brain
centres, the governments, do not notice
this. Two world wars are fought in thirty
years, wars the more bitter because they
are between different parts of the same
system. It would wrong the slaughtered
millions to say these wars did no good.
Old machines, old ideas were replaced at
unusual speed. Science, business and government quickly became richer than ever
before. We must thank the dead for that."

Monboddo glanced at Weems, who stood up and said solemnly, "This is surely a good time to remember the dead. There are hardly any lands where men have not died this century fighting for what they thought best. I invite all delegates to stand with me for two minutes and remember the friends, relations and countrymen who suffered to make us what we are."

"Bloody farce," muttered Odin, gripping Lanark under the elbow to help him rise.

"Soon be over," whispered Powys, helping at the other side. The whole great circle gradually rose to their feet except the black bloc, who stayed obstinately seated. There was silence for a while; than a distant trumpet sounded outside the tent and everyone sat murmuringly down.

"What's the point of this speech?" said Odin. "It's too Marxian for the Corporate Wealth gang and too approving for the Marxists."

"He's trying to please everyone," said Powys.

"You can only do that with vague platitudes. He's like all these Huns—too clever for his own good."

"I thought he came from Languedoc," said Powys.

"As I reach our present dangerous time [said Monboddo, sighing], I fear I have angered almost everyone here by a perhaps too cynical view of history. I have described it as a growing and spreading of wealth. Two styles of government command the modern world. One works to reconcile the different companies which employ their people, the other employs the people themselves. Defenders of the first style think great wealth the reward and necessary tool of those who serve mankind best; to the rest it is a method by which strong people bully weak ones. Can I define wealth in a way which lets both sides agree with me? Easily.

"At the start of my talk I said wealth was a surplus of men. I now say a wealthy state is one which orders its surplus men into great enterprises. In the past extra men were used to invade neighbours, plant colonies and destroy competitors. But the liquidation of unprofitable states

by warfare is not practical now. We all
know it, which is why this assembly has
been a success: *not* because I have been
a specially good chairman but because you,
the delegates of states big and small, have
agreed to order onrushing history, onrushing wealth, onrushing *men* by majority decisions reached through open and honest
debate.''

Weems started clapping again, but Monboddo talked vehemently over him.

''Believe me, this splendid logicalness
has been achieved only just in time! More
men have been born this century than in
all the ages of history and prehistory preceding. Our man surplus has never been
so vast. If this human wealth is not governed it will collapse—in places it is already collapsing—into poverty, anarchy,
disaster. Let me say at once that I do not
fear wars between any government represented here today, nor do I fear revolution. The presence of that great revolutionary hero, Chairman Fu of the People's
Republic of Xanadu, shows that revolu-
tions are perfectly able to create strong
governments. What we must unite to prevent are half-baked revolts which might
give desperadoes access to those doomsday machines and bottled plagues which
stable governments are creating, not to
use, but to prevent themselves from being
bullied by equals. No land today lacks desperadoes, brave greedy ignorant men who
can no longer be sent to work in less busy
parts of the world and are too ambitious
to join a regular police force. No modern
state lacks irresponsible intellectuals, the
enemies of strong government everywhere. Both types seem anxious to break
the world down into tiny republics of the
prehistoric kind, where the voice of the
dull and cranky would sound as loud as

the wise and skilful. But a reversion to barbarism cannot help us. The world can only be saved by a great enterprise in which stable governments use the skills of institutional knowledge with the full backing of corporate wealth. Council, institute and creature everywhere must work together.

"The fuel supply of the present planet is almost exhausted. The food supply is already insufficient. Our deserts have grown too vast, our seas are overfished. We need a new supply of energy, for energy is food as well as fuel. At present, dead matter is turned into nourishment by farming, and by the consumption of uneducated people by clever ones. This arrangement is a failure because it is inefficient; it also puts clever people into a dependent position. Luckily our experts will soon be able to turn dead matter directly into food in our industrial laboratories—*if we give them access to sufficient energy.*

"Where can this energy be found? Ladies and gentlemen, it is all around us, it streams from the sun, gleams from the stars and sings harmoniously in every sphere. Yes, Mr. Kodac! It is time for me to admit that sending ships into space is not just an adventure but a necessity. That greater outer space is not, we now know, a horrid vacuum but a treasure house which can be endlessly, infinitely plundered—if we combine to do it. Once again the secretaries of the sky will be our leaders. We must build them a high new platform, a city floating in space where the clever and adventurous of every land, working in a clean, nearly weightless atmosphere, will reflect heat and sunlight down to the powerhouses of the world.

"It has been suggested we call this enterprise New Frontier or Dynostar. I suggest the Laputa Project. . . ."

Monboddo's speech had hypnotized Lanark. He listened open-mouthed, nodding in the pauses. Whenever he understood a sentence it seemed to say everything was inevitable and therefore right. Yet his body grew less and less easy; his head buzzed; when Monboddo said "a high new platform, a city floating in space," he seemed to hear another voice, harsh and incredulous, say, "The man's a lunatic."

Even so, he was appalled to find himself standing and shouting "EXEXEXEXEXEXEX" at the top of his voice. Powys and Odin gripped his wrists, but he wrenched them free and yelled, "EXCUSE ME! EXCUSE ME but Lord Monboddo lied when he said all the delegates agreed to manage things through open, honest debates! Or else he has been lied to by other people."

There was silence. Lanark watched Monboddo watching him woodenly. Weems stood up and said quietly, "As host of this gathering I apologize to Lord Monboddo and the other delegates for . . . for Provost Lanark's hysterical outburst. He is notorious for his lack of control in civilized company. I also demand that Provost Lanark take back these words."

"I'm sorry I said them," said Lanark, "but Lord Monboddo has deliberately or ignorantly told us a lie. I pissed off a bridge, but I should not have been locked up before I had spoken for Unthank! Unthank is being destroyed with no open agreement at all, jobs and homes are being destroyed, we've begun hating each other, the Merovicnic Discontinuity is threatened—"

He was deafened by a babel of laughter and talk. A row of black-clad men stood behind Weems and Lanark saw two of them walk around the tent toward him. His legs trembled so much that he sat down. Voices were shouting for silence somewhere on his left. Silence fell. He saw Multan of Zimbabwe standing up, smiling at Monboddo, who said shortly, "Speak, by all means."

Multan looked round the table then said, "The Unthank delegate says this assembly has not held free and open debates. That's not news to the black bloc. Is it news to anybody?" He chuckled and shrugged. "Everybody knows three or four big boys run the whole show. The rest of us don't complain, why should we? Words by themselves are no good. When we get organized big, we'll complain and you'll listen. You'll have to listen. So this Lanark is very foolish to speak like he does. But he tells the truth. So on this side of the table we watch what happens. We laugh because it don't matter to us how you claw each other. But we watch closely what happens, all the same."

He sat down. Monboddo sighed and scratched his head. At last he said, "I will answer the Zimbabwe delegate first. He has told us, with admirable modesty, that he and his friends are not yet able to share the work of the council but will do so when they can. That is very good news; may the day come soon. The Unthank delegate's case is less clear. I gather the police arrested him in the circumstances where his exalted rank was not apparent. He has missed our debates, but what can I do? I leave Provan one decimal hour from now. I can grant him a brief personal interview. I can promise that anything he says will be recorded in the assembly minutes for everyone to read. It is all I can offer. Is it sufficient?"

Lanark felt everyone watching him and wanted to hide his face again. He glanced over his shoulder and shivered at the sight of two black-suited men. One nodded and winked. It was Wilkins. Monboddo said loudly, "If you wish this interview, my secretaries will escort you to a convenient place. Otherwise the matter must be dropped. Answer, please, there is not much time."

Lanark nodded. He stood and walked from the tent between the secretaries, feeling old and defeated.

CHAPTER 44. End

As they crossed the wide dim floor Wilkins said cheerily, "That was great fun; you scared the shits out of old M."
The other man said, "These intellectuals have no staying power."
"Lanark has been around for a long, long time," said Wilkins, "I think he deserves a three-syllable name, don't you?"
"Oh, he certainly deserves it," said the other man. "There's nothing wrong with a two-syllable name, I'm called Uxbridge, but Lanark has earned something more melodious. Like Blairdardie."
"Rutherglen, Garscaden," said Wilkins.
"Gargunnock, Carmunnock, Auchenshuggle," said the other man.
"Auchenshuggle has four syllables," said Wilkins.

They went through a narrow door, climbed a dingy stair and crossed a small office into a slightly larger office. It was lit by a neon tube and the walls were hidden by metal filing cabinets, some piled on others. There was a metal desk in the corner. Without much surprise Lanark saw Monboddo sitting behind it with hands clasped patiently on the waistcoat over his stomach. "Bilocation," said Monboddo. "I would be nothing if I did not duplicate. Sit down."
Wilkins placed a straight wooden chair before the desk and Lanark sat.
"Wilkins, Uxbridge, go away. Miss Thing will record us," said Monboddo. Lanark saw a girl exactly like Miss Maheen sitting between two filing cabinets. Wilkins and Uxbridge left. Monboddo tilted his chair back, looked at the ceiling and sighed. He said, "At last the Common Man confronts the Powerful

Lord of this World. Except that you are not very common
and I am not very powerful. We can change nothing, you and
I. But talk to me. Talk to me."

"I am here to speak for the people of Unthank."

"Yes. You wish to tell me they have too few jobs and homes
and social services so stupidity, cruelty, disease and crime are
increasing among them. I know that. There are many such
places in the world, and soon there will be more. Governments
cannot help them much."

"Yet governments can fire great structures into space!"

"Yes. It is profitable."

"For whom? Why can't wealth be used to help folk here and
now?"

"It is, but we can only help people by giving less than we
take away from them. We enlarge the oasis by increasing the
desert. That is the science of time and housekeeping. Some
call it economics."

"Are you telling me that men lack the decency and skill to
be good to each other?"

"Not at all! Men have always possessed that decency and skill.
In small, isolated societies they have even practised it. But it
is a sad fact of human nature that in large numbers we can
only organize against each other."

"You are a liar!" cried Lanark. "We have no nature. Our nations are not built instinctively by our bodies, like beehives;
they are works of art, like ships, carpets and gardens. The possible shapes of them are endless. It is bad habits, not bad nature,
which makes us repeat the dull old shapes of poverty and war.
Only greedy people who profit by these things believe they
are *natural.*"

"Your flood of language is delicious," said Ozenfant, yawning
slightly, "and can have no possible effect upon human behaviour. By the way, it was not clever of you to get Multan speaking
for you. He is no enemy of the council, he is a weak member
plotting to become strong. If he succeeds his aim will be my
aim: to manage things as smoothly as possible. His only enemies
will be people like you—the babies."

"I am not a baby."

"You are. Your deafness to reasoned argument, your indifference to decent custom and personal dignity, a selfishness so
huge and instinctive that it cannot even notice itself, all make
you the nearest thing to an adult baby I have ever encountered.
And now you may retaliate by calling me as many foul names
as you please. Nobody will know. Miss Thing cannot hear what

is irrelevant to the business of the council."

Lanark said coldly, "You want me to lose my temper."

"Yes indeed," said Monboddo, nodding. "But only to cut short a useless argument. You suffer from the oldest delusion in politics. You think you can change the world by talking to a leader. Leaders are the effects, not the causes of changes. I *cannot* give prosperity to people whom my rich supporters cannot exploit."

Lanark put his elbows on his knees and propped his face between his hands. After a while he said, "I don't care what happens to most people. All of us over eighteen have been warped into deserving what happens to us. But if your *reason* shows that civilization can only continue by damaging the brains and hearts of most children, then . . . your reason and civilization are false and will destroy themselves."

"Perhaps," said Monboddo, yawning, "but I think we can make them last our time. What have you recorded, Miss Thing? Tell us, please."

The secretary parted her lips and a monotonous voice slid out between them:

> *"Greater Unthank Addendum to General Assembly Minutes: Provost Lanark referred to Unthank's serious employment, housing, health and pollution problems. Chairman Monboddo related them to the supranational crisis in these areas and intimated that the solution of such problems must await the primary solution of the worldwide energy famine. Provost Lanark called for a more urgent approach to local difficulties insofar as they affect the 0–18 spectrum. Chairman Monboddo suggested the outcome of difficulties in this spectrum was less disastrous than Provost Lanark feared."*

Miss Thing's mouth clicked shut. Monboddo slapped his brow and said, "Cryptonite! I forgot the Cryptonite deposits. Put them in, Miss Thing; it will let us end on a cheerful note."

Miss Thing opened her mouth again.

> *"Chairman Monboddo suggested the outcome of difficulties in this spectrum would be less disastrous socially than Provost Lanark feared as the development by Cortexin of the Unthank*

mineral resources was well on the way to putting
prosperity within the grasp of everyone.''

Lanark stood up and wrung his hands. He cried out, "I am
useless. I should never have come here, I did no good to anyone,
not to Sandy, Rima or anyone. I need to go home."
"Home?" said Monboddo, raising an eyebrow.
"Unthank. It may be bad but the badness is obvious, not gilded
with lies like here."
"You are severe. But I will help you. Open the bolthole, Miss
Thing."

There was a grey woollen rug in front of the desk. Miss
Thing knelt and pulled it back, uncovering a round steel plate
sunk in the linoleum. She put a thumb and forefinger into
two small openings at the centre and lifted it easily out, though
it was two feet across and four inches thick. "The way home,"
said Monboddo. "Look inside. You will recognize the interior
of a familiar aircraft."
He stood up and rested, hands in pockets, on a corner of the
desk. Lanark stooped and stared for a long time into the round
hole. There was a cavity under it lined with blue silk. Monboddo
said, "You do not trust me. But you will climb inside because
you are too reckless to linger. Am I right?"
"You're wrong," said Lanark, sighing. "I will climb inside because I'm too tired to linger."
He stepped into the cavity, sat down and straightened his legs.
The space lengthened and narrowed to fit him. He lay staring
up at a circle of cream-coloured ceiling surrounded by blackness. He heard Monboddo murmur "Bon voyage," and a round
black shape slid sideways across the circle of ceiling and eclipsed
it with a low clang. Then the space he lay in dropped.

The drop was a long down-rushing swoop stopped by a
jarring jerk. Then came another drop. With an indrawn scream
he knew he was going down the great gullet again. The tiny
office, the great round table, Provan, Greater Unthank, Alexander, cathedral, Rima, Zone, council corridors, institute had been
a brief rest from the horror of endless falling. Monboddo had
tricked him back into it. He screamed with hatred. He pissed
with panic. He writhed and his face came out into a rush of
milky mist. He was plunging downward in the bird-machine.
The panic changed. He was the mind of this bird, an old bird

in poor repair. Each wingstroke tore out feathers he needed for landing and the land was far below. He kept falling as far as he dared, then levelling in a thrash of pinions which thinned and flew back like darts. His bald breast and sides were freezing in the fall. The misty air thinned to black and the black map of a city lay below, the streets dotted lines of light. Bits of the map were on fire. A big red flower of flame drew him down to it. He saw a flaming glass tower, a square of statues, engines and seething heads; he heard roaring and sirens, tried to level and crashed sideways on cracking wings through sparks, heat and choking smoke where a great dim column swung at him, missed, swung away and swung back like a mace to strike him down.

He woke, sore and bandaged, in bed with a tube running into his arm. He lay there dreaming and dozing and hardly thinking at all. He assumed he was in the institute again but the ward had windows with darkness outside them, and the beds were packed together with hardly a foot of space between. The patients were all very old. All cleaning and some nursing was done by those fit enough to walk, for there was a very small staff. The light fittings were peculiar. Electric globes hung from the ceiling by slim rods which were parallel to each other but slanted toward a corner of the ward. When a nurse took the tube from his arm and changed the bandages he said, "Is the hospital sloping?"
"So you've found your tongue at last."
"Is the hospital sloping?"
"If that was all, we'd be laughing."
The meals were mainly beans and this pleased him, though he couldn't remember why. The doctor was a hurried, haggard, unshaven man in a dirty smock. He said, "Have you any friends, old man?"
"I used to have."
"Where can we contact them?"
"They used to hang around the cathedral."
"Were you one of Smollet's mob?"
"I knew Ritchie-Smollet, yes. I knew Sludden too."
"Best not to mention that, Sludden is far from popular at present. But we'll find if Smollet can take you. We have to evacuate this place, there's going to be another shock. What's your name?"
"Lanark."

"A common name in these parts. We had a provost called that once. He wasn't much good."

Lanark slept and wakened to screams and shouting. He was sweating and sticky. The air was very hot and the ward was empty except for a bed in a far corner; an old woman sat in it crying, "They shouldn't leave us here, it isn't right." A soldier came in, looking carefully round, avoided the old woman's eye and edged toward Lanark between the empty beds. He was a tall man with a sullen, handsome, slightly baby-ish face and did not seem to be carrying a weapon. His only insignia was a badge on his beret shaped like a hand with an eye in the palm. He stood looking down at Lanark, then sat on the edge of the bed and said, after a moment, "Hullo, Dad."

Lanark whispered "Sandy?" and smiled and touched his hand. He felt very happy. The soldier said, "We've got to get out of here. The foundation is cracked."

He opened the bedside locker, took out trousers, jacket and shoes and helped Lanark into them, saying, "I wish you'd kept in touch with us."

"I didn't know how."

"You could have written or phoned."

"I never seemed to have time. Yet I did no good, Sandy. I changed nothing."

"Of course you changed nothing. The world is only improved by people who do ordinary jobs and refuse to be bullied. Nobody can persuade owners to share with makers when makers won't shift for themselves."

"I could never understand politics. How do you live, Sandy?"

"I report for movers and menders."

"What kind of work is that?"

"We have to hurry, Dad. Are you able to stand?"

Lanark managed to stand, though his knees trembled. The old woman in the corner bed wailed, "Son, could you help me too, son?"

"Wait here! Help is coming!" shouted Alexander fiercely. He took Lanark's right arm over his shoulder, gripped him round the waist and moved him toward the door, cursing below his breath. They were labouring uphill for the slope of the floor was against them. The screams and yelling grew louder. Alexander halted and said, "Listen, you used to be a sentimental man in some ways, so shut your eyes when you get out of here. Some things are happening which we just can't help."

"Anything you say son," said Lanark, closing his eyes. The arm round his waist gave such a strong feeling of happiness and safety that he started chuckling.

He was helped down many stairs amid loud crying and across a space where his ankles brushed past fingertips and then, though the air was no cooler, an uproar of voices and running feet suggested they were outside. He opened his eyes. The sight threw him off balance and he lost more balance trying to recover it. Alexander held him up, saying, "Steady, Dad." A great loose crowd, much of it children shepherded by women, slid and stumbled down a hillside toward a wide-open gate. But the hillside was a city square. The slanting lamp-standards lighting the scene, the slanting buildings on each side, the slanting spire of the nearby cathedral showed the whole landscape was tilted like a board.

"What happened?" cried Lanark.

"Subsidence," said Alexander, carrying him with the crowd. "There's going to be another soon, a bad one. Hurry."

Whenever Lanark's feet touched the ground he felt a vibration like a continuous electric shock. It seemed to strengthen his legs. He began moving almost briskly, chuckling and saying, "I like this."

"Jesus Christ," muttered Alexander.

"Do I sound senile, Sandy? I'm not. This gate leads to the graveyard, the Necropolis, doesn't it?"

"We'll be safer away from the buildings."

"I know this graveyard well, Sandy. So did your mother. I could tell you a lot about it. This bridge we're coming to, for instance, had a tributary of the river flowing under it once."

"Shut up and keep *moving*, Dad."

In the dim cemetery folk crouched on the grass plots or dispersed up the many little paths. From the height of the hill a loudspeaker was telling people to keep clear of high monuments. Alexander said, "Rima should be up at the top, can you go on?"

"Yes, yes!" said Lanark excitedly. "Yes, we must all get to the top, there's going to be a flood, a huge immense deluge."

"Don't be stupid, Dad."

"I'm not stupid. Someone told me everything would end in a deluge; he was very very definite about it. Yes, we must go as high as possible, if only for the view."

As they climbed the steep little paths Lanark felt more and

more energetic and cheerful. He tried to skip a little.

"Are you married, Sandy?"

"Steady, Dad, I wish you'd call me by my full name. No, I'm not married. I've a daughter, if that's any consolation."

"It is! It is! Will she be at the top of the hill too?"

"No, she's in a safer place than this, thank goodness. Do you hear the guns?"

There was a distant snapping sound.

"How can men fight like that at a time like this?" said Lanark, his voice squeaky with indignation.

"The Corquantal Galaxy are trying to liquidate their Unthank plant but Makers, Movers and Menders backed Defence Command in supporting the One-Wagers against them, so the council rump have sent in the Cocquigrues."

"I understand none of that. What are Cocquigrues?"

"I'll tell you when there's time."

Buildings burned in the city below. The glossy walls of the tower blocks reflected flickering glares upon a small knot of people between the monuments and the summit. Lanark couldn't see them clearly because tears came to his eyes. It struck him that Rima must be an old woman now and the thought was an unexpected pain. He muttered "Must sit" and settled on the edge of a granite slab. The vibration through it irritated his backside. He made out a nearby knot of men wearing armbands and stooping over an old-fashioned radio transmitter. Beside them a stout woman in a black dress waved to Alexander, then came over and laid a hand on Lanark's shoulder. He gazed up, astonished, into her large-eyed, large-nosed face with small straight childishly serious mouth. Though a little weary, and the glossy hair slightly streaked with grey, this seemed exactly the face he had first seen in the Elite Café. He said, "You aren't Rima?"

She laughed and said, "You always found it hard to recognize me. You've grown old, Lanark, but I knew you at once."

Lanark smiled and said, "You've grown fat."

"She's pregnant," said Alexander glumly. "At *her* age."

"You don't know my age," said Rima sharply and added, "I'm sorry I can't introduce you to Horace, Lanark, but he refuses to meet you. He's an idiot sometimes."

"Who is Horace?"

Alexander said dourly, "Someone who doesn't want to meet you. And a rotten wireless operator."

Lanark stood up. The vibration in the ground had become a strong, almost audible throbbing and Rima said tensely, "I'm frightened, Alex, don't be nasty to me."
The throbbing stopped. In a great quietness the hot air seemed to scald the skin. Lanark felt so heavy that he crashed on his knees to the ground, then so light that he rose in the air. When he came down again the ground was not where he expected. He lay listening to rumbling and shouting and looked at the firelit pinnacle of an obelisk; it leaned so far over him that he knew it must 'crack or topple. He got heavy, then light again, and this time only his head left the ground and fell back with a thump which dazed him slightly. When he next saw the obelisk it pointed perfectly upright and the glow on it was very strong.

"Tell me what's happening, please," said Rima. She lay curled on the ground with her hands over her eyes. Everybody lay on the ground except Alexander, who knelt beside the radio transmitter earnestly turning knobs.
"The ground is level again," said Lanark, getting up, "and the fire is spreading."
"Is it horrible?"
"It's wonderful. It's universal. You should look."
Behind the burning building was a great band of ruddy light with clouds rising into it from collapsed and collapsing roofs. There were no other lights. "First the fire, then the flood!" cried Lanark exultingly, "Well, I have had an interesting life."
"You're as selfish as ever!" shrieked Rima.
"Be quiet, I'm trying to contact Defence Command," said Alexander.
"Nothing can be defended now, I hear the water coming," said Lanark. There was a faraway rushing mingled with faint squeals. He hobbled between two monuments to the edge of a slope and gazed eagerly down, holding himself erect by a branch of a twisty thorn tree.

A blast of cold wind freshened the air. The rushing grew to surges and gurglings and up the low road between Necropolis and cathedral sped a white foam followed by ripples and plunging waves with gulls swooping and crying over them. He laughed aloud, following the flood with his mind's eye back to the river it flowed from, a full river widening to the ocean. His cheek was touched by something moving in the wind, a black twig with pointed little pink and grey-green buds. The colours of things seemed to be brightening although the fiery light over the roofs had paled to silver streaked with delicate rose. A long silver line marked the horizon. Dim rooftops against it grew solid in the increasing light. The broken buildings were fewer than he had thought. Beyond them a long faint bank of cloud became clear hills, not walling the city in but receding, edge behind pearl-grey edge of farmland and woodland gently rising to a faraway ridge of moor. The darkness overheard shifted and broke in the wind becoming clouds with blue air between. He looked sideways and saw the sun coming up golden behind a laurel bush, light blinking, space dancing among the shifting leaves. Drunk with spaciousness he turned every way, gazing with wide-open mouth and eyes as light created colours, clouds, distances and solid, graspable things close at hand. Among all this light the flaming buildings seemed small blazes which would soon burn out. With only mild disappointment he saw the flood ebbing back down the slope of the road.

Rima came beside him and said teasingly, "Wrong again, Lanark."
He nodded, sighed, and said, "Rima, did you ever love me?"
She laughed, held him and kissed his cheek. She said, "Of course I did, even though you kept driving me away so nastily and so often. They've started shooting again."
They stood awhile listening to the snapping and crackings. She said, "Defence command have called Alex over to maintenance. It's very urgent, but he says he'll come back for you as soon as he can. You're to stay here and not worry if he's late."
"Good."
"I'm sorry you can't come with me, but Horace is an idiot sometimes. Why should a young man like him be jealous of you?"
"I don't know."
She laughed, kissed his cheek and went away.

After a while he hobbled back to the space between the monuments and sat once again on the edge of the granite slab. He was tired and chilly but perfectly content to wait. There was nobody about, but after a while he heard the crunch of a foot on gravel. A figure approached him wearing the black and white clothes and carrying the silver-tipped staff of a chamberlain. Lanark had trouble focusing on the face under the wig: sometimes it seemed to be Munro, sometimes Gloopy. He said, "Munro? Gloopy?"

"Correct sir," said the figure, bowing respectfully. "We have been sent to bestow on you an extraordinary privilege."

"Who sent you?" said Lanark peevishly. "Institute or council? I dislike both."

"Knowledge and government are dissolving. I now represent the ministry of earth."

"Everything keeps getting renamed. I've stopped caring. Don't try to explain."

The figure bowed again and said, "You will die tomorrow at seven minutes after noon."

The words were almost drowned by a squawking gull turning in the sky overhead, but Lanark understood them perfectly. Like a mother's fall in a narrow lobby, like a policeman's hand on his shoulder, he had known or expected this all his life. A roaring like a terrified crowd filled his ears; he whispered, "Death is not a privilege."

"The privilege is knowing when."

"But I . . . I seem to remember passing through several deaths."

"They were rehearsals. After the next death nothing personal will remain of you."

"Will it hurt?"

"Not much. Just now there is no feeling in your left arm; you can't move it. In a moment it will get better again, but at five minutes after noon tomorrow your whole body will become like that. For two minutes you will be able to see and think but not move or speak. That will be the worst time. You will be dead when it stops."

Lanark scowled with self-pity and annoyance. The chamberlain said, respectfully "Have you a complaint?"

"I ought to have more love before I die. I've not had enough."

"That is everyone's complaint. You can appeal against the death sentence if you have something better to do."

"If you're hinting that I should go in for more adventures, no thank you, I don't want them. But how will my son—how will the *world* manage when I'm not here?"

The chamberlain shrugged and spread his hands.

"Well go away, go away," said Lanark more kindly. "You can tell the earth I would have preferred a less common end, like being struck by lightning. But I'm prepared to take death as it comes."

The chamberlain vanished. Lanark forgot him, propped his chin on his hands and sat a long time watching the moving clouds. He was a slightly worried, ordinary old man but glad to see the light in the sky.

I STARTED MAKING MAPS WHEN I WAS SMALL
SHOWING PLACE, RESOURCES, WHERE THE ENEMY
AND WHERE LOVE LAY. I DID NOT KNOW
TIME ADDS TO LAND. EVENTS DRIFT CONTINUALLY DOWN,
EFFACING LANDMARKS, RAISING THE LEVEL, LIKE SNOW.

I HAVE GROWN UP. MY MAPS ARE OUT OF DATE.
THE LAND LIES OVER ME NOW.
I CANNOT MOVE. IT IS TIME TO GO.

GOODBYE

TAILPIECE: How *Lanark* Grew

Hullo again. When Canongate published *Lanark* in 1981 I was 45 and thought the book would become famous, when I was dead. A London publisher told me *Lanark* might get a cult following in the USA and would do less well in Britain. But since 1981 it has been steadily reprinted here, and I have often been asked the following questions.

Q What is your background?

A If background means surroundings: first 25 years were lived in Riddrie, east Glasgow, a well-maintained district of stone-fronted corporation tenements and semi-detached villas. Our neighbours were a nurse, postman, printer and tobacconist, so I was a bit of a snob. I took it for granted that Britain was mainly owned and ruled by Riddrie people – people like my dad who knew Glasgow's deputy town clerk (he also lived in Riddrie) and others who seemed important men but not more important than my dad. If background means family: it was hardworking, well-read and very sober. My English grandad was a Northampton foreman shoemaker who came north because the southern employers blacklisted him for trade-union activities. My Scottish grandad was an industrial blacksmith and congregational elder. My dad fought in the First World War, which made an agnostic Socialist of him. He received a stomach wound that got him a small government pension, worked a cardboard-box cutting machine in a factory that survived the 1930s depression of trade, and in 1931 married Amy Fleming, a shop assistant in a Glasgow department store. She was a good housewife and efficient mother who liked music and had sung in the Glasgow Orpheus Choir. Dad hiked and climbed mountains for a hobby, and did voluntary secretarial work for the Camping Club of Great Britain and the

Scottish Youth Hostel Association. Mum had fewer ways of enjoying herself after marriage and I now realise wanted more from
life, though she seldom grumbled. So they were a typical couple.
I had a younger sister I bullied and fought with until we started
living in separate houses. Then she became one of my best friends.

Q What was childhood like?

A Apart from the attacks of asthma and eczema, mostly painless
but frequently boring. My parents' main wish for me was that I
go to university. They wanted me to get a professional job, you
see, because professional people are not so likely to lose their
income during a depression. To enter university I had to pass
exams in Latin and mathematics which I hated. So half my school
experience was passed in activities which felt to my brain like
a meal of sawdust to the mouth. And of course there was
homework. My father wanted to relieve the drudgery of learning
by taking me cycling and climbing, but I hated enjoying myself
in his shadow, and preferred the escapist worlds of comics and
films and books: books most of all. Riddrie had a good library. I
had a natural preference for all sorts of escapist crap, but when I
had read all there was of that there was nothing left but good
stuff: and myth and legend, and travel, biography and history.
I regarded a well-stocked public library as the pinnacle of
democratic socialism. That a good dull place like Riddrie had one
was proof that the world was essentially well organized. I realize
I am talking here about my life from 11 years onward, after the
Second World War. During it, with evacuation in 1939 to a farm
in Auchterarder (an experience I used in *The Oracle's Prologue*) in
the mining town of Stonehouse, Lanarkshire (which I used in
1982 Janine, my second novel) and Wetherby in Yorkshire, life
was not under the almost total jurisdiction of the Scottish Education system with my parents' full support, so not at all dull.

Q When did you realize you were an artist?

A I did not realize it. Like all infants who were allowed
materials to draw with, I did, and nobody suggested I stop. At
school I was even encouraged to do it. And my parents (like many
parents in those days) expected their children to have a party
piece — a song or poem they would perform at domestic

gatherings. The poems I recited were very poor A A Milne stuff. I found it possible to write verses which struck me as equally good, if not better, because they were mine. My father typed them for me, and the puerile little stories which I sent to children's magazines and children's radio competitions. When I was eleven I read a four-minute programme of my own compositions on Scottish BBC children's hour. But I was eight or nine years old when it occurred to me that I would one day write a story which would get printed in a book. This gave me a feeling of deliriously joyful power.

Q What sort of things did you draw when you were a child?

A Space ships, monsters, maps of imaginary planets and kingdoms, the settings for stories of romantic and violent adventure, which I told my sister when we walked to school together. She was the first audience I could really depend on in the crucial years between seven and eleven. If you have read *Lanark* you will notice how much of Book 1 – the first half of the Thaw section – draws upon my childhood. It does not show how much help and sympathy my mum, dad and sister gave me. I took it for granted as something natural and ordinary because so did they. When I came to use the material of my childhood in that novel what I remembered were our quarrels – they were more dramatic than the support I took for granted.

Q When and why did you want to make a story of your life?

A Surely everyone wants to be a hero or heroine? I'm sure all children do, probably when they stop being babies and find they have very little power over the world, apart from the power they imagine having. Books contained worlds I could grasp and manage through day-dreaming. The complete plays of Bernard Shaw and Henrik Ibsen stood on the middle shelf of a bookcase in my parents' bedroom beside Carlyle's *French Revolution*, Macaulay's essays, *The History of the Working Classes in Scotland* and *Our Noble Families* by Tom Johnson, a Thinkers Library volume called *Humanity's Gain from Unbelief*, an anthology of extracts for atheists called *Lift up Your Heads*, a large blue-grey bound volume with *The Miracle of Life* stamped in gold on the spine. This contained essays on the Dawn of Life, What Evolution Means,

Life that has Vanished, Evolutions as the Clock Ticks, The
Animal Kingdom, The Plant Kingdom, Man's Family Tree,
Races of Mankind, The Human Machine at Work, Psychology
through the Ages, Discoverers of Life's Secrets. The 476 pages
(excluding the index) were half given to black-and-white
photographs and diagrams. The middle shelf also held Shaw's
Quintessence of Ibsenism and *The Adventures of a Black Girl in Search
of God*, and I believe the last was the first adult narrative brought
to my attention, though I cannot remember it. I remember first
reading it with pleasure and excitement in my middle teens, but
years later my father told me he had read it to me when I was wee
– perhaps four years old. The story presents an evolutionary view
of the human faith through the quest of a black girl through the
African bush. Converted to Christianity by an English missionary she sets out to find God, not doubting he can be found on
earth, and encounters in various clearings the gods of Moses, Job
and Isaiah, then meeting Ecclesiastes the Preacher, Jesus,
Mahomet, the founders of the Christian sects, an expedition of
scientific rationalists, Voltaire the sceptic and George Bernard
Shaw the socialist, who teach her that God should not be
searched for but worked for, by cultivating the small piece of
world in our power as intelligently and unselfishly as possible.

The moral of this story is as high as human wisdom has
reached, but I cannot have grasped it then. My father told me
that I kept asking, "Will the next god be the *real* one Daddy?"
No doubt I would have liked the black girl to have at last met
the universal maker like my father: vaster, of course, but with an
equally vital sense of my importance. I am glad he did not teach
me to believe in that, for I would have had to unlearn it. But my
first encounter with this book was in a pre-history I have forgotten or
suppressed, though I returned to it later. It was a beautifully
made book with crisp clear black woodcuts decorating covers,
with title-page and text in a style reminiscent of Eric Gill. Like
the text it convincingly blended the mundane and exotic.

This was all on the middle shelf of our Riddrie bedroom
bookcase. The shelf above was blocked by the orange-red spines
of Left Wing Book Club, four-fifths of it being the collected
works of Lenin in English: dense text with no pictures or conversations in it at all. The bottom shelf was exactly filled by the
Harmsworth Encyclopaedia, because the bookcase had been sold
along with the Encyclopaedia by the publisher, who owned the

Daily Record in which they were first advertised. This contained many pictures, mostly grey monochrome photographs, but each alphabetical section had a complex line drawing in front, a crowded landscape in which an enthroned figure representing Ancient History (for example) was surrounded by orders of Architecture, an Astronomical telescope, glimpses of Australia and the Antarctic with Amundsen, and an Armadillo and Aardvark rooting around a discarded Anchor. I gathered that these volumes contained explanations of everything there is and had been, with lives of everyone important. The six syllables of the name EN-CY-CLO-PAED-I-A seemed to sum up these thick brown books which summed up the universe, so saying it gave me a sense of power confirmed by the pleasure this gave my parents. But the four colour plates showing flags of all nations and heraldic coats-of-arms gave an undiluted pleasure which was purely sensuous. I was fascinated by the crisp oblongs and lozenges holding blues, reds, yellows, greens, blacks and whites combining in patterns more vivid and easily seen than anywhere else, apart from our Christmas decorations.

Healthy children exercise their imaginations by playing games together. I was not healthy. My imagination was mainly exercised in solitary fantasies fed by films and pictures and books. From these I sometimes got the feeling that life could be glorious, a feeling often inspired by sexual episodes in books and not always the best episodes. I felt it in *1984* when Winston saves the girl he detests from stumbling in a corridor in the ministry of Truth, and finds after she has given him a note saying, "I love you"; also when David Copperfield gets the courage to propose to Agnes, who then tells him she has always loved him. Also in *Peer Gynt*, when his mother Aase and fiancée Solveig save him from The Great Boig by ringing the church bells and that vast foggy enclosing force dissolves saying, "He is too strong for us – he has women behind him." I also felt it in the climax of *The Portrait of the Artist as a Young Man* when Stephen Dedalus sees the young bare-legged girl paddling on the beach, and she accepts the worship of his glance, and with a heartfelt "Holy God!" he turns and walks toward the sunset knowing he will be an artist, which is the greatest sort of priest. Also in Joyce Cary's *The Horse's Mouth* when Gulley Jimson, fatally injured in the destruction of his mural painting, is carried off laughing in the ambulance because he knows he was doing his best work right up to the end.

And Joyce Cary's novel brought me to the books of William Blake because Gulley Jimson kept quoting him. The Glasgow Mitchell Library had facsimiles and originals – and Blake's work in verse and picture and prose struck me then and strikes me now as true, beautiful and good. The airy freedom of his naked figures felt like liberation. So did the elaborately clothed, slightly perverse figures of Aubrey Beardsley. And in case this all sounds too high-minded I was terribly stimulated by the highly coloured American comics which first came to Britain in the late 1940s when I was in my early teens. They showed Wonderwoman, Sheena the Jungle Girl and other females with figures and faces like glamorous film-stars of that time, but wearing much less clothing, and since the representation of normal sexual practice was forbidden by the USA moral code their adventures involved them in capture and bondage instead. Such fantasies compensated for my own sexual timidity.

Q This spate of information about the fiction you enjoyed suggests a terrible lack of interest in the life around you.

A Not lack of interest but lack of anticipation. I misled you if I suggested I had no friends of my own. I had several, especially one I called Coulter in the novel. We went on discursive walks and sometimes bicycle rides together. But I could not take part in the sports he liked (running, and watching football) and nights out at the Dennistoun Palais. His accounts of his social adventures fascinated me like stories in books I read. I had no social skill apart from *tête-à-têtes* and haranguing people at the school literary and debating society – the skills of Adolf Hitler. I wanted to be part of it, wanted to be an exciting, welcomed person in other people's lives – especially in the lives of girls who attracted me. Nothing like that seemed possible till I got to Glasgow School of Art in 1952, a few months after my mother died. All that is described as I remember it in *Lanark*. Memory is an editing process which inevitably exaggerates some episodes, suppresses others and arranges events in neater orders, but nobody assumes that of their own memory. I don't.

Q So how autobiographical is *Lanark*?

A Book 1, the first half of the *Thaw* section, is very like my life until 17½ years, though much more miserable, as I explained. Also the hostel for munition workers which my dad managed during from about 1941 to '44 was in Wetherby, Yorkshire. I shifted it to the Scottish west highlands to preserve some national unity and bring in some references to Scotland's Calvinist past, though the Wee Free clergyman is sheer invention. I have never met such a man. The second half of the *Thaw* book is true to friends I made at art school and some of my dealings with the staff, for I filled notebooks while there with details to be used in my Portrait of the Artist as a Young Glaswegian. But unlike James Joyce's portrait I intended my artist to end tragically –

Q Why?

A Young artists couldn't make livings by painting easel or murals in 1950s Scotland. Nearly all art students became teachers, apart from a few who got into industry or advertising or became housewives. I supposed I would have to survive by some kind of compromise like that, but I had no intention of letting Thaw do so. Which is why I made him dourer, more single-minded than I am. His inability to attract women, and sexual frustration would also help push him towards madness. The episode with the prostitute, by the way, was sheer invention. It struck me as the sort of thing that would likely happen if I went with a prostitute. So I never did. In 1954 I was so sure of my *Thaw* story that, instead of taking a summer holiday job like most art students, I got dad's permission to stay at home and write it. Having rapidly filled notebooks with ideas and descriptions I felt able to finish a novel in ten weeks. At the end of that time I had written what is now chapter 12, *The War Begins*, and the hallucinatory episode ending chapter 29, *The Way Out*. I had found I did not want to write in the gushing emotional voice of a diary, but in a calm unemphatic voice readers would trust. This is not my normal reading voice. To make it a normal written voice I had to continually revise

Q But where did *Lanark* come from?

A From Franz Kafka. I had read *The Trial* and *The Castle* and *Amerika* by then, and an introduction by Edwin Muir explaining

these books were like modern Pilgrim's Progresses. The cities in
them seemed very like 1950s Glasgow, an old industrial city
with a smoke-laden grey sky that often seemed to rest like a lid
on the north and south ranges of hills and shut out the stars at
night. I imagined a stranger arriving, making enquiries and
slowly finding he is in hell. I made notes for that book. I wrote a
description of a stranger arriving in a dark city, in a train on
which he is the only passenger. But the *Thaw* novel had to be
finished, I thought.

Then one day in Dennistoun public library I found Tillyard's
The English Epic and its Background, which I will not attempt to
describe in detail, but the lesson I took from it was this. The epic
genre can be prose as well as poetry and can combine all other
genres – convincing accounts of how men and women act in
common and uncommon domestic, political, legendary and
fabulous circumstances. Nothing less than an epic, I decided, was
worth writing, and was helped to the decision by remembering
how much I enjoyed works that mingled different genres;
childhood pantomime, *The Wizard of Oz* film, Hans Andersen's
stories, Amos Tutuola's *Palm-Wine Drunkard*, Hogg's *Confessions
of a Justified Sinner*, Ibsen's *Peer Gynt*, Kingsley's *Water Babies*,
Goethe's *Faust*, *Moby Dick*, Shaw's *Adventures of the Black Girl in
Search of God*, classical myths and some books of the bible. All
these mingle everyday doings with supernatural ones.

I now planned to put my journey through hell in the middle
of my Portrait of the Artist as a Frustrated Young Glaswegian. In
some chapter before Thaw went mad he would attend a drunken
party and meet an elderly gent like himself but thirty or forty
years older who would tell him a queer fantastic story, enjoyable
for its own sake. Only when the readers reached the end of *Thaw*
would they see the interior narrative was a continuation of it. The
design of the book now hung in my mind like a scaffolding put
up for the erection of a large castle, with a few towers (that is,
chapters) completed or partly complete. Most of what happened
to me before the novel was finished provided me with building
materials that I stored in notebooks until I could construct the
other towers and connecting walls.

For example, chapters 7 to 11 describe an institute, a
province of hell in which modern professional middle-class folk
are the devils. This derives from both other writers and my own
experience. The architecture of the place partly derives from

H.G. Wells's Selenite empire in *The First Men on the Moon* and 21st-century London in *The Sleeper Awakes*, but mostly from the afterlife hell in Wyndham Lewis's *Malign Fiesta*. This was part of a trilogy, *The Human Age*, later published as novels, but the last two books were first written as plays for the BBC Third Programme and broadcast several times around 1955. I heard one such broadcast while in Stobhill hospital then, an experience that also gave me material for chapter 26 – *Chaos* – which describes the experience from a patient's point of view. I had been sent there with what our family doctor called 'stasis asthmaticus', and which I ascribed to my quarrel with a very nice girl who only liked me as a friend, whereas I wanted her to be my (A) lover and (B – later of course) wife. In the institute chapters I describe it from a very poorly qualified doctor's viewpoint, and mingled atmospheres and details from Wyndham Lewis's hell, Stobhill hospital, the London underground railway system and the London BBC television centre. I experienced the last when I had plays produced or commissioned there in the middle and late 1960s. But chapters 7 to 11 were written in 1969 and '70, by which time Lanark's story was becoming greater than Thaw's, and I had decided to put the last inside the first.

That large change came about because in 1961 I married and, in September 1963 became a father. The most significant part of my life no longer seemed my eccentrically frustrated youth. The toils of later life which I shared with many other folk now looked as important.

Q Are you telling me that the fantastic and grotesque events in books 3 and 4 are also autobiographical? How can they be? Lanark becomes Lord Provost of Unthank. You were never a figure in the local politics of Glasgow.

A I know, but experience allowed me to generalise. A writer whose play has been chosen for a TV production is very like a politician chosen for an important position because he has made a speech that appeals to widespread sentiment. He then discovers he depends on a host of directors, producers, dramaturges and technicians to whom he is a temporary creature, of use in assisting their work if he does not tamper with the notions it suggests to *them*. The writer of what was once his script may feel good if the production is finally applauded: will certainly be blamed if it is not, but his part in the business may strike him as one that could have been done as well or better by someone with less or very different ideas. TV production taught me all about politics.

Q In what sort of order were the parts of the book completed?

A Book One was completed in its present form before my son was born. My wife and I were living on Social Security money then so I sent the completed part to Spenser Curtis Brown's literary agency because I felt the book good enough to stand alone, though I would have preferred to complete it in the big way I had planned. But Mr Curtis Brown rejected it so I did complete it as planned. By the mid-1970s I had completed book Three and linked it to Book One with my Oracle's Prologue. I had a good agent who liked my work by that time, Frances Head, a London lady. She showed it to three London publishers, who tried to persuade me to split the *Thaw* and *Lanark* narratives in two and make separate books of them. They said it would be dangerously expensive for them to risk publishing so big a first book by an unknown novelist. But my first marriage had collapsed in an amicable way, I had no need of money and was greedy for fame instead, so I refused them.

Books Two and Four were written side by side – I moved from completing a chapter in one to a chapter in the other with an increasing sense of running downhill. In 1975 and '76 I was carrying manuscripts around and working on them in all kinds of places. I remember waking up on the livingroom floor of my friend Angela Mullane's house after a party where I had fallen asleep for a usual Scottish reason, and resuming work there and then because it was a quiet morning and none of the other bodies on the floor were awake. I couldn't do that now. I was then a young fellow of forty or thereabouts.

At the end of July 1976 the whole book was completed, typed and posted to Quartet Ltd, the only London publisher Frances Head had been able to interest in it. She, alas, had died of lung cancer. Quartet books turned it down for the usual reason – it was too long for them to risk the high cost of printing. I sulked for half a year then posted it to Canongate, the only Scottish publishing firm I knew. Five or six months passed before I got an enthusiastic letter from Charles Wilde, the Canongate reader, saying the Scottish Arts Council would probably subsidise printing costs. Chapters had appeared in *Scottish International*, a short-lived but widely read literary magazine eight or nine years earlier, so north Britain was more ready for it than the south. I finally signed a contract with Canongate on the 20th of March 1978.

Q *Lanark* was published three years later. Why did it take so long?

A Canongate arranged a joint publication with Lippincott, an old well-established firm in the USA; but before the book was printed Lippincott got swallowed up by Harper & Row, another old well-established/USA firm. This caused delay. Then American editors proof-read the book, decided my punctuation was inconsistent. I told them that I used punctuation marks to regulate the speed with which readers took in the text — some passages were to be read faster than others, so had fewer commas. There was more delay while I restored my text to its original state. However, the delays gave me time to complete the illustrative title pages and jacket designs.

Q Were you relieved when *Lanark* was finally off your hands?

A Yes. For a while before I held a copy I imagined it like a large paper brick of 600 pages, well bound, a thousand of them to be spread through Britain. I felt that each copy was my true body with my soul inside, and that the animal my friends called Alasdair Gray was a no-longer essential form of after-birth. I enjoyed that sensation. It was a safe feeling.

Q So you the time spent upon *Lanark* over so many years was time well spent?

A Not entirely. Spending half a lifetime turning your soul into printer's ink is a queer way to live. I'm amazed to recall the diaries I wrote when a student, often putting the words into the third person as a half-way stage to making them fictional prose. I'm sure healthy panthers and ducks enjoy better lives, but I would have done more harm if I'd been a banker, broker, advertising agent, arms manufacturer or drug dealer. There are worse as well as better folk in the world, so I don't hate myself.

Selected praise for *Lanark*

"A quirky, crypto-Calvinist Divine Comedy *[that] should be widely read."* New York Times Book Review

"An ambitious and marvellously inventive novel."
Malcolm Bradbury

"This book is more than a provincial or regional classic. Lanark's *ambitions are large and so are its achievements: it's rare to come across a novel so rooted in a particular city and yet so accessible to those outside."* William Boyd

"A quite extraordinary achievement, the most remarkable thing in Scottish fiction for a very long time. It has changed the landscape. That in itself is astonishing. No one with any claims to be interested in or concerned with the state of our culture can ignore Lanark.*"* Allan Massie, *The Scotsman*

"When dawn comes up and retires in dismay, we find ourselves in the presence of an overpowering surreal imagination. A saga of a city where reality is about as reliable as a Salvador Dali watch."
Brian Aldiss

"The landmark post-war Scottish novel. It fuses sci-fi, quasi-autobiography, and an apocalyptic vision into one of the wittiest, darkest, most readable books of the last fifty years." Magnus Linklater

"[Gray] is that rather rare bird among contemporary British writers – a genuine experimentalist, transgressing the rules of formal English prose . . . boldly and imaginatively."
David Lodge, *New Republic*

". . . [the] masterful evocation . . . of an adolescence and young manhood in post-1945 Glasgow, of early friendships and first love, of the stirring of artistic genius and its frustration, and of the subtle social prejudices that had to be learned as one grew up . . . In a larger sense, the novel is an attempt to expose the ills that threaten modern society, an elaboration on a text in one of Gray's plates: 'Let Glasgow flourish' – any and all Glasgows – by telling the truth." Gordon A. Craig, *New York Review of Books*